CROSSING
EDEN

CROSSING
EDEN

A NOVEL
BY MONTE SCHULZ

FANTAGRAPHICS BOOKS · SEATTLE

Fantagraphics Books, 7563 Lake City Way NE, Seattle, Washington, 98115 | Editor: Gary Groth. Cover Design: Michael Heck. Editorial Assistants: Kristy Valenti, Sam Chattin, Kara Krewer and Ao Meng.. Production: Preston White. Associate Publisher: Eric Reynolds. Publisher: Gary Groth. Interior graphics by Gavin Lees, Marie Profant, Eric Reynolds, Nicole Starczak, Rich Tommaso, Zuniga, Geets Vincent, and Jenny Catchings. *Crossing Eden* is copyright © 2015 Monte Schulz. This edition copyright © 2015 Fantagraphics Books. All rights reserved. Permission to excerpt or quote material from this book must be obtained by the author or publisher. To receive a full-color catalog of comics, graphic novels, prose novels, artist monographs, and other fine works of high artistry, call 1-800-657-1100, or visit www.fantagraphics.com. | ISBN 978-1-60699-891-5. Also available in eBook format: ESBN 978-1-60699-918-9 | Printed in South Korea.

For Wesley and John Henry, inheritors of all this.

The World was all before them, where to choose
Thir place of rest, and Providence thir guide:
They hand in hand with wandring steps and slow,
Through *Eden* took thir solitarie way.
— John Milton
Paradise Lost

PROLOGUE
CHARLIE PENDERGAST

TIME WAS, WHEN WE WERE YOUNG. A morning far from heaven whose sunlight in our bright faces gleamed. Father and Mother still in their room, a drowsy milkman at the kitchen door. Our streets were lively with elms and squirrels, miles of sidewalks trampled by pets and children and lightning rod salesmen. Those dusty old planks led to every corner of God's earth, but we did not know it then. We were too busy with community. A doctor down the block brought the first motorcar to town. She's plenty shiny, people joked, but can she find her own way back to the barn at dusk? When the ice wagon stopped coming, progress seemed wicked and cruel, a blight upon the world. Until it meant electricity and radio. Most of us get by with one foot in yesterday and the other in tomorrow, but some refuse to admit it. The calendar gave us a perfect blueprint for living. Under hazy autumn skies we gathered field crops and stole our neighbors' gates at Halloween. Each winter brought sled riding and Yule trees, frost and oranges. Spring breezes filled our nostrils with the scent of blossoms from Eden and the promise of a new earth. By summertime, where boys and old men fished through the long hot lazy afternoons, youth courted beauty by the river. Seasons came long and short, like people and tempers. I never heard my father cuss, but when Mother caught cousin Bebbins and me wrestling in her prize gladiolas I learned a new word. She blamed it on her upbringing across the tracks. Those who believe we are made whole by prosperity too often regard the downtrodden as cripples. Some wore finer shoes than others, but we each delivered our children in the same fashion. When we were young, a nickel bought a handful of peppermint candy and red-hots were a dime. It was not hard to feel rich as Rockefeller. Our day brought more changes to living than the dreamer ever divined. Grandma heard the phonograph when she was a girl and thought it was an echo from next door. More than a few cheered Lincoln and Lindbergh in the same holy span of three score and ten, while Thomas Edison rivaled Jesus Christ as the greatest figure in human history. We were thankful to witness so many miracles in our time. A seed planted in fertile soil sprouts prodigiously, root and vine. We survived world war, influenza, and the arrival of the Volstead Act. We suffered little poverty of spirit. We felt triumphant in our day. This was us. This is our story.

AMERICA

1929

KANSAS CITY

HARRY HENNESEY SHIFTED IN BED as the blonde beside him rolled over and switched on the lamp. A drab yellow light filled the small room, exposing the cracks and water spots on the roseate wallpaper. Still nude and smelling of sex and liquor, the girl got up from the old iron bed and walked across the room to the window and cracked open the blinds for a peek at the paved street below. It was raining outside, pattering on the glass, blown about by a rising wind. She looked over her shoulder at him lying on the bed.

"How old are you, Harry?"

"Forty-three and fit as a fiddle." He tried to sound enthused, but he knew middle age was already creeping over him. "Why, don't I look it?"

"Oh, I think you're terribly handsome. You're just as trim and muscular as my kid brother, and you still got a cute baby face."

"Thank you, dear." He'd been lucky to hold practically his same weight since college without having to go to a gymnasium every week. Most fellows he knew fell apart at thirty.

She smiled. "So how long you been coming here?"

"Long enough to know better, not often enough to worry about," he joked, mimicking those lunchwagon wiseacres he had been listening to all week, fellows who loved talking about girls they'd dated up and those they were still chasing. He sat up and grabbed the blonde's pillow, suddenly appalled at how flip he had become about sinning in a chintzy hotel room while his wife put their children to bed hundreds of miles away. If she knew how he spent some of these evenings on the road, she would likely never let him out the door.

In the next room, a loud thump shook the wall. The blonde let the blinds close. Her lipstick had worn off and her curls drooped. She wasn't the hot tomato Harry had bought a cocktail for six hours ago. Down the hall, a toilet flushed, rattling the pipes up and down the floor.

"Say, darling, do you want to marry me?" she asked, a half-smile on her lips. "I can't boil an egg, but I can drive a car all night long."

The wall thumped again at his head. Voices, barely audible, tittered laughter. Harry had agreed to this hotel because the rates were reasonable and it was walking distance to the train station. Besides, when he had met the blonde at the billiards room, she had told him there were worse places to sin in this city.

The blonde came back to the iron railing at the foot of the bed. Her breasts sagged, but her nipples were still rosy and firm. She lifted the sheet off his feet and kissed his toes. Her tongue tickled and he wriggled away.

"Honestly, I wouldn't want a wife who can drive," Harry told her, pulling the sheets up over his waist. A sudden desire for modesty had come over him and he felt embarrassed. "Who knows where she'd go?"

As a matter of fact, his darling wife was scared silly of auto smashups, and therefore had no interest in learning to motor. She could scarcely ride a bicycle. Her Uncle Harlow still drove his old Stanley Steamer over town, and her mother enjoyed referring to the modern automobile as a bedroom on wheels. Harry always thought of Marie's family as hopelessly backward and he hated going out to the Pendergast farm for Sunday dinner. He was sick of chicken feathers and horse manure and hearing them quote that idiot Billy Sunday. He just could not stand them and knew they despised him, too. No doubt her family had poisoned their marriage union. Once Marie took his ring, the welcome smiles he had been shown through their courtship turned cold and indifferent. No more cigars or invitations to card games in the den. Truly he had come to believe Byron was correct in maintaining that all tragedies are finished by a death, and all comedies are ended by a marriage.

Outside, two car horns sounded in the street. Storm drains had been flooding since dusk and Harry had seen the city streets becoming somewhat precarious. He watched the blonde stroll over to the sink opposite the bed and primp her hair before the mirror. She ran the water to wet her fingers and repaired a curl beside her left ear. Then she turned to face him, unabashedly nude. He stared at her pubic hair, clotted from sex.

"Am I beautiful, Harry?" She traced the outer curve of her lolling breasts with her fingertips. "Don't lie now. I want the absolute truth. Am I?"

"No, darling, you're not." She had a swell figure and a nice bosom, but she was certainly no Venus. Girls he had made love to at State were much prettier, but more reluctant to shed their drawers; probably few of them knew the first thing about sex. Not like Gloria here who seemed to know even more than he did. If only she didn't drink so much. Gin-soaked sex wasn't half as much fun.

She frowned at him. "You need a good spanking, honey bunny. Do you know that? A good long spanking."

The wall thumped half a dozen times in succession, ending in a loud squeal from next door. Above the bed, one of the picture frames containing a cheap faded copy of Gainsborough's *Blue Boy* angled forward on its nail. The lamp flickered.

"It's cold in here," said the blonde, wrapping her arms tightly around her bare bosom, pushing her breasts up. "Are you cold?" Her nipples were stiff and red.

"No," he replied, stifling a yawn. "I'm swell." Except that his stomach had been grumbling for the last hour. Maybe he'd eat a snack on the train.

"Well, honey bunny, I'm freezing," she told him, with a scowl.

He shrugged. "Put on a sweater."

She went over to the window again and pried open the blinds with a thumb and forefinger. "I don't think it'll ever stop raining. Somebody better call Noah."

"Oh, I wouldn't worry. So long as garbage floats, this city'll be safe." He stared at her naked bottom and wondered if he was indeed through with her. He felt himself stir beneath the sheets. Maybe he ought to stay a little while longer, after all.

"Why, it's awfully swell here in the springtime. I love marigolds."

Harry told her, "They give me hay fever."

A loud bang shook the wall, knocking *Blue Boy* from the wall, deflecting off Harry's head like a sharp hammer blow. "Christ almighty!"

He felt his skull for a wound. It hurt, but not seriously. Maybe this was what he deserved for what he'd been doing all evening. Marie would probably say God dropped it.

The blonde ran to the wall and pounded with her fist, yelling, "Goddammit you sonsabitches!" She picked the picture up and ran her fingers through his hair. "Aw, I'm sorry, honey bunny. Are you all right? Those sonsabitches." Her breasts bounced as she banged the wall again with her fist. "You sonofabitches!"

"I'll live," he told her, rubbing his skull. The sharp corner of the picture frame had raised a welt. Did that really fall on his head? Good grief! He checked for blood with the tips of his fingers. "Can you get any ice?"

"Oh, you poor dear. Let me see."

Harry got up and went to the sink and held his head forward into the light, parting a patch of hair to expose the wound that was starting to throb. Marie would notice this when he got home and ask how he was injured. What would he tell her? That he bumped his head getting on the trolley? "I need some ice, dear."

The wall thumped behind him.

"You bastards!" the blonde yelled, and kicked the wall with her heel, denting the plaster. A squeal of laughter followed another loud thump.

"Ice?" asked Harry, tenderly patting the rising lump. He expected to have a roaring headache soon.

"Gee, darling, I don't know where I'd scare any up this time of night. Are you sure you need it?"

"If I wasn't sure, I certainly wouldn't have asked."

"Maybe just running cold water on it'll help."

"How am I supposed to fit my head under the tap?" Studying the wound in the mirror, Harry found a slight trickle of blood on his scalp. My God, now what? "Look here, I'm actually bleeding."

"Does it hurt a lot?"

"No, but I'll certainly have a headache for the rest of the night."

"I'm sorry."

Harry ran the faucet, splashing water on a washrag and using it to dab the patch of blood in his hair. He felt silly complaining about his injury, but it did hurt. "It's not your fault, dear."

After cleaning the wound, he rinsed out the washrag and folded it over the tap. He doubted Gloria had sobered up enough to make it down the flight of stairs to the icebox, anyhow. What if she fell and broke her neck? With his luck, he'd wind up in the tabloids with Reverend Hall. Wouldn't that give the Pendergasts something to chew on? Shutting off the water, he saw the blonde standing over at the window again, still nude, staring out through the open blinds. She was pretty, but not beautiful. In Chicago, she might even go unnoticed in a dance crowd of younger girls. Ferguson had told him once that cowtown dames look like mules. Bed down with one, you'll wake up with fleas. Or worse. Thank God for rubbers.

Next door, the rhythmic thumping continued, less violently now, accentuated every so often by a peal of laughter or a soft giggle. Sometimes he thought the walls of these sorts of hotels were made deliberately thin so that everyone could know everyone else's business. Harry walked over to the bed and picked the picture frame up and hung it back on the wall, making certain it was straight. Crooked pictures disturbed him, a trait passed down from his mother; she held orderliness as the pinnacle of virtues.

"Darling, I think you ought to stay for breakfast." The blonde slid up behind him and wrapped her arms around his neck, kissing him on the shoulder. She reeked of gin as she pressed her soft breasts against his back and she reached between his legs. "I'll buy you a grapefruit."

"I can't."

"Why, sure you can, honey bunny. Don't be a rat."

The thumping next door stopped. Harry removed her hand from his manhood, and pulled away. Deciding this was a good time to go, he asked, "Where's my shirt?"

The blonde slid around beneath him onto the bed and tried to pull him down on top of her. "Aw, don't go yet, darling. It wouldn't be square." She parted her pale thighs and offered herself with a seductive pout. "Pretty please? Honey bunny, I'm cold. I need a warm body beside me."

He held her off. Whether from guilt or fatigue, he had suddenly become frightfully anxious to get out of the hotel. He'd had all the romance he needed; now he felt restless and desperate. If necessary, he would wait on a bench at the train station. No reason to compound his mistake. "Where's my shirt, dear?"

She arched up to kiss his chin and ran her fingers through his hair. "Why, you don't need it just now, do you?"

Harry angled away from her to look under the iron bed. He felt agitated now. "Where are my shoes?"

She wormed out from underneath him and got up as he put on his underwear. "Quit acting like a human icicle."

"Don't be rude."

She stuck her tongue out. "Aw, you're no fun anymore. You know that? Absolutely no fun at all."

He spotted his overcoat and one black leather shoe between the bed and the nightstand and picked them up, laying the coat flat on the bed sheets. He saw it was wrinkled. Swell. He'd have to get it pressed aboard the train. Otherwise, Marie would be suspicious. She knew he hated wrinkles.

"Don't run along yet, honey bunny," the blonde said, as Harry stood to dress. She stroked the inside of his thigh with the back of her hand. "I'm hoping you'll get fresh with me again."

In the next room, voices rose, bickering loudly now. Harry went to the window where his pants were draped over a chair. He looked outside at the cold rain, blown by the winter wind off the northern prairies, pouring down steadily since his arrival in the city. Sad and ugly weather, and home still a long train ride away. Five weeks on the road, suitcases empty, his pockets barely half-full. Meager wages for groceries and gifts. One more trip like this and he'd be washed up. Had Marie ever understood the sacrifices he made for her and the children? She wasn't the only one who felt unaccountable despair. It was sheer torment being gone from Cissie and Henry. Even the thought of their nasty moods became endearing when he was on the selling road away from the tumult and joy of parenthood. Because he was a father, after all: their dear old Dad.

Two shouting voices echoed loudly in the wall. Harry took his trousers off the back of the chair and put them on. Suddenly, he felt the need to get away this very minute.

"Listen to that," said the blonde, her head pressed up against the wall to hear better. "I swear the bird's got no brain. Rule number one, honey: Never let a deadbeat into your room."

"Darling, where's my shirt?" Harry asked, pretending not to hear the dispute next door. A principle to which he adhered religiously involved minding one's own business. What good would come of his interfering? Fastening his trousers, he looked about for the missing shirt. Outside, the storm flung rain hard at the side of the building. Pedestrians down below sloshed along the sidewalks as gutters overflowed. Streetcars shuttled off to the next stop. If he hadn't already engaged a seat on the night train, he'd be forced to wait out the storm overnight. By now, few if any of the roads leading out of town would be much more than miles of muddy sinkholes. Thank goodness he had planned ahead.

"My shirt, please?"

"Under the bed, you old dope."

"Thank you."

As he knelt down to peek under the dust ruffle, a terrific impact at the wall behind the bed knocked down all the picture frames on Harry's side. In the next room, a woman screamed. Harry's door flew open and the blonde dressed only in a Nile-green silk kimono ran out. Terrified, Harry located his shirt under the bed and snatched it up. He quickly put it on while looking for his socks. The woman screamed again. Doors opened down the hallway, footsteps hurrying in Harry's direction. Then a gun, popping like a .38, discharged in the next room. The floor became quiet. His heart leaped as he finished tying one of his shoes. He heard someone knock next door, then the blonde shouting, "Carrie? Are you all right?" A pause, and another knock. "Carrie?"

A small crowd was gathering out in the hall. Harry considered stepping out for a look, but changed his mind when he heard footsteps thundering up the staircase and the distinct clicking of twin hammers drawn back on a double-barreled shotgun. A bald fat man wearing a sleeveless undershirt strode by. Harry grabbed his coat and rushed to the window. There was a crash against the door in the next room. A fellow's voice from inside yelled a curse and the .38 went off again. Chaos in the hallway. Someone kicked the door and the frame cracked. Another kick and the door fell off its hinges. More shouts inside and out, then the roar of a shotgun firing.

BOOM!

BOOM!

Then the blonde's voice shrill and hysterical, screaming to her sister, again and again. Frightened half to death, Harry flung open the window above the alley and crawled out onto the fire escape into the rain. Using his leather suitcase as an umbrella, he negotiated the iron ladder down to the next floor. It was slick with grime and his shoes resisted traction on the wet rungs. Looking down through the rainy dark, the distance from the third floor fire escape to the street seemed twice what it had in the daylight. Up above him, one window to the left, he saw faces crowding the room. Ignoring a longtime fear of heights, Harry worked his way down the fire escape to the alley and hustled away from the hotel. A siren shrieked across the night air.

Safely around the corner into the next block, he stopped to catch his breath. His hands were still shaking. Good God, did that fellow back there shoot his date? He must've gone insane. Now what? Harry's watch read a quarter past eleven. Assuming the train was running on time, he could still get out of town by midnight. Marie worried when he was late. If she knew he was coming in at night, she would take the blankets and wool comforter off the bed and sit on the porch, gazing half-asleep in the direction of Foster Avenue and the Rose Line trolley that brought him home to Cedar Street. At least once each winter she caught a cold waiting up for him, yet it never dissuaded her.

A damp wind tore at his clothes as he sidestepped flooded potholes six blocks from the hotel, heading into the district of lightless street corners and boarded up storefronts, dark alleyways half-submerged in rainsoaked garbage, less subtle signs of decay. He was alone now, motor traffic departing back where the city lights sparkled in the cold rainfall. Crossing Main at 31st Street, he entered Penn Valley Park, half a mile east of the Kansas River. Fallen branches and leaves littered the ground, and the walking paths were muddy and black. Overhead, storm-drenched elms swayed in the wind. Keeping the city cemetery just visible on a knoll to the east as a landmark, Harry hurried through the park. He felt scared and foolish, risking his life like this for one more tawdry sexual encounter. What was wrong with him? Hadn't he any control over himself? Each time he went to another woman, he swore she would be the last. Why couldn't he have kept alone to himself at a decent hotel, studying appointment ledgers for better opportunities, concentrating on work to better the lives of his wife and children like most other men? What fellow gets ahead in this world by chasing skirts? Shouldn't he have been home playing a game of marbles with little Henry before tucking him into bed, reading stories with Cissie, sharing a quiet hour of true love and affection with his dear Marie after dark? Sheets of rain poured down harder. His shoes sank in the mud, soaking the smell of rain-dampened earth into his socks. His feet grew numb from the cold and they ached. Had he not been alone, he might have chosen to stop and rest. There were iron benches beneath the elms throughout the park, dry protected places to sit and consider his life barely a stone's throw from the cemetery. If he sat for even a minute, though, he imagined he'd see Gloria in the dim hallway, her face pressed to her sister's door, listening to a client's revolver discharge inside the room. Sure, he felt horrible for having left her there alone, but what good could he have done? Without a gun, he might have gotten himself shot, too. Then where would he have been? Found dead in a woman's hotel bedroom? One day his lucky streak was going to end. Harry shuddered at the thought and kept walking. The park seemed empty, but he knew vagrants slept in the surrounding bushes to keep out of the rain. They would be watching him as he passed, eyeing with curiosity the leather suitcase he carried along. Picturing his corpse dragged out of the cold Kansas River at dawn with its throat slashed, Harry hurried his pace. Wind gusted hard in the trees and the rainfall thickened. No bum lurched from the foliage to assault him. Somehow, he had survived another evening of sin and foolishness. On Dr. Prideaux-Brune's blackboard at State was scribbled: *"Idleness is the emptiness that leads to a thousand evil consequences, while business is the fullness of the soul."* The fact was, if Harry had any desire to set a grand example one day, this evening had to be his last indulgence. Nobody ever got rich by draping his trousers over a stranger's bed frame.

Half an hour later, he left Main to reach the Union Station. Across the street, the big Chevrolet sign stood out on a black and rainy sky. Electric lights on the corner pole were darkened beneath it. In contrast, the interior of the huge train station glowed brightly. At eighteen minutes to twelve, Harry Hennesey walked inside, secured his ticket, and sat on a wooden bench just beyond the departures platform and waited for the connection to Chicago and the Burlington Pullman that would take him home.

FARRINGTON, ILLINOIS

THE BRASS MANTEL CLOCK above the parlor fireplace rang once
for the half hour. A corner window was cracked open to the
evening breeze, and a pleasantly warm draft redolent of fresh spring
blossoms circulated throughout the downstairs. Outdoors, only the occasional automobile rattled along Cedar Street during the supper hour
and the sky was darkening.

"More potatoes, please."

Harry Hennesey held his hands out to receive the blue porcelain
bowl from his wife. Marie had cooked a pot roast with gravy, potatoes
and lima beans. She cooked to please him, a gratifying fact. Doesn't
every fellow marry his best girl for just this reward?

"More gravy, too?" Marie asked. "I'd rather not see it go to waste."

"No, thank you." He worried a good deal lately about indigestion.
Since Kansas City, his stomach had been troubling him. He knew it
was nerves, aggravated by decisions he'd been forced to make, a sharp
detour he believed was necessary to better their lives, or at least to save
what they still had. In any case, there was a lot to talk about tonight
and he didn't need any fussy interruptions. He certainly wasn't the sort
to call out from the toilet.

Marie frowned. "I'll just have to throw it out. Are you sure, dear?"

"Yes." Harry took a drink of water, then dabbed his lips with the
cloth napkin.

"I baked a pie for you," said Marie. She smiled at the children.
"Your favorite."

"What's that, dear?" Harry asked, ladling the leftover gravy from his plate onto the potatoes. He noticed how agreeable Marie seemed. Perhaps she would be in a good state of mind for what he needed to tell her. A husband is the head of his household, so his word stands, for better or worse. Yet he also knew that domestic harmony thrived on agreement, particularly when things were rough. If Marie resisted what had to be done, it was very likely everything would go to smash. So he strove to be delicate, as well as forceful and honest.

"Apple butterscotch."

"That's my favorite, too," said little Henry. On the seven-year-old's plate was a pile of lima beans, mashed potatoes and roast, sloshed together to resemble a spring mud puddle. The boy made a game of everything and had boundless energy. Harry's youngest hadn't sat still since the day he began walking: the best little boy in the world.

"Maybe a little slice, darling." Harry nodded, with a pleasant smile. "I'm practically full up, but you know I can't resist." Honestly, he was about to burst and the thought of any pie at all turned his stomach. However, it wouldn't do to be contrary. Marie had a delicate temperament and Harry knew that soothing her with compliments would be the wise thing to do. Marriage was a high-wire act of caution and considerations, and only the clever survived. If he had any desire to keep his status as head of this household, he had better start paying attention.

Out in the street, a motor roared past, backfiring from one end of the block to the other.

"Only a small slice?" Marie asked, sounding both surprised and deflated. "Are you sure?"

"I got lots of room," Henry announced, shoving his messy dinner plate to the side. "I love apple butterscotch!"

Ten-year-old Cissie in pigtails quickly corrected her younger brother. "You ninny! You can't love a pie. You can only love people, pets and our Lord Jesus." She smiled. "Isn't that right, Momma?"

"Yes, dear." Marie gave her sweet daughter a pat on the head as she went to the kitchen to retrieve the pie. Those two might knit together, or fight over the laundry. Mothers and daughters were a great wonder.

He adored them equally, his beautiful girls.

"Although I love Ozma, too," Cissie reminded her father, enjoying the book she'd just borrowed from the Farrington library that afternoon. She revered reading. In that, Cissie was her father's daughter. They'd begun by reading Grimm's fairy tales together at bedtime when she was not yet three and, within two years, Cissie had been able to read along aloud, a fact which gave Harry immense pride, a great sense of paternal accomplishment. What sort of father would he be had he not taught his precious children the joy of books and reading?

"Here we are," Marie announced, as she placed the pie on the table. She had already sliced it up and handed Harry a piece that was twice what he asked for. No matter. He would eat every last bite and raise no complaint.

The kids dug in, too, consuming dessert like ravenous pets.

Stirring his fork through the apple butterscotch filling, Harry felt impatient. He decided he wouldn't wait until bedtime. When supper was through, he would simply go ahead and explain to Marie his revised plan for their future. He had no illusions about how she'd react upon hearing that he'd just put the house up for sale, and that everything she counted on in her day-to-day routine would shortly go bust. It would be the bitterest moment in a life that had seen more than its share.

Finished with the pie, Harry wiped his mouth with a cloth napkin. "I suppose I'll go outside for a while," he told Marie, pushing his chair away from table. "This was a wonderful dinner, darling. Thank you."

"Are you sure you won't have another slice? We really have too much."

"No, I guess I've had my fill."

"Can I have your piece of pie, Daddy?" asked Henry.

Cissie stuck her tongue out. "Greedy face! Greedy face! Eat too much to run a race!" She smirked, ever the defiant bully to her baby brother.

"Cissie!" her mother warned.

Harry gave Marie a kiss on the cheek as he passed by on his way out of the room.

— **2** —

The neighborhood was quiet now and cicadas droned in the grass and hazel bushes on both sides of the house. Moths pattered at the porchlight and a faint breeze carried the scent of dooryard lilacs across the alleyway, rustling the leaves of the old shagbark hickory whose branches hung over the front sidewalk. Standing beside the porch swing, Harry listened to the clanging of a late night car departing the Foster Avenue trolley stop and thought about taking a walk to the cigar store. It was only four blocks away and he could be back by the time Marie finished with the dishes.

He enjoyed spring evenings outdoors. With the weather more agreeable, you could put away your winter clothing and go about in a sleeveless sweater. Next door, you might hear a ball slap into leather mitts as the Helten boys played catch out on the sidewalk. At the green craftsman house on the corner, there would be cocktail laughter from those convivial spirits engaged with Jim Villela's bridge game. Four doors away, Louis Maxwell had just put in a new Stewart-Warner radio cabinet and invited neighbors passing by to listen in on the *Camoah Mystery* microphonic drama from NBC. There were five million illiterates in America, most of whom listened to radio broadcasts. Harry took after his father in preferring the newspaper, even when he didn't believe much of what was dished up. Maxwell always had a wise line or two, but Harry generally thought he went flat when conversation got natural. The really popular man is the one who has learned to interest other people, and Harry could just as easily quote a strategy from *Nation's Business* as spring a gibe from a funny column.

But this was not the evening to trade wisecracks on the street corner. A man's duty pointed to his family's welfare, particularly when things soured in the outside world. They counted on him to keep the doors locked and the house warm and safe, a source of great pride to every able husband and father. So, instead of walking to the cigar store, he stayed on the porch, listening to the cicadas and the breeze in the spring lilacs, and waited for Marie.

After washing the dishes and seeing the children to their rooms, she came out onto the porch, still warily cheerful. Harry was certain his wife sensed something was out of order. She told him, "I saved you another slice of pie in case you change your mind. It's in the ice box."

Harry smiled. "Thank you, dear."

Be as pleasant as possible, he reminded himself. Lately, their marriage had cooled somewhat in ways Harry found difficult to contemplate. Despite his stupid indiscretions on the road, he believed he loved his girl as much as the day they married. What fellow doesn't notice a pretty skirt on Main Street? Does that mean he can't still adore the lovely face he wakes to in his own bed each morning? Is it really so hypocritical?

After taking a few moments to smell her star jasmine swarming the trellis, Marie walked over and sat beside Harry. She smoothed her dress. "A friend of yours stopped by yesterday. Lawrence Hopman."

Hopman? That sonofabitch! What train did he fall off? Harry stared out toward the evening street and tried to pretend he didn't recognize the name. Nor had he any interest in discussing anything this evening other than his plan for their future. "Don't know him."

"He said you went to school together in Texas. It seems he's been living in Richmond for the past six years, but hopes to be able to come here and open a furniture store."

"Is that so?"

"I told him you'd be glad to introduce him to your friends on the business council when he decides he's coming."

Drawn reluctantly into the topic, Harry replied, "Do you think we need two furniture stores here in Farrington? George Tunney's already having trouble with business gone sour. Cut a rotten apple in half and what do you get?"

"Worms?" Marie smiled.

"That's very clever, dear."

"I was just teasing."

Harry shook his head. These sorts of conversations held no joy for him. Earning capacity is the foundation of progress in wealth. Everyone has within him the ingredients of success, but few own the formula for distilling its elements. Trouble was, his dear Marie understood quite a bit more about pyrographed pillows and quince blossom than she did Crowell Cash or the new tariff debates. He told her, "Opening a new business is a serious proposition, darling. Only a fool goes into it without investigating the territory beforehand."

"Lawrence said he's visited here before. I'm sure he's quite acquainted with things."

"Not if he's planning to open a furniture store, he isn't. There'll be no market for him. Believe me."

"Well, maybe you should see him and tell him for yourself. I'm sure he'd appreciate your advice."

Harry frowned. "The only advice I could give him would be to stay where he is, or to go look elsewhere. Farrington's a closed market. Period. I ought to know."

"But you will talk to him, won't you?"

"No."

"Harry! For goodness sakes!"

"Look, darling, if you want to feel decent about it and do this Hopman fellow a favor, why not be frank and tell him just what I've told you? I couldn't write it out plainer than that. Why, you'll save the man a small fortune, and be a hero both to him and George Tunney in the bargain."

Marie shook her head. "He'll probably never stop by here again."

Harry stared off down the street. "I'm sure the roof'll stay on."

His wife rapped her heels on the hardwood porch like she did whenever she was upset. Click-CLICK. Click-CLICK. Click-CLICK. Harry ignored her. What else could he do? Hopman was an idiot and a louse. Sure, Harry remembered him. Some thirty years ago, Larry Hopman was the meanest kid in grammar school. Nobody in Bellemont liked him much at all. He was lots bigger than other kids his age, an advantage he used to lord over everyone. At lunch, he would strut around the schoolyard like Napoleon at Elba, investigating what the other kids had brought to eat, and when he found something that appealed to him, he'd force a trade. You were lucky to get half an apple in return. He was a bully and a cheat. Only when puberty allowed the other kids to match him in size and strength did he back down from his ugly tactics of intimidation. By high school, he was hardly noticed any longer. That Larry Hopman had left Texas was news to Harry. But, then again, who would have missed him?

Upstairs, Cissie was singing, Henry shouting. Harry listened for a bit. He smiled. *I hear in the chamber above me, the patter of little feet, the sound of a door that is opened, and voices soft and sweet.* They always gave the children a while to settle down in the evening, after which it was Marie's job to remind them of the hour and see them to bed. Before going to sleep himself, Harry would look in on them, give them each a kiss and be sure that Henry was tucked in properly. Often he'd watch from the threshold until they fell asleep. My goodness, he loved them so.

A shiny green two-tone Buick motor sped past toward Foster Avenue, kicking leaves up in its wake.

"Did you speak with Eustace yet?" Marie asked. Her click-CLICK, click-CLICK slowed.

"Concerning what?"

"The yard."

"What about the yard?"

"Hiring Eugene to take care of it for us."

Now his conversation with Marie would begin. His stomach fluttered as he told her, "We can't afford to hire anyone."

"Eustace assured me Eugene would do it for five dollars a week. I thought that was more than reasonable for the amount of work we need done."

"We still can't afford it. Anyhow, fixing the yard up isn't important now."

Marie stopped rocking her feet. Harry drew a breath, anticipating her response and the dialogue that would follow, one he had been preparing for a month, knowing the blame fell on him alone. How unfair to this dear woman was her husband's sudden decay. He felt sick to his stomach.

"I don't follow you," she said. "Crabgrass is eating our garden to pieces, the fence needs mending, the lawn has to be re-seeded. You promised we'd have it done for summer."

Harry's gaze fixed toward darkened Cedar Street, defeat in his heart. He told her flatly, "We'll be selling the house, darling. We can't afford to live here any longer."

Harry did not have to look at his lovely wife to know the color had gone out of her face. Her body had become perfectly rigid beside him.

Calmly as possible, he added, "You see, darling, there's just not enough work out there for me to keep us in this house. If we sell it, we can take the money, maybe eat for another year or so, keep the children in clean clothes and away from public charity. We've got to move, though. I'm sorry."

Marie spoke slowly, the shock evident in her voice. "Move where?"

"Down to East Texas. At least between whiles. Just you and the children, actually. I telephoned Mother yesterday afternoon. You'll stay with her in Bellemont until I can revise my situation with Transfer & Storage, go to the city, maybe save up some money this summer, then find us a nice place of our own again." Did it sound reasonable, this plan of his? Was it not a plausible direction toward a better future for all of them? Could he find his way in the Big Town? If not, there was nothing facing them but disaster.

"I'm not so sure I want to move," Marie told him. "This is our home. We've always lived here. The children grew up in this house. How can we possibly sell it?"

"We need the money," said Harry. "That's all there is to it. We can't go on, otherwise. We either sell the house or let the bank come and take it from us. Jack Ramsey's got a buyer coming out from Urbana on Monday to have a look."

He felt Marie trembling beside him. He had known this news would pierce her heart. She cherished their house. Cissie was born upstairs where poor little David's bedroom would have been. Those notches on the doorframe to the pantry marked Henry's growth. Gosh, he loved this house, too. Didn't she know that? There were memories here that gave him courage to be a father. Hadn't he picked it out himself and driven Marie down from St. Paul for her approval? Packing up and departing would feel utterly cruel, but this was the ugly part of his plan for the future.

"Why didn't you tell me this sooner?"

Shamefaced, he replied, "Frankly, I didn't know until this last trip. I thought that maybe if I reorganized myself, finagled a few more clients and made some rapid advances, that I'd finish high enough to keep us pointed up." He shook his head. "I'd really hoped to do something in a big way, darling, but honestly, it was no good. I almost had to take a billposting job just to buy groceries last week."

He knew Marie cared nothing for the numbers of business, only the three meals a day it placed on her table. Yet he hoped maybe by convincing her that what she knew in her daily life was now past, she would accept the inevitability of his decisions. She was his wife, after all.

"Who else knows?" she asked, quietly.

"Nobody, except Mother."

"The children won't understand, you know. They'll ask why we're leaving Grandpa and Grandma and Auntie Emeline and all the rest of the family, and I'll be forced to tell them a lie."

"Well, don't. Tell them the truth. We're not royalty. I'm sure they've figured that much out for themselves by now."

"Harry?"

"Yes?"

"Do you still love us?"

His heart contracted. This was what he had become afraid of. For quite a while now he feared his marriage was suffering that mean decline to a sad mediocrity. How long had it been since he and Marie last enjoyed marital relations? Two months? On Valentine's Day, he'd arranged for a babysitter and taken Marie to dinner downtown and bought her a bouquet of roses. Later on, with the children in bed, he'd kissed her while she sat at her vanity and fluffed up her pillows when she turned out the light. Not that the result had led to skyrockets, even then. Those romantic sparks had long since quieted. They made love that night with a solemn urgency and a tender embrace afterward. But then they had both gone to sleep without any of the playful teasing that used to be part of it. Possibly both had come to believe that hearts and flowers were for youthful mating, that gorgeous fever which, for most men and women, runs its natural course by the arrival of the first born. For Harry, marriage these days meant security, consistency, continuity: three words that described the needs of modern adulthood. Where love had once meant slow canoe rides on summer lakes, now it described all those sweet and bitter corners of a life lived for others. Those occasional pleasures found in a squalid hotel room could never supplant that. Sex was not love. His guilt at those encounters was effectively reduced by the knowledge that he rarely visited the same room twice. Moreover, in his own mind, that fellow who made love to wayward women on the selling road was not the one Marie recognized as her husband.

"Of course I love you," Harry replied, soberly. How could he break her heart, this beautiful girl who once held his trembling hand in the summer dark on Cedar Lake not that long ago. "Very much so. Gosh, you know I do. That's why I'm asking you to understand why we have to make this sacrifice. I'd never move you out of Farrington if I had any choice, but I'd also rather we leave here willingly, than be sent packing by the bank."

"Perhaps we ought to talk to my father, or Uncle Cy."

"Or your mother?"

Marie sighed. "No."

"Why speak with them at all?"

"Well, darling, there's just so much room out there on the farm, and Rubin's old carriage garage would make a lovely cottage. I'm sure the children — "

"No, thank you."

Marie frowned. "Why not?"

"Because I'm a businessman, not a farmer."

"You wouldn't be working there."

"I have no intention of living on a farm, at all. I didn't work as hard as I have at getting away from the odor of manure in the morning to begin smelling it again. Not on your life."

"Harry?"

"I tell you, there's no discussing it. We're not moving out to the farm."

Marie touched his elbow lightly with her fingers. "I've always been proud of you," she murmured. "Do you know that?"

Staring out across Cedar Street into the shadows that shrouded the leafy sycamores in Fred Dodd's front yard, frustrated by the very necessity of his unhappy plan, Harry wondered how they had been brought to this point: by turns of fortune, or mistakes of his own making? Admitting the latter, however true, also meant conceding he had failed in the one proposition a man promises his family, which was security: food on the table, respectable clothing, and a sturdy roof over their heads, uninterrupted season after season. Frankly, once he sold the house and sent his family by train to his mother's home in East Texas, he was scared to death that he would feel as foolish and pathetic as the child whose parents are forced to give away a pet their child has been too young and irresponsible to care for.

In the dark across the street, behind Dodd's lot and Willard Marion's, the woods sloped into a ravine where children played during the day and young lovers sought courting privacy. The ravine was perhaps sixty feet deep, wild with vegetation and a shallow brook that wound a quarter of a mile through a double horseshoe curve that led eventually to the Mississippi River. On evenings after Harry had finished a book and found sleep particularly elusive, he would sneak out of the house and walk across Cedar Street into the trees, descending a narrow footpath alone into the shadows by the wild brook, studying peculiar thoughts that plagued him in the night. *What sort of man have I become? What sort of husband and father? As good and decent as my own? When had my father ever uprooted his own family and sent us off to a strange place? When had my father's business gone so sour he needed to develop a plan for the future that brought his family to tears? What cheap rail hotels had my father frequented in the night when he was away from home?* Now and again, Harry considered that the grand passenger trains carrying him away from Illinois each month invited the boy to step out of the man, dividing the two of them, allowing the boy to pretend he was not responsible to that Harry Hennesey whose loving family slept beneath the roof of the pretty blue frame house at 119 Cedar Street in Farrington, Illinois. This fiction had infected his heart almost seven years now. Its dishonesty led him down into the ravine.

"I'll be upstairs, dear," Marie said, squeezing his arm once more. "Please don't stay out too late."

Harry felt her get up from the porch swing. The front door opened and shut again. He was relieved to see her go. What else could he have said once he'd broken her heart?

Soon he grew tired of sitting, and walked a couple blocks down along the sidewalk in the dark to the trolley stop at Foster Avenue where he heard a motor horn honking in the distance and saw George Mercer out with his Labrador. He counted off the business arrangements he had made for inventory space at City Transfer & Storage, the opportunities he had lined up for the purpose of getting his life back on track. A reverent faith in one's own abilities ought to be absolute, he believed, even in the face of failure and disappointment. Selling his home and moving the family to East Texas for a while would be a small sacrifice compared with the eventual dividends it could pay. Harry was no genius, but he had ideas and the confidence to realize them. Tonight, he prayed that fate and fortune would give him the chance.

Sunday morning, after sunrise service, he would drive Marie and the children out to the Pendergast farm for Easter dinner. During the time they spent there, he would answer dozens of questions about distant train trips he had taken, clients he buffaloed, prospects for future rackets. About the latter he would lie, as usual. Either that or skate around the truth to avoid revealing his private humiliations of the past few months. Afterward, he would pile his dear family into the Plymouth and bring them back to Cedar Street to begin packing. Certainly, Susannah Pendergast would find out the house was for sale. Gossip in Farrington traveled faster than Hermes with a hotfoot. Yet maybe by Monday it would be too late for persuasion, and then he would be through with that bunch. It was worth hoping for.

He walked back home. Up and down Cedar Street, houselights went out one after another. The street became quiet and empty for the night. Harry Hennesey sat out alone on the porch until his bedroom window went dark overhead, but it was not until three hours later that he put his reading away and went upstairs from the den, and he was still wide awake an hour past sunrise.

FARRINGTON, ILLINOIS

ALVIN PENDERGAST STOOD OUTDOORS behind the old Farrington auditorium in an Illinois breeze swollen with fresh crab-apple blossoms. The farm boy had a fifty-cent ticket in his hand to see the dance derby, but felt too blue to be inside. Orchestra music filtered out into the motor parking lot and across the spring twilight. He had walked alone three miles from the farm late that afternoon with a meat sandwich and a pocketful of Aunt Hattie's lemon cookies in his jacket and hadn't yet eaten a bite and it was past suppertime now. Tall carbon lamps were lit against the dark and clouds of tiny moths fluttered in and out of the pale light. Leaning against a thick maple tree a dozen yards from the back door, Alvin watched a pair of Model A Ford automobiles rattle into the side parking lot where a crowd his own age got out laughing. The pretty bobbed-haired girls were wearing short skirts and sparkling jewelry, while the boys dressed in white flannel, straw hats and spats. Some were smoking cigarettes. Coughing into his fist, the farm boy watched them hurry off into the noisy auditorium.

He ate his sandwich and one of the cookies. After a while, a flatbed truck swung into the parking lot and a young man Alvin's age jumped out and hurried to the back porch, shouting, "Patsy! Patsy!"

A stout fellow in suspenders and a straw boater held the door open for an attractive girl in a polka dot dress who came out to greet the young man. Her brown hair looked snarled and her street makeup was smeared with tears.

The young man bounded up the steps, shouting, "I'll kick that goddamned sonofabitch's head off if it's the last thing I ever do!"

Alvin's jaw dropped as he saw the girl slap the young man across the face.

The fellow stumbled back against the railing. "Hey! What's that for?"

The girl took a wad of chewing gum out of her mouth and threw it at him. "Nuts to you, Petey. We're finished!"

"Aw, honey," the youth whined, rubbing his cheek, "I know you're sore, but I swear that no-good guinea sonofabitch told me my house was burning down! No kidding! I had to go clear downtown and telephone Elmer to find out it wasn't true!"

"So long, Petey. Lay an egg!" The girl brushed past the stout fellow on her way back indoors.

"Aw, gee whiz, Patsy," the youth called after her. "Can't you see I'm still full of pep? Why, we'll show 'em who can shake a hoof. You bet we will!"

An older fellow in a brown plaid wool worsted suit and a snappy new fedora came out onto the porch, a lit cigar in hand. "Not tonight you won't. I tell you, kid, you're through."

The youth frowned. "Says who?"

"Says I. Now, scram! We don't need any more dumbbells around our derby." He turned to the fellow in the suspenders. "Gus, see that this here lug of Patsy's beats it."

"Yes, sir."

A smart Tiger Rag started up within the auditorium, promoting a raucous cheer from the grandstand audience. The youth spoke up. "Look here, Mister Cheney, let up on that, will you? Me and Patsy'll win the sprint tonight if you'll only give us the chance. We aren't the troublemakers in this derby. We got sponsors, loads of 'em, I tell you, who think we're pretty swell. What do you say?"

Alvin almost laughed out loud when he saw the man in the fedora exhale a cloud of smoke into the youth's face, then follow Patsy back indoors. This was lots better than dancing.

The stout fellow wearing suspenders closed the door, and turned to face the young man. "Sorry, kid, but if the boss says you gotta scram, then you gotta scram."

The youth jerked loose his necktie and flung it off the porch. "It's not fair, Gus! Not fair at all! We'd a won, me and Patsy. Bet your hat on it. I tell you, somebody greased that guinea sonofabitch to gyp us out of our thousand bucks."

"Sure they did, kid, but if you don't shove off now, you'll just queer yourself for the next town."

Alvin edged closer to the rear of the auditorium, hoping like hell to see some fireworks. Why not? Just last week, a shoe salesman from Cleveland had gotten shot four times in the head out behind the smokehouse on Wilson Street. A boy Alvin knew from the high school football team had found the body and told everyone how much blood he'd seen. His name was printed in the morning newspaper.

"Gee whiz, Gus, even if we didn't win, Patsy and me was hoping for a spray that'd get us enough for a ticket to St. Louis."

"Go back to squirting soda."

"Aw, I don't have the poop for that anymore."

"Well, I say a fellow oughtn't to plug himself up for a big shot in a rotten business like this unless he knows he can put it over often enough to eat regular and keep some kale in the bank."

"I know where I stand, Gus," said the youth. "Cheney does, too. I've learned the steps. You bet I have. Two hundred and thirty-six hours of picking 'em up and putting 'em down, and I'm still fresh as a daisy. Never gone squirrely, neither. Not once. And you ought to see the nifty stunt I planned to put over tonight. Why, it's a panic, I tell you. Look here, I'd be a big shot, Gus, if only the derby was fair and square and Cheney did his duty by some of us."

"Keep that under your hat, kid."

Alvin watched the youth stiffen his back, teeth clenched as if he were about to have a fit. Here it comes! Now he'd see something! Every fight started with a mean pose, like dogs and alley cats.

"Don't lecture to me, Gus. By God, if I ever amount to anything it won't be thanks to bums like Cheney."

The fellow in suspenders stepped forward and slugged the youth hard in the mouth, knocking him backwards off the porch into the dirt below. "Who's the bum, now?" roared the fellow in suspenders. "Eh?" Then he went back indoors, slamming the back door closed behind him.

Electrified, Alvin stole to the edge of the shadows, hoping to see the youth get up and start a ruckus. He'd witnessed plenty of school-yard scraps. Nobody really got hurt from a good sock in the head. He walked out from under the maple tree into the pale carbon light where the youth was sobbing like a baby. When Alvin called over to him, the youth lifted his chin a few inches off the ground, face caked with dust like a lump of cookie dough, his bottom lip bleeding into the dirt. He looked like a clown. Alvin stifled a laugh, even as he was trying to be polite. "Say, you ain't hurt there, are you?"

"Huh?"

"I said, that fellow didn't bust your jaw or nothing, did he?"

"Shove it along."

Alvin stopped where he was, his smile fading to a frown. People just weren't friendly anymore. He shot back, "Well, I guess you ain't too handy, are you?"

"You go to hell, too," the youth snarled. He rose up on one elbow and dabbed his lip with the tips of his fingers, tasting blood. "Lousy hick."

"Yeah?" Alvin veered away toward the front of the auditorium. Skipping off backwards, he shouted at the youth, "Well, I ain't the one busted up, neither. Dumbbell!"

Alvin Pendergast had lived all nineteen years of his life on a farm five miles from the Mississippi River in the pasture country of western Illinois. He and his sisters had been born there, and six of his cousins, three uncles, five aunts, his father and grandfather. His mother and most of his other relatives had grown up on farms between Farrington, Illinois and Beldenville, Wisconsin. Only a few lived in towns, and those in and about Farrington came out to the farm after church each Sunday for dinner. That was tradition. Ham, corn and sweet potatoes. Fried chicken, mashed potatoes, gravy and dumplings. Grace recited by Grandpa Pendergast at the long oak

*table draped in lacy white linen. While eating, Uncle Carl told jokes about drunken
Indians. Uncle Rufus argued county politics with Uncle Henry. Alvin's father condemned race music and lantern-slide entertainments, X-ray experiments and the*
Universal News Weekly. *The women at the table chattered among themselves
concerning Sabbatarians and housework, charity bureaus, fussy neighbors, mail-
order houses, and the evils of inebriety. Children invented paragrams and tittered
laughter and received scoldings every few minutes or so. After dinner, the men snuck
down into the basement to smoke cigars and sip bourbon, while the women gathered
in the kitchen for dishwashing and more earnest gossip. Unless it was storming,
the children were sent outdoors to play by the creek until sundown. Too young for
the basement and too old for run-sheep-run, Alvin had no part in any of it except
eating, and believed therefore that not one single Pendergast, Hamill, Chamberlain,
Rutledge, Halverson or Gallup cared less for tradition than did he.*

 *Farm life was a drudgery of frost and manure. Boys wore the stink of it to
school. By horse and walking plow, acres of wild grass became cornrows and hayfields. Corncribs and chicken coops were built with hand-sawed lumber. Cookstoves
heated the kitchen at dawn. Nobody got rich nor went to the County Home. Some
girls slung grain and mended petticoats, others got knocked up in the rafters of a
barn. George Pendergast lost a leg in the mechanical reaper. Cousin Oscar went
crazy from a pig-bite and chased possums at night for the Morris widow down on
Greenfield Road. Snowdrifts buried old Harold Mitchener's duck pond one dark
Christmas and Roy Gallup lost three fingers on his right hand to frostbite when he
fell through the ice chasing a buck across the fenceline. His brother Rudy drowned.
Spring floods stole Auntie Ella's porch and a basketful of kittens. Drought took the
field crops a year later and Alvin's father sold his Ford. Uncle Carl became a barber
and bought a house on Maple Avenue in Farrington. Aunt Marie married a salesman from Texas and raised her children on Cedar Street two blocks from a trolley
stop uptown. Most of the family stayed on. Who else would mend the fences and
curry the horses, asked Granny Chamberlain? A leatherbound Bible inscribed with
five generations of family history sat on a walnut shelf above Aurora Pendergast's
piano, which Alvin passed by in the dark each cold morning before breakfast on his
way to the barn Grandpa Harlan had constructed from timber felled himself three
years after the Civil War. Both the Bible and the barn smelled ancient.*

 *Four years ago, a week before his fifteenth birthday, Alvin Pendergast developed
consumption. It came upon him like a change of seasons, a vague malaise that*

mimicked nothing worse than a persistent cold, unrelenting fatigue in the mornings, a low fever at night. His family thought he had contracted the lazy habits of adolescence and disregarded his complaints. If he worked hard enough, put his heart into the farm like everyone else, the backache he worried about would soon go away. Keep the old beak against the grindstone, Uncle Henry told him, you'll get somewhere. His father growled at him for chores completed too slowly, his mother and sisters pointed out how skinny he looked. Alvin lost ten pounds to a diminished appetite and could no longer lift Aunt Hattie's bushel basket of peaches. His night-sweats worsened and his skin became sallow and waxen and he caught a cough that troubled him for weeks. One morning after a spell of hacking and violent expectoration, he noticed streaks of blood in his handkerchief. Then the doctors came to the farm and diagnosed him as consumptive, infected with pulmonary tuberculosis. They put Alvin on a train and sent him away to a sanitarium. He wept the first week from fear and loneliness. His ward smelled of feces and formaldehyde. He hardly ate at all and had a bellyache for a month. His breathing was so shallow and labored he often thought he was suffocating. He coughed up blood. He was given cold sponge baths and rubbed with alcohol and taken out of doors to sit in the sunlight when the weather permitted. He consumed milk and eggs and calomel and saline laxatives every few days to aid his digestion. He lost another twenty-five pounds. The nurses brought creosote in hot water for his cough and syrup of iodid for his anemia and hypophosphites of lime and soda to reduce his expectorations, and every day cod liver oil, cod liver oil, cod liver oil. The doctors took X-ray photographs of his lungs and pronounced his condition curable. Still, he grew melancholy and refused to speak to his nurses for a month after enduring the artificial pneumothorax treatments. Then his throat became ulcerous and he suffered horrible headaches and sat in bed for another eight weeks and needed the commode and utter silence and nearly forgot who he was or where he had come from. Only his mother was permitted a visit and he scarcely remembered seeing her, though he was told she came often. Finally he began to walk again and converse with his fellow patients out of doors. He learned pottery and basket-making and how to say a few words in French, and eventually his cough went away with the fever as the tubercles dried up, and his breathing returned to normal, and a year after entering the sanitarium, Alvin was put back on a train one morning and sent home.

With the orchestra gone downtown to a late supper, an amplified radio console was broadcasting a lively Turkey Trot when Alvin climbed the wooden bleachers to the circus seats with a bag of hot popcorn. A stinking gray haze of cigarette smoke drifted above the dance floor, obscuring the lettered banners suspended across the upper auditorium.

FARRINGTON DANCE DERBY — 24 HOURS DAILY!!!

DANCING, MUSIC, & SURPRISE ENTERTAINMENTS

WARNING!!! THIS IS A PLACE OF REFINED AMUSEMENT:

NO WHISTLING, STOMPING, CATCALLS!

DO NOT TOUCH CONTESTANTS!

TWO SPRINTS TONIGHT!!

GENTLEMEN: REMOVE YOUR HATS!!!

Alvin hurried to find a seat as a bell rang, ending the rest period. Last night a dancer from Knoxville had gone nuts and tried to strangle a floor judge after being disqualified during a pop-the-whip. Maybe somebody would get shot tonight. Down on the parquet floor, the surviving dancers were barely hanging onto their partners, shuffling disconsolately about in a dreamy rhythm. Behind the orchestra stage, a large scoreboard read:

COUPLES REMAINING: 13
DAYS DANCED: 9
HOURS DANCED: 237

Alvin and Cousin Frenchy had attended the start of the dance derby when the floor was still jammed with fresh contestants. That night all the dancers had kicked up their heels and twirled around and yelled and laughed and danced like crazy while the hot-eyed spectators in the bleachers cheered and cheered, and the master of ceremonies in a red polka dot tie announced that this would be the greatest dance derby of the year and anyone in town who didn't buy a ticket would be missing something pretty swell. Straight away, a pretty redhead wearing a green plaid skirt and shoes dyed gold caught Alvin's eye. She had lovely painted eyelashes and a tiny rosebud mouth whose smile gave him the flutters. Her dance partner was skinny as a candlestick and had oily hair. They did the Charleston and Lindy Hop like a pair of whirly-gigs and won a sprint and took a bow to a fine applause and earned a spray of silver coins from the dollar loge seats. The girl's name was Dorothy Louise Ellison, and she was from Topeka, Kansas. This was her fifth marathon and she'd hoped to win the grand prize in order to go to college out in California where her aunt and uncle owned a lemon grove. Her partner was a homely plumber from Kentucky by the name of Joe Norton. Alvin desperately wanted to take Joe's part with Dorothy. Trouble was, he could hardly dance a two-step without a manual and lacked the stamina in his lungs, and if Dorothy truly needed to win the contest to attend college, she'd want a better partner than a sickly farm boy with two left feet. So Alvin sat under the **NO SPITTING!!!** sign for more than eight hours watching Dorothy and Joe waltz about the dance floor with fifty-six other couples. When Alvin left with Frenchy at half past three in the morning, Dorothy and Joe were still arm-in-arm, dancing a drowsy Fox Trot, and feigning youthful romance for smiling patrons seated on pillows in the loge seats.

Tonight she was gone.

Sitting up in the sweltering grandstand high above the orchestra, Alvin had a good view of the entire auditorium, dancers and spectators alike. He watched Joe Norton come out of a dressing room hallway late from the break with Patsy on his arm and looked at the scoreboard and counted thirteen couples and noticed that all the other dancers were paired up and Dorothy wasn't on the floor. *That plumber sonofabitch got rid of her,* Alvin imagined as his heart sank. *She was probably too good-looking for him.* He considered leaving, but didn't have the pep for much more walking tonight. Besides, where would he go?

The radio program changed to a cheerful waltz.

Most of the dancers were too hot and exhausted to pick up the new rhythm. A floor judge in a referee's pinstripe shirt clapped his hands to speed them up. Behind the loge seats on the far end of the floor, a large hillbilly family stood up to leave, carrying picnic baskets and milk bottles.

Alvin slid down the plank row behind a pair of fat Chevrolet salesmen eating cold fried chicken out of a metal lunch bucket. They smelled like grease. Alvin watched intently as the master of ceremonies, dressed in black top hat and tails, strode onto the orchestra platform and grabbed the microphone. He had a pencil-thin moustache and slicked-backed hair. His assistant, a slinky blonde dressed up in a cowboy hat and spangles, switched off the radio. Behind the emcee, Jimmy Turkel's five-piece orchestra, back from supper break, filed onto the stage. The drummer performed a brief introduction as the lethargic dancers slowed to a shuffle. Applause erupted from the grandstand. Alvin glared at Joe Norton and worried that maybe Dorothy had been injured or taken seriously ill during the week he'd been away at the farm. Why had she chosen that dumbbell Norton in the first place?

"LADIES AND GENTLEMEN! HOW ABOUT A BREAK FOR THESE COURAGEOUS KIDS! AREN'T THEY SWELL?"

The audience cheered loudly.

An elderly man tossed a handful of coins onto the floor from the side railing. A young dance pair dressed in matching blue sailor suits scrambled over to collect it all up while a crowd of college-age fellows gave them a boisterous hip-hip-hurrah.

More people cheered.

The emcee waved his arms to get everyone's attention again. At the rear of the stage stood Arthur Cheney, the derby promoter from Omaha Alvin had seen on the back porch, still puffing on a fat cigar. *Why hadn't Petey taken a poke at him,* Alvin wondered, digging again into his bag of popcorn. *A fellow who blows smoke in your face is just asking for a good crack in the jaw.*

"LADIES AND GENTLEMEN! LADIES AND GENTLEMEN!"

The thirteen dance couples milled about together in the middle of the floor, hardly moving now. The farm boy watched one of the collegiate fellows giving advice over the railing to a blonde in worn-out slippers whose hollow-eyed partner was sagging off her torso.

The emcee tapped the microphone with his fist. "LADIES AND GENTLEMEN! THESE KIDS ARE SO COURAGEOUS, AREN'T THEY? HEROES, EVERY LAST ONE OF THEM! RIGHT OUT OF THE TOP DRAWER! AND THEY AREN'T DONE YET, ARE THEY? YOU BET THEY AREN'T! NO SIRREE! THEY KNOW HOW HARD YOU'RE PULLING FOR THEM AND THEY'LL DO THEIR BEST TO SEE THEY DON'T LET YOU DOWN! YOU CAN COUNT ON IT!"

Spectators in the grandstand rose to give the dancers a big ovation, several of whom appeared bewildered by the cheering. Since Dorothy was gone, Alvin hardly clapped at all. He didn't much care who won now.

The emcee grinned brightly as he spoke into the microphone again. "WHY, THEY'VE SURE GOT A LOT OF GUTS, ALL RIGHT, THESE KIDS OF OURS, DON'T THEY?"

Alvin felt the wooden planks rumble under his feet from the roar that swept the auditorium as the orchestra struck up a boisterous "Yankee Doodle Dandy." The emcee raised his voice. "BUT HONESTLY, LADIES AND GENTLEMEN, HOW LONG CAN THEY LAST? I ASK YOU, HOW-LONG-CAN-THEY-LAST?"

Across the floor, a knot of people in the loge seats began clapping. More coins showered the sluggish dancers. Alvin watched a homely nurse come out from the dressing room with a bottle of smelling salts. The orchestra played a couple bars of "Dixie."

"NOW, LADIES AND GENTLEMEN, WE PROMISED YOU THESE KIDS WOULD DO THEIR BEST ON THE FLOOR, AND BELIEVE YOU ME, LADIES AND GENTLEMEN, THEY HAVE. OH, YOU BET THEY HAVE! NINE DAYS, LADIES AND GENTLEMEN, NINE DAYS, THEY'VE BATTLED NOT ONLY EACH OTHER, BUT FATHER TIME HIMSELF TO KEEP GOING BECAUSE, WHY, THEY JUST KNOW YOU'RE ALL BEHIND THEM! SURE, THEY'VE GOT BUNIONS AND

BLISTERS, BUT OH, THEY'VE GOT MORE THAN ENOUGH GUTS, TOO, TO STICK IT OUT TO THE VERY END AND WIN THIS GREAT DANCE DERBY FAIR AND SQUARE FOR THOSE OF YOU WHO REALLY CARE TO SEE 'EM DO IT! WHAT DO YOU SAY ABOUT THAT?"

The farm boy almost toppled over as the old bleachers shook under the ovation.

"WELL, LADIES AND GENTLEMEN, IT'S TIME TO TURN ON THE HEAT AGAIN, SO PICK OUT YOUR FAVORITE COUPLE AND GIVE 'EM A BREAK BECAUSE THEY'LL NEED ALL THE BOOST THEY CAN GET!"

The emcee motioned to another heat judge waiting just off the platform. More people were crowding into the next row above, shoving along toward the center of the bleachers. Alvin felt like a sardine in his own row and considered switching seats to somewhere higher up.

"MISTER CLARK, ARE YOU READY?"

The bald heat judge nodded.

A buzz swept through the audience.

The emcee drew the microphone close while raising his right hand into the smoky air. "LADIES AND GENTLEMEN, ARE YOU READY?"

A further deafening cheer shook the building. Alvin craned his neck to see through the pack in front of him. A stout woman to his left jammed her elbow into his ribs to make room. He pushed back as the emcee announced to the auditorium spectators, "WELL, THEN, LADIES AND GENTLEMEN, LET'S SEE HOW LONG THESE BRAVE KIDS CAN LAST! MISTER CLARK, HOW ABOUT A SPRINT?" He turned to Turkel. "MAESTRO, GET READY TO GIVE!"

The heat judge walked into the middle of the dance floor where a painted oval marked off a racetrack for the competitors. Alvin felt someone shove roughly into the row beside him.

"Sorry, kid," the fellow said, as he wedged down between Alvin and the stout woman. He was wearing a felt fedora and a smart blue cassimere suit. "Some local yokel kept stepping on my foot up there."

He smelled like whiskey and hair tonic.

"Ain't a lot of room here, neither," Alvin muttered, watching the dance couples tie together for the sprint. He hated getting shoved, particularly when he didn't feel well.

"You got a favorite?"

"Huh?"

"This derby's hired some real cutie pies, don't you agree?"

Alvin shrugged. "I seen a doll last week, but she ain't here no more." He watched Joe Norton fasten a belt onto Patsy's waist for the sprint and give her a kiss on the cheek. Alvin hoped they'd both trip and break their necks.

"Maybe some fellow bought her off the floor and married her afterward. What was her name?"

"I don't know," he lied, figuring this fellow probably didn't care, anyhow. Besides, he thought of Dorothy as his girl and that wasn't anybody's business but his own.

The dancers were packed together behind a white ribbon at the starting line, jostling for position. Another trio of floor judges came out from behind the grandstand. All three looked like sourpusses. Some people booed and hissed when these judges took their places on the dance floor.

After the emcee backed away from the microphone, Turkel's orchestra struck up a rousing "Stars and Stripes Forever" as the audience stood to watch the sprint. Joe Norton and Patsy were tucked so far back now Alvin could hardly see them, but in front of the pack were a sweetheart couple from Ohio lots of people seemed to be boosting and a slick pair of Mexican dancers nobody much cared for at all.

The fellow spoke into the farm boy's ear, "I got a sawbuck says I can predict which couple's out after this sprint."

"Oh yeah?" said Alvin, his attention fixed on the heat judge whose arm was raised at the starting line. *If Dorothy'd been in this sprint*, he thought, *she'd be out front where everyone could see how swell she looked.*

The fellow dropped his voice. "Don't you know most of these marathons are a slice of tripe? Why, oiling one of the floor judges'll give you the dope on who wins and who gets the air any night of the week."

"Says who?" Alvin growled. He wanted the sprint to start so he could watch Joe Norton and Patsy fail miserably before the whole auditorium. Maybe somebody would even throw a tomato at 'em.

"Says I."

"Yeah, how do you know?"

The fellow laughed. "Well, for starters, I've seen a million of them, that's how. Why, marathon dances were standing them up in Chicago all last summer."

The heat judge's whistle shrieked and the sprint began, thirteen dance couples galloping through the ribbon like the start of a horse race. Spectators howled with excitement. Six couples hit the first turn in a thick pack, scrambling for the lead. Turkel's orchestra played a fast and spirited "California, Here I Come," while the audience down by the floor urged their favorite couples to greater speed. Tied together with a belt, whichever partner had the most pluck and fortitude after nine days of dancing dragged the other around the oval, panicked and invigorated by the knowledge that the team finishing last would be cut out of the derby. All about the auditorium, people screamed and shouted for their favorite contestants to go faster and faster, and razzing those they didn't like. Couples stumbled and fought to regain balance. Those who fell hurried to get back on their feet again. Round and round they went, faces horrid with agony. Alvin rooted for Patsy to take a spill or Joe Norton to drop dead. One athletic-looking boy got wobbly-knee'd on the far turn and his partner, a tiny brunette, jammed her shoulder underneath his arm and began dragging him onward, screaming in his ear while the spectators roared for them to keep up. The parquet dance floor became slick with sweat. Desperate couples skidded and slipped. Turkel's orchestra played a fast Peabody and the emcee grabbed the microphone and exhorted the beleaguered dancers to "HURRY! HURRY! HURRY! TIME'S RUNNING OUT, KIDS! DON'T FALL BEHIND! DON'T FALL BEHIND!"

Alvin felt an elbow nudge him in the ribs. His new friend leaned over close to his ear and said, "See those two in the blue sailor suits?"

The farm boy nodded. Those were the Italians from Indiana. "What of it?"

The emcee announced with undisguised glee, "THREE MIN-UTES TO GO, KIDS! THREE MINUTES! HURRY, HURRY, HURRY!"

"Well, they're getting the air."

"Says who?"

"One of Cheney's stooges caught 'em having a lay under the bleachers. I hear the birdie had a flask of gin in her skirt. Some dick from town wanted to prefer charges."

"That's a good laugh," Alvin said, as Joe Norton and Patsy lunged past a couple wearing athletic shirts and shorts soaked in sweat. The dance floor was a frenzy of roughhousing competitors pushing and shoving, male and female alike, battling frantically for position on the final few laps of the sprint. All the spectators were standing now and Alvin found the clamor deafening. He was getting a headache.

The fellow beside him raised his voice above the racket. "You just watch and see if I'm not right."

"Sure I will."

The buoyant emcee cried into the microphone, "ONE MIN-UTE TO GO, KIDS! ONLY ONE MORE MINUTE! HOLD ON! DON'T QUIT NOW! HURRY, HURRY, HURRY!"

Around the track went all thirteen dance couples, struggling to keep upright, racing desperately for the finish. Joe and Patsy were in the middle of the pack just behind the sweetheart couple, but Alvin didn't know how many laps they'd taken. That's what mattered. Whichever team did the most laps won. Fewest laps meant disqualification. Falls earned deductions, too. Joe and Patsy'd had two, but some of the other couples had more than that. All were badly played out. "THIRTY SECONDS, KIDS! ONLY THIRTY SECONDS! HURRY NOW! HURRY!"

Alvin looked for the Italian dance pair wearing sailor suits and saw they were far ahead of Joe and Patsy, just three couples off the lead and heading around the near turn. The oily Mexican pair were dead last and fading, but nobody had sponsored them, anyhow. From where Alvin was standing, it seemed that the sweetheart couple were set to win if they didn't trip up.

Turkel's orchestra finished playing just as the heat judge blew his whistle, ending the sprint. Half of the couples on the dance floor collapsed. Spectators cheered wildly with appreciation while a crew of trainers in white hospital dress rushed out of the dressing rooms, dragging several iron cots for those competitors most badly stricken with exhaustion. Alvin saw Patsy and Joe sitting on the railing near the orchestra platform. Patsy hung her head on Joe's sweaty shoulder. The skinny plumber's eyes were shut. A smartly-dressed Negro sitting just behind them in the loge seats was patting Joe on the back. Alvin guessed he didn't know about Dorothy.

A crowd was gathering near the microphone. The bald heat judge had climbed up from the dance floor and met Cheney and the emcee. Turkel watched for his cue to begin the music that would announce the winners of the sprint.

"Now you'll see," said the fellow beside Alvin. He snuck a silver hipflask from his jacket and enjoyed a quick nip. Then he chuckled and hid it away again. "Why, I doubt any of these marathons are on the up-and-up."

Alvin frowned. "Go on, tell me some more."

"Fact is, the dance derby's just another dirty goldbrick game."

"Oh yeah?"

The fellow took out his bag of peanuts. "I tell you, it's crooked as all hell."

"Says you," Alvin growled. He hated hearing bunk like this. Uncle Henry knocked the derby himself all through dinner last Sunday and he'd never been to one in his life.

The fellow grinned. "You think I'm a joykiller, huh?"

"You said it." *Why didn't this fellow go take a hike?*

"Well," the fellow replied, eating a handful of peanuts, "it wouldn't bust me up to be wrong, but if I am, I'll eat your hat."

The emcee took the microphone in hand. "LADIES AND GENTLEMEN!"

A big cheer went up from the grandstand.

He raised a hand to quiet the audience. Cheney stood in close behind him with the contingent of derby sponsors flanking both men.

"LADIES AND GENTLEMEN! PLEASE!"

Alvin saw Joe Norton shaking hands with the Negro at the loge seats. Patsy was moving forward to the orchestra platform. Joe Norton followed her past the iron cots. Elrod Tarwater, a policemen Alvin knew from downtown, stood at the corner of the orchestra next to that stout fellow Gus who'd punched Petey in the mouth out back.

"LADIES AND GENTLEMEN, AREN'T THESE KIDS WONDERFUL?"

Another big cheer jolted the auditorium.

"YOU BET THEY ARE! AND WE'RE NOT FINISHED YET! NO SIRREE! NOT BY A LONG SHOT! THESE KIDS HAVE PLEDGED TO KEEP ON GOING SO LONG AS YOU COME OUT AND PULL FOR 'EM JUST AS HARD AS YOU'VE BEEN DOING ALL THIS WEEK! LADIES AND GENTLEMEN, WHAT DO YOU HAVE TO SAY ABOUT THAT?"

The audience thundered their approval.

"NOW, OUR FINE TEAM OF FLOOR JUDGES … "

A flurry of boos cascaded down from the upper bleachers.

" … HAVE TABULATED THE OFFICIAL LAP RESULTS OF THIS EVENING'S SPRINT AND I MUST TELL YOU I'VE NEVER WITNESSED A TRUER EXAMPLE OF COURAGE AND PERSEVERANCE! THESE KIDS CERTAINLY PUT IT OVER FOR US, AND I TAKE NO JOY IN HAVING TO ELIMINATE ONE OF THESE BRAVE TEAMS, BUT, LADIES AND GENTLEMEN, RULES ARE RULES. THEREFORE … " The emcee reached into his vest pocket and withdrew a small white card. "FOLKS, LET'S GIVE A HEARTY FAREWELL TO OUR LOVELY FRIENDS FROM THE GREAT STATE OF INDIANA … BUDDY AND EILEEN ROMERO!"

Alvin sucked in his breath as a spotlight from the rafters high above the platform flashed down through the smoky haze to illuminate two contestants wearing blue navy sailor suits.

"Ha!" Alvin's friend cried. Wadding up his empty peanut bag, he began clapping with the rest of the auditorium. "Well, kid, can you feature that?"

Buddy and Eileen Romero looked shocked, tears falling now.

"Aw, what do you know?" Alvin mumbled, both angry and mystified. *Who got this wiseacre told the derby wasn't on the level?*

From the platform, the emcee called down to them. "COME ON UP HERE, KIDS! TAKE A BOW FOR ALL YOUR FRIENDS!"

Buddy Romero barked at a floor judge who quickly turned his back. Eileen Romero stumbled into one of the iron cots. Loud applause from the grandstand persisted. Both were showered with silver from the best-dressed people in the loge seats. Neither seemed to notice and continued forward without stopping to retrieve the coins.

Still clapping, the fellow told Alvin, "See, it really gets me how these sapheads won't play the game fair and square."

Gus came to the front of the platform with another pair of trainers and helped Buddy and Eileen Romero up from the dance floor. A spray of coins greeted them there. The emcee waved to Turkel whose orchestra struck up a lively few bars of "Blue Skies."

Alvin saw Buddy Romero receive a certificate and a handshake from Cheney while Eileen Romero wept. Gus escorted them to the back of the platform to a loud ovation. Then the emcee signaled Turkel for a drum roll. Cheney lit up a fat cigar. Those dance couples not passed out on iron cots milled about looking flummoxed and wan.

"Sorry, kid," said the fellow beside Alvin, dumping the empty peanut bag under his bench seat. "I told you, it ain't copacetic."

"Aw, phooey on you, too." He was feeling sick again. His head hurt and his stomach was queasy.

Now the emcee spoke into the microphone with a big grin on his face. "LADIES AND GENTLEMEN! LADIES AND GENTLEMEN!"

Alvin saw Petey in a crouch next to the platform bunting. What was he doing there?

"WELL, WE'VE HAD A REAL SURPRISE TONIGHT! THAT SPRINT WAS QUITE A GRIND, WASN'T IT?"

Joe Norton and Patsy were on the far side of the platform now. Alvin watched a photographer take a flash picture of them with one of the businessmen from downtown.

"YOU SEE, ALL OF OUR KIDS PROVED THEY'VE GOT THE PLUCK TO EARN A PRIZE IN THIS DERBY, BUT LADIES AND GENTLEMEN, TONIGHT ONE TEAM REALLY SHOWED THEIR TRUE COLORS WHEN WE TURNED ON THE HEAT!"

The popular sweetheart couple stood arm-in-arm on the dance floor directly in front of the platform, all pep and smiles.

"LADIES AND GENTLEMEN, LET'S MEET OUR WIN— NERS … "

Another drum roll was summoned from Turkel's orchestra as a shower of silver coins rained over the beaming sweetheart couple.

" … FROM LEXINGTON, KENTUCKY AND JOHNSTOWN, PENNSYLVANIA … JOE NORTON AND PATSY McCARDLE!"

The audience roared with delight. A cloud of balloons was released from the rafters. Firecrackers exploded here and there.

"Hey, they didn't win!" Alvin shouted. "That ain't fair! I tell you, they didn't win!"

"What'd I say?" The fellow beside him laughed aloud.

Down on the littered parquet dance floor, the sweetheart couple was still smiling for their sponsors, displaying the good sportsmanship and sunny dispositions they knew paid dividends in the long run. A woman wearing a gingham apron dress rose and blew them a kiss. Maybe they didn't win tonight, but the marathon was far from over, so the couple from Ohio persisted in waving brightly to their staunchest supporters. Alvin saw Petey sneak up onto the platform while everyone else's attention was drawn to Joe and Patsy crossing the stage past Elrod Tarwater under a blazing spotlight to the microphone where Arthur Cheney stood with his master of ceremonies and a shiny gold trophy. Alvin thought there must have been two dozen people up on the platform now, crowding closer and closer to the microphone, swarming about Joe and Patsy and Arthur Cheney and his emcee. People around the auditorium were shouting and whistling and stamping their feet as Joe raised the trophy high over his head and Patsy gave him a kiss for the cameras and Cheney lifted his own cigar in triumph. Through the crush of celebrants under the hot lights of the auditorium, Alvin saw Petey shove close enough to swing a small pocketknife in a balled-up fist hard down onto the back of Arthur Cheney's neck. Both Cheney and Petey disappeared into the crowd as the promoter fell. Tarwater knocked over the microphone. Alvin thought he heard Patsy scream. More policemen and trainers rushed forward from backstage.

Then the platform collapsed and the rest was pandemonium.

The evening breeze carried a honey scent of fresh blossoms from a shady home orchard in the next lot as Alvin watched ambulance attendants carry the injured on stretchers from the auditorium while dozens of police and firemen and newspaper reporters and derby patrons milled about.

The smart-mouthed fellow in the blue cassimere suit lit a cigarette in the shadows. He and Alvin had departed the auditorium together through a side door under the old bleachers just ahead of a panicked crowd. Alvin held onto his sack of popcorn and ate a salty handful as his new friend tossed the dead match away into the scruffy grass. *Maybe this fellow ain't half bad*, he thought. *He didn't charge me a dime to find out the derby was a cheat. Now I got something to tell Frenchy he probably don't even know.*

Cousin Frenchy.

He'd slipped Alvin the dope about Doc Hartley coming out to the farm for a chat with Alvin's mom and pop. *Everyone knew Alvin didn't look too good. He'd lost weight and color, and wasn't he coughing again? He couldn't work hardly at all in the fields, got tired too soon, wasn't even strong enough to push a loaded wheelbarrow from one end of the yard to another. He needed treatments again. He was having a relapse. If he didn't go back into the sanitarium, he might not be around for Christmas.* Alvin had no intention of returning to the sanitarium, even though when he woke during the night, his bed sheets were damp with sweat and sometimes he coughed so hard he choked. But the sanitarium doctors had promised him he was cured, that all he needed was lots of sunshine and fresh air and a little rest from time to time. They had lied to him, so he didn't trust them any longer, and if he was going to croak, he didn't want it to be in one of those cold wards that had already stolen a year of his life.

Alvin watched as one of the ambulances left the auditorium for Mercy Hospital downtown. A gust of wind rippled through the dark maples overhead. More people came outdoors.

"That was a close shave," his new friend said, flicking ash off his cigarette.

"That kid Petey's off his head."

"They're all cuckoo, if you ask me."

"You ain't by yourself."

The fellow approached him with a smile. "Say, we haven't really met, have we? My name's Chester Burke."

He offered a firm handshake, which Alvin accepted.

"Alvin Pendergast, sir. Pleased to know you." That was sincere, too. He liked this fellow because he'd been friendly, unlike most people Alvin knew.

"I guess you're local, aren't you? Live in town?"

Alvin nodded. "We got a farm three miles north of here off Wasson Road. It ain't that far."

"Gee, I'll bet that's hard work," Chester said, after a drag off his cigarette. Another ambulance arrived.

"Sure it is," Alvin replied, watching several attendants hurry out to meet it. They reminded him of those fellows who helped carry the dead out of the consumption wards in the sanitarium.

"My uncle hired me onto his hog farm one summer when I was about your age, but I funked it after a month and went home."

"Slopping hogs don't stir you up much."

A tiny woman in a net frock stood behind the attendants as another of the injured was hoisted into the ambulance.

Chester chuckled. "You aren't sore on farming, are you?"

"Naw, it's a panic." Of course he hated it, and everyone in the family knew it, too. They said he was just lazy even when he wasn't sick, which was sort of true, but who's got a smile and a jump in his step for something he can't stand?

"Well, I learned myself a long time ago that it can go pretty hard with a fellow who supplies the sweat on somebody else's safety valve."

Alvin watched Chester take out the silver hip flask again, unscrew it and tip it toward his mouth. Nothing came out. Chester frowned and shook it over the grass and saw it was empty. Then he grinned at Alvin. "Say, is there any place a fellow can get a drink around here?"

Another loaded ambulance left the auditorium, siren wailing across the windy night. Looking over his shoulder, Alvin told Chester, "See this road here?"

"Sure."

"Well, if you follow it down two blocks to an alleyway just past a big blackberry patch, you'll see the old Wickland house on the corner there. Go past it all the way to the end of the alley where you'll find a little gray shack under a big hackberry tree. It belongs to a lady named Marge Bradford, and it's the only place you *can't* get a drink in this town."

Then Alvin laughed.

So did Chester. "That's a swell joke, kid. I like you. I suppose not all farmers are hicks, are they?"

"My uncle Rufus says farmers raise corn, corn makes whiskey, whiskey makes Prohibition agents, and Prohibition agents raise hell."

Chester laughed again. "Why, that's a good one, too."

Alvin grinned, starting to feel better somehow. "He's a jokey old bird."

The thick maples swayed in a cold wind gust. Chester asked, "Have you had any supper tonight, kid?"

"I ate a sandwich." He didn't have much appetite today.

"Well, are you still hungry a little? Reason I ask is, I thought maybe you and me'd find a night lunchroom somewhere and have ourselves something to eat. If you've already had your supper, I'll set you up to a piece of pie. What do you say? I haven't eaten since noon and I'm getting an awful bellyache."

Alvin smiled. "I like pie."

"Well, then, let's shoot the works," Chester said, disposing of his cigarette. "Follow me."

He had parked under a ragged oak at the upper corner of the parking lot. Alvin saw a shiny tan Packard Six hidden in the shadows.

"Gee, this is a pretty swell auto."

Alvin had never seen a Six in the flesh before, only a magazine advertisement that named Packards *"The supreme combination of all that is fine in motor cars. Ask the man who owns one."*

"It's nifty, all right," Chester said, unlocking the door. He climbed into the driver's seat, and reached across to open the passenger door. "Come on, kid. Hop in."

"Sure."

The farm boy climbed into the car as Chester fired up the engine. The interior smelled like cigarettes and gin. A pair of old leather valises were jammed in front of a bunch of boxes in the backseat. Alvin had never been inside of a fine motorcar. He liked it.

At the stop sign on the corner, Chester asked, "Where should we eat?"

"Well, tell the truth," Alvin confessed, "there ain't really nothing open 'round here after dark." Where was he going, anyhow? It'd be a hell of a long walk home by moonlight and he had already begun to feel weak. He sure didn't want to come home wheezing and have everyone in the family see how bad off he was.

"How about the other side of the river?" Chester asked, letting another automobile pass by before he went right.

"I guess so. There's a flock of hotels."

"Should we drive over?"

Alvin shrugged. "All right."

Chester turned at the stop sign, then drove quickly west along Buchanon Street. Most of the framehouses still had lights on, but the sidewalks were empty and the neighborhood was quiet. Alvin knew he had to feed the dairy cows in the morning and replace the floorboards in one of Uncle Henry's barn stalls and help fix his old disc harrow. He also knew Doc Hartley was coming out to the farm tomorrow afternoon to give him another once-over and maybe decide it was time for Alvin's folks to buy another train ticket on the Limited back to the sanitarium. That spooked him something fierce.

Chester asked, "Ever been across the Mississippi this time of night?"

"Not by motor."

"Well, you see, I've got appointments in Hannibal and New London tomorrow. Maybe we ought to hire a couple of rooms, stay over a night or so. What do you think?"

"I ain't got any money."

"We can tackle that tomorrow," Chester said, steering around another corner. The bridge was up ahead, rising out of a cypress grove. "Say, maybe you can help me out in New London. I could sure use a partner who's willing to put in an honest day's work."

"What would I have to do?"

Chester laughed. "Well, you wouldn't be slopping hogs."

Alvin felt his face flush. Now he was really scared. This fellow was asking him to quit the farm, which he hated, without letting anyone know about it, and by noon everyone in the family would say that poor sick Alvin was too dumb to understand just how important it was that he begin his pneumothorax treatments all over again.

Chester swung the Packard onto the bridge that led west across the Mississippi River. Both windows were open and a draft swirled through, cold and nightdamp.

"Well, what do you say, kid? I won't kick about it if you say no, but you have to choose now. I got supper waiting for me on the other side of this bridge."

Life was strange, Alvin thought, as a sort of weary exhilaration came over him. He had walked three miles to the derby and that was a long haul when he lived on the farm, but last week his only true ambition had been to go fishing Saturday morning with Frenchy, maybe lie on a summer hammock afterward by a hackberry grove near the creek. So he said to this fellow he hadn't even known an hour ago, "I guess I'll take that pie."

Chester put the Packard back into gear. "You sure you're not going to pull out of it? It's pretty easy to get bitter if somebody goes back on you."

"No, sir."

"You're a brick, kid."

"Thanks."

INTERLUDE
CHARLIE PENDERGAST

ROUTE 66

WHEN I WAS A BOY, Uncle Henry still walked behind a horse and plow to plant his cornfield on the Pendergast farm in northwest Illinois. Most of the family lived on farms, but we owned a house on Maple Avenue in Farrington where the summer elms were shady and the trolley rolled past out front. My father was a barber. He had a shop downtown on Second Street with Uncle Monroe and another fellow named Lloyd Neumann. It was a three-chair operation with a shoeshine porter in the back corner, and it was often busy: men sitting on the bench chatting or reading magazines while waiting to get a haircut. Father charged thirty-five cents, and that might not seem like a whole lot, but a movie ticket cost thirty cents, a dime for kids, and popcorn was a nickel, so we knew the value of a dollar and learned not to spend our money unwisely.

My mother was a kind woman with a gentle voice who wore clean freshly pressed dresses, and made sweet pastry rosettes at Christmas and a wonderful lemon pie with a delicate crust that everyone agreed was about the best in the whole world. We had a small, simple home with two bedrooms upstairs and a basement below the kitchen, and a backyard just big enough to throw the ball around or make a little ice rink in the winter. I was an only child, but I had cousins to play with and no lack of amusements. Every other Sunday, Mother and Father and I went out to Uncle Henry's farm for dinner. Most of the family would be there and cousin Bebbins and I always made a game of chasing about the barnyard, though the big dogs Uncle Henry owned scared me to death and our older cousins enjoyed shoving us down in the manure or pelting us with filthy corn cobs. One Sunday, cousins Rubin and Russell pushed me from the hayloft and I broke my wrist, which made Mother so angry she refused to go back out to the farm for almost a year. I suppose she spoiled me when I was young, but who can resist being babied by his mother?

When I was nine, we went to California by motor car. How it happened was this: most Fridays, we would drive out to Uncle Harris's house on Seward Road so my parents could have a game of Five Hundred with him and Aunt Lottie, while Bebbins and little Shirley and I would play in the basement or listen to the radio in the kitchen. One night, we heard our folks talking about Uncle Monroe's adopted boy Howard who caught t.b. and how Auntie Leah wanted to take him to the California desert where the dry climate would be better for him than the sanitarium cousin Alvin had gone into. Mother and Aunt Lottie came up with the idea that we ought to go out there to the desert to keep them company, and Father thought that was all right by him. He could cut hair and smoke his cigars anywhere. He told Mother that Lloyd Neumann had already been hinting about a couple of fellows from Pontiac who were looking for a barbershop to hire. Uncle Harris worked for a creamery as a milkman and said he guessed people out in California needed their milk delivered, too. He'd go if we did.

The next day we drove out to Aunt Clara's tumbledown house on a tall embankment at the edge of town to see what she thought. Clara was Mother's favorite great-aunt and spent most of her day smoking cigarettes and puttering about a decaying orchard out back. She was supposedly in her late seventies, but nobody knew for sure and Clara refused to tell her age or wear her false teeth except at the supper table. Once after she'd locked herself out of the house, I remember Father asking her why she didn't just go to the old folks home. She told him, "Well, you gotta to be old to go there."

"Well, how old do you have to be, Clara?"

"Oh, I don't know," she said, "about a hundred, I guess."

When we arrived at her house, it was empty and all the windows were open and the rooms had filled with flies. Father went next door where the fellow there told him Clara had gone to town. Mother decided we ought to buy some bug spray to kill the flies, so we piled back into the Ford and drove off. Near town, we spotted Clara coming down the road barefoot in a flowered cotton dress and a big elephant leaf hair-pinned to her head. Father pulled over and asked Clara what that leaf was doing on her head and she told him she had to do something to keep the sun out of her eyes. Then she climbed into the backseat with me and we brought her home. When Mother asked Clara why she'd left all the windows open, she said it was because of the morning sun on the roof. "It got so hot, honey," Clara told her, "the sparrows laid on their backs and blew on their feet."

She fixed a pot of coffee and put out some peanut butter cookies for me and Mother, while Father explained about the plan to go to California to be with Monroe and Leah. Clara didn't care much for Uncle Harris and said she wouldn't ride with him to heaven in Ezekiel's chariot, but if my mother felt a need to take a trip, why, that's what she ought to do. Father agreed and when we left to drive back to town, Mother decided we would go to California. She sent a telegraph to Auntie Leah telling her we were coming, and a couple of weeks later Uncle Monroe wired back about a nice house on a street corner in Needles they'd found for us. At the farm on Easter Sunday, the family gave us all a swell send off with ham and sweet potatoes, cake and ice cream, and nobody threw dirty corn cobs or pushed me and Bebbins into the manure piles behind Uncle Henry's barn. Auntie Eff took our home on Maple Avenue while we were gone, and Lloyd Neumann got the barbershop squared away with those two fellows from Pontiac.

The next day we left Illinois: cousin Bebbins and his family in Uncle Harris's De Soto, and us in our 1928 Ford. The trip took two weeks on Route 66, and it was one of the most remarkable episodes we ever had. Back then, most of the roads were just gravel and Father couldn't drive much over thirty-five miles an hour. There were no motels, so each night we slept in tents and Mother cooked our meals over a little portable gas stove. Uncle Harris had bought a whole set of fountain pens in various sizes with a sort of glass point and told Father that wherever we stopped for groceries, we could sell the pens for two dollars a piece because the points were unbreakable. In those days, if you dropped an ordinary fountain pen, and it landed on the point and bent it, the pen was ruined for good. But Uncle Harris claimed his glass point pens were revolutionary, and each time we stopped for groceries or gas, he and Father would demonstrate the pen points by banging them down on a counter top to prove the pens still wrote, which they did except for the time Father accidentally broke one of them at a Phillips 66 gas station in Oklahoma. Of course, Bebbins and I borrowed one of Uncle Harris's glass point pens one night at a tourist camp in New Mexico and had no trouble at all breaking the point on a rock. Little Shirley thought the shards looked so pretty sparkling in the moonlight that she brought Aunt Lottie to see them and wound up with a spanking, just after our own.

The year before our trip, a Cherokee Indian by the name of Andy Payne had won the "Bunion Derby," a footrace along the entire length of Route 66, and it seemed incredible to us driving west on the same road that anyone could have run that distance. Aunt Lottie brought her Kodak and made Uncle Harris pull off the road every so often to let her take a picture of some interesting sight. In Missouri, we visited Fisher's Cave where it was so dark, Mother said she felt like lying down and having a nap. There were auto smash-ups to look at now and then, lots of trees and bridges and filling stations, oil wells and cattle herds, Indian tepees in Oklahoma. Father laughed and honked the horn every time he saw the red Burma-Shave signs:

"DOES YOUR HUSBAND"
"MISBEHAVE"
"GRUNT AND GRUMBLE"
"RANT AND RAVE?"
"SHOOT THE BRUTE SOME"
"Burma-Shave"

Bebbins counted up all the snakes and armadilloes flattened on the road in Texas. Mother picked flowers wherever we stopped to do a toilet. Aunt Lottie took a Kodak of every church we passed. We kept up a good pace the whole way except when Uncle Harris got stuck in the mud for three hours one morning at the Jericho Gap, and the bowl of chili Mother fed me in Albuquerque kept us parked for another four hours. I remember how the Rocky Mountains looked like clouds in the distance the morning we first saw them from our picnic table at a tourist camp in New Mexico, and how excited Father was to rap his knuckles on a log in the Petrified Forest, how little Shirley cried when Aunt Lottie told her she couldn't really adopt a jackalope because there was no such thing, and how upset Mother got when I threw up in the backseat of the Ford halfway through the twisting grade to Oatman, Arizona. We were happy to cross that final bridge over the Colorado River into California, but we also knew we'd done something pretty remarkable driving from Illinois, and I remember Mother crying her happy tears that warm evening when she finally saw Auntie Leah on our new front porch.

METROPOLIS

HARRY HENNESEY STOOD under the bright neon-lit marquee of the Orpheum Theater at 10th Street and Roosevelt Boulevard, three people from the ticket window, watching thousands of raindrops sparkle on the night sidewalk. A strong wind off the river ripped and tore at umbrellas belonging to crowds of pedestrians emerging from the 9th Street subway. Fancy-dressed women in fur-trimmed coats and cloche hats and high-heels and chic silk scarves skirted widening puddles. Men in gray felt fedoras and dark overcoats hurried past or hid under arched doorways, smoking cigarettes and exchanging subtle glances with passing strangers. Streams of glittering automobiles thundered by, motor horns roaring.

An attractive woman in a wool fox-grey coat purchased tickets for herself and a little boy in a black rain slicker who huddled beside her gripping a sack of Jolly Time Pop Corn. A burly fellow in the long brown overcoat ahead of Harry put away his umbrella as he shuffled up to the box office. The great electric sign flickering atop the Orpheum marquee gilded the oily sidewalk puddles. Feeling chilled, Harry put his back to the damp wind and enviously watched a determined crowd of young collegiates in smart raincoats rush by toward a brightly lit spaghetti parlor up the street. A pretty blonde seated in the box office tapped at the ticket window to gain Harry's attention. She smiled sweetly as he approached. "Good evening!"

"One, please." He paid with a couple of coins. "What do you think of the show tonight? Is it worth all this? I may not be able to eat later on." He gave her a cheerful wink.

"Oh, it's as good as they make 'em!" She handed him the ticket. "I'm sure you'll enjoy it."

"I'm sure I will. Thank you, dear."

The grand theater lobby was decorated with oriental carpets and potted palms and Venetian crystal chandeliers, and smelled of perfume from the ladies' powder room. Harry unbuttoned his damp raincoat while reading lobby cards that announced the daily program and the organist: a Mr. Richard Reutlinger. Theater patrons wandered in and out of the auditorium. Not since Kansas City had Harry been to a revue or a photoplay house. Lately, most of his evenings were full up with scheduling business engagements aimed at reorganizing himself. His desk at Transfer & Storage on 83rd Street was cluttered with opportunities and memoranda, many requiring immediate replies. Sometimes he wished he had taken an instruction course in speedwriting. Often after supper, he would listen to dinner music on NBC radio up in his apartment while revising strategies, scouring the late edition for fresh ideas, tomorrow's biggest racket.

Down in Bellemont, Marie was still bitter about his selling the house on Cedar Street, and his mother felt crowded by the children. He had tried explaining to his dear wife by letters and long distance telephone that things weren't so wonderful here, either. The big warehouse where he had hired his space was old and gloomy, and the fellows working beside him there weren't exactly out of the top drawer. The rich industrialist who owned the building popped in every so often for a word with some of them, but rarely had more than a nod and a smile for Harry. In the past, that sort of slight would have wormed into his disposition, leaving him dour and worried that his competitors were gaining an edge on him. But these days he simply hadn't the luxury of looking over his shoulder. Once you divide your family geographically for economic considerations, your obligation to them becomes paramount and that drive to succeed accepts no distractions. Harry needed to earn several thousand dollars in the next few months if he had any hope at all of restoring Marie's confidence. And that wasn't even half of it. Nobody wants to be associated with failure, and anyone doing business with Harry needed to know he was one of the hurry-come-ups if that trust in him had a dollar value. Every successful fellow in America these days had a certain sparkle in his eye, recognizable to clients and colleagues alike. That sparkle was earned in the marketplace, and proven on the bottom line.

Trouble was, too much work left him worn out, his spirits flat. Even Rockefeller himself had written how, "every businessman ought to have a hobby. It refreshes him, braces him to meet the strains of business while offering a resource to fall back upon after he has left business behind." During college, Harry swam and boxed in the gymnasium for exercise. When he was older and employed at the stockyards, he went to ballgames with several of his clients. At St. Paul, he played billiards three or four times a week. That was fine for small amusements, but what he really wanted was to take a long holiday abroad. In his entire life, Harry hadn't been anywhere except down to the Gulf of Mexico, when he still lived in Texas, and up north to Winnipeg and Quebec City on a handful of selling trips. But Canada doesn't count as a travel destination when what you really want to do is swim the Hellespont. More than a few of the fellows he knew at State left for Europe after graduation and came back in the fall with stories that made Harry sick with envy. Willard Stanton and Tom Carleton bragged about making love to a pair of English schoolgirls inside the Parthenon; Abner Knapp and George Arnett told a wild story about a month spent drinking absinthe at sunset on the Bay of Naples with a Florentine Countess and her four promiscuous daughters; Parmer Haynes rode the Orient Express alone from Paris to Constantinople where he fell in love one evening and married a Turkish girl whose maiden name nobody in Texas could pronounce. God, Harry hated every last one of those lucky bastards, because it was just all so romantic and wonderful, a world of blue seas and mysteries far beyond his own horizon. For years afterward, whenever Harry went down to Galveston and looked out over the windy Gulf, he imagined himself stowing aboard a freighter bound for North Africa or Bombay and waking up in a port where nobody spoke a word of English. He might be that traveler you meet somewhere who seems to know the customs of every place on earth, and whose opinions you really do take note of. But you can only lead one life and once Harry took his first high-paying position at St. Paul, that freighter sailed without him. Then he married and had children, and Byzantium was lost to him forever. All he could do was draw a circle around his day-to-day world and try to pretend nothing of any real importance existed outside of that. Otherwise, he'd likely drink himself to bed every night.

The auditorium lights were down when he was shown to his seat near the railing in the upper balcony by a skinny usher whose red cap kept sliding off his head. Harry's black leather shoes and the bottom half of his trousers were soaked from the rain and gave him a chill. He took off his raincoat and draped it across the scuffed mohair seat beside him. He was used to going to theaters alone. Marie never cared much for picture shows. If he bought her supper downtown she would agree to see a movie, but only with his assurance that it would make her laugh. She seemed to lack that certain wonder for appreciating the art and cunning of modern photoplays, while he found them to be amusing diversions at the close of a long hard workday. And with the right girl, of course, a seat in the balcony was an adventure in itself.

The Orpheum was less than half full this evening, movie patrons scattered about the darkened auditorium whose faded indigo ceiling twinkled under the false starlight and drifting clouds of a Moorish night sky. Water stains and cracked plaster reliefs disfigured the gilded rose and amber wall murals. Tiled Alhambra fountains on the main floor had gone dry and lifeless, and the old theater stank of tobacco and persistent misuse. Harry came into the auditorium close to the end of a silent photoplay featuring romance and deception in the Great White North. The organist in the center of the orchestra pit played a dirge on the grand American Fotoplayer as the clattering projector flashed images of a deep forest blizzard, wolves and wilderness, a solitary cabin in a snowy mountain clearing. Harry watched intently as the first costumed forms flickered across the screen, a woman huddling with two ragged waifs, trapped and starving, eyes on the merciless blizzard out of doors. Both food and hope are gone. Look of sadness and worry, a child's silvery tear for proof. Snowdrifts rise higher and higher outside the cabin. Wolves howl. Nightfall brings darkness, only a crude oil lamp to illuminate a pale angelic face. O bitter cold! Death lurks nearby. Children slump into a mother's weary bosom. Sleep, deep and eternal, arrives. Suddenly, the face of a brave Canadian Mountie in the icy snowdrift at the window, horror in his eyes! The door crashes in! A rescue! A kiss and a swoon! No blizzard is an obstacle to faithful love. Two faces encircled in a heart. Fade out to black with a lovely organ melody.

A girl's voice giggled from several rows back of Harry, "Aw, ain't that sweet?"

Someone behind her called back, "Shut up, toots!"

The ceiling lights dimmed momentarily and the organist began playing a ballad. After a brief pause, the projector lit the screen once again with a cartoon featuring that funny mouse Harry's children liked so much. A peal of laughter from somewhere down on the main floor followed the mouse's silly hi-jinks on the movie screen. He leaped and dove and rolled about. The girl behind Harry giggled and whistled as the crazy mouse jumped and fought, and finally persevered. When the cartoon ended, most of the audience gave a cheer. Then the organist began playing a brisk version of "I Wanna Be Loved By You."

Up behind Harry, the girl called out, "I tell you, I'da had that cat bumped off!"

"And I'm telling you, toots," a fellow's voice retorted, "to button up your face!"

"Says who?" the girl called back at him.

"Says me, and I ain't gonna warn you again!"

"Or what?" The girl laughed out loud.

"Or I'll knock your block off, girlie! You bet I will, and I don't mean maybe!"

"Gee, I'm shaking!"

"You better be!"

Ignoring both idiots, Harry searched in his jacket for the bag of chocolate drops he'd bought at a candy store up the block. He took out a handful and popped one into his mouth. Whenever he went to the movies at home, he saved some chocolate drops for the children. They would pretend to be sleeping to fool Marie, but as soon as he peeked in on them, their eyes would open and he'd sneak them each a piece of candy with a goodnight kiss. He adored their little game. It was one of the nicest gifts of fatherhood.

Back behind him again, the girl called out, "Say, wouldn't it be the limit if Herb Hoover got thrown out of a speakie for getting fresh with a bird like me?"

She hiccuped loudly, and two fellows seated near Harry got up and walked out.

Giggling, the girl shouted at them, "I'll call for you boys after lunch tomorrow! Toodle-loo!"

Assuming she was drunk, Harry resisted looking back at her. Minors and liquor were a rotten mix. On the train from Illinois, supper had been interrupted by a crowd of drunken collegiates, dancing the Charleston through the dining car, snatching napkins off the tables, scuffling in the aisle, and singing glee club tunes at the top of their lungs. It took four porters and the conductor to move them along. By then, practically everybody had lost his appetite. Several of Marie's nephews were even worse, shiftless and ignorant, running about the Pendergast farm lit to the eyebrows on corn liquor, particularly her shady cousin, Frenchy, an absolute louse if ever there was one. The less Harry saw of that family, the happier he was.

The projector glowed to life and the organist switched to a leisurely "Aloha-Oe" and the title of the next feature appeared on the screen:

Drums of the Seven Seas

Two girls, dressed South Seas native, hula-hula across the screen to a clinking tropical rhapsody. Palm fronds sway in the trade winds. On the ocean horizon, a proud sailing ship flying the Union Jack off the top mast, a man o' war from the King's Navy. From the shore, a burst of smoke and flame, cannon fire from an island summit. A miss! A second shot. A hit! The ship's magazine is violated and the *Lion of the Sea* explodes and burns. Wreckage on the waves. No survivors in sight. A flag goes up from the island heights, a skull and crossbones. A celebration of cutthroats and ne'er-do-wells. Nightfall. A bonfire and a feast. Then, on the beach, a body tossing unconscious in the dark surf, washed up on the white sand. In the village of the natives, lamplight reveals two people inside a grass hut, a pirate and a pretty girl quarreling. The pirate strikes the girl. She huddles in tears. He towers over her and she flees out into the night and the jungle and down to the beach where she sees a handsome fellow struggling to escape the merciless surf.

The clattering projector went dark.

At first, nobody spoke. Mechanical breakdowns were fairly common in old theaters like the Orpheum, so why kick about it?

But then the girl behind Harry shouted out, "Say, what's the big idea? That ain't the finish!" and someone on the main floor tossed a tomato at the screen, which prompted the organist to launch into a rousing version of *"Stars and Stripes Forever."* As the ceiling lights came up, a young usher rushed onto the stage. A second overripe tomato sailed over the head of the organist and struck the carved proscenium arch high above him, spattering into pulp. The organist, a short balding fellow wearing a red velvet smoking jacket and owlish glasses, quit playing and ran off. Several patrons were on their feet now, shuffling along the aisles toward the exit. Harry listened to whistles echoing across the auditorium and a pack of fellows down below cursing like sailors. Sneaking over to the railing, he looked out across the auditorium when a youth near the front row removed another tomato from his pocket and hurled it at the screen. Harry saw it strike the keyboard of the American Fotoplayer left of center and splatter into a soggy mess. Then another youth dressed in work overalls jumped up onto the stage and ran across to one of the side exits and out of the theater.

And then that idiot girl spoke into Harry's ear. "There won't be no more show tonight, handsome. It looks like they played us for suckers. You like coffee? I got ten cents if you got a quarter. Between us, we could get a couple cups of coffee, maybe some doughnuts. You like doughnuts?"

She crawled over into the seat beside him. Was she a nut? Nothing irritated Harry more than being approached by random strangers. Why couldn't people mind their own business? This was a movie house, not a train station.

The doors to the lobby had been opened, admitting a cold draft from the rainy street. The curtains hanging above the gilded proscenium flapped and threatened to flutter loose.

The girl shuddered. "Brrrr! I'm getting a chill. Maybe we ought to have us a coffee, what do you say?"

Unable to resist, Harry turned to see who was pestering him. The slight doll-faced brunette leering back at him wore a dark Clara Bow hat and a wool scarf, a grown woman's overcoat and a lovely cherubic smile. She had violet eyes and smelled like fresh lemon blossoms. Harry would've wagered a month's salary she wasn't a day over fifteen. Shouldn't she be at home doing schoolwork?

"I'm Pearl," the girl announced, leaning close. "What's your name?"

Raised to be civil, he told her. "Harry."

"How do you do, Harry?"

"Just fine, thank you," he mumbled, shooting a glance back toward the stage where the organist had reappeared with a hand towel. Apparently the show really was over for the evening. Suddenly realizing that he and the girl and another short fellow in a derby hat and belted raincoat sitting in the top row were the only patrons left now in the auditorium, Harry grabbed his own hat and raincoat. Who makes his mark in the world sitting at a picture show?

"Excuse me, dear." He got up to go, but quickly discovered Pearl following him along the aisle.

"Say, you and me ought to go uptown," she suggested. "It's still early enough, we could see a show at the Fox. Gilbert Roland and Norma Talmadge in 'The Dove.' Or, gee, maybe we ought to go out to Laswell's Circus at Grant Park. Wouldn't that be a panic? 'Marvels and Mystery Sideshow!' Why, I ain't been to the circus since I was a baby. How's about it?"

Harry frowned. She was quite likely either a con-artist or a pro— stitute. He almost felt sorry for her, though she was undeniably pretty. How often had she been kissed this week? Probably more than he had.

She persisted. "Say, you ain't ascared of dames, are you? I tell you, some fellows won't go nowhere unless they're with a pack of fellows. Girls make 'em nervous, I guess. Do I make you nervous?"

"Not at all. Why would I be nervous?"

"Well, then let's get us a coffee and a doughnut. If you're flat, maybe I'll buy."

An usher came down the aisle from the lobby. "Sorry, folks," he told them. "No more show tonight. Projector's broke."

Harry nodded, grateful to have this stupid conversation interrupted.

Pearl asked the kid, "Is there a payback?"

"Nope," the usher replied. "Program was half over, anyhow."

"Well, that ain't jake."

The usher shrugged. "Take it up with the boss."

"Where is the fat rat?" she growled.

"In his office."

Harry escaped down the lobby staircase. Getting a refund on the ten cents he'd spent for the movie didn't interest him, particularly if he had to haggle with the theater manager over it. Down on the stage, the organist began doodling a Broadway tune from *Kid Boots*. Harry heard the pretty girl's shrill voice echo upstairs and shook his head.

He put his hat on and fastened his coat buttons and went out into the rainy night where motor traffic was noisier than ever. Somewhere down on the river a ship's horn sounded and another horn blared in response. Traffic on the waterway was ceaseless, merchant ships and barges from a dozen states and many foreign nations, plying wares in and out of the great gray city. Night in and night out, the river drifted by, dragging sediment and refuse deeper into the dark. During rainstorms, the waterline rose in the lee of bridges and abutments, flooding campsites and night shacks of the poor and indigent who had traveled hundreds of miles from the countryside for the privilege of wallowing in the foul muck of a modern metropolis. Decent citizens mostly avoided the river.

Rain continued to fall in the flooding streets while the flow of motor traffic rumbled by and the elevated trolleys clanged and the subway discharged more people from underground, clogging the night sidewalks. The cold wind swirling off the river made Harry feel like dunking himself in a tub of scalding water. When he was a school-boy in East Texas, rainy winter mornings gave his mother fits because Harry hid under his blanket, refusing to come out for breakfast. After word got out that a clothes salesman named Phil Algernon had got-ten fried by lightning on College Avenue, suddenly every kid in town decided he had a lightning bolt with his name on it just sailing around the heavens for that one stormy day when he'd be walking to school. Later on, however, Harry realized you can't blame nature for civiliza-tion going to pieces.

Buttoning up his collar, he felt a tug on his raincoat. Whirling about, he found Pearl urging him out from under the neon-lit marquee into the pouring rain, giggling as she shouted, "Ain't this dump a load of baloney?"

He pulled loose. "What do you think you're doing? Let go of me!"

"Aw, come on," she fussed. "Won't you let a dame buy you a cup of coffee? I ain't no dumb Dora. I got a brain. There's lots we can talk about. Honest there is!"

Was she crazy? All he had wanted to do was see a picture show. Now he had this funny business to contend with. Worse yet, passersby were staring.

"What do you say? One cup of coffee. After that, you can give me the air if you like. I won't cry."

She tugged on his arm again, fluttering her eyelids like Betty Boop. She hummed a couple bars of "Let A Smile Be Your Umbrella," then playfully nuzzled his shoulder, acting tipsy.

Embarrassed by her idiot behavior, he said, "Don't you have any-one else to bother?"

"Why, I got the feeling you wanted to bother me!"

"What?"

Did she actually think he had his eye on her? Sometimes he felt he was oversexed, but this was ridiculous. Not that she couldn't find him attractive. Once he had undressed a lovely secretary from Cleveland in a Pullman car on the Union Pacific who said he looked like John Gilbert, but with devilish eyes and an angel's sincerity. She refused to explain what she meant, but you certainly don't argue sex appeal with a naked woman.

He saw Pearl's attention diverted to the street corner where a patrol car was stopped in traffic waiting for the light to change. Rain gusted into her face. Last week, gangsters shot up a gin mill only two blocks from the Civic Repertory on Commerce Street, killing a pair of lovely young flappers who had managed to walk in front of a Tommy gun-armed torpedo dead-set on murdering a rival bootlegger. Harry had seen their photo in the tabloids and fallen in love. Too bad he'd never meet them. He watched the patrol car turn right at the corner and motor off into a stream of traffic toward the river.

Once the cops had disappeared into the rainy dark, Pearl said, "Don't high-hat me, mister."

"I beg your pardon?"

"I guess you think I'm a gold digger, don't you?"

Feeling a nasty chill coming on, Harry tucked both hands into his coat pockets and turned away from the wind and this child who seemed either vagrant or mentally ill.

"Well, I tell you," she insisted, "I'm not."

He strolled away from the Orpheum with the girl right on his heel. When he increased his pace, she matched him. He hustled up to the corner and turned down the block and she kept pace with him as if tethered to his waist. Just past by a drugstore, he stopped. "Are you insane? Why are you following me? Are you expecting a handout? Because I have no intention of giving you a nickel!"

A green Ford roared up the street toward them and Harry stepped back nearer the brick buildings whose roof overhang provided some shelter from the rain. Her persistence flabbergasted him. He should have whistled to those policemen when he had the chance.

"Well, let me tell you something, big shot. I ain't a gold digger," she snarled, sticking close beside him by the wall. "If I was, why'd I want to be with you? You ain't got that much dough. Anyone can see that."

"Is that so?"

"You bet it is."

Pearl danced out toward the curb. She didn't seem to mind the rain. Her hat was soaked black and her overcoat was streaked and stained. Her hair hung limp at the corners of her face. Perhaps she was just a silly flirt, although Harry had to admit she was extraordinarily attractive. Marie often commented on how girls nowadays overdid their paint, but Harry liked that look. He thought it smart and modern. Pearl reminded him of the brunette on a recent cover of *Spicy Stories*. Not the sort of girl a fellow takes home to his family, at least until she puts some clothes on.

He tried easing away while Pearl was distracted by a flashy tan La-Salle on the boulevard heading up town. When were the rich ever bothered by nasty weather?

She caught up to him at the end of the block and hooked her arm into his, trying to change his direction by nuzzling her breast against his elbow. "Honey, take a right up here at Lerner's."

"I said, let go!" Harry slipped her grasp. There was something fishy about this girl. She had one of those eager and confident faces you regret in the morning once you realize it's not true love. Good grief, what if she chased him back to his room?

"Hey!"

Panicked, Harry rushed across the street, barely avoiding a run-down from a black Ford sedan.

"Hey!" she yelled again, checking for traffic, then scampering to catch up. "I said, we oughta — "

Frustrated now, Harry stopped in front of a radio store advertising in its show window the new RCA Radiola Super-Heterodyne cabinet sets. "Now that's enough! For crying out loud, I don't know how to make myself any clearer, but I have no interest in sharing my evening with you. I'm tired and cold, and what I want to do is sit in a hot bath and read a good book. I appreciate your invitation, but if you'd please go off and find yourself another friend, I'd be very grateful. Thank you very much!"

Then he raced off, doing all he could to avoid stepping in puddles. My God, that girl must have been a nut. He was lucky to get away when he did. Who knows what might have happened otherwise? Halfway up the block, he shot a quick look to the rear. She was gone. Thank goodness! Sex had dictated to him long enough. Who was the boss here, after all?

Satisfied he was free of her, he turned the corner at 14th Street in the direction of Columbia Avenue. The steam whistle of a coal barge howled in the rainy dark. Just last winter in the middle of the night, a freighter collided with a log raft killing seven bootleggers onboard the makeshift craft. They had been chased down to the river by police and sought to cross to the far bank where a stolen milk truck had been waiting to transport them out of the state. Failing to provide even a cheap kerosene lamp on a pole for a warning light to other traffic on the river out of fear of being spotted from the bluffs, they rowed through the current directly across the path of the steamer and went under in hardly more than a few seconds. It was a story recounted by city officials mostly as a warning for children foolish enough to consider raft crossings at twilight an adventure worth entertaining.

Nearer to Columbia Avenue, the lights of the great high buildings illuminated the falling rain and those streams of water flooding out of grimy alleyways and side streets where storm drains and gutters had backed up from dead cigars, soggy paper wrappers, and other refuse. A cascade of filthy water splashed by a passing taxicab drove Harry back from the street. A young woman in the backseat waved at him as she went by. He watched the taxi skip the light at 16th and Oxford. Three blocks ahead shone the bright lights of Portland Street where he could catch a trolley to take him back to his hotel on Jackson Street. Enough fooling around tonight. He had work to do. A year ago, he'd been shooting billiards at a pool hall in St. Louis and chatting up the hat check girl who had just gotten a divorce from a fellow who had beaten her senseless for flirting with the milkman. She had eyes like blue sunflowers and a honeysweet voice that whispered her apartment address in his ear as he collected his coat to return to the hotel. He wound up getting her all night long and missed his first three appointments in the morning and cost himself nearly two hundred dollars. Well, that behavior wouldn't do any longer.

Now he hurried along the wet sidewalk, dodging around puddles here and there. Motor traffic greeted him, and roared off into the rainy dark. Up ahead, the next city block was crowded with more automobiles parked along the curb, but most of the street and porch lamps were out and the sidewalk empty. Halfway to the corner on Baker Street, Harry was startled by someone whistling to him from a descending iron-railed stairwell on his right. He stopped and peered down into the stoop. A familiar face greeted him with the faint echo of a jazz orchestra from an underground basement.

"Thirsty?" Pearl asked, raising her smile up into the light from the corner street lamp. She winked salaciously. "Come on down here with me to Merle's Soda Club, and I'll buy you a drink."

Then she darted down beneath the stone stairs to a small basement door.

Harry was flabbergasted. He couldn't get rid of her! Was she going to follow him all night? Good God!

"Honey, I'm growing a beard here waiting for you." Another taxi drove by as the wind picked up. "What're you waiting for, sweetheart? Hurry up!"

Harry could clearly hear the music and hilarity from the heart of the liquor party. Since the start of the great Alcoholiday, he'd done his best to avoid running foul of the booze laws. Whether conditions in America were better or worse under the Volstead Act wasn't any of his concern. He had never been much of a drinker, anyhow, only a cocktail or two at dinner every now and then. Back at Cedar Street, Louis Maxwell's crowd gathered on Fridays in the den of a fellow named Melcher for a booze-up on Canadian whiskey and jackass brandy, during which they'd play poker and share smutty stories of the girls in the local steno pool. Harry was able to go along with most of that, so long as he didn't have to get his nose painted like the rest of them. Ben Poindexter knocked himself senseless one evening after bashing his skull on the toilet bowl and had to be run home to his wife in the backseat of Fritz Morton's Pontiac coupé. Throwing away the cork suited that bunch more than it did Harry and soon enough he found himself conveniently out of town on Fridays. Every so often, though, he missed the toasts and commotion. You could find speakeasies on every block of the city now if you happened to miss out on your morning cocktail at home. Faceless and noisy as they were, Harry didn't care for them much when he first came to the city. Then he grew restless and irritable staying to his room at night and began considering one of the downtown gin palaces where orchestras played and businessmen collected to share leads and dance with rosy-cheeked girls. Last week, a noontime walk in the park got him out of his office, then a steak later at Eckleburg's on Roosevelt Boulevard where bankers dined. Tonight, he had the picture show, and this crazy invitation to a basement gin palace. Maybe the girl was a nut, after all, but he could certainly keep his hands off her and his face out of a whiskey barrel, couldn't he, no matter what his lovely wife thought? Maybe he'd even have a big time for a change. What's so wrong with that? Marie could go cook a potato. Whose life was it, anyhow?

Seeing Harry start down the steps, Pearl leaned forward and rapped on the door. A slot opened and a gruff voice called out, "What's the password?"

She giggled. "Ish gibbibel."

The slot closed. Harry stopped on the bottom step. A few seconds passed and Pearl rapped on the door again. "Aw, come on, Frankie! Do we look like Izzy and Moe? Let us in!"

The door opened a crack and a fellow with a long face peeked out. "Full of skyrockets tonight, aren't you, sweetheart?" He took a look at Harry waiting behind Pearl on the bottom step. "Say, darling, who's the long shot in the old hat?"

"Who's asking?"

"Maybe you and your papa there ought to run along home, get you tucked into bed." He gave her a lewd wink.

Harry hid his face in the shadows, though he knew it was already too late.

"What's the matter, Frankie?" Pearl growled, giving the door a rough shove. "Got something in your eye?"

"Say, I hear a dame talks least in February because it's the shortest month." Then he slammed the door shut.

Pearl shouted, "Cut the chatter, Frankie, and let us in! It's cold out here!" She kicked hard at the bottom of the door, then looked back at Harry. "Sorry, honey. He'll let us in. Don't you worry."

"Oh, I'm not worried at all." He enjoyed hearing someone give her the business.

The slot snapped open. "By the way, sunshine, I just seen a nice little jane from uptown leave here on the arm of that sporty-looking gent you were ogling last week. I guess that'll teach you to get fresh with somebody else's sweetheart, eh?"

"Aw, I'll bet she wasn't nothing but a ring-tailed bazoo." She laughed. "Now, let us in, you big flop, or I'll see that Merle deports you with his next load of Canadian whiskey."

Harry watched a coal truck rumble past on the street above, splashing rainwater onto the sidewalk. The bathtub in his apartment was still waiting for him if this didn't pan out. Besides, he loved seeing this girl's stupid bluster fizzle before his eyes. Harry's younger sister, Rachel, had the same annoying urge for insisting the world jump to her command. When they were children, she wouldn't eat a meal unless everything was cooked to her desire. If her carrots were underdone or the meat too tough, she'd throw a fit and send her plate back to the kitchen, refusing to eat a bite until Mother remedied the problem. And Rachel was perpetually unreasonable on practically every subject. Why do I have to feed the cat? Why can't that Wallace boy from down the street sweep out the chicken coop? Who decided that church has to be on Sundays?

Pearl leaned up on her tiptoes to the closed slot where she whined, "Please, Frankie? It's awful cold out here. If you let us in, I swear I won't make google-eyes at you no more."

Just like that, the door swung open and the long-faced fellow stood aside to let Pearl and Harry pass. He was dressed in a tux and black tails, and gave Harry a sneering nod as the Soda Club's two newest guests entered the riotous basement gin mill. Pearl smiled. "You're a pip, Frankie. Do you know that?"

The doorman leaned forward and kissed her on the cheek. "Keep your nose clean, kid."

Before Harry could take off his hat, Pearl dove away into the stuffy crowd. The bright speakeasy was hot and noisy, and reeked of liquor, sweat and nickel cigars. Every table was packed like a razzle-dazzle jamboree of men and women in the middle of the smoky room. Dozens more high-bottom drinkers were jammed shoulder-to-shoulder like sardines at a long mahogany bar. In the next room, a loud Negro jazz band entertained a boisterous party of fellows in smart evening suits and over-painted girls in shingled hair and metallic fringed dresses, all sipping cocktails and dancing tight-packed in front of the stage. He spotted Pearl by the bar with a highball glass in her hand. She shouted something he couldn't hear above the din, but he nodded anyhow and she blew him a kiss, then swallowed her drink in one gulp and ducked into a wild crowd next to an old cast iron card machine. When he made his way there, she had already vanished into the boozy mayhem. That was fine because without her worrying him to pieces, he could do whatever he liked. Back in Kansas City, he had gone to a blind pig half a block from the river with a couple of salesmen who bought and sold skin ointments. They claimed that going on the water wagon was bad for one's constitution, but since abstinence looked good to the little lady whose husband had difficulty finding his way home at night, the ointment they dredged up in a tiny Appalachian burg supposedly kept a fellow sober as a judge when applied before having that first drink. Rubbing a sample onto his stomach before tipping a glass of brandy, Harry couldn't help laughing. The concoction reeked of goose shit and turpentine. No matter, he spent the rest of the evening flipping cards in a back room and left with thirty extra dollars in his pocket and the admiration of a dozen fellows who were astounded by how clear-eyed he'd remained. His secret was that he never took more than a sip or two each hour while trading glasses with the salesman seated next to him who got so pigeon-eyed he didn't notice Harry's sleight of hand. That rare ability to fit into the company of many different men was a source of pride with Harry, because it was something not all of us can do.

The bartender with a drooping handlebar mustache and weary eyes called over to him, "How'll you have it, pal?"

Behind him on the mahogany back bar, dozens of cloudy brown quart bottles of rum, gin, bourbon, and whiskey lined the shelves, a greater collection of liquor than Harry had seen in years. A throng of drinkers at the table behind him were slurping beer from big glass mugs. Clearly, Prohibition agents had little interest in raiding this booze party. Harry guessed that half the pay checks in the metropolis these days were cashed in underground saloons. Probably the mayor himself was skulking about this crowd or another, imbibing a tall mug of flip.

"Are you drinking or not?" the bartender asked, already impatient.

"How about a Hanky Panky?" Harry sneaked a look around the room. The girls were ravishing.

A short fellow wearing a belted raincoat and derby hat just off Harry's shoulder spoke up. "He's a snooper, Joe. They never drink. You know that."

The bartender glared at Harry. "Is that so, pal? Are you a snooper?"

"Of course not. Don't you know anything? If I were, I'd have knocked back a couple already. But, gee, I guess everyone's an expert these days, aren't they?"

After downing a shot of gin, the fellow in the derby hat replied, "Says who?"

"Says I," Harry replied smartly.

"Oh yeah?"

"Yeah." You have to keep them off balance, especially the gasbags.

"Well, maybe I oughta knock your block off."

"Oh, that's rich!" Harry laughed now. This little fellow was half his size. Who did he think he was? Popeye?

"A smart mouth, huh? What do you say we step outside, you and me, see how handy you are?"

How many idiots am I going to run across tonight? If this fellow wants trouble, I won't let him off. "Lead the way, pal."

"You said it."

Back in his senior year at State, nine different fellows from his dormitory had tried Harry in the gymnasium ring and wound up on their keesters. He had no idea how tough this one was, but there was always a time to find out. He wasn't all that afraid — unless, of course, this idiot had a gun, in which case he'd run like a bandit. Then he realized this was the same short-stack he'd seen in the top row of the balcony at the Orpheum Theater. That was odd. Maybe he was a regular here and spent his life stumbling from one amusement to another. Liquor made bigger fools out of those who had little sense to begin with. The picture hadn't closed down half an hour ago, and this fellow already had a load under his skin.

Harry stepped away from the bar as his opponent put down the glass of gin and stood up. He hoped this wouldn't take too long. One or two pops on this fellow's rosy nose ought to settle things. Seeing Harry unbuttoning his cuffs, the short fellow laughed. "Fraid I can't make it, sweetheart. I guess you'll have to go solo. Don't wear yourself out."

"Scared, huh?"

"You don't know nothing about it."

"Is that so?"

"Yeah."

"Well, keep your opinions to yourself next time," Harry warned. "I wouldn't want to start this over again."

"Sure, pal. Whatever you say." Then the short fellow put his back to Harry and shoved his glass toward the bartender. "Fill 'er up, Joe. I'm dry as an Arab."

Relieved he hadn't actually gotten himself into a stupid scrap, Harry looked around the room for Pearl. Listening to the din and guzzling all about him, his conscience whispered another warning regarding that flirty little girl. He had better keep himself on a short leash.

"Here you go, pal." The bartender slid Harry his cocktail and palmed the cash. Harry took the icy glass and headed away into the crowd, sipping his drink as two more men in damp overcoats shoved past him to the bar. The first one said, "Shoot me over a couple of whiskeys, Joe."

The second fellow added, "Me, too."

In the next room, a lovely coffee-brown Negro girl dressed in white feathers and silk strolled out in front of the orchestra and began singing, "Don't Advertise Your Man." Her voice unfurled across the crowded tables in every corner of the dimly lit speakeasy, that tender soulful melody traveling ear to ear, arousing more than a smile of recognition with both sexes:

> *"Open your eyes, women be wise,*
> *And don't advertise your man.*
> *It's all right to have a little bird in the bush,*
> *But it ain't like the one that you got in your hand."*

The willowy chanteuse looked frail upon the stage in the hazy light, a sad amber nightingale. She sang and sang, and hearing her, Harry felt tears welling up briefly, regretful and mild. He drank more of his cocktail and experienced that endearing flush. Liquor can be a tonic for many moods. Yet even sweet vermouth is a meager joy. As the song ended, Harry's spirit flagged. The chanteuse closed her eyes and stepped back into shadow. During the applause that followed, Harry spotted Pearl across the room, emerging from a crowd of giggling young B-girls decked out in chiffon velvet frocks. She opened a door at the far end of the room and went through alone.

Tossing back the last of his cocktail, Harry slipped away into the noisy crowd, jostling past the tables and ducking under a lamp that had come loose from the crossbeam overhead. It swung free now, shoved into motion by people dancing or just passing by. The light it cast made odd shadows on the basement walls. Fuzzyheaded from his vermouth, Harry felt women leering at him from every corner of the room. Gin made them lustful. He could easily park himself at a table and take one of these beauties on his lap and give her a good long kiss. Wasn't that what they were here for? He smiled at a crowd of darling brunettes in chic silk crepe and metallic cloche hats, one of whom winked back. A thrill danced up his spine. It was getting to be sex o'clock, twenty-four hours a day now. He ought to buy a new watch.

Harry came to the door Pearl had used and went through into a narrow hall reeking of liquor, tobacco smoke, and perfume. The hall had four doors, two on each wall. All closed. Love rooms. Harry tiptoed down the hall, listening to bedsprings squeaking, men grunting, girls squealing delightedly. His old pal Paul Exeter had scribbled out a grandiose list of city joy spots and drink-dice-dame joints when he, Harry, and the Foster brothers were aboard the *Century* last autumn. Exeter boasted about visiting each at least once, except for Martha's Lighthouse near the old stockyards where the stench was unbearable. Harry took his copy of the list back to his sleeper, then crumpled it up and tossed it out the window for fear Marie might stumble across it somehow. He didn't recall any mention of Merle's Soda Club.

He considered knocking on one of these doors, hoping to catch Pearl with her bare bottom in the air. Wouldn't that be something? On the other hand, he didn't need a punch in the nose if he chose the wrong room. He listened for a few moments and looked around. Maybe she went out that door at the end of the hall. A girl like her would be just the sort to snatch a drink off someone's table and run out. Harry went up a short staircase and jiggled the knob. When it opened, he found himself outside in a long dark alley framed overhead by window balconies and iron fire escapes. A couple inches of water flooding in from the sidewalk gutters floated garbage the length of the alley. Ahead, intermittent flashes of light from passing automobiles illuminated the street. Music filtered down from a radio in an upstairs window, Rudy Vallée crooning:

> *"You'll do it someday, so why not now?*
> *Oh, won't you let me try to show you how.*
> *Think what you're missing, oh it's a shame,*
> *You miss the kissing and the rest of the game."*

"Are you following me, mister?" Pearl's voice echoed out of the dark. He saw her by the brick wall, half-hidden behind a stack of trash cans, cigarette in one hand, a small hip flask in the other. Even rain-soaked, she looked absolutely adorable in the dank light. Good grief, she was going to be trouble.

"Don't be a smart-aleck." That was another thing. He hated talking to minors. There was a boy at the A&P grocers where Marie shopped who couldn't bother to be pleasant. He was always smoking a cigarette behind the store and regarded Harry with less respect than a common vagrant.

She took a sip from the hip flask, then stuck it into the folds of her dress and leaned back against the wall, listening to the music in the dark. After sneaking a puff off her cigarette, she asked, "Don't you just love Rudy Vallée?"

"Who?"

She nodded up toward the radio in the window. "The fellow singing, you old dope."

"A man who sings like a girl? I'll take Jolson, thank you."

"Oh, I just adore Rudy Vallée," she said, taking another smoke off the cigarette and flicking the burning ash into the water at her feet. "Ain't he the bee's knees, the cat's nuts?"

"Why do you talk like that?"

"Like how?"

"Those silly expressions. What do they mean, anyhow?" He detested slang. What was so wrong with ordinary speech?

"Aw, you're all wet," she growled. "Besides which, I'm carrying a torch for Mr. Rudy Vallée."

"I should have guessed." Harry chuckled. "But honestly now, think about this for a second, dear. Really do concentrate. Can you manage that?"

Pearl took a puff off her cigarette, exhaling smoke into the rainy air. "Sure, honey."

"Now, why in heaven's name would somebody as famous as Rudy Vallée be interested in a nutty little girl like yourself? Can you possibly imagine a fellow with all that money, the fame and opportunities available to him, ladies by the score, and I mean adult young women, not babies like yourself, possibly bothering to pay you any mind at all? Even for half an instant as his auto drove past? Well? Can you?"

Pearl tossed the final inch of cigarette into a flooded trashcan beside the brick wall as a cold draft from the street swept into the alley. "Why are you such a hardboiled egg?"

Harry fastened the collar buttons on his coat against the drizzling rain. He'd about had enough. "I have no idea what you mean by that stupid remark."

Taking out her hip flask again, she smiled. "Ain't you never been in love?"

He frowned. "How's that any of your business?"

"You got jilted, huh? Gee, I'm sorry." A noisy delivery truck rumbled by the alley entrance. "Still cut about it, aren't you?"

"Darling, somebody ought to put you over his knee and teach you some manners."

"Somebody already did," she shrieked, "and I didn't mind it one bit!"

"Why, you little — "

She flew off like a bird down the alley, chirping back over her shoulder, "So long, honey! Don't wait your supper!" Her laughter echoed into the street.

Harry watched her sail out to the sidewalk and dart away out of sight. My God, it was really astonishing. Her upbringing had obviously been a colossal failure, both parents probably enfeebled by alcohol or mental retardation. The poor thing had no future at all. Maybe a truck would run her down one day and put her out of her misery.

He refastened his collar. She'd almost lured his pants off, and that scared the dickens out of him. Walking out to the front of the alley, Harry saw Pearl cross 17th Street during a lull in traffic and disappear into Washington Park under the dark billowy trees. Now where was she headed? The lamplights stung his eyes as he reached the flooded street. Heading off north up the sidewalk to Columbia Avenue would lead him back to his hotel. Going south led down toward Crane Street and the riverfront. Ahead, the park receded into rainy shadows. That stupid girl had gone in alone: a witless child tempting fate. Almost inconceivable brutalities occurred nightly in the city's park system. Maybe she really was an imbecile, after all.

He stared across into Washington Park. He was cold and tired, yet terrifically intrigued by that peculiar young girl. Why had she latched onto him at the picture show? This was all so confusing. The feminine variety had a mysterious way of insinuating themselves into a fellow's life whether they were invited or not. When Harry had first arrived at St. Paul after college, his housemate Ferguson introduced him to a straw-haired telephone girl named Virginia Sweetwater who drove a worn-out Saxon "Six" around the city like Barney Oldfield. She presumed that most fellows went for a girl who was stork mad and took chances, and maybe some did, but neither Ferguson nor Harry thought her romantic enough to get fussed over. True enough, both of them laid her down and brought flowers to her afterward, but then a couple of weeks later, she climbed up the rose trellis at Ferguson's brownstone and pried open Harry's window and agreed to go with him for the rest of the year, whether he wanted to or not — and he did not. The police had to be called to get her out of the house. She broke a window in Harry's Ford a week later and scribbled a nasty rumor about him on the bulletin board at the YMCA. Fortunately, her mother came west from Connecticut to bring her home and Harry never heard from Miss Sweetwater again. Thank goodness, because once she was gone, he bumped into Marie Alice Pendergast at the boathouse on Cedar Lake and fell in a big way at last. To be fair, of course, not every girl who crossed his path was as frantic as Virginia Sweetwater, nor calm as Marie. And both Harry and Ferguson had episodes themselves that left their own sanity open to question. Harry thought he knew why love brought him so often to the brink of disaster, yet more than two decades after stealing a bashful kiss from Caroline Walker in the basement of her father's store, the opposite sex was still a mystery to him.

A black delivery truck roared past on the street where he stood watching Pearl fade into the drizzling dark. He thought about going in after her. Was he crazy? His cocktail hadn't been that strong. What did he expect to do? Make love to her under a wet bush somewhere? His heart raced and he felt terrified.

He crossed the street into Washington Park.

Overhead, elm and hickory branches swung wildly in the wind, scattering down twigs and leaves that blanketed the soaked and muddy grass. He searched the darkness ahead for the girl, and saw only frantic shadows. The brick walkway swam a serpentine path through the rainy park. The damp cold stung his face and he was forced to keep both hands jammed deep into his coat pockets for warmth. He knew this was absolute madness.

A quarter of a mile into the park, his head still cloudy with vermouth, Harry stopped to rest and survey his surroundings. Stone statuary frozen in poses of studied consternation stared from lawn insets carved out of dense shrubbery and branch-heavy willows. Atop an iron signpost, a small gargoyle cast a baleful gaze toward the river. Rain blew slantways along the path ahead, washing clean the old bricks even as a gusting wind scattered down more leaves. Harry knew he'd gone completely sex-crazy, chasing a girl out here when he ought to have been back in his room at the hotel, soaking in the bathtub and finishing Lawrence Willson's, *"The Cats In Zanzibar."* Who could possibly dissect what had come over him? A pretty little girl had given him the fast eye and he hadn't looked away. Instead, his heart beat faster and he longed to give her a hug.

He wandered deeper into the rainy darkness. One sign led toward the closed gates of the Zoological Gardens, another to the Boat House. Whispering prayers of conviction, Harry chose the latter, traversing the stone arbor, which led onto a wide promenade encircling an artificial pond bordered by brick and mortar walls and denser foliage behind. Its old filters sodden with refuse, the dead waters of the pond were green and brackish, smelling of dung and mildew. Even amphibians and wild fowl appeared absent in this late season of decay. Almost astride the path ahead, a gabled Victorian garden shed stood naked to the wet storm, its hingeless doors flung wide, framed windows vacant, random sections of tin shingled roof fallen in or rusted away. Rain fell lightly on the waters of the pond, dappling the murky surface. A soft gray mist clinging to the cold air like eldritch vapor infiltrated the thick willow trees all about.

Nearby a familiar voice hummed off-key.

Harry called back, "You can come out now!" His echo raced across the black water into drizzling foliage behind.

A soft giggle echoed in the dark close by. Then a familiar voice sang, *"I was oh, so blue till you came along, just to make my life a wonderful song."*

More laughter.

"All right, darling, I'm going back to my hotel."

"Don't get wet, honey!"

Another giggle.

He swung back around, and shouted, "Folly is bound up in the heart of a child!"

He'd learned that from Reverend Pheby at Sunday School after snickering during the story of Jesus and the moneychangers.

"Says who?"

"Proverbs 22, verse 15!"

Pearl stepped out of the old shed, drenched head to toe, yet looking adorable as ever. "I ain't read the Bible. Are you a preacher?"

"No, darling," Harry replied, more quietly. "As a matter of fact, I'm a business man."

Shivering with cold and desire, a curious duo, he remembered one of his favorite old maxims that one does nothing carelessly or in a hurry. Obviously, he no longer believed his own philosophy. Good heavens, he was behaving like an idiot. Ferguson would tell him to either kiss her or run. He really had no idea what he was about to do.

"Is it your business to chase Broadway beauties around in the middle of the night?"

"What makes you think you're a beauty?"

"Men like following me."

She walked to the edge of the pond and gazed into the brackish water. He stared at her. This girl was so unconventional, yet beguiling, that Harry maintained his distance, scared of being liberated from his conscience. There are only so many mistakes we can make without tipping ourselves over. Why had he drunk that stupid cocktail?

"Say, honey, I know a place we can go," she said, easing back into the night beside the shed. "It ain't far. I'll show you."

Harry watched her scramble up onto a black stonewall draped in damp elderberry. Don't be a damned fool, he told himself. You can't make any good of this episode by catting after her. Go back to your room and hide under the bedcovers.

And maybe he would have done so had it not been for something Harry glimpsed dimly through a copse of willows just past the Boat House, a vague figure strolling in his direction, barely obscured in a wet gusting breeze. Last month, all the city newspapers ran headlines in bold regarding two college students out on a date who were shot to death in cold blood at the base of Walt Whitman's statue, less than a quarter mile from where Harry stood now. The boy was from Vermont and his fresh-faced girlfriend was a New Yorker, both nineteen years old, students in the Natural Sciences department. The killer had not been identified, but the newspapers were calling him "The Plugger," and a vigorous citywide manhunt was persisting with warnings by the police advising caution in all the city parks after dark. Was this "The Plugger?" Muddled by sweet vermouth, he just couldn't be sure, so he decided to be safe.

Harry climbed up onto the wall and shoved through the elderberry. He saw Pearl and went after her. By now, she was already past the Child's Garden topiary. As Harry dashed behind her, she led him on a wild chase across the park in and out of black cherry trees and red cedar and thick magnolias, past more statues and blackened lamp-posts, and down a broad brick promenade that entered an arboretum in whose center had been erected a great rotunda constructed of iron girders and emerald-hued glass with Ionic columns of polished Algerian marble: **Athena's Dome**. Its massive front doors were bolted shut for the night, but hurrying to the rear Pearl drew Harry to a small window at the base of the foundation hidden by oleander and flowering trumpet vine. There she removed a pane of cracked glass from its frame and prepared to crawl through.

Setting the glass panel aside, she told him, "It wasn't me that busted it, honey, if that's what you're thinking."

"No, you just happened to notice that someone had pried the glass loose. Do you have your mashing parties here?"

"You think I got hot pants, don't you? Well, just because a dame stays out after dark don't mean she's looking to pet with somebody. So if you've got in your mind to treat me that way, honey, maybe you ought to go back to your room and forget we ever met."

"Don't worry, dear. I'm not running that sort of temperature."

She crawled through the iron frame into the building. Once he heard her drop to a cement floor below, he squatted down to peer into the dark after her.

Pearl's voice echoed indoors. "Honey, it ain't raining in here. Come down, see for yourself."

Harry felt cold rainwater dripping down his back, making him more miserable by the minute. This was so absurd.

"Don't be a flat tire. I know you're freezing up there. Climb down."

Rain fell harder. He looked behind him for signs of "The Plugger." Maybe no one had been there at the boat pond, after all. Maybe it really was only the vermouth, but would it please his wife to hear that her husband had been shot to death trying to stay out of a young girl's arms? He was tired and wet, anyhow. How could he make love like this?

Harry dropped down into the basement of the rotunda.

Pearl stood by a cement wall, her arms wrapped under her bosom. She smiled. "Don't you feel like a baby now?"

"Do you break in here often?"

"A girl's got a right, don't you think?"

"Sure, she does," Harry agreed, peering out into the cement corridor. It was still chilly where they were standing. "Where does this lead?"

"To my favorite place in the whole world. Let me show you!"

Pearl took him by the hand and led him a hundred feet or so into the darkness where the corridor was interrupted by a cast-iron spiral staircase that wound up out of the basement. Next to the staircase an iron door opened onto the interior of the rotunda whose domed emerald glass panels sparkled where rain droplets shimmered in reflection of the city lights. Harry followed Pearl across the marble floor into the center of the great dome. A cold draft swirled down from high above. Designed by Gilbert Irving Gedge, late in the 19th century, Athena's Dome was one of the most famous monuments in the city, yet its purpose seemed vague and undefined, clouded in artistic speculation. Perhaps it had been constructed as a cenotaph for a long forgotten statesman or wealthy aristocrat held at an earlier age in great reverence, its iron doors intended to be shut for all time and eternity.

"I slept in here once last summer during a full moon," said Pearl, her gaze focused high on the ceiling. "I seen moonbeams shining down like rainbows through the glass all night long."

"I have no doubt," Harry remarked as he strolled about under the emerald dome, studying the artistry and engineering of its construction. One hundred feet in diameter and another two hundred to its ceiling apex, the glass pantheon qualified in his view as one of this city's true architectural marvels. *"In Xanadu,"* Harry gently quoted, *"did Kubla Khan a stately pleasure-dome decree."*

"Huh?"

"Coleridge."

"Who's that?"

He saw Pearl lying flat on her back on the marble floor of the dome, legs extended toward the ceiling, a silly grin on her face. She wiggled her toes and giggled. Seeing her in that pose made him want to lie on top of her.

"What are you doing?" he asked, warily.

"Ain't you never?"

"Haven't I ever what?"

"Danced on a glass ballroom floor."

"How much liquor did you drink tonight?"

His voice trembled with a rising lust as he felt his own cocktail wearing off.

"Why, I haven't had a drop." She giggled and her legs swayed off-balance to the right. "Well, maybe a couple."

"At least that." One thing he wouldn't do was make love to her if she were drunk. He'd be a worse louse than he was already. "Now I understand why you dragged me through the speakie."

Pearl let her legs drop to the floor and she sat up. "Aw, you're just sore 'cause I wouldn't let you kiss me back at the picture show."

"Oh, is that so?"

"I saw you giving me the fast eye, honey. That's how come I let you date me up tonight, in spite of us hardly knowing each other."

High above, rain thundered down on the glass surface of the dome as Harry considered escape into the dark. He couldn't know for certain how old she was and there were serious laws against choosing the wrong chicken. Pete Baxter put the boots to a little number he met at a skating rink in Evansville last winter and wound up in county jail for six months when her folks preferred charges against him. Trouble was, nobody dressed her age these days and honesty went out the window with good whiskey.

Pearl took a cigarette out of her purse. "You got the habit?"

"Not that one."

"It ain't so bad if you can afford 'em." Standing again now, she gave Harry a once over. "Say, are you all right? You don't look so good. Maybe you got the flu or something. You seeing a doctor?"

"I don't know why you'd say something like that. There's nothing wrong with me, at all. In fact, I'm in mint condition."

"Oh sure, that's what they all tell you. Then you wake up the next morning and find 'em lying there beside you, stiff as an old board."

He studied her closely, too. This was very important. Some indulgences were sheer lunacy. "How old are you, darling?"

"Nothing doing, honey." She stepped sideways. "Besides, a gentleman doesn't ask a lady her age."

"Well, you're not a lady. You're a girl, and I'll bet my hat you're not a day over fifteen."

"That just shows how smart you are, Weisenheimer, because I'll be twenty-two in January, so stick that in your hat!"

Harry almost choked with laughter. "Oh, come off it! Why, a young lady named Maggie in our steno pool is nineteen and fresh out of secretarial school, and she looks twice as old as you."

"Says who?"

"What?"

"Aw, you don't know nothing about it."

"Yes, that's what I thought."

Feeling sober now and anxious, he went to try a door on the far end of the room. He rattled the knob, but the door was locked. He felt a tap on his shoulder. Before he could draw another breath, Pearl grabbed his arms fiercely, swung him around, leaned up and kissed him deliriously for a couple of seconds, then let go.

Absolutely shocked, Harry gasped, "Why did you do that?"

Pearl gleefully rubbed his hand. "Gee, you're a swell kisser!"

"Good grief, I'm old enough to be your father."

"But you ain't."

"Well, I'm married!"

"Is she a fancyface?"

"Yes, my wife is very pretty," he said, still tasting Pearl's rosy rouge. Did she just kiss him on the mouth? Her lips felt beautiful. They really were extraordinary. This was becoming desperately unsafe. You could try all you like to be deliberate and indissoluble, even stubborn, and love would still have its way with you. Denying it is almost worse than self-indulgence.

"Do you want to give me the business?" She puckered her lips for another kiss.

Honestly, he wanted to throw her down and make love to her that very instant. I'd undress her from the top down, he thought, scatter her clothes across the dome, then drop my own trousers and teach her a few things. He felt dizzy, detached, scarcely sober. But since he hadn't actually gone nuts yet, he fought off those sexual convulsions and told her, "Look, dear, this really is wonderful, but I think I'd better be going. I've got appointments in the morning, and I ought to get some sleep. Can't afford mistakes, you know. Not these days."

"Sure you do, honey." She nodded. "I can tell you got lots of deals cooking."

The scant light of the dome lent her pale skin a moony glow. Was she really old enough to make love? Marie was hardly more than a girl when he first kissed her, and hadn't a clue where to put her hand on their wedding night or even how to receive him. Some of us are biologically versed in the act of mating, Harry believed, while others seem incapable of achieving the simplest pleasure. Marie had the softest bosom he had ever held and a flowery pure scent that was hers alone. They had made love countless evenings and yet he was reasonably sure she had never experienced the ecstasy he noticed so often with other women. That had always troubled him, yet what could he do?

He said, "I'm sorry to skip out on you like this, dear. You're very sweet." He wished he could change his mind. How often did a fellow his age have the opportunity to take a young beauty in his arms and kiss her like Valentino?

"Aw, you don't have to say nothing like that. You're an important fellow. A big cheese. You don't got time to love up a crazy dame like me."

Venereal urgency raced through his brain. His mouth was dry, his hands felt clammy.

She stroked his hand calmly. "If you really got to scram, honey, I'll take you out through the basement. It's a shortcut."

"I'd appreciate that, dear. Thank you."

He'd never felt so relieved in his life. You tell yourself over and over again to behave, and you end up wondering how it's possible to be deaf to your own advice.

Without another word, Pearl led him back out to the spiral staircase where cold air rose from the underground and he couldn't see anything but stone and iron beneath the third bend in the stairs. Her shoes clanked on the iron steps as she hurried downward. Harry kept close behind, holding one hand on the cold damp railing and taking each step with care. His patent leathers were slippery and he worried about breaking his neck. At the bottom of the iron stairs, he followed her east into a black murky brick tunnel submerged in several inches of horrid smelling water. Sloshing blindly forward in a clumsy effort to keep up with her, Harry fought the discomforts of cold and fatigue and the greater unpleasantness of claustrophobia. The tunnel walls felt cold and grimy. Reaching up, he could touch the ceiling where water dripped on his hat. What if she dumps me down here? At least Floyd Collins got his name in all the papers before croaking in that cave. Feeling his shoes becoming ruined in the sloppy filth, he pondered why he continued to do such idiotic things. Only last summer, he had allowed Myrtle Krause to persuade him to make love to her on the fire escape outside her bedroom window at high noon two blocks from Halstead Street, drawing a telephone call to the police from a prudish neighbor across the way. More recently, a silly flirt named Edna May Greenleaf ran off nude into the back garden of her family's home on Euclid Avenue with Harry's trousers wrapped about her waist, daring him to tackle her outdoors, which proved a stupendous lapse in judgment when the gardener appeared. Recalling his past idiotic episodes always embarrassed him, yet here he was with a stupid little tart in a storm drain under the city.

If Marie ever discovered the truth about these ridiculous indiscretions of his, not only would it break her heart, but she would think he was a damned fool, and probably take off with their lovely children and never look back. Then where would he be? Chasing floosies in rail hotels?

He heard Pearl splashing ahead through a bend in the dank tunnel. He shouted for her to slow down before he got lost. It was dark as sin and, worse yet, smelled as if he were wading through a sewer of filth, probably rat infested and diseased. Pinching his nose shut, Harry felt a chill of worry and doubt again. His clothes were soiled, another evening wasted in a foolish girl spree. What does that fellow say to posterity who spends his life in selfish pursuits only to end up tired and alone in a cold hotel room? *Could we but know the land that ends our dark, uncertain travel?*

Then he heard a foghorn and a freighter's droning response, and saw Pearl silhouetted in a slant light at the mouth of the passage. Apparently she had guided him to the river, emerging from the dank underground a hundred feet or so ahead of him. The soggy waif stood on the brick bulwark staring out across the dark water, another lit cigarette in one hand, her silver hip flask in the other. When Harry came out of the drain tunnel into a cold drizzling rain, his nostrils filled with wood smoke and the stink of rotting fish and human sewage strewn in the garbage and mud by the river's edge. From the great brick bulwark, he saw below him, like some vast encampment of a defeated army, hundreds of shabby tents and poorly erected lean-to's littered about the muck and mire of the gray city, and a thousand ragpickers stooped beside small fires in the cold night, huddling like forsaken souls awaiting passage to a brighter shore. Out on the wide river, two barges passed, guide lamps signaling in the rainy blackness. Soaked to his skin, ears aching with cold, Harry watched in silence, while beneath the bulwark, voices bellowed in hoarse wordless rage at meaningless slights or cruel impositions, malevolence directed outward to any within earshot.

He noticed Pearl eyeing him. She tipped the hip flask once, returned it to her coat, then took a last drag off her burnt cigarette and flicked it over the bulwark.

"I don't know none of these people," she remarked, strolling over toward him. "I only come here once in a while, and when I do, I just sit up here by myself. A girl can't be too careful nowadays."

"Why do you come here at all?" he asked, astonished by the sheer number of figures wandering in the shadows of firelight. Were these the vagrant legions of dispossessed he read about each morning in the city newspapers, those dangerous misfits the high mucky-mucks argued were the raw source of crime and ill-fortune everyone else endured? While Harry watched, somebody put a boot into one of the fires near the water, shooting a great blaze of sparks out into the dark above the river. Alighting, they glowed briefly like floating stars in the swirling current.

"They don't mean no harm," Pearl remarked, as if she knew what Harry had been thinking, and perhaps she did. "They just don't got nowhere else to be after dark. I guess they get lonely, too, and feel like being with other cutbacks like themselves. I don't know. It's tough these days." Rain dripping from her soggy Clara Bow hat, she rubbed her nose with the side of her hand. "I don't talk with 'em too much. They stink."

As the rainfall lightened to a slow drizzle, Harry watched the wake from a late fishing trawler wash ashore like luminescent foam. His face had grown numb from the cold and he hardly noticed any longer how damp his suit of clothes had become. Everywhere below him fires seemed to glow in the blackness along the riverfront, yet he felt no rising warmth.

Stepping up close beside him, Pearl asked, "You ever been stuck on a dame who wouldn't give you the time of day?" She shifted her feet on the bulwark, sideways to the chilling wind.

"Well, I've known women of all sorts in my life," he told her plainly, trying now to be kind and conciliatory. At last, he felt sorry for the girl. Obviously she didn't know any better than to chase after strange men in the dark. Besides that, this whole sex gambit of his seemed pathetic and embarrassing, unbecoming of a fellow his age with a darling wife and two beautiful children at home.

Down along the black strand, somebody struck up a lively banjo tune, an Irish jig of some sort, mostly obscured by the wind and rain. Rude voices joined in song. A ship's horn echoed across the long water.

"I seem to know more fellows than ever these days," she confessed, her brow furrowed as if her own statement puzzled her. "Not one of 'em says I'm a fussy pants, so how's about you taking me back to that hotel of yours tonight? What do you say? I won't kick at all."

Harry blanched. Invite her to his room? My God, was she insane? He'd have her there for a week and never get any work done. Then, after she left, he'd probably jump off a bridge. "Look here, darling, it's awfully late, and I need to get to bed. Like I said before, those morning appointments."

She kicked at the muddy brick underfoot, her eyes teary in the cold air. "Honey, you don't got to give me the run-around. Go on, tell me to scram, if you like. I can take it."

How does someone get himself into these situations? Every morning we wake up with the world at our feet. Eat a boiled egg or a bowl of cereal with a piece of buttered toast and drink a glass of grapefruit juice, maybe read the paper, then go outdoors with the simple expectation of pleasing ourselves or others with a confidence that arrives once we discover that we are not alone in our decisions.

Harry stared out across the river where a loaded coal barge fought to make headway on the black current. A tugboat trailed a quarter mile behind. Rain swirled about on the wind. "Look, dear, honestly, what's this all about? What did you have me out here for?"

"If I told you, honey, you might not want to come back."

"Pardon?"

"Sorry, I guess we ain't in love, after all."

This time, Harry pretended he hadn't heard her across the echoing wake of a distant steam whistle. How do you answer those sorts of questions, anyhow? There's a certain narrowness to emotions that can't be neglected, and sometimes their demands are impossible. "Listen here, it's been a terribly long day, and I really do need my rest."

"Sure you do," she mumbled, "like I need a million bucks."

"I beg your pardon?"

"You see that bridge?" She pointed to a footbridge arching over a roadway in the drizzling shadow of a solitary street lamp past the bulwark two or three hundred yards upriver.

"Yes."

"If you go east back into town from there, it'll blow you straight onto Columbia Avenue. You can find your hotel easy, then."

"How do you know where I'm staying?" He hoped she was joking.

Pearl laughed. "Honey, don't be such a sap! You ain't the only one with a brain out here tonight."

"What's that supposed to mean?"

Holding her tiny hands out palms up toward the wet black sky, she giggled, "Ain't the rain romantic?"

Then, blowing him a kiss, she rushed off across the bulwark and disappeared downriver into the windy darkness.

HADLEYVILLE, MISSOURI

WHEN ALVIN PENDERGAST WAS THIRTEEN, *two years before the consumption, he and Cousin Frenchy sneaked a ride one Saturday night on a melon truck driving south to market in Macomb. They figured on traveling a while before jumping off in the next county and hitching a ride back on Sunday. It was summer and the night was warm, so they just lay back and counted stars and gabbed about girls and fishing until they got sleepy and nodded off for a few hours. When they woke up, they found themselves parked behind a blacksmith shop next to a backhouse and a chicken coop full of squawking hens and a pack of children collecting eggs for breakfast. Alvin and Frenchy crawled down off the melon truck and walked out in front of the store to have a look-see, take the "lay of the land" as Frenchy put it. Not that there was all that much to see: a long dirt street, all the buildings on one side, shade trees and huge blackberry bushes on the other. Men sitting in chairs out front of the stores. Wagons parked at the curb. Horses reined to hitching posts. No automobiles anywhere. One sign on a post draped in trumpet vines across the road leading into town told them where they were:* Hiram, Ky. Pop. 132. *If they hadn't just recently gorged themselves on melon, they'd have been in trouble because neither possessed more than sixteen cents in his pockets. Alvin had a peculiar feeling, walking down the middle of Hiram's main street with Frenchy, trying to ignore the thought burning in his brain that he might never see home in Illinois again — an awfully black thought for a thirteen-year-old. Men stared at them from the storefronts clear down to the end of the road leading out of town. Alvin didn't see any women at all. The heels of the shoes Frenchy wore kicked up a trail of dust behind him, disturbing swarms of black flies off the horse apples in the dirt. Past a livery stable, the road bent left and went up a hill lined with more blackberry bushes. The* *boys followed it, hoping to find a county highway and another truck driving north to Illinois. Coming down the slope toward them was a preacher dressed all in black and carrying a leatherbound Bible. Back in Illinois, Alvin's mother attended church every Sunday, but his father never went, claiming the Lord knew how he felt about Him and didn't require a weekly recitation of those affections. Sunday School was where Alvin learned all about slingshots and miracles, which he preferred to sitting with the adults where everybody talked about loving the gospel while they farted all morning. Church was fine so long as it didn't last more than a couple hours and Momma cooked dinner afterward, but this particular Sunday in Hiram was different. The preacher had a little boy alongside dressed just the same as he was: black frock coat and suit, wide-brimmed hat, leatherbound Bible and comfort shoes. He had eyes like a crow and a face white as a spook. Man and boy shared the same gait, a purposeful stride that brought them straight down the road to Alvin and Frenchy. Probably they'd have walked right on by had Frenchy not whistled at the boy once they passed. Both preacher and disciple came about together just a few yards past Frenchy and Alvin. The boy wore a scowl like a wolverine. The preacher's face was mild but stiff. Alvin was terrified. Frenchy whistled again.*

"You mock those bringing the Lord's word," said the little boy in a fluty voice, "and He'll see a visitation upon your house. Ask old Pharaoh if that ain't so."

"I ain't got no house," replied Frenchy, puffing out his chest, "and I ain't got no silly-looking hat like yours, neither. And I wouldn't wear one if I did." Alvin smiled. Frenchy hardly ever showed much respect for anyone smaller than himself. He was always puffed up about all sorts of things and let you know about it, too.

"Blasphemer!" said the boy, eyes narrowed in fury. "Jesus'll burn you up! You just —"

The preacher cuffed the boy, knocking his hat off. "You hush now. The Lord's got no tolerance for curses spoken in His name."

Then he walked on up to Frenchy, his face hardened, while the boy bent down to pick up his hat. Tears filled his black crow's eyes, and the little one bowed his head.

The preacher looked down at Frenchy. "You boys look lost." His voice was thick and hoarse, like he'd swallowed gravel for breakfast.

Frenchy shrugged. "We're just walking."

The preacher held a firm countenance. "The road to the Lord is long and confusing. We all need a guide to take us to its proper end."

Frenchy shuffled his feet in the dirt. Alvin hadn't the guts to look the preacher in the eye, nor did he know just what he and Frenchy were supposed to say.

"The Lord provides in Jesus a road map for all our lives," the preacher continued. "Did you know that?"

"Jesus can see into your heart," barked the little boy. "You can't lie to Jesus."

"Hush up."

"They're sinners, Papa," the boy said, backing up. Tears streaked his cheeks and his lips quivered, but he spoke firmly. "Liars and sinners, both. I reckon I smelled 'em when I got up this morning. I know I did."

In the blackberry bushes, birds twittered and squawked. The sun was rising quickly on the morning sky. It would be a hot day.

"The Lord offers salvation in multitudinous forms," said the preacher, "and He does so without want of recompense or gratitude. It's His gracious heart that redeems us. Without our Lord's guiding hand, we'd all walk in constant night, utterly lost and confused."

"We ain't lost," said Frenchy, hardly a quiver in his voice. "We're just going fishing, is all. We like to start early."

Alvin always admired Frenchy's talent for smart-mouthing, another one of the reasons Alvin liked knocking around with him. Also, Frenchy rowed the boat whenever they went fishing and didn't complain about it.

"I don't see no fishing poles," said the little boy, sounding somewhat bolder himself. "Hard to catch fish without no poles." He stepped closer to Frenchy and shook his Bible at him. "Jesus was a fisher of men, but I expect He'd just throw you two back."

Before the boy could crack a grin at the joke he'd made, the preacher backhanded him across the face, knocking him down again into the dust.

The boy lay there whimpering as the preacher looked Frenchy square in the eye. Scared, Alvin backed up some, keeping one eye on the preacher and the other on the boy who lay flat in the dust, hat off, blood trickling from his nose. Alvin thought maybe he and Frenchy would have been better off staying in the melon truck.

"I ought to take you both home with me," the preacher said to Frenchy, "set you to work learning about the Redeemer and the path He walked. I know you boys are lost. There's no sin in that. We all find ourselves lost now and again. Jesus Himself spent forty days in the wilderness. His suffering lent salvation to all men."

"I told you," said Frenchy, narrowing his eyes to meet those of the preacher, "we ain't lost. We're just going fishing, is all."

The preacher's boy was on his knees now, grabbing his hat and fixing the brim. Tears and blood mixed in the dust. Flies buzzed across the road.

"The path to righteousness is the Lord's inspiration. You boys ought to study on that before you commence to walking any further. There's only one road worth following, and it's the Lord's. You remember that now."

With those words, the preacher strode past Frenchy and Alvin, scooped the little boy up by the crook of his arm, and headed on down the road. Alvin watched them go, his knees shaking.

"Amen," Frenchy said, and gave them one more whistle. Neither preacher nor little disciple looked back. Near the curve at the bottom, they passed out of sight.

Alvin swatted a fly off his face. Frenchy tossed a stone into the blackberry bushes, stirring up some bees. It was a long walk up the road, but Alvin was so afraid to follow the preacher back into Hiram they headed off just the same, deciding to walk home to Illinois if need be. Five hours later, God rewarded them with a ride north courtesy of a businessman from Galesburg, who had been visiting an acquaintance down in Bowling Green. When they reached Farrington, both boys received an enthusiastic whipping with a hickory rod in the tackroom of Uncle Henry's barn, followed by a lecture whose chief message was that life's highway holds extremes of danger and delight and only sinners and fools tempt its fancy.

Chester Burke's tan Packard Six was parked in a grove of old oak and black walnut trees on a shady bluff above the Missouri River a couple of miles from a small town called Hadleyville. Chester sat behind the steering wheel, reading a morning newspaper whose pages riffled in the morning breeze. Alvin Pendergast stood a few yards off in the sunlight, combing his hair and studying his look in a small hand-mirror. His face was sallow and thin, and he had a cough and a slight fever. Back home, he'd be in bed, sweating up the sheets, or maybe riding a train to the sanitarium. Far below to the east, a steamboat plied the wide green swirling current upriver.

Chester called over to him. "Look here, kid: the Babe hit another one. Rupert's gold mine. Greatest drawing card the game's ever had. I tell you, nobody stands 'em up like the Bambino. I saw him at Comiskey last year, swaggering around outside the clubhouse with a bottle of beer in each hand and it wasn't yet breakfast. Well, wouldn't you know it, he hit about a hundred balls out of the park in batting practice, went three-for-four in the game, then left with a dame on both arms! Can you feature that? Of course, Cobb was the real showman — get a hit, swipe a base, knock some poor dumb bastard on his keester. A genuine sonofabitch. My kind of ballplayer." Chester folded the paper to read the next page. He looked back over his shoulder. "Not much of a baseball fan, are you?"

Alvin stuck the comb and mirror into his shirt pocket. "I don't like games at all. They're for babies." Also, he hated getting sweaty from running about in the hot sun. Sports were for dumbbells.

"Don't be a philistine, kid. Baseball's great for the country. Keeps us square and healthy."

"Sure it does."

"You're smart, kid. Anyone tell you that before?"

"Nope."

"Well, it's true. Stick with me, you'll go far."

"Thanks."

"You sick or something?" Chester asked, looking Alvin in the eye with a worried frown.

The farm boy turned away, scared of being found out. "No, sir."

"Got the Heebie-Jeebies?"

"Maybe a little."

"Don't let it stir you up too much."

"I won't," Alvin said, strolling off to the edge of the river bluff. At home, he might have been finishing up with his chores right about now, getting ready to go fishing with Frenchy. They had a spot all picked out for springtime, a little shelter dug into the riverbank by the winter storms on the Mississippi where they could sit in the shade with a tree branch dangling trotlines in the current. Frenchy had been collecting bait for a couple of months, ten dozen nightcrawlers in one gallon fruit jar alone. Frenchy hated fishing alone, so without Alvin there he'd call on Herbert Muller who didn't know a catfish from a groundhog, but who wanted to pal around with Frenchy, hoping to line up some work in the summer. If Alvin ever went home, he planned on crowning Herbert Muller with a rock.

Looking downriver, he thought about Doc Hartley coming out to the farm to see if the consumption had returned. He hadn't traveled to the sanitarium with Alvin, nor had he ever visited. He hadn't told Alvin or his folks about the artificial pneumothorax treatments or how the wards smelled of formaldehyde and death. During that first month at the sanitarium, Alvin watched two brothers no more than nine or ten years old die in the ward together, side by side, like two little pasty white ghosts, hacking their tiny lungs out. Alvin had expected to die himself. He'd thought that's why he had been sent away: to spare his sisters the pain of seeing him croak at home. He saw sixteen people die in his ward during the year he spent at the sanitarium. How could his folks think he'd ever go back there? He'd rather jump off a bridge or dive under a train. If they were intending to send him back to the sanitarium, maybe he wouldn't ever go home again at all.

Chester honked the motor horn.

Alvin spat over the bluff, then returned to the auto and climbed in. Man-sized sunflowers flanked the ditches on both sides of the road and swayed in the draft of the Packard as Chester sped off toward town. There was no traffic for miles. Nobody on the highway at all. It was a funny day, Alvin thought. Not even many birds whizzing through the air. After a while, they ran by the Hadleyville city limits sign. It was almost noon. Shade trees lined the road that led through the back neighborhoods. Flowers bloomed on the white fencelines that marked a few dooryards. A sign read: **Lots for Sale — Easy Terms.** Chester kept the automobile in low as they motored toward the center of town. The quiet sidewalks shimmered in the heat. A couple of blocks farther on, Chester pulled the car over into a Dixie filling station under the shade of a huge weeping willow and let the motor idle. Alvin looked around. Storefronts and flags. Leo Brooks Boots & Shoes, Franklin Bogart's Grocery Emporium, Barton Brothers Clothing and Furnishings, a Ford agency and repair garage, and a furniture store with a fluttering advertising banner: ***Let us feather your nest with a little down!*** Half a dozen automobiles were parked across the street, a few pedestrians strolling about. It was a nice town.

"Why're we stopping here?" asked Alvin, watching a small hound dog chase a bird across the street. He was feeling jumpy all of a sudden.

Chester shut the engine off and climbed out. "You thirsty, kid? There's a lunchroom right around the corner. Come on, I'll set you up to an ice cold dope."

Alvin grabbed his cap and stepped out of the car. The sun was warmer than ever. Most of his family had the constitution for heat; his sisters sat indoors in the kitchen until high noon, then went out past the barn to play dolls in the tall grass meadows while he'd be hiding under an old shagbark hickory whenever he wasn't working, keeping to the shade. The family said it was his red hair that made him burn. Fishing at the river with Frenchy, he had to wear a floppy hat and a long-sleeved shirt buttoned to the collar. The hat made the girls along the shore think he was bald. He already suffered his affliction; now he had the hat, too. It was humiliating. *My dear son, we all have our crosses to bear,* his mother told him, but what did she know? She worked in her garden everyday and hardly ever needed a sunbonnet.

The attendant came out of the filling station, a freckle-faced tow-head hardly older than Alvin himself. "What'll it be, fellows?"

"Shoot some gasoline into our tank," Chester said, handing the boy a couple of dollar bills.

"Yes, sir."

"We'll be back in about ten minutes."

"Yes, sir."

Chester gave Alvin a nudge. "Let's go, kid."

They entered a narrow one-room building across the street where three men in suspenders and blue overalls sat hunched over a game of checkers at a table by the front window. The one kibitzing was smoking a three-for-a-nickel stogie and held a punchboard on his lap. Except for the old fellow in the white chef's hat, reading box scores from the morning sport sheets beside the cash register, they were the only people in the building. Six empty tables were arranged along one wall parallel to a short order counter that ran from the front of the building to the rear. Chester chose a seat at the table next to the back door. Alvin took the chair across from him and studied the lunch program hung on the wall behind the cash register: meatloaf, lamb, beefsteak, roasted chicken, baked ham and tomato soup — each dinner for 50¢.

"Do we have time to eat?" he asked, feeling a queasiness in his stomach that was either nervousness or hunger, probably both. He'd crammed down five hardboiled eggs, smoked bacon, a plate of toast and three cups of coffee for breakfast, but was already hungry again. His appetite was strange since he had gotten sick. Some days he never felt like eating a bite; the next day he couldn't keep his belly quiet.

"Nope." Chester took a package of Camel cigarettes from his vest pocket. He called to the man at the cash register. "Say, dad, how about a couple of Coca-Colas?"

The old fellow nodded and went to get the drinks from an icebox under the counter. They had drawn the attention of the men playing checkers. Chester lit his cigarette and gave them a friendly wave. The old fellow in the chef's hat brought two opened bottles of Coca-Cola and set them down in front of Chester. "That'll be ten cents, please."

Chester dug into his trousers and came up with a nickel and a handful of pennies, which he sprinkled out onto the counter. "Take your pick."

After the fellow had gone, Chester took a sip from one of the Coke bottles. "See those three onionheads over there by the window?"

Alvin nodded. In fact, he had been trying to ignore them. He didn't know much about folks in Missouri and what they thought of strangers. Were they friendly here?

"Well, I'll lay they're trying to figure out whether we're bootleggers or drugstore cowboys," Chester continued, "and we both know they couldn't tell a bootlegger from Hoover's grandmother. But what they're worried about are their birdies. That is, whose we'll be loving up this afternoon and whose we'll be ignoring. Trust me, kid. Losing their dames is the first thing folks get muddleheaded over when fellows like us come into town. We could go out and rob them blind, and while they'll be plenty sore, they'll start forgetting about it in a month or so. But if we were to drive off into the sunset with a couple of Hadleyville's sweeties, they'd hunt us down like animals, shoot us full of holes, and cut our carcasses up for the hogs."

Four more men wearing denim overalls came into the lunchroom and said hello to the old fellow at the cash register and took the table beside the checker players. One of them looked over at Alvin and Chester, and murmured a few words to the fellow beside him. The others seated at the table began talking among themselves.

Chester leaned across to the next table and grabbed an ashtray for his cigarette. Alvin felt a bellyache coming on. Chester had brought him here to Hadleyville to help him take some money out of the First Commerce Bank on Third Street. He'd told him so just after breakfast when he paid the bill. *"It'll be easy as pie," Chester said, handing Alvin a note that read:*

To whom it may concern: My nephew here is come to get his inheritance which is one thousand dollars. Please let him have it.

Signed, Hazel Reese

"You're going to present this to one of the tellers," he said.

"Don't joke me," Alvin replied.

Chester laughed and told him to get into the car because they had to reach Hadleyville by noon. "Don't worry, kid," Chester said, while they were driving along the highway. "You'll make the grade, all right."

Alvin asked, "You sure we ain't got time for a couple of pork chop sandwiches? I'm awful hungry."

Chester took a quick drag off the cigarette. "I'm sure."

His eyes were bluer than any Alvin had ever seen. He shaved each morning. Smelled like cologne. Wore fresh collars and a swell suit. Had his shoes shined before breakfast. Smiled at everyone he met. Never seemed scared, neither, Alvin thought. Now that was something worth learning. He could do a lot worse than taking after a smart fellow like Chester Burke.

A raucous cheer came from the checker game as somebody won. The old fellow at the cash register clapped. Out on the sidewalk, two rag-tag boys on bicycles rode past carrying fishing poles. Alvin felt envious; that's where he ought to be going. He could probably show 'em a good thing or two. The twelve o'clock whistle at the shingle mill across town shrieked, signaling the noon hour.

Chester snuffed out his cigarette, then drained the last of his Coca-Cola. "Let's go, kid."

Alvin studied the men at the checker game. Did they have any suspicions? Before today, he hadn't done more than carry Chester's suitcases for him and sit around the hotel lobby in New London while Chester finished his appointments; after changing a flat tire at Hannibal, Alvin didn't even have to leave his room. Ten dollars a day he'd earned, seventy dollars since the dance derby, more dough than he'd had in his hand all year. Once he hit a thousand dollars, he could buy his own motor and get a shoeshine every morning, too.

Out on the sidewalk, Alvin asked Chester, "You ain't going to cut me out, are you?"

A black Essex sedan rushed by toward the downtown.

Chester smiled. "Of course not, kid. I'm a square shooter. Trust me. There'll be kale enough for the both of us, you'll see." He stared up the street toward the middle of town while lighting another cigarette.

Alvin watched a group of women come out of Bogart's Grocery Emporium, burdened with packages. They were smiling brightly. Another automobile went by and a dog chased across the street, barking in its dusty wake.

The farm boy followed Chester back up the sidewalk to the Dixie filling station where he bought a stick of chewing gum to settle his stomach. When he came out again, Chester reached into the backseat of the Packard for a gray brim hat and gave it to Alvin. "Here, put this on."

Alvin frowned, but took off his checked cap and tried the hat on. It felt tight. He looked across at the garage window to see his reflection. He shook his head. "It don't fit. I prefer my own better."

He took it off.

Chester said, "Put it back on. You'll wear it to the bank. Throw the other one in the car."

"Well, what's it all about?"

"It's part of the gag."

"Oh."

Chester grabbed Alvin's cap and tossed it into the Packard, then climbed in behind the wheel. Before Alvin could get around to the passenger side, Chester stopped him. "You're going to have to walk there. It's only a few blocks or so. This is First Street. Follow it to Chapman, take a left, go to Sixth, take another left. You'll see it on the corner by the town square. First Commerce Bank. You can't miss it." He checked his pocketwatch. "We'll meet inside at a quarter till. Don't be late."

Then Chester put the car into gear and drove off.

The freckle-faced towhead inside the filling station watched through the plate glass. Alvin gave him the bad eye so he would mind his own business. He hated people staring at him. For half a year after Alvin had come back from the sanitarium, he'd felt like a sideshow freak, people looking at him wherever he went like they'd never seen someone return from the dead. When the towhead pulled a linen shade down against the sun, Alvin really felt alone, so he began walking down the sidewalk past the corner of the lunchroom and across the intersection into the next block of shade trees and modest lumber houses and smaller shanties of corrugated iron that looked more like fancy car garages. He took the stick of gum out of his shirt pocket and stuck it into his mouth. A couple of Fords rattled by. People across the street walked in and out of stores. He ignored them all, pretending like he walked down that sidewalk each day of his life and had every right in the world to be there. *Don't act like a hick that ain't never been to town*, he reminded himself. *Folks notice that. They can tell when you're somewhere you never been before and don't belong.* He chewed vigorously while he walked and held his head up so nobody would think he was timid. He smelled the blossoming home orchards behind the houses and spring flowers that grew beneath butterbean vine along picket fencelines in the shade where the dark earth was damp from recent rainshowers. The concrete sidewalk was cracked here and there, and tufts of grass grew in the fractures. Towering elm trees and poplars and cottonwoods arched overhead. More motorcars passed and the I.G.A. store across the street gave way at Williams Street to a neighborhood of elegantly fretted wood houses and gardens. Alvin heard hose nozzles hissing, piano scales from sunlit parlors, a hammerfall on steel echoing across the warm noon air. *It ain't so bad,* he thought. *Why, a fellow could get used to a new place like this in a hurry if he needed to.* To hell with the farm and everybody treating him like an invalid. He'd thrown all of that over and was done with it. His confidence growing by the minute, the farm boy walked ahead with a fresh bounce in his step.

Two blocks on, Alvin paused in front of a large two-story frame-house whose dry, ratty lawn covered most of the square lot. A lovely magnolia out front, a thick white oak in the side yard, and two black cherry trees toward the back fence provided shade for a lot where nearly everything had died from neglect. Even the paint on the fence pickets out front had peeled and vanished in a drier season, some-body's initials carved into the wood. The place looked abandoned and it wasn't only the lawn. Nearer the house, just under the shade of the magnolia, dozens of children's toys lay broken and scattered in the scruffy weeds — alphabet building blocks, tin bugles, wooden soldiers, wingless aeroplanes. Back along the side of the house where coralberry grew beneath the window boxes, an old tire hung down from the branch of the oak tree on a short length of rope. When they were kids, Alvin and Frenchy would go twirling in a tire they had hung inside Uncle Henry's barn. The stunt was to get as dizzy as possible, then play wirewalker along the tops of the stalls from one end of the barn to the other without falling off. Strolling out of the barn without stinking head to foot from horse manure was considered the game's supreme merit badge.

Feeling adventurous, Alvin opened the gate, keeping an eye on the front door whose screen was still closed, and crossed into the yard, staying under the overlapping shade of the blooming magnolia and the old oak. As he moved along the fence to the rear of the house, the farm boy saw more junk thrown about: cushions, shoes, an old lamp, a wicker chair without its seat, a rusted bed frame, torn pillows. He decided that either somebody had been doing spring-cleaning and had forgotten to bring everything back inside or the people living in the house were hillbillies. He came up to the swing and gave it a shove. The rope curled above the tire and twisted into a mean knot where it looped over the branch. Alvin stared at the house. Lace curtains were hung in the window frames, hiding the interior like a shroud. Back of the house, the trashcan had fallen over, spilling its contents all over the walkway between a tool shed and a weed-eaten vegetable patch.

Now he was curious what the indoors looked like, how high the garbage was piled elsewhere throughout the house. A short porch led up to the back door. If it wasn't locked, well, he might just take a quick peek inside. He walked up to the door and reached for the knob, then stopped to reconsider. If someone came to the door, how would he explain his presence in the back yard? Thinking on his feet was not one of Alvin's greatest strengths. All he could say was that he was lost and needed a drink of water and he'd already tried the front door and nobody had answered so he had come around back. Who could get bitter about a fellow asking for help? Alvin reached for the knob again.

"BOO!"

He stumbled backward and nearly fell over. Somebody laughed. Alvin hurried down off the porch, took a few steps backward, and stared up at the kitchen window. He listened for half a minute or so, then took half a stride toward the porch.

"BOO!"

More laughter.

The voice hadn't come from the kitchen, after all. The farm boy stepped back a few feet further and craned his neck upward to a second story window.

The voice, in a guttural murmer, said, *"No! Not there, either!"*

"I see you!" Alvin called out.

"No, you don't!"

Alvin hurried over to the swing and faced the window there above the thick coralberry. Imagining he saw the curtains move, he took a few steps closer. Was that a shadow there behind the glass? He walked close to the side of the house and got up on his tiptoes to see inside. "You're in there, ain't you? I just seen you!"

Laughter echoed into the yard. *"Nope!"*

"I'm going to come in there and clean you out!"

"No, you won't!"

"How about I give you a good pop in the nose?"

"All right, you win," the voice sagged. *"I'm down here."*

Along the foundation below the window box, a patch of coralberry parted, revealing a narrow crawlspace covered by a lattice grate propped open now. Alvin knelt for a look. Divided from the glare of the noon sunlight, the entry was black as cellar pitch. He'd sooner dive headfirst into a brick well than crawl through that hole. As a kid, Alvin'd had a nightmarish fear of the old boogey-man his sister Mary Ann told him lived in the dirt crawlspace beneath his bedroom floor. She said it snuck in out of a storm one night and favored the house so much it decided to stay. *It ain't no wild beast, neither. It's smart. Real smart. And patient. Boogey-man'll camp out down there for years, eating bugs and mice, stray cats, biding its time till it gets what it come for: a nice fresh little boy. Boogey-man'll wait till some poor little boy walks past by hisself and then it'll snatch him. Take him way down into the earth, so far no human being'll ever see him again, and make him a slave, or eat him, depending on how hard the boy works. You be careful, now. Wouldn't surprise me at all to find it's been working on them boards below your bed, trying to loosen 'em up, so's it can sneak in one night and snatch you while you're sleeping!*

"Hello, hello, hello!" the voice called out to him. "You're not afraid of the dark, are you?"

" 'Course not."

"Well then, come on in!"

A pair of hands and arms became visible in the gloom, small and frail, like a child's, followed by a large head wearing a smiling face that was not a child's at all, but in fact a dwarf's.

"Don't be a dilly-dog," the dwarf urged as pleasantly as possible. "Come on in. It's nice and cool."

Alvin stared at the dwarf, utterly unprepared for this encounter. The only such creature he had ever seen away from a circus was at the sanitarium, a diminutive juggler in clown paint who turned somersaults and chased the nurses about with a wooden paddle. He was shocked. It never occurred to him their sort lived in houses like regular folks.

The dwarf smiled up at him. "I won't bite you. I swear."

Alvin hesitated, preferring to remain out in the sunlight where it was safe.

"Oh please," the dwarf begged. "It's not half as dark as it seems. Why, I'm blind as a tick and I don't have any trouble at all getting about down here. What do you say?"

Alvin looked back across the yard to the street. Except for a pair of birds chirping somewhere up in the magnolia branches, the yard was dead quiet in the early afternoon.

"How about it?" Squinting in the sunlight, the dwarf thrust his head out of the coralberry. His hair was thin as cobwebs and nearly as white. "We'd have an awful lot of fun."

"I ain't sure I'd fit."

"Oh, of course you will. If you don't mind me saying, you're awfully skinny. You're not sick, are you?"

"Hell, no."

"Please?"

Alvin shrugged. "All right."

What did he have to be scared about? This little fellow was only half his size. If need be, he could probably throw him down in a second.

"Wonderful!"

The dwarf backed out of the opening, pushing the tiny grate aside as he went. Leaving Chester's hat behind in the grass, Alvin got down on his knees and pointed himself toward the dark square in the side of the house. Shoving the bushy coralberry apart with his hands, he crawled forward into the shadows.

It was a tight fit. His trousers threatened to catch on the latticework frame as he slithered by, while his knees scraped the foundation and his back struck the upper edge of the grate. Once in, though, he was able to sit up without much trouble. A crawlspace roughly four feet high separated the dirt foundation from the floor of the house above him. Plenty of room.

"Name's Rascal," said the dwarf, scrambling over beside him. "What's yours?"

"Alvin."

"Glad to know you, Alvin." Rascal sat down in the dirt and crossed his legs. He was dressed in a small boy's blue one-piece romper with black button shoes. Alvin had never seen anyone like him before in his life, but tried not to stare.

Ducking a spider web, the farm boy asked, "How long you been under here?"

"Since I lost my marbles last Saturday," said Rascal, drawing closer. "It's black as sin, isn't it? No trouble at all cracking your head open. Don't worry, you get used to it. Actually, I think it suits me. I find myself perspiring less down here."

"What's that smell?" asked Alvin, noticing for the first time a distinctly unpleasant odor, sort of fruity and damp, rotting. He thought he might gag from the stink.

Rascal sniffed the air. "Hmm. My guess would be honeydew melon. Sorry, I've been burying the rinds under the porch over there," Rascal gestured in the direction of the front of the house, "but some nocturnal creature keeps digging them up when I'm in bed. Very troublesome situation. Unsanitary to say the least."

"Maybe you ought to put them out with the garbage."

"Oh, except for collecting my groceries, I rarely go outdoors anymore." The dwarf jumped up, his head stopping just short of the support beams. "Do you care to play some marbles? I found a few of my aggies this morning. There's a place all smoothed out under the kitchen." Rascal grabbed Alvin by the wrist. "Come on, I'll show you."

"I can't. Got an appointment downtown in half an hour. Sorry." He wondered what Chester was doing just then, where he'd gone off to. He never saw fit to tell Alvin anything that mattered.

The dwarf tugged. "Please? It'll only take a minute."

"Oh, all right. But I ain't got all day." Reluctantly, Alvin rose as high as he could without hitting his head, and followed the dwarf on a crooked path between the support pillars and foundation blocks from one end of the house to the other, dodging clots of spider web and gunny sacks stuffed with dirt and assorted broken toys like those lying about in the grass outside. The stink under the house worsened the farther in they went. More than rotted fruit, the stench of a summer outhouse whose wooden walls and damp soil collected and preserved the odor. Alvin shuffled behind Rascal until they came to a narrow hole crudely hacked out of the floor overhead.

The dwarf stopped and smiled. "That's my bedroom up there. Would you like to see?" He pulled himself up into the opening and disappeared. Alvin heard his footsteps scrambling across the floorboards. A drawer opened and shut. Something heavy was dragged across the floor. Trying to follow Rascal up into the hole, Alvin only managed to get his head through. He saw Rascal staring at him.

"Aren't you coming?"

"I can't fit."

"How come?"

"My shoulders are too wide."

Alvin swiveled his head to get a better look at the room. It had no window and only two doors, one of which opened to a small closet. There was a small iron bed, a common oak dresser, and a low nightstand with a kerosene lamp. Clothes were jumbled up at the foot of the bed, Post Toasties cereal boxes stacked together beside the dresser, fruit jars filled with preserves on top, six water jugs next to the closet, Big Little books piled on the nightstand. Odds and ends collected beneath the bed: rubber galoshes, mousetraps, used-up pencil tablets, a shoe stretcher, and a pocket spyglass. Rascal dove into the shallow closet and began rummaging through the clothes and assorted junk that had piled up, tossing things out onto the floor behind him. After a couple of minutes, he came out dragging a little old leather suitcase.

"Maybe you ought to go open the back door," said Alvin, "so's I can come in and sit down. This ain't all that comfortable."

Rascal played with the latches on the suitcase, trying to flip them up. "Door's locked."

Alvin bent his knees slightly to ease the pressure on his shoulders. If he were a foot shorter, he could have been standing straight up with his head in the hole. "I know, I tried it. Just go open it from the inside."

"I mean, my bedroom door's locked, too," said Rascal, pointing over his back. "That's why I had to pry a hole in the floorboards with a butter knife. Auntie locked me in and took the key before she left. This used to be a pantry until my behavior last year apparently warranted a change of scenery." The dwarf banged the suitcase hard on the floor. "Dammit!"

"Can't you force it open?"

"I'm trying," said Rascal, banging the suitcase a second time even harder. The latches appeared jammed shut with rust.

"I mean your door."

"Nope." Rascal dropped the suitcase and scuttled back across the floor into the closet. More clothes came flying out behind him: shirts, stockings, a fancy pair of riding boots and a big white ten-gallon William S. Hart cowboy hat. Rascal slid out on his hands and knees carrying a pair of pliers. "She's padlocked all the doors in the house, front to back. So I'm stuck here."

"You could crawl out and bust a window," Alvin told him. "That's what I'd do if I was you. It's your house, too, ain't it?"

"You mean throw a rock?"

"Or use a stick. It don't matter which if you got to get inside."

The dwarf shook his head. "No, I'd feel like a crook and there'd be glass everywhere. What if it rained? I'd have an awful mess to clean up and when Auntie returned, she'd throw a fit."

"Well, suit yourself." Alvin shrugged. "But why'd she lock you in here, anyhow?"

"Doesn't trust me," said Rascal, attacking the suitcase latches with a vengeance, using the pliers to tear out the mountings. His face reddened with the effort.

"Where'd she go?"

One latch broke and popped free. "To a medicine show in Dayton, Ohio. She's addicted to brain tonics."

Rascal worked the pliers on the other, tugging furiously at the lock.

"How long's she supposed to be gone?"

"Three weeks." The pliers snapped and fell apart at the joint. "Oh, for the love of Pete!"

The dwarf spun around and hurled the broken pliers under the bed, then got up and kicked the suitcase against the dresser. When it still didn't open, he ran back into the closet and began digging through his collection of junk again.

Alvin let his head drop out of the room and squatted in the dirt. Sunlight flickered into the shadows through the baseboards that encircled the house, but the only genuine entry was the small lattice grate. Listening to Rascal bang on the suitcase latch, Alvin admired the extensive junkyard the dwarf had created within the crawlspace. Whether from anger or boredom, he had strewn garbage into every corner of the underside of the house; a family of raccoons couldn't have done a better job. It'd take days to clean it all out, digging up what scraps he'd buried and carting it off with the rest of the trash. Alvin wondered what Rascal's aunt would think when she discovered all he had done in her absence. Maybe that's why she didn't trust him alone with the run of the house.

The dwarf quit hacking at the suitcase. Hearing the latches snap open, Alvin stuck his head back up through the hole in the floor just in time to witness the dwarf tip the suitcase upside down and spill a huge stack of papers out onto the floor. Ignoring the loose sheets, Rascal dug hurriedly into the larger pile, sifting to the bottom. When he came up with a thick stack of postcards bound in string, he leaped to his feet. "Aha! Found 'em!"

"Found what?"

"Let me by," said Rascal, straddling the hole. Alvin slipped back down under the house again and the dwarf dropped through the hole, carrying the postcards. He sat in the dirt and handed half of the postcards over to Alvin. "My Uncle Augustus mailed these back to himself from France during the war. When he died, I inherited them with a box of his old correspondences."

"Naked ladies," said Alvin, shuffling through the cards one by one. He'd had no idea this is what the dwarf had busted open his suitcase to retrieve.

Rascal giggled. "Grand, aren't they? If Auntie knew I had them, oh boy!"

Every card featured a different woman, a different pose. More than a couple gave Alvin that hot feeling down below his stomach. Frenchy had these sorts of photographs once when he was living out back of the barn. Some were belly-dancing girls in lacy get-ups with funny tassels on their tits and belly-buttons showing. Others had colored women from Dixie lying on metal cots, posing without smiles or clothes of any kind, completely naked, hair between the legs and all. Frenchy charged his cousins a penny a peek, nickel for half an hour, and bought a bottle of liquor every Saturday night with the earnings.

Alvin shuffled through the cards, the stick in his pants getting bigger by the second. Hurried by the dwarf's stupid grin, he zipped to the bottom of the stack and handed the French postcards back to their owner.

"You like them, don't you?" said the dwarf. "Me, too." Rascal stuck the cards up through the hole and laid them on his bedroom floor. "I used to take them out every so often. Not every day, of course, but I'd have to say three or four times a week. Auntie would say I'm sinning, but what does she know? She's never married."

Feeling an attack of claustrophobia coming on, Alvin looked away from the dwarf toward the exit framed in sunlight across the dark underside of the house. He coughed, and his ears rang.

"I suppose you're late for your appointment," the dwarf remarked, sounding disconsolate. "I'd sure hate you to get in trouble for visiting me."

Through the grate in the crawlspace, Alvin watched the bottom branches of the white oak swaying in the afternoon breeze. "Yeah, I guess I ought to get along pretty soon."

"I wish I had a job," said the dwarf, sitting down against one of the support pillars. "Something stimulating, yet profitable. Perhaps in a department store or a rollercoaster park. Do you know of anything fitting that description?"

"Not today."

"I suppose I should study the newspapers, prowl the pavement, ring doorbells. How else can I expect to gain employment? Can you read?"

"Sure." Scarcely more than labels and street signs, if truth be told, but Alvin didn't feel like admitting one of his worst shortcomings to a stranger. The year of school he had missed being sick set him back so far that he never caught up and didn't care any longer. He hated reading.

"I try to study ten thousand words a day. That's in addition to the fifteen new ones I memorize out of Webster's every night before I go to bed. I also read philosophy and the natural sciences. I've always believed in bettering myself through learning. 'Education has for its object the formation of character.' That's a credo of mine. Do you have one?"

Before Alvin was forced to embarrass himself by asking what exactly a credo was, Rascal leaped up and ran across the dirt to a small hiding space under the veranda where the slats between the front steps afforded a discreet view of the sidewalk.

"Do you see this fellow out here?"

Alvin crab-walked to the steps, then knelt down and angled for a look. He saw a tall man in a gray suit pacing the sidewalk in front of the dwarf's house. "What of it?"

"Well, I'm convinced he's either one of Auntie's gigolos or a cat burglar planning to rob us. I've seen him out there now three days in a row and I confess it's beginning to spook me. Last night, I actually slept with a candle lit. It was quite humiliating."

Alvin didn't think that was anything to get cut up about. Men like him came out to the farm all the time, mostly to take a look at the girls and talk up some bargain that didn't amount to nothing. "Maybe he's just one of those fellows selling soap flakes."

"Oh, I don't know. He doesn't seem very friendly."

They both watched the man, who did nothing but pace up and down. Alvin had no opinion about his character, so he kept quiet. What could he say? The dwarf studied the fellow with a persistent frown. Then the guy broke one of the old fence pickets with a hard kick and walked off.

When he had gone, the dwarf slid away from the steps. "I'm sure he'll be back."

Alvin crept out from under the steps behind him. "If he's a regular burglar, it'll be a knock if he don't."

"Well, I won't stand it. I have a pistol, you know."

"Don't blow off your toe."

"Oh, I'm a sure-shot," the dwarf boasted. "When I was younger, I used to practice on Auntie's empty Cascara bottles nearly once a month."

Alvin remembered his appointment at the bank. "I ought to go."

"Do you have to? Really, entertaining is so much fun. If only I had more room."

"I don't want to be late." In fact, he was afraid of what Chester might do if he didn't show up on time. He had a temper that didn't need showing to be taken account of. Alvin saw it in his eyes. He could be mean if he had to, and Alvin knew it.

"Where are you going? If I may ask."

"First Commerce Bank downtown. Do you know where that is?"

"Of course I do. It's at Sixth and Calhoun," the dwarf replied. "Why, that's where Mr. Sinclair works."

"Who?"

"Harrison B. Sinclair. An old friend of the family. He and Auntie are quite close. You'll like him a lot. He can be a very pleasant fellow, particularly if you have any money to invest."

"Well, I ain't never been there before."

"Oh, it's only a short walk from here," the dwarf explained, "I could take you, if you like. I really haven't been out of doors in almost a week. I miss the air. A good walk now and then makes for a fine con-stitutional, don't you agree?"

Alvin thought about that, bringing the dwarf with him. He imag-ined Chester standing outside even now, checking his watch. How sore would he be if he saw the dwarf? Alvin told Rascal, "I ain't sure I can take you along. It's private business."

"Oh, I wouldn't be a bother. What sort of business?"

"I ain't supposed to say."

"Is it a secret?" The dwarf broke a sly grin. "I adore secrets."

"Sure it is."

"Well, I wouldn't tell anyone. Cross my heart."

Alvin took the note out of his shirt pocket and showed it to the dwarf, figuring it didn't give away much. Besides, he thought, the note's a lie, ain't it?

Rascal laughed when he finished reading. He said, "This is very clever."

"That ain't my real uncle."

The dwarf smiled. "Did you compose this yourself?"

"My partner did," Alvin told him. "He's pretty smart."

"How long've you been in cahoots with this fellow?" the dwarf asked, as he read over the note again.

"Well, I ain't saying."

Rascal looked up. "Beg your pardon?"

"We ain't in cahoots," Alvin said, feeling somewhat awkward now. Maybe he shouldn't have shared Chester's note. Deciding he ought to put the dwarf off the track, Alvin told him, "He's just a fellow I met to do some business with. See, he owns a box factory in Kenosha that makes a new sort of pasteboard and he's looking for folks to work there. I seen his ad in the *Daily News* when I was up north to a show at the Chez Paree, so I sent him a telegram with all the dope about myself, and here we are."

The dwarf laughed. "Oh, I hardly think so. Truth is, you're both here to rob the First Commerce Bank, aren't you?"

Alvin frowned. "Quit your kidding."

"Look, any fool can see this is a decoy note," Rascal said, enthused with discovery, "and not a very persuasive one, either. If you give this to any of Mr. Sinclair's tellers, you'll be a jailbird by suppertime. Let me help you write another."

"Huh?"

"Wait here." The dwarf straightened up, his head still easily below the floorboards. "I've just had the most marvelous idea!"

He dashed off toward his bedroom.

"Hey there!" Alvin called after him. "I got to get along!"

But the dwarf had already climbed up through the hole and disappeared. Alvin crawled under the house toward Rascal's bedroom, afraid he was going to be late now to the bank. He heard the dwarf rummaging through his closet, tossing more things about. It occurred to Alvin that the dwarf bore his cross better than anyone he'd ever known in his life. Had anybody else come to visit Rascal beneath the house in the time he'd been locked indoors? Did he have any friends? Alvin promised himself that if he ever came back through Hadleyville again, why, he'd take Rascal out fishing. The poor little fellow had probably never even been in a boat before.

After a few minutes, the dwarf dropped down through the hole in his bedroom floor, carrying a small black leather doctor's bag. He took a slip of paper from the pocket of his romper and gave it to the farm boy to read.

"This is a much grander plan," Rascal assured him, as he put down the doctor's bag. He wore a big grin. The note read:

> Gentlemen: The bearer of this letter has a dynamite bomb in his satchel. Please deliver into his possession the amount of two thousand dollars or he will fix this bank of yours for good!
>
> Signed, Al Capone

The dwarf said, "We might've asked for more money, but then they'd have to count it out by hand and that could take more time than we'd want. The police station is only four blocks away."

Alvin was flabbergasted. He knew he shouldn't have said anything about his appointment at the bank. Now what was he supposed to do? If the dwarf was right about Chester intending a stick-up, wouldn't changing the plan now make things even worse? He was scared and confused, and felt his bellyache returning. He coughed again and his eyes watered.

He told Rascal, "Look, I ain't asked for your help. What if they got a bank dick? I could get shot in the head."

"They do and his name's Elmer Gleason and he's only got one eye. He lost the other fighting with Stonewall Jackson at Chancellorsville. If he draws his revolver, just remember to keep to his left."

The dwarf laughed.

Alvin scowled. "That ain't so funny."

"Nobody'll shoot you. I promise."

The farm boy grew more desperate. "What if my partner ain't robbing the bank, after all? I'll look like a damned fool."

"Oh, there's no mistake, I assure you. I've read more accounts of bank robberies than you can shake a stick at and anyone who'd deliberately choose to hand your partner's note to one of Mr. Sinclair's tellers, well, I'd have to say he hasn't got the sense God gave an oyster. Now, tell me this: what sort of motor car did you fellows drive to town?"

Feeling resigned to the dwarf's intentions, Alvin said, "It's a Packard Six. Sort of straw-colored."

"All right, listen," Rascal said, unfastening the latches to the doctor's bag. He handed it to Alvin so he could see what was inside. "This is what we'll do."

Downtown Hadleyville felt quiet in the noon hour. Motor traffic was intermittent. Birds flew noiselessly from treetop to flagpole. Children and mothers sat together picnicking on the summer grass. Dogs chased after fluttering leaves.

Alvin waited across the street from the bank. A clock tower on the square indicated he still had a few minutes to run off and avoid the necktie party when the dwarf's plan went on the bum. Chester was inside the bank already, his automobile parked in the alleyway behind Orrey's jewelry shop. Frenchy told Alvin once that *"It ain't what you got, it's what you can get away with,"* but everyone in the family knew he was kind of a half-crook and nearly always in trouble. Frenchy couldn't drive through downtown traffic without skipping a light or two, and always thought it was a swell gag to walk out of a five-and-dime with some hot stuff in his pocket. Just last summer, in fact, he'd been to jail for stealing watermelons from a Mormon market down in Nauvoo. He spent six weeks there mopping floors and scrubbing toilets. One night, the convict he shared a cell with popped him in the mouth and knocked Frenchy's tooth out. When Alvin was younger, before the consumption, he had given hell himself to truant officers and gotten sick on corn liquor and stolen molasses candy and penny chocolate drops every so often from Smead's drugstore, but he had been afraid of the punishment for getting caught to do anything much worse. Robbing a bank was different, more than a germ of youthful anarchy or a one-horse beer racket. This would put a smut on his life. Yet when the clock struck a quarter till, Alvin Pendergast carried the small doctor's bag across Third Street and entered the First Commerce Bank of Hadleyville, Missouri.

It was stuffy indoors, a musty odor of perspiration and dried-out leather. Electric fans suspended from a plaster Greek Revival ceiling high overhead spun dust motes lazily through the sunlight. The wood floor creaked underfoot. Chester stood by the wall opposite the merchants' window, scribbling on a sheet of paper and chatting up a pretty girl in a yellow bloomer dress. Seated in a white wicker chair beside a potted palm was an old man wearing a faded butternut gray Civil War uniform with a navy Colt .44 revolver hanging off his belt. He was sound asleep. Three clerks worked behind the cage. A door leading to offices on the second story was open and voices echoed in the stairwell. Except for the rhythmic tapping of a Monroe adding calculator downstairs and a typewriter clacking upstairs, it was even quieter than outdoors.

Remembering his instructions from Rascal, Alvin went to stand in line behind the other customers at the teller's window. He made eye contact with the young man at the adding calculator and nodded a greeting. Chester and the girl stepped into line behind him. One of the bank officers went upstairs carrying a large sack of coins that chinked with every step he took. The elderly bank guard began to snore.

As the first customer in line finished his business, Chester tapped Alvin on the shoulder. "Pardon me."

The farm boy turned around. "Yes, sir?"

"Would it be too great an inconvenience for you to allow this young lady to go ahead? She's in an awful rush."

Blushing, Alvin looked at the girl behind Chester. Her brown eyes were wide and glossy, and Chester gave him a look that told him to let her past, so Alvin nodded. "All right."

He stepped aside to allow her through to the teller's window. She offered a pleasant smile. "Much obliged." A keen scent of Violet perfume trailed behind her.

"Sure."

"That's a swell valise you got there, " Chester remarked, clapping him on the shoulder.

Alvin mumbled, "It's my daddy's."

"Well, it's a knockout."

"Thanks."

Chester smiled and stepped forward to stand with the slender girl. Alvin had to admit he was slick. Chester hadn't shown the slightest recognition when they'd greeted each other. Presumably, he'd done this so often that fooling people had become natural to him.

Nervous as hell now, Alvin watched a pack of young loafers outdoors, lagging along the sidewalk by the barbershop. A paneled cargo truck drove past in a cloud of exhaust smoke. His bellyache worsened. Alvin stood three customers from the window now and the doctor's bag felt heavy in his hand. He tried to concentrate on fishing to calm his gut. Instead, he recalled an old saw Grandpa Louis used to quote whenever the subject of life and labor arose: *"Get the money — honestly if you can."*

When the girl arrived at the head of the line, Chester stepped off to one side to let her do her business. He winked at Alvin. A pair of fellows in striped brown suits came into the bank and went straight for the executive offices at the rear where one of the fine walnut desks had a tall brass spittoon beside it. The prim bank officer wore pince-nez and a fresh blood carnation on his lapel. Alvin wished he could get a glass of water. His knees felt weak. The pretty girl finished her business at the teller's window and stepped aside. She smiled at Chester. He tipped his fedora as she walked past him out of the bank.

Dropping his voice, Chester murmured to Alvin, "Use your noodle, kid."

Then he, too, walked off, farther down the counter to the merchants' window where a notice from the Advertising Association was hung on the back wall.

"May I help you, sir?"

The farm boy stepped up to the teller and set down the black doctor's bag, scared half out of his wits now. The teller was a fellow maybe Chester's age with oil-slicked hair and a gray wool suit that was probably from Montgomery Ward & Co. He looked drowsy. Alvin handed him the note.

A cool draft swept into the bank from the corridor leading to the rear entrance. Somebody had just walked in through the door leading out to the alley. Voices from the stairwell went silent. The back door swung closed with a bang.

The teller looked confused. "What is this?"

Alvin narrowed his eyes, trying to stave off panic. He kept his voice low. "Can't you read?"

"You have a bomb?"

Alvin picked up the doctor's bag. "Right in this here satchel. Just like it says in the letter."

The teller's face flushed. "Is this some sort of joke?"

"I ain't laughing, am I?" Alvin replied, utterly numb below his neck.

He heard murmuring behind him from a man and a woman waiting in line.

"This is against the law," the teller offered, trying to sound calm while his chin trembled.

"What of it?" Alvin replied, annoyed now. Somehow, fear and fever emboldened him. He raised his voice. "I ain't feeling too good and I might be contagious, so give me the money, you dumbbell, or I'll blow us all up."

"Oh, my Lord!" the woman behind him cried. "He's got a bomb!"

"A bomb!" somebody else shouted. "That boy there's got a bomb!"

When Alvin turned to address the commotion, his teller disappeared beneath the counter. Two men ran out of the bank. Another woman by the bank guard fainted. Old Elmer Gleason still hadn't awakened. The bank officers were staring at Alvin. Unsure of what to do, he opened the doctor's bag and stuck his hand inside. "I ain't joking you. I'll blow us all up. I swear it!"

"Somebody please do something!" another woman cried. "He'll kill us all!"

"Not unless I tell him to!" a voice called out from the rear of the bank. The dwarf emerged from the back door hall dressed in a gray single-breasted boy's corduroy knickerbocker suit that looked spick and span after his grimy under-the-house attire. Even his cornsilk hair was combed and his shoes polished. "Mr. Sinclair! May I see you a moment?"

Another fellow in the teller's line behind Alvin snuck out of the bank and ran off. The bank officers who had been hiding in the stairwell came down into the lobby behind the dwarf who marched over to the cages and got up on his tiptoes to counter level. "How's my money doing?"

The prim fellow in pince-nez left his desk. Keeping an eye on Alvin, he asked, "What's this all about? Do you know that young man over there?"

"Of course," the dwarf replied, steely-eyed. "He's an anarchist I hired to bring that bomb here this afternoon."

Alvin felt everyone staring at him. His bellyache had gone, but his knees still rattled. The handle of the bag was damp from his sweaty palms. He considered running away.

"I don't understand," Mr. Sinclair said to the dwarf. "Where's your Aunt Esther?"

"She's in Dayton on business. I'm in charge of things while she's away. Is my money still here?"

The bank officers looked at each other, surprised by the question. "Of course it is," replied Harrison B. Sinclair. "Why, your aunt is one of our most valued customers."

Alvin saw Chester mumbling to the teller at the merchants' window. The teller nodded and began opening the stack of drawers just beneath the counter.

"Sure she is," replied the dwarf, "but it's not her money. It's mine. May I see it?" The dwarf pulled himself up onto the edge of the counter. "I've decided to take some of it with me today."

The merchants' teller in front of Chester had a large sack open and was shoveling money into it. Alvin glanced at the street outside. Sidewalks were mostly empty, no motor traffic.

The bank officer told the dwarf, "That's not possible without your aunt's approval."

"Why not?"

"Well, she's your legal guardian. Her power-of-attorney in this case extends to withdrawal of funds from the trust your late parents, God rest their souls, set up on your behalf."

Rascal looked briefly in Alvin's direction and frowned. Was he really surprised to hear this, Alvin wondered. "That doesn't seem fair," the dwarf said. "Is it legal?"

"Perfectly."

Both bank officers smiled.

"So, even though it's my money, I can't have any of it."

"Not without your aunt's signature," said Mr. Sinclair. "I can show you the figures, if you like."

"Figures don't lie," the dwarf remarked, "but liars can figure. I'd prefer to see my money."

"Look, son," Sinclair said, confidently, "I'm not sure why you came down here today. It's always been my understanding that you were perfectly aware of this financial arrangement, and that it was quite acceptable to you. Now you're asking us to remove a considerable sum of money from our vault just so you can see that it's there. If you'll pardon my being blunt, but that seems a little childish, don't you agree?"

The dwarf slipped down off the counter and shook his head, looking hangdog. "I thought we were pals, Mr. Sinclair. At least, you said we were. Remember when you told me that? It was on my twenty-first birthday, and you and Auntie were up in her bedroom and I was hiding in the closet, spying on you two? Remember? And afterward, you said if there was anything I ever needed, I could come right down here and ask, and you'd do whatever I wanted, no matter what. You said that! Remember? Anything!"

Harrison B. Sinclair's face became a deep crimson, both angered and embarrassed. "I have no idea what you're talking about."

The dwarf turned to Alvin. "Tommy, please bring me the satchel."

The farm boy carried the doctor's bag over to the dwarf. He could barely walk and wondered when this would all be over. He noticed the bank guard was just waking up. Keep to his left, Alvin reminded himself.

"Thanks," Rascal said, a grave expression on his moony face. "You can run along now."

Chester snatched a sack from the teller and whispered something else to him. As discreetly as possible, Alvin walked back across the bank lobby. Chester left the merchants' window and headed for the door. Mr. Sinclair asked the dwarf, "What are you intending to do?"

"Well," Rascal replied, reaching into the doctor's bag, "I ask myself just that question everyday." He drew out a handful of rocket-sticks, tied together and painted up to resemble dynamite.

"Good grief!" one of the bank officers shouted. "He's really going to blow us up! For Christsakes, Harry! Do something!"

The dwarf took out a match and lit the fuse attached to the stack of rocket-sticks. "If I can't have my inheritance, then nobody can!"

Alvin slipped out the front door of the First Commerce Bank.

Inside, a woman screamed and a huge BANG! echoed throughout the building.

His heart thumping wildly, Alvin hurried down the sidewalk to the corner and around back to the alleyway behind the jewelry store where Chester's Packard was parked beside a board fence swarmed with hollyhocks and sunflowers. He threw his hat into a rubbage barrel, and climbed into the automobile. There, he watched Chester rush up the alley, carrying the sack of money. "Here, kid, stick this in the backseat."

Alvin grabbed the sack and tossed it into the car.

Chester asked, "How'd you come across that bomb idea?"

"Me and that little fellow. We thought it up together."

"Where'd you bump into a nut like that?" Chester asked, as he went around to the trunk. "He's bugs."

"I don't know," Alvin lied, feeling confused now and dizzy from his sudden adventure.

Chester removed his hat and brown coat and threw both into the trunk, then grabbed a new blue coat and hat from his valise. "Well, you put it over just swell. They lapped it up."

Thrilled by the adventure of it all, Alvin felt brave enough to smile. "We gave 'em the works, didn't we?"

"You sure did." Chester put on the blue coat and hat, then handed Alvin the keys to the Packard. "I'll meet you on the sidewalk next to Lowe's furniture store. Don't be late."

"I won't."

Once Chester had gone off down the alley again, Alvin reached back into the Packard and shoved the sack of money under a pile of clothes in the rear seat, then got in and started the motor. Before he could put it in gear, the dwarf came out the rear of Orrey's jewelry store with an old leather suitcase in hand.

"Wait!" he yelled, struggling to reach the car. "Don't go yet!"

"What do you want?"

"Take me along!"

Alvin let his foot slip off the gas pedal and the dwarf dropped the suitcase into the dirt beside the Packard.

"Everything I said went," the dwarf told Alvin, opening the passenger door. "Now they want to kill me. You have to take me with you."

"It ain't my motor."

"Please? I won't be any trouble at all. You have my word."

What was he supposed to say? Without the dwarf, he might be in jail now. Alvin shrugged. Chester could decide what to do with him once they got out of town. "All right, get in."

The farm boy put on his old cap and drove out of the alley and turned left on Fourth Street past the Postal Telegraph office. It was a short run to Main Street at the end of the block. Rolling toward the town square, Alvin's stomach flip-flopped. The sidewalks on both sides of the street adjacent to First Commerce Bank were crowded with people milling about and gesturing in every direction. Alvin slumped low in the seat and drove by without slowing. Both bank officers were outside talking to a local policeman who had just arrived. Elmer Gleason was also out on the sidewalk, lying with his back against a lamppost and receiving treatment from a nurse. His revolver had been drawn and lay next to his leg on the pavement.

A muffled voice from the rear seat mumbled, "Where are we?"

"Hush up," said Alvin, driving now down to the end of the town square.

A strong breeze rippled the flags on the storefronts. Slowing further, Alvin drove by Chase Esquire's Insurance, the Palace movie house, and Johnson Murray's Hardware. As he passed Lowe's furniture, he saw Chester stroll out of M. K. McDonald's wallpaper emporium. Alvin stopped the Packard at the curb just long enough for Chester to come around and jump into the passenger seat. A young woman wearing a rosy porch dress and a straw-bonnet tied with a pink bow under her chin leaned out the store's front door and shouted, "Eight o'clock sharp now!"

Chester waved with a grin. "You said it, sweetheart!"

Alvin checked the mirror. Nobody was coming yet, but he held the Packard in gear just in case.

"Don't be late!" She fluttered her eyelids.

"Oh, I won't!" Chester said, waving to her again, the smile frozen on his face. Then he turned to Alvin and growled. "Step on it."

The woman blew Chester a kiss, "Bye-bye, Charley!"

Alvin accelerated up the street toward the town limits. The road was clear in both directions. No flags or stores. Just a broken-down harness maker and a closed berry crate factory. Hazel bushes and zigzag rail fences and nanny goats in a small old cornfield. Passing a farm tractor parked on the outskirts of town, he asked Chester, "Who was that lady?"

"Just a dame."

"She invite you to supper?"

"You bet she did. I honeyed her up for almost an hour."

"What for?"

Chester laughed out loud. "What for? The old haha, kid. If I got pinched back there, she'd have sworn on a stack of Holy Bibles I was sitting in her lap the whole afternoon."

"Oh."

After crossing over a plank bridge, they drove past a square wooden sign reading **Come back soon to HADLEYVILLE, MO.** Ahead stretched the road west to Kansas or Oklahoma or wherever they chose to go. The afternoon sky overhead was blue clear up to heaven. Alvin slipped the Packard into high gear and leaned back. How far away was Farrington, Illinois now? Farther than yesterday.

As the farm boy drove up the highway between the vast wheat fields, he asked, "Where're we headed?"

Chester laughed again. "Where do you want to go, kid? Name your poison."

Just then the dwarf popped up from beneath the coats and suitcases in the rear seat and leaned his gnarled elbows on the leather seatback. There he announced, "Well, fellows, I don't know where we're going, but we're on our way."

MAY

THE HOUSE IN BELLEMONT had a broad sunporch whose middle staircase faced due west, keeping those sitting out in the wicker chairs warm late into the day. Five wooden steps led up from the wide dirt street, inviting people to stop and share a glass of lemonade or iced tea. Conversation was entertainment in Bellemont. Maude Hennesey had a small circle of ladies who passed three afternoons a week on her porch, playing Hearts and whist and discussing those who were absent. Though the wind blew dust up and down College Street, Maude kept the windows open day and night, circulating the air indoors behind storm screens and allowing sidewalk conversations to be overheard from most any room.

Marie Hennesey and her two children were given Harry's old bedroom on the west end of the house, where a pretty chinaberry tree beside the window frame provided a cooling shade and barely disturbed their view of the backyard and the grassy fields behind the Jessup's house next door. Expressed in the room assignment was an understanding of impermanence. Harry was gone on a business venture to the city where he'd taken a hotel room for this season and the next. When he had earned enough to return, he would find his family another home of their own. Somewhere far from East Texas. Until then, Marie and the children were guests of her mother-in-law.

"I expect you'll need all the drawers," said Maude, studying the old walnut chiffonier she had been using for those clothes she hadn't worn in several seasons. "I just don't know where my things'll go. This house is so small."

She looked at her daughter-in-law, as if hoping somehow Marie might volunteer to manage the children's clothes and her own wardrobe from the old steamer trunk. Laying Cissie's worn-out copy of *The Emerald City of Oz* on the bed, Marie avoided Maude's gaze and walked to the window. What could she say? It wasn't her fault the house wasn't bigger, and they weren't taking Maude's bedroom, anyhow. This one was barely larger than Marie's old sewing room on Cedar Street. If she and the children could make do in such a tiny space, Marie felt Maude ought not to complain. Besides, this had all been Harry's idea. If Maude was unhappy, perhaps she should write her son a letter and tell him so.

Outdoors now behind Maude's house, ten-year-old Cissie had discovered the long fields of bluebonnets under white oaks and dogwood and was halfway over the fence marking the property line, her little brother in tow. The sky was becoming gray in the late afternoon, clouds entering the landscape from the southeast. A wind swept the fields and stirred up dust in those places where the Jessup's livestock had cropped the rye grass down to the soil.

Maude remarked, "What sort of arrangements did Harry make for you and the children?"

"Pardon me?"

"Five dollars a week would be fair and helpful."

"Well, I've always believed in pulling my own weight. I'm sure Harry would tell you that I have no fear of work. I thought I'd find a position downtown," Marie said, her eyes fixed on the children crossing the fields of clover and wildflowers toward the grazing horses. Henry, dressed in denim overalls, fell in the wild grass and Cissie picked him up and brushed him off, then hurried on into the wind. Their young hearts were as wild as her own. "Just a few hours a day."

"Won't many people hire someone for part of a day's work. Can you do anything useful?"

Marie felt like throwing her clothes down and walking out. She had no desire to feel subservient in this household. The Pendergast women never kowtowed to anyone and she wouldn't be the one to start. She was much too modern. Why on earth hadn't Harry warned her that his mother would be so obstinate in receiving family into her home? Now this was a fine start they'd gotten off to. What was next? Boxing ears?

"I can sew," Marie replied, trying to sound confident against Maude's withering assault, though this was all so terribly unsettling. Why couldn't she just go outdoors and work in her garden? "My mother taught me when I was a little girl. She worked four years as a seamstress in Milwaukee before marrying my father."

Maude opened the top drawer of the walnut chiffonier and emptied its contents onto the bed. "Most folks here can sew. Not much need to hire out for something practically everyone knows how to do themselves."

Keeping her voice as pleasant as possible, Marie replied, "Well, I run a typewriter, too. Fifty-five words a minute. And I've run a cash register. I plan to go downtown tomorrow and see what I can find. Five dollars a week will be no trouble at all. You needn't worry."

Marie turned her attention once again to her children outdoors. Seven-year-old Henry stopped a dozen yards or so from the horses, regarding the animals with curiosity and awe. Her little brother watching from a dozen yards off, Cissie tiptoed up to the sorrel and placed a palm on its flank. The horse ignored her. She motioned Henry closer, but he shook his head. The cautious member of the family, Henry slowly circled the horse at a safe distance. He'd been afraid of the pony at the county fair last summer until Harry plopped him on the animal's back.

"What about the children?" Maude gathered up the pile of clothes from the chiffonier drawers and dumped them into the basket she'd brought with her. "I hope you're not expecting me to watch them every day while you're gone. My babysitting days ended when Harry and Rachel grew up. Every other Monday and Friday my ladies club meets at Trudy's until four. Tuesdays and Thursdays, the club ladies come over here at three sharp and we entertain until five. After that, there's supper to fix. I've simply got no time for children. I'm sorry."

"Mrs. Hennesey," Marie said plainly, "I don't expect you to look after my children. They're not your responsibility. I know that. We're guests in your house, and we appreciate your hospitality. I intend to find employment here in Bellemont as soon as I can. Once I have my hours settled, I'll make my own arrangements for the children. They won't be any burden to either you or Rachel. I promise." So mad now she could spit nails, Marie wondered if she could ever forgive Harry for subjecting her to this indignity.

Maude Hennesey replaced the top drawer and picked up the two empty ones. "Don't misunderstand me, dear. You're family, so we're more than glad to have you here." She slid the drawers back into the old chiffonier and took up the laundry basket. "Rachel comes home at half past five. We like to eat by six. If there's anything you need for yourself or the children, just let me know. It's been ages since I've had young ones in the house, but I don't doubt we'll manage."

She walked out of the room, closing the door behind her. Feeling utterly defeated, Marie sat on the iron bed, her gaze returned toward the window, thankful that conversation with Maude was over and done with. Harry had warned her that his mother might be gruff and difficult at first, but being a man, he'd understated the threat. Nothing Maude had said or done since Marie and the children had stepped off the evening train had made them feel the least bit welcome. But Marie refused to blame her mother-in-law. After all, this was her home they were invading, her peace of mind the children would disrupt. Presumably, Harry had gone over all of this with his mother long before and she had agreed to take them in. Truth was, so much would be new for all of them, adjustments would need to be made, tempers controlled. Farrington on the Mississippi was behind them now, the house on Cedar Street taken by strangers, the home where her children had been born reconciled to memory. Though leaving still made Marie sick of soul, her anger at Harry was at least beginning to diminish, day by day. Recriminations were wasteful now. Poor Harry had his own fears, which Marie understood much better than Harry thought she did. *Life bestows bounty and burden upon each of us*, Granny Chamberlain had lectured, *it's how we receive it that sets us apart from our neighbors.*

Both children had climbed the fence on the boundary of the pasture and were running out into the grassy fields in the distance. While she watched, Cissie's white dress, fluttering brightly against the gray landscape, dwindled as she and Henry ran far into the northwest. Dust clouds kicked up in the yard. Marie got up off the bed and went outdoors.

Maude was hanging linen on the line below the back porch that billowed wildly as the wind gusted. The street out front was empty. Thunderheads moved on the horizon to the south. *Rain before seven, clear by eleven.* Marie walked down the short path between the Hennesey house and the fence bordering the pasture and entered the open field through the Jessup's gate next door. Stepping carefully to avoid soiling her shoes, Marie walked out across the scrub grass in the direction her children had taken. She loved being in the country, feeling the grass beneath her feet. Not Harry. His idea of a lawn would be to cement it over. The country was not in his blood. Little wonder he had left. Back at the house, Maude was calling for her. The wind caught her words up, swept them away. Marie pretended not to hear them at all.

She neared the sorrel by the fence line on the north. Henry was out of sight, but Cissie's white dress reflected enough light to remain visible through the tall oaks. They were both laughing, a pair of squealing voices echoing across the spring fields of rye grass and bluebonnets. Henry had slowed his stride so his older sister could catch up. Freedom was meant to be shared. Slowing her own pace, Marie smiled because when she was a little girl, freedom had belonged only to her male cousins. Trust, responsibility, and a shiny new Ford automobile to test it with. Drive up to Chicago to see some shows. Spend every hard-earned dollar chasing around after girls whose mothers didn't care what barn their daughters spent the night in. Never had Marie owned a car, never had her chair at the supper table sat empty for a night, never had she slept beyond the echo of her mother's voice: a perpetual child until she married Harry.

Folding her dress, Marie climbed through the fence. *Go east, go west, go north. Any direction is right. Wherever you're headed, it'll get you there. Just don't stop to answer questions.* Advice to her cousins, courtesy of her father. Why not for her? How long did he think she'd be sitting at his table? Until the Lord returned? Well, he was wrong.

Behind her, Maude's house and the Jessup's shrunk back into the pinewoods that marked the town limits of Bellemont. Ahead, the sky looked as big as the whole world.

Cissie had stopped chasing her brother. Now she was dancing slowly in a circle, her skirt held by fingertips away from her body, singing aloud. Henry had gone on another fifty yards or so, arms flailing wildly in fatigue. His voice carried on the wind above his sister's, "Ya, ya, ya, ya, ya!" A chant of his own creation. A boy-child's song of joy.

Walking closer now, Marie realized Cissie's song was one Harry had taught the children the night before he put them on the train to Bellemont.

"The monkey married the baboon's sister. Gave her a ring and then he kissed her. Kissed her so hard he raised a blister … "

Cissie wore a wondrous smile as she sang loud enough for her brother to hear. Henry, hurrying in circles round and round, raising his own dust storm amid the wildflowers, screeched in laughter, and ran faster still.

On the horizon, great black thunderheads flared lightning in the southern sky, but Marie did not hurry her children to safety, not while Cissie still sang and Henry ran. Instead, Marie took off her shoes and danced lightly barefoot in the soft grass, danced a two-step to a little girl's song in the rhythm of her children's footsteps.

"The monkey married the baboon's sister. Gave her a ring and then he kissed her. Kissed her so hard he raised a blister. She set up a yell."

— 2 —

Rachel Hennesey put down the spring fabrics copy of *Vogue*, danced over to the radio console, dialed up the volume, then took another peek out the window. Sitting at the piano with Cissie on her lap, Marie listened to rain drumming on the roof. She found it comforting, somehow. It was raining so hard the street had become almost invisible from indoors. Mud swamped the sidewalk out front. Roof gutters drained like Niagara Falls. Since sundown, the thunderstorm had dumped three inches of rain onto Bellemont and the surrounding countryside.

Summer resorts on the Gulf Coast were already flooding.

Rachel came away from the window, bother on her face. Stopping by the piano, she said, "He knows I can't stand to be kept waiting. How long could it take to hire a room at the aerodrome?"

Marie offered a hopeful smile. "I'm sure he'll be here any minute now." She thought Rachel, at twenty-six-years-old, was perhaps the most attractive young woman she knew, sure to have her choice of a proper beau. She was nearly as tall as Harry with high cheekbones, the prettiest green eyes Marie had ever seen, and lovely blonde hair bobbed in the most up-to-the-minute fashion. Secretly, Marie was envious because she knew Harry wished her own look were more modern. She knew he was unhappy with her these days, but how would changing her hair change his heart?

Rachel said, "He does it to be contrary."

"Oh?"

"No fellow wants a girl to believe he can't find something better to do on a Saturday night than take her out dancing. They want us to think we're no better than third or fourth choice. I don't know why we put up with it."

Marie ran her fingers lightly over the keys, trying a short scale. With the radio console playing jazz from a Birmingham ballroom, she knew it was pointless to attempt anything else. Apparently the piano had gathered dust since Rachel brought the Crosley set into the house. Now only professional entertainment was worthy of her attention, and Maude was too busy to play much herself. The front parlor was the biggest room in the house with space enough for a piano and side chairs, a lovely old horsehair sofa by the fireplace, three tapestry Morris chairs, and several side-tables and shaded lamps. Marie thought it was adorable. Perhaps when she had a house of her own again, she'd borrow an idea or two.

"Of course, I don't mean to suggest we ought to do away with their entire species," said Rachel. "I'm sure I wouldn't want to inherit the digging of ditches and such. And they do remember special occasions every so often with lovely gifts."

"That they do."

"Let me guess: Harry sends flowers."

"Yes, he does."

"Carnations?"

Marie blushed. "You know your brother too well."

"Well, fact is, he's always been too cheap to send roses. Every birthday I had between six and sixteen, he'd buy a bouquet of white carnations and have them delivered. He didn't fancy having anyone see him carrying sissy flowers down the street."

"He sends me red ones."

"Oh, he does, does he? Well, that's a surprise!"

"White carnations are pretty, too, though."

"I prefer roses," Rachel replied, fingering her string of beads. "Any color'll do." A car rumbled past out front, splashing water against the steps. Rachel hurried over to the window again for a look. "I'll give him five more minutes."

"It's still ten minutes lacking the hour," said Marie, amused by Rachel's impatience. "He'd be early." In her own girlhood, she'd known more than one boy who made her wait for a dance. She had always fought the tears and tried to be cheerful, believing no boy enjoys sobbishness on a date.

"That's not the issue." Rachel stood at the windowsill and parted the curtains with the back of her hand. "A boy ought to show more enthusiasm for his date. Sidney Carlyle was always early. Mother had to entertain him for at least half an hour before I came down to leave. They'd play three or four hands of gin rummy for pretzel sticks and Sidney'd usually let her win."

"Why did you stop seeing him?" Marie asked, as she helped Cissie fit her fingers to a D chord.

"He smelled like chicken feathers."

"I beg your pardon?" Both Marie and Cissie giggled.

"His clothes, hat, shoes. Everything he wore smelled like smelly old chicken feathers. Even Mother noticed after a while."

Maude stuck her head into the room. "The boy worked at a chicken farm, dear. What did you expect?"

Rachel laughed. "He might've washed a little more diligently, wouldn't you say? Was that asking too much? My own clothes were beginning to smell."

"That was your fault for sitting too close."

"Mother!"

"Well, it's God's own truth."

"Nonetheless," said Rachel, turning her attention back to Marie, "there are some things a girl cannot be expected to endure."

"He was the nicest boy you ever stepped out with," offered Maude. "In my opinion, of course."

"Of course."

"And he had sweet eyes."

"And he was a Baptist," Rachel added with a smirk.

"The closer to God we are, the more beautiful we grow."

"He smoked cigars, did you know that?"

"So did your father, dear," Maude replied. "You can't hang a man on what he smokes. What he does on a Saturday night isn't half as important as what he does on Sunday."

"He got himself juiced every Saturday night down in the cellar at Frankie's Café, is what he did. And every Sunday morning following, he'd sleep it off in the back pew by the open window. I doubt he heard word one of Whitaker's old sermons in the month we saw each other. He was nothing but a plain stinking drunk, Baptist or no."

"Nevertheless, in God's eyes … "

"God isn't blind, Mother! For heaven sakes!"

Rachel let go of the curtains and went over to the front door. As she opened it, a gust of rain blew inside over the threshold and onto the carpet.

"Would you mind closing that door!" Maude shouted, coming out from the kitchen. Rachel stepped out onto the porch, pulling the door closed behind her. Marie leaned forward from the piano so that she could see out to the front steps where Rachel was standing now, scouring the street for signs of her suitor. She wondered what position Harry would've taken in this dispute between his mother and sister. He despised these sorts of petty disagreements with which he believed women were obsessed. Half the time, he thought Marie's concerns were silly when she knew they weren't. He could be strict in his thinking, not a flattering habit in Marie's opinion. She often wondered how they managed to get along.

"Even if that boy's got to get here by rowboat," said Maude, taking a look outside for herself, "he'll be here, mark my words. I don't know why she lets herself get so worked up. It's plain as the day is long that the boy's crazy about her."

"Maybe he got stuck in the mud," Cissie said. "It looks awful deep out there." Then she thumped a note on the piano.

"I expect he'll be here any minute. Never known him to be late."

"What's he like?" asked Marie, curious of her mother-in-law's opinion. She took hold of Cissie's right hand and positioned it to play a C chord on the piano.

"Well, he's Catholic," replied Maude, and walked back to the kitchen, closing the door.

Cissie gently played her chord according to Marie's design. A motor horn honked and a car pulled up out front, and Marie heard Rachel's voice above the wind. The headlights went dark and a car door slammed shut. Marie shifted Cissie off her lap, and stood up. The door opened to a draft and Rachel came inside again, her date in tow.

"Good grief, is it pouring out there," she said, shaking her head. Water droplets beaded up in her hair. She went immediately to the bathroom and closed the door.

CW remained on the threshold, trying his best not to drip any water on the floor. He was a tall fine-looking young man with dark brown hair, soft blue eyes, and a strong patrician face. Marie had no difficulty seeing why Rachel was so taken with him. He spoke to her with a distinctly elegant Southern drawl. "Well, it's rather wet out tonight."

Marie nodded. "So I've noticed."

He smiled. "My hired Ford leaks a bit, too."

"Oh?"

"Needs a new winter top." CW moved forward a bit farther into the room, taking care to avoid the throw rug. "I ought to get it replaced, I suppose."

"Yes."

"Haven't had the time." He grinned as he took his hat off, brushed the rim across his coat sleeve, and hung it on the hallstand. His dark hair was trimmed razor-sharp and slicked with oil. "I've been busy as a beaver this season, flying all over the place."

Marie raised an eyebrow. "Even tonight?"

"No, ma'am, I'm not crazy."

"Do you fly in an aerial circus?" Her Cousin Bonnie actually flew an airplane out in California, an undertaking Marie much admired even though Harry always thought her foolish.

CW laughed. "Not on your life! Aeronautics is much too serious an enterprise to be wasted doing loop-de-loops over somebody's barn. That's called a nut sundae in this business. Actually, I have a contract taxiing businessmen all over the South, picking them up in one town, setting them down in another, making certain they make their appointments on time. It's the newest thing. Have you heard of Jake Mollendick?"

She shook her head, woefully ignorant about flying. "I don't believe so."

"Well, he's considered by many to be the founder of our modern commercial aviation. Why, just last year when I traveled to his Swallow factory at Wichita to buy my airplane, I was shown a future vision of the very heavens filled with commerce, argosies of magic sails, pilots of the purple twilight dropping down with costly bales."

"Oh my."

"Stirring, isn't it?" CW grinned. "Well, I'm absolutely convinced this new aviation game is the future."

"I'm sure it is." Marie offered her hand. "By the way, I'm Rachel's sister-in-law. Marie Hennesey." She smiled sweetly, and blushed. He was fine-looking, indeed.

"Of course you are," CW replied with a mock-seriousness. "And I'm very pleased to make your acquaintance. CW McCall, professional birdman, at your service."

CW took off his raincoat, folded it once, and hung it on the hallstand below his felt hat. He was wearing a smart gray metropolitan suit underneath. "Flying's much more reliable than train service. Quicker, too."

"I don't doubt that."

"Have you ever flown in an airplane?"

"No, I can't say that I have."

CW smiled. "Why not?"

"I suppose I've just never had the opportunity. I'm no coward."

"Then you're not afraid of it, like most people?"

"Are most people afraid of flying?" she asked, coyly.

He nodded. "I believe so. Why, I read recently that more than seventy percent of businessmen would use the air if they had the opportunity, but their wives won't allow it. The very idea frightens them. Jake Mollendick believes we need to teach air-mindedness if we hope to see real growth in this industry."

"Well, I wouldn't be at all afraid." Which was true. Harry hated flying because he had a fear of heights, but Marie had climbed trees on the slightest dare when she was a girl and never minded looking down. She always had more heart for risk than Harry did, except for a deathly fear of drowning in deep water which she did not understand because she loved riding in canoes.

"Would you like to take a flight one day?"

"Certainly." The very idea of it filled her tummy with butterflies.

"Then we'll do it. I promise. One day soon."

"Good."

Rachel came out of the bathroom. She'd powdered her face for the third time since supper. Marie noticed that Rachel's lipstick had also received attention. Cissie slid off the piano bench and went to the window, drawing back the curtain for a peek out into the rainy dark.

"Well, nighty-night, Mother," said Rachel, leaning around the doorframe to the kitchen. "Don't bother waiting up." She winked at Marie. "We'll be back late."

Maude's voice followed from inside the kitchen. "You be careful driving out there."

"Of course we will. I'm sure CW's just as capable on the road as he is in the air."

CW got up from the window seat. He pretended to look puzzled.

"Where're we going, darling?"

"To the dance, silly," said Rachel. She offered her cheek to CW for a kiss, which made Marie blush. Harry rarely kissed her in public. He called it embarrassing and un-Christian. "Did your little head fill up with rainwater on the way over here? Goodnight, Mother!"

Marie watched Cissie draw swirls and curlicues in the condensation on the windowpane. Her art mimicked the rhythmic drumming of rainwater on the porch roof just beyond the glass.

"Let's go," said Rachel, urging CW toward the door. "I do not wish to be the last to arrive."

"You won't," said CW. "The roof fell in half an hour ago. Whole floor's under a foot of water. The dance got canceled. Everybody's gone home."

Rachel's face blanched. "You're lying. I ought to slap your face."

"You can go see it for yourself, if you like. A great big hole right there in the middle of the auditorium, like a Bertha shell dropped on it. Thank goodness it didn't cave in a couple hours later. People might've been killed."

Rachel sat down next to Marie on the piano bench, disappointment filling her eyes. "Why didn't somebody tell me earlier before I bothered myself dressing up for nothing?"

CW shrugged. "Nobody knew until it happened. Roof just caved right in. One moment it was fine, the next — KABOOM!"

Maude came out of the kitchen, a dishtowel in her hands. She walked over to the radio and clicked it off. "If you're not listening to that noise, would you please do me the courtesy of leaving it off." She pretended to despise the radio, except for her favorite show: H.J. Seidenfaden Funeral Home in Kansas City, Missouri, with organist Harold Turner, whose Sunday morning program featured mostly religious music. "You know, I've been saying for years that old hall ought to've been torn down. Everybody knew the roof was rotting away. Anybody who tells you they're surprised is just plain lying."

"I think it was done deliberately to ruin my evening," Rachel said, removing her shawl and laying it on the piano top. "There are so few joys in my life and dancing is one of them. Now what am I supposed to do, go fishing?"

Cissie swiveled her head away from the window. "Momma, I see fish swimming in the street. Lots of them."

CW said, "Well then, what do you say we go out and catch a couple of them?" He turned to Marie. "Have you ever fished in the road before?"

She shook her head with a smile. "I can't say that I have. Is it safe?"

"It's crazy," offered Rachel, staring hard at CW. "Why do you want to get all wet? Those are your good dancing clothes. And what about me? I didn't dress up to play in the rain."

"Only a fool'd pass up a chance to do some road fishing," replied CW. He winked at Cissie. "Besides, these trousers need to go to the cleaners, anyhow. Might as well get my money's worth."

"Don't expect to come traipsing back in here later on," said Maude. "I have no desire to scrub these floors again this week."

A thunderclap rolled across the fields, rattling the windows. A lightning strike followed somewhere off to the south. Henry came running out from the back bedroom, eyes wide as saucers. "I saw it, Momma! I saw it!"

"Saw what?" Marie took her son into her arms for a welcome hug. He felt warm and slithery.

"Lightning! I saw lightning!"

"And you want to take these children outside," Rachel said to CW, "to splash about in the road? Your brain must've been struck by lightning on the way over here tonight."

"Oh, it's not dangerous at all. Lightning doesn't strike in the road. It's trees and houses that attract it. Have you ever seen someone knocked dead in the middle of the road by lightning?"

"With my luck," said Rachel, "I'd be the first."

The rain increased to a thunderous downpour, beating furiously against the windowpanes, creating a minor waterfall off the porch overhang. Marie released her little boy to have a look outdoors. He was terrified by stormy weather and she knew he'd cuddle up beside her in bed tonight, but she wouldn't mind at all. Maybe Cissie would join them and they'd all nestle together.

"I've never had such a collection of fools under my roof before," said Maude, peeking out the window over the top of Cissie's head. "It's storming out there, and you want to go play in the street? Don't expect me to come looking for you when you get yourselves swept away into the river."

Rachel laughed. "Mother, that's more than half a mile from here."

CW said, "In the flood of '27, Uncle Edmund's plantation was thirty miles from the delta levee at Cabin Teele when the crevasse broke open to the Mississippi. The next day his gallery was ten feet underwater and there was a cow carcass and a family of sharecroppers on his roof. My own daddy took a boat across seventy-five miles of flood from Vicksburg to Monroe and never once saw dry ground."

"Well, I don't think I've ever seen more than a few inches of water in our streets," said Rachel. "It wouldn't be sensible to live here otherwise. Only an idiot builds in a flood plain."

Maude shot back, "Don't fool yourself, young lady. We've had floods here before. Terrible ones."

"And when was that, exactly?" Rachel asked, a mocking skepticism drawn on her face.

"Well, I'd guess the last one would've been when I was your age," her mother answered, "on a night just like this one. The river rose up like a fox and stole our cows, the chickens, your father's old hound dog, and swept them clear down into the Gulf. It wasn't until morning that we saw they were gone."

"Were y'all drunk?" asked Rachel, heading for the closet. She drew out her raincoat. "I think if they were my chickens, I'd have at least been out there waving good-bye as they were floating off. That'd be the decent thing to do."

Maude turned on her heels and walked back into the kitchen. Then, loud enough for everyone to hear, she said, "*Folly is a joy to him who has no sense.* Proverbs 15: 21," and closed the door.

Pretending to have been deaf to that dispute, Marie pulled Henry onto her lap and mussed his hair. She said to Rachel, "Maybe we ought to stay indoors."

The downpour had abated slightly, but Marie worried the worst was yet to come. She hated storms, too, ever since she was a little girl and her favorite calf drowned in a ditch.

"No, let's go out," Rachel replied. "I can't abide Mother quoting the Bible. Besides, if I can't go dancing, I don't care what we do. Maybe the fish'll appreciate how I look."

"Now you're talking," said CW. He gave Rachel a sweet kiss on her cheek, then pulled his raincoat on and grabbed his hat off the hallstand. Rachel put on her own coat, then took up an umbrella and looked at Marie who was still occupied with Henry in her lap. CW opened the front door and went out. A moment later, he came around to the window in front of Cissie and rapped his knuckles on the glass. Giving Marie a grin, he disappeared again into the dark.

"Aren't you coming?" Rachel asked, waiting at the door. "I'm sure the children want to."

Marie frowned. "I'm not sure it's safe out of doors in this storm. Those floods your mother was talking about — "

"Absolute nonsense," said Rachel. "She's just telling you that to keep you inside with her. Floods like she's talking about would've floated this whole sorry town away, but we're still here, aren't we?"

"I suppose so." Actually, she did want to go out and play in the rain. Why not? Harry wasn't here to fight with over it, not that she required his permission to enjoy herself.

Rachel opened the door. "Get your coats on and come on out. Have some fun for a change." She went out onto the porch, closing the door behind her. Marie leaned over the window for a look outdoors. CW was down in the Ford, fiddling with the headlamps. Rachel stood on the bottom step of the porch laughing, rain dripping off her head. It looked like fun.

"Can we go out?" Cissie asked. "Please?"

"Yeah, Momma, can we?" Henry chimed in. "We won't get drowned or nothing, we promise."

Both tugged at Marie's blouse. How far was the river? Half a mile? Could it really flood so close? Who was right? Whose part should she take? Maude remained in the kitchen, rummaging in the cupboards. She'd dispensed her opinion and now busied herself with rearranging the pots and pans and other assorted utensils, long piling up beneath the countertops. Marie understood quite clearly the wisdom in avoiding conflict within the household, particularly when it involved choosing sides in strife between Rachel and Maude. The radio was a good example. On evenings when they were both home, Rachel cranked the volume up as loud as it would go so she might hear her radio shows in any room of the house. Despising modern music, Maude repeatedly dialed it down in favor of accompanying herself on the piano now and then to the first four bars of "Beautiful Dreamer." Each time she quit the piano, Rachel would sweep back into the room and dial back up the volume which would send Maude back to the piano again, *Beautiful Dreamer, wake unto me. Starlight and dew drops are waiting for thee.* This contest continued sometimes until bedtime, a war of dissonance night after night that drove everyone in the house crazy. Not that Marie ever complained. What would Harry say? Never injure hospitality with disputations.

Henry tugged on Marie's skirt. "Can we, Momma? Can we go out with Aunt Rachel?"

She relented for the children's sake. "Go get your raincoats and boots."

With a cheer, they dashed for the bedroom. Marie got up off the piano bench and went to the closet for her own coat and a pair of umbrellas. Maybe she could keep them dry.

Maude's voice came from the kitchen. "Bring the children back inside through the kitchen when they're done. I'll have some towels warming."

Marie put on her coat, then answered, "Thank you."

"No sense in the little ones catching pneumonia just because Rachel's dance got canceled. Keep an eye on my daughter and that Catholic boy if you can. There'll be another thunderhead following right on the tail of the last one."

"I will," replied Marie. "Thank you."

The children came running out of the bedroom, smiles wide on their faces, raincoats flopping behind. Marie opened the door and ushered them onto the porch where a damp breeze gusted across the threshold.

"Isn't Grandma coming?" asked Cissie. Henry ran down to the bottom of the steps out into the falling rain. He arched his neck backward and stuck out his tongue.

"Grandma's busy," said Marie, fastening the buttons on her coat. Up the street a hundred yards or so where the road ended, the muddy earth was indistinguishable from cloud-blackened fields. Hardly a tree was visible in the rainy dark.

Rachel giggled. Leaning headfirst into CW's automobile, her skirt and bare legs were exposed to the rainfall. CW gave her a sloppy kiss. Marie recalled a time when Harry was still that bold.

"When do we fish?" Cissie asked, tugging on her mother's coat.

"I don't know, honey," Marie replied, having no idea what was planned for them. "Soon."

Henry stepped off the porch and straight into a pothole, drowning his left boot with a splash. Rachel slid backward out of the automobile, then leaned in to give CW one last kiss after which he reached across the passenger seat to pull the door shut. Rachel stepped away and looked up at Marie. She giggled. "Isn't he adorable? He'd make love to me in a hurricane if I'd allow it. I think I may have myself a couple of children, after all."

CW started the engine. Exhaust vapor billowed out into the cold, wet air. Both feet in the mud now, Henry leaned out and touched the front fender.

"You be careful, honey," Rachel said. "Don't get yourself run over now."

"Henry!" Marie shouted. "Get away from the car!"

"Aren't we goin' fishin'?" he asked, trying to free his one foot from the muddy pothole. He wriggled it violently back and forth.

CW put the automobile into gear and rolled away from the house. Henry's boot came free with a sucking noise.

"Where's he going, Momma?" asked Cissie, letting go of her mother's coat. CW swung his automobile out into muddy College Street, honked once, then drove off toward downtown.

"He'll be back," said Rachel, a smile on her face. She sat down on the bottom step and covered up her legs with the edge of the raincoat. "Come on down. Sit right here beside me so we're close to the street."

Henry sat on the far end of the steps away from Rachel, leaving room for his sister and mother. Cissie made her way carefully down the wet stairs and slid in next to Rachel. Marie could still hear the automobile in the next block. A shiver ran up her back and she folded her arms close to keep warm. The rain had lightened to a soft steady drizzle in the yellow porchlight.

"Aren't we gonna fish?" asked Henry.

"We're going to play 'Galveston'," said Rachel, wearing the grin of the cat that ate the canary. "Make sure your coats are all buttoned up tight."

"I don't understand," said Marie, opening her own umbrella. Her children sat huddled up tight six steps below, big smiles of anticipation on their faces. Did they know something she didn't? Harry wasn't much for surprises, and neither was she. What sort of game was this?

"Nothing to understand," said Rachel. "All you have to do is come on down here and have a seat with the rest of us."

A wet gust swirled the slow drizzle in under the porch, dampening Marie's face. She blinked her eyes clear and went down to the bottom step where she had a look in the direction of downtown. Mud blanketed the road that extended ten blocks into the dark cover of billowing shade trees. Then, beginning as just a dot of light in the rainy distance, a car came on toward her.

"You best sit now," said Rachel. "He's coming back."

CW's automobile made a whooshing noise in mud and water and trailed a fantail twice the size of the car. He came on fast.

"Sit down!" Rachel said, urgency in her voice.

Cissie pulled Henry close under the umbrella. "He's coming!"

The headlights illuminated the rain in the road ahead of CW's automobile. His horn honked twice. A hand waved from the driver's window.

"Cover your faces!" shouted Rachel.

"Momma!" Henry cried, tugging at the hem of Marie's raincoat.

Rachel shrieked, "GALVESTON!" as CW's automobile roared

past the porch, splashing a great wave of muddy water over all four seated there on the bottom step. Safe beneath the thoroughly drenched umbrella, the children squealed with laughter. Marie was soaked, head to foot, as she hadn't gotten her umbrella up over her face in time. Water dripped from her head and mud stung in her eyes. Good grief! She felt like a fool, but everyone else was up now, shaking off, laughing more loudly. CW's automobile made a U-turn, and headed back again toward downtown.

"Galveston!" yelled Henry as CW drove by. "Galveston!"

Maude shouted from the window, "Rachel, for goodness sakes, what did I tell you last year? Have you lost your mind?"

Rachel called back over her shoulder, "Good grief, Mother! It's just a game!"

"Tell that to your Uncle Palmer the next time he visits!"

"Mother, please! You're spoiling the children's fun!"

"Just you wait! The Lord remembers those who grieve not for the deprived."

The window slammed shut.

As the water dripped from her brow, Marie asked Rachel, "What did she mean by that?"

Rachel laughed. "Oh, Mother's so dramatic. She thinks our playing out here is a disservice to Uncle Palmer's sister-in-law and her poor family who were swept away with their house on Bath Street and drowned in the Gulf during the great Galveston hurricane. Of course it was a frightful tragedy and all that, but to think this game's got anything to do with that horrid disaster is plainly ridiculous."

Marie used the back of her hand to wipe her eyes. Cissie stood three steps up, patting her face dry while trying to stop giggling. Rachel waved to CW. His automobile disappeared again into the trees down on the next block with a last burst of the motor horn echoing across the rainy night.

Rachel looked up at Marie, muddy water dripping off her nose. "We've been playing 'Galveston' since the first automobiles came to Bellemont. It's the only thing to do around here when it rains."

"Why do you do it at all?" Marie asked, trying not to sound critical, though getting splashed by a passing automobile was not her idea of a rainy evening's entertainment. They'd tricked her into playing this game, but maybe it wasn't the most awful thing in the world.

Rachel wiped her own nose. "Excitement's hard to come by in this town, and anything's more enjoyable than listening to Mother singing 'Beautiful Dreamer' and quoting the Bible."

Feeling a slight chill, Marie folded her coat back over her knees and watched her children, both soaked and giggling.

"Besides," Rachel added, "CW loves driving by here and showing off. He'd race past all night if I'd allow it."

"It seems a little silly to me," said Marie, still blinking water from her eyes. She smiled and felt foolish for getting mad at first.

"Of course," Rachel admitted with a giggle, "but isn't it fun?"

Henry stood a few feet out in the muddy road, sunk up to his shins, peering in the direction of downtown. Cissie had an arm curled around the railing, watching her brother. Both wore enormous grins. That alone gave Marie sufficient reason for staying outdoors.

"He's coming back!" Henry shouted. The children went into hysterics, laughing and disengaging themselves from the mud, lunging for the bottom step of the porch, sitting down and covering up.

"He'll really let us have it this time," said Rachel. "Second pass is always the best."

Marie scrambled for her umbrella. She felt like an idiot. "I don't think I'm — "

"Just cover yourself up and tuck your head in tight," Rachel rolled her head in close to her chest, "like this. You'll be fine. Honest to Abraham."

"He's coming!" shrieked Henry. "He's coming!"

The swoosh of rapid tires in mud and water came out of the north again, engine droning behind. Rain fell harder now in the road. To the south, lightning lit up the sky as CW's automobile roared toward the house. Marie ducked her head and covered up.

"GAL-VES-TON!" screamed Rachel and Henry and Cissie in unison as the automobile flashed by, closer than before, sending up a

wave of muddy water that splashed high up onto the porch, engulf-
ing the four spectators on the bottom step. An instant afterward, a
thunderclap bellowed overhead in the blackened sky. The reverbera-
tion rattled windows up and down the street as CW's automobile ran
off into the dark.

When the echo of the thunderclap cleared, both children were
screaming. A genuine cloudburst followed, rain falling so hard Marie lost sight of the cottonwoods across the road. Cissie and Henry
leaped up off the bottom step. Rachel hurried from the porch into
the road, appearing disoriented by the thunder. Henry and Cissie,
arms wrapped tightly about each other, climbed up onto the next step.
Maude was on the top step calling to them as lightning flashed again
to the south. CW's automobile came past, headlights blinking on and
off. Rachel shouted at him to stop, but thunder roared once more in
the sky and she returned to the cover of the porch. By now, Cissie and
Henry were up on the top step with Maude, huddling together inside
her arms. Seeing that her children were safe, Marie waited for Rachel,
then hurried up the stairs herself.

Rain cascaded down, transforming the road out front into a glistening lake.

"I told you it was foolish," Maude said to Rachel, as her daughter
reached the top of the stairs, "but no, you had to go out and be a show-
off to these little children."

"Not now, Mother."

"You could've been struck by lightning," said Maude. "Or worse."

Rachel laughed as she dripped water from every part of her body.
"Mother, what could possibly be worse than getting hit by lightning?"

"Never you mind. Just stay on the path you're heading and see what
happens. And don't say I didn't tell you so."

"Where's CW gone?" asked Henry. "Is he comin' back?"

Wind swirled the rain about, driving it under the porch overhang.
Shaking a bit, Marie brought her coat sleeve up to dry off her face.
Cissie huddled close to her brother.

"I expect so, dear," said Rachel, though the look on her face indicated she wasn't that certain. Lightning flashed bright blue to the

southwest. An instant later, a great boom shook the house, rattling the windows so hard the sunshade fell off its holder in Maude's bedroom, knocking her cactus flower off the bottom sill and cracking the glass.

"Good Lord!" cried Maude, grabbing for the porch railing. Cissie started crying. Henry broke free and ran to Marie, wrapping his arms about her waist. Rachel flew to the bottom of the stairs and stared out down the road toward town where CW had gone.

"Get back up here!" Maude shouted to her. "Have you lost your senses?"

"Cissie, over here!" said Marie, trying to ignore the storm in favor of gathering up her children. Harry would be furious if he saw them now. "Come quick!"

Cissie joined Henry in wrapping her arms around their mother's waist. They both hid themselves behind Marie, all three shivering from cold and fright. Maude yelled for Rachel. Her daughter ignored her, venturing instead farther out into the road for a better look.

"Take the children inside for me, will you?" Marie asked Maude, nudging them toward the open door. Lightning was a worry now she'd prefer to dispense with for her children's sake. "Henry, Cissie, go with Grandma! This instant!"

"Aren't you coming?" Cissie asked, stepping indoors with her little brother in tow. Anytime either she or someone else went somewhere, she'd ask that question. On the night Harry had set his family on the train to Bellemont, Cissie put that question to him at least twenty times. Knowing Harry's answer a week beforehand, Marie felt her heart break a little each time Cissie asked.

"I'll wait out here with Auntie Rachel until CW comes back," replied Marie, trying to sound brave though her heart was all aflutter. Why on earth was she such a coward? Harry would've laughed to see her like this. Not that he was any brave soul! At the sight of a rat in the cellar, he'd telephone the exterminator and lock the door.

"*He in the company of a fool ...* " said Maude, taking both Cissie and Henry by the hand and leading them to the door.

"I'll be all right," Marie said, and gave her children a little wave as Maude shut the door behind them. Rachel sloshed about in the middle of the road, restless with anxiety. Her hair hung limp and her face was streaked with mud, yet her attention remained focused in the direction CW had driven. Marie assumed he'd return shortly. Each previous run had taken no more than a few minutes. He was overdue now, but not by enough to worry about. Another lightning strike flared in the sky to the east. Four or five seconds later, the thunderclap boomed, though less ferociously than the last. Maybe the storm was passing on.

"He's coming!" shouted Rachel. She waved both her arms wildly, and slid her feet in the mud back and forth. Feeling a little bolder, Marie ventured to the bottom of the porch once more and cupped a hand over her brow to see beyond the rain pouring in her face. A dim pair of headlights glimmered down at the far end of College Street, bouncing as the automobile negotiated the dozens of ruts in the muddy road. Rachel kept waving as she sloshed a path back to the porch. Were it not raining so hard on the roof of Maude's house, the engine noise would've been audible as the headlights neared. Seeing the automobile trailing a large rooster tail of water, Marie climbed back up three steps. She'd gotten wet enough, thank you. Rachel came up onto the porchsteps beside her, still waving. Seconds later, CW roared by, kicking another wave onto the stairs. His Ford went into a sloshing 180-degree spin just at the end of the block, splashing water and mud in a wide half-circle before righting itself and starting back toward the house. He pulled up next to the steps and honked the horn. Rachel ran down to greet him. CW rolled down the passenger window and she leaned inside. He was shouting excitedly. Rachel popped back out of the window and yelled to Marie, "Tell Mother CW says the school's on fire!"

"What?"

"The school's on fire! Lightning set the school on fire! Go tell Mother!"

Marie turned to go inside, but instead the front door opened and Maude stuck her head out. "Trudy's on the phone! There's a fire downtown!"

Rachel yelled, "We know, Mother! CW was just down there!

He says the school's on fire! It got hit by lightning! Whole thing's burning up!"

"Well, what did I tell you?"

Rachel leaned back inside the automobile.

"Just like I said," Maude continued, directing her attention now to Marie. "People have no business being out on a night like this. It's dangerous. You can see now how right I was."

Marie nodded, wondering why she hadn't heard any sirens. Bellemont wasn't so big that the fire could be that far away. Maybe the town didn't have a fire engine. But that would be silly.

Maude called down to Rachel, "Was anybody killed?"

Her daughter pulled back out of the automobile. "I can't hear you, Mother!"

"I said, were there were any injuries or deaths?"

Rachel shrugged. "CW says one man got himself burned pretty badly. He doesn't know about anyone else."

CW said something to Rachel. She nodded and yelled back up to Maude, "He says there's a whole lot of people down there trying to put the fire out, but it seems the whole school's a wreck. If anyone's still inside, they're probably dead." Rachel leaned inside the automobile once more to say something to CW. Then she came back out and said, "CW thinks we ought to go down there and have a look for ourselves. He says it's quite a spectacle."

"Not on your life," said Maude, both children peeking out from behind her now. "You tell CW if he wants to go, he's more than welcome, but I won't have my daughter running around in the middle of the night chasing fires."

Rachel opened the door and got in. "Bye, Mother. We're going." She looked up at Marie. "Would you like to come along? We have plenty of room. Chasing fires is the best entertainment there is in Bellemont."

Rain dripped into the front seat dampening the carpet at her feet.

Marie shook her head. "I should probably stay here with the children. I'm sure they're scared to death."

"Mother can watch them for you." Rachel called up to Maude,

"Can't you, Mother? If Marie comes with us, you can watch over Cissie and Henry, can't you?" She looked back at Marie. "Sure, she can. They'll be fine. We'll just drive down, have a look-see, and come on back."

The rain had lightened again to a steady drizzle, and the wind faded, suggesting that the storm was moving off across the prairie. Marie looked up at Maude and the children. She wanted to go. It'd been years since she'd gone to a fire. There was always so much excitement. Why shouldn't she go?

Maude called down, "Just you make sure to keep your distance. A building like that's likely to fall on your head when it goes."

"Will you be all right here with Grandma?" Marie asked her children.

"Can't we come, too?" Henry cried. "I want to see the fire."

"Me, too!" said his sister. Marie knew Cissie was old enough, but since Henry wasn't, they'd both have to stay home or she'd never see the end of Henry's tears.

"Not tonight. You go inside and keep Grandma company 'til we get back, all right? You be good now. We won't be long."

"They'll be fine," said Maude. "You watch out for Rachel for me, see that she doesn't drag you into any nonsense."

"I promise," said Marie, retreating to the bottom of the stairs. "Thank you."

She waved once more to her children, and climbed into the backseat of CW's automobile. The cushion was wet. Rainwater leaked in through the canvas roof along the edges of the back window, dampening the fabric and soaking through clear down to the floorboards.

"Let's go see us a fire!" Rachel whooped and gave CW a lover's kiss right in front of Marie who blushed to see affection expressed so boldly. My goodness! Were they going to make love here and now? Marie tried to hide a smile. Harry thought this generation lacked decency and proportion, but Marie remembered her mother remarking once how Granny Chamberlain believed no good could come of a boy and a girl alone in a buggy after sundown. Indeed, Marie always wished that Harry would kiss her on the porch now and then when people were passing by.

After Rachel finished nibbling at his ear, CW jammed the automobile into gear and stomped on the gas pedal. They drove away from the house toward downtown, which was hardly more than ten blocks walking. Marie had found that out when she'd gone looking for a job the day after arriving in Bellemont. The town had no streetcars or busses or taxicabs. Most people either went about by automobile or on foot. All the roads leading into Bellemont except the main highway were dirt, but College Street downtown from Broad to Sixth was brick, laid in during the War. There were plenty of shade trees and stores and gas stations where one could stop and buy a cold soda pop and sit awhile. Downtown had benches here and there for mothers and older folks. Marie planned to interview at the Cochrane Building and City Hall for typewriting.

"I tell you, it's just burning like crazy," said CW, veering off from the route Marie took to downtown. "Rain's had no effect on it at all. Wait'll you see."

"Good God!" Rachel exclaimed. "First, the auditorium and now the school. It must be the Lord's visitation on us for all our liquor and sex-madness. Dear, is your steering gear on the blink?" she asked, pointing ahead to the right past a darkened Texaco station. "The school's that way."

"No, it isn't."

"Sure, it is!"

"Why, sugar, I ought to know," replied CW, "I was just there not ten minutes ago."

"Well, I ought to know, too. I spent six years in that old building. Now, turn this heap of yours around."

Instead, CW drove faster down a sidestreet, mud flying like sheets off the tires. Marie felt the leak dripping down the back of her coat. It was raining hard, obscuring the windshield. CW had the wipers working, but they weren't helping much.

"Would you please slow down?" she called out from the backseat. "Good grief!" If CW crashed into a pine tree and killed them all, then what? Marie was frightened of auto smash-ups. Harry thought she was silly, but she'd known three people killed in motorcars and was too terrified to drive herself and had no desire to learn.

"Why, dear, don't worry," Rachel said, smiling benignly, "CW's a terrific driver. I doubt he's had an auto accident in his life, isn't that true, darling?"

"Yes, dear, it is!"

"Well, then, it won't do to have one tonight, would it?" Marie said, closing her eyes as CW swerved around a large fallen tree branch in the road. "Please slow down? You're scaring me to death! I'd rather get out and walk than be killed in a smash-up."

Rachel laughed. "Well, of course, dear! Who wouldn't?"

"There she is!" said CW, swinging onto a side road. "What'd I tell you?"

Up ahead, Marie saw flames reaching high into the rainy night above the gutted wreck of a building sitting in a clearing of old pecan trees. Cars and people were scattered all around the structure, and a line of Negro men were passing buckets across the road from a pine-shrouded creek.

"That's the colored school," said Rachel, relief clear in her voice. "Not ours."

CW ran the automobile up close and slipped it between two trees and shut the motor off. Marie sighed in relief.

"See there?" said Rachel, indicating houselights through the pine woods across the river. "That's Shantytown, where the coloreds live. This is their school. Ours is back the way we came, about a quarter-mile east of us. Thank goodness."

She flung the door open and climbed out. CW followed, holding his door for Marie. Smoke trails drifted in and out of the pecan trees, wet black ash swirling about in the wind and rain and clinging to the soggy leaves. Marie could hear the wood crackling as the building frame was consumed beam by beam. If the rain had helped to slow the fire, it hadn't been by much. Only the front of the school whose wall contained a porch and two windows was completely intact. Nothing from the rear of the structure remained and the east and west walls were in the process of collapsing.

"Good Lord," said Rachel, as she and CW and Marie approached.

"There's hardly anything left to save. It's really a shame."

"Why isn't there a fire engine?" Marie asked, seeing nothing but an old-fashioned bucket brigade in the clearing. One night when she was a little girl, she'd watched Uncle Boyd's barn burn down, and she'd cried and had fire nightmares for years afterward. It had horrified her.

CW shrugged. "Maybe it broke down."

"That's absurd," Rachel replied, taking care not to step in the mud. "Why, I saw Percy driving it through downtown only last Saturday afternoon and it was running just fine."

"How old is this school?" Marie asked, feeling tears welling up in her eyes.

Rachel shrugged. "Older than Moses. Daddy had classes here when he was Henry's age. The Negroes took it over when the new school went up."

Walking closer, Marie saw that the bucket brigade consisted exclusively of Negroes in a long line furiously heaving water on those sections of the school least affected by the blaze. None spoke, laboring instead with urgency, catching one bucket and sending it on, catching the next, hardly spilling a drop on the muddy earth. They were not all men, either. Boys, too, carted buckets up from the creek fifty yards off in the dark and passed them on. Mothers and daughters used wet rags to slap down sparks floating out from the center of the fire. Nobody from white Bellemont carried either a bucket or a wet rag. Three police cars were parked in a stand of pines sixty yards back from the fire. Half a dozen patrolmen sat on the hoods of those cars, watching and socializing in the fire shadows. More than a hundred people had come out from Bellemont to spectate. Conversation buzzed like the drizzling rain.

"One would think," said Rachel, "that all this rain would just drown the fire right out."

"It's burning inside the wood," CW replied, "cooking the oil they used to treat the beams with, like a grease fire on your stove. You have to suffocate it."

"That's why our new school was built in brick. I doubt it can burn at all. Look there, honey," Rachel said, directing Marie's attention to the north side of the school where those Negro women not flailing away at sparks held dozens of small children close, huddled against the cold and the storm. "Those poor children," she said, shaking her head. "They ought to be home in bed. Seeing this'll just bring them nightmares, if not pneumonia. Mother would have a fit."

CW strolled closer to the fire for a better look, hand-in-hand with Rachel. Marie's own face and hands ached from the dampness that had soaked clean to the bone. The sight of small children waiting in the rainy dark for the schoolhouse to collapse pierced her heart. What if it had been Henry's school?

"We ought to get some buckets and help out," said CW, letting go of Rachel's hand. He stepped out from under the safety of the cotton-wood back into the downpour. Rachel grabbed his arm. He shook her loose and walked a few feet closer, rainfall drenching him.

"I agree," Marie said, joining CW. She watched the Negroes passing buckets one to another across the darkness. "It's shameful to watch it burn down without raising a hand."

"Then let's not," CW said, striding toward the fire. "I'll be damned if I'm going to stand here like some cold-hearted jellyfish."

"Let's put it out," said Marie, fully determined to fetch a bucket and join the line of Negroes. Furious with the men by the parked cars, she called back to Rachel, "If those men over there are too cowardly to help us, we'll do it ourselves! Maybe seeing us in the bucket brigade'll bring a few of them to their senses."

"You can't help people who won't ask for it," said Rachel, chasing them into the rain. She grabbed CW's arm. "Honey? Please don't!"

CW tried to free himself from Rachel's grip. He yelled at her, "What's wrong with you?"

Rachel shouted back, "Leave them alone, for Christsakes! It's not your concern!" Then she looked Marie in the eye, adding, "Besides, it's too late anyhow. We ought to let it burn to the ground before somebody else gets hurt."

An instant later, heat exploded the glass in the windowpanes on the front wall and the support beams gave way and the north end side of the building toppled over, nearly crushing a group of black men and boys who had been struggling to tear the porchsteps free as salvage. Screams filled the air. The crowd swept back under the trees as millions of blazing sparks flew to heaven. Another beam cracked in half and collapsed into the middle of the charred classroom. Marie watched a great plume of flames explode high into the dark, causing the bucket brigade to pause for a few seconds. Resuming with an increased ferocity moments later, they attacked the flames two and three buckets a shot, understanding that what they saved now would be the foundation for rebuilding. It was a small schoolhouse. Marie decided Uncle Henry's new barn was probably a third bigger. Rachel's brick-and-sandstone school downtown two blocks from the courthouse square was at least twice as wide and long and two stories taller. How did these poor Negro children find room enough to study? Two to a desk? How many grades to one room? How many teachers for the one school? Marie tried to picture her own Cissie and Henry sitting in those desks memorizing the alphabet and arithmetic tables and the story of George Washington who never told a lie.

She saw a Negro woman crying now, wailing somewhere back by the trees where the sparks and flecks of glowing ash were swatted down and extinguished in the greasy mud. The long brigade kept on its rhythm, pass and pour, pass and pour. A child, then another, joined the woman wailing by the pine trees. The back wall collapsed, hurling thousands more sparks skyward. A blast of heat forced the spectators from Bellemont to back up a few steps. Marie shivered with fear and sorrow. She wanted to help, to go join the bucket brigade, but now she felt afraid. She didn't know this town, or these people. What was her place? How was she supposed to behave here? How would she be thought of if she went off to help the Negroes? How would she be treated? And her children? What would Harry say? She was no coward.

While the rain fell harder, Marie reluctantly followed Rachel and CW off under a tall cottonwood back some from the fire where a man wearing a black slicker coat nodded and tipped his sou'wester hat. She started to offer a greeting when rain hissed in the burning timber. A bitter smoke clouded the darkness.

"It's sure something, ain't it?"

Marie turned to see a husky fellow in muddy denim overalls come out of the rainy dark. The railroad cap he wore was tipped slightly askew. His face looked grimy and swollen.

"Well, hello, Lucius," Rachel said, offering a pleasant smile. "You look soaked to the bone. Did you lose your umbrella?"

"Idabelle swiped it out of my closet at lunchtime."

Rachel laughed. "And you couldn't scare up another? Honey, it's been raining since dusk."

Lucius looked sheepish. "Well, I borrowed this hat from George Blake. It's kept my head dry enough."

"You're a cut-up, dear."

"I know it."

Rachel asked, "Lucius, have you met my sister-in-law?"

"No, ma'am."

"This is Marie," Rachel said, brushing raindrops off her forehead. "She's a Yankee from Illinois."

Smiling, Lucius offered his hand to Marie. "How do you do, ma'am?"

"Just fine, thank you," she replied, her own hand lost in the fellow's immense grip. She noticed a smell of gin on his breath. "I've never been south of St. Louis before."

Lucius laughed. "I expect you'll see a lot here to admire."

Rachel told him, "She's looking for a job downtown. Have you heard of anything? The poor dear's worried about going broke. It seems my brother's resolved to let his wife earn her own keep."

"Sweetheart," CW interjected, jerking his thumb in the direction of the police cars, "are the local cops here putting over a whoopee club?"

Marie watched another squad car roll in under the rainy pines, motor lamps shining.

Rachel frowned. "That's Gene Coulson. Why, I don't believe I've ever seen him out after dark. How peculiar! I'll bet he's just come out here to put the bee on one of the coloreds for starting this fire." She turned to Marie. "Gene takes after his father who was notorious for raking hell all over Shantytown. Mother said once that Tom Coulson was so low he could kiss a mouse without bending his knee."

"Everyone ought to have a hobby," Lucius said, staring off into the woods. Water dripped from his railroad cap. "Trimming niggers is always easier than chasing crooks."

"Now that just tells me piss and swill go together," CW remarked, as the policeman climbed out of his automobile into the drizzling rain. He appeared amiable in the crowd of fellow cops. CW told Rachel, "Maybe we ought to go look into this high-hat mob, dear. What do you say?"

Most of the Negroes had returned to the fire now, working industriously through the smoldering wreck of the schoolhouse, drenching the flames with buckets of water. Marie felt queasy and dispirited. She wanted to go back to Maude's house and sit with the children for a while, perhaps write a letter home, or another to Harry whose letters lately seemed content, though Marie believed he missed his family more than he was willing to confess.

Rachel asked her, "Will you be all right, dear, if CW and I take a little walk? We won't be long."

"Of course." Marie adjusted the angle of her umbrella to the cold raindrops. "I'll just wait here."

"We'll be back straight away, I promise." Rachel took CW by the hand. "Honey, come with me."

They walked off toward the collection of police cars, leaving Marie alone with Lucius. She watched a group of Negroes tear apart a pile of burning timber with pickaxes, stirring through the hot cinders, scattering sparks into the night.

"It's so awful," Marie heard herself remark, and that was truth. She felt ashamed for not having helped with the bucket brigade. Why had she let Rachel talk her out of it?

Lucius held his hat out into the rain to rinse the ash off the rim. "The niggers had a still in the cellar."

"Pardon me?"

"Gallon jugs of kerosene oil and molasses moonshine, parked right down there under the hot stove, likely hidden inside a stack of straw and old sodden boxes or some such. Way that roof blowed off, I'd guess their hootch was better'n ninety-proof. Probably a lightning bolt snaked itself down the chimney, and BOOM! Hello, Jesus! Just like Kehoe done to that Michigan school."

"What will the police say?"

Lucius shrugged. "Not much now, I'd expect. The evidence is all floatin' 'round heaven."

"My goodness."

"Say, honey, you ought to come downtown tomorrow and have a talk with Jimmy Delahaye. He's always looking for help in the restaurant. I'll bet he'll give you a job."

"Do you think so?" She was hopeful. She needed to find work, needed to belong.

"Oh, I'm sure of it. Enid quit last week and we ain't found nobody else to take her place at the register."

Marie smiled. "Why, thank you. I'll do that. I'm sure I'd enjoy being with people much more than typing in an office."

Nauseated from the smell of ash and cinder, she excused herself from Lucius' company and headed back to CW's Ford. She no longer noticed the rain drenching her clothes, chilling her skin. She focused her eyes straight ahead and weaved her way under the dripping pine trees toward the automobiles parked along the muddy lane. Two of the squad cars rolled out onto the road, then rattled off. She noticed a pack of grim-faced men hurrying for another automobile parked near CW's. They piled into a Dodge touring car and roared away into the dark. As Marie reached CW's Ford, she heard her name called from the damp pine grove behind her. She turned to see Rachel and CW rushing through the trees toward her.

"Hurry, dear!" Rachel shouted, excitement drawn on her face. "Get in the car!"

Another automobile farther up the road pulled out into the rain and roared off.

Marie climbed into the rear seat of the Ford and pulled the door closed behind her. CW jumped into the front seat and started the engine after Rachel slid in beside him. As he put the automobile in gear,

Rachel turned to Marie. "Something awful's happened."

The river was black and cold and wild in the rainy dark. Tall cottonwoods arched over the swirling water and swayed in the wind. The grassy soil was soaked and muddy, smelling of rot and humid undergrowth. Marie followed Rachel and CW through a wet thicket of buttonbush toward the riverbank where she saw a dozen men or more on the embankment, police and civilians alike, occupied with a grisly discovery in a backwater beneath a grove of willows at the river's edge. The body of a small boy lay drenched in mud, his skull crushed by a violent blow. His name was Boy-Allen.

"He lived just down the street," said Rachel, edging close to the water just upriver from the crowd of men surrounding the body. She clung to CW's arm, oblivious to a drizzling rain. "The poor thing delivered our morning paper."

Marie stood quietly nearby, ill at the sight of the poor child. She secretly hoped his death had been an accident, a pathetic fall perhaps or some other unfortunate circumstance. Isn't guilt over steps not taken preferable to the helplessness of the unknown? Her own tragedy of burying a first born had taken years to subdue. But now she'd overheard the police trading opinions of a deliberate killing, a murder, and felt sick to her stomach.

"It's what we've come to these days," CW suggested, water dripping from his gray felt hat. "Slaughtering our young."

Rachel frowned. "What a horrid thing to say."

"Well, I believe it's true," CW argued, "this moral arrogance of ours notwithstanding. Modern thinking would have us convinced that a new electric Frigidaire in every kitchen will free us of all evils, as if profit and convenience were signposts along the road to heaven. For Godsakes, unless we learn to behave a lot better toward each other, I'd say we're pretty well fixed to be damned, and this sad child is the proof of it."

Heartbroken for Boy-Allen's mother, Marie watched a doctor stride grim-faced out of the rainy gloom with a pair of attendants trailing behind, while one of the policemen waded into muddy backwater up to his knees. Directing several electric lanterns close above him, the doctor knelt low beside the tortured corpse of Boy-Allen and began his examination. Dialogue among the concerned diminished. The river lapped at the reedy shore. In all her life, Marie had never believed that those dark angels who haunt this world have authority over the weak and tender-hearted. Both goodness and evil have consequences. Virtue is chosen, not endowed, while pleas for mercy ring in our ears like the beckoning of old church bells. We hear, or do not, according to our own unceasing struggle with compassion and piety.

The rain persisted almost till morning.

A NICKEL ARCADE

HARRY HENNESEY could sell green cheese to the man in the moon.

Confidence was his mark in life.

His gift.

The basis for his prosperity.

He had a simple philosophy: *If you don't have what they want, make them want what you have. Make them happy. A happy customer is a repeat customer, and repeat customers put bread on your table.*

The past year, however, had been peculiar. Business ought to have been bright enough for everyone in the Republic, boosted to dizzying heights by the great Bull Market. Fortune beckoned daily, and the eager crowds swelled. Many had forward-looking ideas and got rich. Others plainly did not, and not even Herbert Hoover knew why. There were salesmen Harry knew along the road who spoke of being treated like pariahs, carriers of the plague, fallen angels. Bitterness infected their voices, soured to clients and wholesalers alike. Life carried descriptions of ash and frost. In crowded Pullman cars, late into the traveling night, he overheard whispered predictions of the death of the profession. Among all those whom the glittering market had left behind, despair was rampant. True believers kept to themselves, or sat alone and pretended to read day-old newspapers while keeping an eye out for any change in the weather. Consolidation was on the horizon. One man's fortune became another man's horror. Harry Hennesey was no shark, but blood was in the water and only a fool ignored the truth. He had sold the house in Farrington not only to keep afloat, but to stay in the hunt. This he had done in the most earnest confidence that market shares fluctuate according to faith and perception, indicating patience and persistence as the guiding principles of salesmanship: a true businessman prefers small profits and certain returns to large profits and uncertain settlements. With cash in the bank from the sale of the house on Cedar Street to back him, Harry determined to snare whatever advantages were still to be had.

Six weeks after arriving in the city, he awoke to a gray dawn and resolved to secure a profit for his day's labor. He threw off the blanket and sheets, and went to the toilet. It was cold in his apartment. For the past week, he had been told the radiator would be repaired and so far it had not. Harry was certain the Warsaw Hotel was run by numbskulls. Bohunk Joe, a dice addict whose charge it was to keep the pipes and furnace shipshape, made a crap joint out of the basement. Likewise, the night clerk, Mortimer Watt, was a psychosomatic health nut who paid more attention to his private pharmacy than who telephoned or ran in and out of the hotel. Back when Harry first took his room, an Irish trio of cold prowlers posing as pill salesmen snookered Watt into lending his pass-key so that every medicine cabinet in the building could have a bottle of Dr. Murgatroyd's Famous Blue Pills. Instead of wellness sweeping over the hotel, jewelry and other valuables seemed to fly out of the building until one of the burglars was caught crapping on the toilet in 5A with a stolen gold watch on his wrist. Nor did the property manager, a prig named Horace McDonald, do better than setting foot on the premises once a month, and then only to collect the rent and escort lavender boys to his attic playground.

Were the hotel rates not so reasonable, Harry might have given notice and found lodging elsewhere. Marie would have been horrified. His fourth floor apartment was barely adequate: a tiny bedroom with a dresser and nightstand behind a thin curtain, a kitchenette and a sitting room with space for a sofa and a writing desk and a stuffed easychair, a porcelain sink, tub and toilet in a narrow bathroom: comfortable, but nothing to celebrate. The old brick hotel looked out over noisy Jackson Street. From his sitting room window, Harry would sometimes count auto traffic on the Washington Bridge and listen to the great steamships on the cold river at night. Coal trucks and delivery vans rumbled by at all hours, and the Ibbetson Street elevated trolley rang at the station two blocks away.

After his toilet and shower, Harry brushed his teeth and dressed in a gray worsted suit and straightened up his desk. There was a batch of dunning letters and other correspondences to sort through. Marie had written to thank him for the flowers he'd wired on Mother's Day and to say that she had found a cashier position in downtown Bellemont with James Delahaye, a shrewd fellow Harry knew from school who claimed to have been on his way to France with the A.E.F. until Elrod Hughes drove a flivver over his foot. That she had to find employment at all disturbed him. Sure they'd been having troubles, but that didn't mean he had quit on her and the children. *"Do you know, dear, when I got my salary the other night, I felt like a boy putting his first penny into a tin savings bank, knowing that some of this will go towards making my darling Marie and myself happy, and that this will go on as long as life will last."* Guilt over selling their house on Cedar Street chased behind him like a black cloud. Just the same, he might argue that Marie and the children would probably benefit from the experience of making do in a tough circumstance, and might even, in fact, discover inner qualities of resourcefulness and adaptability they'd never know under the comfort and sheltering wing of the Pendergasts in Farrington. He only hoped they still had faith in him, too.

Anxious to get on with his day, Harry took the elevator to the lobby and hurried out to buy a newspaper and get something to eat. After a breakfast of buckwheat cakes, bacon and coffee at a café on Webster Lane, he caught the trolley at 21st Street and rode north along Columbia Avenue, where cook smoke drifted in the wind from the pushcarts and box stands of fishmongers set up above the river. The streetcar let him off two blocks from the loading docks at mid-river where huge warehouses consolidated product from a thousand merchants to be distributed throughout the city. He rented office and inventory space there from City Transfer & Storage at 83rd Street between Diever and Powell and handled his business each morning by telephone. His products were piled high on wooden pallets near the back of the cavernous warehouse where they did not conflict with those of the larger clients. Seeing as how his rent was significantly lower than his competitors, if it took an extra hour or so to remove a shipment of, say, lampstands or half a dozen boxes of Javanese peacock feathers, that was just one of the tradeoffs necessary to the agreement.

He had occupied this office since March after relinquishing the same arrangement at Gateway Transfer & Storage, a space he had leased for six years. Some of his best work had been accomplished in that old building overlooking the Kansas River. Harry had always been somewhat of a tinkerer, an inventor. He enjoyed toying around with ideas for diminishing life's small labors. He had invented the "rubber thumb" for riffling through voluminous stacks of paper. It won him a hundred dollars and a notice with the U.S. Patent Office in Washington D.C. He had a plaque to prove it and had bronzed the original "thumb" to show friends and visitors at home in Farrington. On another occasion, he had come up with the slogan, "*Safety Is No Accident,*" and won a 21-jeweled watch and a few more dollars and the immortality that follows a useful phrase. Whenever he saw his words repeated in print, whether inside a factory or on the back of a delivery truck, he felt a measure of pride and accomplishment at having rendered a service, however modest, to posterity. *Let him take pleasure in his business, and it will become a recreation to him.*

When Harry walked into the warehouse at eight o'clock, only a pair of longshoremen in denim and a little man wearing a green celluloid eyeshade were up and about, fiddling with a pallet of wooden crates marked "FRAGILE" and labeled for Sault Ste. Marie on the Canadian border. He didn't recognize the little man and gave only a slight nod before heading to his own office near the rear of the building. None of Harry's competitors were about this morning and he was glad of that. Joe Phelps was a guinea from Boston who traded with his fellow Italians on St. Bonaventure Street. He was always worming through everybody's inventory, hoping to swap his pathetic finds for something valuable he could turn a profit on in his old neighborhood. Harry almost boxed Joe's ears one afternoon when he caught him loading a pair of French oil lamps into the business end of a delivery truck. Both lamps had Harry's markers on them in plain sight. *"Honest to God, I wasn't trying to run 'em out of here behind your back. There's this fellow, Dorelli, over on North Frederick, put a notice up for one of these, and I told him to call you, and when he tried, you were out, so I thought I'd show 'em off myself, do you a favor. You know I wouldn't think of putting the shake on you. We're pals, you and me. I hope you know that."* As a matter of fact, nobody had any real friends at Transfer & Storage, least of all Harry. Most of those fellows had been there a couple years or more, and knew the territory better than he did, and saw no reason to cut him in, not that he ever expected to be one of them, or particularly wanted to. Stanton Kelsey was a communist and a dope fiend. He did his business in plain sight of anyone who recognized those hypodermic syringes he kept in the top drawer of his desk. Once when Kelsey saw that Harry noticed the hypo behind a thick ledger, he tried to persuade him that it was for his niece Lily who required insulin injections to treat her chronic diabetes. After that, Harry made it a point not to see Kelsey alone in his office for fear being labeled a needle fiend himself. Then there was Phil Fermer, who held a natural science degree from Northwestern University and strutted about like Albert Einstein, when in reality he barely knew the difference between lightning and lightning bugs. Fermer ran a low-rent furniture racket out of Cameronville that seemed to rake in the dough despite the fact that most of his inventory was flea-bitten and utilized replacement pieces stolen out of the back of department store trucks. Every fellow at Transfer & Storage knew this, and each pretended not to, remembering that oftentimes feigning ignorance makes a day endured. Being in the city wasn't a popularity contest. There was serious work to do, profit to be uncovered. Sharing a beer and a few laughs with his natural competitors was not one of Harry's deathless dreams.

When business was good, his own desk was buried under stacks of order forms and invoices, shipping manifests and customs declaration sheets. Today it was mostly bare, only a note he had written to himself lying beside the In/Out mail cage. He picked it up and read, "Contact Mr. Hiram Johnson at 8:30." A telephone number was underlined below the name. He had arranged a morning appointment and forgotten completely about it. One of his favorite mottos was, *If you give your customers fair treatment, friendly service, and good merchandise, they will remain your customers.* Well, he could still keep the appointment, provided he didn't dawdle with the other odds and ends requiring his attention. He picked up the telephone and dialed the number in front of him. Hiram Johnson had a shipment of pocketwatches he preferred distributed by someone other than himself and had obtained Harry's name by chance at a United Cigar Store a month before. He was offering a substantial percentage of the revenues if all the merchandise could be disposed of within the week. Harry accepted the challenge, realizing the profit margin in this instance encouraged the pursuit of miracles. He let the phone ring fourteen times before replacing the receiver and sitting back. Probably the man was still in bed. Not everyone was willing to see a sunrise in order to make a dollar. Opportunity had its followers, but they were not legion. Even given the desperate straits in which most men labored, sloth and ignorance provided ample avenues for the avoidance of life's offerings, however golden and bright. Because Harry was strict in keeping his engagements, he always found it pathetic to see how horribly the families of these men lived, how little they received of life's daily necessities, and how carelessly they treated this challenge.

He dialed the number again.

By nine, he resigned himself to the loss of his client. Possibly Johnson had reconsidered and chosen instead to handle the distribution himself. Then again, maybe the shipment had been part of a heist and this Johnson was a faker for some gangster racket in stolen goods. Or maybe it was on the level, after all, but had gotten hijacked on its way here. Anything was possible these days. Harry got up and went out into the warehouse, back to where his products were stacked high on the old pallets. It was part of his daily routine to count each boxed item and note it on an inventory tablet. Too many people came and went during the day and night, too many items walked away unannounced. With nobody but a half-wit night-watchman named Oscar Higuera to count these comings and goings, Harry didn't trust anyone but himself to know what he did and did not have available to market on a day-to-day basis. Besides, any fellow worth his salt preferred to be at the head of his own business.

On the way to his rental space, he saw a man enter the far doorway, framed by the fresh white glare of morning sunlight.

"Hennesey! You're here!"

Now this was something, all right. Charles Algernon Follette, industrialist, corn and wheat investor, steel and oil stockbroker, sole-owner of the warehouse. Dressed in his smart silver-gray silk suit, a pink carnation on his lapel, Follette charged forward, a big grin on his face.

"Good to see you, old man." Follette strode up to shake hands.

"Good morning, sir," Harry said, barely managing a grin of his own. "How are you doing?"

Follette made him extremely nervous. The great man owned an Italianate mansion on Mulberry Avenue and a summer cottage with sixteen rooms overlooking the blue sea at Newport. The old warehouse was just another of his many investments, City Transfer & Storage probably a tax dodge for his own American Prometheus Corporation on the 99th floor of the Empyrean Building downtown. Harry's concern was how to talk to a millionaire without acting like a fool.

"Well, I have to admit I'm doing just fine," Follette replied, confidently. "Just fine, indeed. And yourself?"

"Oh, I can't kick, I suppose, things being as they are these days."

"Now that's the spirit." Follette beamed like a winner at the carnival. "Look here, Hennesey, I need a favor and I believe you're just the fellow for the job."

"What do you have in mind, sir?"

"Well, it's like this, old man." He draped his arm over Harry's shoulder. "Let's go back to your office and have ourselves a little pow-wow."

Harry cleared a space at his desk for Follette and pulled up a side chair. Compared to the wealthy industrialist, he dressed like a bank teller. All he had brought with him to the city were a few ordinary suits: brown cassimere, navy blue serge, and gray virgin wool. That they had been purchased from Montgomery Ward & Co. hadn't been any great concern until two minutes ago. He also noticed Follette wore a great smelling cologne that fixed him up like nobody else. The rolling chair creaked as the millionaire leaned back and lit up a fat Cuban cigar. Flicking the burnt match over his shoulder, Follette said, "First off, Hennesey, I need your help."

"You do?"

"Yes, indeed, and it's no lark, either. This will be a terrific challenge. Are you game?"

"Certainly, sir. What can I do?"

Follette puffed on his cigar. "Do you have a family?"

"Yes, sir, a wife and two wonderful children. I'm very lucky, if I do say so."

"That's good, very good. A family is a great thing to have. I find it difficult to trust those fellows who don't. Where's their foundation? Their commitment? Knowing he has little ones at home who need that warm bottle of milk at bedtime is usually enough to put a spark in a fellow's shoe leather, I always say."

"I agree."

"Now, I ought to tell you I've never married. Not that I have anything against the grand institution, mind you. I'm all for it, and always have been. Just haven't found my best girl yet. No sense in confusing the flutter of an eyelid with a dive into the matrimonial sea, is there?"

Harry smiled. "No, sir." Another unmarried, marriage expert.

"You see, my sister Caroline tied the knot when she was sixteen and split the blanket after a year when her husband, a shiftless auto repairman from Boston, fell off the wagon one night and cracked her head open with a sugar bowl. Terrible thing, just awful. Poor Mother held Caroline's hand at St. Joseph's and made her swear out a warrant against that sonofabitch, which she refused to do because he shined up to her once when nobody paid her any notice at all. Can you feature that? He smacks her silly and she won't tell it to the judge? Well, thanks to some persuading, she's unhitched now and won't do it again, I'm here to tell you."

Harry nodded cautiously. "I should hope not. What a terrible thing to have happen." He hoped Follette wouldn't expect him to share his own laundry. Keep business and home life separate; never share too much private information; a colleague or a competitor can always find a weakness in how your lawn is mown or to which morning paper you're subscribed; let them prefer gossip to knowledge.

Follette leaned forward, setting his elbows on the desk, and looked Harry straight in the eye. "Hennesey, how far would you go to bring a wayward member of your family back into the fold?"

That was an odd question. He had to allow for a certain lack of precision here. "What sort of family member? A black sheep, or someone of that sort?"

"Oh, no, nothing like that at all. Just an innocent little girl who was lost in a bitter dispute over a worthless estate. A poor innocent victim of pettiness and greed. My dear niece-once-removed, Olive, whom I haven't seen since her third birthday, was declared mentally defective by a scoundrel of an uncle and shunted off to a hospital from which she apparently escaped last year and is rumored to be wandering the streets of our great city, completely unaware of those of us who still love her and long to bring her home again."

Follette dragged a glass ashtray close and tapped his cigar over it. His face bore an expected sadness that seemed studied, rehearsed, or at least often told. Harry wasn't sure what to make of it. Obligated to the great man for rental space that kept his financial situation afloat, he had to be circumspect in how he responded. These fellows aren't like the rest of us, he reminded himself. The rich and powerful have means and influence to bear their inferiors along like a river washing debris in a mighty tide to the sea. That doesn't mean we're helpless, nor are they omnipotent. We're each aware of our own mortality, after all.

Trying to be interested, Harry offered a sympathetic word. "Children should never be lost."

"No, they shouldn't."

"So how can I be of help?"

"Well, let me tell you," Follette said, firming up. He reached into his coat pocket and drew out a sheet of paper. He slid it across the desk to Harry. "Look there. You see, it's all we know about her, but maybe it'll be enough to bring our little darling home again."

Harry skimmed from top to bottom: *Olive Blanchard (no known middle name) was born in 1913, making her roughly fifteen or sixteen years old today; she likely had blonde hair and bluish eyes. Height and weight unknown, but likely or-dinary.* Not much to go on, he thought. No wonder they haven't turned her up yet.

Follette obviously read the doubt on Harry's face. "I'll admit it's pretty thin, and there could be a thousand girls in this city matching that name and description, but only one of them is our dear Olive, and I'm offering five thousand dollars to the fellow who turns her up."

"Five grand? My goodness, that's a lot of money."

"She's very important to me."

"Certainly."

"We believe she's in the city, but we're not entirely sure. There are complicated circumstances which have led us to that conclusion, al-though you don't need to know what they are. Naturally, we're looking elsewhere, too."

"You must have an army looking for her."

"Yes, I know a lot of people." He puffed vigorously on his cigar.

"Well, you're very generous with this offer. I appreciate it."

Follette smiled. "I've had my eye on you, Hennesey, since you hired this space. Heard a lot about you, too, from the other fellows. They tell me you're an up-and-comer, a real boomer. So I figured I'd toss your name in the hat and see if you can ring the bell for me. A heartache like this can't last forever, can it? Help me out, Hennesey, and I'll see to it that you make the grade like you never thought possible. What do you say?"

Honestly, he felt like a pot of gold had just dropped into his lap. His head was spinning, his stomach churned. Follette's offering me the moon, he thought, and for nothing except some snooping around.

"I'll do everything I can to help you, sir," he told Follette, with a booster's glee. "You'll get my best effort, I swear. Sure, this is a big city, but I know a lot people, too, and maybe I have a few ideas that you fel-lows haven't quite thought of. I promise I won't let you down."

Follette gleamed. "See, I knew I could count on you!" He stood then, offering his hand like a true partner. "I wasn't certain you'd be willing to take on this responsibility, Hennesey, I must admit. You work hard, and keep firm hours, and that's the attribute of a fellow who in-tends to get ahead. But what separates the well-do'er from the rest of the bunch is that extra kick that keeps the desk lamp burning when everyone else is fast asleep. You see, there are ten million men in America lacking the gumption they need to get out there and earn enough to feed their own children, and most of them spend more time dreaming up slipslop schemes for gouging their fellow man than pounding the sidewalk for an honest dollar. And don't for one second think that men like myself don't notice it, either. There's a view from the top drawer not many of you have a clue about, and that's not your fault. We're up here and you're down there, and it's how things have been since Moses was in diapers. But now and then, you fellows get an inkling of what it takes to get out of the crowd, and maybe you grab for it, and maybe you don't, but once you do, suddenly you realize that all you really needed was another hour or two a day of a routine that produced a little more thought and a little more sweat to get that payoff you've been dreaming of since you saw your first top-hat in a gilded carriage."

Harry beamed. My God, when had he last heard a speech like this? Maybe Follette had his eye on him all along. Wouldn't that be something to secure a position that earned both a higher salary and greater prestige, all because of selling the house on Cedar Street and coming here to the city? Stranger things have happened. Joe Dalton at the insurance agency once told Harry about a shoeshine boy who gave such a spit and polish to some high insurance mucky-muck that the big shot took the boy on permanently. Thirty years later, when the insurance fellow died, he left the boy a million dollars. Of course, Harry didn't believe the story, but the principle was instructive. Work hard and stay alert, because the weather's always changing.

"Oh, I just remembered," Follette said, brightening again. "It's the reason I came down here to see you today. It's a small job, a favor for a friend. Are you interested? It'll earn you a few dollars and make us both happy, what do you say?"

"Certainly, sir. Anything you want."

At eleven, Harry found himself along the waterfront at 112th and Chapman Avenue in the old factory district seated beside a tired-looking youth in the cab of a small black delivery truck, rolling past one vast damp and dreary structure after another, searching for a specific address among the dozens of industrial behemoths erected during the latter stages of the previous century. Heaps of garbage were stacked in the lee of brick walls and alleyways, mortar itself dislodged and fallen to refuse hiding the sidewalks, mold gathering on the bricks, soot on the mold, filth and negligence spreading outward block by block into the great city beyond. Only men of ambition could detect fortune in the smoke and rubble by this lapping tide that brought ships from all over the world to the busy waterfront, magnates like Follette, J.W. Leggett, Foster Meriwether, and Adolph Baer, whose giant industries contributed to the ceaseless growth of this mighty Republic. Maybe Follette sees some of that drive and aptitude in me, Harry reflected, and this is his way of nudging it out into the open. Not a test, exactly, but something like an invitation to join him and the other go-getters who gather scraps and make a fabric for the rest of us to use. Did Harry Hennesey have what it takes? Well, if you don't believe in yourself, who will? Once this appointment was handled, Harry decided to get straight after Follette's niece and see what he might come up with. That's the first step. Earn the man's confidence and trust. Show him what you're capable of accomplishing on his behalf. Five thousand dollars was a plenty decent reward, but climbing that ladder to the 99th floor could be worth a hundred times that, and more.

Suddenly he wished this stupid kid would drive faster.

"There it is," said the boy, pointing with the cigarette toward a building just up ahead on the right. "I been here before."

"Oh?"

He drove the truck through the main entrance. "Yeah, some German fellow runs a butcher shop out of the back. Claims he's Kaiser Bill's uncle. If you ask me, he's a nut."

The boy shut off the engine once they were indoors. Harry climbed out. The floor was wet where his shoes touched down, and a disagreeable odor of grease and rot mixed in the building's interior. Machinery whined and pounded in his ears. The boy bounced out of the truck and walked off across the building, passing under a double section of steam pipes, wheels and rotors, and into the dark toward the rear.

Harry looked up. The ceiling was barely visible through the structural supports and conduits: just a number of cracks and holes in the corrugated iron roof that admitted enough light to reveal a gray sky above the factory.

Harry walked around to the back of the truck and untied a rope over the tarpaulin covering his wares. Follette had persuaded him to empty Harry's entire shipment of shoes in fifty-seven cardboard boxes off the pallet at the Transfer & Storage warehouse and load them onto this truck for delivery to a fellow named DuFort. The financial arrangement was fair and equitable and posed no difficulty for Harry at all. Actually, he was pleased that Charles A. Follette had thought enough to consider the exchange in the first place, seeing as how Follette's profit was minuscule. In any case, the shipment of plain black calfskins had been gathering dust for two months now and Harry had begun to worry about their ultimate disposition. If this man DuFort wanted the shoes at a respectable price, he was more than comfortable selling them.

A steam whistle screeched from somewhere deep inside the building. Harry wandered over to the office near the loading entry and peered in through the glass. Papers were stacked up on the sloppiest desk he had ever seen. How could someone run a business from so disorganized a desk? It was astonishing. Even the filing cabinets were left open to whomever desired a peek. He tried the doorknob and found it unlocked.

"Hello!" Behind him, a voice called out across the factory. "Mr. Hennesey!"

Harry looked back over his shoulder and saw a short, stocky fellow in suspenders and spats jogging toward him. "Sorry to keep you waiting." The fellow wore a friendly grin on his dark sweaty face. "Good morning," he said, stopping in front of Harry and offering his hand. "I'm Gus DuFort."

Harry shook it firmly, trying to be pleasant. "Harry Hennesey."

"Glad to know you, Harry. Charley Follette said you were a regular fellow. A clever and industrious fellow. An entrepreneur after his own heart."

"He said that about me?"

"Well, sure he did." DuFort wiped the sheen of sweat from his balding scalp. "Isn't it true? I find Charley Follette to be a damned good judge of character."

"Oh, I'm just surprised to hear it, is all," Harry said, embarrassed now. It's always a surprise to discover you've got a reputation. "I suppose I've done all right."

"I'm sure you have," DuFort agreed. "We both know it's a tough dollar these days, and any fellow who can go out and earn one on his feet has to have some of that good old-fashioned know-how. At least, that's how I see it."

A draft swept into the factory from the river, stirring up dust and grime from the cement floor. Harry coughed and drew a handkerchief from his vest pocket to cover his mouth before he coughed again. When he looked up, DuFort was holding a clipboard out toward him, pen attached. "Well, Charley says you've got some shoes for me."

Harry put the handkerchief away and nodded. "Fifty-seven boxes of the finest black calfskins I could locate. Genuine Goodyear welt construction. They're awfully impressive."

"I'm sure they are."

"Are you in the wholesaling business?"

DuFort laughed. "No, not at all. It doesn't interest me in the slightest. Manufacturing is my game. You name it, I can get it made. I know everybody in the city. May I see the shoes?"

"By all means." Harry led DuFort back around to the delivery truck where he folded open the tarpaulin, exposing the shipment stacked up along the side panels. "I've been tempted to take a pair for myself. According to my buyer, the soles are constructed out of the finest Spanish leather."

"Is that so? I never heard of such a thing." DuFort climbed up into the back of the truck and grabbed one of the boxes.

"Neither had I, but my fellow is darned reliable on these matters."

DuFort opened the boxes and removed a pair of black calfskins and turned them over in his hand, smelled them, slid a pair of fingers down inside one of the shoes, studied the stitching on the soles, smiled to himself, then laughed out loud. "They're magnificent!"

Harry felt buoyant. "I told you so."

"I assume they are all of equal quality?"

"Certainly." His day-long train ride to Kenosha had paid off, after all. Stu Vincent's crowd had laughed when he told them about tracking that shoe store ad. Let's compare ledgers now, wiseacres. "You see, I selected each pair by hand. Tough work, but absolutely necessary to insure I got a fair dollar's worth. Service is the poetry of business, I always say."

"Stupendous," DuFort enthused, sticking the sample pair back into their box. "Simply stupendous. I'll buy all you've got."

"Done!"

They walked shoulder-to-shoulder back across to DuFort's office where the stocky man opened the top drawer of his shabby filing cabinet and drew out an invoice sheet and a payment form. Sitting on the edge of the desk, DuFort riffled through the form until he reached the current dispensing papers and scribbled a set of numbers and a brief notation. The smell of cheap hair-grease filled the small room. A printed sign on the wall beside the window read:

No Goods Exchanged After Being Taken Away

Studying the office now from inside, Harry was less perturbed by the disarray he had seen through the window. After dealing with DuFort face-to-face, he saw the mess as a sign of vigor and energy, an indication of success, and thought perhaps he'd allow his own desk to gather more clutter. He could learn something from this fellow. You can't say high intentions require spit and polish. While DuFort finished filling out a check for the shipment of the black calfskins, Harry remarked, "They are quite wonderful shoes, aren't they?"

"Just swell, " DuFort replied, with a pleasant grin. "Better than I hoped."

"So, tell me, do you have a buyer lined up already, or do you plan on advertising? I ask because I've found wholesaling shoes to be fairly difficult, particularly ones as fine a quality as these. In other words, do you have contacts with the shoe industry, agents and such?"

DuFort laughed and shook his head. "Honestly, I don't know a damned thing about shoes."

"No?"

"Nope," DuFort said, tearing the check off the leaf. He handed it to Harry. "I'm not a shoe man. I just wear 'em."

Harry took a quick glance at the check, and slipped it into his vest pocket. Two hundred and forty dollars wasn't a fortune, but it wasn't half bad for a morning's work. After lunch, he might even wire Marie with the news, let her know he was sending along fifty dollars of it by a money order so that she could buy a new dress, maybe a book for Cissie and a toy for Henry, other household odds and ends. Yes, that's just what he would do.

Buoyed by his modest profit, he remarked brightly to DuFort, "I assume your purchasing agent is with one of the shoe distributors, then. I'll just bet he'll be pleased."

DuFort shook his head. "No, this hasn't anything to do with shoes at all."

"Well, then, what does he want with fifty-seven boxes of them?"

"I guess he'll cut 'em up for scraps," DuFort replied flatly, as he scribbled into his daily ledger. "Sell the leather. It's damned nice quality. After that, who knows? I don't ask, they don't tell me. That's how it is in my work."

"I suppose you're kidding, aren't you?"

"How come?"

There has to be a joke in here somewhere. What sort of business was this? "Let me tell you, DuFort, those are the finest shoes I've been able to secure in three years."

"Sure they are. Like I said, they're damned nice."

Harry felt utterly flabbergasted. "Well, for God's sake, the thought of them being sold for leather scrap is appalling."

"Yeah?" DuFort shut the ledger back into his desk drawer. "Why's that?"

"Well, I just never considered that they weren't to be offered in a department store or some such."

"Follette didn't tell you?"

"No, he did not."

DuFort laughed as he stood up. "Aw, Charley's a card. A hell of a businessman, but a little shady, if you ask me. That's how come the rich get where they are. They think differently from us regular Joes. Always got an angle on everything from gasoline to golf balls, working one deal into another like a corkscrew. Frankly, I wished I had the guts for it, but I don't. I'm just a buck in the middle."

As they walked out of DuFort's office, Harry felt completely deflated. He was always clear and explicit in making a bargain. He had scoured the Middle Border several years now for a shipment of the finest affordable men's shoes and though DuFort had scribbled Harry a check that compensated him well enough for his efforts, the idea that his beautiful shoes, calfskins that they were, would be ripped apart for scraps seemed horrible and demeaning. Harry Hennesey was not a junkman.

"Look here, friend, it's all commodity and profit," DuFort said reassuringly, putting one hand on Harry's shoulder. "Leather, thread, glue. Who cares what they look like when they're put together? We're businessmen, you and me. We're not creating something here. We're selling it. We ain't artists, are we?"

"I don't know." DuFort's amiable suggestion left him more hollow than ever, quite a comedown from the elation Follette's first request had raised.

"Well, you're a real go-getter, Hennesey. Glad to know you. So long now."

He gave Harry a friendly pat on the back and marched off across the factory, whistling an old Stephen Foster tune off-key while Harry trudged back to the truck where the boy was sitting up behind the wheel waiting to drive him back across town to Transfer & Storage. "Son?"

The kid's head perked up when Harry tapped on the driver's door. He'd been dozing lightly. "Yes sir?"

"Look here, you go ahead and drive yourself back to the warehouse. I have several errands to run up here."

"You like me to wait for you?"

"No, thank you."

As Harry stepped back, the kid started up the truck. Sticking the gearshift into reverse, he leaned out the window. "Say, what do you want me to tell Mr. Follette?"

"About what?"

Discouraged, Harry walked up past the factory district toward the next streetcar stop and used his transfer to purchase a ride back downtown. Standing in the open rear platform of a mostly empty electric trolley, watching the factories recede behind him, he considered what DuFort said about their place in the grand scheme of business and knew it was dead wrong. He was certain that good taste did count for something in this world. He was no Babbitt. No matter what his colleagues believed, profit margins were not the sole arbiters of success. How and what one sold was equally as important as how much one earned. After all, didn't the fellows who sold Renaissance art and Egyptian antiquities ride in finer motor cars than those who sold stock in lowly pig knuckles and breakfast cereals? What did he intend as his legacy who earned and spent every penny without thought of how posterity would view his contributions to society? Harry wanted to be remembered as a wise and valuable member, kind and generous, clever and bold, worthy of a monument someday perhaps. That wasn't impossible, was it? With the best urges and good work habits, who could say that our boldest ambitions have limits? But you can't achieve greatness through the simpleminded buying and selling of commodities. No, there need to be contributions made, progression, artfulness, deliberate good taste. If not, he thought, I'd work for a Ford agency.

Along the Avenue of the Republic now, patches of bright sunlight broke through the clouds and warmed the morning air. Thousands of people crowded the sidewalks and street corners as the trolley made its stops, heading toward those grand tall buildings of midtown. By a Red Ball Grocery Store at 71st and Waring, a woman carrying two great bags shuffled onto the streetcar with three small girls clinging to the hem of her skirt, clamoring for peppermint candy. Please? Please? Two men wearing blue serge suits came to the rear beside Harry and smoked cigars and talked about the Stock Exchange and the baseball leagues and a pine cottage on Sumner Bay where they intended to pass the weekend in the absence of wives gone to visit relatives in Cincinnati. Martha hates fishing and won't set foot in the boat unless I've put a cocktail on the hatch cover. Keep quiet about that because I told Gladys we'd be at the polo grounds Saturday and out to Uncle Everett's for the church picnic on Sunday. I thought he went to Havana. Yes, but Gladys still thinks he's sold on Christ and I'd appreciate her not finding out he's thrown that over for Ethelyn's housekeeper Isabel until we're ready to tell her. Listening, Harry kept his back to them and gazed out at the city. He was beginning to feel better just being out here again in the middle of everything that mattered. It truly electrified him, riding on this simple streetcar through the heart of the great metropolis. Conversations swirled about him wherever he went. People ran every which way, flushed with hurry. Exchanging glances with strangers when the opportunity presented itself, once more he felt part of a grand civilization in its golden instant. Perhaps this is how it was to cross Rome by chariot in Christ's youth, or to stroll the Nile River Valley in the gleaming shadow of the newly erected pyramids. An age could pass in the twinkling of an eye, only serendipity exacting significance from the common man. America held the torch of history now, eloquent in her demands for greatness. Would any citizen deliberately deny himself the opportunity to share in her fortune? Not Harry Hennesey. Not by a long shot.

Ten blocks south of Columbia Avenue near the river, he disembarked and bought a piping hot sausage from a scabrous East Indian and brought it with him to an iron railed bench atop the great brick bulwark facing the broad waterway below. Anchored in front was a fence of ornately scrolled wrought iron four feet high, topped by spear points of Fleur de Lys. Pigeons gathered where breadcrumbs were scattered. Children played on the brick plaza and ran in and out of the benches, while passersby commented on the change in weather. A swath of sunshine heated the wooden slats, keeping Harry warm as he looked out over the river. He ate slowly while considering the black calfskins sale and his place in the world. Maybe that hadn't gone so badly, after all. Not only had Follette given him an opportunity to move up in the world with that lead on the missing girl, but there'd been a few dollars he needed as well, money to help Marie and the kids. He watched a slight woman park herself on the next bench upriver and fold a large indigo scarf across her lap from which her little boy snatched handfuls of popcorn. Harry sighed. He did, after all, long for his own darling children. He wrote them both a letter each week to say how much he missed and adored them. He had gotten six letters back, which he kept in a stack by his family photographs on the nightstand. Sometimes he could hardly endure being away. His little Henry was shy with strangers and took his scoldings with a pout that lasted for hours, but he was also relentlessly brave and inquisitive, and laughed more than any child Harry had ever known. Cissie, on the other hand, was a tyrant and a spitfire rolled into one. She loved to read and tease, boss her friends, and defy her mother's request for peace and quiet in the afternoon. What pleased him most was how his lovely daughter refused to close her eyes for bed each night until her dear old dad tucked her in with a poem and gave her a soft angel kiss on her forehead. *When thou art a man, my darling, still the children will be there.* No one knows how deep a father's feelings can be for his children. Just imagining them often brought tears to his eyes. He loved them both so very much. Had they amusements enough to endure the long Texas summer? Did they show respect for the swift river current? Were they eating Mother's cooking? Were they still a family? If not, then what was all this for?

A gust came up and swept a newspaper clean out of the hands of a fellow standing by the bulwark. Harry watched it flutter down toward the shore. River craft slipped past in opposite directions, flatboats and white steamers and passenger ferries plying the cold waters. Farther down the bulwark, a gnarled vendor came walking along with a large load under canvas strapped to his back. Harry watched him stop by the iron railing overlooking the great river, slip the load off, and mop his brow with a handkerchief as a flock of pigeons alighted to the brick for bread crumbs scattered from the hand of an old woman in cotton shawl and hand-basket. The vendor untied the canvas cover, exposing a leather sack that he untied and opened, removing rubber tubing and various items of metal. Then the vendor took to assembling the items he'd withdrawn from his sack, constructing some sort of peculiar contraption. A truck rumbled by, kicking up dust and smoke when the driver changed gears. The shiny Franklin Airman motorcar behind it honked loudly in protest as the cloud of exhaust smothered the intersection. Harry drew his handkerchief to cover his mouth, and decided to have a look at the vendor's contraption. Being a student of curiosities, he was intrigued by the damned thing, whatever it was. Approaching the vendor, he tried to appear only marginally interested in the contraption. That was his normal tact, a device he'd practiced since college. Don't let them know you're fascinated. Be calm and cool. Let the other fellow think he's got it over you. The vendor perked his head up and offered a hand in greeting. "Good afternoon, sir!"

"Hello," said Harry, shaking hands for politeness sake. "How do you do?"

"Fine enough," the vendor replied, standing up. He puffed out his chest with a show of confidence Harry had seen a thousand times over. These fellows always think they're about to show you the crown jewels. "Would you like a demonstration?"

"What is it?" Harry asked casually, studying the odd contraption that appeared even stranger up close. He wondered what on earth he was looking at. Maybe he ought to have enrolled in more engineering classes at State. Parmer Haynes could probably explain this entire business in half a minute. Who else could've reconfigured Dr. Chesnut's office telephone so that it rang on the quarter hour?

The vendor told him, "The Gadget Poledoric, sir."

"Pardon me?"

"It's been suggested over the centuries that our human machine has infinite capacities, but with this creation we've met our rival."

Pretending to understand more than he actually did, Harry gave it a quick once-over. There were polished gears and wooden paddles connected by copper wire to four steel boxes mounted by screws and surrounding what looked for all the world like a simple dairy milk can. How it worked or what it did, if and when it worked, eluded Harry completely.

"A mere twenty dollars!" the vendor announced proudly. "None like it anywhere in the modern world."

"I don't doubt that," Harry replied, still flummoxed. "But what does it do?"

"Well, that would depend, wouldn't it?" The vendor grinned as Harry studied the contraption more closely. Although the drive gears and polished copper wires seemed well-connected, what method of engine cast them into motion? Electricity? Steam? Gasoline? Didn't there have to be a source of energy?

"Twenty dollars," the vendor said, his voice deepening. "Take it or leave it. That's the best I'll do. Unless you're a relative. You ain't, are you?" The vendor squinted his eyes and gave Harry a hard look, studying him head to toe. Then he gave his contraption a pat. "There ain't no better example of this here wonder any place a man can buy a cup of coffee."

"Well, make it do something," Harry said, finally, looking the vendor in the eye. When you do business with someone on the up-and-up, you always look him straight in the eye, because nobody can successfully advertise a dishonest product. Of course, his father also told him a fellow's got to have the facts, and he's got to think honestly. That careful habit of mind alone will keep him prosperous — unlike those idiots who chose to spend two hundred dollars a session with Harry's favorite fraud, Doctor Abrams' miracle cabinets for diagnosing the dead. It still made him laugh. Who could have guessed that Longfellow died of syphilis and Lincoln was secretly a Negro?

"I hope I haven't misjudged you, sir," the vendor said, frowning now. He grasped Harry's hand. "You know a grand opportunity when one presents itself, don't you? Investment in the future, shades of Fulton's paddle wheel and the infernal combustion engine!" His wormy eyes twinkled as he spoke. "I've been on the Continent and in darkest Africa, you see, marketing my wares and exploring the cracks in the timber, searching for the arcane and wonderful. The Gadget Poledoric emerged from just that sort of expedition, sir. Yes, it did! A study of Cleopatra's doxology on papyrus of gold-leaf. An inspiration waiting to be revealed. My invigorated brain proved to be the correct receptacle for the Pharaoh's secret and the Gadget Poledoric was reborn into our age. Truly a miracle! Could any intelligent man stand unimpressed before it? That I do not believe! A share in immortality for twenty dollars, then. Twenty dollars! Hesitation cost Napoleon an empire. I trust you, sir, are wiser than he."

Harry had no idea what the vendor was babbling about, but he knew the whole contraption was a humbug if it wouldn't pop or blow smoke. He pulled back. "Honestly, I can't afford to invest in your machine, whatever you call it. Thank you, though, and good luck."

The vendor shot back, "Don't be penny-wise and pound-foolish, sir. True opportunity is rarer than a snowflake in Egypt."

"Sorry." Harry decided the fellow was probably insane. "Good day."

It was already a quarter of one and he hadn't made half his calls yet. Why was he wasting the day gabbing on street corners?

Behind him, he heard the vendor yell, "You thieving bastard!"

He quickened his step.

The vendor shouted after him, "THIEF!"

Frightened that his rush to get away from the vendor might be misconstrued by bystanders, he stopped. Good grief, now what? The vendor strode in his direction, fury in his eyes. Why couldn't he just enjoy a normal afternoon? Before Harry had to decide whether or not to pop the fellow in the nose, the vendor stopped and smiled broadly. "You, sir, may now purchase the astonishing Gadget Poledoric for a mere fifteen dollars! What do you say? I want to do you a tremendous favor! No? How's about ten dollars? A swell deal just for you!" His voice dropped to a plaintive mutter. "Look here, pal, I'm in a tight corner. I tell you, I ain't ate a decent meal in weeks and I ain't got a bean to my name. Help me out, will you? Lend me a buck."

— **2** —

Harry bought a haircut at a small barbershop on the corner of Hayes and 53rd Street. Foot traffic outdoors was busy, sidewalks crowded with men and women looking over the stores for needful bargains. Streams of motorcars and trucks roared by, choking the afternoon air with clouds of exhaust. Indoors, the barbershop smelled of bay rum and fresh linoleum. Harry sat in the chair near the far window where it was bright and cheerful. Back in St. Paul, he had gotten his hair cut at the Family Barbershop on North Snelling by a cigarsmoking German fellow whose young son drew funny little pictures. In Farrington, he went twice a month to the barbershop downtown on Second Street operated by Marie's older cousin, Carl Pendergast. He firmly believed in the old saw *It pays to look well,* and considered a fine haircut an important part of that equation. He also enjoyed the masculine atmosphere of a good neighborhood barbershop, vibrant with conversation, a faithful meeting place where men from all walks of life shared opinions on the world as they saw it. Getting a haircut was like a bull session back at State, a chance to relax and pretend to be smarter than you really are.

"Backtalk is a woman's backbone," remarked the chubby fellow in the next chair. He was loud and brash, and Harry had smelled gin on his breath when he sat down. "Many's the time Martha's stayed up to give young Tommy a piece of her mind when she could've just walloped him with her momma's old frying pan. I tell you, he's a lucky fellow."

A barber named Ray snipped around Harry's ears with a pair of clippers. The older man operating the chair closest to the front door added, "My missus says Martha makes Bebe Daniels look like seven cents. Poor old Tommy got the eye first time he seen her."

A slight mustachioed fellow sitting on a bench across from the three barbers spoke up from behind his copy of *Life* magazine. "Well, it must've been her beauty because I sure don't see the brains."

The man in the third barber chair laughed. Harry chuckled, too, though he had just heard the same wisecrack at a lunchroom the day before yesterday. Everyone in the city was a comic now. He thought about a joke he'd heard involving a clown and the farmer's daughter, nearly laughing out loud as he recalled the punchline.

"Aw, go jump in a lake," said the chubby fellow. He rustled his chair cloth as the barber brushed around his collar. "Maybe Martha's a little slow on the uptake, but she never asked that boy to buy her a lot of pretties, only that he stayed home to supper every so often and didn't go riding with strange dames."

"Is that so?" the fellow on the bench replied. "See, I always thought she was a little tart."

Harry's barber agreed. "Likewise."

"Ray, don't kid about that," the chubby fellow growled. "My Elsa's gotten so heartsick from this whole mess, she's keeping me awake nights."

The fellow on the bench put down his magazine and lit up a cigarette. Then he said, "Well, speaking strictly for myself, I'd like to look up a piece of fluff like that. See, first thing I'd do is run her out to a necking nook and — "

The chubby fellow leaned forward in his chair. "Shut up, George, or your teeth'll be down your throat. Get me?"

"Says who?"

"Says I, that's who. And I ain't kidding around, neither. Don't forget, when I clean 'em, they stay pressed." He grinned at his own barber in the mirror. "Ain't that so, Mick?"

"You said it."

The barbershop door opened and four men dressed in double-breasted suits walked in. They looked Italian to Harry's eye, olive-skinned and brash. Not that he knew many Italians except Phelps and his bunch. Immigrants started low on the totem pole until they proved themselves to be regular trustworthy fellows. It just seemed to Harry that most of them preferred bootlegging to going out and earning an honest dollar. Anyone could see how tough it was to get started in America, but why be a louse?

Hanging his fedora on the hat rack by the door, the husky fellow in front called out with a big grin, "Well, what do you say, boys?"

Harry's barber raised his scissors in greeting. "Hiya, Frank."

So did the other two barbers.

"What do you know, Frank?"

"Say, Frankie, what's cooking?"

While two of the men who came in with him went over to sit at a table piled high with magazines, Frank pulled a cigar out of his vest pocket and bit off the end. The fourth fellow stood in the open door, looking out on the late morning street packed and noisy with sidewalk traffic and passing motorcars. Harry watched him, curious what he was looking out for. Gangsters always had someone after them.

Lighting up his cigar, Frank said, "Louie, shut the door so's the bugs don't get in."

"Sure, boss." He shoved it closed just as a large delivery truck roared by, spewing smoke.

"It's good to see you gents," Harry's barber said, dipping a comb into a jar of water. "I guess you pulled through, after all."

Harry watched the mirror as his barber guided the comb through his hair. He always favored a clean sharp part. He enjoyed the fresh look it gave him, like a smart crease in new trousers. If I survive the next few minutes, he thought, maybe this'll give a good turn to my day.

"The cops were trying to sweat us, all right," Frank said, puffing on the cigar, "but it just turned into one long razz about Cooney Arnett doing things in a big way out in Southport. Everyone knows that's the lousiest mob that ever ran a beer truck." The Italian wore an oversized liquor grin as he strode about the barbershop like Caesar, jingling silver in his pocket. His partners at the table were occupied with a bag of Planters Salted Peanuts and flipping through fishing magazines. One of them tore a page out and stuffed it into his pocket. "So how the devil are you birds doing?"

The barber down by the door away from Harry replied, "We're making do, Frankie. Paying the back-bills. Getting along, all right. It's a living. Cecilia'd like me to take her down to Florida next year. Her sister Alice lives in Coral Gables where she goes swimming every single day of the week. Isn't that something?"

Frank laughed. "She's lucky she don't get eaten by an alligator."

"Cecilia says Alice's husband just bought her a new Pierce Arrow. Thornton's an engineer with a building firm in Miami Beach and earns a salary that'd make Hoover weep. Well, now Cecilia wants me to buy her a new motor, too, one with lots more pick-up than the Ford. Trouble is, she already drives like mad and the tires won't stand up to it."

Harry watched Frank stroll over to the barber chair. He had the gait of a fellow who was used to getting his own way. Men like that made him nervous. They didn't know the word conciliation and had little appreciation for how today's actions might affect tomorrow. "It'd pay you to telephone Ernest Lamb at that General Tire agency on Vernon Street, the one behind the old firehouse. You can remember me to him if you like. He'll give you a swell deal and make a liberal allowance for your old tires. It's sure-fire."

"Thanks, Frankie. I'll call him first chance I get."

Puffing on his cigar, Frank studied the customer seated before him. "Say, Al, who's this knucklehead in my chair?"

Harry watched the barber lift the straight razor away from the man's neck. Here's where it starts. Bullies like this one just can't let well enough alone. "He's new in town, Frankie, just got here from Buffalo. Isn't that right, mister?"

The customer grunted, his face all lathered up.

Frank exhaled a big cloud of cigar smoke. "Is that so?" He extended his hand. "Well, put it there, pal. Frank Dinucci."

Harry watched Al's customer fidget briefly under the cloth, reluctantly working his hand free. "John Bradford." He shook hands with the Italian, but didn't look him in the eye. That was a mistake. Always look a fellow in the eye and treat him like a friend, particularly if he's a thug.

Frank let go with a big laugh. "Hey, did you boys see that? This bird gave me the icy mitt!"

His partners sitting at the table laughed, too, the one blocking the door sporting an ugly grin. Harry panicked. Why can't this Ray fellow finish up and let me go? These numbskulls are sure to start something any minute now.

The barber smiled gently. "I guess he's just a little shy, Frankie, not knowing the ropes and all. You know how it is when you're a newcomer."

"Sure I do."

"Well, how about letting me finish up with him, then I'll give you the works? What do you say?"

The Italian blew a rude cloud of cigar smoke toward the customer. "You're a fresh fellow, aren't you?"

With an edge to his voice, the fellow in the chair replied, "I don't know what you mean by that. I always try to be polite, particularly to strangers. It's the decent thing to do."

"Well, that's mighty white of you."

Harry gasped. Here we go.

"Look here, friend, if you're putting in a kick about my taking your chair, well, for God's sake, you'll just have to be patient, that's all. I'll be through here soon enough."

The Italian lost his smile. "I tell you, you're through now." He leaned forward and yanked the chair cloth off him. "Go take a smoke."

Harry felt his legs quiver. Thanks to this stupid fellow from Buffalo, now they were all going to get shot.

"Aw, Frankie," the barber moaned, "I'm not done with him."

"Don't mind about that, Al. We'll put some polish on him for you." Frank motioned to the men sitting at the table. "Boys?"

The man sat up in the chair, fury on his brow. "Say, what is this? Some kind of crackerjack?"

Harry was sure Bradford was about to get himself killed. Can't he see these fellows are gangsters? Good grief, what do they teach in Buffalo?

"Out of my chair, pal."

"I won't do it."

"Oh no? Well, these sporty-looking gents ain't eaten any dinner yet today, and they ain't *gonna* eat till I get a shave and a haircut, and they're plenty hungry already, you get me?"

"Come on, Frankie," Al urged the Italian. "Leave the poor guy alone, will you? He doesn't know what he's trying to pull off here."

The man stepped out of the barber chair as Frank's partners approached from the back of the shop. With the cloth removed, Harry saw that Bradford was hollow-chested and frail, certainly no match for the Italian and his partners, a complete idiot. The poor fellow narrowed his eyes. "If you mean to insinuate that these associates of yours intend to beat me up over a silly haircut, well, I tell you, I won't take it lying down. I'll go to the police. Don't think I won't."

Harry decided Bradford must be an immigrant, or a mental defective.

Frank took another puff on his cigar and laughed. "Sure thing, pal. I'll paste that in my hat. Now, go on, beat it out of here!"

His partner Louie opened the barbershop door.

Harry watched the Italian grab the fellow by his arm and push him roughly toward Louie who gave him another stiff shove out onto the sidewalk, and a kick in the rump for emphasis. Then he slammed the door.

Harry was horrified. Of course, the Italian's behavior was disgraceful, but the other fellow must have gone off his trolley, risking his life for a stupid shave and a haircut.

"What a mossback," Frank said, with a laugh.

"Oh, for crying out loud, Frankie," the barber moaned, "you didn't even give him a chance to pay up, and he was a new customer, too. Things aren't that rich I can afford to chase 'em away."

Climbing into the barber chair himself, the Italian said, "You don't need lice like that, Al."

"I'll try telling that to Wertman when the rent payment's due."

"Aw, you fellows worry too much," Frank replied, as the barber tossed the chair cloth over him. "Me and Louie here'll round up some of the boys up on Donovan Street and send 'em over here for a trim once a week. What do you say? Would that make us square?"

The barber shrugged. "Sure, Frankie, whatever you say. Sounds like a racket, though. Don't die 'til some of this comes true."

Scared of these fellows now, Harry murmured to his barber about some appointment he needed to attend to in the next five minutes, hoping he'd get the hint that Harry was anxious to pay and get out.

"Sure thing," Ray replied, slapping Wild Root onto the back of Harry's neck. "No trouble at all. Have you out of here in a flash."

Settled into his own barberchair, the Italian began glad-handing the other customers. "Frank Dinucci," he said to the chubby fellow in the chair next to him.

"Wally Haas. Glad to know you, Frank."

"Likewise."

"My pal over there hiding behind the magazine is George."

Frank nodded, "Hiya, George."

The fellow on the bench looked up with a timid smile. "Hello."

Trying to flatter the gangsters, Wally said, "I tell you, I sure appreciated that story about you and your boys trimming the cops. Gee, I wish

I had the nerve. Me and a couple pals of mine got pinched in a shine parlor last year and it cost us a fair dollar to stay out of the slam."

Frank's barber added, "You can fix anything if you got the right fixers, isn't that right, Frankie?"

The Italian laughed. "That ain't the half of it, Al."

Now what were they talking about? Fixing things? Did that mean putting the slug on some witless sucker? Bullet-ridden bodies were turning up all over these days. The country was safer when anarchists were throwing bombs. Harry's barber finished brushing off his neck, and removed the cloth. Thank goodness! Now he could get out of here without bleeding. But when he stood up from the chair, the Italian looked over at him. "Hiya, pal."

Trying his best to sound polite, Harry nodded a friendly greeting, "How do you do?"

"Just swell," the Italian chuckled, "so long as my friend Al here don't cut my throat."

Harry smiled as he paid his barber. Make them think you're a regular fellow. They're practically human, aren't they? Thanking Ray for the haircut, Harry started for the door, hoping to get outdoors before he drew another breath. No such luck.

From his chair, Frank Dinucci called to him. "Say, what's your racket, mister?"

Harry stopped in mid-stride, hands sweating. Just watch what you tell him. Don't be a dope like Bradford. Remember, you have a family. "I have rental space at City Transfer & Storage in the old factory district uptown. I'm in the selling game."

"On 83rd?"

"Yes, it is. Between Diever and Powell. Do you know the building?"

"Why sure, that's one of Charley Follette's. You work for that high-hat mob?"

Follette's mob? Were they rivals? What should he say now? Gangsters were constantly murdering each other over territories. He didn't want to get involved in some criminal dispute, just because he happened to choose today for a haircut. "I hired a space from him. That's all."

"Well, Follette's no piker, so you must be doing swell. Gee, maybe I'm in the wrong racket." He turned to his partners sitting at the table. "What do you think, boys? Either of you know anything about selling the goods?"

One of them replied, "What goods is that, boss?"

The other said, "I sold a crate of dead soldiers last Tuesday to that Rexall over on 33rd, and it didn't take a lot to put it over."

"Oh yeah?" The Italian raised an eyebrow. "Well, I guess that's swell for a side line, but I bet if you boys'll hang your ears close, this fellow here'll tell you how to really clean 'em and give 'em the car fare home. Won't you, pal?"

Good grief, now what? He thought about making friends by involving them in Follette's search for his missing niece, but decided to hold that card up his sleeve. Besides, he didn't really want to share the profit, and who could say how Follette would respond to hearing that Harry had invited gangsters into his private affairs. He chose to play it safe by saying, "I'm not certain what you mean, but I started out in the old stockyards at Kansas City and worked my way up. I tell you, it's a long road to success and there're no shortcuts. Believe me."

The Italian smiled. "Say, I just got a flash. How's about I hire you to teach the boys here a thing or two. Show 'em the works. They wouldn't know Billy Durant from a bill collector, see, so you can lead 'em around by the nose. What do you say, pal? Are you on?"

Harry shuffled his feet, wishing he'd snuck out sooner. This was getting worse. Now they think I want to be partners. Well, I'm not that big a fool. "Honestly, I'm awfully busy these days, at least a month of appointments booked already, and I've got a family to support. Got to stick on the job."

The Italian's eyes narrowed. "What sort of appointments?"

Don't play games with this fellow. "Well, for starters, I'm seeing a client this afternoon at the Sheridan Hotel on Hammerick Street who says he's interested in a collection of rubber typesets and stamps I came across in Indiana last year."

"What's so hot about that?"

"My profit margin's nearly three hundred percent."

"Well, I'll be damned! Did you hear that, Louie? All it takes is a little shoe leather and pretty soon you're another Rockefeller."

"Sure, boss."

Trying to be agreeable now, Harry told him, "If you'd like, I'd be glad to draw up a summary of the strategies I've been employing lately. You might find them helpful. Do you have a mailing address?"

The Italian laughed. "Well, that's very square of you, pal, but never mind. These cut-ups can't read. Besides which, if you don't cop plenty of cush right from the jump, it's Katy-bar-the-door, ain't it?"

"Pardon?"

The Italian looked Harry in the eye as Louie opened the door to the sidewalk. "Here's what I always say: if they offer to let you in on the ground floor, tell 'em go climb a tree. Then take the elevator to the top."

— 3 —

Near sundown, Jacob's Ladder flared a brilliant orange above the river, warming the cold waters leading out of the city to the east. Scattered clouds drifted by overhead. Wind blew through the alleyways. Harry Hennesey ate supper alone at a restaurant on Peake Street, one block from the trolley stop at Jefferson Square. Motor traffic was lighter now and the voices of passersby echoed in the twilight. This had been a peculiar day so far. Certainly, Follette's proposition intrigued him and he intended to get straight after it, do anything he could to find that little girl and prove he wasn't washed up. But he needed to charge himself up first. When he finished eating, he planned to take the interurban trolley out to the big amusement parks at Shepherds Island, try to have a little fun for a couple of hours. On Ferguson's way out the door those lazy afternoons at Lake Harriet, he used to say, *A little work, a little play, to keep us going.* Back then, Harry considered his old housemate something of a lay-about. You could sit around all evening exchanging ideas with Ferguson on job opportunities with law offices or bond houses and find yourself exasperated when he interviewed at a golf club and quit a week later so he could drink at night. But after marrying Marie and struggling as a husband and father to earn a decent wage in a dollar world, Harry had come to see the truth in that old adage that it's not so much the hours a fellow puts in as what a fellow puts into his hours.

Dipping his spoon into the Mulligan stew, Harry thought again about those gangsters he met in the barbershop, a rotten and arrogant lot. They'd tossed that poor fellow from Buffalo out the door without the least regard for plain civility. He wondered what made such men imagine their stature rose through the deliberate injury of others. Nobody expected a surfeit of polish and refinement in the day-to-day intercourse of society, particularly in this modern age. Yet even as goodness and virtue circulated throughout the world like sparks from heaven, those blessings seemed held in such disregard by some that one might have supposed there were no gain at all to be found in common decency for its own sake. Only a week ago, a simple office clerk and his two little children had been killed outside Renwick's Dry Cleaners, less than six blocks from where Harry sat now. They had gotten caught in a mean crossfire of lead between rival bootleggers and Tommy-gunned to shreds. The next morning, a crescendo of outrage inflamed the editorials in each of the city's dozen newspapers. For a solid week, letters were written, speeches given at City Hall, suspects rounded up for questioning. The funeral services for the victims garnered hundreds of sympathetic visitors, one of whom, an elderly woman, suffered a massive heart attack during the recitation of common prayer and dropped dead on the spot. So it had gone all year long. There were immigrant precincts many citizens refused to cross at any hour, sooty tenement neighborhoods where children shouted obscenities at passing automobiles, where women dressed in flagrant denial of accepted standards of decency, where dogs and drunks dirtied the public sidewalks, and young fellows barely in high school had that unmistakable glint of homicide in their eyes. Bombings, racketeering, murder and mayhem. Gangland warfare and public corruption on a horrendous scale. National Prohibition left few thirsty, but many wounded. Gin mills and hospital operating rooms ran twenty-four hours a day. Music played and people danced and drank, while city streets became increasingly precarious. Society trembled, yet life went on.

— **4** —

Harry took a seat by the window as the Pelican Coast Short Line left Jefferson Station. Beside him, a woman with a small boy occupied the only remaining seat on the trolley to Shepherds Island, and as they traveled she fussed with her street make-up in between mumbled words of reproach to her fidgeting son. She did not appear much older than Harry's sister Rachel, her skin a pale opalescent in the early evening moonlight. The boy, who was roughly little Henry's age, wore a navy blue cap that partially hid his face, preventing Harry from deciphering the youngster's mood. Though if the boy and his mother were headed for the great amusement parks tonight like he was, how could the child not be ecstatic? Last June, Harry took his children on the train to the Breakers Hotel overlooking the beach at Lake Erie where they spent three days on the run about Cedar Point, hurrying from the Amusement Circle to Bluebeard's Palace, Tilt-A-Whirl, Leap-the-Dips, a Water Toboggan beach delight, and the great Cyclone roller coaster, a great family holiday together. Being there with them, those eager young smiles, reminded him of R.F. Outcault's observation that *the greatest forces in this world are those we cannot see, that Wonderland is all about wherever we may look, the soul which sees still more, and the heart that loves.* Maybe when I get home tonight, he thought, I'll telephone and surprise them. Mother won't be happy, but it's awfully lonely being away like this.

The trolley clicked along the tracks beyond Jefferson Square and the broad lamp-lit boulevards. Motor traffic lessened and the show window storefronts and restaurant neon gave over to grand old residences of yesteryear with lovely tree-shaded sidewalks, then on to blocks of modest framehouses linked by dirt alleyways and truck gardens and tin garages, grocery stores and freight sheds, roadhouses, filling stations, and auto agencies. Passing the quiet neighborhoods of Kingsfield and New Milford, the interurban crossed a narrow tributary of the river at Lincoln Creek and left the metropolis for the swampy meadows surrounding Harper Woods where cottonwoods and sycamores and river birch rose unrestrained by men, and thick brambles spread wildly as nature reasserted her claim to the earth. Even birds sailed more gracefully across these skies than back in the noisy canyons of the city. It was nice to get out of the Big Town every so often, away from concrete and smoke stacks. Harry let a window open to admit fresh air. He took a deep breath and sighed. Summer in the good old countryside, a scent of Eden at twilight. He slipped one hand out into the draft and felt the clean warm air encircle his fingers. He ought to hire a cottage on Sumner Bay himself one of these weekends, go fishing for a day or just sit on the porch and read a novel.

The motorman rang his bell as a green Templar sedan darted across the tracks just ahead of the trolley. Next to Harry, the young woman whispered in the small boy's ear, then stood and walked off to smoke a cigarette at the back of the car. Left alone, the youngster fiddled with a red yo-yo. Did he know what awaited him on Shepherds Island? Not a traveling carnival came to Bellemont that Harry hadn't chased through in the dark. Threats of lightning storms or hickory switch whippings in the woodshed were no deterrent. When the sparkling carnival lights lit up the prairie, every boy in town ran out of doors and stayed past curfew for one more ride on the carousel, one more throw on the midway, one last peek at the Princess of Borneo. *O, for boyhood's time of June, crowding years in one brief moon.* Feeling enthusiastic himself, he asked the child, "Are you and your mother going to Nightingale Park, Starland, or Thebes?"

The small boy jammed both hands deep into the pockets of his trousers and shrugged, eyes lowered to the floor at his feet. Harry smiled. And here he thought Henry was shy among adults. Some children take a while to decide whether grownups are actually people they can talk to. Being gentle helps, but often enough a special trick works better yet. Changing his tone slightly, he told the boy, "I've heard all three parks are fabulous. Have you ever been there before? I haven't. Do you suppose I really can buy two red-hots for a nickel?"

The boy shifted in his seat, obviously jittery with strangers. Animating his voice, Harry tried something else. "Is it true that seven men are required to embrace Jolly Trixy, the Fattest Woman on Earth?"

A faint smile rose on the corners of the boy's mouth. Pleased now, Harry recited a well-known quote from a Starland billboard: *"Holy smoke, she's fat! She's awful fat!"*

The boy giggled.

Harry added, "And Princess Wee Wee?"

The boy giggled again, then sneaked in a child's profanity, "She's got no pee-pee!"

Sharing the boy's little joke, Harry offered a schoolyard rejoinder. "She needs no pee-pee to wee-wee!"

The giggles that followed turned heads up and down the aisle. Then, seeing the boy's mother returning to her son, Harry shushed the boy with a smile. Happy again, he looked out the window toward the electric glow of Shepherds Island only a few minutes ahead now.

At Pelican Station, Harry lost track of the mother and boy amid the vast teeming crowd when the interurban discharged its passengers onto the mile long Sand Avenue promenade. In his coat pocket was a guide to Shepherds Island given to him by a business acquaintance before the World War. Its faded cover featured flag-topped minarets and laughing ladies, balloons and beach-goers, young and old, rich and poor, fun and fancy in their eyes. Tens of thousands of park-goers, colorful flags and banners of all sorts, costumed street performers, nickel sideshows, and exhibits featuring every conceivable amusement. *Henderson's Burlesque Opera! Clam Chowder 10¢! The Original Turkish Harem! Freaks!*

Entering the boardwalk, Harry heard barkers calling out above the roar of the passing crowd "HUR-RY, HUR-RY, HUR-RY!" while the aroma from dozens of food stands sifted in the evening air. He saw skyrockets go up over the dark water, bursting into the night sky like fragments of a rainbow. He felt buoyant and laughed aloud and waved his hat in the air as a gaggle of pretty girls skipped past. He fought his way to Nathan's Famous *(STOP HERE! This Is The Only Original Nathan's Famous in Shepherds Island)* and bought a hot frankfurter and a soda pop, and watched the crowds thicken. Thrilled by the carnival spectacle, he followed the rollercoasters at Starland and Nightingale Park — Dragon's Gorge and the Mile High Sky Chaser, Drop the Dip, Flip-Flap, Red Devil Rider, the Cyclone and the Human Toboggan — as they rattled and roared, transporting hundreds of shrieking riders high into the evening air, while farther ahead beyond the great Iron Tower and the Streets of Delhi, the strange and exotic Elephant Hotel stood stoic and proud. *What bawdy pleasures await within her mighty flanks!* He wondered if he'd ever have the guts to take a woman there. Braving a rising wind, he went to the iron railing and looked out onto the beach where a few lusty couples still sparked beneath blankets near empty bathhouses, and the smell of fresh roasted peanuts carried toward the cold water. Sometimes he wished he were twenty years old again with nothing more serious to do than finding a girl who didn't mind kissing a fellow she'd just met. That insightful philosopher Ferguson, after four glasses of brandy one evening, suggested that youth was a blessèd optimism with paths leading everywhere and no signposts for guidance. (You could always get something good out of Ferguson with fine liquor.) There are so many lives we could lead. How can we ever know which path to choose? Our steps can never be retraced. The rest of our lives we ask ourselves: Is this where I meant to be? Harry fastened the upper buttons on his coat and stared south past the curve of the land toward the distant city lights, silver-blue on the horizon. He watched the tide wash in from passing river craft heading north past the Jordan Recreation Pier toward Pelican Bay and found a lone motor dory on the dark water, a lit kerosene lamp mounted on its stern, a man and a boy with fishing poles in hand, crossing to the far shore. Up on the boardwalk, a concertina played a dancing tune across the twilight, melodic and spirited, drawing Harry's attention back again to the Sand Avenue promenade where he re-entered the noisy crowd.

Outside the Pavilion of Fun, the cool night air was a blur of wicked and feathery scents. Harry dodged a gang of boys sprinting down the promenade toward the ball-throwing booths and duck-shooting games, neon carousels, smoke-haired gypsy fortunetellers, estimate-your-weight concessions. Hurrying along himself, giddy for amusements, he stopped just briefly to admire the floating gondolas on the watery Canals of Venice and felt his stomach flip-flop as the Wedding Ring tilted and rose, and the great "Wonder Wheel" slowly revolved in the purple sky above.

But Harry's startling adventure that evening at Shepherds Island really began with a voyage out into space. As both child and adult, he had a fantasy about extraterrestrial flight. In the darkest of nights, he dreamed of sailing through the stars to far-flung destinations, greeting otherworldly races as a gentle ambassador from Earth and sharing the natural advantages of democracy and capitalism with our galactic neighbors. Not that he ever told anybody, certainly not Marie. She thought the novels of Jules Verne and H.G. Wells were too silly to bother with and Edgar Rice Burroughs was suitable for little Henry, perhaps, but not his father. Going to the moon? Impossible. Utterly ridiculous. In Starland, however, fantasy was transformed into reality by the magic of industry and invention, and this evening, without Marie to scold his childish imagination, Harry purchased a ticket for "A Trip to the Moon."

Of course, he didn't journey alone. Thirty other intrepid souls accompanied Harry Hennesey into the *Luna III*, a great airship with huge flapping wings and tiny portholes for viewing flight through space. Securing himself a place at one of the portholes, Harry prepared for the lunar journey. He was terrifically excited. A thunderous sound signaled disembarkation from Starland and the walls were suddenly bright with projections of flight high up into the cloudy blue sky. A steady sensation of pitch and sway gave the passengers the impression of acceleration and direction. Suffering a touch of vertigo, Harry gulped and grabbed for a railing by the porthole and forced himself to stare out into the black void of space where innumerable stars shimmered in the immense etherean beyond. The airship entered an electric storm. Flashes and thunderous booms rattled the walls of the ship. The storm ceased and the moon came into view, a glowing white sphere in the void, growing larger by the second. Harry watched the craters and mountains, vast prairies and deep canyons, of the lunar surface sweep by beneath the ship. The *Luna III* prepared to land on the moon. Harry could hardly contain himself as the hatch opened to silvery moonlight. Everyone proceeded down the ramp, exiting directly into a shadowy green cavern. A cool draft blew toward them from the lunar darkness ahead. Strange sounds echoed in the low chamber. Soft voices murmured. The travelers from Earth entered a narrow iridescent cavern whose low twisting passageways created subtle disorientations. Harry heard whimperings among his fellow travelers. A pair of dressy girls in cloche hats and rabbit fur clutched together like Siamese twins. The tall fellow behind them in the serge suit and wool fedora nearly jumped out of his socks as a purple midget in loincloth and laurel leaves and wielding a golden scimitar popped up suddenly from a secret hiding place along the cave walls, shrieking maniacally. A purple companion leaped out of the shadows behind the first, both taunting the voyagers from Earth before ducking back into the darkness. Just ahead, the ceiling elevated and a pasty white giant strode into the middle of the cavern bellowing like an Indian elephant. The group shrank back. Then a trio of friendly green maidens bearing golden sabers appeared and chased the giant off into the dark.

"HURRY! HURRY! HURRY!" they shouted. A dozen yards on, another giant thundered in the passageway. A stout woman next to Harry shrieked and dropped her hanky. He retrieved it for her with a sympathetic smile. The lunar illusion was fabulous. More green maidens materialized out of the darkness, each swinging a wicked saber. They charged the giant and drove him off a small precipice into a bottomless pit, his baleful cries echoing to nothingness. Passing the pit, Harry heard a low spate of laughter and wished he had a flashlight. Soon a spiraling passageway led down into a vast rainbow grotto beneath a huge crown of stalactites where the great Man-in-the-Moon himself, surrounded by dancing lunar maidens, sat upon his tall golden throne. In a peculiarly musical voice, he addressed his guests, "WEL-COME, VISITORS-FROM-EARTH! WEL-COME-TO-THE-MOON!"

A dozen green moon maidens swarmed toward Harry and his fellow earthlings, greeting each with a curtsy and a kiss, then leading a grand tour of the rainbow grotto while the green-skinned Man-in-the-Moon stamped his feet, clapped his hands, and laughed like Santa Claus. Next, a parade led out of the grotto into a circular green chamber where, reminded by the pretty moon maidens that the moon was made of green cheese, each visitor from Earth was permitted to snatch an edible chunk of the lunar real estate as a souvenir of their grand voyage. Finished now, the group was guided over a frighteningly narrow rope bridge that led across a windy chasm and out through a black door to the bright, electric Starland promenade once again.

It was during this final passage that the most peculiar thing happened. Harry heard his name echo from deep within the lunar cavern.

"Haarrrryyy!"

Halfway across the bridge, at the back of his group, he paused, steadying himself as the rickety plankwalk trembled and swayed. He looked back. The green moon maidens were gone. While Harry stopped to figure out whether or not he had really heard his name called, the last of his fellow space travelers crossed the rope bridge and disappeared into the gloom ahead.

That same voice, distorted by the cavern echo, called out again. *"Haaarrryyy, help me!"*

It belonged to a girl, and sounded terribly familiar, but he couldn't quite place where he had heard it before. He leaned over the bridge, staring down into the black chasm below.

Nothing.

He shouted back into the darkness, "HELLO? WHO'S THERE?"

"Nobody, pal. Show's finished."

Harry saw one of the purple-faced midgets from the cavern-attack, waiting at the end of the rope bridge, still bearing his golden scimitar. Proceeding away across the unsteady planks, Harry said, "Look, I'm certain I heard a girl calling my name back there."

"Beat it, pal, the show's over," the midget growled, raising his scimitar. "Don't make me cut off your noodle."

Reaching a wooden platform at the end of the rope bridge where his fellow travelers had gone, Harry frowned as the purple midget glared at him. *A dollar a week doesn't buy much for brains, does it?*

"I tell you, I heard a girl."

"Didn't we all."

"Look here, I'm serious!"

The moon midget snatched a horn off his belt and blew a loud harsh note into the cavern. Harry heard a flurry of footsteps from the other end of the bridge and watched a gang of sturdy-looking pirates appear across the chasm. Shackled by chains in their midst was that lovely baby vamp who had kissed him in Athena's Dome last month. Terrified, she shrieked, "HARRY! HELP ME! PLEASE!"

In the same instant, the purple moon midget hacked through the ropes binding the plank bridge to the platform. With a dull thwang, ropes broke on both ends and the flimsy bridge collapsed into the abyss.

"My God!" Harry scrambled back from the edge and the buccaneers on the far end of the chasm roared with delight. Then they dragged the poor dear off into the dark, her screams echoing through the lunar cavern.

Behind Harry, the purple-faced midget vanished into ether, leaving only a scrap of paper on the wooden platform where he had stood.

Utterly flabbergasted, Harry picked it up and read a note scribbled on the back:

IF YOU WANT TO SAVE HER LIFE, RIDE THE STEEPLECHASE

Back out in the fresh air of the Starland promenade, he tried to gather his wits. What had he just witnessed in the lunar cavern? While he had certainly never expected to see that fresh young girl again, she hadn't been easy to get out of his mind. Pearl! Good heavens, he'd tasted her kiss for days and worried that he had become infatuated. Thank God he was so rundown that night or she might have ended up in his bed. It seemed incredible that she was actually being held now against her will. Had they kidnapped her from the Trip to the Moon, or snatched her somehow off the promenade and dragged her indoors? Obviously he had to find a policeman and get some help, but he was afraid he would be accused of drinking or pulling a boob stunt and find himself tossed from the park.

"I swear on my father's grave, I saw her dragged off by moon pirates!"

"All right, wiseguy, which is it? Are you a softhead or a stewed fruit?"

Wind stirred the smells of roasted popcorn and red-hots, cigar smoke and perspiration. Harry passed a tent show featuring the hootchy-kootchy dance and another starring a fortune-telling fakir whose disembodied head advertised advice on stock tips and modern romance. Scores of people streamed by toward the Mountain Torrent and the Whirl-of-the-Wind, laughing and shouting. Debating his options, Harry watched a clown in greasepaint juggling bananas for a pair of young girls who tittered laughter. The clown pretended to drop one of the bananas. Bending down to retrieve it, he lifted one of the girl's skirts and peeked up at her bottom. She screamed and tried to strike the clown on his head with her handbag, but he did a giant handspring and bounced away into the roaring crowd.

Perplexed by this fantastic situation, Harry decided simply to follow the note's instructions and see what might happen. What else could he really do? If he didn't try to help her, and she wound up floating in the river next week, he'd feel like an awful coward.

Steeplechase was a mechanical racetrack of undulating iron rails that ran half a mile around the interior of Starland. The ten-cent admission bought you a ticket aboard a metal horse pushed along by gravity from one end of the track down to the other. Both sexes found it a great thrill, especially if you rode with the right partner. Still having no idea why he had been directed to come here and ride the attraction, Harry joined a line of people atop the pavilion and awaited his mount. **"HALF A MILE IN HALF A MINUTE"** boasted one of the signs, and **"DON'T BE A GLOOMSTER! BE A STEEPLECHASER!"** Word had it the heaviest mounts went fastest. Girls stood about in packs seeking a jockey to share their ride. Harry was alone, but didn't solicit a partner. Nothing in the note mentioned a confederate. At any rate, whom would he get? He didn't know a soul in Shepherds Island, besides which, the responsibility for saving that poor little girl seemed to be his own. But why him among the tens of thousands swarming the amusement parks this evening? Harry had wracked his brain with these questions on his way to Steeplechase and had come up with nothing that made any sense at all. She'd interrupted him at the picture show and invited him to that basement speakie on Baker Street, after which he followed her into Washington Park and down a sewer to the river. Sure, he'd also kissed her in the Dome, but what could that possibly have to do with her being kidnapped?

He supposed there was no good choice but to climb onboard and see what happened next. When his turn came, Harry stepped forward and mounted the mechanical steed. This was certainly one of the nuttiest things he had ever done. Couples lined up beside him, left and right, men hugging their metal horses' necks, girls hugging the men. Then Harry felt someone climb on behind him, a stout fellow reeking of fresh sauerkraut. "If you hang on to the reins, Harry," the fellow spoke in his ear, "we'll take this nag to the finish in jig-time."

Before he could utter a syllable, the lever was thrown and the race was on.

The big fellow pressed Harry onto the metal horse's neck as they shot out of the gate and down the first chute. The sensation of speed on the small iron steed was breathtaking, something like his first automobile ride in Frank Gallagher's Peerless down Williston Road to Excelsior Boulevard on two pints of beer. Shrieks of excitement from the other riders rang across the mechanical racetrack. As they swept around a turn, Harry's companion shouted, "IF YOU WANT TO SAVE THAT BIRD OF YOURS, HARRY, YOU BEST PUT THE SPURS TO THIS NAG!"

"How do you know who I am?" Harry called back as the pack of metal horses headed into a row of sinuous dips and rises. This was insane! "Who are you?"

The stout fellow laughed, and directed Harry's attention to the far left lane. "DON'T LET HER GET AWAY, HARRY!"

"What?"

"THERE SHE GOES!"

Bracing himself for a dip in the track, Harry craned his neck just enough to see the horse on the inside lane take over the lead, ridden by two stocky fellows in pirate costumes sandwiched around Pearl. "My God, it's her!"

He heard Pearl scream for help as her mount dropped from view. Hundreds cheered from the Starland promenade.

"We have to catch her!" Harry shouted, frantic with confusion. Where were they taking the girl? Why wasn't anyone else helping her? For God's sake, was he the only one who could see she was frightened out of her wits?

His companion laughed. "IT'S A HORSE RACE, ALL RIGHT!"

Pearl's horse seemed fast as the wind, gliding around the long turn at mid-track, two, three, four, five lengths ahead of the mechanical field.

The stout fellow yelled out, "FASTER, HARRY! FASTER!" His weight pressed on Harry's back as the metal horse sped forward, closing the gap a bit. "DON'T LET 'EM GET AWAY!"

"Good grief!"

How could Pearl's horse go so fast? Starland seemed to speed past in a great electric blur. His huge companion leaned over him, nearly suffocating Harry with his dreadful breath and enormous weight. Another pair of competitors drew even, then swept by, whooping with delight.

"SHE'S GETTING AWAY, HARRY! DON'T LET HER GET AWAY! FASTER, HARRY! FASTER!"

Spectators lining the promenade roared their approval as the lead riders streaked ahead toward the finish line at the great pavilion. Harry's horse was too slow. The race seemed lost and he knew it. His shoulders sagged. "Damn it all! We can't catch her!"

"DON'T QUIT NOW, HARRY!" The fellow hiccuped with laughter. "CATCH HER! GO! GO! GO!"

A pair of giggling young ladies shot past, the girl in back blowing Harry a kiss as they went by.

"For God's sake!" he shouted back at his companion, "Will you please tell me what this is all about? Who the hell are you?"

Trumpets blew as the lead mounts crossed the finish line into the pavilion shadows.

"I think they've beaten us, Harry."

"We didn't have a chance," he growled, his spirits desolate now as the metal steed headed for last place. "This stupid horse was too slow! How were we supposed to catch her?"

"Luck's a chance," the stout fellow chided as they slid toward the finish, "but trouble's sure, my friend, if hope pulls out."

When the metal horse glided to a stop inside the noisy pavilion, the big fellow dismounted, beet-red and puffy from the exertion of the Steeplechase ride. He told Harry, "When you meet that little fellow with the electric paddle, tell him you just seen Fat Ollie. He'll point you straight. That cutie ain't lost yet."

Then he lit a cigar and hurried through a side door.

You could have run Harry through a cyclone and he wouldn't have been more disoriented than he was in the next instant, swept with the racing crowd down a narrow corridor and onto the dazzlingly bright stage of the Insanitarium in the famous Blowhole Theater. Stacks of unsteady barrels tipped toward him, rude bursts of air shot up from the floor, inflating the skirts of the girls crossing just ahead. Gales of hilarity descended from the laughing gallery just beyond the stagelights. Flummoxed by the light and noise, Harry didn't notice the dwarf in the green and yellow polka dot clown suit sneak up from behind and shock his bottom with an electric cattle prod. The bleacher audience howled with delight. Harry stumbled forward and lost his hat to another burst of air from the stage floor. The nasty little dwarf stung him viciously with the paddle and bounced away before Harry could grab him. People were laughing hysterically. Staggering toward the stage exit, he was shocked again by the dwarf's cattle prod. Then somehow he remembered the stout fellow's advice and shouted at the loathsome creature, "FAT OLLIE SENT ME! FAT OLLIE SENT ME! GOOD LORD!"

The pasty-faced dwarf stopped chasing about. He puffed up his tiny chest and spat on the floor next to a sign that read:

As a Matter of
F · A · C · T
most of our troubles
amount to very little
when in
STEEPLECHASE

Rude whistles filled the Blowhole Theater while Harry rubbed his throbbing rear-end.

The dwarf bared a rotten-toothed grin. "Your dame's sniffin' sulphur at Hell Gate, Harry, but she won't be there very long, so don't dilly-daddle. Oh yeah, I'm supposed to tell you this, too: *Let he who rules the dungeon escape, but play no games of hazard.* Now, choose your exit and beat it, you dirty dog!"

The dwarf brandished his electric cattle prod once again and thrust it toward Harry's groin.

The audience howled.

Flustered and humiliated, Harry rushed off.

Hell Gate was one of the more popular attractions in Nightingale Park. As the advertisements said, people enjoyed being frightened, and they liked feeling a little naughty, too. Breathless from his frantic sprint between here and Steeplechase, Harry rested beneath the giant bat-winged sculpture of Lucifer at the crowded entrance to Hell Gate. That experience in Steeplechase had shaken him badly. His boxing coach at State had always told him to take fifteen deep breaths to fight off the panic of a ferocious bout. A shot of gin, he decided, would be more useful now. He could only get so far on effort, after all, and nothing he'd seen in the past half hour was even half-believable. Was this all a game? He felt like a damned Ping-Pong ball. Nearby, two fellows wearing painted sandwich boards passed out gift coupons, while another on stilts shouted through a cardboard megaphone: "HUR-RY! HUR-RY! HUR-RY! DRAGON'S GORGE! CANNON COASTER! WILL SHE THROW HER ARMS AROUND YOUR NECK AND YELL? WELL, I GUESS, YES! HUR-RY! HUR-RY! HUR-RY!"

Above the Hell Gate box office, a sign read:

YOU WHO ENTER HERE ABANDON ALL HOPE

Purchasing his ticket, Harry found Dante's Inferno re-created in plaster and papier-mâché. Sulphurous odors of brimstone filled the darkness where shrunken heads hung on wooden stakes, and the Drinker, the Adulterer, the Thief, and the Gambler were featured in frightful dioramas of sin and punishment from darkest Hades to the medieval torture chambers of the Inquisition. Freaks beset with atrocious deformities lurched from blackened crevices. Still confused about what he was expected to do next, Harry wandered about the nether regions, studying one grievous vignette after another. What's his stunt here supposed to be? Does he throw himself into the River

Styx? There ought to be a map for a fool's errand. Next to an exhibit of Marie Antoinette upon the guillotine, he caught his reflection in a wavy mirror and was shocked at how worn-out he appeared, how lost and pathetic. He *looked* like a fool. Nothing like this had ever happened to him before. Oh sure, he'd suffered plenty of high-jinx at college — snipe hunts, hot hands, shit licks, and so forth, but nothing where a girl's life was at stake. What would he need to do to save her? Kill somebody?

Behind him, a tubby woman screamed as a demon lifted her cotton skirt with his pitchfork. Her skinny date laughed when the woman kicked the demon in the shins. A flurry of girls rushed past them both to the trembling rock of Sisyphus and down a crag that hung over the Pit where Lucifer himself sat on his throne surrounded by a thousand centuries of naked sinners and demonic minions. Crimson flames of cellophane flickered while the guilty moaned in agony.

Something poked Harry in the back.

"Here's a philanderer, if I ever seen one."

Now he found himself flanked by two demons with sharp pitchforks. He backed up to the wavy mirror mounted on the rocky wall. Good grief, what was *this*? He presumed it was pointless to tell them what he was here for. But he tried, anyhow. "Look, fellows, maybe you can help me out, what do you say?"

The demons laughed. "He's a horse from another merry-go-round, all right."

His companion agreed. "Oh, he's delicious! Let's take him."

Grinning maniacally, they poked Harry in the ribs with their pitchforks.

"Hey! Watch it, that hurts!"

The demons shrieked with glee. "Why, that ain't nothing, pal. Wait'll the boss gets hold of you!"

Another jab of the pitchfork and Harry stumbled backward into the mirror. It folded over becoming an open coffin. Then the demons rushed forward, shoving him inside and slamming the lid shut. He felt the coffin tip once again and begin to slide down a long chute, shaking him side to side in a rapid descent. Frightened of suffocating, he held his breath. Only a few seconds later, at the bottom of the chute, the casket lid popped open to a vile stink of smoldering brimstone where Harry faced half a dozen more leering demons in the fiery crater of Lucifer. One of them strode up and yanked him from the coffin. The other wingéd demons cheered as Harry stumbled out into that great chamber of flame and misery. A rain of fire to the north, scalding streams of blood and severed limbs to the south, the black pit of fanged serpents to the east, and Lucifer, Ruler of Hell, seated on a throne of human bones to the west. All about this dismal abyss where the woeful screams of the doomed echoed high and low, Harry saw the criminal and the scorned chained to cliff and crag, writhing in agony's bitter embrace. There were also girls, lots of them, half-naked like those gorgeous young women illustrated on the covers of *Bedtime Stories* and *Stolen Sweets*, shackled and roped about the smoky cavern, their bare breasts gleaming in the fire glow. He felt as if he had slid down into some great brothel of the damned.

"You're late, Harry!" Lucifer shouted to him across the smoky veil. "She ain't here no more!"

On a rocky ledge above the Prince of Darkness, the beaten Minotaur heaved and groaned while Harry sidestepped a rivulet of bubbling lava and crossed the Pit toward Lucifer. Lesser demons taunted him with rude insults. Naked girls squirmed and moaned. Harry tried to ignore them, but a curvaceous redhead chained to a steaming boulder was a real knockout.

"Where is she?" Harry called to Lucifer, hoping to bluff the fellow out. He suspected there was some funny business going on with all this, but he just couldn't quite figure out what it was. The whole kidnapping incident felt peculiar.

Folding back his leather wings, evil Lucifer leaned forward from that monstrous throne. "They took her away, slowpoke. I guess she wasn't old enough to learn the ugly truths of life."

Suspended from a thick chain on another rocky outcropping just over Harry's head, Napoleon Bonaparte rattled the bars of the iron maiden that held him prisoner. A bare-breasted girl chained below cackled at him.

"It's absurd," Harry said, as he approached Lucifer's throne. Jets of steam erupted from hidden crevices. "I've been chasing her all night and I'm not a step closer. What's this all about? And how does everyone know my name?"

Lucifer cracked a vile grin. "If you let me out of here, Harry, I'll help you find her. I think I know where she is, but you can't get there without me."

"A bargain with the devil, is that it?"

Lucifer laughed. "You wouldn't be the first."

Now Harry smiled. If this really was a game of some sort, why not play along? What did he have to lose? After all, he could just throw it over and go home, couldn't he?

He asked Lucifer, "What guarantee would I have? Nobody's been the least bit trustworthy tonight. I feel like I'm on a snipe hunt."

"I seen her, Harry, and she's a swell dame. A real cutie! Get me out of here and I'll help you be a hero."

Deafening cries of anguish from King George and Jefferson Davis swamped in an oily pool of flame gave Harry a start. A flock of demons drew near as a trio of blonde half-naked lovelies screeched with delight. One of the blondes with a droopy eyelash had a familiar look. That hotel on Roxbury Street? Two glasses of brown sherry and a jaky gin?

"What do I have to do?" Harry asked, feeling even more uneasy with this crowd of misfits staring at him. "Why can't we just leave?"

"Because I got a contract that says Satan's got to sit here fourteen hours a day, six days a week. If I miss a turn, Sharkey'll give me the air."

"Is that so?"

"Yeah, but the way I figure it, see, from up there," Lucifer pointed to the uppermost crag, jammed now with visitors to Hell Gate, "nobody can tell Beelzebub from Adam so long as the fellow sitting in this chair's got the right pair of horns and a big pitchfork. What I need is a stand-in for a little while."

"All right, then, let's get one."

"It'll cost you ten bucks."

Now Harry was sure this had to be some sort of grind. "Are you joking me? That's a full day's work anywhere in the city!"

"Maybe so, but on the other hand, a girl's life could be on the line. Don't be cheap."

"You're serious, aren't you?" He still couldn't believe a word of it. Would those pirates actually kill the girl? For what possible reason? Who was she to them? And why did they assume he'd want to save her?

Lucifer called out to one of the crimson demons lurking in the smoky shadows nearby. "Scotty!"

Leviathan's desperate roar echoed across the chamber as two red-hot dragon's eyes glowed through clouds of smoke in a cave on the far side of the Pit. A phalanx of demons marched over to keep the awful beast at bay. A full-bosomed Medusa beckoned from a charred bramble of thorns nearby, sticking her tongue out at Harry and pinching her bare nipples.

"Go ahead and pay him, Harry," Lucifer instructed, getting down off his throne. Bones crunched underfoot. He shed those immense leather wings, then removed his helmet of spiral horns and traded it for the lesser demon's smaller headpiece.

Harry took out his billfold and reluctantly counted off ten dollars for the lesser demon, deciding he really had lost his mind sometime after sunset. "I worked a good deal for this money, I'll have you know."

"It'll be worth it, Harry," said Lucifer, handing over the giant pitchfork to his replacement. "Trust me."

"I'll bet you a doughnut they got her in the volcano," Lucifer told Harry as they hurried from Hell Gate. A gang of lovely girls waiting to ride the Alpine railway pointed and giggled at the devil's costume. A cold breeze rippled across the flags of the Swiss cantons and littered the manicured flowerbeds with torn ticket stubs and hotdog wrappers.

"Are you sure?"

"Only if she's alive."

"Good grief!"

"I told you, Harry, this is serious business. There's no kidding around with these fellows. So hurry up and get born. We need to be there before the top blows off."

The "Fall of Pompeii" dramatized the eruption of Mount Vesuvius and the demise of forty thousand Roman citizens. Lucifer offered no particular explanation as to why it made perfect sense for the girl's kidnappers to hide her in Pompeii. Harry had read Edward Bulwer-Lytton's famous novel as a boy and built his own volcano out of mud behind the stables and burned it up with a gallon of kerosene and remnants from his mother's sewing bag. He imagined Pearl being ejected from the mountain in a fiery explosion, and riding the steaming lava flow to the Bay of Naples like some incandescent Shoot-the-Chutes. Anxious to see the famous paroxysm up close, Harry wormed up near the stage. Then the famous volcano erupted, the audience shrieked with horror, and everyone in the Roman city perished. But Pearl never made her appearance, neither atop the fiery mountain nor among the doomed populace below.

Lucifer just shrugged, offering neither excuse nor explanation.

When Harry persisted, the devil just waved him off. What more was there to say?

So they went elsewhere.

Deferring to Lucifer's insistence and his own baffled curiosity, Harry witnessed "Johnstown" washed away in great torrents of water from the South Fork dam, and the tragic sinking of the "Lusitania" by a German U-boat. He saw the defeat of the "Spanish Armada," and the surrender of the "Mexican Army" at Vera Cruz, and watched Admiral Dewey sail out of New York harbor to sink the combined navies of the world.

But no Pearl.

Harry followed Lucifer in and out of Dr. Couney's "Infant Incubator" and behind the stage at Wormwood's Monkey Theater. He rode through the Great Deep Rift Coal Mine of Pennsylvania and down the River Styx.

He didn't see Pearl anywhere.

"You lied to me!" Harry finally accused his infernal companion as they passed under the Elevated Promenade by the Japanese Tea Gardens. "Admit it! You haven't the least idea where she is, do you?" This damned fellow's duped me out of ten dollars, Harry thought, and I fell for it like a lamb. Either that or he's in on the kidnapping, somehow, and this is just some stall he's putting over to keep me out of the game. At any rate, I'm through with it.

Lucifer shrugged, apparently unconcerned with the exhausting failures of the past couple hours. He told Harry, "Those fiends who snatched her are more devious than I thought. We're going to need some help."

Like anyone who leaves his mother's womb, Harry Hennesey had been lied to on many occasions throughout his life, but never with such unmitigated gall. If this was a snipe hunt, it was a mean-spirited one. He felt like popping this Lucifer fellow on the jaw. He even tried baiting him. "What makes you think there's still a chance to save her? It's been almost three hours since I saw her at the Steeplechase. Good grief, she could be out of the state, for all we know."

"You got to trust me, Harry. Her life depends on it."

"I have trusted you! I've trusted you from one end of this blasted park to the other! If I trust you anymore, I'll need a new pair of shoes!"

"Don't be a wiseacre, Harry. That won't do her any good. They know we're hot on her trail, so my guess is they're moving her around. We're just a little slow, that's all. You should've ridden faster at the Steeplechase. I tell you, that's where we fell off the track."

"Thank you. I knew somehow this would all be my fault."

"We'll go see my pal Jack Johnson," Lucifer added. "He'll know whether she's still in the park or not."

"And where do we find this fellow? Under Cleopatra's lagoon in Thebes?"

"Naw, he's just over on the midway by the nickel shows. Come on, I'll introduce you. He's swell."

Lucifer started off into the crowd. Harry refused to budge. He was tired and frustrated. He had come to Shepherds Island for an evening of amusements and wonder that had become instead a Gordian knot of deceptions. How much further did he expect to pursue this farce? And if it wasn't a farce, could that poor girl even be saved at this late date?

"Harry!" Lucifer called to him from beside the packed Eden Musee. "He won't be there all night!"

A trio of jugglers rolled by on unicycles. Electric lights pulsed above the sparkling minarets and garden parapets. Disgusted with himself for being such a fool, Harry considered returning to his apartment and going to bed. He had never seen himself as much of a hero, anyhow. One summer afternoon near Fort Snelling, he had allowed a pair of hooligans to steal a picnic basket from a crowd of ladies without so much as a harsh word, fearing that one of the bastards might have a pistol and shoot him in the head if he intervened. After those two young thugs ran off, he was forced to endure the unmistakable look of disgust on the faces of the offended women when they noticed him under the shade trees by the river, standing by idle and useless. But, after all, he was no Sergeant York. Couldn't they have seen that?

Lucifer shouted, "Come on, Harry! Hurry up!"

The painted sign read "**COON BALL**" and another beneath it advertised "**THE AFRICAN DODGER**." It was a booth like any other in a nickel arcade: a plank counter top, cheap prizes collected on wooden side shelves, the game at the back. Piles of baseballs were stacked on the counter and a canvas draped over the rear wall of the booth was painted with concentric circles out of which popped the bruised and swollen skull of a grinning Negro.

"Harry, say hi to my pal Jack Johnson."

More dubious now than ever, Harry nodded to the colored fellow. "Hello."

"Howdy." The Negro smiled warmly.

"Jack's an oracle, Harry," said Lucifer, picking up one of the baseballs. "There's nothing he don't know. Take one of these balls and pop him on the bean, he'll tell you anything you want. Three for a dime."

"No, thank you." Not since those carnival sideshows in the East Texas of his youth had Harry seen this contemptible sport. 'Nigger ball' was what they named it back home. Only the peanut brains bought tickets.

Lucifer laughed. "You can't afford it, eh? Need a loan?"

"As a matter of fact, I've done well enough for myself this year, not that it's any of your business."

"Flying high, eh?" Lucifer smirked.

Before Harry could reply, he heard a delicate woman's voice behind him. "Have you forgotten, Mr. Hennesey? *Play no games of hazard.*"

A stubby feather-winged angel stood beside him in a flowing white gown and blonde wig and pearl-buckled slippers, her doughy face smeared with gold paint and glitter. She smiled sweetly as the wind gusted, blowing dust about the midway.

"Beat it, Billie!" Lucifer growled. "I found him. He's mine."

"She's crazy for you, honey," the angel told Harry, in a soft murmuring voice. "Don't let her down."

"Oh, trying the old sob stuff, eh?" Lucifer laughed. "Well, lay off! Harry's no fool. He knows the ropes and he ain't buying it. Are you, Harry? Go on, tell her."

Flummoxed by the angel's odd appearance, Harry stammered. "What's this all about? Who are you?"

"I'm your guardian angel, Harry, and I've been sent by that poor dear girl to retrieve you from this loathsome fellow's company." She pointed a gold fingernail at Lucifer. "He's been deceiving you all night long. It was never his intention for you to find her."

Lucifer put a hand on Harry's shoulder. "Don't listen to this dame, Harry. She's off her nut. Why, just look at her wings: they're molting."

The angel ignored Lucifer, speaking instead to Harry in a delicate voice, "Beware now, lest the honeyed words of the deceiver betray thee into danger and nothing further be revealed. Indeed, only with the blessings of heaven shalt thou gain thy cause."

Lucifer growled back, "God's an old woman, Harry, and she's lost her mirth. I wouldn't trust her to fry potatoes. Here, take this." He offered a baseball to Harry. "Come on, give it a go! Plunk my pal Jack here on his noggin and he'll tell you exactly where that little girl of yours went. Sure he will." Lucifer spoke to the Negro, still perched in the center of the bulls-eye. "You'll feed Harry the right dope, won't you, Jack?"

The Negro grinned like a pumpkin. "You said it, boss."

Harry felt angry and confused, caught between fork-tailed Lucifer on one shoulder and a dumpy tattered angel on the other. What was the point of all this? Maybe Follette had cooked the whole thing up as a test of Harry's dedication to tracking down that young niece of his, the old razzle-dazzle to get his head spinning. If that was so, it was going just swell.

As the cold wind blew across the hectic midway, the angel gently took Harry's hand, her golden face serene in the electric light. "Honey, let the companion of thy journey be honest as well as brave."

"Tell her to beat it, Harry," Lucifer said, glaring at the frumpy angel. "She's giving me the creeps." He rubbed Harry's shoulder. "Besides, we don't need her to find that sweet dish of yours, do we? We got our own club, and this old hussy ain't included."

His patience exhausted at last, Harry shrugged Lucifer's hand off his shoulder, and told him, "I despise you."

Lucifer laughed. "Sure you do! Who doesn't? But that's no reason to quit the game, Harry. Come on, let's have another go at it. What do you say?"

"Good-bye."

Wind ruffled the white gown and feathered wings of the guardian angel while she and Harry proceeded along the electric promenade toward Nightingale Park. Her name was Billie Fry and she had come to Shepherds Island from St. Louis. "Mother's a monologist with Barnum," she told Harry, as they passed the Dragon's Gorge. "She says her stage is polished so well you could eat your dinner off the floor. We write to each other every day."

"I've been traveling a good deal myself lately," Harry remarked, growing more comfortable in her company — although anyone would make better company than Lucifer. "Sometimes I think our Republic is hardly more than a nation of vagabonds."

Smells of cigars and steaming sauerkraut traded on the wind. A chorus of screams chased a roller coaster clattering through the Swiss Alps nearby. The angel said, "My brother and I used to wrestle in the basement when we were kids. Now he's in the fight game and we don't hear from him unless he's knocked out and his manager telegraphs to Mother letting her know he's not too badly hurt."

"I wouldn't mind seeing somebody clean up on that mouth-artist back there in the devil costume."

"Oh, he's so queer about me," the angel said, stopping beside the yawning entrance to Cupid's Tunnel of Love. "I've done nothing to wrong him, yet whenever he catches sight of me, he pretends to be outraged by all the laws of God and men. I guess it's his nature."

"Never did nature say one thing, and wisdom say another."

The angel smiled sweetly. "Your faith in humanity is startling, honey. What on earth did that dear girl do to earn your attention?"

"I believed she was in danger," Harry replied, watching scraps of wastepaper blow along the midway. Purple and gold banners flapped atop the lighted parapets. "That might sound like a flat thing to say, but it's God's honest truth."

"And you hoped to rescue her?"

"If possible."

"Honey, would you please buy us two tickets to the Tunnel of Love?"

Harry looked up at the red Valentine façade decorated with dozens of rosy Cupids in flight.

"What for?"

"Don't you trust me?"

He shrugged. "Should I?"

Folding her arm into his, the stubby angel told him, "Not every heart is wicked, Harry."

A flat wooden boat carved like a pink swan carried Harry and his lazy-winged angel through a flooded subterranean chamber lit by rose-red lanterns. Lovely music from Pan flutes and violins played in the dark. A waterfall of rose petals cascaded over a granite arch. Drifting farther on, the swan-boat descended from the top of the flume with a rush of foam and rode a crest of water into a narrow tunnel where Harry saw two naked young water nymphs nuzzling each other on a cloud-pink rock. Shadows of cherubs armed with bows and arrows danced about. The chubby angel squeezed Harry's arm. "Isn't it beautiful?"

"Wondrous." Really, he felt tired enough to nap in the boat.

"Your madness is complete now."

"Pardon?"

A red-feathered arrow sailed by overhead and stuck on the far cavern wall, quivering like a bird. A pale cupid in laurel leaves and a white silk sash swung down from the ceiling to fire another scarlet arrow across the bow of the swan-boat.

"Love the gods captive holds, shall mortals not yield to thee?" the guardian angel murmured in Harry's ear.

He frowned. "I have no idea what you're talking about."

"She's here, Harry." And the tattered angel kissed him gently on the cheek as the swan-boat passed into stygian darkness. "So long."

The boat tipped slightly. Harry steadied his grip and cold water splashed lightly against the hull. A cool draft, fragrant with violet and honeysuckle, breathed across his face. Somebody climbed into the swan-boat and sat down beside him. Before he could speak, Harry was hushed by a pair of slender fingers upon his lips. Up ahead, a rosy light lit the cavern as Harry drifted toward a fleet of pink swan-boats, each floating serenely through a sunny meadow of olive trees and wildflowers. Serenaded by a symphonic recording of "Clair de Lune," tiny pink cherubs played tag among the pussy willows while crimson papier-mâché hearts fluttered down like autumn leaves from a hazy blue sky whose smiling clouds peeked over the enchanted meadow below.

When his own swan-boat entered this corny lovers Elysium, Harry turned to see who had snuck aboard in the dark. That was when he found Pearl seated there beside him, her blue silk frock and cloche hat dripping wet from the misty Tunnel of Love.

She gave him a quick peck on the cheek, then squealed delightedly, "You came for me, honey! You came for me! Oh my gosh, you really did!"

— 5 —

On Sand Avenue outside Nightingale Park, a damp breeze swept inland off the dark water, fogging the lighted arches along a busy boardwalk, thinning the noisy Bowery crowds and bringing cold night to Shepherds Island. The photographers and Mah Jongg players, bathers and lovers, were gone, the human pyramids, leap frog races, beauty parades, checker tables and penny spyglasses, peanuts and popcorn, forgotten until tomorrow. Only small birds remained, descending from a blackened sky to scavenge supper in the foaming tide.

Thoroughly exhausted from running back and forth across the park, Harry leaned on the iron railing and watched a pilot boat navigate the oily current a quarter mile or so downriver. A clock tower perched within the spires of a Byzantine minaret rang the half hour. Harry intended to catch the 12:45 train at Pelican Station. It was chilly out, numbing his face and hands while he waited for Pearl who had gone to the ladies toilet. She'd offered no fair explanation about her strange abduction, nor her captors' purpose in dragging her about Shepherds Island, other than to tell Harry over and over how wonderful he was for rescuing her. In fact, he was dead tired and his feet hurt. His canonization would have to wait. First, he needed a cup of cocoa and a hot bath. Looking down Sand Avenue toward the Bowery, he saw someone who looked awfully familiar sitting on a bench, nibbling from a sack of popcorn in his lap: that pipsqueak from Merle's Soda Club who'd tried to start a scrap at the speakie the night he met Pearl. Good grief, what on earth was he doing here? If it was to square accounts, to hell with him. That'd really be the limit. Harry put his back to Sand Avenue. He didn't need any more trouble.

Pearl came back out onto the boardwalk a few minutes later, wearing a black cloth wrap over her frock and carrying a smart glass-beaded evening bag. She looked pleased. Harry had already volunteered to escort her back to the city. Despite his being flabbergasted by the entire experience, he still found her plenty adorable. He just had to wise up and get home while he had the chance.

"We've got seven minutes to catch the train," he told Pearl, as she strolled toward him. "It won't do to be late. I've got business early in the morning."

She stroked his arm. "I guess a girl needs her beauty rest, too, don't she?"

"I suppose she does," he replied, trying not to stare. She was far lovelier than he remembered, her girlish figure more mature, her violet eyes utterly entrancing. Walking quickly together up Sand Avenue toward Pelican Station, he wondered if she wanted to kiss him again as she had in the dome that night. Then he asked himself why he entertained that thought at all. Motorcycle policemen rumbled side-by-side down the dusty boardwalk. A pilothouse whistle echoed from the cold river. A derby-hatted fellow wearing a sandwich board advertising a shirt sale at Goldstein & Co. passed in the opposite direction. Harry watched scores of shouting young boys rushing in and out of the Bowery. He was pleased not to see that short fellow again at all.

The Pelican Coast interurban waited at the station, admitting late-night passengers. Harry's cheeks were flushed from the cold, his eyes watering.

"See, honey? We ain't late," Pearl told him, stepping up to the electric J.G. Brill car. "We got lots of time."

Harry nodded. "Sure we do. Now let's try to find a decent seat."

They waited their turn to board at the rear of the interurban. Harry took the window and Pearl slid in warmly beside him, still fragrant with a honeysweet perfume. She sat close enough that their legs were touching, and her warmth radiated into him, stealing his breath away. He wanted to kiss her. He wanted to put his arms around her, hug her to his chest, and kiss her deliriously. He decided he needed a straitjacket. The conductor rang the bell, and the crowded trolley left Pelican Station. Harry took one last look back toward Sand Avenue where Edmund Tingley's perpetual Wonder Wheel glowed in the windy darkness above Starland, performing revolution after revolution for anyone willing to buy a ticket and climb aboard. After having a mind-boggling adventure, here he was riding home with a beautiful girl. Was this a dream or a wicked hallucination? He supposed that all depended upon how this finished up.

That didn't take long.

A mile or so down the tracks past Roanoke Creek and the lights of Bascom township, Pearl leaned over and whispered in his ear, "Want to hear a secret?"

Lost in a reverie of lust and bewilderment, Harry wondered how these things happened to him? Was he really that fellow who can't keep his eyes to himself? These are the sorts of distractions that lead to big mistakes.

"It's about you," Pearl told him, gently kissing his earlobe.

With a shiver, Harry perked up. "How's that?"

Lips to his ear, she murmured, "It ain't love if you don't got to be there."

"Pardon?" His heart tensed. *Who was in love?*

"I seen a pretty sunset today from the corner of Peake and 60th."

"What are you talking about?"

Her smile widened. She was gleaming now. "I been with you, honey, ever since you came out of your hotel this evening. I seen you button your collar and fix your hat. I seen you sneeze and blow your nose with that new handkerchief of yours. I seen you eat your Mulligan stew, and I seen you on the train with that little boy. I even seen you make him laugh. That was darling." She giggled.

Not certain he fully grasped what she'd just said, Harry sat up. "You've been following me around this evening? Is that what you're telling me?" The fog was blowing out of his head, and he had a terrible intuition of trouble. This wasn't what he expected.

Her smile faded. "Oh, don't get sore, honey. It was only since before suppertime, and you didn't notice 'til you seen me with those fellows from the Queen Anne's Revenge. I didn't know if you even cared, and now we're sitting here together like a pair of lovebirds. Ain't that wonderful?"

Lovebirds? Now he realized what she was trying to say. "Wait a minute! You knew those pirates who kidnapped you?"

Suddenly Pearl looked startled, as if caught in a transgression of immense proportion. She blinked and her eyes became watery.

"Well?" Harry persisted angrily. "Did you or didn't you?"

He should've known all along. For God's sake, nothing was on the up-and-up anymore.

The lights of a crossroads washed the interior as the interurban flashed by Milbury Lane. Pearl bit her lip, then whimpered, "I swear it wasn't all my idea, honey. Why, Gene and Ned came up with the big idea of proving whether you cared or not, and you put 'em wise, all right. Sure you did."

He was stupefied. Gene and Ned? Co-conspirators? "Good grief, why, you weren't in trouble at all, were you? This was all a farce concocted to make a fool out of me! Those idiot pirates and that blubber-belly at the Steeplechase, the stupid dwarf with the cattle prod, that Lucifer fellow, and your silly angel friend. They were all confederates of yours, weren't they? Go on, say it straight!"

Pearl blanched. "Gosh, no, honey! That ain't so! Why, sure, all right, I knew 'em before, but I didn't go to fool you tonight, honest I didn't!" She grabbed his arm, desperate tears welling up in her eyes. "Oh, honey, you got to believe me!"

His blood boiling, Harry shoved her hand away. He hated being duped by anyone, much less a child. "Why, you're nothing but a liar and a cheat."

"Honey, don't say that!"

He shook his head, thoroughly disgusted. "You make me sick. Go sit somewhere else. I don't want to have anything more to do with you. Get out of my sight."

"No, I won't! Please, honey, I didn't mean to bust you up! I swear I didn't! You got across swell tonight, and I was so proud of you, won't you see that? Why, those fellows tried to turn you every which way, but you didn't let nothing put you off. Rocky thought you were licked when he took you to Jack Johnson, but you showed him plenty, didn't you? Why, sure you did! That poor dope thought he had you played for a sucker, but you smashed that plan. Ned says Rocky flooded the room when he saw you beat it out of there with Billie Fry without even throwing one ball! I hope to tell you, honey, it was splendacious!"

This was worse than he had imagined, by far the stupidest escapade he had been involved in since college. And here he'd supposed Follette drummed up the entire charade as a test of character. God almighty, if old Charley found out how easily he was tricked, Follette'd probably cut him out of the game altogether. And he'd be right to do so. Clearly,

Marie had married a complete idiot.

For the next few miles, Harry stared out the window toward a stream of automobiles on a distant motor road entering the darkness from East Mallon. Those fellows he had encountered in Starland and Nightingale Park were seasoned con-artists, all right. They had put it over on him pretty thoroughly. But so what? After all, he had chased his tail for half the night out of a noble desire to rescue some poor innocent girl from what seemed to be a deadly situation. For once, he had actually been a hero, right? Let's face facts: that Lucifer fellow did all he could to lead him astray and failed miserably. Harry hadn't succumbed to greed and tossed those balls at the colored fellow. Quite the opposite. He had shunned the devil and chosen the best path. In truth, what turned the game in his favor was the virtue of his purpose. He saw that now very clearly. They attempted all manner of ruses to distract him, but in the end, the biggest failure was theirs. Honestly, what was there to feel humiliated about? He had gotten his girl. If this *had* been a test devised by Follette, well, he'd certainly passed with flying colors.

Rapidly warming to this reevaluation of his adventure, he told Pearl, "The truth of the matter is, I don't rate that scheme of theirs very highly at all. Sure, I'll admit it tied me up for a few minutes, but it wasn't all that hard to see where it was going. I was more concerned with your welfare than spoiling their silly little game."

Wiping a tear from her eye, she gladly agreed. "I knew those cut-ups couldn't put it over on you, honey. I told 'em so, too. They just didn't believe me."

"That Lucifer fellow's a real louse, isn't he? I didn't care much for him from the start."

"Oh, Rocky'll be crabbing about you 'til Christmas," Pearl replied, with a giggle. "Nobody ever run him off like that before."

"I guess I gave him a little skull practice, after all, didn't I?"

Pearl brightened. "Sure you did, honey. You were all aces!"

"Well, I suppose all's well that ends well, right?" His mood warming now, Harry felt a little sorry for having yelled at this poor girl. Besides, he had another idea percolating wildly in his brain, a darned swell scheme for putting his evening's humiliation to a greater advantage. He should've thought of this earlier. Maybe this was serendipity, after all.

"So, what do you say we get you home, safe and sound? How would that be, darling?"

She rested her head on his shoulder. "Gee whiz, honey. You're the cat's meow."

Disembarking downtown from the Ibbetson Street trolley, Harry walked with Pearl the two blocks back to the Warsaw Hotel where she promised to telephone for a taxi. A trio of noisy, foul-smelling coal trucks rumbled past followed shortly by a paper delivery truck from the *City Sentinel* and a police car that flew down Jackson Street in the direction of Columbia Avenue.

At the hotel, Harry stopped beneath the canvas awning. He was about to try out his new proposition on her, when Pearl put her back to the wind and asked, "You got a toilet upstairs?"

She rubbed her arms vigorously, too, letting Harry know it was cold in front of the hotel. She had such beautiful eyes. He knew what she was asking, but how could he resist?

"Yes, I do," he replied. "Do you need to use it?"

"If you'd prefer me to be a lady."

This might not be smart, but he supposed he could invite her up for a few minutes. Maybe she'd be more comfortable there, anyhow, more receptive to his idea.

They entered the hotel and went upstairs by elevator.

While Harry fished the room key out of his coat pocket, Pearl waited back at the elevator door beneath a single bulb dangling from the ceiling by an insulated wire. She leaned against the iron cage as Harry fumbled with a recalcitrant lock. His hand was shaking when he flicked the knob and stepped back, letting the door open into the front room. He nodded at Pearl, "After you, dear."

She shoved off from the elevator frame and swept past him into the apartment. Down the hall, a friendly book salesman, George O'Hara, had his radio tuned to the NBC "Slumber Hour Ensemble." Listening just briefly, Harry followed into his own apartment and shut the door behind him. Pearl already had the light on in the bathroom. The sink faucet was running water and she was fussing with her silk frock while

Harry went to the window to lower the shade. She closed the door.

Light from the streetlamps helped illuminate the front room, but often kept him awake at night. Had he been willing to pay another fifteen dollars a month, he would have been able to hire an apartment with overhead lighting, but since he was generally in bed early, the extra money seemed better spent elsewhere. Winning Follette's five thousand dollar missing-niece-sweepstakes would change all this, of course, and that's where Pearl came in. Hearing her describe the confederacy of deception that suckered him at Shepherds Island gave him the idea of using her crowd to his own advantage. How many of those sorts of fellows did she know in the city? He thought there had to be dozens, if not hundreds. And they were smart, too, particularly that crafty Lucifer. Really, how else were they able to fool him? What if somehow he were able to enlist their talents and manpower to the purpose of uncovering Follette's niece? He wouldn't need to give them all the dope on who she really is, or even what amount of reward lay in it for himself. Any story should suffice so long as he had Pearl taking his part, shoving them along the straight and narrow. Naturally, this had to be undertaken with a great deal of finesse, offering just enough details to keep them in the game without getting anyone's curiosity out of hand. A smart fellow keeps his designs and business from the knowledge of others. Handling Pearl's bunch would be tricky, but that image of her cronies fanning out across the city, sticking their noses into every crack and crevice for his benefit, was terribly appealing. He decided it was a wonderful plan. All he needed to do was get this little girl onboard.

Pearl flushed the toilet, and ran water in the sink. Then she came out, fiddling with her cloche hat. "Say, this ain't such a bad dump you got here. Kinda cold, though, don't you think?" She frowned. "Maybe you ought to get the radiator fixed. How much they got you paying for this joint?"

"Actually, I prefer the heat down somewhat at night."

Pearl went to the window overlooking Jackson Street and shoved the shade up with the back of one hand, peeking out underneath. "Say, you got a pretty swell view up here, too."

After switching on a lamp, Harry glanced at the clock atop his desk: it read half past one. He had an eight a.m. appointment with Bell Telephone about improving the quality of the wire in his office. Later on, he hoped to meet with a fellow by the name of Newcomb to discuss a crated shipment of Mikado pencils and Slip-On shades. Newcomb was a vacationist, just this week landed from the *Aquitania*, who had wired Follette a radiogram from sea promising to instruct a couple of the salesmen at Transfer & Storage on how best to make one's fortune in wholesale merchandise. Harry didn't place much faith in miracles, but he certainly intended to hear what the fellow had to say. Why let Phelps or Kelsey make the score?

Pearl strolled over to his writing desk and touched the papers piled there with the tips of her fingers, disturbing none yet increasing Harry's anxiety. She was so incredibly lovely, he felt almost frightened with lust having her there in his apartment. He didn't trust himself. He had made love to girls who weren't half as pretty, and none of them had followed him back to his room. This was very dangerous. If he were smart, he would go ahead and pitch his plan to her as quickly as he could, then telephone for a taxi. She stopped at the photograph of his family on the verandah in Farrington, studied it momentarily, and moved on without comment. Harry returned to the window, repositioned the shade, then bound its cord fast to the latch.

"Are you glad we met tonight in Nightingale Park?" she asked, a faint tremble to her voice. Beside the lampstand by Harry's sofa, she averted her eyes, pretending to be unconcerned with what she had just asked. He knew better, of course. A girl won't introduce how pleased she is to be in your company unless it's really so. This one gave herself away the moment she spoke. He could see affection plainly in her eyes. She was already fond of him.

"Well, it was certainly a surprise," Harry teased, keeping his voice calm. Drawing a breath, he boldly added, "Though, all in all, I suppose not an unpleasant one." He was aware of becoming aroused and felt absurd. He caught himself staring at her bosom and wondered if he would be able to talk to her about his idea regarding Follette's niece. If not, he thought, I'm in a lot of trouble.

She strolled over toward him, that certain gleam in her eye. "Even after you found me, I kept expecting you to tell me to scram."

"Oh? Why's that?"

"Aw, you know how it is," she said, fingering her shawl. "Soon as a girl gets a crush on some fellow, he starts giving her the run-around."

Harry felt as if he were floating out of his own head. "Do you have a crush on someone?"

She stopped just inches in front of him. "You were so sweet to rescue me, honey." She played with his lapel, and let her fingers slide down his coat sleeve to take his hand. She drew it up to her lips and kissed it, then pressed it to her bosom. She was so soft he could hardly speak. Then he didn't need to, because she raised up slightly on her tip-toes and kissed him passionately on the mouth. Her breath tasted like peppermint. He kissed her back. Her rosebud lips were warm and opened slightly and he kissed her more deeply. He could smell honey perfume in her hair, and her breast swelled in his hand as she pressed her body against his and whimpered like a kitten when he kissed her neck. He felt overwhelmed with desire, and slipped a hand beneath her camisole to feel her ripened nipple. Her next breath came like a shortened sigh and she sagged in his arms. Then her eyes closed as she fainted and fell to the floor.

He was absolutely certain she had died.

A horrid future of police investigators, doctors, prosecutors, tabloid reporters, prison guards, divorce lawyers, decades of shame and humiliation, flashed across his brain. He carried her to the couch and laid her down. Christ, if she were dead, he would have to throw himself out the window. His flat was four stories up, so he assumed the fall would kill him. Why had he brought her here, anyhow? What was he thinking? Did he despise his life so much he was willing to throw it away for a girl he barely knew? For God's sake, what on earth had gotten into him?

Her eyelids fluttered.

She coughed, then burped.

She was alive! Thank God in heaven!

Her violet eyes opened. When she saw him leaning over her, concern on his face, she smiled. Pressing the back of one hand to her forehead, Pearl said, "Gee, honey, I'm feeling tipsy all of a sudden, and I ain't hardly had a drop all day."

Relief surging through him, he asked, "Do you need a drink of water?"

She shrugged. "I ain't sure. Maybe."

"Let me get you a glass, dear."

His hands quivering, Harry walked over to his desk and opened one of the bottom cabinets and took out a drinking glass. He brought it into the bathroom and closed the door behind him. Running the faucet, he set the glass on the sink counter, then stood over the commode, letting the running water in the sink hide the sound of his urinating. God, he was lucky! If she had really dropped dead, who knows what might have happened? Look here, he was still shaking! Why had she fainted, anyhow? Was that her orgasm? He'd heard stories of that sort of thing and had always thought they were nonsense. Good grief, he had hardly touched her! Was it really possible to climax so quickly? Well, regardless, the fact was, he had to get her out of here while she was still breathing. Follette's search could wait. Harry felt now as if fate had just given him a miraculous reprieve and he'd be damned if he wouldn't take advantage of it. He also worried that another tenant had seen him escorting Pearl to his apartment. Gossip traveled like electricity through the walls. Reputations were ruined with a whisper and a nod. Better to be careful than apologetic. Who would understand, anyhow? Certainly not Marie.

When Harry was finished, he returned to the sink, filled the drinking glass with water, shut off the faucet, then flushed the toilet. As the water in the commode swirled away, he heard Pearl's voice call out from the other side of the door, "Honey, I been wondering, how come they call it 'Nightingale Park'? I didn't see no birds there."

Harry switched off the light above the toilet. From the dark, he quoted a visitor's pamphlet to Shepherds Island, *"The nightingale's sweet song persuades us that miracles are not yet ceased."*

He came out of the toilet, water glass in hand, and saw Pearl lying on his bed in the next room, propped up by a couple pillows, nude as the hour she was born.

"My God!" he murmured, and dropped the glass.

INTERLUDE
CHARLIE PENDERGAST

CHAUTAUQUA

THE FIRST PALM TREE I ever saw in my life stood in a vacant lot across the street from our house in Needles. Uncle Monroe had sent us postcards from California with lots of pictures of palm trees and orange groves and sunny blue skies. Mother carried a juice squeezer all the way from Illinois so we'd have fresh orange juice for breakfast every morning, but we never saw one orange tree.

Needles was a desert town. Most often it was hot, and sand blew in the streets. A few people here and there about town had grass lawns, but we just had sand. Father had ordered me a Hawthorne bicycle from Montgomery Ward's before we left Illinois, and Uncle Harris had gotten one for Bebbins, too, and we rode all over town. There wasn't much else to do. Uncle Monroe had found a small empty building to rent as a barbershop, and he and Father took a garden hose to it one afternoon, washing out spider webs and wasp nests, cleaning the floors and fixing it up. We all pitched in one weekend with wall brushes and buckets of paints, and by Monday morning it was open for business.

Bebbins and I went to school for two months in an old green building on the other side of town. Every morning we rode there on our bicycles and played jacks on the sidewalk when we weren't in class, and did little else but play. Neither of us paid much attention to our lessons. I wrote stories instead of doing homework, and Bebbins wasn't very bright and liked to wrestle, and more than once Aunt Lottie took a belt to him for a scrap he'd started with one of the other boys in class. Some of those kids were poor as Job's turkey. They lived in shacks and came to school each morning, covered head to toe with dust and smelling like spoiled milk. There was one pretty girl named Marie Holland who had dark curls and skipped rope faster than anyone I'd ever known. I saw her one night out in front of our house playing on the sidewalk. I think we ran down the street together and back again a dozen times and made a funny game of it. I liked her quite a lot, but I had no idea where she lived and I was afraid to ask her. She won a diploma for being the smartest in our class and I remember one of the other girls pushed her down one day at recess and said something nasty to her, which made Marie Holland pee her underpants and start crying in front of the whole school. I just watched along with the other kids and felt so badly about it afterward that whenever she smiled at me in class or out on the sidewalk, I looked away. I was glad when school finally let out for the year.

Most summer evenings we went over to the house Uncle Harris and Aunt Lottie shared with Uncle Monroe and Auntie Leah. It was bigger than ours and had a large front porch where we could sit outdoors and watch the wind blow in the palms across the street. Uncle Monroe drank beer and so did my father and Uncle Harris (though not half as much as Monroe), and they talked about fishing and eating frog-legs and what the relatives were doing back home. Little Shirley napped with Howard, whose health was already improving, while Bebbins and I tramped around in the dust outdoors. Mother and Lottie and Auntie Leah did the washing and baked pies in the kitchen after the sun went down, and played three-handed bridge until it was time to go home. Now and then, Father and Mother and I would drive up onto the desert to feel the night breeze and just sit there for a while. Sometimes we would be out so late, I'd fall asleep in the backseat and Father would drive back to town and Mother would rub my shoulder, saying, "My sweet baby-boy, are you sleeping? Wake up now. We're home."

One night, my father took me to a movie in downtown Needles. We walked in when the theater was dark and we couldn't see a thing.

I remember it was a cowboy movie and the theater was crowded and we only stayed for a few minutes because Father got disgusted when he couldn't find us the seats we wanted, so he took me out and we went home. Another day, Bebbins and Shirley and Howard and I went downtown once with Mother and Aunt Lottie to get ice cream cones. We stopped at a little store and went in and ordered our ice cream and the fellow behind the counter gave us each a double dip ice cream cone and said, "That'll be ten cents a piece."

When Mother and Aunt Lottie expressed great surprise and horror that an ice cream cone should cost ten cents, the fellow replied, "Well, after all, it's a double dip, you know."

Mother said, "Yes, but where we come from, ice cream cones are only a nickel."

He told her, "Sure, but like I said, you got a double dip, didn't you?"

When I look back on that funny incident now, ten cents doesn't seem like much, yet I suppose when my father was only making fifteen or twenty dollars a week, ten cents for an ice cream cone was a lot of money, as was twenty cents to see a movie when there was no decent place to sit.

It was Auntie Leah's idea to attend the Chautauqua at the Colorado River. She and Auntie Eff had gone to one on Lake Harriet during the War where they'd taken classes on *Bible Miracles & Modern Science*, heard the Ontario orchestra and a stirring lecture about the Yellow Menace, and watched a Slavic magician make a horse and buggy disappear before their eyes. It cost a dollar for the week, more than a fair price for Moral Progress and the diffusion of civilized knowledge. One morning, Mother read a handbill in downtown Needles advertising the arrival of the circuit Chautauqua and Auntie Leah insisted we go. She said there'd be a boy's club for Howard and Bebbins and me, a girl's club for Shirley, and a tasty barbecue in the afternoon for everyone with a paid ticket. Uncle Harris didn't hold much for education, sixth grade was as far as he'd gone in school, but when Auntie Leah told him there would be banjoists and a yodeler from Switzerland, that was enticement enough. The announcement of a sermon on alcohol by the Temperance Union at the Chautauqua persuaded Uncle Monroe to stay home. Since the start of summer, he'd been making raisin wine in his cellar. I can still see the raisins floating up and down in his jugs of wine as it was fermenting. I don't think Father and Mother drank too much, but Uncle Monroe did, and said he had no desire to be preached to on his day off.

Early the next morning, we drove out east of town to a tabernacle of great brown canvas tents near the river. There were hundreds of people and more automobiles than trees. We heard a glee club performing "Onward Christian Soldiers" from the center tent and Auntie Leah wanted to march right in and sing along. Aunt Lottie preferred to visit the fortune telling booth, while my father and mother favored attending a lecture on juvenile delinquency, and Uncle Harris wanted to go spin the prize wheel to win something nice to take home with him. Straight away, Bebbins and I left Howard and Shirley with Auntie Leah and ran to the taffy stand. We each spent a nickel there, then went off to find the lyceum for scientific demonstrations. Back in Illinois, Bebbins had gotten a microscope for Christmas one year, which he used to look at ant feelers and snail slick. Bebbins always pretended to know more than he did, and I wasn't fooled; he used to think that if you took a wet dishcloth and wiped it over a wart on your hand, then buried the cloth in the backyard, the wart would disappear. This was valuable to know because Bebbins had lots of warts. Actually, I didn't care much for science at all. What I really wanted to do was go to the storytelling tent and hear about Geronimo from a genuine Apache warrior. We'd seen some Indians the last evening of our trip when we had our campfire set up maybe fifty yards from the road, and a bunch of them came by in a Model-T and suddenly drove off the road and the whole thing tipped over. Uncle Harris went to have a look, and when he came back, he told us they were all drunk. Since Bebbins was afraid of Indians, I went to hear the story of Geronimo by myself.

It was hot underneath the canvas tent. People cooled themselves with paper fans and wet handkerchieves. All the chairs were taken, so I had to sit in the sawdust by the tent wall. After a few minutes, a flap behind a podium at the rear of the tent parted and an ancient Indian with long grey hair wearing a wide brimmed black hat and black frock coat came in. His brown face was dried and wrinkled, his eyes dark. I thought he was the oldest man on earth. When he spoke, his breath exhaled like a rasping wind.

Geronimo, he told us, was a medicine man with great powers of magic. His people were the Chiricahua Apache who hunted and fished in the mountains and streams of the Arizona territory long before the white man knew there was such a place. They were betrayed by the greed of those whose god commanded, 'Thou shalt not covet thy neighbor's house, nor anything that is thy neighbor's.' Back then, the scalp of a single Chiricahua warrior was worth a hundred dollars to bounty hunters. Geronimo's mother and wife and children were murdered by Mexicans for less than that, but the great medicine man himself was more difficult to kill. His magic helped him outfox his enemies. When the other Apache surrendered to become farmers, Geronimo and Naiche and one hundred and fifty warriors escaped into the Sierra Madre. The Chiricahua wanted to hunt, not farm and raise cattle. Five thousand soldiers could not find them. They chased him for years through the mountains. He was impossible to capture. Finally the white soldiers enlisted Apache scouts to track down Geronimo and bring him back to the reservation at San Carlos. They promised if he surrendered peacefully, he and his people could return to their land at Fort Bowie. Weary of hiding, Geronimo agreed in order to prevent the extinction of his tribe. He surrendered at Skeleton Canyon. But they lied to him, and sent Geronimo with his people to Fort Marion in Florida. It was foreign to them. Where were the mountains and the deer and the streams? Many died of malaria and yellow fever. Their children were taken from them and sent away to the north and never came back. The Chiricahua were held captive at St. Augustine and Mobile for eight years until the Kiowa and the Comanche allowed Geronimo to bring his people to their own reservation in Oklahoma where the great medicine man died of pneumonia in 1909.

The old Apache stopped speaking. He stared at his audience under the tent, sweeping us with an eagle's gaze. Then he said, "When I was a boy, I walked with Geronimo. He taught me to move like the wind.

Like a warrior. We fought for our land, and lost, and we can never go back to that life. It is gone forever. I am older now than Geronimo was when his powers of magic were great, and there are no more soldiers to outfox. The hunt is finished, but our people have peace."

Then he walked out the back of the tent. The ladies continued fanning themselves, while men here and there checked their watches and spoke about what to do next. Soon we all got up to leave. I went out into the sunlight and looked for Bebbins. Maybe he'd gone down to the river. I headed off in that direction around behind the tent, and saw the old Apache seated on a low wooden stool, smoking a cigarette and staring at the ground. I remember thinking how exciting it must have been chasing around with Geronimo. Did he still have the rifle or the bow he used as a boy all those years ago? I wanted to ask him, but lacked the nerve. Before I could step back behind the tent, though, the old Apache saw me. His eyes narrowed. I was so scared, I thought my heart would fly right out of my chest. He took a drag off his cigarette, and raised his chin skyward, and put his fingers across his mouth and made a sound like, "Woo-woo-woo-woo," sending smoke signals up into the air. Then he smiled at me, tossed his cigarette down, stamped it cold, and went back into the tent for the next audience.

HARRISON, KANSAS

ASEA OF PORCUPINE GRASS, tall and golden in the mid-afternoon sun, surrounded a small white farmhouse and a ramshackle barn. Parked in back of the farmhouse was a tan Packard Six, deliberately hidden from the road. Alvin Pendergast stood by the iron pump watching the dwarf bathe in a water trough. Rascal had just dropped his knickers and kicked them aside, then stripped off his union suit and jumped in. He sank himself up to his chin and splashed water at Alvin.

"Why, it's not so bad," the dwarf remarked. "Hardly smells at all."

"Horses drink out of it," the farm boy said, plugging his nose. "You could get a disease."

Rascal dunked his head. Water stopped splashing over the sides of the trough. Submerged, the dwarf freed small air bubbles from his nose. Then a single finger broke the surface like a periscope, made a circle, and disappeared. All about the farm, wild grass in the empty fields swayed lazily. Crows yakked on the fence-posts. Alvin listened to bedsprings squeaking behind the window at the middle of the house where Chester entertained a girl from town. Every so often, Chester's head bobbed up into view, a nasty grin stuck on his face. The brown-haired girl beneath him squealed off and on while a portable Victrola that Chester had dug out of a closet played "Waiting For The Robert E. Lee."

With a great splash soaking Alvin's shirt and pants, the dwarf emerged from the depths of the trough. He leaned forward, both arms hung over the wood.

"Do you have any soap?" he asked. "I still feel grimy."

Alvin looked at the water stains on his shirt and pants. "You got me all wet."

"Maybe you ought to climb in here and wash off."

"I guess I'm washed enough already."

The farm boy watched Rascal rub his scalp with the tips of his fingers, scrubbing diligently. The old pump filled the wooden trough to three-quarters full, but nobody had bothered to clean it out in a while. Horsehair floated on the surface of the water and stuck to Rascal's upper arms and chest. It looked filthy. Not a hundred dollars could get him swimming in there alive and willing.

"Of course, a sugar bath would be much more refreshing."

Alvin frowned. "A what?"

"Sugar bath."

"What's that?"

The dwarf wore an expression of incredulity. "You've never had a sugar bath?"

Alvin shook his head. "Never even heard of such a thing. Are you joking me again?"

The girl under Chester shrieked as the iron bed frame slammed against the back wall, rattling the window. Chester grunted a response, then laughed out loud. The song quit and he replaced the needle. *Way down on the levee in old Alabamy...*

"They sound like dogs," said Alvin, trying unsuccessfully not to listen to Chester rutting with his honey pie fifteen yards away. "I bet she's hating every minute of it."

"I bet she's not," the dwarf replied, continuing his scrubbing. His white hair was plastered flat on his scalp, almost invisible in the bright sunlight. The thick blue veins on his chest and skull made the skin look translucent. If Rascal had been outdoors at all since winter, Alvin thought, it must have been on a cloudy day. The dwarf dunked his head again, while the farm boy's ears went back to the window and the sassy girl squealing beneath Chester.

Half a day's drive from Hadleyville had led them across the Missouri border into Kansas where, after nightfall, Chester drove to the outskirts of a small town named Gridley and sent Alvin on foot to buy the three of them some supper. The road into town was dark and muddy and twice he tripped, negotiating the sinkholes between ditches. The sole restaurant in Gridley offered steak and onion dinners for forty cents, including tapioca pudding. They ate on a blanket in the wet grass under a sky threatening rain, then drove on to a tourist camp north of Abilene. Only Chester got much sleep those first few nights out of Hadleyville, taking his own cabin and staying to himself, as usual, and not being too talkative, as if something had put him in a foul mood. Meanwhile, Rascal kept Alvin up for hours, chattering endlessly about famous individuals he'd met: Lincoln's bastard nephew, Napoleon's barber's granddaughter, Teddy Roosevelt's wet nurse. Each episode ended with somebody offering Rascal a trip to Egypt or Norway or full-shares in a new railway venture financed by J.P. Morgan, rejected by the dwarf in favor of tending his award-winning vegetable garden in Hadleyville. Whether the dwarf actually believed his own stories Alvin didn't know, and once he had heard them each a dozen times, he didn't care much, either.

After twelve days of eating from paper sacks, they decided to stop for breakfast at Charlie Harper's Restaurant & Glassware Emporium in a little town called Harrison. Cheap soda glasses etched and fluted to resemble expensive Viennese crystal were mounted high on the walls with calligraphic tags beneath each one describing its stylistic lineage. Only the crudest hicks from the sticks could have been fooled, but Alvin managed to embarrass himself by asking how long it took to ship glasses like that across the ocean. The dwarf laughed so loudly the manager came out of the back room carrying a club. After eating, Alvin and Rascal went outdoors. Chester followed a few minutes later hand in hand with the darling brunette waitress and announced she'd be spending the afternoon with him. Her name was Rose, and her recently deceased Uncle Edgar owned a farm five miles south of Harrison. Since the day he'd gone into the ground, Edgar's house had sat empty, so they would all be more than welcome to sleep there overnight. She looked only slightly older than Alvin's sister Mary Ann who had her fourteenth birthday the week before Easter, but Chester didn't seem to care in the least. He told her his name was Calvin Coolidge III and that he'd made packs of dough in the oil game. After giving Alvin and Rascal a few dollars to buy groceries, he swept Rose off her feet and deposited her into the front seat until it was time to head out to the farm. Once there, they retired to Uncle Edgar's bedroom where they remained for the rest of the day, playing records, sipping gin from a hipflask and rolling in bed.

Rascal stood up in the trough and splashed water on his waist and legs. Out of modesty, he kept his back to the bedroom window. He told the farm boy, "A pound of powdered sugar mixed into a bath nourishes the skin. I try to take a sugar bath at least once a month."

The dwarf climbed out of the trough. His splashing had made a muddy quagmire of the immediate area. He grabbed his white union suit and tiny brown knickers and put them back on.

"Sounds dumb to me," said Alvin, keeping out of the mud. He heard the girl giggling now. What the hell was Chester doing to her? The farm boy hadn't taken that girl for a floosie when they first met.

Rascal wrestled his cotton shirt and red suspenders over the damp skin of his upper body. "That's just because you've never tried one."

"I wouldn't want to. Sugar's for eating, not washing."

The dwarf worked the pump to clean off his hands. "Don't be so sure. Sugar's just another one of God's gifts we're to use as we see fit."

"Then I'll stick to sprinkling mine on hotcakes, thank you very much."

The iron bed stopped squeaking. Rascal put on his black button shoes and slicked his hair with the wet palms of his hands. He smiled at Alvin. "That was thoroughly refreshing."

The record ended as Chester raised the bedroom window and stuck his sweaty face out into the afternoon air. Alvin saw Rose get up off the bed behind him bare-naked and head for the bathroom. Seeing her lolling breasts got him going again and he tried to put her out of his mind, doubting that Chester would share her with his partners.

Chester called out, "Anybody hungry?"

"I am," replied Alvin. "I'm starving." That was a fact, too. His stomach was rumbling fierce.

"What do you want to eat?"

"Anything."

"All we have are eggs and potatoes," the dwarf announced. "Have either of you ever tried an Idaho soufflé?"

Chester disappeared from the window. Alvin could hear him talking to Rose about cooking. He didn't usually consult with them about meals. They ate where he chose and did what he said. That was swell with Alvin who didn't have many ideas these days, but Rascal voiced his opinion on everything from filling stations to petting parties. When Chester had first seen the dwarf in the backseat of the Packard, he hadn't raised his voice at all in ordering Rascal to get the hell out of his motorcar. Nor had he started shouting when the dwarf refused to do so on account of having planned and executed the better part of the bank robbery all by himself without even asking for so much as a red cent in profit. Chester kept driving, and after the argument quit a dozen miles down the road, he made it clear that Rascal would be allowed to ride along and take part if he was able to prove his worth in one fashion or another. This suited Rascal just fine. He had plenty of helpful ideas. Bootleggers and cutters and hold-up men intrigued him, and whenever Chester was off somewhere, the dwarf would philosophize about the nature and purpose of criminal behavior in modern society. Little of this discourse made sense to Alvin, though Rascal's enthusiasm for their adventure was infectious. For his own part, Alvin avoided Chester as much as possible, afraid of getting the bad eye, or a bawling out for having invited the dwarf along. Mostly, Chester had been pretty swell to Alvin, picking him up a sturdy old Montgomery Ward suitcase and a fresh pair of shoes as if they were best pals for no reason the farm boy could figure. After all, he wasn't doing anything special, just lugging trunks and looking after the auto. Anybody could have done that. What did Chester have him along for, anyhow? Maybe he'd gotten sick of driving around on his own. He had a smile for every occasion and treated Alvin better than anyone else ever had. But one evening when Alvin tried asking Chester where he grew up, he got told in just such a voice to mind his own business, and that was that. Besides which, later on that same night, Alvin's night sweats returned and his breathing became labored and he knew he was getting sicker again, and didn't want Chester to know it for fear of being put out on the road himself. So far, he was content to ride along a while further, if for no other reason than to see where they might end up. And where else did he really have to go besides back into the sanitarium?

"Do you prefer your boiled eggs with pepper or salt?" Rascal inquired of Alvin. "I ask this because I've become quite fond of pepper recently, much more so than when I was younger. I just used to detest it, while Auntie would sprinkle it on practically everything she served, even pie and puddings. One of her more despicable habits."

"I hate boiled eggs," said Alvin, stepping over to the pump. His hands were as dusty as his shoes. If it weren't for Rose, he might have stripped down and jumped into the trough himself. All the driving they'd done the past two days had made him feel smutty as hell. No doubt he stunk pretty badly, too. He drew water from the pump and splashed it onto his bare arms and face, ladling water onto the back of his neck and letting it run down his shirt. That felt good. Rascal headed for the barn while Alvin finished washing off. Indoors, Chester's voice carried across the farmhouse as he and Rose walked in one room and out another discussing supper. Hoping to avoid being dragged into the debate, Alvin followed Rascal into the barn. Chester had told them to sleep in the stalls in order to keep an eye on the Packard after dark. The dwarf had quickly made a bed of moldy straw and left Alvin wondering whether sleeping in the hayloft violated Chester's instructions. All the livestock were long since gone, and dried rat dung littered the floor. Wasn't there any room at the farmhouse?

Alvin called for Rascal. When he didn't hear back, the farm boy went looking for him out behind the barn where the fence was broken down. It had been some time since a plow had entered the field and the grass had grown tall. Maybe a dozen yards beyond the rail fence, the tips of the grass rustled, indicating where Rascal had gone tramping about. Sparrows sailed by overhead, darting high and low. Insects buzzed in the grass. Rascal giggled. Alvin lay down and closed his eyes and listened to the insects and the birds and the dwarf. When he and Frenchy were kids, they were always running out into the cornrows at twilight and playing hider-seeker with big sticks, which they used to slap the stalks and taunt each other. After dark, they'd huddle together with a kerosene lantern and dig for fishing worms in the black loam.

Alvin heard the grass rustle nearby. The dwarf sat down next to his shoulder and asked, "When's supper? I'm famished."

"I hope soon. I'm hungry as a horse."

A door slammed shut back at the farmhouse.

Rascal sighed. "I wish I were a farmer. I love animals."

"You love spreading manure, too?"

"If need be. I'm not afraid of work."

Alvin rolled onto his shoulder and spat in the grass. "You think you know what farm life's all about, but you're just a dumbbell. There ain't nothing swell about it at all, and if you grew up on a farm like I did, you'd hate it like the dickens, and that's a fact."

"I doubt that very much," the dwarf replied. "One man's cross is another man's lintel. You ought to try locking yourself in a closet for a couple of weeks if you don't think that's so. See how that suits your fancy."

"Well, I'd rather live underneath that ugly old house of yours for twenty years than spend another day shoveling chicken shit."

Rascal plucked a stem of grass and stuck it in his mouth to chew on. "When I was young, I had a chicken named Evelyn. Auntie sewed her a dress to wear when she went outdoors. I made her a bonnet with a red bow. She'd fetch buttons and thimbles all day long if you coated them with maple syrup or peppermint."

"A chicken?"

"Yes."

"Fetching like a dog?"

"Yes."

"I don't believe you."

"Well, it's true. She was the cutest thing you ever saw, all fancied up like a society lady out for a stroll. I'd hoped to have her taken to a taxidermist when she died, but that ugly dog from next door, Mr. Bowser, cornered Evelyn under the porch and chewed her up so badly we couldn't find enough of her to stitch together. It was very sad."

Alvin looked the dwarf straight in the eye, astonished at his story-telling audacity. "You are the goddamnedest liar."

"I am not!"

"You are so!"

Chester called out across the grassy fields. Alvin picked himself up and headed for the farmhouse. He found Chester standing by the water pump, ladling water into his hands which he used to slick his hair back just as Rascal had done. He was dressed handsomely for town: blue jacket and trousers, a new felt hat. His shoes looked newly polished and spit-shined. Rose sat on the raised windowsill, her legs hanging down, bare feet swinging above the dirt. All she wore was a white silk envelope chemise. Her hair was damp and stringy with sweat, her blue eyes dark and hollow.

"I've got some business to put over in town for a few hours," said Chester, eyeing the young farm boy. "I'll be back later on. Rose'll fix some supper for you and the midget if you like. She's a swell cook."

"I'd rather go with you into town, if that's all right."

"Well, it isn't. You're staying here until I get back."

"There ain't nothing to do."

Chester worked the pump once more, drew a handkerchief from his back pocket, and dried his hands. He told Alvin, "Another hour or so, the sun'll be down. Nobody's supposed to know we're staying here, so keep the lights out. Don't go running around, either. If someone sees you, they're likely to come give us a once-over. I won't be gone too long, so be a sport and keep your eyes peeled. Get some sleep, too. We'll be driving out of here at dawn." Chester lowered his voice. "Keep an eye on this birdie for me, will you? She'll do anything you tell her to do, just make sure she doesn't try to go anywhere until I get back." He looked over at her, still sitting motionless on the windowsill, her brown curls fluttering in the breeze. "She'll be coming with us tomorrow."

Rose smiled.

Alvin gave her a small wave.

Chester walked over to the window, kissed Rose once on the mouth, ran his hand through her hair, then walked over to the Packard and climbed in. As the engine started up, Alvin saw Rascal standing by the barn door, nearly invisible in the shadow. The tan Packard rolled out from behind the farmhouse and down the dirt road leading to the highway. Chester beeped the horn twice as he turned in the direction of Harrison.

They sat in the kitchen, watching Rose fry up the eggs and potatoes on an old wood-burning stove. Outdoors, the sundown sky cast burnt shadows all across the dusty yard. Rascal had removed a stuffed pillow from the front room sofa and used it to raise the level of his seat at the table. Alvin played with the tarnished silverware Rose had dug out of her uncle's boxes in the cellar. He also had his eye on Rose in her white chemise. Something inside him stirred when he studied the curves of her body and the milky-white skin of her neck and shoulders. Her dark hair was long and curly, fussy from her afternoon under the sheets with Chester. She had a musky odor, too, not entirely unpleasant. When she looked at him, he could hardly breathe. Maybe he loved her. Back at the restaurant when they were all hungry and tired from traveling, Alvin wondered why Chester had invited her out. Now, alone with her in the kitchen, he knew clear as a bell that if he had the guts Chester had, he would date her up himself. If he had the guts.

"I can still scramble 'em if you'd prefer," Rose said, turning from the stove. Her face was sweaty from the heat and it made her even prettier. "You just tell me what you like."

"If they're not boiled, I don't care how you fix them," replied Rascal, rubbing one eye.

"Can't boil an egg without a pot," Rose said. "You didn't see one out in the barn, did you?"

"No, I didn't."

"Then, there you go. No boiled eggs."

"Fried eggs are swell, too," said Alvin, feeling like a hick all of a sudden. "If I was cooking, that's how I'd fix them." Why couldn't he spit out a quick word or two to catch her eye? A fellow can't expect much if he won't deliver nothing. Frenchy always told him that and he was right.

Soon enough, Rose slid the fried eggs and potatoes onto three plates and sat down at the table with Alvin and Rascal.

"Shall we say grace?" the dwarf asked.

Rose looked over at Alvin who shrugged, wholly ignorant of the topic. She told the dwarf, "Go on, if you like. I don't trust God. He don't listen to me much."

"All right." The dwarf bowed his head. "O merciful Father who hath turned our dearth and scarcity into plenty, we give Thee humble thanks for this Thy special bounty, beseeching Thee to continue Thy loving kindness unto us, to Thy glory and our comfort, through Jesus Christ our Lord. Amen."

His stomach grumbling, Alvin picked up his fork. "Let's eat."

"You said it," added Rose.

"Is there anything to drink?" the dwarf asked Rose, as he dug into the fried potatoes.

"Icebox's dry as a bone, but there's water in the well."

"Are there any glasses?"

"Not anymore," replied Rose. "Just some tin cups in the cabinet back there." She motioned toward the pantry.

The dwarf shoved his chair back from the table.

"Bring me one, too," Alvin said, his mouth drier than a hole in the ground.

"If I get you a cup, will you pump the water?" asked Rascal. "I have an awful pain in my shoulder."

"Nope, I ain't that thirsty." Why the hell should he do all the work? Chester wasn't here.

"Thank you very much."

Rascal glared at Alvin and headed for the pantry. After a few minutes of rummaging around, he came out with a tin cup and crossed through the kitchen and out the back door. The screen slammed shut behind him. Alvin listened to him trotting across the yard to the trough pump. It was dark out now. Crickets sang in the bushes by the rear porch. The pump creaked as Rascal drew water from the well. Alvin stuck a forkful of eggs into his mouth and tried his best not to stare at Rose's titties. Her knife scratched the plate as she scooped some eggs onto her fork. While the dwarf worked the pump over and over, the farm boy felt his passion coming back again.

"You come out here very often?" he asked Rose.

"Only when I need a fellow."

She said this without changing expression, still shoving eggs and potato into her mouth. It stabbed at Alvin's heart. His face flushed and his own appetite faded.

"You got a girl back home?" Rose asked, setting her fork down for a moment.

Alvin swallowed a chunk of fried potato and shook his head. The truth embarrassed him. "None in particular. How come you ask?"

"My daddy thinks I'm a whore."

He stopped chewing. "Is that so?"

She leaned close, her eyes sparkling. "Do you think I'm a whore?"

What was he supposed to say? He shrugged. "How should I know?"

"When we met back in my daddy's restaurant, and you first saw me, did you think to yourself, 'She sure looks like a whore'?"

Alvin felt his face redden deeper. Rose's attention was fixed hard on him. He was sure he smelled Chester's gin on her breath. "I thought you were pretty swell-looking."

"Are you jealous of Calvin?"

"Huh?"

The pump stopped outdoors and the dwarf's footsteps scurried back through the dirt toward the house. Rose said, "Me lying down with him, instead of with you? Are you jealous?"

Alvin shrugged. "Sort of, I guess." Sure, he was jealous as hell, but what could he do about it? He didn't hardly smile at her in town. Who knows what she thought of him back there?

"Don't be," she said. "It ain't account of you that I'm with him. It's 'cause of my daddy. He's scared of Calvin. The second he laid eyes on him, he told me to stay away from him."

Rose put down her fork and napkin.

"Do you love him?" Alvin asked, afraid of her reply. If she said yes, he'd likely throw up.

"Who?"

"Calvin."

"Of course not. I don't lie down with fellows I'm in love with. I don't flirt with them, neither, though I have to say I'd rather be thought of as a whore than a flirt. But this's got nothing to do with love. No girl with half a brain and an ounce of self-respect would consider it."

"I ain't following you."

"That's 'cause you're not a girl, and you don't know my daddy, neither."

The back door opened and Rascal came inside with his tin cup in one hand and a small brown feather in the other. Quietly, he sat down at the table, took a drink from the cup, laid the feather on the side of his plate, and began eating once again. Alvin watched how the dwarf held his fork funny, twisted nearly backward in his hand, making him bring food to his mouth in a strange looping motion. The farm boy wondered who taught him that.

Rose got up from the table and went to the back door. She opened it and tossed her leftover eggs and potatoes out into the yard. "My cooking stinks."

Then she laid her empty plate on the counter and walked out of the kitchen. Rascal continued eating. Alvin listened for Rose. She had gone into the bedroom. The bedsprings squeaked as she plunked herself down onto the mattress. Alvin finished his own food and got up, setting his plate on the counter next to Rose's. The dwarf had his head down, methodically shoveling egg and potato into his mouth, one forkful after another. Alvin went outdoors to relieve himself.

A cool wind had come up in the past hour, blowing dirty feathers off a mud hen carcass all over the yard. A dozen or so floated in the water trough. A sweet hay smell filled the evening air. The farm boy walked across the yard to the edge of the field by the barn and unfastened his pants. He was feeling a little better. The summer grass rustled and swayed before him as he pissed into the dirt and stared out across the prairie. Farrington was not so flat, so vast and empty. Here in Kansas, the wind played through the grass like the fingers of God. In the daylight, every contour of the prairie justified property lines divided according to high ground and low. Sunlight made visible the particulars of slope and expanse. Darkness erased them, creating an endless flatland beneath the tips of the tall prairie grass. The wind in Alvin's face blew across a hundred miles of fields.

The back door banged in the wind. Alvin finished pissing and buttoned up. Rascal appeared in the doorframe, staring off into the dark. A moment later, the light went out in the kitchen. Rose had assured Chester that the farm still had electricity, but the only room with working electric lights was the kitchen. All the others required kerosene lamps after sundown. A yellow glow behind the window shade in the main bedroom indicated that Rose had lighted hers already. A small shadow moved in front of the shade, the dwarf visiting her for conversation. Rather than going back indoors, Alvin decided to eavesdrop at the window, hoping he'd overhear some conversation concerning himself. Nobody ever spoke honestly in the presence of the person they were discussing. When Alvin was a boy, Granny Chamberlain had told him that any fly on the wall hears more truth spoken in half a minute than any man in his lifetime. She said this with the conviction of a woman who had held secrets deep in her heart for more years than her family had been alive.

He crouched beneath Rose's window. The dwarf was speaking, his hushed voice barely carrying past the glass. Alvin peeked over the windowsill and saw Rascal seated on the bed beside Rose, holding her hand in his. Alvin sank back down again, astonished. Was Rose allowing herself to be wooed by the dwarf? Maybe that silver tongue of his made up for the peculiarities of his appearance. Rose giggled loudly. Rascal's voice became slightly louder, enthusiastic, chirping like a bird. It was too much for Alvin to bear outdoors, so he crawled along the side of the house to the kitchen door and slipped inside.

With the lights out in the kitchen, he had a difficult time negotiating his way from the back door to the hallway dividing the bedroom from the front of the house. Once there, however, the lamp Rose had lighted guided him in her direction. The door was partway open. He tiptoed up to it and craned his neck around the edge to have a look inside. She and the dwarf were still sitting side by side in the middle of the bed, her hand in his, both smiling. Chester's hipflask was on the nightstand.

"I don't believe a word you're saying," Rose giggled. "It's a lie, all a lie!"

"Palmistry is one of the ancient sciences. I learned it from my Uncle Augustus who was taught by a lovely Egyptian woman at Alexandria where it's been practiced for thousands of years. I've been fascinated by mysteries of the occult since I was a child. I intend to see the famous oracle at Delphi one day before I die."

"My daddy got his fortune read once by a gypsy who told him he'd die a rich man. He says it's all hokum."

Rascal ran the tip of his forefinger down the middle of her palm and across to the base of her thumb. "Belief, like beauty," the dwarf replied, in a solemn voice, "exists in the eye of the beholder. Truth, on the other hand, is unwavering and eternal. Your own flesh reveals it. Doubt not that which you know to be true."

Then Rascal giggled, too.

The bedroom stunk of liquor and sweat.

Alvin walked in. A flickering yellow light from the single kerosene lamp danced lazily on the bare walls. The portable Victrola sat mute on a wooden chest by the footboard. Rose and the dwarf ignored Alvin completely. He cleared his throat to get their attention, but Rascal continued to chatter on as he stroked the palm of Rose's left hand with his forefinger, tracing a circuitous pattern between her thumb and little finger.

" … and so your children from this marriage will be lost in a ballooning accident in the Congo only to be captured by a tribe of pygmies and ransomed for a herd of goats to a family of Quakers and returned a year later to America where they'll become doctors, healing the poor and destitute of Philadelphia."

Rose laughed and withdrew her hand from Rascal's. She fell back onto the pillow behind her head. She winked at Alvin. "Will they remember their dear old mother every Christmas?"

"No," replied the dwarf. "In fact, the ballooning accident will cause a rare form of amnesia that destroys all memory of their former lives. It's very tragic."

"Are you sure?"

Rascal nodded. "I'm sorry."

"Then I'll need to have more children."

"And so you shall," said the dwarf, a moony smile on his face.

Rose jumped up off the bed. "Oh, goody!"

She took the hipflask and had a sip, then wiped her mouth with the back of her hand. She crawled back across the bed to open the window on the yard and stuck her head out for a look. "I think it might rain tonight. I hope you'll be all right in the barn. My uncle had trouble with the roof leaking. It can get awfully wet and cold out there."

"Maybe we ought to stay in here," said Alvin, looking at himself in the silvered mirror over the dresser. "We could throw down some blankets and sleep on the floor."

Her eyes looking boozy now, Rose replied, "I don't guess Calvin'd appreciate that much company tonight."

"Well, that's fine," said Rascal. "Actually, I prefer the outdoors. There's nothing like fresh air, I always say."

"It's freezing in the barn," said Alvin, sitting down on the bed next to Rascal. "Probably catch cold out there if we don't get our toes chewed off first by the rats."

The dwarf stiffened. "Rats?"

"There's always rats in an old barn, crawling around in the hay. I saw one this afternoon, in fact."

Rose twisted her head back toward the dwarf. "This boy's just pulling your leg. Ain't no rats in my uncle's barn."

"You calling me a liar?" said Alvin. Of course, he hadn't really seen a rat, but then again who was to say there weren't any hiding in the straw? Frenchy was always finding rats up in Uncle Henry's hayloft. He'd kill them, and cut off their tails for fish bait. Frenchy said, "*The fish ain't been born who can tell the difference between a rat's tail and a fat worm flopping off a hook.*" And he was right, too, because they caught a lot of catfish using rat tails.

"Although I am not afraid of rats," said the dwarf, "it is a well-known fact that they carried the Black Plague throughout Europe in the Middle Ages and were nearly responsible for the destruction of our entire species. They're very dirty creatures. I wouldn't care to be bitten by one while I'm sleeping. Rabies, I hear, is a dreadful disease."

"It kills you in a day or so," Alvin said. "You choke to death from foaming out of your own mouth, like a sick dog."

"There ain't no rats in the barn!" Rose repeated. "I swear I'd sleep out there with you myself if it wasn't for Calvin. And I wouldn't be scared at all, so don't you be."

She sat down on the bed, sipped again from Chester's flask, and curled up with her back against the headboard. Rascal gently slid over beside her and took her right hand and traced his forefinger once more across the middle of her palm. Feeling a little queasy, Alvin got up off the bed and went to the open window, prepared to lean outside and upchuck if necessary. His forehead felt slightly feverish and he guessed another sweat was coming on. Turning about, he found Rose staring at him while the dwarf stroked her palm. What kind of girl was she? Could he yet kiss her?

"Where're y'all headed from here?" she asked.

Alvin shrugged. "Maybe the Dakotas, California. Who knows?"

"You go where Calvin tells you to go, don't you?"

"Only when there's money involved."

"Oh yeah?" Her eyebrows arched in surprise at his answer. "What made you decide to stop in Harrison?"

He felt insulted again. "Why are you such a busybody? Who told you to come out here and lie around in this bed all afternoon, huh? Something tells me you take orders pretty damn well yourself."

Rose grinned. "Well, of course I do, sweetie pie. Been doing it my whole life. Daddy tells me to clean out my closet and throw away my old dolls, I go do it. He tells me to shine his shoes and wash his shorts, I do it. He tells me to sit in his lap and sing 'Good-bye Liza Jane,' I sit there and sing till he tells me to stop. Nobody in Kansas takes orders better than Rosa Jean Harper."

"Aw, quit your sniveling," said Alvin, shaking his head. His opinion of her was diminishing by the minute. "I ain't never got a break from my daddy, neither, but it don't bust me up none."

"Did he tan you?" Rose asked, after sipping again from the hipflask.

" 'Course he did. What of it?"

"My daddy calls me his little princess whenever he's squiffy."

"Your lifeline indicates royalty in a previous lifetime," said Rascal, taking her free hand once again. "Perhaps the servitude you provide in this life offers atonement for sins of indulgence committed in another."

"Probably," said Rose. "Some days, I feel awful bossy. It's just that I can't seem to find anyone to boss around in Harrison, is all."

"I'll be your slave," offered Rascal. "Command me!"

"All right," said Alvin, his fever rising now, "choke it. She knows you ain't on the level." He walked over to look in the closet. Maybe there was something he could steal.

"Envy doesn't become you," replied the dwarf, putting his back to the farm boy.

"I told you both, it's Calvin my daddy don't trust," Rose said, re-adjusting the pillow at her back. "Says he's a shady character. But I think he's just more polished than people around here, and I like that. Makes me feel polished, too. Like a real lady. My daddy'd like his daughter on a leash that's just long enough to wait on his customers and get the cleaning done upstairs and down. He's scared of somebody like Calvin coming along and sneaking off with his little girl."

"Where's your momma?" Alvin asked, kicking over a stack of empty hat boxes.

"She run off with a shoe salesman when I was four. Daddy called her every name in the book. Of course, I say if it makes him feel better to think of her as a whore, so be it, but I guess he's still plenty sad about her. Every one of us got feelings, and when you get treated bad, it hurts, no matter how much you go around telling people it don't."

The dwarf said to Rose, "Did you know that once you were a handmaiden to Cleopatra, serving her in a slave barge on the Nile after being led into captivity from Babylon the Great where you had been a queen?" His eyes were wide as saucers. "It's truly amazing to chart your palm. An honor, if I do say so myself."

"Calvin wants to bring me with him when y'all go tomorrow," said Rose, closing the hipflask. "He knows my daddy's giving me hell. Said if I go with you, I'll eat steak every night of the week. You think I ought to believe him?"

Alvin was beginning to feel sick and stupid. Rose and the dwarf talking like they were stuck on each other didn't seem right, like they were lying about things and spreading gossip. Aunt Hattie told him once that talking behind people's backs was like whispering secrets in the devil's ear.

"Is Calvin Coolidge III a gentleman, in your opinion?" asked the dwarf, releasing Rose's hand. "Is he honorable?"

"Well, he kissed my hand before lying down here next to me. He even asked permission to take his clothes off. I liked that. It shows class."

"A man well-bred is rarely ill-led," said Rascal.

"Pardon me?"

"Don't pay him no mind," said Alvin, frowning at the dwarf. He went over to the Victrola and spun the record. "He's just spouting off."

Rose shrugged. "Well, I just wish my daddy understood that a girl can't spend her whole life washing floors and sewing on buttons." She straightened up. "Do either of you fellows know how to dance?"

Alvin wandered back over to the window for some fresh air. "Dancing's for sissies," he said, sticking his head outside. The stuffy room made him feel faint. He needed to lie down.

"I had lessons when I was six," said Rascal. "Miss Angelina taught me all sorts of fancy steps. I was her star pupil. I believe I even won an award once."

"I can do a swell Charleston," said Rose. "Watch!" She hopped off the bed and began dancing furiously in the middle of the room. In mid-step, her stocking feet slipped on the throw rug and she tumbled forward, landing on her face and slamming her chin hard on the wood floor. "Oww!"

She rolled over, bleeding from a gash on the jawline. "Goddammit!"

Rascal slid down beside her and cupped his hand over the wound. Alvin remained at the window, more amused than worried by her injury. The dwarf reached back and dragged a corner of the sheet off the bed to use as a compress against Rose's bleeding chin. "Hold it here."

After placing Rose's hand on the sheet covering the cut, Rascal dashed out of the bedroom. His tiny footsteps pattered through the house into the kitchen. The screen door swung open and closed with a bang. Alvin shifted his position to catch sight of the dwarf at the pump, working it quickly, a long white rag wadded up beneath the spout. Water gushed out onto the rag, soaking both it and Rascal. The dwarf stopped pumping and ran back toward the house. Then the door opened and shut with another bang and a moment later the dwarf burst into the room, dripping water all over the floor.

"Here," he said, removing the sheet from Rose's chin and replacing it with the wet rag. The girl moaned in pain. Rascal said, "We have to get you cleaned up. Infection is an ugly consideration with any injury. I once got lockjaw from a rusty nail in my closet and couldn't speak for a month."

"Who was sorry about that?" asked Alvin, feeling nasty now.

"It hurts," Rose moaned, as the dwarf swabbed the wound and the skin surrounding it. "Oww!"

"Be brave," Rascal said, wiping off the blood that had trickled down her neck. "Is there any alcohol in the house?"

"Of course not," Rose answered. "Kansas's as dry as Arabia these days."

"No hootch in the cellar?" asked Alvin. "You sure about that?"

"My uncle never touched liquor in his life. He didn't hold with drinking. He was a good Christian gentleman until the day he died."

"A regular flat tire, huh?" Alvin said, the smirk on his face growing minute by minute. Realizing there wasn't a chance in hell of bedding down with her allowed him to say whatever he felt. He liked that. Speaking his true thoughts for once made him giddy. Love was for the birds.

"Liquor leads men to ruin," said Rascal, fashioning Rose a bandage wrap from the rag. "It lies at the heart of all our foibles."

"Women, too," replied Alvin, "but at least the bottle won't chew your ears off."

Rose said, "My uncle maintained that liquor was evil and he'd rather burn in hellfire than allow even a drop of the contentious fluid to touch his lips."

"Good for him," said Alvin. He watched Rascal wrap the bandage around Rose's jaw from ear to ear and pull it tight. Maybe he ought to choke her next.

"Oww!"

The dwarf tied it with a bow at the back of her head. "I'm sorry."

"I feel stupid," said Rose. She stood up and checked herself in the mirror. "It looks like my jaw's wrapped for a toothache."

"Vanity must always follow utility in the world of medicine," the dwarf explained. "Have you a needle and thread handy? We ought to properly close that wound. Otherwise, you'll have a scar for a souvenir."

"No, thanks," said Rose. She took a step back from Rascal and covered her chin with the palm of one hand. "I don't mind scars. I got plenty of them already. One more won't spoil my beauty."

"Of course not," said the dwarf, and he gave her arm a light pat.

"I'm going to bed," Alvin said, sliding off the window frame. "This is just too damned much excitement for one day."

"Calvin'll be back soon," said Rose. "Don't you want to sit up a while?"

"What for?"

"I'm staying," said Rascal. "Rose says I can hide under her bed and listen to the fireworks so long as I keep quiet."

"Calvin'll break your neck."

"He won't know I'm here. I won't make a sound. I can play dead better than a dog if I have to. Ask Auntie. She called the funeral parlor one afternoon when I pretended to have a stroke. I held my breath for three minutes and made my face turn blue. She got so scared, I thought she'd have a stroke of her own."

Looking at Rose, Alvin said, "Well, then maybe I'll join you under the bed and we'll both spy on Calvin. I can keep pretty quiet myself."

"Nobody's hiding under my bed," Rose said. "I'd never allow it. Privacy's important to a girl. Being men, you can't understand that because y'all got to boast about what you do and who you done it to. We girls got too much dignity to go around sharing our most intimate, private activities with the whole world."

"You'll get no argument from me," said Rascal. "I wouldn't think of intruding on your privacy."

"You little two-faced Judas!" Alvin growled. "Why, you just said you were going to hide under the bed and listen to everything she did."

"Only if I were invited to do so," replied the dwarf, showing Rose his broadest smile, "and seeing as I'm not," he got to his feet, "I'll be on my way to the barn." He took Rose's hand and planted a kiss on the knuckle of her wedding finger. "I thank you for the opportunity of reading your fortune. Good night."

Then he walked out of the bedroom.

Rose crawled up onto the bed and stretched her legs. Alvin heard the kitchen door open and close again. He looked over at Rose. She smiled. "Nighty-night."

He nodded.

She whispered, "Don't tell him I said so, but I think your pal's the cutest little fellow I ever saw. If he were another foot taller, I'd bed down with him in a minute."

Stopping at the water trough to wash his face, Alvin worked the pump, studying the horizon for headlights. Chester had been gone quite a while now. Whatever business he had was keeping him longer than Alvin had expected. Of course, he'd probably eaten supper in Harrison, maybe steak and potatoes, pie for dessert, a beer in the basement of a scratch house downtown, afterward. Why the hell had he gone alone?

Alvin stopped pumping and wiped his hands dry on the tails of his shirt. A wind swept out across the fields of grass and chilled the skin on the back of his neck. He felt a peculiar vibration in his bones, but it wasn't fever. Kansas spooked him. The wind carried a smell with it, musty, dry, dead. A spook's breath, stale and dirty. Older than dirt itself. Without a doubt, Alvin believed Kansas was populated by ghosts and haunted like a vast grassy cemetery. He was scared that if he stayed too long, somehow he'd become fertilizer for the same grasses that whispered to him now in the windy darkness.

The farm boy walked to the barn. He heard Rascal singing up in the hayloft. The dwarf loved music, although he could barely carry a tune. The top of his head bobbed just above a bale of hay where he danced in time to his own song.

I found a horseshoe, I found a horseshoe.
I picked it up and nailed it on the door;
And it was rusty and full of nail holes,
Good luck 'twill bring to you forevermore.

It was an old railroad song Uncle Harlow used to sing whenever he came back from the depot. Rascal had mangled the tune such that he'd probably helped chase out the spooks. Alvin headed for the ladder to the loft. If not for the lamp hung there, the interior of the barn would have been black as pitch. The dwarf was on his hands and knees, digging into a moldy old bale of hay with a rusty screwdriver.

"What're you doing there?" Alvin asked, looking around. The wood at the dwarf's feet was crisscrossed in scratches made by the screwdriver he was holding.

"Hunting."

"What for?"

"Rats." Rascal jabbed at the bale of hay, stabbing randomly here and there. "They make nests in the hay. I have to flush them out and kick them in the head." The dwarf stood up over the bale and jabbed furiously down into the top of it, zigzagging his attack from one end to the other. His tiny hand was a blur above the hay.

"Get any of 'em yet?" the farm boy asked. He had never heard of anyone hunting rats with a screwdriver. Uncle Henry stuck them with his pitchfork and Frenchy shot one with a pistol after it chewed up his boot. Best was to smoke them out and club them when they ran for it.

"I'd appreciate some help," said Rascal, jabbing at the sides of the bale now. Sweat dripped off his forehead. "After all, they'll bite you, too."

"There ain't no rats in here."

The dwarf quit chopping at the hay. He twisted the screwdriver in his fist and looked up at Alvin. "You lied?"

"Sure I did."

The dwarf sat back against the bale. "Why did you lie?"

Alvin shrugged. "I didn't care none for how you were whooping it up with Rose, telling those stories and getting her going. It made us both look like dumbbells."

"The fool and the wise man often reflect a common image."

"Huh?"

"Envy doesn't become you," said the dwarf, poking the screwdriver into the bale of hay. "Rose appreciated our attention. She's sad and lonely. We made her smile."

"She's just joking us, is all. I didn't care for that, neither."

"Joy has its own rainbow. I'm satisfied that, however we did it, to-night was quite special for her."

"Says you."

"I do."

"I'm going to bed," the farm boy said, with a yawn. He was sick of jawing over that girl.

"You're not planning to wait up for Chester? I'll bet he has a story of his own to tell. Do you know why he went back into town?"

"No, do you?"

"Yes, but I'll wait for him to tell you all about it. I'm sure it was very exciting."

"What if he don't come back here at all? What if he throws us over and goes off by hisself?"

"We'll buy a train ticket to Wichita."

Now that was a spooky thought. A shiver ran through Alvin's heart. "I ain't never been there before. What would we do?"

"I'm sure we could hire a decent flat in a roominghouse and find ourselves work with the cattle trade, no trouble at all. Uncle Augustus brought me out to the Dakotas one summer when I was a boy and I learned all about working on a ranch."

"Sure you did."

"Well, it's the truth."

"You think Chester robbed the bank?" By now, of course, the farm boy knew his boss was some sort of gangster, because of the associa-tions he seemed to have wherever they went. Alvin just wasn't sure what all Chester did at night while they were sleeping.

"Of course not. There's much more profit today in booze-traffic. Every town in this great republic of ours has its own speakeasy. Who do you think keeps them stocked with demon rum?"

"I never seen a drunkard or a saloon downtown this morning."

"Did you notice the soda fountains and drugstores?"

"What of it?"

"Well, they're selling more than soda pop these days. Why, I'd wa-ger you'll find overnight liquor in milk bottles on half the stoops in

Kansas tomorrow morning."

Alvin mulled that over. Cousin Frenchy kept quart bottles of whiskey hidden in Uncle Roy's root cellar and had a drink habit he couldn't crack. Uncle Cy believed half the population of Farrington was misusing liquor. "You think Chester's a rumrunner?"

The dwarf replied, "He's no snooper."

"Well, I ain't for squealing on nobody, neither, but I'll bet you there's plenty of homebrew outfits in these parts. I seen empty gallon jugs packed in straw and sodden boxes in that kitchen cellar. I smelled kerosene and molasses down there, too. Don't tell me that uncle of hers wasn't an old soak."

"Auntie imbibed Coca Cordials while she was sending dollar bills through the mail to the Reverend Dr. Wilson in support of National Prohibition, and seeing a revenue officer from Peoria, too."

"Well, my Aunt Clara makes cider with a kick, but it ain't kitchen brew."

"Laws are made for men," said the dwarf, "not men for the law. Who can be made moral by legislation? Persecution causes a crime to spread. *This ought ye to have done, and not to leave the other undone.* I'm sure there are temperate uses of alcoholic drink, but until they're commonly understood, gangsters like Chester are certain to knock heads with the Volsteadites, leaving the rest of us caught in the middle."

"Well, I ain't interested in getting pinched over some stall to sell a few bottles of hootch."

Rascal got up and walked to the ladder. He put the screwdriver aside and went backwards down the first few rungs. Stopping halfway to the barn floor, the dwarf said, "These are dangerous times, my friend. Very dangerous. We must keep our wits about us, if we wish to survive."

Alvin got up, too, and followed the dwarf to the ladder. "What's that supposed to mean?"

"The heart of the adventurer is sly," Rascal said, as he descended to the floor of the barn. Stepping away from the ladder, he looked back up at Alvin. "Even in his dreams, he is alert."

Rascal disappeared into one of the stalls directly beneath the hayloft.

Alvin sat down on the ledge beside the ladder. He felt drowsy and ill. Below him, the dwarf shuffled about in the dark, fixing his bed for the night. After a few minutes, Alvin climbed down the ladder and looked in on the dwarf. He was hard to see, buried in the straw with only the bald top of his head visible in the yellow lamplight. With each breath, little puffs of dust blew free from his mouth. Alvin noticed the light in Rose's bedroom was extinguished. She, too, had given up on Chester, and had gone to sleep. The farm boy took the lantern off the ladder and walked to the back of the barn where he had chosen his own stall. He hung the lamp on a post nail. The night wind hissed in the long dry grass. Trying to ignore the fever chill in his bones, Alvin spread his bedroll out over the straw and lay down on his back. If anyone was worrying about him at home tonight, he was sorry, but they'd intended to send him back to the sanitarium, and that was a lot meaner than him running off. Like his own daddy used to say, *"A man finds his own road one day and starts walking. He don't argue an east fork into a west one, and he don't set hisself facing backwards, neither."*

After ten minutes or so of looking for bats in the upper rafters of the barn, Alvin fell asleep. *Out on the Mississippi with Frenchy, fly casting into a swift green current, sunlight on the water, catfish tapping at the underside of the skiff, inviting themselves to get caught and fried up for supper. Frenchy had trotlines baited with rat tails. The skiff had a hole in it, leaking water in at Alvin's feet. Baling with his right shoe wasn't working, so he removed his left and used that, too. A catfish as big as a pig flew into the boat, landing in Alvin's lap, knocking him over. The skiff capsized. Swimming underwater, Alvin found himself caught in Frenchy's trotlines. Freeing himself just before drowning, he rose to the surface. The river was black. Stars flickered overhead while up-stream, fireworks exploded in the night sky above the Illiniwek Bridge where a crowd had gathered to witness another suicide like Mable Stephenson, jilted by her college geography teacher, who did her lover's leap at high noon on Christmas Day in front of a hundred people, landing headfirst on a frozen log and breaking her neck. Alvin swam in that direction. All along the shoreline, giggling voices rang in the bushes. Rose was atop the bridge, her arms spread wide, the hem of her white chemise blowing wildly in the wind. As Alvin swam close, she leaped away from the bridge and* something blunt struck Alvin between the eyes, waking him, and a voice he didn't recognize, ordered, "Get up, you little sonofabitch!"

Alvin felt cold steel pressed to his forehead and opened his eyes. A dark figure stood over him. A rifle barrel extended from Alvin's forehead to the hands of the man standing in front of him. "Nobody robs Charlie Harper, you little double-crossing sonofabitch!"

"Huh?"

"You think I couldn'ta guessed who done it?"

The barrel dug into the skin between Alvin's eyes, hurting more now that he was waking up.

The man yelled, "ROSA JEAN!"

Off to Alvin's left across the barn, a small shadow darted through the railing of the last stall and slipped outdoors.

"Get up," said Harper, nudging Alvin in the butt with the toe of his boot. He pulled the old Sharp's rifle back a few inches from Alvin's face. "ROSA JEAN!"

The farm boy climbed to his feet as slowly as possible while searching the barn for something to use as a club if the opportunity to fight presented itself. His head spun with vertigo. A cough rattled out of his chest. With the lamp extinguished, most of the barn was black.

"ROSA JEAN!" Harper poked Alvin in the ribs with the rifle, directing him out the barn door toward the farmhouse. "Get on out there, and don't try nothing, you little shit-heel!"

They walked out of the barn in tandem, connected by the length of rifle. A cold wind swirled in the yard, sweeping dust about and scattering stems of dried grass from the empty fields beyond.

"ROSA JEAN!"

The back screen door banged open and shut in the wind. Rose's bedroom window was raised an inch or so, the drapes closed. Nearing the trough, Alvin wondered if she was watching.

Charlie Harper prodded Alvin in the back with the rifle and shouted again. "ROSA JEAN!" Water dripped from the pump. The kitchen door banged hard. Alvin took three more steps, and Harper called out, "ROSA JEAN!"

Then another voice, just off Alvin's right shoulder, said, "Stop right there."

Harper stopped, and the rifle barrel left Alvin's back.

Chester's voice spoke once again, "Go on, dad. Put that rifle down."

Alvin swiveled his head to see Chester, rising from a hiding place beside the trough. His .38 revolver was held at arm's length and pointed directly at Charlie Harper's head. Chester cocked the hammer back. "No cause for trouble now. Just do like I say."

The kitchen door flung open and Rose came out into the yard. Her hair blew wildly in the wind, her white chemise billowing up. Alvin's hands and feet felt cold. He studied Rose's face for indications of fear or surprise or anger, and saw none. He was terrified himself.

"They robbed us, Rosa Jean," said Harper, whose attention was not on Chester at all, but rather on his daughter. "They snuck in after closing and robbed us blind."

"I don't want to shoot you, old man, but I surely will if you don't set that rifle down."

"They're crooks, Rosa Jean. Scoundrels. They took every last cent in that safe."

Rose stood perfectly still, maybe thirty or forty feet from Alvin, teary-eyed in the wind and dust, staring past her father toward Chester who began slowly to circle behind the old man.

"They don't care nothing about people like us, Rosa Jean," said Harper. "They come here to hurt us, is all. They're nothing but goddamned liars and cheats."

"Come on, dad, put the rifle down," Chester said, his voice flat and nerveless. "Let's be friendly here. What do you say? No sense in getting hurt over a little misapprehension."

"Daddy," said Rose, walking now toward him, hair blowing across her face. "Please put the gun down."

"They're thieves, Rosa Jean. Don't trust them."

Chester had circled clear around Harper, standing just behind his right shoulder. Harper's rifle still pointed toward Alvin's back. Rose stopped fifteen feet from the water trough, her arms held out imploringly to her father. "Daddy, please!"

Out of the corner of his eye, Alvin caught a glimpse of Rascal standing motionless by the rear corner of the house, watching from the shadow of the eaves. Then he heard Harper release the hammer, and a moment later the barrel of the Sharp's rifle struck the dirt behind his feet.

"Goddamned sonsofbitches!" said the old man, and sunk backward to sit down on the trough. Rose walked forward another three steps, muttering something under her breath indistinguishable in the wind, and got close enough to her father to have her dress sprayed with blood an instant after Chester placed his pistol against the back of Harper's head and pulled the trigger.

The blast echo circled the yard and chased out across the fields. Charlie Harper's body lurched into the trough with a large splash. Stink of gunsmoke filled the dark.

Paralyzed with shock, Alvin found himself utterly transfixed by the sight of Charlie Harper bobbing in the black water. As Rose drew near, she whispered, "Daddy?" and leaned over the trough.

"Well, I guess that plan was a dud," said Chester, his gun still held out in the air where Harper's head had just been. "A fellow really ought to cut out boozing after work."

Dust stung Alvin's face, forcing him to look away from Rose and the water trough. He sought out the dwarf by the north side of the farmhouse and found that Rascal was gone. Chester jammed the pistol back into his waistband. He grabbed the handle of the pump and jerked it twice to draw fresh water from the well. As Chester ladled it into his cupped palms, sucking a drink, Rose grabbed up her father's rifle from the dirt beside the trough. Cocking the hammer, she swung the barrel around to Chester's direction, but he had already drawn his revolver again.

Alvin watched dumbfounded as Chester calmly took aim and shot Rose through the chest.

She fell away from the trough, landing flat on her back, a small black stain from the wound soaking the hole in the front of her chemise. Her eyes were wide open, staring up into the night sky. Her left foot twitched for a couple more seconds, then stopped altogether.

Another gunshot echo faded across the dark.

Chester stared at her a little while, revolver drawn and pointed, then shook his head, put the gun away again, and washed his hands clean under the pump spout. He rubbed them hard, scraping and scrubbing with his thumbs and fingertips.

Alvin had lost all feeling in his limbs.

The rising water floated Harper's body to the rim so that his hands appeared determined to try and grip the edges. A vile taste crept up into the back of Alvin's throat and he coughed harshly. Vertigo came and went. That section of Charlie Harper's face disintegrated by the exit wound remained underwater.

Chester let go of the pump handle before the trough could overflow. He took a handkerchief out of his breast pocket and used it to dry off his hands. Then he told Alvin, "She'd have killed us both. We're lucky I saw her."

Alvin stared at Rose, lying just below him. The dead held no particular fascination for him, having seen over the years his Uncle Otis, old Grandpa Chamberlain, his second-cousin Leroy, and a traveling salesman give up the ghost right before his eyes on the farm in Farrington. Funerals followed harvest celebrations as the most popularly attended ceremonies in the county. None of the casket dead resembled themselves. Faces all waxy and pale. Lips and brows painted. Eyes stitched shut. That was the difference. Here, Rose looked prettier in death's shadow than she had sitting on the bed indoors. It spooked Alvin. If he leaned over her, she'd be looking him right in the eye. The stain had quit, just a damp soiled patch on the fabric, requiring only a good scrubbing with soap and vinegar. Her eyes needed closing, though. Otherwise, she wouldn't get her reward. At every wake, Granny Chamberlain said, *God's sweet smile is too glorious to behold with white eyes revealed.*

As Alvin bent down to close Rose's eyes, Chester leaned forward and grabbed him by the wrist. "Don't touch her. Don't touch either of them. Just leave them where they are."

Then Chester walked off toward the back door, his blue suit jacket fluttering in the wind. Thoroughly terrified, Alvin looked once again for Rascal. The dwarf had been by the rear of the farmhouse, watching everything. Afterward, he had run off like a scared rabbit. Alvin went over to the rail fence for a look into the fields. It seemed even darker now than when Harper had led him out of the barn. Trees only a few dozen yards away were all but invisible, just big hazy shadows somewhere out beyond the fence. Alvin stopped breathing and listened to the wind hissing through the grass on the dark Kansas prairie.

The back door slammed shut and Chester came out into the yard, carrying the thirty-dollar Victrola under one arm and a flat piece of wood under the other, a narrow shelf from one of the white kitchen cabinets. He walked over to the trough and placed the wood upright against the pump. Then he took a pocketwatch out of his vest, checked the hour, and headed to the Packard, announcing that they had to go. Rascal walked out of the barn loaded up and ready to depart, his wool blanket in one hand, Alvin's bedroll in the other. He went only as far as the middle of the yard, where he stopped and waited for Alvin to pay his last respects at the trough. Back around the rear of the house, Chester started up the car.

Both bodies looked like genuine Farrington farm corpses now, dead as yesterday. Wind had partially covered Rose's hair and fingers in dust, and clouded her eyes. If she hadn't yet beheld the Lord, she surely would in the next hour or so. Alvin came around the trough and found himself facing the board Chester had laid up against the pump. It was a message scribbled in charcoal, intended for whoever found Rose and Charlie Harper. It read:

> We was attacked by a band of
> wild niggers. They killd this
> poor man and his little girl.
> Im chasin them to Missouri.
> Send help
>   Signed Calvin Coolidge

JUNE

BY EARLY SUMMER, Marie had taken a job as cashier at Delahaye's Restaurant in downtown Bellemont. She worked half a day from eight until two in the afternoon, which allowed her to share the expense of boarding at Maude's house on College Street. The children played all about the neighborhood with youngsters their own age and were happy to be out of doors. So far, nobody had been arrested for the ugly murder of Boy-Allen, a circumstance that troubled Marie and many other mothers across town. Detectives traveled from Houston and Dallas to help with the investigation, but left without solving the crime. The newspapers worried Marie with talk of further killings, then quit discussing the story entirely. A month passed and the fear engendered by Boy-Allen's death faded to rumor and gossip. Only mothers kept a suspicious eye on shadows after dark, Marie among them. This disconcerting journey into the South was trying enough, but to have a murder occur practically in her backyard so soon upon arrival was horrifying. At night with the children asleep beside her, Marie was haunted by the blackest thoughts: Henry drowning in the river or trampled under hoof, Cissie tumbling off a roof or disappearing somehow into the twilight like poor Boy-Allen. What parent lacks these fears? Her marriage troubled by her husband's inscrutable behavior, Marie's heart wrapped about her children and refused to let go.

Life went on.

Maude enjoyed the company of her club ladies three afternoons and one evening a week and did her laundry and housekeeping in peace. Rachel went to work at the insurance office and paraded out

in the evenings on CW's arm when he was in town, and with friends
when he wasn't. Each morning after writing letters, either to Harry or
her family back home, Marie walked beneath the elm trees and cottonwoods that led downtown, stopping to exchange pleasantries with
the invalid Mr. Gray seated on his shady porch at Third Street, and
Dora Bennett, who knew her way around Bellemont and offered Marie
fine advice and fresh vegetables from her garden at Church Street. If
Marie worked hard and earned her keep, Harry would be proud of
her — not that she needed his approval, mind you. She would do her
job well and honestly because that was how she had been raised. A
husband's opinion had nothing to do with it. Still, she could not deny
that effort and ability had always been Harry's constant hallmarks
to success, attributes Marie hoped she also possessed — even as she
tried to forgive Harry for sending her here. At the cash register she
felt calm as a fish, despite the noise of shouting men and banging billiard balls upstairs. The men who frequented Delahaye's were mostly
hard-smoking roughnecks from the mills and oil fields, or those who
held no job of any sort and had too much time on their hands. Most
were lonely, showing hurt in their eyes while they joked about skirts
and bumpy mattresses. Listening to their chatter, Marie guessed life's
capriciousness had somehow stolen the lightness from their hearts.
Men bear shame differently than women who talk teary, but make
themselves agreeable without being scolded. Harry quoted after John
D. Rockefeller that if a man believes himself rich and has everything
he desires and feels that he needs, then he is really rich, even if he has
only ten dollars. Poverty of confidence and hope drags men downward, sinks them in despair and bitterness. No good ever comes of it.

Marie sat at the cash register beneath a sign that said: **In God We
Trust, All Others Pay Cash.** She counted and numbered receipts
as quickly as she could while ringing up customers through the haze
of cigar smoke. She was proud of how quick she was. Automobiles
rattled past outdoors. Men came and went. In the corner office upstairs, Jimmy Delahaye was yelling into the telephone, complaining
about something or other. Ordinarily, Marie refused to pry into other
people's concerns or eavesdrop on conversations that did not directly

involve her. Here, she found herself tipping an ear in one direction and then another, trying to learn what she could about her new neighbors. She was awfully curious about this character and that, who was trustworthy or not, whose heart had been broken by whom, who hoped to travel abroad if that oil well ever came in a gusher. More than once she bit her lip before suggesting a solution to some nasty contention because she felt like a guest in town and determined to keep her place until she became more comfortable. She offered opinions only when asked and avoided all manner of disputes. At home, Harry often thought her timid, and there was some truth in that, but Marie also believed the tongue can be an unruly member and not every point of view needs airing in public.

She took a pair of dimes from the man at the counter and dropped them into the till. "Thank you, sir."

"Yes, ma'am," the fellow said, touching the tip of his hat and walking off. Marie reached into the drawer beneath the cash register for a rubberband to bind the receipts. She felt confident today.

Idabelle Collins came out of the kitchen, wiping her hands clean on the white apron she wore. Her red hair was in a net and beads of perspiration dotted her forehead. She was the skinniest woman Marie had ever known, but pretty in a country way. She was the first friend Marie had made in town, and Harry had warned she was a gossip, which made her all the more enjoyable. She was also desperately oversexed, and eyed every fellow that came and went.

"Jimmy wants to see you upstairs before you leave."

"Oh?"

"Now don't get yourself all worked up," Idabelle said, seeing worry rise in Marie's face. She took off her glasses. "He's thinking about offering you another few hours work."

"I'm not sure I ought to take on any more hours than I already have. Did he mention what sort of work it would be?"

Idabelle shook her head. "But a body can't be choosy when the offerings are slim."

"Well, I have my children to consider. They already spend half the day without me. I can't imagine working until suppertime." She was also deathly afraid of the children running all over creation while she was away downtown and Boy-Allen's killer remained at large. Trying to be brave, and actually doing so, was still beyond her capacity.

"Sweetheart, ideals won't put a patch on little Henry's trousers," Idabelle said, her voice rising at the end of her thought. She whistled the same "Yankee Doodle Dandy" she always did whenever she chose to leave her audience hanging, then gave Marie a smile and sat down behind the cash register just as another pair of customers came up, cash in hand. "May I help you gentlemen?"

"Good-bye, Idabelle." Marie smiled. "And thank you very much for the advice." Regardless of the objections she raised, Marie knew she needed the money.

"Of course," Idabelle replied, holding a hand out to the man standing in front of her. "Your bill, please?"

Money was always on the table to be worried over. Not forty-eight hours passed after Marie's arrival before Maude took the opportunity to remark how quickly her sugar had run out. The children loved it on their oatmeal and Maude knew this. Also, though, Rachel poured it in her tea and coffee like an addict and Maude rarely did more than raise an eyebrow. It wasn't at all fair, but Marie refused to complain. Instead, she hustled downtown to the market and bought enough to last all summer. Intrigued by the idea of earning another dollar or two a day, Marie followed the bar to the back of the restaurant and up the rear staircase to Jimmy Delahaye's office where a sign on the door read:

BE BRIEF, WE HAVE OUR LIVING TO MAKE!

The windowless hallway was dark and musty, smelling of tobacco and old wood. Delahaye had several framed photographs hiding cracks in the wallpaper just above the wainscotting, none of which could be appreciated in the dim light. Supposedly the pictures portrayed members of Delahaye's family in an earlier time, although the resemblance was not apparent.

Delahaye's office door was cracked open, so Marie walked up to the threshold and stood patiently outside until he noticed her. Delahaye was busy talking on the telephone. "See, I got myself a delivery problem. Y'all aren't delivering me nothing."

He nodded at Marie and directed her to an old horsehair sofa under the window that overlooked Main Street. Delahaye had a cigar smoldering in an ashtray on his desk and a stack of papers piled beside a plate of day-old lemon cookies baked by Idabelle. His office was cramped and disordered and stuffy with the odor of cigar smoke and Canadian whiskey everyone knew he drank after hours when the building was closed. He was just a year younger than Harry, slender and tall, and wore up-to-the-minute suits and collars and a razor-sharp haircut. According to Idabelle, he was as fine a looking gentleman as there was in the county and had a great lot of sex appeal. Marie agreed that Jimmy Delahaye had a firm jaw and a blue twinkle in his eye that no doubt kept his dance card full on Saturday nights. She didn't mind at all sitting in his office.

"Yes, yes, and then?" Delahaye spoke briskly into the phone. "I tell you, we've got that beaten flat. Yes sir, forty per! ... Oh bushwa! A lot he cared for those chuckleheads. They were chasing around like the Rebel cavalry while his sonofabitch brother cleaned up over ten grand in Rooney's cotton mill... No, Perry made that dough square and he wasn't born with any phenomenal intellect, either."

Jimmy Delahaye cupped his hand over the mouthpiece. "I'll be through in a second, honey. You just sit tight."

Marie smiled and pretended not to notice how handsome he was, though she felt like a schoolgirl whenever he smiled at her. Once upon a time, Harry had produced that effect on her, too. There were long-ago afternoons canoing on Cedar Lake and picnics beneath the river bluff north of Farrington where he strummed the ukulele, rather badly, and brought a smile to her lips that made her feel like a woman when Marie doubted she'd ever lose her girlhood. Remembering made her feel lonely, so she looked out the front window over Main Street where a tattered and sun-faded Confederate flag above the courthouse fluttered in the wind. The children had gone to the river after breakfast with their little friends from down the block. Henry had taken one of Harry's father's old fishing poles with him, swearing to bring back catfish for supper, although he'd never caught one in his life. Harry had never cared much for fishing. On the one occasion he went out with Frenchy and Cousin Alvin to the Mississippi, Harry lost a pole in the current and groused about a pair of shoes ruined in the muck at the river's edge. Frenchy called Harry a milquetoast and got a laugh from the rest of the Pendergasts who knew it to be true and tried in vain to steer Marie into Buddy Theale's embrace instead. No such luck. She'd have nothing to do with a fellow who stuffed birds for a living, and told her cousins to butt out. Were her children not the darlings they turned out to be, perhaps she might admit she'd chosen poorly. But love has its own authority and won't be ignored.

The handsome Jimmy Delahaye spoke again into the phone, "Like I said, this bird knows his way around, all right. What he did was grab a sheet of paper and wrote down a figure so small I had to take out a spyglass to read it. I says to him, 'Listen friend, is this supposed to be funny? Are y'all clowning around here?' So he blows out on me. The next thing I know he's got a lawyer and a date in court. It's a wonder I'm still in business…. How's that?" Delahaye laughed. "Well, bumping him off'd leave me four hundred in arrears. I got obligations, see: room rent, back rent, and a monkey suit to hire for the Fourth. So strike that off the record…. Huh? … I said, *Hoffman!* Try taking the cigar out of your ear. He's the little fellow with a nutcracker face, that squirt in George's speakie who puffed himself up about all the jack he made in Houston after the War." Cupping his hand over the phone again, Delahaye told Marie, "I'll be right along, honey. Have a cookie if you like."

He shoved the plate across the desk and winked. She knew he liked her, but shook her head to the cookies, having sampled one yesterday morning when they were still fresh. Besides, her stomach was too tickled with nerves to eat a thing. She tried to hide a smile. When he offered her more hours, she might agree if he asked her sweetly. Had he kissed any girls this week?

"Well, listen, pal," Delahaye continued, "there's a lot to admire in that combine, but hiring all those niggers of his'd put me in a flat spin, so I got to say no…. Sure, that'd be swell…. Thanks, pal. So long."

Delahaye put down the phone and leaned back in his chair. He said to Marie, "Well, sweetheart, I got a proposition for you."

He grinned and lit a fresh cigar. His flirting eyes gave Marie a pleasant shiver. She felt herself blush.

"A proposition?" Had she heard him correctly? Her throat tightened.

"Yes, ma'am," he said, "a proposition. See, I like you, honey. You work hard. You're on time. You don't steal from me. I like that."

"Well, I can't imagine stealing from anybody." Marie had found a purse once when she was a girl and taken the money and spent it on ice cream cones for her friends. When she'd told her mother about the purse, she was forced to go house to house until she found the owner, then to pay back the money she had stolen out of her own allowance, a lesson she never forgot.

"I know you can't," he smiled. "You're honest as a lamb, and I like that, too."

Gaining her confidence, Marie raised an eyebrow. She didn't intend to be meek. "What do you mean by 'proposition'?"

Just uttering that question came off as fresh to Marie. What on earth had gotten into her?

Delahaye leaned forward across his desk. "Well, you see, honey, I've never had a secretary. Fellows I deal with from Galveston to San Antonio, Texas Rockefeller-sorts, have their own personal secretaries taking dictation and opening boxes, sorting mail. I started thinking, things going so swell lately, maybe I ought to get me one, too."

"I'm sure you'd find a secretary very helpful." Was she flirting now, too? Her knees trembled and she felt a pleasant flush. She was enjoying this. Harry would've been furious, but he could go take a flying leap into a rose bush for all she cared at this moment.

"So what do you say?"

"You'd like to hire me as your secretary?" Harry had once hired a stenographer from Joliet back when he was still working in Farrington, despite Marie's insistence that she was more than capable of doing the job herself. After the girl had dropped a Multigraph machine on her foot, he'd let her out and hadn't bothered interviewing another, nor had he given Marie a chance. She'd felt bitter about it for months afterward, yet never said a word.

"Yes, ma'am, I would." He showed his teeth through a wide smile, and bit down on his cigar. "What do you say?"

"Well, I don't know. I've just learned the register."

Delahaye laughed. "You like ringing up customers, do you? That's sweet."

Marie felt herself blush again. Delahaye had a way of making her feel awkward and girlish. He was so very handsome. My goodness! How many girls had he kissed? Did he want to kiss her, too? What might she do if he tried? Well, she certainly wouldn't run!

"I just meant that learning another job, well, perhaps I wouldn't be any good at it. I've never worked as a secretary for anyone before. I'm not sure I'd know what was required of me."

"Aw, there'd be nothing to it." Delahaye took a couple puffs off the cigar and leaned back in his chair again. "I can train you in a couple days. We'll put Idabelle on the register while you're learning and Lucius behind the counter. If I hide his liquor, he'll do just swell. And if you like, I'll give you a few hours downstairs every week, too, just so you don't feel lonesome for the register. What do you say?"

Before Marie could answer, a tremendous noise thundered from the street below, then the crash of shattering glass in the dining room downstairs.

Delahaye ran to the window. "Good God!"

He rushed out of his office.

Marie hurried to the window and looked out at the wreck of a black delivery truck tipped on its side in the middle of the street and spewing steam into the noon air. Knocked half onto the sidewalk was the mangled heap of a two-tone brown Dodge sedan impaled upside-down on the lower half of the streetlamp in front of Delahaye's restaurant. The driver of the delivery truck hung out the door, blood streaming from a deep gash across his forehead. Marie saw people running down the sidewalk toward the accident. Frightened for the drivers, she hurried downstairs where she found confusion reigning. The upper section of the streetlamp had been sheared off by the careening Dodge and hurled through the plate-glass window, cascading glass throughout the crowded dining room. Dust and smoke clouded the air. The Dodge was smoldering, its lifeless driver hanging through a jagged fracture in the windshield. Lucius Beauchamp yelled for buckets of water. Marie rushed behind the cash register to the end of the counter where Idabelle had just risen from cover, shock drawn on her face. A small cut to the cheek dripped blood onto the front of Idabelle's blouse. Determined to stop the bleeding, Marie went straight into the kitchen to fetch a cloth. She ran water onto it and brought it back out to Idabelle and dabbed the cut clean of blood. Everywhere in the restaurant the smell of gasoline was strong and Marie heard Delahaye outdoors yelling frantically for somebody to call the firehouse.

"Heavens, I feel faint," Idabelle said, sitting on the stool behind the register.

"I think we ought to go outdoors into the fresh air," Marie said, keeping one eye on the smashed automobile and the gasoline leak. She was terrified of the motor exploding. Steam from the punctured radiator issued out from under the dented hood in a swelling hiss. She kept her attention away from the body of the driver. Death's intimate posture, sudden and incontrovertible, gave her a touch of vertigo. She hooked an arm under Idabelle's left shoulder and lifted her to her feet. Men left the dining room through the smashed front window, water buckets in hand.

Marie helped Idabelle around the bar toward the front door, preferring not to cross the threshold of broken glass where more men were gathering with water buckets. Before she reached the door, a great BANG echoed through the restaurant. Her heart skipped a beat and Idabelle fainted, crumpling to the floor.

"Explosion!" someone from outside yelled. "It's blowing up!"

The crowd on the sidewalk beside the front window rolled back like the tide on Lake Michigan as smoke billowed up from under the twisted hood of the Dodge.

A man standing next to Delahaye dropped his bucket and ran out into the street.

Scared half out of her wits, Marie looked at the automobile and saw Delahaye and Lucius Beauchamp swatting at the engine hood with wet towels. Delahaye yelled at the men who had retreated into the street, "GET THE HELL BACK HERE!"

Marie cradled Idabelle's head in her hands, stroking her cheeks, trying her best to bring the woman back to consciousness even as her own legs were shaking. Delahaye saw the two women and tossed his towel aside and hurried over.

"What the hell happened to Ida?"

"She fainted," Marie said, looking up at him. "The noise scared her. She'll be all right."

"Is she hurt?"

"Just her cheek. It's only a small cut." Marie couldn't stop shaking. Was she about to faint, too? Good grief, it seemed as if the world was coming to an end. Where were her children?

"Let's get her out of the building," Delahaye said, grabbing Idabelle and hoisting her up. He yelled out to the men in the street. "Throw some water on the hood, for Christsakes!" As he slung Idabelle over his shoulder, Delahaye muttered, "Goddamn cowards."

A fire engine arrived. As she followed Delahaye out of the building, Marie watched the truck discharge hoses, which were quickly attached to the hydrant two stores down from the restaurant. Idabelle had been taken across the street to recuperate in the shade of the willow trees. A crowd encircled both the smashed front window and the injured truck driver who was still in the cab holding a wet towel as a cold compress to his head wound to stanch the bleeding. Marie heard a siren approaching from across town. She hoped it was an ambulance.

A high afternoon wind twisted the smoke rising from the smashed Dodge into wispy funnels. The crowd had grown to more than a hundred, swelling across the street onto the other sidewalks, the atmosphere almost festive with excitement and danger. Children wandered on the fringe, giggling and hiding, worry and joy on their tiny faces. Still jittery with fear, Marie searched for her own children, hoping if they were about, they would have sense enough to remain at a safe distance. Cissie was born nosy and adventurous, a wearying combination. She'd drag timid Henry along just to be contrary. But the very fact that Marie hadn't seen Cissie sitting atop the fire engine or poking her face into the ruined Dodge meant she was off somewhere else.

Jimmy Delahaye emerged from the gaping hole in the plate-glass window, waving his arms and shouting for everyone to get away from the building. A pair of firemen came down toward him, hurriedly dragging their hose along toward the Dodge. People on the sidewalk began backing up. A second engine, siren wailing, rolled to a stop in the middle of the street a dozen yards or so from the wrecked truck. Three firemen ran a hose from the hydrant on the next corner down the sidewalk and up to the front of Delahaye's. More smoke poured out of the Dodge and again the crowd retreated into the street. An ambulance roared toward the restaurant from uptown. Marie found herself standing only a few feet from the tipped-over truck, just a couple of yards behind the rear bumper where the man she had seen hanging out of the wreck only a few minutes ago was lying flat on his back by the curb. He had suffered an awful laceration to his forehead and another Marie had not seen to his left shoulder. One leg was twisted oddly away from his torso, trouser-leg soaked in blood. His face was gritty and raw as sunburn, his eyes glassy. A trio of men, one of whom Marie took to be a doctor, were speaking to the driver and attending to his agony while awaiting an ambulance. As Marie inched forward, shoved by the crowd at her back, she heard the man moaning over and over, "Mable! Won't somebody please call Mable!"

— 2 —

When Marie returned from downtown, she found Rachel playing the piano alone in the sitting room. All the windows in the house were flung open and a pleasant breeze swept back the curtain lace and chinked the dangling prisms on Maude's glass table lamp. In the mid-afternoon, indoors was cool and smelled of fresh flowers. Marie listened to the casual way Rachel fingered the piano keys in a slow, almost arrhythmic rendering of "Beautiful Dreamer." Marie had thought only radio programs held Rachel's musical interest. Harry had owned his own piano in Farrington and played most evenings when he was not occupied with business or billiards. He performed lovely ballads with the lightest touch on the keys and rarely required sheet music, while his voice was strong and natural. Listening to him play while she did housework upstairs or puttered in the garden warmed Marie's heart. After their first-born's death that awful gray afternoon at Lake Calhoun, Harry sat at the piano every evening for a month, refusing to speak a word while Marie suffered little David's drowning in guilt and silence; for a season, she believed his playing had helped heal them both, but as the years went by she saw that was not so.

Marie slipped into the sitting room by increments, hoping not to disturb Rachel. She leaned against the doorframe and watched Rachel's fingers glide across the keys. She played more softly than did her brother, extracting from the instrument her own distinction. Marie listened until Rachel finished, then remarked, "You play wonderfully."

Rachel frowned, swiveling on the piano bench to face Marie. She was wearing a pale rose frock and she was barefoot. She was still lovely as ever. Little wonder CW had fallen for her. "I despise this instrument. I wish Mother had never persuaded me to take lessons."

"Why do you say that?"

"Because I play like a cow. Nothing ever sounds like I want it to. I feel as though I could do as well banging on the keyboard with my elbows. Harry is much better. He plays like an angel."

Marie smiled. "Yes, he does."

"Did he sell the Bösendorfer?"

"Yes."

"That's a shame. It was a beautiful piano." Rachel got up and walked over to the raised window and nudged the curtain lace open a few inches with the back of her hand and looked out to the street. A brief draft swept into the house, fluttering against her frock and the frilly antimacassars on Maude's walnut side table.

Marie said, "Harry told me it was foolish to choose between a piece of furniture and winter clothes for the children."

"He called the Bösendorfer a piece of furniture?"

"Yes."

"Hmm."

Reluctantly, Marie added, "Well, he really hadn't played all that much recently, so I suppose he didn't feel about it quite like he had when your mother gave it to him."

Actually, the past year or so, she'd noticed that Harry hadn't touched the keys at all. He seemed indifferent to music, or sweet pleasures of any sort. She had no clear idea why, but she supposed it had something to do with what he did while he was away. Her mother once told her that our smiles fade for one even as they bloom for another. Marie hoped that wasn't true with Harry, because she wasn't ready to let go. Everything else aside, for better or worse, she still loved him so much.

Rachel let the curtains close and walked over to the Crosley set, switched it on, then sat down on the couch and relaxed. A sweet ballad from the station in Austin filtered into the room. She said, "I remember the look on Harry's face when he came in and saw it sitting here. I swear we thought he would cry for joy. He'd never responded like that to a gift before. To think he'd sell it as furniture now is almost beyond belief. Mother would have a fit."

"You won't tell her, will you?"

"Heavens, no! She'd disown me and throw us all out into the street. That piano cost her more than … well, I'm sure you have an idea."

"Yes, I suppose I do." Harry, too, spoke often against needless spending. Marie's mother thought him something of a skinflint, but Marie believed he was frugal for his family's benefit.

"Anyhow, I hate playing and wouldn't be sad in the least if Mother sold ours as well."

Marie went to the piano and sat down, running her fingers lightly over the keyboard, though not depressing any of the keys. Dust had gathered in between the black and ivory. She'd take a cloth to it later on. Maude dusted, but not as thoroughly as Marie who learned from her own mother how to spit and polish.

"You'll be coming with us to the circus tonight, won't you?" Rachel asked. "CW'll be here at half past seven to pick us up."

Marie shook her head. "I promised your mother I'd stay home and keep her company. The children'll go, though. It's been two years since they saw the circus. They'll have a wonderful time."

"You shouldn't feel you have to stay home with Mother. She always has hundreds of things to do, besides which her club ladies are coming out this evening, so I doubt she cares one way or the other."

"Well, she asked me to."

"Oh, really? That's queer. I wonder why. Did she say?"

"No, only that she'd appreciate the company." Also, Marie knew it was important to try and please Maude by being friendly and helpful whenever she could.

"I wonder if she's having her change of life again." Rachel laughed, then caught herself.

"I don't mind staying home, actually," Marie said, lying slightly. "I've been to the circus dozens of times. It's lots of fun, but I'm sure there'll be others. I'll go next time."

"Of course you will," Rachel replied, shaking her head. "Mother's got you all knotted up, doesn't she? Why, I'll bet you haven't the faintest notion what you should and shouldn't do."

A scowl on her face, she walked over to the front door and opened it and looked out into the dusty street as a noisy Ford rumbled by. Marie got up from the piano and joined her. Rachel went out onto the porch and took a seat in the wicker settee and fanned her face with her hands. Marie followed and sat in the chair beside her. She told Rachel about the motor accident outside of Delahaye's restaurant.

"My goodness! I'll bet you liquor was involved. When isn't there with a smash-up? Was anybody arrested?"

"I haven't the least idea. It was a horrible mess. I'll probably have nightmares." Hardly anything gave her more fright than auto smash-ups.

"We're supposed to be dry, you know, but I don't doubt we have more drunks here on our streets than anywhere else in Texas. We've probably never been wetter. Mother's club ladies served a pitcher of lemonade last week that was nothing less than alcohol drained from lemon extract frozen in a cake of ice. Trudy refused to admit it, of course, but I've seen bottles of pear extract in her pantry and I know her cats don't imbibe."

Marie laughed. She couldn't imagine Maude drinking liquor on the sly.

Rachel asked, "Has Idabelle offered you a chock beer yet?"

She shook her head. "I've never even heard of such a thing."

"Go on!"

Marie blushed. "Well, I haven't, although I presume it's some new sort of fancy bootleg liquor. Is that right?"

Rachel giggled. "Why dear, you are bucking the times, aren't you?"

"Pardon?" Why hadn't Harry told her these things? She felt like such a fool.

"Well, you ought to know that Lucius and Idabelle drive to Dallas once a month to buy a carload of booze that's nothing more than water, old blackstrap molasses, old yeast, and old cornpone stirred together and left to stew for three weeks. It's sold all over town. They claim it's got a swell kick, although I've never been that thirsty. CW says he's heard of people in New Orleans poisoning themselves with the same cheap liquor. Of course, I'm sure that's just gossip."

Rachel smiled.

As they sat for a few minutes in silence, Marie thought about the man injured in the wreck, that horrid fear in his eyes, his plaintive voice; and the poor fellow in the brown Dodge who hadn't survived. Had the consumption of unlicensed liquor been his end? Marie knew the advantages of temperance went mostly unheeded in a country sopping with rum. Yet she also tended to believe it was the portion and right of every man to walk a crooked path if he so chose. Both virtue and calamity lie in wait. A foundation of optimism is often the only remedy for these trials. Though all our lives are encumbered by tragedy, the courageous heart looks forward and persists.

Rachel sighed. "It's dreadfully hot today, don't you think? I sometimes wonder why I've continued to live here. There must be somewhere else more appealing."

Marie smiled. "There are attachments." Although she'd left Illinois, she wasn't sure how long she'd be able to stay away. Every night she dreamed of the farm and her old cat.

Rachel dismissed the notion with a wave of her hand. "Why live somewhere you despise just because you were born there? That makes no sense whatsoever. Look at Harry. Do you think for a minute he'd come back here? Not on your life! He couldn't stand this one-horse town, absolutely despised it. Mother would deny that, of course, but believe me, it's the truth. Harry couldn't wait to leave. Once Daddy died, that just sealed the bargain. I'm surprised my brother sent you here, truth be told. I don't know what sort of difficulties you were having, and I'm not asking you to tell me, but it must have been quite serious for Harry to make this kind of decision. I know that ordinarily he'd never have considered it. Mother was thrilled, of course, thinking that Harry would be coming back, too. She misses him terribly, though she's never said a word."

"I'm sure that's so." Marie always wondered how Maude felt about this entire arrangement. Harry had made it sound as if she'd be thrilled to see her grandchildren, which may have been so, but that opinion had not yet crossed Maude's lips. Did she really favor Harry above Rachel? Would Maude still favor her son if she knew Harry's sins the way Marie did? Maude had never traveled north, not for the wedding, nor David's funeral. There were always reasons upon reasons, none more convincing than her own desire to stay home to her life here in Bellemont. Harry wrote and cajoled and begged, but Maude remained steadfast; if she was to be a grandmother, the children would have to be placed on her lap. And so it went. *Family*, Aunt Hattie once told Marie, *is a strange concoction.*

A two-door Chevrolet roared past, exhaling a foul cloud of exhaust into the afternoon air, stirring dust and leaves into small whirlwinds.

"She admires CW, I think," said Marie, once the dust had settled and the draft faded.

"Who does?"

"Your mother."

Rachel gave a sarcastic laugh. "Why, I doubt she approves at all! In fact, I'm quite sure she loathes him. I know she hates the very idea of us making love out on her wonderful porch for all the world to see. Not that I care, mind you. If there's anything I've learned to hold onto as my own, it's my relationship with the gentlemen I see. Mother understands that, or at least she's aware of what sort of trouble it causes whenever she even considers interfering."

Rachel got up and strolled to the end of the porch and leaned against one of the posts.

Marie said, "Is it his religion she objects to?"

"Will a cat eat liver?" Rachel replied. "Of course it is, among other things."

"Such as? If you don't mind my asking."

"She thinks he's too big for his Catholic britches, to put it bluntly. She thinks he's got snooty ideas and a fast tongue and no true sense of morals and decency. To tell you the truth, she believes he's a sex fiend."

Marie frowned, shocked at the inference. "She said that?"

"Well, of course not," Rachel said, "she doesn't need to. I know how Mother thinks. CW might just as well be Chinese for all her purposes in discussing his behavior. She has no appreciation whatsoever for anyone or anything that exists outside of this town. She'd feel the same about you, if it weren't for Harry. I'm sure you've figured that much out by now. Having you here only reminds her that Harry isn't. Maybe she even resents you for reminding her, I don't know."

"Well, I — "

Rachel interrupted her. "Look, the fact is, Mother's quite narrow-minded and doesn't seem to mind it a bit." She fanned her face with her hands. "Oh, I don't know why I bother discussing her anyhow. I've trained Mother to leave me alone, and she still makes me so angry sometimes I could just throw myself in front of a truck."

Marie saw a parade of dusty children and animals spilling out of the cottonwood grove across the street, her daughter Cissie at the head of the pack leading a gray swaybacked pony by a short rope.

"Well, look at this!" she said to Rachel, and burst out laughing.

"Isn't he beautiful?" Cissie remarked proudly, tying the pony to the backyard gate. The other children milled about the sidewalk: Henry beside blonde Lili Jessup from next door; a scrawny youngster with thick eyeglasses named Abel Kritt who lived down the street and had hold of a cocker spaniel by a cloth leash; and two tiny Negro girls, Eva and Caroline, barefoot and dusty in floral flour-sack dresses, daughters of the handyman Maude hired to repair the storm gutters after the last rain. Cissie told her mother, "His name's Mr. Slopey and he's a race horse."

"Is that so?" Marie studied the old swayback, its mangy tail, ugly and hopeless, precisely the sort of animal her daughter would rescue and fall in love with. Cissie was always bringing animals home. A stray dog, a basket of kittens, a chicken, a bullfrog, a wounded robin, all recipients of Cissie's unconditional compassion. Cissie loved animals of all kinds. In Farrington, she'd belonged to 4-H and had entries at the October Fair. Last year, her lamb Twinkle won third prize. Her attachment to it was so dear that Twinkle was allowed to live out her natural years in the Pendergast back pasture, safe from the carving knife. Marie smiled, her sweet lovely daughter, Florence Nightingale to the animal kingdom.

"We found him by the river and he followed us home," Cissie explained. "He was awful lonely. Isn't that right, Lili?"

The Jessup girl nodded while Caroline and Eva fooled with each other's dark braids. Little towheaded Abel Kritt let a black bug scurry out of his hand as Marie turned her attention to Henry who was trying to hide behind the old pony, his overalls muddy and wet, water dripping still from his cowlick. "Henry Albert Hennesey! What on earth?"

He cracked a sheepish grin. "I been swimming, Momma."

"He fell in the river," Cissie corrected, "chasing after a silly little catfish. I warned him to stay on the riverbank, but he disobeyed me. He ought to've drowned. That'd taught him a lesson, don't you think?"

"Cissie!" Her daughter found sympathy to be a trying task, choosing instead to pick on her little brother at every turn. Marie scolded her constantly, but saw scant improvement. Perhaps she took after her father.

"Well, he never does a thing I tell him. He's awful!"

"It was polliwogs I was collecting, Momma," said Henry, chiming in on his own behalf. "And whales! Bigger'n our whole house!"

"And alligators, too?" Cissie asked, snidely. "Big awful green ones who swim 'round looking for stupid little boys?"

"That's how come I swum like a frog," Henry explained. "I went underwater and kicked out and swam — "

"Like a rock," Cissie interrupted, fingering her braids. "That's how he swam, as usual. If it wasn't for a pine log he bumped into and our friend Julius swimming out in his good clothes to save him, Henry'd be a goner." She snarled at her little brother, "Not that we'd miss him all that much, the little scamp. I told Henry the next time he disobeys a direct order from me, I'll leave him for the wolves."

"Oh, Cissie." Marie shook her head, exasperated with her daughter. What she needed was a good spanking. Where was Harry? At least in those mournful years after David's drowning, he'd taught the children to swim, thank goodness. Now Cissie streaked through the water like a fish, while Henry, despite his sister's critical eye, did a very passable dog paddle. The thought of her children playing at the river made her terribly nervous, but she also knew they just couldn't be kept away. Thanks to Harry, if worst came to worst, they'd have a fighting chance. Nothing in life was safe, yet it had to be lived, not withstanding. Perhaps she ought to learn a simple dog paddle herself, if only for another gray and blustery afternoon.

Lili Jessup reached under the fence to pick up her little gray kitten. Henry swatted a pair of flies off the swayback's rump. Little Abel sat down on the curb to wipe off his eyeglasses. Caroline and Eva traded flower petals from the white aster bouquets they had picked in the woods.

Cissie asked, "We can keep him, can't we, Momma? He won't be a bother. You promised I could have my own horse."

Rachel spoke from the porch railing, "Mother'll flip her wig."

"We won't tell her," Cissie suggested. "We'll hide Mr. Slopey behind the barn and feed him after dark when Grandma goes to bed. She won't suspect a thing, I promise."

"A kind-hearted fraud, huh?" Rachel laughed. "Well, I expect we'll have to talk that over later, dear."

"It'll be up to your grandma, honey," Marie said, reasonably sure Maude would be sympathetic. She seemed to adore animals more than people. "We're guests here, remember."

"But we will keep him, won't we?" Cissie pleaded. "Oh, he's the sweetest horse I ever met. And he can do the swellest tricks."

"I don't doubt that for an instant."

"There's Julius now," Rachel said, directing Marie's attention down the street where the tall black man emerged from the cottonwood grove, his work clothes damp as Henry's, his boots caked with mud. Following him out of the woods was a small Negro boy in overalls carrying a fishing pole and a brown sack. Eva and Caroline hurried off down the dusty sidewalk, squealing with delight. Julius Reeves greeted them by hoisting both up onto his husky shoulders.

Rachel waved and called out to him. "Hello, Julius!"

Marie gave a pleasant wave, too. She'd known too few colored folks in her life and believed in kindness as a bridge between the races. Besides, Julius Reeves was the most congenial fellow she'd met in Bellemont, clear testimony to the pure idiocy of prejudice.

"Momma, Julius risked his life to save Henry," Cissie told her. "He was so brave. We were absolutely certain they'd both be swept away. I called for Lili to come and bring help, but she and Abel were too busy trying to capture Mr. Slopey who just slipped his rope and wandered off by his ownself. I guess he didn't want to go swimming with us." Cissie broke off a chunk of carrot she'd just pulled out of her pocket and guided it into Mr. Slopey's mouth. The swayback greedily devoured the carrot and sought another. "He's very spirited."

"I'm sure he is."

"See, that's how come I left Henry by himself, Momma," Cissie explained, "'cause I had to help Lili and Abel find Mr. Slopey. Only when I told Henry to stay away from the water, he disobeyed me. I told you, Momma, he oughtn't to be allowed out of the yard. He's entirely too young."

"Am not!" Henry yelled.

"Are so!"

"Children!" Marie glared at them both, embarrassed by their behavior. "Please!"

As Julius Reeves arrived in front of the house, he let his little girls slip back onto the sidewalk to play with their flower bouquets. Then he smiled at Rachel and Marie and tipped his hat. "Afternoon, Mrs. Hennesey. Afternoon to you, too, Miss Hennesey."

"I wasn't scared, Momma," Henry insisted, coming over and standing next to the black man. "I swam all by myself and held onto the log 'til I saw Julius coming for me. Then we both swum out of that old river together, him steerin' and me kickin'. Isn't that right, Julius?"

The black man smiled down on him. "Yessir, Mister Henry."

"Ain't no reason to drown on a sunny day, is there?" Henry asked, smiling up at the handyman. Nothing ever seemed to douse that grin. He was the happiest child Marie had ever known. Cousin Emeline argued that a sweet disposition follows a boy raised on sweets, and fed him cookies at every turn, but Marie believed her little Henry was just born happy.

"No, sir, there ain't."

"I'm sorry you had to get your clothes all wet," Marie said to Julius, "but thank you very much for rescuing my son."

"He's a fine boy," Julius replied, with a friendly smile.

"When he's not causing a stir," Cissie snapped.

"Don't take much for boys to get themselves into trouble," Julius said. "No, ma'am. Got one of my own right here. Willie, say afternoon to these nice ladies."

The boy lowered his eyes, sheepishly. "Afternoon, ma'ams."

"Hello, Willie," Marie said. "I'm very pleased to know you."

Cissie added, "Momma, Julius calls Eva and Caroline his 'rays of sunshine', don't you, Julius?"

The handyman nodded. "Yes, ma'am. I expect I do."

Marie watched a flight of yakking crows sail low over the summer trees, eastward across the blue sky toward the river. Abel and Henry ran out into the empty street to give chase. Abel chucked a stone that barely reached the switchgrass. Willie let his fishing pole dip until it dragged in the dust. Then he followed Henry and Abel to the blackberry thicket across the street.

Rachel came around to the front steps, descending to the sidewalk. "I've always thought those were the two prettiest names I ever heard — Eva and Caroline."

Julius nodded. "Thank you, ma'am."

"You're so lucky to have girls in the family. I've always believed that boys are troublemakers," Rachel added, sitting down on the bottom step and smoothing out her skirt. She made a sunshade for her eyes with the back of her hand. "Avoiding them at all costs should be the female aim in life. Not that it's possible, of course. Soon enough they grow up to be men and our entire sex humiliates itself falling all over them. Isn't that right, Julius? Why, I'll bet you had women worrying you to pieces when you came back from France."

"No, ma'am," the handyman replied, clearly embarrassed by Rachel's question. "That ain't exactly so."

"Oh, I'm sure you're just being modest." replied Rachel. She turned to Marie in time to take the breeze flush in her face. "He's our town's grandest hero of the war, you know."

"Is that so?" Marie asked, cheerfully. She admired his manners and dignity. Why couldn't more men be civil and glad?

The handyman shook his head, pearl beads of sweat gleaming on his skin in the noon glare. "Naw, that ain't so at all."

"Oh, of course you are," Rachel persisted. "Everybody knows it, too. You're just being modest again." She told Marie, "He hasn't an ounce of boastfulness, unlike some of the men around here."

Marie said, "Well, I'm sure everybody's very proud of him."

Julius looked down at his boots as his daughters hid behind him. "Ain't nobody more hero'n another once the shooting starts. Just plenty scared folks praying they gonna get home again. It ain't much to be proud of."

"Well, have it your own way. Modesty's silence deprives truth's consecration," said Rachel. "I'm sure if anyone from Bellemont had shot sixteen Germans and rescued a dozen or more American doughboys all by himself, we'd have another holiday here to celebrate." She turned to Cissie with the swayback, and Lili Jessup who sat up on the fence now chewing on a long stem of dried grass in her mouth. "Wouldn't you kids like that? A grand parade with lots of flowers and horses?"

"Could I be in it with Mr. Slopey?" Cissie asked, her eyes wide and blue.

"Of course," Rachel replied, giving Marie a wink. "Why not? He's family now, isn't he?"

Cissie threw an arm around her pony's neck and gave him a hug, saying, "Did you hear that, Mr. Slopey? You're family. So why'd you try to run away, Mr. Slopey? Didn't you know we love you?"

"That fishin' man was awful mean to him," little Henry said, back from across the street where Abel and Willie were poking long sticks into the blackberry thicket. Henry stroked the pony's mane. "I think he hurt Mr. Slopey's feelings."

"Which man was that?" Marie asked, somewhat nervously. Two mothers on Finch Street steadfastly refused to let their children out of doors unattended until the fiend who murdered Boy-Allen was apprehended. Marie wasn't terrified like some, but she had her worries. Who knew where the killer lurked? "Where was he?"

"By the river where we found Mr. Slopey under the cedar trees," Cissie answered. "He said that Mr. Slopey was ugly and that the only race he'd win was to the glue factory, so Lili got mad and called him a dirty liar, and that's when the man said Mr. Slopey wasn't going to be a champion of nothing except to the dog that ate him for supper."

Marie gasped. "Good gracious! What an awful thing to say!"

"Yes, ma'am," Cissie confirmed. "I think it made Mr. Slopey feel bad, and that's why he ran off like he did."

"Well, I'm sure he's feeling better now," said Marie, glad that her daughter had so much love in her heart. "After all, it's what's inside that counts, isn't it? And I'll bet he's a fine horse."

"I'll show him at the fair one day," Cissie said, "and he'll win a blue ribbon."

"That man said Mr. Slopey'd fit in better at the circus," Henry said, "with the three-headed turkeys."

"Did you hear any of this, Julius?" Rachel asked. "What they're talking about?"

"No, ma'am. I didn't see nobody but these three when I come back from fishing with my boy."

"It was earlier," Cissie corrected, "before Henry went in the water, and farther up the river where there was sand and rocks to sit on. I even dipped in myself, after removing my shoes, of course. It was awful pretty. And there were the loveliest birds singing, Momma. You ought've heard them. We were all having a good time until we met that horrible man. When I told him about Mr. Slopey likely winning a blue ribbon at the fair this year, he said I was a crazy person who ought to be locked away in the bughouse."

"Well, I can't imagine who'd say something like that to a child," Rachel remarked, fanning away a fly. "You don't think it was somebody from away, do you Julius?"

"Oh, those vagrants that fish by the river don't live 'round here. They just camp down there and get orn'ry when they can't catch nothing. I seen 'em all the time. I expect most of 'em are hopped up on liquor."

Marie asked, "Near Shantytown, you mean?" She hoped there weren't vagrants within shouting distance. Good grief! She'd be afraid to let the children out of the house.

Julius told her, "This side of the river, too, close enough I been telling my own youngsters to watch out so's they don't go too near 'em."

"Well, somebody ought to be notified of the danger, in any case," Rachel said. "It's our civic duty to keep the community safe for children, especially after that horrible tragedy with Boy-Allen. Wasn't he killed near there? Perhaps the police ought to be called out to investigate that fellow. Who's to say he's not the one we're looking for? If I had a child of my own, I don't know that I could cope these days. There seem to be cutthroats and ne'er-do-wells behind every bush in the country now." She turned again to Marie with a frown. "Wait until Mother hears about it. She'll certainly give somebody at City Hall a piece of her mind. She thinks the police've been dragging their heels about looking for suspects. I'm sure she'll find this whole mess absolutely disgraceful."

It was hot in the road and flies buzzed as smells of decay and manure traded about on the summer breeze. The old cat two doors down lolled its head out into the sunlight just under the dooryard foundation, dreaming in the afternoon heat.

Julius said, "Well, I expect I better get back on the job." He looked down at Henry who was patiently holding the rope Lili Jessup had wrapped around Mr. Slopey's neck. "You be careful now, Mister Henry, next time you decide to go swimming in the river. Won't do nobody no good chasing you down into the Gulf, you hear?"

Henry nodded.

"We're going to the circus tonight," Cissie told Julius. "Soon as the sun goes down."

The handyman smiled. "So I hear."

"Eating cotton candy on the Ferris wheel is just about my favorite thing to do in the whole world," Cissie said. "I love the circus! Won't you come along with us? We'd have an awfully good time together." She looked at her mother. "Can't Julius and Eva and Caroline and Willie come with us to the circus tonight? I'm sure CW has plenty of room. I could ride in the rumble seat. I wouldn't mind. I'm sure it'll be warm out tonight."

Before Marie could reply, the black man said, "I appreciate the invitation, but family's got us occupied elsewhere this evening. You know how it is."

"Oh, I suppose so," Cissie replied, disappointed. "Family always comes first. That's what Momma tells me whenever we have to go out to Uncle Henry's for Sunday dinner. His mean old dogs try to bite me whenever I pet them. I never have a good time there. I hate my cousins. They're always awful to us, but Momma says it's important we go."

"It's not that bad," Marie explained to Julius. "I guess they just don't get along particularly well." Cissie didn't care for her relatives at all, but Marie always felt she picked it up from her father who hated the farm and refused to keep his opinion quiet, even around the children.

"They throw corncobs at me," Henry announced, a deep frown on his face. "I got a black eye once."

"And they make fun of us for living in town," Cissie added, "as if playing in manure every day makes them so wonderful. Just thinking about it makes me mad."

"No wonder Harry kept y'all in town," Rachel laughed. "He just despises getting dirty."

"I expect we'll be going along now," Julius said. "It was nice to see you again, ma'am."

"Thank you," Marie replied. "Have a pleasant evening."

"Children." His tiny daughters rose from the sidewalk where they'd been playing patty cake and brushed each other off. Julius smiled up at Rachel. "Good-day, Miss Hennesey."

"Good-bye, Julius," said Rachel.

"Bye-bye!" the children shouted.

After Julius had crossed the street to fetch his little boy, Marie said to Rachel, "What a nice fellow."

"Yes, he is."

Rachel stared toward the falling sun on the dusty horizon. Lili Jessup climbed the fence and ran to the barn to prepare a stall for the swayback while Cissie took her brother by the hand and called for little Abel to join them in the corral. Wind drove Rachel back indoors, but Marie decided to stay out a little longer, noting flora and fauna in the brush across the street for the letters she would write to relatives in Farrington. Few members of the Pendergast family understood why she'd moved away. Prying into each other's lives was not casual to her family. Life in Farrington passed quickly enough without disrupting its harmony with impolitic inquiries and sly accusations. Though her mother despised Harry for selling the house on Cedar Street and stealing her grandchildren away, her father had wished her godspeed, given her a kiss, and squeezed her hand. By memory's grace, her home in the Pendergast heart was assured, however distant from Illinois she and her children were committed to travel.

— 3 —

At twilight, crickets chirruped in the shadows between houses while restless dogs wandered the half-empty streets and backyards, barking distractedly at hidden enemies. On the north end of town, bursting Roman candles brightened the purple evening horizon.

"That's the circus, Momma!" Cissie announced, looking out one of the sitting room windows of Maude Hennesey's house. "That's the circus!"

"I can see, dear," Marie replied, gathering up the tablecloth after supper. The smell of fried pork chops, steamed greens, and hot gooseberry pie remained in the air. They'd had a fine supper and Marie had helped cook half of it, which made her feel useful and happy for once. When she was a girl, her mother had told her that no man who tasted her cooking would leave her side. Now and then, as Harry's business trips became longer and more frequent, Marie wondered if she'd lost her touch in the kitchen. But what did baking have to do with love?

"Won't you come, too?" Cissie pleaded. For emphasis, she tugged on her mother's sleeve and sagged toward her. "I want you to come along with us."

"You know I have to stay here, honey. I promised your grandma I'd help her out tonight."

Rachel walked out from the kitchen after finishing washing dishes. She switched off the radio, then crossed to the window and gazed with Cissie toward the north where another round of skyrockets lit the sky. "When CW gets here," she said, "we'll light the sparklers and wave them from his automobile as we drive across town. Everybody'll come out to watch."

"I want my own," Henry called from the piano bench, flipping a buffalo nickel off the back of his left hand into the air and letting it fall to the carpet. He checked to see which side landed face up, then fetched it off the floor. Harry taught him that, and pitching pennies, which Marie had not found the least bit amusing. Gambling was a sin of sloth and avarice, and Harry knew it.

"They'll be so pretty," Cissie said. "People might follow us to the circus just to get their own."

"They might at that," Marie said, hoping her children wouldn't burn their fingers. She had warned Cissie to be careful and hoped her daughter listened for a change.

Rachel added, "We won't let them, though. It'll be our special trick."

"Can Mr. Slopey come along, too? He'd love to visit the circus."

"Of course not," Rachel said. "Mr. Slopey has to stay here and keep the chickens company. They get awful lonely in the evening when we go away."

"They do?" Henry asked. "How come?"

"I don't know," Rachel replied, looking to Marie for an answer. "I guess they just do. You'll have to ask them yourself."

"May we go outside, Momma?" Cissie asked, already halfway to the living room door.

"Yes, let's all do that," Rachel agreed. "It's too stuffy in here."

Marie agreed and they all went onto the porch where a breeze washed the sweet perfume of nightblooming jasmine across the evening air. Marie listened happily to the voices of children running throughout the neighborhood, merriment and enthusiasm rising for a visit to the circus in the summer dark. Fear of Boy-Allen's mysterious killer was mostly ignored by children who preferred to chase a thousand amusements out of doors rather than hide away in their bedrooms from barely imaginable notions of kidnapping and murder. Maude rattled pans in the kitchen as she straightened things up after supper. Automobile lights flickered in the trees down the street.

"Are you sure we can't persuade you to come with us?" Rachel asked Marie. "I don't see any reason at all for you to stay home and entertain Mother. It's not as if she requires company, you know. I doubt she'd even notice you were gone."

"Yes, yes, yes!" Cissie pleaded, jerking once more on Marie's sleeve. "Pleeeeaaassse, come!"

Henry flipped the coin off his thumb out into the road, and dashed down the steps after it. Marie shook her head with a smile. "Besides, I have all sorts of letters to write home. If I don't hold up my end of the correspondence, they'll forget me. Maude and I may play a two-handed game of Hearts until her club ladies arrive."

Rachel laughed. "Mother cheats, you know. She's hoping to win enough money to buy a new stove."

Maude's angry voice broke in upon them from the kitchen. "That's a bald-faced lie!"

Rachel called back at her, "Oh, you do so, Mother. Why, everyone in town knows it."

Maude came to the open window, her face just visible behind the screen, wearing a scowl. "I've never cheated in my life and anyone who says I have is a liar and a thief."

"A thief?" Rachel asked, puzzlement drawn on her face. "Why, I don't get you." She winked at Marie.

"You just stop telling fibs about me," Maude said, striking the screen with the flat of her palm. "I won't stand for my own daughter defaming me in the middle of the street."

"A guilty conscience is the deceiver's own purgatory," Rachel remarked. "I just thought Marie ought to be warned if she chooses to stay home with you instead of driving out to the circus with the rest of us."

Marie moved off down the steps after Henry who had wandered out into the dark street. She looked for automobiles, afraid of seeing her children run down by one. Jinny Branson had been struck by a Ford and killed just outside her gate not three blocks from the house on Cedar Street. Rosemary Branson's wailing had sounded like the ambulance siren across the trees. That memory always gave Marie a case of the shakes.

"She can go if she chooses," Maude replied. "I have plenty to do on my own."

"Why, there," Rachel said to Marie. "You've just heard it for yourself. You're free to come with us if you like. Mother has released you from any obligation you might have felt." She raised her voice, "Isn't that right, Mother?"

"I believe I've just said so."

Henry was on his knees, raking the dirt with his fingers in search of the coin he'd somehow lost in the road. Dust blew into his eyes, and he covered them with one arm and searched like a blind man with the other. Cissie stood in the porch shadows poking her index fingers into her cheeks while staring north toward the fairgrounds where another skyrocket had just burst orange on the black sky.

Marie told Rachel, "Well, I've already made up my mind to stay." She snatched Henry out of the dirt by the crook of his arm and swatted the dirt off his rump. She looked back up at Cissie whose fingers were jammed deeper still into the hollow of her cheeks. Marie frowned. "Honey, what on earth are you doing?"

Cissie let her hands fall away. "Making dimples, Momma. Lili taught me how."

A noisy automobile barreled in their direction. The motor horn honked and the driver stood up in the seat and gave a grand stage salute. Cissie shrieked with excitement as she and Henry returned CW's wave. Passing the house, CW brought the car around in a wide circle and rolled curbward to a stop and shut the engine off. He bounced out of his Ford like an acrobat and bowed to his audience. Both children cheered.

"Why do you show off like that?" Rachel called out, feigning anger. "You know I'm not impressed."

"He's a daredevil!" Cissie shouted, bounding down off the porch. "The bravest in the world!"

"Then somebody ought to get him a stick and a tall hat," Rachel groused. "I think he's a silly old show-off, and I won't set foot off this property unless he promises to quit fooling around."

CW strode to the porch railing. "Aw, you don't mean that, honey. I know you don't." He pursed his lips for a kiss. Rachel had told Marie when they first met that CW was a splendid kisser, which had made her blush. Now she was almost used to these overbold displays. Once upon a time, Harry had made the Pendergasts blush when he called on her after dark. It was pure jealousy on Emeline's part to suggest his manners were lacking when the truth was she longed for a fellow of her own to nibble on.

"Believe your ears," Rachel replied, turning her back to him. "I do so mean it. If you've got your heart set on going to the circus with me, I guess you'd better swear an oath this instant or I'll just go inside and spend the evening with Mother. She's not well enough to come out tonight with the rest of us." Rachel dropped her voice. "She's been suffering a deal from indigestion, you know."

"Really?"

"That's a lie!" came Maude's voice from the window. "Why, I'm fit as a fiddle! I've just got too much to do, that's all. The Lord's got me coming and going tonight. My club ladies will be here in an hour to play cards, and then I've a letter to write to Mrs. Reece in Killeen and another to Enid Todd in Stephenville."

"Oh, my heavens!" Rachel gasped, "That'd be the limit! Why, I couldn't bear it! I'm sure I'd faint dead away from the excitement of it all!"

Ignoring her daughter's sarcasm, Maude continued, "And then I have laundry to take in and a shimmy to sew for Clara Conklin."

"Oh, heart flutters!" said Rachel, and laughed out loud.

CW knelt down in front of Henry. "I saw some boys just your age walking back from the circus, and do you know what they were eating?"

"Cotton candy?" Henry asked, his eyes widening.

"Yessiree. A whole bale of it."

"Wow!"

"Don't tease the child, dear," said Rachel. "You're in enough trouble as it is."

"As God is my witness," CW said, crossing his chest. "I — "

"Are there many people downtown?" Marie interrupted, as a breeze scattered dust and leaves across the steps. She loved company and having lots of people about.

"Not any longer, but did you know there was a motor accident on Main Street this afternoon?" CW asked. "A Dodge sedan was smashed to smithereens by a truck. One man died and another was seriously injured. Bennie told me it was quite a sight."

"Of course we know," Rachel said. "Our own Marie was at the Delahaye building during lunch hour. She's already told us all about it."

"You were there?" CW asked, astonishment in his voice. "Great Scott! How did it all happen?"

"I was upstairs speaking with Mr. Delahaye," Marie said, keeping her voice low as possible to spare the children the awful details. "We heard a terrific collision from down below and went to the window. A truck and an automobile had struck each other and the automobile flipped over onto its back and caught fire. It was just horrible."

CW said, "I would imagine so! Did you see either of the victims?"

"Only the man driving the truck. He was out in the street. The other died inside his automobile before it caught fire." Marie still felt a shiver when she pictured his eyes.

"They ought to arrest someone," Rachel said, "and if it were up to me, I'd start with Newton Devlin, who is without a doubt the biggest horse's ass we've ever had sitting in the mayor's office. I don't know how many complaints he's received about people automobiling like that on Main Street and he's ignored every last one of them."

"You should write a letter," Maude remarked from behind the window screen.

Rachel walked down the length of the porch and looked in toward the kitchen. "Mother, I just said that hasn't done any good. I seriously doubt the man can even read. He ought to be lynched."

"A letter well-composed persuades when passions rise and reason fades."

Henry tugged on Marie's dress. "Let's go, Momma!" he whined. "I want to go to the circus!"

Marie freed his hand. "Patience, please!"

CW leaned into the backseat of the Ford and drew out a sparkler, which he lit with a wooden match. It flared to life with a smoky burst of blue and orange sparks that caught everyone's attention. Waving the sparkler above his head, he announced, "All aboard who's coming aboard!"

Both children shrieked with delight and leaped into the backseat. Marie looked up into the dome of the night sky where millions of silver stars were visible overhead, light from heaven.

"I've decided I'll have a sparkler of my own," Rachel said, climbing into the Ford. CW gave her a soft kiss on the cheek, closed her door, and hurried around to the driver's side and got in and started the engine. Then he reached under his seat, drew out three more sparklers, lit all three and passed them to his passengers, one by one.

"It's a go!" he shouted, tipped his cap to Marie, and slipped the Ford into gear.

"Bye-bye!" Marie called, as the Ford rolled away. "Have a good time!"

A dancing rainbow of sparks flickered and glowed in the dark as they headed off, Cissie and Henry twirling the sparklers above their heads. Their laughter echoed in the twilight and the Ford was swallowed up by the shadows. A last long wailing of the Ford's horn carried backward to Marie before the street was quiet and dark once again.

Maude finished preparing a batch of hard sugar gingerbread cakes for the quick oven, and came into the front room where Marie knelt before the small bookcase, studying her choices beyond *The Sunny Side of Life*, *Pep*, *Church Socials and Entertainments*, a collection of *Ford Smiles* and Dr. Eliot's Five Foot Shelf of the Harvard Classics that Harry had mailed from Illinois last Christmas.

Setting the silver coffee-service down on the card table, Maude said, "I never seem to find the time to read. It's very distressing. My husband was quite the reader, although you'd never have known it by first impression. He presented himself as uneducated and plain. He said it gave him an advantage over more sophisticated men who would be disposed toward underestimating him, which many of his competitors did." Maude sat down on the sofa across from Marie and folded her hands in her lap. "Yet I've never known a more clever, intelligent man as long as I've lived."

"Harry says reading makes a well-informed and gentlemanly salesman. I'm sure he learned that from his father."

Maude smiled. "Jonas believed in bending the twig when it's young. Now, of course, Rachel won't read anything besides those addle-brained *Photoplay* magazines at Hooker's drugstore, but Harry was forever running downtown to the library, utterly convinced that all the books he hadn't yet looked over were about to disappear from the shelves. Unlike most of the boys he knew at school, Harry refused to allow his horizon to be limited by foolishness. Jonas considered him a rare child. He was very proud of his son."

"Cissie adores books, too," Marie remarked, "thanks to her father who's guided her footsteps since she was little, although I must say Cousin Emeline and myself are avid readers, as well. In fact, my family has always believed in the value of education. Granny Ruth went to college in Wisconsin and taught Latin and mathematics before she married my grandfather. And my mother wrote poetry when she was a girl and had each of us recite one canto from 'Hiawatha' after Thanksgiving dinner as a matter of tradition."

"Now, you see, that's precisely the point I was trying to put across to Rachel last night," Maude explained, as a motorcar rumbled by outdoors. "This snarling youth nowadays have too little appreciation for tradition and standards. All they care about is having a good time. For heaven sakes, can you imagine my daughter or any of her fast-stepping friends joining us around the fireplace to hear our opinions on anything modern? Scarcely! Yet we're accused of sobbishness when we describe the heartscald of seeing our children coming home on the milk train at six o'clock in the morning, sick from liquor and sin. I believe this willingness of theirs to ridicule our ideals and counsel will lead us all to the break-up of the family unless this younger generation recognizes its fault and changes its habits. And I mean sooner than later."

The curtains flapped lazily behind the storm screens, drawing a cool draft into the front room. Marie wondered what her own children were doing that moment at the circus, if they were enjoying themselves and were safe out in the dark of the fairgrounds where Emmett J. Laswell's Traveling Circus Giganticus had raised its tents. Until Boy-Allen's killer was caught, a threat persisted, and Marie couldn't help but worry. Who could be safe? Maybe she'd made a mistake in not going with them. What sort of mother leaves her children outdoors after dark? Of course, they were with Rachel and CW, but how responsible were those two? Rachel had no children of her own and wouldn't likely have one at all, except by accident. Listening to her talk about men, Marie suspected it might only be a matter of time before she got herself in trouble. CW seemed quite mature and responsible, but he also let Rachel push him around, not a good sign for a fellow just starting off with a girl as willful as her. Were the circus not on the other end of town, Marie might just have jumped up and hurried over there that minute. After all, what was more important than her children's well-being?

The doorbell rang and a flurry of voices issued from the front porch.

Maude looked at the clock on the fireplace mantle. "Are you sure you won't join us?"

Marie smiled and shook her head. "No, thank you. I have reading and letters to catch up on while the children are out. But I appreciate your asking. Thank you."

She was pleased, indeed. This was the first time Maude had invited Marie to join her club ladies. Were they becoming friends at last? She doubted it, yet stranger things had happened, and Reverend Whitehead always preached the theme of the lamb lying down with the lion. Perhaps anything was possible in this age.

Maude stood. "Will you look in on my gingerbread cakes every so often? Trudy refuses to touch one if it's overdone and that old stove is utterly unreliable. I believe next month I may actually buy a new one, after all."

"Certainly."

The doorbell rang again amid a tittering of laughter. As Maude went to answer it, Marie located a volume of Longfellow and made herself comfortable in the plum tapestry Morris chair in Maude's sewing room away from the card game. While she re-read "Hiawatha," voices excited and agitated carried to her across the house.

"You needn't shuffle more than once!"

"I'll shuffle as often as I please, thank you!"

"What a rotten hand! Just rotten to the core!"

"I do believe I may win this round!"

"Emmy, I'll thank you to keep your eyes to yourself!"

"Cheaters never prosper, Maude!"

"Well, I'll have you know, the prosperous have no need for cheating! Here, take this!"

"Oh, bother!"

"My, oh, my! Luck has deserted this poor old girl tonight! Heavens!"

"If you hand me one more heart, Trudy, I'll slit your throat!"

"Beatrice!"

"I win again!"

"Why Maude, you're nothing but a wicked old witch! I doubt I'll ever play this game again. Trudy, you shuffle this time. I do not trust our hostess! She's much too sly!"

Laughter echoed through the house.

When the hour had passed, Maude came into the room and invited Marie to have a cup of tea and a gingerbread cake with the club ladies. The cards had been put away and doilies arranged on the mahogany tea table, cups in each place setting, one extra for Marie. The house felt lively.

"That Trudy is such a cheat," said Beatrice, winking at Emily. "I cannot win if she is included in the game. It is utterly hopeless."

Marie sat down on one of Maude's tufted oak side chairs. The club ladies were the most pleasant women Marie had met in town, although they seemed to have little use for anyone outside their little circle and gossiped shamelessly about everyone in the county. Yet people in Bellemont treated them with a peculiar deference explained by rumors about each having gold buried in her back garden and a controlling interest in the bank.

"Don't believe a word that woman says," Trudy replied, with a scowl. "Beatrice is nothing but a sore loser. Always has been. Why, I remember back in school — "

"Don't you dare bring Bobby Watson into this conversation!" Beatrice cried. "You've sullied both his reputation and my own for more years than I can count with that silly story of yours, not a word of which is true!"

"Story? Why, you old — "

Beatrice covered her ears with both hands and shouted, "I am not listening!"

"Of course you're not!" Trudy cried, "You're as deaf as an old shoe! Everybody in town knows it. Bobby Watson knew it before the rest of us, which is why he stepped out with Mary Pearson under the Harvest Moon and you stayed home with your momma and baked a dozen pounds of sweetcake that nobody ever ate and — "

"I'm going home," Beatrice announced, and got up from the table. "That woman is crazy as a March Hare and tells vicious lies all over town."

As she reached for her shawl, Maude came into the room carrying a tray of tea and gingerbread cakes. "Beatrice!"

The woman at the door stopped and turned around, tears brimming at her eyes. "I will not stay and be insulted by you people on my only night out! Maude, it isn't fair."

"Fair's got nothing to do with it, dear," Maude said, her voice calm but a touch louder than normal. "I spent most of this afternoon preparing these cakes and I'll be — " she shot a quick glance across at

Marie " — disappointed, if you don't stay and try them. Let bygones be bygones, I always say. Shall we? Ladies?"

"Well … " Beatrice took her hand off her shawl. "As long as you've gone to the effort, I might forgive her just this once." She walked back to the tea table, pausing to cast a cold eye upon Trudy before seating herself on her side chair.

"Emmy?"

"Honey and lemon, please." She reached forward and snatched a cake off the tray and placed it on her plate. Maude handed her the honey jar from which she poured a couple of drops into her tea, then took a lemon slice and put it next to the tea cup. "Thank you, Maude."

"You're welcome. Marie?"

"Honey, please."

When Maude finished her tour of the table, she returned to the kitchen, leaving Marie with the club ladies. No further words were spoken regarding either game conduct or rules or past indiscretions, and once Maude returned all were laughing together over a word of blue humor overheard downtown.

"Emily Haskins, you devil," said Trudy. "How dare you repeat that in public!"

"Why, this isn't public, it's Maude's house. Isn't that right, Maude?"

"I've heard worse," she replied, grinning wryly, "when Jonas was alive."

Beatrice asked, "Then you agree that it is possible for a man to perform that, uh, feat?"

Before Maude could respond, laughter erupted once again.

"Ladies! We have a guest present!"

"Oh, I'm sure she's heard worse, too, haven't you, dear?" Trudy asked Marie. "Northerners haven't as well-developed a sensibility for the silliness of gentility and manners as we do. Your people aren't nearly so stuck on petty proprieties, are they, dear?"

Marie had no idea at all how to respond to Trudy's suggestion. Did she mean that among Northerners politeness had less value than in the South? If so, then the woman was wrong and ought to be correct-ed. Basic manners and civility were certainly not determined by the boundaries of the Mason-Dixon line. Yet, on the other hand, if Trudy meant that perhaps the North did not adhere to outdated customs and etiquettes, well, Marie had no quarrel with that. She told them, "I grew up with four older brothers and thin bedroom walls and uncles who drank corn whiskey on the porch outside my window at night when we children were supposed to be asleep, so I've long understood how men tell stories."

She smiled.

To that Beatrice added, "They are crude creatures, aren't they?"

And everybody laughed again.

By half-past ten, the club ladies had gone and Maude returned to her laundry at the rear of the house. The wind had grown stronger, banging the Jessup's storm-shutters next door. Marie peeked anxiously out through the curtains and saw the stars had disappeared behind a layer of black clouds drifting east toward Louisiana. She heard Maude open the back door and go out. A few minutes later she came back in with a basket load of laundry. Marie got up and went to help her with the sorting.

"It'll rain by midnight," Maude remarked, folding linen. "I hope those fools don't keep the circus open much longer. It wouldn't do to have the children caught in a storm."

"I'm sure Rachel has an eye on the weather," Marie said, picking out her children's clothing to sort and fold. "I trust CW, too. I'm sure he'll keep them out of trouble. He seems to be a reasonable young man, don't you agree?"

"He's a character," Maude said, emptying the basket and setting it beside the linen cabinet. "Driving around like a fool's advertisement. I sometimes wonder if he's got half the sense God gave a groundhog."

"Rachel is quite taken with him, isn't she?" She loved telling Marie when they were alone how she and CW made love here and there, and how they were too modern to worry about who was watching. Marie always pretended to be shocked, when in truth she was a bit envious. Marie couldn't imagine Harry interested in making love out of doors. He hated the very thought of dust on his trouser cuffs.

Maude frowned. "She's afraid to death of men, always has been. That fear distorts her judgment, makes her choose the wrong fellows to run with. I doubt Rachel really knows how she feels about this one. The fact that he's a fancy-pants from New Orleans with a sack of money to throw around gives her cause to believe Cupid's sitting on her shoulder. Piffle!"

Maude picked up the laundry basket and carried it into her bedroom. Marie went out onto the back porch. A bedroom lamp was lit at the Jessup's, which meant Lili's father was home from the oil fields, sixty miles away. To the north, Marie could just make out the lights of Laswell's circus. She wished she had been able to go with her children, see that they ate something besides cotton candy and ice cream, and didn't get into trouble. Harry would've gone. He adored playing with the children, taking them to the zoo or a movie matinee. He often complained that she had no interest in silly things, but he rarely invited her out anymore, so how could he know? There's a child's heart in each of us.

Finished with her laundry, Maude came out onto the porch. She stood by the railing facing south. "Perhaps it won't rain tonight, after all. There's much too much wind. Those clouds'll pass on by midnight and we'll have a beautiful sunrise, mark my words."

"I hope so," Marie said, as she studied the black sky, noting how the air held a dry grassy smell not at all like that which presaged summer rain. She thought of Illinois and her apple tree in the dooryard. Who would tend to it now that she was gone?

Maude added, "Watch for heat lightning tonight when you're in bed. You'll see it to the south and east. It won't bring showers, though. I've lived here my whole life and I can feel the sky on my skin and know which way it'll turn. I've never been wrong." When a gust ruffled Maude's apron, she held it down with both hands and put her back to the wind as she stared out into the dark. "Dear, your children will have to know that this is not Illinois, that there are considerations one must pay service to."

"Pardon me?"

"The colored children from Shantytown." Maude's eyes were steely and gray, her expression firm. "I do not say this to disturb you, nor as an apology for those of us who have always lived here. What is in our hearts has been there since birth and we have not denied our inheritance. It is a fact and, though not all of us embrace it, we nevertheless accept what is, and will likely remain, part of our lives here. As much as possible, we stay on our side of the river, and they stay on theirs. This is the accommodation we've arrived at, and everyone understands it. Will you explain this to your children, or would you rather I did so?"

Her heart pounding, Marie gazed out into the dark, not quite certain how to respond. During supper, Cissie had recounted her adventure at the river, the excitement of it still evident in her voice. Henry, too, had been taken by the events and rattled on about flailing in the current and the strong Negro hand that had rescued him. In the years they had been married, Harry regaled Marie with thousands of stories of growing up in Texas, the people he had known, those he had cared for, those he had despised. Race had only now and then been part of those tales, even by inference. Nor had the issue arisen in Marie's imagination about his life in Bellemont. Prior to the moment she and the children disembarked from the train in Bellemont, she had never set foot in the South. Her grandfather had fought with Burnside in the War Between the States, but that was a distant memory now, a forgotten conflict. Yet nobody who read the newspapers was entirely ignorant about the South. The Ku Klux Klan had infiltrated Indiana only a few years back. Cousins Frenchy and Alvin mentioned fishing near colored people along the Mississippi every so often, saying they had come upriver by barge and caught fish to feed their children because it was preferable to buying in town where they might not be welcomed. She never heard anybody else in Farrington express that sentiment aloud. It would have been considered vulgar and ill-mannered to do so, beneath one's dignity and demeaning to all. In church, she was taught that all people, regardless of the color of their skin, were an expression of divine inspiration, and that one's standing before God had nothing to do with race. If it was true that fortune lent its grace more broadly upon white people than dark, that was more a result of worldly constructions than whispers from on high. Implied was the notion that Negroes suffered misfortune derived from a coincidence of birth and that here on earth their station was muddled by inconsiderate and evil people like D.C. Stephenson whose fears overwhelmed the grace God had planted in their hearts at the beginning of time. Only when hurt and suffering and wrongdoing went out of the world would the Negro's stature rise. Yet those lurid and ghastly tales of rape and lynchings in the Deep South that Marie occasionally read about in the newspapers made her debate what she had learned. How long was it necessary for the Negro to wait upon his white neighbor's education of the heart? She was not shocked the night the colored school had burned down in the rain outside Shantytown, not taken aback by the indifference shown the Negro bucket brigade by the white citizenry of Bellemont, nor insulted by Rachel's offhanded remark about not offering help to those who refuse to ask for it. That night, Marie understood how many state lines she had crossed by train, how far south she had traveled with her children. Indeed, the colored man who rescued Henry in the current likely taught the children a better lesson than most people in Bellemont would ever know. Whose side of the river, after all, was more blessed?

In her calmest voice, she told Maude, "I've never told them whom to play with and whom to avoid. Neither has Harry. My own mother raised me to believe the heart sees truths our eyes deny." Marie stared off down the street. "But I am not such a Pollyanna as to think everyone feels the same way. I know this isn't Illinois. Yes, indeed I'll speak to the children this evening before bedtime."

"Thank you," said Maude. "Well, I have to take a bath. Good night, dear."

"Good night."

Somewhat depressed now, Marie turned down the beds in her room and went outdoors where the dizzying fragrance of honeysuckle from the Jessup's fence blossomed with the rising humidity and made her drowsy. To the north, a distant glow of electric colors gradually dimmed and winked out as the circus closed down for the evening. Marie herself felt deflated at not having gone. Once when she was a girl, a wagon circus had stopped for the night a mile outside of Farrington and put up a campfire performance for the local children

who'd collected to see the elephants and clowns and fire-breathing giants. Marie had come down Willitson Road from the farm with her
cousins Emeline and Violet and hid together in a stand of willows
where they could spy on the circus animals and spangled acrobats
without being seen. Huddled in the shadows, Marie saw a pretty girl
perhaps younger than herself with crow-black eyes flung to the stars
by a pair of strongmen only to somersault safely back to earth. She
watched a tiny fellow in a golden suit stand upright in the mouth of
a man-eating lion and sing, "Nearer my God to Thee." Terrified of
freaks and wild animals, Violet ran home after that. Emeline lasted
just long enough to see a silky blonde mermaid emerge from a briny
tub to puff rose blossoms off her fingertips for the gathering audience.
Marie preferred to stay behind, hoping she might be caught, perhaps
even kidnapped, and stolen away to a foreign land somewhere where a
kindhearted gypsy would teach her the Arabian belly-dance and how
to stand on her head atop the great death-defying highwire. Instead,
she fell asleep in the bushes and awoke to an empty clearing and had
to walk home alone to a severe scolding by her mother who told her
that no adventure on this earth compares to that which a woman un-
dertakes by marrying a man she loves and raising children in a home
of her own. True enough, but aren't females permitted dreams beyond
dishes and bed linen? Time was, Marie frolicked in the summer woods
by moonlight. Why not now?

A gentle breeze swirled in the road. Noisy motors droned far away,
then went quiet. Marie walked down to the front gate and stared off
past the cottonwoods toward downtown. Her feet were restless. She
went out onto the sidewalk and strolled along to the end of the fence.
Nights like this led her wandering. Harry had no idea. Now and then,
he'd go to the cigar store after supper or slip out of bed in the dark and
take walks across Cedar Street down into the vine-clogged ravine. His
secret little adventures. Yes, she knew all about them. But she had her
own, though not at night when the children needed her; rather, during
the afternoon when Emeline volunteered to watch the children play
in the yard. Then Marie might take the trolley across town, or board
the Limited and ride to Danleyville and back, just to see the sights, be

a stranger somewhere, observe other lives in other places. She did so want to go.

Not a block and a half away, she saw the shadow cross behind a cottonwood, a shape in the trees. Startled, at first Marie didn't believe she'd seen anything at all. It was a trick of the eye, she thought, a phantom revealed by the wind. She stared at the figure motionless in the dark, afraid to take another step. Then he became a man, and her arms went cold. She stood very still herself. Was she being watched? The longer she stared, the less she believed her eyes. Many times in the woods at night behind the farm, she'd see strange sights and scare herself half to death and need to run home. Then in the daylight there'd be nothing but birds on branches. She guessed this, too, was nothing and began to walk down the sidewalk, one foot after the other. She had the jitters now, and wanted to turn about and go back to the safety of Maude's yard. Instead, plain as day, she called out, "Hello?"

Her voice carried down the street, which startled her. She'd hoped to be discreet. There were people in bed, after all, Maude included. Regardless, she drew no response from her mysterious phantom. Emboldened by her own voice in the summer dark, Marie took another six steps along the sidewalk, still sticking to the fenceline. What if this were the killer of Boy-Allen? Had she considered that? How reckless was she prepared to be? Just being out after dark under these circumstances would have Harry thinking she'd gone off her nut. He would sit her down and ask if she drank liquor like her cousins, to which she'd laugh and make him angry and they wouldn't speak for at least three days.

Marie moved further along the fenceline, and saw the figure dart off into the woods. She heard the brush crackle and the snap of a large branch. Her breath caught in her throat. What on earth had she just seen? Well, by God, she had no intention of going home now. Acting on some impulse she'd never known before in her life, Marie hurried down the sidewalk to a spot just across the street from where that man (of course it was a man, what woman runs away into the woods?) had escaped into the darkness. If she'd had a whistle, she would have deflated her lungs blowing it. That was Boy-Allen's killer, she was sure.

Who else would hide like that, spying on houses from the shadows? Of course, every town had a peeper. At home, it was William Winningham, a pathetic creature whose mother and father had burned up one night in a terrible fire, leaving him destitute and disturbed. For years, he wandered the neighborhoods of Farrington, sneaking into dooryards and peeking through hedges, more pest than threat, until one night when he stumbled into a potato cellar and broke his neck and wound up in a sanitarium where his Uncle Edgar claimed he was much happier.

So why was Marie crossing College Street now and pursuing her phantom through the dark? She had no desire to enter the brush; she wasn't that impulsive. A month ago, she would have turned on her heel and gone back to the house. That was then. Now, she walked quickly to the corner and took Cordelia Road toward the river, guessing that this fellow, whoever he was, would either disappear into the woods, or emerge somewhere on this road, and if he did, then she'd see him. Then Marie slowed, eyes fixated on the trees ahead. Her legs felt jittery and the skin on the back of her neck crawled like a swarm of bugs. She shuddered. A cool breeze wafted across the dark, carrying a scent of cedar and damp grass.

A moment later, perhaps a hundred feet away, someone crossed the road from the underbrush and passed into the alley between the houses fronting College Street, some lit still before bedtime, others dark. The figure passed so quickly and silently, had Marie not been focused directly ahead, had her attention been drawn away in that instant, she might not have noticed.

She called out, "STOP!"

And her voice echoed back across the sultry night, idiotic and misplaced. What was she thinking? If he hadn't known before that she was chasing him, surely now he did. A trash can banged in the alleyway and a dog began barking in a back garden. Marie hurried across the road. A porchlight came on four houses away and she heard a low voice grumbling. She thought about calling to whomever had come out to attend to the dog, but was afraid of drawing the wrong sort of attention to herself. What would she say? There was a strange man running away from her in the dark? She peered into the dirty alleyway lined with plank fences, absolutely black now in the night. Why hadn't she gone back indoors straight off and borrowed one of Rachel's electric lanterns? Harry would tell her that was the smart thing to do. Whenever they had raccoons in the yard, or boys playing pranks in the neighborhood, Harry fetched his flashlight from the closet and went out to have a look. He rarely called from the upper window, and never went out empty-handed. Fine, so he was right about being prepared. Well, fiddle-dee-dee, he wasn't here now, was he? And this was her chase, her problem to solve. What did she intend to do now?

A man she didn't recognize leaned out a wooden gate halfway down the alley. In the lamplight from the porch, he looked puffy and unshaven, and when Marie drew near, she could smell burning tobacco and a hint of beer on the breeze. She stepped back into the shadows, and knew she was being silly but had no thought of revealing herself. Just ahead, her phantom figure darted past a stack of cordwood and a Ford truck near the end of the alley.

The fellow at the gate called out in a crude voice, "Who's there? You goddamned kids get the hell out of here now! I ain't fooling!"

Another dog began barking down the alley and a cat shrieked.

Trapped between exposing herself as a nasty sneak and losing track of her phantom, Marie wasn't sure what to do. It was all so thrilling. What would Maude think? Or her own children? The wooden gate closed and the gruff fellow went back indoors. Marie stepped out of the shadows and tiptoed past his yard. She'd certainly lost her chance to catch the phantom now, but hurried on down to the end of the alley, anyhow. There were more voices somewhere off in the dark in the next block or the one beyond, and she noticed how completely her fear had gone. Something had come over her now in the dark, a strength she hadn't anticipated. Indeed, she felt braver than ever before. Common sense told her now was the time to go back to Maude's house and wait there safely for her children to return. She did not. Instead, Marie came out of the alley onto Hardin Street and went across, and on into the shadows. She felt like a hunter now, stalking her prey, unafraid. The night buzzed about her, music from indoor radios, errant voices from sheltered porches, angry dogs here and there. None of it frightened or dissuaded her. She walked ahead, determined to find her phantom.

The town was a warren in the summer dark. Narrow dirt streets and cluttered alleyways led every which way, and she chose her route with only slight discrimination. She crept past a livery stable and a hog pen and several tin garages where anyone who chose might hide and let her by. Here and there, she peered into the shadows with her sternest gaze. She refused to rush. Twice, Marie imagined footsteps nearby and stood still as a tree until she was sure nobody was there. She followed a dirt road that paralleled College Street where she smelled lilac from a dooryard and imagined the river was near. Beside her now were the thick woods and darkness. If a killer waited in ambush, he could drag her off and dismember her body and nobody would know until daylight — if then. She felt a chill. Fear crept into her toes. Marie was sure Boy-Allen's killer was watching her that very instant, poised to strike. What on earth would she do if he did? Back on the farm when she was a girl, her male cousins were forever scrapping in the dust and wrestling. She held her own with Frenchy and once gave Cousin Bert a shiner when he tried to pitch her into Uncle Henry's watering trough. *It's wrong to worry over anything before it happens.* Cissie's motto, borrowed from Oz. She clenched her fists, drew a deep breath, and moved straight ahead along the road.

Then she was a block from downtown and there were autos on Main Street closeby and nobody had jumped out. If she'd lost her phantom, well, at least he knew she meant business! Marie walked toward Keister's blacksmith shop, eyes focused on the sign over the rear entrance, still in the shadows, but only a dozen yards from a lamplit porch on the corner.

She heard him step out behind her and the hair stood up on the back of her neck, and her heart froze solid. She felt as if she were walking in mud, her legs numb and useless, like in a dream. He was so close, she smelled the tobacco stink off his jacket. Too frightened to turn and face him, too scared to run, she did nothing at all. Not even breathe. Directly behind her now, he seemed omnipresent, swelling up like a beast, occupying all the alley space between fences. Crossing her brain in the instant before he grabbed her shoulder was the thought that she'd never been brave at all in her life, never anything more than reckless and foolish. And now she'd pay a dear price for that failing.

His hand was big and strong. It closed over her shoulder and she felt feeble beneath that grip. She ought to have screamed or kicked out backward like one of Uncle Henry's mules. Instead, she sagged, almost fainting, and found herself held upright as she slumped, expecting a painful, wrenching death.

But nothing hurt at all. Instead, even as he breathed a stink of gin in her ear, she heard a gruff yet pleasant voice say, softly, "Looking for your cat?"

Then Jimmy Delahaye was staring Marie in the face, that wry smile pumping blood back into her limbs.

"I haven't got a cat," she stammered, feebly. "I don't know what I'm doing."

Even to herself that sounded absurd. She must truly have gone out of her mind. Delahaye stared at her like she was crazy, so maybe she was. Harry would think so. She felt like an idiot.

Delahaye asked, "Are you lost? It's awfully dark out here."

She shook her head. "No, I just went this way because it seemed like a shortcut. I guess I should've stayed in bed."

"You got out of bed to take a walk in the middle of the night?"

Now she was confused. Maybe she had lost her head, after all. "No, I was waiting up for the children. Rachel took them to the circus this evening. I stayed home with Maude to help with her club ladies."

"So, you weren't in bed?"

"No." She folded her arms as Delahaye became more visible in the shadows. He had his eye on her, and she wasn't sure how to behave. Not every woman goes out walking in the dark. It just wasn't done. What did he think of her?

"Are you headed anywhere in particular? Nothing's open downtown. It's kind of late to be out and about."

"Well, I was thinking about going home, if truth be told. I'm expecting the children any minute." That sounded silly, and she knew it, but was much too flustered to tell a better fib.

"Would you like me to walk you back? I'll show you a better short-cut, if you prefer."

Trying to sound sane for a moment, Marie replied, "That would be just fine. Thank you very much."

"My pleasure."

Delahaye offered his arm, and Marie took it as if it were the most natural thing in the world, hoping to preserve what shred of dignity she had remaining. He led her out of the alleyway, past the blacksmith shop, then up the old plank sidewalk on Morgan Lane under the dusty willows. A pleasant breeze sighed across the dark and Marie felt herself calm down enough to tell Delahaye about the phantom she'd seen skulking in the brush.

"I have no doubt whatsoever that he was Boy-Allen's killer. Who else would hide in the bushes, peeping on the Jessup's. How he ran from me gave it away."

"Did you see his face?"

"Of course not," Marie said, as if the question were somehow impertinent. "He was far too clever to let himself be seen that clearly. A vile murderer like that would never allow himself to be caught so easily. We'll just all have to be far more vigilant now that we know he's still with us."

When they reached Maude's house again on College Street, Delahaye let Marie in through the front gate, but stayed behind on the sidewalk. In a tone Marie hadn't heard from him before, Delahaye warned, "I think you ought to be more careful yourself. You know, I'd hate to lose my secretary to a lunatic."

He smiled.

Rachel and the children hadn't come home yet, and the house was dark but for a light on in Maude's bedroom. There was no pressing reason for Marie to go indoors just now, so she didn't. The clouds had parted and the air was warm and moist. It made her feel carefree somehow.

"Did you see me tiptoeing down the alley?" Marie asked, keeping her voice low. She realized what a stroke of luck it was that Delahaye had been there.

"I thought you were a cat on the prowl," he told her.

"That's not a bit funny. I nearly ran myself into one of those ash-cans."

"If you wanted company, you ought've rang me up. I'd have been over here in a flash."

"So you weren't at the circus?"

"Earlier, for a while. But I had some papers to look over downtown and when I finished, I thought I'd take a walk."

"I guess I'm fortunate that you did." She felt herself blushing. What was it about this man that had such a terrible effect on her? If only Harry knew — not that he was so awfully private with his own wandering eye, as if he imagined she didn't know how women looked at him, and how he looked back.

"Well, I suppose I'd better drag myself to bed," Delahaye said, casting a long gaze off down the street. He sounded weary, or pensive. Marie wasn't sure which.

"I'm grateful," she murmured.

"Don't mention it," Delahaye said, suddenly focusing his eyes directly on Marie. They had the faintest twinkle, she was sure. He tipped his hat. "See you soon."

"I hope so."

And she did, too.

— **4** —

At half past twelve, CW's automobile parked in front of the house. Maude had long since retired, leaving Marie to compose letters by lamplight in the sitting room off the kitchen. She wrote to Harry about the smash-up on Main Street, recounted Henry's accident on the river, and Maude's angry opinion of the Boy-Allen investigation, then asked his advice regarding Delahaye's offer. She told Harry how terribly she missed him and wished he'd come to visit soon. Knowing he, too, must be lonely, she signed it with an extra kiss and a hug. Maybe she lied a little about how she felt, and ought to have been more honest with her feelings, but what good could come out of that? Nor had she any intention of telling him about how handsome she'd found Jimmy Delahaye, nor one word regarding her exciting adventure tonight. Some things these days needed to remain her own. Marie had just begun a note to Emeline regarding Cousin Alvin's peculiar disappearance from the farm when the sounds of giggling and auto-doors slamming drew her attention. She put down her pen and went out onto the front porch where the children were dancing circles in the road and waving Japanese modesty fans about over their heads. CW wore a straw hat ringed with a garland of laurel leaves; Rachel's blouse was draped in boa feathers.

Seeing their mother, the children let out a shriek. "Momma! Momma! We won! We won!"

"Shhh!" Marie came down the porchsteps to the windy street. "Grandma's sleeping."

"But we won!" Cissie cried, only slightly less loudly than before. She held a stuffed lion for her mother to see. "We won a prize for each of us! Well, *we* didn't win, exactly. CW did, throwing balls at wooden ducks, and he was so good that the man there told him we could each have anything we wanted if he would only stop throwing and go home! So I chose Ali Baba here and Henry got a crocodile and Rachel got some unicorn feathers and CW took Caesar's old hat and each of us got to keep one of these beautiful fans! Isn't it wonderful?"

"I rode on the Ferris wheel, Momma," Henry announced, "and I wasn't scared at all!"

"It was a marvelous evening," Rachel said, climbing out of CW's Ford. "We all had a grand time."

"I expect you did," said Marie, smiling as Henry twirled his paper fan about like an airplane diving and arcing back up into the air. "Did everyone get enough to eat?"

"A bellyful," Cissie said, patting her stomach. She stopped twirling. "I'm so full up, I may explode any minute now."

"The children had packs of fun," CW said, coming around from the driver's side of the Ford. He had a ticket in his hatband and his flannel trousers rippled in the wind. "There was so much to do."

"I even touched a monkey, Momma," Henry said, the paper fan flying out of his hand into the dusty street. The wind blew it away from him and he gave chase.

"My gosh!" Marie smiled. "What do you know about that."

"No, he didn't," Cissie corrected. "He gave it a piece of Cracker Jack, even though the sign said not to feed the animals."

"Sure I did! He was awful hungry," Henry explained, snatching up the paper fan again. "He wanted some Cracker Jacks."

"Henry stuck his hand right through the bars. I was sure that monkey'd bite his fingers off."

"Did you do that?" Marie asked, amazed at her son's bravado. Ordinarily, he was afraid of loud dogs and hissing cats. To picture him offering Cracker Jack to a strange monkey, well, Texas apparently had its spell on all of them.

"He wasn't at all mean, Momma," said Henry. "I liked him."

"There were a million things to see," Cissie said. "I could've stayed all night and not seen them all."

"I believe she's telling the truth," agreed Rachel. "Your children ran us ragged trying to keep up. We had to be pitched out so Laswell could close for the night."

"I liked the show under the big top best of all," Cissie said.

"The clowns!" Henry cried. "They were funny!"

Cissie said, "One of them had a flower that shot water into the audience as he rode by on a giant unicycle. Everyone around us got wet and no one was mad. Then a group of baby clowns —"

"Midgets," Rachel corrected with a shudder. "Why, I've never seen so many in my life. They gave me the heebie-jeebies."

"Well, they looked like babies, Momma, I promise they did! And they all ganged up on one big giant clown and hit him with orange clubs and bouquets of exploding flowers and a powder puff the size of a pumpkin until he fell over and pretended to be dead and shushed us all so we wouldn't tell the baby clowns that he wasn't really dead, only fooling so they'd quit picking on him. I've never laughed so hard! And then the trapeze people came out on the high wire! Oh, Momma! There was a girl my age named Jenny Dodge and she was so beautiful and not a bit scared to be up so high and she crossed the wire without looking down once and she smiled and waved when she got to the other side and everybody clapped and then she went back the other direction, only this time she stood on her head in the middle of the wire and made a somersault and a turn on one toe and then dove off!"

"Into mid-air?" Marie asked, trying her best to sound incredulous. She was so pleased at her daughter's joy, she could scarcely resist giving Cissie a big warm hug.

"Yes, only another one of the trapeze boys also dived off the platform just above her and as she fell toward us, he caught her, and then someone else caught him and all three of them swung back and forth smiling and waving until they got tired and climbed down to the ground where everybody clapped! I was so scared I thought I'd faint, but I didn't, and I decided, Momma, right then that one day I'm going to join the circus and climb the trapeze and be the first in the world to do a triple flip-flop! Isn't that a wonderful plan, Momma? Isn't it?"

"I should say so, dear."

"Me, too!" Cissie agreed. "And you will all be invited to watch me perform."

"And so we shall," said Marie, "but first, you and your brother'll have to get off to sleep. It's hours past your bedtime."

"But Momma! I want to write a letter to Daddy and tell him all about my wonderful circus plan!"

"You can do that tomorrow, dear," Marie replied, already exhausted by her daughter's excitement. "Enough's enough for tonight. Both of you, this very moment, run along to bed!"

"Aww — " Cissie's voice trailed off. Confronted with the hopeless reality of the situation, she grabbed her brother's hand and led him up the porchsteps. She turned to the adults below her. "Thank you for taking us to the circus tonight. We had a wonderful time." She showed a brilliant smile and nudged Henry for the same.

"Thank you," Henry said, looking disconsolate now that his circus evening was finally over.

"You're very welcome," CW replied with a bow. "It was our pleasure."

"Night, kids!" Rachel added. "Sleep tight!"

"I'll be in shortly," Marie said. "Don't wake your grandma."

"May I mix a glass of malted milk to take to bed?" Cissie asked.

"Me, too!" Henry squealed.

Marie sighed. "All right, dear. Now hurry along, both of you."

After the children had gone inside, Marie said, "That was very kind of you both to take them to the circus. They truly enjoyed themselves."

"I'm sure we'd have stayed all night if it had been up to them," Rachel replied. "They were just a pair of little spitfires, on the run from the ticket box to the moment we dragged them out the gate."

"I hadn't been to the circus myself in years," CW said. "I'd forgotten how fabulous it can be."

"And dirty, too," Rachel added. "Those people who work there? Ugghh! I like to died! That Laswell fellow must hire them right out of a cave. I doubt one of them can read or write. And not only are their manners atrocious, but the language they use with one another! I was embarrassed for the children. If it had rained insect powder, there wouldn't have been enough decent folks among us to bury the rest. One would think Mr. Laswell would have better sense than hiring ignorant good-for-nothings like that. Then again, perhaps that's why his vile little circus is no Barnum & Bailey."

"Aw, quit crabbing," CW growled. "You're not being at all fair. Why, it's a swell circus. Sure, those fellows working the midway are a little rough. I won't gripe with you about that. But, gee whiz, there was so much to see and do there, well, for a small wagon circus, I was quite taken."

"And I wonder why Mother is constantly drawing your good taste into question."

CW laughed. "Now, darling, you're just sore because you had a chance to win that beautiful crystal vase and you missed the bull's-eye!"

"Crystal?" Marie exclaimed. She had no idea they offered such prizes. "Oh my!"

"It was certainly not Viennese crystal," said Rachel, "probably just ordinary glass, and the darts that ugly man gave me were bent. No one on earth could've thrown them straight. I was cheated out of my prize."

"Poor sport." He kissed her cheek as two boys rode past on bicycles, one carrying a stuffed dog and the other a half-eaten stick of cotton candy. Wind chased them off into the dark. Hadn't they any thought at all of Boy-Allen's killer and the threat that hid in the woods?

Marie felt a chill and wrapped her arms tightly about herself. It was late, too, and she was growing drowsy. Were the children in bed yet? She'd give them another couple of minutes, then go indoors to be sure.

Slipping an arm about CW's waist, Rachel told him, "Well, you needn't sound so smug. After all, I consider myself at least partially responsible for your winning."

Marie turned to CW. "Did you win many games on the midway?"

"He was the greatest champion of them all this evening." She kissed him softly on the cheek. "My hero! You should have seen him pitch those baseballs. I believe he ought to try out for a professional team!"

"I did all right," CW admitted, blushing visibly even in the dark. He drew her close enough to briefly nibble her neck. "But that colored boy's the one who could really throw. My goodness! What an arm!"

Rachel pulled free of CW's grasp. "Oh, quit talking about him. What's done is done."

He caught her hand, trying to pull her back to him. "Well, dear, it was just plain rotten."

"What are you two talking about?" Marie asked, utterly perplexed by their bickering.

"A Negro boy," said CW, "with a wing like a Springfield rifle. He knocked down every single one of those milk bottles, just popped them off the shelves one after another fair and square like Sergeant Alvin York at a Tennessee turkey shoot, and what did he win? Not a blessed thing."

"No, that's not true at all," Rachel argued. "He was given a prize. Every winner got a prize."

"Yes, an old clothespin," CW said to Marie, "given only to humiliate the boy. To put him in his place. What did that fellow behind us call it? 'A nigger prize!' I was ashamed to witness such disgraceful behavior." He shuddered in disgust.

"I was surprised to see so many of them there tonight. Usually they come in after most of us have left. I know they prefer it that way." Rachel slipped loose of CW's hand and moved off.

"How do you know that?" CW said, following her. "Have you ever asked a colored person?"

"I don't need to," Rachel replied, testy now at being challenged. "It's understood."

"Well, I understand, too," CW said, "but I'm not sure I'd like it if I were one of them. Humiliating and venal, is what it is."

"And you don't have such restrictions in New Orleans?" Rachel inquired, the edge to her voice growing steadily.

"Of course we do! And such proprieties are just as rotten there as they are here. Rotten and despicable! Why we choose to continue inflicting this shame upon ourselves simply mystifies me. It's the social blight of our age." CW tried to catch her, but Rachel strolled away from his reach.

"Oh, snap out of it, can't you!" She turned to Marie. "CW suffers so for the downtrodden and put-upon of society. It's a wonder the Catholics tolerate him."

"Empathy for the unfortunate is considered commendable in most civilized societies," CW said to Marie. "Wouldn't you agree?"

Trying to be neutral yet honest, she replied, "Well, all our lives are diminished by the suffering of others. We learn that in church."

"Did you hear that, dear?" CW turned to Rachel who refused to let him near. "Now, what do you have to say for yourself? What is the Baptist response to human suffering and indignity?"

Rachel steeled her eyes, then said, "We pay the same nickel at the entrance to the Hall of Freaks as you Catholics." She turned to Marie. "Or you Methodists, or the Pentacostals or the Congregationalists, or anyone else for that matter. And then we go inside the tent and stare for as long as we're allowed because the horrid Turtle Boy reminds us that, but for God's sweet grace, the freak's misfortune might just as well be our own. Therefore, my dear, we Baptists are thankful! That is our response. What else could it be?"

— 5 —

Marie lay in bed listening to the wind as it swept across the piney woods blowing storm clouds toward dawn. Nearby, a small electric fan whirred in the dark where her children breathed quietly and slept well, thoroughly exhausted from the thrills and enchantment of a visit to Emmett J. Laswell's Traveling Circus Giganticus. She knew they would dream of spiraling aerialists, sequins, spangles and sawdust, cotton candy, tumbling clowns and cascading fireworks illuminating a purple sky at twilight: a world come and gone in one summer evening. Across the faint light, she watched Henry's eyelids flutter and jump, Cissie's lips form a silent laugh, a squeal of whispered awe. The wind banged the storm-shutters on the rear of the house, tore at the laundry line, and kicked up clouds of dust that dirtied the chinaberry tree and rattled on the siding next door. A thousand miles away from her husband, in a house she barely knew, Marie Hennesey lay on her back and closed her eyes, remembering her girlhood and the dreams she'd herself had late at night after an evening at the circus.

Across what tightrope had she tiptoed in golden slippers to reach this place? What dangers lay before her still? Everyone has fears that toss with sleep and steal into our dreams. Back across the highwire was her home on Cedar Street in Illinois, unreachable now, lost for good. But whose good? This was not her bed, nor her room. Her children were orphaned from familiar surroundings. She slept in sheets that bore no scent of her husband. Where did he sleep now? And by whose scent? *When we have the least reason for getting into trouble,* Cissie learned from the Tin Woodman, *something is sure to go wrong.* The sad fate of Boy-Allen was not her only warning. She had to watch her step, and her children's, too.

Then soon Marie slept, and dreamed of home.

HIGH SOCIETY

IT WAS SATURDAY MORNING late in June, and Harry Hennesey felt better than he had in months.

A dollar more than yesterday in his pocket, thanks to a buyer from Pittsburgh who had relieved him of the peacock feathers he had kept in storage for a year and a half, Harry hurried along Columbia Avenue in a thin rain with a fresh bounce to his step. Despite the damp and dreary weather, people were out by the thousands. Streetcars fully laden with those freed from the city's industry for the day clanged past. Foul-smelling two-ton trucks rumbled by, bumper to bumper with honking taxicabs, red motorcycles, auto-busses, flashy cream-tinted foreign automobiles, errand boys on bicycle. Near the river, hungry pigeons scoured the bulwarks for soggy bread crumbs, shelled peanuts, fallen popcorn, while along the wide avenues noisy crowds flooded the dampened sidewalks, innumerable black umbrellas providing shelter for the quick and artful. Where Columbia Avenue intersected Beresford Street, a small newspaper boy, perhaps eight or nine years old, stood unsheltered on the corner, shouting, "Extra! Extra! Read all about it! Murder in the Ice House!" His shrill voice carried a block away, reaching Harry as he crossed the busy avenue from the bulwark. The newsboy's brown knickers were drenched, his cotton shirt and flat brown cap dripping crystal beads of rainwater as he hawked his stack of soggy pink newspapers to passersby. Evading a taxi as he reached Beresford Street, Harry saw a bright little face, made ruddy and raw by the cold morning.

Dodging several puddles, he hurried across the street, two pennies for the newspaper in his fist.

"EXTRA! EXTRA! READ ALL ABOUT IT! MURDER IN THE ICE HOUSE!" The boy faced uptown now, away from the windy river, shouting his tiny lungs out above the din of traffic while waving the *Daily Clarion.*

Harry took a peek at the headline: more gangsters and murder. Bootleggers ambushed in an old ice house on Banyon Street across from the Daughters of Israel. Half-a-dozen machine-gunned to death and impaled on steel hooks. Police baffled as to the identity of the culprits. Stories like this certainly gave the newspapers a lift, although Harry was becoming tired of raw sensationalism. What good did it do to read something over your toast and corn flakes that brought on a case of indigestion? Even so, he bought a newspaper every morning because he still enjoyed the funny pages.

"I'll take one, son."

The newsboy spun about, eyes bloodshot and weary. Harry felt sorry for him, a child working the city streets all morning long when he ought to have been off somewhere playing with his friends. Selling anything on a Saturday morning in a drizzling rain was certainly no fun.

Trying to be friendly, he asked the boy, "How much?"

"How's that?"

"For the paper? How much?" He loved joking with kids. Roll a fifty-cent piece across your fingers or slide the ace of clubs out of a shirt pocket and you're more popular than the Easter bunny. Kids adore a little fun with a grownup. Didn't Henry love to play with his dear old dad for just that reason?

"Say, mister, you just get off a boat or something?" A sneer curled across the newsie's mouth. He screeched again, "EXTRA! EXTRA! READ ALL ABOUT IT! MURDER IN THE ICE HOUSE!"

Ignoring the wisecrack, Harry told the boy, "I sold papers myself when I was your age. I had a bicycle route, delivering all over town. Thought I'd make my first million!" He chuckled lightly.

The boy sold a paper to a man in a black overcoat, and turned back to Harry. "Say, you want a paper, mister?"

"Well, sure I do," Harry replied, holding his temper. "Why else would I have crossed the street?"

"Then why ain't you bought one?" The boy turned away again, waving his papers in the direction of traffic stopped now along the crowded avenue. Harry watched two terrifically beautiful women cross the street as the newsie hollered out, "EXTRA! EXTRA! READ ALL ABOUT IT! MURDER IN THE ICE HOUSE!"

"Well, maybe, I won't take one after all. You ought to think about how you talk to your elders."

"Aw, stick it in your ear! If you ain't buyin' nothing, shove off! You're scaring away my customers! EXTRA! EXTRA! READ ALL ABOUT IT! MURDER IN THE ICE HOUSE!"

Harry wanted to grab the boy and throw him over his knee. Really, he had just tried to make the poor kid feel better about his stupid job. Being nasty was bad policy.

"Say, mister, ain't you got no sense? I tell you, I'm about ready to give you a sock on the beak!"

The newsboy bared his rotten teeth, a youngster's sneer the likes of which Harry hadn't seen since grade school. Rainwater dripping off the boy's soggy cap reinforced his nasty countenance, giving Harry cause to retreat a step or two. For all he knew, the youngster concealed a knife somewhere in his shabby clothing.

The boy advanced toward Harry, still waving his papers at passing traffic. "Thought I was a sweetpea, huh? Why, I oughta… !"

As the newsie raised a fist, Harry stepped backward off the curb with a splash into Beresford Street, drowning both shoes in the cold gutter stream.

"Go on, you big sap! SCRAM! Beat it while I'm feelin' generous!"

Then he spat at Harry's feet and raced back to his spot beside the iron lamppost, calling loudly into the street, "EXTRA! EXTRA! READ ALL ABOUT IT! MURDER IN THE ICE HOUSE!"

Delany's Café at 23rd Street had the lights on over the busy lunch counter, and cigarette smoke hung in a gray haze above the room. Conversation roared. Plates clanked. Swinging doors leading in and out of the kitchen flew open and closed. Six pretty waitresses in white aprons rushed from table to table, taking and delivering orders, laughing with familiar customers. Harry sat in a booth by a window, an order of ham and scrambled eggs, plain toast, and a steaming cup of black coffee on the Formica table in front of him. Outdoors, the rain had slowed to a light mist. As he slipped his fork under a bite of eggs, his lovely young dining companion spread raspberry jam onto a slice of toast. Pearl's owlish eyes glistened under a rakish peekaboo hat sewn from metallic cloth and beads. Wrapped in her usual cheap brown Ulster, her soft lips painted a rich carmine, she looked like a fledgling huddled over a stack of hot cakes and Cream of Wheat. Harry did his best not to imagine her nude beneath those clothes. It was too early in the day for that. Dropping that glass in his apartment when he discovered her naked in his bed had helped him resist behaving badly. But it had been rough. The shock of seeing a young girl exposing herself like that nearly threw him over. Lying there atop his blanket, she reminded him of a rosy Maxfield Parrish cherub. She'd begged him to make love to her, then flew into a silly rage when he reminded her that he was married. *Well, she ain't here and I am!* Pearl shouted in complete disregard for his neighbors. *Say it straight, honey, are you a man, or aren't you? You really got the nerve! You have me up here, and then you don't have me. What gives?*

That was when he decided to fill her in on his scheme for Follette's missing niece. What else could he do, anyhow, other than toss her out into the hall? Naturally, he didn't mention the great industrialist at all. That was a certain detail he just knew was better kept to himself. In his version, young Olive Blanchard was a rattlebrained hatcheck girl from the Blackstone Hotel in Omaha who had run off with the overcoat of a big shot from New York City. Sewn into the lining of the coat was a bank draft for a thousand dollars. Harry happened to hear about the fellow through a mutual acquaintance who found out the check hadn't yet been cashed. That meant the girl still had the funds in her possession. A posted reward for the bank draft's safe return offered ten percent. Harry told Pearl he would be willing to work a three-to-one split with her. She argued for sixty-forty, and he agreed. Once he pitched the idea of Pearl involving her gang from the pirate escapade, she became greatly enthused and kissed him, then apologized for acting like a horny hussy, claiming liquor had dulled her judgment. That night, he had let her sleep on the sofa in the front room of the apartment after she promised not to peek through the curtains to his bedroom.

Feeling generous the next morning, Harry bought her a month of transfers on the Belvedere streetcar line. Soon he began to visit her most afternoons at Market Lane where the fishmongers and fruit vendors gathered to sell their product, or the occasional evening in sultry Chinatown in the midst of a gay dinner crowd. Appearing suddenly from the ether of her curious and filthy netherworld, she would tap his shoulder while whistling one of those idiot Rudy Vallée melodies she found so endearing. Expecting to keep his nose to the grindstone for these next few months, instead he began quitting work early to spend more time with her. That was deeply troubling, mostly because Marie wrote weekly from Texas of the children's adventures in their new home and her own need for stability, which meant more money from him and a reassurance that this situation really was only temporary. Truth was, he ought to have held the purse strings tighter last year, not let the budget budge. Standing off the bank for another shingle was a big mistake, as was straddling the market for months on end. *Speculate when you have more money than you need, never when you need more money than you have.* Playing with the milk money is not how a man helps his family. Now he had let himself get fussed up over a girl half his age who probably didn't know the cat from the canary.

Yet she had already been helpful. A couple of weeks after taking her clothes off in front of him, she had burst into his apartment, waving a slip of paper that bore the telephone number of a fellow named Elmer Thurston who was seeking a barrel full of peacock feathers for a garden party at a mansion on Penn Avenue in Pittsburgh. Harry rang Thurston that morning and made the sale before supper, earning enough on the transaction to pay a month's rent on his apartment and still wire another three hundred dollars down to East Texas. The next morning, Pearl took Harry down to Berkeley Corners to meet a girl named Olive who vaguely matched Follette's description: the age was correct, so was her rough physical makeup, except her eyes were brown and her last name was Porter, not Blanchard. A similar disappointment arose with a fourteen year-old urchin who lived in a flat by the stockyards near Onion Street. This Olive was a Symmes, not a Blanchard, either, but she had brown hair with blue eyes. In her case, what failed to pan out, besides her last name again, was where she was born and raised. She came from Medford, Oregon and hadn't been east of the Rockies until this past January when she rode out on a train with her aunt who was raped and murdered in a side street alley off Regency Boulevard the day after they arrived. Before this, Harry would have guessed searching for a teenage girl with the name of Olive was statistically improbable. With Pearl helping, he decided he actually had a pretty fair chance, because she seemed to know half the people in the city.

This morning, she'd telephoned the front desk at the Warsaw Hotel with a message to meet her at Delany's Café. He hoped she had some good news for him, but so far all she'd done was gab on and on about the silly little inanities that described her life. News flash: a kid handed her a fresh red rose down on Third Street, then stuck his hand up her skirt when she whirled around to see a car skid into a newsstand; two cute dames she met out in Bartlett Park caught a dose from a pair of Harvard boys who were in town for a tennis tournament; a Rexall druggist on Carson Street tried making her by slipping knockout drops into her soda pop; also, had Harry seen that photograph in the *Evening Sentinel* of the manhole blown sky high from a busted gas main on Jefferson Avenue? She thought the fellow whose head got knocked off might have been one of Harry's business acquaintances because the newspaper said he worked up on Diever Street.

"No, dear, I saw the picture, but I've never met the poor fellow. Now, are you going to eat, or just talk my ear off this morning?" He poured sugar into his coffee and tasted slowly. It was atrocious. "And what did you call me for, anyhow?"

Pearl asked, "How come you don't eat so much, honey? You ain't got cancer in your boiler, do you?"

"Of course not." He looked past his scrambled egg to the window. Did he look that bad? "I'm in tip-top shape."

Across the avenue, umbrellas were being put away, clouds breaking up, sunshine on the brick pathways. Soon a grand morning rainbow would arc brightly above the river bulwark while children chased about waving colorful flags, and trolleys delivered more passengers to the festive bulwark. Since his first years of working a steady job, Harry had come to believe that leisure rightly belonged to those whose daily labor provided all of us with sustenance and vitality. Play strengthened a worker's heart, restored vibrancy to his soul. American industry owed its prosperity to each of those whose sweat and diligence allowed the nation's great turbines to keep churning. A day off for golf or bowling or fishing on the river was only fair. Months on the selling road had always worn him down: those all-night train rides back east or across the Middle Border. Hours of solitude in the parlor cars led inevitably to depression and despair, his heart no longer able to bear the demands placed upon it by his own stupid commitment to fortune as virtue. But a sunny afternoon at the zoo with his children, or solving a new crossword puzzle during breakfast, just playing a couple rounds of Mah Jongg with Marie after supper, seemed to lighten his spirits, and wasn't contentment, more than profit, life's truest recompense?

One cold autumn evening at Milwaukee about eight years ago, Harry was asked by a fellow salesman named Bill Dunbar to go with him to a spirited I.W.W. meeting. There were maybe twenty or thirty men roughly Harry's age gathered in a small hall decked out with slogans such as: *When Labor Hangs by the Neck, Liberty Hangs in the Balance,* and *America: Where Labor is Strong and Valiant and Beautiful.* Harry took a seat in the middle of the hall expecting to hear how much better his life would be in Soviet Russia, or that salesmen like himself were dupes of capitalist greed. And he did hear some of that, of course, and would have been disappointed if he hadn't. But an hour or so into the meeting, his friend Bill Dunbar went up to the podium and began arguing that each one of us plays the role of victim and oppressor from time to time. It's as natural, he explained, as watching rain falling from the sky. We feel within our rights to complain when it rains too much or too little, but does that sort of rebellion get us anywhere? There are laws guiding our behavior that were established long before Noah built his ark. Unfortunately, we can't seem to face a few simple facts about how the world is meant to be organized. In Bill's own household, for example, labor was divided among himself, his wife June, and his three teenage sons. Being husband and father, Dunbar explained, he was naturally expected to bring home a paycheck substantial enough to allow June to buy groceries at the A&P every Thursday morning, while his wife's duties involved shopping, cooking meals, and keeping their wonderful home neat and tidy. As the Dunbar boys have grown up, they've been taught to have their rooms clean, trim the hedges, take out the garbage, and keep the family dog fed and brushed. Whether the division of labor was equitable or not, this was how the Dunbar clan succeeded. Certainly he and his wife bickered every once in a while over what amount of money they ought to risk in the market, whether or not their old Ford was worth replacing, or if the dining room needed new curtains. Most choices were made by putting both their heads together and arriving at a sensible decision, but Bill was the head of the household, and always would be. June had no dispute with that, nor did their sons who understood that someone always had to have the last word, and he was that person whose responsibilities were the greatest. If I lose my job tomorrow, Dunbar told the hall, my family knows we'll be out in the street in nothing flat. Likewise, if Henry Ford loses his shirt, and his auto company goes under, a lot of fellows in Dearborn'll be out of a job, too, maybe for good. But if those thousands of autoworkers walk out on him, and he can't drum up anyone competent enough to take their places, he'll lose his shirt, just the same. And if June decides I spend too much of my time speaking at meetings like this or having a drink on Wednesdays after work in the storeroom at Woolworth's, and she takes the boys to her mother's house in Beaver Falls, why, I'll be just as bad off as Henry Ford. I can't sew and my cooking stinks, and I doubt Mr. Ford can assemble one of those shiny new automobiles by himself. You see, a man's household and his country work best when everyone works together, respectful of what each of us puts into the pot. We have floods in Idaho and drought in Kansas, and we can't switch places — no matter what the Communists might say. We just cannot share everything equally, nor are we meant to. Certain laws have come down to us from the blue skies above, and we succeed when we recognize those laws for what they are and adapt to them as best we can. This is the simplest explanation as to why things have come to be as they are. Once the meeting let out, Bill Dunbar drove Harry back across town through a thin snowfall to a frame boardinghouse where they had hired a second floor room together to save a couple of dollars. Using the washbasin while Harry sat in bed trying to read, Dunbar said that the biggest trouble labor has these days is persecution, and he didn't mean the Palmer raids. Give two men a pair of shovels and tell them each to dig a hole four feet deep. Let them know that whoever finishes first will earn six dollars. Once they're both finished, the loser will likely complain that the other fellow had some sort of advantage with his shovel or the quality of dirt he was digging in. Either way, he'll hate that fellow's guts for having beaten him. Ask the winner if he'd choose his pal to help dig a ditch with him for twelve dollars and he'll tell you he'd rather hire someone with more spunk. Pay them both equally and you'll see how the loser will be happy, while the winner will ask himself why he bothered to work so hard. This might seem hard for you to understand, Hennesey, but I lied to all those fellows at the meeting tonight. The anarchist doesn't throw his bombs because of failures he's suffered; he throws them because he's had to suffer the success of others. People hate each other whether they're treated equally or not. Worse yet, they resent the fellow who hires them unless he pays the highest wage for the least amount of work. Envy drives the world, Hennesey, not hunger. Harry put down his book. I don't believe that, he told Dunbar, because it would mean no one values work at all, and that's just not so. In fact, it's contrary to human nature. Some of us want to succeed, no matter what the other fellow does. We may well be persecuted for our efforts, but we're certainly not the least interested in bothering with, much less persecuting, those who strike it rich or fall off the track of their own accord. Bill Dunbar finished splashing water onto his face, then toweled off and sat down on the bed. Well, that's just where you're plain wrong, he told Harry, but I can't prove it to you tonight. You're too stubborn to hear me out, and we've got a train at six in the morning.

All I can tell you is that one day you'll see that none of us are ever good enough to each other. It's just not our instinct, whether we pretend to dream it or not. We all have too much ambition.

Pearl put down her fork. "You ain't flat no more, are you, honey?"

"I beg your pardon?"

Now he was distracted by a fancy black Lincoln sedan discharging four rather sullen-looking young men in long wool coats at the curb fifty feet or so down the street from Delany's Café. The shortest of the four, wearing a black derby, walked back around to the driver's window and spoke briefly there before joining the others on the damp sidewalk. At first, he thought the short one was that same fellow from Sand Avenue he'd seen again a couple of days ago out front of the Rexall Drugstore on 23rd when he took Pearl to buy some toothpaste. But it wasn't.

Pearl tapped his hand with her spoon. "Pick your chin up, honey. Things'll be cozy soon, you'll see. I just know it." She gave him a gentle nudge under the table.

A tray full of empty coffee cups rattled past his head as one of the busboys hurried toward the kitchen. Steam billowed up from the grill in back. Harry's redheaded waitress shouted a nasty word at a customer departing the lunchroom. She had a lovely figure with a nice round bosom and a pretty face and sparkling green eyes. She was adorable. Sipping his coffee, Harry told Pearl, "I have no doubts about the future whatsoever. I do appreciate your help, though. Thurston gave me a pretty square deal."

Of course, if he hadn't been so short of money, he would never have given a fellow like that the time of day. There is just something about certain people that makes you despise them as soon as you say hello. Thurston was one of those. He had shifty eyes and talked money as if he had a cool million in the bank when it was clear he was at best a third-rater.

"You know, him and me go way back," Pearl remarked, spreading more jam onto her toast. "I let him buy me a pair of shoes once and a new hat." She took a bite from the middle of the toast, and put it back onto her plate. "You sure you ain't sick?"

"Stop quizzing me about my health. I've never been fitter. In fact, this morning I walked nine blocks along the river in both directions. I'd like to see you try that."

"Aw, I get around plenty." She coughed harshly, then grabbed for a glass of water and took a gulp. Her eyes teared up briefly and she smiled, wiping her mouth with the back of her hand. "Gee whiz, maybe I'm the one ought to see a doctor."

"Look, at any rate, I wish you wouldn't whisper my name in the ear of everyone you meet. Reputation means a lot to me, and I've built mine up over quite a few years now. Word of mouth travels in both directions, you realize."

"Sure it does, honey, and, like I said, I got the word out about you all over the place." She raised her coffee cup, slurping from the edge. "And we're going to turn that little dame up in no time, see? But, if you ask me, this sales racket of yours is a lot of hooey."

"Oh yes? How's that?" Good grief, you could never get enough opinions from young people. They imagine every thought that crosses their tiny brains is worth publishing in *Colliers*.

"Now, don't get me wrong, honey. Why, I bet you're the swellest salesman there is. But a fellow like you ought to be on top. You might think I'm nuts to say so, but you could be an all-time all timer if you'd only put it over like them other fellows."

"And how might that be?"

"Well, it's a racket, ain't it? Just like any other. It ain't so much what you got as who you know, right? Like I knew Elmer Thurston, and I knew you, and I worked it so's the two of you got yourselves stuck in the same room together and when you came out, Elmer had a bunch of feathers and you had some dough in your pockets that wasn't there before. Do you get me?"

"Yes, I appreciated the arrangement." Harry took a piece of toast off his plate. He should never have accepted Thurston's number from her in the first place. "But please, darling, don't send any more fellows my way."

"I was just trying to help."

"I know you were, and I'm thankful. We made a nice arrangement. But let me tell you, dear, it's not wise to do business with someone you don't care for. It just doesn't pay in the long run."

Wherever you go, people will tell you there's money for the taking and nobody does anybody a favor if he expects to get ahead. But what you won't hear as often is that business by definition ought to involve some measure of pride and dignity, fondness even for the selling profession. Merchants from Marco Polo to the East India Company once spread civilization's grand and indisputable wealth across the globe by exchanging goods and learning with peoples vastly different from themselves. Trade achieved without artifice or deception led eventually to true progress and advancement benefiting all peoples. But try explaining that to a fellow like Thurston who only cared about how much dough he could stuff into his pockets. Had Harry not despaired of ever ridding himself of the musty old peacock feathers, he'd have thrown Thurston out of his office the minute they met.

Pearl lightly touched his cuff. "Honey, that ought to be you over there showing off how much dough you got."

"Pardon?"

Harry looked out toward the street where half a dozen elegant horse-drawn carriages, polished Broughams and Laundalettes, had parked along the far side of the avenue, discharging a flurry of smart-looking passengers above the morning river. A crowd of gorgeous women sported white parasols and wore long white dresses with strings of pearls and white silk scarves wrapped loosely about their necks to catch the breeze rising off the water. Several held trained Airdales on silver leashes and greeted each other with bright smiles and Continental kisses. The handsome men who accompanied them were also dressed exclusively in white: tailored Corsican suits and Panama hats and well-polished spats that reflected the fresh sunlight and drew attention from the less affluent visitors along the bulwark. Traffic along the avenue slowed as drivers gawked at the row of fancy old carriages, while pedestrians stopped to stare or skirted around the flood of white, disinterested in another meretricious display of elegance and wealth.

"If those swells can make good, honey, there's no reason you can't, too."

"Thank you, darling."

Harry had never really met anyone as rich as that outfit, and he doubted Pearl had, either. Most people don't know the true meaning of high class. Money doesn't raise our social status; the best money can do is disguise it like lip-rouge. But even the ignorant and naive can often arrive at simple truths, that ability to take an honest measure of hearts, which is all that really matters.

"Now don't start glooming on me, honey," Pearl said, rapping his knuckle with the back of her fork. "I know you think you're all in, but we got lots of time to get you square again."

He picked up his spoon and ladled a little sugar into his coffee cup. As he began to stir the spoon, the doors to the lunchroom swung open and those four young fellows Harry had seen out on the sidewalk earlier walked in, the short one with the derby taking the lead. The derby-hatted fellow called out to someone seated at the counter, "Hey, Eddie! Say cheese!"

A scruffy mousy-looking man wearing a cheap suit and a paper bib beneath his bowtie whirled around, more anger than surprise in his eyes.

"Why, you dirty sonsabi — "

POP!

The short man in the derby shot Eddie in the neck with a revolver. A faint gurgling noise issued from the mousy man's lips.

POP!

A small black hole appeared in his cheek.

Harry dropped his spoon into the coffee cup, knocking it over. A moment later, the short man's three companions stepped forward and drew out Tommy guns they had concealed within their long coats and began firing. Afterward, Harry would recall the sound as a great Wurlitzer organ roaring in deep timbre, the counter exploding in a thunderous fury of dust and glass and blood as if ripped apart by a summer tornado alighting within Delany's Café. The mousy man vanished in a cloud of pink mist and cheap threaded fabric. So did those poor fellows seated on either side of him and Harry's pretty red-haired waitress who had the misfortune of arriving with a pot of coffee just as the four gunmen entered the lunchroom. Harry ducked as best he could below his own table, ears ringing, adrenaline igniting every nerve in his body. The lights dimmed inside the café, something heavy crashed to the floor, people screamed.

The shooting ceased.

Harry saw Pearl under the table, too, a thrill of action and mortal danger on her pretty face.

POP!

POP!

The derby's revolver discharged twice more. More screams of shock and fright drowned out a general whimpering throughout the lunchroom. Then Harry heard the doors fly apart with a bang. Pearl lifted her head to peek over the windowsill. She yelled, "THEY'RE SCRAMMIN'!"

Terrified, Harry rose from his cover just as the black Lincoln sedan roared away from the curb, tires squealing. People came racing toward the café from every direction, and a police siren wailed. Then another more pathetic sort of wailing began within the lunchroom. All that was left of the luncheon counter where the mousy man had sat were splintered fragments of wood and glass, shards of broken plates, refuse splashed about in pools of coffee, cream, water and blood. A small crowd gathered about the mangled remains: a surviving waitress bawling profusely, two cooks trying to console her, the dazed and horrified men who had been seated near those who died, others luckier still who had managed like Harry to dive under tabletops when the Tommy guns thundered. Gray smoke drifted in the bright light of the crowded lunchroom like dense fog on the morning river, smell of cordite and blood swirling about.

My God, those fellows must've been lunatics!

Harry worked himself out from under the table, then grabbed Pearl by the arm and pointed her toward the exit. "Let's get out of here."

"Huh?" She, too, was shaking like a leaf.

"This way, dear." He took particular care not to gaze too long at the butchered bodies of the mousy man or the waitress and her two innocent customers as he steered Pearl around the carnage and out of the café.

Outdoors, the morning was warm and clear. They huddled together on the sidewalk by the window near the booth where they had just been sitting with a pleasant meal only five minutes ago. It seemed almost impossible. With Pearl clinging madly to his arm, Harry resisted the temptation to look back indoors. What was the point? The very thought sickened him. To see people killed like that before his eyes? It was horrific! Three police cars arrived and Harry heard an ambulance racing nearby. Reporters from the *City Sentinel* and the *Daily Gazette* and the *Metropolitan News Dispatch* began collecting now, too, at the entrance to the café, furiously shouting questions at Delany's customers as they stumbled half-dazed out onto the sidewalk. The whole scene resembled a madhouse, but nobody was running off just yet.

Harry asked Pearl, "Did you know those monsters?"

She shook her head. "Fancy pants fellows like them don't associate with dames like me."

"What do you mean by 'fancy pants?' Is that supposed to be funny?"

Pearl poked her finger at Harry's shirt. "Look, honey, you spilled coffee all over yourself. What a klutz!" She giggled, then stifled her laughter with a hand over her mouth.

Harry watched the ambulance arrive to the curb, white-jacketed attendants spilling out of the rear, carrying a stretcher and several black medical bags. More police cars roared up, sirens shrieking. The audience of spectators had already grown tenfold. Across the avenue, none of the beautiful crowd in white remained. Their grand and elegant carriages were still parked across the wide avenue, but the men in Panama hats and the women with their Airedales and bright parasols had all gone off to pursue whatever amusements and intrigues had lured them to the morning river.

One of the victims came out of the lunchroom now on a stretcher, a blood-soaked sheet covering the body. Was that the mousy man? *Good God,* Harry thought, *I'll hear him in my sleep for the next year!* He felt Pearl tug on his sleeve.

"What do you say we go somewhere, honey? Suddenly I ain't feeling so peppy anymore. I'm awful sick. How's about it?" She slumped against his arm.

"All right, dear."

Two more bodies came out of Delany's Café by stretcher. Tabloid reporters were swarming everywhere. Seeing one from the *Star Herald* approach with an eager smile, notepad flipped open, Harry tried to steer Pearl away, but the reporter caught them.

"Say, fellow, did you happen to see any of the shooting?"

"No," Harry told him.

"You bet we did," Pearl cut in quickly. "In fact, we was in the joint when that chump got hit. It was the awfullest thing I ever seen!"

"Can you describe the shooters?"

"Sure, they was all about your size, see, with cheap black pots on their heads and brown bennies to hide the Tommy guns. I never seen them before in my life, but I'll know 'em next time. Those sonsabitches almost gave us the works. I hope the cops pinch 'em, and soon. Put 'em all in the hot chair, I say."

The reporter scribbled like mad, recording Pearl's description of the gangsters. Harry thought she was crazy for giving him details like that. For God's sake, what if the gangsters got wind of her?

"And what about you, pal?" the reporter asked Harry directly. "Is that what you saw, too?"

"Honestly, I can't be sure. It all happened so quickly and once the bullets started flying, I have to admit I ducked under the table. I didn't even see them leave."

"Well, I did," Pearl went on again. "And I tell you, they highballed it like nobody's business. They had a Lincoln parked up the block, and I seen 'em take an out at Porter Street. Who knows where they blew to after that."

"And I guess you didn't recognize the poor sap they shot up?"

Harry shook his head. So did Pearl, who couldn't help adding, "He wasn't a prize package, I can tell you that."

— **2** —

At Legion Park, a couple of hours later, Harry sat on a stone bench near the cascading Olympia Fountain, still trying to rid himself of the hideous images from Delany's Café, while Pearl waded barefoot in the waters of the great marble fountain, one hand holding the hem of her skirt and scooping up coins with the other. Amused by how oblivious she seemed to the impropriety of what she was doing, he told her with a smile, "They're going to arrest you, dear. I hope you know that."

"Aw, clam yourself, honey. I ain't killing no one, am I?"

"People made wishes with those coins. Maybe they won't come true now."

"Mine will," she replied, tucking another handful into her purse. "When I got up this morning, I wished for that swell pair of pumps I seen in the show window at Paget's last week." She laughed.

Harry was impressed at how little seemed to disturb her. "I suppose you don't care that it's stealing, do you? What if everybody did it?"

Pearl climbed out of the water and snatched her shoes off the rim of the fountain. "You're a peach, honey. Anyone ever tell you that before?" She dried her feet with one sleeve of her Ulster.

"Thank you."

When Harry was young, he'd never had the nerve to go with girls as pretty as Pearl. He really wanted to take this one to bed, if only to make up for all the lost opportunities of youth, those girls he had desired and never made. He hadn't actually counted up his infidelities in quite a while now, but he suspected the number was absurd, and he certainly felt guilty about it, particularly when he was home with one of the kids on his lap and Marie doting on him like a lovesick schoolgirl. She could be awfully sweet when the mood struck her. How many girls will say you're the most wonderful man they have ever known? After a couple of Bacardi cocktails one afternoon, Joe Phelps confessed to Harry, Kelsey, and Fermer that he only married his wife because he got her in trouble, and being Catholic he hadn't any other choice, but if he had it to do over again, he would've gone out of town and not come back. *You don't know what I put up with, boys,* he told everyone. *She wears me down and I tell you, I can't take a good deal more. She's a mean bondage.* Well, that's where Harry knew he had it different from men like Phelps, because he always considered himself lucky to have a wife who generally did her utmost to please him. She was no tyrant and neither was he. Some of the greatest happiness he had ever known was in her company. Sex was certainly an anxiety, but all these years, he'd never yearned for another dear heart. If only marriage weren't so damned complicated.

Deliberately ignoring a brass signpost that expressly forbade the pilfering of flowers, Pearl picked a lovely lavender rose, broke off most of its stem, and slipped the bud into the silk band of her little Clara Bow hat. Then she took a cigarette out of her purse and tried to light it with a bad match. She really was a living wonder. Harry got up and took a stroll east of the fountain where blue jays chattered in a stand of sycamore trees and a clock atop a tall cast-iron pole indicated noon was approaching. Shade provided by the trees attracted older men and women seeking a restful ambiance for their morning constitutional. Harry nodded as he passed one elderly couple after another, smiling when greeted with a sultry wink by one wrinkled old woman dressed in agéd fox fur and crinoline, ambulatory only by the aid of a stout cane. Embarrassed as he was by her not-so-sly flirtation, he was flattered, too. Women of all ages seemed to like him. He caught them giving him the glad eye all day long. Even at Calvary Baptist last month, a young woman with a child on her lap batted her eyelashes at him while her husband was taking communion. Really, he knew this nonsense ought to stop, but it was difficult to see how.

There were actually a great many things about life these days he just could not understand. Where he was walking now in this park, for instance, despite the horror of witnessing an unparalleled atrocity during breakfast, somehow the sky seemed more beautiful to him than ever. Why did he not feel more shock and guilt and horror? Certainly the act of seeing that poor mousy man and the red-haired waitress torn to pieces by the Tommy guns left him nauseated. Yet here the sun shone brightly in the warm gardens, birds sang in the summer trees, people meandered about smiling, Eden in hearts regained. How do we manage to reconcile both worlds: the beautiful and the profane? Am I some moral imbecile? he wondered. Shouldn't I be despondent over those poor people's deaths? Is something wrong with me?

Reaching a reflection pool in a bushy arbor beside a marble statue of Narcissus leaning over the still water, Harry noticed his own glassy reflection and saw another thing to be disturbed about these days. His hairline receded season by season and he needed glasses to read the morning newspapers without squinting. He was getting old, all right. How many yesterdays ago had he first felt manhood coursing through his veins? How many tomorrows awaited before he, too, like the crone in black crinoline and fox fur, required a stout cane and a steady hand to go about? An unanswerable question: Time passes, as it will. He wondered if school age boys in Bellemont still raid Hutchinson's watermelon patch by moonlight in July. Do they climb the apple trees in Joe Miller's orchard to hide from Lila Kipfer and her club of girls? Do young men and young women yet float canoes on the river at twilight in August to play ukuleles in the soft grass at Homer's Bend, or sneak up into the shadowy hayloft of Leland Galway's round barn in early September to court and spark after dancing all night at the old pavilion? His summers as a boy had long since come and gone. His youth was lost forever. Would he give all he ever knew and owned to have one summer back again?

Pearl's squealing voice echoed across the park from nearby in the shrubbery surrounding the limestone Temple of Isis. He saw her flitting from tree to tree, like a wayward shadow. Escaping into a shady bower framed by cisterns growing lemon trees, Harry passed under a pergola fashioned from green holly branches and found himself on a circular lawn upon which stood a sundial whose gnomon of polished brass tracked the sun's arc across miniature bas-relief silhouettes of the ancient Hellenistic deities: Olympus rendered in bronze at high noon. About its stone base was a carved garland of rosebuds and Greek sailing ships, and the Homeric inscription: *Tell of the storm-tossed man, O Muse.* Sculpted into the column of the sundial was elegant Penelope herself, patiently unraveling a robe woven by her own hand, trading time against hope, honor for love — a tale that had broken Harry's heart since boyhood. Who, after all, but lovely Penelope held romance in such esteem as to await its return for twenty years? Would his own Marie linger so long? Did faith in love's gentlest promise steel her dear heart? Would she even believe him worthy of such faithfulness? Or had she, in fact, easily seen through his constant deceptions all these years, only her fear of dramatic consequences dissuading her from exposing his careless infidelities? *"My dear Marie, look what you have made out of that sedate and cautious young man who first began his courting by taking the young lady boating, then walking her back to the hotel from the lake, a quiet chat in the parlor, sitting together on the couch, then our first kiss and good night. Ah, my darling, what happy times we have had; and so the little seed has grown and born fruit in mutual confidence, love, and esteem, so that I could promise as I did last night that I would remain true to you as if we were already joined by the marriage ties."*

"She really must have been a silly girl, don't you think?" spoke a soft voice from behind Harry. Turning about, he noticed the old woman at the entrance to the bower, a sly smirk on her withered face. She walked forward under the pergola. "Love," she added, with a sigh. "A grand illusion for which poor sweet Penelope suffered so greatly."

She paused briefly at the lawn's edge, allowing her cane to rest on the grass a few inches beyond her toes. "Are men exempt from such foolishness?"

"Of course not." Harry smiled. What a fool he himself had been these past few years.

"Oh, I should think they most certainly are," she said, slowly crossing the lawn to the sundial. "While sad Penelope wept, Ulysses braved the wine-dark sea for glory's own reward."

"And returned home," Harry reminded her. He'd read Homer more than once. Dr. Collingsworth had seen to that after a couple of awful term papers on The Iliad.

"Eventually, yes," she agreed, her ancient eyes gray in the pale bower light. "Yet for whose sake? Aeolian winds bluster and storm, but always the heart provides a rudder and sails."

The old woman stopped at the pedestal just a few feet from Harry, fixing him with an uncertain gaze as if he were momentarily incomprehensible to her, some curiosity she had chanced upon while out for a stroll this sunny day. In a watery voice, she asked, "What part sorcery behind fair Circe's wand divined the truth within the soul of the bewitched? Indeed, for whose trusting heart did dear Penelope wait so long?"

"I doubt even Homer knew the answer to that," Harry answered, pleased to have met someone today who studied more than the city tabloids.

Brushing her fingers gracefully across the face of the sundial, and offering a friendly smile, she said, "Charles Whitaker Hastings always was quite fond of Homer. I think this must have been his favorite corner of the gardens. I remember my mother hushing me as we passed by here on our daily stroll because 'Mr. Hastings is enjoying his privacy in the bower.' He would sit there beneath the laurel leaves," she gestured toward a marble bench in a shady nook across from the sundial, "for precisely one and a half hours every afternoon, eating his sandwich and reading Homer's verse. My mother admired Charles Hastings immensely but was never able to summon up the courage to speak with him. She was quite shy and he was an extraordinary man. When I became old enough to understand how fear rises and humiliates, I felt so very sorry for her. Of course, by then both she and Dr. Hastings had already passed away, and I'd discovered my own fears and sorrows." She shook her head, sighed again. "Cruel Penelope, your triumph has become our burden."

A breeze rippled through the bower, fluttering in the laurel leaves and the holly. The old woman left Harry by the sundial and wandered over to the marble bench where she sat, resting her cane beside her on the grass. She fixed her gaze at the entrance to the bower where casual passersby were visible on the brick walkway. Harry wondered if someone had broken her own heart in the long, long ago, what irreplaceable treasure she had lost. *I cannot love as I have loved, and yet I know not why/ It is the one great woe of life to feel all feeling die.*

"It is quite beautiful, isn't it?" she remarked, her eyes waking once more.

"Yes, it is," Harry replied, distracted by the elegance of her demeanor. Moreover, he'd always envisioned Charles Hastings to have been as aristocratic as any American. His architectural and design achievements rivaled Saint-Gaudens, Olmstead and Sullivan, and made him one of the true giants of his day. That this old woman knew him, even when she was a child, was all the more incredible. He took off his hat and leaned against the sundial.

She said, "Did you know he sailed to Europe on commission to study the gardens at Villa Lante and Isola Bella and Vaux-le-Vicomte for his inspiration? Not that Charles required much beyond his own genius. Quite the contrary! When I was a little girl, this was all swamp and thicket. Carriages had to be paid extra to travel here from Columbia Avenue in the rainy season. Men rode out by horseback to shoot wild game along the warrens near the water. Wanted criminals hid in gypsy camps buried deep inside the woods. It was all very romantic and dangerous."

In the branches of a weeping willow, blue jays chirped excitedly. The old woman craned her neck upward. "You hush now!"

Harry laughed. Had she ever read Pope? *Hear how the birds, on ev'ry blooming spray, with joyous musick wake the dawning day!*

The old woman added, "These birds are inveterate eavesdroppers and gossips, with simply atrocious manners."

"I'm sure they find us equally amusing," Harry remarked, watching the blue jays cavort in the leaves overhead. "Why else would they bother coming here?"

He tried to be smart and friendly by sharing her whimsy; he was almost embarrassed by the fun they were sharing as complete strangers.

"Of course, Charles was a naturalist, so you see his passion for wildlife. These gardens, indeed all the city parks and arboretums, even such monuments as the Court of Honor and the Victory Memorial, suggest his refusal to accommodate those who would have extended the hideous city bulwark and metropolitan thoroughfares from Shepherds Island to the Burlington Lighthouse. In fact, he so despised the concrete avenues and gateways, I doubt he ever used them."

"Commerce trades on convenience," Harry quickly pointed out. "Necessity demands it. We can't all meander our way from appointment to appointment." That wasn't quite what he intended, but it was too late to take back.

"Oh, Charles cared nothing for business. He had no use for its casual greed and shameless manipulations. Rather, the simple pursuit of beauty guided his hand. Could you even conceive of these enchanting gardens arising from a cold banker's fancy? Ridiculous! Charles Hast-

ings personally supervised the dredging of the swamps and the impor-
tations of native and European shrubbery, the cultivation of flower
beds and shade arbors, and the laying brick by brick of the lovely
promenades we've strolled today."

"I would imagine, though, he was paid quite well for his attention.
Wasn't it Emerson who said the beautiful rests on the foundations of
the necessary?" While Harry was sympathetic to the aesthetic ideal, a
dollar earned was, after all, a dollar earned, and he doubted Hastings lent his considerable talents to the city free of charge. Honestly, he hadn't meant to be crass, but was this woman so removed
from the commercial world that she failed to recognize how the
wheels are oiled?

Rising carefully from the marble bench, the old woman frowned,
disappointment evident in her eyes at Harry's apparent cynicism. "A
philanthropic heart is born," she replied, "not hired. Any compensation Dr. Hastings received for his bequest to our posterity was quite
paltry, I assure you."

Walking slowly back across the lawn toward the pergola, she asked,
"Have you been here in our city long?"

Harry stood by, hat in hand, humbled by his own mouth. "Only
a few months. I have rental space at City Transfer & Storage in
the upper warehouse district. I'm a salesman, or at least that's the
rumor I've been spreading." He tried to smile. "My banker might
disagree."

"How nice. Then I should imagine you've scrutinized most of our
gilded finials by now."

"Pardon me?"

She paused under the holly branches where the arc of the pergola
shaded the bower entry. There she leaned on her cane and looked
back at Harry. "I don't know your name, do I?"

"Harry Hennesey." He felt ashamed to tell her. Like losing a game
of pin the tail on the donkey at six years old, he had just become the
ass named Harold.

The old woman offered a thin smile. "Well, Mr. Hennesey, for every
gilded finial there is elsewhere in this city a black, filthy rat hole. If

you truly wish to venture an appraisal of Charles Whitaker Hastings' struggle and achievement, I suggest you indulge your courage."

Then she walked out of the bower and was gone.

Pearl stood behind a nickel telescope at the end of a sloping lawn overlooking the river where an old garbage scow loaded halfway to heaven plowed the current south to deeper water. Back under the shade of the drooping elms, a dozen or so olive-skinned Hungarians in summer costume had unfolded a large checkered blanket and put down a lunch of fruit and bread and sausage: the laughter of their children running on the grass and the bright music from their accordions and their singing women carried to the river bluffs and beyond.

"Ain't this scarf cunning, Harry?" Pearl released her grip on the brass telescope and lightly fingered the delicate silk. She arched one of her painted eyebrows.

"Did you steal it?" he asked, only partly in jest. His eyes wandered farther downriver where a loaded flat barge just entered the wide stream, smokestacks billowing clouds high into a china-blue sky. He chuckled. "I promise I won't tell."

Pearl walked away from the telescope to the iron fence dividing the park from the bluffs. She stood with her back to the river and fussed again with her scarf. "You got a mean sense of humor, honey, you know that? Here I got us invited to a swell party tonight and all you do is make wisecracks."

"What party?" He imagined drunks and criminals and vagabond children carousing in some damp black underground chamber.

"You don't know the half of it, darling. Why, I was about to tell you at Delany's until those ginks shot up the joint."

She walked over to him, slipped her hand inside his coat and stroked his belly obscenely. He pulled her hand out and gave it a playful slap. "Well, as it so happens, I've already made other plans."

"No, you ain't," Pearl argued. "You want to go to the ballgame this afternoon, and that's swell, but we still got us a date tonight and you're stickin' to it."

"Oh, is that so?" A group of small children dressed in blue sailor suits hurried out from the rose gardens toward the river bluff, shrieking with joy. There is another world out here, isn't there? "And why would that be?"

Pearl retied her scarf. "Because you ain't like all them other fellows who sweet-talk a dame, then give her a line just when things get cozy."

A late middle-aged man and woman, both in bright holiday attire, followed the children out of the gardens. The man had on a smart vanilla dress suit and an old-fashioned straw boater, and smoked a cigarette from an ivory holder; the woman wore a pale silk frock and a wild honey-colored Joan Crawford hat and held a tan leather handbag and a gold leash fastened to a Great Dane. They gestured extravagantly as they spoke to each other and strolled casually along as if the lawn belonged to them and they were alone in the world and had no obligations and nowhere else to be. As they came down the wide lawn, their children veered off from the fence at the dirt bluffs and ran laughing in Harry and Pearl's direction toward the cement telescope platform. Missing his own children again, Harry wanted to watch them play for a while. It felt important. Somehow once you start pretending you are not that man who mows his lawn on Saturdays and tucks his kids in bed at night, they take it as if none of that means anything to you. Yet it means everything. You toss your own problems aside and tie a tail to a kite and race your little boy across a field with the wind at your back and nothing can touch you. It's the most wonderful thing in the world. It's all that really matters.

Pearl grabbed him by the arm. "Come on, honey. I hate kiddies. Let's scram. Besides, I still got something swell to show you."

At the far eastern edge of Legion Park, under the shade of fragrant cedar trees where sprinklers dampened the summer grass and sunlight illuminated a million water droplets, Pearl stood in the Gate of Eternity with her arms outstretched, her fingers reaching toward the curved walls of a perfect red earthen brick circle built into an eight-foot-high gray stone wall, a portal dividing these beautiful gardens from all the world beyond.

"Ain't it keen?" She waved her arms up and down the arc of the Chinese moongate.

Atop the wall, a set of small steps arched up to a tiny seat, suitable only for a child, engraved with the initials **CWH**. At the base of the stonewall, just beside the portal, a bronze plaque read:

Love is a circle that doth restless move
In the same sweet eternity of love
R. Herrick

Pearl stepped out of the portal, a corn muffin in her hand. "Ain't it just wonderful?"

"It's very interesting," Harry agreed, already tiring of this afternoon holiday in the park. It occurred to him that those appointments he had arranged earlier this morning regarding a quartet of cane chairs and a Cecilian portable phonograph were all he had on his calendar for the weekend, and he owed McDonald fifty dollars for rent past due. He saw a gap between that ever-present hope he cultivated and the hard facts of his bank balance. Well, there's nothing he could do about it right this moment. Maybe he'd go knock on McDonald's door after supper, explain himself. He was a salesman, wasn't he?

Standing closer now to examine the meticulous brickwork that created the circle, Harry noticed that each brick adhered to and supported the other without benefit or need of common mortar and sand, an intricate, almost seamless, construction in arrogant defiance of gravity — or perhaps, rather, in acceptance of gravity's immutability, an elegant circle built upon faith in the unrelenting weight of the world.

"A fellow ought to kiss his best girl in the gateway, don't you think?" Pearl asked, pursing her lips.

"Why's that?" Harry asked, his eye drawn just then to a short fellow emerging from a grove of willow trees about thirty yards away across the lawn. He was dressed in a shabby brown wool suit and a derby hat. That same fellow from Sand Avenue! *Is he following me? Good grief, if he's still burned up about that stupid scrap at the speakeasy bar, he's insane. Why, I didn't even touch him.*

"Ain't you listening to me, honey?"

"Sure I am." The bricks were fragrant of moss and damp earth. He grazed them with his fingers.

"Well?"

"Well, what?"

"Don't you want to make love to me in the gate?"

"Why would I do that?"

"Because it's romantic. Ain't you romantic, Harry?"

She ate a chunk out of the muffin, and pursed her lips again for a kiss. Did she expect him to think of her forever? About three years ago, he had met a girl named Della Brice at a restaurant in St. Paul who was so adventurous she'd persuaded Harry to love her up that night on the smoking platform of an interurban trolley in the dark woods near Lake Minnetonka. He had bent her over the railing and at his climax nearly toppled them both off the car. She claimed he broke her rib, but was healthy enough an hour later to perform fellatio on him in a downtown phone booth. Perhaps the gin she drank all evening had dulled the pain. At any rate, she tried to hire a lawyer to prefer charges against him. Fortunately, he'd given her a fake name and hotel address.

Pearl leaned forward and kissed his cheek.

Harry looked over at the small fellow across the damp lawn. He'd gone to sit on a stone bench under a gorgeous weeping willow where he smoked a cigarette. It couldn't be sheer chance that he was here, could it? Flustered, Harry drew out his watch and checked the hour. The ballgame at Highland Park would just be getting started, the first batter kicking his spikes into the dust of the batter's box at home plate. He told Pearl, "Look, dear, I really do have to get along now."

"Aw, honey, don't say that. You know I hate it when you give me the air."

"Oh, I'm sure you'll find other activities to amuse yourself." She really was so lovely. Maybe he ought to kiss her in the moongate, after all. What could it hurt? If only that fellow weren't watching. Who is he, anyhow?

"Gee, honey, how come you're acting so tough all of a sudden?" She looked completely worn out. "Don't you care for me anymore?

Darling, when a girl gets a crush on some fellow, she needs to hear him say she's a hot number, even if she ain't. Why, even him just giving her a line's better'n getting the run-around. If that's what you're doing, go on, I can take it. Honest I can." Tears began to well up in her pretty violet eyes.

He really had enough of this nonsense. What did she think they were going to do, anyhow? Run off to California? He imagined Marie spying from behind one of the cedar trees. Trouble wore a thousand disguises. He wondered if maybe that small fellow sitting over there was a private detective she had hired to see what he was up to. It would certainly make sense given that Harry had only seen him when he had been with this girl. It's funny how you begin to notice things all of a sudden that have been staring you in the face.

Pearl went over and sat down in the brick moongate, her cheap stockings drooping to her ankles, frock and scarf fluttering in the draft of rushing motorcars from the boulevard at her back. She sagged visibly, her eyes dark now. "I guess you just ain't much for surprises, are you, honey?"

He told her, "No, actually I enjoy chasing kidnapped girls around amusement parks all evening."

She giggled. "Gee, wasn't that fun?"

"Look, dear, why can't we just get this over with? What do you want?"

Just then, another fellow came along the garden path of bricks and lavender roses and sat on the bench next to the short one. This man in the smart brown suit looked half a foot taller and wore a smart gray fedora and mustache like Douglas Fairbanks. He borrowed a cigarette from the small fellow and stared in Harry's direction. The small fellow nodded as he lit a match for his companion. Now there're two of them, Harry thought, and if they're not private detectives, then the other one is probably here to help his pal beat me up. Well, I could probably handle that short fellow by myself, but the other one's bigger than Jim Corbett. If they pick a fight, I may have to run.

"Honey?"

"Yes, dear?"

Pearl wiped her eyes with a sleeve, blinked hard, offered him a kind smile. "I'm a pushover. You know that. I'll tell you about the party. Why, sure I will. I just wanted you to be surprised."

He sighed. "All right, darling, thank you. We've made great progress today. Now, what sort of party is it, and where?"

"Maybe you won't believe me."

"Well, we won't know until you try, will we, dear?"

"All right, it's some big cheese up on Edison Heights," Pearl confessed, a coy smile struggling through her tears. "Ain't that the tops?"

"Are you joking now?"

How on earth could a stupid little girl like Pearl be invited up there for any kind of party that didn't risk a police raid? Good grief, this couldn't be on the level, could it? Several years ago on a week-long selling trip here to the city, he and a fellow named Tarnstrom hired a motorcar for a Sunday drive. They motored up the long winding boulevard to the Heights and spent an afternoon admiring the great brownstone mansions whose front yards were bigger than most town squares. Great thick cedars divided one estate from the next: stone columns fifteen feet tall heralded the driveways: elaborate rose gardens scented the sidewalks from one end of Mulberry Avenue to the other. If you stood in the middle of the block at almost any time of day, you could see any sort of beautiful automobiles roaring in and out of the long driveways where stylish men and women lunched on the upper terraces or played croquet on the rolling lawns. It was something to think about before you invested your life savings in your uncle's oil well. Reading over the morning society columns, he couldn't help memorizing those exasperatingly fawning descriptions of elaborate garden parties and grand soirées involving the rich and influential, the amorous and fabled. Hadn't some of these parties degenerated into nude bacchanalian orgies? What if he were actually invited to an orgy in the middle of the night?

He asked, "Are you sure this isn't one of your silly games? Because if it is, I'm not going to like it."

"Cross my heart and soul, honey. I'd never lie about such a thing."

"A party at a real house on Mulberry Avenue?"

"Honest to God!" She crossed her heart again.

Harry almost laughed out loud. He had no faith in her silly party invitation, but thought it might be fun to see her squirm when she fell on her face. He told her, "I suppose I'll have to hire a cab. You realize, of course, it'll be fairly expensive coming back afterward. I've done well for myself, but I'm not one of that crowd. Not yet, anyhow."

"I'm sorry, honey. Why, if I had the dough, I'd get us a carriage to wait all night."

Harry glanced back across the lawn toward the bench where those two peculiar fellows were sitting. Something about them bothered him, but he couldn't quite put his finger on it. He watched as the tall fellow checked his wristwatch and took another puff off his cigarette, looking distracted. The short one was talking in his ear and not getting much play for it. Maybe they're here because of the café shooting, Harry thought, some of the gangster's pals, trailing witnesses, or some such. Maybe it was just a coincidence he'd seen the short one so often recently. Well, if he had to, he'd just plead amnesia. After all, he was under the table when the shooting started, wasn't he?

"Say, honey." Pearl tapped his arm. "Now that I think about it, the Heights ain't that far. You and me could take the trolley from Riverside Avenue to Empire Boulevard and hike up the hill. Why, I tell you it's a cinch! How's about it?"

Harry shook his head. "No, darling, that's too much trouble. I can afford the fare. You just be sure to have the address for the cabby." Another snipe hunt or not, the sooner he agreed, the quicker he could get out of the park and away from those two fellows over there.

Pearl leaped forward and gave him a kiss on the cheek, then bounced away, waving her scarf about. "Thank you, darling! Oh, I'm so excited!"

— 3 —

Along the waterfront, near the industry district, city streets narrowed and the blue sky diminished. The grand sweep of busy avenues and towering skyscrapers and twelve-story Art Deco hotels and Gothic cathedrals and office buildings and great department stores declined into drab three-story brick tenements lining streets of aging Reuss block and wheel-worn cobblestone. Half a century of factory soot and grime blackened façades roughened by wind and water. Electrical wires sagged and wash-lines stretched across sidestreets, fluttering white linen on a relentless draft that stunk of kerosene and sour vegetable markets and stirred dust into the gray air made filthier by coal trucks that trundled along day after day after day as phantom dogs and cats sifted trash with the lost and dispossessed for low rewards in narrow alleyways.

But there was grace here, too. In the summer, hydrants sprayed water over screeching children, sidewalk organ grinders played music for pennies, and just as elsewhere in the city where men's and women's paths crossed daily, couples strolled arm-in-arm or sat entwined on the shaded stoops of sweltering apartment buildings and high upon iron fire escapes. From Sprague Street to York, Jews and gentiles traded in butcher shops and dry goods stores and bakeries. Here, the tinsmith was Jewish; there, a wedding photographer was Catholic; shop window bridal portraits featured Presbyterians and Lutherans and Greek Orthodox Christians. Day in and day out, these holy streets echoed the cries of rope-skipping girls and penny-pitching boys in knee-pants, the garbled Yiddish of old men in Sabbath suits, the voices of day laborers dodging delivery trucks and water wagons and baby carriages. By law and custom, the city's commerce intersected with its people's needs, and bargains were struck on stores and rent and protection, the price of physical and spiritual sustenance, a dubious moral gambit wherein virtue and profit were locked in a hopeless struggle mistaken by the foolish as a romantic embrace.

Harry Hennesey stepped off a streetcar at the corner of Baskin Street and Havesham Avenue, four blocks from the big ball field at Highland Park, where a sweaty organist in suspenders and a brown bowler played "Baby Face" for a pack of barefooted children and a slender blonde in a flowery dress. Nearby, a newsstand attracted its own audience, men perusing copies of the *Saturday Evening Post, Collier's, the Atlantic Monthly, Life, the New Yorker, Time, American Mercury, True Confessions, Evening Graphic.* Beneath them, half a dozen small boys sat reading the comics from newspapers spread flat on the hot pavement and held down with empty seltzer bottles: *Moon Mullins, Krazy Kat, Bughouse Fables, Polly and Her Pals, Mutt and Jeff, The Nebbs, Happy Hooligan, The Gumps, and Barney Google.* A horse-drawn wagon piled high with furniture was parked across the street, a handsome young Swede at the reins, two older Swedes, perhaps in their late fifties, attempting to wedge an upright piano into the rear of the flatbed. They gave constant voice to their frustrations, much to the amusement of two gorgeous red-haired Irish girls drinking orangeade on the shaded stoop of the next tenement building. Down the street, where a lively stickball game was intruded upon by passing grocery trucks, the rhythmic clanging of a sledgehammer on steel echoed across the sweltering air, and a small boy rode past one-handed on a bicycle hugging a tawny kitten to his chest. Men wearing sandwich boards walked up and down the sidewalks. Destitute flower urchins scrambled about offering red carnations to anyone with a penny to spare. Fruit and oyster peddlers called out prices to customers. Harry bought a ripe peach from a peddler's cart just down the block from the trolley stop and hurried along while he ate, fascinated by all he saw. Here were more foreigners than anywhere else in the city, desperate immigrants from those failed empires of southern and central Europe and the Bosporus: shabbily attired, weary-eyed, proud-faced, shouting, joking, pleading, crying, boasting, laughing in more languages than he knew existed, Babel on Baskin Street, each individual shopkeeper, bricklayer, teamster, packer, hauler, painter, carpenter, handyman, baker, cook, clerk, window-washer, mortician, haberdasher, solderer, dry cleaner, musician, printer, inventor, chimney sweep, choreman, husband and father, wife and mother, eager for fortune's warmest welcome. Indeed, if Providence had not brought these people to America, then why were they here?

— **4** —

Sitting under the grandstand thirty rows up from first base, Harry Hennesey shelled a handful of peanuts and watched the ballgame played on an emerald-green field dotted by men in gray uniforms. Behind them, a tall fence advertising Marcus the Hatter, C.C.A. 10¢

Cigar, Bennett Brothers Clothiers, Woodhill's Café, Regal Shoes, Bilko Lumber & Millwork, Orienta Coffee, Tiptop Drycleaning, Dr Pepper, Yellow Cab, and Coca-Cola, separated the outfield from bleachers filled with thousands of white-shirted spectators. On the black scoreboard above centerfield, the grand old Flag of the Republic and a string of victory pennants fluttered over a painted advertisement for Red Fox Ale. The wooden benches were splintery and hard, crowded, too, where fans cheered for the home team winning by one run in the fifth inning. Next to Harry, an immense fellow named Cy sat with his young son roaring at every pitch. His breath bellowed whiskey into the air, but this fellow was a friendly drunk, harmless in public, comical in his gargantuan manner, clownish and crude. Harry felt only sympathy for Cy's young boy who pretended not to notice his father's overboisterous cheering. He really wished his own little Henry had taken an interest in going to the ballgame. A couple of years ago, Harry had ridden him by train to see the White Sox, and his best little boy had whined the entire time, begging to go see the bears at the city zoo, instead. The whole day had turned into a terrific disappointment for them both, and Marie hadn't helped by asking later on why he could not just have shown Henry to the zoo right from the start. Well, good heavens, what father doesn't want to take his son to a ballgame?

A batter from the home team rocketed a line drive over first base that curved deep into the right field corner. Fans in every corner of the park rose and cheered a dashing slide into third and the umpire's emphatic call of "SAFE!"

While Harry applauded, Cy boomed, "ATTAWAY, ATTAWAY!" When everyone sat back down again, Cy's little boy was still standing on the green bench, his cheering carrying out under the grandstand like a bird screeching. Cy took a cigar out of his pocket and lit it, then gave Harry a nudge on the shoulder. "How do you like that, eh? We're gonna trim 'em today! Whatta ya think?"

Sweat beaded on the man's brow, his fat round face puffy and red, a moony grin.

"I'll say so," Harry agreed, enjoying the atmosphere. Last summer he'd gone to see Ruth and Gehrig knock a pair into the seats of Sportsman's Park at St. Louis. You couldn't forget the smell of roasted peanuts and hotdogs, the fresh grass and dirt of a modern ball-field. There was nothing quite like it anywhere else. Most of the men with whom he did business were baseball fans, trading ideas and discussing future transactions while at the ballpark for the afternoon. Even those Harry knew who had no interest in athletics of any sort purchased tickets to doubleheaders when business was slow and clients wary. Dialogue was the lifeblood of commerce, he had once read, and such intercourse depended upon familiarity and common interest. Baseball often provided that middle ground on a lazy afternoon when other inroads were absent. It had the additional benefit of acting as a tonic for what one stock trader called indigestion of the soul, when customers became difficult and profits scarce and life's grand rainbow of promise seemed to lose its clarity and luster. That's why you went out to the ballpark, whether to get away from the pressures of business or your household, just good clean fun, and no doubts about anything for a couple of hours.

Cy cheered a ball dropped in foul territory behind third base. His boy stamped his feet on the bench. Harry cracked open another handful of peanuts, deciding he would share them if asked. Cy's not a bad sort, he decided, once you got past the liquor.

With the pitcher holding the ball again, Cy gave Harry another nudge and a wink. Leaning close, he spoke conspiratorially into Harry's ear, "I got a sawbuck on this one."

Harry smiled back. "Oh?"

"Why, sure! It don't take no Einstein to know we'll trim these bums today. Our club's got loads of punch and that boy of theirs on the mound spent all last night on Clancy Street. Woke up there, too. What's that tell you?"

"Where did you hear this?" Harry was curious about the innuendo that chased ballplayers and show performers from city to city. He had met a girl once from St. Cloud who swore she had gotten hitched to a different ballplayer in every city of the American League. It sounded absurd until she showed Harry her stack of marriage certificates and divorce notices. When he asked why she had taken the vows rather than jazzing around like most girls, she told him: *A girl's got to feel respectable, honey, even if she ain't.*

A ground ball dribbled over second base into center field and the runner on third hustled home to score another run. Cy cheered with the crowd. When he sat back down again, he told Harry, "They got some pretty sweet dames down on Clancy Street who'll jump naked in the river on Christmas Eve if the price is right. They ain't no Gibson Girls, you understand. A buck's a buck to them birds, but most of 'em got loyalty, see? Root, root, root for the home team, eh? Why, it's the oldest jig on the block." Cy laughed and neatly exhaled another smoke ring across the lower benches.

A pop fly high over home plate landed in the catcher's mitt and the homeside was retired. Cy's little boy tugged at his father's sleeve, whining for a bag of popcorn and a soda pop. Cy put a couple of coins into the boy's hand and set him free to find a vendor. As the boy passed in the aisle, Harry saw that his right ear was heavily bandaged and his tiny cheek scarred: a frightening wound. Good gracious, what could have caused that?

"Rats," Cy explained, noticing Harry's interest. "I got rats. Every night, I hear 'em scratching in the walls and under the floor. Pretty soon, my wife's yelling in my ear, 'Cyrus, the baby! The baby!' Well, Sammy's a good kid. He got bit pretty good and hardly complained. Didn't cry a lick. My boy! 'Course, Mary's afraid of Sammy getting infected so we took him down to Mercy General and had him looked over. Ugliest bite I ever seen. Clean through the earlobe, like from an ice pick. Bloody as all hell. Them scratches you seen on his face? Big brown rat trying to get hisself loose when Sammy woke up and figured out what was hurting him."

"That's awful!"

The first gray-jerseyed hitter struck out swinging and received a healthy jeering from the left field pavilion as he returned to the visitor's dugout.

"ATTABOY, BOBBY!" Cy cheered the hometown pitcher. "Great kid, huh? He's got arms like legs. Wait'll you see his high hard one. Great kid! Yessirree!"

Harry agreed, and offered Cy some peanuts.

"Don't mind if I do." Cy grabbed a handful of peanuts and stuffed them into his mouth as the next hitter stepped into the box. "Nasty business, having rats. Hell, I seen 'em in the grandstand here last week right under these benches. They got a little runway going from the cheap seats to the dugout. I hear some of the ballplayers been complaining about gloves getting chewed on and finding toothmarks in some of their bats."

A lazy fly ball drifted out into centerfield and was easily caught. Cy's little boy returned with a bag of popcorn in one hand, an orange soda pop in the other. With a cute boyish smile, he squeezed past Harry to sit beside his father once more and cheer another out. Cy stole some popcorn from Sammy's bag, winked at his son, and remarked to Harry, "See, I'm a night watchman over at Fernald Manufacturers. Now, that's one of the oldest brick factories in the city, so we got rats on the board of directors."

Both Harry and Cy craned their necks to follow the path of a long fly ball that arced deep into the left field corner toward the bleachers before hooking out of play just short of the foul pole.

"Well, I have an office at City Transfer & Storage off Diever Street at 83rd," Harry cut in as the batter stepped out of the box. He wanted Cy to know he was no fresh face to this city. "That's less than four blocks from the river. I haven't seen a rat yet, but I've overheard complaints from some of the teamsters."

"Oh, you've got 'em, all right." Cy laughed. "I know the joint. That close to the river? I'd keep my feet up on the desk if I was you." He laughed again. "Just don't go poking at 'em with a stick. A Canadian fellow by the name of D'Invilliers who owns a piano store across the street from us trapped one in an old closet and tried to stick it to the floor. Filthy little thing used his umbrella like the Brooklyn Bridge to run up his arm and bite him in the lip."

"Well, I wouldn't think of doing anything like that." Harry shuddered. "If I saw a rat anywhere near the office, I'd run out and call fumigation."

A line drive back to the mound ended the visitors' turn at bat and the home team came in from the field to hit again. Rising to applaud another well-pitched inning, Cy told Harry, "We got a cellar at Fernald that's underwater most of the year. It's connected by an old drain tunnel to Stinson's slaughterhouse and the poultry markets on Polk. Take a lantern down there, you can see all the rats you want swimming in the sewers, big brown rats, bigger'n Sammy's cocker spaniel. They come into the city off them foreign ships tied up at Pier Nine, cocky as all hell. A shoremaster told me once he seen 'em prancing down the gangplanks like royalty."

Harry watched a shallow pop fly float over second base and drop free into the outfield, giving the home team a runner on base. Cy grabbed another handful of popcorn from his boy's bag. He clapped for the bloop single, then leaned back toward Harry. "See, this whole damned city's built perfect for 'em. Under the streets with all them tunnels, it's a regular Hades. Worse probably."

A ground ball back to the mound was turned into a double play, bringing a loud groan from the grandstand.

"Actually, I've been in the storm drains," Harry interrupted, "two months ago, during the rains. It was awful. I wouldn't want to make it a habit."

"I'll say so! One night on Schiller Street when I was working the market district, a pack of 'em got into a chicken house and ripped the throats outa maybe two, three hundred chickens in an hour and a half, and only ate a dozen of 'em. Just killed the rest 'cause they was there to be had. Another night, they chewed a hole in the wall at Watson's Produce and vandalized a shipment of grain sacks. Ate holes in every one of 'em just enough to ruin it so's it wasn't no good anymore for people to eat. Ugliest thing I ever seen. You smell 'em in the warehouse?"

"I'm not sure whether I do or not," Harry said, as the next home team hitter took ball four with the bat on his shoulder, and trotted down to first with a big cheer from the bleachers. A chorus of boos cascaded down upon the pitcher as the on-deck hitter strolled to home plate. "I certainly wouldn't be glad to find out I did."

Grabbing another handful of popcorn from his son, Cy said, "When Fatty Maxwell got rid of all them feedlots and stables down on the waterfront, that helped some. Then he hired this Mitchell fellow from Baltimore to gas 'em or poison 'em, I don't know which, but they're a whole lot smarter'n he was. Fatty's boys found him down in one of them tunnels, deader than John Brown's dog. His hands and feet and ears were chewed clean off, the poison not even touched."

Cy patted little Sammy, and grimly shook his head. "Traps don't work much, neither. Rats just spring 'em and laugh. Over at Fernald we been using glueboards 'cause nothing gets off that, but you gotta burn 'em all up afterwards, and there ain't enough shingles in the whole city to catch as many rats as we got under our feet right here today. Fellow I work for says the whole stinking city oughta be burned to the ground, buried over, and forgot about."

Harry watched the visiting pitcher struggle to find the plate again, running the count to three balls, and wondered if the kid was drunk. How difficult could it be to throw one down the middle? He told Cy, "Well, you can't expect to get more out of anything than you're willing to put in. Vermin thrive on unsanitary conditions. If City Hall and the Health Department would simply address the causes that lead to these infestations — "

"You can lead a horse to water," Cy interrupted, a black smirk on his face, "but you can't make a Polack have a bath."

The home batter walked, chasing his teammate to second and bringing another hitter to the plate. A buzz rose in the crowd now. Sammy was on his feet, clapping as the home team's big slugger trudged from the dugout to the on-deck circle, three bats in his grip. Cy dropped his cigar on the cement at his feet and stamped it out. Wind swept across the diamond, whipping dust from one foul line to the other. The pitcher stepped off the mound to clear grit from his eyes.

Cy told Harry, "See, I grew up six blocks from the waterfront, so I seen what it was like before, and it wasn't no paradise, but it was a hell of a lot better'n it's been since those ships started leaving 'em all off down there at Matthiessen Park."

"Leaving who off?" Harry asked, shelling a couple of peanuts. He reminded himself that not everyone's interested in hearing another's opinion. All they want is to have their say and hear you tell them how right they are.

"Polacks, gypsies, guineas, you know the sort. Don't get me wrong, now. I ain't against people having a decent place to live, raising their kids, earning a fair buck on the up and up like the rest of us. This is America, after all."

The batter slammed a pitch over third base that barely curved foul as it fell into left field. A loud groan replaced an incipient cheer. In the distant bleachers, the crowd was standing for the next pitch. Cy asked, "You ever find a rat's nest in some old cellar wall?"

"No, I can't say that I have," Harry replied, as the batter looked at another ball low and outside. If this kid on the mound hits the batter in the head with his next pitch, maybe Cy'll get distracted and keep quiet for five minutes. He ought to have brought Pearl to the game. She wasn't much more ignorant than this fellow and could probably talk his ear off, which begs the question why know-nothings always have so much to say.

The next pitch thumped the batter in the ribs. He buckled over and dropped the bat. The batboy ran out from the home team's dugout and huddled beside him for a few moments, then picked up the bat and returned to the dugout as the injured batter limped up the line. Spectators in the pavilions along first base stood and gave him a nice ovation, a cheer that grew louder as the next hitter ambled to home plate. Harry shoveled a handful of peanuts into his mouth. This is probably my own fault, he thought. I should've changed seats two innings ago.

Cy clapped for the batter, gave little Sammy a pat on the head, then told Harry, "See, you got Bohunks and Polacks living sixteen to a room on Crawford Street by the river. Same with them guineas on York. I went in there one night with a fellow from Northside Sanitation. Filthiest place I ever seen in my life. You'd a bet not one of 'em ever thought of cleaning nothing since they got off the boat. Sinks were blocked up with slop, they'd stuffed all their stinking garbage in the floor vents like they guessed it led to the city dump or something. One of 'em used his closet for a shitter. Not even the coloreds up on Ashford Street ever sank that low."

Harry really wanted to stuff a fistful of peanuts into Cy's mouth. So now we're going to get the straight dope on the problems with immigration, is that it? How all that foreign riff-raff is bringing down the highest standard of living on earth. What pack of idiots built Ellis Island, anyhow? S.O.S.! Ship or shoot 'em, is that it? For crying out loud, why can't this fellow just watch the ballgame like the rest of us? Doesn't he know he's ruining the day for his little boy?

The home team's cleanup hitter took a wild cut at an in-shoot drop and fouled it back into the grandstand. Most of the fans behind home plate had risen, cheering more loudly with each pitch. Harry angrily shook another few peanuts into his palm and watched the pitcher work over the new baseball. He was resolute in refusing even to look at Cy, who told him now, "When we were kids, we didn't think nothing of walking to the ballgame from my old neighborhood at Elliot and O'Connor. People were friendly back then, mostly Irish and German families, hardworking people, clean, honest, trustworthy Americans, even if they hadn't been here all that long yet."

The visiting pitcher threw a fastball right past the slugger. Even up in the grandstand, Harry could hear it smack into the catcher's glove at home plate and the umpire call, "STEEE-RIIIIKE!" The crowd groaned. Sammy kicked at the bench and socked a fist into the palm of his other hand. Cy fished another cigar out of his shirt pocket and lit it up. Breathing noxious fumes into Harry's face, Cy said, "See, nowadays a fellow like you or me walking Baskin Street after sundown's likely as not to get his throat cut and wind up in the river like them poor soldiers they drug out from under Washington Bridge last week. Christ, I hear there's guinea kids, little Sacco and Vanzettis, no older'n my boy Sammy, carrying stilettos now who'll carve your eyes out sooner'n say hello. They got no respect for nothing, those people. Cops won't even come 'round here anymore when the sun goes down. They say, 'Let 'em kill each other, it ain't worth it for no one else.' Now, that's a damn shame, but decent folks know that's the straight of it, too."

The next pitch sailed wide of the plate. The slugger held a hand up to the umpire and backed out of the box. He tapped his cleats with the bat and flexed his arms, then stepped back in to face the pitcher. Wind rippled across the sea of white shirts in the sunlit bleachers. Cy exhaled a cloud of smoke and coughed. Leaning over Harry's shoulder, he announced loudly, "Mark my words, pal, someone downtown's gonna wake up one fine morning and realize what a mistake they been making on Baskin Street, letting those goddamned greaseballs run our old neighborhoods into the ground, then you'll see something. Boy oh boy! 'Course, it'll be too late by then! You think we got a big problem with rats? Hell, that ain't half — "

A thunderous roar from both pavilions followed a crack of the slugger's bat at home plate that sent a fly ball rocketing high and deep into right field, rising now, higher and higher into the warm summer air above Highland Park as the gray-jerseyed outfielder raced back across the grass, deeper, deeper, clear to the painted Coca-Cola sign where he stopped and watched the ball sail above the fence and the white-shirted bleachers, far beyond the playing field while Harry desperately craned his neck with twenty thousand fellow spectators cheering the ball farther and farther across the hazy blue distance, and down, finally, toward the cold river.

— 5 —

By nightfall, the city was illuminated in silver. Strings of electric lights draped like holiday swags on the towers and cables of the great bridges spanning the river sparkled like constellations above the dark. Downtown, lamp poles along four miles of the Avenue of the Republic served as glowing beacons inviting the restless city populace to step out into the evening streets in a spirit of Saturday's gaiety and joy. Sidewalk cafés emitted smells of roasted coffee and garlic and hot cinnamon. Jazz played in high curtained windows. Loud radio shows filled the airwaves, *Good evening Mr. and Mrs. America and all the ships at sea!* Shiny automobiles raced from swank restaurants to blue-lit nightclubs across the city. A soft summer breeze blew among the stars.

Harry Hennesey sat beside Pearl on the buff seat of a black taxicab that sped by the crowds of beautiful women on the Avenue, veering in and out of traffic, dodging auto-busses and foolhardy pedestrians. Pearl knew the driver and pleaded with him to go faster, while Harry urged restraint. Who wants to be killed in a motor smash-up on his way to a party? He tucked himself against the seatback as downtown's bright lights passed in a blur. The taxi bore southeast away from the river, driving up a slight grade into quieter neighborhoods. Leafy trees on narrow sidestreets arched overhead. Lamp poles were fewer, but more elegant. Motors seldom passed now. The only people about were mostly older couples out walking dogs through the moonlight. Gardens and carriage gates multiplied as the drive ascended gradually along a stone wall off Harry's right shoulder beyond which reflected the dark distant waterway streaming through the low plain of the sleepless city.

The taxicab stopped at the bottom of a steep hill. Harry listened to the cost of the ride, then fumbled his payment into the driver's hand and thanked him for his service. When the draft from the departing taxicab quieted, he stood alone with Pearl looking up the long slope of a narrow sidewalk bordered by a great ivy-draped wall rising forty or fifty feet above them now, tapering off to a lesser height at the top of the hill. He felt desperately anxious to get to the party. This could be the most important night of his life.

"I still don't see why that fellow couldn't have driven us up to the gate," he remarked, watching Pearl check her makeup for the thirtieth time. She angled a small brass compact under the street lamp, illuminating by turns each corner of her face. Satisfied, she closed the mirror and tucked it into her handbag. She wore a fox fur over a two-piece crepe frock with a marine-blue blouse and knee skirt, pale stockings, flat shoes. When they rendezvous'd at Brooklyn Circle, he'd felt bold enough to remark how lovely she looked, but she pretended disbelief. *"Aw, you're just saying that, honey, so's I won't ditch you at the door, but thanks for noticing. It's sweet of you."* Marie wasn't half as vain, he thought, and she was undoubtedly prettier, albeit in a more mature fashion. No girl can truly compete with a grown woman, and vice versa. Any fellow knows you can't reasonably choose between them unless you have something specific in mind.

She smiled coyly. "It ain't that far, darling."

"Are you certain? Somehow, I neglected to dress for athletics." He already felt foolish in his hired tuxedo and spats.

"I tell you, honey, it ain't that far. Oh, I'm so excited!" Pearl seized his hand and dragged him forward up the sidewalk. "Let's hurry! Please?"

"Don't tug. I can get along on my own."

"Then hurry up, you old goat!"

She let go and ran on ahead, giggling while Harry tried to estimate the height of the hill. By any measure, it would be a rough hike to the top. Gosh, he'd let himself go since college. He ought to join a gymnasium, after all, really try to get himself fit again.

"Harry!"

Pearl gave a shrill whistle that echoed across the street.

"Stop that! I'm not a horse!"

"Hurry up, darling, I'm bored!"

Head down, knees bent to the slope, Harry jogged up the sidewalk as quickly as his wind would allow. It was a trial, all right. His knees ached, his lungs burned. Good grief, he might as well take his retirement tonight if this was the best he could do. Near the top, he stopped to catch his wind. Where was she?

"Say, mister, you got a light?"

A slender hand holding a cigarette thrust out from a narrow recess in the gray stonewall just behind him. There, Harry found Pearl sheltered in a grotto of ivy, half-hidden by shadow, a small gate at her back.

"I walked right past you." He was panting like a dog.

"Sure you did, honey," said Pearl, sticking the cigarette back into one of her coat pockets. She reached through the iron bars of the gate and lifted the latch, then slipped through. Her melodic voice issued from behind the wall. "Ain't you coming?"

"Where?"

"To the party!"

Confused, he took a quick look down the street where a blue Marmon Eight had arrived at the bottom of the hill, turning to ascend in his direction. Feeling exposed out on the sidewalk by himself, he pushed forward into the ivy. Pearl grabbed his hand and pulled him through the garden wall. Behind him the automobile roared past, exhaust cloud trailing in the cool night air.

Pearl giggled.

Harry heard an orchestra playing in the distance, a popular fox trot. His heart raced. Pearl closed the gate behind them and fastened an old rusty padlock across the latch. Then she kissed him.

"What's this?" He grabbed the lock and gave it a shake. He couldn't reopen it. "Is this some sort of stunt?"

"You're a gatecrasher, honey," she told him, giggling again. "How's about that?"

His thrill vanished. "Darling, you said we were invited."

"Shush!"

Harry lowered his voice, resisting the urge to shout. "You lied to me!"

"Aw, we're here, anyhow, ain't we? Don't crab the evening." Then she raced off under the dripping eucalyptus trees that shrouded this corner of the estate.

Furious, he kicked over a pot of hydrangeas. Good grief, you certainly don't expect to be humiliated as soon as you arrive somewhere. There ought to be a decent interval where a cocktail is offered, maybe a cheese sausage and a compliment to precede the bad news. He could see it now, a crowd of swells popping champagne corks as he was tossed off the grounds.

Somewhere close by, he heard Pearl whistling another of her stupid jazz melodies. Feeling wan and disgusted, he pursued her into the foliage.

They were on the lower quarter of a terraced lawn about a hundred yards southeast of a Palladian brownstone mansion in a topiary garden of manicured flower beds and cleverly hewn hedges arranged to complement Roman stone urns and classical statuary on pedestals of Belgian marble encircling cold lily ponds. The grass was damp from a recent watering, and a rhythmic bleating of frogs nearly overwhelmed the gay orchestral music up above. Harry saw the lighted arch of a grand portico across the lawn in the direction of Mulberry Avenue, the entrance legitimate guests no doubt were using. Motor traffic outside the front sidewalk was busy, seven passenger sedans and sleek roadsters easing up and down the drive from the auto-gate, discharging guests. From beside a bubbling fountain, he watched eager men in top-hats and tails exit a pair of glorious J Duesenbergs and a Bugatti Royale. Bright cheerful laughter filtered across the night. Downtown at DiCostanza's Ristorante last month, he had overhead someone ask Victor Hauer's chauffeur if Mulberry Avenue was dry. The fellow replied that it depended upon whether you were sitting inside or outside the limousine. Harry wondered whose party he was crashing tonight. Knowing your host is one of those important pieces of information you really ought to find out before you barge through the door.

Pearl whistled as she ran up ahead, ducking briefly behind a granite sculpture of Persephone, and chasing away again beyond a marble sundial into a grove of oleander and rising cypresses. He ignored her, utterly convinced the poor dear ought to be institutionalized. Meanwhile he felt himself drawn toward the sparkling lights and gaiety. As he climbed the wide lawn, choosing an ascending brick path from terrace to terrace, other guests gradually came into view, gliding between potted firs and young pine trees, sitting on the stone balustrades between the gushing fountains that framed the grand stairway from Mulberry Avenue; dozens of gorgeous women in evening gowns of chiffon, velvet, metal brocade, shawl collars and cuffs of white hare, chic cloche and bengaline hats with metallic stitched brims, silk stockings, bobbed hair, glittering jewelry; handsome men wearing dress-suits with Arrow, Covington or Welsh-Margotson collars, slicked-back hair, polished spats. None paid Harry much notice at all as he strolled out of the dark into a small courtyard, dressed as he was in comparable fashion. On the balcony above him, a crowd of pretty girls smoking cigarettes tittered laughter and acted tipsy. He waved and one of them blew him a kiss and he pretended to be in love until suddenly they all disappeared. In front of him, water trickled from a statue of Demeter draped with grape ivy in a sculpted niche carved from the retaining wall. Seized with enthusiasm for the occasion, he cupped his hands under the waterfall to give his own hair a good slicking. Satisfied by his little fraud, he followed along the wall beneath the balustrade of stone urns to join a crowd of recent arrivals on the wide stairway to the upper terrace.

Indoors, the orchestra played a lively "Ukulele Lady." More lovely women streamed casually in and out under the gilded filigree arch and façade of the grand entrance. Harry was certain he saw Pearl slip inside as he came up the steps. Where does she find the nerve? Two stolid gentlemen in tuxedos flanked the marble entry pilasters, unaffected by the hilarity surrounding them. The interior was ablaze with light and excitement. Holding his breath, Harry strode ahead as if urgently expected. Nobody said a word. Somehow if you walk into any room projecting that nose of confidence, you'll be accepted, whether you ought to be or not.

Strolling away from the foyer, he entered a long glittering mirror chamber whose curved ceiling floated a hazy blue Florentine tromp l'oeil of billowy clouds and golden sunrays and flying cherubs dragging garlands of roses and laurel wreaths across the high arc of the Olympian heavens. The marble floor was wild with enthusiastic men and women flowing about toward the ballroom or the stone terrace, cocktails in hand, or joining the lines in front of a dozen buffet tables covered with white cloth and red napkins where etched serving trays of Spanish silver held steaming racks of lamb, golden roast turkey, and baked ham in spicy molasses, tins of mashed potatoes and candied yams and English puddings and flat silver platters offering a variety of delicate hors d'oeuvres. Scattered among the buffet were Chinese porcelain bowls filled with sliced fruit and petit fours and peppermint candies. Behind each table stood an aproned woman wearing a Martha Washington cap and a willing smile.

Too excited to eat, Harry crossed to the grand ballroom, a vivid expanse of white and gold, lit by crystal chandeliers and brass torchéres, where hundreds of colored balloons tied with fancy ribbon floated near the gilded ceiling and the orchestra played loudly and the revelry was vibrant. He walked between two large potted palms, narrowly avoiding collision with two staggering young flappers, one in a light-blue satin frock and the other wearing a gold and white beaded chemise, both splashing champagne from finger-glasses as they lurched for the exit.

"Why, Clara, you stumbling drunk," said the one with yellow curls, her glassy eyes working to focus on Harry. "You almost wet this poor fellow's suit."

"Oh, I did nothing of the sort." The brunette's head bobbed back and forth. "I couldn't imagine doing such a thing to good old Stanley here. Why, he and I go way back, don't we, dear?" She wiggled her eyebrows at Harry and offered a sloppy grin. "Paris, two years ago, wasn't it, darling? Stingers at the Montparnasse?"

Harry had no idea who these two girls were, but he was certainly eager to meet them. "Actually, I had Beaujolais and a biscuit," he answered, with a jaunty smile.

"Yes, that's true, you did!" She burped. "I must have forgotten! I really do have a rotten memory." She giggled.

"Of course you do, darling," the blonde agreed. "You forgot your underwear this evening, remember?" She leaned on her companion, her eyes drilling Harry lasciviously from head to toe. "Say, he's a swell fellow, isn't he? Right out of the top drawer."

"Why, Stanley and I made love on the poop deck of the Ile de France on our way home." She addressed Harry. "Didn't we, dear? Wasn't it just awfully romantic?"

"Are you sure?" The blonde giggled, her eyes still focused on Harry's trouser buttons. "He seems so shy."

"Oh, not at all," the brunette replied. "Why, Stanley's a beast! Watch here!" And she kissed him square on the lips, a sloppy kiss that tasted of gin and cigarettes. Harry felt people watching him and knew he was blushing as the orchestra began an irresistible Fox Trot:

> *"Toot, Toot, Tootsie goodbye,*
> *Toot, Toot, Tootsie don't cry.*
> *The choo-choo train that takes me away from you*
> *No words can tell how sad it makes me*
> *Kiss me, Tootsie, and then*
> *I'll do it over again."*

"Go on, Winnie, get hot!" the brunette called above the merry-making din, flinging herself free of Harry. She finished her drink and tossed the glass into a potted palm, then danced a couple slick Charleston steps and feigned a swoon, and let herself fall into Harry's arms. When he caught her, she swung about and kissed him again. He propped her up and kissed her back. Men who had been standing about the wet bar set down their drinks to dash out onto the parquet dance floor with women they had an eye on. Those already dancing raised the pitch to a higher key.

This nutty girl in his arms, Harry felt flushed with excitement and began tapping his toe like everyone else. He decided he ought to have a cocktail. The brunette grabbed Harry's chin. "Kiss me again, Stanley. I'm lonely!"

"Why, you're such a flirt, Clara!" the blonde cried. "I'm sure Stanley really isn't the least interested in a pair of dolls like us, are you, Stanley? Go on, darling, say it straight."

Before he could reply, a young man with lightly oiled hair and a well-tanned complexion squeezed a path from the dancing throng, an arm raised high overhead. "Oh, Winnie! Clara! Say, there you are!"

"Why, Stoddard! You poor dear!" The blonde tipped the last of her champagne and rushed toward him, sagging into his arms and kissing him passionately on the lips. Catching a breath, she asked, "Where ever have you been? Clara's been flirting like a streak."

He studied the brunette wrapped up in Harry's arms. "Going the pace, has she? Well, I trust you've kept a keen eye on her, then." He gave Clara a wink. "We certainly can't have her running amok. Why, Sylvester would throw us all out into the street."

"Oh, Stoddard, darling, you simply must fetch me another drink," Winnie insisted, dropping her own glass into the same potted palm and tossing a free arm over the young man's shoulder. "I'm feeling awfully faint and my poor heart's beating like a steam engine."

"Well, we can't have that, can we, dear?"

"If you're really willing to go," Clara said, "Please bring a bottle of champagne back for Stanley and myself, won't you, dear?"

"Say, I don't believe we've met," the young man addressed Harry, offering his hand. "I'm Stoddard Platt."

Clara snatched Harry's hand away before he could extend it to the young man. "Oh, don't bother, Stanley. I'd much prefer the two of you didn't become friends. You see, Stoddard owns all the gossip money can buy, and I'm sure he'd poison you against me."

"Don't be a prig, Clara!" Stoddard laughed. "Great Scott! If I had that much on you, I'd have written a popular novel and earned my fortune by now."

"Don't believe him, Stanley," Clara countered, confusing Harry even further. "His people are inveterate liars. I met his mother once at a garden party in Charleston and she assured me her children were not only clever as ghosts, but capable of almost anything. Why, he's been frightfully mean to me lately. I'm sure I'll never trust him again."

Stoddard laughed loudly, and clapped Harry on the back. "Well, Stanley, in that case I should say, it's my distinct pleasure not to have met you!"

"Likewise, I'm sure," Harry replied, smartly. He liked this young fellow. Probably Harvard or Yale and a strong position with a brokerage firm somewhere.

The blonde cut in on the conversation. "Stoddard, darling, didn't you just promise me a drink?"

"Why, I don't recall, Winnie. Did I?" He winked at Harry who had removed his arms from Clara's waist. He felt he was already overdoing things, but she didn't seem to notice.

The orchestra quit playing momentarily and the dancers relaxed. Conversation and airy laughter cascaded about the ballroom. Clara murmured in Harry's ear, "Are you aware, Stanley, that half the stags at this party get lit to avoid being kissed?"

"No, I wasn't aware of that at all," he replied earnestly, hoping to avoid seeming stiff to this crowd. "Is it true?"

"Of course it's true," she told him. "But some of them are homos, so they don't count."

"Is what true?" Winnie inquired, flustered now from thirst. "Clara, you simply must stop wearing so much paint. It spoils your color."

Stoddard frowned. "Oh, don't clip her wings, Winnie. Clara's quite sympathetic just as she is. Although, true enough, she's ruined many a good man in her time." He smiled at Harry. "Don't take that as a warning, Stanley. After all, you might be marking a turning point in her life. Clara's been rather unsteady for quite some time now, haven't you, dear?" He tickled a forefinger under her chin. "Didn't I warn you both about going to Antibes? That Spaniard painted you girls nude to get you into the bathtub with him, not vice versa."

"Aw, go cook a radish!" Winnie snarled.

The orchestra began a fresh Charleston. The mash of dancers picked it up, and again a lively music flooded the ballroom. Clara wormed her arm into Harry's again and gave a gentle tug. "Take me to the billiards, Stanley. We'll have an old-fashioned romance." Then she stuck her tongue out at the young fellow. "So long, Stoddy! Don't forget to brush your teeth!"

"Why, Clara, you're funny as a goat," said Winnie. She released her hold on Stoddard and transferred it to the brunette. "Oh, take me with you, dearie. I've finally decided to give Dohrman a tumble. Otherwise, I'll just go to pieces."

She blew the young man a kiss, then turned her back on him. Clara urged Harry into the crowd of dancers, Winnie chasing just behind.

"Say, don't leave me flat, girls!" the young man complained, drawing a cigarette from his shirt. Seeing they didn't intend to wait for him, he tossed the cigarette away, unlit. "Aw, for the love of Mike!"

All four of them chased a ragged path across the ballroom, scarcely avoiding collision with dozens of bouncing couples. Harry apologized repeatedly, offering a bemused smile and a shrug. He had no idea where they were heading, but hoped it was somewhere more private where perhaps he and Clara might get reacquainted. He wanted to kiss her again, let her know he was no old stiff. He felt dangerously off-kilter about her, but couldn't help himself. Unlike young Pearl, Clara was almost mature, which meant she would know what she was doing. He hadn't loved up a girl her age in years. They could talk your ear off about sex during the physical act itself and not pay it any notice. You had to be on your best game to keep up with them. If this one wants to make love in a goldfish pond, Harry decided, he might just take off his shoes and wade in after her.

Apparently the ballroom sat approximately in the center of the mansion, eight doors leading out of it in cardinal directions. Stoddard took them through the one on the northwest corner of the room, departing into a dim narrow hallway of Circasian walnut panels, gold Pompeiian ceiling stencils, and blue oriental carpet-runners leading to a staircase rising with floral reliefs and carved oak balusters. Elegantly framed and hand-tinted chromolithographs lined the walls, depicting domestic portraits and wonderfully exotic locales: on safari in the dry African bush and Serengeti; mountaineering atop the snowy Alps; exploring the Colosseum ruins at sundown; aboard a dahabieh moored along the banks of the beautiful island of Philae in Upper Egypt. Each setting featured the patriarch, Horton Sylvester, his wife, two sons and a pretty young daughter: an adventurous family on holiday. Were Harry not so rushed by his new companions, he would have studied each picture in detail. An education abroad! Did those children appreciate their marvelous fortune? What had he been telling Marie for years? Couldn't he just imagine his beautiful children wading in the Mediterranean Sea one morning off Gibraltar, vivid Africa lurking across the strait? *I travel for travel's sake. The great affair is to move.*

Stoddard paused at the foot of the stairs where the two newel post statues, bronze sculptures of Venus and Minerva draped in silk tunics, supported globes lit by electricity, each glowing a dull amber. He asked the girls, "Say, do you suppose anyone's got into the bedrooms upstairs? I hear Elinor screeches like a peacock."

Winnie giggled. "Stoddy, I believe the question ought to be: Whom do you suppose has gotten into somebody upstairs?"

A sound like a cheap party noisemaker came from the hallway overhead. Riotous laughter followed. A thump on the floor. A glass shattering. Someone running. Doors slamming shut.

"My goodness!" Stoddard looked delighted. "Why, I've heard Elinor's a bum hump, but she sounds awfully exciting to me."

Clara grasped Harry's arm, whimpering shamelessly, "Stanley, I'm frightened. Suppose they're not Elinor at all, but horrid spooks. Hold me, darling. Don't let me go." She gave him a sloppy kiss on the cheek, and pressed her pretty head against his chest. She smelled like orange blossoms. Feeling crazy for her, Harry stroked her cheek and she mewed like a kitten.

Stoddard burst out laughing. "Good God, Stanley, now see what you've gotten yourself into! Why, Clara dear, you do need a stiff drink after all, don't you?"

Escaping the ghosts of the upper mansion, Stoddard led Winnie, Clara and Harry on a hasty tour through three high-ceilinged rooms arranged in a square, divided by doorless arches hung with tasseled French portières. First was the library, high-shouldered and prim, redolent of ten thousand leather bindings, and fit with overstuffed armchairs, mahogany side-tables, scrolled brass astral lamps, Chinese carpets, and a ceiling fresco depicting Alexandria in the time of the Ptolemies: a diorama of the famous Library, the Mouseion, and the ancient wonder of Pharos alit beside the crowded harbor in a purple Mediterranean twilight. Swept along with his new friends, Harry gave a polite nod to the guests gathered at an immense ebonized and gilded firemantle: three balding, weighty gentlemen cheerfully intoxicated by brandy snifters and an arcane discussion of sidereal physics and the plausibility of moon travel.

Next came an unlit music room rendered in pale emerald and radiant gold leaf beneath a plaster cove containing hand-painted Egyptian cartouches and classical figures from the Bronze Age, curving up toward a painting in an oval ceiling panel that described the vainglorious struggle of Prometheus on Mount Elbruz. A few Louis XV chairs and sofas were all the furniture in the room, no rugs or tables, save an exquisite grand piano at a tall double window where a group of men, roughly Harry's age, stood together behind a companion at the keyboard, arms wrapped collegiately about each other's shoulders, singing by moonlight.

> *"Once again I'll say I love you,*
> *While the birds sing all the day*
> *When it's springtime in the Rockies,*
> *In the Rockies far away."*

Winnie clearly thought this scene hilarious and snickered as she crossed the polished floor, urged ahead by a scolding Stoddard. Clara echoed the piano tune quite easily, her pitch clear and melodic, merely amused by the quaint posturing of these older men (which was to say, the absence of any liquor or feminine companionship), or so she whispered in Harry's ear while he was recalling the smart barbershop harmony his father had taught him almost thirty years ago. No one at the piano even bothered to acknowledge the intrusion.

A single Turkish oil table lamp burned low in the salon next door. Whispers uttered from shadowed cozy corners, giggles, panting, a rustling of clothes. Entering behind Clara, Harry smelled liquor and perfume, cigarette smoke and sex. In here, the woven portières were drawn closed, lending the impression of an elaborately ornamented Moorish evening bazaar or Chinese opium den: Persian rugs underfoot, tufted sofas with large stuffed pillows, a plush mulberry ottoman in the center of the salon encircling a tall Kentia palm. Where the flame from the oil lamp flickered and illuminated a small section of the painted ceiling above, Harry saw peacocks and papyrus reeds, acanthus leaves, griffins and wild poppies on an indigo background of golden stars.

"Oh, Stanley dear, I can't see a thing!" Clara whined, narrowly avoiding a clay amphora filled with dried bulrushes. "Help me, please?"

She stutter-stepped sideways across the fringed carpet, exaggerating her blindness. As she stumbled awkwardly into the ottoman, Harry eagerly grabbed her waist from behind to hold her up, and a male voice called out of the dark, "Look here, you bastards, this isn't Central Station! Why not kiss or get out!"

"And how!" added a shrill female voice. "You're crabbin' the party!"

"Aw, go love a monkey!" Clara shouted back, regaining her balance. She swiveled her head to give Harry a kiss, thumbed her nose in the direction of the offending voices, and hurried to the exit where Winnie and Stoddard waited beside an onyx pedestal supporting a granite bust of Nefertiti. As a large shadow rose against the back wall of the salon, all four slipped through the silk portière into the smoky billiard room.

Drunken hilarity in a lavish and stuffy art gallery was Harry's initial impression: the wild heart of the party. Twenty or thirty young men and women the age of his new acquaintances danced and drank to scratchy jazz records played on a corner table Victrola, or stood nose-to-nose in flirtatious conversation along the rosewood walls next to gilt-framed naturalist paintings and grand Portuguese tapestries, or gathered in play around a large nineteenth-century Brunswick billiard table under a great coffered ceiling whose octagonal rosette suspended a six-lamp bronze gasolier with tinted-glass shades that diffused the smoky light and lent a ghostly pallor to the grinning faces of those underneath.

Straight away, a smiling young man in a black flaring suit and dressy peg-top trousers raced up from the green billiard table, champagne glass in one hand, cue stick in the other. "So!" he cried, raising his glass to the arriving quartet. "The restless return! How splendid!"

"Say, let me have some of that!" Winnie cried, relieving him of his glass. "Here's lead in your pencil." She put it to her lips and tipped it over.

Stoddard laughed. "Winnie's been disenchanted lately. She simply refuses to speak to anyone unless first bribed with liquor."

The curly blonde flopped into a padded jersey easychair and adjusted her hem. "Oh, you men pretend to be so blasé about everything, when it's perfectly obvious you're just aching to be called." She found a match on the side-table and lit a cigarette. "It's all such a silly howl, isn't it?"

Clara slipped off Harry's arm and sprawled on a sink-down sofa nearby. Delightfully engaged now, Harry was set on joining her until another pair of young men came over, champagne glasses and cue sticks in hand. An awfully pretty and petite young woman with copper-colored hair and a fashionably thin white dress remained at the billiard table sitting on a stool, her attention fixed pointedly on Clara.

"Say, darling," said the young man with arched eyebrows and a neatly trimmed mustache, "I'd imagined you'd deserted us for good."

"Why, Jay darling, you should know there's not a man at this party who throws me like you do."

"Muriel over there thinks you've been deliberately cruel this evening, Clara," the other young man interjected, taking a deviled egg off a plate on Winnie's side-table. He was highbrowed and clean-shaven, but pale as a sheet. "I assured her you're not a bad sort, once she looks past the gin."

"Oh, Clarence, you're a high one," Clara replied, with a silly laugh. "I suppose you think I'm having a perfectly rotten time tonight, don't you? Well, I'm not." She located Harry standing by himself and slapped her palm on the seat beside her. "Oh Stanley, darling! Put it down here!"

His heart bounced. "Thank you, dear." Feeling gleeful, he went over and sat beside her as if they were engaged. He was conscious of his achievement and intended to play it up.

"Oh dear," Clarence said, staring at Harry, "she's got another victim!"

"I met Stanley in Paris," Clara explained to the crowd, "at Fouquet's where he was drinking Armagnac with Cole Porter. You see, Stanley was a hero in the war and he's got letters of introduction all over the world."

"Which is obviously how he wound up on your lap, darling," Clarence remarked, barely disguising a smirk.

Clara frowned at Muriel. "Say, honey pie, if you can't keep your eyes to yourself, I'll have to ask you to marry me."

Giggling again, she shifted her position on the sofa and took Harry's hand. He squeezed her fingers. She was more fun than these stupid boys who seemed rash and exaggerated.

"Clara's all a ridiculous pose," Jay observed, tipping back his glass of champagne. He wore a sour grin.

"Why, I'd say she's too drunk to pose," Stoddard remarked. He glanced over at Harry, nodding sympathetically. "You're welcome to join the fray if you like, Stanley. We'll call a brief armistice for your benefit."

"Stanley's been patiently observing our nastiness," Winnie announced from her easychair. "I think he's a darn swell fellow, even without a drink in his hand."

"Oh, he just prefers to keep clear-eyed tonight, that's all," Clara responded on Harry's behalf. "Don't you, Stanley dear?"

Harry smiled awkwardly. Perhaps this crowd was too young for him, after all. He adored the girls, but these fellows seemed damned nervous. "Well, frankly," he told them, "I only drink at work. Why spoil the memory of a wonderful party by forgetting what you did there?"

"See?" Winnie tittered. "Isn't he disarming?"

"Thanks to Stanley here," Clara declared, "I've decided to dance nude this winter at the Folies Bergère. I've never been so excited in my life. It's quite a spectacle, you know."

"I thought Djuna Barnes already booked your passage," Clarence remarked with a suitable sneer. "Didn't she persuade your father to pose you in feathers last year for Al Johnston?"

"Stanley *is* her father," Jay offered, waving his cue stick. "Can't you see the resemblance?"

Clara kicked at him with her shoe. "You must be talking about yourself, Jay, one masher to another. Why, Stanley here hasn't bought his own drink at the Ritz bar since you were in diapers."

"You've stayed at the Ritz?" Stoddard asked Harry, incredulously.

"Certainly!" Harry nodded with the confidence of a good lie. "When I wasn't elsewhere."

Clarence said to him, "Oh, well then, you must know Coco Chanel."

He couldn't resist. "No, but I do admit I've always preferred tea or coffee."

Clara laughed far out of proportion to the joke. "Honestly, isn't Stanley just the tops?"

"Yes, darling," Jay agreed, "he's one in a million. Now, would you please act your age?"

Dohrman picked his cue stick up off the divan. He asked Harry, "Do you enjoy billiards, old boy? Three-ball carom?"

Harry nodded. "Why, sure. It's a beautiful game." He adored billiards. It was practically all he did at St. Paul.

"Well, then, what do you say?" Dohrman passed him the cue with a friendly smile. "Come on, have a whack at it."

"All right," he agreed, getting up off the sofa. He smiled back at Clara. "Will you excuse me, dear?" It was freshman year all over again. Here was his chance to prove he was no dub.

"Show 'em how, Stanley!" She leaned over in Winnie's direction. "Oh darling, come park your girdle over here. Please? We'll kibitz together."

Harry walked over to the billiard table. Actually, he hadn't played in months, nor had he any sense what sort of players they might be. But at least he was sober. That ought to give him an edge with this crowd. He doubted one of them could roll the ball straight anymore.

Muriel slid her stool back a few feet, and folded her arms beneath her lovely bosom, an expression of distinct unhappiness on her face. Trying to be pleasant, Harry nodded a greeting and she forced a brief smile. Winnie picked up a glass of champagne and crossed the carpet to sit beside Clara. Stoddard went to the wall rack mounted beneath a dark oil painting of Napoleon-at-Elba to choose a cue.

As Harry finished chalking, Stoddard told his friends, "Honestly, I really do prefer to stag these sorts of parties, you know. It's all so tiresome otherwise."

"Oh, that's idiotic," Dohrman argued. He picked up the red ball and rolled it softly against the rail. "Do you see that wonderful little fluff standing next to the Degas with those two fellows? Well, I've had my eye on her all evening."

Placing the ball beside the two white ones, Harry studied the girl in question and agreed she had a very nice fanny.

Dohrman added, "Why, I have half a mind to walk across this room and make love to her right now."

"Oh, that'd get it started," Clarence agreed, sitting on a stool beside Muriel. He leaned over and kissed her cheek.

"A hot dispute," Jay agreed, filing the tip of his cue with a small strip of sandpaper. He had a good long look across the smoky room where those three huddled under a panel of the ornamented ceiling painted to represent a range of English birds and wildflowers in springtime. Cornered by the two young men, the tiny blonde was laughing delightedly.

Stoddard said, "Why, I'd say they both seem quite stuck on her."

"Well, so am I, damn it," Dohrman countered, sounding more testy by the second. "And, I'm worth twice what they are sold together. She ought to be told the difference." He grabbed the cue ball and flung it across the table.

In another corner of the room, a fresh record was put on the table Victrola, a slow waltz.

> *"I wonder why you keep me waiting,*
> *Charmaine, cries in vain.*
> *I wonder when bluebirds are mating,*
> *Will you come back again?"*

Meanwhile, Clarence began play like a tyro, breaking with a hard long shot that knocked both object balls carelessly astray. Harry watched Jay chalk his cue and study the scatter. His own open table shot that followed was equally ill-considered, a foolish carom that left both red and white balls beside the end rail and the cue ball less than a yard away. These fellows didn't know the first thing about billiards. When Harry's own turn came, he'd show them a thing or two.

"Oh, that's keen, Jay," Stoddard commiserated, giving him a pat on the back. "A darned nice foozle."

"Well, you're not much of a help," his opponent grumbled, sitting back on a stool. "You ruined my cue last round."

"Would you prefer to trade?" asked Stoddard, offering him his own cue stick. Jay shook his head, and walked off to the rack.

Approaching the table now, Harry watched with glee. These boys played like idiots.

"Go ahead, Stanley," Clarence said, tapping Harry on the arm with his cue stick. "You're next."

"Are you sure?" he asked, trying to appear timid.

Stoddard laughed. "Stanley's a bit nervous, I'd guess." He put a hand on Harry's shoulder, gave it a playful rub. "Don't mind that, Stanley. Do your best. Don't forget, you have our dear Clara in your corner tonight." He turned around. "Isn't that right, darling?"

Lighting a cigarette, Clara glanced at Winnie, barely stifling a giggle. "Oh, Stoddy, darling, shouldn't you be in the toilet?"

"Why do you say that, dear?"

"Your fly's open."

Both Clara and Winnie burst into hysterics. While Stoddard checked his trousers, Harry wondered how Clara would be to make love to. For some reason, he imagined her giggling the whole time.

Clearly irritated by Clara's childish humor, Stoddard gave Harry a nudge. "Go on, Stanley, have a turn. It seems our dear Clara's having her monthlies."

With fine confidence, Harry fingered the cue and lightly drew aim on the object ball and let fly, rolling a dead draw shot to the end rail that just nicked the red one and gave the white carom ball a soft kiss, leaving all three grouped together. That drew a gasp from his audience. He straightened up proudly as Jay whistled and Stoddard clapped Harry on the shoulder. Even Clarence applauded from his stool beside Muriel. "That's a damn splendid shot, Stanley!"

"Yes, indeed," Stoddard agreed. "Well struck."

As a matter of fact, it wasn't the least bit difficult. Any decent billiard player would have played it just as easily. These poor fellows obviously didn't know much about the game at all. Harry re-chalked his cue as he walked around the table to position himself for his next try.

Over on the couch, Clara and Winnie lay in each other's arms, laughing hysterically. By the Victrola, the dancers had given over to fatigue, although the record droned on. Behind Harry, Jay and Dohrman discussed a mutual female acquaintance. "Oh, I made her at Nantucket last New Year's," Jay said. "Of course, I'd love to say it was a swell start to the year, but she was no good."

"I hear she's a fresh little smack," Dohrman said, his attention still stuck on the girl across the room. "Anthony claims Emmy's got the eyes of a cow. Look, what kind of girl is she, really?"

"Nice as the damned strain she gave me," Jay confessed, looking across at Muriel who averted her eyes immediately.

Choosing his next shot, Harry decided to really show off. Having already developed a decent feel for the tightness of the cloth, he leaned against the table, arched high over the three balls, his cue vertical to the spread, setting up a strenuous massé shot. Ferguson had taught him this one years ago at St. Paul when they used to pass a couple of evenings each week inside Hespersen's billiard hall. With a light thrust directly downward, he struck the cue ball on the side toward the cushion, drawing it back along the rail, so that it just slid past the red object ball, barely "grazing the glisten" before tapping the white carom ball and stopping again in a mirror set of the previous spread. Harry did his best to stifle a huge grin. A damned swell shot, he thought proudly, if I do say so myself.

"Great Scott!" Stoddard cried. "Stanley's a king pin! We're finished!"

"Thank God we didn't have any money on the table," said Jay, admiring Harry's last leave. "Why, I'd be forced to beg a ride home."

"Whoever sized Stanley up needs a fresh pair of cheaters." Clarence chuckled. "Of course, we'll all have an eye on him from now on, won't we." He pointed his cue toward the girls on the couch. "Clara, darling, you should know we're holding you personally responsible for any damage Stanley inflicts upon us this evening."

"Maybe Muriel can sell her pearls," Clara laughed, holding Winnie in her arms.

Harry glanced at Muriel and saw she had her eye on him. When he smiled at her, she looked away with a rosy blush.

The crimson portière from the salon parted and another couple slipped through, arm in arm. Both were considerably older than those already in the billiard room, the man several years Harry's senior, his evening suit perfectly tailored, his black hair combed back rather than slicked with oil and showing a distinguished hint of gray; the woman's white evening dress slightly more elegant and tasteful, less exuberant, her hair fashionably curled more than bobbed. They approached the table, each carrying a little sandwich of hot crab meat and melted cheese on toasted bread.

"Hello, boys!"

"Why, Parkman, you old snake!" Stoddard laid his cue on the table and rushed over to the new arrivals. He shook the man's hand and gave the woman a polite kiss on her cheek. "Edith! So nice to see you! Francis hasn't been swilling highballs all evening, has he?"

"Certainly not," she frowned, raising an eyebrow like a Hollywood queen, her voice smooth and assured. "Why, he knows I despise that sort."

"And yet it's still quite a show off with the popular crowd, isn't it? Good old Scott thinks so."

"If you're referring to that loathsome inebriate Fitzgerald and his silly wife, don't let on you find them the least bit intriguing. I'll see you thrown out of here on your head."

While Harry stood alone by the billiard table, Parkman greeted the restless girls on the sink-down sofa, both still rosy-faced from laughter and cocktails. "Clara! Winnie! I see you've been enjoying yourselves."

"Oh, we don't rate this party much, but I suppose we've had the best of what there is to be had." Clara's voice was slurred, almost languid now. She tapped cigarette ash into a fluted crystal vase. "Of course, absolutely everyone's been stewed since dinner." She winked at Harry.

Winnie raised her champagne glass. "It's been perfectly mad."

While Edith strolled over to chat with them, Parkman turned across to the table. "So, you boys are still at this damned game, are you?"

Stoddard cocked his thumb toward Harry. "Stanley here's just handed us our heads."

"Oh, he has, has he?" Parkman laughed and introduced himself. Harry reached across the table and shook his hand. "Glad to know you, sir."

"Showing the boys here a thing or two, eh?" asked Parkman, slipping the last bite of the crabmeat and toast into his mouth. By the look of his eyes, Harry guessed the old fellow was a bit fizzed up himself from a cocktail or two.

"Why, Stanley's a damned whiz!" Clarence complained, giving his sullen Muriel a hug. "It wasn't a bit fair."

"Is that so?" Parkman studied the leave Harry had set up. He chuckled. "Why, the old rail-nurse, is it? Flocking the ivory sheep?"

Harry was pleased. It seemed Parkman was another billiards enthusiast. You wouldn't ordinarily expect to meet one in a crowd like this. "You play, then, I assume?"

Parkman shook his head. "Christ no, I'm far too clumsy," he admitted. "I saw Frank Ives, though, at a tournament in '94 execute an anchor run of four hundred and eighty-seven. His genius persuaded me to give up the game for good."

Harry decided he liked this fellow. Parkman seemed intellectual, which was more than he could say for the rest of this bunch. "Genius is the capacity for hard work," he remarked. "I've heard nobody practiced more diligently than Ives."

"What line of work are you in, Stanley?" asked Parkman, picking up one of the billiard balls as if the game were already done.

"Well, in fact," Harry stalled, debating in his mind how much of the truth to shade, "actually, I'm in business with Charles Follette."

"The industrialist?"

"Yes." Of course that was a lie, but there was no reason to talk himself down in front of these fellows. Everyone inflates his own reputation now and then. It was no great sin.

Clarence asked Harry, "Say, then, you wouldn't happen to know any of the bootleggers here tonight, do you?"

"Are there bootleggers here?" Harry replied, both startled and curious as to the reasoning that connected Follette to criminals.

"Oh, I should say so," Clarence asserted. "Not that I've made their acquaintance, mind you. I'm much too cowardly for that. Nor would Muriel permit it, would you, dear?"

The pretty girl smiled pleasantly, then looked away, clearly bothered by this scene. Harry noticed Clara giving her the bad eye, but Muriel didn't reciprocate.

"Stanley ought to try his luck against Hollister," Stoddard said, coming back from a side-table with a slice of chocolate cake and a butter pastry, which he handed to Jay. "Wouldn't you agree?"

"Who?" Harry asked, setting the cue stick against the tableside.

"Graham Hollister," Jay replied. "He's a whiz at just about anything he tries."

"Of course, he high-hats everyone, too," Clarence observed, stroking Muriel's neck with his fingertips. "Why, he hasn't a friend in the world who doesn't owe him money."

"I've never heard of him," said Harry. He took his pocketwatch out and checked the time: a quarter past midnight. No wonder he was feeling drowsy.

"Oh, Graham's one of the smart set who summer on Lake Como

390 | MONTE SCHULZ

and winter at Santa Barbara," Parkman explained. "They're all horribly allergic to snow, you see."

Stoddard added, "His family owns a swell old beach house a couple of miles from the Miramar."

"Naturally, it's quite beautiful," said Jay.

"Not a beach house," Parkman corrected, playfully. "A bungalow!"

"Why, I hear he sleeps on palm fronds," said Stoddard, licking chocolate off his fingers. "Florence told me he's become brown as a Honolulu beach boy."

They all roared with laughter.

Clarence added, "Graham spends half the year surfboarding and riding horseback at Sandyland."

"Crashing parties at Montecito."

"Playing hide and seek with naïve little schoolgirls in the orange groves," said Jay.

"Then luring them up for a drink on those sultry California evenings," added Dohrman, still occupied staring at the girl across the room.

"A very tall drink!"

"Several, in fact!"

"Of course," Stoddard remarked, "the Mann Act has prevented any of us from ever meeting his little Sirens, as much as we'd like to."

Everyone laughed again. Then, out of the blue, pretty Muriel said, "But he's got awfully wicked eyes. Don't you agree?"

"Pardon me, darling?" Clarence looked surprised, as if he wasn't accustomed to hearing Muriel speak in public.

"Why, you dear little girl!" Jay laughed. "You do get out after all, don't you?"

By now, Clara and Winnie had gotten up off the sofa and come to the table with Edith. While Winnie went over to Dohrman and kissed his ear, Clara floated around behind Harry and stroked his neck with her fingers, giving him a wonderful shiver as she said, "I want to see Stanley show us his stuff."

"Oh, I think I've shown off enough," Harry said, feigning modesty. Hadn't he gone the limit already? True enough, girls adored a good act. It was the quickest way into bed.

"Oh, please, Stanley," Clara pleaded. "Why, I love a show-off. Do another trick!"

"Go on, Stanley," Stoddard urged. He gave him a light clap on the back. "Show us a trick."

While the crowd cheered him on, Harry took the cue stick again, then reached over and grabbed up the red ball in his right hand and curled it up behind his wrist. With the other hand, he raked the cue across the table, gathering the two white balls together and drawing them near. Then he switched the cue to his right hand, and let the red ball slide down out of his left sleeve.

"Oh my!"

"Why, it's magic!"

"Gee, he's a clever guy!"

"Great stuff, Stanley!" said Parkman, as everyone clapped. Harry rolled the red ball across the table and gave a short bow. Before the cheering ended, however, Dohrman was already embroiled in a heated exchange with Winnie. "What's your idea in bringing that up? I didn't love her."

Winnie looked hurt for an instant, then threw herself forward and kissed him. "Come on, honey. Please? Let's you and I go upstairs and have a party."

Dohrman grabbed her wrists, shoving her back. "Oh, now you're trying to show me a good time, are you? That's a laugh."

Clara took her glass and hopped up onto the billiard table near Harry and kicked her feet out. To no one in particular, she announced, "I'm awfully afraid that if I went off with Stanley tonight, when I came back I wouldn't be pure." She leaned over and kissed his ear. He blushed. Should he kiss her back? Is that what she expects?

Stoddard came around to Clara and placed his hands on her pale thighs. "Why, I used to be pure, darling, until I met you." He knelt forward and kissed her on the kneecap.

"Oh, no you don't, Stoddy!" She kicked him back with her heel. "That's closed for the evening." Clara shook her head in mock disgust. "Men!" She giggled. "Not a thought in their silly heads except the one that didn't need learning."

Stoddard feigned anger. "Why, Clara, an hour ago you were dying to make love."

"Clara's just talk, isn't she?" said Jay, taking a sugar pastry off a small plate, then setting the plate on the edge of the billiard table next to Parkman and Edith. Now the spacious room was mostly empty, and felt dark. Harry wondered if the party was ending, or moving upstairs.

"That's perfectly ridiculous, Jay." Clara laughed. "Why, you know I'd rather make love first and have a conversation after." She turned to Edith on the other side of the table. "It's always such an intolerable bore when they begin telling you about their mothers."

Dohrman strolled out from under the gasolier, away from Winnie, still staring resolutely at the pretty blonde. One of her suitors had departed, allowing her to stand even closer to the other, apparently enraptured by his presence. Harry watched Dohrman grab a nearly full glass of champagne off a French console table by the wall and quickly drink it to the bottom. He glared back across the room at the pair kissing passionately beside the Degas. "I tell you, this whole idiotic business of romance has got me balled up."

"Oh, Dohrman, forget about her," Winnie pleaded, reaching for him. "Let's fill up a bathtub with champagne and have a party. You can teach me how to swim."

"Say, that reminds me," Clarence began, taking a pastry of his own, "I was fined thirteen dollars last spring for wading nude in George Audsley's birdbath. Muriel was so humiliated she refused to see me for a month, isn't that so, darling? It simply played the deuce with our wedding plans."

"Look there now!" Dohrman fumed as the young man nuzzled the girl about her ears and neck. "That idiot hasn't any idea how a decent fellow ought to act. Why, he's probably a gatecrasher. Sylvester ought to ask for references at the door."

Harry choked. If he were somehow exposed as a phony now, good heavens, he'd need to leave town.

Winnie glanced there briefly. "Why, I'd say she seems quite taken with him."

"Well, I couldn't disagree more. I believe she's just getting wrong, and I intend to tell her so this very instant."

Dohrman took off across the room. Parkman and the others called for him to come back, but he ignored them and barged in between the pretty blonde and her suitor. Flabbergasted, Harry watched the intoxicated Dohrman grab the girl and kiss her flush on the mouth. She broke free, and slapped him. Surprised, Dohrman backed up a step. The suitor shoved him. Dohrman turned and slugged him in the mouth, knocking the fellow down. When he got up off the floor bleeding and tackled Dohrman into the nearest davenport, the group from the table dropped their pastries and champagne glasses and cue sticks and rushed over. Seeing Clara and Winnie rush to join the fray, laughing like hyenas, Harry suddenly realized how absurdly he had been behaving, kissing Clara and encouraging her to flop all over him. This was all ridiculous. He was creeping closer and closer to that line. Before he went completely to pieces, Harry flipped his cue stick onto the table, excused himself from Edith Parkman's company, and left the billiard room to find Pearl.

Of course, he had no idea where to look. The immense brownstone was a labyrinthine warren of doors and angled hallways. Dozens of Sylvester's remaining guests gathered in vestibules and stair landings, oiled with liquor and lewd flirtations. Roaring jazz and slurry voices chased throughout the mansion. Joining those swells in the billiard room had given Harry the confidence to meander about without fear of being turned out as a fraud. Popping into the kitchen briefly, he stole a couple of fried crab cakes and a glass of champagne. No one paid him any notice at all as he nodded to the waiters gathered there and ducked back out again, grinning like a fox. To think that four hours ago he was filling out a request sheet in his apartment for tungsten flashlights and four boxes of Pittsburgh stogies.

Leaving the kitchen, Harry found a short staircase that led to the second floor landing. Imagining Pearl upstairs chasing about and getting into things, he went there to look for her. At the top of the stairs was a wide hallway lit brightly by brass wall sconces with a thick blue oriental carpet that ran from where Harry stood at one end of the hall to a third floor staircase at the other. He heard voices issuing from a room near the far end of the corridor. These fellows speaking were certainly not from the boozy crowd who ran amok downstairs. The tone was serious and firm. Harry could make out fragments of a conversation regarding the next gubernatorial race and Charles Follette's chances to attain the esteemed office. That was interesting. How often did one of the high industrialist mucky-mucks run for public office? Follette for governor? This was news, all right. Since the door was open, Harry chose to walk past and have a quick peek. Naturally, he had to look as if he either belonged up here, or was lost. Maybe he ought to whistle a tune as he passed. No, just firm up your shoulders and stroll by.

Approaching the door, he heard a stern voice say, "I tell you, he's licked in November if we don't get this sorted out, and we're running out of big ideas here. You fellows simply have to do a better job of piecing this together."

"If you ask me, we ought to call in some of Mason's boys. They know the territory and don't need to give any buildup or sprinkle the flowers, for that matter. It'd be cheaper, and I tell you we'd have our pigeon before you know it."

"Not on your life. Bringing that outfit into the game now would be a hell of a risk, and I know for a fact the boss wouldn't like it one bit, so that plan's out, and I mean to tell you, plain as day. If I hear any rumors about Mason or Schumacher or any of those hotshots poking their noses into this business, you'll be selling apples out in Westbrook. Get me?"

Harry passed by just then, sneaking a casual glance into the room where he saw two men standing face to face by a big oak desk: a thin gray-haired fellow wearing a tuxedo, and a short fellow in a blue serge suit — that same idiot from the speakeasy who'd been following him all summer! So, too, was the tall one who had joined his pal today at Legion Park, smoking a cigarette over in a corner by a bookcase; Harry recognized his gray fedora and neatly trimmed Fairbanks mustache. What on earth were they doing here? Stepping quickly by to the marble staircase at the end of the hall, Harry took the carpeted stairs that curved up around the corner out of view. He stopped to let the air out. Seeing those two from the park shocked him. Had they trailed him here? What the devil for? Follette running for governor was a big story, all right, but how did those two characters figure into it? Maybe seeing them at the park today was just a coincidence. Maybe this had nothing to do with that gangster shooting at Delany's Café or confronting the short fellow at the Soda Club that night in May. Lots of people go to speakies, don't they? Why should that be a surprise?

Deciding he needed to have a second look, Harry eased down the stairs. There was another door just past the office. If he had to, he might be able to duck in there and have a good listen. He slipped back into the hall. Passing the office again, he took one more peek at the men inside and saw without a doubt those two were the same fellows he had spotted on the bench this afternoon at Legion Park.

"Now, let me tell you one, pal. It'll be fifty tomorrow and another fifty at the end of the week," Harry heard the short fellow say, "or me and Fred are taking a vacation."

"You'll get paid."

"Says you."

"Tuttle's got your money. You can drop up to see him in the morning. He'll be expecting you."

"You bet he will."

Finding the door unlocked, Harry sneaked into a small room of files and boxes with a mimeograph machine and tickertape and a pair of typewriters facing each other across an oak desk. He left the door slightly ajar so that he could hear more clearly. He could always claim to be drunk like everyone else and gotten lost looking for the wine cellar. Thrilled at his little caper, Harry finished the glass of champagne, then hid behind the door and listened to the short fellow saying goodnight. The older fellow replied with some remark about avoiding the crowds down in the foyer and taking the service entry out to the garage.

"I got no idea where that is," the short one said. "I'd need a map to find my way out of this joint."

"Well, it's easy. I'll show you. Come on."

"Fred?"

"Check."

Harry set his empty champagne glass on the desk. This was exciting. He heard the men walk past, one of them jingling a set of keys. Counting backwards to sixty, he pressed his ear to the wood. Sleuthing was a tricky affair. If one of those three hadn't gone with the others, Harry could be exposed as a sneak, regardless of his excuse. He decided to wait in the dark another minute or two, just to be safe. This business of Follette was damned confusing. So what if he was running for governor? Men in his position could do what they wanted. Politics cost a fortune these days, but certainly Follette had the bankroll to buy the State House. Of course, why he would bother with a job like that was another question. Harry figured Follette had enough on his plate without spending half the day glad-handing, nor did he need a governor's influence to get the legislature to see his way on most issues. Everyone in the city knew that if Follette wasn't exactly steering the ship of state, he was at least navigating. So what were those fellows talking about in Sylvester's office? Trouble with the Follette candidacy? That could mean anything from a reluctant campaign contributor to some kind of blackmail. What else worries a politician?

Emboldened by the champagne, Harry decided to take a look in that office across the hall. Curiosity always diminished the risk. Easing the door open, he saw the hallway was still empty. Five quick steps took him out and into the other room. This was Sylvester's personal office, all right, the sort Harry had dreamed of when he was young: a great marble fire mantle, oriental carpets, leather armchairs, polished brass lamps, a lawyer's oak desk, and wall-mounted eight foot mahogany bookcases topped by a frieze of Egyptian hieroglyphics that framed a grand ceiling fresco of Apian's star chart. Harry felt as if he were in a museum. On the desk were family photographs, books, a couple of thick ledgers, correspondences, and stacks of folders directly in front of the desk chair, one of which lay open. Reading it over quickly, Harry discovered a record of observation, indicated by hourly notations:

```
Olive Subject 42 (brunette, blue eyes, 5 ft 2 in approx):
June 29th
7:48 A.M. -- spotted at Union St Florist.
8:10  -- takes 13th St trolley to Ju-Ju's Black Bottom
          on Commerce St
10:03 -- takes trolley to Columbia Ave
10:26 -- buys popcorn from vendor on Park St
10:32 -- talks to old lady on bench
10:51 -- enters Delany's Cafe
11:07 -- joined by unidentified white man, (late-30s approx)
11:31 -- Fiori's hitter burns up Eddie Kahn, (r.i.p.)
12:08 P.M. -- shares taxicab with man to Legion Park and
               stays with him at park
11:39 -- subject leaves joint with same man
1:43  -- leaves Legion Park alone through Sheridan Gate
1:58  -- stops at lunchwagon on Patrick Henry Ave.
2:06  -- Meets unidentified lady (redhead, 30s approx).
2:14  -- goes with lady in Dodge auto to Leslie St. millinery
5:12  -- leaves millinery. Takes trolley to Humbert St
5:29  -- walks to Lorelli's piano factory, goes in
6:00  -- factory closes for the day. Contact with subject lost.
```

Good grief, how could he be such an idiot? Those fellows weren't after him at all! He put her sheet aside and picked up the one beneath it. Same sort of thing: *Olive Subject 31, tracked down at a grocery store on Manchester Street, followed to Harkin and over to a fish market at Belevedere, sold flowers under a lamppost till sundown.* And another, *Olive Subject 17, picked up at Waterfront Avenue in a crowd of fishermen and trailed across the river on a barge to Easthaven and back with a couple of boys holding the sacks of potatoes she confiscated from the A&P market on Lowell.*

Harry flipped through more than a dozen such reports and shook his head. Unless there were real top-drawer detectives out somewhere pursuing definite leads, this whole search was being undertaken by a low-rent shotgun method, targeting as many girls fitting the name, age, and description as humanly possible. These two fellows spying on Pearl didn't seem much more than cut-rate spotters, which probably meant she wasn't a hot lead. Also, since her name wasn't even Olive, regardless of what was written on that report sheet, they were trying to pull a fast one on Follette's outfit. Still, the fact that they thought she was worth following at all gave Harry a strange feeling. Was this all a setup? And why was Follette so anxious to turn her up before the election? What difference did that make?

Then he heard voices again in the hallway, approaching the office. He searched the room for another exit. There were just two doors in

Sylvester's office. He tried the one across the room and found the toilet. No place to hide there. On the far side of the office, another door opened to a coat closet. Harry quickly ducked inside there behind a thick gabardine topcoat.

"Now, last night Kitty told me it's Paris or nothing, and I'd rather go jump in a lake than spend another miserable summer traipsing up and down the Rue de Rivoli with her and that idiot sister Doris. All those horrid little cafés they like so much are for the birds, if you ask me, and I've never cared a damn for Josephine Baker and her jungle show, or any other jazz, for that matter. It's all obscene over there. So, to answer your question, yes, I guess I'll be solo at Grossinger's like everyone else."

Harry heard the door close.

A second man's voice said, "Well, I don't mind letting Hazel off for a couple of weeks, because, frankly, she's a terrible pester when the weather warms up and won't even try to be agreeable unless she's with her own bunch. So I agree. Good riddance."

"You ought to know Willoughby's apparently hired a carload of dollies from Albany, and Waldo claims not a one of them can tie her own shoe without a manual."

"Who's footing the bill for that?"

"Merriam, so long as he gets first pick."

"Well, I suppose that's fair."

"I'd say so."

They both laughed. Harry thought one of the two voices belonged to the older fellow who was in the room before. The other he didn't recognize at all. How long would he have to stay concealed in the closet? The air was stuffy and one of his legs was beginning to cramp.

"Look here, these boys that Charley's got canvassing the neighborhoods talk a good game, but I don't for one minute believe they're onto anything more than a girl-spree with our cash. This little fellow Cobb I just had in here is a case in point. Ten days after Follette brings him into the sweepstakes, he's already picked out some common street tomato because he thinks she fits the bill for Charley's little Olive Blanchard. Of course, nobody but he and his pal Fred

Markle have seen her, and I'm not sure I'd trust either of them to watch a fire hydrant. Truth be told, I had half a mind to throw them both out of here, but look at these files — we've got more girls than Ziegfeld and only one of them could be Follette's bastard. So how can we know Cobb hasn't actually turned over the genuine ticket? We started this three months ago, and we've gotten nowhere. It's absolutely maddening."

Follette's bastard?

"I tell you, we go to Rosenthal at the *World-Telegram* and make a deal to put out a want ad that details a certain girl for a modeling job that'll let her collect, say, fifty dollars if she comes across as right for the part. Word of mouth is bound to bring in ten times the girls your boys have got in those folders."

"All right, so then what? Say she shows up and we're able to determine she's the girl we're looking for. You know the papers are going to want to write up her story and take her picture. Then we pay her and drive her off into the sunset. Is that your idea?"

"Correct."

"Well, get this: Egan wants her dumped into the river. That's the latest. I just got off the telephone this morning from Herb Belding and that's what came out of the meeting at the Seventh Heaven Club last night. Get rid of her. Make her disappear."

Harry gasped.

"You're not serious."

"Yes, I am. Their best opinion was that Charley's got plenty of troubles already out in Loughridge and Hopkinstown without some bastard daughter showing up in the middle of this campaign. Can you fathom what Grace Morley's bluenoses at the Decency League would say? They'd fry our hair. We couldn't run him for dog catcher."

Bastard daughter? What on earth are they talking about?

"I see why we can't involve the papers."

"Yes."

"Has Horton been advised on all this? I'm sure he'd like to offer his two cents worth."

"It's my understanding that John Bartlett wired Claridge's this afternoon. Apparently, Horton was out with his family at Westminister. I haven't heard anything further."

"Arthur, this is a very serious matter, disposing of that girl as Egan proposes. I must tell you, I have grave doubts about the wisdom involved with his decision. Horton's too close. It's one thing for Charley to feel he can't be exposed to the scandal of a bastard child at the start of a gubernatorial campaign, but Horton ought to consider his own position. Aside from the advantage he gains with Charley voiding the Amalgamated Steel contracts, what's his profit in all this?"

"Well, there are more than steel contracts involved here, remember. General Motors and Edison have a stake in that game now, and Morgan Bank, too. Horton can't afford any sidetracks. Not at this late date."

"But the risk, man, the risk! Egan's not seeing over the horizon. One slip up, a loose word, some unforeseen misfortune, and Horton's tied, at least indirectly, to the murder of an innocent girl. Can you possibly imagine how that would play out in the public mind? He'd be ruined. We'd all be ruined. And one of us could fry."

"Well, I can't disagree with you there. Egan's crowd has always been brash, perhaps to a fault, and — "

"I tell you, somebody's got to advise Horton to exercise caution here. And I mean now, tonight. Or tomorrow at the latest. Before somebody lays a hand on that poor girl. Restrain Charley's thugs until all the angles are covered. It's only prudent, don't you agree?"

"I'll see what I can do. It's no good telephoning Egan, Belding or Sherman. Those fellows aren't reasonable like we are. Once they make a decision, it's cut in stone. But maybe I'll shoot over to Reggie's tonight. He'll still be up. I doubt he takes more than a catnap, anymore. That girl he's been seeing won't let him."

"Will Horton take his call? I heard they were having a spat."

"Do you mean that nonsense with the yacht? Nothing to it. Just gossip, probably out of Kittridge's office, hoping Reggie'd drop his lawsuit against them. He won't. Clark can go to hell as far as Reggie's concerned, and Horton won't take sides."

"I hope you're right."

"Well, I am."

"It still confounds me why Charley gave up on locating the woman first. After all, he knew what she looked like and there were connections to her that just don't exist with the girl."

"She's gone, that's why. Completely vanished. After eight months of kicking over every rock in this part of the country, Drew Bosley found three different Maggie Blanchard's and not one of them was Charley's old flame. They decided it was a dead end. Besides, the courthouse in Sagamont County burned to the ground fourteen years ago, so there are no records, no trails, nothing. That's why we've moved onto the girl and we'd better turn her up or it's curtains for this whole episode."

"Then why don't you drop over to visit Reggie tonight and I'll finish here and go have a word with Parkman. Did you see him downstairs? He and Edith arrived about an hour ago. Leonard says she's in a foul mood, but he doesn't know why."

"I should imagine it likely has something to do with that crowd of junior inebriates Parkman fancies. He simply can't keep his eyes off the debutantes. I don't know how Edith stands it."

"Be sure Reggie understands the gravity of this situation. Don't let him off the hook."

"I won't."

Then Harry heard the office door open. The air inside the closet had become stifling and he felt suffocated. Had they both gone? He listened for a few moments. No, one of them was still at the desk, shuffling folders. Good grief, he'd be dead before this fellow finishes. Harry shifted his position behind the topcoat. A telephone number was being dialed.

"Lyman? Drake here... Yes, fine, just fine. And you?... Well, we both know that can't be helped, can it? We're not in college any longer... Pardon? No, she's doing very well, thank you. I'll tell her you asked... Right, well, it's simply this: I just spent the past half hour trying to get a fix on where this business with Charley's headed and I have to tell you it's become a damned muddle and it's getting worse. A lot worse. I think it's turning into a racket now and we're not going to be served well staying involved much longer. If you don't believe me, give Egan a call and listen to what his crowd came up with last night. It's astounding, really... No, I'd rather you hear it from him personally... No, I don't want to say another word. Just telephone over there and let him explain... Well, I'm going over there tomorrow morning. You can reach me after breakfast... Certainly... All right, I'll speak with you then... Thank you, Lyman... Yes, good night."

Harry heard the telephone placed back in its cradle as the fellow cursed to himself. Something had definitely gone to smash with Follette and his so-called niece. How many people were involved with this? Dozens? Who knew what, and how much? A desk drawer slid shut and a key clicked into a lock. The fellow mumbled something, then the lights went off and Harry heard the door close. Thank goodness!

Caution suggested he wait a few more minutes just to be sure. This was incredibly baffling. So Follette's niece wasn't his niece at all, but a bastard child from some cheap affair years ago? My God! And that short fellow, Cobb, thinks Pearl's his ticket to Follette's five thousand dollar grand prize. No wonder he's following her. But what makes him think she's the one? Pearl's too old to be that girl, her name's not Olive, and she doesn't have blonde hair. Does she know people are following her? It seemed fantastic that a silly nobody like her could possibly bring hell to a candidate for governor, particularly a great man like Charles Follette. It was something you just wouldn't believe unless you heard it spoken aloud.

A couple of more minutes passed, then Harry eased the closet open to the dark office. He crept across to the front door and listened. When he was certain the hall was empty, he slipped out of the office and went back downstairs.

By half past two, the orchestra had stopped playing. Throughout the brownstone mansion, guests were departing, the finely appointed rooms vacated. Heading for the front door like everyone else, Harry saw cigarette butts and liquor bottles and food of all sorts spilled on the oriental carpets, furniture inelegantly rearranged, a Tiffany lamp broken. In the narrow hallway where the Sylvester family portraits hung, he noticed a young man lying flat on his back, a balloon glass of Canadian ale held to his lips by a rather homely girl kneeling beside him in a torn emerald dress. The grand ballroom and mirror gallery were littered with napkins and crushed flowers, shattered champagne glasses, discarded bows and ribbons, and party balloons slowly deflating on a quiet floor.

Out on the terrace now, the night air was delightfully cool and fragrant with summer flowers. Harry stood with his back to the balustrade of stone urns, watching the great mansion empty. He was desperate to find Pearl, so he decided to wait for her outdoors where he could see her leave the mansion. Those guests who had not yet gone to their autos milled about the brightly lit entrance or flirted in the shadowed gardens below. The orchestra was packing up for the night. Trying to relax, Harry watched the musicians file out casually, flushed with merriment. A handsome trumpet player walked out arm-in-arm with a lovely young brunette. As they strolled across the brick terrace toward the stairs, the musician put the horn to his lips and played some sassy jazz notes. After several engaging bars of "Sugar Blues," he lowered the horn and gently kissed the young woman on her cheek. Harry clapped for the impromptu performance.

The pale trumpet player bowed. "Thank you, sir."

"Very nicely done," Harry said. "Really, your entire orchestra was delightful tonight."

The trumpet player draped his free arm around the brunette, and raised the horn with a grin. "We's the best!"

"Oh, Buster, darling." The pretty brunette pinched his ribs. "Your humility always rises to the occasion, doesn't it? Is that why I love you so?"

The trumpet player gave her another kiss on the cheek. "My dear Marion, you know the song's in my blood." He raised the trumpet again and played a jazz riff that hurtled across the night.

The smiling brunette shook her head. "Never marry a trumpet player."

Waving good-bye, they walked off together down the wide stairway toward Mulberry Avenue. As Harry watched an older gentleman, roughly Parkman's age, stroll alone across the terrace to a shadowed section of the balustrade perpendicular to his own, he considered how lucky he was to have gotten into this grand brownstone at all. You could go through your entire life and never see inside one of these homes — if you could even think of something this outlandish as a home. Marie always mused about the people who inhabited these sorts of places. She invented little fictions about tea parties for hundreds, and hidden passageways, and eccentric relatives who came for a rainy weekend and ended up living in the attic bedrooms for a century or two. Frankly, Harry doubted she would have found much to amuse herself tonight. Marie hated drinking and sex language and certainly did not appreciate such shameless flirting. It wasn't her fault. The Pendergasts were a family who seemed to despise any behavior that didn't mimic their own. The whole lot was provincial and dull. He was glad to be rid of them for a while. What had they ever done for him, anyhow, but mix things up?

His nerves settling somewhat thanks to that last glass of champagne, Harry watched the older gentlemen in the shadows across the terrace light a cigarette and stare out toward the city. He seemed thoroughly calm and content, not a care in the world. Men like him are miles above me, Harry thought. I'm just a pipsqueak to them. That could change, certainly, if he managed to put the arm on Follette's bastard. Then he'd be a big shot, the hero that saved the day. Perhaps they would have him out to the Huffaker Lounge for lunch one sunny afternoon and a round of golf and a fair whack at his own gold key to the Seventh Heaven Club. Wouldn't that be something? Of course, the privilege of that advancement might involve helping to get an innocent girl murdered. But isn't that how it always starts? They dangle that precious bauble one inch from your nose and expect you'll ignore all the whispering going on behind you. You'll be ruined either way. They just hope you don't realize it before you've made your choice.

Beneath the terrace, a girl's sudden laughter, bright and clear, echoed up from a stand of Italian cypress. Angling sideways between the stone urns for a look, Harry heard glass breaking on cement, then a shriek and a loud splash from one of the marble fountains.

"Stanley!"

Harry turned about and saw Parkman wave to him. He was alone and mopped his brow with a white handkerchief as he came across the brick toward Harry from the grand entrance. Behind him, another group of people came out of the mirror gallery, drinks still in hand.

"That was quite something back there, wasn't it?" said Parkman, approaching the balustrade. His handkerchief appeared almost luminescent in the moonlight. He looked distressed.

"Not unexpected, I suppose," Harry replied, trying to be casual. "Though an excellent argument for temperance, wouldn't you say?" Being a little fuddled himself from the champagne, he decided against letting on that he knew anything about Follette's drama. After all, who could say what role, if any, Parkman might have in that mess?

The old fellow chuckled. "It's true young Dohrman tipples like a damn flounder. Always has. Restraint of any sort is certainly not in the boy's character. He's been acting like a fool all year, and it seems to be contagious. Indeed, his whole crowd's plagued by prosperity indigestion. Why, I've come to believe their entire generation views silly behavior as a virtue."

"Well, certainly that boy's friends aren't the only ones guilty of imprudent conduct." Harry did his best to describe the disarray he had seen on his stroll from the billiard room, omitting his excursion to the office closet. "Why would Sylvester tolerate it?"

Parkman laughed. "Horton's at London on summer holiday with his family. He never attends any of his own large parties. They don't interest him in the least."

"Then why give them?" Harry could scarcely conceive of inviting a house full of guests to his home on Cedar Street and not being there to welcome and entertain them. Perhaps it was different for the wealthy. How many in this crowd tonight were actually close to Sylvester? Do the rich have any true loyalty to anyone but their banker?

Parkman drew a cigarette from a silver case in his jacket. "Well, Horton appreciates his many friendships, and chooses to reward them through demonstrations of conspicuous excess. He finds they enjoy it and come back again." Parkman lit his cigarette and exhaled smoke into the dark. "As a host, Horton Sylvester's held in the highest regard, you know."

The excitement at the fountain resulted in a beautiful girl being led sopping wet from the dark garden, her dress ruined, her sequined Clara Bow hat dripping water. Nevertheless, she wore a big smile on her face, swooning into the arms of her escort as she reached the lighted stairway, kissing him deeply, giggling afterward. She was extraordinary. Harry wondered if she had a sister.

"I see Howard's still with us," Parkman observed, lowering his voice while nodding in the direction of the older gentleman by the shadowed balustrade. "In body, if not in spirit."

"Who?"

"Howard Guiberson. You've never met?"

"No," Harry replied, once again eyeing the older gentleman as he smoked his cigarette in the dark, his pose stoic as the Sphinx. Somehow he didn't appear to belong to this riotous crowd.

"Well, Howard was on the *Titanic*, you know."

"You're joking." Harry turned to face Parkman, his interest suddenly piqued. "Aren't you?"

"An absolutely tragic story. Just horrible." Parkman settled back against one of the stone urns. He took a short drag off his cigarette, and tapped the ash off into the urn at his elbow. "Of course, you remember that Howard Guiberson and Horton Sylvester were roommates at New Haven."

"Is that so? Yale men, eh? That's a crowd, all right. " Long ago Harry aspired to an Eastern education. Sadly, he was neither rich nor smart enough.

"Yes, indeed," Parkman nodded, proudly. "Members in Wolf's Head, the Lizzie, football captains, rakes about campus. They were quite close, back then. Best of friends. Absolutely inseparable. In fact, after taking their degrees, they traveled together through Suez to Java and Peking in '00 on summer holiday and found themselves fighting side-by-side with Captain Jack Myers and the American Legation at the Tartar Wall during the Rebellion. Later, when Horton married Phoebe, Howard served as his best man, a favor Horton returned for Howard the next spring when he married Lydia Chase at Stamford. As the Sylvester family owned a fair interest in White Star Line at the time, Horton's wedding gift to Howard and Lydia was a first class booking on the maiden voyage of the *Titanic*."

"Good grief!"

Parkman shrugged, and flicked more ash into the stone urn. "Passage was reserved a year in advance, and there were no clairvoyants in the booking office." He smiled, wanly.

"I suppose not, but for heaven sakes. It's just incredible to think back on it now."

"Yes, it is." Parkman nodded. "You see, by the January following their marriage, Lydia had given birth to twins, Ariel and Corrina, at London where she and Howard had been living since shortly after the wedding. He had employment with an investment firm on Threadneedle Street while intending to return triumphantly to America aboard the *Titanic* with his new family in April. Horton had even arranged a gala homecoming for Howard and Lydia at Newport for the evening after their arrival. Nearly everyone they knew had expected to attend."

Parkman finished with his cigarette and snuffed out the butt. He stared across the terrace at Guiberson, who had taken on the appearance of a dark specter haunting the upper balustrade in the pale moonshadow of the Palladian brownstone.

Lowering his voice, Parkman said, "Horton had secured a stateroom for Howard and Lydia on the 'B' deck with most of the smart crowd who were returning from holiday in the Mediterranean. J. J. Astor himself and young Madeleine Force had just been in Cairo. It had been a wonderful spring, and all agreed that a crossing in the *Titanic* was quite the way to end the season abroad. Of course, this made for another simply marvelous party. The Wideners and Ryersons were there, remember, and Archie Butt, Clarence Moore, Francis Millet, Henry Harris, Washington Dodge, Guggenheim, many others of the old register. Every evening, the best crowd would gather in the dining saloon. Although it was April, and quite cool, the passage was calm and clear, very accommodating for Lydia who was, in fact, deathly afraid of the sea. On the first day out of Queenstown, she'd made the acquaintance of Mrs. William Graham and her daughter Margaret, and passed much of the voyage with them in the Palm Court and the writing room. Meanwhile, Howard paraded about like a schoolboy from the smoking room up to the Boat Deck and the gym, returning to the lounge for a round of bridge with Butt and Moore and Ryerson, then dashing down to the racket court where he thrashed a variety of opponents for three days running. Every afternoon following dinner, he and Lydia joined the Ryersons and the Grahams for one of Wallace Hartley's concerts; Lydia particularly loved Franz Lehar's 'Merry Widow Waltz' and Hartley's orchestra played it for her everyday."

Parkman drew another cigarette from the silver case and lit it, flicking the match into the stone urn. "That Sunday, the fourteenth, Lydia came down with the sniffles after singing hymns in the dining saloon and decided to take supper in the stateroom. Failing to persuade Lydia that he ought to stay with her, Howard went off to attend George Widener's dinner party with Captain Smith, the Thayers, Archie Butt, and the Carters. Indeed, all the smart crowd appeared, and the sumptuous meal made for a splendid evening of high spirits and revelry. After dinner, Howard looked in on Lydia and the children who'd fallen asleep, then joined everyone in the Louis Seize lounge on 'A' deck where the orchestra was giving a concert, 'Les Contes d'Hoffman.' The night was quite beautiful, you may recall: moonless, brilliant with stars, utterly clear. When the performance of the barcarole was concluded with a rousing ovation, Howard followed Widener and Moore and several others to the smoking room for cigars and a few last stories. Highballs were generally the order of the hour, but as it was late, Howard satisfied himself with a hot lemonade, and after staying well past eleven just to hear another of Clarence Moore's extravagant adventures in the mountains of Virginia, he retired to the stateroom."

Parkman took a drag off the cigarette, exhaling slowly, and tapping ash into the urn. He continued, his voice somber now. "Howard had been in bed reading from Kipling's 'Recessional' when the iceberg was struck. He hardly felt it, nor did many others of the early-to-bed crowd on 'B' deck: just a rumble of sorts, a queer vibration from the starboard side. Neither Lydia nor the children awakened. Curious, Howard threw an overcoat atop his pajamas and went out to investigate. Though the night was clear, by now it was also bitterly cold on deck, yet Howard saw passengers from steerage frolicking about the starboard well deck with chunks of ice. He also joined a crowd supposedly watching the guilty iceberg itself disappear to stern. No one thought much of it. After all, what sort of damage might a silly piece of ice inflict on the mighty *Titanic*, eh?

"After half an hour or so of exploring about, discussing with several members of the crew and his own crowd when the ship might get underway again, Howard returned to the stateroom where he found Lydia awake, tending to the children, both of whom had apparently caught her sniffles. While they debated whether or not to summon a physician, their steward came to the door and asked if they might put on their lifebelts and join everyone on the Boat Deck. Lydia resisted the idea, arguing that the cold would harm the children and that she herself had a fever. When Howard explained, however, that the ship was listing and it might actually become necessary to leave her, Lydia was persuaded to dress and go up. Although she was frightened, Lydia helped Howard bundle the twins into her own sable stoles and together they carried them up to the Boat Deck where practically everyone they knew on board milled about in various states of fine evening dress augmented by winter clothes. As Howard and Lydia arrived on deck, the first rocket went off from the starboard side of the bridge."

Parkman puffed on his cigarette while staring across the dark at Guiberson who had yet to move from the far balustrade. A light breeze stirred in the cypress. Harry only vaguely recalled what came next. It seemed so long ago.

"Of course, as everybody knew what rockets at sea meant, Lydia herself began to weep, and asked Howard to take her back to the stateroom. That he refused to do, which only made matters worse. Fortunately, Hartley's band had set up in a corner of the lounge nearby and began a spirited ragtime melody that seemed to provide the necessary calm and allowed the stewards to begin loading the lifeboats with a minimum of fuss. Howard brought Lydia and the children to boat Number Eight, and kissed her good-bye. She refused to leave without him. However, the steward for Eight, John Hart, pointed out that no men would be allowed in the lifeboats until all women and children were safely loaded. Lydia argued with him, as did many of the other women, and only when Howard assured her that he'd step into the first available boat did she consent to go. Even then, with a seat waiting in the boat beside Margaret and Mrs. Graham, Lydia persisted in not stepping foot off the *Titanic* until Howard left to find another boat. With that last promise secured, they embraced and Howard kissed the children, and Lydia, once again, and hurried to stern.

"As Howard crossed the promenade to starboard, he saw the last of the rockets go up. Steerage passengers were coming up on deck now, wandering aimlessly about, nobody to guide them. Howard took it upon himself to escort a group of young Irish ladies to the aft lifeboats, then proceeded forward where he saw J.J. Astor and Madeleine sitting on a pair of mechanical horses in the gymnasium examining a lifebelt that Astor had sliced open with his penknife. Ahead, Colonel Gracie and others were struggling with one of the collapsibles and not having much luck. Lifeboats Seven and Five were already in the water. Number Three was sliding down. Although Howard saw men in each of these boats, he hurried back across the promenade to port to see that Lydia was safely away. All the while, of course, Hartley's band continued to play cheerful ragtime airs which, remarkably, kept spirits up. Howard saw Harry Widener there chatting at the railing with William Carter. Both Eight and Six had already gone. Widener informed Howard that Archie Butt, Moore, and Ryerson had gone back in for a round of bridge. The rest of the old crowd, Astor, Yates, George Widener, Ben Guggenheim, were still about somewhere intending to 'go down like gentlemen.'

"Trusting that Lydia and the children were safe, Howard returned to the starboard Boat Deck determined to find a seat in one of the boats. Indeed, collapsible 'C' was just lowering when he arrived at the bow. Fortunately, Quartermaster Rowe gave Howard permission to climb aboard, then waved the Engelhardt free of the ship."

Gently sobering up, Harry kept his eye on Guiberson who had shifted his attitude slightly to the gray balustrade, his gaze focused somewhere into the cypress grove at the rear of the brownstone.

Parkman spoke even more softly now. "The sea was calm and black. Howard's Engelhardt pulled easily away from the *Titanic* as the great ship dipped forward lower and lower into the water, her bow lights disappearing while Wallace Hartley's extraordinary orchestra played 'Autumn,' and those who hadn't found space in the boats watched those who had from the railings. Eventually, you'll recall, the stern rose nearly to vertical and everything not fixed in place within the ship collided with a great roar, and hundreds of desperate souls threw themselves overboard into the icy waters, and the unsinkable *Titanic* foundered."

Parkman took a brief drag off his cigarette, and coughed harshly before continuing. "While debate raged in the Engelhardt over the wisdom of attempting to rescue those in the water — cries for help were all anyone could hear now — Howard watched the sea nearby for lifeboat Number Eight. Naturally it was futile, due to the dark. After the voices from the water died away one by one, there were so many corpses in the waters about the Engelhardt that, for awhile, it became all but impossible to row. Boats drifted here and there during the night. Quartermaster Rowe led a prayer. Every so often, Howard tried calling to Lydia, without success. Even in the boats, people died of the fierce cold well before the *Carpathia* arrived. That most did not seems almost remarkable now. In fact, a fellow survivor in the Englehardt with Howard was none other than J. Bruce Ismay himself, Chairman of White Star, who was, of course, quite vilified later on for failing to do his duty and perish with the ship as had Captain Smith and so many of his valiant crew.

"At dawn, Howard and collapsible Engelhardt 'C' crossed the great ice field and reached the *Carpathia*. Several other boats were there already. Immediately after being helped up on deck, he began inquiring about Number Eight. He circled the *Carpathia's* deck twice before coming across Gladys Cherry and the Countess of Rothes, both of whom he'd seen in Eight when he'd left Lydia and the children. They told Howard, and Margaret Graham confirmed this an hour later, that Lydia had decided not to leave the *Titanic* without him, and had simply taken the children and gotten off. That was the last anyone remembered seeing her."

Parkman drew a deep breath and stared at Guiberson once more across the shadowed terrace, his stony figure posed against the balustrade. "His belovéd Lydia had most likely returned to the stateroom and waited for Howard to come back to her. She and the children had gone down with the ship."

Until that moment, Harry hadn't really ever felt himself stirred by people from another world. It was too pleasant to think they were so different he needn't be sympathetic. Now he felt graceless and faintly dissipated, reminded somehow of his own fluffy narcissism.

Parkman shook his head sadly. "Howard spent two years at a sanitarium in Connecticut. Only when Horton finally came for him did he begin to make appearances again. In the seventeen years since, he's never remarried, nor has he ever returned to sea, though on each of Horton's crossings, at longitude 50 degrees, 14 minutes, west, Phoebe tosses a garland of roses overboard on Howard's behalf."

Parkman snuffed out his cigarette on the rounded edge of the urn and let it fall inside. He looked Harry in the eye. "The truth is, one couldn't count the times we've said to Howard, 'Pull yourself together, old man. You've got to buckle down and get on with it.' But, of course, it's never any use. As Horton said to a group of us just last Christmas, 'Though Howard Guiberson's heart has continued to beat all these years, surely his life ended with his dear Lydia's that night aboard the *Titanic*.'"

Thoroughly silenced by Parkman's story, Harry sought out Guiberson once more in the shadows across the terrace and saw that he had finally left the balustrade of stone urns and wandered off toward the rear of the mansion, a solitary figure strolling through the dark cypress grove, a bleak shade.

Brightening somewhat, Parkman nudged Harry, directing his attention back to the front of the brownstone where Stoddard Platt had just come out of the gallery. "Well, what do you suppose we're to make of this?"

The champagne fading away now, Harry watched the young man hurry over, hair all a mess, jacket disheveled. Stoddard spoke in a loud, frantic voice. "Dohrman's just gone to pieces, Francis! He's all in!"

Stopping to catch his breath, he noticed Harry behind Parkman at the balustrade. "Oh, hello, Stanley. Good to see you again." He reached out and shook Harry's hand as if they had just met. Immediately, his attention reverted to Parkman. "A filthy muddle is what it is, Francis. Why, that stupid fellow's nose isn't half as badly broken as he's claiming, yet he's called for a doctor and a lawyer. Dohrman'll be lucky to avoid spending the rest of the night in the klink. Oh, it just burns me up!"

Parkman remarked, "Well, you know, if young Dohrman persists in imagining himself as Frank Merriwell, all the while acting like an ass, he'll soon find the need for a lawyer of his own."

"But that's just it, Francis!" Stoddard complained. "That damned fellow intends to send the law after Dohrman. All for a stupid little scrap. Why, it's just idiotic!"

Glancing back at the stairway terrace, Harry noticed a young man hurriedly departing, Dohrman's pretty blonde beside him holding a towel to his face. Harry asked, "Isn't that the boy now?"

Both Stoddard and Parkman turned to look. Stoddard frowned. "Well, I don't understand this at all. Why would that fellow choose to leave before the fireworks begin? I ought to find out."

Stoddard raced back toward the mansion where Harry noticed Parkman's wife waiting beside an entry pilaster.

Parkman saw her then, too, and called loudly, "Edith!"

She smiled, and gave a brief wave. Just then, Dohrman himself came sailing out of the gallery, dodging a crowd of men in black coats and tails, and charged down the wide stairway toward Mulberry Avenue. Stoddard, who hadn't yet reached the entrance, instantly changed directions and chased after him while Parkman hurried over toward Edith. Alone again, Harry moved along the balustrade for a better view, though the foliage of the lower terraces prevented him from seeing anything more than Dohrman's dress jacket flapping in the lamplight midway down the stairs to the grand portico. He was amused by the boy's stupid urgency. Couldn't he see how ridiculous he was? And what exactly *was* Parkman's connection to that crowd of young fools?

Harry caught a chorus of strident voices shouting above the stream of guests awaiting automobiles at the circle drive. He watched Parkman and Edith descend the first level of steps, their own eyes riveted on the lower terrace. Next he heard a woman's shrill cry from below the portico, then a single gunshot, and a hideous scream. A cluster of men smoking cigars by the grand entrance hurried forward. Parkman and Edith disappeared into a flurry of guests rushing down the stairway. After that, he recognized only confusion beneath the portico, a tidal swell in that direction, true pandemonium. He stood at the corner urns for a long while, watching until the first sirens echoed across Edison Heights. The crowds from up and down the avenue intensified, buzzing and frenzied. He wanted to go down there, give someone a swift kick in the shins. Instead, feeling a burgeoning liquor headache from all the evening's champagne and tumult, Harry left the brick terrace and followed the zigzag of the long balustrade to the rear garden of the brownstone where Guiberson had disappeared.

He had somehow forgotten about Pearl.

Behind the mansion, moonlight splintered into shadows and a cool breeze drifted through the rising cypress like whispers upon the summer air. As he strolled across the short patio onto a manicured lawn, Harry saw an empty glass atrium erected in the shape of a summer gazebo and attached to the Victorian conservatory off the east wing. Beside the patio was a tennis court, net sagging on the grass, and a lovely grape arbor left untended for the season. Harry looked briefly for Guiberson, but he had gone elsewhere. That was fine, as Harry suddenly realized he had no idea what he would say to the poor fellow if they met. Eight summers ago, he had lost his own little David to the blustery waters of Lake Calhoun on a gray windy afternoon. Harry hadn't been there when his first-born drowned, busying himself idiotically instead with a dull client at St. Paul, one of those hopeless regrets. Not until five o'clock in the evening had he been informed. Even now, he found it difficult to speak David's name aloud and often found himself weeping unaccountably. That dear boy's beautiful smile wafted resolutely through his days and nights, an irrepressible sadness. But no one really survives the death of a child, does he?

Crossing the lawn to a flagstone wall at the back of the estate, it occurred to him finally that these people he had met this evening, flirted with, entertained, studied, and spied upon were not at all what he had anticipated in the taxi ride up from the Avenue of the Republic:

neither stodgy nor impossibly dignified, nor egotistical and rapacious, nor overly well-behaved. Somehow his mood brightened as he stopped at the ivy-covered wall. If this was indeed part of that vivid crowd in white he had seen on the morning bulwark, perhaps he had not so far to climb, after all. Even the foolish and risky intrusion he perpetrated in Sylvester's office no longer held him in dread. Let them toss him into the street; he had already seen and heard all he needed to. Now, high atop Empire Boulevard, half a block from where he had gotten out of the taxi, Harry rested his elbows on the stonewall and looked back toward the bright city where his evening had begun. As he watched a loaded ferry chugging upriver in the distance, a soft familiar voice spoke to him from the cypress grove nearby.

"Ain't the party a riot, honey?"

Pearl walked out of the shadows, chewing gum. She adjusted her cheap fox fur. "I seen you with them ritzy dames. I bet you had a swell time, didn't you?"

"Where have you been?" Harry asked, greatly relieved to find her. "I didn't see you all evening." He wondered if Cobb even knew she was here at the brownstone. Just the thought of her being followed by that stupid fellow angered him.

She parked herself beside Harry on the wall, took his hand and entwined their fingers. "Oh, honey, I just wanted you to have a swell time, that's all. And you did, didn't you?"

"Yes, darling, I certainly did," he replied, squeezing her pretty hand. "Thank you." Somehow he had a greater affection for her now than ever. Maybe that threat from Cobb led to this urge he suddenly had for expressing how he felt. Let someone dear to you be attacked, and watch your heart respond. Drop my girl into the river? I'd like to see them try.

"It's a swell joint, ain't it?"

He gazed into her violet eyes. "Very beautiful."

"Here," Pearl said, raising her arm up to his face. "Don't I smell sweet?" A scent of gardenia perfume led him to wonder how she passed the evening, or in whose company. "Honey, I tell you I'm made for love."

"Well, you look very pretty tonight." For a while back there, Harry was certain he loved Clara. Yet his dear Pearl was so fresh and lovely, none of the other girls he had seen inside the brownstone were her equal. Tonight, she was no child. What was he going to do with her? Who's on her side in all of this? What if by some strange happenstance it comes out that she truly is Follette's child? Good grief, she'd be doomed.

Pearl blushed. "Honey, you don't got to lie to me. I know I ain't no hot number like them other birds you seen in there."

He smiled. "Look here, darling, I appreciate you inviting me to the party. I had a wonderful evening."

"Me, too." She faked a hiccup. "They got a swell wine cellar."

Worried to death for her, Harry sighed. "I suppose we ought to find a taxi, don't you think? It's getting quite late." He took out his pocketwatch. A quarter after three. He had hoped to attend services in the morning. It had been a month of Sundays since he last went.

"Don't stall, honey," Pearl whispered close now. She brushed his arm with her fingers. He could feel her breath on his face, a warm honey scent that aroused him. "You know how I feel."

She kissed him flush on the lips. He returned her kiss, pulling her toward him. She tasted like liquor and peppermint. He was seduced by her perfume in the dark. He kissed her neck and felt her breath rise and fall. She kissed him deeply and he saw a dreamy look on her face.

She murmured, "Oh, darling, tell me you love me. Please? I won't tell nobody. Just once, what do you say?"

His heart leaped, he felt numb, scandalous. How could he tell any girl other than Marie that he loved her, even this one? For heaven sakes, the very idea was crazy! How could he possibly love her? She was too young. He was married. She knew nothing of the world. He had obligations, responsibilities, and two beautiful children who adored and cherished him. In any case, what sort of fool falls in love with no plan for the future? "You see, darling, I — "

"Why, sure you can, honey, please?" Pearl tilted her head, offering her kindest, misty-eyed smile. Her young bosom swelled. "Please, Harry? Tell me you love me? Just this once? Please? I'll never ask you again, honey. I swear it."

She eased forward, rising gently on her tip-toes until she was just below his chin, her face up, lips puckered, eyes closed, waiting for him to kiss her and say he loved her.

Harry Hennesey had no idea if uttering those three little words might bring her heart, or his, to the awful verge of something grand or ruinous.

But finally he did.

STANTONSBURG, NEBRASKA

THE DWARF WADED AT the shady creek bottom in cold water up to his kneecaps, the suspender straps to his short denim overalls hanging loosely at his side, insects buzzing about his sunburned ears. Overhead, cottonwoods rustled and shook, fluttering leaves and dry bunchgrass down into the creek bed behind a narrow two-story frame-house on the great Nebraska prairie. Alvin Pendergast tossed his cap and farm shoes and socks underneath a fallen cottonwood log, then rolled up the cuffs of his work trousers and dangled his feet off the log into the narrow stream. Cold water numbed his toes and they tingled when he withdrew them from the current. Brushing a shock of hair off his forehead, he watched Rascal squat in the creek like a duck and fish the sand with his fingers, sloshing in quick circles, making paddling motions and humming to himself. Chester had taken the Packard and headed back up the highway to Stantonsburg: pop. 1328. He had told them to wait down in the creek bed until he came back. By Alvin's guess, that was two hours ago. Feeling a little better today than he had all week, Alvin wanted to go over town himself, buy a soda pop and have a look around, maybe find a pretty girl to jolly at the sweetshop, get her going with a nifty Ford joke or two *("Why is a Ford like a bathtub? Because you hate to be seen in one!")*. He liked that idea. What was the use of traveling around, he thought, if you don't go nowhere?

"The flora and fauna of our Republic," said the dwarf, "are quite fascinating when one takes care to observe them in their natural habitat. I once kept a grand collection of lady bugs in a Mason jar for a season of breeding." He bent further and sunk his elbows into the water, dredging a trench in the creek bottom and rising up with two handfuls of mud. "Creatures of a lower order have always been a great interest of mine."

"My cousin Frenchy eats crawdads cold," said Alvin, dunking his toes again. "Don't ask me why."

The water felt better now, less icy. The farm boy sunk his legs in up to his calves and sloshed around. It was hot out. The creek bed was cooler than up on the prairie, but Alvin still found it generally stifling. If the water had been deeper, he'd have already dived in and had himself a swim. He splashed lightly with his feet, watched the ripples expand. He liked fooling around in the middle of the day. Work was for saps. Water bugs skittered across the surface. A moldy odor of decaying vegetation on the muddy banks floated in the air. He asked the dwarf, "Can you swim?"

"Actually, I've never tried."

"Scared of drowning, huh?" Alvin smirked, picturing the dwarf flailing his arms and sinking like a rock. Alvin himself had learned to swim when he was three, taught by old Uncle Henry who couldn't swim a lap in a bathtub anymore.

"Of course not. In fact, I'm sure I could manage quite well. My Uncle Augustus once swam across Lake Michigan in a rainstorm. He assured me buoyancy runs in the family."

"I didn't ask if you float or not," Alvin said. "I asked if you ever been swimming."

The dwarf's hand shot down into the water. "Ahhh ... there ... devil, devil, devil!" It came up empty, three tiny streams of soggy sand leaking between his fingers. He looked over at Alvin. "Do you suppose there are any snapping turtles hereabouts?"

"I never met nobody before who couldn't swim," Alvin remarked, letting his legs slide down a bit further off the mossy log. Sunlight sparkled on the current. Maybe he'd just go ahead and jump in. His cotton shirt and brown trousers were filthy, and needed washing. "Seems like something everybody ought to be able to do. Like walking, or riding a horse."

"When I was a child," replied Rascal, "we owned a stable of race horses down in Kentucky. People came from as far away as India to buy them from us for all the great competitions around the world. I believe we won the Queen's Steeplechase on more than one occasion."

"I'd go swimming everyday in the summer if I didn't have chores to do," said Alvin. He splashed water in the dwarf's direction, hoping to soak him. Half the time he and Frenchy went fishing, they wound up giving each other the works and riding home in Uncle Henry's Chevrolet dripping wet. "My cousin and me'd go swimming in the Mississippi Saturday mornings and be back home for supper. Swam all the way across once, like Johnny Weissmuller. Dove off the Illiniwek Bridge, too. Just to scare people who never seen someone do it before."

Rascal waded across the creek to study a pool worn by erosion into the far bank. "Do you see these bugs here?" He flicked his fingers lightly on the murky water lapping against the bank. "If I had a jar, I'd collect some and take them with us. Do you know, none of them have ever been more than a foot or so from this spot in their entire lives? It's a fact. They're born, grow up, mate and perish right here in the mud by this little creek. What do you suppose they know about life?"

"They're bugs. They don't have a need to know nothing."

"So you say."

"So I know." Alvin dropped off the log into the cold creek water, making a big splash. He really wished Chester had taken him into town for a hotdog and a soda pop.

Plucking violets off the embankment farther downstream, the dwarf remarked, "Are you aware that amphibians are the precursors of modern man?" He dipped his hands into the stream, letting the current wash over the pretty wildflowers.

Alvin began kicking about, digging his feet in the sand. "Pardon?"

"Well, millions of years ago, we crawled out of the primordial swamp to establish civilization, while our cousins, the amphibians, remained behind."

The dwarf released the wild violets into the stream and saw them float away into the splintered shadows. Alvin watched Rascal wade off down the creek, exploring the bank as he went, dipping his hands into the water when he saw something of interest, letting the sluggish current wash over his bare legs.

His own two legs growing numb from the cold, Alvin sloshed his way back to the damp sedge and climbed up onto the grass. Threads of sunlight like silver spider webs shone through white poplar leaves. He felt drowsy now, and hungry. All he'd eaten were buns for lunch. Chester had refused to let them visit a café. Clearing a place to sit amid leafless stems of scouringrush, the farm boy told the dwarf, "I guess I wouldn't mind lying in the mud all day. What makes us so smart? Maybe we ought to've stayed right where we were. Been better off. Most of us, anyhow."

"Evolution is not a matter of choice." Rascal refastened the shoulder buttons on his romper. "Rather, I believe, it's a form of destiny."

"Favoring frogs and salamanders, huh?" Alvin laughed. Aunt Hattie had always maintained that evolution was a hokum which denied God's bitter miracle of life. She believed Noah strolled out of the ark on December 18th, 2348 B.C. and that's when the modern world began. Who's to say she wasn't right? Nobody had even half the answers. Life was too damned confusing.

"I collect them, of course," said the dwarf, wading back toward the shore. "Studying one's past is invaluable for understanding one's place in the world. Do you think we'll eat soon?"

A dozen yards downstream, Rascal sat down in the soggy sedge and rinsed the mud from between his toes. Alvin climbed back up onto the rotting log. Balancing on one foot, the farm boy picked his nose. Meadowlarks chattered in the cottonwoods. Leaves fluttered down into the creek bed. Alvin walked to the end of the log and balanced above the stream. His sister Mary Ann could turn a cartwheel on a worm fence without falling off. Alvin searched for stream minnies in the creek bed. He watched the dwarf scramble up from the water and sit down in a pretty patch of blue verbena that grew near a thicket of sandbar willows where he put his shoes back on. Rascal said, "If I lived around here, I'd want to have lots of neighbors close by."

"You mean, shouting distance?"

"If you will. Only through a life of society do men truly flourish."

"Not me," said Alvin, turning a circle on the log, careful not to slip off. His bare feet didn't offer much purchase on the damp moss. "I'd keep people about a mile off, so's I wouldn't have to hear 'em yammering all day long. Most folks talk too much."

"I can recite by heart the inaugural addresses of nine Presidents of the United States. Uncle Augustus taught me when I was only six."

"That'll earn you a living."

The dwarf pulled his legs up under his chin and rocked backward. "I've often thought I ought to be a newspaper man, perhaps a city editor. I'm sure I have many of the correct qualifications. I can read quick as the wind and my grammar is excellent."

"Why not just be President?"

"I've considered it."

"You'd have to wear one of those tall black Lincoln stovepipes, you know? Think they got one big enough for that head of yours?" His laughter echoed loudly down the creek. He liked joking the dwarf. It passed the time.

Rascal frowned. "There's no cause to be cruel."

Tired of the creek, the farm boy paced to the end of the cottonwood log and hopped off into the long grass. He picked up his cap and went to put on his shoes. "I'm going up to the house and have myself a glass of lemonade."

"Wait for me!"

Up on the Nebraska prairie, a light wind pushed across dry fields of Indian grass and flowering thimbleweed and bush clover, trading hay scents and dust. Overhead, the summer sky was blue and clear. The old gray framehouse was sheltered by a dense grove of common hackberry trees and a thick bur oak in the front yard. Red berries of a bittersweet vine draped the downstairs sleeping porch, and the backhouse under white poplars by the creek was shrouded at its rear in wild grape and poison ivy. A one-horse shovel plow and a Mayflower cultivator lay beside a dusty tractor near the barn, and a collection of milk pails and peach baskets were piled like junk next to a perforated bee-smoker beneath an old plum tree. Alvin thought maybe the fellow who owned the farm used to be more prosperous. Maybe life had given up on him.

The gravel driveway out to the county road was empty.

The farm boy listened to the bleating of sheep from somewhere across the fields. He walked under a sagging laundry line to the rear of the house where the kitchen door had been left ajar. His shoes kicked up dust wherever he strode. A familiar stink like rotten crabapples traveled here and there on the breeze. He brushed a curious bumblebee off his forehead and went over to study a tall wire birdcage framed in wood planks that stood almost as high as Alvin himself. There were still piles of dried shit on the dirt floor, but a foot-long section of chicken wire was ripped away near the bottom and he guessed some slick old fox had torn into it one night and had himself a snack.

Chester had told them the fellow who occupied this house was an old pal of his from Black Jack Pershing's army, but he also made them promise to stay hidden until he got back from town, so Alvin guessed it was another lie. Chester had driven the Packard up to the front door and invited himself inside for a drink of water. Hadn't bothered to knock or call out. Just went in like that. He came out five minutes later, rolling a Walking Liberty half-dollar over his knuckles and whistling a tune. He said he was going downtown to fix himself up with a shampoo and shave, then settle some business arrangements for the afternoon. *"It's the roving bee that gathers the honey,"* Chester had told Alvin as he got back into the Packard. Then he had driven off and left them.

To Alvin's eye, the house looked poor, or maybe the owner was just tired. Then again, maybe he was occupied most of the day smuggling corn whiskey and Chester had come to help him out of a fix. But if Chester had a plan doped out, he wasn't sharing it yet. Since Kansas, he'd just driven them around, visiting storehouses in small towns, cutting hootch in swill tubs, selling Scotch whiskey through the backrooms of pool parlors in old beer-jugs, and joyriding through the countryside in a hired liquor truck. For helping with the loading and unloading of whiskey barrels, and changing a flat tire now and then, he had paid Alvin fifteen dollars a week, and given the dwarf another thirty dollars for putting over a pretty fair applejack recipe and devising a scheme that involved the construction of pineapple bombs. There hadn't been any further talk of bank robbery since Kansas. Chester hadn't allowed it and both the farm boy and the dwarf knew how to hush up. None of them mentioned Charlie and Rose Harper at all. Lately, though, Alvin had been having bad dreams, and they weren't just fever.

The narrow sleeping porch was screened-in, but the back door leading to the kitchen was flimsy and rattled loose when the wind gusted. Alvin heard the dwarf thrashing up through the leafy milkweed above the creek, so he went inside.

The house was dark and cool. He listened to a mantel clock ticking in another room. Floorboards creaked underfoot. The pale lime-green kitchen smelled of coffee grounds and pipe tobacco. The latest issue of *Farm & Fireside* lay open on the table in the middle of the room. Filthy plates and cups were stacked in the sink. The ceiling was cracked and water-spotted. Window curtains were soiled. He looked in the icebox and saw only a bottle of milk and a chunk of cheese. Not much to eat. Except for a few canned goods and cornmeal, most of the pantry shelves were empty, too. Didn't this fellow ever go to the grocery store? Probably he was a bachelor, or a widower like Uncle Boyd, Alvin thought, as he opened a cupboard next to the cook stove in search of a clean glass. No woman would let her kitchen look this sore. He found a glass and brought it to the sink and ran cold water from the tap, then had a drink. He felt strange being indoors without having been invited. He had already been partner to a bank robbery and the killing of a fellow and his daughter, and he felt sick and lousy about it. He hadn't known any of that was going to happen. Over and over Rascal said it wasn't their fault, yet even though Charlie Harper had stuck a rifle in his face, Alvin still felt awful guilty. If the Bible was true like Aunt Hattie claimed, then he was probably going straight to hell when all he had wanted to do was stay out of the sanitarium. He might've jumped off a train and joined some workers at a tent colony or hired himself a cheap boardinghouse room and slung hash in a buffet flat. It needn't have amounted to much. Trouble was, he was getting sicker now and worried that sooner or later he'd have to see a doctor for the consumption, and he knew what that would mean. He supposed his daddy was burned up about him skipping out on his chores and all, while his momma sobbed after supper now and then. Alvin presumed his sisters were probably fighting over who'd be getting his room. He hadn't meant to run off for good. That was certainly a mistake, but what was done was done. Now he wished somebody would come along and tell him what he ought to do next.

He drank another glass of water, and belched.

The dwarf was in the yard outdoors, fooling with the birdcage. Alvin could hardly see through the dirt-smudged windows, but he heard him plain as day. Rascal had crawled into the cage where the fox had torn a hole and was fiddling with the dangling perch, making it swing.

A small door just outside the kitchen pantry led down to the basement and a quick peek from atop the stairs showed it was darker than a cow's innards, so Alvin left the kitchen for the dining room, telling himself again there wasn't no harm done just looking around. He wasn't a thief. One day if he ever got healthy enough to work again, he'd own a house of his own, and if somebody ran in while he was away and didn't do nothing except have himself a glass of cold water, why, that'd be all right. A mahogany sideboard across from the dining room table displayed a set of small porcelain jars with flowers painted under the rims and a silver tea service beside the jars. Dust covered everything and Alvin guessed the fellow didn't drink much tea, nor had any use for little jars with flowers on them. He opened the top drawers to the sideboard and found white lace table covers and linen napkins neatly folded one on top of the other. He saw a fine set of silverware, too, then shut the drawer to prove he wasn't tempted. He listened briefly to a pair of catbirds chirping in the hackberry. Wind clattered at the backyard door. The interior of the house smelled musty. Alvin went into the front room where the mantel clock was ticking.

This reminded him of Uncle Henry's parlor on the farm: a couple of shaded table lamps, two easy chairs and a fancy green velour Morris chair, an old phonograph console beside a long sofa, a Windsor upright piano, a blue Axminster rug in the middle of the floor, and a crystal set on an oak Bible stand near the fireplace. Alvin considered switching on the radio, but thought better of it. His sisters did nothing except listen to radio shows, hour after hour at home. They favored those fellows that sang and played the ukulele and cracked jokes. He didn't care for none of that. He and his daddy and Uncle Henry only tuned in when there was a horse race or a boxing match. One night they heard Jack Dempsey knock a fellow out quicker'n lightning. Uncle Henry jumped up out of his chair and shook a fist at Alvin and his daddy, cackling, *"Now you see it, now you don't! Now you see it, now you don't!"* Alvin's daddy had bet fifty cents on the other guy.

He picked up one of the magazines piled on a walnut table and riffled through it. He stopped at a lingerie advertisement for Hickory Shadow Skirts and gave a good once-over to the smiling girl posed in her undergarments. *"Begin to know the comfort, beauty, and style of Hickory. Ask for Personal Necessities by Hickory. At your favorite notion department."* Almost before he knew it, he'd torn the page out of the magazine, folded it up, and stuck it into his shirt pocket. Then he slipped the magazine under the bottom of the pile and pretended he hadn't noticed it was there at all.

He went over to the staircase. There was a cob pipe left on the newel post, half-full of tobacco as if its owner had intended to bring it with him, but had forgotten. Alvin could hear a shade flapping at an open window upstairs. Family photographs decorated the stairwell, rising to a stained glass window at the top of the steps. As the farm boy mounted the staircase to study the portraits, he heard a squirrel land on the rooftop from one of the shady hackberry trees. Then the dwarf came into the house through the kitchen, letting the screen door bang closed behind him. When Rascal called out, Alvin went upstairs.

At home, his bedroom was in the rear attic with a window facing over his mama's vegetable garden toward the pinewoods north of York's peacock farm. He'd painted a sign that ordered his sisters to keep out. Though Alvin protected his own privacy, an irresistible curiosity sent him up these stairs to the top where a short hallway led to three bedrooms and a toilet closet. He felt jittery. It was scorching under the eaves, airless and humid. Wind had sucked the bedroom doors shut, so the hall was dusky beyond the stained glass window. He paused outside the nearest door and listened to the window shade flapping in the draft. Downstairs, the dwarf was wandering room-to-room, calling out Alvin's name as if they both belonged in the house. The radio came on, spilling orchestra music into the silence, then switched off again. Alvin opened the door in front of him and peeked inside. It was a young boy's room, cluttered with cowboy paraphernalia and wooden aeroplanes and toy soldiers. There was a single bed and a nightstand and a writing desk beneath the window. On the wall above his bed was a large movie photograph of Tim McCoy from *War Paint* and several others of Douglas Fairbanks and Rod La Rocque and Rin-Tin-Tin and Mickey Mouse. The boy's writing desk was covered with paper thumbnail sketches of automobiles. His bed was carelessly made and a pair of denim overalls lay on the floor by the closet. Alvin went to the open window and lifted the shade and took a look outdoors where he could see clear to the grassy horizon, miles and miles away. Nebraska seemed almost as lonesome as Kansas. Old farmhouses. Silos and barns. Dirt and sky. Wind probably most days. On the way here, he had seen a remarkable sight: fields of cornhusks unattended to, stalks wilting, wildrye and hound dogs chasing through the empty rows, ash barrels stuffed with fodder, the dust of wheel-worn roads blowing to heaven. *No point in owning the land,* his daddy once told him, *if you aren't willing to do nothing with it. Work it, or it'll go tired on you. Won't grow nothing, won't feed your children. A man who won't work his own land, deserves to live in a house built by strangers.*

Alvin heard the dwarf at the bottom of the stairwell, so he went back out into the hall. He knew it was wrong sneaking around like this, yet he couldn't help himself. At least he hadn't stolen nothing. Chester hadn't told them not to go indoors. Besides, they'd gotten thirsty sitting in the creek bed and it was hot as blazes out. What did he expect? Alvin went down to the room at the end of the hall. Inside was nothing but a common iron bed with brass knobs and a mattress with a green blanket and a feather pillow, a plain oak bureau, and a small chamberset table and lamp. No rug on the floor. Bare walls painted white. Like living in a stall, Alvin reflected, without the straw. There ought to at least be a pretty picture or two on the walls. He had a few swell boat pictures in his attic room and a racy tabloid photograph of Peaches on her honeymoon that Frenchy had gotten for him in Chicago. Alvin didn't hold much for decorating, but he knew what he liked.

Stifling a cough, the farm boy went back across the hall to the next room just as the dwarf arrived on the second floor landing. From the door, a smothering odor of sweet lilac filled Alvin's nostrils. Inside, he found a shade-drawn bedroom jammed with lavender draperies and gilt curtain bands, a grand chamber suite in carved black walnut: bed, chiffonier, dresser, washstand and mirrored wardrobe, a marble top center table with an ormolu kerosene lamp, brass cameo miniatures, and a blue china vase stuffed with frayed peacock feathers. The bedroom walls were adorned with wire-hung paintings and floral lithographs and the floor covered by a crimson tapestry rug. Velvet pincushions and stuffed pillows were piled upon the bed under a fringed gauze turnover canopy. Awed by the elegant clutter, Alvin wasn't sure he ought to go in. He'd never seen such a pretty bedroom in his whole life. Aunt Emeline had some fancy stuff all right, and so did Granny Chamberlain with her porcelain dolls and papier-mâché, but how a lady in a house as plain as this could fix out her room so swell, he couldn't figure. No doubt somebody had some pretty high coin.

Promising himself not to bust anything, Alvin walked into the middle of the bedroom. The ceiling overhead was painted like the summer sky outdoors, fluffy clouds drifting about here and there, tiny swallows on the wing. A vine of stenciled ivy encircled the outer border. If he hadn't known better, he'd have thought the lady who slept in here was a queen. On the dresser were Ivorette hairbrushes, and hair combs and tuck combs, nail files, lingerie clasps, perfume bottles, skin lotions, Pompeian night cream, a powder puff box, a pair of bevel glass bonnet mirrors, and a Mavis 3-piece set. How could anyone on earth ever use all that?

The dwarf came into the bedroom behind him, holding a cloudy glass of lemonade.

Alvin frowned. He hadn't seen any lemons in the kitchen.

The dwarf asked, "Why didn't you answer when I called?"

"I didn't hear you," Alvin lied, checking his look in the dresser mirror. His freckles were nearly hidden under the dust on his face. He felt hot and grimy and knew he needed a bath. Maybe Chester would hire a couple of rooms in a hotel later on after supper.

"Wasn't the creek refreshing?" the dwarf asked, strolling across the rug, a dreamy look of contentment on his misshapen face. He sipped from his glass of lemonade.

"It ought to be," the farm boy replied, as he sorted through a pearl button collection in a corner of the dresser top. "That water's cold enough to freeze the whiskers off a brass monkey." He stared at the dwarf's drinking glass. "Say, how come you didn't fix me up with a lemonade?"

"You didn't wait for me," Rascal said, walking over to the dresser. He plucked a Japanese fan from a dry rosewater and glycerine bottle, and carefully unfolded it. "He's a widower, you know."

"Who?"

"The fellow who lives here."

"How do you know that?"

"I read a note of bereavement downstairs," the dwarf explained, replacing the fan. "His wife Annabelle passed away a year ago Christmas. Apparently it was quite unexpected." He put down his lemonade and opened a top drawer, rummaged around a little, then took out a jewelry box and sprung the clasp, revealing a splendid assortment of scarf pins, rings, lavallieres, necklaces and silver thimbles.

"Don't steal nothing," Alvin warned, suddenly protective of the late woman's possessions, though he had no idea why. He didn't even know what she looked like.

"Do you think I'm a thief?" Rascal drew out a gold Daughters of Rebekah pin. "Why, I've never stolen anything in my life. I couldn't imagine stooping so low."

"Says you."

The dwarf returned the enameled pin to the jewelry box. "What in the dickens are you talking about?"

Alvin found a matchstick in a silver child's cup and stuck it in his mouth to chew on. He smirked at Rascal, and gave him the bad eye.

That prompted the dwarf to grouse, "I suppose this is what I deserve for traveling with a no-good like you."

Alvin shut the jewelry box drawer. "Lay off the wisecracks."

The dwarf picked up a brown bottle containing pure sweet spirits of nitre. "Here, try some of this. It'll fix you up all right."

Alvin scowled, sure this was a gag. He grabbed the bottle, anyhow. "What's it good for?" Reading the label didn't offer much instruction. He didn't recognize half the words.

The dwarf giggled. "Whatever ails you, and if nothing ails you, it's good for that, too."

"Aw, cut that stuff," Alvin growled, putting the bottle of nitre back on the dresser top. The heat upstairs had begun to irritate him. "If you weren't so cuckoo, I'd take out my cast-iron knucks and knock you flat."

Rascal smiled. "There's no need to offer alibis. Why, I'm more than willing to rough it up a bit. Uncle Augustus taught me several nifty wrestling holds when I was younger. If I were you, I'd think twice about who you'd be scrapping with."

Alvin heard a motorcar coming up from the county road. He went across the hall into the plain room to look out the window, and saw Chester's tan Packard Six rolling to a stop by the front of the house. "He's back."

The dwarf darted out of the woman's bedroom, and hurried off to the stairwell.

"Hey!" Alvin shouted, rushing after him.

The dwarf bounded down the stairs.

Alvin followed him to the first floor and went outside through the kitchen door, while Rascal left the house by the front porch. Wind kicked up in the driveway, sweeping leaves from the hackberry trees and stirring dust about the yard. Chester stood beside the automobile, his foot on the runningboard as he lit up a cigarette. The dwarf had engaged him in conversation before Alvin reached the plum tree on the side of the house. Chester flicked the burnt match away. His eyes were bright blue in the sunlight. Alvin guessed his pow-wow in Stantonsburg had come off all right. Maybe he'd even found another girl downtown to play post office with.

When Chester noticed the farm boy, he smiled and called across the wind, "Well, we made a ten-strike today, kid!"

"How's that?"

"It's like I've been telling you right along. Some fellows furnish the manure while others grow the flowers. They tried to cut in on us, but I wouldn't let 'em because they're all a lot of damn four flushers and they know it."

Alvin hadn't any idea what Chester was talking about. He coughed into his fist.

"Well, they weren't half through before I gave 'em the raspberry and put on my hat. That's when one of them got the big idea that we were all set to throw everything over and go home unless they came around pretty damn quick."

Chester opened the passenger door and took out a small black traveling bag. Then he slung it through the air over to Alvin. The cowhide bag skidded in the dirt at the farm boy's feet. "Go on, see for yourself."

Rascal scampered over as Alvin undid the latches. Inside, the bag looked stuffed with greenback bills.

Chester told the farm boy, "With what we got there, you could buy that whole hick town of yours and make yourself mayor."

"Like Al Capone!" the dwarf enthused, reaching in and riffling through a handful of bills.

Chester frowned. "Don't be a wiseacre."

Alvin just stared at the dough. Chester had told them if he cashed-in downtown, they'd be able to settle some obligations. He hadn't said anything about striking oil. Too scared to touch it, the farm boy stepped back from the bag.

Holding up a fistful of bills, the dwarf grinned. "This is quite a fortune!"

Chester tapped ash off his cigarette into the dirt. "It'll make out all right."

Rascal stuffed the cash back into the bag. "May I ask you a great favor?"

"What's that?"

"Well, I'd like to have a photograph taken of myself in bed with this money that I could mail to Auntie in Hadleyville."

Chester shook his head. "Just bring the dough back over here."

Alvin saw a small truck out on the county road coming from the east, lifting clouds of dust on the blue summer sky. Rascal closed the leather bag and lugged it over to the Packard where Chester stuck it into the rear seat once again. He told them, "Keep this under your hat. We need to beat it up to Des Moines without giving anyone the dope on how big we put it over. You get me?"

The dwarf nodded. "Of course."

"You fellows stay out here. I need a drink." Chester looked Alvin in the eye. "All right, kid?"

"Sure."

Chester flicked his cigarette into the dirt and went inside by the front porch. After the door closed, Rascal walked down to the small barn where the farm tractor was parked.

Looking back out to the county road, Alvin noticed the small truck slow at the approach to the driveway. Butterflies churned in his belly. Every so often, he'd heard about trespassers getting shot in Illinois. He considered hurrying indoors to fetch Chester, but decided against it. Maybe he was expecting this fellow and just get sore that Alvin had come into the house when he had already been told not to. On the other hand, maybe this fellow wasn't expecting to find a pack of strangers at his door at all.

Alvin had an idea.

He went over to the Packard and undid the radiator filler cap and raised the hood.

By then, the dwarf had noticed the truck, too, and gone to hide inside the barn. Alvin knelt behind the Packard until he heard a noisy truck motor drawing near and the crunching of tires on the dusty gravel. Chester still hadn't come out of the house. When the truck rolled to a stop half a dozen yards away, Alvin rose from his hiding place, hands apart. A cloud of dust stirred up from the driveway swept over him. He coughed harshly and waved it out of his face as a tall scrawny man in work overalls and an army-style hat climbed out of the driver's door. A small boy seated on the passenger side remained in the truck. The man said, "Who are you?"

Alvin shuffled his feet in the dirt, mute.

A wary frown on his brow, the man studied the farm boy up and down and gave the Packard a quick once-over, too. He asked, "You broke down?"

Alvin forced a nod.

"Radiator?"

He nodded again.

"There's water in the pump and a iron pail." The man gestured toward the other side of the house, well shaded in hackberry. He added, "It'll pay you to use a spout. I got a can back over yonder in the barn by the feed cutter."

Alvin mumbled a thank you, still scared enough to faint.

The man turned his attention to the boy seated quietly in the truck. "Arnie, get along into the house."

The boy climbed out of the truck, holding a tiny jackknife. He was wearing a pair of denim trousers and a red-checkered shirt and black cowboy boots. His light hair was freshly combed with a well-oiled cowlick that resisted the wind. He stared at Alvin, eyes clear and curious.

"Go on now," the man told him.

The boy walked past Alvin without a word, up the steps and into the house. Alvin guessed the kid was just as scared as he was. Then he remembered who was still indoors and his belly went cold. Why had Chester chosen this fellow's house? It didn't make sense.

"It's my son's birthday today," the man told Alvin. "I just brought him into town for a haircut and a root beer."

Urging himself to speak up, the farm boy said, "He's a swell kid."

"What're you doing out here?"

His brain gone dead as wax, Alvin persisted with the same lie, "We're broke down."

The man fixed him hard with a stare.

He's no dumbbell, Alvin thought. *He knows I ain't being square with him. If he had a shotgun handy, he'd probably knock me out of my shoes.*

The man walked over toward the porch and found a stick in the dirt and brought it back to the Packard. Keeping an eye on Alvin, he poked the stick down into the radiator, then drew it out again. Wet.

He said, "Where's the other fellow?"

Alvin didn't know how to answer that. He felt like a dirty crook and knew he wasn't smart enough to make up another lie. A warm gust of wind kicked up dust and left grit in his eyes. As he rubbed them clear with one hand, he heard the man hurry away toward the house where his boy was calling from indoors.

Alvin saw the dwarf emerge from the corner of the small barn and walk up as far as the tractor.

The front screen door swung shut with a bang.

He had no idea what to do now. He felt rotten as hell. He thought if he wasn't such a coward, he'd probably run off down to the county road and hike back to Illinois. He heard voices briefly inside the house. Alvin closed the hood of the Packard and put the radiator filler cap back on.

Then he waited.

Several minutes went by. The dwarf left the farm tractor and crossed the yard to the side of the house near the plum tree. Dust swirled about. Then the screen door swung open and Chester walked out onto the porch carrying a box of glass canning jars. He paused at the top of the steps and called down to Alvin, "Do you like peach preserves? I just found these down in the cellar."

Alvin shrugged. "I ain't all that fond of 'em."

"No?"

"Nope."

Chester smiled. "Me neither."

Then he threw the box off the porch upside down.

The din of glass shattering brought Rascal from around the side of the house.

Chester was already down the steps by then, striding toward the Packard. He motioned Alvin to get into the automobile, and slid in behind the wheel. When he started the engine, the dwarf rushed over and climbed into the backseat. Then Chester put the Packard into gear and quickly steered the motorcar around in a circle, aiming it back down the gravel drive. Just before mashing his foot on the gas pedal, he said, "Let me tell you, boys. Hospitality's not what it used to be."

Then they were hurtling down the road toward Stantonsburg, a great hot cloud of dust trailing in their wake. Part of Chester's morning newspaper billowed up and out of the backseat of the Packard. It alighted once in the middle of the road, and flew off like a kite into the fields. Along the roadside, switchgrass stood taller than the Packard and swayed in the draft as the automobile sped by. Alvin saw dozens of sparrows perched on telegraph wires, crowding one another for room, hardly paying notice to the roaring motor. Only a few people were about anywhere he looked: a man on a tractor off in a cornfield to the east; three women standing under the porch eaves of a tall white farm-house to the west; and outside a small house next to the road, a little girl with pigtails chasing a black Labrador through billowing laundry in a windy yard.

After driving about three miles, Chester spoke up again. "Listen up, kid, here's how I've doped this out. I arranged a four o'clock appointment at the Union Bank over in Stantonsburg. We'll be meeting a fellow there named Jerome. When I telephoned this morning, I told him about a young pal of mine whose uncle just kicked off and left him a load of dough and that he'd like to start up a bank account."

"Who's that?" Alvin said, somewhat desultorily. He felt thoroughly demoralized over what had just happened back at the farmhouse, and thought if he weren't such a yellow-bellied coward, he'd jump out of the auto right now and kill himself. That'd cure his cough for good and all, and who'd miss him, anyhow? Nobody, that's who.

"You."

"Huh?"

"Your name's Buddy McCoy and you just inherited a bag of money from your dear old Uncle Homer. You're rich now, see, you're getting up in the world, and you want your dough in a safe place, so you asked me to set you up with a bank downtown. You heard they're a fine lot at Union, and you're sure they'll give you a square deal, but you want it to be confidential. That's why you came up with the big idea of running in after hours. If they want to take charge of your money, it'll have to be at your convenience. When I had him on the wire, Jerome told me he'd be delighted to have you call today at four if that'd make you happy. He seems like a swell fellow. Of course, once he lets us in, we'll clean 'em out. Swell gag, isn't it?"

"It's a wonderful plan," the dwarf acknowledged from behind a Texaco road map he was studying. Alvin glared at him. Chester drove faster, bouncing across the dips in the road, swerving here and there to avoid sinkholes. A quarter mile farther on, he ran the Packard straight over a dead fox.

The whole idea scared the hell out of Alvin. He didn't want to go inside another bank at all. If he were lucky, he'd get shot and it'd be over and done with. Hanging his arm out the window into the hot draft, he said, "Maybe I ain't made for this sort of thing. I hate lying and I ain't very good at it, neither."

"Nobody lies better than I do," the dwarf remarked.

The farm boy agreed. "You're a bag of wind, all right."

"Perhaps I ought to play the role of the wealthy nephew," Rascal argued, ignoring the jibe. "All you'd need to do is give me my lines. I'm a whiz at memorization, and I can be utterly convincing."

Chester shook his head. "Not on your life. We couldn't put that over in a bughouse. Who'd leave his fortune to a midget?"

The Packard struck a sharp dip in the dusty road, jolting the dwarf off-balance, bouncing him backward into the seat.

"I'd rather stay with the car," Alvin persisted, worried like the devil now. "I ain't cut out for selling this stuff. It gives me a big bellyache and I ain't ashamed to tell you."

"I don't need you in the car," Chester barked. "I need you in the bank acting like a lucky plowboy whose rich uncle just fell down a well. So stop squawking. You can put it over, all right. Just don't act nervous. Remember, they got to listen when they know who you are."

Stantonsburg was shady and quiet in the afternoon, sidewalks mostly empty, shops all closing up in the four o'clock hour, both roads leading out of town clear of traffic.

"They're having a rutabaga festival today over at a fairgrounds across town," Chester said, as they rolled through the center of Stantonsburg. "What the hell's a rutabaga?"

"The rutabaga is a large turnip with an edible yellow root," the dwarf explained. "Auntie and I once grew them in our garden. One year, we even won a blue ribbon at the Hadleyville Fair for best of show. Rutabagas are quite tasty if you know how to prepare them."

"Momma used to cook them on Sundays after church whenever Reverend Tyler'd come for dinner," Alvin added.

"Aren't they swell?" said the dwarf, smiling.

"No," Alvin replied. "They taste like boiled shoes."

"Cut the chatter," Chester interrupted. "Fact is, thanks to the festival, downtown's closing early today, so we'll be the last customers doing business at the bank. They'll lock the doors behind us and we'll have all the time we need. You just keep your mouth shut and let me do the talking, we won't have any trouble."

Chester steered over to the curb between Rexall Drugs and Foote's hardware, a block and a half from the Union Bank. He stopped the car and turned off the motor. The air was dry and smelled of cornfields. Chester climbed out of the Packard, stretched and yawned. Alvin got out, too, then jerked his thumb in the dwarf's direction. "What about him? What's his job?"

Without looking at Rascal, Chester replied, "He's staying in the car, and keeping his mug out of sight. I doubt they have a lot of midgets around here and if they see him with us, you can be sure they'll remember."

"I could disguise myself," said the dwarf, still sitting low with his Texaco map in the backseat. "I was in a play once."

"Well, that won't go around here. You're sticking with the car, see?" Chester added, "We'll be back in about twenty minutes, so I'm telling you straight: no monkey business. After this, we're pulling out."

He reached back into the Packard and grabbed the black leather bag. He handed it to Alvin. "All right, kid, let's go."

They headed up the sidewalk toward the Union Bank. Most of the blinds in the upper windows on Omaha Street were shut. Birds perched on the rooftops surveyed the empty sidewalks below. Already, the hair on the back of Alvin's neck bristled. He searched the elm trees for black crows, a sure omen of death. Probably he ought to have borrowed Granny Chamberlain's corncob Cross of Jesus out of

Momma's chifforobe and brought it west with him. That old crucifix, his momma had maintained, held sway against all manner of jinxes and evil. Granny Chamberlain lived to be eighty-nine so far just by hanging it on a nail over her bed and whispering the Lord's Prayer before sleeping every night. She prayed for Alvin when he was in the sanitarium and he came home cured, so everybody knew its power was genuine. Of course, he had also gotten sick again, which just proved nothing was on the level anymore.

As they came up to the Union Bank, Alvin saw a fellow in a blue pinstriped suit with a white carnation on his lapel waiting behind the glass at the front door. He dangled a set of keys on a large iron ring in his left hand and cracked a big smile as he stepped outside to greet his new customers.

Chester tipped his hat to the guy. "Afternoon, sir. Are you Jerome?"

"Indeed, I am. And you're Mr. Wells, I assume?"

"Yes, sir."

They shook hands.

"Well, did y'all have a nice lunch?"

"We sure did."

The fellow stuck his hand out to Alvin. "My name's Walter Jerome. You're Buddy, I presume."

Alvin nodded, the phony greeting stuck in his throat. He coughed and turned away.

"He's a little nervous," Chester explained. "First time in town and all. Forgets himself with excitement. You know how it is."

"I surely do," said Mr. Jerome, and offered his hand again to Alvin.

Alvin's arm began quivering, and he felt like a dumbbell. "Glad to know you, sir," he mumbled, eyes watering as they shook hands. He hated fibbing like this.

"Glad to know you, too, Buddy. Quite glad, in fact." He took Alvin by the crook of the arm. "Come on in out of the sun."

Jerome led Alvin and Chester into the shadowy interior of the bank whose dark wood and fabrics lent a somber tone to daily financial transactions. There were no windows, except for those facing out on Omaha Street. The large safe sat against the rear wall behind the teller stations. Beside it on both sides were the bank officers' desks and a small door leading to the president's office. It was closed. Only Mr. Jerome and a single bank clerk were still working.

"Let me take that for you," Mr. Jerome said, reaching for Alvin's bag. "Howard! We have a deposit to make. Could you give us some help?"

The clerk behind the teller's window got up from his desk and came around to the gate dividing the lobby from the offices and unlocked it. Mr. Jerome walked through with the black bag, which he handed to the clerk. Then he turned back to Alvin and Chester with a smile. "Howard here'll take good care of you."

"This is a straight deposit, I assume," said the clerk, adjusting his eyeglasses.

"Yes, it is. We'll be watching over this young man's fortune until he decides what investments he'd like us to make for him."

Having no idea what they were talking about, Alvin smiled and pretended to be content with the arrangement. The clerk reminded him of a chemistry teacher he had at Farrington High School, Mr. Fisher. Both wore old-fashioned bowties and striped suspenders and were skinnier than matchsticks.

Chester asked, "I assume the rate of interest he's receiving will be commensurate with the amount of cash we're leaving off today."

"Of course."

The clerk set the bag onto the desk behind him. Mr. Jerome twirled the ring of keys on his forefinger and smiled at Alvin. "This is the best decision you've ever made in your life, young man."

The farm boy mumbled, "I sure hope so."

"Now, if you two gents'll excuse me," said Mr. Jerome, "I have to be running along to the fair. My son's showing the biggest rutabaga this county's seen in forty years."

Walter Jerome stared at Alvin a moment, as if studying on something in his mind. Then he switched his attention over to Chester. "A thought just occurred to me. Do you two have any plans for supper? I ask because my wife's planning a feast this afternoon in celebration of the blue ribbon we're certain Jonathan'll be bringing home from the fair and, well, you'd be more than welcome to join us, if you'd like. We'd be dining at half past five."

Alvin nodded his approval, hoping that eating a meal would make him feel better.

Chester agreed. "That's swell of you. We'd be pleased to join you and your family. Thanks a lot."

"Well, we live out on Route Four, north of town. Just drive in that direction three miles or so and you'll see us up on a rise to your left. Big white house and a red barn next to it."

"I'm sure we'll find it."

"Wonderful!" Mr. Jerome took Alvin's hand and gave it another shake. "Thank you again, Buddy, and we'll see you soon."

Alvin nodded. "Sure."

Then Mr. Jerome shook hands with Chester and headed for the door. Before stepping out into the street, he called back to the clerk, "Howard, be sure they get the proper papers and all that, will you? Receipts and such?" He winked at Alvin. "I wouldn't want young Buddy here forgetting where he put his money." Then he laughed and wandered out into the sunlight.

The clerk took the bag over to a desk beside the safe. Chester strolled through the teller's gate behind him. "You'll be keeping the money here, is that right? In case he wants to pay it a visit one of these days?"

"A visit?" the clerk asked, somewhat startled by Chester's presence in the office area. "I'm not sure I know what you mean by that."

Chester put his hand on top of the cowhide bag, preventing the clerk from opening it just yet. "What I mean to say is, you keep your money right here in this safe, don't you? It's not all sent away somewhere a fellow can't get to it if he chooses."

Still waiting on the public side of the teller's window, Alvin watched the clerk wipe his forehead with the back of his hand. It was hot inside the bank, stuffy and humid. The clerk said, "Of course, we invest some of what's deposited here, but our customers always retain adequate means to withdraw their funds. Certainly."

The wall clock above the safe chimed four o'clock.

Waiting until it finished, the clerk said to Chester, "Excuse me a moment," and went over to his desk, pulling open the top drawer and taking out a ring of keys similar to Jerome's. "It's that time of day," he said, smiling at Alvin as he passed through the teller's gate. Chester sat down at the desk beside the safe and unfastened the latches of the black bag while the clerk locked the front door.

"Now, ordinarily," the clerk called from over by the front door, "we don't allow anyone inside the bank after hours, but seeing as this is a unique circumstance, Mr. Jerome thought it best that … "

The clerk's voice trailed off as he saw Chester counting a stack of bills he had taken out of the bag. He finished locking the front door. "Perhaps you ought to allow me to … " The clerk jammed the key ring into his pants pocket and hurried back into the teller's cage. Before he could get there, Chester had already stuck the money back into the black bag and closed it again.

"This is a lot of kale," said Chester.

"Yes, it is," said the clerk, taking the bag off the desk. "But it's in good hands here with us. You can be sure of that."

"Oh, I am."

"Great! Then let's just take this." The clerk unlocked the back office.

"Say, what are you doing?" Chester interjected, as the clerk opened the door.

Pausing in the doorway, the clerk looked back. "Pardon me?"

"Well, shouldn't that go into the safe?"

The clerk shook his head. "Opening the safe after hours is strictly forbidden. Therefore, I have to put this in Mr. Jerome's office overnight. Rules, you know?"

Chester frowned. "So that's your racket, eh? Why, young Buddy here brought that money a long way today to see it put in your safe. If you're telling us now it'll be spending the night in some desk drawer, well, I guess we'll just have to take it back home, maybe find another bank for it."

"I assure you it'll be perfectly secure in Mr. Jerome's desk."

"No, I think we might have to take it with us. Sorry."

Chester stared the clerk in the eye. It was a standoff. Alvin studied the clerk's face, indecision apparent in his eyes. He had a twitch in one of his eyebrows and sweat beading on his upper-lip. What would he do? And what did Chester have in mind? His plan sounded fishy.

"Oh my," said the clerk, glancing at the black leather bag. "I don't know."

"Why not just open the safe and put the money away," said Chester, "Nobody'll get wise to you and it'd make us happy."

"I can't do that."

"Why not?"

"Bank regulations."

"They're for hicks."

"Pardon me?"

Chester glanced up at the clock. His expression was changing now, the sunny disposition he had worn into the bank dimming as quickly as the light outside. Alvin watched him unbutton his coat and look the clerk straight in the eye with the same expression he had shown Charlie Harper that night by the water trough in Kansas. "Open the safe."

"I've already told you, I can't do that."

"Sure you can."

The frail clerk shrunk back into the office doorway. "I'd lose my job."

"Well, here's the lowdown," Chester said, exposing the revolver tucked into his waistband. He offered the clerk a big smile. "I'll kill you if you don't."

The clerk looked at the gun, then quickly over at Alvin, himself surprised by Chester's sudden abandonment of the stunt they'd been putting on. "I don't understand."

"Sure you do, pal," Chester growled. "And don't kid yourself. I've taken care of plenty of birds like you. Now, open the safe."

"I can't," the clerk whined. "I tell you, I'll lose my job."

Chester lunged forward and grabbed the clerk's left hand and forced his three middle fingers backward until the clerk's knees buckled and he tumbled into the doorframe. Chester urged the clerk's fingers back further until they fractured with a loud crack. As the clerk slumped to the floor, eyes bulging from pain and shock, Chester seized him by the collar. Then he jerked the .38 revolver out of his waistband and pushed the barrel up under the clerk's chin. "You're not the brainiest fellow in the world, are you? Snap out of it and open the safe, or I'll take this gat and blow your brains out!"

Too scared to move, Alvin watched Chester drag the clerk over to the safe, then pick up the black bag, set it on the desk again and flip open the latches. With his left hand firmly planted on the clerk's collar, he began tossing the neatly stacked greenback bills out of the bag with his right, dumping them onto the desktop. When he finished, Chester balled the clerk's collar up in his fist, and rammed the man face first into the safe, shattering the clerk's nose on the steel door. Then Chester jerked the sobbing clerk by the collar again, and positioned him eye level with the big combination lock on the front of the safe. Chester jammed the revolver into his ear. He dropped his voice. "Well, sweetheart, this is your last chance. What'll it be?"

Simultaneously moaning and mumbling, the clerk raised his good hand and began dialing the combination. Keeping an eye on him, Chester called over to the Alvin, "Come over here, kid, and help me stack the cash."

His legs trembling, Alvin took another look out into windy Omaha Street. It was still mostly empty, although here and there, a few people passed in or out of those shops not yet closed up for the day. Hoping the Stantonsburg police had gone off to the rutabaga festival with everyone else, the farm boy walked around to the teller's gate and let himself into the office area.

Chester yelled, "Come on, make it snappy!"

The safe swung open. Chester shoved the sobbing clerk aside and began grabbing stacks of orangeback bills piled up on the middle shelves. Trying to keep his eyes off the clerk, Alvin hurried over to the desk and picked up the bag and held it open for Chester to shovel the money into. The clerk crawled off toward the back office doorway and lay on his side against the frame, cradling his fractured fingers in his lap while blood streamed from his broken nose. By now, his face had swollen grotesquely and the odd, mewling noise that came from his lips gave Alvin the chills.

"Let's go, kid. Hop to it," Chester urged, trying to fill the black bag as fast as possible.

There were bonds and safe deposit boxes lining the top and bottom shelves, but Chester ignored them in favor of several smaller stacks of large-denomination bills. Besides, the leather bag had only so much space in it and his plan had been for ironmen, nothing else. Alvin stacked the bills as fast as he could, filling the bag to the rim. He was scared to death, but tried not to let on. For all he knew, Chester might crack him in the skull, too.

"All right," Chester said, straightening up. "We're done. No sense being greedy."

The farm boy closed the black bag and refastened the latches. The clerk was watching him with squinty eyes, puffy and black. Alvin felt guilty as all hell and pretended not to notice. Chester looked around, searching the office area for something. Then he grabbed Alvin by the sleeve.

"Say, slip me that cushion over there," he told Alvin, pointing to one of the teller's stools that had a small blue cushion on the seat. The farm boy went over and fetched it off the stool. "All right, now beat it out of here. Wait for me down on the corner. I won't be long."

Alvin stole one more look at the clerk who had lapsed into shock. The swelling had changed his features so much that Alvin had a hard time recalling exactly what his face had looked like when they had entered the bank a quarter of an hour ago. He felt awful enough for him, all right, but what could he do?

"Wait a minute, kid!" Chester shouted. "Here." He threw Alvin the key ring. It flew past the farm boy's head and slid into the door. "Just go ahead and leave the keys in the lock. I'll take care of them when I go."

Alvin picked up the key ring and unlocked the door, leaving the keys hanging from the cylinder, and hurried out of the bank into the late afternoon sunlight. The wind had risen outdoors now, sweeping dust along Omaha Street, flapping through the store awnings. Alvin hurried down to the corner by the lamppost and waited there while a man and a woman came along the block toward him, heading in the direction of the bank. The farm boy felt lightheaded from fear and guilt, shocked at Chester's viciousness, and ashamed of his own culpability. He felt short of breath and dizzy, barely able to walk a straight line. He was afraid he might keel over right there on the sidewalk. The man nodded a greeting that Alvin ignored. After they passed, the farm boy walked down the sidewalk another dozen yards and got sick in the gutter.

An amber sunset reflected in the crystal glassware of the dining room facing west through a bay window. Streams of patterned color washed intermittently on the floral wallpaper of the room and across the ivory-hued linen tablecloth and porcelain china. Steam from the kitchen clouded the mirrors behind the sideboard while a breeze from an adjoining foyer cooled the front of the room where the diners sat.

The teenage girl was both fascinated and appalled by the dwarf. It was clear she had never encountered such a creature and found his presence at her supper table intriguing. They sat across from each other, beside Alvin and May Jerome's father, catty-corner to her mother, and Chester Burke. Pork roast and sweet corn, mashed potatoes, brown gravy, rutabaga and biscuits occupied the center of the table.

Rascal talked and ate simultaneously, half a biscuit in one hand, a silver fork in the other. "Well then, after he showed me the medal he won at San Juan Hill, I brought him into my bedroom and took out my collection of Indian arrowheads dug up at camp one summer on the shores of the Belle Fourche River. He was so impressed, he shook my hand and promised me a certificate of merit if I ever visited Washington."

"How wonderful!" said Mr. Jerome, a big cigar in his hand. "Your family must've been very proud. I hear Teddy cut quite a figure in his day."

Rascal nodded. "Yes, indeed. In truth, he and I got along famously. Had he lived longer, I'm certain we'd have become great friends. We had so much in common."

The dwarf took a sip of lemonade and chewed off another piece of biscuit. He smiled at May Jerome, and she blushed. Alvin listened, but he had no appetite of his own. The dwarf didn't know yet what had occurred inside the bank. Alvin did, and it made him sick and desolate, afraid even to speak for fear of revealing his revulsion over what he had witnessed. He had let Chester bully and beat that poor clerk without offering a word in the fellow's defense. He had proven himself gutless and was thoroughly ashamed. If God worsened the consumption for his complicity, Alvin wouldn't kick about it. Even coughing his guts out would be less than he deserved.

"You must tell your Teddy Roosevelt story to our boy when he gets home," Mr. Jerome said to Rascal. "When Jonathan was growing up, the president was one of his heroes. I remember when he was about six or so, he cut a section of tail off my wife's favorite roan to fashion a mustache, which he glued to his upper lip. Naturally, she did not find it amusing," he smiled at Mrs. Jerome, "but the rest of us were in hysterics for a week. Jonathan looked so darling."

Rascal leaned forward and snatched another biscuit off the serving plate and put it on his plate. Buttering it, he offered another anecdote similar to Mrs. Jerome's, substituting Teddy Roosevelt's mustache for Kaiser Wilhelm's. Everybody laughed but Alvin who had already heard the story twice before. Instead, his interest was distracted now by May whose olive-green eyes bored holes in his heart. The late sunlight sparkled in them, and glowed on her pale skin. Even riddled with guilt, he thought he might be falling in love.

"Look here, Buddy," Mr. Jerome began, looking Alvin in the eye, "I must say, the idea of you working that farm by yourself does my heart good. The pioneer spirit's in some decline today, but a young fellow like yourself taking on that sort of responsibility makes me feel mighty encouraged."

The farm boy barely mumbled, "Thank you, sir." His enthusiasm for prolonging Chester's gag had evaporated and he wished Jerome would forget they had ever met. In fact, he'd rather not say another word about that bank business for the rest of his life, however brief that might be.

Mr. Jerome puffed at his cigar. "No, I thank you, young man. Pride's a divisible commodity, isn't it? I like to think that your good fortune's an inspiration we can all share."

Buttering his biscuit, Rascal added, "A man is more fairly measured by his efforts than his accomplishments." Then he stuffed the biscuit into his mouth.

"Well spoken," replied Mr. Jerome, flicking the ash off his cigar onto a small dish beside his dinner plate.

"Actually, Buddy plans on selling if he gets a good price," Chester said, removing the cloth napkin from his lap and dumping it on his supper plate. "Fact is, the boy's sick of farming, but didn't want his uncle to know it. Now that the old fellow's dead, what Buddy'd like to do is move off the farm to the Big Town while he can still wash the smell of chicken shit off himself. Pardon my French."

"My goodness," Mrs. Jerome muttered, clearly shocked at Chester's language. May averted her eyes while suppressing a grin with her napkin. Rascal winked at her and swallowed his fifth biscuit. Staring out into the backyard where a chicken strutted about in the dirt, Alvin considered excusing himself to go outdoors. He needed to piss.

Chester eased his chair back from the table.

"Is that true, Buddy?" said Mr. Jerome, putting his cigar down, "You're planning to sell? Why, I wouldn't advise — "

The doorbell rang.

"Excuse me," May said, then leaped up and hurried out of the room through the folds of the crimson portière.

"Are we expecting someone, dear?" Mr. Jerome asked his wife.

She shook her head. "No, I don't believe so."

At the window, a string of crystal prisms suspended in front of the glass clinked lazily together in the draft from the hallway. Rascal grabbed another biscuit and buttered it. Chester took the watch out of his pocket, flipped it open, and checked it against the wall clock. Alvin played nervously with his soupspoon, tapping it softly on his plate. His heart was thumping and he felt vaguely feverish and wanted to lie down. He muffled a rattling cough with the cloth napkin. Maybe he'd die tonight.

The tasseled portière divided and May walked back into the room. "Daddy," she said, "Mr. Hancock's here to see you. Shall I ask him in?"

"Certainly."

She left again.

"George Hancock's got an insurance business down the block from your new bank," Mr. Jerome told Alvin. "He's a swell fellow. I'll introduce you."

"Why would he come all the way out here so late in the day?" Mrs. Jerome asked her husband. She still looked disturbed by Chester's remark.

"If you'll sit there a moment, dear, I expect we'll find out."

"These insurance fellows," Chester chuckled, looking Mrs. Jerome straight in the eye. "You sure got to hand it to 'em. They get their split, all right, though it beats me how they do it. Maybe I'm stepping in too deep, but when I look at their rake-off at the end of the month, sometimes I think I'm in the wrong racket."

He checked his watch again as May was followed into the dining room by a thin, balding man wearing a striped-brown worsted suit. Mr. Jerome shoved his chair back and stood up. So did Chester. The dwarf whispered something to himself, and set his butter knife down.

"Hancock!" Mr. Jerome said, grabbing the man's hand and shaking it. "What brings you out here tonight?"

"Perhaps you ought to introduce our guests, dear?" his wife suggested. She smiled at Rascal, and sipped from her water glass. The dwarf had sliced his last biscuit into five identically sized triangles and arranged them on his plate in the shape of a star.

"Of course. Hancock, this young man here," said Mr. Jerome, pointing to Alvin, "is Buddy McCoy, our newest customer, and his business associates Mr. Wells, and, uh, — "

"Name's Rascal," said the dwarf, bouncing up. He stood on his chair and reached forward across the table to shake hands with Hancock. "Pleased to meet you, sir."

"Likewise," replied Hancock, disconcerted somewhat by Rascal's odd choice of clothes and general appearance. He looked back at Mr. Jerome. "Wally, I'm afraid I've got some terrible news."

"Oh?"

"Your bank was held up this afternoon," Hancock glanced at the women, then lowered his voice, "and whoever did it killed Howard, shot him in the head."

"Good God!"

Mrs. Jerome let out a gasp and sank into her chair. May, who'd been whispering with Rascal, went silent. Alvin felt the blood drain out of his face. His eyes watered and he stared down at his plate. He thought he might puke again. Chester lifted a toothpick from a vest pocket.

Hancock said, "The safe was cleaned out of cash. All they left were stocks and bonds."

Chester jumped up. "Good grief, that's Buddy's inheritance! Five thousand dollars!"

"Now, wait just a minute!" Mr. Jerome said, confusion on his face, "Let me think a minute here. When did this happen?"

"We were there until a quarter past four," said Chester, "and we didn't see anybody at all. Your fellow locked up after we left."

"The back door wasn't locked," Hancock countered. "Edna was supposed to meet Howard outside at four-thirty. When he wasn't there, she tried knocking, then found the back door unlocked and went right in. He was in your office, face down, a pillow covering his head, blood all over the floor."

"Lord Almighty!"

Alvin felt like choking now. His fingerprints were all over Chester's crime. This was the end of him, for sure, and he deserved it.

Hancock said to Mr. Jerome, "The marshals are driving over from Kelsey. Meanwhile, we're advising folks to stay indoors and keep an eye out for strangers riding around."

"We're expected in Norman by noon tomorrow," said Chester, sliding the toothpick into his mouth. "We've got a business appointment at National Bank. A late arrival would put us in a jam."

"Howard's dead?" asked Mr. Jerome, apparently the fact of it not yet settled in his brain. He looked at Alvin, who lowered his eyes and looked away. The farm boy felt like a snake in the grass.

"Shot in the head," Hancock affirmed. "Killed like an animal on the floor of the bank."

Mrs. Jerome excused herself from the table and left the room, her daughter in tow. At the supper table, Chester complained about the lack of security at the bank and the loss of "Buddy's" family's hard-earned funds. Rascal offered to send a telegraph back to New York City for summoning detectives from the Pinkerton Agency, men with whom his family had dealt for years on a variety of secret cases. Then he left the table and disappeared into the rear of the house, presumably to the water closet behind the kitchen.

Alvin slipped away outdoors.

It was almost pleasant now. Along the prairie horizon, twilight darkened the Nebraska sky. A barking Irish setter chased a chicken into the barn and shot away again, on the run elsewhere. May came out onto the porch and sat in a wooden swing, looking west toward the prairie. Alvin walked over toward her and stared across the yard. This ruse was cruel and he felt ashamed to be part of it, but was too afraid to admit his guilt, so he said nothing.

"I'm sorry you lost your money," May told him as she swayed gently in the swing. Her eyes were soft with tears. "I'm sure my father will do everything he can to get it back for you."

Alvin nodded and leaned against the porch railing. The sky was a reddish-purple on its western edge, lingering color before the dark. In the distance, a flock of sparrows soared over the prairie toward a grain silo on the next farm.

"I think stealing is awful," May continued, "particularly when it's from people who've worked their whole lives to save up. My father says those aren't men at all, but mad dogs who ought to be rounded up and hung like horse thieves. He says violence is all their kind understand. Fight fire with fire."

Alvin nodded again, having no real idea what to say. He watched the dusk-wind flutter in her hair, saw the sunlight at the end of the day glisten in her eyes. The Irish setter barked out back of the barn, howling at drifting shadows in the empty fields.

May got up off the swing and went forward to the railing just away from Alvin. She watched her dog cross under the fence and romp into the wheat. She shouted to him, "Max! Maximilian!" Hunting in the wild fields, the setter ignored her, preferring to run.

"I got a dog at home," said Alvin, after May stopped calling.

"You do?"

"He's a bloodhound, chases squirrels and rabbits. Or at least, he used to. He can barely shuffle down off the porch nowadays. He's getting on, I guess."

"What's his name?"

"Red."

"That's nice."

"My daddy picked it out, on account of Red's got big old red eyes."

May nodded and looked back out to the west. "I love animals. Mother and Father do, too. That's why we moved out here from town. I wanted to have a horse, so Father bought me Tillie. She was a Paint. I rode her everywhere — to town and back, over to my friend Nellie's, everywhere. She just died last year. We buried her over there behind the barn."

"I seen men riding horses across the Mississippi in the dark once."

"How cruel!"

"Pardon?"

"I mean, those poor animals. They must've been terrified."

"I don't know." Alvin shrugged, feeling a strange chill. "It was dark."

Both May and Alvin put their backs to the wind. When Alvin turned his head again to cough, Rascal was walking out from behind the house with a chicken in his arms. The dwarf was humming to himself while scratching the chicken's beak with his right forefinger. Just outside the barn door, the chicken leaped from the dwarf's grasp and ran for the fence. Rascal gave chase. Scared by his pursuit, the chicken changed direction and flew back into the middle of the yard. Rascal ran hard after it, knees bent almost to the dirt, arms outstretched wide, clucking with his tongue, acting crazy. He dove at the chicken and missed. It scurried across the yard and up onto a fencepost, screeching with fright.

The screen door opened and Chester came out, followed by Hancock and Mr. Jerome. He put his hat on while surveying the yard out front and told the farm boy, "We're leaving."

Hancock drew a pocketwatch from his vest, checked the hour, and mumbled something to Mr. Jerome that Alvin was unable to hear. Chester turned back to the other men and shook hands with both of them. He flicked the toothpick away and walked down the steps and headed for the Packard.

"I guess I got to get along," Alvin said to May, reluctant to leave. He decided she was the prettiest girl he had ever met. He tipped his cap. "Pleased to have made your acquaintance."

"Nice meeting you, too."

"Well, so long now."

"So long."

Alvin swung his legs over the railing and dropped down into the yard. A breeze gusted again, sweeping up clouds of dust, forcing Alvin to cover his face as he followed Chester to the automobile. The dwarf was already there, perched up in the backseat, a long chicken feather stuck in the thinning white hair behind his ear. Back on the porch, May leaned forward, her elbows on the railing. Mr. Jerome stood side by side at the top of the stairs with Hancock, both staring west into the late sunset. Chester steered the Packard out of the yard.

They drove about four miles along the narrow highway to the west, riding in silence through the warm evening. Alvin sat back in the seat, one arm out the window, and daydreamed about going fishing with May. *She'd have hold of his hand, her tiny fingers entwined in his, sitting on the riverbank, maybe whistling an Irish folk tune or two. She'd be quiet and listen while he talked about working with Frenchy on his daddy's farm, riding to dances on a buckboard and home again by moonlight. He'd tell her about the consumption and she'd take him in her arms and tell him how badly she felt about his sickness, her skin milky white in the darkness under the cottonwoods, her young eyes reflecting starlight, her lips redder than —*

The dwarf poked him in the back of the head. "Someone's coming after us."

"Huh?"

Alvin twisted in the seat to get a better look as Chester checked the mirror. About a quarter mile back, an automobile, headlamps glowing bright, raced toward the Packard.

"He's driving like a rocket," observed the dwarf. "He'll catch us in a minute."

"Can we outrun him?" Alvin asked Chester, certain it was federal marshals the instant he saw the approaching headlights. Instead of speeding up, however, Chester slowed the Packard to less than twenty miles an hour. The other automobile roared up from behind, closing until its headlamps illuminated every strand of white hair on Rascal's head. Its horn beeped twice and Chester ran the Packard over to the side of the road. A blue Nash "400" sedan pulled up alongside, George Hancock behind the wheel. He sat there a few seconds, staring at Chester and his two traveling companions. Then he eased back on the throttle, quieting the motor.

"I know what you fellows did," said Hancock, hands falling to his lap. His eyes met Alvin's for a moment, and moved on to the dwarf and back to Chester, fixing each as if for memory's sake. "We're not all hicks from the sticks out here."

Chester fidgeted with the gear lever and the button at the bottom of his shirt. Alvin tried to slow his racing heart by taking measured breaths, in and out, in and out. The dwarf sat rock-still just back of his shoulder. Chester squinted his eyes and looked across at Hancock. "What's your game, mister?"

Dry stalks of corn on both sides of the road shook as a breeze gusted and dust blew up over the hoods of both cars in its draft. No one blinked.

His face to the wind, Hancock said, "I saw you and that kid there go into the Union Bank this afternoon. I saw you both come out again, one after the other a quarter of an hour past closing time. I also saw Edna Evans go around back, looking for her husband at four-thirty. I never saw anyone else. Before or after."

Chester steeled his gaze at Hancock. "Is that so?"

The wind gusted again in the cornrows and rained dust across the windshields of both vehicles.

"I'll shoot square with you, Wells, or whatever your name is," Hancock said. "I didn't care for you from the moment I laid eyes on you. Oh, I've been to Chicago, all right, and I've seen plenty fresh fellows of your kind, swaggering through fancy restaurants, throwing money around like Carnegie, pretending to be respectable. You might've fooled Walter, but you didn't fool me. I know what you are. I didn't say so back at Jerome's out of fear for his family's lives, but I'm saying it now because I'm not afraid of you. Not one iota. Oh, I guess you're pretty tough when you've got the upper hand on somebody who's — "

"Look here, Hancock," Chester interrupted. "I'm afraid what we're having is a case of misapprehension."

"You're a liar, too."

"No, sir," Chester replied, "Not at all, and I'll prove it to you. Let me ride with you back into Stantonsburg. We'll put everything square."

Chester smiled at Hancock who eyed him back in return, clearly taken off guard by Chester's offer. Warily, Hancock asked, "Yeah? What about these two fellows?"

Chester shrugged. "Buddy here and the midget can drive on alone to Norman tonight. I'll worry about catching up to them once you and I've worked out our little misunderstanding."

Hancock studied him. "The marshals'll be at Stantonsburg in half an hour. I plan on driving straight into town to take it up with them. What do you say to that?"

"I'd say that'd be swell by me. I'd like to get this baloney cleared up in a hurry."

Chester opened the door and stepped out into the road. Only the irregular humming of twin automobile motors disturbed the quiet.

"All right, get in the car," Hancock said, flipping open the passenger door. "And don't try pulling anything. I know a few tricks of my own." He folded his jacket open to show a revolver in the waistband.

Chester smirked. "I'm sure you do. Just let me get my hat." Reaching into the foot-well of the backseat beside the dwarf, he murmured to Alvin, "Forget Norman. You boys drive on through to Council Bluffs and hire us a couple rooms at the Dakota Hotel. I'll meet you there at eight in the morning."

Then Chester snatched his hat up and crossed the road, jumping into the seat next to Hancock. He gave Alvin a wave and shouted, "Take care of my auto, kid!"

A moment later, George Hancock spun the blue Nash around in a half circle and accelerated back down the long empty road toward Stantonsburg. Alvin and the dwarf watched until the exhaust cloud spun into ether and the red taillights were swallowed up in the broadening dark.

INTERLUDE
CHARLIE PENDERGAST

THE BALLOONIST

AUNT EDITH HAD NEVER been in love until she met the tal-cumed-faced balloonist at Barstow. Mother assured us this was true because only love makes people do silly things and she believed Edith hadn't done anything more ridiculous in her life than setting foot in Professor Laburum's gondola for the final ascent that day in July. There had been other fellows in her life, of course. Aunt Edith had gone to college and owned an automobile and won a ribbon at a beauty show in Cleveland one summer. Her sister Florence tattled to the family about Edith's sordid escapades, how far she'd fled from Jesus. Shame, Florence argued, reveals the sour wisdom of experience, though the truth remained that Edith had always had more boys to go with than Florence who soaked herself in Mavis perfume until no one could tolerate being in the same room. Mother said Edith spoke about some of these fellows offering diamond rings and furs and trips abroad in exchange for her hand in marriage, but Edith had no intention of becoming a "yes, dear," kind of wife. She threw over one suitor after an-other, then went to Hollywood and had her picture taken in a mink coat.

The balloon ascent was held in a grassy field half a mile from Route 66. Uncle Harris had the idea we ought to go when he read a handbill outside the grocery store in Needles and Father agreed. Mother and Aunt Lottie telephoned to Aunt Edith, and on Saturday the next we piled into the Ford and drove out to see the hot-air balloon. Admission to the field was fifty cents. Racing across the dusty grass, Cousin Bebbins and Shirley and I imagined floating high into the clouds above earth, although Father had already told us we wouldn't be allowed to go up. There was a small carnival beside the balloon with a refreshment stand and a juggling clown and a pony ride and a Navajo snake handler. The balloonist had his own khaki wall tent with a brand new 8-cylinder Cadillac parked behind it. Until Aunt Edith arrived from Glendale in her own new automobile, Professor Theodosius Laburum, Aerialist & Scholar, hadn't set foot in the sunlight. Mother told us he hailed from Carpathia. Uncle Harris believed the balloonist was either a Jew or a Pentacostal -- who else traveled with snakes? Before Aunt Edith arrived, Bebbins and I bought ice cream and Shirley rode the pony in a circle and a noisy crowd gathered about the balloon. It cost one dollar per seat in the gondola and five people could go aloft at a time. The first flight was advertised for ten o'clock. Edith stepped out of her shiny tan Dodge roadster at five minutes lacking the hour, wearing a smart coat of honey-beige ermine and a leather helmet with goggles. Aunt Lottie hurried over to greet her with a big kiss and a hug. Mother kissed her, too, and summoned Shirley and me and Bebbins. We each got a big kiss on the cheek that left us stinking of gardenia and rose red lipstick. The crowd cheered as Professor Laburum emerged from his tent, and Bebbins and I ran to the balloon.

Shirley thought Professor Laburum was a ghost. His face was pasty-white with talcum powder, his hair slicked back with oil. He wore a waxed moustache that curled up toward his cheeks and a long black coat with tails and boots with pointed toes. He held a cane with a golden knob and greeted the ladies with a kiss on the hand. Edith remarked that Professor Laburum was the handsomest fellow she'd ever seen. She blew him a kiss when he entered the gondola and giggled when he smiled back. Father and Mother changed their minds about going aloft as the wind gusted. Those who did climb into the gondola seemed to Bebbins and me the luckiest people in the world. Flames burst from a firebox above the gondola. Professor Laburum released a pair of sandbags. The balloon rose. People shouted and waved. The balloon ascended higher and higher until a length of rope fastened between the gondola and an iron stake behind the Professor's tent became taut. It was a grand sight as the balloon drifted slowly here and there. Bebbins and I ran about underneath, hoping to see the floor of the gondola collapse and the people inside come tumbling out. Father lit a cigar and sat beside Mother on a bale of hay. Uncle Harris smoked a cigarette and drank a beer. Aunt Lottie and Mother and Aunt Edith waved to Professor Laburum, who saluted back. When the balloon descended to earth again, he invited all seven of us into his tent where he had a tray of biscuits and a tea urn and a porcelain music box from Vienna. The Professor sparked Edith to a fair you well. He gave her a rose and kissed her hand and sat beside her on his fancy divan while he spoke to us about ballooning with the King of Denmark. He had a soothing voice and a peculiar way of saying certain words that sent a chill up my spine. Edith giggled like little Shirley and drank a shot of schnapps and told the balloonist how Aunt Lottie climbed a tree behind the church one Sunday without her bloomers. Bebbins and I thought it was the funniest thing we'd ever heard, but Uncle Harris got up and left the tent. Then Shirley knocked a flower vase off the Professor's table and Aunt Lottie gave her a spanking, and Mother and Father decided it was time for us to leave. Only Aunt Edith remained behind.

We waited half an hour before Professor Laburum came out for the next ascent. His face was white as snow from talcum and his lips were rouge red. We waved to him as he went to the balloon and climbed in. While the clown ushered the next five riders into the gondola, Mother decided to see what Edith was doing in Laburum's tent. We watched the balloon rise into the summer sky to a great cheer. Bebbins tried to pull on the rope tether and was shoo'd off by the clown. Mother came out of the tent and told Aunt Lottie that Edith was smoking a cigarette on the Professor's divan and drinking another schnapps while she was waiting to go up in the balloon. Uncle Harris laughed when he heard that. He said Edith was so afraid of heights she wouldn't go near a stepladder -- what made her think she had the guts to ride in a balloon? Aunt Lottie thought it was liquor that gave her the guts and Mother agreed because everyone knew Edith drank gin with her grapefruit in the morning and kissed the mailman afterward. Granny

Gallup once said Edith had an unquiet heart.

By late afternoon, the crowds grew tired and began to disperse. A wind came up and blew dust around and the sun reddened the horizon. All day long the balloon had gone up and come down again and Mother had steadfastly refused to allow Bebbins and me to go aloft, while Edith stayed in the tent eating biscuits and drinking schnapps and playing the music box. After Professor Laburum retired to his tent once again, the clown led the pony away to a trailor, which made little Shirley cry. Then the Indian snakehandler drove off in a Model A Ford, and Father and Uncle Harris decided it was time for us to go, too, but Aunt Lottie expected Edith to have supper with us and said she couldn't possibly leave without her. She went inside the tent to fetch Edith while we waited by the automobiles. Father lit a cigar and asked Uncle Harris if he'd ever handled a snake and Uncle Harris said not since he'd thrown that paperhanger off the porch for blowing a kiss at Aunt Lottie when he thought nobody was looking.

Bebbins and Shirley were already asleep in the backseat of the Ford when Aunt Edith and Aunt Lottie and the balloonist came out of the tent. Edith was wearing her leather helmet and goggles and held a rose in one hand and her bag in the other and walked like she was tipsy. Aunt Lottie told Mother that Edith intended to have a ride in the balloon and that when she came back down again, we'd all go to supper. Professor Laburum said the atmospheric conditions for an ascent were best at sunset and thanked us for taking the trouble to drive out to watch. He shook hands with Father and Uncle Harris, then called for the clown to prepare the balloon. I let Shirley sleep, but woke Bebbins. The wind was hot and dusty as the sky darkened and I felt scared somehow to see the balloon prepared to go aloft one last time. The Professor and the clown helped Aunt Edith climb into the gondola, which shook in the gusts. Then the balloonist climbed in and Edith blew a kiss to Mother and Aunt Lottie. Professor Laburum ignited the firebox, released the sandbags, and the balloon slowly ascended. The clown held the tether rope until it became taut and swung against the wind when the balloon was high above us. A rose sailed down from the gondola and Edith's voice was lost in the wind. Then Professor Laburum signaled to the clown who untied the tether from its iron stake and let the rope chase the balloon up into the air. We were astounded. Father and Mother and Uncle Harris stood with their mouths agape watching the balloon rise higher and higher until it wasn't any bigger than a penny against the sky. Then Aunt Lottie shrieked like a bird and ran about in a circle beneath the balloon, calling for Edith to come back. Bebbins threw a rock into the air. Father and Uncle Harris watched as the balloon grew smaller and smaller until it drifted east toward the moon and finally disappeared. The clown drove off in Professor Laburum's Cadillac.

Mother wept in the front seat of our own automobile as we followed Uncle Harris home that evening in Edith's roadster. Father didn't say a word. We never saw Aunt Edith again. Aunt Lottie believed she'd flown to New York, or maybe even to Europe, and passed the rest of her life in theaters and bistros. Uncle Harris said she'd probably gotten drunk and fallen out of the balloon somewhere. Bebbins thought she'd sailed to the moon. I didn't know what to think, but Mother told me the heart has its own map and its own destination, and more than likely our dear old Aunt Edith had at last found hers.

JULY

LATE ON THE MORNING of the Fourth of July, Marie Hennesey stood in the warm sunlight at the bedroom window folding linen. In the kitchen, still wearing a checkered apron from rolling pie crust after breakfast, Maude finished cleaning the pan she'd used to make puff-paste for a blueberry pie and ran a cotton cloth under the faucet while Rachel flitted about the front room, dusting the walnut side tables and bookcases, and listening to a musical radio program from Wichita. A parade in celebration of the Glorious Fourth was scheduled for noon through downtown Bellemont and Maude insisted the house be tidied up beforehand.

"What on earth for, Mother?" Rachel argued loudly enough for Marie to listen in. She didn't seem at all to mind sharing her disputes. "Are you expecting the parade to make a detour through our sitting room?"

"It's how we show respect," Maude answered, quickly polishing the blue porcelain enamel on her new Windsor range. "What the heart conceals, the face reveals."

Marie heard Maude shake out the floor mat by the kitchen door and replace it on the back porch. Henry had been playing in the stalls since sunrise and stomped dirt all over the porch when he came in for breakfast. Marie apologized to Maude for the mess, but secretly she was happy because it meant that Henry wasn't tiptoeing about; instead, he was acting like he did at home, silly and carefree. Maude could stand a little of that herself.

"I assume you won't mind then if I wear my spangled skirt to the parade," Rachel called to her. "It has Uncle Sam written all over it. CW thinks it's very patriotic."

"My dear," Maude cautioned, "if you walk out of this house in that costume, you may just as well keep walking. I'll disown you and have a yard sale with all your possessions. I may even rent your room to a stranger."

"Oh, Mother!" Rachel laughed. "How thoroughly dramatic! Have you ever thought of traveling to Hollywood for an audition in the squawkies?"

"Never mind about that," Maude replied, picking up a stack of mail-order catalogues Rachel had left on a chair by the rear door. She took them into Rachel's room and put them on the bed. "You just remember what a wonderful country you live in, and show your respect for those who've come before. Our inheritance is their glory."

"Well, hallelujah, then!" Rachel cried. "I'll be sure to wear my Jefferson Davis button to the parade."

Marie heard Cissie laughing around front. Looking out the bedroom window, she saw Lili Jessup run up the sidewalk from next door, her arms loaded with straw. Maude had gone from Rachel's bedroom to her own, closing drawers and fussing about. After folding the last of the bedsheets, Marie slipped them into the bottom drawer of the dresser and walked out to the shadowy sitting room where Rachel lay on the sofa, her arms splayed limp in a pose of utter exhaustion. On the radio, an orchestra played a brisk Paul Whiteman number. A summer breeze fluttered in the curtain lace. Marie sat down at the piano, her favorite place in the room. Her feet were sore and she was weary. The draft clinked at the glass beads hanging from one of Maude's lamps. She told Rachel, "If you're half as tired as I am, I pity you. I can hardly keep on my feet."

"Well, I can't for the life of me imagine why," Rachel replied, her voice languid, almost drowsy. "I doubt there's a rooster anywhere in this town who wakes before you do. CW and I both feel you're suffering some rare affliction."

Marie laughed. "Oh, I enjoy mornings. It's so quiet, and I can get everything done I need to do without worrying about crossing anyone.

I find it simplifying somehow." Back home in Illinois, Harry hated waking up early and generally stayed in bed while Marie bathed and dressed. She thought it strange not to wake at sunup, but was loathe to tell him so, knowing he'd likely ask why it was any concern of hers. She always felt it was important for a husband and wife to share the basis for these small incompatibilities with each other, in order to be better understood and get along more easily. Harry had no interest in that, which Marie came to believe was a grave fault in any marriage, hers included.

Maude called out to Rachel from her bedroom. "There, what am I always telling you? You just listen to her, dear! Trudy says that Vivian's been exercising at half past seven each morning to a radio class in pyjama calisthenics, and she was just raised to thirty dollars a week. I don't imagine it would hurt you to rise an hour or two earlier every day."

Rachel dismissed the suggestion with a wave of her hand. "Oh, apple butter! Why, I've no interest at all in eating the early bird's worm, Mother. Besides which, CW hates mornings and has to be routed out of bed himself. If we're to be married, I might just as well accustom myself to his schedule — it's the chief duty of wifehood, remember? Right after dishes and didies."

"If you don't watch yourself, young lady, you won't become anyone's wife."

Rachel leaped up from the sofa and went to the hallway where she shouted, "Don't you dare try and put the bee on me today, Mother! I simply won't allow it!" She came back into the sitting room with a wicked grin on her face. Fanning herself by the window, she said to Marie, "It's horrid in here, isn't it? Since Mother bought that idiotic stove, she's been broiling us out of house and home. I don't believe I can stand it another minute."

"Maybe we need an air conditioner," Marie suggested, patting the perspiration on her own cheeks, "or at least a new electric refrigerator to sit next to. Idabelle says they sell them on time now at Heywood's." She found the heat of East Texas utterly horrid, but the children raised little objection at all. Perhaps a small body is more adaptable to adverse circumstances than a big one.

"Of course they do," Rachel replied, taking out a cigarette from a patch pocket, "but anything I show a fondness for, Mother automatically disregards as utterly unnecessary. Fact is, we'd all better brace up for another unbearable summer, and that isn't bluff."

She crossed to the front door and went out to take her smoke.

Marie rose from the piano bench and followed. She felt antsy, ready to shake out the cobwebs. A warm draft had come up in the past half hour, drying the morning air and chasing dust and leaves from one end of College Street to the other. Marie brushed the hair back off her forehead and strolled around to the side porch where she could look down at Cissie's project under the fig tree: the construction of an authentic three-ring circus in doll-size scale. Naturally, the idea had come to her that night after visiting Laswell's circus. It was all Cissie had talked about for several days until one morning when Julius Reeves passed by the house pushing a wheelbarrow piled high with scraps of canvas and colored string and a fractured old wagon wheel he'd planned to cart away to the dump north of town for a couple of dollars in salvage redemption. Cissie stopped him and requested a thorough examination of the booty he'd collected, explaining that, seeing as how her mother had not permitted her to run away and join Laswell's wagon circus, she'd decided to build one of her own in her grandmother's front yard where anyone could stop by and be entertained for a penny. In a few minutes, Cissie persuaded Julius not only to give her half of what he'd planned to take to the dump that day, but to provide her with further materials until she completed the circus, at which time he'd become part-owner and share in the profits she was certain would exceed the value of any materials he could turn up. A portion of her own profit, she and Lili determined, would go toward daily flowers for Boy-Allen's grave. A handshake had sealed the bargain and, since that afternoon, with the help of Henry, Lili Jessup, and Abel Kritt, a big top was erected with several smaller tents housing the animal exhibits and the Freak Show (old dolls of Lili's beheaded or similarly crippled by Henry) along the midway and other exotic attractions.

"Cissie?" Marie called out, looking for her daughter. She saw Cissie's new brown elk sandals lying atop a small rabbit cage. Her daughter had no less a penchant for trouble than any other child, and she was more clever than most. Harry joked that one day she'd become a criminal genius, but Marie saw little humor in the notion. There was trouble enough in the world.

Henry crawled out of the tiny tent they had built from Julius's canvas. "She ain't in here."

Little Abel stuck his head out, too, his thick glasses cloudy with dust.

"*Isn't* in here," Rachel corrected, studying the layout of the circus grounds where Lili's worn-out dolls lay about in varying states of amputation and paint. Henry and Abel had been experimenting with dark-shaded dyes in order to create a more frightful flavor to their collection of freaks. "I'm afraid that living here in Bellemont has had a deleterious effect on your children's grammar, dear. Sorry."

"Henry, where's your sister?" Marie asked, craning her neck to search the grounds back of the circus and below the porch overhang. Lili's voice, raised in laughter, echoed somewhere nearby.

"She's collectin' wild pigs," Henry announced, getting up, his trousers dusty and worn at the knees from crawling about under the Big Top. "I'm s'posed to build the cages, but I can't find any wire. Do you think Grandma's got some me and Abel could borrow?"

Rachel said, "I think your children have gotten into Mother's medication cabinet."

"That's not at all funny," Marie replied, concerned that it might be true. One afternoon in her own girlhood, she had tried to paint her nails with mercurochrome and Cousin Violet licked the bottle cap and threw up all over them both. "Henry, where's your sister?"

"I told you!" he whined, stamping his foot in the dirt. "She's collectin' wild pigs for the circus!"

Frustrated, Marie called out, "Cissie!"

She heard a spate of giggles nearby, then a muffled reply. *"Over here, Momma!"*

Rachel said, "Why, I believe she's under the house."

"Oh, for goodness sakes!" Marie hurried down off the porch, joining Rachel by the corner of the house where a broken section of lattice revealed an entry to the foundation. This was just what she needed! Good gracious! What would they get into next? Marie leaned down to the black rectangle outlining the entry and called out. "Cissie?"

Her willful daughter's voice came out of the dark, *"Yes, Momma?"*

Marie could hear some shuffling in the dirt closeby. As firmly as possible, she said, "Come out from under there this instant."

"I can't," Cissie's disembodied voice replied. *"I think I'm stuck."*

Lili's distinctive giggle carried to Marie from the shadows. Marie asked, "Is that you, Lili?"

"Yes, ma'am."

"Is Cissie stuck somewhere under there?"

"Yes, ma'am." Lili tried unsuccessfully to muffle another giggle.

Maude's summer jasmine blooming along the lattice breathed a pretty scent as the morning breeze rose and fell. Out in the street, a new black Studebaker rattled past, chalky clouds of dust billowing up in its wake. Next door, the Jessup's collie began barking.

Cissie called out, *"Momma?"*

"Yes, dear."

"You don't need to wait. I'm sure I'll be free before the parade."

Her patience waning, Marie said, "Young lady, I'd prefer you to come out of there now and get cleaned up."

Lili giggled again.

"Where is she?" Rachel inquired, leaning down for a better look. "Can you tell?"

Lili answered, instead. *"We're by the chinaberry tree. I can see Mrs. Hennesey's bedsheets from where we're sitting."*

Rachel frowned. "Why, the girls aren't even by this side of the house."

"Well, for goodness sakes," said Marie, getting to her feet. She hurried around to the sideyard, ducked under the laundry line, and knelt beside an old wicker basket Maude had thrown out when its bottom tore free. She called again, "Cissie?"

"Yes, Momma?"

"Am I close?"

"I can see your shoes," she giggled. *"You're getting dirt all over them."*

"You can touch her foot if you stretch out." Lili appeared at the bottom of the foundation, peeking from the darkness with a smile.

Rachel knelt beside Marie. "It's been years since we've had a man out here to exterminate the rats."

Marie pulled back, astonishment drawn on her face. "Rats?"

"Yes, isn't that awful?" Rachel said, "If I've reminded Mother once, I've reminded her a thousand times. Of course, she's much too old to reform. We're lucky the Public Health Service hasn't come to board up our house. I can hear them at night, gnawing on the floorboards beneath my bed. I expect eventually to fall through and be eaten alive."

Marie frowned. She detested rats. Frenchy used to kill them in traps, then chase her and Emeline around the yard with the mutilated carcasses. "You're joking, of course."

"Ask Mother! She's heard them! Harry, too. He used to tell me they were leprechauns building a ship to sail back to Ireland. Some nights it does sound as though they're sawing and pounding nails."

Marie ducked back to the foundation and called out, "Cissie?"

"Yes, Momma?"

"Where are you stuck?"

"Right here! Can't you see my shoe?"

Marie inched her face forward, pressing her cheek to the dirt and staring sideways into the dark beneath the house. First Lili Jessup in pigtails, then Cissie, became visible in the shadows. Lili was sitting up against one of the wood supports, her arms folded about her knees, while Cissie lay on her side wedged between two other supports. They were no more than four or five feet from Marie, and both wore grins. Marie saw nothing amusing at all in this circumstance.

"Lili?" she asked, trying to remain calm. "Can you push Cissie from behind if I grab her feet and tug?"

"Don't hurt me, Momma," Cissie pleaded. "I'm really stuck."

Henry came up and kneeled in the dirt next to Marie, sticking his face into the dark. "I can help," he suggested.

"You just stay right here," Marie said. "I'd rather not have to call the fire department."

She slipped her arms under the lower wall and reached forward and grabbed Cissie's ankles. "Ready?"

"Yes, ma'am."

Marie pulled, gently at first, then more firmly when she realized how much more force was needed. Under the house, Lili groaned with the effort of shoving Cissie forward. Marie tugged a little harder. Cissie yelled for her to stop.

"My dress is tearing!" she cried. "It's stuck on a nail!"

"We can sew your dress," Marie said.

Another flurry of whispers passed between the girls, then Cissie called out to her mother, "Oh, swell! It's torn already. Go ahead."

Marie gripped her daughter's ankles more firmly, gave a sharp tug, and pulled Cissie clear, ripping the dress clear down the inseam, but freeing her daughter from the support posts and sliding her out from underneath the house. Lili crawled out after her. Both girls were filthy and Cissie's rose plaid gingham hung torn from one shoulder, soiled with grime of all sorts, spider web in her haircurls.

Marie took one look at her daughter, grabbed her by the arm without saying a word, and took her into the house, the screen door slamming behind them. Marie led Cissie to the bathroom and closed the door. "Now get out of that dress this instant and don't squabble!"

"Momma!"

"You heard me," Marie bent down to stick the plug into the bathtub drain. She swiveled both spigots and water began to run into the tub.

"I don't feel like a bath," Cissie protested. "I won't take one."

"Yes, you will. Now get out of that dress, young lady. I won't ask you again."

"But I didn't do anything wrong!"

"I haven't said you did," Marie corrected, testing the temperature of the water with her fingers. Who claimed daughters were neater than sons?

"Then why do I have to take a bath?"

"Because I say so." With Harry gone, both children were constantly testing her patience and she was not at all pleased. If they persisted in doing so, there'd be trouble ahead. She'd had more than her share of agitations this summer already.

Cissie unfastened the buttons of her dress with dirty fingers. "You always side against me. You know you do."

"Sides have nothing to do with it. Just have a look at yourself in the mirror. Good grief! What do you think your father would say?"

"That I'm filthy. Then he'd clench his teeth and ask me what the devil I thought I was doing under the house."

"No smart cracks, young lady."

There was a knock at the door.

"Yes?"

Maude peeked her head in.

"We're taking a bath," Marie said, somewhat embarrassed at her daughter's plight.

"Momma?" Cissie frowned. "My feet stink."

Maude came in, shutting the door behind her. "Grab her ankles."

"Pardon?"

"Go ahead, dear. Do as I say."

"All right." Somewhat confused, Marie bent down and grabbed Cissie by both ankles as Maude slipped her own arms under Cissie's shoulders.

"Now, lift her up over the tub."

"Momma!" Cissie cried.

"Hush!" Maude looked Marie in the eye and nodded for her to begin lifting. Somewhat reluctantly, Marie raised her daughter up to horizontal, and helped Maude maneuver her above the water. "Now, give her a good shake."

Marie frowned. "Pardon me?"

"Honey, do as I say!"

"Momma, help!"

Maude twisted Cissie by the shoulders vigorously back and forth, up and down. Seeing she had no choice, Marie did likewise. Cissie shrieked out loud, but Maude continued until Cissie's clothing fluttered above the water. Cascading filth in the form of dust and web fragments filtered down to the surface of the water. Another few vigorous shakes, and Maude motioned Marie to carry Cissie away from the tub where they set her back on her feet.

"Now, dear," said Maude, "have a look at what you got yourself into crawling around under there. Fleas! The kind that fester in the wounds of dead vermin and make life miserable for everyone in the household once they're brought indoors."

Both Cissie and her mother leaned over the tub. If there were fleas, they resembled dark particles of dust floating on the cloudy water. Maude reached down and pulled the chain on the plug, draining the tub. "We'll refill the bath when you get out of those clothes." She showed Cissie a scowl. "Go on now. Hurry up. Take off your dress. The parade'll start soon enough and I'm sure you'll want to go."

Cissie reluctantly pulled the torn gingham dress over her head and stood humiliated beside the old tub in her white cambric drawers.

Maude looked at Marie. "If we hadn't shaken them off her clothing, we'd have had to burn it. Nothing less would have removed the eggs laid in the time it took her to come indoors, not to mention germs of all sorts, which Beatrice says are our constant associates. She was a nurse once in Houston, you know."

"I had no idea," Marie said, embarrrassed at her own ignorance of pests.

Maude leaned down around the side of the tub and drew out a porcelain pitcher and basin. She filled the pitcher with water from the bath spigot and used it to wash the filthy water, fleas and all, down the drain as the bath emptied. Replacing the plug, she dialed up the hot water and allowed the tub to begin filling once more.

Marie said to Cissie, "Honey, take your drawers off, too. They're filthy."

"Momma?"

"Melissa Jean Hennesey! This instant!"

Cissie began whimpering.

"Listen, dear, it's as much my fault as yours," Maude said, replacing the pitcher and basin. "I ought to have known you children would find a way underneath the house. Rachel and her friends used to play under there every Saturday morning until her father caught a rat the size of a Chihuahua in the rose bushes by the steps. Pestilence is the Lord's opinion of the ignorant. I'll wash these clothes this afternoon."

Maude scooped up Cissie's soiled clothing and left the bathroom.

"I'm sorry, Momma," Cissie said, climbing into the tub. "I was only looking for mice to invite into our circus. If Grandma or Auntie Rachel had told me there were rats under there, I'd never have let Lili persuade me to go."

The water rose to her belly as she sat down in the lukewarm water.

"I know, dear," said Marie, grabbing a bar of soap and a washcloth as Cissie dunked her head underwater. "Rats!"

She shuddered and began to lather the soap.

Farrington, Illinois
June 28th, 1929

Dearest Marie,

It is now two months and a day since you've been gone from us. We all miss you so horribly. Granny Chamberlain thinks you're off to St. Paul on holiday and will be back next week. Were it only true! Had your letter when it arrived here not been carried around in the pocket of our forgetful postman's mackintosh, an answer would have reached you sooner. But such is life in the northern farms, and when Mr. Giroux is headfull of buying a house and thinking of his future-intended, you can easily excuse such errors.

Now it is Saturday. My spoiled little bottle-baby has been such a worry this week that I gave a call to Auntie Emma. She came here fast as lightning and seems heaven sent, as always. What would we do without her? I wish you could see what a darling the baby has become since Easter. Roy is already pestering me for another! He fusses when I accuse him of sex-madness, but it sure keeps him hopping! Yesterday I was out to Galesburg to buy a new hat and a pair of gloves, letting the house struggle along without me. Strange to say, Roy and Uncle Boyd managed very well, and I found the kitchen all intact upon my return. It was a perfect day and I enjoyed myself to the limit, though my head was full of plans for a fall garden, and how best to finish my arduous duties today. Tomorrow is Sunday and as yet we have no teacher. Last Sunday we picked up Mr. Vernon H. Cowsert, a Methodist minister from Peoria, and enjoyed the lesson almost as much as if you had been there with us. Who is to teach tomorrow I don't know. Maybe another Methodist minister floating around, in which case it will be all right. I rather hesitate to attempt to teach or even lead a discussion myself. Seems too much like a blind leader of those who see. No, this is not modesty, but a candid recognition of facts as they are.

Bonnie and I went out to Mrs. Milo's to a young ladies missionary society meeting and waited on them. Such appetites! We were all decked out in white aprons and caps. Edith had one the size of a postage stamp. Bonnie nearly cut herself in two trying to put one of Dorothy's aprons on. Everything went off splendidly, especially the pineapple ice. Corrine Frank sang for us and they all left at the seasonable hour of 9:45. Harlow's automobile was in great demand, but too many girls were too much for the engine, and it broke a couple of ball-bearings, corresponding, I suppose, to a heart. It only returned in time to take Dorothy home, together with Edith and Corrine.

You spoke of my library being untouched, but you are wrong. I finished *Middlemarch*, but have been too busy to write anything about it. I am reading Hawthorne's biography evenings, and Shakespeare Sunday afternoons. So you see I am not neglecting my education. I can't afford to do that, for I need it so much. By the way, that was a good joke of yours, though I had not eaten breakfast and my internals were roaring like the little pigs going to market, much to Roy's amusement.

But here I am filling up these pages with the chatter which is becoming natural to me. I wish I had your ability to glorify the commonplace, and mix in a little of the sublime. As it is, I can only keep on in my own way, or be accused of being sentimental. News is scarce.

I love you bushels.

Your loving cousin,

Emeline

— **2** —

By half past eleven, people were wandering about the sidewalks in the direction of downtown or sitting up on shaded verandas along the parade route. Smelling of fresh Barbasol and hair tonic, CW arrived on College Street, four flags of Old Glory fluttering from antennae mounted on the corners of his Ford. Across both the driver's and passenger's doors, he'd draped larger flags, folded and hung like bunting. Idling, the engine dulled to a hornet's hum.

"Why, dear, I believe you could enter the parade and not appear at all out of place. It's absolutely grand!" said Rachel, stepping out of doors behind Marie who walked to the porch-railing.

CW tipped his straw hat. "Thank you, darling." He shut off the motor and bounced out of the automobile. Rachel greeted him at the gate and gave him a kiss much too intimate for a public sidewalk at midday. Soon Marie expected to see them making love with the top down on Main Street. What would Harry say? He used to have that spark of sex in his eye. Maybe Rachel wasn't overbold, after all. Why couldn't everyone be so daring?

Wind blew in the street and rippled the flags on CW's car. It was warm out, tending toward a hot afternoon. Henry dashed down the steps and bounced into the rear seat. "Let's go now!"

"We won't be taking the automobile, dear," Marie said, "even if it is quite spectacular."

"Why, I think we ought to," Rachel argued. "Who says we can't? A parade is for everyone, isn't it? Can't we join? Don't we count in that crowd?"

"But it's much nicer to walk, don't you agree?" Marie suggested, anxious to stretch her legs. "More festive?" She could walk downtown, even if she had to do it alone. Being housebound all morning left her feeling both wan and restless. She needed the society of neighbors to perk up. Apropos of that spirit, Marie had dressed for the parade in a lovely French blue silk flat crepe frock, and felt very up-to-the-minute, even if Harry might not agree it was modern enough. .

CW laughed. "Don't forget, dear: Rachel absolutely despises exertion of any sort. Why, she'd take a trolley from her bed to the breakfast table every morning if she could."

Maude came out onto the porch, fastening her Sunday bonnet and squinting into the sunlight. Already, the distant rhythms of a marching band carried across the afternoon air. Children squealed with joy, dancing and waving small flags in the middle of College Street. A dog with a patriotic ribbon tied to its tail ran past in the direction of the children, barking loudly. Motor horns honked constantly.

"Mother, why are you wearing that silly old bonnet?" Rachel laughed, taking CW's hand. "The parade doesn't lead to church."

"It's no concern of yours what I wear." Maude sniffed as she studied Rachel's skirt a moment or two. "Though I don't see how dressing like a harlot honors the birth of our country."

"Mother, if you're dyspeptic this morning, chew a stick of Beeman's." Rachel laughed again. "I'll have you know this dress is an exact copy of the one Martha Washington wore on the night she visited Thomas Jefferson while his pal George was away at Valley Forge. How can one be more patriotic than that?"

Cissie came out of the dooryard arm-in-arm with Lili Jessup, skipping into the street. Henry and Abel Kritt ran to catch up with them. Marie looked down the sidewalk and saw dozens of people strolling toward downtown. Overhead, the sky was clear and blue, a fine day for a parade. With the children running on ahead, the adults were hoping to find a nice shady place on the lawn of the courthouse square from which to view the grand procession. They walked beneath the dense green canopy of cottonwoods and willows and waved at neighbors drinking tea and lemonade on screened verandas and shaded stairs. Maude called out a greeting at each address and touched her bonnet, which elicited an equally gracious response. Marie exchanged holiday pleasantries with Mr. Gray, whose wheelchair, high on his shady porch, was swathed in Old Glory, and shared a fine recipe for rhubarb pie with Dora Bennett out tending her lovely summer roses, too busy for any old parade. Rachel and CW strolled side by side, nuzzling each other affectionately as they went, teasing with whispered flirtations. Glad to be out and about, Marie watched the children darting in and out of the tall shade trees, playing tag and kick-the-can with a rusty Campbell's Soup tin. Two men dressed in Confederate gray and bearing shiny sabers rode quickly by on horseback, late for parade formation. Closer to the square, Marie passed several women carrying fringed mulberry parasols and American flags and a full-skirted young girl with a trim little figure pushing a wicker baby carriage. All were chatting casually in the shade of the weeping willows as they walked along.

Marie and Maude, Rachel, CW and the children found the court-house square filled with people wandering about admiring the decorations and waiting for the parade. American flags of all sizes rippled in the breeze, while barking dogs and popping firecrackers echoed across downtown.

"Can we light some firecrackers, Momma?" Henry asked, hopefully. Standing behind him was little Abel, a look of mischief on his face. "Please?"

Marie frowned. "Why, I don't know. Where on earth would you find any?" Harry had taught his son a love of fireworks that Marie found distressing. They scared her half to death.

He gave a shrug. "Maybe there's some lying 'round somewhere. Me and Abel could go lookin', if it's allowed. I guess they ain't too hard to find."

"*Aren't* too hard to find," Rachel corrected, as she gave CW a kiss on the cheek and sent him off across Main Street to Hooker's drug-store. She followed Maude onto the lawn.

Marie turned to Henry's little friend, Abel. "Honey, what does your mother say about playing with firecrackers?"

The quiet towhead adjusted his glasses, and shrugged. "She don't mind if I ain't popping them off in the house."

"Thank you," said Marie, pausing with the children. "Henry, I suppose it would be fine for you and Abel to have a look around, so long as you promise not to set any off without my permission."

"We will," Henry promised. Then he called to Cissie and Lili petting a black Labrador on the lawn next to the sidewalk. "Momma says me and Abel can go find firecrackers!"

"Oh?" Cissie called back from beside the Labrador. "Momma, is that true?"

Marie nodded. "You can go, too, if you keep an eye on your brother and promise not to get into trouble."

"Well, I'm not sure I want to blow up any firecrackers," Cissie confessed, rising to her feet. "They hurt my ears. Besides, Lili and I'd rather go see the horses saddling up."

Henry stamped his foot. "I want to blow up firecrackers!"

Little Abel came up beside him, wiping his glasses off again on the back of his sleeve. His brown moleskin knickers were already dusty and his hands caked with dirt. He and Henry were a pair, all right.

"Oh, go to it, you little ninny," Cissie snapped. "What in the Hades do I care?"

Marie blanched. "Cissie! Would you like to go home right now?"

"No, ma'am."

"Well, then, you'd better change your disposition, young lady. You've been flip since breakfast and I won't have anymore of it, do you hear me?" Her daughter had been trying Marie's patience for days now and this was the limit. She had much too much on her own mind to be sorting out Cissie's nasty behavior on such a pleasant afternoon.

Cissie brushed grass off her skirt. "Yes, ma'am."

"Now, are you going to go with your brother or not?"

She looked at Lili still kneeling on the lawn beside the panting Labrador. "We'd rather see the horses."

"Well, you suit yourselves." Marie turned to Henry. "Honey, you and Abel be careful, all right? And don't forget to be back here before the parade ends. Dinner's at two."

"Yes, Momma."

Marie watched a flock of sparrows sail past as the midday heat swelled and men and women all about downtown fanned themselves briskly with hats and handkerchiefs. There were scores of Shantytown Negroes among the Main Street crowd, as well, young and old alike, waving crisp flags of the Republic and carrying on in the spirit of the hour. Did public events restore God's intended gravity to the world, Marie wondered, that holy equity inspired from Eden? Kindness is easily reciprocated without need of plot or hidden motives. Tolerance instructs the soul and soon the heart warms to it as naturally as love. Seeing grand holiday smiles on so many black faces along Main Street gave Marie herself a delightful shiver of sorts, soft as sleep.

A band struck up a lively John Philip Sousa march as CW cut through the crowd and hurried across the street carrying two strawberry ice cream cones already melting in the heat. Marie saw Rachel and Maude beside the flagpole and worked her way through the vibrant crowd to reach them.

"Now and then," she heard Maude say to Rachel as she approached, "perhaps the less we know, the longer we live."

"Pardon me?" Marie said, hoping to catch the thread of conversation as a flurry of motor horns honked across town. "Did I miss something?"

"Boy-Allen's mom," Rachel replied, as she directed Marie's attention across the street to a slight young woman in a shabby peach housedress and dark scrambled hair, half-hidden in the alleyway between the Electric & Battery Shop and Lippincott's Dry Goods Company. "I was just telling Mother, I believe this is the first I've seen Loretta out of doors since the funeral."

"Perhaps she's been keeping a solitude," Marie remarked, still disturbed by the memory of the little white hearse rolling under the cottonwoods that grim and windy afternoon. To her eye, the woman appeared frightfully woebegone.

Fanning herself with her hands, Rachel added, "Boyd Powell says Loretta telephones downtown every morning at eight o'clock to ask if the killer's been caught yet. It's obvious she's been driven into great extremes. I expect it'll be tough going for her in the future."

"There's your clue," Maude remarked. "Well-being is more than seeming to be well. Do you remember my commenting on how slim and proud she used to be? That was only last summer. Why, I doubt a girl her age has the wherewithal to cope on her own. I blame Fred Stevens equally with Boy-Allen's killer for wrecking that poor girl's outlook. To hear Trudy tell it, Loretta was completely devoted to that man. She fell for him like a ton o' brick and when he chucked her, well, you can see for yourself."

"She does look awfully worn out," Marie agreed, as she watched a cluster of red and blue balloons float sluggishly off into the midday sky from the rooftop of the First State Bank. The clamor of a large marching band drew nearer. A Negro man had been arrested just last week for Boy-Allen's murder, then released the next day when the court at

Henderson admitted they'd been holding the same fellow in jail the night Boy-Allen died. Where was the true killer? Had Marie seen him across College Street that night of the circus? It was both frightful and maddening how close she'd come to identifying his face, if that indeed had been him.

Rachel said, "Mother, I'm going to write your life and include all the correct living habits that you and those dirty old snoops of yours like to paw over the rest of us for lacking. It's sure to be one of the biggest volumes in the world."

Maude scowled. "Oh, horsefeathers! Fact is, Trudy says that boy was always full of hop and crying for trouble, and I agree. A lot he cared for Loretta or that poor child. I saw him hiding under his hat at the services and I doubt he shed one tear. Why, I'll lay his heart wasn't even chipped."

"Whose heart?" CW asked, arriving now with the strawberry ice cream cones. A thundering of bass drums caused a great stir in the crowd along the sidewalk. Children shrieked and rushed for the curb. Marie craned her neck, looking for the parade to start. She loved the horses and the drums.

"Thank you, darling." Rachel took her ice cream cone from CW and gave him a kiss on the cheek where perspiration droplets beaded from the heat. "Mother insists that Fred Stevens' making love to one woman after another is the moral equivalent of murder."

"I never said that," Maude protested.

A flurry of torpedoes burst loudly on the sidewalk behind the bandshell, giving Marie a start. She hoped Henry and Abel weren't involved with that.

CW asked, "Who's Fred Stevens?"

Rachel licked her strawberry ice cream, then replied, "Boy-Allen's father and a notorious rake-hell who could pick out any sweet girl he wanted when he was still fit. For ten years he pretended to be a devoted husband, then he quit her cold last September and now most people in town think he's just a fat-headed dub who only married Loretta because he got her caught while out tomcatting one night."

CW laughed. "Well, you can't blame a fellow for trying to make love at sight, can you? It's in our blood. Sure we'd like to duck it, but quite frankly we can't."

"Hmph!" Maude snorted. "I tell you, Fred Stevens had no genuine fondness at all for poor Loretta, and his absence since Boy-Allen's murder has made that plain as day."

"Oh, so he's beaten it, has he?" CW said, licking his own ice cream cone. "Lit out for the territories like Huck Finn?"

"A rolling stone gathers no whiskers," said Rachel, turning to the north end of the block as a great cheer went up. Marie heard a chorus of brass horns and a raucous clash of cymbals. Maude moved forward to get a better view of the street as the Panola Citizens Marching Brass Band came into view. Fourteen men in spit-and-polished blue uniforms, trumpets and flutes and trombones and drums playing for the assembled multitude, each earnest member wearing hats with feathered plumes and tiny flags of the Republic. The crowd cheered loudly as the brass band passed in revue. The Women's Relief Corps followed in flowing white dresses with flower-rimmed parasols and bonnets. Marie recognized Beatrice and Trudy and heard Maude give a cheerful yell as her friends passed by. Behind them came a long marching column of stern-faced war veterans, rifles at shoulder arms. At the front were half a dozen elderly men in long white beards wearing butternut gray and carrying a faded battle flag of the old Confederacy, trailed by a youthful bugler playing "Dixie." While kiddies with flags and horns chased along the curb, many a straw-hatted fellow gave these weary veterans a solemn salute. Marie's own heart contracted as she recalled great Uncle Philander who helped chase Braxton Bragg across Stone's River with the 19th Illinois Infantry, despite losing his left thumb to a Rebel bullet, and survived to march in the regimental colors each Glorious Fourth until he passed away on Hattie's porch after supper one spring evening in 1924.

When a flurry of young maidens wrapped in flags of the Republic tossed garlands of rose petals and daisies in the footsteps of the old soldiers, Rachel remarked, "Isn't this the most disgusting display of garishness and bad taste you've ever witnessed? Surely no Northern town debases itself so thoroughly as do we here in the South."

"Don't be so sure," Marie replied, her attention on the parade. "We're all proud of our heritage, don't you agree?"

"If you say so."

Rachel took out a handkerchief to wipe her mouth as she finished her ice cream. CW cheered as soldiers from the War with Spain followed down Main Street, half a dozen infantrymen with rifles and horns and two saber-clad Rough Riders on horseback recalling Teddy's First Volunteer Cavalry from the camp at San Antonio whose mounts wore war's grand regalia of pomp and patriotism. Each offered a brisk and dignified salute to Mayor Devlin and Bellemont's city council as he passed the courthouse grandstand and the colorful display of American and Republic of Texas flags hanging there in the midsummer heat.

"We have parades in Illinois," Marie remarked, raising her voice above the thundering drums, "and I don't recall them being much different than this. I always enjoy them, in fact. Don't you?"

"Not since Mother forced me to march down this very street dressed up in a tiger costume that attracted every dog in Texas. I was bitten on the ankle and laughed at from one end of Bellemont to the other. I'd never been so humiliated in all my life."

"Well, you can't blame that on the parade."

"Of course I can," Rachel replied, "and I do, every year at this time. My foot swelled up fat as a pumpkin. I refused to leave the house for a week."

Cissie and Lili had wormed a path through the skirts and dark suits and crossed over to the far side of the street where they waved to Marie and clapped for the sixteen brawny doughboys from Black Jack Pershing's A.E.F. when they came into view. The crowd roared. The brass band played "Over There" and an old Confederate cannon in the empty lot behind Hooker's drugstore boomed a loud salute. Marie recognized one of the doughboys as Wilfred Morrison, who worked the butcher's counter at Metcalf's Market, and another as Maude's dentist, Dr. Carl Holt. Both looked fit and proud in smart overseas caps and uniforms. She wondered how many of their classmates hadn't returned from France. Tears spoiled the face-paint of more than one on Main Street this sunny afternoon. Pride and sorrow wrestled with the past. *Memorials may warm the heart now and then,* Granny Mae once told her, *but the terrible quiet of an empty chair abides forever.*

CW came up beside Marie just as a hired brewery truck transporting a dozen or more Uncle Sams arrived on Main Street playing the fiddle and singing an enthusiastic chorus of "The Yellow Rose of Texas." He said, "Rachel's not telling you that silly tiger costume story of hers now, is she?"

"You hush your mouth, mister know-it-all," Rachel snapped back. "Dignity's forfeiture abides not reason nor calendar. All Mother cared about was participating in the parade without actually having to set foot in the street herself. I ought to've had her arrested for scurrility."

CW's response was drowned out by a particularly boisterous section of marching tuba players leading a procession of fraternal orders in triumphant precision, then a men's glee club, a barbershop quartet in old-fashioned handlebar moustaches, fifteen foot-racers in tights, and Bellemont's volunteer fire brigade.

"Well, your personal suffering notwithstanding," Marie said, angling to see past a portly woman holding a large fringed parasol, "I think it's a grand parade."

— 3 —

The kitchen screen door banged shut as Henry rushed dusty-faced out onto the back porch. Down the sidewalk, little Abel Kritt was called home to dinner by his mother. Having changed out of her glad garments into a more practical gingham, Marie busied herself about the kitchen while Maude set the dining room table. Potatoes hot and mealy simmered on the stovetop; fishcakes sizzled in a pan beside them. Though Rachel had argued all morning for lettuce sandwiches and iced tea, Maude insisted on a warm meal for the children who would have happily settled on Grape-Nuts with cream or a dish of Beech-Nut orange drops. After rinsing water glasses in the sink, Marie put on a pair of mitts and took Maude's blueberry pie out of the oven. She had to concede this new range was a fine improvement over the old one; both the firebox and reservoir were larger and the whole range could be cleaned with a soft cloth. She had already written about it in a letter to her mother whose own cook stove was just about worn out.

"You're a marvel," Rachel said to Marie, as she came into the kitchen from the sitting room. "Do you know that, dear?"

Marie smiled. "I'm not sure what you mean."

"Oh, this divine urge with which you attend to us, your dizzy relations." Rachel giggled. "You've helped us get out of our rut by removing the ruts. I don't know how we ever managed before."

"There's no need to idealize her," Maude called out from the dining room. "It ought to be enough to say Marie's a credit to her family, and leave it at that."

Rachel sniffed over the hot fishcakes. "Why, I don't idealize her at all, though she must have the patience of a flea-tamer to spend all day with you, Mother." She winked at Marie. "Daddy always said you can choose your friends, but you can't choose your relatives."

The telephone rang.

Rachel shot off into the hallway where Marie heard her shout, "Don't touch the phone, Mother! It's for me!"

"How do you know that?" Maude asked. "I'm expecting a call from Trudy."

"Mother, please!" Rachel caught the telephone midway through the second ring. "Hello?"

Marie gently placed a red-checkered cloth over the steaming blueberry pie. She made it a point never to answer the phone here herself unless asked to do so.

"Oh, how are you, dear?" she heard Rachel speak into the telephone.

"Who is it?" Maude asked, impatiently. "If it's Trudy, I won't — "

Rachel snapped back, "Mother, would you please sit down before you burst a blood vessel! It's not for you! It's Sophie and she has news from Robert in Port Arthur. Now go on! Shoo!"

"Piffle!" Maude walked back into the dining room.

Marie returned to the stove. Of course she was pleased by Rachel's flattery. *Let another praise you, and not your own mouth*, Aunt Hattie always said, though Emeline was often boastful, and Violet, too, when she was alive. Marie was proud enough to see that she had made herself useful this summer, that she and her children had been no heartscald for Maude or Rachel in a trying circumstance. She imagined Harry would be pleased, regardless of their difficulties. He had told her that it was always harder to make others believe better of you than you believe of yourself. From fear and apprehension she wept one night after packing, but that was all. Afterward, a mother's sacred responsibility gave her strength enough to endure until she saw the miles and miles of pretty bluebonnets from her sleeper car window; then she knew they would survive, and whatever duties were required of her in that household she could perform without reticence or complaint.

Marie heard Cissie yelling at Henry outdoors. She put down the spatula and went to the back door. The children had returned to work on the circus. Cissie proclaimed herself ringmaster and began delegating tasks to her brother and Lili Jessup in hopes of completing construction on her Big Top and midway by the end of the week. Several children they had met at the parade donated the use of worn-out stuffed animals and a box full of paper dolls Cissie intended as spectators under the tent.

Stepping onto the back porch, Marie saw Henry in tears by the Jessup's fence. Lili knelt beside him in the dirt, scratching her old gray cat.

Cissie stood in front of Henry, shouting in his ear. "You are utterly hopeless! I told Momma she ought to have left you under that bridge where she and Daddy found you!"

"Don't say that!" Henry cried.

"I will say it because it's true. Momma told me you were no better'n a silly little groundhog crawling in the mud underneath that dirty old bridge. She and Daddy just felt sorry for you, that's all."

"Liar!"

"Groundhog!"

Marie shouted from the porch railing. "CISSIE!"

Her daughter turned toward the house. "Yes, Momma?"

"Stop telling stories about your brother!"

"I ain't born from a groundhog, am I, Momma?" Henry asked, tears carving thin rivulets through the dirt on his cheeks.

Marie frowned. "Of course not. Your sister's just teasing."

"He ought to know the truth, Momma," Cissie insisted. "Why, I'm sure he's old enough to put up with the shame."

"You hush, young lady," Marie warned, "before I trade you and that smart mouth of yours to Mr. Laswell's circus."

"Oh, would you, please? I have no doubt I'd enjoy myself much more in a cage full of wild animals than I do living with this little urchin. Send me away this instant, Momma! Please!"

"Don't tempt me, darling," Marie replied, watching a pair of motorcars roll by, packed with young people fit out for the doings scheduled in the Bellemont pavilion at twilight. "Now unless you'd like to stay indoors for the rest of the day, stop tormenting your brother. I mean it!"

With that last warning, Marie went back inside where Maude was opening the windows to admit a draft in the warm afternoon. "That too-clever daughter of mine is turning into a little gangster," said Marie, attending once more to the stove. "I've half a mind to send her to bed after dinner." Next time she wrote to Harry, she intended to ask that he put a word or two of caution for Cissie in a future letter of his own. She believed that was the least he could do for being away so long.

"Truth be told, she takes after her father," Maude remarked with a smile. "When Harry was her age, he was so full of vinegar, he made us wild. He was flip and careless, and I didn't think Jonas or myself could ever bear it, yet we all made out, and Harry grew into a fine man, which told me plenty about the heart of a child."

"Then you don't think there's much to worry over with Cissie? You can see she's been quite a caution."

"I expect you'll both pull through just fine," Maude replied, disappearing into the pantry. "I have no great concern."

Rachel hung up the telephone and came back into the kitchen, wearing a smirk. "Sophie says Robert's been running around with a doll named Grace who traveled to Japan last year. It seems she owns a fortune in stocks and can buy whatever she pleases. Robert says her aim is to retire soon and spend the rest of her life knocking about the world, going where the jazz is the thickest! Isn't that remarkable? He says she's just got that certain air about her."

"Is she decent?" Maude asked, taking the potatoes off the stove.

Rachel frowned. "Oh, I'm sure she smokes cigarettes, Mother, and drinks gin with her eggs in the morning and hasn't been to church since Harding died. Good grief! According to Sophie, Grace gave Robert a man-sized hickey when they went out sailing one afternoon in the Gulf. Do you suppose that makes her cheap?" She grabbed a dishtowel and wiped off a puddle of water on the countertop.

"Don't snipe, dear," Maude answered. "I just believe it's easy for a girl to get in wrong these days, all the more so if she's rich and spoiled." She turned to address Marie. "It's always dreadful when a defect of character alters the course of a human life."

"Yes, it is."

Rachel rolled her eyes. "Mother, who said she was spoiled? I just told you she's been investing in the market for all it's worth and earning a king's ransom doing so! Playing the high and the low these days is no dip in the river, you know."

Maude stuck a fork lightly into the potatoes. "All the same, Robert's Miss So-and-So ought to be careful whom she decides to run with. Breaches of moral law don't exist for men. Beatrice says Helen told her that Rose Foster went to a nudist colony last year in the company of three oil barons from Dallas. Imagine that, if you will! Well, Helen claimed Rose was the picture of death during the Easter Egg Hunt at Hunziger's farm, and I couldn't disagree, though I refused to say anything as raw as that."

Rachel laughed. "Oh, of course not. You're much too polite, Mother. You'd never say anything against a neighbor, would you?"

Rinsing the fork, Maude told Marie, "I've never held for low insinuations. I believe it's bad manners."

Rachel cracked a mischievous grin. "Still, dear, wasn't it you who told Roland Butler he ought to take care picking a right girl because a bad one's like a viper swollen with poison?"

"Honey, I merely suggested to him that bringing a young lady back from Matamoros might prove to be a difficult proposition, that's all.

Marriage is serious stuff, I told him. Why collect fresh fish for all the old cats to feast on?"

"Yet he and Yolanda are getting on gloriously, aren't they? That good-for-nothing Roland — that waster, as y'all used to call him — seems as if he's been married since the first day he shaved. He wasn't ruined at all. In fact, he's well thought of now and making good, and most of us agree he's got Yolanda to thank for that."

Maude sniffed. "Well, that may be so, but Trudy tells me Roland's people still don't think much of her."

"Oh, for crying out loud, Mother, that's ridiculous! Where'd she get that hooey?"

"Why, I believe Lois confessed it over tea last month."

Rachel laughed out loud. "Well, then, Trudy's landed the real low-down, hasn't she? You people just burn me up! Why won't you concede that — "

The doorbell rang.

Rachel threw down her dishtowel and dashed off to the front room.

"I think the fishcakes are done," Marie said, removing the skillet from the stove. Maude made room on the counter next to the pan of potatoes.

"Perhaps you could fetch a bottle of milk from the ice-box, dear," Maude said.

"Certainly," Marie replied, heading into the pantry.

"Could you bring more sugar, as well? We'll need to refill the bowl. Rachel practically emptied it onto her corn flakes this morning. I'm surprised her teeth haven't rotted away."

The pantry was cool and dark and Marie had to switch on a light to find the sack of sugar on the middle shelf. Emeline once left hers on a bottom shelf and woke one morning to find it swarmed with ants. *Draw a line with chalk across the threshold and along the baseboards*, Aunt Hattie suggested to them both, *and no ant will cross it.*

Marie came out of the pantry just as Rachel walked in carrying a bouquet of red roses.

"Isn't this frightfully romantic?" she announced, smiling broadly. "Why, I do believe CW McCall is today the finest gentlemen in the great state of Texas. That is, if I'm allowed to utter such flattery in the presence of ladies less fortunate than myself."

"Of course you are, dear," CW said, entering the kitchen behind her, straw hat in hand. "It's a holiday."

"They're beautiful," Marie said, admiring Rachel's flowers. She turned to CW, "Where in heaven's name did you find them?"

"Why, I don't know," he replied, feigning ignorance. "One moment, my hands were empty, and the next I had this wonderful bouquet to give to my sweet patootie lamb. Didn't I, dear?"

Rachel kissed him square on the lips. "I had no idea men were capable of such displays of affection." She turned to Marie. "Isn't he a surprise?"

"You're a lucky girl," said Marie, smiling. "I'm sure if it weren't for Harry I'd be quite jealous."

"Oh, luck's got nothing whatsoever to do with romance," Rachel said, dancing through the hall to the front room where she stroked the piano keys lightly with one finger. "A girl knows when she's special. Even if she just can't see it in her vanity mirror, every man on the street'll let her know when she walks by. It's God's apology to Eve for His temper that horrid morning in Eden."

"Trust a woman to remember," CW remarked. He leaned over to smell the fishcakes and smiled. "My oh my!"

"Only by love doth the heart reveal its most innocent desire," Rachel called out. "Our Heavenly Father ought not to have intruded upon Eve's privacy. You'd think He'd have better manners than that."

"I'd be careful what I say, young lady," Maude scolded, as she walked back into the kitchen. "It's been more than a month since you've attended Sunday service. The Lord's neither deaf nor blind, and His memory is — "

"I know, Mother," Rachel interrupted. "Greater than all Creation."

"Well, that's a fact."

"Honest to goodness, Mother. Why do you ever have anything to do with me at all?" Rachel giggled, then sniffed her red rose bouquet. "I must make you awfully bitter."

Maude went into the pantry and came out with a bowl of carrots.

"I've learned not to remember your faults, dear." She smiled at Marie.

"That seems sensible," CW remarked. "I wonder if I'll develop the same patience."

"Well, it's certainly not too late to pull out, otherwise," Maude added, rinsing the carrots under the faucet.

"I resent that, Mother," Rachel said. "Why, I've received gifts from men and been admired at one time or another on nearly every single day of the year. A gentleman told me once that he found me even more charming on Sunday mornings than on Saturday nights."

"Who might that have been?" Maude asked, doubt etched in her expression. "Herbert?"

"Who's Herbert?" CW asked. "A former flame? A schoolyard sweetheart?"

"A most suitable beau," Rachel answered, "provided that I were struck on the head by a boulder and rendered insensible for the rest of my life."

"He's addled?" CW asked.

"Blissfully ignorant of life's drama and grandeur."

"The town idiot," Maude corrected. "Why his people allow him to wander the streets alone is beyond me. I've often held that Herbert's entire line must be afflicted, each to his own dark angel. Truth be told, I wouldn't be at all surprised if the solution to Boy-Allen's mystery were to be found with that seedy lot."

"That's cruel, Mother," Rachel argued. "Herbert's no Edison, but he's a decent enough boy who has a perfect right to walk on public streets. If he is the laughingstock of the community, why, we ought to have more laughingstocks in Bellemont. Herbert has a good heart. You should know that as well as anyone, Mother."

"The fact that the boy can perform simple tasks is no excuse to allow him out and about at all hours."

"Mother, he helped you out of the mud and carried those packages of yours half a mile in the rain!"

"And I offered to pay him for his trouble, if you'll recall."

"Mother!" Rachel cried. "For goodness sakes. Herbert doesn't know the difference between a dollar and a dog bone. You might've invited him indoors, at least until it stopped raining. Would that have been so great an imposition? Honestly now?"

"We've had this discussion before, young lady," Maude replied, her voice becoming testy. "I won't allow you to draw me into any further argument concerning my behavior towards that boy. I acknowledged his good deed and offered a more than generous compensation when, in truth, I'd found the entire incident quite embarrassing. In hindsight, I'd have been better served to leave those packages where they fell. Beatrice and the other club ladies thought I'd lost my mind."

Rachel burst out laughing. "Why, Mother, how ever could they tell?"

A motor horn blared just outside.

Rachel went to the front door for a look. Marie heard her shout, "My God! That idiot ran the child over! Somebody call a doctor!"

Rachel went out, CW directly behind her.

Marie rushed onto the back porch and down around to the front where she saw a green Franklin cabriolet stalled at the curb and a pudgy fellow climbing out from behind the wheel, waving his derby hat.

When Rachel screamed Henry's name, Marie felt a chill sweep over her and she felt faint for half an instant. Then little Henry crawled on his hands and knees from underneath the front bumper of the automobile, dirt and oil covering him head to toe. Cissie ran out of the yard from beneath the fig tree and grabbed Henry by the wrist, jerking him away from the motorcar. The man yelled at her, "Goddamn kids! Are you crazy? Christ Almighty! Why, I ought to — "

Rachel rushed straight out the gate to the man, and slapped him. "How dare you speak to a child like that!"

Stunned, he took a step backward, staring at Rachel with amazement, his cheek crimson from her blow.

"How dare you!" she shrieked.

Scared silly, Marie ran up the sidewalk to Henry who was crying, hugged tightly by Cissie, his grimy face streaked with tears. Kneeling beside the children, she found one of Henry's elbows was skinned raw, his new trousers torn at the knee, but he was not seriously injured. Marie felt her own legs. She realized she was crying and hadn't even known it. Cissie was weeping, too, and Lili had raced to the fence carrying an armful of headless dolls, her eyes wide as saucers. Harry had warned her about letting Henry run in the street, as if that was at all necessary. She knew about autos and children, thank you very much, dear!

"Oh, honey, you're all right. You're just fine." She hugged Henry close and tried not to let him see her tears. Her hands were shaking. She looked up at the driver. "What on earth happened? Didn't you see him?"

By now, Rachel stood nose to nose with the driver of the green automobile, rage flush on her face. She shouted, "Are you insane? Why, we ought to have you arrested this very instant!"

"Aw, you're nuts, lady! That youngster run right out in front of my new motor. I damned near broke my ankle stomping on the brake. Y'all ought to be the ones apologizing to me."

"Good grief," Marie shouted up at him, her tears abating. "You almost killed my son!"

Rachel became furious. "Shut your mouth, mister crazy man, or I'll slap you silly!"

The man backed up another step. "You hit me again, darling, and I'll see you in court."

"You'll be lucky to get there!" CW shouted, arriving onto the sidewalk just behind Rachel, his fists clenched. "I'll gladly finish this right now! What do you say?"

"You stay right there," the man warned weakly.

Maude came out onto the porch, still wearing her apron. As frightened as she was angry, Marie huddled with her children, trying both to console Henry and discover what exactly had happened. All he had done so far was mumble about one of Lili Jessup's dolls running away from the circus. Rachel moved toward the man who immediately backed up against the Franklin, his eyes flicking back and forth from Rachel to CW and Maude.

The man drew a handkerchief from his vest pocket and used it to wipe the sweat from his brow as Maude said to him, "I'd appreciate an explanation, sir."

He blew his nose into the handkerchief. "Ain't nothing to explain, ma'am. That youngster there run under my car and almost got himself killed."

"The man's insane, Mother," Rachel asserted. "First he nearly ran little Henry down like a dog, then he had the fat nerve to curse the poor child, scaring him half to death. I'm sure we have grounds to have him thrown in jail. Mother, go put a call into Sheriff Lloyd before this lunatic tries to escape. I know he'd be properly furious."

"You ought to get married, honey," the man shot back at Rachel. "Learn yourself some manners."

"Maybe I'll teach you something myself," CW said, bluffing forward.

"I refuse to converse with a raving maniac," Rachel added, turning her back. "Mother?"

Wind riffled Maude's apron and fanned more dust into the yard. "I suppose we ought to put a call into the sheriff," she said. "Raising voices just turns sense into nonsense."

"I've heard my share of nonsense, all right," the man said, sliding back behind the wheel of the green Franklin. "You're all nuts."

Maude turned to Marie and asked, "How is the child, dear? Is he injured?"

Still shaking with fear and relief, Marie looked at Henry and wiped a patch of axle grease off his forehead with her fingers, then gave him a warm hug to reassure him that he'd survived to enter the three-legged sack race at the fairgrounds later on that afternoon. "He's just fine. Aren't you, dear?" She hugged him again as he whimpered. "We'll put a little Unguentine on his scrapes and he'll be good as gold. He wasn't hurt badly. Just frightened."

"That's good."

Angry now, too, Marie added, "I just think everyone drives too fast on this street. It scares me half to death. It's not safe to walk the children."

"I'll go put in the call myself," Rachel said, gleefully. "Nobody should be allowed to drive like that."

"Aw, let's just forget it," the man said, pulling the door closed. "I ain't got time to talk with your cops. I got appointments in Wichita tomorrow. I wasted enough of the day in this damned town as it is. If the kiddie's not hurt, I say let bygones be bygones. I got no more beef about it, so long as my auto's not damaged."

He cranked the engine over and started it up.

"Mother, don't let this reptile drive off like that," Rachel protested. "He's a criminal. He ought to at least be forced to spend the night in jail." As the black exhaust cloud rose, she covered her mouth with the back of her hand and turned her head away.

"Come on indoors, honey," Marie said, helping Henry to his feet. "Let's get you patched up."

"Well, I suppose there's no further issue to take so long as Henry's fine and this man's willing to forgive and forget," Maude remarked, glancing at Marie once more. Then she lowered her voice and spoke directly to the man in the Franklin. "Children remain near and dear to our hearts here in Bellemont. Their health and well-being concerns us greatly. You'd be strongly advised to consider that the next time you hurry down one of our streets. The speed limit here is ten miles an hour and not all our citizenry are as disposed toward reason and sensibility as myself. Good day, sir."

Then Maude reversed herself and walked back up the stairs into the house.

"Good riddance, you old windbag," the man mumbled, sliding the car into gear. As the motorcar rolled forward, Rachel darted up and gave a kick to the rear fender.

"Hey!" the man shouted, leaning out the window. "Cut that out!"

— **4** —

Half-a-mile east of town, past P&B's cotton mill near the pinewoods along old Langston Road, lay the Panola fairgrounds in a grassy meadow of white oaks and shady cottonwoods. By late afternoon, when Marie arrived with Maude from College Street, hundreds of people already crowded long picnic tables and chow lines half-hidden in cook smoke under the leafy trees. Rachel and CW had driven over with the children at four o'clock, hoping to enter a few of the field contests. There were mud pits for tug-of-war teams dug out near the rodeo corrals, and chalklines cut and drawn for sprints and sack races and hammer throws. Cissie had won a sack race on Field Day at Brookfield School in Farrington the week Harry came home to sell the house on Cedar Street. She skinned a knee and her elbow and still won a blue ribbon. Today, she intended to win another. Likewise, Henry hoped to enter the three-legged race with little Abel, if he arrived in time. Telephoning Mrs. Kritt's house on Ninth Street after dinner, Marie was told that little Abel had gone off outdoors somewhere and hadn't yet come back, despite his favorite apple dumplings waiting on the table. Marie carried this worry with her to the fairgrounds.

Under the shade of a broad oak, she watched anxiously as Cissie stepped into a shabby gunny sack for the race she planned to win. Other children with equally worn gunny sacks lined up beside her, yelling and bragging of past triumphs. Rachel nervously lit a cigarette. CW clapped loudly. Maude fanned herself with a handkerchief. A skinny fellow in a striped shirt whom Marie remembered from Hooker's drugstore raised a pistol at the starting line.

"ON YOUR MARKS!"

Children in the crowd leaped and squealed.

"GET SET!"

Marie stood up, her heart fluttering with excitement. She nearly fainted whenever her children competed.

"GO!"

At the crack of the pistol, twenty-three valiant young sack racers were off. Dust flew violently along the track. Straight away, six children went down all together in a hilarious collision. The crowd of adults roared. Marie saw Cissie lunging forward among the lead pack, her pigtails flopping in the air. She shouted, "GO, HONEY! GO!"

A freckled-face boy stumbled and fell. A dark-haired boy tumbled to earth just beyond him. The leaders resembled Mexican jumping beans. Marie heard herself laughing and was surprised. Was she so excited for her daughter to win? Beside her, Rachel stamped out a smoldering Chesterfield and shouted encouragement while CW called for more speed. Half the pack was lost now in the dusty track, given over to defeat and laughter, rolling about hysterically like big June bugs. Cissie chugged forward, nearing the goal. A last boy collapsed as a pair of towheaded twins fell through the tape side by side at the finish line, a tie for the victory, Cissie just behind in third. The race was over. Everybody gave a big cheer for the contestants. Parents hurried to their children. Marie and Rachel and CW reached Cissie in time to help her struggle to her feet where she'd fallen just past the chalk.

"I lost, Momma!" Cissie moaned, as she rolled over in the grass, grimy sweat on her face. "I lost!" She kicked at the gunny sack to free herself.

"Oh, you did fine, honey! Just fine!"

A handsome man in a blue worsted suit and felt hat hurried to congratulate the two winners, all smiles and innocent bravado. The umpire, too, hustled toward them, blue ribbons in hand.

"Oh, don't get sore, dear," Rachel said, lifting Cissie out of her torn gunny sack. "It's just rotten luck. You did awfully well."

Marie brushed the dust off Cissie's shoulders. "You were wonderful, darling! Absolutely wonderful! Your father'll be very proud. You won a ribbon!" She gave her daughter a kiss.

"It was the race of the century!" CW enthused.

"Aw, phooey," Cissie grumbled, giving the dusty old gunny sack another kick. "Let's never talk about it again."

Rebuffing the umpire's attempt to give her a white ribbon, Cissie shot off in a huff toward the rodeo corral. Knowing her daughter's temperament, Marie let her go. Harry, too, hated to lose; whether ping-pong or billiards, it made no matter. When he lost, she had learned to avoid him for at least an hour or so. Only that and a warm cup of Horlick's malted milk soothed his bitterness.

"The poor dear," Rachel remarked, watching Cissie disappear into the great crowd. "I had no idea she'd be so cut up about losing a silly race. It's not as if there were scads of dough on the line."

"That's because you're no competitor," CW replied, biting the end off a five-cent cigar he'd had in his vest pocket. "When that fellow from Plaquemine beat me nine up last month at Springhaven, I was so sunk, I nearly threw my new Spalding clubs into the river."

"How childish," Rachel scolded. She turned to Marie. "Don't you agree that's silly?"

Marie smiled. "Well, my Uncle Boyd always says we ought to hope for the best, be prepared for the worst, and bear resolutely whatever happens. I can't imagine quitting something I enjoy just because I haven't done particularly well one day."

CW lit his cigar. "Oh, I haven't quit. On the contrary, I just learned Bobby Jones' overlapping grip, so I'm all geared up for another whirl next week with that same fellow. I've even placed a bet for a thousand berries, just to prove I'm no dub." He blew a smoke ring into the air. "I tell you, I can't lose." He darted forward to kiss Rachel on the ear.

"Oh, I can't bear it any longer," Rachel snapped, dodging a second kiss. She shook her head in disgust. "CW's skull's so big he'd tell the devil how to stoke a furnace." She took Marie by the arm. "Dear, let's go have some fried oysters. I'm really done in. CW can shift for himself."

"Aw, cut it out," CW laughed, lurching forward to take Rachel's arm. "You know I don't give a hang about anything but romance, don't you, darling?" He gave her a kiss on the cheek.

"Don't overplay your hand, dear," Rachel warned, squirming away, "if you have any desire to make love to me today. I have too much fondness for wealth and charm in a husband-to-be, qualities I've somehow yet to find in you."

"Now, darling — "

"And another thing — "

The midsummer heat lingered, slowing the pace of celebrants to a drifting passage from one entertainment to another. Cissie had gone off to see the rodeo ponies with Lili Jessup; Henry won a pair of nickel balloons at the penny pitch and popped them both straight away. Marie located Maude at the pie booth, chatting with Emily Haskins and sipping lemonade from a porcelain cup. She bought a lemonade for herself, and went off with Maude and Rachel who led CW about from contest to contest, pitting his skill against Bellemont's finest in games of strength and skill, praising his courage in competitions of all sorts. Somehow Marie felt reassured in the summer crowds, confident that she and the children were growing comfortable here and discovering true affections in those they met. If only Harry would come down to see them. She smiled, watching Rachel with CW. They were both happily afflicted with sex-madness. Once long ago, she and Harry had been, too, and though she had feared being inadequate to the task of womanhood, neither had her husband bounded out of bed in disgust. She watched Rachel now with CW and saw two young people with most of their lives ahead of them, and discovered she was secretly envious, for once she, too, had felt playful and joyous on a summer holiday. Where had it all gone?

"You must admit he's game for most everything," Marie suggested to Maude as CW removed his coat and joined a crowd of young men at the Test of Strength pole. "I admire his pluck."

"Pluck's got nothing to do with it," Maude sniffed. "Rachel's never content until she's proven to every other bachelor in this town that her choice in rejecting each one of them was correct. I feel sorry for the poor boy. If he's not willing to stand up to her, she'll have him driven to his own grave by sundown."

Marie watched Rachel hold CW's coat while he struggled to raise the sledgehammer. She kissed him for luck, then stood back as her beau swung down hard, launching the weight only halfway up the pole. CW laughed at the feeble result and took his coat back from Rachel who looked somewhat disappointed. They kissed again, more passionately than Marie's mother might have approved of, and walked off arm-in-arm in the direction of the shooting gallery.

"Love encourages him, I think, as it does us all, wouldn't you agree?"

"Rachel doesn't know the first thing about love," Maude said. "She flirts and curtsies for men she hardly knows, and when they're granted an audience with her, she treats them like children begging for candy. Never in her life has she offered herself with sincerity to a boy whose affections are genuine. If she were truly to fall in love, as a young woman ought to, I doubt she could bear the burden. She'd be petulant and scared. She'd cling to the poor fellow like a cat caught upside down in a tree and frighten him half out of his wits. In any case, it's not love Rachel wants at all. The responsibility would terrify her."

"Well, my mother always warned me that love's obligations can poison the heart against itself. She told me, 'To be true to another, we should first be true to ourselves, accept how we feel about the one we love and treat him always as we would have him treat us.' I've always regarded that as wise advice."

"Oh, I doubt Rachel sees herself as obligated to anyone but herself. When she's in love, it's Rachel around whom the world revolves, every affection directed naturally to her, every little kindness. I can't recall the last time she sent one of her gentlemen a gift of any sort, nor if she's ever written her affections to someone in a letter. Pure unconcealed selfishness guides her every action, and I'd be surprised to hear her gentlemen argue otherwise."

"And yet CW seems to be quite taken with her, wouldn't you agree?"

"I imagine he's infatuated beyond hope. Half the time he acts like a lovesick schoolboy," Maude replied, reaching into her bag for a handkerchief. "Mark my words, though, one day he'll come to his senses and that'll be the last we'll see of him." She blew her nose, then put the handkerchief away. "It's foolish for them to step out with each other, anyhow. For the life of me, I don't know what Rachel was thinking. After all, she knew he was Catholic."

At dusk, skyrockets showered the sky above the fairgrounds with color and noise. The crack of explosions echoed overhead as splintered rainbows arced across the evening, while children squealed with delight and adults wandered about in the dark and the voice of the figure-caller for a plain quadrille echoed from the pavilion: *Honor your partner … corners the same … head couples right and left through … promenade across … promenade back … change your ladies now!* A faint wind brushed across the meadow, bending stalks of dry grass and tossing in Marie's hair, carrying, too, a scent of summer she had forgotten since Farrington. A smell of fresh grass and wildflowers were loose in the warm summer night. As she watched Rachel and CW take the children to the chow line for barbecued hotdogs and potato salad under the boom and glare of bursting fireworks, Marie wondered where Harry was this night, if perhaps he might be thinking of her. Did he miss her, as she still

missed him? She knew Harry was no saint. Her heart did not permit
her that foolishness. No man has eyes only for the woman he marries.
Every so often, rumor and dark intuitions troubled her dreams and
gave her worry. Now and then, she grew angry and jealous and had
ugly thoughts that shocked her in the dark. Marie had read once in a
magazine that infidelity arises out of some unnamed hollowness in the
heart of the unfaithful. She had also overheard her own mother say
that a man who strays even once has a lump of coal in his chest where
his heart ought to be — something Marie did not believe was neces-
sarily true, at least not when applied to her Harry. His heart was good.
Not perfect, but kind and decent. When he was home, his eyes never
strayed from hers. The trust they shared between them was complete,
even when love's passion dimmed. What he did while away, she did not
know, nor did she care to know: moral sins, imagined or confirmed,
mortally wound a jealous heart. As often as she could, Marie tried to
believe in the good a man brings to a woman when he arrives on her
porchstep, flowers in hand. Her mother thought her foolish and naïve. She hadn't cared for Harry from the day they met at the Lake of
the Isles. She cared for him even less when Marie told her about the
selling of the house on Cedar Street and the proposed move to Bellemont. Her fury astounded everyone. She urged Marie to return to
the farm and swear never to see Harry again. She begged for the sake
of the children, for Marie's sake, and the entire Pendergast family.
Marie walked quietly out of her mother's house to the barn where
she asked Cousin Frenchy to drive her back into Farrington so that
she could begin packing that very afternoon. At the rail depot, the
morning Harry sent them to Bellemont, Marie tried her best to say
something kind to Harry, words to make this separation pleasant and
fair. She refused to cry and so she did not, even when he whispered a
last affection in her ear as the train whistle sounded. Her own anger
abated by apprehension and sorrow, she squeezed his hand softly
and closed her eyes and kissed his cheek and allowed her arms to fall
around his waist to let him know he was loved and would be missed
as much by his wife as by his children. As hopeless as it often seemed
these days, Marie understood that love had come into her world

by this man's yearning heart. Somehow, in her compassionate moments, Marie still believed she was meant to care for him her entire life, excusing his weaknesses, tolerating his vanities, encouraging her own love for him to grow daily, despite the distance. Was it cowardly to love simply for well-being? Perhaps, but Marie saw no dignity in loneliness for pride's sake.

The skyrockets flared brightly again on the purple summer sky, raining color down across the stars and disappearing near the evening horizon. A series of booming echoes followed and the crowds roared with delight while Marie wandered out across the grass, letting it brush against her skirt as she walked. She paused long enough to see a string of fire balloons ignited and set aloft by the Ladies Auxiliary, glowing orbs ascending slowly, slowly into the night sky, rising, drifting above the fairgrounds like sparkling fairies come to earth for a midsummer celebration. As the fire balloons disappeared high and faraway into the starry dark, Marie, alone now, beyond earshot of her children, strolled off under the leafy cottonwoods. The dance orchestra struck up a song back at the gaily decorated pavilion, and laughter swept out into the dark. A breeze brushed the dry tips of grass and washed across Marie's face, a pleasantly warm breeze, scent of sweet wildflowers and honey. Her girlhood was long behind her; nevertheless she felt young this evening, younger than she had in years, wayward while alone, yet not lonely. If Harry rode a train all night to see her, she would welcome him back into her arms gladly, whisper old affections in his ear, greet him with a kiss and a tear. He was her husband, and she wanted to love him dearly. Yet if he did not come back to Bellemont at summer's end, did not return to her and the children by harvest, still she would go on confident that life had not forsaken her. Therefore, as she strolled about in the summer grass, love's oldest music played in Marie's ear, a sweet sentimental melody of quiet confidence and private longing, a lingering song of hope and desire, fear and comfort, that rang in her heart all these years. Listening to this music, Marie was reminded why she had allowed Harold Louis Hennesey to take her hand in the cool darkness and lead her out behind Uncle Harlow's barn and steal a tender kiss under the autumn moon. In her life, love meant this to

Marie: a belief in beauty and tenderness and the everlasting good that comes from a gentle smile.

"There you are, dear!" Rachel cried, seeing Marie walk in under the electric lights outside the grand pavilion. "Mother was afraid you'd wandered off into the woods and become lost. We were just discussing a search party."

Marie felt herself blush. "I hadn't realized how late it was. I'm sorry." Had she been gone so long? She had enjoyed her freedom. It wasn't often she managed to rediscover it.

"Oh, it isn't late at all," Rachel enthused. "Why, I haven't even danced yet and my card is full."

CW held up a glass of fruit punch. His eyes looked weary, his straw hat tipped slightly askew. "Would you like me to get you something to drink? Rachel's been sending me back and forth to the punch bowl all evening just so I won't notice the recruiting for her dance card."

"Oh, I have not," Rachel argued. "I'm not that kind. In fact, I've turned down many more offers than I've accepted." She turned to Marie. "CW's quite the jealous sort, you know. If I'd known six months ago, I doubt I'd have encouraged his attentions."

"Is that so?" Marie laughed.

"Wait 'til I marry you, darling," CW said, leaning over to give Rachel a kiss, "then you'll really see the mess you're in."

The evening wind was rising now, scattering flecks of dried grass. Marie looked up at the grand old dance pavilion, constructed like a wooden carousel with a shingled cupola on top and a balustraded gallery with broad white staircases at the four cardinal points of the compass. Banners and Independence Day flags and pennants flapped wildly along the rooftop overhead. Wherever she looked, people crowded the gallery railing. Marie felt festive and lively herself.

"Where are my children?" she asked, brushing a strand of hair off her face. "I hope we haven't lost them." Given half a chance, Cissie would be on a train to Timbuktu. Somehow the joyful atmosphere of the fairgrounds had beaten back her worries over Boy-Allen's killer, but that didn't mean she'd entirely forgotten.

"Well, your lovely daughter's been eating sugar cookies hand over fist with Lili Jessup by the punch bowl," Rachel replied, taking CW's glass for a sip. "I thought she'd be full as a tick from the hotdogs and chunks of cream pie she ate for supper, but apparently I was wrong. And last I saw, poor little Henry was sleeping in Mother's lap at the Ladies Auxiliary. I expect they're both ready to go home soon."

Indoors, the orchestra began playing "Waltz Me Around Again, Willie" to a great ovation.

"Let's go inside," Marie suggested, when the wind gusted once more. "Shall we? I hear the decorations are wonderful." And she desperately wanted to see the dancers and hear the music, be with people now, gay and laughing.

"Now that's a swell idea," CW agreed, taking Rachel by the arm and hugging her tightly to his side. "I'm in just the mood to tickle the floor. Darling, do you hear what the band's playing? Why, that's our theme song."

"Isn't CW a fine boy?" Rachel remarked, as they walked through the grass toward the east staircase. "And he dances like Vernon Castle."

"Before his smash-up, of course," CW corrected, a gleam in his eye.

"I have no doubt he can waltz with a glass of water on his head," Marie remarked playfully. Just ahead of her, the wide stairs were draped in bunting and gleaming with new white paint. She could scarcely wait to go inside. Was Jimmy Delahaye here tonight? She felt breathless and bold once again. Perhaps she would dance if asked. Harry might not approve, but he wasn't here, was he? And it had been years since he'd waltzed with her. Despite everything else, she had a right to smile, didn't she?

"Now, promise you'll keep that under your hat, won't you?" CW told Marie. "I wouldn't want the other girls to cut in on my sweet. Doesn't she look radiant tonight?"

"Of course she does. You'd better keep your eye on her. There are wolves all around here tonight. I think both of you ought to watch out."

Rachel giggled. "That hideous Amy Keene and her gang of thieves already gave CW the once-over by the punch bowl just to stir me up, though he's much too swell for the chewing-gum set."

"And, boy, were you sore!" CW observed, reaching the bottom steps under a tall glowing lamp pole. "I thought you were about to clean up on her."

"Oh, I was not," Rachel snorted. She turned to Marie. "He's utterly wrong, you know. I was just queening my public, that's all. Why, I'm perfectly harmless this evening."

"Like a black widow spider!" CW laughed, as he marched them both up the staircase through the gallery crowds into the noisy pavilion.

On a humid evening long ago, a gentle silver light shone upon the dark waters of Lake Minnetonka where seventeen-year-old Marie Alice Pendergast stood by the dock station at Excelsior watching the summer moon rise over Big Island Park. Tickets to the steamer "Minneapolis" were ten cents apiece for the trip across to the amusement park and back again, and Harry Hennesey purchased two while Marie listened to the careening rollerskaters in the rink above the promenade and the shrill ferry boat whistles out on the lake. Crowds of tourists from the Hotel La Paul mingled about the docks, men in strawboaters smoking fat cigars, women chattering together like birds in a thicket. Marie had already enjoyed the forty-minute ride from downtown St. Paul on the electric railway through the swampy woods of Deephaven and Purgatory and Vine Hill, with those pretty cottages on the inlets, and distant ferries ablaze with electric lights. Harry had given cheerfully casual handwaves to people along the tracks and comforted a teary-eyed child with a jam-stained blouse by sharing his sack of lemon candies. He looked so brash and handsome in his new navy-blue serge suit, Marie found herself smiling from St. Paul to Excelsior Station.

Aboard the "Minneapolis," Harry performed a clever coin trick for a family of tourists from North Dakota and declared lovely Marie Pendergast his inspiration. She blushed and felt her shy young heart pierced with joy. This season already, Emeline had boys call on her all the way from town, riding to the Chamberlain farm on horseback with a fistful of daisies and chocolate drops that Aunt Hattie ate after she'd sent the boys away. All spring and summer, Violet snuck out after dark to kiss Orson McCardell under the old apple tree on Falls Road. But until Harry had come into her life by the boat docks at the Lake of the Isles, Marie had no boy to swoon over, no dreamy thoughts of tender reassurance at bedtime. That left-out feeling evaporated with Harry's quick and confident smile, the pluck in his step, the innocent flutter of his eyelids as he handed her a bouquet of red carnations and kissed her blushing cheek.

At Big Island Park, Marie persuaded Harry to break from the flossy crowd on the Main Walk to stroll under the trellised pergola where light from the great Electric Tower splintered and dimmed, and dance music from the casino bandshell serenaded the wooded dark. As they walked about, Harry directed her gaze across the lake waters to the distant lamplit façade of Lucian Swift's summer home, Katahdin, and the elegant grounds of Frank Peavey's Highcroft at Breezy Point. He described the history of the northern woods and the clever Indians who camped and hunted along the shores of the big water, then guided Marie to a bench at Point Charming where he held her hand and expressed his genuine affection for the girl she was and the woman he declared she'd one day become. Fretful of uttering a silly word, or acting too proper, Marie sat quietly by his side, trembling like a dove, one hand warmly entwined with his, the other grasping the red carnations close to her breast as she prayed he saw her strength, a serene and considered devotion to one who would care for her and keep her forever close at heart.

Amber light from dozens of Japanese lanterns flickered high in the rafters of the Bellemont pavilion above all the people Marie Hennesey knew in town, knotted on the crowded dance floor or beside the busy punch bowl, drinks and cookies in hand. The orchestra from Shreveport played leisurely. Across the buffed pine floor, Idabelle Collins did a shuffling Fox Trot with a newsdealer from downtown named Clinton Morrison whose teeth bore the unfortunate stains of tobacco smoke. Behind them, Lucius Beauchamp shamblefooted with Verna Grieg from the beauty salon on South Main. Near the bandstand, Rachel and CW danced cheek to cheek, exquisitely in love. Marie sighed. Henry had gone home for the evening with Maude, while Cissie and Lili went back with Mildred Jessup who told Marie she was licked from carving up chickens all afternoon for the barbecue and thought she might have a touch of ptomaine. Alone now in a gay crowd of Civic Garden Club ladies by the south exit, Marie sat in a cane chair by the wall and tapped her toe to the jazzy rhythm of the orchestra. If only …

"Would you care to dance, honey?"

Looking up, Marie found Jimmy Delahaye beside her, dressed like a gentleman in a tux with a white boutonniere on his peaked lapel. He smelled of Wildroot hair tonic, a hint of gin on his breath. His jaw was firm, his bearing confident. Truth be told, Marie thought him the handsomest man at the pavilion. Her heart fluttered.

"That is," Delahaye added, a twinkle in his eye, "if you're still spry enough."

"Why, Mr. Delahaye, how nice to see you," Marie stammered, her throat tightening. Was he serious? Should she? "You know, I haven't danced in years. I'm sure I'd be quite an awful partner."

"Nonsense," he replied, smoothing his hair. "I'd be honored."

She bit her lip. "Are you sure? I wouldn't want to trip you up." Perhaps she couldn't dance a step any longer. Perhaps she ought not to try. What would Harry think if he found out? Did she even care? No, not tonight she didn't.

He arched an eyebrow, then offered a firm hand. "Please?"

"Well, if you insist." She blushed like a schoolgirl as she rose to her feet, knees trembling. She was excited. "You are my boss, after all."

"Yes, ma'am."

On Delahaye's arm, Marie waded hesitantly into the sea of dancers, her feet unsure of the new steps. Timid and embarrassed, she glided into motion with her handsome partner. He felt strong and certain, and in his arms, her own confidence grew. Overhead, the paper lanterns glowed like yellow moons above the revolving dancers. Jimmy Delahaye's hands were firm and warm, his eyes alight, perspiration visible on his brow and upper lip as he slid easily from step to step, maneuvering them away from the band to where the light was dimmer, the din of the pavilion crowd less pronounced. Her anxiety increased, even as desire bloomed within. Delahaye drew her closer to his chest and she felt her heart warm, too.

"Honey, you step like an angel," he said to Marie, as he led her about the floor. His breath was hot, but not unpleasant.

"Thank you," she replied, feeling intoxicated by the orchestra. She adored music. On Cedar Street she played the Victrola while cleaning house and sang aloud to herself in the attic. Emeline took piano lessons when she was a girl and Violet played the organ at church on Sundays. Both made a joyful sound, yet just as often Marie felt blue when the music was the loveliest, a strange and subtle discomfort inexpressible as a butterfly tickling her heart.

"I have to confess that I paid Frank Merritt ten dollars to keep his band playing as long as I stay on my feet tonight," Delahaye told Marie, guiding her back toward the crowded middle of the pavilion where a hundred dancers blotted out the pine floor. She loved dancing with him. She loved his firm grasp, how his hand felt on her lower back, how they seemed to glide in step together here and there about the floor. It had been years since she and Harry had gone dancing. Marie supposed it no longer interested him, business concerns flooded his life now, but whenever a waltz or a Fox Trot played on the radio set, she thought about those wonderful ballrooms he used to take her to, all the music and dancing they'd enjoyed together.

She told him, "Idabelle says you caught cold yesterday. Are you sure you ought to be here at all?" She peeked up, offering a coy smile. Could he see how she enjoyed his touch?

He danced Marie about in a gentle arc. "Tell the truth, I've been slugging quinine since breakfast to work it off."

Marie smiled. "Is that wise?"

"Idabelle doesn't think so," Delahaye replied with dusky eyes, his speech almost languid. Marie liked it, though, almost as if he were murmuring to her alone in the dark. "When I showed her the bottle this morning, she laughed so hard I thought she'd lose a filling."

Across the floor, CW and Rachel abruptly quit dancing as the orchestra began a waltz. Rachel walked ahead of him without looking back so Marie guessed they had taken a disagreement over another triviality and were heading out of doors to quarrel again. A pack of young men in black waistcoats rushed gleefully through the pavilion and out the south exit. Where were they going?

Changing his step for the waltz, Delahaye spoke softly in Marie's ear, "Honey, I've been busting to dance with you all evening."

His breath tickled, and she blushed. "You're teasing, aren't you?"

"No, ma'am," Delahaye replied with a smile. "Smartest thing I did all year was hiring you to the restaurant."

Marie's heart skipped as they traversed the crowded dance floor. She felt crazy and fluttery. Her knees wobbled as she danced. Her breath felt short, her eyes watered, and she was smiling widely and knew it. When had she last felt this flush with Harry? "Well, I have to tell you I'm very grateful. Everyone's been terribly decent to me since I began." That wasn't at all what she wanted to say, but it was what came out. Now she was a bashful schoolgirl again, afraid to look that charming boy in the eye and say she liked him.

"Lucius and Idabelle adore you."

"Oh, they've both been ever so sweet," Marie said, locating Lucius with Verna Grieg across the pavilion at the punch bowl, then Idabelle and Clinton Morrison waltzing with a crowd of older dancers in the lantern shadows. Everyone seemed so congenial together. Why was she alone so nervous? "I realize my half-a-day's have been inconvenient to all of you."

"Don't give it another thought," Delahaye said, his thick voice growing huskier. "You know it's your brains I'm paying for, not your hours at the desk."

A fellow in a checked coat with a wide-brimmed straw hat came up and tapped Delahaye on the shoulder. "Cut in on the pretty lady?"

Delahaye shot him a fierce glare. "On your way, Bob."

"Sorry."

As the fellow slunk off to try his luck elsewhere, Delahaye drew Marie close enough to his chest that she could feel his breathing and the heat off his skin. "I refuse to share you tonight. Do you mind?"

She smiled. "Not at all."

Marie glanced away just as Delahaye leaned his face near and whispered beside her ear, "You have lovely hair, honey." He drew a deep breath through his nose. "Smells like what my sister Edith used to wear, gardenia or some such."

"Lilac," Marie corrected, feeling herself close to swooning. He'd aroused her unawares and she was shocked to discover how she felt. Yet she remained close in his arms, not relaxed but comfortable, and far too happy to pull away. Where was her heart tending? Too often

Harry had made love to her when she felt cold and tired; too often he was unwilling to give her desire a chance to rise and meet his own. When had she last felt so feminine as she did tonight?

Delahaye hovered closer still. "Harry's a damned lucky fellow. It's not easy working close to you."

Marie felt his gin breath on her bare neck as he spoke and thought he was about to kiss her and imagined that if he did, she'd likely faint and cause a scene, so she began humming the orchestra melody as if it were the most natural thing in the world to do just then. She dared not look Delahaye in the eye, because she felt feverish with desire and desperate to be kissed.

"Go with me to a picture, won't you?" Delahaye asked, gently squeezing her hand. "Maybe one night this week?"

When she felt his lips brush her forehead, she raised her chin ever so slightly as her own lips quivered. She looked into his eyes, saw them gleam. Woozy and confused, she sighed. "Oh, I don't — "

"Look, I'm not trying to get fresh with you, honey," Delahaye said, offering a boyish smile. "You know, I just thought you might like to get out of the house some evening, go downtown with me and shoot the moon. Where's the harm in that? We'd have a good time, and it wouldn't cost you a bull nickel."

Marie had no idea what to say. Why had she agreed to this dance? What did she think she was doing now? Did she want to kiss him or not? She was terrified by the pounding of her own heart. What should she say? "Well, the children have been such a share lately," she offered, meekly. "I'm afraid Maude hasn't had a moment to herself this entire month, so you see I swore an oath yesterday we'd stay out of her hair all week long." Now that she'd thoroughly humiliated herself, she peeked up at him to see the same disarming smile. She believed he was staring straight into her heart. She felt both panicked and flushed with sexual passion. She had no idea where she was any longer.

"Then we'll make it some other time, all right?" Delahaye suggested, his blue eyes glistening in lantern light as he danced her in a slow circle. She was too frightened to speak. Did he think she was lonely this evening, so wanting of a man's touch, his whispered affections, his kiss? Was she so obvious? How humiliating that would be! Was it true?

And did Jimmy Delahaye imagine that Harry, gone off alone to the city, had gone, too, from Marie's heart? Surely not. She realized now that she ought to offer a word or two to Delahaye, something clever or wise to express clearly both her appreciation for his sweet affection and her faith in Harry's return. That failing, Marie was quite certain she would need to walk away from the pavilion very soon now and lie down beside her children in the small bedroom by the chinaberry tree where she knew she belonged. *Oh, Harry! Where are you?*

Honeymoon couples in rented canoes stirred the moonlit waters off Big Island Park where Marie and Harry strolled the lakeshore, trading glances across the summer dark. Loons cried in the marshes. Inland, a gala crowd swarmed the rollercoaster and the noisy shooting galleries. Marie hoped desperately to dance with Harry at the casino. One spring night, Violet had run away to a tea dance at the La Salle Hotel and done the two-step with a suave young Jewish dramatist from New York who lent a sympathetic ear to romantic yearnings. When she'd told her story in Marie's bedroom after dinner the next day, Emeline had refused to acknowledge that embrace of courtship belovéd of choreography and rhythm, but Marie had understood very well: the heart seeks proportion in all things; unobserved, love has less gravity, while blesséd touch rekindles the divine order.

Late that evening, she and Harry crossed the tree-shaded lawns of Big Island Park toward the bright casino, stopping briefly for orange soda and popcorn at a refreshment booth where they watched the lighted rollercoaster rasp and rattle up the steep track, high into the night sky, packed with screeching young riders. Marie hummed a dance melody for Harry as music from the bandshell beckoned, and hinted her desire by shameless flirtation. She needn't have begged, after all. Finishing his soda pop, Harry took Marie by the hand and led her through the wild crowd to the casino pavilion, sweeping past the potted palms and the orchestra in the bandshell and out onto the dance floor, his hand hardly pressing her fingers as he brought her to the center of the pavilion under the crystal chandelier and into harmony with the other dancers whirling about the floor to a brisk Viennese waltz Marie had never heard before but whose beautiful melody she could hum even now.

What dreams come true? Dance after dance late into that summer night, hardly a whisper passed between them: Harry too proud for words, Marie hushed by a secret peace deep in her heart. By midnight, the lights had dimmed and the other dancers had either departed Big Island Park by steamboat or retired to the damp lawns to be intimate while she and Harry remained in the center of the dance floor, close in each other's arms, even as the orchestra quit playing for the evening and the musicians packed up and left. All Marie could hear was distant laughter from beyond the casino and the soft scraping of Harry's shoes on the polished wood floor. Alone in the ballroom as the ceiling lights winked out one by one, Harry Hennesey whispered ardent affections in her ear, words she'd expected to hear, words she hadn't, promises he'd keep, ones he would not. Aboard the last ferry boat crossing Lake Minnetonka for Excelsior and St. Paul that night, Marie Alice Pendergast made a promise to herself as well, a promise to which she would swear to hold true wherever she went with his name, a vow of fidelity and trust to keep her own heart honest, her affections pure, so long as thoughts of that summer night at Big Island Park reminded her of precious romance first discovered.

Marie stood on the pavilion's south gallery facing into a pleasantly cool breeze. Delahaye had developed a stitch in his rib and tugged at his linen collar with a complaint about the heat indoors, so they'd quit the dance floor and went out together. Rachel and CW hadn't returned from their squabble and Marie supposed they'd already left the Panola fairgrounds for home. Many other dancers had also wandered off the floor as a draft passing in and out of the pavilion tussled with the Japanese lanterns and the strings of electric lights. Marie could see people down in the shadowy meadow. Somewhere nearby, a gaggle of young teens shared a joke, voices tittering laughter on the breeze. She felt a sudden shiver as Delahaye stepped close beside her. A gust stirred in her hair and her dress fluttered. She held the skirt down with the back of one hand and brushed the hair out of her eyes with the other.

Delahaye remarked, "Lucius came to work today smelling like a distillery. He's probably been in with the gents most of the evening. I'll bet you Verna's gone home with Archie Pollard. He doesn't have much gumption, but he's straight as a rule. Spends every Sunday reading the Bible, which never has made him a big hit with the ladies. Verna thinks Lucius needs a good jacking-up and she knows Archie won't try to make love to her."

"I imagine I ought to be getting home, too," Marie told him, as she considered the hour. How late could she be out? What was expected of her in this place, a married woman residing with her mother-in-law? "I'd guess it's awfully late, and I wouldn't care to be locked out. I'm still a guest in Maude's house." Sunday morning, she'd sing hymns between Maude and Rachel in the fourth row of pews, raising her voice in song to the Lord in appreciation of all the joy in her life. Harry had a good strong voice himself. That was something she'd noticed straightaway.

Delahaye said, "Did you know Lucius used to give Harry a hell of a razzing when they were in school? Sometimes he laid it on pretty thick, too, but Harry wouldn't get bitter. He told everyone Lucius was all right, except for that one bug. Harry was an awfully good sport. I suppose he always knew that Lucius was all beef and no brains, and that he'd wind up a mediocrity. Of course, some of the boys around here thought Harry Hennesey was swell-headed because he wouldn't go out and raise a lot of Cain like the rest of us, though I can see now that was just a misapprehension on our part. Truth is, a fellow of his type had to get out of here to make good."

"Don't feel that way about it," Marie said, staring off into the evening wind. Her stomach fluttered, her knees still trembled. What if Delahaye took her hand now? What if he kissed her? "Why, it's such a foolish thing to say. After all, Harry's father had just passed away, and you know they were very close. I remember Harry suffered quite a deal over his decision not to return to Texas. He's always spoken fondly of his life here and the friends he grew up with."

"Oh, cut it out, honey," Delahaye chuckled, as he took a cigar out of his vest pocket and bit off the end. When he smiled at Marie, his eyes sparkled in the lantern light. She believed he was the handsomest fellow in town. "Harry's never been full of sentimental prune juice. He knew there's something doing all the time in the city, and he worked like a nigger to get there. I admire him for that. I don't know that I could make the grade where he's gone. I'm probably too thick in the head. Even if he overplays his hand one day, I'll lay you he won't come back here. And why the hell should he? Any fellow that's ever grown up in this town's wanted to strike it off his record, get himself elsewhere someday. Of course, that's hard to do because usually no place else wants him. He can't fit in. He's stuck being a simple fish from a bum little town. But not Harry Hennesey. He knows his own mind, and he'll never come back. Not in this life. You can't make a steamroller out of a racing car."

"Well, I believe he's still very strong for all of you," Marie persisted, knowing as she spoke that if Delahaye chose to kiss her, she might let him. If he took her hand, she'd wrap her fingers in his and lean close so he could smell her perfume.

Delahaye lit the cigar. "Don't bet your teeth against it."

Marie watched him exhale a ragged smoke ring into the breeze. She felt excited and lonely together. She wished Delahaye would lead her off somewhere into the dark to kiss her under the cottonwood trees, yet she also wished she were home writing letters or lying in bed with her children. Why had Harry left her here like this? Why didn't he love her like he had so many years ago? What was so wrong with how she'd loved him all these years?

Somewhere in the dark meadow, beyond sight of the gallery, a sudden peal of laughter fluttered across the night, a girl's voice carrying uninhibited joy, a summer giddiness. *When Marie was young, she and Violet and Emeline would sneak out after midnight in the summer months to play in the deep pinewoods surrounding the farm whose branches were filled with songbirds and noisy squirrels. Just across the creekbed, up a short rise and behind a dense thicket, Violet had discovered a hidden meadow, a secret clearing of clover and wildflowers shrouded in pine branches where wild cats hunted and three pretty young fairies slid off their nightshirts and slippers to dance together naked hand-in-hand in a perfect circle, swearing oaths to romance and beauty and eternal sisterhood. Binding tiaras of snapdragons and daisies into each other's hair like ancient wreaths of laurel, their bare skin nearly translucent under the silver moon, they would share stories and private confidences until dawn shone faintly in the treetops. Then all three girls would dress hurriedly and race back through the dry creek and the thick dark woods, across the wheat fields that led home again before sunrise. Their special game was a confidence Marie never in her life shared with anyone else — not her family, not Harry. Nor did the other girls ever speak of it once the game was over and they'd each grown up. In fact, poisoned by a hidden spider in an old sugar bowl, Violet took their secret to her grave in the summer of 1916. Emeline never mentioned it, either*

— even alone with Marie up in her uncle's attic on the morning of Emeline's wedding to Roy Gallup. So many summer nights spent in that pretty meadow, a perfect secret preserved forever like perfume on parchment, a childhood trust never broken.

Marie gazed out across the dark meadow where the summer grass bent low in the warm evening wind and wondered how much of that sweet fairy-child still dwelled in her heart. Did she yet hold adventure and romance in such esteem? Was there somewhere in her life a gold heart-locket waiting to be opened, its lovely inscription still to be read? A quick breeze swirled up dust into her face, causing her eyes to water. Suddenly she felt as though she ought to take off alone, run again in the long grass, remove her shoes and feel the earth between her toes, listen to the wind blow in the trees across the fields nearby, listen for songbirds and the low rustling of wild cats in the thicket, laughter of fairies at play under the summer moon.

"How about taking a walk?" Delahaye asked, gently resting a hand on her shoulder.

Marie felt her heart leap. She trembled and her mouth went dry. What should she do? Was it wrong to let herself behave like this? Could she be forgiven for longing to be a girl once more in the summer dark? Why was love so fleeting and mean? Incredibly, she told him, "Yes, I'd like to."

They went down from the pavilion for a stroll in the grass under the cottonwood trees. They crossed into the shadows where the breeze rustled through the branches above. Marie had never felt so anxious in the company of a man. Had many people seen them go? Once Morris Farwell had taken her on a buggy ride by moonlight out past Mitchener's duck pond. When she saw him tie off the reins, she knew he intended to kiss her and became so nervous she started laughing, which led him to take her home unkissed. But she wouldn't laugh to-night. She was sure of that.

Delahaye didn't speak for the longest while. He smoked his cigar and guided Marie with a hand gently on her lower back. Her head swam and she felt almost feverish. They walked for about five minutes farther into the dark under the cottonwood trees, then stopped and listened to the breeze crossing the evening air. Harry was a thousand miles away tonight, Marie thought, as she felt Delahaye put his arms on her shoulders to draw her close. The breeze ruffled her skirt. She smelled the tobacco on his breath when he brought his face to hers and he was smiling. She kissed him.

Just once.

A schoolgirl's kiss, brief yet not entirely chaste.

Then she hid her face. He kissed her forehead and held her close to his chest and murmured something she couldn't hear and they stood together for a long while letting the evening breeze wash over them across the dark. Marie felt both relief and shame. She did not say a word. Why had she done this? A man who was not her husband, not Harry, had kissed her and she'd kissed him back with scant hesitation and had not run off afterward. Neither had she extended any further affection to him, but merely allowed herself into his arms. What would become of her now? Had one kiss led her astray? She wondered why her wandering heart felt so anxious and alive. She might stand here in the dark all night and watch young lovers hurry by toward a distant rendezvous and know something about their urgency she'd forgotten until a few moments ago. Why had she waited so long to remember? When would she wander off into the dark again? Would Harry go with her? Perhaps she'd invite him, but only once more. And if Jimmy Delahaye called? She might answer again.

Soon enough it grew late and Marie found herself feeling thoroughly self-conscious and missing her children and told Delahaye she ought to go.

"Well, let me drop you at home, honey," he offered, as she stepped away from him.

"Oh, that's not necessary," Marie replied. Her passion subdued by the hour, now she felt sad and weary, ready for sleep. It had been a long and fitful day, and she was glad it was over. "It's not far and I know my way."

"Say, I hope you don't feel I was doing Harry dirty by trying to drag you off to a picture show."

Marie shook her head, embarrassed by her own timidity and her foolish flirtations. What on earth had gotten into her? "Of course not."

"Honey, let me run you home." Delahaye flicked his cigar off into the dirt. "Please? I don't care for the idea of you out alone so late by yourself. I'll bet Harry wouldn't either. Nobody knows what the hell happened to Boy-Allen, whether it was a nigger or some maniac, but until we do, well, you never know what can happen, do you? I say, there's no sense guessing."

Marie smiled. "Well, all right. It's sweet of you to offer. Thank you."

— 5 —

Near midnight, Delahaye let Marie off by the curb at Maude's house and motored away alone into the dark. It was quiet now, the street empty, only crickets audible in the summer night. Marie opened the small gate to Maude's backyard. A breeze fluttered through the wash that hung on the line, items Rachel had forgotten to bring indoors. Bits of dry grass skittered across the ground at her feet. She could hear Mr. Slopey shuffling inside his stall. The Jessup's collie began barking as Marie ducked under the linen she would have to re-wash tomorrow for Maude and went to the back steps where she removed her shoes, lifted the latch on the screen door, and stepped quietly up into the kitchen. Indoors, the air was humid and still. Marie loosened the top two buttons on her blouse and went to the sink, guided by moonlight that reflected off the glass cupboards and rows of Mason jars along the wall beside the pantry. Sometime since dinner, Maude had baked sweetcakes and gingerbread; their warm and spicy scent filled the small kitchen, reminding Marie how long she had been absent that evening. She ran the cold water and slipped her hands under the faucet, letting them soak nearly to a chill. After drying them on a cotton towel beside the sink, a turn in the hallway past the kitchen brought Marie to her bedroom where she saw a note beside the door. She picked it up and brought it back to the kitchen and switched on the light above the sink. The note read:

> Mrs. Kritt tells us that Abel had been lost in the woods but is safe at home now, though he doesn't seem to be himself just yet. They intend to see a doctor tomorrow. She thanks us for our concern.

This gave Marie a peculiar feeling which sent her quickly to the bedroom. Easing the door open, she peeked in and looked at her children as they lay there together in the bed beneath the open window, arm-in-arm, cuddling like tired kittens. Henry's soft breath feathered his sister's hair; Cissie dreamt, her eyelids stirring. Marie wondered what happened to little Abel, and what his poor mother must be feeling just now. All she prayed for each night was that her children be safe and happy. Too often in the modern world that simple desire seemed elusive. How would we ever survive if our children were not able to be safe at play? And who was that phantom haunting this town? That dark angel? If only she'd caught a glimpse of his face that night.

Gently, Marie closed the door and tiptoed ahead to the front parlor where she decided to read for a while until sleep called her to bed. Although she had danced all evening and walked more than three miles since dinner that afternoon, Marie felt more woozy than fatigued. She also felt strangely nervous, anxious somehow. Why had she gone off under the cottonwoods with Jimmy Delahaye? She'd kissed him and felt shameless and thought she might do it again if the opportunity were right. Or maybe not. Was it awful, what she had just done? Why had she done it? What had come over her? Rainbows of skyrockets and Japanese lanterns and elegant dancers swirled maddeningly in her head as she went to sit by the window where Maude had left an oil lamp burning on a stand against the night. There, cooled by the evening draft of nightblooming jasmine, Marie heard voices murmuring just a few yards away.

"A gentleman wouldn't hold such an opinion," came Rachel's petulant voice. "You only say that to injure me. Innocence offends the guilty heart. Why else would you persist with such petty viciousness?"

"Don't be childish, darling," CW drawled, his voice slurred with liquor.

Looking through the lace, Marie saw CW braced against the post, Rachel only a foot or so away. She saw CW kiss her, then slide away. Were they having a lover's tiff?

"If you use that word with me again this evening, I swear I will slap your smug little face. I will not be insulted on my own front porch."

A match flared in the dark. Moments later, cigarette smoke wafted in at the curtain lace. Rachel's voice followed, "Besides that, it's just not fair. Not fair at all."

"Oh, now I'm the villain, am I? That's a hoot!"

"I have no idea what you mean by that remark," said Rachel, flicking the burnt match into the rose bushes. "Why, I've defended your character on more occasions than I could possibly count, and to whose benefit? Certainly not my own. You have no idea how often I've had to explain your intentions away as innocent flirtations in order to preserve my reputation among my other admirers."

"Why, that's just it, isn't it? You're ashamed of me!"

"Of course I'm not!" Rachel folded her arms and put her back to CW.

"Why, you most certainly are!" CW cried, his voice barely under control. "You're so afraid your reputation is becoming soiled by being seen in my company. That's why you were reluctant to dance with me tonight. That's why we left early and followed that filthy alley most of the way back here afterward. It was fine to be escorted by me to the pavilion with your mother along beside you, but the moment she left, you became terrified that somebody might conclude you'd stepped out with me in earnest, and we both know what sort of gossip that would incur, don't we?"

"If you choose to speak without any consideration as to my feelings," Rachel replied, "then I'd rather not discuss this any longer. I've never heard such rudeness."

Rachel faced the street and blew smoke from the cigarette into the night air. Hooking her little finger about the bottom of the lace, Marie nudged it aside for a better view. She was curious to know how these two fought, because it revealed how firmly their hearts were, or were not, bound to one another's. CW held a small silver flask in his right hand, unscrewing the cap slowly with his left. Both he and Rachel were staring into the road.

Across the room, Marie heard Rachel's radio set playing with the volume wound low, filtering Gershwin's jazz into the dark from some distant station on the Gulf Coast. CW took a drink from the flask, then spoke flatly. "Rachel, dear, I want to say something to you that is terrifically important, and I want you to listen very carefully. This has gone quite deep with me, do you understand?" He glanced across at her. "You see, I believe there are Negroes who enjoy more consideration in the vilest parishes of Louisiana than I've ever received in this household." He sipped from his flask. "Do you deny that?"

Marie was shocked, scarcely able to believe her ears.

Without raising her own voice in the slightest, Rachel replied, "That is the most disgusting thing I have ever heard, and a filthy lie as well. If you don't apologize this instant, I'll never forgive you."

"Darling, you know I'm no milquetoast, and I've no intention of getting down on my knees when I've never been treated as anything more than a stuffed coat in your mother's house."

"Then you can go climb a rose bush for all I care."

"Sweetheart, she despises me for reasons of religious conviction, a prejudice I find inexcusable for any true Christian man or woman. Were it not for the promise of our engagement, I'd hardly be able to tolerate her slurs. I'm surprised she hasn't accused me of murdering Boy-Allen as part of some ritualistic Catholic conspiracy."

She turned to face him. "What an ugly thing to say! Only your — "

"Rachel, I love you dearly, but love has its limits, shame being one of them. I'd never thought of myself as pious or reverential when conversation turned to religion. Spirituality, I was raised to believe, deferred to privacy and personal belief. No one has the right to judge another on matters of faith. I certainly would never have asked you to quote chapter and verse in defense of your own interpretation of the Lord's desire. Therefore, it's not fair for you to insist on my doing so, either for your benefit or your mother's. And, in any case, I won't."

Marie watched CW tip back his flask once more, then replace it in his jacket pocket. She was astonished at what she just heard, yet she couldn't entirely argue against all of it, either. Bellemont's religion was not her own, the witnessing of their faith foreign to her understanding of scripture. No God who preferred hellfire to the mercy of a tender heart would hear her prayers in the dark, nor those of her children. What part of Bellemont's piety involved love?

An automobile rolled past slowly, the driver's window open, a hand waving a lighted cigar out in the draft. CW walked down to the bottom step and stared off up the street.

Rachel said, "So that's how it is? You don't love me, do you? Perhaps you'd prefer not to visit here any more. Perhaps you'd rather have nothing more to do with me." Her cigarette had burned down to the butt, so she flicked it into the honeysuckle. "You see, I only ask because if you have no further interest in pursuing this courtship, I'd rather know tonight. Mother has invited several of her club ladies over to a tea tomorrow afternoon and I promised her we'd attend so that you might regale them with stories of New Orleans at Mardi Gras. They've never had the opportunity of attending and Mother assures me they're all quite intrigued to hear about it."

Indoors, the latest radio melody ended and for a few brief moments the house became silent. Marie shifted her position on the chair, terrified she'd be caught spying. Ordinarily, she detested eavesdropping, but tonight she found the urge irresistible, if only for catching this glimpse into her sister-in-law's heart of hearts. A fresh ballad issued from the radio, a soft melody composed for lovers dancing late into the night. Marie wondered what made Rachel and CW feel the need to be so brutal. Was this how she and Harry sounded? Had the children heard them through the walls in the dark? She hoped not, but knew it was likely. How stupid and cruel.

His eyes locked on Rachel, CW said, "Darling, I believe we ought to marry as soon as possible."

A gust of wind blew through the wisteria, rippling in the curtains by Marie who, for the second time, was stunned by CW.

Rachel replied, "Pardon me?"

"Well, you know yourself the longer we delay, the greater pressure your mother brings to bear upon the differences between us, those meaningless incompatibilities that most people use as excuses to remain apart. I'd rather not have that happen to us. I love you, and I believe we ought to marry. No later than summer's end."

"That's impossible," Rachel said, decending to the next porch step. "Even if Mother approved, which she wouldn't, I don't favor in the least the idea of a wedding thrown together with so little thought given to its arrangement."

"Well, I've spent considerable time thinking about it," CW said. "In fact, I've hardly had anything else on my mind since I arrived here this morning."

"A man's notion of time is quite different from a woman's," said Rachel, "especially in terms of planning for occasions of importance such as this. A wedding is worth a lifetime of consideration. I wouldn't dream of ruining mine through rash behavior."

"And you think that marrying me this summer would be rash?"

"I don't expect you to understand," she replied. "A man's heart is simply not conditioned for such sensitivities. Don't be dismayed. It's not your fault."

CW laughed and drew his flask out for another sip. He tilted his head back and drank, then laughed once again, his voice echoing out into the road. Marie sat back, afraid she'd be seen as her sister-in-law glanced toward the house. She felt badly now for both of them, and wished she had the courage to intercede, even warn them of the heartbreak they were instigating for no good purpose.

"Shhhh!" Rachel hissed at CW. "You'll wake Mother!"

He waved the flask at her, then wandered down to the bottom of the stairs. "My goodness! Wouldn't that be a crime! Maude Hennesey, the grand dame of Bellemont Baptists, awakened in the dead of night by a drunk Catholic proposing marriage to her lovely daughter! What would people say!"

"That you've become very ugly in the past half hour, so much so I can hardly believe I ever surrendered my heart to you. I must have been insane."

"Love's wondrous intoxication leads us all to the brink of lunacy. Come down here and share in my delirium!"

He held a hand out to her with a crazy smile. When Rachel failed to budge from the porch, CW removed his straw hat and tried bending down on one knee to offer his hand again. Instead, he lost his balance and toppled over into the dirt. "Nerts!"

"For heaven sakes, you *are* drunk!"

Marie stifled a giggle of her own. He did look very funny.

Prone in the dust, CW grinned up at her. "Blissfully spifflicated by your beauty, my little sunshine!"

"Don't insult me."

"Let's marry tonight! We'll fly to Baton Rouge. Simon Beauregard's father is a justice of the peace there. He'll perform a civil ceremony for us free of charge. We can cable your mother from the aerodrome and tell her the good news. Have you ever been to Cuba? I'll fly us there for our honeymoon tomorrow evening. Dining in Havana! Wouldn't that be romantic? What do you say?"

"I'm going off to bed now. I expect you ought to as well. I'll write you a letter tomorrow and try my very best to forgive your ugly behavior this evening."

CW struggled unsuccessfully to get back on his feet. Balancing precariously on hands and knees, he cried, "Aw, sweetheart! Don't be like that! I love you!"

"Then please say goodnight."

Hearing Rachel's hand on the doorknob snapped Marie to her senses, aware that she was about to be caught. She rose from her chair at the window and tiptoed quickly to the rear of the house. As the front door opened, Marie grabbed her shoes off the laundry stool and darted out onto the back porch and down the steps. Outdoors, she heard CW's plaintive voice still calling to Rachel as the front door closed with a muffled thud. Marie tiptoed up the steps, and shut the rear door behind her. She heard Rachel cross the house and enter her own bedroom on the west side. A yellow glow from Rachel's hand-painted Japanese vanity lamp shone briefly onto the chickencoop, then extinguished.

Marie slipped her shoes on and eased down the steps into the yard where the hard corners of fenceline, shed and water trough, appeared clearer now in the pale moonlight than when she had arrived home earlier. A pair of brown bats chased above College Street. Marie watched until they'd gone, then crossed to the gate, craning her neck for a look around front. CW was seated behind the wheel of his Ford, smoking a cigarette and tapping the dashboard with his other fist. The engine was rattling loudly, exhaust billowing up like coal dust from the rear, ruin on his face.

The Jessup's collie bounded around a corner from their backyard and leaped up against the fence beside Marie, panting with excitement. Marie opened Maude's gate and went out onto the sidewalk. CW saw her and flashed his headlamps once. A chill came over Marie as she closed the gate and headed up the sidewalk. She hoped nobody was watching from indoors. She felt sneaky and bold. What would Rachel think if she saw her? Who was the bigger flirt tonight?

CW stumbled out of the Ford, but left the door hanging open.

As Marie approached the automobile, CW dropped the lighted cigarette into the road at his feet, stamped it cold, then tipped his hat to her. "Good evening, ma'am."

"Hello," she said, brightly, hoping she was doing the right thing. Would Rachel say she was butting in where she didn't belong? Probably, but Rachel was also too proud to admit when she was wrong.

"Out for a constitutional?"

Marie lowered her voice. "I suppose it's rather late for that, wouldn't you agree?"

"Yes, it is. How are you?"

"Very well, and yourself?"

CW leaned toward the bumper of the Ford to catch his balance. "Actually, I'm lit to the eyebrows."

Marie smiled. "I can see that." Though she didn't entirely approve of liquor, she found CW's condition amusing tonight. Rachel could be such a share, perhaps CW needed a drink now and then to be pleasant. Often Harry's behavior led to her thinking about wine tonics. Maybe one day soon she'd consider a glass of something to make her dizzy for an hour or two. Marie saw no great moral wrong there.

"Your company's always a pleasure, of course." He bowed, striking his forehead on the car roof. Marie barely stifled a laugh. He looked very funny.

"Oh my!" CW rubbed his head. "I am squiffy, aren't I?"

Marie giggled. "Yes, I'm afraid you are. Perhaps you ought to go to bed."

"If thou wilt ease thine heart of love and all its smart, then sleep, dear, sleep," CW recited aloud.

The Jessup's collie jumped against the gate next door and began barking at something across the road. Marie looked down the empty street, then stole another furtive glance at Maude's window. A tea kettle whistling at dawn would rouse her with little trouble. A peculiar shiver ran up Marie's spine. CW forced a smile and tried once more to stand upright without aid of his automobile.

"Rachel's gone to bed," said Marie, unsure of what else to contribute. "I suppose she'd have a fit if she knew you were still here. I'm sorry." Marie couldn't mend her own wounded heart tonight, much less his. Truth was, she hated hearing them fight with such bitterness. It seemed so utterly wasteful and pointless. Too many nights she and Harry had gone to bed with cold shoulders and what good had come out of it? Did they kiss more often afterward? She knew better than that.

"Oh, don't be. We've had our glittering evening out, and now she thinks I'm a skunk. It's all a mess. I was just preparing to depart."

"You don't intend to fly back to New Orleans tonight in this condition, I hope."

An expression of incredulity crossed CW's face. "Why not? It's a birdman's evening. No clouds. A beautiful moon to guide me home. Once the take-off is dispensed with, there's really very little danger to be had. Other than landing, of course."

Marie smiled. "Of course." She thought CW overbold, and liquor made him worse. She worried for him. "You will be safe, won't you? I'm sure Rachel would be worried sick to have you fly off like this."

CW swayed outward, then staggered back against the automobile. He burped softly, and chuckled. "Did you know she and I intend to marry later this summer?"

"No, I hadn't heard," Marie replied, wondering what Maude would think if she heard that. "How nice!"

CW leaned forward, supporting himself on the driver's door. In a low voice, he said, "Her mother may not be attending, however."

"Oh?"

CW shook his head vigorously. "No. You see, rumor has it the Pope himself intends to perform the ceremony, in which case any Baptist in attendance would burst spontaneously into flames!"

His laughter echoed into the dark.

Down the street now, a motorcar's lamps shone in the pitch-dark shadows beneath the tall cottonwoods. The automobile came quick as lightning, engine roaring, dust and exhaust trailing like a black tornado. Top down, all heads and arms from driver to rumble seat, singing and shouts rising above the engine noise as it drew nearer. Instinctively, Marie backed up close to the sidewalk, having little desire to be run down like a dog in the road. Since Henry's frightening incident this afternoon, Marie was doubly concerned about the children's safety out here. CW, on the other hand, seemed to wander away from his own automobile toward the middle of College Street, drifting like a boat cut loose from its mooring. A block away now and closing, the oncoming motor let loose with its horn, loud and long. Marie called to CW, but her voice was drowned out by the steady honking. He stood at military attention now, near the center of the road, one arm at his side, the other pressed to his brow, locked in a sober salute. Headlamps illuminated his tan suit as the automobile drew closer. Scared silly now, Marie shouted for CW to give way, but he remained resolute in his determination to greet this company of late-night revelers up close. The driver laid on his horn less than fifty yards off, zooming toward the Jessup's where he flashed the headlamps once more. CW's gaze remained stern, unwavering, his salute firm. The motor roared forward, past the Jessup's, toward CW, caught now in the glare of the lamps, lit like a monument statue, fully aglow — when Marie saw a strong dark hand reach over his shoulder from behind and jerk him out of the way of the speeding automobile, pulling him down into the dirt as the motorcar raced by, horn wailing, voices hurling vulgar epithets to CW's stupidity, disappearing on ahead into the dark, the horn echoes tailing off with the headlamps at the town limits.

"Oh my goodness!" Frightened to death, Marie rushed forward to see if CW had been injured.

As she did, a window flew open on the side of the house, and Maude's voice issued forth. "Good gracious sakes alive! What's all that racket! Who's out there? Is that you, Rachel?"

Her words carried across the street. Knowing Maude would not be able to see around the blooming honeysuckle and wisteria, Marie crept beside the running boards of CW's motorcar and remained quiet. By now, CW had risen from the dirt and slid back behind the wheel of the Ford, dust covering his jacket, clouding his hair. His straw hat lay crushed in the street. CW ran a hand over his forehead, smoothing his hair back, then reached over and pulled the driver's door closed with a bang. He seemed to have survived. Thank goodness for that!

Maude called out, "Rachel?"

CW leaned across the passenger seat toward the open window. He said, "Good night, Mrs. Hennesey."

Then he straightened up, looked at Marie. He dropped his voice. "Give my regards to Rachel. Please let her know I'm still nuts about her."

Putting his motorcar in gear, CW drove slowly away from the curb and headed off down the dark street.

As the Ford puttered away into the dark, Marie walked out of the road, back onto the sidewalk, just out of Maude's sight. She heard Maude say, somewhat testily, "Rachel, we'll discuss this in the morning."

Then the window slammed shut.

Straight away, Marie looked for the fellow who had tugged CW from traffic, and discovered him in the shadows by the east corner of the house, her attention drawn to the scraping of his shoes on the sidewalk. "Julius!" she whispered.

"Yes, ma'am."

Dressed in work-soiled overalls and a flat brown cap, he was nearly invisible.

"How nice to see you," she remarked, noticing the wheelbarrow parked behind him under the fig tree Cissie had adopted as the site of her grand circus. It was filled with more of the same sorts of scraps from the junkyard Julius had been bringing since Cissie conceived her summer project. She added, "Thank you for saving CW's life. I thought for sure he would be run down by those hooligans. I doubt he appreciated the danger he was in."

Who had been scared worse, she or CW?

"A body needs to keep moving."

"Pardon?"

Julius smiled. "Just somethin' my granny told me when I was a youngster. 'Don't never stop movin'.' When she was one hundred and four years old, she'd be walking along the river by moonlight, callin' after them catfish to give themselves up so's there'd be breakfast come morning for all her grandchildren. She never quit taking them walks of hers, died on her feet coming out of the hen house one afternoon, chicken in one hand, hatchet in the other. Bless her sweet heart. She passed on with the love of Jesus-walkin'-on-the-water plain on her face."

Marie wandered another few steps up the sidewalk away from the front porch. Nearer to Julius, she saw some of the scraps he brought for Cissie's circus: an old wire bird cage, six balls of binding string, a cracked apple crate, cotton balls, dried corncobs, chicken feathers, a wagon wheel, and a mildewy collection of old coffee cups whose place in the grand scheme only Cissie knew. Still in the wheelbarrow were a pair of Mason jars filled with cloudy dark water and peculiar drifting shapes like frogs in formaldehyde or an ancient wizard's shelved homunculi that Marie was unable to discern in the pale moonlight. In any case, she assumed they were intended for Henry and Abel's House of Frights.

A train whistle shrieked across the darkness from somewhere beyond the river, most likely a freight headed for the Gulf. Both Marie and Julius looked in that direction, although the tracks were more than two miles east of Bellemont and visible only from that side of the woods. Marie could hear the train whistle howl again across the distance. She stood perfectly quiet with her arms folded and listened while Julius stepped back into the shadows, emptying his wheelbarrow of the Mason jars.

"Thank you," Marie said, finally. "Cissie's in love with her circus."

"It's nothing but a joy for children to play at making a game out of something they love."

"Well, it's very generous of you, to say the least." She let her eyes roam across that part of the circus already completed: part of the Big Top rendered by gunny sacks and old canvas, a trapeze erected in thread and fishnet, the revolving Ferris wheel constructed out of an old bicycle wheel, booths along the midway cut out of old coffee tins turned upside down, lion cages made of cheese graters. "I'm afraid to say that Cissie has an extravagant imagination. I'm not sure where she gets it from, perhaps her father. Harry's always had a fanciful outlook."

She smiled, remembering all the evenings her husband had spent reading to Cissie and Henry from *Grimm's Fairy Tales*, crossing his heart and swearing every word was fact.

Julius told her, "In all God's creation, nothing got more magic wrapped up in it than a sweet child's heart. Sees things we can't. Hears 'em, too. Ain't our fault neither, that's just how it is."

Marie studied Cissie's circus rising from the weeds beneath the fig tree like the most natural thing in the world. Julius set the last of the Mason jars side by side next to the half-finished tent and backed the wheelbarrow out of the weeds.

Marie asked, "Do you think the children will complete this by the end of summer?" She desperately wished some dreams this summer might yet come true. In each of our hearts reside wishes for joy and contentment above all else.

Julius put his cap back on, then smiled and shook his head. "Circus ain't never done, Mrs. Hennesey, never finished. Can't be. Got too much hidden up in it to see one time around. Got to come back again, buy another ticket, have another look-see. Circus always got something you never seen before, always something new. Ask your children if that ain't the truth. No, ma'am, circus ain't never done. That's why it's still here."

Then, whistling a tune Marie didn't know, the black man steered the old wheelbarrow about and rolled it off into the summer night.

UTOPIA

ONE MORNING IN EARLY AUGUST, Harry Hennesey sat beneath an olive tree on University Hill daydreaming about Utopia.

The idyllic nature of this campus that surrounded him invigorated his thoughts, sharpened the great Ideal he considered, Elysian Fields and Oneida reinvested in his imagination. When Harry was at college, many afternoons were spent debating such questions as: Did virtue and goodness enter the world by Providence or choice? Was grace revealed by intentions or works? Were all men and women guided equally toward Beauty and Truth? In those youthful years at State, Harry held that neither potion nor persuasion could lead an honest man astray, that wrongdoing arose from misunderstandings and false assumptions, poverty from misbehavior. If only the benefits of cooperation and moral rectitude were fully appreciated, he believed, the march of progress toward a truly civilized world would not have struggled with such hardships. Meanwhile, semester after semester, his roommate Albert Eliot had argued that temperance and Christian values pursued with vigor and enthusiasm were all the tonic a healthy individual required to achieve both grace and forgiveness in this life. Furthermore, he maintained that success in all worldly ventures followed therefrom in God's perfect logic. Dollars from decency, was how Albert put it: an honorable road rewards its faithful traveler. Yet, if Albert were correct, would not John D. Rockefeller and Andrew Carnegie have been canonized as saints? Did their vast fortunes result from earlier virtuousness? Harry's professor in Classical Languages and Philosophy, Dr. Ellwood Collingsworth, lectured that only the provincial mind expected financial recompense for a moral life. He often chided those students from the business school by requiring them to wear classical Latin epigrams upon their lapels as they went about during the semester. Harry's had read: *Sollicitae tu causa, pecunia, vitae.* Each Tuesday morning, Collingsworth argued that all truths were universal, excepting no man. What stood for pure virtue in ancient Athens and Imperial Rome was equally true at modern St. Louis. It was architecture and fashions that had changed over the centuries, not the human heart.

You, money, are the cause of an anxious life. As he sat under the olive tree, Harry had a bank draft for one hundred dollars in his coat pocket ready to be mailed to Bellemont. His mother had written that week of her need for the money and Harry was obliged to fulfill her request. Marie worked her dear heart out at Delahaye's restaurant, but she and the children had needs unmet by a half-day's salary and Harry understood how it was unfair for his mother to shoulder the extra burden. Honestly, his own financial situation was becoming somewhat precarious. McDonald asked almost daily for rent payment on Harry's apartment, and his reserve from the sale of those shoes to Gus DuFort in May and the peacock feathers to Ollie Thurston last month was dangerously low. Sure, he had a contract to deliver a pair of rebuilt Aeolian Co. pianolas to the Lyceum Theater at Clancy Street, a deal that would fetch nearly five hundred dollars. Also, the sudden death of Bertha Matson, a childless widow on the second floor of the Warsaw Hotel, had secured him a closet full of perfectly fine tea gowns and Japanese silk kimonos for which he already had a buyer. So, even without winning Follette's phony five thousand dollar "missing niece" sweepstakes, there was no thought of becoming destitute, not tomorrow at least; but he had responsibilities, obligations both to his family and himself, goals that needed to be met and secured before he could go forward confident in the future. At Transfer & Storage, all the fellows spoke of was this big Bull Market and its myriad possibilities, investing in America and all that — getting aboard. Indeed, the great Stock Exchanges were all abuzz these days with fortunes to be made. Yet Harry was leery. In his opinion, trading in stock shares had little do with the actual life of business as he knew it. They hardly represented the worth of a nation whose labors supposedly translated into growth and comfort, a better life for the common man. Speculation represented fortune, not security, and it was for the latter that most men rose in the dark blue dawn and followed the milk wagons along a thousand cold streets to work each morning, surrendering the diurnities of their lives for vital wages, hours they would not get back. At night in kerosene-lighted kitchens they would eat supper and mull over those hours and those wages, knowing labor held no guarantee of joy or fulfillment, nor much profit when all was counted out and numbered. Industry was no substitute for yearning, yet each day following they would rise once again in the darkness and go out the door into that cold morning convinced this was what the world intended for them all along.

Harry climbed the grassy hillock toward the towering brick campanile whose bells would soon ring in the noon hour. At the crest of the slope, he paused to look back toward the distant river glittering in bright sunlight beyond the great city. He could hear birds chattering in the tall trees about campus, watch the wind rise in the leafy green branches, smell the freshly mown grass and fragrant flower beds that lined the stone paths between lecture halls. When he was eighteen years old, obliged by financial considerations to hire a small furnished room in an old roominghouse four blocks from State campus, Harry had placed his desk at a third-story window shaded by a great elm tree that overlooked a brick sidewalk, affording him the opportunity to study passersby late into the night, puzzling the differences of one to the other. Why did one fellow stroll along with a hip flask in hand, the next weighted down with a pair of milk bottles and a sack of groceries? Why did one woman wear an elegant raincape, the other carry a ratty old fabric umbrella? As a freshman at eighteen, he saw little in those passersby that resembled himself. He had plans, after all.

In those years, everyone he knew went about quoting from the "Rubaiyat of Omar Khayyám." Harry's favorite quatrain read:

"Come, fill the cup, and in the fire of Spring
Your winter garment of repentance fling;
The Bird of Time has but a little way
To flutter — the bird is on the wing."

Non scholae sed vitae discimus. During college, Harry joined the debating society and Glee Club, boxed and played ball in the spring, made love to darling young co-eds, went on wild automobile rides in the night, endured secret initiation into a smart fraternity, indulged his intellect by chewing the rag over political and philosophical questions, rallied for Roosevelt and Taft, crammed for exams by gaslight in the upper corridors of the campus library, roughhoused in the roominghouse hallways, pledged eternal loyalty to the friends he had made, earned his Baccalaureus Artium diploma, then graduated to law school where, after half a semester, he suddenly decided a life of dusty volumes and endless debates held less fascination for him than the vibrant challenge of the marketplace.

We learn not for school, but for life. This morning he found himself wondering how life rewarded the curious and thoughtful. Standing in the warm sunlight, Harry watched men in black and brown rumpled coats stroll across the upper lawns of the university carrying books or briefcases, each face a stern portrait in cerebration. His old professors at State had lectured daily against sloth and ignorance, their bespectacled eyes vigilant, clever, and far wiser than those whose tuition paid their teachers' rent. In Dr. Collingsworth's office one afternoon, Harry sat for two hours listening to the tale of Heinrich Schliemann's desperate search for fabled Troy on the windswept plains of Asia Minor just forty years before. *Possunt quia posse videntur — They can because they think they can.* Afterward, Collingsworth asked Harry what he intended to accomplish for himself when college was over, to which passions he would dedicate his own heart. Only a year after graduation, bound to an inventories desk in a small office overlooking the stockyards of Kansas City, Harry had tried to pretend that numbering entries in a ledger for men rich enough to purchase his entire hometown was itself a progression in the world, a rising gradient that defined wealth as success, and success as virtue. Then he left Kansas City and traveled to Minneapolis-St. Paul where one April evening by the boat docks at Cedar Lake he met pretty young Marie Alice Pendergast. *Tanta potentia formae est.*

Of all God's creatures, in this life only man seeks the sublime. Dr. Collingsworth had been a child of Oneida and upheld his belief in the Utopian Ideal, that of reasonable men arriving at long last upon the halcyon crossroads of commerce and community wherein competition would be tempered by compassion, and intellect soothed in the gentleness of the heart's true spirit as cooperation in life's least endeavors revealed God's unwavering presence and advocacy in the common world of men.

So great is the power of beauty. In fact, from his marriage to Marie, Harry had himself learned the healing benefits of negotiation and compromise. She taught him that grace arises from concern for another's prosperity, that love offers redemptive gifts of far greater and lasting value than any sum of merchant bank drafts, and that so long as he lived, goodness freely delivered was all he would ever require of Truth. *Virtus praemium est optimum — Virtue is the best reward.*

— 2 —

Pearl shaded her eyes as she stared up at the red brick campanile whose bell tower rang across the noon air. "Ain't it just like the singing of angels?"

She set the small picnic basket on the grass beneath an elm tree, then folded her skirt and sat down. She unwrapped one of the meat sandwiches she had bought at a lunchwagon down on Rector Street below the Hill and handed it to Harry as he sat down. Her girlish skin was mild in the sunlight, lovely dark wisps of hair hiding her ears, those darling lips rosy and fresh. He trembled whenever he thought of kissing her, that sleepy, violent fever persisting day after day unrestrained, while her violet eyes tickled his dreams. Some might call it love.

"You like olives?" Pearl asked him, opening another paper wrapping.

He inhaled a tranquil scent of summer flowers on the breeze. "Certainly."

She passed him a cup filled with green olives, and a handful of crackers, afterward. Then she fished a hip flask out of her bag and unscrewed its lid and took a sip. She hiccuped, and offered Harry the flask with a wink. "Say, how's about we get tight? Shot of rye?"

He smiled. "I thought we've talked about this. Didn't you tell me you were through with liquor?"

"Aw, keep your shirt on, honey. It ain't nothing but soda pop."

Harry sniffed at the lip of the hip flask while Pearl stuck a pair of olives between two crackers and ate it like a sandwich. Besides the olives, her basket held a dish of pickles, lemon wafers, a deviled ham sandwich, and a box of Uneeda biscuits. This morning when Harry saw what a sweet picnic basket she had packed, he swept her into his arms and gave her a wonderfully exuberant kiss that left them both dizzy. If this beautiful girl were indeed Follette's illegitimate daughter, and she had a reservation at the bottom of the river, how could he even consider tossing her over to him? There is a price to pay for selling one's soul, and it's certainly not five thousand dollars. She just had to be protected. He read the newspapers each morning for stories about girls dragged lifeless from the cold river. Who could say what that Cobb fellow might do if he thought he could put one over on Follette? These days, it seemed wherever Harry looked, there he was: Cobb at a florist on Hoag Street across from a crowded hash-joint where Harry and Pearl ate one afternoon; Cobb reading a tabloid on the stoop of the Hines School of Physical Culture at 29th Street by a corner A&P grocery store Pearl preferred; Cobb three doors down from the Dunhill candy store when Harry bought a sack of lemon drops for Pearl and a box of assorted chocolates to mail down to his children in Texas. One evening Harry noticed both Cobb and his pal Fred Markle outside a dress shop next door to the Lyric Theater where he and Pearl had gone to see Betty Compson and George Bancroft in *The Docks of New York*. What the devil was that little fellow's strategy?

"This smells like ginger ale," Harry said, sniffing at the flask again, surprised he couldn't detect a hint of liquor.

She smiled. "I just told you it's only soda pop."

"Well, I've heard that ginger ale with gin added is a popular cocktail among young people these days."

She took a biscuit and another pair of olives. "I'd say Scotch highballs are lots more popular." She stuffed the biscuit into her mouth.

"Now, darling, did you see Lancaster, as I asked you to?" Harry plucked a lemon wafer and a pickle from the picnic basket. A week ago, he had spoken with a fellow by the name of George Lancaster, who occupied a small office half a block from Transfer & Storage, to see if one of the flower stalls he owned along Columbia Avenue needed a girl. Harry had done all the work arranging the interview; Pearl had only to be on time and Harry was assured she would be given fair consideration for the job.

She swallowed another Uneeda biscuit. "Aw, I got the rottenest luck."

"You didn't see Lancaster?"

"Well, it's like this, honey," Pearl said, before popping a pair of olives into her mouth. "I'm flat, see? Not a red cent. You know, a girl's got to be careful where she's walking these days. This city ain't safe no more."

"Are you trying to tell me you missed your appointment with Lancaster because you lacked change for the trolley? Why, I gave you five dollars just last Saturday. That ought to have lasted a week, unless you've been back to that blind pig on Pressley Street. Is that what happened? Be straight with me now. I want the truth."

She put on a pout. "Aw, honey, how come you're always high-hatting me? I ain't been drinking if I said I wasn't. Why, I've been sober as a penguin since Tuesday."

"But that five dollars —"

"I had to eat, didn't I? Look here, ain't I a stick, though? Have a heart, will you, dear?" She took a pickle and jammed it into her mouth, chewing vigorously.

Good God, she's such a little cheat!

"Darling, I saw a sign in Kelso's diner on 17th Street advertising 55¢ dinners, and they weren't Chinese, either."

"I ain't eating any more steamed clams, Harry."

"In fact, they offered Welsh rabbit with a potato, and a piece of blueberry pie or a slice of pineapple for dessert. All for 55¢."

Pearl took a sip from her silver hip flask, and screwed the lid back on. After eating the last lemon wafer, she told him, "Honey, I've been doping out a plan since last week with a couple of fellows I met down at the Cook Street pier in Chinatown."

"What sort of plan?" Harry asked, as a light breeze rippled across the lawn. He studied that lovely shadow of Pearl's eyes and wondered how beauty could be so young. "Did you find another girl?"

Two weeks ago, she had led him to a new Olive over on Zion Street, a girl who had grown up just outside the city in East Matson. The young lady was roughly the correct age and there was some question about the identity of her father, since she had been raised by her maternal aunts. Where it all fell apart was her last name. It was Bernstein and her family was Jewish.

"Well, I can't tell you now. It's a secret. You wouldn't want to spoil it for me, would you?"

"Oh, of course not."

"Ain't I a dollface, honey?"

"I beg your pardon?" Her conversation shifts really did confuse him. She could flirt and be silly, regardless of context, probably knowing he was already drawn to her by love's irrational opinion. Most girls know instinctively when a male has a superabundance of interest in them and rarely will they let that advantage escape.

"See, I know I ain't that pretty, but there's lots of fellows who'd follow me home if I let 'em."

"I have no idea what you're talking about."

"My momma'd sure like to meet you, Harry. Did you know that? I told her all about you, and she said that the next time I came to see her, I ought to bring you along. What do you say? She's awful darling."

Mother? Now that was a surprise! For some reason, he'd assumed she had no family, at least none she saw any longer. That wouldn't be so unusual these days. The city was awash with those like her: orphaned, destitute, living from dawn till dusk on idiot schemes, constant

hose older and cleverer than themselves. More than a few
ιp under the Lincoln Bridge.

ι'll be a sport about it, won't you, honey?" Pearl asked, rising
to brush the grass off her dress. "She's expecting us this afternoon."

"Is that so?" He watched Pearl put the Uneeda biscuits back into
her picnic basket. "How come I don't recall you mentioning her before? Aren't girls obsessed with their mothers?"

"Most fellows don't want to hear nothing about a girl's family. It
makes them think she's trying to tie them down or something. I know
it ain't the same for you, but I was scared you'd tell me to scram and
I'd never see you again."

"Do you really think I'd be so rash?"

Pearl shrugged. "You're a strange fish, honey. I never met a fellow
like you before. You interest me, even though you're kind of bossy.
That's funny, huh? Because sometimes I think we're made for each
other. I guess that's why I love you. But you know, a girl's got to be
careful not to let her heart get broke."

"Yes, that's true," Harry agreed, his eye on her frock where it folded
at her knee and across the bare curve of her shoulder, her pale smooth
skin. Somehow she reminded him of a girl he had seen in Bellemont
once when he was a boy, a strange and pretty girl from away whose
blue-dark eyes were sad and lovely, who wandered the summer roads
of town alone, speaking to no one, her dress a simple floral print that
fluttered in the warm wind as she passed, a thin smile on her lips.
Rumors whispered on porch fronts across town had her an orphan,
an idiot, a harlot, a gypsy, a ghost. By summer's end, she had gone
forever, only the memory of her sunlit hair and calm quiet smile left
for the curious.

Intrigued now, and feeling confident, he added, "But why do you
love me, darling?"

She squealed. "Gosh, honey, don't be crazy! That's like asking a girl
to tell you her age. I won't do it. A girl's got to have her secrets."

"Then I'll have to ask you again tomorrow."

"Oh, you're just awful, honey." She kissed him, delicately, brushing
his cheeks with her tiny fingertips as she retreated. "What do you say

we go to the picture show at the Lux on 101st Street. They're showing *West of Zanzibar* with Mary Nolan and Lon Chaney. I seen the ending last Saturday night. Why, it's a scream."

Harry shook his head. Actually, he had a much better idea for her. "Only the lazy and the rich spend their afternoons in the dark." He stood and brushed off his trousers. "Have you ever been inside a library?"

— **3** —

Sunlight glowed in the upper windows of University Library, illuminating a vast interior of fluted stone columns and carved pilasters and black ornamental wrought-iron railings rising four stories high to a vaulted ceiling whose lacunaria were painted aquamarine behind gold stenciled ornaments. More than two million volumes were stored here and the library was quite busy even on a late summer afternoon. Standing on a gilded compass rose, Harry could hear the collective whispers of people passing in and out of the stacks. He adored libraries.

Pearl asked, "How come you brought me here, honey? I ain't read a book in my life."

"Well, darling, in our home, we believe that education is one of the four Foundations to Success. My daughter Cissie read a hundred books before her eighth birthday and was delighted by each one. She's a smart little girl. I'm very proud of her."

"Well, I don't give a rap about reading." Her hard-heeled shoes clanked lightly as they climbed the iron staircase to the next floor. "A girl like me's got lots more important things to do."

"That's nonsense."

"I tell you, I'd rather put on my glad rags, honey, any night of the week than sit home reading a dumb book like some old Wilmer."

Ignoring her stupid comment, Harry counted the fluted columns ahead on the second floor. A young fellow carrying a stack of books under each arm eased by. Harry noticed the boy sneak a look at Pearl's bottom as he passed. Did everybody have sex on his mind these days?

She asked, "Do you think I ought to get a dancing job? I seen a notice at the Shamrock Theater last night advertising for hoofers. If I had a couple lessons, I'll bet I could put it over big."

"It's just up ahead there," Harry said, avoiding her last remark. He had a point to make with Pearl and intended to see it through, whether she liked it or not. This was for her own good, after all. You can't really be helpful to people by indulging their pride for accomplishments that aren't true accomplishments. "See at the corner? Take a right past those shelves."

"Aw, honey," she complained. "A girl like me ain't cut out for books. Can't you see that?"

"Didn't you ever attend school?" He stopped her beside one of the literature aisles. "I'm sure you were compelled to learn to read and write along with every other child. It's the law, you realize."

He stepped into the aisle to take a quick look at the old titles.

Pearl strolled in behind him. "That old hag Miss Swanson hated my guts, worse than I hated hers. She tried to choke me once after school when everybody else went home. If I hadn't brained her with a coal shovel and run off, maybe I wouldn't even be here today."

Harry took down an old volume whose spine had cracked, its gold title letters all but worn away. He searched inside, riffling the pages slowly until he found what he wanted.

"Listen here." He read, *"The good want power, but to weep barren tears/ The powerful goodness want: worse need for them/ The wise want love; and those who love want wisdom."* He smiled. "I suppose you don't care for poetry, either?"

"Why, sure! *Of all sad words that now are roared/ the saddest are these/ he bought a Ford!"*

She laughed so loudly, Harry became afraid the librarian would toss them both out of the building. People in the upper stacks were already staring. He must've been out of his mind to bring her here.

"Didn't you like it, honey? I learned it from Johnny Angelino at Emerson Hall grammar school. I thought it was so funny I let him kiss me right after he told it."

Harry sighed. Maybe she really was a hopeless case. After all, you can only do so much when people refuse to see that opportunity is not seasonal. For most of them, life's sweetest rewards come and go unheeded. Patience and intuition are rare commodities, even when success is tied to both. He could easily picture this girl in her adult years as one of ten thousands whose noses are pressed against the plate glass of those grand show window displays downtown along the Avenue of the Republic, peering with envy at everything they cannot have. Often he considered flipping open his billfold and giving her money enough to help her get along, knowing all the while that a handful of dollars alone would not substantially change the direction her life had taken. No, if she hoped to survive, she'd have to do a lot more than steal liquor and go to picture shows.

Reluctantly, he slipped the volume of poetry back into its place on the shelf. Books had enriched his life since he was a boy. When Harry was thirteen years old, his father had him nominated to the National Geographic Society. Once his magazines began arriving, he would read a section of each issue before going to sleep at night and dream about Victoria Falls and black Calcutta, the wild jungles of Borneo and those forbidden palaces of imperial China. Reading offered him dreams that life had not. His own modest library at Cedar Street once held a fine collection of those authors whose works uplifted his spirits. Walt Whitman was one he liked quite a lot, Emerson, Kipling and Whittier, too. Marie preferred Henry Wadsworth Longfellow and Robert Burns; occasionally she would quote "Hiawatha" for guests after supper and always draw a fine round of applause. A successful life, he had heard once, ought to be a life of study as much as balancing household needs, for we cannot soak in wisdom from the sunshine and fresh air.

"I tell you, honey, this joint ain't too lively," Pearl remarked, perched at the iron railing looking down on the main floor. "And I ain't feeling so peppy no more, neither."

"Why do you always say that when you're unhappy?"

"Say what?"

"That you're ill. Whenever I suggest us doing something you don't want to do, you tell me you're suddenly under the weather. Don't you know how maddening that is?" He replaced a well-thumbed copy of Shakespeare's sonnets. Growing more frustrated by the second, he found it tough keeping his own voice down. "Just stop being so childish. I brought you here for your own benefit, you know."

"Says who?"

"Good grief, aren't you the least bit interested in bettering yourself?" This was the same argument he had with Marie when they'd first met. No matter how often he talked to her about Thomas Hardy and John Galsworthy, Jack London, Tolstoy, William Dean Howells, even Mark Sullivan, she seemed to have no interest in reading anything but stocking ads in the Sears-Roebuck catalogue. Later on, he discovered that she read more often than he did, but had kept it to herself, afraid that he wouldn't approve of the writers she admired. Well, he had nothing against Burns, Longfellow or Emily Dickinson, and told her so.

Pearl wandered back out of the aisle to the railing. She craned her neck to look up at the people in stacks on the third floor. "I'm taking a dancing audition. Why, someday I'll be bigger than Mae Murray."

He almost laughed. "Why not just elect yourself queen? Show-business popularity is nothing to bank on, darling. Just think about that."

"Oh yeah? Tell it to Miss Mary Pickford." Pearl gave a wave to somebody up above, then giggled. "Why, she's got a joint out in Hollywood that makes this dump look like a hatbox."

He persisted. "Why won't you trust me for an hour or so?"

"Because I ain't going to read a book, honey, and that's all there is to it."

Thoroughly exasperated, Harry quit. He was no Pygmalion, after all. Too many of us believe in shaping people to that comfortable image of ourselves. He studied the surrounding shelves: so much to learn, so many benefits to be had. In these few volumes alone, she might have discovered answers to questions she had not even yet asked, found prayers of promise and comfort for bleak nights, simple dreams and intuitions she had herself known, yet was unable to express. If she were patient, a new world would be revealed to her. If she were patient. He relented with a sigh. Honestly, what else could he do? "Look, dear, I promise you won't have to read a word, if you don't want to."

"Then you got yourself a deal, sweetheart." Pearl left the railing and came back to him, puckering her lips for that reward.

He kissed her once. "All right, now, come along with me. There's still time for you to learn a few things."

At the University Museum of Art and Antiquities, whose exhibits in glass cases and sculpted wall niches described the progress of civilization from Uruk to Victorian London, Harry led Pearl to a plain stone sarcophagus in which lay the three-thousand year old remains of a young Egyptian woman from Thebes. Nearby, a small boat of reed papyrus from Heliopolis lay beneath a lithograph of the Sphinx and the Great Pyramid at Gizeh. Beside it, a plaque of hieroglyphics was translated as: *"The Sektet boat receiveth fair winds."* Harry reminded Pearl of Howard Carter's incredible discovery in the Valley of the Kings in '22, and described the significance of Champollion and the Rosetta Stone. Farther on, in the Hall of the Bronze Age, he showed Pearl a plaster model of the Oracle at Delphi on Mount Parnassus and explained why the miracle of Greek civilization was reduced now to sad ruins scattered about the beautiful islands of the Aegean Sea. While Pearl gawked at gold jewelry and polished gemstones uncovered at Pergamum and Ephesus, Harry marveled at how the ancients could have believed that anything at all lasts forever.

De nobis fabula narratur. For an hour and a half, Harry patiently guided Pearl through the Imperial Roman exhibits from the Gracchi to Caesar Augustus, Marcus Aurelius to Nero, Christ, and Constantine, the Appian Way to Hadrian's Wall and the Salarian Gate, then led her onward to Byzantium, Medieval Europe, the Renaissance, and the Age of Enlightenment. He did his best to explain to her about the Golden Horn and Gothic cathedrals, the horrors of the Black Death, the Crusades, Islamic caravans, Venetian merchants and Marco Polo, Gutenberg's Bible, Da Vinci, Columbus, Torquemada's Spanish Inquisition, Mozart, George Washington, and the Age of Machines. But approaching the end of the Hall of History, all she really wanted to know was how Louis XIV was able to balance his flamboyant hats as he marched about the royal gardens of Versailles, and whether or not Harry would have jousted for her honor against England's Black Knight.

Naturally, it got worse. In the granite Science & Natural History building, whose shadowy halls smelled vaguely of formaldehyde and sulfur, Harry brought her to an exhibit of Indians and the wilderness of the Americas thousands of years before the Europeans arrived. They weren't there five minutes before he had to put a stop to a rain dance of hers that looked suspiciously like the Lindy Hop. Next he tried teaching her about life in the Far West when pioneer flatboats navigated the Mississippi, and buffalo herds swarmed over the Great Plains before modern man, in his vanity and ignorance, hunted them to near-extinction. Beneath an oil painting of the Ohio Valley, where the vanished passenger pigeons once flocked by the millions darkening the autumn sky during their southwestward migration, he showed her a bronze plaque that quoted Henry Ward Beecher: *The philosophy of one century is the common sense of the next.*

When he finished, she told him, "Honey, I seen one of those same pigeons on my window sill a couple of days ago."

"Well, given that they've been extinct now for about fifteen years, I doubt that very much."

"I tell you, honey, I really seen one."

"Thank you, dear."

Persisting, Harry led her back outdoors through a shady grape arbor to the University of the Republic's Hall of Astronomy whose entry corridor housed exhibits of old meridian telescopes, a 16th-century brass astrolabe, armillary spheres, a gilded quadrant and heliometer, a 17th-century octagonal brass orrery, Ptolemaic, Tychonic and Copernican planetary systems and star charts, arcane experiments in magnetism, and an expository panel describing the histories and characteristics of the sun and moon and the eight planets of our earth's solar system. Directly in the center of the hall, suspended from a ceiling painting of Bartholomaeus Anglicus' 15th-century astrologer's sky, a long Foucault pendulum attached to the great silver

Globe of the Universe swayed in and out across a circle of the Zo-diac, demonstrating how the earth rotated on its axis. He told Pearl that everything known in this world emanates from the cosmos and what we do on earth is only a pale imitation of what occurs among the stars.

"You mean stars like Clara Bow?" she laughed, twirling on the marble floor like a vagrant ballerina.

"Yes, exactly like that."

At the end of the gallery was the planetarium whose double doors were closed for the afternoon. A sign on the wall read:

LEANDER ILLINGTON PLANETARIUM

MORNING SHOW 9AM — EVENING SHOW 6PM

ASTRONOMER: DR. MARTIMBEAU

ADMISSION 5¢

Pearl cracked the door slightly and took a peek. Barely stifling a giggle, she slipped inside. Though there was no show scheduled for that hour, for some reason the empty planetarium was dark and the Zeiss star projector illuminated, filling the great aluminum dome with a magnificent display of the evening sky arcing forty feet overhead, star-flung and glittering.

Pearl took a seat in the nearest row. "Gosh, I never seen nothing so beautiful in my whole life."

"It's extraordinary," he agreed, sliding in beside her. "Breathtaking."

A gibbous moon was rising in the heavens now, brightened by the thousand-watt bulbs of the great projector. Both Venus and Mars were shining, too, and a streaking comet was visible to the east as the false sky continued its slow rotation across the starry dome. Harry found himself pleased at seeing Pearl in awe of the planetarium splendor. It indicated a heart still willing to receive wonders beyond the delirium of daily existence. Without such spec-tacles of the extraordinary and divine, the human spirit withers and recedes, lost to both this life and the next. He took her hand, braided her tiny fingers to his. Resisting her felt so hopeless. Men

are born to adore the opposite sex, the flutter of a delicate eyelash, a gentle voice silk-soft, honey-pure skin scented of morning
gardens. He wanted desperately to make love to her right there in
the planetarium. Her lips were tiny rosebuds. He longed to kiss
her again. The cotton frock she wore barely disguised her youthful
bosom. He'd almost forgotten how young Marie had been when he
first took her hand in a canoe on the Lake of the Isles. She'd had
a gentle laugh and a freshness he had been unable to live without.
But how quickly faith in matrimonial love had deserted him. Sex
proved a tyrant. His forever vows did not last four years before reckless passion provoked a vain and shameless disregard for the values
of marriage. Every so often he heard suspicion in her voice when
she telephoned at night to his hotel, whether in Kansas City, Cleveland, Knoxville or Altoona. Once she actually referred to a steno
girl named Ina Gleason as his girlfriend, and he hadn't even spoken
to the young lady. But you really can't feel dismal when someone
so dear loves you with all her heart, especially when you've done
so little to fulfill that love. Then again, what if you no longer cared
what anybody thought? Once you've swallowed the apple, you can't
go back, anyhow, can you?

Pearl set her picnic basket aside and curled toward him, whispered
a sweet valentine in his ear, then snuggled close with a sigh. Harry
felt a rising warmth as the projector produced a rosy sunrise on the
lower quarter of the dome. He kissed her and she slipped a hand onto
his trousers. He cupped her breast and kissed her ear and heard a
sigh when he touched her more intimately. They kissed deeply and
drew closer still. Then he heard footsteps on the marble floor of the
gallery approaching the planetarium. Stirred from that cloud of lust,
he managed to give Pearl a gentle nudge. Quickly she rose, slipped
past him, and had a peek at the door. Putting a finger to her lips, she
waved him over beside her. Both pressed their backs up against the
wall behind the door as someone entered the darkened planetarium
and hurried up the aisle to the console. The moment the intruder's
back was turned Pearl and Harry ran off down the gallery, ignoring
shouts behind them.

— **4** —

Close to four o'clock, they were hurrying down a narrow cobblestone street lined with cherry trees planted during the Hayes Administration. Pearl carried a single American Beauty rose she had found for her mother on Knapp Avenue just below the hill while Harry nibbled on a crescent roll he purchased at a lunchwagon. At the bottom of a thick sloping wood, a quarter of a mile southeast of the University, Drinkwater Street led between several old derelict four-story Second Empire brownstones on Harry's left and a six-foot concrete embankment topped by the long row of cherry trees to his right. The height of the mansard rooftops and the thick woods above the sidewalk splintered sunlight even at midday. Harry and Pearl walked along toward a large ivy-shrouded brick building that blocked the end of the street behind which lay a vast ravine of salt marshes and decaying lime deposits, a sunken riverwash sealed off almost a century earlier during the construction of the city bulwark. Neglect marked this once-elegant corner of the city. The sidewalks were cracked and broken in several places. The iron lampposts that lined the street were in dire need of painting. Even a sign above the stoop on one of the brownstones that read Jordan Mission was flaked and peeling.

As they arrived at a brick building at the end of the street, a breeze swirled up out of the riverwash and fluttered in the chestnut trees that flanked a pair of griffin statues perched on marble plinths. The façade of the building was rendered in Gothic Revival but entirely sober and restrained, bereft of ornament or beauty. A stone plaque cut flush in the architrave read simply:

WINTERHILL

Now Harry understood that Pearl's mother did not live in a cozy room somewhere by herself, unattended to and alone except for a gorgeous young daughter whose brief visits were likely all the joy she knew anymore. Instead, he was standing outside of the city's most famous sanitarium, home to those who had no other, who were wanted nowhere else, who were no longer able to go about freely as common citizens in this great Republic. Off in the distance, Harry heard the bells of the university campanile ringing in the hour. Pearl had already hurried up the stairs to the iron doors within a gray sandstone portico, waiting just long enough to see that he still intended to accompany her before passing indoors. Looking back down Drinkwater Street, past the row of cherry trees and sullen brownstones, Harry could see traffic roaring up Knapp Avenue, people hurrying by, vibrancy abounding. He heard birds, too, singing in the summer woods below University Hill.

The Reception Hall was a cheerless, high-ceilinged foyer with a large wooden desk in front of one wall, a glass case and a simple wooden bench across from it. The sanitarium air was cool and bone-dry, smelling of wood varnish and recent disinfectant scrubs on the sea-blue linoleum floors. Short walnut-paneled corridors led off to the east and west wings of the building and a staircase just left of the oak desk headed up to a second floor. Hundreds of voices urgent yet indistinct echoed from deep within the interior of the institution. Pearl stood at the front desk in conversation with an elderly nurse. Familiar smiles passed between them as Pearl took a pen in hand and scribbled on a sheet of paper attached to a clipboard. A white-jacketed attendant came down the stairs carrying a chart-book and hurried off down the east corridor where a woman had just begun shrieking. Pearl came over to Harry. For once, she spoke plainly. "Momma's late today so we'll have to wait to visit her. It won't be too long. She's still got to eat supper at six."

"That's fine, dear."

Wondering what it must be like to be confined here, Harry glanced down toward the west wing just as a group of people came around the corner there, an older gentleman accompanied by four reasonably attractive women and a pair of small children, a boy and a girl, each dressed smartly as if for church on Sunday. The prettiest of the four women was crying, consoled by the other three. The man's expression was firm, both children idle in their own thoughts. Behind them followed a stocky balding doctor in a long white coat and a nurse with a tin water pitcher and a small empty tray. The doctor was attempting to converse with the man who would have none of it, proceeding relentlessly instead toward the front exit.

"You simply must appreciate the seriousness of her condition, sir," the doctor persisted. "Psychopathic symptoms and melancholia are not taken lightly by Eastlake Court. The sad fact is, we've had no choice in the direction of our treatments. None at all. Indeed, it's what the law demands."

At the iron doors, the man stepped out and held the right door open for the women and the children to pass. When they had gone down the granite steps, he came back in and let the door close, then turned to the doctor, his face grim and resolute. "Veronal?"

"In small cachets, it's perfectly therapeutic," the doctor replied, somewhat defensively.

"Tappings? The 'pack'? Morning and night?"

Noticing Harry by the desk with Pearl, the doctor lowered his voice. "Quite common procedures for her condition. Not the least unusual. If it's your worry that Sophia's been mistreated, well, I assure you that's patent nonsense. Indeed, her hydrotherapy — "

"My sister was kept on that table downstairs for a week! Good God, man! Who's calling whom cuckoo? No wonder she's suffered hallucinations! The very idea of it boggles the mind!"

"Had we been informed prior to Sophia's admittance of the pellagra, there'd have been no need for this misunderstanding. Any competent physician — "

"Would not send a patient here for treatment if he entertained any hope of improvement, much less a cure! Who exactly are the deranged at Winterhill, doctor? Tell me that!"

"Sir!"

"Listen here!" the man interrupted, barely containing his fury. "I'll have the proper dismissal papers delivered to your desk no later than ten o'clock this evening, at which hour I expect to hear from your office informing me that Sophia's private clothing and belongings have been restored to her and that she is ready to be released into my charge."

"I will not! Her condition is far too grave to permit movement at this time. Logic absolutely forbids it!"

The man's face darkened further, his jaw tightened. When he spoke next, his voice quivered. "Logic's requirement, doctor, does not suggest personal choice in this matter. Otherwise, I'd see you and your entire staff dragged out into Drinkwater Street this very afternoon and flogged like mules! Even Judge Cowherd's law doesn't demand brutality in the name of medicine! My goodness!"

With that, the man flung the door open and hurried out under the portico. The iron door slammed shut again, and the echo reverberated down the corridors. Muttering to herself, the nurse with the water pitcher walked past Harry and went upstairs. The doctor stared at the door for another few moments, then came over to the front desk. There, the older nurse offered her two cents worth. "I knew that girl would be a headache when we admitted her. A family like that."

Disgusted, the doctor shook his head. "The man's an idiot. I don't doubt we'll see him in here one day. Undoubtedly in the basement with the paranoiacs."

The nurse handed him another chart-book. He flipped a few pages forward, glanced at them briefly, nodded. Finally he turned to Pearl and smiled. "Hello, dear. How are you today?"

"Just swell, doc."

"Come to see your mother?"

"Yes, sir."

"Well, she's doing just wonderfully. We're very pleased." He gave Pearl a pat on the shoulder, then took a pen and scribbled a notation in the chart-book. When he finished, the doctor noticed Harry waiting quietly beside the desk. "May I help you, sir?"

Pearl answered instead. "This is my pal Harry. He's here to see Momma, too. She's been asking about him all summer."

"Oh yes? How nice!"

The doctor tucked the chart-book under his elbow and offered Harry his right hand. "I'm Doctor Cornelius Bloom."

"Harry Hennesey." They shook hands. "Pleased to meet you, sir." Somehow Bloom's name sounded familiar. Maybe he'd seen it in the newspapers, or mentioned in a newsreel.

Meanwhile, the doctor returned his attention to Pearl. "I trust

Katherine's told you that your mother is still occupied with her kinesia therapy?"

Pearl nodded.

"Well, it oughtn't to be long," the doctor continued. "I know she's quite anxious to see you." To the woman at the desk, Bloom said, "Would you ring Seven, please, and let Miriam know her patient's daughter has arrived? Thank you."

The doctor smiled pleasantly at Pearl. "You're welcome, of course, to wait for your mother in the Gallery. We've just put in a row of new benches this morning."

Pearl grinned. "Sure, that'd be swell. What do you say, honey?"

Before Harry could reply, Bloom interrupted. "Actually, being that Mr. Hennesey's not family, he'll have to be sent for once your mother's ready to receive visitors. I'm sorry, but those are the rules."

"Oh, that's fine," Harry said, not wanting to intrude on Pearl's appointment. Better to let her have some privacy with her mother. "I'll just wait here until you're ready. No trouble at all."

"Are you sure, honey?" Pearl asked, as another pair of white-jacketed attendants came down from upstairs and hurried by toward the west corridor. "It don't seem fair."

"Really, darling, it's perfectly fine. You go ahead and call me when it's time. I'll be here."

"Gee, honey," she said, with a smile, "you're a peach!"

After darting forward to kiss him on the cheek, she rushed off down the east corridor humming a Rudy Vallée tune as she disappeared around the corner.

Once she had gone, the doctor remarked, "A very interesting girl. Remarkable, in fact."

"Yes, indeed," Harry agreed, still blushing from her kiss. He wondered what the doctor thought. Maybe she shouldn't have kissed him, but love isn't easily hidden. Once taken root in the heart, his mother used to say, it flowers for all to see.

"How long have you been acquainted with her?"

"Honestly, I'm not entirely certain that I am," Harry conceded with a smile. "She's quite a case."

"Yes, she is," Bloom agreed.

The telephone at the desk rang and the nurse answered it, and held up a forefinger to the doctor indicating the call was for him. As Bloom took the receiver, Harry strolled across the lobby to the glass case where several old photographs and sketches of Winterhill and its original environs were on display for visitors. In an early daguerreotype, the sanitarium alone occupied this knoll atop the riverwash, looking stark and austere. The city had not yet risen around it; Drinkwater Street was hardly more than a dusty footpath. Below, in a grainy ferrotype made on some bright spring afternoon, Winterhill appeared to be the terminus for a grand parade of carriages and patriotic garlands, gaily decorated floats and costumed children proceeding in formation, genuine exuberance in the air. A more recent one revealed a similar view of the sanitarium's façade in wintertime, snowdrifts burying Drinkwater Street, only the granite heads of the twin griffins visible and an icy stillness surrounding a solitary human figure posed within the gray portico in dark greatcoat and cane. The caption was scrawled out in cursive by ink and pen, and read:

Doctor Emerson Peerbolte at Winterhill, 1883

"Sir?"

Harry turned away from the exhibit as Doctor Bloom approached from the desk.

"As it happens, there's been an unforeseen delay with Mrs. Stelinger. I trust you won't be overly inconvenienced. Visiting procedures are often quite complicated to coordinate."

Harry took out his pocketwatch and checked the time. Nearly a quarter past four now. This was becoming inconvenient, after all. He snapped the watch shut. "Well, I do have late appointments uptown."

"Where do you work?"

"I have an office with City Transfer & Storage," he replied, slipping the old watch back into his pocket. "At 83rd Street between Diever and Powell near the river."

"Follette's warehouse?"

"Yes, it is. Do you know him?"

The doctor cheered up. "I certainly do. Charley and I shared a dormitory room for a semester and a half at Princeton in '88. He was somewhat of a dub with the books, but quite the ace on a tennis court. A fair match for Tilden, I'd say. Very popular fellow, too, high-spirited and extremely wicked, at least when supplied with bourbon and girls. I'd often wondered what a dedicated phrenologist might have made of his case. Of course, he's done quite well with himself since, hasn't he?"

"Yes, he has."

Bloom shook his head and chuckled, clearly reminded of youthful days filled with unbridled fun.

"He and I have done business together since late January," Harry remarked, trying to sound important. Bloom didn't need to know he was just renting a space.

"And yet you've still got your shirt?"

Harry chuckled. "Follette's got a keen enough mind for transactions, no doubt. Really, though, we hardly see him. His desk has been piled high with ledgers all summer. A man named Pennington takes care of that part of the business for him."

The doctor laughed, too. "Well, I've never known old Charley to sit still long enough to throw a shadow. The crazy fellow's too busy earning money to relax and enjoy it."

Bloom checked his own gold pocketwatch and reopened the chartbook. He turned back to Harry. "Look here, I have my afternoon rounds to make now. But if you'd care to see a bit of the institution, you're more than welcome to accompany me. It's somewhat out of routine, but I always enjoy a good diversion, and unless your backside is made of cast iron, you won't find that bench over there particularly inviting. Katherine'll notify us when Mrs. Stelinger is ready for her visit."

"Thank you," Harry said, pleased now. "I'd enjoy a tour."

"Well, come on along, then," Bloom said, heading up the stairs. "We'll begin on Ward Three. One of my favorite patients is expecting me. I think you'll find her quite intriguing."

So Pearl Stelinger's her name, Harry thought as he followed Bloom, not Olive Blanchard. Cobb and his pal Fred are on the wrong track, after all. That's wonderful news, but you can't drop your apprehension without studying the thing forward and back. Unless Cobb was a complete idiot, he must have trailed Pearl here more than once to find out whom she was visiting. Let's say you're him. What do you do? You go to the desk and ask for a name. You don't spare a word. Get every piece of information you can wring out of that nurse. Loot one of the drawers if you can. Anything that might help. But you don't leave until you're satisfied.

Harry decided to ask Bloom about this as soon as he could.

Ascending the broad staircase just behind the doctor, he heard voices issuing from the sanitarium interior like the hum of electricity within the walls. On the second-floor landing, a hand-painted signpost indicated the direction of the four wards. Six windows looking out onto Drinkwater Street were shaded and barred, creating a dusky atmosphere. Several attendants hovered about a curiously obese patient in a wheelchair down to the west, while a nurse walked arm-in-arm with an old man as he proceeded carefully along the linoleum floor.

"Am I correct in assuming you've never been to Winterhill before today?" the doctor asked Harry, strolling down the corridor toward the attendants with the wheelchair.

"Yes, that's true," Harry nodded. "In fact, I hadn't even the vaguest idea of its location. Of course, I'd heard of Winterhill from newspaper stories and idle conversation." Frankly, rumor had the place being a cesspool of degradation and hopelessness, a sort of calcimined dungeon into which societal rejects were tossed to keep them out of public view. So claimed the editorials.

"Well, there's no doubt the public has a singularly jaundiced opinion of us, though I should say entirely undeserved. I'm perfectly aware that we're thought of as either a jail or a hospital, depending upon which of our patients is being discussed on any given occasion. In truth, we're neither. Winterhill is an institution whose express purpose is the care of individuals whose place in society has been forfeited to the circumstance of incurable illness. We house neither criminals nor treatable invalids."

Bloom led Harry down the dim corridor to a door with the nu-
meral 3 mounted in brass below a glass transom. Stepping aside to
allow Harry past, he said, "Less than three-dozen patients of the two
thousand or so admitted to this institution since Peerbolte and Mc-
Naughton revived Winterhill as a sanitarium have left here alive. That
fact disturbs a small circle of politicals downtown who truly believe
our purpose here ought to be convalescence and rehabilitation. However, it is my view that they are themselves victims of pathological self-
loathing, social architects whose interest in the welfare of the infirm
extends only to the depth of their own guilt for suffering the need of a
Winterhill in their shining city."

Inside, Harry was reminded of the drab recreation hall in Bellemont's old Alamo auditorium: plain card and game tables and straight-
back chairs randomly situated here and there, wooden benches against
the plaster walls, nearly all taken up by the dozens of patients in the
room just then, most of whom wore either pajamas or bathrobes and
bedroom slippers. Each was engaged in some form of activity. Who
could complain about this? Were these sorts of remedies so terribly
dismal?

"Recreation is a tonic to superior mental hygiene," Bloom remarked, surveying the room. "Without it, I've no doubt all of us here
would become hopelessly maudlin, succumbing to precisely those
symptoms of melancholia that have brought many of our patients to
Winterhill these past several years."

Fascinated by so much activity, Harry did his utmost not to stare at
the patients busying themselves with bridge tournaments and knitting,
solving anagrams and crossword puzzles, drawing, reading, or chatting
amiably with fellow patients or one of the half-dozen attendants passing in and out from the hall. A Ping-Pong table sat in the middle of the
room, busied by a young woman dressed in pink pajamas and involved
in a lively game with one of the male attendants. Proceeding at his
own pace, the doctor greeted patients, exchanged pleasantries, listened
to complaints, lent a cheerful word then moved on, arriving after a few
minutes at one of three square checker tables where a microcephalic
girl in yellow polka dot pajamas sat hunched over the board, constant-

ly shuffling the red and black checkers about in no order Harry was able to discern.

"Good afternoon, dear," said Bloom, pulling up the chair across from the girl. "May I join you?"

She nodded without looking up.

"Thank you, dear," Bloom said, sitting down. "Gilda, I've brought a friend who would very much like to meet you. His name is Harry."

Eyes averted, she quickly thrust her right hand upward across the table toward Harry, while continuing to slide the wooden checkers around the board with the other. After they shook, she blinked and a single tear rolled down her cheek. Rather than wiping it off, she rapidly undid the big pink bow at her collar with the same hand she had offered Harry, then immediately re-tied the ribbon with astonishing dexterity. Another pink ribbon, this one knotting a little tuft of blonde hair on top of her tiny head, dangled loosely down the back of her neck. Her facial skin was pallid and mottled, her lips dry. She had an awful overbite, but a sweet angelic smile.

"Shall we play a game, dear?" Bloom asked the girl, sliding his chair a notch closer to the table. He placed the chart-book on his lap.

The girl nodded, her face tucked even lower now. Behind Harry, one of the attendants had both hands on the shoulders of an older fellow, shaking him awake. The patient grumbled a crude imprecation, and waved his own arms at the attendant, driving him off. Without even bothering to look, Bloom remarked, "Post-prandial naps are frowned upon here. Not even a brief snooze. No therapy is suitable for lay-abouts. Only the strictest regimen of proper sleep and wakefulness obtains in this sanitarium. Do you prefer to play black or red today, Gilda?"

Shuffling the checkers in a blur, the girl divided red from black, and gathered the red checkers toward her into a neat pile. Next, Harry watched her deliberate over the placement of each red checker in its proper location across the board. Doctor Bloom set his up more casually, chatting with the girl about the sunny weather and somebody named Lucretia. To Harry, the girl's murmuring voice sounded impossibly reedy and frail, her words mostly indistinguishable. However, the doctor seemed to have no difficulty at all understanding her.

"Well, I'm sure she'll write to you soon, dear, then you'll feel much better about everything," said Bloom. "Remember what I told you last week: Oft the pangs of absence are removed by a letter."

The doctor finished lining up his black checkers and sat back. Looking up at Harry, he observed, "Gilda is the most marvelously gifted checkers player I've ever challenged." He smiled at the girl. "Aren't you, dear?"

She hid a sly grin behind her forearm, while fidgeting with one of the wooden red checkers from the king row. Her eyes were focused intensely upon the board, her brow furrowed with concentration. Harry wondered how her thoughts were organized, whether by logic or instinct. Can the idiot be a genius, or vice versa? He hadn't a clue how to answer that.

"You should know that I was college champion at Princeton," said Doctor Bloom. "Yet in the three months Gilda's been with us at Winterhill, I've never been able to defeat her. Go ahead, dear. Your move."

The girl just sat still, fiddling with her red checkers. After a few moments, Bloom said to Harry, "Gilda has an extremely well-developed ethic of fair play. You see, she won't allow me to grant her the advantage of moving first because she knows the rules require black to start. If I had red and went first, she'd refuse to continue the game unless I backed up and allowed her to go first. Of course, since she's refused lately to play any color other than red, I am always obliged to begin the game." He smiled. "Good for you, dear." Then Bloom shoved a black checker forward. "Here we go."

Harry looked up from the game just as a male patient in a blue bathrobe at the back of the room threw a small book at one of the attendants, hitting him in the head. Immediately the young woman in pink pajamas at the Ping-Pong table attacked the book-thrower with her wooden paddle. There was a scuffle as she struck the book-thrower about the neck and upper back. Both she and her adversary had to be restrained by another pair of attendants who rushed in from the corridor. Bloom did not take his eyes off the checkerboard. When Harry glanced down again, fully half of Bloom's twelve black checkers resided in the microcephalic girl's possession, while three of her own red checkers sat in the adverse king row already crowned.

His fingers folded under his chin, Bloom commented, "Patients run amuck up here on a regular basis. So long as their rampage is contained to this ward, we're forgiving. Triple bromides and prolonged baths usually solve the problem. If somebody goes truly haywire, restraints may be required, or perhaps dope-pills. Of course, on certain occasions a period of isolation is often required as well. Just last evening, for example, we were forced to send a young woman to what we call 'the nursery' for attempting to throttle one of our assistant superintendents. Her hallucinations insisted that he'd been sneaking into her ear canals at bedtime for the sinister purpose of eavesdropping on her prayers."

The girl jumped a pair of Bloom's black checkers, then crowned another of her own reds as the game proceeded toward its inevitable conclusion. Her sweet eyes lit now, incapable of disguising her glee, the girl collected still another black checker from Bloom. Yet a smile crossed the doctor's expression, too, pride evident in his patient's nearing triumph. Two more offerings from Bloom were each swallowed up by the girl's response. Soon she collected the doctor's twelfth black checker and stacked it atop her capture pile, a wry grin on her lips.

Harry was speechless. Someone ought to be told about her. Not the tabloids, of course, but somebody. What a splash she'd make onstage at the Adelphi Opera House. Despite her freakish appearance, she'd be worth a fortune. In any case, you certainly couldn't conceal her talent from the public forever, could you?

"Well played, dear," said Bloom, rising from his chair. He removed the gold pocketwatch from his white coat, checked it, and smiled. "Unless I stall, in which case Gilda will quickly become agitated and quite unpleasant, no game between us lasts more than five minutes. Indeed, I've recently begun to suspect that she plays to finish rather than to win. She seems to enjoy seeing the board clear of all the black checkers as it is now."

Bloom and Harry looked back down at the checkerboard where only the red checkers remained. As they watched, Gilda ran the fingers of her left hand rapidly over the red checkers, touching each once lightly then moving on to the next while tying and untying the big pink bow at her collar with her free hand. Bloom remarked, "Do you see anything recognizable there in the pattern of the red checkers?"

Harry shook his head. "Not at all." Nor had he any idea what to look for.

"Neither do I. Yet I'm convinced there is one. My theory is that Gilda plays to clear the board of all the black checkers in order to reveal a specific arrangement of the red checkers. She wins because that is the fastest route to achieving her goal."

"Won't the patterns change with each game?"

"Presumably."

"Then why play at all?" Harry asked, somewhat perplexed now. He hated mental contests like this. "Why not just arrange whichever checkers she likes in the way she prefers?"

Bloom shrugged. "Well, of course I've asked Gilda that question at least a dozen times, haven't I, dear?"

The girl cracked a subtle smile, and continued to dance her fingertips over the red checkers.

"Perhaps the process of playing an actual game establishes the final pattern of red checkers," suggested Bloom. "Perhaps she requires an opponent to meet her goal of order and arrangement, whatever that might ultimately be. Or perhaps random play itself divines a pattern for her."

Stumped, Harry admitted, "It's all very confusing."

Bloom smiled again. "You see, many of our patients here at Winterhill have nearly indecipherable twists and complexes. One may spend decades determining the nature of any single patient's obsession or delusion. Gilda is a marvelous enigma whose solution is likely contained in an abstruse arrangement of red game disks on an ordinary checkerboard. Quite fascinating."

Doctor Bloom bent down to touch the microcephalic girl gently on her left shoulder. "Thank you for the game, dear. Shall we play again tomorrow?"

The girl nodded slowly as another glassy tear rolled off her cheek. Yet she, too, was smiling.

In another corridor on the south end of the sanitarium, Harry waited while Bloom spoke on a wall-telephone with the nurse downstairs at the reception desk. His voice sounded weary. The chart-book was folded open and he scribbled all the while they spoke. Behind him, two attendants led a man wearing only a sagging diaper and a pair of bedroom slippers past toward the stairs midway down the corridor. The man was alternately weeping and cursing, and reeked of warm urine. Harry wondered how Bloom survived in this peculiar environment. Where does the doctor find hope? He was certain he'd lose his own mind after a week, or take a club to someone. He also wondered where Pearl's mother was, and what sort of affliction kept her here. The girl seemed utterly transformed just crossing the threshold. This wasn't the place for wisecracks, was it? My God, how had she managed to keep this a secret from him? And why?

Harry wandered over to one of the windows and parted the drawn shade to peer out over the vast riverwash ravine whose withered salt marshes seemed more barren and desolate from within the sanitarium. A plaintive wail issued from somewhere downstairs and persisted for more than a minute. An attendant stopped to speak with Bloom. Harry studied the sunny grounds at the rear of the sanitarium where he saw groups of patients dressed in white, wandering the expanse of grass or sitting on tarnished lawn chairs under holiday umbrellas. A net had been strung up near the dogwood trees in one corner of the lawn and several patients and attendants batted a volleyball back and forth. Harry noticed other patients in the garden walking single file among the rose bushes. You could go all over this city today and not find a more sympathetic picture.

"Sunshine is God's sparkling restorative," said Bloom, arriving at Harry's elbow and glancing outside as well. "Between June and September, we forbid our patients to use the gymnasium unless we're having a cloudburst. From noon dinner until supper at six, we escort them out of doors in groups small enough to monitor and allow them as wide a range of activities as their general health and behavior permits. Our attendants organize daily programs for croquet or lawn bowling, pitching horseshoes, poetry readings, even the collecting of summer blossoms and butterflies if they like." Bloom chuckled lightly. "Of course, as I'm sure you've already observed, many of our patients are barely ambulatory these days. In their case, just being helped out into the sunlight for an hour each afternoon provides vital assurance that they are indeed still with us."

Harry saw one of the patients standing at the tall ivy-wrapped iron fence that divided Winterhill's manicured grounds from the empty ravine. He was staring off into the breezy distance. One of the attendants stood beside him. Soon another attendant arrived and the man was led away from the fence.

"Well, come along, again," said Bloom, folding his chart-book shut. "Ward Nine awaits." The doctor smiled at a nurse passing by. She winked at Bloom and he blushed. Inside the recreation hall, somebody began singing aloud:

> *"Pussy, where have you been to-day?*
> *In the meadows a-sleep in the hay.*
> *Pussy, you are a lazy cat,*
> *If you have done no more than that."*

Though it felt unsettling to be strolling along within the walls of the sanitarium, Harry followed Doctor Bloom to the end of the corridor and around two attendants conversing at the corner, then on to the staircase in the east corridor. Those wailing voices he had been hearing became more strident. The crying resonated in the dark paneled stairwell as he and Bloom descended.

"You see, the welfare of our patients is of the utmost concern to all of us at Winterhill," the doctor said, taking each step downward with care. "Each attendant is keenly aware of the shame these poor souls experience in being confined here. That virtually all our patients, even the chronic neurasthenics, suffer some incurable malady lends a bleak perspective to any procedures or treatments we might elect to pursue, which is precisely why our work these days is so greatly misunderstood outside of the institution. In truth, Mr. Hennesey, Winterhill is a sanctuary. The grounds of the sanitarium provide an anesthetic to the heartache and despair many of our patients endure merely by rising from their beds each morning. Our darling Gilda is just such a case. Left here on our doorstep by a circus troupe one evening in May after a brutal assault by persons unknown, Gilda nearly bled to death before one of our night attendants discovered her huddling in the juniper. She was catatonic for the first twelve days. The gravity of the injustice done her that night cannot be overstated. Yet within six weeks her injury had fully healed, as well as her spirit. One morning afterward, Gilda herself drew me to the checkerboard, introducing there this strange riddle of her genius."

Bloom reached the door at the bottom of the stairs and held it open for Harry, allowing him to enter the noisy hallway ahead where a dozen or more attendants and patients shared the corridor like Saturday afternoon traffic along Columbia Avenue. Following Harry into the hallway, the doctor continued, his tone darker now. "Last week, an examination revealed a cancer in dear Gilda's blood which will soon take her life. Were she my own daughter, I'd be no more disheartened. Yet, look here — "

Harry knew now why she wasn't on stage at the Adelphi. Her story was more tragic than that: neither fame and fortune, nor salvation in this world. Perhaps somewhere across the veil she can wish for pleasantness and have some expectation of reward.

Bloom opened the first door on the left and let Harry peek inside a ward whose beds occupied a room larger than the old gymnasium at Bellemont Normal School. Lowering his voice, the doctor said, "In this Sick Hall, each patient you see before you is dying of some cancer or respiratory disease. None are likely to be with us at Christmas. Fate is already rid of them. Their futures lie now solely within our keeping."

As he leaned further into the room, a septic odor reached Harry's nostrils. Disgust turned his stomach before he held his breath. Bloom, seeming entirely unfazed, added, "Restoring to these patients some measure of dignity, or extending a daily kindness, is the obligation of every member of our staff, one that has been accepted with grace and dedication as long as I've been here. Much of our work at this sanitarium consists of programs — moving pictures, concerts, ballroom dancing, lyceum bureaus — that attempt to inspire enthusiasm in our patients for each day of life still remaining them. In addition, we do everything we can to address the spiritual needs of these patients. Each Sunday afternoon from three to four, for example, divine service is held in the Chapel, and is always well-attended. I myself bring Gilda because she seems lately to enjoy the hymns so very much."

Bloom walked over to the bedside of an elderly woman who had just spilled a glass of orange juice down the front of her pajamas. She was weeping silently, either from frustration or embarrassment. Bloom removed the glass from her lap, then grabbed a hand towel from a side table and gingerly dabbed the spilled juice while speaking softly to her. As he finished, she squeezed his hand. Six beds away, a dark-haired young girl began shouting for somebody to come administer iodine to her genitalia. Behind Harry, a nurse and a pair of male attendants entered the Sick Hall carrying bandages and linen. Leaving the elderly woman's side, Bloom scribbled briefly into his chart-book, then directed Harry back out into the corridor where another attendant with oily black hair came up to the doctor and handed him a clipboard. Harry could still hear the girl calling for iodine, her pathetic voice pained and urgent.

After examining a notation on the clipboard, Bloom turned to Harry. "Mr. Hennesey, it seems a minor emergency in Ward Four requires my attention. I've asked Desmond here to escort you to the Gallery where Mrs. Stelinger is seeing her visitors today." The doctor took out his pocketwatch and checked the time.

"Is it five yet?" Harry asked, concerned now about the lateness of the hour. "I do have those appointments." He felt terrifically anxious, too, to escape this sad, dissipating place. *Why are we so often compelled to see terrible things when nothing can be done about them? We can't cure a bleeding tumor with love and sympathy, can we? Lungs fail and hearts give out whether we cry, hope, or do nothing. Men like Bloom must be saints.*

"I have ten 'til five," Bloom replied, cheerfully, "but you shouldn't be here much longer. Mrs. Stelinger will have to eat supper at six, regardless. I'm sure you'll be well on your way before that."

Just then, Harry's attention was drawn to a man being wheeled out of a room down the corridor. The fellow was strapped flat on his back aboard a metal gurney, his head immobilized, tape and cotton sealing his mouth shut. Yet his eyes were frantic, his fists clenched, panic or terror or fury clear in his expression. Attendants pushed his gurney farther down the corridor while a small group of patients in the company of another nurse followed a few yards behind.

"Mr. Hennesey?" Bloom offered Harry his hand. "It was very nice to have met you. Although life at Winterhill is certainly far from humdrum, I do always welcome the diversion of chatting with visitors such as yourself. I trust you've seen that our patients here at the sanitarium are receiving the finest care and attention possible from a dedicated staff. All we ask of you is that these unfortunate souls, such as our dear Gilda, not be forgotten." They shook hands. "You'll give my regards to Charley Follette, won't you?"

"I certainly will." Harry nodded. "But, listen, may I ask you one more thing? It's an odd question, but it's important."

"Certainly."

"You see, there's a fellow I'm wondering about, whether he's been up here or not." He gave Bloom a brief description of Cobb, mentioning only that he seemed obsessed with Pearl's family.

Bloom laughed. "Back in May, in fact. He was here one afternoon pestering my staff about anyone with the last name of Blanchard. We told him there hasn't been a patient here with that name in six years, not since a longtime friend of ours, Simon Blanchard, passed away with chronic tuberculosis. Apparently your fellow didn't believe us, and tried to bully Katherine into admitting him to Records & Statistics, something she had no authority to do, and told him so. Eventually, I had to ask a pair of our larger orderlies to throw him out the front door," Bloom chuckled, "which they did with great enthusiasm, I might add. And he hasn't been back since."

"Do you keep extensive records for all your patients?"

"Case histories, of course, which are invaluable, but not personal files. Those are destroyed once the patient passes on. I've always believed in the sacrosanctity of privacy for the deceased." Bloom glanced again at the clipboard. "Is there anything else I can help you with? Please let that dear girl know she needn't worry about Mr. Cobb coming back here. He's not permitted to set foot in this building again. Next time he'll be arrested."

"Yes, I'll tell her that." Harry grinned. "She'll appreciate it. Thank you very much."

"Well, good day, sir," said Bloom, cheerfully. "Enjoy your visit with Mrs. Stelinger." Then the doctor turned on his heel and hurried off to the staircase.

Harry removed his own watch to check the time again, and Desmond gently directed him out of the path of a small East Indian boy whose head was partially wrapped in bandages. Eyes shut tight, the boy proceeded slowly along the corridor by brushing the fingers of his right hand against the wall. As the boy passed, Harry heard him buzzing like a housefly. What sort of disease brought that on?

"Follow me," Desmond said, starting down the corridor in the same direction the gurney had gone. Harry kept pace, hoping his visit to Winterhill was nearing its end. If he were ever so unfortunate as to come back here one day as a patient, he hoped someone would smash his head with a brick. When he and Desmond reached the double doors, a hideous scream echoed in the building from somewhere down below. A few moments passed, then another scream came forth, more prolonged and frightening, certainly someone suffering profound agony. Passing through the doors behind the attendant, Harry inquired timidly, "Is anyone seeing to that?"

"Seeing to what?"

"That fellow yelling. It sounds as if he's in quite a lot of pain."

Ahead, the corridor dead-ended at a freight elevator, dividing east and west into unlighted back halls. Desmond grabbed the iron gate to the elevator and wrenched it open for Harry to enter ahead of him. As he came in and closed the gate, the attendant pushed a shock of black hair off his forehead and told Harry, "Don't pay it any mind. That's just Christopher." He rotated the hand crank and the elevator began descending. "He's one of the hummingbirds."

"The what?"

Another bloodcurdling scream issued from somewhere beneath the descending elevator, raising the bristles on the back of Harry's neck.

The attendant brushed his shock of hair back again. "Likes screaming his lungs out even when there's nothing the matter with him. Just to hear himself. We're supposed to let all the hummingbirds downstairs howl like wolves at midnight. Psychoanalytic cranks like Bloom won't let us treat them like the other maniacs in the basement because someone decided they're suicide risks. Everybody hates them."

"I don't see why," Harry chuckled, nervously. Where on earth were they going? Three stories of brick sanitarium were sitting on top of him. If it collapsed, his body wouldn't be found for months. Who'd tell Marie and the children? The elevator stopped at the basement floor. Desmond stepped forward and pulled the iron gate open for Harry. Unlike the upstairs of Winterhill, the walls here were exposed brick and the floors a cold cement. The low ceiling was also brick, clearly dating from the old city. A series of electric ceiling bulbs caged in wire provided only adequate illumination down here where the temperature was much cooler than on the sanitarium's upper floors. It also felt damp, leading him to suppose that a subterranean tributary of the river diverted somewhere beneath Winterhill. Not that the sound of flowing water could possibly be heard in these cold corridors today. All those voices that Harry had been hearing in the old walls of the sanitarium since he arrived seemed to converge and resonate at the precise spot where he now stood: moaning, shrieking, pleading, cackling, wailing, bickering, like the tonal hallucinations of a vulgar nightmare.

"Everyone's hungry," said Desmond, motioning Harry to follow him into the corridor ahead. They both began walking. "Even the manic-depressives start acting like wild animals in the hour before supper. It's the same in the morning. We wake them up at six and breakfast isn't until seven. It doesn't take an hour to get them dressed and ready to go, either, but by half past some of the patients get so cracked they won't settle down enough to wash unless we bring them toast and coffee — or prunes. Last month, Bloom admitted a pair of congenital idiots who won't get out of bed at all in the morning if they're not fed a snack of milk and crackers and told a bedtime story. Isn't that sweet?"

His skin crawling, Harry strode quickly beside the attendant down a corridor lined with solid iron doors, cells whose tiny barred windows allowed only a peek through. Behind these apertures spoke many of the lunatic voices that surrounded him now:

"Georgy-boy knows he's been a bad, bad fellow, but if you don't come in here now and fix his zipper, he swears he'll give Little Audrey more candy than she cares to eat!"

"Bring me boiled potatoes, breaded chops in tomato sauce, powdered soapstone, collodion, tripe, baloney, hooey, propho kits, females, chimpanzees, doctors!"

"Dear Edna, if you can hear me, let the cat out at eight and tell the milkman two quarts. I'm coming home tonight."

Hearing each so close-by gave Harry a singular fright. Why was this fellow Desmond walking so damned slowly? Up ahead, the corridor split like a brick warren, dividing the floor into smaller segments, housing still more cells. The dampness gave him a faint chill. There was a nasty odor here, too, like soiled wet bed clothing. An iron door slammed shut with a loud bang in the distance. Closer, a portable electric generator buzzed to life and somebody began to whimper.

"Why did you bring me down here?" he asked Desmond as they approached an open room whose entrance was flanked by a pair of large sturdy-looking attendants, both seated in wooden chairs. He felt thoroughly spooked now and on the verge of panic, but he knew that you don't antagonize your guide unless you're willing to go off on your own, which he certainly was not.

Desmond told him, "It's a shortcut to the Gallery from the Sick Hall. Bloom said you were in a rush."

"Stepping out a tenth story window is a shortcut to the sidewalk."

"Huh?"

"Let's just hurry, can't we?" *So what if this fellow thinks I'm a coward? It wouldn't be the worst opinion anyone's had.*

From within the room, a familiar scream shot forth. Arriving at the open door, his guide stopped beside the other two men and removed a pair of Turkish cigarettes from his shirt pocket and handed one to each. Harry peeked around the threshold and saw the most extraordinary sight: a square room painted entirely in white, with perfectly smooth walls, floor, and ceiling, entirely devoid of fixtures or furniture except for a post-less bed bolted to the floor in the middle of the room and covered with a rubber bedspread as white as everything else. Upon the bed, flat on his back, completely encased in wet wafer-thin sheets, wrapped so tightly he could scarcely flex to breathe, lay a young man with an ice pack on his head. Here was Christopher the hummingbird, held in an extraordinary trap. As Harry stared at him, Christopher shrieked again like a mad rooster at dawn.

All three attendants laughed. Then so did Christopher. In fact, he seemed to Harry to be enjoying himself immensely, much more so than the attendants who were watching over the poor fellow. Although moisture dripped off the patient's head beneath the ice pack, he did not appear to be suffering any particular discomfort. Indeed, the opposite was true; his face was relaxed, his demeanor oddly calm. He howled again. A few moments later, a distant voice howled in mimicry of Christopher. Then another from elsewhere. Now a third, and a fourth, ringing out almost in chorus.

"My God!" Harry exclaimed, fully disturbed now by the murky dreariness of the lower sanitarium, Dante echoing in his head, *Let us not speak of them, but look, and pass on.*

"Damned imbeciles," said the attendant nearest the door. He banged the wall with a metal plate, making a racket of his own.

Across the way, one of the patients barked like a hyena, and laughter filtered down the corridor. Somebody whistled, and an angry shouting match ensued just four cells away. A bright soprano voice rose above the din, singing clearly,

"Arm and arm we will rove
Thro' a sweet orange grove
Far away in California
Like a bird I mean to fly West again
And I'll hold her close to my breast again."

"Your sweetheart's calling, Desmond," one of the seated attendants remarked. "Leopold told me last night that if you don't put on one of his camisoles or take him dancing soon, he'll knock his head on the wall. He claims you've been unfaithful."

Desmond scowled. "That bastard fruitcake actually mailed a letter to Molly last Thursday. Van Leeuwen swore to me he wouldn't let any of that sort of mail get out of the hatch. You can't trust anyone around here." He noticed Harry hiding by the door. "Come on, let's go. We're late."

As Desmond led Harry off, the other attendant called after him, "What'll we tell Leopold?"

Desmond's reply was a crude obscenity.

They traversed the brick labyrinth in a few more minutes, though the rising clamor from the patients made the walk increasingly frightening and claustrophobic. Drinkwater Street seemed distant now. Reaching the elevator on the eastern side of the basement floor, Harry saw a boy curled into a corner in fetal position, sucking his thumb, and mewling. Three attendants stood over him. Snot slid out the boy's nose. His pupils appeared dilated. One of the attendants held a syringe, another a pair of handcuffs and a lit cigarette. The attendant with the syringe called to Desmond and he went over to help. Across from the elevator was a room with a tiled floor and a huge bathtub within. Beside the tub stood an old man, fully nude, entirely hairless, scalp bald as marble. Water ran into the tub, steam rising from its surface. While Harry watched in horror, a doctor came into view behind the naked man and guided him over the lip of the bathtub and into the water. Placing a rubber pillow under the man's head, the doctor plugged the patient's ears with cotton, ran the hot water a little longer until it reached the level of the man's chin, then switched off the spigot and took out a thermometer to test the water temperature. Satisfied, he slid a chair next to the tub and sat down. The man in the bathtub stared at the ceiling overhead, his face expressionless and dumb.

"Sexual deviant," Desmond explained, nudging Harry toward the elevator just as the lights went out in the tiled room and the door swung closed. "Tattletale, too. Bad mixture. Makes the other patients despise him all the more." Desmond stepped ahead of him and pulled the iron gate open and let Harry enter. When they were both inside, the attendant closed the gate and cranked the elevator switch.

"What was the trouble with that boy in the corner?" Harry asked, feeling more courageous with the elevator ascending. How many people really knew what went on in these rooms? You could see the old brick sanitarium from Roosevelt Boulevard during the day and think nothing of it except perhaps that City Planning had forgotten to raze those old buildings. You could use your best intellect to try to guess what was up here, but there is nothing logical about the miserable indignities that so often occur under the strain of attempting to do good.

Desmond leaned against the gate. "He hallucinated last month that he was Gabriel with the trumpet and jumped out of a third story window at Chapin Place. Landed upside-down on an apple cart. Hopeless case. He'd have been luckier if he'd missed the cart and killed himself. Now he thinks he's a kitten sucking his mother's teat."

The elevator came to a stop on the main floor of the sanitarium's west wing, and the attendant jerked the iron gate open for Harry. "Even kitty-cats won't find a lot of sympathy in the basement here at Winterhill."

After giving Harry simple directions to Ward Six, Desmond stepped aside and let him out into an empty corridor. Then he rotated the lever and descended into the basement once again.

With one last shudder, Harry proceeded through a pair of double doors into a quiet lobby at whose desk sat a tiny woman behind a thick bound ledger. She looked up with a smile. "Hello."

"How do you do?"

"Very well, thank you," the woman replied. "How may I help you?"

"I'm here to visit Mrs. Stelinger. Dr. Bloom gave me permission."

"Certainly," said the woman, who then shifted in her chair just enough to ring a bell on an electric board behind her. She handed a fountain pen to Harry and indicated where he ought to sign his name in the ledger. "Is it a very pleasant day out?" she inquired once he'd scribbled his name and the date into the visitor's column.

"Yes, it is."

"I thought so. It seemed very nice when I walked out my door this morning."

Well, I wish I were taking a walk outdoors, too, Harry thought. How could anyone normal endure this day after day without cracking up? Many years ago, he had briefly imagined himself capable of performing selfless works among the poor and dispossessed, beloved by the crippled and insane thanks to his enduring willingness to forsake personal opportunities in favor of a higher good. *There, but for the grace of God, go I*, was to be his motto, that superlative ideal. Of course, nothing came of it. Like most of us, he was too great a coward, too fearful of those he secretly despised. Instead, he averted his gaze whenever the ugly and hopeless appeared. Once when he was at State, his crowd of fraternity brothers drove out after dark across the railroad tracks to pay a visit on a pair of Negro girls whose yellow eyes were fixed upon oversexed young men. The room they inhabited was barely a cabin with two iron beds and a wood floor that shook when the mattress rocked. A single oil lamp gave enough light for each fellow to find his trousers once he had finished and a window open to the evening air washed out the stink of sweat and soiled linen. Harry took his turn like everyone else, then rushed outdoors afterward and watched a couple of State's finest scholars pissing furiously against the siding under the open window while complaining about venereal disease and nigger whores across the humid night. The next day, both fellows claimed to have been drunk, but that loud indignation in their voices signified a bitter truth that Harry learned by experience some years later: we shame ourselves when we pretend to be better than those whose services we require, whose needs we refuse.

A few minutes passed, then a door opened across the lobby and an attractive brunette-haired nurse, perhaps Marie's age, came toward the desk carrying a worn chart-book and a fresh white hand towel. "Mr. Hennesey?"

"Yes?"

"I'm Miriam Kaye, Mrs. Stelinger's nurse. Would you please come with me?"

She led Harry out another pair of doors that connected the lobby to a sunlit hallway farther ahead. The near perfect quiet in this wing stood in odd contrast with the perpetual noise elsewhere in the sanitarium. This delighted Harry, of course, whose nerves had suffered greatly during the basement crossing. He also found Miriam Kaye delightfully pleasing to the eye. He wondered if she was involved with someone. In her stature and graceful bearing, she also reminded him somewhat of Marie. Or at least it pleased him to think so.

"Margaret's kinesia therapy went quite well today," the nurse remarked. "You may even notice her improvement."

"Actually, we've never met," Harry confessed as they walked. He eyed the chart-book where he noticed the name "Stelinger" and wondered if she might let him look it over. "Her daughter invited me along for the visit this very morning, though I had no idea it would be here. Can you imagine my surprise?"

"You're not a friend of Mrs. Stelinger's?"

"No, only the daughter. In fact, to be honest, until today I hadn't even known her family name." He felt awfully tempted to ask this woman about Mrs. Stelinger's family. What was her secret? Who was she really?

Just beyond the turn in the hallway, they reached a set of double doors with translucent glass panels. Here the nurse stopped and faced Harry. "May I assume you know why Margaret Stelinger is at Winterhill?"

"No, actually," he admitted, "not at all." Now he felt humiliated. How had he failed to ask Pearl such a basic question? That was one of his serious faults, rarely asking people how they were doing or really anything about themselves at all. Marie often complained he gave people the impression he had little interest in them, but why should he pry into the concerns of others? Wouldn't they just tell him if their worries were that great?

The nurse frowned. "My goodness, Mr. Hennesey. Most of our visitors here are familiar with the patients they've come to see. This illness is understood by each as a share of life's promise, however dispiriting at times. In their hearts they feel the epidemic was simply a departure from wellness, not the end of hope."

"Epidemic?"

Miriam Kaye opened the doors for Harry. Ahead stretched a red brick corridor almost the length of the sanitarium, lined with park benches and potted palms, brightened by shafts of warm sunlight pouring in through glass clerestory windows. Near its far end stood dozens of white robed figures, singularly and in groups, each silent and immobile like fine sculpted statuary in a pretty summer garden.

"Encephalitis lethargica," replied the nurse, proceeding forward into the Gallery where the whisper of voices from attendants and visitors barely disturbed the quiet.

"The sleepy-sickness?"

"Yes."

"My God," Harry murmured as he followed just a step behind, his eyes glancing from one rigid patient to another. He had no idea so many victims of the epidemic were brought here. Not having given much thought to it either way, he merely assumed that most of the afflicted had just disappeared into local hospitals, or died quietly at home. "Her daughter's never mentioned a word about it."

"Mrs. Stelinger's been a patient at Winterhill since the 13th of April, 1922, when she was admitted following a series of negative disorder crises that left her virtually absent from our world. I was assigned to her three years ago by Dr. Bloom and have passed much of that time attempting to penetrate the hideous Parkinsonian veil that has hidden her away from us for so long."

Harry searched now for Pearl in the crowd of visitors who had gathered close to loved ones in the sunny Gallery, encouraging faces whose murmured remarks surely bore more comfort than reality. Who, after all, among the afflicted here would likely ever again walk out of Winterhill under his own power? If Purgatory existed on earth, thought Harry, it undoubtedly lay in this sad wing of the sanitarium.

The nurse said to him, "Although you'll find Mrs. Stelinger clearly destitute of initiative and vitality due to the constraining Parkinsonian aboulia, do not confuse this with a lack of perception. I firmly believe that she is still quite functional in the sense of awareness for her misfortune. Only her inability to shed this strange catatonia enough to communicate the depth of her isolation truly separates her from the living. God knows, it is against this unfathomable solitude that Margaret and I have struggled so together."

Passing by the closest group of patients, Harry marveled that anyone could be so cruelly deserted by life. If Fate were this capricious, this mean, little wonder so many people sought joy above all else.

"Margaret very much appreciates Visitors Day," the nurse added, stopping to open her chart-book. "I'm sure you'll see it in her eyes. They still brighten with kind words and affections."

Harry let his own eyes skip through the crowd ahead until at last he caught sight of Pearl seated on a tall wooden stool with her back to the farthest window, slowly brushing the long black hair of the lovely woman posed in warm sunlight before her. Margaret Stelinger stood motionless in the bright afternoon light, her slender figure even in the white sanitarium gown dignified and elegant, her smooth hands held outward palms up as if awaiting another's embrace.

"Would you sign this, please?" The nurse handed Harry the chart-book and a pen with which he quickly scribbled his signature. Just then, a male attendant entered the Gallery from the far end, motioning to Miriam Kaye. With her attention diverted briefly, Harry furtively skimmed the top couple pages. What he saw halfway down page two gave him a terrific shock. On a line describing <u>Parents: Deceased</u>, were written the names, *Thomas and Mary Ellen Blanchard*. Below that line read <u>Children</u>, and Harry saw the name, *Olive May*.

Good grief! It was impossible! That bastard Cobb had her right, all along! How the hell could he have known? Or was it just a guess? The hair color was wrong, her eyes, too. Maybe he's still not sure. Isn't that possible? There was a fierce tightness in Harry's chest as he realized Pearl's existence had completely changed for him with one glance at that damned chart-book.

"Thank you, Mr. Hennesey. The patients you see here in the Gallery today are very special to us. Not only have they survived a most dreadful illness, but the courage they've shown in persisting with their struggle has been an inspiration to all of us at Winterhill."

Taking back the chart-book, the nurse said a pleasant good day, leaving Harry to proceed ahead by himself to the end of the bright Gallery, absolutely staggered by his discovery. He had no thought of what to do. There had to be a million people scattered across the city this afternoon who would kill each other for the payoff on what he'd just found out. He imagined a lot of things, but none that stimulated any true solutions. What should he do now? He really ought to have let well enough alone, but it was much too late for that. You can't run away from anything you know. All you can do is pretend to know something better.

Pearl noticed him as he came out of the crowd nearby, and let the brush fall through her mother's hair once more. Leaning forward, she said softly, "He's here, Momma."

"I'm sorry, dear," Harry muttered, walking up beside her. He did his best to hide the tremble in his voice. "I didn't intend to be so late. As it turned out, Bloom and one of his attendants gave me a grand tour of the institution. It's quite a remarkable place."

What else could he say? Every part of her story was a tragedy now.

Pearl smiled. "Momma, this is my friend, Harry. Ain't he swell?"

Margaret Stelinger's angelic face glowed like alabaster in the late afternoon light. Her violet eyes were clear and moist, her gaze slightly uplifted toward the sky. What her thoughts were, or what her heart desired in that sunny moment, only she would know, as her countenance never wavered, her pose never changed, even as Pearl began humming a tune Harry knew from years ago, a lovely melody whose lyric went:

> *"Bright stars are gleaming high in the Heavens,*
> *Softly the moon floods the earth with her beams;*
> *Night spreads her mantel, all nature is sleeping*
> *As we journey in slumber to the land of Rose Dreams."*

— 5 —

Just after dusk, Harry sat in a green high-back leather booth beside
Pearl in the tropical Palm Court of the Zanzibar Club on Belvedere
Street downtown. Wooden fans whirled in the shadows overhead;
brass torchères mounted on mahogany pilasters issued a gas flame
that diffused light amid the lush foliage between booths; olive-skinned
waiters dressed in red fez and white jackets rushed here and there.
Conversation hummed inside the restaurant, and in the glittering Cairo ballroom across the lobby, a lively dance orchestra played "Oceana
Roll." A lovely gathering, except for Cobb and his partner Fred Markle sharing a booth across the room. They each had highballs and a
plate of noodles. Markle wore his napkin like a bib. What were they
doing here? Cobb had apparently located Pearl sometime after Winterhill and chased her around until Harry met her for dinner when
he finished with his appointments on Ludden Street. Harry had gone
there directly from the sanitarium to arrange for the delivery of some
rebuilt Philco sets on consignment from a radio shop, then headed off
to a third floor apartment two blocks away and around the corner on
Dixwell to see a man named Cosmo who had telephoned about those
Japanese silk kimonos. The elevator was out of service, so Harry had
to walk up three flights of stairs to the apartment at the end of a long
dimly lit hallway. The pudgy fellow who answered the door was the
very picture of Madame Butterfly. He wore a lavender tea gown and
more face paint than Pearl. Harry assumed Cosmo was a fairy until
he called for his wife Myrna, who strolled out of the bedroom with a
lit cigarette and a copy of *A Preface To Morals*. They offered to pay four
hundred dollars for the half-dozen kimonos and celebrated Harry's
acceptance of the deal with glasses of sherry. Half an hour later, he
greeted Pearl on the crowded sidewalk outside the Zanzibar Club and
escorted her indoors. Cobb strolled into the restaurant just after they
were shown a booth in the Palm Court and placed a telephone call
from the lobby, presumably to his pal Fred who showed up about ten
minutes afterward like a late date. Those two took a booth under a
scrawny palm across the crowded room and pretended to be out to

dinner like everyone else. Harry almost laughed. Those fellows were so sure they're minor geniuses, they probably thought they were invisible.

Ladling a spoonful of gravy over a portion of roast chicken, Harry tried to ignore them as he listened to Pearl recount the miserable circumstances of her mother's confinement.

"Well, then I told them that Momma hadn't been sick a day in her whole life, and me neither except for the measles when I was five. She just didn't eat a whole lot anymore and had lost all her pep, but I still thought it was because of the mutt that bit her foot. Everybody in the neighborhood knew Snowy had rabies. I guess it was just plain old lousy luck."

Harry watched Pearl stir a teaspoon of salt into her beef broth. Her pretty eyes sparkled in the gaslight. She had a lovely, quizzical arch to her dark eyebrows he found irresistible. Why had she chosen him among all the fellows in the city? That night at the Orpheum Theater, he had been sitting with his back to her. What had brought her down the aisle to badger him for coffee and doughnuts? He tried to recall what day of the week that had been, imagining perhaps she had just come from visiting her mother and was feeling especially lonely that night. Her mother. God, that horror she suffered! He felt stupid and vain now for having scolded Pearl so often over such silly faults. You just cannot expect someone to be at her best when tragedy makes her incapable of normal behavior. If she's disagreeable now and then, maybe her eyes simply cleared long enough for her to see things as they really were.

Pearl forked a soggy mushroom out of her soup and dropped it into the glass ashtray. Two attractive women with purple eyelids and glittering emerald brooches elegantly attached to flamingo-pink silk gowns strolled past, chatting loudly enough about gin and sex for everyone to hear. Harry watched them cross to the far end of the Palm Court where they took a booth beneath a wall mural painted to represent a jujube grove in the tropics. A stout man wearing a swallowtail suit and carrying a cigar and a half-empty bottle of White Rock in the other joined them. Now there's a lucky fellow, Harry mused, unless he's their brother.

Pearl tapped his hand with her spoon. "Honey?"

"Yes, darling?"

"Like I was saying, when she was a girl, Momma danced at the Blue Onion club." Pearl chewed the end of a celery stick. "Daddy said she was the cat's meow."

This evening was becoming difficult to manage. Pearl demanded Harry's focus, but he was too distracted by Cobb and everything else swirling about the dining room. It was maddening. He asked, "Did your mother have notices in the newspapers?"

"I suppose so," she replied, drowning the celery stick in her soup. "Why?"

"Well, dear, lots of theater people keep a scrapbook of their reviews, and I just thought it might be nice to see some of your mother's." He really did want to learn more about them both. Maybe something he'd discover would help to save her later on. You just couldn't tell.

She shook her head. "No, honey, Momma didn't save nothing like that. She always said she didn't care much for being on stage. She told me those stagedoor johnnies only came to the show to squeeze her peaches. Daddy made her quit when they got married."

"That's too bad."

Pearl shrugged. "She didn't seem so awfully cut up about it."

"Well, I'm sure she was happier being a wife and a mother. I understand that life in the theater can be awfully rough. Not everyone's got the stuff for it."

Harry heard lots of stories about dance girls and their sexual appetites. A fellow he met in Cincinnati a couple of years back claimed he took three of them from Jolson's revue and a bottle of brandy to his hotel room and didn't leave for a week. After hearing that, Harry began going to more shows.

A thousand blue lights were swirling now in the Cairo ballroom across the Zanzibar lobby where Harry could see giddy couples doing a ferocious tango. At the booth next to his, a tray of steamed clams in a porcelain bowl and a serving of Welsh rarebit were delivered to a man and a lovely woman dressed in summer evening clothes. The man handed the waiter a folded note. Half a minute later, a freckled-face

Western Union messenger boy appeared at the booth with a telegram. The waiter returned with a bicarbonate of soda, a basket of corn muffins, sliced pineapple, and a glass of ginger ale. The man handed the bicarbonate of soda to the Western Union boy and gave him a dollar as well. Meanwhile, Cobb had gotten up from his booth and gone to the telephone again. His partner fussed over his plate of noodles and gazed absently in Harry's general direction, trying not to be apparent. Was he drunk?

Waiting for Pearl to finish a spoonful of soup, Harry remarked, "Look, darling, I don't quite understand how your mother was allowed to remain at home when she was obviously so ill. Didn't your father see the seriousness of the situation?"

"Daddy wasn't living with us no more when Momma got sick, so he didn't have nothing to do with it. I took care of Momma by myself. We didn't need nobody else."

She broke a cracker over her soup and stirred it deeply into the broth. A smell of cooked cabbage wafted over from the next booth.

Harry frowned. "Well, that seems ridiculous."

"Aw, we did just fine, Momma and me. A girl don't need nothing anyhow but a good egg on her shoulders to get by these days. Go look it up."

"And when your mother became too sick to remain alone at home with a child? What then?" He sawed off a slice of boiled red potato with his knife. The food in the Palm Court really was quite good. The newspapers were truthful about something, after all.

Staring briefly toward the noisy ballroom, Pearl explained, "I told them Momma didn't want to go nowhere without me."

"But Winterhill isn't for healthy children, is it, dear? So you weren't allowed to go with her. Did you have any idea why? Were you able to ask?"

At the front of the Palm Court, a slender young man in a white suit and tortoise-shell glasses handed his tan fedora to the pretty hatcheck girl, then gave her a kiss on the cheek. One of the fez-topped waiters hurried over and clapped him on the shoulder and mussed his hair. All three laughed out loud. Fred Markle got up and went out to the lobby. Harry watched him tap Cobb on the shoulder, say something, then leave the Zanzibar Club while Cobb went back to his telephone conversation. Markle had left half his plate of noodles untouched.

Grabbing another celery stick to dunk in her soup, Pearl went on with her story. "The same day Momma went to Winterhill, see, I got stuck at Longfellow Home with a bunch of other saps that didn't have nobody to take care of them, neither." She averted her eyes to the tablecloth and stirred her soup with the celery stick. She looked hurt now. Back out in the lobby, Cobb hung up the telephone and walked over to the Cairo ballroom. The orchestra there was loud and vibrant.

"I assume you're referring to an orphanage here in the city," Harry said, trying to be considerate as he raised his voice above the raucous jazz across the lobby. "There weren't any relatives to take you in? Where was your father?"

Pearl sagged backward, misty-eyed. "Aw, Harry, I'll go all pop if we keep talking about this. Have a heart, will you?" She let the celery stick sink into the bowl of soup. There was a long pause. Then she said, "Say, how's about me and you seeing a show later? They got Ronald Colman and Vilma Banky at the Ferguson Street Odeon tonight. Why, I hear — HOLY JEEZ!" Pearl shot up from the booth seat.

Harry glanced toward the jujube grove mural just in time to see one of the two young women in flamingo-pink gowns rise from the booth, flame bursting off her hair from the lit torchère. "GOOD GOD!"

The poor girl was on fire. She screamed like a hyena and her companions fled as she rolled onto the table, scattering food and drink into the aisle. A waiter ran over with a pitcher of water and splashed it onto the young woman's head. Smoke hissed from her burning hair. The tablecloth was aflame. One booth after another emptied, terrified diners dodging every which way in the excitement. The stout fellow in the swallowtail suit rushed from the Palm Court. Smoke still billowing off her head, the young woman shrieked for help. Another waiter splashed a bowl of soup onto the burning tablecloth.

"WHY AIN'T SOMEBODY CALLING A DOCTOR?" Pearl shouted, bolting from the booth. Harry chased her. A riot was breaking out, people shouting hysterically as a nasty pungent odor filled the restaurant. The teary-eyed hatcheck girl rushed by carrying a bottle of aromatic spirits of ammonia and a glass of water.

Pearl yelled again, "WHY AIN'T SOMEBODY GETTING THAT DAME A DOCTOR?"

"Let's get out of here," Harry said, grabbing Pearl's elbow while two of the fez-topped waiters wrapped the burning woman's smoke-blackened head with a collection of sopping wet towels. When they lowered her from the table to the floor, the young woman's girlfriend burst from the crowd of onlookers and dove to her side, wailing hysterically. Then lights in the Palm Court dimmed as the gas torchères were extinguished by the Zanzibar management.

Harry saw Cobb jammed up with a huge crowd of rubbernecking looky-loo's from the Cairo ballroom. "Come on, dear, we have to go."

"No, honey, I want to see what happens!"

"Do you want to wait for your skirt to catch fire?" He pushed Pearl toward the kitchen. "If we don't go now, we could both burn up."

Seeing Cobb trapped in that maelstrom by the lobby almost made Harry laugh. Maybe they'd get lucky and he'd be trampled. Harry led Pearl out into a narrow alley beside the restaurant just as an ambulance flew to the curb in front of the Zanzibar Club, siren howling. Two fire trucks and a police wagon approached Belvedere Street from uptown. Clots of Palm Court diners spilled out into the street, blocking motor traffic and creating a greater uproar. A fist-fight started under the near lamppost, and a small dog was kicked by a drunk with a sooty face.

Harry hustled Pearl away up the alley toward the hectic Avenue of the Republic where taxicabs whizzed by across the summer night. Turning onto Madison Street, they passed beneath the roof gardens of the Kingston Hotel whose giddy fourth-floor patrons splashed champagne like raindrops onto the hordes of passersby. Two blocks on, the Forbidden Palace offered authentic Chinese meals at 35¢, chop suey or fried eggplant and sweet potatoes for a quarter. Feeling free now of Cobb for a few moments, Harry smiled as he accepted a fortune cookie wrapped within an advertisement from the lovely Oriental hostess posted in the doorway wearing a black crimson kimono and gold slippers. Everywhere the city glowed exuberantly.

"Please, Harry, have me a gin?" Pearl begged, worming a path through a smartly dressed crowd outside the ritzy Parakeet Lounge on Hampton Lane, a dozen blocks now from downtown. "I won't get tight. I swear it."

Did she torture him deliberately? What was it about liquor that caused fanaticism? Look up at any apartment building in the city after dark and you will likely see someone sitting at a window having a drink. Now think about night after night being nourished on a vague expectation of that inconsequential splendor. You just couldn't count on a more self-indulgent equation.

Across the lane, an elevated electric trolley sparked a violet flash from the night damp rails. Street lamps flickered. The klaxons ceased. Refusing the bait, he steered her away liquor-free toward 61st Street where the crowds thinned and the streets darkened. As they strolled through an elm-shaded neighborhood of brownstones toward the lights of Federal Boulevard, the city seemed to Harry incomprehensibly vast, its grand avenues endless strips of asphalt and gilded concrete monuments, its beautiful parks a pre-Columbian wilderness. Thousands of voices echoed in and out of the metropolitan night. A million lighted windows rose into the sky where the great city displaced even the stars.

At a newsstand a block and a half from the boulevard, Harry bought an evening edition of the *City Sentinel* and took it with him to a bench where Pearl sat unwrapping the Forbidden Palace advertisement from the fortune cookie. She seemed to have forgotten about her gin. Cracking open the fortune cookie, Pearl read aloud, *"By gentleness, the hardest heart may be softened."* She smiled. "Say, honey, maybe this ain't such baloney after all."

"Pardon?" A breeze had risen in the quarter-hour and fluttered the newspaper as Harry folded it into quarters and quickly skimmed a short section called *Business Connections*. He found his own notice at the bottom of the next page. It was an advertisement he had composed himself and placed last week. It read:

I have sold goods for 18 years. I know how to sell
any worthy product to jobbers, to dealers, to department stores. I have done it successfully for 18
years in my own business and for others. Now I
prefer a selling opportunity principally in the metropolitan district… although I have no objections
to short trips. Married, 43, with substantial references. Box 14, Warsaw Hotel, 254 Jackson Street.

Smiling, he removed the advertisement section of the *Sentinel* and
folded it inside his jacket.

Pearl crumpled the Chinese fortune and tossed it under the bench.
"Honey, it's the neck of the evening and we ain't been nowhere yet."
She popped the other half of the cookie into her mouth, then rested a
hand high up on his shoulder, fiddling with his coat collar.

He smiled as she tickled his ear. "Then perhaps you've been too
rash."

"How's that?"

Feeling reckless and irresistible, he took Pearl in a romantic clinch
and kissed her firmly on the lips.

Her violet eyes watered. "Gosh, honey, I didn't know you cared."

Aroused by her exquisite smile, he kissed her again and gave her a
hug, and felt a flush of another sort. She was that gorgeous.

"I love you, Harry," she murmured. "You're so sweet."

"Well, I love you, too, dear. But if you'll recall, three hours ago
when I left Winterhill, you promised that if I were to buy you supper
at the Zanzibar Club tonight, afterward you'd show me the neighborhood where you grew up and the house you lived in." He withdrew his
pocketwatch and checked the hour. "It's already half past nine. Are we
anywhere nearby?"

She got up with a pout. "How come you always make me feel like
a skunk, Harry?"

"Because we need to keep our word. I learned that from my own
mother when I was little. I won't tell you what happened if I broke a
promise back then, but, believe me, it wasn't pleasant."

The breeze gusted in the elm branches above, fluttering leaves
down across the street where a woman and a young boy on the op-

posite sidewalk approached from the boulevard walking a sleek Irish Setter.

Pearl asked, "You ever heard of Stuyvesant Street?"

"No, I can't say that I have," Harry replied, his eye on the boy who was dressed in a cap and long coat, very much like his own little Henry on any autumn evening back in Farrington. The woman wore a stylish tweed suit and French button hat, and resembled no one Harry knew in the city. As they drew near, the small boy glanced across the street at Harry and Pearl and reined the dog in close.

"We got to take the Blue Line there," said Pearl, fumbling in her bag for a compact. "It's a long ride."

Across the street, the woman leaned down to whisper in the boy's ear as they passed, refusing to meet Harry's gaze. Once they disappeared into the elm shadows, Harry remarked, "Well, then, I suppose we ought to find the proper trolley depot, shouldn't we?"

— 6 —

Along Federal Boulevard, cast-iron lamp poles supported electric globes that glowed white beneath the dense ash and bur oaks bordering the asphalt motorway. Only half a dozen automobiles passed in either direction while Harry and Pearl walked to the rail depot at East Empire Street six blocks ahead. On the opposite side of Federal Boulevard where it bordered the south rose gardens of Legion Park, a group of elderly pedestrians strolled together in pairs, arm-in-arm — men with men, women with women — each protected in long coat and hat against the brisk evening breeze. Doubtless, they perceived themselves safer together than alone, although Harry had read so many sensational crime stories in the newspapers this summer, he wondered if that were even true. Just this morning, for instance, a Mr. and Mrs. Gaddis had been shot to death on the stoop of a fine brownstone on Chandler Street. The late edition of the *City Sentinel* reported no suspects, no witnesses, despite the crime having occurred just after sunrise in plain view from the street in the hour of milk trucks and delivery wagons.

Violence seemed commonplace. Overzealous Prohibition enforce-ment agents murdered, and were themselves murdered, almost weekly now, the "dry" killings occupying increasingly more space in the edi-torial columns than on the front page where they sensibly belonged. Respect for life and property were in steep decline. Even advertise-ments for new parking garages addressed the current problem of how automobiles parked innocently in certain neighborhoods had become playgrounds to the younger inhabitants of the sidewalks. Hundreds of dollars for the repair of ugly scratches and bent fenders had led to this booming new trade, a clever business venture. But did profits derived from fear truly serve the public good? Watching this group of elderly citizens pass under the gateway into Legion Park, Harry wondered upon whose ledger the moral life of the Republic would be measured.

The East Empire Street depot was empty when he and Pearl reached the top of the concrete stairs. There were wooden benches on the platform and Pearl went immediately to have a seat. While she smoked a cigarette, Harry strolled out closer to the tracks and had a look into the distance. After ten minutes or so, the blue and gold inter-urban arrived out of the dark from the south track, its arc headlight blazing white in his eyes. A hissing from the copper wires overhead and the shriek of the traction motors preceded the electric J.G. Brill car to the platform where Pearl and Harry waited to board. At the rear of the trolley, a mustachioed conductor in a rumpled blue uniform cau-tioned them both to step lively, then collected their fares and pulled the signal cord for departure. A plump middle-aged woman sitting by the door with a large grocery sack in her lap forced Harry and Pearl to step around her when they entered the interurban car.

"End-seat hog," Pearl muttered, and led Harry down the carpeted aisle to the middle of the trolley. She chose facing walkover seats be-neath the baggage racks. A man in a brown suit and derby hat stood beside the conductor on the smoking platform as the motorman sounded an air horn and the electric trolley left the East Empire depot. The polished mahogany glistened in the electric light. Overhead, the ceiling of the car was covered with advertisements: *Schuler Bros.* "*We Buy False Teeth*" — *Tiffany & Co. Clocks* — *Reach for a Lucky instead of a*

Sweet! — *INSECT BITES Don't scratch, stop the miserable stinging itch with a light touch of RESINOL!* — *"I'll tell the world they satisfy" CHESTERFIELD CIGARETTES "and the blend can't be copied!"* — *Insurance Agents & Brokers Geo. A. Derrick* — *The Great Atlantic & Pacific Tea Co.* — *"You, too, can have a skin you love to touch" Woodbury's Facial Soap* — TARRYTON COUNTY ELECTRIC TRANSIT ROUTE.

Beneath the interurban trolley advertisement was painted the words, *"Come unto me, all ye who labor and are heavy laden and I will give thee rest."*

"I ain't been out here since I was a kid," Pearl said, kicking her left foot up onto the seat next to Harry who sat facing the front of the trolley. "It gives me the heebie-jeebies."

"There's no reason to worry," he told her, glad they were onboard at last. "Don't you think this visit will rekindle many fond memories of your old neighborhood?"

"What if I ain't got none?"

"Nonsense." He laughed. "We each have little thoughts from childhood we keep to ourselves. It's what makes us individuals. You're no different, darling, no matter what you may think."

"Says you."

"Yes, that's right."

Electric fans whirred noisily, laboring to keep the interior cool while the open window brought a pleasant draft scented by trees and summer wildflowers as the interurban ran northeast beyond Federal Boulevard and Legion Park.

Pearl brightened. "Say, honey, how come you don't got your own jalopy?"

"Well, I suppose mostly because I haven't any garage to store one, darling, and also I prefer riding the train. It's more convenient for getting about in the city. But thank you for asking."

She stuck her foot out and rubbed his ankle. "Well, I think you ought to buy a rubberneck wagon so's me and you can go all sorts of places whenever we like."

"Something tells me that wouldn't be a good idea," he replied, gazing out the window at a home orchard of persimmon trees that whizzed by. Gallivanting about in a roadster? What if they became involved in a smash-up? He could just imagine a lurid tabloid photograph winding up in Marie's lap at breakfast one morning. Wouldn't that be a case?

The interurban tilted slightly around a curve, nosing side to side, the "click-click" of the rail increasing in volume as they crossed the truss over an inland tributary of the river. The man in the brown suit and derby hat walked past Harry toward the motorman's compartment in the front of the car. He had a silver pocketwatch open in the palm of his right hand, an unhappy expression on his face. He knocked on the compartment, and held up the pocketwatch for the motorman to see. Outside, a blue-white flash lit up the trackside when the racing trolley-wheel lost contact briefly with the wire. Riding the trolleys was one of life's simple pleasures. Certainly Harry understood why the electric railways were being overturned by the automobile, but his preference for the familiar old trolley held firm. On what motor road could a driver read the morning newspaper, converse with fellow passengers, watch the scenery pass in comfort, or casually nap in transit? We can grow very fond of activities nobody else cares about, and maybe we'll get accused of being dull or pathological, but those nice thoughts make up for any interval of snide remarks from those who don't share our pleasures. It's how we live best.

The interurban passed a series of block signals and rolled to a stop in a quiet neighborhood of small framehouses and dirt streets. The plump woman with the grocery sack rose and left the trolley. The man with the brown suit and derby hat came back from the motorman's compartment and told the conductor he wanted a fare reduction since the trolley had already bypassed his stop. Out on the platform, a yellow Labrador sat alone barking into the darkened woods across the tracks. Harry rose from his seat and crossed the aisle.

Pearl told him, "This ain't our stop, honey."

"It isn't?" He looked out at the brick depot. A single lamp burned in the office window where the shade was pulled flush to the sill. He had never been this far out into the city's rural suburbs. "Where are we?"

"Oakley Road." She tugged him gently toward her and kissed him on the nose. "We get off at the next station, honey. It ain't that far now."

"I'm glad, because it's getting late."

"Honestly, I ain't tired at all," Pearl said, letting go of his arm. She got up and strolled off down the aisle. At the back of the car, a young man in a flat cap, cotton shirt, suspenders and gray trousers paid a fare to the conductor and climbed on board. He carried a metal lunch pail in one hand and looked exhausted, his face smudged with soot. A younger boy equally worn and dirty followed, carrying a wooden toolbox, and they took seats on opposite sides of the aisle near the back of the car. Meanwhile, the man in the brown suit refused to allow the conductor to pull the cord for departure. He produced a token for the conductor and showed him the hour on his pocketwatch. He flung the token to the floor of the car and crushed it under his shoe. When the conductor shook his head and reached for the cord, the man in the brown suit lit a cigarette, puffed on it briefly while listening to an explanation of fare regulations, then blew smoke in the conductor's face and went out onto the smoking platform. When the door shut, the flustered conductor pulled the cord for departure.

The trolley rolled into motion, and Harry looked out the window once more and saw a small boy in denim overalls come up onto the platform and seize the Labrador by the collar. Both dwindled into the distance as the interurban accelerated down the tracks lined by yellow wildflowers. Pearl came back up the aisle and plunked herself down next to Harry. "Say, honey, I just got wised up to the fact that maybe it ain't safe to be riding out here after dark."

"Is that so?" Harry stared out into the warm rural night. Clouds filtered across the sky now; the moon was gone. All he could see was intermittent lamplight from the small framehouses flashing past on the narrow roadside. Where on earth was he going tonight? What did any of this have to do with selling goods and feeding his dear family? He was not so young anymore that he could do this or that according to the same whim with which he ordered dinner off a restaurant menu. His best hope was that age would finally settle him down, disarming these threats of his own making. Because when we imagine ourselves free to do absolutely anything that seems intriguing, we invite the worst possible sort of consequences, and even those that do arrive are almost certain to surprise us.

"The motorman told me a couple of maniacs came on board last Sunday for a hold-up. Some poor sap kicked one of them in the teeth and got himself stabbed. He's dead now. Ain't that a shame? If the cops pinch 'em, it's the hot seat."

"It's terrible."

"I hope they fry."

"I'm sure they will, darling."

— 7 —

The sign at the depot said **Tarryton Crossing**. Harry stood at the end of the platform watching the trolley wire sway in the wake of the just-departed interurban. Dust and ozone and hot grease drifted in the night air. The clanging of cross bells echoed down the tracks. There was nobody else around when Pearl came out of the toilet and checked her makeup under the lamp pole by one of the dusty flyspecked windows of the small depot. Harry's mood hadn't improved much. Riding along that last mile or so, he'd come to the conclusion that if he thought he could protect this adorable young girl, he was insane.

"Stuyvesant Street's this way," she said, directing him up the road away from the tracks. Tall plank fences lined both sides of the dirt road leading into the neighborhoods flanking the depot. They walked arm-in-arm ahead into the dark, Harry listening to dogs rooting through garbage cans and scratchy phonograph music and radio shows playing behind curtained windows. A boy catcalled from the dark one street over. The stink of manure from nearby stables breathed into the alleyway, and Harry remembered being a boy again behind Hoot Wickson's livery.

"There ain't much here," Pearl said, turning the corner onto a dirt street rutted from a week-ago rain. Sumach bushes and ragweed forced through the slats of the old plank sidewalks and fences. Telegraph wires sagged overhead. Across the street, a woman in a frilled muslin dress came out onto the bracketed porch of a square white two-story house and emptied a pitcher of water into a flower balcony of lavender pansies below the railing.

Pointing Harry down the old sidewalk, Pearl said, "I ain't been back since Momma got sick. Did I tell you that?" Her mood felt dampened and sober, much like she'd been at the sanitarium.

"Yes, dear, you did."

"Momma used to say there wasn't a fellow in Tarryton Crossing who wouldn't steal your last rubber nickel if he got the chance."

The narrow streets seemed more warren than neighborhood. Gardenia and honeysuckle drooped off the slatted fenceline. Screen doors banged shut, a motor horn honked loudly and drew an angry shout, a newly born infant cried in the upstairs of one of the weather boarded framehouses. Tarryton Crossing mostly reminded Harry of rail towns he had visited on the traveling road whose existence depended upon an industry that cared little for the community's natural life. Railroads meant boom or bust, fortune or failure. He had seen plenty of small towns shrivel and die when commerce diverted elsewhere, when grass and wildflowers grew in the tracks. Here he imagined the relentless dynamo of the city lured away much of the town's youth, drawn to the machines of prosperity that lay beyond these kindling-wood houses and tin garages, beyond the distant railyards and suspension bridges and factory smokestacks, toward those great skyscrapers of modern corporations that glittered brightly above the hard steel-gray of sky and water.

Pearl led him down to a street corner where the sign read **Stuyvesant St**. She stopped and stared across at a plain gray two-story house that had a dirt front yard and a small porch with a wicker chair beside the door, a pair of sash-and-weight side windows in a square bay downstairs, and a single shuttered window upstairs beneath the pitched roof. A honey locust shade tree flanked the house to the left, a small garage to the right. In the upper window behind a fabric shade, a light was on.

"Is that it, darling?" Harry asked, tired of walking. It was really too late to be out like this. At the house just behind them, a screen door closed, leaving behind a faint odor of burning pipe tobacco in the night air.

Pearl pointed to the window below the gable. "That was my bedroom. I lived up there all by myself until Momma got sick. It was a swell room, too. I had my own closet and a desk and a lamp with a calico shade Momma and me sewed together all by ourselves."

The house walls were old clapboard, set upon now by ivy and tall weeds. Grass grew in patches between the house and the garage. Empty flowerpots collected next to the porch steps. A pair of apple crates was stacked just inside the garage.

"I see it ain't all that swell a house now, but I didn't know better back then. I guess I been wised up since."

Looking down the street in the direction they had just walked, Harry noticed a policeman swinging his nightstick. He was alone, patrolling the neighborhood. Harry watched him greet a middle-aged couple out for a late evening stroll. Everyone seemed pleasant.

Pearl left Harry's arm to cross the street. She stopped at the splintered fence, staring up at the lighted window under the eaves. She looked so darling and forlorn, Harry quickly crossed to join her. When he drew near enough to be heard, she said quietly, "Daddy came home foxed every night. 'Cause he'd be too late to eat with us, Momma'd tell him to cook his own supper. Sometimes I'd hear him fiddling around with the stove, trying to get a fire going under the skittle so's he could heat up some beans. Drinking made him hungry. He'd come home from fixing boats at the canal and fight with Momma and she'd go to bed and he'd make supper and sit on the sofa listening to radio shows until he fell asleep."

Pearl's eyes were fixed on the upper window. She folded her bare arms against the breeze and huddled close to Harry. In her old neighborhood, that boldness was gone, the wisecracking confidence, the silly jazz in her voice. Now he felt he loved her more than ever. All he could think of was taking her home and tucking her into bed. This was a terrifically complicated situation. There's not a thing you can change, he reminded himself. Don't start imagining otherwise.

She told him, "Daddy got the flu with a lot of other people in town at the end of the War. Momma kept him in my room upstairs and had me sleep with her in the downstairs bedroom and we both took care of Daddy until he got better. He didn't have any liquor for a whole year and we thought he was happy and everything was swell again. He even took me fishing with him on the canal." She shuddered. "Gosh, I hate worms, but Daddy taught me how to bait a hook and cast without getting caught in the cattails. He said I was his 'precious little pearl and he loved to watch me grow.'" Her violet eyes shone. "Then Momma caught him drinking gin in the garage one night and told him to pack up and scram. She told me he smacked her in the lip, so she didn't ever want to see him again."

Somebody passed in front of the shade in the gable window and the light went out. Pearl shuffled her feet on the sidewalk, took Harry's hand and squeezed it tightly. He felt a chill coming on. Farther up the street, a man walked out from one of the yards and left a garbage can at the curb. Pearl blew her nose into a handkerchief with her free hand. The cool night breeze rose in the trees above, tattering like rain in the leaves.

When she cleared her throat, Pearl said, "Daddy came upstairs when I was sleeping that night and woke me up and said he had to go away somewhere because Momma didn't love him anymore."

She abruptly dropped Harry's hand and left him at the gate, moving off down the sidewalk to where the fence ended. There she entered the yard in the direction of the garage, just a few steps in, gazing into the dark behind the house. He was afraid to follow. At the end of this, he imagined he would have to do something wonderful for her, but he had no idea yet what that would be.

Looking back at him, she said, "Daddy promised he'd come back to see me as soon as he could, but he never did. Momma got a job at Dollinger's boardinghouse cleaning rooms and cooking in the afternoons. She gave me ten cents a week to spend on myself however I liked. She didn't go nowhere except to Dollinger's and the market on Fourth Street. I went to the nickel shows and rode the trolleys all over. I met lots of people and had lots of friends who invited me to parties and picnics and canoe rides on the canal. We put on our own shows with a stage and curtains right here in this yard for a penny a day and all the kids in town came to watch. They said it was the best they ever seen. Momma called me an awful share, but Mr. Otis who ran the steamboat told me I was the prettiest, most talented little girl in Tarryton Crossing. How do you like that, honey? Ain't it a swell thing to say?"

"Yes, dear, it's very nice."

Pearl knelt down to retrieve something from the weedy grass, a wooden toy aeroplane whose wing was fractured, its tail rudder missing. Harry bent over the fence for a closer look, mindful of how he was sneaking a peek into this private yard. He heard voices in the dark somewhere down the street and grew anxious. Why had he come here with her, after all? Didn't he already love her so much that he really no longer cared who she was in those dear dead days? What do yesterdays matter, anyhow, if they were never going to happen again?

With Harry beside her now, Pearl spoke even more softly. "The night Momma got sick, I was at the canal with Billy Hawkins sinking milk bottles in the mud. We didn't have enough money to see a movie so we were just clowning around until suppertime. When I came home, the potatoes were boiling over on the stove and Momma wasn't doing nothing about it. She was just sitting at the kitchen table talking nonsense to herself. Doc Drury couldn't come out to see Momma until Thursday, so I got her undressed and put her to bed and got supper for myself. I wasn't scared at all, honey. Not even a little, 'cause I thought Momma was going to get better."

She set the toy aeroplane back down in the grass, and stared quietly into the dark between the house and garage. Harry murmured, "But she didn't, did she?"

Pearl shook her head. "Nope."

"So that's when they took her to Winterhill, and you were put in the orphanage?" He ached so badly for her he could hardly stand it. Never had he been given to such a plaintive devotion and he felt almost irritated with the ineptness of fate.

"A man came to the house on the day the doctors sent Momma to Winterhill. He said that since Daddy was gone and Momma was too sick to see after herself, and since I didn't have no aunts or uncles to take me in, I had to go to the orphans' home with all the other kids that didn't have nobody that wanted them."

Truly, this world is crueler than any of us can imagine. We pretend the sins we commit against each other aren't really sins, but, in fact, virtues that let us get on with the more important things in life that really aren't important at all.

"Didn't anyone attempt to locate your father once your mother became ill?"

Pearl turned toward him with sweet damp eyes. She shook her head. "The year before she got sick, Momma told me Daddy got killed on a steamship in the China Sea where he had a job fixing things that broke. She heard it from Lenny Hargis. He knew Daddy from the barbershop and working at the canal. Momma had a stack of letters Daddy wrote to her. I seen them once. They said how much Daddy still loved us, and that Momma knew it. Sure she visited with other fellows after Daddy left, but they didn't love Momma like Daddy did and she didn't love them, neither. She just got lonely, that's all."

Pearl came close to the fence, brushing against Harry's shoulder. She asked, "Do you ever get lonely, honey?"

"Yes, dear, I think we all do."

"It's hell, ain't it?"

"Yes, it is."

Soon they left the house and walked ahead into the shadows up Stuyvesant Street whose gray framehouses sat dark and still in the late summer night. The breeze rose to a cold wind and they walked close together where the old elms and black willows swayed overhead and dust blew in the narrow rutted street. Eventually the sidewalk ended at a freight road bordered by scattered shacks and brown marshes. Smoke from old stovepipes curled up into the stiff wind as Pearl led Harry along the route that divided Tarryton Crossing from the empty wetlands. It smelled like rain coming.

A quarter of a mile down the road, Pearl strode through a patch of gooseberry bushes to pick wildflowers, mostly white violets and wood

cress, wrapped in skunk cabbage to form a small bouquet. Harry tested the damp sedge with one foot, determined not to wade accidentally
into the marshy bog. Just a few dozen yards away, a dilapidated steamboat lay half-sunk in the muddy canal, its decks rotting, funnels rusted
out. Pearl came back onto the road, knotting her bouquet as Harry
debated whether the brackish waterway was yet navigable. Cold wind
rippled across the tall oat grass.

Walking along the freight road in the dark beside the canal, Pearl
told Harry a story about a sad girl at the Longfellow orphanage who
was loved by no one, who had no friend or family in the world, who
cried herself to sleep every night on the fourth floor of the girls' dormitory. Her name was Lilah and she was a mute. The other orphans
taunted her horribly. She was teased and spat upon, bound up in filthy
laundry. Often she ran off and hid in the custodian's basement to escape her tormentors. She had a secret place no one could find, a drain
tunnel beneath the central orphanage that led a quarter mile to the
river. One evening in May after Lilah was forced by one of the older
girls to swallow a black spider that had crawled out of a crack in the
wood floor under her bed, Pearl found Lilah's teardrops on the cement
in front of the old steam boiler and climbed in behind her and saw the
rift in the iron wall and Lilah's blue nightgown hanging from a short
brick ledge just beyond. The next night they escaped together, saying
no good-byes, bringing nothing with them. They stole fruit on lower
Baskin Street at dawn for breakfast. They beggared crescent rolls and
sweet butter from a restaurant on Hancock Street for supper. They
raided spring wagons and pickle stands and chased milk trucks all up
and down Highland Avenue. For weeks they slept in the Doyle Road
car-barns and snatched clean laundry off backyard lines in the neighborhoods near the river, hiding in livery stables or weedy alleyways
if they would see a policeman coming. When Lilah became ill with
a horrid diarrhea, Pearl stole cream bottles off the marble stoops on
Franklin Avenue and sold them for two cents apiece on Plasster Street
to buy medicine and toasted crackers and soup for her friend. Soon
they discovered that the ragpickers who camped along the lower city
bulwark would gladly share food and shelter with them in exchange

for favors like stealing cigarettes, coffee, dry socks and bread from the stores on Baskin and Havesham. At night, Pearl and Lilah would huddle together under a pair of cotton blankets in an old A.E.F. tent listening to smutty stories, Jew's harps dueling in the dark, loud ugly fist fights by the river's edge. Then, in September, four months after escaping the Longfellow orphanage, Lilah crawled from her blanket during the middle of the night, climbed the darkened bulwark, and crossed the Washington Bridge alone to the far shore. Pearl never saw her again. A week later, emboldened by fear and loneliness, Pearl herself ascended the bulwark at Columbia Avenue and melted into the city where nobody questioned her purpose any longer.

The damp wind swept across the marshlands. To the east, Harry saw a pink flutter of lightning in the black sky illuminating the old grain elevators on the distant horizon. Pearl tossed her wildflower bouquet into the muddy canal. She waded out of the tall soggy oat grass with her hands held above her waist. Harry had not traveled to the city to chase skirts. He honestly believed that tangled anarchy held no sway over him any longer. Yet here he was in the middle of the night with a breathtaking young female whose unsullied gleam and vulnerability pierced his heart so deeply he could scarcely hear those cautionary whispers reminding him that love respects no boundaries.

Pearl's silk scarf ruffled in the cold gusts as she accompanied him down the dark empty road. "I sold roses in summer hotels," she told him, "and worked in a button factory and a flour mill and a meat-packing house and a soup kitchen, and lots of other places. I swept sidewalks and helped wash clothes in a Chinese laundry for a nickel a day. I emptied slop pails and baked blueberry pies for a couple of swell old colored ladies on Ashford Street, and sold pineapples and walnuts and Dutch cleanser from a pushcart. I wasn't some dumb Dora, and I wasn't a pushover, neither. When I worked as a coat girl one winter at the Westchester Hotel, I met a parlor snake named Leo who had more dough in his pockets than Johnny Rockefeller. He bought me a ritzy pair of red shoes with runover heels just so's I'd get hot with him in the Jupiter Ballroom. I guess he had a crush on me 'cause when I got thirsty he let me trade him a smooch for a glass of champagne. He smelled like Corona-Corona. When we went up to his room for a shot of Green River whiskey, he told me he wanted to make whoopee and I said, 'Sure, for a cool million!' so he knocked me down and said I had syphilis and that I better scram or he'd call the night clerk." She shivered at another damp gust rippling through the oat grass. "Life ain't easy, honey. It can drive a dame cuckoo if she's got too much smarts to be a tramp. I know you ain't ever going to see me in a Gibson Girl calendar, but I swear I never done nothing Momma'd be ashamed of me for."

Harry's eyes watered as he stared out across the brown marshlands. Pearl was shivering worse now beside him. He slipped his arm gently around that beautiful waif, drew her close, gave her a rather humble kiss. He was such a fool to get involved in all this. It just seemed so useless, so shoddy, but what else could he possibly do? In any case, they were probably both doomed.

There were lights ahead in the windy darkness that indicated an intersection with a highway that led back toward town. They hurried on. Soon, Harry began to see patches of small shacks again, telegraph poles, the headlamps of automobiles farther down the road, a lighted filling station, and just past that a roadhouse whose glowing sign on a shingled roof read: **AVALON**.

— **8** —

There were three automobiles parked out front, two Fords and an old black 1912 Reo, trading an odor of gasoline fumes on the damp draft. One of the Fords had the top down and its owner had parked under the roof overhang against the possibility of later rain. Already, though, Harry heard the swish of tires on wet oily pavement where a blue Stutz Bearcat raced by toward town. Across the road, he saw gray ash rising from burning rubbish piles in an empty lot, hot sparks flickering in the gritty wind. Harry held the door open for Pearl to the noisy conversation from within. He hoped someone had the furnace lit. He was freezing.

"Aw, he ain't no stew!" argued a thick, ruddy-faced man behind the counter as Harry and Pearl entered the roadhouse. He had a towel slung over one shoulder and a collection of drinking glasses on the countertop in front of him. "That poor kid never touched a bottle, and he ain't a dope, neither! Why, Bill's sister had him goggle-eyed all summer until he couldn't stand it no longer. Then, when he tried to make her, she had him canned out of the joint. If you ask me, that girlie's the one oughta been given the air."

A stout blonde in caked-on makeup sitting at one of the tables near the counter shuffled a deck of playing cards. She answered back, "That boy's a nut, George, and that's all there is to it. If you ask me, his whole crowd of so-and-so's got nothing but a load of alibis in place of common sense."

As Pearl undid her wrap and chose a table away from the window, George called out from behind the counter to Harry, "There ain't no program tonight, mister, except that one there."

He pointed to the bill of fare pinned on the wall back of the cash register next to an old cameo lithograph of Maude Adams. Steam rose from the kitchen behind the dining counter where the cook, a small Greek, paced back and forth looking perturbed.

After a quick study of the menu, Pearl said, "Get me a chicken sandwich and a cup of coffee." Harry held the chair for her as she sat down. Her cheeks were still rosy-pink from the cold outdoors, her violet eyes teary. Harry thought she looked lovelier than ever. Terrifically anxious to get home now, he settled on a cup of coffee of his own and a biscuit. He hoped to eat quickly and take her back to the city with him before it got too late. *No matter where Cobb is,* Harry thought, *we'll both be safer at my apartment.*

Near the cash register, a scrawny little man with day-old whiskers sat on the last stool, a punchboard at his elbow and an evening newspaper folded open in front of him. Directly left of the counter at a table along the far wall with his back to them was a fairly tall fellow roughly Harry's age wearing a gray pongee suit and smoking a cigarette. Facing him was an attractive redhead in a fine blue silk dress, both laughing as they drank Scotch highballs.

Seated at one of the quartet tables in the middle of the room were two middle-aged men with slicked-backed hair, each wearing a suit — one gray, the other blue — with Dutch collars and striped neckties, both men dressed as if for an evening at the theater. The man in the blue suit had squinty eyes and a puffy face like Herbert Hoover and barely more hair. The one in the gray suit had a small narrow face and a pencil-thin mustache and wore bifocal glasses. They traded casual conversation with a boy and a pretty girl sitting at a smaller table by the window behind them, while picking over the remains of mutton chops, roast chicken, baked potatoes and bean soup.

Those two young people, Harry guessed, owned the Ford roadster, as the boy still had on a linen auto-coat, and the girl a fancy gray rain-cape over a yellow accordion-pleated dress. She wore a black cloche hat with a silver feather and reminded Harry of Mary Miles Minter. Both kids spoke brightly amid giggling laughter. A steaming tureen of soup in the middle of their small table sat hardly touched.

George brought two cups of coffee to Harry's table. "Cold out, ain't it?"

"Yes, it certainly is," he replied, folding a napkin in his lap. His hands were numb from the damp wind. He had been rubbing them together since sitting down, but it hadn't seemed to help much yet.

"It's a cinch it's going to rain," said Pearl, after sipping from her cup. "We just seen lightning."

To the right of the counter, a sign reading **CLOSED** hung on a chain over the swinging doors to the dance hall. Next to the doors was another sign indicating the toilets. Above that was a placard reading: **IF YOU SPIT ON THE FLOOR AT HOME, YOU CAN DO IT HERE!**

"Say, Ada, listen up!" The scrawny man at the counter read aloud from his newspaper: *"Mrs. Edward Courtade, 40, of Great Neck, Long Island, a summer resident of Bantam Lake, who last night won an automobile at a church carnival, was killed today when another automobile driven by her husband crashed into an embankment.'* Now, ain't that a shame?"

The blonde shook her head as she shuffled the cards. "Why, I'd bet the fellow was driving reckless, or else he drank himself a flock of highballs and was stewed when he took the wheel."

"It ain't always liquor, sweetheart, that's the root of discord," said the man with the Hoover face.

"Now, that's a hot one, coming from you, Ralph," Ada retorted, "seeing as how there ain't a forenoon gone by that George hasn't had you a shot of gin or filled that hip flask of yours with Chartreuse!"

The boy and girl both laughed out loud. The scrawny man with the newspaper added, "I and the misses seen old Ralphie with the blind staggers outside of McGrew's last Saturday night. The misses says to me, 'Ezra, that one's a real case, ain't he?'"

Harry stifled a laugh. This crowd took him back to his father's mercantile and those jokey old farmers who would talk for hours and rarely buy a thing.

"Say, what're you trying to pull off?" Ralph asked, somewhat peevishly. "Why, Louis here'll tell you that misses of yours ain't no Queen of the Temperance Union herself. Get what I mean?"

"Aw, don't be sore, Ralph," said Ada, dealing herself a hand of solitaire. "Ezra didn't mean none of that in earnest. He's just hungry." She smiled up at the scrawny man. "Ain't you, dear?"

Ezra folded his newspaper over to the next page. "Well, I guess so." He turned to George who was still wiping off glasses. "The eats here is pretty darned good."

"How's about another chicken pie?" George asked, putting down the towel. He walked to the kitchen opening. "Say, Victor, how's about setting our old pal Ezra up to another chicken pie? He's awful hungry."

Pearl took a sip from her cup of coffee, and murmured in a low voice, "Honey, these folks are dumbbells. I say we eat, then beat it out of here. I'll bet we can find something else to do." She gave a lewd wink, and stroked his knee under the table.

"Shhh!" Harry wondered what these people thought, seeing the two of them together. They probably thought he was her father. At any rate, he was too cold to go outdoors now. A quick look to the window told him it would really be coming down soon, and who knows how long it took to get a taxicab out here. Maybe he would telephone after they finished eating.

The pretty girl in the rain-cape shoved her chair back and stood up. She giggled at a remark by Ralph's companion Louis, then excused herself and walked across the room, heels clicking on the hardwood floor. Her features were pale and smooth, her eyes brown as a wild fawn's. As she passed by Harry's table, she told Pearl, "That's a swell hat, dearie."

Then she winked at Harry and continued back toward the toilets. Pearl stuck her tongue out when she thought Harry wasn't looking, but the men in the room clearly admired the girl's walk, grinning to each other after she had gone. Louis smoothed his hair back with his hand, adjusted his bi-focals, and whistled softly. He remarked, "She sure's a pip."

"You betcha," agreed Ralph, straightening his tie and pretending to be fussed by the girl's presence. Harry doubted any of them had ever made love to such a pretty girl, which puffed him up all the more for sitting here with Pearl who was at least as attractive, if not more so.

Folding his newspaper again, Ezra added, "That little dame'd make Lillian Gish look like Mrs. Gump."

With a maudlin sigh, Ada scooped her cards up to reshuffle. "Honestly, I guess I ought to reduce. Of course, I ain't got time to go gadding like I did when I was a girl."

Behind the counter, George grabbed a tray with Pearl's chicken sandwich and Harry's biscuit. "Who says you need to reduce? Why, that's a lot of hooey." He winked at her.

She smiled while dealing herself another hand of solitaire. "Aw, ain't you a flatter."

"The poor fish," Louis said.

George brought the food to Harry's table and set it down. Both he and Pearl thanked him, and Harry took a long gulp of coffee. Nothing tasted better after an hour outdoors in the cold air. In a way, they were lucky to have the weather go bad like this because it lessened the chance of anyone following them. Who wants to go out in the rain?

The bartender said to the others, "Now, I knew all about Ada before I took her out, so I can't kick, besides which if she ain't a genuine sweet patootie, why, there ain't no such thing in Tarryton Crossing."

Ada turned to Ralph and Louis with a broad grin on her face. "How's that for a T.L.?"

Ralph frowned. "Ain't that making it a little strong?"

"Well, what of it?" Ada grinned even wider while counting cards. "Say, why ain't you giving us the dope about that dame I seen you stepping out with last month?"

"You wouldn't be meaning that silly Stella Cordell?"

"Yes, I guess I do," said Ada, sticking the ace of clubs on her scoring rack. She appeared to be ahead of the game for once. Harry quit it last year when he got tired of losing every hand.

"Well, it's cold," said Ralph, sounding disgusted with the memory of it. "She was just blah. Didn't even bathe daily." He shook his head. "I'd had to been under ether to step out with her again."

Louis agreed. "You don't know the half of it!"

"And they ain't going to, neither," said Ralph, sticking his fork into the last bite of his mutton chop. The boy in the auto coat hiccupped with laughter. Across the room, the man and woman seated together along the far wall had their fingers entwined, gazing romantically into each other's eyes. Presumably they had just made love and were out for a drink to celebrate. Harry cut his biscuit in half and dipped part of it into his coffee. He looked at Pearl who quietly ate her chicken sandwich. She was so adorable. He loved kissing her, particularly when she giggled and acted girlish. Marie had always been a good kisser, but sometimes Harry felt she took it too seriously. Why not have fun with sex and romance? Why can't men and women share a good laugh every so often?

"Say, listen here!" Ezra called out from the counter. He read from the evening newspaper again. "'*Mrs. Louis Greenberg, 48, of New Rochelle, New York, was injured fatally in an automobile accident between Batavia and Le Roy today, caused by her husband's losing control of the car when a bee flew into his face. Mr. Greenberg was injured slightly and the three other occupants were unhurt. The car left the road and crashed into a telephone pole. Mrs. Greenberg suffered a broken neck and died twenty minutes after being taken to a Batavia hospital. The party was bound on a vacation trip.*'" Ezra laid the paper down. "Now, ain't that rotten?"

"It's a wallop, all right," said Louis, passing a plate of butter to Ralph who slid a bowl of bean soup back to him. George brought Ezra a steaming hot chicken pie with a clean fork and a napkin. Ezra leaned close to sniff it. Satisfied, he stuck the fork through the browned crust, wriggled it, and came out with a piece of chicken.

"I was stung by a bee once," said Ada, sorting through her cards. Evidently, she was close to losing, after all, her expression turned vaguely sullen. "It was quite wicked. See, I was roller-skating at the Barnum Hippodrome when a bee flew straight down from the rafters and stung me on the nose. My face puffed up like a big fat balloon. Mother scolded me as if I'd personally invited that ugly bee to sting me."

"Why, my girl's just bugs over roller skating," the boy announced, rising briefly to shed his auto coat. "In fact, that's where I met Grace just last month. At the old Hippodrome."

"I won't patronize that dump no more after my bee sting," said Ada. Deciding her latest game was lost, she swept the cards together in a pile to be reshuffled. Harry heard someone playing a jazz on the piano back in the closed dance hall. Both the man and woman romancing across the room looked in that direction, pleased as if the music had been requested for the two of them. When Harry saw the fellow's face, he almost fainted.

It was Fred Markle.

Good grief! What on earth was he doing here? It was impossible! And who's that woman? Was she the emergency that rushed him out of the Zanzibar Club?

Pearl noticed Harry watching Markle and his date. "Say, honey, how come I don't ever hear none of that babytalk from you? Ain't I pretty enough?" She puckered her lips.

Harry said, "I really think we ought to leave."

"Well, I ain't done eating, yet. Besides which, it's raining outside. I don't want to rust."

"Why, it's barely a drizzle. I tell you, we really ought to go now before it begins to pour down. Look, darling, not five minutes ago you told me nothing would do but that we get out of this dump."

Pearl sipped her coffee. "Well, a girl's got a right to change her mind, don't she?"

Harry took a bite from his biscuit, and peeked over his shoulder. Maybe Markle was only here to date up this woman and it was just a terrible coincidence that they bumped into him.

"Listen, darling, I really do think we ought to go."

She scowled. "Are you sitting on a tack, honey? I ain't even finished my coffee! Hold your potatoes."

"Well, good grief!"

"Say, here's one for you, George," Ezra called out, reading another filler item in the newspaper: "*Miss Gertrude Sanford, New York Society girl who has just returned from a hunting expedition in Abyssinia, found herself greatly embarrassed when a native chief presented to her four baboons and three sprightly mountain monkeys as a token of gratitude for a bottle of cognac. Abyssinian headmen, Miss Sanford said, know nothing about Prohibition, but they know good liquor from bad.*" Ezra shook his head with a grin. "Now, ain't that cockeyed?"

"What, knowin' good liquor from bad?" George asked, walking over to have a look at the story for himself. "Why, I'd bet even Andy Volstead's kiddies learnt some alky cooking! Where's the dispute in that?"

"Well, it ain't no snap," argued Louis, "unless you're drinking your lunch every day, like Ralphie here." He cracked a wide grin. "Ain't he a life-size highball?"

Ralph threw down the piece of bread he was chewing on. "You old cheese! Why, I've stood ace high with you for years, haven't I? Particularly with that Myrtle dame who was a drag on you, the one who left you popeyed and all. Well, listen to the thanks a fellow gets! Worse than a crack in the eye, is what it is!"

Louis smiled, "Aw, Ralphie, I just meant that as a boost for George here, that's all. Don't be a tough egg."

"Well, don't overstrain yourself complimenting your pals, neither."

Scared of Markle and sick of listening to these idiots, Harry told Pearl, "Look, dear, just finish your coffee and let's go. I think the rain's quitting now and we can get back to the trolley stop without swimming."

Pearl didn't bother raising her eyes. "Says you."

"How's that?" He shot another glance across the room. Markle wasn't paying attention to anyone except his date and that highball in his hand. Maybe he'd fall under the table and they could just walk out of here. Harry wondered if the fellow was carrying a gun.

The young girl came out from the toilet, humming along with a different melody from the piano back in the dance hall, a maudlin old ballad to which Harry actually knew a few of the words:

> *"You have loved lots of girls*
> *In the sweet long ago,*
> *And each one has meant Heaven to you.*
> *You have vowed your affection to each one in turn,*
> *And have sworn to them all you'd be true."*

"Grace, darling!" the boy called over to her. "Please tell them about our roller-skating introduction, won't you, dear?"

Smiling as she sat down again, the fawn-eyed girl replied, "Why, I just adore skating. It's a marvelous time. And Johnny's as fast as the wind."

The boy told Ada, "Of course, we hadn't had a proper introduction, you see, because Grace's mother hadn't come along. Not that it mattered, as we got along wonderfully, anyhow, isn't that true, dear?"

Grace explained, "Mother'd just received a telegraph from my father whose train was arriving from Albany that very hour. We were all to greet him at Central Station. But I'd already taken the trolley to Thelma's house and couldn't be reached there as the Grierson's telephone was out of order all day long." She smiled at the boy. "Why, it does seem awfully like fate now, doesn't it, Johnny?"

"Grace's family's well-invested in comestibles. She hopes to attend University in the fall."

"Well, what do you know about that?" said Ada, reviewing her playing cards once again. She gave Ralph and Louis a wink. "Ain't that swell, boys?"

"Why, sure it is," Ralph agreed, folding his napkin and placing it on his plate, done at last with the meal. He took out a cigarette. "Who'd rather work in a fish market than go to college?"

"My father and mother own a grocery store in Littleton," said Grace, ignoring the inference. "Although, did Johnny tell you he'll be at Dartmouth next month? It's a tradition in his family. Both his uncle and father earned degrees there, so Johnny knows the inside ropes, don't you, dear?"

The boy shrugged. "It's very expensive, of course, but as my father holds quite a lot of stock in RCA, Postal Telegraph & Cable, and United States Lines shipping, I'll have no trouble at all. Why, father's investments have already earned half of a million dollars just this summer alone."

"And speaking of ships, Johnny's family sailed to France at Christmas just last year aboard the *Aquitania*!" said Grace, brightening with enthusiasm for the topic of her new beau.

"Me, too," said Ralph, tapping cigarette ash onto his dinner plate. "Except it wasn't France and it wasn't a ship and I couldn't go to my Aunt Ethel's, after all, on account of the rain and the squeegees busting on my old Reo. I had to lay it up for a week at the garage and missed Christmas altogether. Now, ain't that a shame?"

Ada stopped dealing herself cards long enough to listen to rain falling harder on the roof, then said, "Well, I've plainly refused to ride about in an automobile when it's raining since I and Lottie had that awful collision with the trolley."

George nodded as he wiped off a section of the counter with a wet towel. "Ain't nothing skiddier than car tracks."

"Oh, Johnny's an expert driver," said Grace, rubbing the boy's left hand. "I always feel quite safe in his Ford."

"Gee, dearie," Ada said, smiling sweetly at Grace while she swept her playing cards into a big pile. "This date of yours sure is a fresh one, ain't he?"

"Oh, he's as good as pie!"

"Well, I hope you gave him the third degree," said Ralph, wrinkling his nose at the water he had just drank. "Most fellows'll try anything to put themselves over with a dame as pretty as you."

Feeling like he could crack-up any minute now, Harry watched George bring the pot of coffee and a pair of cups over to Markle and his date along the far wall. The red-haired woman smiled at George, a lit cigarette in one hand. Maybe they hadn't made love yet, after all.

If that was the case, Markle probably wasn't concentrating about any-thing but the skirt in front of him.

Grace said, "Well, that's what decided me about Johnny. He hasn't such a line as the others I've gone with. Why, he's the most honest boy I've ever known. And so debonair."

Dealing herself another hand of solitaire, Ada agreed, "He's a peach, all right."

"You see, my family's third generation Mulberry Avenue," the boy explained, as if in defense of the girl's adoration. "Great-Uncle Jeremiah put up the first mansion on the Heights back in the seventies. Why, there's really nobody of importance on the Avenue who hasn't attended one of my mother's parties."

"Well, Louis and me got a pile of dough in cold storage and the ritziest suite in the house at Dollinger's," said Ralph, tapping more ash off his cigarette, then removing a hip flask from his jacket pocket. He spiked the water in his glass with the contents of the flask and had a sip. "That's at Main and Third, if you ain't familiar."

"I hate to mix up with some people," Grace remarked, "but Johnny's family has been awful swell to me since the day I met them."

Outdoors, an automobile stopped to park in front of the roadhouse, its headlamps shining in the rain, the engine idling. Harry listened briefly, then nodded at Pearl to finish her coffee. She scowled, but took another sip.

"You see, of course, Grace hasn't the entrée that she ought to," the boy explained, "though I like her ever so much. Being the silly sex they are, most girls end up as 'mighthavebeens,' don't you agree, darling?"

Grace smiled sweetly. "Johnny's promised to send me three night letters every week until the holidays, when he'll have me to Dartmouth by train."

"I've asked my sister to fit her out for the Winter Carnival — "

"So long as it's not too daring." Grace blushed.

Outside, the motor quit and the headlamps went dark. Harry heard a car door slam shut. Who's that now? For God's sake, if it's Cobb…

Reaching for the coffee cup, Harry found his hands were shaking. He was angry with himself for not having a plan in case something like this happened.

Finished with his fresh chicken pie, Ezra shoved the plate away and called out from the counter, "All righty now, here's one for you, Ralphie: *'Robert O'Brien, 16, son of a Birmingham manufacturer, died early today of shotgun wounds received late last night while in a watermelon patch with two men. S.E. Burnett told deputy sheriffs that melons had been stolen from his patch and he was on guard last night with a shotgun loaded with buckshot. He said he fired when he saw three men carrying off melons. Burnett was not arrested.'"* Ezra laid the paper in his lap. "Now, you ain't mixed up in any of that mess, are you, Ralphie?"

Ada and Louis both laughed out loud.

So did Pearl before Harry could hush her up.

Ralph frowned as he exhaled smoke from his nostrils. "Why, you're a real funny duck, Ezra. Now, why don't you beat it before I throw you out."

The roadhouse door swung open and a tall man walked in, his hair and brown overcoat and old flat shoes dripping wet. He had a short crowbar in his right hand. As he looked the dining room over, George called out to him from behind the counter, "Hello, Jimmy!"

Seeing it wasn't Cobb, Harry relaxed.

George's greeting was ignored when his customer quickly found what he had come to the roadhouse for. His attention solidly fixed on the red-haired woman in the blue silk dress whose companion, Fred Markle, had just burned his tongue on a sip of hot coffee, the fellow said, "I stayed to dinner, Ruthie, just like you told me to. Why ain't you never turned up?"

"Don't scold me, Jimmy," the woman calmly replied, as if expecting his arrival. "Why, I haven't had such a big time in months."

He scowled at her. "I guess I'm an old stick in the mud, ain't I?"

The fellow looked furious, but the woman didn't seem to pay it any mind.

Sounding amiable, Markle spoke up. "You're all out of sorts, Jimmy. Why not let us have you a highball and be decent about this?"

No one else in the roadhouse said a word. Harry watched Jimmy tighten his grip on the crowbar. There was going to be trouble of some sort. He just knew it. Behind him, Johnny whispered briefly to Grace, then stood to put on his auto coat. His eye still on Markle and the woman, Jimmy warned the boy, "Don't try to go nowhere. I ain't through here yet."

Harry felt a shiver run up his spine. Nobody moved. Even Pearl seemed startled to silence, her eyes blank and wet.

Ruthie took a long drag on her cigarette, and laughed. "Well, ain't you an interesting study, Jimmy." She addressed her companion in the gray pongee suit. "Fred, your brother's been seeing too many picture plays. He believes he's Hoot Gibson."

His brother? Good grief, here we go!

"Jimmy ought to be sleepy as a dog," said Fred, raising his voice for no apparent purpose. He smiled at the rest of the room, but sounded less confident as he spoke up. "Why, it's already hours past his normal bedtime."

Ada folded her cards flat onto the table. Ezra wrinkled the evening paper. Ralph and Louis both sat like statues, Ralph's cigarette burning close to his fingers. Grace and Johnny moved close together, holding hands. Harry noticed the Greek cook lean into the room from the dance hall, grab the wall phone, and crank for the operator.

Jimmy crossed the room, stopping just beside the small table by the wall. "You ain't been foolin' me none, Fred," he said, arching over his brother. "I known about you and Ruthie all summer. I ain't believed it, of course, 'cause all she used to tell me was how she couldn't hardly stand you coming over Sundays to eat with us and why didn't I never give you the air or say something to you about stayin' home to yourself."

"Why, that's a lie!" the woman shouted. "Jimmy, you shut your mouth about that!" She looked at his brother. "Fred, that isn't a bit true."

Jimmy stared Ruthie in the eye. "Didn't you never tell me about Fred here, sayin', 'Aw he ain't so much! His hair's scraggly and he ain't peppy enough for a decent girl to marry!' Didn't you never say that, honey?"

"Look here, it's no good discussing this now," said Fred, tossing his napkin onto the table. "Ruthie's suitcase is already planted at my house, Jimmy. She's through with you." He shoved his chair back. "Come on, Ruthie. Let's go."

As Fred stood, Jimmy brought the crowbar up and slammed it into his forehead knocking him to the floor. "You ain't going nowhere, you double-crossing sonofabitch!"

Ruthie shrieked in horror. As George attempted to come around from behind the counter, Jimmy shouted, "Don't come near me! This ain't your concern! Don't nobody come near me!"

Then he swung the crowbar at Ruthie, too, striking her beside the ear, driving her backwards into the wall. Dazed and bloodied, Fred tried to rise from the floor. Jimmy slammed him again hard on top of the head, cracking his skull.

Ada screamed. Grace and Johnny ducked under a table. Jimmy stepped forward and slammed Ruthie square in the face with the crowbar, while yelling, "You ain't but a common tart, Ruthie!"

Then he slammed her in the head again. Harry wished he had the guts to leap out of his chair and grab that fellow and throw him down, maybe save that woman before Jimmy killed her, but he was scared out of his wits.

Only George moved to help. He tried once more to come out from behind the counter but was warned off by Jimmy. "Stay back, you sonofabitch! This ain't no concern of yours!"

He slammed Ruthie on top of the head with the crowbar once more as Harry looked away.

A dark pool of blood spread under the chair where Fred had collapsed. Ada began whimpering. Ralph and Louis both sat frozen in shock. Johnny and Grace huddled together beneath their table by the window. Ezra was behind the cash register now, only his head visible above the countertop. George just stared at Jimmy who hovered over Ruthie and Fred muttering something to both of them Harry couldn't hear. Good God, he thought, maybe this lunatic'll go away now. He's counted them both out, hasn't he? What else could he want?

Pearl wept softly.

Then the roadhouse door swung open and a policeman came in soaking wet, revolver drawn. He yelled, "Jimmy Fagan!"

Victor the cook came out from the dance hall, but hid by the door to the toilet. Jimmy turned to face the policeman who slowly entered the room. "I guess I killed my wife, Mac." Most of the rage had drained from his voice. "She went sour on me."

"All right, Jimmy, keep your shirt on."

"It was them hot books of Fred's that done it to her."

The policeman said to George, "Tell the Greek to call Doc Earling. He'll be at home. The number's Drexel 1452. Tell him to get out here on the double."

Jimmy said, "I got wise to the fact that he was dropping up to see her when I was at the factory earnin' the dough that paid for all them fancy new dresses of hers."

"Put that iron down, Jimmy."

"Sure, Mac," Jimmy replied, lowering the crowbar to the floor. "Anything you say."

"I got to arrest you."

"I know it."

The policeman holstered the revolver. He walked over to Jimmy. As he removed a pair of handcuffs from his belt, Jimmy swung the crowbar up from the floor and slammed the policeman in the jaw, knocking him over backwards into the table next to Ada's. Then Jimmy dropped the crowbar and quickly wrestled the revolver free from the unconscious policeman's holster. He stood up and rotated the cylinder to see it was loaded properly.

Harry saw the door to the dance hall swing shut. He was convinced they were all about to be killed and there was nothing they could do to stop it. For God's sake, why didn't we grab him when he had the crowbar? Now it's too late. None of us have a chance with a gun. He's going to murder us all. And for what? Ruined with tears, Pearl leaned toward him and squeezed his hand.

Holding the revolver at his waist, Jimmy turned toward the counter. "How's about having me a whiskey, George?"

"Why sure, Jimmy." George's voice cracked. "Anything you like."

Jimmy approached the counter. "I'm awful tired."

"It's been a long night."

"Yeah."

While George dropped beneath the counter, Jimmy parked himself on one of the stools. Then he brought the revolver up to his ear and pulled the trigger.

— 9 —

Rain drizzled lightly on the cold breeze. Harry stood in the tall oat grass near the canal. Pearl knelt a few yards away in the damp sedge beside the muddy water, wiggling her fingers in the slow current. Far behind them, the burning headlamps of a dozen automobiles parked haphazardly in front of the Avalon roadhouse lit the rainy gloom along the narrow motor road. Yet Harry looked east instead across the brown marshlands toward the grain elevators on the cold horizon where the cloudy black sky would bring morning soon. Miles from the pretty olive trees atop University Hill, and twenty-four years since the lecture hour for Classical Languages and Philosophy at State, Harry found himself recalling Dr. Collingsworth's favorite passage from Wordsworth, five brief lines of "The Prelude":

> *"Not in Utopia, subterranean fields,*
> *Or some secreted island, Heaven knows where!*
> *But in the very world, which is the world*
> *Of all of us — the place where, in the end,*
> *We find our happiness, or not at all!"*

ALLENVILLE, IOWA

SIX MILES EAST OF ALLENVILLE, an hour toward twilight, the farm boy and the dwarf found matching headstones beneath a shady oak tree in an old pioneer cemetery and sat down to watch the sunset on the prairie horizon. The plots were laid out on a mound, rising thirty feet or so above the great expanse of grass and wildflowers that led to the edges of the sky. Below the mound, down a path that wound through an old stand of white oaks and bitternut hickory and across a narrow creek bed, was a ramshackle house facing a road that ran east, perhaps even as far as the Mississippi River. The August sky was windless, stems of surrounding grass and leaves of the trees under which the dwarf and the farm boy sat were quiet in the soft roselight at the end of the day. The dwarf curled his legs under himself and leaned back against the tombstone while the farm boy stretched out his own legs through white larkspur almost to the next headstone. No one had been buried on the mound in many years and the wooden gravemarkers scattered haphazardly about the finer granite tombstones were weathered nearly blank, their testimony and witness to the dead long worn off by wind and sun.

"I, myself," said the dwarf, "would prefer a simple grave, perhaps in my garden beneath the pear tree, there where another child might till the earth above my corpse and plant tomatoes in my belly, let my legacy be quickened fertilizer come season." He frowned. "Of course, Auntie would never permit it. We're all to be entombed together in a great marble cenotaph overlooking the Missouri River by a grove of willows where everyone who passes by will comment on how pompous our family must have been. I've often considered an anonymous death, perhaps being run down by a train out of state somewhere, in hope of avoiding an eternity of humiliation."

The dwarf played his fingers through the petals of purple morning glory between his knees. Sunlight, reddened by the hour, shone on the pallid skin of his face and lit his eyes as he stared directly into the sunset, smiling an unspoken thought. The farm boy had rolled over onto his belly and traced the carving on the tombstone in front of him with a forefinger, scratching flecks of dirt away with an overgrown nail, slowly marking by touch the immutable dates of birth and death.

OLIVER HEDDISON HENDRICK
BORN
JAN. 23 1853
DIED
JUNE 8 1877
NATIVE OF OHIO
AGED 24 YR'S SIX MO'S 15 DA'S

In this green land, his heart found peace,
In God's sweet arms, his soul now sleeps.

The farm boy said, "It don't matter much to me at all where I go afterward. Once I'm dead, I'm dead, and I don't figure I'll be caring all that much."

"Oh, I disagree," replied the dwarf. "In truth, Auntie assured me long ago that as we're all signed and sealed over to the afterlife, the choices we make in the here-and-now bear directly upon how much we'll enjoy God's offerings in the Great Reward."

"Huh?"

"Whose day our Lord saw fit to bless, receives at dusk a finer rest."

"Well then, I guess you and me got things all twisted up, don't we?"

The farm boy stood and took a long look into the west, shading his eyes against the sun, and spat. On this mound, the long prairie grasses grew fully and wildflowers bloomed free of plow and scythe. Tall soft tails of switchgrass leaned up just slightly higher than the lanky farm boy's belt buckle. Below the mound, a soft breeze swept across the fields like the gentle swells of a sundown sea. If he looked far enough into the west, he could glimpse the painted grain silos of the farms encircling Allenville where boys like himself labored in the day's end, counting the minutes down to supper and then maybe a few hours of freedom afterward in the dark.

The dwarf got up, too, wandering across the cemetery to another plot of headstones, these ringed in ornamental wrought iron and set upon by weeds and stems of yellow goatsbeard. The gate to the plot was missing and the surrounding rail had rusted and broken in several places and the headstones themselves were fractured by intruding vegetation both crossways and up from the gravesites. Although the dates of birth and death were yet legible on the old granite, the names were gone, weathered into anonymity by sixty long seasons.

The dwarf murmured, "In daydream we recall what our hearts thought buried."

His thin white hair glistened in the sunlight and his skin appeared almost limpid. He turned to the farm boy. "Are you much disposed toward recollection?"

Ignoring the dwarf's question, the farm boy strolled over to a wood marker stuck in the dirt within a patch of prairie rose and knelt down for a closer look.

Shielding his eyes with the back of one hand, the dwarf walked toward the western edge of the mound, parallel to the farm boy, staying within earshot for conversation sake. Just ahead, a small stone angel was posed in shawl and rose wreath atop a granite block, eyes gazing south, look of contentment carved onto a cherubic face.

Staring up at the statue, the dwarf recited another old rhyme, "When a mother dies, young forth to bring, her soul is borne on angel's wings."

Now the farm boy came up behind him to have his own look at the stone angel. "That thing must've cost some high coin." He circled it slowly, looking for an inscription that was absent. "Spend all that money, you'd think they'd include a name or something to let folks know who they're looking at and all."

When he came around to the front again, the farm boy noticed the dwarf was rocking back and forth on his heels like he did when he was occupied with himself. His eyes were glassy, a half-smile of sorts on his lips, arms akimbo.

"Does she look like some person you been acquainted with?" asked the farm boy. He took another look at the stone angel. "I guess she's sort of pretty."

The dwarf stopped rocking and coughed once. His eyes watered from the effort and he shook. After clearing his throat of the dust they had both been inhaling on a dozen back roads leading out of Nebraska, the dwarf drew a clean breath and remarked, "My mother passed away granting me life. Auntie said she suffered greatly giving birth to me, but refused to cease her struggle until I came forth. She lost consciousness an instant after I drew my first breath in this world and her valiant heart stopped before she ever saw my face. Auntie told me the midwife heard a faint flutter of wings above my dear mother's bed as she died." The dwarf looked up at the farm boy. "Do you believe in the unseen?"

Having no answer for the dwarf's question, the farm boy shrugged and studied instead the stone angel whose expression seemed to change ever so slightly in the angle of the sun's path across the sky. In Farrington, he had witnessed a cow choke to death trying to swallow an apple whole, witnessed a hound dog get his rib cage crushed running blind under the iron wheels of a loaded hay wagon. He had seen a stroke take a traveling salesman on Uncle Henry's front porch and a heart attack steal away Grandpa Chamberlain, interrupting him at Sunday dinner with his mouth full of sweet potatoes, and how Uncle Otis's eyes twitched and his tongue lolled about when he broke his neck falling drunk off the barn on the Fourth of July in the summer of 1921. The only wings Alvin had ever heard during the dying were those belonging to his momma's chickens flapping in the yard out of doors. In his experience, when God came for you, be it quick or be it slow, it was done in silence. One moment you're here, the next you're gone. Wink of an eye. Neither was it wondrous or beautiful. Dead squirrels smelled up the woods in summer. Cows and dogs stunk, too, even worse if they weren't gotten rid of soon enough. Grandpa Chamberlain owned a particular odor in the casket he never had in life. The consumption wards at the sanitarium reeked of antiseptics and gloom. Death drew a peculiar shade down on the living, not just putting out the light, but changing the color, too, into something waxy and pale. Something ugly.

"My mother had eyes blue as the sea," the dwarf told him. "She played the piano and sang after supper for people passing by out of doors. Auntie said she danced on the front porch in the dark before bedtime and wrote poems to everyone she knew. I'm told they were quite beautiful."

"When I get the call," the farm boy muttered, "I hope they nail the casket shut and not let anyone have a look-see at all. I'd like to be recollected as a living person, not some hollowed-out scarecrow in a black box."

Now late sunlight gave the stone angel a pink hue as a cool breeze swept slowly through the grass. Insects tossed and spun in its wake. Below the cemetery, a solitary flock of sparrows sailed east across the prairie.

"Sacred is the breath of life in our lungs," the dwarf recited, "God's precious gift by death now undone."

The farm boy sat down in the grass beside a patch of black-eyed susan. He pulled his knees up to his chest and lowered his eyes. The dwarf walked around back of the stone angel so that the statue blocked the last rays of sunlight from the red west. Then, in the shadow of the angel, he whispered a prayer for himself and the farm boy, and waited for evening to fall.

Along the road to Allenville was a tourist camp in a sheltering wood of black walnut and sycamore trees. Alvin Pendergast sat on a narrow spring-cot in one of the small cabins, listening to rain and thunder in the summer dark. He had just awakened from a nap and was alone. The one-room cabin was drafty and his cotton mattress smelled

moldy and worn out. Next to the camp was a roadside stand popular
with motorists. Because it was a weekend, plenty of automobiles were
parked out front. Alvin heard a couple of fellows slosh past through
the mud singing, *"How pleasant is Saturday night when you've tried all the week
to be good."* Both were drunk.

From his cot, Alvin stared out into the dark where a gust rippled
through the leafy sycamores. Water leaked into a corner of the cabin,
dripping steadily into a pot they had borrowed from a family traveling to the Badlands. Dampness clouded his lungs. Alvin grabbed his
shoes from beside the iron cot and put them on. He felt rheumy and
vaguely depressed. The dwarf had gone out at twilight, just before
the rain began, and left him alone to sleep. A round of thunder had
awakened him from a fitful dream in which he had been cornered
behind a downtown show window by federal marshals and shot down
mercilessly like a dog. His mother had been there, too, and he had
cried for her to hold him as he bled. He had such dreams often in the
sanitarium, cloudy black nightmares of drowning and doctors dressed
as undertakers pushing squeaky-wheeled gurneys through unlit wards.

He coughed harshly and put his cap on and went outdoors into the
drizzling rain. There were people all about, some sitting on the stoops
of the small cabins, others crowded into touring tents or huddled under blankets in automobile beds. Across the camp, Alvin saw a pack
of grimy children splashing gleefully in the mud and wondered where
their folks were. He smelled wood smoke on the humid rain-washed
air and a chicken roasting on a barbecue spit nearby. Electric lights
glowed on a tall wire from one end of the camp to the other. He heard
a concertina playing and walked in that direction. Rain dripped from
the sycamores. Voices rose and echoed across the darkness like the
ceaseless chatter of the sanitarium hallways that had kept him awake
night after night when he was his sickest. A motor horn beeped and
Alvin looked just quickly enough to see a liquor bottle shatter against
a thick black walnut tree. A lucifer match flared and a woman laughed
from the rainy shadows behind one of the cabins. She called out and
the farm boy stopped and stared into the dark and a big derby-hatted
man came forth soaking wet and stared back at him. Alvin almost gave

him the raspberry, but knew he wasn't fit enough to scrap with a fellow that husky. The cabin door opened and a woman in curlpapers stuck her head out, saw the derby-hatted man, and shouted a dirty word at him. Alvin watched him zip open his trousers and piss across the mud toward the cabin door as it slammed shut again. Then the man closed his trousers and barked his own filthy obscenity and Alvin went off into the dark without looking back.

He sloshed past the middle of the auto camp where the sewer on the other side of the registration hut smelled ugly and foul. When the gang of soggy children ran by, Alvin kicked mud at them and they squealed with laughter. Rain poured down harder and a gusting breeze shook the wire of lights. Somewhere ahead, a pitchman called numbers for a beano game. Then Alvin saw a tent ringed with electric lanterns and picnic tables under the canvas roof and a crowd bigger than ever, the dwarf among them.

"93, LADIES AND GENTS, 93!"

The caller stood atop a makeshift podium with a megaphone, drawing game numbers scribbled on small wooden disks from a cigar box. The dwarf was sitting at a table with five other tourists: a ruddy-faced man in a squam hat and a slicker coat, and four women Alvin's mother's age in rainproof cotton or gabardine twill coats and hats. Each had a game card and a pile of dried beans beside it.

"Come in out of the rain, young fellow!" the ruddy fellow called out. "Pull up a chair!" He held a cheap stogie cigar between his teeth.

"Is this him?" one of the women in gabardine asked the dwarf. She wore a mesh net in her hair and a stick of punk behind one ear.

Rascal fiddled with his beans, then looked up with a smile. "Why, yes it is. Although I didn't think he'd ever wake up."

Still muddleheaded from his nap, Alvin walked in under the tent covering while the pitchman called out another beano number.

"15, LADIES AND GENTS, 15!"

Water dripped on the table from his cap as Alvin shuffled himself into a folding chair. He felt as if everybody at the beano game had their eye on him and worried what the dwarf had told them. Alvin was used to keeping things confidential himself and didn't trust the dwarf not to feed them the wrong dope. He knew Rascal would tell a lie for a piece of toast.

"Want a card?" the older fellow asked him. "We'll get you one up front."

Alvin coughed again and shook his head, not feeling much like playing games tonight. He hated beano, anyhow. His aunts played it at the Farrington auditorium once a month for a nickel a card and Uncle Henry thought it was a smart racket, even though Aunt Clara told Hattie that beans were for eating, which Alvin thought was pretty funny.

"We're from Ashtabula," said the woman with the punk in her hair. Did she just give Alvin the glad eye? "My name's Margaret and these are my friends Alice, Hazel and Bertha. We're Couéists on a pilgrimage."

"Day by day, in every way, I'm getting better and better," the dwarf chirped, quoting Émile Coué's famous auto-suggestion.

"Indeed, we are," Margaret enthused.

"Glad to know you," Alvin said, politely, although truthfully he didn't really care one way or another. He had met quite a lot of people on the road since Easter and could just as soon have given them all the raspberry. He felt his forehead for a fever and found it warm. He knew he ought to go back to the cabin and lie down again, but he also wanted to see what sort of stunt the dwarf was putting over on these dumbbells.

"I told you, this ain't no roadside pulpit," said the man with the cigar. "How about we just play the game and let this little fellow finish his story."

"Certainly," Margaret agreed.

The other three women smiled sweetly at the farm boy. One of them down at the end of the table wearing ear puffs gave him a wink. She reminded him of the old nurses he knew at the sanitarium who fed him cod liver oil five times a day and made him walk up and down the halls with his bottom showing and joked about it when they thought he was asleep.

Thunder rumbled in the rainy distance and Alvin saw lightning flash. He sniffed the damp air and decided it was warmer than before he had taken his nap, which meant a thunderstorm rising. Alvin wondered what everyone was doing out here playing beano under a tent in this weather. If a tornado blew through this tourist camp, that'd be it.

"42, LADIES AND GENTS, 42!"

"Where was I?" the dwarf asked, sliding a bean onto his card. He seemed preoccupied, distracted by an errant thought. Alvin wondered if Rascal had a worry in the world besides where his next meal was coming from. Not a damned thing since Hadleyville had seemed to trouble him.

"Mosquitoes of the foreign tropics," the ruddy fellow said, tapping ash off his cigar into the mud behind him. He smiled at Alvin and gave him a friendly nod. The farm boy looked away.

Margaret interjected, "Speaking of which, I've been bitten so often this summer I feel like a dartboard. Isn't that true, Alice? Our tourist sleeper hasn't proven to be bug-proof at all, has it?"

"No, dear," the woman seated across from Margaret replied. "Not at all. We need a shower of Flit."

She wore eyeglasses that had fogged up in the rainy air. How she could see her card well enough to play was a mystery.

"You ought to've bought a good wall tent like I suggested," said the woman with ear puffs. Alvin noticed that her card already had three beans horizontal on the middle row. "You know, Hazel and I haven't had any bother whatsoever with mosquitoes."

"Well, Bertha, I should say you've been very fortunate, indeed," Margaret remarked, forcing a smile. "They've given us thunder this entire trip."

"Yes, but Hazel and I also prepared well."

"I tell you," Alice insisted, "we ought to have brought along some Flit."

"9, LADIES AND GENTS, 9!"

"Actually, my mother's used oil of cloves for years," said Hazel, fixing her own elastic hair net, "and she's never been mosquito bit. Not once."

That explained the spicy odor Alvin had smelled when he sat down at the table.

Putting a bean on his card, the ruddy-faced fellow said, "When I was with the First Nebraska at Manila in '98, we seen mosquitoes the size of hummingbirds. If you got bit by one of them, you were finished. It's the sickliest place on earth."

"I detest mosquitoes of all sorts," Margaret said, with a shiver. "They're despicable pests."

"Well, thanks to the mosquito," the dwarf said, trying to maneuver himself back into the conversation, "poor Uncle Augustus was virtually addicted to quinine for the final thirty-three years of his life. He never recovered from the recurring spells of malaria he contracted on a secret mission for Queen Victoria to Java."

"Where?" the farm boy asked, hoping to get under his skin. Whenever Alvin felt sick, he enjoyed sharing his misery with others. Easiest was making his sisters cry. Mary Ann acted like a baby whenever she got teased. Everyone in the family hated that.

"The Dutch East Indies."

"Never heard of it," Alvin said, with a practiced sneer and a fake giggle.

The dwarf clucked his tongue. "Well, it's very far away in the Java Sea, south of Borneo. You know, you really ought to consider studying geography some day."

"Says you."

"44, LADIES AND GENTS, 44."

Margaret shifted a bean onto her card, then told the dwarf, "My friends and I hope to travel around the world one day."

"We believe all roads lead to Rome," said Bertha, winking again at Alvin.

"You ever been to Borneo?" the ruddy fellow asked Rascal after a puff on his cigar.

The dwarf shook his head. "No, but twice dear old Uncle Augustus circumnavigated the globe. He was the bravest man I ever knew. His photograph was taken on six continents and I saw each of them on the walls of his library when I was a boy. At every supper, he led us in a toast to the seven seas, '*Sail and sail, with unshut eye / Round the world for ever and aye.*'"

"He ought to've been with me and Dewey at Manila in '98. Now, there was something to sing about."

"I want to hear this little fellow's story about Queen Victoria," Bertha said, playing with her beans.

"Yes," Margaret agreed. "Let's hear his story."

"Are you certain?" the dwarf asked. "It's quite frightening."

"Are there ghosts involved?" asked Hazel, a slight tremble in her voice. Alvin almost laughed aloud. Now he knew these folks were dumbbells.

"No," Rascal replied, "but there'll be many horrible deaths. I had nightmares for a month after I first heard the story myself."

"Oh, I adore a good nightmare!" said Alice. "Do tell your story."

"Sure, go ahead," the ruddy fellow agreed.

"All right." The dwarf smiled. "Well, in April of 1883, my Uncle Augustus and a fellow from Stepney by the name of Louis Hurlburt hired onto a tramp steamer as firemen sailing to Java. Apparently, the Queen was quite worried about Dutch intentions concerning Singapore and wished to discover how earnest its colonial regents had become. Uncle Augustus said Java was a wonderful paradise of the most lovely orchids and ancient temples, yet also terribly dangerous in those years. Why, a grown man might be gored to death by a wild ox, drown into a dark mangrove swamp, or earn his fortune in oil and rubber according to the whims of fate."

"Gee, maybe I'd ought to go hunting there one day," Alvin interrupted, as thunder rumbled in the distance. The rain had lightened to a steady drizzle, hissing in the cottonwoods nearby.

"Oh, I should think you'd be fortunate not to be eaten by a royal tiger. It's one of the most perilous jungles on earth."

"36, LADIES AND GENTS, 36!"

"I wouldn't be at all ascared. I shot a bear once from my bedroom window."

"Now, that takes some doing," the ruddy fellow remarked, placing a bean on his card.

"Sure it does."

"Well, having devoted considerable study of my own to the Dutch

East Indies," the dwarf continued, "I've always been astonished by the course Mother Nature took in that strange corner of the earth. Did you know there are wild fig trees in the forests of Java whose branches droop downward to become roots for even more trees? Its leaves are so large, the Javanese natives use them as plates for their meat. And there are great bats with wings five feet or more across. I've read authentic reports of sleeping babies snatched from their bamboo cradles and whisked away into the dark by those infernal creatures."

"My goodness!" Margaret exclaimed. "That isn't true, is it?"

Alvin shook his head. " 'Course it ain't. He's just pulling your leg."

"Look it up in the *Geographic*," Rascal said. "Only a month after sailing into Bantam Bay, Uncle Augustus saw lemurs hunting birds at night with eyes that glowed red as coals. Why, he personally killed a wild hog and six Java musks for food when he became lost in the jungle by the Vale of Poison at Butar, where he nearly perished in a fog of deadly carbonic acid gas after rescuing two hundred Javanese native children from Dutch slavery inside a secret diamond mine."

"Well, I'll be switched," said the ruddy fellow.

"What a marvelous story!" Alice remarked.

"56, LADIES AND GENTS, 56!"

The dwarf studied his card for a moment. "Oh, it's only the beginning. You see, Java is called the 'Land of Fire' because of its many volcanoes. Above the blue sea, in the Straits of Sunda, one of these fire towers, Mount Perboewatan on Krakatau, began spewing smoke and steam. Naturally, my uncle and Mr. Hurlburt were somewhat concerned, but after the Queen wired a secret message ordering them both to remain in Java, there could be no thought of departing. Posing as Pieter Van Dijk, a coffee and tobacco grader from Amsterdam, Uncle Augustus traveled all summer from port to port within the Straits, while hot volcanic ash rained down upon the sea and a huge black thundercloud of smoke spread out from Krakatau. In the meantime, Louis Hurlburt had secured a position as a stoker aboard the Dutch mail steamer *Governor General Loudon*, which was ferrying interested parties back and forth to the volcanic island for scientific observation. Uncle Augustus sailed there in late May and was quite astounded by the smoke clouds and the constant hail of stones and fire. He went ashore with a crew of engineers. The wide beach was buried under a foot of thick pumice and two feet of ash. All vegetation on Krakatau had disappeared, only bare stumps and a few leafless trees remained and the air smelled of sulfuric acid. Uncle Augustus gathered up a small collection of black pitchstones when he left Krakatau. In fact, I have one of them in my bedroom at home. It's a wonderful souvenir."

"19, LADIES AND GENTS, 19!"

"Oh, I'd love to see it one day," Bertha said, then checked her card. She sighed.

The dwarf smiled at her. "Perhaps you shall."

At another table, a woman rose with a child in her arms and walked off into the rainy dark toward the roadside stand. She was crying. Alvin saw a fellow in suspenders and a felt hat jump up and start after her. The pitchman left the podium and caught the fellow at the edge of the tent and had a few words with him. Some people at another table began hooting for the pitchman to go back to the podium.

The dwarf said, "Well, by August, Mount Danan on Krakatau had also erupted and all the Straits were cast into utter darkness. On Sunday the twenty-sixth, Uncle Augustus crossed from Prinsen Island north to Telok Betong at Sumatra where he had a dinner appointment with a Dutch admiral who much admired good cigars. The admiral's daughter, Elise Van Leeuwen, who also attended, negotiated a trade with my uncle involving a crate of South American coffee for a collection of lovely Java sparrows Miss Van Leeuwen had recently purchased at Katimbang. By now, ships had arrived from all over the world, maneuvering in the Straits to witness the great paroxysm. Lightning flashed in the black clouds over Krakatau. Earthquakes rumbled across the islands. The admiral's daughter grew fearful and left dinner early for a steamer heading back east across the Straits to Anjer. After she had gone, Uncle Augustus began proposing a toast to the glory of Dutch rule in the East Indies when a tremendous explosion thundered across the Straits. Uncle Augustus rushed from the saloon with the admiral to watch a great black cloud rise into the dark heavens from Krakatau. He knew he ought to quit the port, as well, but a morning telegraph from Anjer had stated that the *Loudon* was already en route to Telok Betong, and Uncle Augustus felt duty bound to wait for Mr. Hurlburt. The admiral, however, decided to leave immediately aboard the gunboat *Berouw* to evacuate both his wife and daughter for Batavia on the northwestern coast of Java. After saying good-bye to his worried host, Uncle Augustus went to have one last glass of whiskey at the Bergen Hotel near the River Koeripan."

The pitchman quit arguing with the fellow in the felt hat and went back to the podium where he grabbed another disk. "71, LADIES AND GENTS, 71!"

"An old soak, was he?" said the ruddy fellow, leaning back in his chair. He laughed out loud.

Alvin saw a woman wearing a cotton dress and a blue Sunday bonnet join the pitchman at the podium. She spoke in his ear, which appeared to upset him, because he spilled the cigar box of disks into the mud.

Rascal frowned. "I beg your pardon? Misusing liquor was very common in those days and I'm sure the volcanic rain had quite a lot to do with his intemperance that dark afternoon."

"You said it."

The pitchman climbed down off the podium to retrieve the disks while the woman in the Sunday bonnet shook a finger at him. A gust of wind rippled the string of lights.

The dwarf scowled. "Look here, none of us can imagine in the least what it must've been like to feel the very earth tremble underfoot like Judgment Day. Now, as I was saying, when Uncle Augustus finally left the hotel, he found people dashing here and there, carrying their children and valuables away from the port. Another infernal blast thundered across the black waters from Krakatau and within the hour a rain of ash and stones began to fall. The wind was blowing fiercely from the northwest when Uncle Augustus stood on the pier looking across Lampong Bay for the *Loudon* and saw the first volcanic waves approaching from Krakatau. They rose from the sea much too quickly to permit escape by anyone on the shore. Having nowhere to go, Uncle Augustus ran to the end of the pier and dove into the bay just ahead of the first big sea wave. When he rose again from the deep, he saw the waves had swamped the pier and poured across the postal road into town, destroying the government offices and all the other buildings at sea level and chasing the survivors up to the District Hall on higher ground. The crew of a pilot boat that had ridden out the danger in deeper water found Uncle Augustus grasping a wooden crate. He was given dry clothing and a cup of hot tea and a biscuit and told to stay off the decks as large stones from Krakatau were falling now all across the Straits. Soon, the salt ship *Marie* anchored nearby and signaled the arrival of the *Loudon* from Anjer, and Uncle Augustus persuaded the captain of the pilot boat to ferry him over to the mail steamer."

Once the pitchman had collected the muddy disks, he climbed back up onto the podium and called out the next number: "18, LADIES AND GENTS, 18!" The woman in the Sunday bonnet scowled behind his back.

"Oh, your uncle must've been awfully brave," Bertha remarked. She found a place for another bean on her card. Alvin saw she had three now in a vertical column.

"Of course he was," Margaret said, clearly disgusted with her own card that had no more than two beans side by side anywhere across its surface. "Now, stop interrupting!"

Suddenly, the woman in the Sunday bonnet snatched a handful of disks from the cigar box. The pitchman reached for them, but the woman refused to give them back. As the caller grabbed at them again, she backed away. Alvin heard cackling from another table.

"The sea was rising and falling almost by the minute now. Lightning glowed in the smoke over the volcano and warm pumice littered the water. Aboard the *Loudon*, Uncle Augustus inquired as to Louis Hurlburt and was told he'd left the steamship at Anjer. His companion apparently intended to row north to a secret telegraph station in a sugar mill near the port of Merak to send a message to the Queen, informing her of the great cataclysm. However, the *Loudon* had already heard from the telegraph master at Anjer, reporting damage at the drawbridge there, boats smashed everywhere, and word that high waves had entirely destroyed the Chinese camp at Merak. Sometime after midnight, Uncle Augustus and the crew of the *Loudon* saw another great wave rise from Lampong Bay and sweep toward the port, destroying the harbor light and the warehouse and a coal storage on the pier and briefly capsizing the *Marie*, throwing the admiral's gunboat *Berouw* from the east side of the pier clear over to the other."

Still lacking a handful of disks, the caller took one from the cigar box. "64, LADIES AND GENTS, 64!"

Margaret scowled over her card. "Oh, fiddle-faddle!"

Shuffling another bean onto his card, the ruddy fellow tapped ash off his cigar, then asked, "Didn't no one there know how to drop an anchor?"

"Yeah, how about that?" Alvin agreed, hoping to see Rascal squirm over this dumbbell story of his.

"Of course," the dwarf replied, adding another bean to his own card, "but the volcanic waves were so enormous, not even an anchor could hold the ships against their fury. Why, Uncle Augustus said he'd never been so frightened in all his life. Blue flames of St. Elmo's fire flew about the sky and the wind that swept over the *Loudon* smelled of hot sulphur like Hades itself. The sea was so rough, Uncle Augustus was obliged to remain aboard the mail steamer until dawn, listening all night long to the explosions from Krakatau becoming louder and louder until half past five when a blast unlike anything Uncle Augustus had heard on this earth shook the *Loudon* and knocked out the ear drums on half the members of the ship's crew. He saw the admiral's gunboat beached high up on the shore and insisted the ship's boat take him back across the bay to the *Berouw* to help his old Dutch friend. Well, of course, the journey was trying beyond faith. The sea was filled with masses of floating pumice, and lightning struck the mast conductor repeatedly, and a furious wind tore at the decks. When the first mate refused to bring the boat any closer than a quarter mile from the port, Uncle Augustus dove into the bay once again and swam alone to shore through the dangerous surf. All was chaos aboard the stranded *Berouw*. Several members of the gunboat's crew had been swept overboard by the wave that had carried them onto the beach and the admiral had been struck in the head by a fallen cocoa-nut tree and knocked unconscious."

Alvin asked, "Were there any wild monkeys in the tree that hit him?"

Bertha and Hazel both giggled.

A scowl on his face, the pitchman took two disks from the cigar box. "58, LADIES AND GENTS, 58! DO WE HAVE A WINNER YET?"

"No, I don't believe so," replied the dwarf, sounding testy now. "Would you mind awfully not interrupting? Poor Uncle Augustus was in a terrible scrape. Why, it's one of God's greatest miracles that he came out alive."

"When does he get the malaria?" Alvin asked.

"Soon!" growled the dwarf. "For heaven sakes, will you please keep quiet?"

"Go on," said the ruddy fellow, "finish the story."

"Thank you, sir. Now, where were we?"

"A scrape in a cocoa-nut tree."

"17, LADIES AND GENTS, 17!"

The dwarf shifted a bean onto the middle of his card, and continued with his story. "Oh, yes. Well, those fortunate souls at Telok Betong who survived the initial sea-waves returned to the village again to gather up their remaining possessions while Uncle Augustus labored furiously with the crew of the *Berouw* to get her back into the bay. More boats were washed ashore from the harbor and Uncle Augustus said the sky was blacker than the blackest night and hot pumice big as pumpkins rained down upon them as they worked. Of course, the effort was hopeless. Within the hour, four more volcanic waves rolled over the port, stranding the *Berouw* farther up on the beach and drowning another half-dozen members of the crew, including the poor old admiral, the captain, and his first navigating officer. Uncle Augustus felt quite terrible. He advised everyone to abandon the gunboat and find safe shelter from the waves and the mud rains and the furious wind. The *Marie* had already pulled up anchor and left for deeper waters. Then came a sound Uncle Augustus described as God Himself clapping His hands together, and the black smoke clouds brightened to a fearsome crimson over Krakatau as the volcano gave a mighty roar and blew itself to heaven with the greatest explosion ever witnessed by mortal man! Within minutes, Uncle Augustus saw a gigantic wave emerge from the briny deep and rush toward the shore. Most of the crew ran in panic for the jungle. Knowing he had no chance to escape on foot, Uncle Augustus hid down alone in the captain's cabin, closing himself in and awaiting his fate in the dark. When the huge sea wave struck the *Berouw*, Uncle Augustus was praying to the Lord for deliverance from the tempest. It washed completely over Telok Betong, leaving nothing but rough seas in its frightful wake."

"47, LADIES AND GENTS, 47!"

"My heavens!" Alice cried. "How dreadful!"

"Everybody was killed, weren't they?" the ruddy fellow asked, looking over his card.

The dwarf nodded, his voice somber now. "Nothing survived. Uncle Augustus recalled the gunboat tumbling over and over in the roaring water, himself hurled about the small cabin like a child's toy until at last he lost consciousness. When he awoke, all was quiet. The great wave had receded, leaving the battered gunboat perched thirty-feet above sea level on the River Koeripan, more than a mile and a half inland. Uncle Augustus crawled from his hiding place and used a rope to climb down off the gunboat. Hot ash still rained from the dark sky. Where once fields of rice had grown, Uncle Augustus saw nothing but mud and boulders. So, too, had all the lovely Javanese villages been washed away. Not even the paroquets cackled in the jungle. When Uncle Augustus called out for help, no one answered. He was quite alone. Having little idea where he was, Uncle Augustus determined to stay put until the clouds broke, so he climbed back up onto the gunboat."

"87, LADIES AND GENTS, 87!"

Hazel added a bean to her card. Bertha frowned at hers.

"The next morning he built a fire, then killed a wild hog and ate it with crackers from the crew's rations. Not until the moon lit the night sky nearly two days later, was he able to see Lampong Bay and walk out of the jungle along the Koeripan to the appalling ruin of Telok Betong. At the first of September, Uncle Augustus took a ferry across the Straits of Sunda to locate Louis Hurlburt. The volcanic island of Krakatau had mostly disappeared, as had the seaports of Anjer and

Merak, along with the Dutch admiral's pretty daughter, her collection of Java sparrows, and more than thirty thousand poor souls. Though Uncle Augustus searched the west coast of Java for a month from Tjeringen to Bantam Bay, he never found his companion, and the malaria he contracted from tramping through those damp jungles of paradise remained with him for the rest of his days."

"12, LADIES AND GENTS, 12!"

Nobody spoke at the table. Rain dribbled off the tent sides, and the electric lanterns shook in the damp breeze. Then the ruddy fellow shoved his chair back and stood up. He tossed his burnt cigar out into the mud and stared the dwarf in the eye and began clapping. The four ladies remained seating, but they joined in, too, with a fine round of applause. Rascal acknowledged their admiration with a stiff bow from his seat.

When they were through clapping, the farm boy remarked, "Well, that's a swell story. Was any part of it true?"

"Of course," replied the dwarf, sliding a bean to the bottom row of his card. He added, "Uncle Augustus wrote it all down in a private diary which was bequeathed to me after a Prussian sniper took his life at Delville Wood. I value no possession of mine more greatly and it's been immensely instructive these past few years. Dear old Uncle Augustus believed that our lives bear irrefutable testimony to the immortal purpose of character and courage in this world, and he held selflessness as the pinnacle of virtues. Indeed, his epitaph on the family mausoleum at Hannibal reads most eloquently: *We owe respect to the living; to the dead, we owe only truth.*"

"13, LADIES AND GENTS, 13." The pitchman's voice sounded weary.

The dwarf slid another bean across his bottom row, then cried, "Why, I believe I've won!" He stood and shouted loudly enough for everyone under the tent to hear, "BEANO!"

Alvin got up and walked off into the rainy dark.

The breeze felt warmer somehow, but the drizzle persisted. When he was sickest with consumption, Alvin had dreamt of angels in gauze masks wandering the halls of the sanitarium in search of those whose failing lungs would lead them to God's bright countenance, or eternal night, depending upon whether the Bible was true or not. Now he wondered how it felt to be carried away by a giant sea wave. He imagined a blast of wind and the sky of stars disappearing, his body thrust suddenly upwards like a bird in flight.

Alvin walked out to the front of the muddy camp where the roadside stand was crowded with motorcars and people. He smelled liquor in the dark and burning pipe tobacco. The woman he had seen with the child under the beano tent sat in the rear seat of a brown DeSoto. She held a cup of coffee to her lips, sipping like a cat. A pack of men in suits and neckties stood behind the automobile just under the rear awning, yammering away about Jack Johnson and Kansas blue laws. Another crowd of fellows in a Ford runabout pulled in off the road, soaking wet and singing "Alabamy Bound" at the top of their lungs. Getting to the short order counter ahead of them, Alvin bought a hotdog and a Coca-Cola from the change in his pocket and went off to the side of the building. A large truck roared by on the wet road. Alvin felt the damp draft on his face as it passed. Stifling a cough, he ate the hotdog and drank his soda pop and threw the empty bottle into a thick growth of sumac. An angry voice cursed back at him from the dark and a sturdy-looking man in mudcaked overalls and a denim jacket came out of the bushes, buttoning up his fly. Looking Alvin square in the eye, he produced the empty pop bottle. "Fill this up with corn liquor, young fellow, and I won't crack you in the head like you just done me." Then he bent forward so Alvin could see a bloody laceration at the hairline.

"I didn't even know you was there," the farm boy said, though he might have supposed in a place such as this there would be someone lurking in the bushes.

"You ain't been around all that long, have you?"

"What of it?"

"You been sick, ain't you? Don't lie to me. I can see it in your eyes. You got the cure, but it ain't made you well, so you gone looking for another and all you found is more trouble, and now you're sicker'n you ever been, and that's the plain truth, ain't it?"

Alvin wiped his nose with the back of a sleeve and shook his head as the rain began to fall harder again. "I catched a cold this morning, that's all."

The man took a sniff of the pop bottle. "I had the whooping cough once, and that wasn't nothing but a sidetrack. Am I better off for it? Well, I can still do a pretty fair buck-and-wing when the fiddler plays, and peddle bananas enough for a suit of up-to-the-minute clothes and a swell lay every other week or so with any little slip-shoe lovey I like, if that's 'better off' in your lingo."

"I ain't said nothing about that," Alvin replied, watching another automobile streak past. The man tossed Alvin's empty pop bottle back into the sumac. He smelled like onions when the wet breeze shifted and one of his eyes sagged unnaturally and Alvin guessed he had a kink from too much back-stall booze.

"Who was it that run you off? Your daddy? Is that how come you're looking all blue? He tan your britches once too often?" The man chuckled.

"What's it to you?" the farm boy answered. He didn't care for this fellow and wished he hadn't begun gabbing with him in the first place. He felt his fever coming on, maybe even a coughing fit.

The man stared at Alvin like he had a bug on his face. "Well, don't pay no mind to that. We all done things we ain't proud of. We like to be held up to our better angels, but it ain't always that simple, is it? Why, I seen men so beaten down with shame that life become just a dark cloud they couldn't see out of no more, and I'm here to tell you liquor don't cure it, neither, though some of us surely believed that's so. Truth is, nobody's wise to how cold-blooded and mean this world can be when a fellow's out of sorts with the straight and narrow and can't see his way back and there ain't no forgiveness waiting up the road."

"I ain't asking no one to pass the hat," Alvin said, temper rising. He didn't care for folks feeling sorry him even when he was hid away in the sanitarium, and he surely didn't need no dumbbell's sympathy.

"Is that a fact?"

"You said it."

The wind gusted hard, blowing wet leaves across the rainy night sky. The young bunch in the Ford runabout swung back out into the road and drove off, still singing like melon vendors. Alvin envied them, wished he'd been invited along.

The man said, "I guess you're a pretty tough egg, aren't you?"

Alvin frowned. "How's that?"

"You don't let nothing stir you up, do you?"

"Well, I ain't no baby."

"Oh yeah?" The man smirked. "Well, answer me this, sonny boy: who's buying your breakfast?"

The cabin door was ajar when Alvin came back from the roadside stand. He peeked through the window and saw Chester beside one of the camp cots with an electric lantern in hand. His suit was smudged with dirt, his felt hat dripping rainwater. When he noticed the farm boy on the stoop, he said, "I got a job for you boys."

A damp gust of wind shook the walls of the small structure and hundreds of tiny flecks of rotted wood cascaded down from the ceiling. Alvin shielded his eyes from the glow of the lantern. "What's that?"

"I'll show you outside."

"Thunderstorm's coming," Alvin noted after smelling the air. Farm life had taught him how to smell a storm on a night wind, hours before it arrived. It was a dandy skill, but didn't earn him much more than dry clothes on a rainy day.

"We don't have time to worry about rain," Chester replied. "Too much work to do tonight."

The dwarf rose from a dark corner of the cabin, suitcase in hand. Illuminated in lamplight, his eyes glowed yellow and his skin looked waxen and old, his hair white as corn silk. Chester directed the lamp toward him. "You can leave that here. You'll be coming back soon as you're done with the job."

Rascal put down his suitcase. "All right."

"Storm's coming up," Alvin said, tucking his shirt in. "Be here soon. Maybe quicker."

"I heard you the first time," Chester said, bringing the electric lantern back toward Alvin, suspending it in front of his face. "I tell you, don't worry about it. Weather's got nothing to do with your job tonight. A little rain won't bother a thing."

"Be more'n a little, I'd guess."

"No matter, you've got plenty of work to do, rain or no rain."

"There'll be rain," Alvin assured him.

"Swell," said Chester, losing patience. "I'll be waiting by the car. Hop to it."

He walked out.

Alvin went to the cabin door where black droplets swirled about on the wind. Close on the heels of an electric flash in the east, thunder boomed across the dark. He took a hard look at the sky. Lightning could strike a man dead in an instant. On the farm, cows and horses got hit now and again. Fried to the bone, carcass smoking, even in Noah's rain. Alvin felt the dwarf beside him, also studying the clouds with a watchful eye.

"Won't pay to get hit by lightning," the farm boy said, holding a hand out into the rain which was falling harder now. His shoes and socks felt soggy.

"I remember being terrified of it as a child," the dwarf agreed. "Auntie had to close my windows and tie down the shades so that I couldn't see it flash. I'd hide under the bedcovers until the thunder stopped and Auntie told me it was safe to come out."

Alvin shook his head. "That's dumb."

"Oh?"

"Everyone knows you can't hide. If it's got your name, you're fixed, and that's all there is to it."

The dwarf stared up into the dark, rain blowing about overhead. "I don't believe in that sort of silly superstition."

"Don't matter if you believe it or not," Alvin replied, watching sheets of rain drench the tourist camp. "It's a fact, just the same. If you doubt it, go on and take a walk out there. You don't need a lightning rod on your head, neither. Just remember: it's not in God's plan to have everybody check out in their sleep."

He smiled, hoping he'd gotten under Rascal's skin a little, stirred him up some.

Another lightning strike lit the sky to the east. The dwarf counted by seconds to nine, then the thunder roared across the prairie. As the echo died away, Chester's voice followed from the automobile parked under a black oak by the road. "Hurry up, goddamn it!"

Standing just out of the rain beneath the big oak, Chester held the electric lantern over the rear seat of the Packard for Alvin to see inside. Pale lamplight made visible a youth's face partly wrapped in gunny cloth and shadows. His eyes were shut and his hands folded into the heavy overcoat that covered him up.

"He's out of the game," Chester said, as if it weren't obvious.

Alvin's skin crawled. "You shot him?"

"He slipped on a banana peel and broke his neck."

The dwarf slid quietly into the front seat on the driver's side for a better look.

Alvin stared at him, heart thumping. The boy wasn't much older than himself.

Chester spoke up. "He had more spirit than brains."

"Huh?"

He handed the lantern over to the farm boy whose legs were trembling now.

"He had a set of keys I needed and didn't care to negotiate for them. He was a stubborn little sonofabitch." Chester smiled. "I liked that."

Alvin directed the lantern again toward the rear seat of the Packard. Chester had hiked the boy's collar up higher than normal to hide the bruising about the larynx, but the swelling showed still in his cheeks and eyelids. Alvin found himself transfixed by the boy, slumped in the seat, looking drunk and passed out, yet in fact deader than last November's turkey. The farm boy pressed his face to the glass and watched the dwarf climb into the rear seat beside the dead boy as if they were old friends out for a ride in a motorcar. Alvin shuddered as rain began to fall in earnest.

Chester said, "He's just some hick. Nobody to concern yourselves over. Go on, jump in and get acquainted. We need to beat it out of here before somebody sees him."

"How come you brought him here, anyhow?"

"Well, I thought you boys could give him a swell send-off."

Half a mile or so from the tourist camp, Chester pulled off the highway onto a narrow road that led east through a soggy wheat field to a dilapidated farmhouse and a sagging old barn. He parked next to the storm cellar behind the barn and got out. Both Alvin and the dwarf joined him there in the rain. Chester said, "Come on, get the kid out of the car."

He took the electric lantern off the front seat of the Packard and switched it on. "Look here, boys, I have to be getting along. I've got an appointment in town tonight and it won't pay to be late. There's a shovel and a pickaxe in the cellar." He handed the electric lantern to the farm boy. "When you're done putting this kid in the ground, go back to the camp and get some sleep, then meet me at the Methodist church in the morning. You remember it? That tall skinny white building with the steeple we passed by this afternoon. If you hurry along, it won't take you more than a couple hours. When you get there, don't go in until the service lets out, all right?"

With the rain pouring down harder, Alvin asked, "Where do you want us to bury him?"

"I don't care."

Then Chester got back into the Packard and started the motor. A great cloudy fog of exhaust billowed out of the tailpipes. He told the farm boy, "Go on, get him out of there."

Alvin gave the lamp to the dwarf, then reluctantly leaned inside the Packard and grabbed the dead boy by his shirt collar and pulled him up off the seat. The boy's corpse smelled like fresh shaving soap; Alvin figured it was still a few hours yet from stinking. He tugged it into the doorframe as the dwarf put the lantern down in the mud and took hold of the boy's legs and pulled. Together, they dragged the stiffening body out into the mud beside the rear wheel.

"All right, now close the door," said Chester, lighting a cigarette. He switched on the automobile's headlamps. "I'll see you boys in the morning."

They stepped back as Chester stuck the transmission into gear and rolled away from the barn, and watched as he drove quickly down toward the county road, honking once before he disappeared into the rainy dark. It was a mean and peculiar road they had been following since Hadleyville, Alvin thought, as that awful sinking in his heart began once again, mostly a lot of winding around and doubling back and traveling the old routes nobody else chose to drive. Tonight and tomorrow it'd be Iowa, and a week afterward Oklahoma, or maybe Nebraska again. All summer long, Chester had been sneaking in among these people like some dark angel on Judgment Day, cleansing the scrolls of those whose sad fortune had drawn them across his path. Alvin knew his own soul had been soiled by complicity and no apology made to the families of the murdered would redeem him. Sick in his heart for what he'd seen since Hadleyville, believing that retribution for the guilty was assured, he had ridden quietly these many miles and raised no conflict with Chester for any of it. Why not? If consumption had sealed his fate like the doctors whispered behind his back, how come he lacked the courage to meet God at the Gate of Virtue? What held him back? If he weren't so afraid of Chester, he would have gone to the police and told them everything. That'd fix him, all right. Sure, Alvin knew he'd probably wind up in jail himself, or get shot, but at least he wouldn't be stuck out in the middle of another wheat field, burying a dead body whose killing he didn't have any part of. Why couldn't he just go and do that? Why was he so goddamned yellow?

Alvin picked up the lamp and held it over the dead boy's face pelted now by rain as he lay in the mud. Wind blew open the boy's collar, exposing the fatal bruise to the lamplight. Feeling a sudden touch of nausea, he turned away and headed across the yard toward the storm cellar to get the shovel. One of the doors fell off its hinge as he raised it open. The cellar was black as tar. Nine steps led downward into the dark. Two of the boards were cracked through with splinters. These steps Alvin maneuvered past by clinging to the cellar walls, lamp suspended in front of him. Old webs clouded the stairwell. The floor of the cellar was damp and smelled horrible. Alvin ran the light back and forth, wall to wall. More webs, junk, boxes, tins and bottles. He spied rat droppings atop several of the boxes. Frenchy had been bitten once, hunting through a dank fruit cellar in the dark where he didn't belong. The howl he had made when a nesting rat bit him in the hand carried clear up to the house where Aunt Hattie was hanging out the laundry. His crazy screaming scared the daylights out of her and when she saw his hand and Alvin told her about the rat, she fainted dead away in the dust.

The cellar was leaking. Alvin's shoes sloshed in the mud as he directed the lamp here and there. A dead mouse floated inside a lidless fruit jar. Scores of eviscerated flies and moths lay in ragged webs suspended beneath the support beams. An odor of wet rot persisted even with the cellar door propped open to the storm. The lamp was mostly useless. Alvin kicked at the junk along the walls from one corner to the next until he finally located the shovel alongside a stack of boards. Holding the lantern with one hand, he slid the shovel out with the other, careful not to disturb whatever might be lurking beneath the lumber. He wondered how Chester knew about it. Maybe this was where he had murdered the boy. What had brought him out here? Was it just to kill the kid? Did he give the poor dope some line about bees and honey to string him along? Alvin decided Chester was the evilest fellow he'd ever met. He wished they'd never said hello. What on earth had persuaded him to cross the river with Chester that night? Was he so sick and lonely that he'd needed the company of a fellow who didn't know him from Adam but offered up a slice of pie if Alvin would walk out on his family? Having consumption clouded his judgment back on the farm, made him tie his shoes backwards and forget to water the chickens. Some days he'd walk out of doors with his fly open or leave the keys to Daddy's auto on the fencepost. He grew tired from hardly nothing at all and had to sit down until he got yelled at. All his decisions seemed confused. Then again, choosing right from wrong wasn't so easy when his fever spiked and he spewed blood with a cough. If Alvin hadn't gotten his relapse, he'd have never run off like he did. Now he had traveled so far from home, he doubted he'd ever get back. How could he? After all he'd seen and done, Chester wouldn't ever let him go; Alvin knew that for a fact. And if he snuck out one night? How would he know where to go that hadn't any spotters or gun mates of Chester's just waiting on him to show his face? How far could he get before one of them caught him in an alley somewhere and shot him in the head? He had no auto to drive, and not enough dough for a train ticket. Too sick to walk more than a few miles, too scared to seek help, Alvin felt caught in a trap of his own stupidity. He was doomed and he knew it. All that was left was to see how it played out, in what dark place or gallows he'd meet his just reward.

Rising from the cellar, shovel in hand, Alvin saw the dwarf sitting in the mud beside the dead body. A cold damp wind replaced the steady rainfall again as the storm drifted. The dwarf carefully refastened the boy's collar buttons, and gently combed his wet tussled hair with his fingers. Alvin's own hands were numb from the cold. Hurrying across the yard, he tossed the shovel into the mud beside the dwarf and seized the dead boy by one arm and heaved him upward. Startled by Alvin's urgency, the dwarf fell backward onto the seat of his pants, then scrambled to his feet.

"We ain't got all night, you know," Alvin said, raising the boy halfway up to his feet. "He needs to be put down good in the ground before it really gets to storming. Otherwise, the rain'll wash him out." He looked at the dwarf. "Come on, help me!"

"Where'll we bury him?" asked the dwarf.

"In one of the stalls," Alvin answered, reaching down with his free hand to grab the lantern, "under the dirt and straw where nobody'll find him."

"Oh, that's very clever."

Rascal wrapped both his arms around the boy's thigh and hoisted one whole leg out of the mud. Meanwhile, Alvin tugged the boy's torso up toward his own chest and began hauling the corpse back into the barn. Wind tore at the boy's coat, flinging it open into the dwarf's face. From an inside pocket, a flurry of papers slipped out and blew free into the air.

"Wait!" The dwarf let go of the boy's leg and ran after the papers, scattering now across the yard.

"Leave 'em be!" Alvin shouted, trying in vain to support the boy alone. His weight shifted, tilting the stiff corpse off balance, which caused Alvin's feet to slip in the mud. The boy fell away from him, landing face down in the mud. Alvin coughed harshly and put the lantern down and called for Rascal to help, but by now the dwarf had chased to the end of the rainy yard, collecting soggy papers one after another and stuffing them down the front of his romper. Across the prairie to the east, lightning stitched the night sky. The rumble of thunder reverberated in the yard. Maybe the storm would pass on by, Alvin thought, dumping a few buckets of rain, then hurrying off somewhere else. If a twister hit now, they'd be finished. Aunt Florence had hid herself in a fruit cellar at Gorham when the great spring tornado of '25 blew that town off the face of the earth. Witnessing one up close gave her a fright she had never forgotten. When the cellar doors blew off, she saw a full-grown milk cow fly over a barn upside down, and a row of chicken sheds come apart and vanish into thin air — boards, wire, nails, chickens, all gone in the snap of a finger. If Alvin caught sight of a whirlwind out here tonight, he'd take off running and never look back.

Black droplets struck him on the head as he stood searching into the dark for the dwarf. Down by the fenceline that ran from the ramshackle house on out to the road, Rascal dashed from post to post gathering up the last of the papers. When he was done, he checked the sky for signs of lightning, and dashed back toward the barn.

"What'd you go running off for like that?" Alvin yelled, as the dwarf reappeared out of the dark.

"The wind blew his letters away. I had to recover them."

"What for? He don't have no more need of them."

"They're his, nevertheless. They belong to him. If you'll recall, the Egyptian pharaohs were buried with many earthly possessions."

The farm boy smirked. "You think he's Egyptian?"

"I doubt it, but the principle is the same — honor and duty regarding the dead."

Alvin watched the dwarf begin stuffing the papers back into the boy's inside jacket pocket. "What sort of letters were they?"

"I didn't read them."

"Why not?"

"It's none of our concern."

"Give 'em over," said Alvin. "Let me see."

The dwarf stopped stuffing and held one hand over the coat pocket. "Of course not."

"Huh?"

"I can't let you see them. They're private."

"He's up there pushing the clouds around," Alvin said. "Who's going to pay any mind?"

"It wouldn't be proper."

Rain began falling harder again. If the storm had indeed drifted south, maybe a few straggling thunderheads had found the farm and released their burden.

"Honor is one of the transcendent virtues," Rascal continued, his face solemn and gray. "Our lives are meaningless without it."

Lightning flashed nearby. Thunder cannoned in the sky. Rain cascaded across the yard in cold black sheets.

Drenched, Alvin growled, "Goddamn you." Then he reached down, grabbed under the boy's arm, and lifted. The dwarf stuffed the rest of the letters deep into the boy's pocket and took his other arm to help raise him up.

"Get the lamp!"

Rascal snatched the lantern, shuffling it into the crook of his arm. Together they dragged the dead boy through the barn door. When he was safely out of the rain, they dropped him and stepped back to rest. The body was caked now in mud, head to foot.

"Might I express an opinion here?" Rascal asked.

"No."

The dwarf frowned. "Well, that isn't fair. I've as much a right to a voice in this as you do."

A fierce cough shook Alvin's chest and his eyes watered. "No, you don't. Chester put me in charge of burying the kid. Not you."

"That isn't so. He told us both to bury him."

"He meant me, though. Hell, you can't even lift a shovel, much less bury someone on your own."

"Why, I've buried several persons."

"When?"

"On that expedition into the Black Hills you'll recall I discussed with that banker's family on our visit to Stantonsburg."

"You mean the trip you took with Teddy Roosevelt?"

"I never said the President was there with us, only that he was impressed with the collection of arrowheads I'd brought back from the Belle Fourche River. Why do I bother carrying on a conversation with you? You never listen to anything I say."

Alvin coughed again. "Tell me who you buried."

"Mary Alexandra Foxweather, a fine woman who sadly succumbed to the spotted fever three days' ride out of Fort Dodge. Mary's husband George decided that as it had been Mary's desire to travel out West, she ought to be put to rest in her heart's country. Therefore, we found a restful knoll just across the river from our camp and laid her in the ground. Seeing as how Mary and I had become so close during our journey, and since George suffered greatly from clavicle arthritis and was under his physician's instructions to avoid physical exertion of any sort, I was elected to perform the duties, which I did."

"Was everyone else crippled?"

"Sarcasm is the last resort of the devil's logic."

Alvin shook his head. "Quit your sniveling and let's get this over with. I'll go bring the shovel."

He walked back out into a soft drizzling rain and stood there several minutes, watching for lightning strikes on the cloudy sky. When he fetched the shovel from the mud and brought it back into the barn, he saw the dwarf had taken a bucket full of rainwater and washed most of the mud off the corpse. He had also cleared a space in the second stall for a gravesite — all the old damp straw piled up to one side and an outline drawn in the dirt. Alvin stared at the boy still lying where they'd dragged him, his jacket buttoned, cuffs folded down.

"He looks swell."

"Thank you."

"Like to do some digging?" Alvin asked, walking over to the stall.

He felt light-headed with fever and wanted to get this over with so he could go back to bed.

"I'd rather not."

"I thought you were the gravedigger here."

"I never said so."

"Well, that's what I heard."

Rascal averted his eyes. The electric lamp hanging from a nail above the dwarf draped a silhouette across the dead boy beside him. A cold gust of wind shook the roof of the barn, cascading more dirt down off the shingles.

"Well, don't trouble yourself," Alvin said, hoisting the shovel, "I'll do the digging. You'd just be in the way, anyhow."

He entered the stall and jabbed at the ground with the tip of the shovel, testing the firmness of the earth. It was muddy and soft only half a foot down; after that, he'd have to work at it. Maybe the exercise would be good for him.

He dug for half an hour.

By then, the storm had passed, leaving only a cold stiff wind behind to shake the barn roof and bring a draft inside. Alvin's shoulders ached from the effort of his work and his eyes burned with fever. When he had dug four feet down below the level of the dirt floor, he quit and climbed out of the hole and rolled onto his side, thoroughly exhausted. Once Alvin's breathing eased and he quit coughing, he said, "Let's put him in."

The dwarf, who had been sitting quietly holding the boy's hand and whispering to him in the dark, crawled now to the edge of the grave and peered in. "Is it deep enough?"

"For who?"

"To shield the deceased from life's grand and awful misery."

"It's deep as it's gonna get unless you do some of the digging."

"I believe we owe him a decent burial."

"And he'll be getting one," Alvin said, struggling to his feet, "soon as you help me put him in the ground." He tossed the shovel over to the wall and grabbed the lamp and held it over the hole he'd dug. Down at the very bottom, water was seeping in from all sides. "It's flooding."

Rascal leaned into the hole for another look. "You must have dug into a well."

"It ain't that deep," said Alvin. "I'd guess it'd be runoff from the storm."

The dwarf stared hard into the hole. "Perhaps we ought to dig another hole elsewhere."

"We?"

"Well, we can't have him floating out of his own tomb."

"He won't," Alvin assured the dwarf. "We'll just bury him quick before the water gets too deep down there. Come on, help me get him over here."

Together, they dragged the boy's body to the hole and dropped it in. The corpse landed with a muffled splash. Water soaked immediately into the edges of his clothing and Rascal removed the lamp from over the hole.

"Well?"

"Well, what?" Alvin said, wiping his hands dry on the front of his shirt. "It's done. Give me the damned shovel."

"We owe a prayer to the deceased," said the dwarf, placing the lamp in the dirt beside the hole. The electric light seemed to flicker. "For honoring the dead even as we cherish the living."

"I don't know no prayers," Alvin growled. "You say something."

"Are you certain? In the eyes of the Lord, performing a recitation of the common prayer in a burial of someone close is held in the highest esteem."

"I never even seen him before Chester brought him here. You just go ahead and do it. I don't have nothing to say."

"If you wish."

"I do."

Alvin picked up the lamp. He was tired and sore and his throat hurt from coughing.

"All right." The dwarf bowed his head and clasped both hands together at his belt buckle, then drew a long deep breath, shivered once, and began reciting, "Unto Almighty God we commend the soul of our brother departed, and we commit his body to the ground, earth to earth, ashes to ashes, dust to dust; in sure and certain hope of the Resurrection unto eternal life, through our Lord Jesus Christ. Amen."

"Amen."

Then Alvin filled the hole and covered the grave under straw. When he was finished, he returned the shovel to the cellar where he had found it, and followed the dwarf by electric lamplight back through the wet cornfield to the county road. By midnight they were both asleep in the tourist cabin again.

An hour or so after dawn, the farm boy and the dwarf ate meat sandwiches and a pair of mushmelons for breakfast at the roadside stand, then left the auto camp and headed down the county road to Allenville. The skies had cleared and the sun felt warm and dried their clothes as they walked along, suitcases in hand. The dwarf kept to the shoulder of the road, while Alvin strolled down the middle, humming a tune his grandmother had taught him when he was a baby. He'd had sweaty dreams all night long about the kid they had buried, but now that his fever was gone, he was doing his best not to remember. They hadn't seen any traffic since sunup when a truck carrying a load of hay drove by heading away from Allenville. The driver honked and gave a wave as he passed and the dwarf saluted in return. The farm boy just watched. None of the roads near Allenville had been paved yet, so the wheel ruts and damp earth made walking arduous. The dwarf seemed unconcerned. He meandered in and out of the weeds along the shoulder of the road and talked unceasingly about people and places Alvin had never heard of.

"Of course," said the dwarf, "had our guide warned me of the dangers of the cave beforehand, I'd have never dared take such a risk, at least not alone. Fortunately, I was able to keep my wits about me and devise a plan to mark my progress until a solution presented itself. Can you guess what I did?"

"No." Alvin was keeping count of black crows on the fencelines from the tourist camp to Allenville. If he reached a dozen, he would stop and make a cross in the dirt of the road ahead.

"Well, I'm sure you recall how Theseus unraveled a ball of string in the labyrinth of the Minotaur. That was my inspiration, but as I had no string, I was forced to improvise. You see, at such depths within our earth, the stygian darkness evolves creatures whose very skin glows phosphorescent, thereby creating visibility where sunlight never shines."

"Glow-worms," said Alvin. "I seen 'em before. They ain't nothing special." He watched a pair of crows take flight several hundred yards up the road. That made six since breakfast, a bad sign. "Me and Frenchy used to fix lanterns out of fruit jars and fireflies when we were kids so's we could fish in the dark. That's what you ought to've done."

"Perhaps," replied the dwarf, "but seeing as how I had no jars, nor were there any fireflies in the cave, a different solution was required. Nor were the creatures I spoke of glow-worms. Rather, they were a peculiar form of fungus that grew along the cave walls. What I did was to secure great handfuls of them for storage in my haversack and I used them to finger-paint arrows along all the maze of passageways leading to a subterranean river where at last I discovered a secret crevice in the cavern wall underwater and took advantage of a favorable current to float to safety. I emerged less than a mile from our camp. Afterward, I was told by our guide, a full-blooded Shawnee, that my escape was most remarkable and that he'd never before heard of such cleverness."

"So you were made chief of his tribe, right?"

"No, but I did receive a genuine war bonnet with eagle feathers in honor of my achievement, thank you."

"Look, don't tell me another one of them stories," said Alvin, kicking at a clump of dirt. He was tired of the dwarf's claptrappery. It gave him a headache. "I don't want to hear no more."

Rascal set his suitcase down and sat on it to rest. Wisps of his white hair fluttered in the morning breeze as he stared out across the fields. Alvin walked across the road and looked into the ditch where last night's rainwater puddled up under the weeds. He saw his reflection in little pools here and there. He looked filthy. It had been two days now since he'd taken a bath. He probably smelled, too. But what of it? Mostly it was just the dwarf who had to smell him and he wasn't no spring flower himself. Traveling was hard. Somehow Alvin had thought it would be a swell adventure, but he hadn't counted on the miles between towns, the empty roads, hours of boredom, and lonesome feelings that came more and more often, especially when he thought of the killings. If he lived on the farm until he was ninety, he didn't guess he'd see half of what he had witnessed since Hadleyville. If he lived.

Alvin looked across at the dwarf, still perched on his suitcase, eyes focused somewhere down the road ahead. "Tell me something," the farm boy said. "How come you never run off before?"

The dwarf shifted to face Alvin, folding his ankles over one another and clasping his hands together in his lap. "That's a very good question."

Alvin nudged a clump of dirt into the ditchwater and watched it sink. He put his own suitcase down and felt his forehead. Since they'd stopped to rest, Alvin guessed his temperature had gone up a degree or so. He still held out hope his clothes would be dry before he reached the church. Walking around in stinking clothes was bad enough without them being wet, too. One of the nurses at the sanitarium had told him that if he ever caught pneumonia, he'd be done for.

"Did you know that I come from a family of considerable means?" asked the dwarf. He left his suitcase and walked down into the ditch on the other side of the road until only his head showed above the dirt. Rascal began picking wildflowers from the embankment and formed a bouquet, which he clenched in his right hand. When he had gathered as many as he could easily hold, he climbed back up and told Alvin, "Auntie always said flowers gild the heart dearly, and that we ought never to go a day without appreciating their loveliness."

Using the stem of one flower, he bound the bouquet, and recited, *"Wildflowers exhale the gentle fragrance of our Lord's sweet breath."* He held the bouquet out to Alvin. "Would you like one?"

Alvin shook his head. "They give me hayfever."

"How dreadful." Rascal slipped the bouquet into his back pocket. "If I suffered such an affliction, I don't know that I'd survive. How would I be able to work in my garden?"

"I guess you couldn't."

"Have you been feeling homesick lately?" the dwarf asked. "It would be quite understandable, given the circumstances of our journey thus far."

Rascal took his suitcase and began walking down the road again toward Allenville. The farm boy kicked another dirt clod into the muddy ditch, then started walking again, too, keeping to his own half of the road. He lied to the dwarf when he told him, "I ain't homesick."

"I've been worried lately about my garden," Rascal said. "I'm sure it hasn't been watered since I left." He shook his head. "Perhaps there've been rainshowers."

"Maybe you ought've stayed put," Alvin said, "not come along at all. Maybe you made a mistake."

"I'm quite certain that if half of all the decisions we make in our lives prove to be correct, we are indeed fortunate. However, hindsight, Auntie always said, is a cat with his head stuck in a milk bottle. Had I remained in that crawlspace beneath my house much longer, I have no doubt I'd have become quite ill by now, perhaps even deceased. Do you miss your family?"

"I don't know." Alvin shrugged. "Why?" He wondered who missed him. He knew his sisters didn't, but maybe his momma or Aunt Hattie. Daddy'd be too mad at him for running off. Did Frenchy? Who had he found to collect bait and go fishing with? That goddamned Herbert Muller?

"I never really knew my family. Did I tell you that?"

"You said your momma died when you were born."

"Yes, she did, and my father left home when I was seven. That was when Auntie came to take care of me."

"Where'd your daddy go?"

"Out West, so I'm told. Auntie says he went to seek his fortune in gold somewhere in Alaska. By all accounts, he was quite successful, as he sent a great deal of money back to Hadleyville until the day he died in a mine explosion."

From the grassy fields ahead, a flock of sparrows suddenly took flight, angling overhead to the west. Rascal hummed a few notes of a tune he'd been working on since Omaha. After a moment, he stopped and said, matter-of-factly, "Auntie's a very wealthy woman. She's invested quite intelligently for many years and now she's one of the richest women in all of Missouri."

"Sure don't show it much, does she?" said Alvin. A bee buzzed his head and he swatted at it with the back of his hand. It'd be just his luck to get stung.

"I assume you're referring to the dilapidated condition of our house. Well, to be truthful, since it doesn't actually belong to her, Auntie doesn't much care about its appearance. We had a gardener for several years, but Auntie dismissed him last June when she took a summerhouse with friends in Mobile. I tried keeping the yard up by myself, but I fatigue quickly in the heat, and, of course, we had an awful winter, which kept me confined indoors for weeks at a time. I suppose I ought to have hired more help, but … "

The dwarf's voice trailed off as he looked down the narrow dirt road. "Actually, I'm a pathetic little coward."

"Huh?"

"Truth is, Auntie's stolen my inheritance and locked me away. The house in Hadleyville, its contents, the fortune held by the bank, were all kept in trust for me by my mother and father. When I contracted scarlet fever several years ago, Auntie had herself appointed executor of my estate in the event I became too ill to manage my own affairs. She's been using my money to finance her investments in expectation of my death which the doctors have always assured her is imminent."

"That don't seem fair." Now he understood why the dwarf had acted so nutty in the bank.

Rascal shrugged. "Since Auntie's my closest living relation, upon my death, everything I now possess, all my estate, becomes hers. Knowing this, I believe she persuaded Mr. Harrison B. Sinclair to gain the advantage of investing these funds in advance of my demise. He and Auntie are crazy about the stock market. Of course, the house and several other properties are another matter entirely. She cannot touch them until I die and their worth far outweighs the money kept in Mr. Sinclair's bank."

The dwarf walked on quietly for a few minutes, but farther up the road he stopped and told the farm boy, "I lied to you back in Hadleyville when I said Auntie locked me in my room because she didn't trust me alone in the house. Before she left for Dayton, we had an awful fight and called each other names and I told her if she spent one more night there I'd burn us both up. Well, you can just imagine! She grabbed me by the arm and tossed me into my bedroom and locked the door. Sometime in the middle of the night while I was asleep, she stuck some bottles of water, crackers and peach jars in a box, and slipped them into my room. Then she went off to the medicine show. I tried to pick the lock, but she'd also taken my Houdini kit while I was sleeping, so I had to pry up the floorboards with that old butterknife and make my escape. I had no idea I'd offended her that badly. Am I so ugly?"

"Well — " the farm boy paused a second. "I guess I ain't never seen nobody like you before."

Ordinarily, human deformities turned his stomach. He had seen patients at the sanitarium whose faces were so encumbered with what he thought were tubercles that their heads looked like big overripe vegetables. Uncle Truman had a stump for a left arm that always gave Alvin the shivers, and whenever he and Frenchy went to the carnival, Alvin steered clear of the freak pavilion because it scared him so to see people with misshapen heads and no limbs and contorted bones and other oddities of nature.

"You mean, a dwarf."

Alvin nodded.

"Well, I'll tell you, Auntie led me to believe that when my father received word of my affliction, he blamed it for my mother's death. However, in those dear dead days before he left to go out West, he never let on that he felt so. We seemed to be quite close."

"Maybe he didn't blame you at all," Alvin suggested, resisting a cough. "Maybe she just made it up to get under your skin." *Why was everyone so damned mean these days?*

"I've considered that. Auntie raised me, you see, with the help of my Uncle Augustus. After his death, however, I was left permanently in Auntie's charge. She hired tutors to educate me, citing my condition to the Hadleyville schoolboard as part and parcel of a chronic health problem that prevented me from attending school with other children. To me, she said it was necessary that I be educated away from wicked boys and girls who would certainly taunt me and break my heart long before I had the chance to strengthen and bloom. Uncle Augustus provided that part of my education which involved the out of doors by taking me on excursions into the wild, and trips out West where I had the opportunity to ride horses and strike fire from flint in the deep woods. We read *The Strenuous Life* together by firelight on the banks of the Belle Fourche River and fished with our bare hands. I think Uncle Augustus had honest affection for me and I loved him like a second father. When he was killed in the World War, I felt his absence greatly. From then on, I had to remain in Hadleyville, studying piano and literature and tending garden at the rear of our yard where Auntie had granted me the favor of a sunny parcel."

The dwarf set the suitcase down again to catch his breath. A warm wind blew across the wheat fields on both sides of the road. Alvin felt himself wheezing and stopped to rest. His breathing had begun to sound funny. He saw an automobile raising dust on another road in the distance and decided to hitch a ride if the opportunity came along. Whether it was good for him or not, he was tired of walking, and his right instep was throbbing like a bone felon.

"Do you read many books?" the dwarf asked.

"Nope."

"You see, I believe I've learned most of what I know by reading. My mother loved to read, or so Auntie told me. Many of the books we own were hers left to me in her will. And Uncle Augustus had a great library in Hannibal, more than ten thousand volumes containing the collected wisdom of our entire civilization. As a child I was left for hours in that room to browse on my own, which I did quite enthusiastically. Have you read much of Oscar Wilde?"

"Who's that?"

"A writer I much admire."

"I already told you, I don't like books. I quit reading soon as I got out of school."

"Well, that's too bad."

"You can't learn nothing about life from a book. None of those books got you away from your aunt, did they?"

"No."

"They didn't get you that money of yours from your daddy, did they?" Before the dwarf could answer, Alvin asked, "You got any friends back home?"

"Auntie wouldn't let me out of the yard unsupervised, but if by friends you mean — "

Alvin interrupted the dwarf. "You ain't got no friends back there because you don't do nothing but sit in that garden of yours fiddling with flowers like an old lady."

"There's no need to be cruel."

"I ain't being cruel," Alvin shot back. "Just truthful."

"I've already admitted to being a coward."

"It ain't just that," Alvin said, feeling anxious all of a sudden and jittery, and no idea why. "You got nobody yelling in your ear to get out of bed in the morning, no chores between you and fishing whenever you like. What do you have to kick about? You got the swellest life I ever heard of. I'd swap with you in a second. Anybody says they wouldn't's a damned liar."

"If someone offered me a job, I would certainly trade places with him. I believe the discipline of manual labor would be instructive and helpful."

"It'd kill you, is what it'd do."

The dwarf waved off a nosy bee. "Look, I don't expect you to be sympathetic, of course, as I haven't had cause to labor for wages a single day of my life. In terms of basic needs, such as food and clothing and shelter, I've never wanted. Auntie made certain of that. We had a cook, and a delivery boy for groceries, and a woman who came in twice a week to clean. Each was under specific instructions to speak to me only when addressed and never to discuss away from our house what had occurred indoors that day. While the delivery boy had a distinctly unfriendly manner about him, I can say, I think quite confidently, that I made fast friends with Bessie, our cook, and Pleasance, the cleaning lady. In the afternoons, when Auntie was gone visiting friends, the three of us would sit together in the parlor and play whist for lemon candies, and in the evening we'd sip apricot brandy and use Auntie's Ouija board to communicate with the spirit world."

"Why didn't you get yourself a regular job?" Alvin asked, his eyes fixed on a grain silo about half a mile to the east. Not since his year at the sanitarium had he had the opportunity of playing cards in the middle of a workday. Even afterward, when he was still sick, his mother made him clean house and wash windows and follow her around picking up clothes after his sisters. Frenchy laughed at him and said he ought to start wearing an apron dress.

"I was discouraged from even considering it," the dwarf replied. "I'd given thought to writing stories for the *Hadleyville Journal* when I was as young as thirteen, but Auntie told me if I sold even one, my photograph would be published by the paper the next day and she'd become the laughingstock of the community, and might even draw attention from the Eugenics Society. I did grow many wonderful tomatoes and green beans in my garden that Auntie sold at market, but Bessie and Pleasance told me later that she always maintained they'd come down river by steamboat from her cousin Percival J. Miner's garden in Festus. I didn't care. More important to me was that people had actually thought enough of what I had grown to buy it and serve it in their homes. The very idea pleased me no end."

Alvin walked ahead maybe a dozen yards or so, studying the sky for rain clouds and crows, tracing with his shoes wagon ruts in the old dirt road. He figured they had walked a couple miles now since leaving the tourist camp. Though the air was cool in the wake of the storm's passing, the sun was rising higher on the morning sky and before long the road would be warm and the walking more difficult. He was surprised that no truck or automobile or haywagons had come by for so long. He looked back for the dwarf and saw him resting on the suitcase. Rascal wasn't like anyone Alvin had ever met before. He seemed to be some character out of a tall tale spun around a campfire at night when everyone had drank too much corn liquor. Sometimes when they were lying out under a tree in the dark beside Chester's automobile, trying to get a little sleep, Alvin would look over and see the dwarf staring up at the stars, a silly sort of grin on his face, his lips curled back exposing his big teeth, and Alvin would wonder if the dwarf knew more about driving around to strange towns and doing what they were doing than he ever let on.

The farm boy slowed his walking to a casual stroll. Allenville was still a mile or so ahead and the sun was rising higher in the summer sky. He watched the dwarf strain to lift his small suitcase. A day ago, Alvin would have been happy to see him suffer, but this morning he felt sorry for him. He called back to Rascal, "Want me to carry that?"

"No, thank you," the dwarf replied. "It's my responsibility, although I believe I'm developing a blister on my palm."

"Those'll kill you."

"I've had my share, thank you. I'm sure I'll survive."

"Suit yourself."

Half an hour later, the farm boy and the dwarf reached the south side of town. The dirt road gave way to plank sidewalks and tall leafy poplars providing shade. Most of Allenville looked plain and ugly, bleached of life and color by the wind and weather off the Iowa prairie.

"I don't believe I can walk any farther this morning," the dwarf said, dropping his suitcase. His red face was sore with fatigue and sweat beaded up on his brow and stained his romper about the armpits. He looked bedraggled. "Perhaps we ought to rest a while."

Alvin saw a circus poster nailed to a telephone pole across the street in front of a motor garage and a telegraph office, and went over to have a look.

The poster was still grimy and damp from the evening rainstorm and the dates had been torn away, so Alvin was left to guess when the traveling circus had actually made its appearance in Allenville.

"A circus," the dwarf remarked, circling the pole. "How wonderful."

"It ain't here no more," Alvin said, trying to get the poster off the pole. He put his own suitcase down and stuck his fingernails under the wire staples and popped one of them loose.

"I love the circus," Rascal said. "Uncle Augustus took me to Hagenbeck-Wallace when I was young. We were given a tour behind the scenes to see how the performers actually lived while on the road. I remember being quite impressed. Everybody was very kind to me and presented both Uncle Augustus and myself with souvenirs before we left."

"What kind of souvenirs?"

"I don't exactly recall, but I'm sure they were lovely."

"Well, I won me a prize once at a carnival throwing darts when I was six years old," said Alvin, prying free another section of the poster. "I still got it, too. A genuine Injun tomahawk from Custer's Last Stand."

"That's nice," said Rascal, as he bent down to collect one of the staples Alvin had popped off the pole. He stuck it into his romper and snapped the pocket closed. "Actually, now that you mention it, I do recall winning a fine crystal vase on the midway by pitching lead slugs into several open milk bottles. The circus people told me that nobody had ever done so well at that particular game. I might've been given a ribbon as well, but I couldn't say for certain. I felt quite proud, regardless."

"Sure you did," said Alvin, tearing loose the last two corners of the poster from the telephone pole. He read it over carefully once more, then folded the poster into quarters and slipped it under his shirt. "Well, I'd sure like to go see the circus again. I ain't been to one since I was a kid. I remember my daddy telling me how them bearded ladies give you the evil eye if you look at 'em wrong, and once they give it to you, your brains are scrambled the rest of your life and you ain't good for nothing but raking leaves. Maybe we ought to find out where this circus went and follow it down the road. It couldn'ta gone too far."

"Perhaps we could make the suggestion to our companion. Everybody loves a good circus," the dwarf said. "Why, even Auntie shared a belly laugh during the clown act last time we went, and ordinarily she has no sense of humor at all."

"I'd like to go," said the farm boy, growing an enthusiasm for the idea. "I won't deny it."

"Then I vote we ought to. It's settled."

"We'll see."

They headed down to the end of the alley at the fenceline that bordered the fields surrounding Allenville, then turned west and walked on for another quarter of a mile or so down a long country lane until they heard hymns from the church at the crossroads just outside of Allenville. In a bell tower atop the steeple, a flurry of sparrows chattered. Whitewash had flaked away from the siding, and a quarter of the shingles were missing on the main roof. Sections of the stained glass along the upper windows were also cracked and in danger of falling out.

"They ought to at least paint it," Alvin remarked, giving the church a good once-over from across the road. "Don't seem right to let it go like that."

"I suppose they haven't the resources," the dwarf replied. "I painted our back porch one day when Auntie was off on errands and was shocked to discover how much everything cost. Had Auntie seen the bill, I doubt she'd have allowed it."

"I guess a church'd be able to afford it," Alvin said. "They don't do nothing except collect money."

"Do you attend often?"

"Not if I can help it." He hated church and didn't ever read the Bible. It was all baloney.

Alvin listened to the singing.

There's a land that is fairer than day, and by faith we can see it afar
For the Father waits over the way, to prepare me a dwelling place there
In the sweet (in the sweet) by and by (by and by)
We shall meet on that beautiful shore (by and by)

Rascal said, "Auntie and I attended services every Sunday morning together until I turned twenty. We went by hired carriage and greeted each of our fellow Christians by name along the route. It made for quite a spectacle, I must admit."

To our bountiful Father above, we will offer our tribute of praise,
For the glorious gift of His love, and the blessings that hallow our days."

The dwarf added, "It was also one of the few occasions where she allowed herself to be seen with me out of doors. At the church, we had our own special place reserved in the front pew and two fine leatherbound volumes of the hymnal."

In the sweet (in the sweet) by and by (by and by)
We shall meet on that beautiful shore (by and by).
In the sweet (in the sweet) by and by, (by and by)
We shall meet on that beautiful shore.

"Singing's the worst part of going to church," said Alvin, listening to the hymn. "Any old bunch of billygoats'll sound about as good as most folks trying to carry a tune."

"I was elected to the choir," Rascal said, "though, of course, Auntie did not permit me to perform for fear I'd embarrass myself in front of our neighbors."

"I hope you thanked her."

"In fact, her fears were quite unfounded. My voice back then possessed near perfect pitch and I'd long since committed all our hymns to memory. I'm sure my performance would have been memorable."

We shall sing on that beautiful shore, the melodious songs of the blest
And our spirits shall sorrow no more, not a sigh for the blessings of rest.
In the sweet (in the sweet) by and by (by and by)
We shall meet on that beautiful shore (by and by).

Alvin stuck his suitcase in the weeds and crossed the road to the side of the church and looked in through the yellow windowpanes.

The pews were packed with people dressed in their Sunday finest. At the pulpit, the preacher was lecturing hellfire and brimstone while the choir behind him nodded grimly. It didn't seem all that different from services Alvin had attended in Farrington. Singing and shouting. Lots of old people acting drowsy, small children getting pinched by their mothers for fidgeting too often. Who paid any mind to what some dumbbell preacher had to say? When Alvin first caught the consumption, Reverend Newbury came to the farm and took his hand and told him Jesus dwelt in his lungs and if he kept faith in the Lord, Jesus would do his breathing for him until the Holy Spirit healed that awful disease. A month later Alvin was in the sanitarium, nearer to heaven than health.

The farm boy stepped down from the window and looked around. He and the dwarf seemed to be the only people nearby not inside the church. Somehow it made him feel truant and guilty, like he ought to go indoors and sit down, maybe sing along for a few minutes or so. Rascal walked along the road a little further, studying a patch of Arkansas rose growing at the foot of the fence that bordered the fields next to the church. Probably the dwarf wouldn't be allowed inside a church with normal folks, Alvin thought, on account of a case like his would make the Lord look bad. Then again, maybe the preacher would just hold Rascal up as an example of what can happen if you don't go to church or say your prayers at bedtime. Being born a dwarf might even be the mark of Cain, for all anyone knew, God's judgment on a wicked man or woman for sins unforgiven. Aunt Hattie always said the Lord worked in sly and secretive ways. He knew everything you ever did, and everything you planned to do, and though you might fool Him now and then, when the last card got thrown down, you'd always know His hand was the strongest. Alvin watched the dwarf pick a handful of purple asters and fold them into his fist for carrying alongside the small suitcase. Somewhere along the line, Rascal's family must have earned the Lord's attention in a powerful way. *How well we bear our burdens*, Aunt Hattie had told Alvin, *marks us in the Lord's countenance, for it was He who bestowed them, after all.*

"It's a beautiful day, don't you agree?" said the dwarf, walking toward Alvin. He offered a wildflower, but the farm boy declined.

"I already told you, I'm allergic."

"Then I'll keep them myself for luck," Rascal said, tucking a blossom into his romper before scattering the remaining handful into the wildrye next to the church. "God smiles on Sundays. I can hardly recall one where it rained."

"Maybe we ought to go inside," Alvin said, tired of waiting around outdoors. He'd like to have been able to stretch out in the back row on a long pew and have a nap. Truth was, he was beginning to think he would have to see a doctor sooner than later.

"Do you think that would be wise? Chester was most specific in his request that we wait until service lets out."

"Well, I ain't standing here all morning."

"I don't mind waiting," the dwarf replied. "Impatience is the devil's lure."

"Shut up."

The dwarf crossed back over the road and picked up his suitcase. Alvin walked around to the rear of the church to look for the back door. Most of the conveyances people had used to travel to the church were parked there, scattered about in no particular order, old buggies and motorcars — including Chester's tan Packard. There was only a short section of fence along the north end of the church separating the lot from the surrounding fields, and most of the horses hitched to the buggies stood in the morning sun, grazing where grass was long enough. As Alvin drew nearer, he saw a homely young girl with stringy brown hair sitting on a wooden fifteen-gallon water bucket, a tattered Bible in her lap. She was fiddling with a partially unraveled ball of lavender yarn, a cat's cradle. The girl's plain thin face was pale as powder and her print dress thread-worn and dull.

"Hey there," said Alvin, easing between two of the horses. The girl looked up, squinting her eyes against the sun. The farm boy asked, "You watching these horses?"

"They ain't watching me."

"How come you ain't in church with them other folks?" Alvin noticed a purple birthmark behind her ear, a sign of misfortune. Also, she had a nose like a russet potato. Poor thing.

She cocked her head. "Why ain't you?"

"I got business out here, that's why." He puffed himself up for her benefit.

"Me, too."

The girl completed the cat's cradle and sat still on the wooden bucket. The morning breeze blew lightly through her hair. Within the church, organ tones accompanied the plaintive voices of men and women joined in song. Alvin studied the girl. She looked drowsy and dim-witted. She was stick thin, but had soft little titties on her chest, so he figured she wasn't more than four or five years younger than himself. Her eyes were cloudy, her face expressionless as a cow's. Maybe she was sick, too. A girl her age had died in the sanitarium the morning Alvin was released, drowned in her own blood. He'd never heard a peep out of her.

"You from around here?" he asked, shuffling his feet in the dust. It was all he could think of to say. For some reason, he grew shy. Maybe she was a little pretty. He'd seen worse.

" 'Course," she replied, fooling with the yarn. "I been adopted by the Lord."

"Where do you live?"

"Inside the church," she said. "Down in the basement."

"You like sleeping in a church?"

"I don't mind. They's worse places."

He nodded. "Yeah, I guess so."

"Jesus didn't never live in any big old mansion," said the girl, unraveling her yarn out through the palm of one hand. "He didn't need all that fanciness to get by."

Inside the church, the organ quit and the singing stopped. Shortly after, Alvin could hear the preacher's voice echoing within, as if everyone listening to him was half-deaf.

"Maybe I ought to go in there and sit down," Alvin said to the girl. "I guess nobody'd mind."

"Don't you love Jesus?" the girl asked, squinting up at Alvin in the glare of the morning sun. Something with her eyes caught Alvin's attention, how they flicked about like squirrels in a tree. *This girl's not right in the head,* Alvin thought. *She's suffered some peculiar condition whereby she can sort of talk all right and even make a little sense now and then, but some part of her is cracked and not even sleeping in a church can fix it.*

"I guess Jesus got enough to worry about." Alvin stroked the mane of the horse harnessed to the buggy. "He probably don't care what I do or where I go. I could get inside there and sit down in a corner somewhere, He might not even notice me."

"His eye is on the sparrow and I know He's watching me," the girl said, quoting from a hymn Aunt Hattie sang in the kitchen on Sundays. "We all been adopted by Jesus, and He loves us no matter what we do 'cause we're His children."

"You get that from a preacher?" Alvin heard the doxology, *Praise God, from Whom all blessings flow,* as the collection plate was being passed through the congregation.

"Nobody had to tell me," said the girl. "I knowed myself it's true. I trust Jesus."

"Good for you."

"You better, too."

"Oh yeah?"

"All sinners need Jesus."

"What would you know about sin? You're just a girl."

He was losing patience now, and decided she wasn't anything worth looking at, after all.

"Why ain't you scared of Jesus?" she asked. "Didn't nobody tell you He's coming soon?"

"Jesus don't scare me as much as some other things," said Alvin, taking a look down the road toward Allenville. He felt a bad cough coming on, maybe even a dizzy fit.

"What other things?" the girl asked.

"That ain't no concern of yours."

"There ain't nobody's business that ain't Jesus'."

"Well, you ain't Jesus now, are you?"

Alvin let go of the horse and walked out toward the edge of the field where the last buggy was parked. Why had he even bothered trying to strike up a conversation with a stupid girl obviously afflicted by some dumbpalsy? He'd just wanted to be a little friendly, and ended hearing another sermon. People weren't nice anywhere these days.

He looked for Rascal. Last he had seen him, the dwarf was digging around by the roadside for more wildflowers. The organ had started up again with another hymn.

Alvin walked along the fence until he came around to the church front and climbed the ten steps (one for each of the Lord's Commandments) to the landing and eased open the large wooden door. With the preacher's voice raised once more to his congregation, nobody noticed Alvin slip inside and take a seat by himself on the far end of the rear pew. He removed his cap and looked for Chester and saw him in the front row on the aisle, felt hat in hand, attention rapt and focused on the preacher perched above him. He didn't notice Alvin. The surrounding congregation wasn't much different from those who sat in the pews back in Farrington. The ladies wore the same frilly sunbonnets and the men smelled of Wildroot and Saturday night liquor. Not one of them did anything but sit like boards and listen to a fellow who looked like every country preacher Alvin had seen in his life: stony-faced, a plain black suit that might've been shared with the local undertaker, eyes like hot-fire.

The preacher's voice bellowed between the pitched and narrow walls of the small church, "FRIENDS, YOU MIGHT THINK YOU CAN CHOOSE YOUR RELIGION, BUT IN TRUTH IT ALWAYS CHOOSES YOU. THE LORD *PRO*VIDES WHILE SATAN *DI*VIDES. IGNORING THAT FACT CAN BE THE GREATEST MISTAKE OF YOUR LIVES! FRIENDS, I AM NOT HERE TO OFFER YOU SALVATION! ONLY THE LORD CAN DO THAT! I AM NOT HERE TO LEAD YOU PAST WORLDLY TEMPTATIONS! ONLY JESUS CAN DO THAT! ONLY THROUGH HIS EYES WILL YOU BE ABLE TO SEE THE SHADOW THAT'S BEEN STALKING YOU SINCE THE DAY YOU WERE BORN! YOU CANNOT MAKE RESTITUTION TO ME FOR ERRORS OF FAITH OR JUDGMENT! I AM NOT YOUR REDEEMER! JESUS IS! BUT I AM HERE TO WARN YOU TODAY: SINCE THE FALL, OUR HEARTS HAVE BEEN BLACKENED BY SINS CONCEIVED AND CONCEALED! ALONE, WE HAVE NO HOPE OF REDEMPTION! ALONE, WE ARE ALREADY LOST

AND GIVEN OVER TO THE FIERY PITS! OUR FATES ARE SEALED, OUR AGONY DELIVERED! THE ROPE ABOVE THE GALLOW SWINGS IN A TROUBLING WIND! *YEA, THE LIGHT OF THE WICKED IS PUT OUT, AND THE FLAME OF HIS FIRE DOES NOT SHINE!* TRUSTING IN THE CERTAINTY OF OUR ANGUISH, WE WALK DEAF, DUMB AND BLIND TOWARD THE PIT! YET, JESUS DOES NOT FORSAKE US! EVEN AS WE HAVE FORSAKEN OURSELVES, HIS GRACIOUS HEART WAITS TO REDEEM US, TO RESTORE OUR SOILED — "

Alvin got up and walked out.

Disgusted with sermons, he sat down on the top step of the porch and watched the breeze wash across the fields of wildrye to the south. The sun was hot now and Alvin unbuttoned his shirt cuffs and rolled up his sleeves. What the hell had Chester brought them here for? What was his plan? The farm boy walked down to the bottom of the steps to look for the dwarf. He guessed that Sunday services were almost done and soon the organ would play its final hymn. He wandered out to the road and discovered Rascal sitting astride the suitcase once again, his bouquet of purple asters in one hand, a black leatherbound Bible in the other.

"What's that you're reading there?"

The dwarf looked up from the page. "The Book of Job. I thought that, as we are not allowed inside the church, and seeing it is Sunday, after all, I ought to study."

"Where'd you get that?" Alvin asked, pointing at Rascal's bible.

"From a thoroughly delightful young lady I just met."

"I hope you don't mean that ugly little thing sitting over there behind the church looking after the horses."

"Oh, did you meet her, as well?"

"Sure," Alvin replied. "She talked my ear off about Jesus. I think she's afflicted."

"Oh? Why, she seemed quite enlightened to me. I was impressed by her command of Scripture."

"She says she been adopted by Jesus," said Alvin, "but she don't hardly know nothing about anything, especially her own self. She thinks she's smart, but she don't begin to fool me."

"I found her quite well-versed in the Scriptures. I wouldn't be surprised if she teaches Sunday school somewhere. She's very bright."

"I think she's dumb as ditchwater," said Alvin. "The day she starts teaching folks about Jesus, Billy Sunday'll be singing polkas with the devil in Hades."

"Well, I wouldn't worry about that," said the dwarf. "Our Lord only calls those He deems most capable."

Inside the church, the organist began playing and Alvin heard the front doors swing open. The dwarf closed the Bible and jumped up, grabbing his suitcase. As the first people flooded the staircase, Alvin followed the dwarf across the road and behind the church where the homely girl was still perched on her wooden water bucket, the cat's cradle yarn in her lap. When she saw Alvin and Rascal, she swiveled on the bucket to face them.

The dwarf gave the Bible back to her. "I'm sorry that I did not get the chance to finish studying Job's plight. I promise to try and locate a Bible of my own very soon and complete my lesson."

The girl smiled. "You been teaching this one here about the Lord?"

Before Rascal could reply, Alvin stepped forward and snatched the Bible out of the girl's hand. "Looky here, sweetheart: he don't need to teach me nothing about nobody! I already learned about Jesus Christ Almighty when I was half this tall, and only dumbbells ever believed there was such a thing, and I don't need no ugly little girl telling me nothing to the contrary! You get me?"

Then Alvin threw the Bible into the dirt and took the dwarf by the crook of his arm and hauled him up to the fenceline on the north side of the church where people filing out to their buggies or automobiles couldn't see them.

"I don't know why you waste your time like that," Alvin said, giving the fence a good shake.

Rascal laid his suitcase against one of the posts and growled back, "I have no idea what you mean."

"That ugly girl."

"Well, you were very rude."

"She wouldn't understand nothing else."

"Nevertheless."

"How long do you figure we're supposed to wait out here?" Alvin asked, taking a look out toward the rear where people were beginning to depart. He felt jittery as hell now. A motor roared to life nearer the road and the backfire caused some commotion with the horses. Alvin heard the girl yapping like a barking dog as she tried to calm them down.

"We just ought to take care not to be seen, I suppose," the dwarf said, down on both knees studying the weeds growing along the rotting plank foundation of the church. "We're to be entirely inconspicuous."

"Pardon?"

Rascal looked up, glee drawn on his face. "I believe there may be field mushrooms growing underneath here!"

"Oh yeah?"

"I tried for so long to grow them under our washroom, but even where our plumbing leaked, the soil conditions were simply unsuited for their purposes. Here, though, even in midsummer, the dirt is moist and sweetened by shadow, ideal for waxy caps." He frowned. "If we only had time to crawl under for a look." Rascal stuck his arm under the foundation.

"You get yourself spider-bit sticking your hand under there like that," Alvin said, having a quick peek of his own. "A black widow'll kill you in nothing flat." He snapped his fingers for emphasis, then coughed.

"I'm quite careful not to disturb their webs."

"That don't matter much to them that like to bite you."

"In fact, most spiders aren't at all aggressive by nature," the dwarf replied. "They're shy to the point of cowardice. They attack only when prodded to action. That includes the black widow. I've never had any trouble."

"Just the same, I wouldn't be poking around underneath there like that, if I was you."

"Well, seeing as you have little or no interest whatsoever in learning about the natural world, I'm sure you wouldn't."

Alvin looked back toward the rear of the church. Buggies and automobiles were rolling off down the road, people heading home for Sunday dinner. Soon, only the homely girl remained out back. While Rascal dug for mushrooms at the north wall, Alvin watched the girl stroll about humming some hymn to herself. After a few minutes, she disappeared. Hearing the door close with a soft thud, Alvin nudged the dwarf with the toe of his boot. "Maybe we ought to go in."

The dwarf swiveled his head to look up. "Pardon me?"

"I think we ought to go inside now."

The dwarf pulled his arm out emptyhanded and wiped the dirt off onto his sleeves. "I'd rather wait out here until we're called."

"I bet he's sticking up the collection plate."

"Oh?" Rascal stopped hunting in the black dirt. "Is that what he told you?"

"He didn't tell me nothing," Alvin replied. "I just figured it out on my own. Why else'd we be here at a church?"

"It doesn't seem to me as though heisting the collection box from a country church would prove all that worthwhile."

"Maybe he knows something we don't."

"I'd assume so," said the dwarf, starting back in again with his one-armed digging. He didn't appear much interested in what was occurring inside the church. Alvin noticed how most of the trip Rascal had been like that, talking about everything under the sun, except what they were doing day after day in these towns they visited. Alvin felt guilt and fear daily, while the dwarf's conscience seemed not to trouble him. It was a plain mystery how Rascal managed to avoid confronting the truth of the crimes they'd helped Chester commit. At night Alvin wondered if perhaps the dwarf actually enjoyed all the misery they'd inflicted, or if everything the dwarf had endured in his former life had frozen his heart to the suffering of others.

A voice echoed across the morning air. "You two there! Come over here!"

Alvin saw the preacher standing down by the corner of the church. The homely girl stood behind him, grinning ear to ear. She pointed a finger at Alvin and raised her voice. "See? That's the skinny one there that don't accept Jesus as fact!"

"How come you two been waiting out here?" the preacher called up to Alvin.

"He's ascared of Jesus, that's why," said the girl, "I believe that's how come he don't want to hear nothing good for him."

"Is that so?" said the preacher, slinging his arm around the girl's shoulder.

"I ain't ascared of Jesus," Alvin called back to the preacher, "and anyone says so's a liar." He glared at the girl. "I just rather be out of doors, is all. I was sick once. That ain't no crime."

Chester came around the corner of the church now, smoking a cigarette. He stopped beside the preacher. "I told them both to wait outside so as not to disturb your service. Truth is, I was afraid the sight of the midget might upset some of the smaller children."

The preacher studied the dwarf, then asked Chester, "You three been traveling together?"

"No, sir, I just happened upon these two young fellows on my way out of Harlan yesterday evening. They were walking alongside the road after sundown, looking all worn out and hungry, so I asked them if they'd like to share a ride. Feeling charitable, I bought them supper. It was clear they hadn't eaten in days. When I asked them where they were headed, they said 'Topeka' where the midget had them hired to a job in a shoe factory. Recalling our Lord's admonition about forsaking our brothers in time of need, I volunteered to drive them. All I asked was that they stay to themselves and be on good Christian behavior when I made my appointments. I'm sorry if this boy here has upset your girl." Chester gestured toward Alvin. "Frankly, he's grown up ignorant his entire life. Ignorant of other people, and ignorant of the Lord. He may even be a trifle slow, if you get my meaning."

The preacher nodded, his face still grim. A gust of wind ruffled his black coat.

Chester added, "I'd be pleased to complete my presentation to you indoors if you'd be so generous as to allow me five more minutes of your time, sir." He pulled out his pocketwatch and checked the hour.

"I need to be running along by noontime, anyhow."

"They comin' in?" asked the girl, sneering at Alvin once more. "I could teach this one how to thank Jesus, proper and all."

The dwarf grabbed his suitcase. Alvin decided that if Chester hadn't been there just then, he would have given the girl a good choking.

"Bring them in with you," the preacher told the girl, then walked back around to the rear door, Chester on his heels. The girl stuck her tongue out at Alvin before chasing after the preacher.

The shadowy interior of the church basement served as a rectory, and smelled like rats to Alvin. Rats and mildew and wet rot. He guessed they'd had a little water leakage from the storm last night. There were three sets of shelves on either side of the door with boxes filled with Bibles stacked up on them, and small cartons with what looked to be bookmarks cut to resemble the Savior. Alvin took one and stuffed it into his back pants pocket, then followed the others into an office with a small pine desk, a leatherback swivel chair, and three other caned chairs along one wall. A painting of Jesus suffering on the bitter road to Calvary hung behind the desk.

The preacher was holding a brass candleholder in one hand and a pewter one in the other, rolling them over, examining both with deliberation and care.

"It's a matter of devotion, I'm told," Chester said, matter-of-factly, a salesboard held against his side. "A question of esteem that reflects how you and your congregation feel about the Lord, what He means to you, what place He holds in your hearts."

"Ten dollars is a lot of money," said the preacher. "I could buy a stack of hymnals for that and a new collection plate."

"Sure," Chester replied, "but you've already got songbooks and a fine collection plate that everybody who's sat in here for the last two hundred and fifty Sundays has seen and admired. What I'm offering is something different, something uplifting and beautiful to dress up the altar of the Lord and give your congregation a feeling of wonder and delight."

The preacher cracked half a grin, barely perceptible. "I got to hand it to you, Mr. Harris. You make an awful good pitch."

"Thank you, sir."

Alvin looked over at the dwarf, seated beside the young girl in the caned chairs, suitcase at his feet, sharing a read in one of the hymnals. Alvin caught sight of the safe in one corner behind a painting of Jesus, exposed slightly by the tilt of the gilded picture frame. Probably Chester intended to rob the collection plate, after all.

"Trouble is," said the preacher, "I just can't see how we could possibly afford those candleholders of yours, as much as I'd like to say we can."

"Well, I understand your dilemma," Chester said, affecting a slight drawl. "Times are hard all over these days. Why, just last week I was passing through a town in the Panhandle where the only bank they'd ever had there, only one that'd come to their town, just shut its doors for keeps. Broke my heart to see what it did to those good Christian people. It seems these days, nobody but bankers and bootleggers can afford much of anything at all, doesn't it?"

"We're just a small church and — "

"But it's times like these I find people are most in need of something to help them forget how terrible life can be," Chester persisted, "something to make them feel good inside, something bigger than themselves."

"How's that, Mr. Harris?"

"If you could afford it, you and your congregation would build the biggest, most beautiful church in the state of Iowa, wouldn't you?"

"We think we have ourselves a pretty nice little church, right now."

"Sure you do," said Chester. "It's swell. All I meant to say is that what I'm offering you are some items worthy of what you've already got here, something to point it up a little."

Chester smiled.

The preacher shook his head. "No, sir, I have to tell you I don't believe in dolling up a house of the Lord. And I have to say, sir, that'll need to be my last word. But I do thank you for stopping by."

Chester's smile broadened. "Well, we all make mistakes, don't we?"

The preacher frowned. "Beg your pardon?"

Chester quit smiling and gave Alvin that look he'd been expecting

CROSSING EDEN | 667

all morning long. "I'm just sorry we couldn't do business, pal. I hate getting up early just to be disappointed."

The preacher walked to the door. "Well, there's nothing to be done about it, but I'm obliged to you for coming to see us, just the same. Let me show you out."

"Why, that'd be swell of you."

As the preacher turned to go, Chester drew his revolver and shot him in the spine.

The preacher struck his head on the doorframe and fell face first to the cement.

Deafened by the revolver's discharge, Alvin couldn't hear what Chester yelled as he grabbed the girl by the collar and shoved her forward into the hall. The dwarf had escaped unseen. Ears ringing, Alvin bolted over the body of the preacher and headed for the back door. Somewhere in the church above, Chester was shouting at the girl who responded with a horrid wail. Alvin looked outside, expecting to see the dwarf running off down the road. Instead, the yard was empty. Filled with confusion, Alvin looked back down the hall toward the preacher where a pool of blood was spreading out from under his black coat. Upstairs, the girl had quit screaming. Alvin wanted to go hide out somewhere. He didn't give a hang about his split or becoming a big shot, nor was he afraid of going back on Chester, because he knew that sooner or later, the cops would get them both, dead sure.

But instead of beating it out of the church, he climbed a narrow paneled oak stairway that brought him up behind the stage backing the empty pulpit where the small church choir had stood during morning service. Only a stack of hymnals remained, and the silence within the building brought a quiver to Alvin's soul. He walked over to the pulpit and gazed out on the quiet rows of pews, and saw the dwarf kneeling in supplication to God, murmuring prayers in a hoarse and worried voice. Somewhere within a room high in the church, a mean thump echoed through the walls.

"How come you run off like that?" Alvin asked, gripping the sides of the pulpit like the preacher himself. His trembling hands rattled the wood. He felt woozy with shock and fear.

"Murder," replied the dwarf, rising to his feet once again. "Despicable and low. Villainous!" He contorted his face to reinforce the words.

"Ain't many killings you can call good," the farm boy said, his legs quivering, too.

"In a house of the Lord!"

"Ain't many good places to get killed, neither." He was becoming sick to his stomach.

"It's so discouraging," the dwarf said, shaking his head. "I'm thoroughly ashamed."

"On what account?"

"I'm sure we oughtn't to have let him do it. His vileness bears witness upon us as well."

"I'd be quiet, if I was you. If we can hear him up there," Alvin said, nodding at the ceiling, "he sure can hear us down here."

"I witnessed the life pass out of a man of God as I stood by in silence."

"You shut your mouth now," said Alvin, fear rising in his gut. Footsteps creaked in the wood overhead as someone crossed from end of the room to the other. Alvin tiptoed away from the pulpit back to a small door behind the choir box. He opened the door as quietly as he could manage and slipped inside another narrow oak staircase, this one leading high into an attic beneath the belltower. Alvin crept up to a landing illuminated by a stained glass window of the Apostles at Galilee. Five steps higher still was another door. Alvin pressed an ear to the wood. When he heard nothing, he nudged the door open a crack and peeked into a small room. Flat on her back in bed, dress hiked up to her chin and naked underneath, lay the young girl. Her eyes were shut tight, face smeared with tears, lips pursed, her arms held rigidly to her sides, legs bent apart and bowed at the knees. Blood from her middle parts stained the sheets. Chester stood at the far window, fastening the buttons of his vest. He was whistling one of those jazz tunes Alvin heard on the radio from Chicago at night. The farm boy eased the door shut and hurried back downstairs where he saw the front door flung open to the sunlight. He went outside and looked around and found the dwarf hurrying away with his suitcase, a quarter of a mile down the road. Was he trying to make a bust for it? Alvin took off after him, yelling for Rascal to stop. Scared of getting left behind, he snatched his own suitcase from the weeds across the road and ran like a bandit to catch up.

It didn't take long. Seeing the farm boy coming, the dwarf quit walking and stared back at the church steeple and the flock of sparrows circling its faded belltower. Still horrified by the shooting, Rascal's eyes were fixed upward, his spirit destitute. As Alvin caught up to him, the dwarf said, "My behavior shames me. I can never go home now."

"Huh?"

"Were my pockets to hold thirty pieces of silver, I could be no less guilty of betrayal."

"What the hell are you talking about?"

"A double-faced Judas is what I am. I ought to have warned the preacher of imminent danger. Because I did not, his death is on my record before the Lord."

Alvin kicked a clod of dirt into the fenceline. "That killing wasn't nobody's fault but his who pulled the trigger. There ain't nothing we could've done." Yet he felt his own eyes filling with tears.

The dwarf began walking again down the road to the south.

"Where the hell do you think you're going?" Alvin called after him. The dwarf walked on. Alvin hurried forward and circled ahead of him and blocked his path. His voice trembling, he said, "I asked you a question. Where the hell you going?"

The dwarf stopped and put his suitcase down in the dust. "I'm not sure."

"You can't run off and leave me out here by myself."

"Of course I can."

"It ain't right!"

"By that I assume you to mean it would be unfair for me to let our collective guilt pass on to you alone. Have no fear. I plan on confessing my own part in this tawdry affair to the proper authorities in due course. And, in any event, I can hardly hide my guilt from the Lord, and it's His judgment, and His alone, we ought properly to fear."

"I don't know no one 'round here, except you and Chester," said Alvin, looking nervously about. He felt scared and cold in the pit of his stomach. "If you run off, what the hell am I going to do? I never been this far from home before, and I don't know if I like it so much."

The dwarf wiped his brow with the back of a sleeve and stared out across the fields to the prairie horizon where the late morning sky was blue and clear. Nearby, in the wildrye beyond the fence, insects buzzed. A warm breeze was on the rise. The dwarf folded his hands together at his waist. In a reverent voice, he said, "Forgiveness is the Lord's, but redemption abides keenly within the guilty and the brave."

Alvin told him, "We got to beat it out of here."

"Would you help me save us both?"

"Huh?"

Hearing the familiar exhaust note of the Packard Six, both the farm boy and the dwarf turned to watch Chester wheel the automobile out of the churchyard and begin driving down the road toward them.

"Yes or no," said the dwarf, picking up his suitcase. "Indecision is itself an act of cowardice."

The motorcar drew near and Chester slowed to pick up his two companions. He wore the identical grin on his face he'd shown just before shooting the preacher in the back. Not a hint of worry at finding his two companions down the road. Before the Packard pulled even with the farm boy and the dwarf, Alvin said, "Just tell me what you want me to do."

Chester stopped the Packard beside him and flung open the passenger door. "Swell weather for a Sunday drive, don't you think? Climb on in and let's go."

The dwarf hoisted his suitcase into the rearseat of the Packard and scrambled in after it. Alvin tossed his own suitcase on top of Rascal's, then slid into the front seat and pulled the door closed.

"What do you say about the three of us getting something to eat?" Chester asked, sticking the Packard back into gear. "I've worked up an awful appetite this morning."

"Sure," Alvin replied, as the automobile sped up. He tried to hide his fear and disgust. "I can always eat." He kicked something in the foot-well and looked down and saw a canvas sack stuffed full of dollar bills.

"What a racket," Chester said, shaking his head. "Why, if I'd had the first idea how much dough these fellows rake in every Sunday, I'd have started my own church years ago. Why bother chasing the saps all over Creation when every Sunday morning they show up on your doorstep, pleased as punch to give you every red cent they own."

"Tithing," remarked the dwarf, "is one part alms and one part penance."

"Where're we headed?" Alvin asked, sticking his arm out into the draft. He felt dizzy.

Chester shrugged as he stepped on the accelerator. "Wherever you like. I'm feeling swell today, so you two go ahead and choose. Anywhere's fine with me."

Hearing that, the dwarf slipped his hand into the farm boy's shirt and fished out the poster Alvin had torn from the telephone pole back in Allenville. Wind blowing in his hair, he told Chester, "We found a circus."

AUGUST

THREE MILES EAST OF BELLEMONT, a late afternoon breeze blew in the summer grass surrounding the old Rickenbacker Aerodrome. The warm blue skies of late August were cloudless on the prairie horizon. Marie stood anxiously beside the open hangar, watching CW push his De Havilland "Gipsy Moth" out of the shadows while Rachel smoked a cigarette nearby and Cissie and Henry played tag a hundred yards off in the middle of the dirt runway. Marie had dressed in a thin wool sweater and a pair of tweed knickers that CW had suggested she wear for her first flight. Although she felt silly, everyone assured Marie her attire was entirely appropriate for the occasion.

"To my eye, she looks just like Harriet Quimby on her way across the English Channel," CW enthused, shoving the airplane into the sunlight. "Isn't this a marvelous day for flying? We're darned fortunate."

"I'm awfully glad to hear that," Marie said, smiling nervously. "I've been worried the clouds would come in and spoil everything." All morning she'd had butterflies in her stomach from the thought of going up in the airplane. But she was terribly excited and absolutely certain she wanted to fly. She had read somewhere that this world was just a big vaudeville stage with some of us sitting in boxes, some in the gallery, and more people on stage than know it. Well, she'd been spectating longer than she wanted to, and now she, too, wanted her turn on stage, even if it weren't entirely safe. Dear God, she hoped the plane wouldn't crash! What would the children do?

"Oh, there's nothing to worry about at all."

"Why, just last night you assured us that modern aviation is a science," Rachel remarked, exhaling smoke into the air. "You said flying about the clouds has nothing whatsoever to do with luck. Well, I ought to have known you couldn't be trusted to tell the truth for fifteen minutes. It seems Mother was right, after all."

CW stopped. Sunlight glinted off the silver fuselage of the "Gipsy Moth" forcing Marie to shade her eyes. He smiled. "My dear, what I meant to say was that flying is an awfully serious enterprise. Up there, a simple puff of air under the wings is all that separates life from death. Yet, when properly applied, an aviator's skill will overcome the most precarious conditions."

"Is that true?" Marie asked. "You know, this makes me awfully nervous."

Rachel laughed. "Of course it isn't! Don't be ridiculous! Why, even Lindy carried a rabbit's foot to Paris with him."

"I doubt that," CW replied, taking a pre-flight walk around the De Havilland. "Colonel Lindbergh would never have attempted that historic flight if he hadn't been confident of success. I met him, you know."

"You did?" Marie asked, suitably impressed. She only agreed to go up after Rachel assured her that CW had the reputation for being one of the very best pilots in Louisiana. "When?"

"He's lying, of course," Rachel interjected. "CW's never met anyone of note in his entire life."

CW held his own smile, while continuing his walk-around. "Actually, it was in '25 at the Carterville aviation field in Illinois where he was performing with Vera Dunlap's Flying Circus. We met in the hangar after the show. I remember Colonel Lindbergh being a very pleasant fellow. Quite personable, in fact, and a true enthusiast. He told me he'd rather fly than eat."

"I've been to Carterville, once when I was a little girl," said Marie, strolling over to the biplane, touching one of the wing struts. Was it sturdy enough? It looked awfully frail. What if it broke mid-flight? The thought of tumbling out of the clouds put a terrible fright in her heart. "It was in autumn and our entire family visited a pumpkin festival in a Lutheran auditorium. I'd never been on a train before, so the trip down from Farrington was very exciting."

"Did you meet 'Lucky Lindy' there, too?" Rachel asked, finishing with her cigarette. She dropped the butt in the dirt at her feet and stamped it cold.

"No," replied Marie, feeling her stomach do flip-flops. "I've never met anyone of note in my entire life." She smiled timidly at Rachel. "Except you and CW, of course."

CW climbed into the rear seat cockpit and disappeared below the lip of the fuselage. Out on the narrow runway, Cissie and Henry danced in a circle, kicking up dust. Marie called to them and they stopped dancing. Cissie waved and Marie called again and the children raced back from the runway.

"I swear I won't fall out, Momma," Cissie pleaded, reaching her mother ten steps in front of her little brother. She tugged on Marie's skirt. "Please? I want to fly!"

"I believe we've already discussed this." She had no intention of letting the children take a flight. Harry would throw a fit, not that she cared all that much any longer. She had the children with her, after all, while he was off galavanting about the country. The responsibility for their safety and well-being was hers now and she was doing just fine. She didn't need him at all — unless the plane fell out of the sky. She wondered if he'd make it down for her funeral.

Cissie threw her arms around her mother and hugged her tightly. "But it just isn't fair! I've never flown in an airplane before!"

"Neither have I," Marie replied, welcoming Henry into her arms. Could he tell she was frightened? She hoped not. There was no reason for them to know how nervous she was. "Nor has your brother."

"I don't want to fly, Momma," Henry said, freeing himself. "It's too scary!"

"Why, you stinky little coward!" Cissie cried, pinching Henry's ear. "You just told me you wanted to ride in CW's lap! You're nothing but a yellow-bellied coward!" She chased him a few feet away, then came back to Marie. "Couldn't I ride in your lap, Momma?"

"Absolutely not," Marie said. "The subject is closed. Now, go over and wait by the hangar until your Aunt Rachel says it's safe."

"Are you gonna fly now, Momma?" Henry asked, creeping near his sister. The breeze ruffled his hair, kicking dust onto his dirty trousers. Henry's laundry was twice his sister's.

"Pretty soon," Marie replied, as CW finished fueling the De Havilland. The aerodrome's sole mechanic, a skinny young fellow Rachel referred to as "Benny Beeswax," trotted out of a shed next to the hangar and handed CW a sheet of paper to sign, a fresh invoice for Red Crown aviation gasoline. Then the mechanic walked off and CW waved for Marie to come back over to the airplane. He reached into the front seat and took out a leather aviator's cap and a pair of goggles. "Here you are," he said, handing them to Marie. "You'll need a jacket, too." He leaned back into the seat and drew out a fleece-lined leather jacket.

"Will it be cold?" She felt her knees weaken. Why on earth had she agreed to this? Had she completely lost her mind? Good grief!

CW grinned. "Well, we'll be flying nearly eighty miles an hour, and perhaps reach an altitude of a thousand feet! Gosh, yes, I should think you'll be glad to have it on."

Taking the jacket from CW, Marie said, "It just seems so funny to dress for winter in August." She laughed nervously. "I'm afraid I'll suffer heatstroke before we leave the ground."

Rachel walked over and helped Marie fit the jacket over her sweater. "You'll be glad to have this once you're airborne. Believe you me, it's cold as the North Pole up there."

"I thought you said you haven't flown with CW."

"Well, I haven't," Rachel replied, stepping back for a look at Marie, attired now for flight. "But his hands always feel like icicles when he arrives from Shreveport."

"Oh, that's not so," CW said, giving a wave to the mechanic. "She's just teasing. In fact, I always wear gloves, so the cold doesn't bother me at all."

"Will I need gloves, as well?" Marie asked. "I already feel like an Eskimo." What would Harry think if he saw her now? Or Jimmy Delahaye? She knew he thought her to be shy and perhaps a bit mousy.

Would this change his estimation of her? Had he ever kissed a girl who'd flown in an airplane?

"No, I don't believe so. If you keep your hands in the jacket, you'll be fine."

Marie watched the children wander inside the old hangar, fading into its shadowy interior. Then the mechanic's shed opened and "Benny Beeswax" trotted over to the airplane.

"Well, here we go!" CW announced, and took Marie's hand. "Are you ready?"

She nodded while her stomach churned and she searched once for Cissie and Henry and saw them standing near the hangar's entrance, barely visible in the brown light. Trembling now, she said to Rachel, "Will you watch the children for me?"

Rachel laughed. "You've already asked me nine times since we left home, dear. Are you sure you want to go? Nobody would blame you for changing your mind. I'd planned to quit work early today, anyhow, so don't feel obligated to risk your life on my behalf."

"Well, yes," said Marie, placing a hand on the fuselage beside her forward seat. "I might be a little afraid, but I'm no coward. I'm ready to fly." She smiled bravely and tried not to faint.

"That-a-girl," cheered CW, taking her free hand and helping her up. Marie stepped over into the seat and slid down into place. It was cramped, but not as tight as she'd imagined it would be. She positioned her legs so that neither was touching the joystick, then leaned back so that she could see Rachel and CW. Her stomach all aflutter, Marie attempted enthusiasm. "Let's go!"

While Rachel walked off toward the hangar, CW took his own seat, fastened his goggles and gave "Benny Beeswax" a brief wave. A light breeze swirled across the field, gently fanning up little whirlwinds of dust on the runway. She heard CW call out, "Fuel on! Mags on! Clear prop!" A moment later, "Benny Beeswax" stood on his toes and gave the propeller a hard tug and the motor roared to life. A cloud of blue smoke puffed from the engine and the entire fuselage vibrated. Marie looked back again to the hangar and saw the children huddled next to Rachel. She waved just as the De Havilland lurched forward and began rolling out toward the runway, bouncing across the rough ground. Every few yards, the engine rattled and sputtered. CW guided the airplane briskly along the edge of the dusty field where the summer grass provided a boundary and the sun angled in Marie's eyes and the heat from the engine caused her to feel faintly claustrophobic.

As they taxied toward a dense stand of pecan trees, CW called to her from behind, "Do you see the stick and rudder pedals?"

Marie swiveled her head to reply. She was almost too scared to look. "Yes, they're at my feet."

"That's right. Well, you'll be able to see me operating them from where you are. They'll look like they're moving all by themselves, but they're not. Just be sure you don't touch them. We wouldn't want to have any confusion as to who's actually flying the plane, would we?"

Marie shook her head. She had no intention of touching anything on the airplane except the part she was sitting on. By now, they were several hundred yards from the hangar, out in the middle of the fields, exposed to the dusty breeze and the afternoon sun. At the end of the runway, the De Havilland spun about abruptly, facing back toward the hangar and the mechanic's shack. Just off Marie's shoulder, an old tractor sat in the tall grass, its iron wheels and rusted rear carriage half-swallowed up by a thick bramble of wild blackberries. She worried it might be the last thing she ever saw on this earth.

"Are you ready?" CW shouted above the rumble of the motor. He laughed as Marie nodded. She was quite nervous now, frightened half out of her wits, in fact. Was this all a disastrous mistake? Harry had once taken an airplane on a short flight across Indiana the summer Henry was born and had passed through a black thunderstorm just south of Muncie. Harry told Marie the plane was battered about so violently even the pilot had gotten sick. What would he think now, his silly timid wife about to go aloft? Maybe she wasn't timid, after all. In fact, maybe Harry didn't know his wife as well as he thought he did. CW shouted for her to keep an eye on the altimeter in front of her once they became airborne. Then the engine roared louder and the "Gipsy Moth" rattled forward down the runway. It was bumpy, yet felt as though the airplane were skipping along the ground as they raced forward. She craned her neck briefly for a glance back at the hangar where her children and Rachel stood cheering.

And then the De Havilland left the ground.

Beneath the airplane, the prairie horizon fell farther and farther away and the sky above it expanded like the interior of a great blue circus tent, raised higher and higher as the airplane gained altitude. She watched the arrow rise on the altimeter and airspeed gauges, and noticed the pedals shifting position slightly and the joystick tilting left as CW brought the airplane about in a long slow circle, returning for a pass above the aerodrome. Then her stomach dropped as the "Gipsy Moth" fell into a lazy dive toward the old hangar. Now only a couple hundred feet above the fields, CW slowed the engine speed and the din lessened and Marie heard him shouting for her to wave and she swiveled her head in time to see the tiny figures of Cissie and Henry racing across the runway as CW brought the airplane on a direct line between the hangar and the runway. He tilted each wing once up and down as they roared over the heads of the children and flew toward the pecan trees, then high up into the blue sky and over the pinewoods north of town. It was exhilarating. In Cissie's favorite daydream, a young wingéd monkey named Clarissa, blown out of the Land of Oz by a great gust of wind, lived in the attic of the house at 119 Cedar Street. In exchange for a plate of lemon cakes and a cup of ginger tea, she promised to teach Cissie how to fly. Whenever Cissie closed her eyes and whispered the secret command of the Winkies, she'd rise above the farmlands of Illinois, up above the clouds, and fly with Clarissa until her mother's voice called her to earth again. Not until CW banked the "Gipsy Moth" over the river toward Bellemont did Marie truly appreciate her daughter's fantasy of flight.

The De Havilland was noisier than she expected, smoky, too, and the fuselage shook and creaked whenever CW wrenched it into a half-loop. Once she even thought the struts were about to break off, flinging them both to the earth in a crumpled mess. Yet, despite an eighty-mile-an-hour wind in her face, and the persistent engine roar in her ears, she felt thrilled. They swept over the mudflats and pine trees and those small gray shacks of Shantytown near the river, sailing smoothly five hundred feet off the ground following the railroad tracks, then over the squat depot itself toward downtown Bellemont. Marie located the green lawn on the town square where she and the children had watched the Independence Day parade, and the white steeple of the First Baptist Church of Bellemont, and the red brick library where Cissie borrowed her Oz books, and the Bijou picture house and Bellemont Normal School and the business district downtown where dozens and dozens of tiny people strolled about the concrete sidewalks she followed every day from Delahaye's Restaurant downtown to Maude's small white house on College Street with the narrow backyard and the white linen on the washline and Lili Jessup's pale brown house next door, the grassy oak meadows beyond.

As CW brought the "Gipsy Moth" into a lazy circle, Marie saw Bellemont as she hadn't before, a small community clustered tightly along the banks of a twisty river in the middle of pinewoods and meadows, a plain rectangular settlement parceled into small sections by irregular fencelines and connected to the country beyond by thin dusty roads and a single stretch of railroad tracks. The De Havilland was rising now, higher and higher, a thousand feet above the earth. Marie tried her best to track a flight of redbirds half a mile away, and wondered how the Pendergast fields and the rolling hillocks of York's peacock farm and Miller's dairy would appear from the summer sky. *In the summer fields of Illinois long ago, Marie and her cousins run in the wake of the mowers, playing hider-seeker among the haycocks, chasing butterflies about with lacy straw bonnets, gathering a bed in the fresh mow upon which to lie back and watch the sparrows and starlings in the blue sky overhead. How sad and clumsy people must appear to birds, thinks Marie, how crude and graceless. In those halcyon years before the World War, all she knows of life are the Pendergast farmlands and Farrington's shady sidestreets and a mile of sandy river bluff along the muddy Mississippi. All the beauty in the world, she knows by touch. Basking in the warm haycocks until sundown, musty fragrance of fresh-mown hay in the summer air, the loud echoing voices of her father and uncles and brothers laboring in the fields until dark, supper by lamplight, later a cool breeze at a bedroom window, familiar whispers in the night. Where will her own children find fields of summer hay to play in? Across the wake of whose mowers will they run?*

CW called to Marie, telling her it was time to return to the aerodrome. She nodded, and the "Gipsy Moth" banked smoothly over the pinewoods east of town. Then the engine sputtered. Marie heard CW curse and instantly felt the plane drop. He cursed again and Marie saw a vapor trail of fuel misting off the back of the airplane. She called to CW, "Is there something wrong?"

He looked back at her in obvious distress. "The gas line's busted!"

"Oh?" She knew nothing about motors of any sort.

Then the engine quit completely and the wings dipped. CW leaned forward, yelling at the plane and Marie became utterly convinced she was about to die. She was a fool for taking a chance like this. The children were going to watch her fall out of the sky and crash before their eyes. She must've lost her mind to go up in the air like this. The biplane swooped into a slow but steep dive to Marie's left and she was so terrified all she could do was watch the earth spinning toward her. Dear God, she didn't want to die! Would it hurt badly when we crashed? How would Harry react to the news? Is this why she'd come to Texas, to die in a stupid accident? What'll happen to the children?

"We're going to try to land!" CW shouted to Marie. "I'm bringing us around in a circle. Hold on!"

Good grief, she was petrified with fear. The plane rolled into a tight left turn that almost tossed her out of the seat. Without the roar of the engine, she could hear the rush of wind and seemed to become light-headed as they swooped down over the cold river beside Shantytown. Trees grew larger and the grassy fields around the aerodrome flattened out wider than ever. She had always imagined airplane wrecks to be loud, but somehow there was no noise at all anymore and now she saw the end coming quickly. This was it, after all. Her life was finished in a silly airplane ride.

"Hold on! We're going in!"

Then Marie saw the runway and watched CW fighting to line up with it. As the biplane descended, the hangar came into focus once more. Marie saw her children hurrying across the runway from the safety of the hangar and the airplane seemed to float down over the flying field, gently crossing the pecan trees and the old tractor in the blackberry bramble, closer and closer to earth, down, down down, then … alighting finally on the dusty runway with a fierce bump that jolted her head. The Gipsy Moth bounced once, twice, three times, lurching left and right, CW yelling loudly, fighting to keep it from flipping over, and then the airplane rolled to a stop, and everything was still. Marie let out her breath. Was she actually alive? She could scarcely believe her eyes. They were on the ground and all in one piece.

"Well, I guess we made it," CW announced, his attempted glee at having brought them in safely sounding more like abject relief. "I haven't the vaguest idea what happened to the gas line, but that sure was exciting, wasn't it?"

Unable to speak, Marie squeezed her hands tightly together so they'd quit trembling.

"Thank goodness you got back safely!" Rachel said, hurrying up to the plane as CW helped Marie climb down out of the cockpit. Waves of heat swelled off the motor. She shaded her eyes to the sun's glare. "I was absolutely certain he'd do something idiotic like flipping the airplane upside-down and tossing you out."

CW took off his goggles and shaded his own eyes to the afternoon light. "Why, I'd never pull a stunt of that sort with anyone on board. I'm no show-off."

"Of course you are," Rachel insisted while giving Marie a brief hug. "Welcome back, dear."

"Why, thank you," Marie replied, still so frightened she could scarcely speak. Nor had she any intention of telling the children what had just occured. "I can hardly believe I did it. CW was wonderful. I've never had so much fun!"

"Good for you!" Rachel kissed her on the cheek. "Now, for the children's sake, I'd advise you never to fly again. It's much too dangerous."

Marie removed the goggles and aviator's cap and the leather jacket and replaced all three items into the forward cockpit. She waved to her children who had been kept back from the biplane by Rachel. Her legs felt wobbly, but somehow she had survived and now had a terrific story to write home about. She grinned like crazy, imagining Emeline's astonishment over her flight. She could hardly wait to tell her all about it. "Why, it was the most marvelous experience I've ever had!"

"Oh, you're just dizzy," Rachel remarked. "You'll be fine again in an hour or so, I'm sure."

"Oh, Momma!" Cissie shouted, rushing forward ahead of Henry and giving her mother a big hug at the waist. "You really flew! I'm so proud of you!"

— 2 —

Maude was standing by the porchsteps, gabbing with the old postman when they arrived home. CW swung the Ford around in a U-turn and parked at the curb where Cissie was constructing her summer circus beneath the fig tree. Marie saw that Maude still wore her sewing thimble on one hand and had the remnant of a scarf tucked into the front pocket of her dotted blue percale apron dress. She'd been sewing for her club ladies since dawn. Her eyes sagged and she looked fatigued. Cissie ran around back to the stables to look in on Mr. Slopey, Henry trotting dutifully after her. After greeting Maude, CW followed Rachel indoors, while Marie remained out in the sunlight where the heat was just beginning to abate and the afternoon air was lightly redolent of jasmine and dusty roses. She was still feeling terrifically giddy over her flight, and proud, too, for doing something she never imagined she'd have the nerve. Were Harry only here to have witnessed it, perhaps he'd see her in a different light. Would that make a difference between them? She could only hope somehow to change the direction his heart was tending, and if that wasn't possible, then she'd show him that she had a lot more gumption than he guessed and that one day soon he'd have to recognize that, for both their sakes. Too little sympathy already plagued them.

Maude thanked the postman for his delivery and watched as he went off. She remarked to Marie, "That's the sweetest man in this town. A saint, if I had the vote to cast. Clarence has been delivering my mail since Harry was in knickers and never has anything but a good word to say. He's outlived three of his own children and both his sisters and it looks as if he'll bury his wife before autumn. Yet he doesn't let on that life hasn't always treated him well and decently."

"Perhaps resilience ought to be counted a virtue," said Marie, passing through the gate, and closing it behind her. *"Has not man a hard service upon earth?"* she quoted, her father's favorite epigram from the Bible. He held little more sacred than constancy.

"Well, if any man were a latter-day Job, it would be that one," Maude replied, watching the old postman fade into the shady cottonwoods down the street. "I do believe we've forgotten how grace delivers the futility of sorrow from our hearts."

Clucking her tongue as she did when lost in thought, Maude removed the remnant of the scarf from her dress and followed Marie indoors.

Rachel already had the radio tuned to a dance orchestra playing jazz from a ballroom in Baton Rouge. Marie watched her waltz about the front room through amber slants of sunlight that penetrated Maude's lace curtains, while CW sat on the piano bench with his back to the keyboard and tapped rhythm on his kneecaps. Swirling about like a child ballerina, her spirits clearly brightened by the music, Rachel danced close to CW, rustled her fingers in his hair as she pirouetted past, kissing his ear and cheek before dancing off again. Marie wondered if Rachel imagined that love would always be like this.

> *I love him in the springtime,*
> *And I love him in the fall.*
> *But last night on the back porch,*
> *I loved him most of all.*

After straightening up another of Henry's messes in the bedroom, Marie went out through the back door intending to bring in the laundry. Seeing it had already been taken off the washline, she looked for the children in the stables and in the chickencoop, then walked around to the front of the house where she found Cissie helping Julius Reeves remove a lazy Susan and an old Victorian table lamp with a beaded fringe shade from a kitbag in his overloaded wheelbarrow. Abel Kritt and Henry sat side by side in a splint chair under the fig tree, Abel cradling one of Rachel's hens like a football, a stray white cat pawing a twig at his feet. Little Abel had gone missing for the better part of a day after the Fourth of July and refused to tell anyone where he had been, though his clothes had been caked with dried mud and he had lost his eyeglasses and had suffered nasty scratches and one of his fingers was bruised and swollen. His frantic mother had put him to bed for a week and brought a doctor to look him over, and a policeman from downtown, too, but not much seemed to have come of it. Mrs. Kritt plainly refused to discuss the trouble and closed her door to prying neighbors, several of whom claimed she went about teary-eyed and angry and talked to herself after dark when the bedroom window was open to the night air. There were dark rumors, naturally, and Boy-Allen's name popped up in conversation along with Abel Kritt's. If there was any consensus at all, it was that something ugly was occuring in Bellemont's shadows and the end of it was not yet in sight. Still, life went on, and soon enough little Abel and Henry were back playing together, apparently cheerful as ever, unmindful of the torment Abel's brief disappearance had caused among those who cared for him, and those who feared for their own children all about town.

Still buoyant from her flight, Marie walked over to the fig tree. In the wheelbarrow was a toy wooden horse head sticking out of a small box. When Cissie noticed her mother, she jumped up. "It's a flying-jinny, Momma! Isn't that wonderful? Our very own flying-jinny!"

Julius looked up at Marie and touched the bill of his old railroad cap. "Afternoon, Mrs. Hennesey. We're buildin' us a fine circus here."

Marie smiled, pleased to see her children occupied with the business of having fun. "You're constructing a merry-go-round?"

"A flying-jinny, Momma," Cissie corrected. "That's what they call them down here. Julius made it out of all these scraps." She got up and went to the wheelbarrow and took out the box full of discarded toys from another era, labeled *Humpty-Dumpty-Circus.*

"Oh my goodness!" Delighted, Marie bent over the box and found more horses of various colors and poses, a pair of giraffes and a donkey, a camel, a lion, a trio of trapeze aerialists, several painted clowns and a mustachioed ringmaster dressed in a red coat and black top-hat.

Under everything were toy stools, pedestals, a ladder, a colored ball and a piece of white cloth stitched with red garlands. Marie looked over at Julius who was busy fastening the lamp to the lazy Susan. "Santa Claus brought me one of these for Christmas one year when I was a little girl. Wherever did you dig this up?"

"There's all sorts of places where things other folks don't want no more been collecting," said Julius, tapping another hole in the lazy Susan. "It's just a case of knowing where to put a hole in the dirt." He pulled a screwdriver from his overalls and drove a screw through the base of the lamp, connecting it to the lazy Susan.

"Why, when Julius gets done putting our flying-jinny together, Momma," Cissie enthused, separating the wooden horses from the rest of her miniature circus menagerie, "I guess we'll have just about the best circus in the whole country, won't we?"

Marie smiled. "I expect you will at that." When Emeline saw Marie's Humpty-Dumpty circus, she was so jealous, she refused to come play until after New Year's.

She bent down and brushed her fingers across the beaded fringe of the Victorian table lamp that would serve as canopy to the merry-go-round. Marie's mother still owned a similar lamp and shade with prism glass, which she kept atop an embroidered lambrequin on a table in front of the parlor's east window where morning sunlight drew rainbows on all the walls and ceiling. Marie thought it was the most beautiful object in all the world.

Julius tapped the final hole into the lazy Susan and screwed the lampstand down tight. Then he hitched up his overalls, grabbed the shade, re-attached it to the lamp, and sat back. "All right, Mister Henry. Throw the switch!"

Henry gave the lazy Susan a push and they all watched the little merry-go-round revolve with only a slight tilt.

"Oh, it'll be so beautiful when we put our horses on it!" said Cissie, brushing the beads as they went by.

"I want to ride a tiger!" Henry cried, grabbing one from the box. He placed it on the merry-go-round. It slid off and Abel snatched it for his own with a big grin. The hen hopped free, scaring the cat. Marie heard Maude call to her from the front of the house.

"Excuse me," she said, getting up.

She walked back around to the front steps where Maude waited in the late sunlight, a letter in hand.

"I think I must be slowly losing my mind," she said, handing the letter to Marie. "This came with the rest of the mail today, dear. It's from Illinois."

"Why, thank you."

Maude went back indoors as Marie read the envelope and saw the return address with Auntie Emma's name. Before Marie could tear the envelope open, Cissie came running past the honeysuckle bush shouting, "Wait, Momma! Wait! It's my turn!"

Marie frowned. "Pardon me, dear?"

Cissie stopped beside her at the stairs, one hand shading her eyes to the late sun, the other held palm up. Her pigtails were as dusty as Henry's trousers. "Don't you remember?" she said, brightly. "You promised the next letter I could read first!"

Marie slipped the paper out of the envelope. "How about if we read it together?"

Cissie shook her head. "No, me first this time. You got to read Daddy's on Tuesday. It's my turn today."

"Well, all right." Marie handed the letter to her daughter, and sat down in the middle of the stairs. "I'll just wait here until you finish, but be quick. We'll be eating soon."

A pair of black automobiles droned past, oilworkers heading east to home in Clementville. One of the drivers beeped his horn and a pair of arms thrust out from the back seat of the second car and gave a wave as they passed. The Jessup's collie began barking and Marie heard Lili yell to it from the backyard. Earlier in the day, Lili had claimed to be too busy giving a bath to a scruffy terrier she and Cissie had rescued from an abandoned well to play out at the airfield, and Cissie worried perhaps their friendship was waning, though less than a week had passed since they'd sworn an oath of eternal affection. Back in Farrington, Cissie had constantly formed clubs and tested her members' loyalty with silly challenges: cross Lovett's creek barefoot in

December, go an entire day with both shoelaces untied, write an anonymous letter to the mayor telling him that Widow Allyson is secretly married to an Indian. Since Cissie had arrived in Bellemont, only Lili Jessup had yet paid her the compliment of following her about, helping her rescue orphaned animals, being her friend. If Cissie's bossiness led to her losing Lili's friendship, she'd be sorry.

Cissie gasped and dropped the letter. Before Marie could say a word, she raced up the steps and went indoors. As the screen door slammed shut, Marie picked up the letter and quickly read it through.

Farrington, Illinois
July 30th, 1929

Dear Niece,

My, how these months have hurried along! Your mother reminded me just this morning that we've been without you for almost half a year now. Of course, we all miss you so very much. Did you know Josie just celebrated her fifth birthday? It is remarkable how the days pass when one works too hard at living to observe the calendar. I'm getting older yet I rarely notice. Do you suppose that means the Lord will postpone my appointment? These are questions I ponder when your mother and Leora are away and I am left to my thoughts.

Last Friday Auntie Eff had the Ladies Missionary Society out to George's farm and we all went. I had a fine time. Abby's young nephew Milton waited on our tables. You ought to have been there and seen him. He had a cap with a little blue bow and he looked pretty as anything. If his hair had been long he would have looked exactly like a girl. There were over a hundred ladies there. George made out that they were a terrible crowd but he was in a foul temper again. Cousin Francis sang. Doesn't she sing dandy? Milton was quite struck with her. He says he is going to the church where she sings some Sunday so that he can hear her again. He also thinks Mattie McCall is fine. Perhaps he'll call on them both. Grandma, Roy, Emeline, Victor and I went out to Uncle Charlie's Sunday. Milton thinks Hazel is awfully cute as well. That boy is a Gallup, isn't he?

Mattie gave Uncle Charlie a white tie for his birthday and sent a letter with it. Grandma thought you would like to see the letter so I am sending it next week with a postal card. Mr. Williams, Aunt Et's nephew, was here the other day. You know he came on the Glidden tour. He wanted to run off with your table. He says it's worth more than a few dollars and if he sells it, there's quite a lot he can buy. Don't worry. He won't be allowed indoors without a policeman standing by! Grandma is doing fine.

Effie's more worried than ever about your cousin Alvin. No one has the least idea where he's gone off to. He has not written nor did he say where he was going. We are all worried and pray for him daily. Doctor Hartley believes Alvin's t.b. has returned and that his running off is very dangerous. If Alvin wishes to do without his family only the Lord can say how he'll end up. Frenchy claims we ought not to worry. He believes only Alvin knows why he has gone off like this and when he is good and ready he'll come back home again where he belongs. We can only hope this is so.

Now for some terrible news. Yesterday when Lottie and Sam went out to the barn to feed the pets, Cissie's little ball of sunshine Punky was nowhere to be found. They looked high and low for hours and when they discovered him under the steps of Uncle Boyd's workshed it became a tragedy. Punky had died in the night. Effie thinks it was poison but nobody can imagine where the poor cat could have gotten into any so we have a mystery with our sadness. Please let Cissie rest assured that Punky will be missed by all of us and that the children gave him a touching burial. I'm so very sorry about this. I trust Cissie will forgive us. Please write soon. We miss you dearly.

Your Loving,

Auntie Emma

Marie folded the letter in her lap. She sighed. Cissie had worried herself to tears over Punky remaining behind on the farm. She insisted he would be unhappy and might even run off. Despite her protestations, Harry had driven Punky and Cissie together out to the farm and seen to it that Cissie say good-bye to the old cat outside Uncle Henry's barn. Necessity demanded sacrifice, Harry had told her on the road home. Regardless, that night the poor dear cried herself to sleep.

Marie got up and went inside where the sunlight had disappeared and the interior was mostly reflection and shadow. Rachel had stopped dancing and now sat in CW's lap on the piano bench, kissing him so deeply Marie blushed to see them. The radio orchestra played an instrumental arrangement of Rudy Vallee's Fox Trot melody "Betty Co-ed." Rachel gave a brief nod to Marie, directing her toward the back of the house, then returned to kissing. Maude was baking cinnamon cookies when Marie passed by the kitchen. Even before she got to the bedroom, Marie could hear Cissie sobbing.

In the shadow of the chinaberry tree, Cissie lay on her side atop the quilted bedspread, tears running down her cheeks.

"Oh, honey," Marie said, sliding onto the bed beside her, "I'm so sorry. We all loved Punky very much."

"I miss him already, Momma," Cissie sobbed into the pillow. "It hurts so bad."

"I know it does." She stroked Cissie's hair. "He was a very sweet cat. We'll all miss him dearly."

"It was my fault for not bringing him with us," she cried. "I let Punky die."

Marie leaned forward and pulled Cissie into her arms and hugged her tightly. "Oh, honey. No, you didn't. It wasn't anybody's fault. Your cousins loved Punky very much and took the best care of him they knew how. Punky had a wonderful life. He was very happy."

"But he died, Momma! He died, and I wasn't even with him! He must've been awful scared." She began sobbing again. Looking out through the window past the chinaberry tree, Marie saw Lili brushing down her horse. The horse's mane tossed with dust swirling in the small corral. The young girl was struggling to finish her chores before sundown.

Cissie murmured, "Momma, I'll never ever love another cat like Punky."

Marie kissed Cissie's cheek. "Of course you will, honey. One day you'll have another kitty you'll love with all your heart."

"How do you know, Momma?" Cissie moaned. "I never had a cat before Punky. What if I found one who wouldn't love me like Punky did? What would I do?"

Marie laughed. "Oh, baby." She gave Cissie another big hug and a kiss. "How could it not?"

Outdoors, the breeze gusted and the chinaberry tree scratched at the window and dropped more ripe berries into the dusty backyard. After a while, Cissie stopped crying and cuddled beside Marie. "Momma?"

"Yes, dear?"

"Where's Punky now? Is he in heaven?"

Marie smiled. "He's in a very special place, honey, where I'm sure he's very happy."

"Did they bury him by the creek under the Indian tree with the other cats?"

Marie nodded. "Probably beside old Mister Stockingfeet."

"That's such a silly name, Momma," said Cissie, wiping a tear off her cheek. "Do you still miss him?"

"Of course," she replied, softly stroking Cissie's hair. "Mister Stockingfeet was the sweetest kitty I ever owned. I cried just like you when he died. I thought I'd never love anything again as long as I lived, but then I had my children and they taught me how wrong I'd been."

Next door, Lili undid the slip knot she'd fixed to the fencepost and led the horse back across the yard to his stall. A rooster fluttered across the dusty ground and skittered under the Jessup's backstairs. Lili's gray kitten chased a leaf through the gate between the two properties.

"Did Boy-Allen go to heaven, Momma?"

"Of course he did, honey. Heaven's a providing place where sadness and hurt are washed away in God's eternal joy, and nobody feels lost or neglected any longer."

"I'm glad, Momma. I'd feel awfully sad if he wasn't in heaven now."

"Me, too."

Thinking about that for a few moments, Cissie said, "Sometimes I still miss David, Momma." She looked up at her mother, eyes still damp and red with tears. "Did he love me?"

"Very much so," Marie answered, somewhat taken aback. Although her firstborn never drifted far from remembrance, since his death a week after his fifth birthday, rarely had Marie spoken David's name aloud. Nor had Harry. To lose a child so young proved an almost unbearable burden, worsened yet by memory's insistent whisper. Time dulled the ache, but that was all. Moreover, Marie had become convinced the Lord did not allow such wounds to heal in the belief that denying sorrow only forfeits love, since both share a common place in the heart.

A blustery wind is hissing off Lake Calhoun, stirring whitecaps out on the cold water. The afternoon sky is grim and threatens rain, perhaps by evening, but Marie has promised David a picnic, so here they are with a basket of fruit and sandwiches. They are not alone. Sailboats drift across the waves and a fisherman guides his skiff by the shore where other people stroll the walkways or relax on park benches and study the clouds. Marie ought to have more company for her excursion today, but Cissie is napping at home with Aunt Ruth while Harry is over to St. Paul on business. Little David doesn't seem to mind at all. He scurries about the grass like a bug, tumbling and laughing, showing off for his mother, having a grand visit to the lake. Marie enjoys a pear and a cheese sandwich, and watches the sailboats flutter like kites on the steel-gray water. The fisherman brings his flatbottom boat to shore, then gets out, anchoring his skiff on the grass with a rock tied to a rope. He hurries off through the trees. When David heads over to the boat, Marie warns him to stay clear of the lapping water. He nods, and kneels to study the knotted rope. Wary of his intentions, Marie rises from the picnic blanket to go fetch him back from the shoreline. As she stands, a terrific gust of wind billows under the blanket, upsetting the picnic basket. Startled by the sight of her napkins and Dixie cups blowing away toward the cycle path, she takes her eye off David. The blanket ripples under the wind as Marie quickly grabs what she can reach. Glancing back toward the water, she sees the fisherman's skiff has come free of its anchor and is drifting out into the lake, her five-year-old David perched at the bow. Marie screams. She runs to the sandy embankment at the water's edge and calls to him as the windblown current carries David's skiff farther from shore. Marie jumps into the water and sinks up to her waist. She shouts frantically for her little boy to come back. Horrified, she watches David climb up onto the bow, and plunge overboard into the pitching waves. He cannot swim. Neither can she. A brave fellow from the shore dives into the lake, but David has already disappeared. Hysterical with fear, Marie splashes toward the skiff, loses her balance, and goes under. By the time strong arms carry her out of the lake, she knows her little boy has been lost, and the suffocating grief lays her unconscious.

Cissie said, "I was just a baby when David died, wasn't I, Momma?"

"Yes, you were," replied Marie, giving Cissie another kiss on her ear while hugging her tightly, "but he'll always be your brother, just as Henry is. We lost him a good while ago, honey, but he's stayed in our hearts all the same, hasn't he?" How strange that Marie could no longer recall David's voice, yet his soapy after-bath scent persisted whenever she remembered him in her arms. What persists for eternity, if not a mother's devotion to her child?

"Yes, Momma," Cissie agreed. She folded her fingers into Marie's and squeezed gently. "That's why I still pray for him every night before I go to sleep."

"So do I, honey."

"David knows we still love him, doesn't he, Momma? Even in heaven?"

"Of course he does," Marie said, watching now as Lili crossed her yard to the backstairs and went indoors, her small gray kitten trailing just behind. "That's why God brought him there, so he'll always be loved, no matter what. His being in heaven teaches us how precious life is, honey. Every single day of it. That's why we'll never forget our dear little David."

"Or Punky," Cissie added, wiping away another tear.

Marie smiled, "That's right. We'll always remember Punky, too."

Then she gave her sweet daughter another kiss and cuddled with her in the small bed beneath the back window until evening's shadows crept out from the pretty chinaberry tree and Maude called them both to supper.

— 3 —

Over Maude's objections, Rachel tuned the radio set to an NBC orchestra broadcast from Kansas City's Meuhlebach Hotel while they ate. Arguing that music aids digestion, she had set the volume so every note could be clearly heard in the dining room. CW didn't seem to mind, but it drove everyone else crazy. Marie knew Harry would've taken the radio and tossed it out a window, nor was she herself exactly pleased to have it playing during supper, but Rachel was obstinate. Between servings of vegetable soup and the veal Maude cooked to resemble pork chops,

Rachel fidgeted with her fork and spoon, tapping rhythm to "The Sheik of Araby" and singing along with the broadcast.

> *I'm the sheik of Araby*
> *Your love belongs to me.*
> *At night when you're asleep,*
> *Into your tent I'll creep.*

The children giggled when her spoon struck the side of the table too hard and flew off onto the carpet. Maude slapped her own hand down beside her plate. "Rachel!"

"Yes, Mother?" Rachel bent down to retrieve the spoon.

"You're behaving like a wild animal. I'm asking you to stop it this instant. It's spoiling my appetite."

"I resent that, Mother," replied Rachel, putting the spoon back onto her plate. "It's an ugly thought. Why, I suppose next you'll be telling me to sleep out in the stalls."

"Don't give me cause," Maude threatened, her eyes steeled to the occasion. "You're acting more childish than these two little ones. I won't stand for it."

"Why, you've just proven Darwin's theory, Mother." Rachel giggled like a clown. "I've evolved from a wild animal to a child in less time than it took Eve to swallow the apple. Somebody ought to wire John Scopes."

"Laugh at the dinner table and you'll cry before bed," Maude scolded. "I'm warning you, young lady."

"Young lady? I thought I was a child. Please make up your mind, Mother. You're confusing me now."

"Rachel!"

In one swift stroke of her left hand, Rachel knocked the bowl of potatoes off the table. It landed upside down on the rug beside Marie's chair. "There, Mother," she said. "Now, that's childish!"

"My heavens!" Maude cried, rising from her chair.

Marie was shocked. Had her sister-in-law gone insane? She told her, "Good grief, dear! You're scaring the children!"

"Darling!" CW leaned forward, clearly shocked. "If you ask me — "

"Well, I didn't ask you!" Rachel seized her glass of water and splashed it between his eyes. "And I refuse to look at your stupid face another instant!"

Then she slid her chair back, got up and ran out of the room.

They all heard the front door slam.

Maude stood at the table. "Why, I believe she's lost her mind."

CW wiped his face with the cloth napkin. Marie looked across the table at the children, both of whom appeared goggle-eyed by the nasty display of adult temperament. She put her finger to her lips just as Cissie began to say something. Henry kept his own eyes down, his fork stuck in a pile of mashed potatoes. The radio played on.

> *While stars are fading in the dawn*
> *Over the desert they'll be gone*
> *His captured bride close by his side*
> *Swift as the wind they will ride.*

CW pushed his chair back. "I suppose I ought to go out and see where she's run off to."

Marie slid her own chair away from the table and picked up the bowl of potatoes, scooping onto Rachel's plate all that had spilled. She felt horribly embarrassed for Maude and the children. What had gotten into Rachel? CW went out the front door. Marie heard him calling for Rachel as Maude came out of the kitchen with a wet rag, angrier than Marie had ever seen her.

"Here, let me do that," Marie offered, taking the rag. "Cissie? Please?"

Her daughter got up and came around the table to help. Henry sat still, intent on finishing his dessert of tapioca pudding that apparently no one else had any interest in.

"I declare I ought to put that nasty mouth of hers out into the street," said Maude, at the window now, her fingers curled inside the curtain for a look outside. Marie scrubbed the rug while Cissie used her fingers to pick up smaller bits of potato. A bright peal of laughter issued from out of doors, Rachel's voice echoing across the early evening dark.

"I don't know what came over her," Marie said, cleaning as best she could. It was an awful mess. What on earth had just happened? "I've never seen her behave that way before."

"You just haven't been here long enough." Maude shook her head in disgust. "If she were destitute even a short while she might learn how to behave. Jonas spoiled Rachel when she was little and now there's nothing to be done with her. Beatrice tells me that practically everyone at Corby & Beauchamp is scared to death of her throwing these sorts of fits. They say she's a holy terror. I presume that's how she's managed to hold onto her job for so long." Maude came away from the window shaking her head. "Even in an insurance office, secretarial is nothing to sniff at, you know. More than thirty girls applied for that position. I'm sure the fact that Rachel was hired proves she's capable of impressing people when she sets her mind to it. What I don't understand is her refusal to accept the notion of courtesy and decent behavior. She ought to realize there are those who will hold it against her one of these days. Nobody is entirely belovéd. Why, even a peacock envies his own reflection."

Marie went out onto the back porch where she heard Rachel and CW busy in conversation. She gently closed the screen door. With a fresh batch of gingerbread cookies in the oven, Maude had gone to draw a rosewater bath for herself, while the children played slapjack across the hall in the back bedroom. Outdoors, the night air was sultry and calm. Moths flapped at the washroom screens. Automobiles rattled by every so often and hordes of youngsters chased about in the next block, their shrill voices echoing adventure and quarrel in the summer dark.

As Marie crossed the yard, she heard Rachel still explaining her outburst at supper. "Well, of course you all were ganging up on me. When don't you? To tell the truth, I've felt persecuted in this house since the day I was born. All for speaking my mind. Am I not entitled to voice my opinions now and then? I tell you, it's just not fair!"

"Now, darling, be reasonable," CW said, kissing Rachel on the cheek. "Say, didn't I let you decide where I'd be escorting you tonight? Ordinarily that would be a fellow's decision, but in the interest of fair play and all, I let you choose, and so we're going to the picture show, aren't we?"

Rachel broke away and wandered over to the fence by the Jessup's corral. CW flipped his straw hat on one finger and strolled after her. The plumbing rattled under the house as hot water ran toward Maude's bathtub. Rachel saw Marie and waved to her, so Marie walked across the backyard to meet up with her and CW beside the Jessup's. She knew Rachel wasn't done fussing yet, although her moods were as changeable as the wind. Harry found his sister impossible to understand and had warned Marie to avoid her as often as possible. That advice seemed silly, and Marie mostly ignored it. More often than not, Rachel was quite endearing. But her behavior tonight had been disgraceful and Marie intended to tell her so. "Hello."

"Is Mother still put out?" Rachel asked, with a grin. "I don't know what came over me. That was such a silly thing to do."

"It was very rude," Marie said, her lips tightened. "I don't see why the children had to witness something like that at the supper table. It's hard enough just getting them to sit down."

Rachel turned her face away, and feigned a shiver in the wind.

Marie refused to indulge her. "Did you hear what I just said? There's no excuse for involving the children in your own drama. It's mean, and you know it."

"I'm sorry, dear," Rachel replied, casually. "I had no idea I'd made such a scene. Were they very upset?"

Marie knew Rachel was trying to soften her up, but she'd have none of it yet. "I'm sure they'll live. That's hardly the point. My dear, you behave sometimes as if you're the only person on earth, and that's very selfish. Why your mother puts up with it is her business, but I'm telling you right now that I won't. It isn't at all fair to the children. They don't understand why you're acting so idiotically, and they shouldn't have to."

"Piffle!" Rachel muttered, shaking her head. She looked away again. "Maybe I'll be run down by a car tonight and solve all your problems."

"Don't be so dramatic, dear," Marie advised, with a frown. "That doesn't help a thing."

Maude opened the back door and set the garbage out on the porch.

Indoors, Cissie was shouting at Henry to stay out of the bath. The screen door banged shut as Maude went back inside.

"Do you know, I feel light as a feather tonight," Rachel remarked, gazing up into a black sky of stars. Then she fanned her face with both hands. "Though, it's so warm out I can hardly breath."

"Actually, it seems quite pleasant to me," CW said, leaning against the fence. "If you think this is hot, you ought to try New Orleans in August, dear. Without an evening breeze blowing off the Gulf, humidity from the bayou makes just getting up off a stool seem impossible."

Rachel stamped her foot. "There! What did I just say? I can't utter a syllable without being contradicted. This engagement is becoming utterly hopeless."

"Well, if you're so put-out with me, dear," CW remarked, "perhaps you ought to go back indoors and bake cookies with your mother. I've already been to the picture show eight times this month alone, and I've got several appointments at Lafayette and New Iberia tomorrow."

"You realize, honeypie," Rachel continued, her voice languid as she brushed her hair back with one hand, "this is precisely why Mother has objected so strongly to our seeing each other all summer." Then she leaned over, kissed CW on the lips, tousled his hair, and giggled. Marie glanced off into the dark, not the least bit interested in watching them make love. Why did they have to behave so? What were they trying to prove?

Breaking from Rachel's embrace, CW flipped the straw hat back onto his head. "Why, I'd say pure viciousness informs her opinions, dear. That, and disgust for people different from herself and those silly old hags she plays cards with. Honestly, I feel sorry for her. How do the narrow-minded find the courage to go outdoors every day among their inferiors? It must be fairly intolerable."

"Shhh!" Marie shushed him. "For goodness sakes, the entire neighborhood can hear you!"

The Jessup's collie came to the fence, wagging its tail eagerly, anxious for attention. CW scratched the collie's snout. A light came on in the Jessup's back bedroom.

Quite pleasantly, Rachel asked Marie, "Did you hear CW's offer to buy us tickets for the show at the Bijou tonight? It's a movie with that funny little man. Do you care to come along?"

"Pardon?" Marie was shocked how Rachel's mood could change so quickly.

"We're planning on having a wonderful time."

"Oh, I wouldn't want to spoil your evening out," Marie replied, still feeling a little testy towards her, not sure she wanted to share Rachel's company. She was tempted, though. Truth was, she'd wanted to go to the pictures all summer long, particularly since Jimmy Delahaye had hinted at asking her to one. In fact, she was fairly desperate to get out of the house for a few hours.

"You won't be spoiling a thing, dear," Rachel said, as a faint breeze drifted through the cottonwoods across College Street. "Why, we'd be glad to have you. Unless, of course, you'd rather stay home and help Mother cook potato soup and discuss her club ladies' theories about who murdered Boy-Allen. Last Wednesday, they chose the Pig Woman. Can you feature that? Call the papers!"

"Well, I don't know," Marie answered, checking back toward the window at the chinaberry for signs of the children. She hoped they weren't making a wreck of the bedroom. "Wouldn't CW rather have you to himself? I'm afraid I'd be a nuisance."

When she'd first peeked out through the kitchen window, Rachel and CW had been embracing each other much too recklessly, in Marie's opinion. She didn't consider herself a bluenose, but there were proprieties, weren't there? Had she and Harry ever been that bold in public? Well, maybe that was one of their problems; they hadn't taken any true risks for the sake of love and romance.

Rachel dismissed Marie's suggestion with a wave of her hand. "Oh, he's not sure any longer if he even wants me at all. CW claims he was trapped for years between whores and chastity. Now I suppose he's found love to be equally tiresome. Just you watch; he'll let me talk myself out, then he'll wash us up and fly home alone."

"Why, dear, you know that's just not so," CW countered. "I've asked you to marry me, haven't I? What greater example of my devotion can I offer? In fact, you're the one who's lost her faith in true love! If a fellow can't please every point of this ideal you've worked up, you throw them over. And on it goes. If you're not careful, dear, you'll end up an old maid, sitting with your mother at the supper table, just the two of you kicking about everything under the sun."

Rachel laughed. "Oh, aren't you vile? Why, honeypie, it hadn't occurred to me that marriage was one of the special favors you dole out to the girls you entertain. How ignorant of me! Have there been any children? I should think you'd make a wonderful father."

"You know, darling, you're even more sarcastic than your mother."

"Oh, Mother's not sarcastic at all," Rachel said, poking her leg through the fence. "She literally means every word she says. That way, her insults are never misunderstood. Fact is, I admire her consistency. Rarely am I able to be so honest. I consider that one of my few genuine faults."

Marie watched in utter amazement. She had no idea what to say. Sister-in-law was a difficult relation, especially with Rachel so petulant and spoiled, yet slyly aware of her own faults. She prided herself on possessing a sharp wit that offered little compromise in a contest of wills. Even Maude struggled to retain her authority over Rachel, while freely admitting that her daughter was old enough to pursue her own path, wherever it might lead. So Rachel skipped church on Sundays when she'd been out late with CW the night before, smoked cigarettes outside her mother's window after dark, performed only those household duties that served her own interests, and asserted her independence by threatening at least once a week to pack up and leave town. For her part, Marie refused to choose sides. Nor did she offer to mediate, as it wasn't her nature to presume her opinion had value in such longstanding disputes. Besides, as the summer wore on, she had become tired of the drama. She wanted smiles and joy now, and felt she deserved it.

"Oh, I'm sick to death of quarreling," Rachel said, pushing off from the Jessup's fence. "Aren't you? I say, let's just forget about everything and have a swell date tonight." She turned to Marie. "Shall we?"

Marie nodded, warily. "Agreed."

Atttending a picture show did seem like a wonderful idea. If it helped keep the peace, that was all the more reason to go. Besides, Harry went all the time and rarely invited her along, believing she had no interest in the movies. Trouble was, he always seemed to choose those evenings when Emeline was off somewhere and there wasn't anyone else to watch the children. What could she do? Maybe if Jimmy Delahaye asked her again she'd go. Why not?

"Resolved," CW then announced, placing the straw hat over his heart, "that this old world is fair as heaven when sweet harmony rather than discord rules the day!" He took his pocketwatch out and examined the time. Smiling, he snapped it closed, and took Rachel by the arm. "Well, three hours from now I turn back into a damn pumpkin, so I suggest we go; Little Charlie's awaiting us at the old Bijou."

— 4 —

On summer evenings in Bellemont, people came out onto galleries to sit in wicker rockers and listen to the crickets' soothing tremolo and watch neighbors pass by along the shadowy sidewalks. It was too hot indoors for sleep. On Second Street, eighty-year-old Widow Shoemaker sat propped up in bed by a cracked window with a cold wet towel wrapped about her forehead and played Mah Jongg with her Mexican nurse and the ghosts of her two late husbands. Over on Arbor Lane, where weeping willows draped branches over picket fences and mosquitoes floated in the damp leaves, four gin-soaked oilworkers sent their wives next door for the evening and stacked poker chips on a card table inside a screened-in back porch and played Seven-toed Pete by the light of an old kerosene lamp. In the third house west from the corner of Hyperion Road and Tenth Street, Wilma Domeier sat on a tufted loveseat in her parlor and counted old valentines from grade school and imagined handsome Lewis McGraw ringing her doorbell with a bouquet of fresh pink roses in his hand and crimson passion for her in his heart. While Rachel and CW strolled arm-in-arm on the sidewalk ahead, Marie listened to the children in the next street playing tag and hider-seeker under the black cottonwoods: *Ready or not, you shall be caught!* Littler ones younger than Boy-Allen wandered unattended about the dusty sidewalks, dragging streamers of colored ribbon or naked dolls, or sat forlorn in rusty red wagons waiting impatiently to be tugged along toward a new game in the next block. Dozens of lanterned bicyclists flew past like falling stars, dinging bells street to street, while voices of all ages spoke from every corner veranda and treeshaded stoop.

Downtown Bellemont was bright and lively. Most stores were closed, but adults sat in the booths of late-closing cafés and restaurants or stood about in the parking lots of a dozen gas stations, hoping that lively conversation and a bottle of ice-cold Dr Pepper might help them forget the evening heat. Cars were parked along the curb in a line to the Bijou where a noisy crowd gathered under the flashing theater marquee.

BIJOU — PHOTO-PLAY HOUSE — MOVING PICTURES

"I tell you, there's no such thing as being late to the picture show," Rachel argued, as they approached the crowd. "Nobody's on stage to be disturbed when people come in after the curtain goes up. It's entirely different."

At the box office, a pretty freckled brunette with a pleasant smile sorted coins and distributed ticket stubs to movie patrons one by one. Behind the glassed-in booth, a lanky youth with a ragged haircut stood waiting. As the line shortened, the girl pointed to the clock inside the box office and smiled for him.

"This used to be a vaudeville theater, you know," Rachel informed Marie, as they neared the ticket window. "All the cleverest acts came here to perform — Harry Lauder, Loie Fuller, Joe Weber, Honey Boy Evans, the Cherry Sisters. Lots of others. It was quite popular. Why, there was even an elephant on stage one evening with a trio of pygmies from darkest Africa."

"I love shows," said Marie, watching the girl exchange coins for tickets. "Farrington had a nice little theater that Harry used to take me to on Saturday nights before Cissie was born. We had W.C. Fields one night, and Irene Franklin and Nora Bayes the next."

"Say, don't you think they ought to put on something more up-to-the-minute?" CW asked, pointing to the marquee overhead where **CHARLIE CHAPLIN in "THE CIRCUS"** was advertised in big block letters. "Why, I saw this in New Orleans two years ago."

"Oh, I doubt that," Rachel snorted. "We feature only the newest photo-plays here in Bellemont. Feel free to look it up at the Chamber of Commerce if you like. It's in our charter."

"Is that true?" Marie asked, studying the playbill. "I wouldn't care to see the same show twice, unless it's John Barrymore. I think he's so handsome." She grinned.

CW stepped forward and paid for the three of them, flirting with the young brunette. "Twenty-five cents a piece! My goodness, that's steep. Why, the last picture I saw only cost me a dime. Is there a reduction for aviators?"

The girl blushed. "Not that I'm aware of, sir."

"Well, there ought to be, don't you agree?"

The girl shrugged, her blush deepening.

"Well, thank you, anyhow," CW said, sticking the ticket into his hatband as he led Rachel and Marie into the theater.

Inside the lobby, an old red velvet carpet was dirty and threadworn, scuffed through to the cement floor in several places, and the gilt ceiling stencils of Turkish arabesques and rose garlands had faded from the accumulated grime of three decades. On every wall, old lobby cards in glass frames reminded visitors of past dancehall nights and vaudeville attractions, while a new one mounted on an easel announced the program for the evening.

Chas. Chaplin
Merna Kennedy & Others
"THE CIRCUS"
&
3rd Episode of
The Serial Sensation

"THE CRIMSON STAIN MYSTERY"

2 SHOWS TONIGHT!!!

The auditorium had already dimmed for the Hearst Metrotone News. Cigarette smoke drifted across the pale blue light from the projection booth high atop the rear of the theater. Down in front and off to one side, a small woman in a print frock played "My Bonnie Lies Over The Ocean" on the piano with her eyes fixed on those black-and-white images that flickered across the silver screen.

"Look there," CW said, leading Rachel and Marie to their seats near the middle of the auditorium, "what've I been telling you?"

Up on the screen, "Metrotone News" featured the Graf Zeppelin's ascent from Friedrichshafen on its flight around the world. After a brief round trip from Germany to Lakehurst and back, Hugo Eckener's great airship would travel east from Germany past Moscow, over Asia toward Tokyo, then across the Pacific to San Francisco and Los Angeles before descending at Lakehurst, thereby completing history's first circumnavigation of the globe by aircraft.

"Six days!" CW remarked, as he sat down. "Incredible! Why, that'll be less time than one needs to steam across the Pacific now. My goodness! The Age of Flight is certainly upon us, wouldn't you agree?"

"Yes, indeed!" Marie said, examining the seats. She hoped they were clean.

"Upon you, perhaps," Rachel sniffed. "I still think it's far too dangerous."

CW kept his eye on the screen. "Oh, that's not at all true. In fact, I'd wager that within a few years anyone who wishes will be able to make the same trip whenever he chooses. Of course, it won't be by airship. No, they're much too slow and ridiculous. Instead, we'll travel by airplane to every corner of the earth. Why, I wouldn't be surprised if one day I fly myself around the world in less time than it takes to sail from New York to London."

"Well, I'd prefer to go by sea," said Rachel. "Besides, it's much more romantic."

"Suit yourself," CW replied, "but soon enough you'll go alone. Why, even your sister-in-law is an experienced aviatrix." He grinned at Marie. "I doubt she'd rather trawl around the globe aboard a silly old steamship, would you, dear?"

Smoothing her skirt as she took the seat beside Rachel, Marie said,

"After today, if I were to travel around the world, I suppose I'd like to fly across land and sail between ports. Then I'd enjoy the best of both." Truth be told, after her experience today, she'd rather fly than be on the water any day of the week. Somehow, she no longer feared aviation as she did crossing a cold dark sea.

CW laughed. "That's very diplomatic!"

"Marie's quite clever," Rachel added. "I'm sure that's why my brother married her. He despises quarreling."

Four young men came down the aisle with bags of hot popcorn from Hooker's drugstore and sat down in the front row. When the pianist finished her song, the clattering noise of the projector filled the theater and the Metrotone News finished with a short segment that featured President Hoover offering encouragement to his fellow citizens from the steps of the White House. Then the screen went dark for a couple of minutes while the pianist played "Me and My Shadow" and the projectionist prepared a serial, *The Crimson Mystery*, which didn't really interest Marie much. Although she adored cartoons, in her opinion serials were for children whose attention spans were short enough to ignore the frustration of endings that weren't really endings. Also, whenever there was a chase in a cowboy serial, kids in the theater would begin kicking the seatbacks to mimic the galloping horses. Henry loved cowboy serials, except when a girl got kissed. Then he'd hide behind the seat. Marie found it stuffy in the auditorium of the Bijou, worsened by cigarette smoke and perspiration odor. In the balcony up above and behind her, voices of Negroes from Shantytown murmured to each other across the dark.

When the serial closed with another deadly climax, the screen went black. Rachel groaned as the pianist began playing "Beautiful Dreamer." Leaning toward Marie, she remarked, "If Mother were here, she'd stand up now and lead a sing-a-long."

Just then, a familiar voice spoke from the row behind her, "Well, who's the fresh number?"

Jimmy Delahaye stood with a sack of peanuts in one hand, a bottle of Coca-Cola in the other. He leaned down over Marie's shoulder, grinning. "So, honey, I see somebody's finally dragged you out to the picture show, after all."

Marie felt her heart skip a beat, a thrill she hadn't enjoyed in a while.

"We kidnapped her for the evening," Rachel replied on Marie's behalf. "She's been awful tired lately. Why, I hear you've been working the poor girl half to death."

"It hasn't been that bad," Marie offered, somewhat embarrassed now. She noticed that people were staring. She also knew she was blushing. Jimmy made her knees tremble.

"Well, she should've said something," Delahaye replied, his grin widening. "I'd have been more than happy to drag her out to a picture myself. She knows I'm that way about her."

He winked at Marie and she hid her eyes. Did he really know how she felt? Was it so obvious? She wondered if he intended to try and kiss her when the lights went down. *I must be losing my mind,* she thought.

"Don't tempt her," Rachel giggled. "Without Harry to hold her hand, Marie's been ever so lonely this summer."

"Rachel!"

"Well, it's true, isn't it?" Rachel giggled even more loudly now. "Everybody knows that a married woman has needs that aren't satisfied by housework or typewriting. For Godsakes, dear, even if he is my brother, I believe Harry's been a fool all summer long, and I hope you know it."

"Thank you very much, for telling the world." Marie prayed the movie would begin. Since being turned down on his invitation to a picture show that night of the Fourth, Delahaye had asked Marie more than a few times and on each occasion she had offered a silly alibi. Now Rachel's teasing was humiliating her. Certainly she wanted to go downtown with Delahaye one night. Perhaps she would soon enough. Husband or not, Harry didn't have a rope tied around her ankles, not forevermore.

"Well, I doubt it's been all that bad," said Delahaye, rising to his feet. "She doesn't seem that lonely to me."

"It's a clever ruse," Rachel asserted. "Trust me."

"I think Rachel talks too much," Marie said, glaring at her now. The fun was over. She wanted to watch the movie and not think about how she might behave with Jimmy Delahaye in the dark. Was she panting?

"I'll say she does," CW added, locking an arm around Rachel's shoulder, drawing her near. He kissed her flush on the mouth.

The auditorium went black.

Beside her, Marie saw Rachel rise wordlessly and slip past, moving toward the aisle. CW followed. Now the pianist began playing a soft lilting melody and the shuttering projector light flickered onto the screen as the credits ran. Delahaye climbed over into Marie's row and took Rachel's seat. He murmured, "Leonard says it'll be another month at least before the Bijou gets that Western Electric sound system. And the Vitaphone's not working, neither. I know living up north you're probably used to the talkies." Marie noticed he smelled like gin and witch hazel, yet she didn't mind at all.

Marie told him, "I haven't been to a picture show since last winter. Harry prefers going alone."

Delahaye chuckled. "Where's the fun of sitting in the dark all by yourself? I couldn't stand it. Not if I had a pretty wife at home."

Marie blushed. Had anyone heard him? What if everyone in town thought she flirted with Delahaye? What then? Delahaye took a cigarette out of his shirt pocket. He leaned close to her as he did, brushing his sleeve against her bare arm. She almost leaned back into his shoulder. Instead, she pretended to look where Rachel and CW had gone. She thought she heard them somewhere along the back row to the right of the door. *Up on the silver screen now, a pretty young brunette swings from the trapeze in the Big Top, soaring above the trick riders on horseback and the silly painted clowns.*

"I hate seeing pictures alone," Delahaye whispered, breathing on her cheek. His breath was hot and stale, but not unpleasant. She felt drawn to him.

"But you did come by yourself, didn't you?" Marie murmured, facing forward again. "I mean, you are here alone, aren't you?" Why had she asked him that?

"Not at all," Delahaye replied with a grin. He dipped a hand into the sack of warm peanuts, drew out a fistful, and dropped a couple into the bottle of Coke. "I'm here with you, honey."

Charlie Chaplin, dressed in his familiar costume as "The Tramp," ambled along the midway between the sideshows. Just the sight of his cane and bowler and his funny walk made Marie giggle. *After a pickpocketing dispute, he's chased into a mirror maze by the cops, then into the Big Top where the show is already started. He hides in a magician's cabinet, upsets the act, causing hilarity in the circus audience and ruining the humor of the real clowns who follow. The circus audience boos them and calls to "bring on the funny man!"*

"I saw you walking down the street with Rachel," Delahaye said, offering the sack of peanuts to Marie. Too nervous to eat a bite of anything, she shook her head politely and looked again for her sister-in-law and CW. Now she spotted them in a corner of the auditorium, nuzzling together in the shadows. Sex, sex, sex. Did Maude really know her daughter?

The pianist changed music, a lovely tune now, strains of sadness. *It's mealtime and the aerialist is hungry, but her boss won't let her eat. Meanwhile, he's decided to hire Charlie as a clown.*

Trying to be bold, Marie asked Delahaye, "Are you telling me you followed us in here? It's awfully peculiar. Why on earth would you do that?"

"Well, I thought you dropped something in the lobby, but when I went in, I saw it belonged to someone else. Of course, by then, I'd already bought myself a ticket, so I came on in and sat myself down. You know, I can't keep away from you." He poured a swig of Coke into his mouth. *Back up on the screen, morning has come and Charlie's boiling an egg in a tin can for breakfast. The poor girl still hasn't eaten and Charlie feels sorry for her and shares a piece of bread.*

Rachel's angry voice echoed across the auditorium. She was eye to eye with CW. Others in the back of the theater were watching her. A woman's voice yelled at Rachel to shut up. Rachel shouted a curse back and the pianist began playing more loudly. Somebody behind Marie blew cigar smoke toward the stage. Marie watched Rachel leave the auditorium, CW at her heels.

On the screen, a card read "The Tryout." *The circus owner is talking to Charlie. "Go ahead and be funny." Charlie plays a skit with a pair of clowns and fouls it up. "That's awful." They try something else, an archery joke.*

708 | MONTE SCHULZ

Now the pianist began playing the William Tell Overture. High in the balcony, the Negro crowd was mostly silent, the faint hot glow of cigarettes burning here and there in the dark. The projector stuttered slightly and the film slipped and blurred.

"Maybe I should go and see about Rachel," said Marie, glancing back up the aisle. Delahaye was leaning over her shoulder now, smelling her hair. She was certain he was about to kiss her and not certain whether she'd kiss him back or not, although she knew if she did, everyone in her family and on her block would think her a fool, and Harry would likely hear about it and probably leave her and the children in Texas forever. Well, maybe he'd take the children.

The rattling projector noise increased and the film smoothed out again. *Charlie disrupts the last tryout act by lathering the ringmaster's face with shaving cream. He's fired. "Get out and stay out!"*

"I'd keep out of her way tonight, if it was up to me," Delahaye replied, folding the empty sack of peanuts into his lap. He shifted his body closer to Marie.

Lucius Beauchamp stopped beside her seat and whispered at Delahaye. "Hey, Jimmy."

"Hey, Lucius! Come on in here!" Delahaye replied, pulling his legs back to make room.

"Excuse me, honey," Lucius whispered, slipping by as Marie folded her own legs inward, allowing him to pass. He stank of liquor and sweat. Idabelle had told her that Lucius brewed corn liquor in his basement and sold it in Longview. He drank all day long, but he was always polite to Marie who assumed liquor anesthetized a broken heart, though Lucius never mentioned a culprit.

The pianist began another sad melody. *Charlie thinks he's seeing his lovely aerialist for the last time. Then, outside the tent, there's trouble with the property men. No back pay. "They've quit." Charlie's hired. He's carrying a stack of plates when a mule chases him in the Big Top. He drops the plates and hides in the magic cabinet of Prof. Bosco - Magician. "Don't touch that button!" Birds, rabbits, geese, everywhere! Thinking Charlie's troubles are part of the show again, the audience roars with laughter. He's a sensation, but he doesn't know it! The ringmaster decides to let Charlie stay on. "Keep him busy and don't let him know he's the hit of the show!"*

Delahaye lit a cigarette and began talking about automobiles with Lucius. Marie decided she really ought to go see after Rachel. Also, she was uncomfortable sitting with Lucius who troubled her when he'd been drinking.

"Pardon me," Marie said, rising to leave. She felt agitated and near feverish from the heat. Or was it even the theater at all? In any case, she needed to get away from Delahaye, if only for a moment or two, so that she might regain her wits and good sense, provided she still had any.

"Don't go, honey," Delahaye said, grabbing her arm. "Picture's not over."

"I have to find Rachel," she replied, easing free of his grasp. "I'll come back." She hurried to the aisle, hoping Rachel and CW hadn't left without her. Delahaye called after her, but Marie walked out of the auditorium.

Except for a youth sweeping the carpet, the theater foyer was empty. One of the doors to the street was propped open and a draft passed throughout. Marie had no idea where Rachel and CW had gone. Across the lobby, a narrow carpeted stairway led up to the second floor balcony. There was a door at the top, half closed. A great roar of laughter issued from the darkness behind it.

"You looking for somebody, ma'am?" the boy with the broom asked. He collected the last of the refuse he'd pushed around into a dustpan.

"Did you see two people leave a few minutes ago?" Marie asked.

"Lady with a temper?"

Marie smiled. "And a tall fellow wearing a blue jacket."

"They beat it," replied the boy, dumping the contents of the dustpan into a trash can next to one of the theater doors.

"Do you have any idea where they went?" Marie asked, listening to the piano music from the auditorium, cheery now and bright. Perhaps Charlie had won the aerialist's heart, after all.

"Nope."

Marie frowned. Had they fought so harshly she'd been forgotten? She wondered what had set Rachel off, or if they'd simply chosen to rehash their earlier debate. The boy walked off toward the office.

Inside the auditorium, the pianist lightly fingered the keys, playing a pretty melody that was followed by a smattering of laughter from the audience. She looked up the stairs. Maybe that's where they'd gone. CW wouldn't have left without telling Marie. He had better manners than that, even if Rachel did not. Were they allowed upstairs? She decided to go have a look. What sort of trouble might it cause? Harry would suggest she mind her own business, but he wasn't here now, nor was the boy with the broom. Could she be arrested? She went up, anyhow.

At the top of the stairs, she stopped to listen at the door. The audience was laughing in the dark. She slipped inside and closed the door behind her. The heat here on the second floor of the theater was more suffocating than Maude's kitchen at midday. Cigarette smoke hung like gray haze. The walls smelled like fresh calcimine. She edged forward a couple of steps so that she could see the full balcony. The clattering projector sounded louder, too.

The lovely aerialist is pleading with Charlie. "Please don't do this!" It's no use. Charlie foolishly heads for the highwire. "You're on!" Above the upturned faces of the circus crowd, Charlie does a handstand, then a one-handed spin. Another trick. His harness breaks, but he doesn't know it! He dances about until he realizes he's balancing on his own and becomes jittery.

Searching the crowded rows, she didn't see Rachel or CW anywhere, but somewhere off to Marie's left, a burly Negro rose from his seat in the back row and climbed over into the narrow aisle. She backed up against the wall again and held her breath. He ambled across the rear of the balcony toward her. The audience laughed loudly. Marie felt him draw close as she lowered her eyes to the floor. Perhaps he'd pass and not notice her. The heat made her feel faint. He stopped a few feet nearby and leaned against the calcimined wall and drew a hip flask from his shirt pocket and took a sip. She saw him staring at her. Flickering light from the old projector danced on the seatbacks in front of Marie. The Negro lit a cigarette and exhaled smoke in her direction. She stifled a cough as her eyes watered. Her stomach felt queasy.

He spoke so closely now she felt his hot breath on her face, but the audience burst out in another roar of laughter, so Marie couldn't hear what he said. A Negro boy and girl seated two rows down in front of Marie leaned toward each other and kissed. The boy slipped his hand inside the girl's blouse. The large Negro mumbled something else she couldn't quite hear above the tittering crowd and slid a step closer, just off her shoulder now. Somebody wearing a porkpie hat down at the bottom row of the balcony lit a cigar and bent forward, propping his elbows on the brass railing.

"Honey, you oughtn't to be up here," the black man's voice murmured in Marie's ear, stink of gin and tobacco on his breath.

"I was looking for someone," she mumbled, as the audience laughed again.

"That's fine," he whispered. "It's just that they could be a misapprehension."

Now she knew how silly her plan had been, how idiotic and senseless. "I'm sorry."

She ran for the small door and rushed down the stairs, across the lobby and out to the sidewalk. She hurried a dozen yards up the street away from the Bijou theater, then stopped, her legs shaking. What in God's name had possessed her to go up into that balcony where she knew perfectly well she was not permitted? She felt both angry and embarrassed. Harry would have called what she'd just done idiotic, and Marie would have had no good counter to that. She remembered her mother lecturing once on curiosity when she was little, explaining that a closet locked is shut for a purpose and if that purpose were hers to know there'd be no need for the lock. She understood, of course, that the Negro hadn't meant to scare her. A woman's fear was both burden and blessing. Running out of the balcony had not humiliated her at all. Curiosity had done that. Probably she ought to have minded her own business and watched the picture show downstairs with her own crowd. Race was not supposed to be her concern. Or was it? She was reminded of what Maude had told her earlier in the summer. *What is in our hearts has been there since birth and we have not denied our inheritance. It is a fact and, though not all of us embrace it, we nevertheless accept what is, and will likely remain, part of our lives here in Bellemont.* Well, Marie also remembered Granny Chamberlain's Sunday dinner admonishment that *"Only a fool inherits the sinner's wisdom."*

It was late and the crowds she had seen downtown earlier had gone home for the night. A cool breeze carried the scent of pine trees and damp grass and the river farther off. The nightblue sky was lit with stars, quiet all about. A green Buick puttered by, an older man behind the wheel. He smiled at her as he passed. She pretended not to have noticed. Where had Rachel and CW gone? Why had they left her alone in the Bijou? Had they expected her to walk home by herself? How could they both be so rude?

Just then, a familiar voice called to her from down the sidewalk. "Darling, what's your hurry?"

Marie turned back toward the Bijou and saw Delahaye strolling toward her, burning cigar in hand. He wore his usual smile and seemed pleased to see her. *Well*, she thought, *at least someone is interested in my company tonight.*

Delahaye said, "I thought you were coming back."

She blushed. "That's right, I did say that, didn't I?" Once again, her heart fluttered felt like a schoolgirl's.

"I got lonely waiting on you when the show was over with and you weren't there." Delahaye gave her a wink as he puffed on his cigar. "They turned the lights out on me."

"Oh, they did not."

"Yes, ma'am. Just lonesome old Jimmy, there in the dark."

"Well, that seems awfully inconsiderate," Marie remarked, barely containing a smile. Suddenly, her evening had taken a turn for the better. "I hope you didn't bump your knee on the way out."

Delahaye laughed as he drew near. "Honey, that's the first nice thing you've ever said to me!"

"Why, that's not true," Marie protested. She felt almost giddy now. "Is it?"

"Cross my heart."

"Well, I'm sorry if it is, but, like most handsome men, you can be very difficult."

Her knees wobbled as she spoke the last of that. Never before in her life had Marie been so bold. She was out on a tightrope now, tiptoing into mid-air. What on earth was she doing?

Delahaye stepped close, looking her in the eyes. His own expression firmed up, his smile fixed and confident. "You make me feel handsome as hell."

Her throat tightening, Marie said, "You don't need any help with that."

"Thank you."

"You're very welcome."

They stood there on the sidewalk in the light evening breeze as a pair of motorcars drove past from downtown. Marie felt crazy and quick, desiring something she hadn't felt in years. A lunatic passion swept through her heart. Everything was racing so suddenly, she had fallen off-balance, lightheaded, confused. The automobiles disappeared and the street became quiet and she didn't notice anyone but Delahaye who asked if she'd care to be escorted home.

"Oh, I don't know," she replied, looking up and down the sidewalk.

"You shouldn't walk home alone."

"I believe you," Marie heard herself say, "but I'm just not sure I'm ready to go home at all. Not yet, anyhow."

Delahaye tossed his burnt cigar into the gutter. He reached out and touched her arm ever so gently. "Well, then, how about we take a walk somewhere?"

Marie needed only a moment to reply. "Yes, let's do that."

The more you fish for what you want, the less chance you have of getting it. Cissie quoted that line from one of her Oz books to Henry at supper last week when he was pestering her for a favor. As Marie strolled the dark sidewalks west of downtown with Delahaye, she wondered what she could possibly be fishing for herself. All her life she had craved that intimate heart to share things bleak and bright. Throughout her girlhood, Violet and Emeline heard her confessions and forgave her faults. On Cedar Lake, Harry swore an oath to take her part through any threat. Now, so much had fallen away, she could hardly recall any of her longings fulfilled. Perhaps her dreams had been misguided, her expectations unrealistic. Marie had never thought of herself as impetuous or flighty. Each decision, she believed, was made with great caution and consideration for all possible eventualities. Yet somehow she had been led to this estrangement from husband and blood relatives, so far from all she held dear, those old desires, how could she possibly find her way back again?

They walked several blocks into a part of town Marie didn't know very well, whose houses seemed large and fit with nice yards and trim fences and tall old trees for shade. This, too, was enlightening, because the very fact that she had neglected this neighborhood in what was a very small town, proved to her, once again, how much of her summer had passed housebound with Maude. Now tonight she felt bold somehow, adventurous, eager. Certainly it was late and she needed to get home to look in on the children, then put herself to bed so she'd have enough energy to face tomorrow, whatever puzzles might arise, but couldn't that wait? There still ought to be another hour just for her. Was that so terribly selfish?

"These homes are lovely," Marie remarked, as they strolled down the narrow sidewalk. She adored tall houses. Cedar Street had many of them, her old blue one at 119 as pretty as any.

"They sure are," Delahaye replied.

"I'll bet they're comfortable, too." She loved having a large bedroom and kitchen, and an attic upstairs to store things away. When Harry called them back to Farrington, Marie vowed to find another house with big rooms and private corners, all her own. "I'd be awfully curious to have a peek inside."

"Even if the owners weren't home?"

Marie giggled. "Oh, I don't know that I'd be that brave. I'd hate to be arrested. What would I say to the children?"

"Who's to say you'd get caught?"

"What if I did?"

"What if you didn't?" Delahaye replied, with a sweet endearing smile. "What if you just tiptoed right up to, say, that house there at the end of the block and snuck inside for a look-see? Who'd be worse off for that? You wouldn't steal anything, would you?"

Marie barely suppressed a laugh. "Of course not!"

"Well, there you go. Why not do it? Right now, in fact." He picked up his pace, heading along the sidewalk toward the house in question, a fairly elegant two-story pale green framehouse with a gallery on both floors and thick bougainvillea blooming scarlet on the sides. Marie hurried to keep up. He was joking, wasn't he? She presumed he was, but her heart began pounding with the excitement of it all. Once they drew near to the old house, Delahaye stopped beneath a towering elm. The window shades were drawn shut and the interior was dark, offering not a hint whether anyone was home.

"All right," he said, lowering his voice to a murmur. "Here we are."

"Are you daring me to go in?"

He smiled. "I'm double-daring you."

"What? Nobody's double-dared me since Cousin Emeline thought I was afraid to eat an earthworm." Marie steeled her eyes. "She paid off with her favorite doll, Baby Margaret."

"Gee, I don't have a doll."

"I'd think of something."

"I'm not worried, because I know you won't go in."

"What if the door's locked? I hope you don't expect me to break a window."

"Nobody locks their doors in this town," Delahaye said, stepping out from under the tree. "Go ahead, see for yourself."

Marie stepped out, too. "Maybe I will."

"Maybe you won't."

With that, Marie did something she never in her life would have believed she was capable of doing. She left Delahaye on the sidewalk and strode through the yard gate, then up the wide stairs to the front door and tried the front door latch.

The old oak door swung open to a dark foyer.

Startled to her toes, Marie almost ran off.

Behind her, Delahaye called out, "What did I tell you?"

"Shhh!"

She stared into the unlit entry, listening for approaching footsteps. She leaned inside for a furtive peek. Delahaye joined her on the threshold.

"Not going in?" he asked. "Too scared?"

Like a ghost, she slipped past him onto the carpet runner that led off into the shadows. The house had a curious odor, neither musty nor florid, but quite pleasant, something like lemon blossoms and wood polish, as if the place had just undergone a visit by diligent housecleaners. Delahaye eased the door closed behind her.

"What are you doing?" she whispered, then held her breath to listen once again for the legitimate occupants. She was scared to death, but excited, too, particularly knowing that Harry would never do anything like this himself. Would he even believe where she was right now?

Delahaye lit a match.

When the light flared, Marie saw how near they were standing to the parlor and a curved staircase up to the second floor. The entry hall led off to the back of the house, presumably to a kitchen, and all of this much bigger than Maude's home on College Street. Her heart was racing. She felt wicked and it thrilled her. Suddenly, she wanted to explore the downstairs, room by room. Perhaps nobody was home, and if they were, well, that made it all the more exciting. She'd be quiet as a mouse and nobody would ever know she was here.

The match went out and everything was black once again. Delahaye put his hand on Marie's shoulder and she felt a flush in her cheeks. Whatever trouble she might be getting herself into, at least Jimmy was beside her to share. Somehow Marie found it difficult to believe James B. Delahaye would do anything that might get him tossed into jail. He seemed too self-assured, too clever for that. She admired his confident demeanor, never letting anyone cross him at work, bending people's will to his own needs. If he thought sneaking into someone's home in the middle of the night was a good lark to pursue, why, by all means open the door! Maybe she needed a little of that herself.

"Are you thirsty?" Delahaye whispered in her ear.

"Hmm?"

"There's a liquor cabinet in the kitchen."

"How do you know that?"

"Come with me," he murmured, gently taking Marie's hand and leading her down the darkened hall.

"This is positively insane," she whispered, stepping quietly. What if the owners were home, after all, and came downstairs with a shotgun? Or they telephoned the police and she got arrested? How could she possible explain any of this to Maude or the children, or Harry, for that matter? He'd think she'd lost her mind, and he'd be right.

Once in the kitchen, Delahaye began searching through a cupboard above the ice-box, and whistling!

"Shhh!" Marie hissed at him.

"Found it."

Delahaye switched on the kitchen light.

Marie's nearly fainted from shock. "Are you crazy?"

"No," he said, calmly. "Why?"

"We're going to get caught!" Marie exclaimed, trying to keep her voice down, though Delahaye didn't seem to care about that. "Good grief!"

He shook his head. "No, we're not."

"No? What if the owners are home?"

"Actually," Delahaye opened the mahogany cupboard directly in front of them and took out a bottle of Scotch, "he is."

Marie frowned, utterly confused now. "Pardon me?"

"He's home this very moment and standing right beside you," Delahaye announced in that authoritative voice he used upstairs in the restaurant office, "and he doesn't mind one bit that you're here."

A trick!

And she'd fallen for it. Good heavens, he'd scared her to death. Delahaye laughed and went to another cupboard and found a couple of shotglasses. Marie felt both embarrassed and relieved.

"I grew up in this house," Delahaye said, as he poured them both a drink. "When my folks passed away, I took it over. I guess it's solid enough to see me off, too, when the Lord comes around. Here."

He handed her a shotglass of Scotch, barely wet.

"Oh, I don't think I ought to," she told him, watching the golden whiskey sparkle under the glow of the kitchen lamp. "I really don't drink liquor."

"Just a nip won't hurt."

"Well, it's awfully late, too."

"It'll help you sleep. Believe me."

Marie felt he was daring her again and wasn't certain she was interested this time. Hadn't she already proven her courage just sneaking into the house? Liquor of any sort gave her a headache, though she'd sipped peach brandy at Emeline's on more blue afternoons than she'd care to recall. Besides, what kind of invitation was Delahaye really offering? She'd gone for a walk with him and now she was in his house. Yet part of Marie didn't care in the least, and that's what gave her the greatest worry. She saw herself reeling out of control and could scarcely put a halt to it. She drank the Scotch whiskey in one gulp, and winked as she handed the shotglass back to Delahaye.

He laughed. "I thought you wouldn't."

"Never predict a woman's behavior. We're very mysterious creatures."

Why was she talking like that? What had come over her? Stepping out with a fellow who wasn't Harry, and drinking liquor after dark?

"Would you like to see some of the house?" Delahaye asked, draining his own shotglass. His eyes sagged from the booze, but he spoke clearly. "I've been fixing it up."

In fact, yes, she did want to see his home, if only to gain a better sense of him. Also, she loved comparing how people lived. Back in Farrington, Marie and Emeline used to make a game of getting themselves invited to homes all over town. Aunt Hazel thought it shameful to pry, and told them so one Sunday in front of the entire family. *We are each of us just where we belong,* she lectured, *and it is our duty to try and find our own duty and not to get into the duty of another.* True enough, yet everyone knew Hazel herself smiled at Hiram Johnson when he was married and was first to offer her condolences when poor Eleanor was run over by a haywagon. *Where was the harm,* Emeline argued, *in counting a neighbor's doilies?*

"If we're quick about it," Marie told Delahaye, a yawn coming on. "I really ought to get home, don't you agree?"

"They got you on a curfew over there?"

"Of course not," she replied, somewhat testily. Did he think she was a milquetoast? "It's just sensible, that's all. I keep my own hours." An obvious lie, simply because of the children. Oh, she was becoming more and more confused now over what to say and how to act.

"Come here," Delahaye said, guiding her back toward the hallway. "Let me show you something."

Though still black as pitch, the big house didn't seem as forbidding to Marie now that she wasn't a burglar. Delahaye led her into the front parlor where he switched on a brass table lamp. It was a lovely room of walnut bookcases, a carved mahogany library table, overstuffed sofas and armchairs, an Eastlake parlor organ, lambrequins covering pedestal tables, a tile-and-wood mantel and beveled mirror, paintings and portraits hung on the walls, lace curtains draping the windows to the street. Not the sort of thing she would ordinarily have associated with a man of Jimmy Delahaye's taste and sympathies, given the look of his office downtown.

"Momma's favorite room," Delahaye told her, by way of explanation for the old-fashioned furnishings and appointments. He smiled. "I wasn't allowed in here until I grew up."

"Your mother must've been a smart woman," Marie said, admiring the old burgundy fabric on the organ stool. "I doubt I'd have let you play in here. It's much too wonderful for little boys."

"What if I told you I was well-behaved?"

Marie smiled. "I wouldn't believe it for an instant."

"Well, let me show something," Delahaye said, going to a cabinet beneath the bookcase on far wall. Marie followed as Delahaye popped it open to draw out a gilded birdcage. He set it on a small marble top table. "Listen."

He tipped it over and wound a small brass key like a clock, then put the birdcage upright once again. Within the cage was a tiny yellow mechanical songbird. When Delahaye nudged a small lever on the lower side of the cage, the hand-feathered bird began to sing.

"Oh my goodness!" Marie exclaimed, utterly enchanted. It was one of the most beautiful things she had ever seen. How on earth could a human hand build a bird that sang so exquisitely? "It's so life-like."

"This was her favorite toy." Delahaye was standing now so close to Marie she could smell the Scotch on his warm breath. "It's pretty, huh?"

"Very."

Then he wrapped her hand into his palm, entwining fingers, squeezing gently. "But it doesn't hold a candle to you, darling."

Suddenly, Marie grew faint, her heart pulsing wildly, legs slumping. *Is this why he brought me here? And why I followed?* Delahaye leaned down to kiss her neck and Marie froze. His mouth was hot as he grazed her ear.

"That bird's in a cage just like you are," he murmured awkwardly.

"What a silly thing to say," she argued, barely able to breathe. "I'm not in a cage." *Is that what he thinks of me? A pathetic captive in my own marriage?*

The bird's delicate song began to fray as the clockwork ran down.

"You just deserve better," Delahaye whispered, kissing Marie's cheek.

Never in her life had she been so frightened. A flush bloomed through her body. Her eyes teared. She yearned to lie down. What on earth had persuaded her to sneak into this house tonight?

Delahaye maneuvered them face-to-face and kissed her passionately on the mouth, and she kissed him back. He urged himself against her, entangling her, kissing her shamelessly now, illicitly. Marie offered no resistance. And why should she? Wasn't this why she was here? How cowardly to flee from one's own seduction!

Delahaye tussled his thick fingers into her hair, kissed her cheek, her neck, her ear. Marie breathed his bitter whiskey odor and held him tightly and kissed his chin. How foolish was she to be here like this? Delahaye mumbled a lustful suggestion into her ear and Marie retreated to the sofa where she flopped back against a pair of soft chenille cushions, preparing to shame herself if that's what Jimmy Delahaye desired. He loosened his tie, then shed it along with his coat, and slid onto the sofa to claim her. His gaze was lopsided but solemn, his lips swollen as he moved to straddle her. Marie lay back in a bewildering trance, her soul gaping and lunatic. Her eyelids fluttered, her fingers felt cool and feathery. Astonished by her wilting resolve to be good, she awaited Delahaye's carnal embrace, and, indeed, prayed he'd be swift and irreverent.

And then —

A crash of metal ashcans clattered onto the sidewalk as a motorcar roared out of the driveway next door. Youthful voices yelled out in drunken laughter.

Marie perked her head up.

And, just as suddenly, she became aware of a face hovering over hers that wasn't Harry's, and a duplicitous romance she needed to flee this very instant.

Marie sighed, sobering up.

Delahaye saw it in her eyes as she squirmed beneath him. Flatly, he said, "You need to go home, right?"

She nodded, guilt flooding her with breathtaking grace. "I really ought to."

Delahaye stepped back to let her rise from the sofa. There was a sudden hush between them as Marie stood and collected herself in the golden lamplight. She felt clumsy, fallen, and yearned for fresh air out of doors. How big a mistake this had been, if at all, did not concern her just yet. First she wanted to escape with her dignity.

Delahaye switched off the table lamp, darkening the front of the house, for which Marie was grateful. He followed her to the door where he offered to walk her home. She asked how far Maude's house was, and when he told her, she said, "In that case, thank you, but I guess I'd rather go alone, if that's all right. It's so close, and I'm not at all worried anymore."

Letting her out onto the shadowed gallery, Delahaye gently kissed Marie's cheek as he whispered, "Honey, don't be ashamed of falling for someone other than Harry. There's nothing wrong with it. Show a little faith in yourself."

— 5 —

Arriving at Maude's house in the dark, Marie found Rachel sitting alone on the bottom step of the front porch smoking one of her modern Tarryton Spuds. CW's Ford was gone. Marie looked at the window beside the chinaberry tree and saw her own bedroom was dark, the children likely sound asleep. Rachel spoke from the steps, her voice flat and low. "I must've been insane to involve myself with that man. He's entirely too arrogant and selfish."

"I looked for you two all over," said Marie, still somewhat miffed at being abandoned at the theater, despite her confusing transgression with Delahaye. Since when had Rachel become incapable of seeing past her own nose? "You left without me. I hadn't any idea where you'd gone."

"I tell you, he's mean-spirited and vain."

"And how was I supposed to know you'd left?"

Rachel tapped cigarette ash into the dust below the step. "Why, he's the most disagreeable person I've ever known. Of course, any chance of an engagement is off. I hope I never see him again."

Marie stopped at the trellis of nightblooming jasmine as a bony white cat dashed across the street into the dark brush beyond. Unable yet to know how she felt about her own evening out, Marie told her sister-in-law, "I just think that was very inconsiderate."

"Of course."

Noticing that Rachel had been weeping, Marie relented somewhat. "I thought you two were in love."

Wiping a tear from her cheek, Rachel shook her head. "Oh, I doubt I've ever been in love. I'm not that big a fool. All men want is somebody to show off for. Someone to listen to all their dirty little lies. Why, not one of them even believes in love."

"Did he say why he left?"

"I asked him to," replied Rachel. She puffed once on the cigarette, then exhaled smoke into the dark and drew a deep breath, trying to compose herself. "He's held a low and ugly opinion of us for as long as I've known him. Well, mostly of Mother, but I suppose he finds me guilty by association. Yet I should say it's he who's bigoted and narrow. Why, I've never harbored the slightest resentment toward any Catholic man, woman or child. I'd be ignorant to do so! In fact, I don't believe I know the first thing about the Pope, and don't care to. It's just not my concern, and I've told CW so on several occasions. But that's not enough for him. Not by a long shot. No, he's got to prove that being a Baptist ought to be legal grounds for having oneself institutionalized. Well, it's plain enough for anyone to see that he looks down on us and that just being here causes him the worst manner of suffering. So, I merely suggested that as an act of mercy I hereby relieve him of any obligation to set foot in this stupid town again."

Despite her own disturbingly indiscrete brush with romance, Marie found herself still upset with Rachel whose selfishness was inexcusable. What was she supposed to say, anyhow? CW wasn't her problem. So, all that came out of her mouth was that same white lie she'd begun with. "I walked back here all alone in the dark. Did you expect me to wait there all night?"

Rachel shook her head. "It's just silly to imagine that a man like him actually cares about someone enough to marry her. Mother was here when we returned from downtown, you know. She saw CW drive off and thought he was behaving awfully cruelly to me. Of course, it was impossible for her to fully take my side. In fact, she had the gall to suggest that I ought to keep a keener eye out for the men I choose to see, as if I deliberately ask to be punished like this. Why, it just burns me up! Sometimes I think I should do like Harry, just pack up and drive somewhere far away and forget I ever knew her. Now, that'd teach Mother a lesson, wouldn't it?"

Rachel extinguished the cigarette in the dirt. She stood and brushed off her skirt. "Well, I simply refuse to pretend any longer that he and I share even the slightest compatibility. I suppose I was blinded by the flattery of his attentions. We each have our own silly weaknesses, don't we? Mother assured me a Catholic could no more be content here in Bellemont than a Baptist in Rome. Of course, she's just as insane as he is. Mother doesn't know one iota more about the Catholic Church than CW does about Baptists, but I simply could not tolerate his hatred of Bellemont. We may be small-minded and ridiculous, but there's no deception to it, and nobody cares what he thinks, anyhow. Who says a Negro from Shantytown couldn't have murdered Boy-Allen? That's utterly absurd! I told him to go fly home to Louisiana tonight and forget he ever called on me. If I never see that man again, I'll be happier than I have been all summer long."

Then Rachel went up the stairs and back indoors.

Except for a lamp lit in the back hall, the house was quiet and dark. Sneaking inside, Marie could smell the gingerbread cookies Maude had cooked after supper. An aroma of cinnamon tea and lemon floated in the kitchen hallway and made Marie desperately wish she had stayed home for the evening, played games with the children, and written another letter to Harry explaining the difficult circumstance of being without him. She crept quietly into the bedroom and checked to see that Henry was asleep. Her dear little one had been awake most of the night before suffering troublesome dreams. Cissie had told him a bogeyman lived underneath the house and that unless he swore never to draw in her Oz books again so long as he lived the creature would steal him away after midnight and either sell him to a thieving gypsy or eat him for supper. Tonight, he slept quietly. So did his cantankerous sister. The window facing the pretty chinaberry tree was cracked open an inch admitting a mild draft that cooled the room. Marie changed into her slipover gown and folded her dress and dropped it quietly into the laundry basket. Walking back and forth from downtown had soiled the hemline with dust. She would wash it tomorrow.

Returning to the kitchen for a glass of water, she heard Rachel fidgeting in her own bedroom. How could anyone be so self-centered? She didn't seem to care about anyone's feelings but her own. What did Rachel even know about love? Still, knowing how difficult love can be, Marie tried to feel sorry for her. A romantic separation was always cruel, and the tears Marie had seen on Rachel's face were genuine. Anger only lessened sorrow; it did not relieve it for long. She knew this to be true from years of bitter disputes with Harry, who rarely allowed his own anger to relent. He preferred his constant solitudes and the festering of grudges that made him mean and selfish.

Marie looked out the back porch window. Next door, a light was on inside the Jessup's house, Lili's mother or uncle moving about, restless in the heat. Marie hadn't met Lili's father, Howard Jessup. He labored in the oil fields a hundred miles to the south and rarely came home. Lately, since Mildred's brother Fritz had come from Tallahachee to live with her and Lili, Mildred didn't act as though she missed Howard much at all. Perhaps it was true. Sometimes love evaporates into a sullen nothingness between two people and cannot be retrieved, eventually passing away forever. After enough time has gone by, both forget it had been there at all. But probably Lili hadn't. She would see herself as proof that her father and mother had loved each other once, yet not fully understand why they no longer did. Perhaps children knew more about love than they ought to.

Marie drank her water, rinsed the glass out and put it up in the cupboard, then tiptoed back to the bedroom. Rachel's light had gone off and Marie heard no more sounds behind her door. On her own dresser was an envelope she hadn't noticed before, a letter from Harry to Maude, left for Marie to read. She took it in hand, and went to her old steamer trunk for something else her strange mood compelled her to fetch, a blue cardboard shoebox of postcards and letters and notes from Harry she had saved since that first summer when she was sixteen and Harry Hennesey was "that most intriguing young salesman from Texas" her cousins fawned over and her mother warned her to avoid. Marie brought the old shoebox and Maude's letter from Harry with her into the front room where she could sit under the reading lamp and not disturb anyone while she read. The letter was brief.

Warsaw Hotel
Box 14, 254 Jackson St.
August 2, 1929

Dear Mother,

I am sending along thirty dollars as per our agreement and intend to send another twenty no later than next week. Charles Follette has been gracious enough to defer my debt to next month in exchange for a percentage of my commission on the sales I've managed recently. He is tough yet honest and I believe we've struck a fair bargain. There's been no hardship on my part. I am well and busy. The Kogan deal is still in the making and may materialize. I'm hopeful because I just received a note today from Mr. McDonald saying that unless I pay at least part of the rent by Saturday next he will have to ask for my apartment. Last week he put a tenant into the street for one month's arrears.

I hope you can help Marie for she is making such a grand fight to make a go of her job. You remember I told you that she thinks that you think she is out of her league. Be sure to let her see how you admire her ability and determination. I really believe she has more to her than any of the women her age in Bellemont. She sees lots of things that the rest of us are blind to. I sure take my hat off to her. Please give her and the children all my love and best wishes.

Your faithful son,
Harry

With a peculiar ache in her bosom, Marie slipped the letter back into the envelope and opened the blue shoebox and began sorting through the other envelopes and carefully folded notes. Harry had pursued her like a crazy schoolboy for six years, arriving by train once a month and staying a weekend at the Excelsior Hotel in east Farrington. He would telephone an hour after checking into his room and visit her on the farm before sundown. When she went off to Stout to study Domestic Science, he called on her at the dormitory by six o'clock every third Friday for two years until she graduated and returned to Farrington where his routine at the Excelsior began again. He had a patience her father found perplexing, and a talent for flattery both Violet and Emeline admired. Flowers and clever postcards. Saturday picnics in the shaded meadows about Farrington. Sunday outings after church with her family. Little affections to seal her confidence. Marie knew Harry loved her. He gave her a thousand reasons to trust her heart, and so when he joined them on Easter holiday at Cedar Lake, and floating her away in the canoe like a yellow water-lily to tell her all that was in his own heart that warm April evening, by moonlight she accepted his proposal.

Marie reached into the box and sorted through several envelopes until she came across a section of newspaper clipped out of the Farrington *Herald-Dispatch* by Cousin Emeline fourteen years ago: her wedding announcement, dated June 17th 1915.

Hennesey-Pendergast

One of the first peony weddings of the season was solemnized last evening at 8:30 p.m. in the home of Mr. and Mrs. Louis M. Chamberlain, 540 Pillsbury Avenue, when their niece, Miss Marie Alice Pendergast became the bride of Mr. Harold Louis Hennesey. A color scheme of pink and white predominated and masses of pink and white peonies were artistically arranged throughout the house. Miss Florence Dow of Chicago, friend of the family, sang, "I Gave You a Rose" and "O, Radiant Hour"... The bridegroom and his best man, Mr. Victor Ferguson, son of Mr. and Mrs. Archibald M. Ferguson of St. Paul, entered together and they were followed by Miss Violet Pendergast, first cousin of the bride, who was a bridesmaid ... Miss Emeline Chamberlain, a second cousin of the bride, who was maid of honor, preceded the bride... The Misses Margaret Rutherford and Lucy Leonard, who were classmates of the bride at Stout Institute, Menominee, Wis. were ribbon stretchers. Receiving with the bride and bridegroom were the bride's parents, Mr. and Mrs. Harlow H. Pendergast, Miss Emma Pendergast, aunt of the bride and Mrs. H.P. Pendergast, grandmother of the bride... Mr. Hennesey and his bride left on a motor trip and they will be at home after July 1, at 119 Cedar Street.

Marrying in the shaded flower garden at Emeline's house had been Harry's desire. He despised the farm where Marie's family had expected the wedding ceremony to be held. Emeline agreed that the delicate floral decorations might spoil in the heat and dust and promised Marie to lend her own bedroom to the bridesmaids. More than a hundred people attended and when Harry whispered his love to her as she took his ring, her heart swelled with joy. Afterward, they enjoyed a lovely honeymoon at the Grand Hotel on Mackinac Island, and when they moved into the pretty blue house on Cedar Street, Marie placed some reminder in each room — a glass flower, a Japanese fan, a handtinted postcard, a sweet notion — that by touch or glance might restore some small hint of that wonderful courtship. Whenever Harry traveled away now on one of his business trips, she would choose a memory in the dark and hold it close, praying that Harry loved her still as she knew he had in that summer long ago.

Marie brushed the curtains back with her fingers as a motorcar clattered by toward downtown. Several autos had passed as she walked home from Delahaye's house and she had taken great care to stay deep in the tree shadows, praying not to be seen. That fear was greater now than any she had of Boy-Allen's killer. Flushed with worry and confusion, Marie rummaged deeper in the shoebox, sorting here and there, glancing at envelopes whose contents she hadn't studied in many years, still searching for one item in particular. She paused at a slip of paper that had lost its envelope, a brief note Harry had sent to her a year ago from St. Paul, his first visit to Minnesota since they had passed a sad season in the upstairs of the Fergusons' grand Summit Avenue residence in the summer of 1920. He had composed it on a piece of fine stationery from the Nicollet Hotel and hired a courier to deliver it by sundown directly to the front porch at 119 Cedar Street where he knew she would be sitting at that hour. It read:

Dearest Marie,

I drove out today by the Lake of the Isles. I stopped at the bridge over the channel into Cedar Lake and looked out over the lake. Then I began remembering. In my vision I saw a canoe and a boy and a girl. He was pretty hopeful, in his opinion, when he began a little story — a story as I remember, of his life and his hopes — and ended with a proposal to that girl. He told her he was proposing when she was too young, but he still hoped.

The lake was still there, but each drop of water is a new one. The blades of the grass along the shore are new. Every fish in the lake is new. But the islands are there and the trees are the same ones. The air is different air. But one thing hasn't changed. That man felt he was with the girl he wanted to be with for the rest of his life. And he still feels the same way. Although more than a decade has passed, he knows that as far as he is concerned, he made no mistake. She is still the object of his love, but deeper and broader than it was then.

I remember the wedding, the days that followed, the weeks, months and years. I remember the joys of anticipated and realized children. I remember, with a sweet but heart-tightening memory that still chokes me and brings the tears, the little fellow whom God let us have for a while. His little self lies not a short distance from where I am and where I expect to lie beside him. And there is no terror about it. It is life …

"Marie?"

Rachel stood in the hall wearing her pink nightgown, tears again on her face. Marie dropped the letter back into the box. Rachel's voice had startled her and her hand shook.

Rachel said, "I'm sorry I left you at the picture show. I was upset with CW, but I know that forgetting about you was inexcusable. Please accept my apology." She lowered her eyes, clearly humiliated by the entire episode.

"I forgive you," said Marie, closing the box. What else could she do? Whose sin was greater tonight? She shifted in the chair to face Rachel. "I admit to being angry myself, but I was also concerned for you both. My mother always says that quarreling worries the heart while solving little and leaving scars that heal too slowly. It does pierce me very cruelly to see either of you hurt."

Rachel walked into the room and sat on the piano bench. She wiped a tear off her cheek, then folded her hands into her lap. She looked tired and sad. "Well, I'm afraid one of us is already hurt. I can't explain why, but I was horribly mean to CW tonight. I lost all sense of proportion and just made a grand to-do out of nothing. I must be crazy."

"You poor dear," replied Marie, offering a sympathetic smile. Who hasn't known heartache and sorrow? "Why, I'm sure he'll be feeling just as badly tonight."

"Oh, I'm sure he doesn't care at all. Why should he? I've treated him as rotten as anyone who's ever called on me. I've no idea how he's been able to stand me for this long, except that he's got the patience of a saint. I've had a horrid temper all summer now, yet he's only raised his voice with me once."

"He loves you," said Marie, trying to sound hopeful. "Isn't it obvious?"

"He's from a fine family, did you know that? Very well-to-do, in fact. Catholic, of course, being third generation New Orleans. They own a grand old home near the Vieux Carré. CW himself lives in a garden cottage that used to be a Creole house built by a family of mulattos. His grandfather owned a plantation and his mother's family were merchants from Amsterdam. Isn't that romantic?"

Though entirely unfamiliar with Louisiana history, Marie smiled. "It's very interesting."

"The point is, CW's family has more money than all the wealthiest people in Bellemont taken together. They're invested in business ventures all across the South and are very well thought of in New Orleans society. CW's told me of garden parties his mother's given where the guest list runs into the hundreds, can you imagine?"

"No, I can't. Where would everybody sit?"

Rachel returned a brief smile, but her unhappiness persisted. "Compared to any girl he's known in New Orleans, I'm hopelessly plain."

"Of course you're not."

"Yes, I am, and Mother knows it better than anyone. Our entire family is common as ditchwater, except for Harry, of course, who had the genius to go away and make something of himself. Why CW ever called on me at all is an utter mystery. The fact that it was I who sent him away and not the reverse just proves the point. He had no business engaging himself to a silly Baptist girl who's nothing more than a stupid secretary in an insurance office. Well, the mistake's been corrected now, hasn't it? I doubt I'll ever hear from him again." Rachel slumped against the piano next to the metronome, tears running on her cheeks once more.

"You love him, don't you?" Perhaps it was more than sex-madness between them, after all.

Rachel nodded, blinking tears from her eyes. "You wouldn't understand how."

"Well, then, if it were me, I think I'd wire him a telegram in the morning."

"Pardon?"

"You know, we've all had words with those we love at one time or another, things we ought not to have said, isn't that true? Ordinarily, you seem quite happy together."

Rachel wiped another tear away, a frown on her face. "Why, I'm afraid these were more than words. I deliberately humiliated him, practically associating him with those Negroes he seems to adore so much. I'm sure any wire he received now from me would go straight into the trash. Nor would I blame him. I've done it and I'll have to accept the consequences. That's all there is to be said."

"Well, of course it isn't," Marie argued, impatience with Rachel rising inside her. "You're being foolish now." Why are lovers so foolish? Is pride more dear than true affection?

"I wish I were."

"And feeling sorry for yourself, too. What does your mother always say? Self-pity is a beggar's vanity."

Rachel forced a grin. "Why, if Mother had her way, I'd spend the rest of my life right here with her, an old maid washing clothes and playing Hearts every damned evening until the day I die. Besides, with Mother pulling against CW since he and I first met, what chance have I had?"

"Wire him a telegram in the morning. Admit you were wrong. Apologize and ask him if he can't fly back on Saturday."

"Oh, I haven't the nerve," Rachel said, getting up from the piano bench. "I'm afraid he'd say no, in which case I'd probably wish I were dead."

Another automobile drove past outside, its driver hollering out a strange profanity that caught Rachel's attention. She went to the window and pulled the curtain aside. After muttering someone's name Marie hadn't heard before, she let the curtain fall closed, then remarked, "I just believe that CW deserves to court a girl who appreciates his good qualities, perhaps someone of his faith, as well, although did you know he hasn't attended Mass since Easter? Well, it's the truth. If Mother had known that, I'm sure she'd have been much happier with my seeing him."

"Listen to me, please," Marie told Rachel in all earnestness. "If you don't at least make the gesture of conciliation, you'll never forgive yourself. If you truly believe he loves you, allow him another chance to prove it."

Rachel wiped another tear from her cheek with the sleeve of the nightgown. She walked across the room to the front door and opened it and looked out into the road. After a few minutes she closed the door, and turned to Marie. "All right, I'll wire an apology in the morning. I doubt he'll respond, but at least I'll have made the attempt, isn't that so?"

"Yes."

"Are you happy now?"

Marie smiled. "Very."

"Then I'm going to bed," Rachel said, heading for the hallway. At the threshold to the hallway, she paused long enough to say, "Thank you, dear."

Marie nodded. "You're quite welcome."

After Rachel had gone back to her room, Marie reopened the blue box and continued searching for her most treasured memento from that long-ago courtship. In her own girlhood, love and romance had occupied her waking thoughts more completely than she had ever dreamt possible. According to dear Auntie Emma, love was a fever in the blood cured only by a sweetheart's kiss. Marie felt sorry for Rachel. Whose broken heart prevails, unmended by a lover's ardent hand? She wondered, did marriage truly provide rescue or relief from the vicis-situdes of romance? Will all worries linger long after those vows are taken?

Near the bottom of the old shoebox, wrapped in a lace handker-chief, a slender blue "book" smaller than her own hand enclosed a typed letter offered to Marie as a gift by Harry on the occasion of her twenty-first birthday. She drew it out, unfolded the lace. On the front cover, lettered in white against the sea-blue paper was written:

To Miss Marie Alice Pendergast
Sept. 17, 1892 ---- Sept. 17, 1913

On several tiny neatly spaced pages, he had composed a typewrit-ten letter of a sort she had hardly expected, even from Harry.

Dear Marie:

Time was when you regarded the age of twenty-one with some apprehension, not unmixed with awe. You could have anticipated nothing more dismal than to have reached that age and be neither married nor engaged. As a matter of fact, though, actual mar-riage itself would have appeared fully as undesirable.

What sort of girl have you come to be? I am going to do a daring thing. I am going to see if I can guess correctly how a young girl has felt in the four years before the present, drawing a conclusion — perhaps — as to how she views things at this mature age.

Do you know, the words of some of these "popular songs" often surprise me, as much as I dislike the most of them. Somehow men seem to have given expression in some of the songs to thoughts that occur to the most of us.

"When I first met you" — do you remember when that was? I do. It was at Cedar Lake during the summer of 1909, when your Uncle Harlow first got his Stanley steamer, the car that was to revolutionize the automobile business. You had just turned sev-enteen. Weren't you young then, though? Yet, you had not gotten

over talking about the husband you were going to have. We were
out riding in the Stanley, you and the rest of the family and I,
only a month before our night at Big Island Park. Try as I will,
I can't remember what was said, but it was something about your
future husband. You suddenly realized there was a 'man' along;
he fitted the description — and you looked fixedly ahead while the
family laughed. Perhaps I blushed. It didn't take much to make
me blush then. Now I am a hardened criminal.

So there you were — seventeen years old. Men? They hadn't entered your horizon in reality, although you read over and over
the 'touching' parts in the novels. You could have told 'him'
just when to draw you to him and enclose your hand in his. But
a real man! Huh! Let Emeline go with 'em, if she wants to. I
don't. They're too much bother.

Am I right?

It was in the spring of 1910, when you were still seventeen,
but fast nearing eighteen, when Violet went East. Do you remember "our" first party? The machine brought our little patrician
in a white sweater to the bridge over the tracks at Lake Poague.
From there we went to the Griffith's where you played the Melody
in F and I told them what it was. I knew the names of about
three pieces in those days and that was one. I know but very
few more now. No one could have suspected my deep-laid plot to
finally settle on the owner of the pretty black hat.

But, alas, my too-frequent attentions brought out a trait
of your nature, peculiar to the age of eighteen. People saw us
together one time. Very well. They saw us together again. Still
all right. They saw us together a third time. They invited us
together at a picnic. Himmel! Do people think he has strings
on me? I'll show him. No, thank you, I'm sorry, and you would
grab Harlow by the arm and say, "Come on, Unc", smiling a sweet
goodnight to me over your shoulder. (Really, though, there is
a period of a boy's life when a rebuff is a good thing. It cul-
tivates patience in him.) This was a real, girlish turndown or
flyaway — not a turndown in the real sense, but a will-o'-the-

wisp sort of attitude that was due to an inward clinging to girlhood freedom — a dislike of even having people say you had a 'sweetheart'.

What kind of a girl were you, then? Now I am on dangerous ground. You wanted the fellows and enjoyed having them come around. Still you objected to being taken for granted and you wanted them only a few times in succession. I learned this from harrowing experience the following winter. One night Roy had asked Emeline to go out with her. I was singing in the parlor and could not see you before it was time to go home. The music over I dashed madly out and got my hat and made for you — who were leaving the Chamberlain drive. I saw you clutch Roy and hurry out the door and if you did not run you did some tall moving, for you were out of sight before I got outside.

Know what I did then? I walked and walked some more. And gradually as I walked my thoughts changed. I would leave you in peace for a month. Still I would be as nice to you as I wanted to be. I could see your reason and the same pessimism that worries Emeline, worried me. I saw a family looking with approving eyes at your 'keeping company' with a deserving young man. And yet I saw with a clearness that was not all a mistake, that to you I was, as any young man so painfully steady would be, an ogre looming upon your girlhood horizon and clouding the sunshine of your youthful imagination.

When I came home that night I had reached my conclusion. I would pay no attention to this. I would be no quitter and in spite of the attitude of rebellion I knew you had, I saw no way to give up to it without also giving way for 'the other fellow'. What mental disturbances impelled you to act that way? Maybe I will get into trouble if I guess. Well, first of all was that objection to being taken for granted and having strings tied to you. You were still very much of a girl — were you not? You preferred to have a fellow around only once in a while and the rest of the time you wanted to be with the family. Then, possibly it was nice to be a little perverse. The folks liked that 'him' too well. You wouldn't fall for it. Then again it was sort of natural, being a girl, to like to prevent 'him' from getting too self-confident. Your time was not to be won so easily.

That was last summer. You turned twenty at the end of it and you started to school at Stout. You have finished a year; you spent another summer; you have turned twenty-one — and without apprehension or awe. Your Granny says, "Marie has improved wonderfully this past year. She has matured. It is very noticeable."

Let this be said: Here is a family of high ideals and love for Christian things. Honor, patriotism, loyalty, reverence, love for home, broadmindedness, willpower, freedom from dissimulation: Will she absorb none of it? Will she be such a snob that she will be called 'stuck up and proud', so that the other girls dislike her? Somehow I think she will be liked because she really won't feel any better than someone else because of anything she has, although she may be better because of something she is.

Listen, girl, this is shallow water, although it may look deep. I refer to things a man and a woman would naturally talk freely about. I speak of the little things that bother and that look big — such things, for instance, as occurred to you when you spoke one night of how a girl would feel to meet the members of her husband's family. I want you to feel free to talk about things like that. I guess I am simply trying to ask you to have confidence in me and not to be afraid to talk naturally for fear I will not understand.

Now what does the age of twenty-one bring to you, who claims so lately to have matured? Do you feel the "soul within you climb to the awful verge of" — something or other that you never felt before? Or do you still feel like a schoolgirl, undecided as to how you are to approach the reality of life and afraid, to some extent, of the seriousness of it?

What shall I wish you first? This — the thing I most desire

for you. That you shall retain the lightness of girlhood that will make your laughter wholehearted and free. This will be only done as you realize that life is not so serious as young people sometimes think. That is what people are telling me and I am passing it on to you. Your brightness is your charm, but not your only one. I would not, for the world, in spite of anything I say, have you lose it.

Next — those day dreams. Do they not clothe friends and more than friends with qualities they may or may not possess? I wish — so very earnestly — that the troubles that come to so many will not come to you. And I don't think they will, for they are mostly the result of wickedness and you are going to be good.

Finally, may another year roll around and you be twenty-two, with a capacity for care, but with no increase of care to test your capacity.

Thus Endeth This Book and Letter.

Harry L. Hennesey

Neatly glued to the rear inside jacket was another, smaller blue envelope encasing a business card. On the card, Harry had these words inscribed:

*and now, dear
little girl, I wish
with all my heart
you were with me
H.*

It hadn't been until after supper that Marie took the opportunity to sneak out to the barn and read Harry's long love letter. Of course, everyone in the family knew she had received it and had badgered her mercilessly about its content. However, none but Violet and Emeline were allowed to read it and their impassioned response had been to warn Marie of the perils a man can bring to a girl's life, and the equal-

ly dreadful solitude she would invite by sending him away. By nightfall, perched in the darkened hayloft of Uncle Harlow's barn, she had
decided that if one day he would ask her to marry him she would say
yes, and since that warm September evening long ago only Harry had
owned her heart. Now sixteen years had passed. Did she yet retain that
lightness of girlhood against the seriousness of adult life? Were her
daydreams yet evidence of qualities she was proud to possess? Would
Harry believe her heart to have been good, after all?

Carefully re-packing each of the letters, folding her wedding announcement into an empty envelope with Harry's touching note from
the Nicollet Hotel and placing it atop the little blue "book," Marie
switched off the reading lamp and went to bed. Lying in the dark an
hour later, she wondered how different her life might have been had
she not stepped into the birch canoe with Harold Louis Hennesey that
evening on Cedar Lake, had not invited him along that bright Sunday
with Uncle Harlow in the Stanley Steamer, had not sworn a blood
oath with Violet and Emeline when she was thirteen that the first man
with whom she fell in love, she would marry. Now Cissie slept quietly.
Henry slept quietly. And gradually falling into dreams herself, Marie
listened closely but heard nothing above the beating of her own heart.

— **6** —

Shading his eyes against the glare of the noonday sun on the office
windows, Jimmy Delahaye shouted into the telephone, "Mistake my
eye! Trust me, they'll take to him like Mabel Willebrandt at Texas Gui-
nan's... Oh yeah? Well, that hopheaded union sonofabitch'll settle up
quick when I get my hands on him or I'll knock his block off."

In the next room, Marie kept typing notes to the stockroom invoices Delahaye had dumped onto her desk after breakfast and tried not
to listen to his conversation. He had been speaking by the telephone
to one person or another since she had arrived, hardly paying her any
notice at all. She looked up at him every now and then, hoping to
catch his eye. What did he think of last night? Had she angered him

by fleeing his company? Was he still interested in their little flirtation? She worried he had given up on her and, amazingly enough, she didn't want him to.

"Oh, for Christsakes, Charlie, don't flood the room. I tell you, it's a faked-up charge … No, that was Logan. Who else had the punch to put over a deal like that? … Oh, he did, eh? Well, I'd play innocent, too, if it came to that. He may be bugs on fighting, but snap a dispossess on him and, trust me, he'll come across. He's nothing but a big yellow louse…. . Yeah, I'll wait, but do it pronto. I got a business to run here."

Delahaye cupped the receiver into the palm of his hand and leaned across the desk. "Honey?"

Marie stopped typing. "Yes?"

"Do you want to come in here a second?"

She put her work aside and got up. Delahaye's office had an electric fan switched on and the temperature felt several degrees cooler than where she had been sitting. She felt herself perspiring unnaturally and was happy to change rooms.

Delahaye winked at Marie as she took a chair, then spoke back into the phone. "Yeah, I'm still here, but I don't have all day to fiddle around … All right, I'll be in the office another hour or so… Yeah, you tell him that for me… Swell!"

He hung up the phone, grinning. "Well, haven't you been a little church mouse this morning."

"Pardon?" She blushed. He was always teasing her, and she knew how to take it. He was always sweet to her, perhaps too much so, considering everything.

"You ought to make a little noise so I won't think you're slipping in late on me or something."

"You were on the phone," Marie said, smiling coyly as she glanced out the window where a light breeze rippled the state flag on the courthouse across the street. "I didn't want to disturb you."

"Honey, you ought to let me take you to the show next Saturday night. I seen the card this morning. They got Mickey Mouse and Lon Chaney both. What do you say?"

Marie blushed. So he was still interested? Now what should she do? How much trouble did she want to make for herself? This was all absurd, and getting worse. What should she say? "Well, Maude always has her club ladies over on Saturdays and someone has to be there to watch the children."

"Let one of them do it," said Delahaye, with a laugh. "They love those kiddies of yours."

"Well, I don't know. It's awfully difficult finding time to get away, what with my children's needs, you understand." She had gone too far last night, and she knew it. They had almost made a dreadful mistake which she had no intention of repeating. What if she accepted his invitation to go downtown with him one night soon and see a picture and let him sit close enough that people started talking? Did it really matter? What would Maude think? Or her club ladies? Well, let them all have their gossip, so long as it all appeared silly and innocent. Besides, Harry had been gone long enough. Surely Maude knew that better than anyone.

She offered Delahaye a partial answer. "Would it be all right if I think about it? See if it's possible?"

He smiled and took a cigar out of his desk. "I hope you do, honey."

Next she had to warn him that nothing like last night might ever happen again. "Of course, you understand I can't stay out too awfully late."

"Sure I do," he smiled. "I'll have you home and tucked into bed plenty early."

She blushed. "Thank you."

And, of course, when the time came, Jimmy Delahaye would also have to understand this wasn't to be considered a date, by any means, just a chance for her to go out for the evening. She should also tell him that Harry was coming down by train to see her and the children, perhaps in a few weeks. If that made him jealous, all the better! Emeline once had three boys courting her and always said it was the best time she'd ever had.

"Look here." Delahaye reached down and opened the drawer beside his leg and drew out a stack of checks. After riffling through them once, he handed the checks across the desk to Marie. "Honey, I need you to run these over to the bank for me. I'd have Lucius do it, but he's been on a bender since Tuesday and I don't think he could find his way across the street this morning. Have Edgar deposit them and write up a bill of receipt for you."

"Certainly." She looked at the wall clock behind Delahaye. It read a quarter to noon. She said, "Would it be all right if I brought the receipt back after lunch? I have to go home to feed the children today. Maude's out for the afternoon. I'll be very careful."

"I suppose so," replied Delahaye. He cracked a grin and lit up his cigar. "I like you, honey. You're swell."

"Thank you." He was so handsome. She couldn't help but feel like a girl again. Was that really so terribly wrong?

"Picture show next Saturday night?"

She smiled. "I'll see what I can do."

"Good enough," Delahaye replied, then picked up the telephone and began dialing a number. Pleased with herself for a successful balancing act between flirtation and sanity, Marie walked out of the office.

Downstairs, the restaurant was just beginning to fill for lunch. Idabelle sat at the cash register talking to a short puffy man Marie knew only as Blind Jack. Most of the regular customers were already seated at their favorite booths or tables, and the young waitress Delahaye had hired that week, a thin brunette Rachel's age named Amelia, hurried from a redheaded businessman in a cheap yellow linen suit to a pair of cotton gin supervisors at one of the middle tables near Idabelle, distributing cups of hot coffee and scribbling furiously on her order pad. Smells of vegetable soup and freshly baked chicken pie and cornbread gravy floated out of the kitchen. Conversation hummed. The revolving glass doors opened and more customers poured in. Idabelle called Marie over to the cash register. "Say, sweetie, how'd you like to earn a couple of dollars? Mister Wonderful here wants to take me on a picnic and I can't get away unless you cover for me."

Blind Jack removed his hat and attempted a grin, but his jaw screwed into an odd grimace instead. Hidden under a black felt derby-hat, his forehead looked lopsided and he hadn't shaved in a week or more. "Do a fellow a favor, honey. Idabelle's been giving me the heebie-jeebies all month. If I don't get her in my jalopy this afternoon, I don't know what I'm liable to do!"

"What do you say, sweetie?" Idabelle begged. "Don't it sound like he's got a crush on me?"

Marie nodded. "It certainly does, dear, but Jimmy just gave me these checks to take to the bank for him, and I told the children I'd be home for lunch, and I have to stop at the five-and-ten for Maude. I just don't think I have time. I'm very sorry."

"Oh, that's all right, honey." Idabelle shrugged. "I wasn't going to let him kiss me, anyhow."

A customer came up and handed his bill to Idabelle. As she rang it up, Blind Jack laid his head on the counter and moaned.

Traffic rolled through town in the noon hour and people sat on benches, either eating lunch, reading the newspaper, or enthused in conversation. Nodding a greeting to a woman with a stroller, Marie crossed the lawn to the Commercial National Bank and went indoors. Overhead, wooden blades provided a draft and the main lights were off, so the interior was felt dark. Only a man in a blue pinstriped suit stood in line ahead of Marie. He carried a leather satchel and a copy of the morning *Pinckneyville Echo-Gazette*. The angle of his fedora gave Marie pause, as he resembled men she noticed in the "Wanted" posters on the wall just inside the door. Harry had written constantly that summer about crazed bootleggers. She watched the man for signs of criminal behavior while trying to imagine what she would do if he were to pull a revolver from his jacket. When he merely cashed a bond from the black satchel, Marie relaxed, completed her own transaction, and hurried outdoors again, the receipt tucked safely inside her purse. She had one more errand before returning home to prepare lunch for the children. On Main Street, she bought Milk of Magnesia and a pair of red peppermint sticks from Hooker's drugstore and a paper of pins for Maude at the five-and-dime. Then she hurried out Tyler Road past the livery stables and feedlots toward the outskirts of town where weeds grew tall and flies buzzed in the heat.

The afternoon train to Longview was preparing to depart when Marie walked past the rail depot. Black smoke cascaded downwind and she coughed from the foul odor of burning coal and hot grease. A steamwhistle shrieked and the telegraph operator from the cable office came out onto the platform and gave the engineer a wave and shouted something to him that Marie was unable to hear above the bell clanging. A quarter of a mile farther on, past the cotton mill, Marie veered off onto a footpath through the cemetery in a mossy grove of oaks and cottonwoods that led to the Tyler Road Bridge. Cissie had learned this shortcut from Lili Jessup early in the summer. Scattered about the shady field were wooden markers and carved headstones.

ELIZABETH
WIFE OF
ELDER W.H.ROBERTS
BORN
MAY 26, 1829
DIED
AUG. 30, 1900
She cannot come to me
but I shall go to her

FATHER
J.C. JONES
AUG.10,1847
NOV.1,1926
Christ is my hope

A shirtless Negro labored with a shovel in the heat and did not notice her crossing. Marie counted here and there names and dates of the deceased, many of whom were children when the Lord called. Boy-Allen himself rested in the shade of the southeast corner where birds chattered in an old cottonwood above. There were roses and daisies on his grave, and a toy automobile beside the headstone. Nobody had forgotten him, even if justice had not yet tracked down his killer. Aunt Hattie would say he wasn't lonely in his everlasting sleep. Every time she used that expression,

Marie wondered if she was actually speaking of little David, lying in the earth alone at the Lakewood cemetery. How long would he await his family whose plots were long since bought and paid for? Sometimes Marie felt more guilty over where her first born lay in the earth than about the dreadful circumstance that put him there. More dark thoughts. Walking among these headstones now, she noticed, too, those poor souls who had vacated this world in 1918, the year of the Flu. All that long summer and fall in Farrington, horsedrawn hearses and black carriages had paraded up and down Calvary Hill, Christian men and women in solemn mourning (her mother held the same black parasol at each burial), gravediggers at work day after day, family lots crowded by the Flu, grieving survivors seeking to interpret God's will in all their sorrow. Marie had lost Cousin Floyd, her aunt Rebecca, Grandpa Gustav, and her little cousin Ruthie on the sweetest blue morning of that summer. At the hour of her death, Ruthie failed to recognize her own mother and passed away humming a song Marie used to sing at bedtime. When the pandemic ended abruptly in the autumn of Armistice, few in Farrington had escaped the tragedy of loss during that long sad season.

A canopy of pecan trees, hickory, and sweetgum arched over the old plank bridge to Shantytown, shading the humid summer afternoon. This was where Maude had warned Marie not to go, the deep flowing water, a dividing line between white and black. But whose decision was this to make, hers or Maude's? All her life, somebody was telling Marie what to do, where to go, how to feel. Having Harry sell the house on Cedar Street and send her and the children down here to Texas ignited a change in Marie's heart. She was tired of being a milquetoast, sick of being treated like a child. If she wanted to take a job in Jimmy Delahaye's office, then that's just what she would do, and if flirting with her boss made the day go by and gave her heart flutters, then so much the better, Harry be damned. And today? She was going to Shantytown. She intended to cross this bridge and break every rule in Bellemont, even if it drew a nasty response from Maude or those gossips on College Street who spoke behind Marie's back when she passed, or her fellow Christians singing praise on Sundays to a Lord whose loving desires they ignored in daily living. Right this minute, Marie was going to walk across the bridge and do for once what she wanted to do because it was her choice and her life now, and everyone else better get used it.

Halfway across the river, Marie stopped to watch the muddy current flow by underneath her feet, cold and silent. She shuddered as that awful thought of submerging crossed her mind, and hurried on where she heard cardinals and bluejays tittering in the woods amid fragrant ivory blossoms from southern magnolias. At the far embankment, the road cut a flat and dusty scar through the pinewoods into Shantytown. By storm season, the water rose here, flooding the bottom floor of the houses nearest the river, carrying off everything not packed up and hidden from the high current. Sewage escaped from toppled outhouses, chickens and rabbits were swept away, disease threatened. Today, the sun glared down and baked the road where Negro children ran about barefoot and played at games familiar to Cissie and Henry. Dogs lolled under porch stoops, bluebottle flies spun circles over rusting tin cans and decrepit barrels and darted away from the lashing tail of a scrawny milk cow tied to a post beside a pig sty. The houses, mostly one-story Creole architecture with low shingled roofs and propped-up foundations under shaded galleries against the eventuality of flood, extended side by side down the long section of road out to the pinewoods and back under the pecan trees. There was no town center, just houses and weeds and dust.

Yet Shantytown was as alive as downtown Bellemont in the noon hour. Everywhere, people went about their business, working indoors and outdoors, scrubbing and digging and hauling, or eating and drinking and talking with one another, few paying Marie much notice as she passed by. Only an old dark woman on her hands and knees in the furrows of a small vegetable garden did so much as look up, offering a smile which Marie gladly returned, then giving her directions to a particular address, as Marie hadn't seen any house numbers so far.

"That ain't but a little farther on, child. Pretty basket of verbena and snapdragons on the porchfront."

"Thank you very kindly."

"My pleasure, honey."

"It's a pleasant day, isn't it?"

"Why, yes, honey, it is."

A flatbed truck carrying empty chicken cages sat in the middle of the road, steam rising from beneath its rusty hood. Three black men huddled around, while another had slid on his back under the engine. A young woman wearing a red scarf about her head spoke anxiously to one of the men and her eyes looked as if she had been crying recently. The address Marie sought was just past the stalled truck, surrounded by a low wire fence and stalks of sunflowers. The siding was gray and splintery, lacking paint or stain, weather worn and old. The porch overhang slumped visibly in the middle and the bottom step was split and broken to the left. The basket of verbena hung just off-center from the steps and a coffee-brown girl, barely younger than Rachel, sat beneath it, a bemused expression on her pretty face. She wore a faded rose frock and a little blue bow in her hair.

"He ain't here," the girl said to Marie, as she stopped in front of the house. She wore a wary expression.

"Mr. Reeves?"

"Been gone with Eva and Caroline since before I woke up. First to Longview, now maybe sortin' about at the dump again. I don't know."

"Well, I have something for him," said Marie, opening her handbag. She felt timid now, and a little flustered. Perhaps she ought not to have come. Maude wouldn't have approved of this walking trip to Shanty-town, yet Marie did just as she pleased these days and if Maude was sore about that, well, so be it.

She asked the girl, "Could I leave it with you?"

"What is it?"

Marie smiled, trying to be polite and friendly. "Well, he's been bring-ing toys and lampshades and assorted discards for a play-circus my daughter's been building and I thought I'd like to pay him for some of it. I'm sure much of what he's found had value in trade somewhere and he deserves some compensation for his generosity." She drew a pair of bills from her pocketbook.

The girl brightened. "Why, you must be Cissie's mama."

Marie nodded. "Yes, I am."

The girl stood, offering a smile of her own. "I'm Lucy Hudson. Julius, he's my brother-in-law. Honey, come sit here out of the sun. I don't bite."

"Thank you," Marie replied, unlatching the wire gate and walking in. Perhaps she had been right in coming, after all.

Lucy backed up onto the porch and brought a wooden chair from the corner for Marie to sit on. Then she dragged another over for herself. "Go on, honey, sit yourself down. I been hearing a lot about you, seems like all summer long. Ain't nothing but 'Mrs. Hennesey this and Mrs. Hennesey that,' and those kids of hers and that little circus."

Marie laughed. "He's been wonderfully helpful. The children just adore him."

From inside the house, an infant's voice cried out briefly, and stopped. Lucy turned an ear to listen for a few moments, then lent her attention back to Marie. "Ain't hardly nothing Julius won't do for folks he likes. That's how he's always been. Sister says Julius always been more generous than most."

"He has a good heart."

"Yes, ma'am."

"Here," said Marie, handing the two dollar bills to Lucy. "I'm sure we owe him twice that."

"Oh, honey, he won't have you paying him for something he done free of charge."

Lucy tried to give the money back, but Marie shook her head and snapped her handbag shut. "He's the nicest person I've met since we've come here. I know that money won't buy kindness nor is it a fair reward, either, but I'd appreciate you giving it to him as a thank you on behalf of the children and myself."

"Well, isn't that sweet of you?" replied Lucy. "Tell the truth, he ain't used to receiving blessings like that from certain folks 'round here, if you understand my meaning."

"I suppose I do," Marie admitted, peeking indoors where a Negro child no more than three or four years old toddled across the floor toward the screen door, blanket in hand. "We've only lived here a few months, but I must say it does trouble me and I've been ashamed of what I've seen and heard, now and then. We're taught in the Bible to love all our neighbors. I've always believed in God's simplest truths. It's what we've learned in church since childhood."

Lucy smiled, touching Marie on the arm. "Honey, they got the same Bible down here. They just read it different, is all."

She studied Marie with eyes darkened by sorrow until Marie looked away, the most peculiar feeling in her heart. The child was at the screen door now, whimpering softly. A young boy's voice called out from farther inside the house and Marie heard running footsteps and then a door bang closed out back. Lucy got up and went to the screen and opened it and scooped the child into her arms. She looked back at Marie. "Do you care to step inside? Baby here needs to go to sleep and I got a child named Willie who won't stop causing commotion. I could get you a glass of lemonade if you like?"

"That'd be nice," Marie replied, getting to her feet. "I can't stay long, of course. My own children are waiting for lunch."

Lucy smiled. "You come here down Tyler Road past the old cemetery, did you?"

"Why, yes. What makes you ask?"

"I find that so strange."

"Oh? How come?"

Lucy giggled. "Our cemetery's about a mile from here, and I never set foot in it."

"Pardon?" She was confused.

The girl gave a mock shudder. "Most colored folks is afraid of ghosts. You ask Julius if you don't think it's so."

Marie smiled. "That's silly."

Lucy laughed. "Yes, ma'am."

Suppressing her own giggles, Marie followed the black girl into the front room where the air was dark and cool and smelled of fried catfish and butter oil. The wooden floor underfoot was covered in part by an old brown hook rug. There were four windows, each of which had a cotton quilt draped over the glass. An old pump organ like Marie's grandmother used to play, sat in one corner beside a burgundy sofa near to the kitchen entry.

"Sit yourself down, honey," Lucy told Marie, "I'll be back directly."

Feeling relaxed now and pleased with herself for coming here, Marie sat on the sofa and counted a number of small clay vases holding an assortment of summer wildflowers and studied a row of old photographs atop the fire mantel. Lucy came out of the kitchen with a glass of lemonade and sat down beside her. Marie took the lemonade thankfully and had a sip. It had been a fairly long walk from Delahaye's to Shantytown and she was parched from the heat.

"Sister Angela's gone away to Knoxville, so Julius and me been left to ourselves with five little ones to worry after. When he goes off to do his business, I've got no patience for all this trouble."

Marie said, "I'm fortunate to have Maude home to watch Cissie and Henry when I'm at work. Up north, it was just me when Harry traveled, though Cousin Emeline liked to babysit from time to time when her own husband was out of town. The children can be a trial."

The black girl nodded. "Ain't that a case."

"Maybe you could find someone to come help during the day."

"Naw, I don't mean like that. We come from Tennessee seven years ago, down here to be with my Aunt Ida and I hated it then and I hate it now. I didn't want to come. Sister made me do it 'cause Julius had it in his mind he wanted to go some place different after the War. So we came here and I just never cared for it."

"I don't understand."

Lucy got up and went into the back of the house. Marie heard her open a dresser and take something out. When she came, she was holding a flat box, which she gave to Marie. "Go on, open it."

Even in the hazy light of the front room, Marie recognized the medals placed there. She had seen both on display in the Farrington courthouse each Independence Day since 1919: the Distinguished Service Cross and the French Croix de Guerre.

"Julius was a hero in the World War."

Marie smiled. "I know. Rachel told us. You must be very proud."

"He got shot up bad saving some boys, so they give him these rewards and told him he was a good soldier, even though back in Knoxville he was still just another colored fellow. Ain't that something?"

"Yes, it is." Marie sipped her lemonade and stared at Julius's medals from the Great War, shining honors for valor and courage. She hadn't any idea he had been wounded. Cousin Rory had lost a limb and the use of his left eye. Maggie Rutherford's brother had been blown to bits his first morning at the Argonne. Both Tommy Layton and Milton Metcalf had been gassed. Each of those who had come back from France had lost vitality and eagerness.

"Julius told Sister that the Army didn't want no colored boys carrying guns in the War, but they was so afraid of losing the war that they made the colored boys throw away those shovels and commence to training just like the white soldiers. Hardly any colored boys knew nothing about no Kaiser or where France was or nothing. They just went where they was ordered to go and did what they was told like any other good Americans. Julius said to Sister, 'Colored soldier love his country maybe more than the white 'cause he spilled more of his blood there. When this War come, all he wants is the chance to show Uncle Sam that he's a man, just like any other.'"

Marie felt embarrassed. She had never heard of such a thing. It was utterly disgraceful. Why hadn't Harry told her? Or Uncle Henry? Did they think she wouldn't understand?

Lucy said, "Over there, they worked harder'n anyone proving what Julius said, especially when the white soldiers started going on about how the coloreds got tails like monkeys and won't do nothing but drink liquor and rape white women. See, Julius come from Tennessee so he got sent into the army with the 92nd Division that had lots of Southern boys, white and colored, and the coloreds even had some of their own officers and that didn't make none of them white boys happy so they wouldn't salute or show respect for the uniform if it had a colored man in it. Then the shooting started up and soldiers were dying and it didn't make much matter what color was giving orders and there was a place where so many boys got themselves killed that Julius wanted to give up and come home like everybody else, but they had an awful battle one night and so many boys being blowed up that he crawled in the mud across the wires and hauled a lot of colored boys back with him in spite of his getting shot in three places, and then he went back into the gas and killed fourteen Germans that tried to shoot him and when he was done and crawled back to his own side again, everybody called him a hero and sent him home, after all."

"Good gracious! I don't know how I could've tolerated that."

Lucy shrugged. "He was sick in the hospital all winter and part of the next spring and only Sister was allowed to visit him. I knitted him a shirt and Papa bought him a new pair of boots and Mama scribbled his name in the family Bible and prayed he'd come back to us like he left.

Then they had a big parade in Knoxville for the soldiers that fought for America over there, and Julius was still sick but he put his uniform on with them medals you're holding and got out of bed to be in it when he couldn't walk more than across the room yet. Well, he ought to've stayed right where he was in bed, 'cause the Army didn't allow no colored soldiers to march in that parade. You hear me, honey? He seen plenty of colored soldiers killing and getting killed for their country that wouldn't let a one of them march in that damned parade. It broke his poor heart. That's why we left Knoxville and come down here."

"I'm so sorry." Marie felt truly ashamed. She detested deliberate humiliations of any sort. If she believed most people here felt that way about their colored neighbors, she didn't know how long she and the children could remain here. Why hadn't Harry warned her? Did he hope she wouldn't notice?

"Ain't nothing you done to be sorry for, honey," said Lucy, taking the box of medals off Marie's lap and folding it shut. "That's just how it is."

"Well, I believe he's very courageous." She drank the last of her lemonade.

The back door flew open, and two small boys barefoot in dusty overalls and carrying old croquet mallets burst in, one chasing after the other, both crying and yelling simultaneously, "Lucy, Lucy! He hit me! He hit me!"

Marie recognized Willie Reeves from that day Cissie brought Mr. Slopey back from the river. The other boy she didn't know at all.

Lucy Hudson put the box of medals on the organ and got up. As Willie and his playmate reached the front room, bawling loudly, Lucy hollered, "First one of you two wants a whipping, come on in!"

Marie stood, too, setting her empty glass on the floor. "I better go along. I'm sure Henry's just as anxious as these two."

The boys had stopped cold, tears welling up, both staring at Marie as if she were a ghost. Lucy ignored them for the moment, saying to Marie, "I appreciate you coming down here today, bringing what you did. He'll be thankful."

"You're very welcome, dear."

The truck was still there in the middle of the road, but the hood was closed and one of the men was behind the wheel working over the starter. The woman in the red scarf had gotten herself surrounded by a pack of scrawny hounds, but didn't appear to mind. The sun burned down hotter than ever.

On the dirt road back to Bellemont, Marie thought about what she might say to Julius when next she saw him. His generosity and kindness toward her children pleased Marie, lent her strength and optimism in Harry's long absence. If in this small town a ray of divine light shone so brightly in one man, Marie wondered, why could it not in others?

She crossed over the cold river and wandered up the narrow road through the pinewoods, listening to the birds chattering in the trees. She felt safe here during the day, perhaps because she was reminded of the thick forest behind the farm at home. An automobile rattled by as she stepped back into the long grass and waved to the driver. Insects flew slantwise on the heated air ahead of her as she walked.

The road came out into sunlight just south of Watson Avenue. Another block and she saw Cissie atop Mr. Slopey, with Henry and Abel Kritt and Lili Jessup trailing just behind. Lili held her kitten and Abel led a small terrier on a leash. When Marie called out, Cissie urged the old swayback forward and another mutt came running out from the bushes nearby and Henry and Lili ran, too.

"I thought you were going to wait for me to come home," Marie said, pausing in the shade. "Aren't you hungry?"

"Grandma told us to go on a picnic today," said Henry, showing his mother the small wicker basket.

"There's lots of people over there now, Momma," Cissie said. "All her club ladies and that man from the airfield, Mr. Beeswax."

"My momma's there, too," Lili added. "I guess it's a party for someone."

"Maybe Mr. Beeswax has a birthday," Henry suggested, taking a thick carrot out of the basket and breaking it in half. He gave the other half to Abel who wiped off his dusty eyeglasses, and fed a small chunk of it to the dog.

"Maybe," said Marie, curious now herself. Maude hadn't mentioned a word earlier that morning. "Well, I'll just go see for myself. You be careful where you have your picnic. Keep away from the road, and if you go to the river — "

"Stay out of the water," Cissie interrupted. "We know, Momma. We'll be good. I promise."

"All right, then. I have to go back to work after lunch, but I'll be home before supper."

"Bye-bye, Momma!"

When the children were safely off the main road and heading toward the river, Marie continued up the street to Maude's house. Two automobiles were parked out front, a green Nash and a tan Chevrolet. As Marie arrived at the gate to the backyard, "Benny Beeswax" from the Rickenbacker Aerodrome came out and climbed into the green Nash and motored off. Marie went into the yard, quickly took her morning linen off the line, and carried it indoors by way of the kitchen porch. The house was filled with voices. Two of Maude's club ladies, Beatrice and Emily, were just walking out of the kitchen as Marie came in, Emily saying, "When I was a little girl, I remember a lightning storm just like that. I was scared to death. Why, I thought I'd be struck dead for sure."

Marie set the basket on a stool beside the pantry just as Trudy and Leila Neal, whom Marie had met one afternoon downtown at Butler's Dry Goods, came in from the bedroom hallway, Trudy saying with a distinct frown, "Heavens, no, she'd only seen the boy since Easter and really hadn't made her mind up about anything. That's just idle gossip and you ought not to repeat a word of it."

When Trudy looked up and saw Marie standing beside the sink, she managed a weak smile. "Hello, honey."

Marie nodded a greeting, and asked, "Where's Maude?"

Her voice plaintive and low, Trudy replied, "Oh, she's still in with Rachel, the poor dear. They've given her two Asafetida tablets and sent for Doctor Bird."

Worried now, Marie asked, "Is she ill? Why, I saw her just this morning and she seemed fine. Did she catch something?"

Trudy's face went ashen. "Oh my goodness, honey, haven't you heard? Why, there's been a terrible accident. Oh, it's just awful. Two aeroplanes collided last night in a storm cloud over Lake Pontchartrain. Dearie, CW's been killed."

INTERLUDE

CHARLIE PENDERGAST

A KINGDOM OF ONE DOLLAR BILLS

YEARS AGO IN NEEDLES, I remember one afternoon sitting on the porch with Uncle Monroe and Uncle Harris, waiting for Bebbins to finish his bath so he could come out and play. It was one of those late summer days where the wind had quit and we could scarcely breath in the heat. They were both drinking beer and staring at the dusty street in front of us, when Uncle Monroe said, right out of the blue, "By golly, I sure wish I had a hundred dollars."

And Uncle Harris replied, "Yeah, I'd sure like to have a hundred dollars."

Back then, I suppose Uncle Monroe thought that having a hundred dollars would solve all his problems. He and my father had a two-chair operation in the barbershop and Father hardly ever said a word about money, though the shop often seemed empty. But while my father still collected rent from his barbershop in Illinois, Uncle Monroe had no other source of income and imagined he'd be better off moving on to Los Angeles. Uncle Cy had just come out to California and told us about an oil well in Santa Fe Springs he was investigating. Uncle Monroe wanted to go look into it with him, but Auntie Leah was still worried about Howard and refused to leave, especially now that the rest of us had arrived and she had lots of company for supper. So long as we were all in Needles together, Auntie Leah had no intention of going anywhere else. Because of that, I think Uncle Monroe wished the rest of us would pack up and go back to Illinois. He'd start drinking and say little things like,

"This whole California business sure isn't what it's cracked up to be" and "We're living in a kingdom of one-dollar bills." He and Auntie Leah had some awful fights. When they'd begin, Mother would send Bebbins and me home on our bicycles, where we could hear them yelling clear down to the end of the block. Sometimes the neighbors would come out onto their porches to listen. A few of them laughed, but most people in Needles seemed to mind their own business.

One night the phone rang in the dark, Auntie Leah calling to tell Mother that she and Uncle Monroe had gotten into it again and that he'd taken the car and driven off. Mother dressed and went over to find out what happened and didn't come back until breakfast. The next day, everyone was upset and mad at Uncle Monroe, who still hadn't returned home. We had a big supper planned for that evening and it would be ruined if he weren't there. Well, he didn't come back for supper, either that night or the next, and Auntie Leah cried and Mother cried, and Father and Uncle Harris drove all over looking for him, without any luck. Nobody knew what to think. Bebbins guessed he'd fallen down a well somewhere and broken his leg. I thought may-be Uncle Monroe had driven out into the desert and gotten lost and was down in Mexico. Then Auntie Leah telephoned to Mother and told her that Uncle Monroe had just come home. We drove right over and there was Uncle Monroe waiting for us on the porch. Auntie Leah was inside getting supper ready on the stove and needed Uncle Monroe to go to the grocery store for a loaf of bread. Mother asked if I could go with him and he agreed, so off we went. As we drove along, I sat quietly, aching to ask Uncle Monroe where he'd gone, though much too scared to do so. He still seemed angry. He gripped the steering wheel hard and stared straight ahead. Then, when we were about a mile from the house, Uncle Monroe spoke up. In a dead flat voice, he said to me, "Whatever you do, Charlie, never marry an Okie. Do you hear me? Never marry an Okie."

I guess Uncle Monroe had become pretty miserable by then, and listening to Cy talk about his oil well made it that much worse. Uncle Harris was already begun talking about going back to Illinois, but Aunt Lottie refused to leave California until she'd seen Hollywood.

Though Uncle Harris hated getting out of bed to deliver milk, Father was dedicated to his barbershop and worked hard. While we were in Needles, Father got a telegram from Lloyd Neumann telling him that one of the fellows renting the barbershop at home had died of appendicitis. Mother thought it meant that we'd need to go back to Illinois, but father told her everything was fine; he'd just keep the barbershop in Needles open another hour or so each evening. Father didn't seem to care much for traveling here and there and, as I look back on it now, I realize that he never did go any place alone.

Yet, I suppose few of us are immune to homesickness. The last month we were in Needles, Grandma Halverson came out by train to visit mother. She had nine children who lived all over and whenever she was away from one of them, she got lonely and went to visit. I thought she was always kind of a helpless old woman because once Grandpa died, she was at the mercy of being supported by her children. Mother said Grandma's pension earned her eighteen dollars a month, which didn't really help all that much, except that she had no expenses to speak of. There was nothing she wanted to buy. She'd end up lending her money to her children who would always say, "Ma, can I borrow two dollars?" When my mother came home from the store or visiting Aunt Lottie, she and grandma would fix a pot of coffee that Grandma drank by placing a sugar cube between her teeth and slurping the coffee through her lips. She said it saved on sugar. In Needles, she sat in our front room most of the day, knitting and listening to the radio that was mostly static. She'd sit there waiting for the hymns, like "The Old Rugged Cross," that played at the close of an hour's program. I remember asking her one afternoon, "Grandma, why do you listen to that awful radio?"

And she replied, "Well, I like to listen to the hymns."

I suppose she wasn't very educated. We had a blackboard that Bebbins and I found at the dump, and one afternoon Grandma and I played school. I was the teacher and she was the student. Her own mother and father only went to the third grade, and I doubt if Grandma even made it that far, so she couldn't spell anything. Each time she got a word wrong, I gave her a failing mark, which pleased me no end.

She had poor vision, too, but claimed she didn't have enough money to buy a pair of glasses, which my father used to say was ridiculous. Things like that drove him crazy. So when Grandma came out to Needles, my mother and I took her downtown one morning and bought her some glasses. She was astounded as she walked along the street to see people's faces for once without squinting. When we went over to the barbershop, she walked in, looked at my father, and said, "Carl, I never realized you were so homely."

She stayed with us for two weeks, then went back east to see my Aunt Marian. I remember us taking her down to the station to put her on the train. I was afraid that while we were saying good-bye to her, the train would pull out and we wouldn't be able to get off in time -- one of those silly childhood fears. Mother told me that Grandma would have to sit on that train for three days until she reached Pennsylvania, where she'd stay with Aunt Marian until she became lonely again for another one of her children. It must have been difficult for her, traveling by herself like that, but love of family kept her going.

I imagine that's how my father and mother were able to tolerate being so far away from our home in Illinois. With Uncle Harris's family in Needles, Uncle Monroe and Auntie Leah, and Cy there, too, later on, none of us could feel too lonely for relatives. We just enjoyed being together. Late that summer, before Father and Mother and I finally left California, I remember all of us piling into my father's Ford and Uncle Monroe's Dodge for a Sunday outing with no idea where we were headed. We kept driving farther and farther into the desert, and we must have gotten lost because soon enough we were driving along in the middle of the nowhere on a washboard-type road -- just a bunch of planks in the sand -- when we came across a filling station and a little grocery store with a restaurant. We stopped to get gas and something to drink. Mother bought Bebbins and me bottles of soda pop and everyone else drank beer, and pretty soon Cy and Uncle Monroe were feeling pretty good, not staggering drunk, but they'd certainly had too much, and I remember Uncle Monroe telling the proprietor that he was a barber. Straight away, Uncle Monroe had the fellow sitting down in a chair and was giving him a shampoo with a bottle of beer. Meanwhile, looking for a ladies room in the back of the restaurant, Mother and Auntie Leah came across a box filled with bottles of vanilla extract, and decided to steal it. What they were going to do with this vanilla, I don't know. I suppose they could use it in their cooking, so they stole that box with all those bottles of vanilla and put it in the back of Uncle Monroe's Dodge, and eventually we left.

It was late at night, then, and we headed down the road, and soon Bebbins needed a toilet so we pulled over to stop, and everyone got out and the next thing I knew, Cy and Monroe were tumbling around and wrestling in the middle of the road. They were always getting into some kind of fight. Nobody ever took it too seriously. Father just lit a cigar and watched while Uncle Harris laughed at the dust they were kicking up. Back by the cars, Auntie Leah and Mother had opened up the box and discovered that those bottles of vanilla they'd taken hadn't anything in them. They were both disappointed because all they had done was steal a box of empty bottles. So they proceeded to do something that gave Bebbins and me great delight. Mother and Auntie Leah began throwing those empty bottles out into the desert in the dark. We could hear them break when they hit a rock now and then, and I remember thinking this was great sport. There was no one else around for miles, only us standing on the side of the road in the middle of the night, throwing those bottles out into the desert.

SEPTEMBER

WASHING OFF A SET of tableware in the sink, Marie looked out the kitchen window to a gloomy late-afternoon sky. Gray clouds roiled on the horizon. A gusty wind blew in the cottonwood grove across the road, perhaps some wayward thunderstorm, she thought, emerging from late summer heat. As she scrubbed the silver clean, cold tap water numbed her hands.

In the dry sunless sitting room, Rachel sat at the piano playing a few brief bars of an old Appalachian hymn. Woefully dispirited since CW's fatal airplane accident above Lake Pontchartrain, the past few weeks she had taken to spending her lunchtime at home with Maude, eating little meat sandwiches cut into triangles and rolling pie crusts for supper.

Bursting with energy, Maude roamed from room to room as she attended to the housekeeping while engaging in a conversation about epileptics and the peculiar fits they throw. From the unlit pantry, she called out, "Now, mind you, infirmity of any sort teaches us the Lord's humility, but when that poor dear girl fell off Edgar Foote's delivery wagon and nearly swallowed her own pigtails, well, it's clear to me how some of us have obviously misunderstood God's intentions in that regard."

Marie rinsed off a handful of forks under the sink faucet. Her hands ached from the cold. She felt tired and wished she could nap for an hour. She heard her daughter's voice carrying across the gusty wind from outdoors where Cissie and Lili and Henry were playing toad-in-the-hole inside the Jessup's smelly old chickencoop. Dust swirled in the empty street. Marie hoped the instructions she had given them regarding soiled school clothing had not been entirely ignored. Twice this week, Maude had administered arnica to Henry's wounds: once on a skinned left knee after he'd tripped over a milk can, and again on his right elbow where he had bumped into a wooden post. The fall school term had started and neither child was happy about it. Already Cissie had brought home a notice from the school principal after cracking a boy named Jerome Winning on the jaw for tugging at her pigtails. Her teacher, Mrs. Jarisch, wrote to Marie praising Cissie's fine reading skills and penmanship while expressing concern for her daily deportment. Henry had begun well enough himself, but then last week, little Abel Kritt and his mother left town. A truck had come in the middle of the night and taken them away with everything they owned, no explanations, and no good-byes except to Henry, who accepted guardianship of Abel's favorite turtle, and to Mary Snell, a close friend of Mrs. Kritt's, who shared with the neighbors Mrs. Kritt's troubling suggestion that children ought to be kept away from the river until iniquity was overcome. Most people assumed she was referring to the unsolved murder of poor Boy-Allen, but rumor suggested there was something more, a shameful hush about those hours little Abel had gone missing on the Fourth of July. Marie worried now whenever the children went into the woods and was glad school had begun.

Rachel's fingers danced once more up the piano scale, tinkling across the upper octaves, then quit altogether. She rose from the piano bench and came into the kitchen hallway where she addressed both Maude and Marie in a doleful voice. "Joanna says Thelma Waller's taken up Science because of Peggy's sickness. She's convinced that right thoughts will cure her daughter and that Mary Baker Eddy's inspired scripture is the key to her own salvation."

Setting a can of condensed milk on the breadboard, Maude snorted. "Beatrice shares Thelma's party line and she says that woman calls her house physician more often than Hooker's drugstore. Why, I doubt there's a soul in this county with a medicine closet fuller than Thelma

Waller's, and I know for a fact she drinks lemon and salt from time to time to dispense with her periods and that she purchased a bottle of White Pine syrup just last week to ward off a silly little cold. Christian Science, indeed. Ha!"

Marie closed off the tap and took a towel to dry off her hands. The pink frock she wore was speckled with soapy water above the waist apron and she dabbed it clean. Her back still to Maude, she remarked, "Cissie tells me Peggy's quite a little darling, her awful affliction notwithstanding. I imagine she's awfully brave, too."

"Well, of course she is," agreed Maude, tying on a yellow checkered apron. "I certainly didn't mean to suggest that any of this is her fault. She's only a child, after all."

Rachel came into the kitchen and fetched a ginger cookie from the Mason jar on the counter top under the cabinets. Enlivened by dispute, she perked up, her tone louder, closer to her usual self. "Oh, for heaven sakes, Mother, she's thirteen years old! Why, Thelma told Joanna that Peggy collects photographs of matinée idols now and pastes them onto the wall above her bed. Apparently she's got an awful crush on Gilbert Roland."

"My cousin Emeline collects teapots and Japanese dolls with painted lashes," Marie added, having a ginger cookie of her own. She hadn't eaten a bite of lunch herself and her stomach felt pained and empty. "I envy her passion for them, although sometimes it does seem a little foolish."

"Oh, I think it's wonderful to be passionate," said Rachel. "I wish I were. Being in the doldrums is so tiresome I can hardly stand it. It's absolutely hateful."

Maude fetched a bottle of milk from the ice-box, then took down a glass from the cupboard and filled it for Marie. She reminded Rachel, "A cheerful heart is a good medicine. You know, dear, I seem to recall your own foolish enthusiasms for a particularly horrid Italian movie fellow who had both you and Francie Powell loafing about Hooker's drugstore in the evening reading *Photoplay* magazines and shaming yourselves with that sodajerker whose language would make a monkey blush."

"Good grief, Mother! Clarence did not have a foul mouth! Why, I doubt he uttered a cussword his entire life!" Rachel turned to Marie. "He was the sweetest boy you'd ever like to meet. Francie hoped to marry Clarence when she graduated school, but a Bertha shell killed him in France six days before Armistice. I helped her arrange a pretty bouquet of orange poppies for his grave."

"That was nice of you. I'm sure she appreciated it. Kindness rarely goes unnoticed."

Maude handed the glass of milk to Marie, and poured one for Rachel. "Yet you weren't nearly so distraught as when that horrible Italian was poisoned."

Rachel burst into laughter. "Spaghetti Valentino was not poisoned, Mother! He died from peritonitis. That rumor was a vicious lie perpetrated by his enemies who were sick with envy from seeing how many millions of people were heartbroken at his passing. Why, I'm still carrying a torch for him." She smiled at Marie. "In fact, I'm sure most women agree he was the most adorable man ever born."

"I never shed one tear," said Maude, putting the bottle of milk back into the ice-box.

"I remember Harry and I watched the funeral on *Metrotone News* at the Gem in Farrington," Marie said, after finishing her ginger cookie. "I'd never seen so many mourners in my life. It was quite a spectacle." Harry thought the entire thing was a shameful waste of money, but Marie secretly envied all those girls who had fallen in love with a fellow they'd never even kissed.

Sipping from her milk, Rachel asked Marie, "Did you know Valentino's casket was draped in a cloth of gold?"

Marie shook her head. "Were you actually there at the funeral?"

"No, she was not," Maude interjected. "Although poor Rachel was so overwrought with grief, she did try to buy a train ticket to New York City. Of course, I refused to let her out of the house until all that nonsense was over with. You can't imagine the fuss she put up. She threw seven kinds of cat fits, and said things that were entirely uncalled for."

"Mother has absolutely no sense of drama," said Rachel, putting the glass of milk down and walking to the back door. When she opened it, a dank draft filled the kitchen, fluttering through the lace curtains above the window. According to the *Bellemont Oracle*, Monday last had been the hottest day of the year. Both humans and animals had suffered heat prostration: nine people had been admitted to the hospital by their doctors and a truckhorse harnessed to an old coal dray dropped dead in the Fourth Street alleyway downtown. After a record stretch of unearthly heat, everyone looked forward to a change in weather. As Rachel stepped out onto the back porch to look at the cloudy sky, Marie heard her remark, "I believe we may actually see some rain today."

— 2 —

Marie sat on her bed staring out past the pretty chinaberry tree to the washing on the laundry line she needed to bring indoors soon. Six months ago in Farrington, she had her own home with a back-yard veranda that looked out onto a garden of flower beds and fruit trees and vegetables where clouds of lightning bugs sparkled in the lavender dusk and feral cats stole by instinct through crape myrtle and clumps of deadly nightshade. Once each week, Cousin Emeline came by for tea and cookies and to exchange mail-order catalogues and idle gossip. She helped prune the rose bushes and urged Marie to register herself by maiden name in the telephone book. When Harry put the house up for sale after Easter, dear Emeline knelt beside Marie in the sunlit parlor filling stacks of packing boxes until each was tied shut and it was time to go. An hour before traintime in May, Marie crept through the cool of the morning garden with a studio photograph of Harry and the children and herself and buried it in a cigar box beneath the gnarled apple tree in the back corner of the yard. Afterward, propelled by steam locomotive through that vast windy emptiness of Missouri and Oklahoma in the middle of the night, Marie dreamt of seedtime and bloom on the Farrington plains, her bare fingers thrust into damp black loam, sweet fragrance of dripping honeysuckle rising on a faint breeze, a million crickets and glowing fireflies swarming a long humid summer twilight and her mother's persistent voice echoing across the starry dark, calling her only daughter home to supper.

There were days now when Marie felt lost and forgotten. Though she dearly loved Harry and trusted his reasoning for packing her off with the children to this distant place, the strangeness of lighted stores downtown whose proprietors she did not recognize on the sidewalks out front worried her lonely heart. Why had he sent her away? How much longer would they need to stay in this place? Would he ever love her as he once did? *"Oh, darling, you told me the story of your sorrow in such a plaintive voice, it seemed to be the voice of wounded love. I shall try so hard to never make such a break again. Oh, my sweetheart, I love you and you love me, and I will try so hard to be your good boy."* How had her life become so difficult? Maude, Rachel, CW, Delahaye, Julius Reeves, Boy-Allen, spinning like a carousel in her head. Why had things taken this course? In the big show window of Kelly's department store, a Majestic set broadcast unfamiliar voices from unfamiliar places performing radio-plays she could hardly make sense of. On Sunday mornings, she stood in a crowded pew next to Maude and Rachel as the Baptist congregation sang hymns whose verses she didn't know. One evening at the community hall, she overheard a woman from the other end of town refer to her as a "Yankee" in the same accusatory tone she had just been using to discuss the foul mystery of Boy-Allen's murder. In each typewritten letter from the city, Harry praised her courage, wrote how proud he was to have such a fine wife whose Christian sacrifice and selflessness lent encouragement both to himself and their children. Marie felt neither brave nor selfless, not in a very long while. Moreover, that sort of pride was a nuisance she could gladly do without if only Emeline would come to tea once a week or her mother would send Cousin Frenchy to fetch her for Sunday dinner in Uncle Harlow's old Stanley Steamer. If the children continued to smile at breakfast each morning, she would attempt to bear up and study patience when her heart spoke sadly, but remembrances often kindle on a sudden breeze and each letter she received unfailingly deepened her longing for home.

Farrington, Illinois
September 1st, 1929

Dearest Marie,

This summer past without you in our midst has been the saddest I have ever known. It's been lonesomer than thunder. Roy and Uncle Boyd both agree that you must come back to us tomorrow or no later than the day after. Do you see how dearly you are missed? Victor bought a secondhand Ford last Tuesday and promises to teach you how to drive if you hurry back soon, as Uncle Charlie has already told him to get rid of it. Auntie Emma and Lottie and Sam and Uncle Merrill came to breakfast this morning. They each send their love.

Yesterday the baby was sick and needed to see Dr. Mahoney who was very nice. I didn't mind going to him at all. Later in the afternoon I went for a walk with Luther in the pinewoods behind Esther York's peacock farm. We followed a narrow path beside the creekbed that led us so far into the thicket I thought we were lost. Did Effie ever tell you the story of how Great-aunt Sara was eaten by wolves near here? Mother says every word of it is true, so help her God. Well, dear cousin, just as I thought I'd need to send that old hound dog back for Roy to save my life, a miracle happened. I found God's sunlight up ahead shining through the pine trees upon a meadow of songbirds and Indian grass where long ago three silly little girls once dreamed they built a fairy throne from a rotting old stump. Do you recall our meadow in the beautiful moonlight? We were wild as cats ourselves with no fear of the dark. Roy keeps a coal oil lamp beside his bed when he sleeps, but I have no need of it. Our precious Violet was scared of wind and lightning and nothing else. In bed, spider-bitten, she swore that when the Lord came for her, she'd not hide. At the last she said to me, "Divine light shineth brightest by night." To this day I believe we ought to have set aside a corner of that pretty meadow for Violet and laid a tiara of snapdragons upon her marker each anniversary. Cor unum, via una. Our secret motto. Do you remember? One heart, one way. If only I could listen to dear Violet play mother's organ once again, perhaps I would not sleep as fitfully as I do.

Now Aunt Hattie has insisted I pass on to you all the latest Farrington gossip, so I will. Dear cousin, Mrs. Craswell died two weeks ago Saturday.

She was about the sweetest old lady I ever knew and I was always very fond of her. What enjoyable visits I had in her home. I don't imagine she had very much besides her Crown Darby and that old walnut chifforobe, but whatever it is I hope her son William gets it because he has grown up to be a fine man. I am glad that he was able to be with her when she went. Her sister Margery doesn't need another penny, anyhow, and she is the most disagreeable woman in this county. Have you written Edith of late? Everett is working for the Bendix Co. so they both have a salary now and are on a week's vacation with pay in Mishawaka. I'm going downtown this afternoon to get some sherbet glasses for Edith. We don't want to spend a lot of money, but we ought to give her something for all the wonderful embroidery she did for Grandma Sayers. Don't you think so? Last Sunday after morning services, Mother had Ida Hawley over for dinner and I went out with Agnes in the afternoon. We went to a "sing" at the auditorium but there was such a crowd that we only stayed a short time, then we went for a ride. Agnes seems to be a very nice woman and I enjoy her. We had a good talk about youth nowadays. Agnes doesn't like the fact that her daughters are going with boys whose names they don't even know, nor the hours they keep. This disagreement is a fair one in my book. When we were girls there were no automobiles so we went to the square dance in a horse and buggy and found our husbands from the boys we knew at school. It was a fine arrangement. We saw the good and the bad in each other and knew what to make of it. When we married there were fewer surprises. How does a girl in Chicago know she is going with a gentleman and not a thief? I am grateful to have been born on a farm.

Well, dear cousin, I must bathe and dress the baby and get to Ruth's in time for lunch. Lloyd is coming out for supper tonight. What would he do without his friends? Read the Bible and water the chickens, says Auntie Emma, which I believe is heaven for her. Do you suppose we'll ever have picnics and fun again on holidays?

Please give my love to the children. We miss you all so very much.

Your loving cousin,

Emeline

— 3 —

After folding the last batch of laundry into a basket and carrying it indoors, Marie crossed the dusty yard to the Jessup's chickencoop. She had noticed on her last trip out of the house that Cissie's chirping voice had been lost in the banging of Maude's old storm-shutters shaken loose by the rising wind. Great gray clouds continued to darken the sky horizon and prickled the hairs on the back of her neck. If rainshowers were coming, she preferred the children play indoors. She called into the chickencoop and heard no answer. She leaned down to peek underneath, catching her hair on a bent nail. As she tugged loose, the Jessup's back screen door slammed and Lili's gray kitten, who had been sitting beside the porch, scrambled under the house. Concerned, Marie called again for Cissie and Henry. Where were they? A side window of the Jessup's house raised up and Mildred stuck her head out wrapped in curlpapers. A pale yellow lightbulb glowed from the ceiling behind her face. She held a cigarette in one hand. Mildred shouted to Marie, "Lost something?"

Marie stood and nodded as the wind gusted in the tall dry grass of the Jessup's yard. Walking over, she replied, "My children. I thought they were playing with Lili in the chickencoop, but they seem to be missing since coming home from school."

"Don't go nowhere, honey."

Mildred disappeared indoors and Marie heard her call to her brother Fritz who had barely set foot outside of the house since arriving four months ago. A doctor named Mulligan stopped by for an hour on Tuesday and Rachel claimed he had looked mad as the devil upon departing. Marie listened to Mildred and her brother shouting back and forth until Mildred stuck her head back out the bathroom window. She told Marie, "They ain't here. Fritz says Lili told him they were all going down to the drugstore to buy candy." She flicked redhot ash off her cigarette in the wind. Maude believed no woman in Bellemont smoked more than Mildred Jessup. "My brother's been swallowing dope pills all week. He ain't well."

"I'm sorry. Is there anything I can do?"

Her face drawn with fatigue, Mildred shrugged. "He come over here from Tallahachee just so's I could take care of him. He gets mean as hell when he's sick and his own doctor don't want to see him no more. Won't go to the hospital neither 'cause they won't serve him liquor in bed. Last winter we lost my sister Harriet to a cancer in her ovaries. None of us even knew she was sick until I got a telegraph from her friend Sophie telling me to come quick to Abilene. When I got there, I says, 'Honeypie, how come you never called for me?' And she says, 'Why, Millie, when we were little you told me I was such a bother.' And that was the truth, too, because when we were girls, I did say she was a bother when she wouldn't stop following me around, trying on my prettiest clothes whenever I wasn't looking, but after the Lord took her home with Him, my heart just broke to think of poor little Harriet lying in bed with all that pain and not one of her own flesh and blood beside her to hold her hand." Mildred Jessup exhaled a lungful of cigarette smoke. "I believe it don't matter what's been said in the past. When you're in desperate need, family ought to take you in. That's why God grows us together, don't you agree?"

Marie nodded, sympathetic to Mildred's plight. "I expect that's so. It's nice to live away from home now and again, but strangers won't bring us soup in the dark."

Mildred leaned far enough out into the air to smell the dampness on the wind, then told Marie, "Honey, if you see my little girl, you tell her to get her fanny home. Supper's at six."

— **4** —

Rain fell two blocks from downtown, dappling the summer dust under the pecan trees. A humid odor ripe with soiled leaves scented the air where Marie hurried along on an errand for Maude who required some soda mint tablets, a fresh tube of dental cream, and a headache bromo. Wet branches swayed overhead. Sparrows flew in and out of the cloudy wood. An elderly nurse stood on the gallery of Mr. Gray's house, wrapped in a patchwork quilt, watching for lightning. In the narrow alley next door, a middle-aged Negro man in stained cotton overalls struggled atop a ladder with a hammer and a broken storm-shutter; by the next block, the sound of his banging was lost on the wind. A trio of passenger automobiles rattled past with windshields speckled by raindrops and left muddy tracks in the street. The last car, a black Model A Ford, had its motor lamps lit. When Marie had passed through here to work in the morning sunshine, she had seen two yellow dogs rolling in the dust and a small Negro boy with a fish-ing pole scooping worms back into a tin can he had just dropped by the side of the road. Down at the end of the block, a red-haired girl in braids, perhaps Cissie's age, skipped rope on the wooden sidewalk for the mailman while singing a child's nonsense rhyme. *"Acka-backa soda cracka, acka-backa boo! If your daddy chews tobacca, he's a dirty Jew!"* Now these tree-shrouded neighborhoods were silent except for a pattering of rain in the summer leaves. Miles of dense clouds blackened above the prairie and a warm damp wind gusted and Marie wondered why she had left the house without bringing Rachel's rose-handled um-brella along.

The ceiling lamps were lit indoors at Hooker's drugstore downtown as Marie peeked in through the plate-glass from beneath the sidewalk aw-ning. Two teenage girls she didn't know sat on stools at the soda coun-ter sipping cherry phosphates from Coca-Cola glasses. Maude's club friend Trudy stood fourth in line at the pharmacist window in front of a man named Mowry who worked in the textile building next to Dela-haye's. Behind him were the buck-toothed Mitchell sisters, both of whom were older than Maude and suffered chronic rheumatism and recurring attacks of St. Anthony's Fire which kept them housebound most of the time. Though she didn't see the children, Marie went in-side anyhow to ask the druggist if they had come in that afternoon. A little bell rang above the door as she stepped through. The pharmacist looked up with a smile. Marie edged over to the soda fountain, hoping to attract the attention of the druggist when he came out of the stor-age room. She felt increasingly antsy about her children and wanted to get back outdoors. The building was stuffy and warm, smelling of medication and rosewater perfume. Marie smiled at the two girls drinking cherry phosphates and they smiled back before continuing a conversation about a high school boy named Jimbo who had just gotten a job cleaning motorcars at a Dodge Agency in Texarkana. A burly man in a tan fedora emerged from behind an aisle near the magazine rack and went to talk with Mowry by the prescription counter. Leora Mitchell fetched a handkerchief from her purse and blew her nose. Her sister Amelia patted her on the back and whispered something in her ear. The bell over the door rang and a pretty Negro girl in a blue cotton dress came inside. Outdoors, a light rain swirled about on the wind. Store lights were visible clear across the town square and more than half of the automobiles downtown now rumbled by with headlamps lit. The Negro girl went to the soda fountain near the candy display and stood behind one of the stools, but did not sit. Neither of the two girls at the counter looked her way and Marie noticed the Negro girl paid them no mind, staring down at the penny candy in the glasscase, instead. By the pharmacy, Trudy paid for a brown bottle of Nux & Iron tablets with change from her small silvernet bag, thanked the young man behind the cash register, and stepped aside for Mowry and the other man beside him.

Tucking the bottle of tablets into her purse, Trudy saw Marie. With a frown, she said, "Beatrice feels we're in for a terrible storm tonight, dear. Worse than that awful evening Boy-Allen was murdered. She's gathered up all her cats and put them in the cellar with a candle and a big plate of tunafish. Has Maude remembered to take her morning laundry off the line?"

Marie smiled. "Yes, ma'am. We did it together when I came home for lunch. Do you really think there'll be a storm? I'm searching for the children. Mildred Jessup says they may have come downtown to buy candy this afternoon, but I'm afraid now they might've gone to play at the river. You haven't seen them, by any chance, have you? The look of the sky worries me."

"Oh, there'll be an awful storm! Beatrice says so. Why, she's been calling all over town this afternoon to let us know there'll be no Mah Jongg this evening."

The druggist came out of the back, wiping his hands with a white cloth towel. He glanced at the Negro girl by the candy display, then gave Marie a smile and stopped at the counter in front of Trudy who remarked, "Albert, your mother is a dirty cheat."

The druggist laughed. "Oh, she is, is she?"

"I should hope to tell you! She hasn't dealt me a fair hand since Decoration Day, and Beatrice has worn down nine pencils just this summer recording your mother's winning tricks. I've always maintained that it is immoral to be selfish with good fortune."

"Maybe y'all ought to find another game to play. Nobody ever beats Momma at whist."

"Well, that's no surprise at all when her dishonesty is taken into account. May I have my tablets with juice in the morning, Albert?"

The druggist shook his head. "Only mutton tea, warm milk, or lime-water."

Trudy turned to Marie with a frown. "It's positively mystifying why the Lord keeps me here when I'm not permitted to enjoy even the least of life's pleasures."

"That does seem cruel," agreed Marie. If she couldn't work in her garden, what would she do? *Simple joys are the best,* Granny Chamberlain always said. *Without them, our time here on earth would remain a fearsome puzzle and gut-mean.*

Albert laughed. "My guess is you've been scaring the bejeezus out of Him for a while now and He won't be calling you home any time soon. He knows there's no telling what you and your club ladies'll do to the Kingdom once y'all get there."

Trudy folded her purse under her arm. "Thank you for the compliment, Albert. I'll remember to save a seat for you in the pew on Sunday." Before departing, she reached over and laid a hand on Marie's wrist. "Dear, please remind Maude to wrap her wicker in wet canvas before dark. Beatrice truly believes there'll be a horrible storm tonight."

The downstairs of Delahaye's restaurant was hectic with roaring oilworkers and stiff-collared businessmen seated in a thick smoky haze of burning cigars and amber lamplight. Ignoring rude catcalls from a corner table, Marie crossed quickly to the cash register at the end of the bar where Idabelle sat tabulating dinner bills. Noise from the busy billiard room upstairs racketed in the rear stairwell. The back door was propped open to the lot behind the building and a swirling draft forced rain into the narrow entry hall. She peeked up the staircase to Jimmy Delahaye's office where she heard him on the telephone. They had gone to the movies twice now and had a fair time. Not alone, of course. Once Idabelle had come along, and another night Lucius brought a young lady from Longview whose voice was hoarse as a man's. Delahaye had been a prefect gentleman in not calling attention to himself and Marie as they sat in the theater. Then he had tried to kiss her again on the walk home that second night and she had turned her head to thwart him, why exactly she didn't know. She had wanted to apologize to Jimmy Delahaye and have him try again, but did not and so he had escorted her the rest of the way home in silence, leaving Marie feeling desolate and humiliated. Perhaps he was simply too handsome and she couldn't trust herself, any longer. How she behaved that night in his parlor worried her half to death. Never in her life had she been so careless. If Maude knew she had gone there, the children might still have a warm bed in her house, but Marie herself would likely be sleeping out back with the chickens. Whatever had come over her needed more attention. She was, after all, married to a man Marie believed she still loved. But then yesterday Delahaye invited her to another picture show on Saturday night, and she had accepted. Why? No good could come from any of this. Wasn't that so? What her heart required these days had become a mystery to her, and raising her thoughts to heaven provided little relief. Yet as she went about her business during the day, whether in haste or calm, she was curiously aware of the faintest change coming over her heart.

Counting a handful of dollar bills into the register, Idabelle remarked, "I declare, honey, you must be some kind of glutton for punishment."

"Pardon?" Marie frowned. "What do you mean by that?"

At the far end of the bar, Lucius Beauchamp wiped off the mahogany countertop with a cotton cloth. Idabelle called over to him above the din of voices. "LUCIUS, HONEY, LOOK WHO'S BACK!"

Lucius saw Marie and waved.

She waved back to the bartender, then asked Idabelle, "Why do you say that?" She never had any idea what was being said about her and half the time she didn't follow the jokes told in her presence, either.

Upstairs, a billiard ball hit the floor and rolled across the room. Raucous laughter erupted into the stairwell next to Delahaye's office. Marie glanced up the stairs and thought about Jimmy. She wanted to go up and see him for a minute or two, but she felt silly and scared. Out front of the restaurant, a motor horn blared as a truck narrowly avoiding crashing into a Ford on the wet pavement. Rain was falling harder now and Marie grew nervous imagining her children at play in the thick woods near the river.

"I just never seen anyone come back to work once she was done for the day," said Idabelle, shutting the cash register. "If I didn't know better, I might think you were sweet on Jimmy, after all."

Lucius walked along behind the bar toward Idabelle and Marie, wiping off the counter with the washcloth as he approached. A group of men from the cotton mill wearing black slicker coats came in from outdoors, rainwater dripping from their hats.

"That's the most ridiculous thing I've ever heard," Marie replied, blushing. "You know I can't imagine being married to any man but Harry." Then, in case those words might be relayed to Jimmy, she added, "Although I do admit that Mr. Delahaye is a fine dancer and an engaging storyteller. I'm sure any girl would find him quite good company on a date." Any girl with the nerve for romance, Marie thought, still ashamed of her cowardice. Maybe she'd go upstairs, after all.

"Not this one, honeypie," Idabelle cackled. "He's a drinker and a flirt."

"Name me a fellow in Texas over the age of twelve who ain't," said Lucius, wiping the counter clean near the cash register. He scratched his beard. "Old Jimmy ain't nothing special in that regard."

"He does flirt quite a lot," agreed Marie, "but what man doesn't? I still think he's awfully sweet, especially for a boss." She adored Jimmy Delahaye's flirtations. Harry flirted, but not with her any longer. Some mornings she wore perfume and he didn't even notice. Where had his heart gone? Too far from her, she worried.

"I won't date a man with roving eyes," Idabelle said. "I believe it's impolite and disrespectful. If he wants to go with me, he ought to have better manners than that."

"That's just it, sweetheart," Lucius told Idabelle. "He don't want to go with you. It's Marie here he's stuck on." He turned to Marie. "Ain't that right?"

She blushed. "I doubt that's true. We've only gone to the picture show twice, and certainly not as anything but friends. Besides, you ought to know I've been terribly busy. I doubt I'd have the time for romance, even if I weren't married, which I am, don't forget. In fact, I expect Harry to come down here by train next month." What balderdash! She doubted Harry would ever come down here unless one of the children got hurt or became seriously ill. But Marie knew it was important that she begin to deflect attention away from herself and Delahaye. This was all so difficult. What was she going to do?

"Don't wait too long to go again, honey," Idabelle advised. "Jimmy's got itchy feet."

A homely fellow in a blue business suit came up to the cash register and handed his ticket to Idabelle with a handful of coins. Marie got a whiff of bay rum and bootleg whiskey and avoided his drooping eyes, gazing instead out through the rear hallway to the grassy backyard where Julius Reeves had just come into the yard through the back gate carrying a shovel. He wore a long brown coat and a floppy cotton hat and his boots were covered in mud, his sooty face half-hidden by the sagging rim of the hat. He walked through the windy rain toward the side of the building where he called up to someone on the second floor. Another round of laughter from the billiard room echoed into the empty stairwell as the cash register rang closed and the homely man walked off.

"Jimmy didn't really call you back to work, did he?" Idabelle asked Marie, sitting back onto her stool. "Because if he did, why, I'd just have to go upstairs and give that man a piece of my mind. It's not right to expect you to come down here all hours of the day when you've got kiddies at home."

Hoping to change the topic of conversation away from her perplexing situation with Jimmy Delahaye, Marie asked, "Have you seen
my children since school let out? I've been looking all over for them.
Mildred Jessup thinks they might've walked downtown to buy candy."

Idabelle shook her head as Lucius slipped behind her, heading into
the back hallway. He went to a storage closet under the stairwell and
took out a mop and a bucket. Idabelle said to Marie, "I'm not concerned. When Rachel and I were little, we'd sneak out after bedtime
and run all over downtown. One Halloween, we captured a raccoon in
an old canvas sack and dropped him down mean old Widow Miller's
coal chute. When he chewed himself free, Widow Miller thought he
was a burglar come to steal her wedding ring, so she took a shot at him
on the stairs with her father's old Confederate revolver and popped a
hole in the basement furnace which started a fire and nearly burned
up her whole house. Three firewagons had to be called. Of course,
that was long before Boy-Allen. I'm not sure I'd have the nerve to go
out after dark these days."

Lucius came back behind the bar with a bucket and a wet mop.
"Looks like Jimmy's got poor old Julius digging a hole to China."

Marie saw Julius laboring with the shovel in the muddy grass a few
feet from the plank fence. Idabelle left the cash register for a look, too.

Marie asked, "Why does he need to do that now? It's raining."

Lucius told her, "Sewer line's broke and there ain't nobody but a
out-of-work nigger that's gonna dig a hole in the ground with a thunderstorm coming."

Idabelle stood alone in the drafty hall watching. Rain fell harder
now, blown slantways on the wind. Julius paused briefly to pull his collar tight on the neck, and jammed the shovel back down into the wet
earth. Marie shuddered. Why persuade someone to manual labor in a
driving rain? She had never heard of such a thing. It seemed a mean
and thoughtless imposition, regardless of the needful circumstance.
Upstairs in the billiard room, Jimmy Delahaye shouted a crude obscenity and a roar of laughter ensued in the hollow staircase. Maybe
Marie wouldn't go up, after all. No, she was much too busy. Besides,
she needed to get the children home.

Strolling back to the register, Idabelle remarked, "I'd take a dime for every hole in the ground old Hardy Hooper's gonna be digging at Huntsville come wintertime."

"He'll be lucky if he ain't occupying a hole of his own," said Lucius, filling the bucket with water from a tap below the counter. He smelled strongly of corn liquor.

"Who's Hardy Hooper?" asked Marie.

"A sweet-talking colored fellow from Longview," Idabelle replied, ringing up a bill left at the register, "who come home last week and shot his wife in the head when he found out she didn't have his supper waiting for him."

"He claimed it wasn't the first time she ain't done it, neither," Lucius added. "Says he was justified 'cause of a contract with her daddy when Hardy married her that said Sallie couldn't never be late with supper or mending rents in his clothes. I guess Hardy didn't have no complaints with that second part 'cause he kept his shoes on the whole time they stood him up before Judge Bass."

Disturbed by the worsening rain, Marie asked Idabelle if anybody had an umbrella she might borrow when she went back outdoors again to look for the children. "I'm afraid they may have gone to the river."

"Now, that ain't too smart," said Lucius, mopping the floor behind the counter where he had spilled a pot of coffee an hour earlier. "Kids oughta know better'n to fool around out there in this weather. Storm comes, that river'll rise quicker'n a snake in a henhouse. They can be wadin' in the sand one moment, then suddenly find themselves floatin' down to the Gulf of Mexico."

"Lucius!" Idabelle scowled. "For goodness sakes, don't scare her!"

Marie felt herself go cold with fear. "I had no idea it was that dangerous. Mildred didn't say a word about floods."

Idabelle turned to Marie. "Honey, nobody's died in the river 'round here in years except Boy-Allen and he didn't fall in on his own. Those kids of yours are plenty smart enough to keep their feet out of the water when it begins to rise. Lili knows better anyhow. She'll see they don't get themselves in trouble. I'm sure they're playing somewhere in town with their friends. There's no sense in worrying. Go home. I'm sure they'll be back soon enough." She rang shut the cash register. "Wait here a moment."

Idabelle went down to the end of the bar and leaned into the coatroom where she grabbed her own umbrella off a hook. Outdoors, the rain had slowed again to a steady drizzle. Looking through the rear hallway to the backyard, Marie watched Julius laboring with the shovel, knee-deep in mud and grass, his clothing soaked, his stern face coal-dark in the rainy gloom. As another group of wet oilworkers entered the restaurant by the front door, Idabelle handed her umbrella over to Marie.

"Lucius'll take me home in his Ford," she smiled, slipping an arm about the bartender's waist. "Keep your kiddies indoors tonight, honey. Momma thinks there's a big storm coming."

— 5 —

Marie peeked out through the sitting room curtains at the cloudy gray sky, waiting anxiously for the children to come home for supper. Where on earth were they? She hoped Cissie hadn't taken them off on some silly adventure. When Marie was a girl, she and Violet and Emeline would get rowboats and go behind the paddle cruisers by the big wheels because they enjoyed the excitement of getting tossed by the waves. It never dawned on them what a terrible risk they were taking, but looking back Marie saw how absurdly dangerous it really was. She hoped her daughter had better sense.

Rain sprinkled in the street and the wind gusted off and on, shaking damp leaves from the cottonwoods. Indoors, a warm odor of toasted cheese filled the house and Maude had the lights on in the kitchen. Idle on the sofa after cleaning out her bedroom closet, Rachel put down Maude's thumbworn copy of *The Man Nobody Knows*, and sighed. "I have to tell you, dear, sometimes CW could be mean as a crab, although thinking back on it now I don't believe that was ever his truest intention. More often than not, he acted his cruelest when he was simply done in by work. You see, he always had quite a bit on his mind, flying concerns and so forth, that gave him fits and worry, and I can't say I was any great up-lifter, either. I honestly don't recall a single visit where I didn't pester him to take me here or there, or put on some silly show of affection to impress Mother who never felt any genuine fondness for him, anyhow."

"Don't remember that about CW," Marie advised, letting the curtain fall closed. She walked over to the sofa and sat down next to Rachel whose eyes still watered when she spoke of her lost aviator. "It's foolish to pierce your heart with misgivings over past errors. Honest to goodness, we trouble our lives so thoroughly by guilt and suspicions of failure, I often wonder what we think we're supposed to be doing. You've been more than adequate to the worst, dear, and I believe you'll make good from all of this if only you'll refuse the bitterness. CW loved you very much. You mustn't forget that."

"I suppose you're right."

"Just don't take on so about these supposed faults," Marie suggested, remembering something Aunt Hattie used to say. "Without windows, I'm sure we'd all look a fright."

Rachel got up and went over to the piano and lightly fingered the keys, tinkling a short scale as the wind gusted against the storm-shutters. She told Marie, "Mother's decided I ought to bundle myself out of doors and devote more time each evening to Baptist youth activities. She believes it'd give me more pep and dispense with what she calls my more vulgar impulses. Of course, Mother can no more refrain from criticizing me than she could quit breathing. It's so tiresome."

"You know, I've always found church fellowship to be inspiring. We weren't meant to walk alone. Belonging to something larger than ourselves offers the hope of the divine. These trials we endure throughout our lives would be fairly intolerable without the mercy of another's hand to hold. Really, as I grow older I'm convinced it's companionship, more than faith, that ties us to heaven."

Dishes clanked in the kitchen as Maude finished sorting her collection of sweet jellies in the pantry and began preparing for supper. Rain drummed on the rooftop. The gray sky seemed darker yet. Looking across the sitting room to the window, Marie noticed a flurry of windblown leaves shower the damp street outside. She was concerned that Cissie and Henry hadn't worn their raincoats out to play after school. She ought to have insisted. Had Boy-Allen's mother worried so for her own child's whereabouts the night he died? Or Mrs. Kritt that terrible afternoon of the Fourth? How can any mother care too much for her child?

Rachel went over to the radio and tuned to a performance of dance music, but kept the volume low. Then she reached into the walnut curio cabinet and drew something out which she brought back across the room to show Marie.

"Have you seen this?" She handed over a small ivory pendant carved in the shape of a figurine, perhaps three inches high.

Marie shook her head. "What is it?" She felt so badly for Rachel. That sweet boy she loved had gone and left her alone. Where would she ever find her true smile again?

"Mother of the Lamb," said Rachel, directing Marie's attention to the bowed head of the Madonna whose arms were folded as if cradling an infant. "CW wore it wherever he flew. When the wreck of his airplane was pulled from the waters of Lake Pontchartrain, the coroner collected it together with the rest of his belongings. CW's mother gave it to me on the morning of his funeral."

"How kind of her."

"Do you think so? I've been terribly afraid she's held a grudge against me in her heart for causing CW to fly away from here that awful evening. Of course, she's got every right in the world to despise me, but I'm not sure I could bear it if I thought she really did."

Returning the solemn icon to Rachel, Marie said, "Tell me, dear: would you live your life any differently if somehow you knew the hour of your passing beforehand?"

Rachel frowned. "Pardon?"

"Well, do you think we have a purpose that keeps us alert to the grim and tender, while preparing our hearts for the world to come?"

Rachel went to the window and drew back the curtain and glanced out on the rain-dampened street. She told Marie, "Since I was little, I've had peculiar suspicions of being swallowed up whole by such a dreadful sadness that sometimes I doubt I've ever been able to believe in the ordinary joy other people feel, and it's terrified me for so long that each morning I've risen from bed expecting to be borne away with grief over some sudden calamity. And then CW was killed, and cross my heart and body, dear, I realized I've lived all my life before in perfect peace."

— 6 —

Dressed in a black slicker, Marie raised Idabelle's umbrella under the veranda and watched a pair of motorcars pass by. She had waited for the children quite a while now and had finally surrendered to panic. While fitting her out in Maude's raincoat and galoshes, Rachel gave Marie directions through the woods to the river where she reluctantly guessed the children had gone after school. Maude telephoned the fire department. As the car lamps disappeared, Marie walked down the steps and crossed the street into the cottonwood grove. For the past hour, storm clouds had grown darker and rain drizzled through the treetops, sprinkling pools of muddy water where Marie trod ghostlike in the soggy earth. Fog swirled up from the afternoon bog like steam in the humid thicket and the slow rain fell soundless under the wind. She found a narrow path in the dense pine thicket and followed it for a while. Thunder rumbled off somewhere to the northeast and the wind rose and rain fell harder. Her shoes sank in grassy mud as she tramped forward, branches whipped about raking her face and arms. Brambles obscured the woods ahead. She stumbled across a fallen pine log and nearly fell. Treetops shook wildly overhead and her umbrella caught in a clump of low branches and tore apart when she pulled it free. Stepping into a narrow clearing without benefit of cover, Marie was soaked in a black downpour barely filtered through the ruined leaves above. Disoriented by this sudden deluge, she stumbled sideways into the thicket of mud and wet leaves that smelled of black rot, her eyes clouded with rain, shoes soaked and muddy, clothing damp and sticky. She shouted Cissie's name, then Henry's and Lili's, calling frantically for the children until a deafening thunderclap shook the muddy earth and the storm surged in the rainy dark treetops and she cowered in the underbrush, listening to the wind roar.

A drifting gust tore at the dripping cottonwood. Marie called to the children, listened, and called again. Rain streamed down from the trees, soaking the earth and leaves. Her clothes were drenched, her face and hands scratched from ragged discarded branches. Another electric flash of lightning lit the black cloudstrewn sky overhead. Harry would have been furious with her for allowing the children to wander off by themselves with a storm imminent, for failing to organize a proper search, for chasing off into the woods alone. He would have given her a lecture about carelessness and not spoken to her for a week — except to mention that cruel afternoon at Lake Calhoun. Again and again and again. Well, good gracious, where had *he* been that day? Did he not think *her* heart broke, too, with every thought of that tragedy? Who walked a longer road with guilt as a companion than she, forever bound to the horrid sight of her firstborn child disappearing beneath the surface of that troubled water? Scolding her year after year was fine and fair. Perhaps she deserved it, but then why wasn't *he* here now to watch over the children who were every bit his responsibility as hers, were they not? What was wrong with *him*?

Rain streamed off her head, flooding her eyes and ears, soaking her dress beneath the raincoat. Under a damp pine tree she wiped her eyes and pushed away strands of wet hair that lay across her face. Frantic now and deafened by a thunderous wind, she trampled a narrow path into the thicket, fending off dipping branches as she hurried her fearful course to the river. She lost a shoe and grabbed it up muddy from the leafy bog and replaced it onto her foot. Boy-Allen had been murdered in these woods during the torrential downpour that bitter evening in May, and Marie heard there were Negroes from Shantytown piloting flat-bottomed skiffs on cloudy nights under the cypress gloom who maintained that poor Boy-Allen still huddled on a brush pile high atop the leafy riverbank clearly visible from deeper water in the smoky haze of hand-held kerosene lamps, his sad eyes phosphorescent like the foamy current, his little slicker and rubber boots perpetually mudcaked and bloody. Did his killer still haunt these woods?

When the rumble of an enormous thunderclap faded, Marie could hear the river rushing by the shore, dragging flotsam along downstream, floating logs and the mud-splashed underpinnings of old fishing shacks torn to splinters in the rising storm. She worked her way past a blackberry bramble atop the riverbank and shouted for her children and searched the muddy sandbar in the gloom and called their names again and again across the steady gray rain while hiding her face from the storm that blew harder still. All she heard was the swollen river flowing past beneath her and the damp wind roaring through the soggy cypress leaves above. Somewhere down below she caught a glimpse of swirling water pitch-black with rotting leaves of lilies and broken saplings and mud. Keeping close to the bluff, she discovered an old fisherman's trail that led upriver through the dark bramble. A narrow footpath dipped below the bluff into a damp patch of blackberries and water reeds where she could smell the river and hear the steady hiss of heavy rainfall on the swift stream and see the ugly storm clouds above, roiling greenish-black with a rutted underbelly like hazy cobblestone. A false step toward the sandbar sank one foot into the muck and nearly threw her off-balance. She felt the spray of the rushing current on her face as she staggered free. Leaves fluttered about on the wind and a child's anxious voice shrieked across the dark gray twilight. She looked up the embankment and saw a dog emerging from the bramble, soaked and frantic, Lili Jessup's collie. An instant later, it disappeared again. Marie struggled forward through the flattened reeds, scrambling toward higher ground, away from the sandbar and the rising water. She heard the collie barking somewhere off in the woods.

Rain fell harder. She sloshed upwards through the mud toward a shelter of pine trees that hung solemnly over the embankment. Across the river, somebody had lit a fire within a garbage can surrounded by human forms in the windy dark. More detritus released by the storm upstream drifted silently past. Reaching the largest pine, she cowered briefly beneath its sheltering boughs. In the thunder's lull, Marie thought she heard a child's cry again, not too far off. She stared hard toward the river and heard a wailing voice once more and knew she was near enough to respond, so she shouted back into the fierce downpour and heard a plaintive yell for help that sounded very much like her own daughter.

Cissie came out of a blackberry thicket above the river like a wild-eyed spook, dragging her little brother by the hand, both drenched in mud. Seeing her mother, she slumped and began to wail. Henry did, too, and Marie rushed to embrace them as a thunderous wind howled across the pinewoods, flailing millions of rain-sodden leaves and cracked saplings onto the river. Marie hugged and kissed them both and held them close and heard herself whimpering during a wind lull and whispered a prayer of abject humility for another prayer already answered.

For a short period, she cuddled with her children beneath a ragged cottonwood, grateful to the Lord for this rescue. Cissie was sobbing quietly while Henry pressed himself to Marie's bosom, both refusing to budge from her care. Rain hissed loudly on the water, dripping, too, from Marie's hair, which clung like damp brown seaweed to her narrow face. Cold and repentant, Cissie explained how she and Henry had wound up drenched and muddy in the river. "It was all Mr. Slopey's fault, Momma! He fell in the water and got stuck and couldn't get out! Then Biscuit started barking at him and he got scared and Lili went to get a rope and it began raining so hard I couldn't see, and then Henry tried to save Mr. Slopey all by himself and he went in the river and that's how he got stuck, too! And I had to swim with all my clothes on just to get him out! Oh, Momma, I never been so scared in my life!"

"Where's Lili now?"

"I don't know, Momma," Cissie moaned. "I called for her to come back to help us, but I guess she didn't hear me."

"I saw Lili's collie in the woods a few minutes before I found you," Marie told Cissie. "Do you suppose Lili was going to Shantytown for help?"

Cissie sobbed. "I don't know."

Still shivering, Henry spoke up for the first time, "I saw Mr. Slopey get drowned, Momma. I yelled at him to swim, but he didn't know how."

Cissie added, "Soon as he got himself unstuck from the mud, the river swept him away. We tried to grab his rope, but I couldn't! It was awful."

"My goodness."

"I'm scared, Momma," Henry whined.

"So am I, honey."

"Can we go home?"

Thoroughly spent from fright and relief, Marie hugged her son tightly to her breast. "Of course, we can, sweetie. Yes, yes, yes."

— 7 —

At the end of town, Maude stood under the eaves on her front porch, looking out toward the low black clouds approaching from the northeast. Lightning flashed here and there. Horses and cattle cornered in wide pastures fled to distant fencelines. A stiff wind swept across ten thousand acres of oak trees and summer grass, and brought more rain as a greater storm drew near. Next door at the Jessup's, storm-shutters banged loudly and Lili's chickens squawked in a dozen wire cages. Behind the open kitchen door, Rachel was shouting to somebody in the backyard when Marie followed her children up the muddy street to the house. A flurry of leaves swirled past the picket fence. Cissie called to Maude, "Grandma! Grandma!"

Rachel hurried out onto the back porch. Marie slowed her pace as both children sloshed off toward the house. Her legs were still trembling. She needed to lie down.

"Where in heaven's name have you been?" Maude cried after one look at the children, both dripping muddy water from their clothing. "For goodness sakes, we've been calling all over town! You scared us half to death!"

"We were scared, too!" Cissie wailed. "Henry fell in the river and I tried to save him and almost drowned myself and then we got lost in the woods until Momma came and found us!"

"Good heavens!"

Rachel came to the back gate. "Oh, you poor dears!"

Maude waited on the porch as Marie came up to the house. Remaining under the porch eaves, she asked her daughter-in-law, "Honey, are you all right?"

"I suppose so," replied Marie, exhausted by the hike through the woods from the river. Rainwater dripped from her hair and Idabelle's umbrella had been blown to tatters. She felt like a wreck, but relieved, too, unburdened by their rescue. "It was quite an ordeal. I'm just grateful we're home."

A strong gust out of the cottonwoods across the street blew rain into the yard. Rachel was staring at the black thunderclouds rolling still closer to town. Her hair curled about her face as she turned back to Maude. "I tell you, it'll be a tornado, Mother, believe me. We'll have to hide in the potato cellar."

Marie's heart went cold. "Tornado?"

"Nonsense!" Maude snorted. "There hasn't been a tornado through here in eighty years. You can ask Beatrice."

Hearing the children's voices in the road, Mildred Jessup raised the window on her bedroom and shouted for her daughter, "Lili, you come home this instant! Supper's on the table!"

Marie hurried over to the Jessup's gate. "She's not here, Mrs. Jessup. The children had an accident at the river and Cissie says Lili went to Shantytown for help."

The window curtains parted and Mildred Jessup leaned out, horror on her face. "What sort of accident?"

Wind swept across the road, fanning leaves into both yards. Speaking above the damp gust, Marie replied, "I'm sure Lili's just fine! Apparently, that old swayback fell into the river and got washed away!"

"Good Lord!" Rachel cried, coming over. "Are you sure?"

Maude walked to the end of the veranda. "Haven't I told you that river's no place for children? Ever since Jimmy McGuire drowned I've stayed away."

"Mother, that was forty years ago. You just can't swim, is all. That's why you don't go to the river."

Rain began to fall harder again as the wind rose in the cottonwoods. Cissie passed through Maude's gate and crossed the yard to the Jessup's where she went to explain Lili's absence to Mildred. Henry stood in the rain with his hands held palms up, allowing some of the mud to wash off.

Lightning flashed in the northeast from the belly of the black thunderheads. The sky seemed darker. Wind blew hard in the street. Shaking her head, Maude left the porch for indoors, letting the screen door slam shut behind her.

Rachel told Marie, "Don't listen to Mother. She wouldn't recognize a tornado if one flew up her skirt. Believe you me, it's coming."

Thunder rumbled across the prairie. Henry went to sit on the porchsteps and watch the rain-gray sky for lightning. Marie looked quickly back toward the horizon where the huge greenish clouds had drifted closer to earth. She felt a prickling up the back of her neck.

"CW flew next to a tornado in Oklahoma once," Rachel said, with an eye on the approaching stormclouds. "His air route took him so close he could see roof shingles from Guthrie spinning in the funnel cloud. He told me it nearly pulled the wings off his airplane when he was still half a mile away. Can you imagine that? Only a fool wouldn't take cover if he knew one was coming." She glanced back at the porch. "Why, I swear sometimes Mother's become dippy in her old age."

Monstrous black clouds filled the sky horizon, lit by electric flashes of lightning. Raindrops blew about on the wind. Next door, Mildred Jessup was yelling at her brother as Cissie hurried back across the yard toward the kitchen. The chickencoop was alive with squawking hens.

"I need to go change clothes," Marie announced. "I'm soaking wet. So are the children."

"Of course you should," Rachel agreed. "I have to let the horses out to pasture before the storm arrives. Just don't dawdle. I've been telling Mother for more than an hour now that we ought to wait in the potato cellar until the storm passes. For the children's sake, at the very least."

"I'll make the suggestion myself," said Marie, and walked off to the front gate, her knees shaking from fear and fatigue. The rain softened again, but wind crackled in the pecan trees down the street and the town looked dark.

Indoors, kerosene lamps provided the sole illumination. All the electric power in Bellemont had gone down an hour earlier and amber shadows from the glass table lamps lent a gloomy cast to the interior of the small house. Cissie was already in the bedroom undressing when Marie came in.

"Honey, where's your brother?"

Cissie shrugged and pulled off her socks.

Marie frowned. She had seen Henry go indoors while she was still speaking with Rachel. He knew she wanted him out of the rain. If Harry were here, her son would not be so difficult.

"May I take a bath, Momma?" Cissie asked, as she stripped off the last of her wet clothing. "I'm awfully cold."

Marie peeked out the window to the backyard where the chinaberry tree shook wildly in the wind. Thousands of dirty leaves blew slantways and rain pelted the roof of the house. Out of the corner of her eye, she saw Henry disappear into the chickencoop.

"Can I, Momma?" Cissie stood beside the bed wrapped in a cotton towel. She rubbed her sockless feet on the rug. "I feel dirty as a monkey."

A light rain blew against the windowglass. Dressed in only a lavender tea gown and one of her husband's old brown fedoras, Mildred Jessup was out in the backyard now, dragging an old canvas tarpaulin out from under her house. Rachel came around to the front and entered by the veranda. The door slammed shut in the draft and Marie heard Rachel open the windows in the parlor.

"Not now," she said to her daughter. She felt fear grow once again in her stomach. "Just put on something dry until later. You can have a bath before you go to bed."

"Momma!"

"Don't argue with me!"

After quickly changing into a dry khaki dress of her own, Marie left the bedroom to go bring Henry indoors. In the kitchen, Maude busied herself peeling red potatoes for a pot of vegetable stew simmering on the stove. A draft fluttered in the open window curtains above the sink. As Marie hurried by, Maude remarked, "We'll eat in half an hour."

From the living room hallway, Rachel called out, "For Godsakes, Mother, this house may be flying over Arkansas by then! Would you please put out that stove and take your shawl! We need to go to the cellar right now!"

Lightning flashed across the ugly green sky. Moments later, a rolling thunderclap shook the Haviland china in Maude's oak sideboard. Rachel cursed at her mother as Marie went out the back door into the wind. Most of the sky was blackened with thunderclouds, miles of summer grass bent low by rain. From the kitchen porch, one might have thought the world was shrinking: fields and pinewoods, old framehouses along the street, drawn into the widening dark and eradicated. Mildred Jessup leaned at the fence between yards. The canvas she sought to cover Lili's rabbit hutch with was torn and useless. Worry over her daughter showed on Mildred's face. Her brother Fritz had come out of the house and stood at the top of the stairs, dressed in a fine gray Sunday suit. His hair was combed nicely and slicked back with oil. A grim expression crossed his lips, though his eyes were keen in the dim gray light as he coughed violently and spoke to Mildred in a husky voice beneath the wind. Rachel raised the bedroom window behind the chinaberry tree, and Marie rushed down from the kitchen porch into the muddy yard directly to the chickencoop where she had last seen Henry. His little voice issued from within. Opening the screen door, she found him by the cages, feeding and watering the screeching chickens. A violent gust of wind shook the small structure and chilled her skin.

After slinging grain into one of the cages, Henry looked up and saw his mother. "Grandma forgot to feed 'em, Momma. They were hungry."

"I know, dear." Marie realized her lips were trembling.

"They're scared, too!"

"We have to go back indoors, honey. It's too dangerous to stay out here. There's a bad storm coming."

"But I'm not done yet!"

Another loud crack of thunder rattled the plank walls of the old chickencoop, startling Henry so that he dropped the pail of grain onto the dirt floor. Looking outdoors, Marie saw streams of water blowing wildly across the yard. Mildred had left the fence to send her brother back up the steps of the Jessup's porch where he stood now with his arms raised under the driving rain. Inside the chickencoop, Henry was on his hands and knees in the dirt scooping the grain he had spilled back into the tin pail. The chickens squawked. Lightning lit the sky overhead. Marie ran to her son and grabbed his arm and heaved him to his feet. "We have to go, honey."

"Momma, no!"

"Yes!"

She pried his fingers off the bucket, flinging it back into the dirt. A huge wind gust nearly toppled the chickencoop. The old door fell off its hinges. Rain blew inside. Henry struggled to pick up the grain pail and finish his chores.

"LEMME GO, MOMMA! LEMME GO!"

Then Marie heard Rachel's voice above the wind, screaming her name from the house. She swept Henry up into her arms and peeked out and saw Maude and Rachel and Cissie descending the back staircase, carrying bundles. The chinaberry tree twisted and shook, raking the side of the house. Across the yard, millions of leaves and broken twigs littered the black sky. Debris from College Street flew past the house. Both Mildred and her brother were gone from the Jessup's yard and the torn canvas tarpaulin blown to heaven. Rachel grabbed Marie's wrist and shouted directly into her face. "FOLLOW ME!"

Carrying her bunny rabbit Lulu-Belle, Cissie hurried by with Maude a few feet away. Rachel took Henry by the hand and led him off from the chickencoop around to the back of the house by the water pump and out to where the potato cellar lay half-hidden in the scrub grass and weeds. Although Marie knew the pasture fence was close by, she couldn't see it. Dirt stung her eyes. Rachel hurried to the cellar and flung the doors open. Both Henry and Cissie were screaming like birds, "GRANDMA! GRANDMA!"

Maude had fallen into the weeds, her hands shielding the wind-blown dirt from her face.

"MAUDE!" Marie went to help her up while Rachel urged the children down into the cellar. A thunderous roar rose on the prairie and the wind blew so hard Marie was certain her clothes were about to be torn from her body. Maude collapsed again into the weeds.

"MOTHER!" Rachel rushed over. She shouted to Marie above the wind, "GO DOWN INTO THE CELLAR WITH THE CHILDREN! I'LL HELP MOTHER!"

Mildred Jessup and Fritz arrived like ghosts out of the windy dark, wrapped in tattered brown cotton blankets. Mildred's face was streaked with muddy tears, her hair blown wild by the storm. Fritz wore a faint smile that offered no indication of fear. Neither spoke as they hurried toward the cellar entrance and disappeared beneath the damp earth. Rachel had Maude back on her feet now and guided her toward the potato cellar. At the top of the stairs, Marie took Maude's hand. From somewhere below, she heard Cissie screaming for her to hurry. Nearly blinded by blowing grass and leaves, Marie led Maude down into the cellar, then went to her children as Rachel let the doors slam shut overhead, exiling them into darkness.

An odor of dirt-soaked potatoes and fermenting fruit and mildew pervaded the dank cellar eight feet underground. Rachel bolted the doors, then lit a smoky lamp. Rain dripped through the cellar doors, which banged relentlessly in the roaring wind. Dust soft as mist from the plank ceiling filled the damp air of the small dirt enclosure. Maude sneezed aloud. Mildred and her brother scuttled to the rear of the cellar. Cissie held hands with Henry, whispering comfort in his ear. Marie huddled beside her children as a noise like thousands of stampeding horses grew louder. Rachel lit a second lamp and placed it on the dirt floor at her feet. The bright flame flickered in a damp draft from above.

"It's a cyclone, Momma, isn't it?" Cissie blurted out. "Like the one that took Dorothy to Oz!"

"Shhh!"

"But it is, isn't it?"

"I don't know, honey." She had never seen a tornado. Auntie Florence had one pass right over top of her at Gorham in '25 and barely survived. It was all she ever spoke of any more.

The cellar doors rattled violently from the wind gusts. Mildred Jessup moaned aloud back in her dark dusty corner. Her brother had his gaze fixed upon Rachel's burning lamp. He muffled a bad cough. Maude watched the cellar doors.

Hugging her bunny, Cissie murmured, "Should we say a prayer, Momma?"

"Of course."

"Will you do it for us, Momma? I'm too scared."

"All right." Unremitting belief in petition was something Marie had never forsaken, having committed dozens of supplications from the Book of Common Prayer to memory for a variety of needs since girlhood. Linking hands with her frightened children, she recited, "O God, merciful and compassionate, who are ever ready to hear the prayers of those who put their trust in thee; Graciously hearken to us who call upon thee, and grant us thy help in this our need; through Jesus Christ our Lord. Amen."

"Amen," Cissie repeated.

Henry sneezed in the shadows.

The rattling of the cellar doors persisted as Rachel murmured something to Maude who quickly shushed her. Mildred Jessup sobbed quietly in her black corner, but her brother Fritz spoke out from the dark in a grim voice, saying, "Once in Ohio, I saw a vision of Christ in a rainstorm where a trestle had collapsed. The river that ran underneath was filled with bodies from a passenger train that went over in the dark. I was up on the bluffs with a couple of fellows waving lanterns where we saw coal still burning red-hot underwater and we thought the engine had sank, and those few that hadn't already drowned were begging us to climb down and rescue them, though there wasn't any good way off the bluffs with the trestle gone. That's when I saw Him standing on the far shore looking like His picture in the Bible except He was naked as a jaybird and held a candle that burned bright as day when the sky was raining pitchforks. I watched the Lord jump into that cold river and swim back and forth from the wreck to the shore until sixteen lucky people were saved from drowning and nobody else called for help and His work was done and He swam off downriver alone."

The cellar doors wrenched hard at the bolt and hinges and the sodden floor beneath Marie's feet began to tremble like the world was about to end. Fritz coughed in the dark.

From the shadows, Maude raised her voice: *"Then the Lord answered Job out of the whirlwind, and said, 'Who is this that darkeneth counsel by words without knowledge?'"*

Rachel said, "Mother, you promised."

"I did nothing of the sort."

Rachel grabbed the lamp and thrust it into her mother's face. "Do not start quoting the Bible in this cellar!"

Marie shouted at her, "Rachel, please!"

Clearing his throat, Fritz spoke above the wind. "Jesus swam in the cold river that night like an ordinary man. Not once did He walk upon the water like He done at Galilee. He saved sixteen people's lives. That was His miracle. I saw a vision of Christ naked on the shore and He wasn't at all wondrous to look at, only what He did that night in the river. He saved sixteen human lives by Himself and swam away without asking for recompense, and I was blessed to witness, which is God's own truth."

The ground trembled as if a burly steam locomotive were crossing the pasture just a few yards away while the roaring of the wind rose to a high keening that suddenly drew close upon the old potato cellar.

"MOMMA!" Cissie shrieked. "MOMMA!"

The bunny wriggled out of her arms.

Then the cellar doors flew apart with a loud bang and both of Rachel's lanterns went out and the cellar became black and Mildred Jessup screamed and the noise from the wind was so great Marie had to pinch Cissie's arm to gain her attention and force Henry down between them both as the potato cellar filled with dust and debris and Marie fought to breathe and thought she could not and believed that she and her children were about to perish right there underground. A deafening roar thundered from outside, screech of metal and wood reluctantly dividing in violent ascension. One of the cellar doors disappeared, drawn up into the sky with the cold lantern from the bottom of the stairs. Marie covered her ears. Rachel screamed and screamed as Maude's newly knit shawl was lost to the voracious wind and Mildred Jessup was struck in the head by an empty Mason jar and knocked unconscious while her brother Fritz crawled on his knees to the bottom of the cellar stairs for a look into the heart of the storm and Marie shut her eyes to the whirling dust and pressed herself against her children and repeated her fearful prayer over and over and over again … until at last the earth quit trembling and rain fell once more into the open cellar and the whirlwind roared off across the pasture like a great locomotive hurtling farther and farther away.

Dust and leaves littered the cellar floor. Thunder rumbled in the distance. Marie felt her children squirm beneath her. Rain fell steadily on the cellar steps. Still terrified, Marie whispered a brief prayer of thankfulness for her life and that of her children and looked about the cellar and saw Rachel and Maude huddled over Mildred Jessup. Rachel held her neighbor's injured head while Maude wrapped the wound with a garment cloth torn from the bundle she had brought out of the house before the storm arrived. Fritz stood to one side watching, his face nearly black with filth from the cascading wind. Another thunderous rumble crossed the yard from somewhere in the distance. The rainfall lightened.

"Is it gone, Momma?" Cissie asking, speaking for the first time since the storm passed overhead.

"I think so." Her hands shook. "Thank goodness." It was plainly a miracle they hadn't been lifted right out of the cellar.

"I was scared, Momma. Really, really scared."

"Me, too." She stroked Henry's hair and peered into his tiny eyes, which seemed empty in the dusty darkness. "Are you all right, honey?"

Her son nodded.

Rachel re-lit the other kerosene lamp as Fritz went back up the cellar stairs to the pasture. Marie craned her neck for a look of her own. She could hear wind blowing across the damp grass. It carried a smell of rain and dirt. The sky was black with clouds. Cissie stood and helped Henry to his feet, then looked about for her bunny rabbit. She found Lulu-Belle huddling in a corner of the cellar and went to fetch her. Marie also rose, seeing to it that Maude did not stumble in the dark, guiding her to the cellar stairs, letting her safely locate the bottom step.

Fritz's voice drifted across the rainy wind from out in the pasture above. Maude proceeded up the stairs. Mildred Jessup moaned with pain as Rachel brought her upright. A light gust of wind sprayed rain deep into the cellar.

"Can we go out, too, Momma?" Cissie asked at the bottom of the steps as she cradled the rabbit. Henry hid behind her, still trembling slightly. The wind fluttered through Maude's dress where she stood at the top of the cellar stairs.

"I suppose so," Marie replied, glancing back at Rachel who was guiding Mildred toward the stairs. She was still too frightened to think clearly. What should they do now?

Maude walked away from the broken cellar doors and disappeared from sight.

"Is it safe?" Cissie asked, only halfway up from the bottom. Henry climbed past her to the next step, his timid focus drawn to the black raindrawn sky overhead. Somewhere up above, Maude uttered a cry.

"Go on, honey." Marie urged her daughter up the cellar stairs. "It'll be all right."

Behind her, Rachel brought Mildred Jessup to the bottom of the steps. The children hurried up out of the cellar into the dark rainy wind. They were already running off toward the back of the house when Marie stepped clear of the cellar. Damp wind blew in her face. She hardly paid notice to the soft rain persisting. Somewhere just past the rear corner of the house, Cissie shouted, "Momma! Momma! Come look!"

The damp pasture of grass and oak trees behind College Street was black under the stormclouds and windblown rain. Marie hurried after her daughter's voice and came around the back corner of the house where the children waited and saw the wreckage of the chickencoop and the horse stalls, heaps of shattered boards and wire and little else to recognize in the rainy gloom, and beyond that where Fritz stood quietly in the mud, only a section of wooden fence and part of the back staircase where Mildred Jessup's house had sat just a quarter of an hour ago. All the rest was gone.

The kitchen door to Maude's house swung shut with a bang. Back at the potato cellar, Mildred shouted across the damp wind for her brother. Marie watched Fritz. He did not turn to answer, nor did he move at all even as Henry slowly approached to stand by the last pickets of the broken fence.

Cissie came over to Marie, asking, "Momma, what happened to Lili's house? Where did it go?"

"I don't know, honey. I think the wind took it away."

Marie looked at Maude's house and saw that all the windows on the Jessup's side had been blown out by the storm and the rough siding damaged by flying debris. Along the foundation only the small chinaberry tree survived of all Maude's flowerbeds and rose hedges. The side gate was also gone and the laundry lines, and Rachel's fresh vegetable garden had been ripped apart. Darting suddenly away from her mother, Cissie rushed through the torn rose hedge toward the road.

"Honey!"

"I have to see about my circus, Momma!" Cissie called back, as she disappeared around toward the front of the house.

Mildred entered the yard with Rachel beside her carrying the burning kerosene lamp. Stepping past the remains of the chickencoop, she gasped aloud, "Oh my Lord!"

Rain tossed about on the soft wind as Fritz stared wordlessly into the thick pile of wreckage that was left of his sister's home. A deep cough rattled his body. Rachel muttered a phrase Marie could not hear. A violet streak of lightning flared across the black clouds to the east. Mildred Jessup fell down in the dirt and began wailing.

— 8 —

Quiet passed over the town when the strong winds died half an hour later. Rain fell intermittently. Voices of the frightened and injured echoed out of the sidestreets. Neighbors wandered about together dazed and curious as night blackened the town and heaven was obscured by drifting stormclouds.

After getting Henry changed at last into dry clothes, Marie swept broken glass from her bedroom into a pile by the door. With Cissie holding a lamp beside the window, she had managed to locate most of the shards of glass and wind debris scattered onto the beds and across the rugs. The frame itself was fractured and needed repairing by a carpenter. Until then, a simple drape of bedsheets and pins would have to do for privacy and comfort. Since she and the children were safe and well, Marie had no complaints. In the kitchen, Maude boiled more water for treatment of Mildred Jessup's head wound after cleaning up cups and plates and utensils exposed to the storm when the ferocious wind flung open the back door. Rachel ignited kerosene lamps in each room of the house, then kept Mildred company in the parlor after attempting unsuccessfully to telephone downtown for the doctor. Lili had still not returned home.

"I'll walk!" Mildred insisted, as Marie entered the shadowy room with Cissie. She struggled to rise from the sofa where she had been resting. "I'll find my daughter without them if I have to. What if she's been hurt?" Then another spell of vertigo struck, and she was compelled to lie back again.

"See?" Rachel observed, adjusting the bandage on Mildred's forehead. Blood had soaked through the cotton swath requiring its replacement twice already. "Honey, you can't go anywhere. Soon as I can, I'll go downtown myself and find out where she is. You just lie still and rest."

"My poor little girl."

"I'm sure Lili's just fine," said Rachel, dabbing off a streak of dried blood. "She's a very clever child. She'd know where to find shelter. I'm not worried in the least."

Mildred moaned.

A damp draft swept into the room as Cissie opened the front door and went out onto the dark veranda. She shouted for Henry, then reached back to close the door behind her. Marie found it peculiar that Cissie seemed so unconcerned about Lili's absence. Had they been fighting earlier? She pulled aside the curtains to look out the window beside the piano. There were men in denim overall suits walking up the road, carrying burning kerosene lanterns. An enormous broken tree limb blocked the motor route to town, but the pack of men ignored it and detoured toward the rainy woods. When they were gone under the cottonwoods, Marie saw little Henry wander out into the dark empty street behind them. She knew she would be frantic if he or Cissie hadn't come home after the tornado struck. What would she have done? She hadn't any idea except to run out looking for them.

"I never seen it storm like that before," Mildred remarked, as Rachel pressed a piece of ice wrapped in cotton cloth to the head wound. "Dear God, the wind took my house away and didn't leave nothing behind. What'll Howard say when he comes down from Tulsa?"

"Do you expect him soon?" Marie asked, moving to the piano seat. Mildred rarely mentioned Howard who seemed more rumor than husband. Then again, Harry was gone, too, so who was she to judge the state of Mildred's marriage?

Mildred shrugged. "Maybe next week. Of course I'll have to wire him now about the tornado. He'll have a fit. We never bought a dollar of insurance. Howard always called it a cheat thought up by Jews."

"Oh dear, what will you do?" Marie couldn't imagine being destitute. How would they survive? Thank goodness Harry had a head for business, no matter what the market.

"I haven't any idea," Mildred replied, sagging on the couch. "Howard owns all the money."

"Well, I think we're very fortunate to be alive," Rachel suggested, squeezing cold water from a damp cloth. "Why, just seven years ago, Austin suffered the same tornado twice within an hour and the newspapers said more than a dozen people were killed. Idabelle's cousin Ray lost his wife Margaret and his home and his filling station and his two Chevrolet automobiles, and had to return to San Antonio to live with his mother."

"Imagine that," said Maude, leaning in from the hallway. She picked up a dustpan and poured its contents into a tin ashcan.

"He was quite humiliated, Mother!" Rachel snapped back at her. "When Ray went back to San Antonio, he was forty-four years old. I don't believe he's ever remarried."

"To his mother's enduring shame, no doubt."

"I didn't say that."

Shaking her head as she picked up the ashcan, Maude sighed. "When your children are small, they step on your toes. When they grow up, they step on your heart."

"Mother, please!"

"Rachel, not now!" Marie spoke up, hoping for a little peace between them tonight. "We've had enough of that." When would their bickering ever end?

Maude went back into the lamplit kitchen. Marie heard the screen door open and soon felt a cool draft sweep into the house as a stiff breeze rattled the shutters outdoors. The sound gave her a shiver. Did tornadoes really return? She worried about that, too.

"Oh, where's my darling Lili?" Mildred cried, shifting to rise once again from the couch. Rachel held her down. "I have to go find her."

"I'll take Cissie and go downtown to look for her myself," Marie offered, stealing another peek through the window. "Rachel can stay here with you." She saw Henry sitting on the fallen tree limb, calling to Cissie across the road. She felt like going out now. For some reason, being in the house made her jittery.

"Oh, honey, would you really do that?" Mildred asked, brushing her hair back. "I'd be terribly grateful."

"Certainly." She smiled at Mildred and touched her hand. "I'd be happy to."

"If she's been hurt, I don't know that I could forgive myself."

"It wouldn't be your fault," Rachel said, dunking the washcloth in ice water again. "After all, we didn't invite that tornado here, did we? At CW's funeral, the priest from Evangeline reminded us that fortune and tragedy follow the same sun across God's blue sky, and that blessed by one likewise binds us to the other. Sometimes we want our lives so justright, we forget that we're not yet in heaven. He said misfortune only gilds the reward to come."

Mildred whimpered softly as Rachel mopped her brow.

Marie went outdoors.

Down the street she saw lanterns under the pecan trees by Weaver Street. The night air felt muggy in spite of the breeze. On the side of the house, she found her daughter's makeshift circus ripped to pieces under the fig tree, her tents and carousels and midway booths torn apart, all the miniature painted toy figures flung about in the grass, the tiny colorful flags gone. Once Cissie saw the damage, she swore to everyone in the household that her play circus would be rebuilt, more gloriously than ever. Both she and Henry were across the road now near the cottonwood thicket. Marie called to them and Cissie waved back. Marie went out through the front gate and called again and her children came running out of the damp shadows.

"Momma, the wind knocked that tree right over," Cissie told her. "We could see the roots where it used to grow."

"I seen a million worms," Henry added, scratching his ear. "Can I go get a jar to put 'em in?"

Marie shook her head. "I promised Mrs. Jessup we'd try to find Lili for her."

"I'll bet she went to Shantytown, Momma," said Cissie, waving in that general direction, still sounding curiously indifferent.

"Well, then, that's where we'll go."

"It's a long walk, Momma," Henry said, an eye on the fallen tree trunk. "What if the cyclone comes back?"

"I think it's gone away, honey. I'm sure we'll be fine."

Rain sprinkled on the road. There were voices echoing farther down the block, urgent shouts rising and falling with the warm breeze. She began to wonder what the tornado had done to the rest of Bellemont. Had more people been injured? With the wires blown down and the telephones out of order, there had been no word from Maude's club ladies. What about Idabelle and Lucius and Jimmy Delahaye? She was afraid for Jimmy and prayed he was well.

Marie told Cissie, "Go get your raincoat, honey, so we can walk downtown. Henry, I want you to stay here and look after your grandmother."

"I want to go, too," he whined, kicking at the mud by the gatepost.

"Auntie Rachel needs you to stay here, honey. Grandma's still scared from the storm and she'll feel better knowing you're nearby, all right?" Marie turned to Cissie, feeling a sudden chill on her face. "Bring our umbrellas, too, will you? I'm sure we'll see more rain."

While the children went indoors, Marie went down the sidewalk as far as the Jessup's front fence to study again the utter destruction wrought by the tornado. Most of the white pickets were missing and the corner post by Maude's house had been uprooted. Mildred Jessup's house was hardly more than a pile of wet broken lumber. Marie found it difficult to imagine this junk as the home it had been earlier that evening. Where were the pretty window shutters and drapes and flower boxes and porch balustrades and raingutters? Indeed, where had Mildred Jessup's interior furnishings and possessions gone? Her appliances and furniture and dinnerware and framed pictures and knitted quilts? Her clothes and jewelry and dearest mementos? And Lili's possessions? Had all that poor child owned in her young life been blown far away into the sky, too? In the breeze off the dark meadow, Marie noticed, too, a smell from what was left of the Jessup's house that was more than damp wood and earth. Drifting across the evening air was an unimaginable mixture of toilet powders, perfume, laundry soap, cooking spices, tobacco, furniture oils, dried flowers, liquor, cedar chests, kerosene and dust conspiring, perhaps, to inform strangers passing by that once this ugly pile of shattered planks had been a home of people.

Mildred's brother Fritz strolled out of the darkness behind the wreckage of his sister's house toward the sidewalk where Marie stood. His suit was rumpled, disturbed by the wind, his hair wet under the drizzling rain. He stopped back of the broken fence in the mud beside Rachel's ruined vegetable garden, urgency of fatigue in his eyes. With a cold voice, he asked Marie, "Do you believe God loves His children?"

He coughed harshly, and wiped rainwater from his brow.

Warily, she answered, "I believe it's faith that cures our doubts."

"My sister called me here to be healed," Fritz said, knotting his hands together as if in prayer. "I've been sick longer than I can remember. I haven't earned a wage in years. I was branded a coward in France and had no dispute with that judgment. My sins are legion and I offer no excuse. Millie would save me, but she believes the Lord extends grace only to those who are most willing to receive it."

"We learn that in church," Marie replied, feeling the drizzling rain on her shoulders. "Christ teaches that many are called, but few are chosen."

"The keys to the Kingdom," Fritz said, as a rasping cough shook his chest. His eyes watered and his posture faltered briefly.

Realizing how ill he was, Marie suggested he ought to go indoors. "Mildred's on the couch now in the front room with Rachel."

Fritz shook his head. "The Lord offers mercy in exchange for obedience, but it's the Lord's bargain, not ours, and His promise to keep, or not to keep, according to His will, which we can only know through faith. Is that evidence enough for supplication?"

"We trust in His goodness," Marie explained, as Cissie came out onto Maude's veranda, "because of Christ's sacrifice on Golgotha. We accept His plan for our lives with patience and gratitude, knowing in His care we'll enjoy life everlasting."

She watched her daughter open the umbrella as she descended the steps to the front walk. By the tattered rose hedge, Cissie called out, "Momma, let's hurry before it starts raining again!"

Backing away from the broken fence, Fritz told Marie, "From the bottom of that cellar where we hid from the whirlwind, I swear to you I saw the face of the Savior on those black clouds that stole Millie's house away. His message has been made manifest, and I believe the bitter storm of His righteousness has not yet passed."

— 9 —

All the streets and alleyways and plank sidewalks leading to downtown were strewn with house debris and leaves and splintered branches dispersed by the tornado. Mr. Gray's darkened gallery was filthy with refuse and Dora Bennett's summer roses were buried under fallen roof shingles. Echoing out of the alleyways at Elm and Jackson Streets were the mournful cries of those who had been unlucky enough to feel the wrath of the tornado. Marie and Cissie saw groups of people with shovels, pickaxes, crowbars and kerosene lanterns, neighbors gathered to sift through the wreckage of homes ripped apart and blown to pieces. At the site of what was once a tall roominghouse on Rector Street, they stood on a debris-covered sidewalk, watching firemen search through the wreckage for a man named Gundersen and his two daughters who hadn't been seen anywhere since the tornado passed over the block. Tenants and neighbors believed both had taken shelter in the basement, a cement pit upon which most of the old rooming-house lay now. A group of small boys Henry's age stood beside a white ambulance where two attendants and a doctor prepared a stretcher. A light rain had begun to fall again. Marie and Cissie huddled under the umbrella at the back of the crowd. Both homes immediately adjacent to the roominghouse were damaged, their owners commiserating with each other. Behind them, a pack of dogs ran in the muddy street, the first animals Marie had seen since the storm hit. She wondered if the horses Rachel had freed to pasture before the tornado were safe. Not a feather was left from Maude's chickencoop, nor had Marie seen Lili's little gray kitten since the terrible whirlwind.

Downtown Bellemont was littered with hundreds of fractured tree limbs and shards of carpentry and broken glass from the shattered houses carried off by the tornado. Crowds of adults from all across town gathered in the square to share anecdotes of the thunderstorm. Marie watched a police car and a firetruck from Henderson roll past uptown. She supposed news of the awful tornado had gotten out across the county by now. Hooker's drugstore was lit inside with candles as the pharmacy doled out supplies to aid the injured. More men gathered at the Standard Oil filling station and across the street in the parking lot of the Ford Agency. A faint breeze blew off the prairie from the south and rain fell intermittently. Nobody appeared to pay it much notice.

"May I go buy a peppermint stick, Momma?" Cissie asked, brushing the hair out of her eyes. The breeze fluttered under her raincoat. She seemed dazed somehow, indifferent to the disaster. Perhaps Marie had made a mistake bringing her downtown.

She told her pretty daughter, "Oh, I think they're much too busy to sell candy, dear. You mustn't bother them." Marie looked into Hooker's drugstore, packed with people almost to the door. Wasn't anybody worried about the tornado coming back?

"I won't be a bother, Momma. I'll wait my turn."

"I don't know, honey." She wanted to go to the restaurant and see if Jimmy Delahaye was there, if he was all right.

A flatbed Ford truck emerged from the alleyway next to the National Bank building, loaded with oilworkers carrying shovels. Its headlamps threw long shadows on the townsquare, illuminating more people in the darkened streets.

Cissie tugged on Marie's coat sleeve. "Momma? May I go? Maybe somebody's seen Lili come back from Shantytown. I could ask everybody who comes in while I'm waiting. Please, Momma?"

"All right, but don't go anywhere else. I have to go over to the restaurant for a few minutes. I'll be right back."

"I promise."

Cissie drew a nickel from the pocket of her raincoat and dashed through the crowd to Hooker's drugstore while Marie went on down the sidewalk. Indoors at Delahaye's, the restaurant was empty. Only a pair of kerosene lamps burned in the main room. Upstairs was dark, too, but Marie heard a water faucet running in the kitchen and Lucius Beauchamp singing "Goodnight Ladies" in the billiard room.

She called out, "Hello?"

Outside, a pair of police cars from Longview drove by slowly, loaded with uniformed officers. Cigarette smoke wafted from the open windows. A group at the sidewalk in front of the mercantile building next door waved in greeting. One of the officers stuck his head out, shouting at somebody familiar.

Marie walked down to the end of the bar and looked up the dark staircase to Delahaye's office and the billiard room. She tried calling out again, "Hello!"

All the lights were extinguished and the doors shut for the night. She wondered where Jimmy Delahaye had been when the tornado struck. The hallway door to the backyard was open, bringing a rainy draft into the building. Marie called out once more. "Hello there!"

She walked out the door onto the back porch and studied the muddy yard where Julius Reeves had been digging in the dirt. There was a slit trench and a large piece of canvas lying nearby crumpled up in the wet grass. Rain fell more steadily now and the breeze felt cool on her skin. Rubbing her neck, Marie heard loud voices somewhere beyond the back fence, men shouting to each other across the dark for help in tearing loose a section of collapsed roof from a wind-damaged shack behind the mercantile building. A woman's voice followed as a distant echo from farther away, plaintive, worried, then dispersed by a gust in the thick pecan trees behind Delahaye's lot. Marie also noticed a strong odor of smoke on the breeze, a house fire, perhaps, ignited during the whirlwind.

"Why, honey, I heard y'all were wiped out by the tornado!"

Idabelle stood in the doorframe behind Marie. The glowing kerosene lantern she held cast a grotesque shadow in the narrow hallway. She was smiling.

Startled at first, Marie accepted a warm embrace from Idabelle. "We survived. It was very frightening, though. How are you, dear? Are you all right?"

"Al Clooney's been running all over town tonight telling folks how Maude Hennesey's house blew away."

The breeze stiffened, fanning rain across the small porch. Marie drew close toward Idabelle who retreated into the dark hallway. She told Idabelle, "I imagine he saw Mildred Jessup's home. It appears the tornado passed right through it. She lost everything she owned. It was quite a shock."

"Were y'all hurt at all?"

Marie shook her head. "Mildred has a bump on the head and the children were scared to death, of course, but we're fine, thank goodness."

"Well, when I heard Al, I didn't know what to think. Ansel Elliot lost a leg when his porch fell on him and George Stevens' mother had a heart attack. Doc Edmunds tried to save her, but she died not an hour ago."

"Oh my goodness."

The wet breeze gusted, sending Marie further indoors. Feeling the jitters again, she listened briefly to those men shouting behind the mercantile building, then told Idabelle what had happened in the woods earlier in the evening and along the flooding river with herself and the children. She said, "Mildred's worried that Lili hasn't come home yet. The children think she might've gone to Shantytown, but that was before the storm."

"Nobody's been across the river yet," Idabelle told her. "Lucius says a sixty-foot cedar tree fell on the bridge at Tyler Road. The busline to

Henderson is closed, too, on account of some cottonwoods that came down on Watson Street. The tornado took the roof right off Mowry's feedstore, but Lucius says it didn't touch a thing inside. I find that so strange."

Marie looked around. "Where's Jimmy?" She had a terrific urge to see that he was all right. She worried that something horrible might have happened and she'd never see him again.

Idabelle shrugged. "He come in about a half hour before the tornado with a pair of fellows from the mill. They went upstairs to his office and called somebody on the telephone. When they come back down again, I guess they went out through here 'cause Lucius said one of them left the door open and got water on the floor that he had to mop up after."

Somebody waving a flashlight walked past the back fence. Marie heard rain drizzling in the muddy yard.

Lucius Beauchamp's thick voice issued from the upper staircase. "There's no going to Shantytown tonight!"

The stairs creaked under his weight. Idabelle craned her neck to see up the steps. "Is that you, honeypie?"

Lucius remarked, "Coloreds got their own trouble without folks from over here sticking their noses in. I say, leave 'em be."

He came down the stairs with a stack of mail-order catalogues under one arm. His overalls and suspenders were damp and his workboots muddy. When he reached the bottom, Marie told him, "I'm trying to find Lili. She hasn't come home yet and Mildred's worried to death about her. Cissie believes she may have gone over to Shantytown." Marie explained again about her harrowing adventure with the children at the swollen river. It sounded worse in the telling.

Lucius remarked, "You ought to ask Julius if he seen her at all."

"Is he still here?"

Idabelle shook her head. "Jimmy told him to go along home early when it got too muddy to dig that hole out there."

"Jimmy had no cause to keep him as long as he did," Lucius said, putting the stack of catalogues on the floor. Marie smelled gin on his breath. "Poor fellow's got two little girls sick from the mumps and a boy with whooping cough. He ought to've been home with them tonight. If Jimmy'd kept him here another hour, he might've been on the bridge when that old cedar fell over. Louie says it about cracked the damn bridge in half and killed a colored fellow named Cooty who tried to run underneath it."

"How awful! Well, I don't know what I should do now," Marie remarked, feeling a slight chill from the drafty hall. "I'd feel terrible having to go back home without any news for Mildred."

A siren wailed somewhere across town, adding to the commotion outdoors. More shouts echoed from behind the mercantile building. A truck engine roared. Marie felt a breeze rise in the drizzling dark.

"Lucius, honey, maybe you ought to go with her," Idabelle suggested, "see if you can't get across somehow."

"I don't see how. Louie says it's all blocked up from that cedar."

Marie said, "Maybe we could call a message across to see if Lili's over there, perhaps find out if she's safe. I'm sure poor Mildred would be happy just knowing that, even if Lili couldn't return until the bridge opens again."

In the amber glow from Idabelle's lantern, Marie noticed how ruddy Lucius' face appeared this evening. His hair was damp and filthy, too, smelling of wet earth. He looked tired, or drunk. And he seemed disturbed, too. But then again, who wasn't tonight?

Idabelle said, "That poor little girl must be frightened out of her wits. Why, I'll bet she's just as worried about her momma as Mildred is about her, don't you think, honey?"

"Yes," Marie agreed, "I'm sure she's just as scared as the rest of us."

Lucius shook his head. "I tell you, there just ain't no way across tonight. Mark my words. Louie said some colored fellows already tried pulling that tree off the bridge with a handwinch and one of them fell in the river and would've drowned for fair if the others hadn't been there to save him."

"But we can ask if anyone's seen Lili, can't we?" asked Marie, trying to sound hopeful. "They'll tell us, don't you agree? I'm sure someone will."

Lucius shrugged. "Can't go out Tyler Road. Tornado went right through there, tore everything up between the depot and the cotton mill. We'd have to angle over to Clevis and Sattley, then go Weaver Street to Finley Road and take the old path along the bluff to the bridge that way. I ain't sure it's safe, but I s'pose we could try."

Idabelle smiled. "There, then! It's settled! You'll take Marie there yourself and help her find out if anyone's seen Lili."

Lucius frowned. "Well, I ain't staying out there all night. If there's a dispute with any of the coloreds, we're coming back."

"All right," Marie agreed. "That's fair enough. It's certainly better than doing nothing."

Lucius picked up the mail-order catalogues. "I'll be in front of Hawley's barber shop in five minutes." Then he walked past Marie and Idabelle and out into the rainy dark of the backyard.

After Lucius had gone, Marie followed Idabelle back to the dining room where they watched another ambulance roll by. She noticed people outdoors now she hadn't seen on the streets of Bellemont all summer, men and women, boys and girls, drinking soda pop and eating sandwiches and showing off odd souvenirs of tornado damage picked up all over town. Apparently the drizzling rain mattered not at all, nor the horrific destruction here and there. Perhaps those truly wounded like Mildred Jessup were hiding away somewhere in the dark attended to by friends or family, while those blessed to have escaped the tornado uninjured felt free to celebrate. Were it not for the electric power lines having been blown down by the wind, closing Bellemont's restaurants and cafés and meeting halls, Marie imagined downtown might resemble Mardi Gras. She wished she could telephone to Harry this evening and tell him everything that had happened and ask him to come down by train tomorrow. She also wanted to pack up the children and go home to Illinois, now more than ever.

"You be careful, honey," Idabelle advised. "This is not a night to be waltzing about."

"Do you believe there's danger still?" What a silly question! Were it not for Lili and Mildred, Marie would be under a warm blanket with her children this very moment.

Idabelle furrowed her brow. "Only a fool ignores clear signs of warning. Myself, I intend to go home and have a warm bath before bed."

Then she gave Marie a hug for luck and let her out the front door.

Marie found Cissie on the crowded sidewalk by the Bijou picture house whose unlit marquee advertised John Barrymore and Camilla Horn in *Eternal Love*. A rambunctious group of high school youths surrounded the closed box office, trading loud bawdy jokes and passing a silver hipflask back and forth, gaiety evident on their faces. The boys had oil-slicked hair and two of them by the theater door smoked cigarettes. All the girls wore short dresses and had their hair bobbed and their faces painted like those silly flappers Marie saw in Rachel's *Vogue* magazines. Both sexes exchanged boldly flirtatious gestures and teased each other with rude expressions. Stirring a peppermint stick in a bottle of Coca-Cola, Cissie seemed eager to hear everything being said around her. She was clearly too sophisticated now to be satisfied with dolls and penny candy. Shortly, there would be boys of her own in white shirt-sleeves and fancy collars calling at twilight, honeysweet perfume on her pink vanity, secrets she'd no longer share with her dear old mother.

As Marie crossed the street, Cissie stood and brushed off her skirt. She slipped a paper straw into the bottle of Coca-Cola beside her peppermint stick and took a long sip while a damp breeze blew in her hair. Clouds drifted restlessly overhead and Marie imagined she heard thunder rumbling somewhere not so far off. More automobiles passed in the street. Cissie went back to the box office and spoke briefly to one of the boys standing there. Something she said made him laugh and he dug into one of his trouser pockets and came out with a coin, which he handed over to her. Then Cissie dodged away through the sidewalk crowd to greet Marie.

She cried, "Momma, look what I just won!"

A truck horn roared behind them both in the street, hurrying pedestrians from its path.

"My goodness! How did you do that?" Marie asked, brushing a wisp of hair off her daughter's face. They needed to find out about Lili and get back home.

"Those boys bet me I couldn't spell 'hippopotamus,' but I did, Momma, so they gave me a nickel to buy another peppermint stick!"

"Do you need another one?" asked Marie, nodding at Cissie's Co-ca-Cola bottle.

"Not tonight, but tomorrow I will. Aren't you proud of me for winning the bet? I told you, Momma, I'm the best speller in the world!"

"How could they ever have doubted you?"

"Oh, those boys didn't know me at all," Cissie explained, walking up the wet sidewalk with her mother. She sipped again from the Coca-Cola bottle. A damp gust rustled through the willow trees by the bandshell. "Do you suppose I'll have lots of parties when I'm older?"

"Of course," Marie replied, as she watched another Ford automobile filled with young men rattle past. "I'm sure you'll be the most popular of them all."

"Oh, I hope so."

A group of men in mud-soiled khaki work overalls and flat caps smoked cigars by the red striped pole of Hawley's barbershop. Lucius was not around so Marie looked about for him, searching the downtown crowds and up the sidewalk. Next to the barbershop was a dark narrow alleyway leading to Fifth Street where she heard more men's voices speaking in the drizzling shadow. Burning ash glowed from lit cigarettes. Debris from the tornado cluttered the passage. One of the men held a dim flashlight. A damp gust of wind swept through the alleyway stirring up a cloud of dust. Several men coughed after a round of cursing. Cissie gave a tug on Marie's arm. "Momma?"

"Yes, dear?"

Cissie directed her mother's attention across the street. "Look, it's Auntie Rachel."

Rachel was on the far sidewalk with her raincoat and umbrella, consternation on her brow. She was searching for somebody in the crowd. Marie thought she appeared frightened, too, or worried. Was Mildred injured more badly than imagined? Marie tried calling to Rachel across the street, but a delivery truck rumbled by and she couldn't see Rachel and when the truck had passed Rachel was already off at the far end of the square walking into the darkness toward Ritter's department store. Lucius still hadn't arrived at the barbershop. Perhaps Marie had misunderstood him. What should she do if he didn't show up? She was afraid to go look for Lili by herself.

"Momma?" Cissie tugged her sleeve. "Shouldn't we tell Auntie Rachel we're here?"

Somewhere far across town another siren shrieked. Marie took Cissie by the hand and led her down the sidewalk past Hooker's drugstore and Bennett's Shoes and the Clothing House and Commercial National Bank and the Lone Star Café. They hurried across the street to Delahaye's where Marie knocked at the door and called for Idabelle and knocked again. A crowd of men in derby hats and long coats stood in front of the Temple Theater at the end of the block talking to Bellemont's chief of police and a pair of officers from Longview. She watched Rachel speak briefly with one of the men there.

"Maybe Auntie Rachel's looking for us, Momma," Cissie said, trying to peek through Delahaye's plate-glass window. The dining room was pitch-black, all of Idabelle's kerosene lanterns extinguished.

Marie looked back up the sidewalk toward the barbershop for Lucius. He still wasn't there, so she said to Cissie, "Would you like to run and ask her if she needs us?"

"May I?"

"Please."

Marie waited in front of Delahaye's while her daughter hurried down the sidewalk to the Temple Theater. It was late now, but strangers and young people were still arriving, flushed with nervous merriment and curiosity. Looking up at the night sky, Marie actually saw stars peeking through rifts of black clouds. The wind had faded to a soft breeze. Maybe the worst of the storm had passed, after all.

At Strebel's Hardware next door to the Temple Theater, Cissie grabbed Rachel by the wrist, giving her a start. She squealed with delight and Rachel laughed aloud and pinched Cissie's ear, and Cissie pointed back up the sidewalk to Marie out in front of Delahaye's. Rachel gave a wave, inviting Marie to come join them, which she did.

"Mildred became absolutely hysterical," Rachel told Marie, once she'd squeezed by the pack of men at the theater entrance, "insisting y'all were lost and that Mother should call out the Texas Rangers to organize a search. I finally had to bring her a hot toddy with a pinch of sleeping powder."

"I'm sure she'll feel much happier when we find Lili," Marie replied, as a window opened on the second story of the hardware store above. "Lucius said he'll help us. We're waiting for him."

"Where is he? We can't wait out here all night."

"I don't know. He said he'd be right along."

A man called down to the chief of police, inquiring about tornado damage to the cotton mill. Marie heard phonograph music playing indoors. Told that no damage to the mill had been reported, the man thanked the police and closed his window again to the street.

"I suppose you've asked all over," Rachel inquired.

"Well, I've spoken with Lucius and Idabelle. It's very worrisome, though I'm sure she's safe."

"Shouldn't we go to Shantytown, Momma?" Cissie asked. "Maybe she's visiting with Eva and Caroline."

"Aren't you afraid to go back to the river?" Rachel asked, sounding somewhat surprised. "I thought y'all nearly drowned."

"Oh, we can't cross," Marie told her, too afraid to try, anyhow. The very thought of cold swirling water in the darkness was terrifying. "Lucius says a tree's fallen on the Tyler Road bridge and somebody was killed."

"Well, I have no burning desire to be mutilated," Rachel admitted. "If it's that dangerous, perhaps we shouldn't go at all."

"I thought perhaps we'd just shout across the bridge to ask if anybody's seen her."

"Now, that's a fine idea," Rachel agreed. "If Lili's there, we can have her stay put until morning. Mildred'll be happy just to know she's all right."

"Won't it be awfully dark?" Cissie asked, a damp breeze tossing a shock of hair across her eyes. "I don't want to get scared again."

"Oh, I guess we'll be safe," Rachel said, as a green Hudson sedan rattled by, exhaust rising like steam in the dark. "I told Mother I'd be back in an hour or so. I think we should go now. We don't need Lucius. I know the way, but we'll have to hurry."

"Are you sure?"

"Of course."

Rachel led them across town past the millinery and Caldwell's furniture store, Doyle's Cigars and the old Masonic Hall, then down a narrow alleyway beyond the old blacksmith shop and livery stables whose desolate structures still stank of soot and dung. Away from downtown now, the night air was quiet except for the damp breeze in the cottonwoods whose wet leaves were strewn everywhere they walked. Peeking through a slatted fence into the backyards of the shabby gray frame-houses on Weaver Street, Marie saw amber kerosene lamps glowing behind drawn roller shades. Cissie kicked at clumps of muddy grass in her path. Rachel's attention jumped about as they walked to the far end of the empty alleyway where it intersected Panola Street near the pinewoods. Tobacco smoke from somewhere nearby drifted on the breeze. Cissie scampered ahead, diverting to a warren of hackberry bushes, squatting down for a peek. "Momma, I think I saw a rabbit!"

"Be careful, dear."

"I will."

The wild grass lining the road smelled sweet in the rain-dampened air. Marie heard birds rustling high in the cottonwoods nearby, no doubt disturbed by the ferocious storm. Rachel stopped to pluck a pale lily from an overgrown patch of wildflowers. Marie thought her behavior in those harrowing minutes before the tornado struck was quite heroic, the way she had gathered everyone together and insisted they all go down into the potato cellar, how she had lighted lanterns and guided Maude to a safe place and been so assured in her manner. Marie felt certain that grace had entered Rachel's heart in that late hour of turmoil and she had proven herself worthy and courageous. She told her that CW would've been very proud of her.

"He gave me a lily on the night he died," Rachel replied, with half a smile. "He knew I was angry with him, yet insisted I take it as a token of his constant affections. I threw it out my bedroom window the moment I heard his automobile drive off and thought nothing of it until the funeral when I saw his casket draped with garlands of the most beautiful Resurrection lilies."

"Oh dear." Marie felt like crying herself at the very thought. She couldn't imagine losing Harry like that, regardless of the sourness that had passed between them these last few years. What makes the heart grow so cold in trying times? Why can't love be more persistent?

Across the breezy dark, Rachel's soft voice trembled. "At the services, CW's mother assured me that love and sorrow are faithful sisters in the heart. She believes we persuade ourselves they are not because we choose to deny that true joy is a gift from God. She says that life is a fair bargain we honor by loving another."

Marie watched Cissie hunting about the wet hackberry bush for her phantom rabbit. Children, she thought, must have a miraculous capacity to quiet the most appalling circumstances in their desire for normalcy. She told Rachel, "My dear old Granny Chamberlain always maintained that grief is itself another medicine."

"Oh, I'm sure that's the truth," Rachel said, raising the wild lily to her lips. "But I still hate it like poison."

Cissie had risen from the hackberry bush, resigned to failure in her brief rabbit hunt. She marched forward down the mud-soaked lane. The damp breeze fluttered through a dense grove of sycamore trees and Marie felt rain sprinkling on her cold skin once again.

Shame-faced in her gloom, Rachel asked, "Do you believe Mother would have ever tolerated CW as family?"

"Because he was Catholic?"

"Of course."

"Isn't a daughter's happiness worth more than opinions of faith?" Once when Marie was a girl, a retriever she owned had died of rabies. Asking her mother if they'd see him again in heaven, she was told very matter-of-factly that dogs most certainly do not go to heaven and that the very idea was silly. Grown up with children of her own, Marie realized what a terrible thing that was to say to a child, whether a Biblical truth or not.

Rachel shrugged. "Mother told me once that God despises ingratitude. For each penny we drop into the collection plate, one sin is forgiven. She says only pride keeps us wealthy Sunday mornings."

Marie remarked, "In Hosea, the Lord says He desires mercy and not sacrifice. If we deny love to one another, how can any of us hope to share His lasting reward, whether here on earth or in heaven to come?"

Perhaps fifty yards ahead, Cissie stopped by the bend of the road. There were at least half a dozen fresh automobile tire tracks in the mud sloshed through the intersection of Panola Street and Finley Road that led toward the river. Cissie darted back and forth across the narrow motor route like a wood sprite. Wet leaves fluttered to earth here and there. A dog barked loudly in the direction of town. The way to the river now was shrouded in darkness. Walking close to Rachel, Marie watched Cissie prance ahead, her little raincoat barely visible through the oily black drizzle. Back toward town, an automobile horn honked loudly twice, then went silent. A faint calling voice in the same direction echoed across the night. Soon, a pair of motor lamps lit the woods. A black Ford sedan drove out of the dark. Cissie stepped back off the road as it clattered past. Rachel and Marie ducked down into the grass as well when the Ford drew near to them. The driver sped by without slowing. Marie saw two men in the back seat huddled over somebody in a thick blanket between them.

"That was Doctor Wharton behind the wheel," Rachel said, watching the black Ford's taillights disappear into the drizzling gloom toward town.

Cissie shouted from the dark for Marie to come quick. Her voice sounded urgent. Farther down the road, another figure emerged from the rainy woods, a youth in tan overalls and a brown floppy hat. He was jogging through the mud, a wet grin on his face. When he came upon Marie, he slowed to a walk, caught his breath, and proudly announced, "We got us the nigger that killed Boy-Allen!"

"Pardon me?"

The boy reeked of corn liquor and sweat. Mud caked his overalls. Rainwater dripped off his grimy face. "Roy and Frankie catched him by the bridge trying to drown a little girl. They're gonna string him up!" The boy giggled with glee. "I just know'd a nigger done it!"

The boy whooped aloud and ran off up the rainy road toward town, yelling wildly into the night. When Cissie called out again, Marie left Rachel by the grass and went ahead down the road. Rachel shouted something nasty back at the grimy youth. Vaguely frightened now, Marie saw other figures in the dense woods, drifting like shades under the dripping cottonwoods and pine trees, and a glow of lights across the dark, flickering dimly through the drizzling rain.

"Momma!"

"I'm coming, honey."

Farther on, Marie saw automobiles parked on the edge of the road, still a quarter mile away from the bridge, while beside the trunk of a ragged pecan tree, Cissie watched small groups of faceless men in ordinary hats and garments soiled by the storm entering the black woods through the thick wet grass. Their voices echoed across the dark, ranting and indistinguishable. Several of them carried rifles or shotguns. Others led hound dogs on long leashes. When the breeze changed, Marie smelled burning firewood in the air. She looked back for Rachel and discovered to her surprise that Finley Road was empty in both directions. She stopped walking and called Rachel's name, but got no answer. She waited and listened, and heard only another automobile in the distance and a faint barking of hound dogs. Rain hissed in the woods. Marie shouted again for Rachel, but she was gone.

Quietly, Cissie crouched beside the pecan tree, one arm on the damp trunk, legs lost in the tall grass. As her mother approached from the road, Cissie asked, "Where's Auntie Rachel? Did she go home? Aren't we going to find Lili?"

"I don't know, honey. Maybe," Marie replied, worry growing in her heart. "I think we should get you to bed. It's awfully late. I'm sure we'll see Lili in the morning."

"Who are all those men, Momma?"

The burning kerosene lanterns carried by the men glowed like huge fireflies through the pines. Down the road, an automobile engine started up and its headlamps came on. Marie took Cissie by the hand and led her away from the pecan tree, a dozen yards deeper into the woods. As the automobile drove by slowly, Marie saw it was a police car. It didn't occur to her to call out for help, nor had she any urge to chase the automobile up the road. A peculiar disquietude infiltrated her heart that told her to take her daughter away that instant and forget she had seen men with lanterns and guns and dogs in the middle of the night. She felt herself shivering. A pale murmur of cool rain in the leaves increased. What did she intend to do? Wasn't it awfully late now? Why weren't they leaving? But she wondered, too, if the little girl the boy yelled about was Lili Jessup herself.

"Aren't we going home, Momma?"

"Yes, honey. Soon."

Another automobile came down Finley Road toward the river, this one rolling slowly, not more than ten miles an hour. The boy Marie and Rachel had encountered hung his head out the back window, shouting obscenities. The driver slapped the side of the car as he maneuvered down the road. Frightened, Marie took Cissie by the hand again and led her farther into the pine woods, parallel to the yellow lanterns, which seemed more luminous now, collecting together a hundred yards or so from the road, near enough for Marie to smell kerosene smoke on the damp air and to hear a man's hysterical protests above yelping hound dogs and the cruelest human imprecations.

Cissie broke free and ran.

Marie shouted for her daughter to stop, but Cissie rushed ahead anyhow through a soaked tangle of sycamore branches and disappeared into the lightless thicket. A man's scream echoed across the darkness of soggy earth and trees and the hounds began barking furiously. A shotgun boomed. Marie saw Cissie burst out of the wet underbrush a dozen yards ahead, not away from the lanterns, but toward them. Bewildered by her daughter's behavior, Marie tried to follow. She stumbled across a gutted log and past the dead trunk of a storm-beaten cottonwood, while her daughter snuck between thick clumps of trees and flickering kerosene shadows toward the shabby group of men whose hounds yelped and yelped at some frightened soul trapped and outnumbered in a damp pine grove ahead. As she drew near, the loud voices became uglier and she saw torches burning and smelled the woodsmoke and kerosene and expected D.C. Stephenson's hoods and robes, but saw instead only dark grimy faces whose particular features were hidden in shadow. In front of them, a shirtless Negro had been tied by wire to a tall pine. Another man was flogging him with a riding whip. When Marie angled past the rear of the grove farther to her left and fought through a wild hedge of hackberries, she saw that the man being beaten was Julius Reeves and that his tormentor was her handsome boss, Jimmy Delahaye.

This scene was so shocking, she thought at first it had to be a terrible mistake. Delahaye must have discovered Julius already bound to that tree and was trying to free him somehow. Nobody she had allowed to kiss her could be so reckless and cruel. Her head swam. She crept closer, just outside the flickering lantern glow, still seeking Cissie in the black underbrush. Fear made her sick to her stomach because she knew her daughter was somewhere nearby, witnessing something unfathomably hideous.

Thirty feet away now, Marie could hear Delahaye's voice above the drizzling rain as he spoke to Julius. Was this the darling fellow in whose office she had sat so many mornings, admiring the strength of his jaw, the man in whose parlor she had nearly made love? Could it be so? He was shouting now, "Do you hear me, boy? I will cut your nigger hide to shreds if you don't tell me how come you killed Boy-Allen and that little girl."

The black man mumbled something and Marie watched in horror as Jimmy Delahaye lashed him across the chest with the whip. Julius raised his head and spat back at him. Delahaye swore aloud and a burly fellow called J.G. Schofield who operated the Texaco filling station south of town stepped forward and punched Julius in the face. Blood and saliva sprayed from his lacerated nostrils. Delahaye fumbled in his coat pocket and drew out a handkerchief, wadded it up, and jammed it past the black man's teeth deep into his mouth.

Marie felt paralyzed with fear and horror. She could neither run nor quit watching. She was crying, too. Where was Cissie?

"Let's just string him up now, Jimmy," said a man named Hawkins who worked mornings at the feed store. He held a large thick coil of rope in his left hand. "We're getting wet out here and I got a hell of a mess in my yard to clean up."

"I want to know how come he done it," answered Delahaye. "That poor kid delivered my paper every morning and his momma deserves an answer." He curled his hand about the riding whip, drew it back, and lashed Julius again across his bare chest, drawing more blood. The Negro's cry was muffled by the handkerchief. Shouts of approval echoed from the large noisy group of men farther back in the pine grove. More faces became familiar, too, men Marie had passed on the sidewalks of downtown or met walking to church on Sundays, men with whom Rachel worked and Maude spoke to by telephone, whom Harry had likely known in school when he was young, whose children Cissie and Henry played with most afternoons when the sun was out: a handful of oilworkers, a pair of Dodge agency and Equitable Life Insurance salesmen, a carpenter, a plumber, a young clerk from Lowe's Department Store, a bus driver, a crowd of pig-farmers and several well-to-do businessmen who had greeted Marie all summer long with Christian civility and pleasant smiles. She was terrified and heartbroken altogether. What had come over Jimmy Delahaye? How could he be so mean? She looked into the woods for her sweet daughter. Good gracious, was she really seeing this?

"Do you hear me, boy?" Delahaye yelled in Julius' face. "I want to know how come you killed Boy-Allen and that little girl."

He kicked the black man hard in the groin with toe of his boot, drawing a stiff grunt. As Julius slumped in pain, Delahaye lashed his shoulders with the whip. "You hear me?"

The black man groaned.

"He ain't gonna tell us, Jimmy," Hawkins argued, wiping rainwater from his brow. The coil of rope in his left hand unraveled. "Come on now. I say we string the sonofabitch up and go home."

His opinion was echoed from the mob. "YOU HEARD HIM, JIMMY! STRING THE NIGGER UP!"

Marie felt herself go faint. What should she do?

Delahaye shouted back, "Not 'til he tells me why he did it!"

"It don't matter why," Hawkins persisted, "only that he done it and he's gonna hang."

A tall gaunt man named Carson who sold Bibles and vacuum cleaners farm to farm on the long empty roads of East Texas slipped out of the pack with a burning torch that reeked of kerosene. He approached

Julius, staring him in the eye. Loud enough for every man there to hear, he announced: "THEN THE ANGEL TOOK THE CENSER AND FILLED IT WITH FIRE FROM THE ALTAR AND THREW IT ON THE EARTH."

He tossed the torch between the black man's feet. Somebody behind Hawkins laughed. Then a ghastly howl erupted from Julius's throat as his trousers ignited in flame.

"You sonofabitch!" Delahaye cried, shoving the traveling salesman backward, knocking him over into the mud. "Goddamnit!"

A dozen yards or so to Marie's right, Cissie burst from her hiding place in the rainsoaked bramble toward the pine tree, screaming, "Help him, Momma! Help him!"

Marie rushed forward into the drizzling light and ran to her daughter, grabbing her before she reached the mob, many of whom were cheering. She snatched Cissie up and held her tightly to her breast, while Delahaye kicked mud and wet pine needles onto the flames. Julius expelled the handkerchief from his mouth along with blood and mucus. He retched violently and vomited as Delahaye kicked more dirt onto the smoldering trousers.

When the fire was put out, Delahaye yelled into Julius' face. "You see that, boy? These fellows don't have much patience for donkey-ass niggers tonight! Now, you tell me why you did what you did and we'll get this over with."

The skin on both his legs burned away with his trousers below the knees, Julius moaned in agony.

Marie released Cissie and rushed to the tree and began clawing furiously at the wire that bound Julius's neck. He wouldn't die. She would set him free herself, everyone else be damned. A strong hand grabbed her arm and jerked her backward.

"Stop that, honey!" Delahaye held her by the wrist, his grip tight and painful.

"Let go of me!" She tried to twist loose, but he was strong as iron.

Cissie screamed, "MOMMA!"

Marie squirmed in Delahaye's grasp. She felt frantic now, crazy with fear and anger. She struck out at him, hitting him in the chest and shoulder, clawing at his face. She kicked him in the shins."Let me go! Let me go!"

He freed her with a shove away from the tree, and she lost her balance and fell into the mud. Cissie ran to help her up, sobbing violently.

Jimmy Delahaye stared at Marie who held her sobbing daughter close in her arms in the crowded pine grove. Delahaye's face was filthy with sweat and mud, his blue serge suit soaked from the drizzling rain. Whatever had made her think he was grand and handsome? How could this be the man who had asked her to dance at the Pavilion on the Fourth of July, that wonderful fellow who had kissed her under the cottonwood tree and nearly made her swoon? This dreadful person?

He look Marie straight in the eye, and told her plainly, "Sweetheart, this ain't your concern. I suggest you take that little girl and get along home." His voice was ugly and cruel. She hardly recognized him as the sweet Jimmy Delahaye who flirted with her every morning in his upstairs office at the restaurant. Now she was ashamed she had ever taken that job, ashamed she had almost given herself to him. Where was Harry?

She fought back tears. "How could you do this? I don't understand. Who says he had anything to do with hurting Boy-Allen, or anyone else? You don't know, do you? No, you don't! None of you know!"

"Honey, there's no nigger in Texas that decided his own future more than this one here," Delahaye answered, wrapping the whip over his fist again. "When morning comes, won't nobody around here be grieving for this sonofabitch."

Julius' eyes were filmy and cold, his head hung low, blood dripping from his nose and mouth; a bitter odor wafted from his direction. Schofield spat tobacco juice into the mud. Hawkins stood near Delahaye, curling the rope in his hand. Two dozen men behind him watched in silence.

Cissie shook with sobs and Marie hugged her daughter tightly. Her heart contracted and she felt frightened half out of her wits, yet still, with her lips quivering, she spoke her mind out loud: "Mr. Delahaye, my husband told me there were men here in Bellemont whose cowardice proved that faith in God has nothing to do with sitting in a church pew on Sundays. We're taught since childhood that it is a sin to judge without mercy. If the least among us can't expect justice and decency from his fellow man, how dare any of us ask forgiveness of the Lord?"

Then she wept unashamed.

The hound dogs began barking and somebody shouted to Jimmy Delahaye from the back of the rainy pine grove where a group of noisy men were retreating from a disturbance in the surrounding woods. Looking up, Marie saw a Negro woman holding an infant emerge from a stand of dark cottonwoods fifty yards away. After a few moments, she was joined by another Negro woman and four elderly Negro men carrying lanterns across the cold evening rain.

Shaking his head, Hawkins said to Delahaye, "What did I tell you?"

J.G. Schofield drew a pistol from his coat.

Dozens more black faces came out of the darkness, old and young, male and female, dressed as if they had walked straight from the supper table to this muddy clearing in the woods. Each appeared soaking wet.

"What the hell?" Delahaye said, refusing to budge from his spot near the pine tree. In no time at all, the woods all about filled with Negroes, not one of whom had yet uttered a word. "Where'd they all come from?"

"Shantytown," said Hawkins, wrapping the rope up under his arm.

"No, sir." Schofield shook his head. "The bridge is out."

"By God," said the traveling salesman, "they forded the river."

"It's a goddamn flood tonight," spoke another man behind Hawkins. "What the hell'd they want to do that for?"

"Likely to set this nigger free," suggested the traveling salesman, "like Moses down in Egypt."

Delahaye frowned. "Well, this ain't Egypt and he ain't going nowhere. He killed Boy-Allen and that little girl and we're gonna hang him and that's all there is to it. To hell with the niggers. They can watch if they like." He shouted into the drizzle, "Y'ALL HEAR THAT? WE GOT US SOME BUSINESS WITH THIS FELLOW HERE THAT AIN'T GOT NOTHING TO DO WITH NONE OF YOU! IT'S AN EYE FOR AN EYE NOW, AND A TOOTH FOR A TOOTH, JUST LIKE YOUR BIBLE SAYS!"

Not one black voice offered protest. Instead, Marie saw nearly a hundred faces staring toward Delahaye from the woods, mostly expressionless and mute: Negro women in wet scarves and long cotton skirts, some rocking children in their arms, a crowd of Negro men and youths whose work overalls were smeared with mud, dozens of Negro girls huddling together, faces golden in the damp kerosene light. The cool drizzling rain dripped evenly from the pine trees. Cissie sobbed quietly at her mother's side.

A light hand touched Marie's shoulder. She turned to see Rachel standing behind her in the shadows. Marie blinked tears away. "Where did you go?" Her voice trembled. She felt lost and defeated.

"Shhh." Rachel put a finger to her lips and shook her head. Marie noticed that her umbrella was gone and her hair was soaked and that Rachel's dress was filthier than her own.

In the pine grove, Jimmy Delahaye spoke briefly to Hawkins who unraveled the rope. Schofield kept the revolver in plain view of the silent Negroes. The larger group of white men with lanterns shrank back away from the woods closer to the middle of the grove, muttering insults to older blacks nearby. Several hound dogs whined to be free of their leashes.

Delahaye approached Julius again. Raising his voice to an ugly tone, he said, "Boy, there's a world of difference between a man and a child, and I don't know why you did what you did to Boy-Allen, or why the hell you did it again to that little girl, but my daddy once told me there's a devil hiding in every nigger and if you don't watch 'em close they're always gonna sneak around getting themselves into trouble 'cause doing right by other folks ain't in a nigger's heart." Delahaye stepped closer to Julius, whose brown eyes flickered unconsciously. "Are you listening, boy? I know you're no hero like they say you are. A nigger with medals? Why, that just doesn't make sense to me."

The Negroes from Shantytown stood like ragged ghosts in the drizzling rain, watching quietly in soiled clothing, some weeping, some not. They seemed to Marie more numerous than the trees. Mystified, she whispered to Rachel, "Why aren't they doing anything?"

"There's nothing they can do."

"Then why did they come across the river?"

Rachel shook her head. "I'm not sure."

Marie had never seen so many colored people in her life. If they hadn't come to rescue Julius, what were they here for? How could they just stand there and do nothing?

Cissie murmured into her ear, something Marie would never forget, "It's true, Momma, what the Scarecrow says. Cruel people are always cowards."

A breeze came up, shaking the dark pine branches overhead. Water dripped off the brim of Schofield's hat. He waved the revolver at a group of sullen Negro youths off to his left. Somebody's dog began barking until his owner stifled him with a kick to the ribs.

"Tommy?" said Delahaye, still staring Julius in the eye.

Hawkins nodded and came forward with the rope and slung it over a thick sturdy branch ten or twelve feet above Julius' head. He pulled a length of it down and began knotting a hangman's noose. Marie hid Cissie in the wet folds of her raincoat, readying them both to depart if the worst should occur. Such venality was incomprehensible to her and she felt desperately nauseous. Blood dripped from Julius' nose. His eyes were shut now, his breathing hoarse and shallow.

Jimmy Delahaye leaned down over him. "We both know you did it, boy, and we know that God don't forgive niggers that sneak around murdering children, so you're gonna burn in hell tonight, you sonofabitch, and nobody's gonna care you're gone."

Julius groaned.

His sister-in-law Lucy Hudson appeared in the dark at the rear of the pine grove, her pretty face stony and cold. *Honey, they got the same Bible down here. They just read it different, is all.* Marie was horrified to see her. How did she expect to watch Julius die so dreadfully? Hawkins finished the noose and slipped it over Julius' head. Schofield walked up to Delahaye and murmured to him under the wind. A pack of men who had been standing with Hawkins came up, too. One of them took out a pair of cutters and snipped apart the wire that bound Julius to the trunk of the pine tree. Hawkins caught him as he slumped forward. The others helped prop him up. Schofield watched Hawkins tighten the noose. Horrified, Marie grabbed her daughter again when Jimmy Delahaye told the men, "Go ahead, string him up!"

As these men raised Julius to the taut rope, a woman's angry voice shouted from the woods. "DON'T YOU DARE!"

Marie looked behind her into the damp black thicket where she heard tramping in the wet leaves. She noticed Rachel smiling. Vague shadowy figures were approaching from the direction of town, speaking urgently among themselves. Within a few moments they came out of the woods single file, four women under raincoats and umbrellas, Maude Hennesey with her club ladies: Emily Haskins, Beatrice Stebbins and Trudy Crouch. Through the drizzling amber glow of the kerosene lanterns, Maude marched with the other ladies up to the crowd of men in the pine grove.

Jimmy Delahaye let the riding whip drop to his side. J.G. Schofield held his revolver at rest, while Hawkins and the men propping up Julius Reeves stood still beneath the dripping pine. None spoke.

Furious, Maude shouted at Delahaye, "My goodness, are you men deranged? Never in my life have I endured such a shock as when my daughter walked into the kitchen not twenty minutes ago to tell me what you fellows were intending to do to this poor man! Is it your desire to humiliate the entire community?"

Delahaye shot back, "He killed a little girl tonight! We got the right to do something about that!"

"Piffle! Why, I've just been assured by Lyman Wharton that Lili Jessup is not the least bit deceased! In fact, I believe she's with Mildred this very moment on her way to the hospital in Longview to have a cast put on her leg. Lyman says he expects her to do quite well, considering."

"Somebody's been telling fibs tonight," Trudy remarked, adjusting her umbrella.

"Rotten lies," said Beatrice.

Emily Haskins asked, "Just how did you intend explaining this to those of us too busy cleaning up after the tornado to come out here and pretend lynching is codified in the law?"

"This nigger killed Boy-Allen!" Hawkins shouted back, jerking the rope around Julius' neck. "And Roy Cooper seen him with that little girl by the bridge just after the twister, didn't you, Roy?"

A damp bulging man in a rainsoaked hat responded from the mob, "Yessir!"

"So if he ain't done it," Hawkins argued, "who did? And if he did do it, why, you're damned right he oughta be lynched! Why the hell not?"

"You ladies oughta go on home to your card games and peppermint drops," said Delahaye, "and let us finish up what we come out here to do."

Marie noticed the Negroes in the dark pinewoods hadn't moved an inch since the club ladies arrived, nor had any of them uttered a sound. Cold seeped into the rainy darkness.

Maude was livid as she spoke to Delahaye. "Since my late husband Jonas brought me here from Waxahachie forty-two years ago, I have refused to be ashamed of any Christian man or woman for the clumsy deceits practiced in this town." She stared at Julius bound painfully beside the damp pine tree, then glanced over at Marie. "I've tried to convince my daughter-in-law that we've inherited this profanity from a different time and that we have too much temper here to dismiss our own wretched inclinations. Too much temper?" She shook her head. "Well, I'm no less a hypocrite than anyone else in Bellemont for having believed that intolerance is no more sinful than drinking whiskey on Sundays. Even the arrangement of property encourages us to contemplate our superiority. Now only an eccentric crosses the river by design. Truth is, intolerance has stolen our good senses and desecrated our virtue, and not one of us has been immune. We've allowed our dignity to jump the track with small appreciation of the peril and now some of us have come out here in the rain to prove to our colored neighbors just how despicable this petty vindictiveness has become. Well, I will not stand here and see this disgrace continue. Turn him loose this instant."

"The hell I will!" Delahaye shouted. "No silly old widows club's gonna tell me I can't string this nigger up like he deserves! Tommy?"

Immediately, Hawkins pulled the rope at Julius' neck, jerking the black man to his full height.

Emily Haskins spoke in a level voice. "Mr. Delahaye, this silly old widow is entirely prepared to go home and tear up your lease on the building she owns if you choose to inflict further injury upon that poor man."

Delahaye frowned. "You can't do that."

"She mostly certainly can!" said Trudy. "Just as I can, and will, tear up your lease, Mr. Schofield, for the city lot which your silly little grocery store and filling station occupies."

"Turn him loose, Mr. Hawkins," Beatrice ordered, stepping forward, too. "Or by tomorrow morning, neither you nor your friends will have employment at the feed merchant, because there won't be a feed merchant on my property to employ you." She redirected her attention across the crowd to a group of men standing silently by with flashlights in hand. "Nor will you, Mr. DeCamp, have a bank to operate, nor you, Mr. Haines, an insurance office. Not in this town, not so long as I'm alive."

"You're all crazy," said Delahaye. "We'll get us a lawyer, Willy Lickliter from Austin who'll — "

"Do exactly as Judge Dakin tells him to do," Maude interrupted, "which will be to ignore the case and stay home. I tell you, times change slowly and we have always lived on intimate terms with our heritage, perhaps too often with pride than reluctance, but maladies of judgment have proven that no one here has been cut out for sanctification and neither is the Kingdom of Heaven built upon contradictions of race." She swept the men in the pine clearing with her fury. "Do you hear me? Our consciences are already sewn with violations of Christian duty, and we've sinned as if it were a natural process that would bring us closer to God. Fact is, we've rarely worried about consequences, and silence is a discipline we've practiced too well. Now it is finished. Mr. Delahaye, as sure as the day is long, we are prepared to evict every tenant and employee here tonight from our buildings and properties unless you turn this man loose right now. Is that clear? If he is not set free this instant, you may just as well go home tonight and pack your bags because come tomorrow morning there'll be no place for you in Bellemont."

"For the sake of truth and common decency," Emily Haskins added.

"And it don't matter to you ladies that this nigger murdered a child?" Delahaye added.

Holding her umbrella firmly overhead, Maude walked up close to the pine tree where Julius was held by rope and hand. She looked Jimmy Delahaye straight in the eye. "It was our very own Lucius Beauchamp who killed Boy-Allen and broke Lili Jessup's leg this evening trying to drown her in the river at Tyler Crossing. He confessed to his crimes in Rufus Palmer's office at the City Jail just half an hour ago, including a very terrible obscenity he inflicted upon poor Abel Kritt in the woods last July. He also admitted it was Julius here who drove him off during the storm and saved Lili's life."

"Lucius?"

"He's apparently a very troubled soul," said Maude, while a damp gusty breeze swept through the grove. "Perhaps you ought to pay him a visit."

Tossing the riding whip into the mud, Delahaye turned away from the club ladies. Hawkins let the rope go slack in his hands. Schofield hid the pistol in his coat. Delahaye walked off alone into the thick dark woods without uttering another word.

Soon enough, the kerosene lanterns went cold and most of those men Marie knew from the morning sidewalks of Bellemont slipped past the gathered Negroes and went quietly home. Rain hissed steadily in the pine grove. Standing with Rachel and Maude, Marie no longer felt the chill. Cissie pressed her small fingers tightly into her mother's hand within the folds of the damp raincoat as Lucy Hudson came unattended through the crowd of those who remained and freed her brother-in-law from the rope under the dripping pine tree and held him in her arms and washed the blood from his face and cried for a very long while.

Bellemont, Texas
September 14, 1929

Dear Auntie Eff,

It is an age since I've written to you. I've tried so often to find time, but could never do it. I hope you and all the rest of the family are well. I have felt very anxious not being able to hear from you for so long. I would use a portion of the day that I usually spend in your society remembering you and praying that we might soon again bake pies together in Mother's kitchen. The children and I are quite well and have seen more of the world than I ever expected. The more I see, the more I feel that "there is no place like home." Auntie dear, I love you and I do so long to see you. It seems strange that one who loves home as I do should be obliged to travel around as I am doing. Although I've had a fine time over here, it isn't like being home with you and Mother. I feel sort of like an outsider and I miss having someone I can depend upon. Do you ever feel that way? I will be so glad when we come back and get into a house of our own again. Harry believes that I ought to have another garden. This is surely going to be the longest week I've spent in a long time.

I got a letter from Florence Francis Haviland yesterday thanking me for the divinity fudge that I made for her. It was the nuttiest letter I ever got. Apparently she is quite gone on Minister Talmadge. Last week she bought some eggs for him when she was over town which she insisted on delivering herself. She brought along her big rooster named Teddy whom she admires very much and wanted to show off with her new Ford. When she left him unattended outside the pantry to visit with Minister Talmadge in his parlor, somehow Teddy flew up the laundry chute and onto Constance Talmadge's lap in the upstairs bath. Hearing his daughter's cry of surprise gave Minister Talmadge such a start, he spilled the fresh eggs onto his new carpet! Thank goodness I don't have to live with Florence or she would drive me crazy.

Oh dear Auntie Eff, Louie's letter has just come and it seems as if my heart would break. I have hoped all the time that my darling uncle would get well and that I should see him again in this world. Often I found myself saying, "The Lord bless thee and bring thee back in safety again." He was always such a dear compassionate uncle, and I love him so. He was such a comfort to me that tearful summer at St. Paul. I shall not forget it as long as I live. But if he is going where "They shall no more say I am sick" and where our dear ones are, oh kiss him for me, give him my dearest love. There is so much of my treasure there.

Now Auntie, I must tell you of one thing that has been running in my mind, the first thing that I thought of upon awaking. There is a man I know named Mr. Gray who has been here about eleven years and has a big corn biz in Albuquerque. His health gave out several years ago, and being paralyzed, he goes around in a wheeled chair. He lives in the third house from ours and I go down every so often when the sun shines and talk with him. He has been so much alone that he enjoys my visits very much. He reads newspapers instead of the Bible and declares that this old world of ours is losing its struggle with politics and sin. Once Mr. Gray was a carpenter who built houses for strangers. He had a fine reputation and earned a fair living. Then his wife was stolen by influenza and he took up drinking and one morning fell off a ladder and broke his neck. Because he couldn't work any longer to pay off his debts, the bank offered his home and property at auction to a family of Presbyterians and he took a room at a boardinghouse for invalids. On the floor above his own lived a Serbian Jewess whose husband had been killed fighting the Austrian cavalry. She had been crippled by an ice wagon after the War and her religious habits and poor speech left her to herself. Often Mr. Gray heard her singing alone in her room after dark, strange and beautiful melodies. One Sunday during evening services a fire broke out in the kitchen and the boardinghouse burned to the ground. As she was not a Christian woman, her name had not been included on the Sunday attendance roll and none bothered to recall that she sat by herself upstairs. Therefore, she perished in the fire. Nor did anyone come to mourn for her. There was no House of Israel in that town, nobody to speak for her faith. The Baptist minister who had attended to the boardinghouse performed a brief service over her casket bitter with pious lamentations that condemned as profane her chosen repudiation of Christ. She was buried in a potter's field with an unmarked plot. The next winter, a rising flood swept her earthly remains into the river, after which she was forgotten by all but those who recalled her lovely voice at night. Mr. Gray told me that our infirmities in this life proceed from the false witness we bear against each other and the burden of righteousness that shame provides. I did not dispute his opinion. Reverence for truth is no riddle to ponder. It is plain as the nose on our face. Intolerance binds us to the grave.

Auntie, I speak the truth of my heart when I say that while I look forward to the future, I do not look for a life of ease and pleasure as much as I look for a life of good works, little kindnesses done. I will try to live down the bad and bring up the good. If God's grace allows, we will enjoy ourselves to the limit and our sweet fortune will be His glory. Oh Auntie Eff, it is so nice to dream these dreams, when we know they will all be realized some day.

And now darling I can't wait until Sunday to see you, so I am going to fix this letter and send it to you. There are the children to be washed, dressed and combed. Cissie has written you a letter and I will send a few lines with it. I hope to start Henry to school with her at Brookfield next week. Auntie, I love you, my sympathies and prayers are with you all the time. I just want to reach out and give you a hugging. If I could only be with you all tonight, but God has not seen fit to make it possible.

God bless and keep you all in the hollow of His hand.

Your adoring niece,

Marie

— **10** —

The house in Bellemont had many windows and many rooms visited with mild breezes, which once bore the scent of summer roses in bloom. Days of joy and sorrow. God's sunlight came and went in the wake of murmured prayers, and the simulacrum of grace collected in dusty mementos. Tears were wept, then forgotten. Tending to gravity's portion and silence ceased. Sparrows darted once more under the shadowed eaves. Meals were cooked and disposed of. Housework had no end. Society persisted. From all across town, ladies visited for tea and ginger cookies, while the radiant laughter of children in and out of doors lent humor and purpose to each tomorrow.

Marie stood by her bedstead in the mid-afternoon shade of the chinaberry tree, emptying clothes from the bottom drawer of the oak dresser into a small open suitcase in front of her on the mattress. Three larger tan suitcases and an old steamer trunk sat nearby on the wooden floor. The room felt hollow. She had written to Harry and told him with utter certainty that she and the children were returning home to Farrington. It was not his decision, but hers. Since he was still in the city, pursuing his own fortune (whatever he thought that might be), whether he approved or not; she didn't care. They were leaving Bellemont. Emeline had already prepared a room upstairs in her home downtown where Marie and the children could live until Harry put them back into a house of their own once again. No longer would Marie live under someone else's heel and order. She still loved her husband, but this summer past had led her to see how necessary it was that she find her own way in this world. How could anyone disagree? And if they did? Her face was already turned.

Peeking now and then through the curtain lace, she watched Cissie play cripple with Lili Jessup's crutches in the backyard as Henry ran with the collie toward the grassy oak pasture. Both had been cautioned not to go too far today. Rachel promised to join them at the train depot before departure at six. Until then she had an appointment downtown to have her hair curled and shingled for an old-fashioned fancy dress ball later that evening in Kilgore. "Of course, if I hate it," she told Marie at the door as she left, "I'll probably blow my brains out." Maude had been laboring the past hour with corn meal and a rolling pin and sugar sweets that smelled of cinnamon and vanilla. Now Marie heard her rummaging through the empty tonic bottles and jelly glasses and white stone-china jars atop the pantry cupboard shelves. Earlier in the morning, Maude had allowed Cissie to choose from a selection of old attic clothing to take back with her to Illinois: two black wool dresses, three basket skirts, a white chambray bonnet, a taffeta petticoat, and a pretty black basque with white collar and cuffs. Though all were much too big to wear now, Cissie had insisted that one day when she was married and lived in a fancy house she would need such wonderful clothing to receive her many visitors. Maude also gave her granddaughter a tiny bottle of Orange Flower perfume and a Spanish comb Jonas Hennesey had brought back from the Gulf of Mexico one summer long ago. From another corner of the attic, little Henry appropriated a brown necktie and one of his grandfather's buggy whips and a corncob pipe and a strip of old crowbait. He was sure it was Christmas come early. Marie packed her son's gifts together into the steamer trunk with a cigar box full of bird feathers and pine needles he had collected in the woods by the river.

"Beatrice had another dizzy spell this morning," Maude told Marie from the hallway, stuffing a cotton-filled comforter into the wall linen closet. "Trudy believes the poor dear is still suffering the effects of smoking Edgar's old medicated cigarettes."

While Marie carefully sorted out Cissie's clothes, Maude shut the hall closet and entered the bedroom carrying a laundry basket full of bleached hemstitched bed sheets and pillowcases. She remarked, "To each his own, I used to say, though I couldn't abide that terrible smell on Jonas, and told him so. He claimed that smoking warded off mosquitoes. That may well be, I told him, but we've none indoors and if he didn't stop the habit, he'd find his next bride at the County Home." She put the linen on the bed. "When he was alive, Edgar Stebbins was more stubborn than a mule. Now Beatrice has adopted his vice to preserve the virtue of his memory. I find it quite mysterious how often age steals our loved ones and our good senses all together."

Glad to be finishing this final chore, Marie placed a pair of Cissie's chambray dresses and a corset waist into the last empty suitcase. She had taken the laundry off the line an hour ago. Packing occupied nearly two full days. Cissie and Henry took the surviving remnants of their circus over to Shantytown to give to little Eva and Caroline and a colored girl Cissie's age named Mae Hudson who cried when she spun the toy carousel. Though both children had thrown fits at having to leave Farrington last spring, now neither wanted to go back. Cissie cried for the better part of an hour in Lili Jessup's arms, her dearest friend forever, while Henry crawled into a corner of the bedroom closet and refused to come out until Rachel promised to mail him one of her roosters named Will Rogers.

Sitting up, Marie told Maude, "My mother's always supposed that our longing for loved ones is a premonition of sorts. If ever somebody in the Pendergast family goes on a trip or becomes ill, she brings fresh flowers to Grandma's marker in the cemetery and sings louder than the choir at Sunday services. Nor will she abide any discussion of recuperation or reunion until it's become fact. She's always insisted that only heaven heals a broken heart. Of course, Harry thinks we're all hopelessly maudlin in Farrington. Although I can't say he's entirely wrong, I do believe we are surprised by jubilance from time to time."

She watched Maude peek through the bedroom window, out past the chinaberry tree toward the cloudless blue horizon. A girl's voice echoed across the empty yard, Lili Jessup calling after her old collie. A tall carpenter named Klingelhofer had come from Henderson to rebuild the Jessup's house. He promised Lili she would sleep in her own bed by Thanksgiving.

Fetching a whiskbroom from the pantry, Maude turned the empty drawer upside down and swept the dust out of it. Then she said, "When Harry was still in knee breeches, Jonas had a plowhorse die of the heaves out in the hayfields and didn't know it until evening when the wind lent a bitter taste to supper. Jonas rode out with a hired man to load the carcass onto the wagon and he brought Harry along to teach him a lesson about mortality. Harry yelled and stamped and swore he wouldn't go, but Jonas refused to quarrel so he put Harry on the buckboard and drove him out there. Well, I didn't get half the dishes washed before I heard a clatter out on the back porch and came to find Harry shivering outside the door, dingy and soiled, his face white as milk and all tied up in knots. Jonas said that when they began loading the carcass onto the wagon, the hired man had a heart failure and dropped dead in his tracks which scared Harry so that he took off like a jackrabbit and ran all the way home in the dark by himself." Maude laughed. "The poor dear hid in here for two days. It was a hard pull just persuading him to come out to eat."

Marie smiled as she shuffled Cissie's dresses to a better fit within the suitcase. "He's never told me that story."

Did she really know her husband? To hear Harry tell it, he had never been afraid of anything, but she'd always known better. Fear guides our judgment and no one's heart is exempt.

Helping Marie fold some of Henry's trousers, Maude said, "Oh, my son is much too proud to admit suffering that fear. I used to tell him, 'Honey, there's a rare day with no threats in it.' When he was a boy, he didn't understand my meaning. Now I believe he does. We each share our humanity in the Lord and none of us are lacking in weakness."

Marie tried to imagine Harry huddled under his bedcovers, terrified by pictures of dark mortality. She wondered what portion of that fear still dwelled in his soul, if somehow it carried responsibility for his selling of the house on Cedar Street or the puzzling solitudes her husband had chosen lately to pursue, those tiresome and endless struggles between the two of them. Was he really to blame for all their misfortune? Could healing begin somehow with her? For a few moments, Marie quit folding clothes and sat on the bed next to the window frame where light through the pretty chinaberry tree diffused in ragged shadow. The afternoon felt quiet and restful.

Eventually, she said to Maude, "I love Harry for more than his virtues. If it were his nature to be only half as strong, I would still love him as much. My children adore their father, and so do I, because goodness and decency, I believe, have always resided in his heart. I don't deny that Harry's absence has been awfully painful for us, and there are certainly times I wish he wouldn't work another day if that meant he'd be home with us for supper each evening, but in all these years I've made no sacrifices unwillingly, and I would marry your son again tomorrow if only the morning train would wait." Was that the truth, after all? Would she really do this all again? Yes, perhaps so.

Maude smiled as she put three pairs of Henry's overalls and a gray cotton wash suit into the last suitcase. Outdoors, Lili Jessup shouted for the other children from a summer hammock that swayed in a light wind between two laundry poles. Marie repacked the children's clothing into the small suitcase, and fastened the latches shut. When next they were opened, she would be back in Illinois. How curious it was to travel so far and see so much and end up where she had started last spring.

Rising to her feet after replacing the bottom drawer into the oak chest, Maude said to Marie, "Well, dear, Jonas was no different. My husband had a good head for business and offered few alibis for his failures. His family predicted he'd end up a wastrel when he quit the farm, yet we wanted for little in hard times and considered ourselves better off than most. Some might hiss and growl and get the heartburn over high grocery bills and sugar ants in the coat closet. Not Jonas. He saw no use in reprimands whose purpose was to criticize and shame imperfection. On our wedding night I promised that if he carved an oak cradle for me, I would give him a son — a bargain we both kept.

When Jonas built this house, Rachel rewarded our joy together. Now I've come to believe the Lord has blessed our days with obstacles to teach forbearance and humility. The morning my husband was laid to rest, I picked a basketful of bluebonnets in the meadow to bind into a wreath for his grave. *The sun also ariseth, and the sun goeth down, and hasteth to his place where he arose."*

With a deep sigh, Maude picked up her laundry basket. "You see, honey, I am reminded daily how this small truth is shared equally by the sinner and the saint. If I have regrets, it is that we gave more worry to poverty than dissolution. My dear, I slept in the same bed with that man for twenty-nine years. After he was gone I could not stand the dark, so I kept an oil lamp burning on the nightstand and another outside my door. Jonas would think me a superstitious old woman, but a widow has fears. I've never been any hand to cry or walk the floor, yet often enough I've trembled awake at night knowing I will never see my husband again in this life, never smell the odor of his clothing after he's worn it, never again hear him breathing beside me. I am alone now with my night dreams and my private thoughts and it is a trial."

Maude retreated to the door threshold where she stopped and looked back to Marie, her eyes softened at last. She said, "Sometimes the simplest life can own the most imponderable riddles, but, honey, I would tell you this: hold close to that which you find most dear to you. It is precious beyond all words."

— 11 —

Now the late summer meadows were windy, and tired old leaves blew across wild grass cropped by horses and cattle. Sunset was coming soon and the afternoon sky was white to the west. The faint odor of livery stables chased on a cool draft that gave Marie's skin gooseflesh. She was long past the fenceline on the footpath her children had run toward the oak cluttered horizon. By traintime, both would be exhausted and Henry would likely sleep clear through Missouri. With each lull in the gusts, Marie heard a tune tinkling on the piano from the house far behind her. Time was, when season upon season, she had learned the meaning of devotion through the trying solitudes of marriage. Now another summer had come and gone, and the mint bed she had planted before Easter provided for somebody else's tea and jelly. *It is human to seek togetherness,* her mother had once said of living on this earth, *but if a woman keeps her children bathed and her husband fed, little wrong can be thought of her.*

Marie watched her children frolic in the grassy meadow where a great blue sky surrounded the whole world. Soon they would be traveling home again and one day she would have another lovely sun garden whose golden zinnias and fine rutabaga would summon favorable notices from all about. Persistence, she would tell her children, reveals the lasting spirit of our convictions. As wind through the summer grass blows, so, too, must we keep our faith in love, true forever.

ICARIA, MISSOURI

AT SUMMER'S END, the farm boy from Illinois stood with a leather trunk and a pile of suitcases under the white arc lights of a small rail station platform in southern Nebraska. It was nearly half past ten and the train was late. A warm evening wind blew through a grove of weeping willows next to the depot and a crowd of young sports from the state college collected about a pair of Ford automobiles, drinking booze from a thermos bottle and joking. Down at the end of the platform beside the ticket office, Chester Burke sat on a wooden bench with a young brunette the farm boy fancied for himself. She was awfully pretty with silver-blue eyes and a melodic laugh that stirred Alvin's heart. She wore thin white muslin and a pink scarf she fiddled with while Chester flirted. Alvin had noticed her first while he and the dwarf were unloading their baggage from the taxicab. When she was alone, waiting by the depot with a brown valise and a hat box, lace hanky in hand and weeping unaccountably, Alvin thought to go up and comfort her, perhaps put his arm around her and listen to her troubles, but he was too shy, so he left her alone. Now all Alvin could do was watch helplessly from across the platform while Chester honeyed her up and made the farm boy feel like a lemon.

The office door opened and the dwarf came out with the station agent, both laughing. A breeze gusted and Alvin brushed a shock of hair from his eyes. Dust kicked up in the oily roadbed. He felt for the ticket in his pants pocket and looked down the tracks again for the late train. He was anxious to leave. He had already snuck out that morning to see a doctor for his aggravating sore throat. Alvin knew he had been getting sicker day by day, but was afraid of mentioning the consumption because he didn't want to be ordered to the hospital, so he said nothing about the persistent cough nor the recurrent night sweats he had endured since Kansas. Still, the doctor detected his anemia and prescribed a dosage of iron and arsenic and ordered him home to bed. Chester had parked the Packard in an old livery stable ten blocks from the depot, hiding it until their return from Missouri where Rascal had found Emmett J. Laswell's Traveling Circus Giganticus in a small town called Icaria. For five weeks now, the dwarf had been hunting Laswell by newspaper and rumor. He had scoured fair bulletins and trade notices, sent off telegraphs, written letters to chambers of commerce by the dozen, encouraged by Chester who paid cash-value for the effort without question. Now, upon the dwarf's recommendation, Chester had purchased train tickets to Missouri because a grimy wagon circus had stopped to put on a show there, though Alvin had no idea why that had him so stewed up.

The farm boy watched Chester take one of the peachy brunette's hands and give it a soft pat as she mooned up at him from the shadows beside the office. Rascal hopped down off the platform to place a nickel on one of the iron rails. The station agent went back indoors to the information desk. In the dark distance, a train whistle sounded. While Chester Burke slipped his arm around the young girl's shoulder and lightly nuzzled her ear, the dwarf hurried from the tracks toward Alvin and the baggage. Clouds of dust moths swarmed the arc light. A family of six dragged suitcases and stuffed burlap sacks up onto the rail platform. Three traveling salesmen in overcoats and felt hats walked up out of the willow shadows past Alvin. A sleepy woman with a small boy holding a hot-water bottle to his ear appeared nearby. The train whistle echoed again, and the blazing electric headlight of the great locomotive flashed down the tracks. The dwarf scrambled back up onto the station platform. Inhaling dust aggravated Alvin's cough and made his head swim. He felt his fever rising and needed to lie down, worrying now that he might not be long for this world.

"I've just spoken with a most remarkable fellow," said Rascal, wiping dirt from the roadbed off his short pants. His blue suspenders were dusty and his white cotton shirt stained by perspiration.

"I ain't carrying your bags no more," Alvin replied, his attention still focused on Chester and the brunette. Seeing them together like that gave him a peculiar bellyache. "It ain't fair."

A man and a woman in evening dress walked toward the station, the man carrying a leather valise and a burning quarter cigar, the woman a longstem red rose.

The dwarf stared intently at the college fellows roughhousing beside their automobiles. Farther down the platform, a baby's fitful squalling was half-drowned out by the station agent announcing the arrival of Union Pacific passenger service to Kearney, Columbus and Omaha. More people crowded the platform, a few casting curious glances at the dwarf in his odd clothing.

Rascal said, "Did I tell you how my Uncle Augustus helped drive the golden spike for the Union Pacific at Promontory, Utah?"

Alvin frowned. "Not yet."

"Well, Dr. Thomas Durant, vice-president of the railroad, had been commissioned to drive the last spike at the grand ceremony, but having been enfeebled the night before by a spoiled bite of mince pie, he directed Uncle Augustus to take his part. I'm told the best engineers were quite impressed by Uncle Augustus' strength and prowess."

"Did he get a medal?"

The dwarf thought for a second. "Why, yes, I believe so."

"Hot diggety."

At last the locomotive arrived in a huge cloud of steam. A conductor and six Negro porters stepped off close to the station agent's office. Alvin looked for Chester through the crowds to get his help with the luggage. A group of college fellows with slicked-back hair and polished spats came onto the platform, reeking of gin.

"I'm very excited," Rascal remarked, watching people getting on and off the train. "Oh, it's been years since I've traveled by Pullman car. Of course, Auntie steadfastly refused to hear of it since Uncle Augustus died, claiming my constitution was entirely too frail for railroad transportation. As often as we fought over this, I was unable to persuade her otherwise. She can be quite stubborn. Did I ever tell you I once operated a locomotive?"

Across the busy platform, Alvin saw Chester draw the brunette toward him and kiss her hard on the lips. When they broke, she was grinning like a spaniel puppy. The farm boy felt ill from fever and nerves. Truth was, he hadn't been on a train since riding back from the sanitarium, another of the reasons he had run off with Chester: to get away from the farm, maybe live it up for once. Frenchy had taken a day-coach to Chicago the day after he graduated Normal School and gotten drunk on Canadian ale at a blind tiger in Cicero and woke up along the windy Lake Michigan shore with only his hat on. When he came home, he told Alvin he'd never had such a high time. Fellows they both knew in Farrington got stewed on hard cider and blackstrap and every so often attended the Odeon picture show after supper or church fairs on Sunday and some got buried in the same old clothes they had worn on their wedding day without ever having left the farmlands of Illinois. *Work and pray, live on hay.* Well, nobody could say that of Alvin, any longer. He had seen a lot of the world this summer, and it wasn't anything to snicker at: roadside stands and barley fields hiding a thousand barrels of hootch, bed-bugs in tourist camps, motor-speeding by moonlight, suitcases full of orangeback bills, girls and killings. Cold-blooded murder. He had seen plenty, all right. Lately, though, he found himself in the middle of the night thinking about Aunt Hattie's hermit cookies and the mullen weeds that grew under his bedroom window.

Two pretty co-eds dressed in chic wool-velour coats and Clara Bow hats stepped off the train into the over-smiling welcome of the college fellows, one of whom planted a wet kiss onto the cheek of the first co-ed. The conductor directed a redcap to help the family of six with their baggage. Chester boarded the train two cars down at a compartment sleeper with the smiling young brunette on his arm. Alvin tugged at the steamer trunk, pulling it upright. He told the dwarf, "Like I said, I ain't fetchin' yours no more. It ain't fair."

The conductor called out "All aboard," and after another few minutes the train whistle shrieked and sparks flew out of the engine compartment as the fireman, black-faced with coal grime, stoked the furnace. Smoke billowed high into the dark.

"I wouldn't think to ask," the dwarf replied, grabbing two of the smaller suitcases and dragging them toward the train and the nearest redcap. Alvin followed the dwarf through a crowded vestibule on a second-class Pullman sleeper whose berths were already drawn with curtains. The narrow aisle was hectic with people shoving past in both directions. Odors of disinfectant mixed with stale tobacco fumes and sweat. A white-jacketed porter hustled by with dust cloths and fresh bed linen and a portable vacuum cleaner.

"I'll need the lower berth, of course," said the dwarf, stopping at number eight. He tossed his suitcase onto the bed and immediately crawled inside. Alvin frowned as a plump woman with a small child shoved past, grumbling about ill-mannered people crowding the aisles. He looked up at the upper berth and decided it was too cramped. The train whistle screeched.

"I ain't climbing up there," the farm boy said, setting his own leather suitcase down. "You take it. I'll give you a boost."

"No, thank you. I prefer where I am." The dwarf pushed a buzzer next to the window as the Pullman car lurched into motion. The whistle blew again and the locomotive chugged slowly forward along the tracks. Down at one end of the car, the washroom door opened and a fellow in a waistline suit and gray fedora exited, a folded newspaper tucked under one arm.

"Yes, sir?"

Alvin found the Negro porter at his elbow, holding a small stepladder. Rascal stuck his head out of the lower berth to watch. The farm boy said, "I ain't getting up there. I want this one down here."

The porter said, "Looks to me like it already been spoken for." He picked up Alvin's luggage to be stowed away.

Just down the corridor, a young woman wearing a flamingo pink silk tea gown stepped out into the aisle from number four. "Oh, porter, could you help me, please?"

"Yes, ma'am." He turned to the farm boy. "Be right back, sir."

Leaving the stepladder at Alvin's berth, the porter moved off down the aisle while the sleeper car swayed gently side to side. One of the conductors entered the Pullman from the front vestibule. Through the window, the last lights of the factory town flickered out of the dark. Rascal rolled over on the bed and closed the curtain.

"May I help you, sir?" the conductor asked Alvin, as he arrived at the berth.

"I ain't sleeping up there," replied the farm boy, coughing into his fist. "It ain't room enough."

"Your ticket, please?"

Alvin handed it over to the conductor who took one quick look and gave the ticket back again. He told the farm boy, "Well, I'm sorry, but there are no other accommodations available on this train tonight. I'm afraid you'll have to make do. Your porter'll help you up. Goodnight."

Tipping his cap, the conductor walked off toward the drawing rooms at the rear of the car.

Rascal stuck his head out through a fold in the curtain. "These berths really are quite comfortable."

"Aw, choke it," Alvin growled, climbing up into his berth.

Soon the electric lights were extinguished and the Pullman car was dark. Across the aisle, Alvin heard a salesman in the upper berth snoring like a sick bear. Half a dozen times, the porter passed by. Twice, the girl in number four summoned his attention. Another short dumpy fellow waddled back from the washroom, stinking of gin and cigars. In his cramped upper berth, Alvin watched the night countryside fly past, lights of scattered farmhouses glowing like tiny stars on the black prairie. He wondered how far east the other passengers were going. St. Louis? Cleveland? Pittsburgh? Washington? All those places he'd likely never live long enough to see. Trains ran all night in America. He wondered what it would be like to get off one in Boston or New York, walk around under a giant skyscraper, eat in a swank restaurant somewhere, attend a movie show with a big crowd, ride a subway car to the waterfront and watch the big ships come in from China, all the ladies of joy flocking to sailors and other young strangers like himself.

Rascal tapped on the underside of the bed. Alvin ignored him. The dwarf tapped again. Somebody passed by in the aisle, scent of bay rum trailing behind. Two men were conversing in low voices at the front of the car with the porter. Rascal tapped again and Alvin stuck his head through his curtain and leaned over the side and pulled open the dwarf's berth. "What're you doing that for?"

The dwarf's smiling face thrust out from the dark. "Shall we play a game of Hearts?"

"Go roll your hoop."

Rascal ducked back into his berth and rang for the porter. The whistle from the locomotive screeched and a few seconds later the clanging of klaxon bells at an empty crossroads echoed briefly through the Pullman car. The porter came down the aisle to Rascal's berth. "Yes, sir?"

"Is there a toilet?"

"At the front of this car."

"Much obliged."

The porter left.

Rascal crawled out of his berth, fully dressed. Peeking out from his own berth, Alvin saw a woman's face and enormous bosom emerge from behind the curtain in number three, curlpapers in her hair. "Good heavens!" She gave a tug on the curtain to the berth above her. "Harold?"

A man's voice answered. "Yes, dear?"

"It's that strange little man again!"

"Close your eyes, honey, he'll go away."

Rascal gave her a polite bow.

The woman shrieked, "Harold!"

Another man stuck his head out of a lower berth. "For crying out loud, would you folks please keep quiet!"

The dwarf closed his curtain and rushed off toward the front of the Pullman. Alvin stretched out. He closed his eyes and tried to forget his bellyache. After a while the salesman in the upper berth across the aisle quit snoring. Alvin listened to the occasional train whistle and thought of the trestle across the Mississippi where he used to fish and swim. *Fact was, nobody knew where he'd gone. Maybe they thought he'd gotten on a truck and ridden to California, or else jumped in the river and drowned. Probably Joe Mitchell would organize a pack of men to drag the current below the trestle and ol' Stewball would throw a couple sticks of dynamite into the water to try and get the body to come up out of the muck, after which they'd go home and eat a chicken dinner and get drunk and probably forget about him in a week or so. Maybe Frenchy would nail up some notices down river and drive Uncle Cy's Chevrolet south to Quincy, but it wouldn't be more than a month before most of them would give up and figure he just bumped off from his consumption somewhere. Poor old Alvin was dead and gone to Jesus. Someone else'll have to feed the cows now and water the chickens. Maybe Mary Ann. She doesn't hardly do nothing around the house but read drugstore magazines and chalk up her face for snooty Jimmy McFarland. If Daddy wasn't feeling stingy, he might order up a nifty stone for the gravesite and maybe Frenchy would get a haircut and wear a suit of black broadcloth and everyone'd come and bawl their eyes out for a couple hours and say a sorrowing word or two about what a fine kid good old Alvin had been when he was alive for tolerating his illness and all, and how much they were going to miss him, and how nobody could ever weed and water a garden as good, and who could forget how he fixed Mrs. Wilkie's worm fence in a day and a half for nothing more'n a jar of watermelon pickles and a glass of cider, and how after hearing that, the preacher might even tell everybody that poor dear departed Alvin Frederick Pendergast was a saint and a credit to his grieving family, after all.*

The train roared past a blackened junction town without stopping. Alvin had finally drifted off to sleep when a woman's voice down the aisle called from the dark, "Good heavens, Harold! He's back!"

Alvin felt the stepladder scrape against the lower berth. The double curtain rustled, and parted briefly, allowing somebody to struggle up onto his bed, nearly pulling the bedlinen off in the process.

"Hey!"

"Shhhh!"

The berth light flashed on and Alvin saw the dwarf propped up near the window-fastenings at the foot of the berth. Rascal held a fistful of bills. "We're rich!"

Feeling wobbly and lightheaded, the farm boy leaned out through the curtain to look down the aisle where the woman from berth three was talking to the porter: "I tell you, he's deliberately spoiling my sleep."

"Yes, ma'am."

"My husband owns fourteen chain stores and I want something done."

"Yes, ma'am."

"Harold!"

Alvin ducked back into his berth. The dwarf had curled up next to the window and spread the bills out on the blanket. The farm boy switched off the berth light, then shushed the dwarf. Somebody grabbed the stepladder. The porter's face thrust into the upper berth. Seeing the two of them together, he smiled. "Why, ain't that something. Looky here."

"Yeah?" Alvin coughed hoarsely. Now he wasn't sure he could get back to sleep.

"I s'pose y'all ain't needing this ladder no more."

"I guess I will tomorrow morning," the farm boy said, rubbing his eyes. He noticed his bedclothes were damp and smelled moldy. "When's breakfast? I'm so hungry I could eat a rubber boot."

"Well, sir, I'd say you're still a few hours shy of a cup of coffee and a doughnut, but I'll come get you, don't you worry. Yes, sir." Then the porter turned to Rascal who was hiding in the corner of the berth at Alvin's feet. "And if I was you, little fellow, I'd keep my eyes peeled. There's a lady we both know who'd like her husband to give you a good old-fashioned lickin'."

"I can't imagine why," Rascal protested. "I haven't done a thing."

"Well, she's awful cranky."

"So I noticed."

"Now, don't say I ain't warned you. 'Night, boys."

"Good night."

When he heard the porter open the washroom door, Alvin switched on the berth light and grabbed a handful of the bills lying on the blanket. He riffled through them, counting haphazardly. "We got better'n two hundred bucks here."

The dwarf switched the light off. "It's three hundred and seventy-three even, and it's not ours, it's mine. I won it fair and square."

"Says you," Alvin replied, still holding a handful of bills. "I ain't had this much cash-money in my whole life. Where'd you steal it?"

"I just told you, I won it playing thirteen unusually trying hands of Fargo Pete with some very sneaky cardsharks back there in the clubcar. In fact, I was fully prepared to be murdered by them when the game was over. A thoroughly nasty fellow named Patch was quite upset with me for emptying his pockets. It's a wonder I survived." The dwarf reached for the money. "Here, give it to me."

Alvin snatched it away. The dwarf lunged across the bed and grabbed at the dollar bills in Alvin's hands, but he was too slow and the farm boy tucked them under his pillow.

"I'll ring for the porter," the dwarf warned.

"Aw, be a sport. Let me have some of it."

"Why should I? You didn't win it, I did."

"Don't be stingy. I ain't feeling good." His pillow was half-drenched in fever sweat.

"Listen here, if you return it to me," the dwarf said, "I'll give you a share."

"Oh yeah?" Alvin coughed. "How much?"

"I won't say until I have it all back."

The train passed a crossroad, bells clanging in the dark. Another prairie town briefly lit the upper berth as the Pullman swayed gently. Reluctantly, the farm boy shoved his handful of bills back to the dwarf. "Well, you better not leave me flat, you old skinflint. Remember, if it wasn't for me, you wouldn't even been on this train tonight."

"Thank you. Now, if you're truly feeling ill, perhaps we ought to call for a doctor."

Alvin shook his head. "There ain't nothing wrong with me. It's just allergies."

"Oh, I doubt that very much. You've been under the weather for weeks now and I'm quite worried. It's obvious you're not well."

"If you say so."

"Look, there's no sense in avoiding a fact of health. You're not afraid of doctors, are you?"

"No!" Alvin scowled. "And there ain't nothing wrong me, neither. So why don't you just tell me how you won that dough?"

Collecting the bills together one by one, the dwarf replied, "I told you, it was Fargo Pete."

"What the hell's that?"

"A card game, you ninny! The rules are quite involved, otherwise I'd teach them to you." Rascal began counting up his money in the dark. "As a child, I used to play for hours on end. I'm an expert Fargo Pete player."

"Maybe we ought to try a hand or two."

The dwarf stifled a laugh. "That's precious."

"Huh?"

"When I was eleven years old, I suffered an awful spell of rheumatism and had to be confined to bed for a week. This was the middle of July, so the upstairs of our house was terribly hot, and, of course, the rheumatism gave me quite a high fever and dreadful sweats and I couldn't move a muscle without enduring the worst pain imaginable. Auntie shifted my bed under the dormer where a breeze provided some comfort. She and Miss Evalena from next door administered salicylate of soda every two or three hours with buttermilk and Dover's powder at night and wrapped up my legs in cotton-batting to ease the horrid inflammation. It was quite hellish, I assure you — that is, until I was paid a visit by the sweetest angel in God's creation. Dear little Betsy Bennett was new to Hadleyville and had no friends before we were introduced to each other by Auntie and Mrs. Bennett, who'd chanced to strike up a conversation at the grocery store. She wore blue gingham and corkscrew curls and a yellow ribbon in her hair and had read every volume of *Chatterbox* I owned, cover to cover. Betsy was the most remarkable child I'd ever met. Naturally, we became great friends. It was she who taught me how to play Fargo Pete, and I must admit that when it came time for Betsy to go home, I was forced to give her my favorite savings bank as penalty for all the tricks I lost. Even so, the very next morning she returned with a basket of hot cinnamon buns and a pair of loaded dice with which she allowed me to reclaim the penny bank. Wasn't that lovely? All week long we shared my buttermilk and told each other riddles and quoted poems and jingles from *St. Nicholas*. She read to me from *Marjorie-Joe* and I read to her out of *Tales of the Days of Chivalry* and *The Little Colonel*. I taught her sailor's knots and

Indian cures and she showed me how to darn my own stockings and to say 'Merry Christmas' to the deaf. Why, I believe it may have been the grandest time I ever knew as a child, despite my painful rheumatism. Unfortunately, Mrs. Bennett was called away by relatives to the mines in California. The last I heard from dear Betsy was a Christmas card she mailed from a tiny gold town in the mountains. She wrote that it had been snowing for a week and she'd seen a bear in the woods behind her house that very morning."

Bells clanged at a crossroads and Alvin heard the salesman across the aisle begin snoring once again. In the dark corridor below, the porter passed by whistling to himself. Rascal folded open the curtain to stop him. The dwarf said, "I'm terribly hungry."

The porter cracked a grin. "Don't I know it."

"I'd like a meat sandwich and a glass of lemonade."

"Well, sir, don't know's I could do that. Kitchen's closed for the night, but I believe the candybutcher's catnapping in the dining car right now and I guess he might have you a snack if you can wake him."

"Splendid! How do I get there?"

"Just follow this aisle ahead through the vestibule to the next car." The porter pointed to the rear of the Pullman. "Go through that one, too, and there she'll be."

"Wonderful! Thank you very much."

"Yes, sir."

The porter walked off.

Alvin said, "I ain't a-going with you. I'm waiting for breakfast."

"I don't recall extending the invitation," replied the dwarf, struggling to re-tie his shoes.

Across the aisle, a thin fellow in nightclothes parted his curtain. "Shhhh! Trying to sleep here."

"Sorry," Alvin whispered, as the dwarf jumped down into the aisle and hustled off.

"Harold! It's him again!"

"Who?"

"That awful little man!"

The farm boy quickly tied his shoes and slid down off the upper berth into the darkened aisle, landing with a loud thud. At once, several people rang for the porter. Murmuring apologies as he went along, the farm boy chased after the dwarf.

A crowd of men in gray wool flannel suits stood in the drafty vestibule smoking cigarettes and sharing conversation with a pair of conductors. Alvin nodded as he came through. Before he reached the door to the next Pullman car, one of the conductors grabbed his shoulder. "Hold on there, young fellow."

"Huh?"

"Do you have a ticket for that car?"

Alvin felt his face flush. "No, sir."

"Well, then, you can't go in there. These cars are fully engaged."

Through the glass, Alvin saw somebody come out of the men's smoking room in the next Pullman. The rhythmic click-clack-click-clack of the gently swaying train vibrated underfoot. The farm boy told the conductor, "I ain't feeling too good. I need something to eat."

"Well, son, I'm afraid it's a little late for that. The diner's been closed for hours now."

One of the men piped up, "Oh, Wilbur, don't be a stiff. Let the poor kid through. The swells won't mind. Look how skinny he is. It's obvious he hasn't eaten in a week. Say, I'll bet Ollie'd set him up to a wienie sandwich in half a shake."

The stocky man smoking a cigarette beside him added, "Why, sure he would. And probably throw in a cup of coffee, too, for a folksy young fellow like this."

"I ain't no hick," said Alvin, his blood rising. As the train swayed, everyone in the vestibule steadied his balance and a touch of vertigo chased behind the farm boy's eyes.

"Do you hear that, Wilbur?" a third gentleman chimed in. "This boy's not some sap from blind baggage. He's an earnest young fellow who won't let you put it all over him just to keep this railroad running on routine lines. If he's sick like he says he is, why not do the fair square thing and let him by? A fellow shouldn't need a lounge suit to get a sandwich."

"Let him through, Wilbur," said the other conductor. "The railroad won't go belly-up on account of a hungry kid."

"Well, I couldn't stand the gaff if it did," Wilbur said, stepping aside to allow Alvin by. "All right, then. Go ahead, son. Have yourself a sandwich, but be quick about it. I'll be through that car in another quarter of a hour, so there'd better not be any monkey business."

"Thanks."

Crossing the threshold, Alvin heard a round of laughter behind him and felt humiliated. Gasbags! Why had that rattlebrained conductor allowed the dwarf to slip by so easily? It wasn't at all fair. He entered the men's washroom and used the toilet. Checking himself in the mirror afterward, his face appeared waxy and sallow. He hadn't any idea he looked so awful. Alvin felt the train rumble under his feet and heard the clanging at another crossroad. He washed his hands, dried them off, and went back out into the empty aisle again in time to see the lights of a Dixie filling station disappear into the darkness. Alvin heard laughter from a compartment near the end of the car. He walked quietly along the aisle to drawing room "A," found the electric light on and the door cracked open, and stole a peek inside. The brunette from the station platform, now wearing a gold kimono, winked at him, then called to someone out of Alvin's view, "Oh, Clarence dear, it seems we have company."

The farm boy backed up into the aisle, flushed with embarrassment. Then the door swung open wide and Chester appeared in a blue flannel robe, holding a plate with a cheese sandwich and a stack of crackers. Seeing Alvin, he broke into a wide grin. "Well, what do you know? Hiya, kid!"

He leaned forward and grabbed Alvin by the elbow and dragged him into the drawing room and shut the door. "Honey, meet Melvin. Kid, say hello to Alma."

Gardenia perfume wafted up as the brunette offered Alvin her hand. "Evening, dear."

The farm boy shook her hand politely. "Hello."

Chester grinned. "Melvin's a corking athlete, footballer with the college at Lincoln."

"You don't say?" she giggled, nudging a soft brown curl off her eyebrow. "Why, he doesn't look at all the sort. He seems like an awful softie and those freckles are so boyish."

Alvin blushed to see her study him like she did. He still thought she was swell, and he'd lay her in nothing flat if he had the chance. Chester sat down and took a bite of his sandwich. The green carpet was littered with cracker crumbs and Alvin smelled liquor.

Chester laughed. "Well, I tell you, he's as rough as they come. Aren't you, kid?"

The farm boy shrugged. He knew how haggard and pale he looked, but what could he do about it? Truth was, he felt even worse. God, how he hated being sick.

Chester went on, "You bet he is! Why, the papers in Lincoln say he's another Red Grange, and I don't doubt it for a minute. Anyone who knows his football can tell he's got the stuff."

The brunette slipped a silver hipflask out from the folds of her gold kimono, took a sip, and giggled again. "Well, what's a hero like you doing riding a train in the middle of the night? Shouldn't you be in a gymnasium somewhere doing calisthenics or throwing a medicine ball around with the other boys on the team?"

"Sure, I guess so," Alvin stammered weakly, trying his best to play along. "I just ain't thought that much about it. Nobody told me what to do today, so soon as my feet started itchin', I went and got on the train." He summoned a feeble smile. Lying didn't seem that tough, anymore.

Chester drew a bottle of Canadian whiskey from his handbag and filled a shotglass on the table beside him. "What he means to say, darling, is that he thinks school's for the birds. Melvin's commercial, see, and he's gotten up a meeting to try for a professional team in St. Louis and believes he can cinch a job so long as his mother doesn't find out. She's something of a trueblood Christer from a rock farm down by Abilene, and more than anything in the world she wants Melvin to get ducked before she passes on to her reward. He's still got a raft of faith in the Old Book, of course, and the importance of church fellowship and all, but he can't just chuck everything to take a swim for Jesus. Well, at any rate, as you can see, the poor kid's feeling awful bum about it."

Alvin saw the pretty brunette staring at him, a bright twinkle in her eye as she took another sip from the silver hipflask. He felt a slight chill from his fever and had to steady himself.

Alma said, "Why, I'll bet you a cookie that Melvin's mommy is darned proud of her boy even if he isn't a Sunday School teacher." She offered Alvin her hipflask. "Here, honey, have a jolt. It'll help. Honest."

Chester grabbed her wrist. "Don't tempt him, sweetheart. When I met Melvin in the lunchroom of that rube burg this morning, I could see the poor fellow was already about to crack. Why, he almost fainted in his eggs, didn't you, kid?"

"Sure I did." The farm boy noticed that the brunette's kimono had parted above the waist giving him a discreet peek at one of her pale pink breasts. Suddenly he felt flushed, and stifled a cough even as his peenie stiffened.

Alma frowned. "Gee, honey, that's awful! Maybe you hadn't ought to've taken that church dope so hard. My momma, bless her heart, baked peach pies for twenty-two years at the Methodist fair back in Kimball and never took her eye off the pulpit until Reverend Waller called her down one Sunday evening for sneaking a gallon of swee-twine into the punch, and him, that mucker, with a cocktail shaker in his office closet and Mabel Hutchins from the choir waiting up in the attic. Poor Momma came home fussing that Reverend Waller didn't have any call to bawl her out like he did, and if the Lord only asked temperance of the congregation, well, forget it! And I tell you, honey, Momma never went back. If you ask me, all religious folks are crabs."

Chester downed his whiskey with a smile. "Gee, that's a swell story, sweetheart, but would you mind awfully taking a smoke in the toilet? Melvin and I have a few things to talk over and that means man to man, darling, get what I mean?" He walked over and opened the door to the washroom annex and jerked his thumb at her to get up.

"Clarence, honey, you know I told you I don't smoke."

"Well, this is as good a time as any to get the habit." He tossed her a package of Chesterfields from the table. "Here, now beat it."

"Hey!"

He grabbed her harshly and gave her a kiss on the lips. When Chester stepped back again, the brunette was smiling. He said to her, "You love me, don't you, darling?"

"Honey, I'd give you a clout in the head if you weren't so nice to pat." She wiggled her fingers at the farm boy. "Toodle-loo, Melvin."

After the toilet door closed, Chester dragged Alvin over to the window and sat down in front of him. "She's a peacherino, isn't she?"

He nodded. "She's slick, all right."

Chester clucked his tongue. "Dumb as a cow, though. For two hours now she's been gassing about some fellow her sister's going with and how he bought her a new electric refrigerator." Chester poured another shot of Canadian whiskey and drank it in one gulp. Then he took a cigarette from his robe and lit up. Flicking the spent match onto the table, he told Alvin, "Look here, you boys are going to ride through to Omaha, then change trains to the Missouri Pacific. I need to run in on someone tomorrow morning at Council Bluffs, so I won't be traveling with you after tonight. When you get to Icaria, there's a flophouse on Third Street owned by a fellow named Spud Farrell. He'll hire you a room for the week. Pay him cash-money. He's an old hellcat, so he'll give you the lowdown on the smart neighborhoods and where the best eats are. If you like, you and the midget can give the circus a once-over before I get there on Saturday. Just don't go till after dark. I'll be staying at the Belvedere Hotel. That's downtown on Main. I'll telephone to Spud when my train gets in. He'll let you know I arrived. All right?"

"Sure."

"Tell the midget if he does anything to put this job on the fritz, I'll pop him so hard he'll need Western Union to tell you good morning."

The farm boy coughed into his fist, then nodded. "I was out looking for him when I walked by your door and seen that girl sitting here. I ain't exactly sure where he is right now."

"I just saw him back there in the smoker playing cards with a flock of bond salesmen. What'll you bet he'll have 'em all busted by midnight?"

As the train passed another crossroad, Alvin heard the girl humming a few bars of jazz in the toilet. Her voice was wonderfully clear and lovely. Chester listened briefly, then took a drag off the cigarette and stood up. Somebody buzzed insistently to enter another drawing room back up the darkened aisle.

Chester told Alvin, "All right, you better scram now and get your sleep. You're not looking that fresh and there's a little song sparrow next door waiting for me to love her up." He led the farm boy to the compartment door. "So long, kid."

Leaving the drawing room, the farm boy bumped straight into the conductor who had blocked him back at the vestibule. One glance at Alvin and the conductor's face went sour. "You? Why, I shoulda — "

"Awww, keep your shirt on, pal," Alvin growled, squeezing past. "I'm beating it already!"

At Icaria, the train station was located in a section of town that had run down when the Singer Sewing Machine Company quit its thread mill contract and the labor turnover sent hundreds to public charity and pauper funds. Worn-out plank sidewalks led from the noisy Missouri Pacific locomotives and the crowded depot, past a potato warehouse and a grimy brickyard and a packing plant into the pathetic neighborhood of scratch houses and shiftlessness. A sudden cloudburst had descended upon Icaria earlier that week, drenching the old dirt roads to mud. Sewer drainage by the train district was dismal, too, the oily stench nauseating as the farm boy and the dwarf carried their suitcases past a row of shabby Negro residences and across the railroad tracks toward Third Street. They stopped for a few minutes to watch a freight train going back light to Kansas City. Sooty-eyed men stared at them from empty Illinois Central boxcars and sagging tarpaper cookshacks. Gray clouds were scattered about the late morning sky and the day was cool. A quarter mile past the tracks, a collection of broken-down flivvers crowded the yard of a squat framehouse on Clover Lane across the road from a blacksmith shop and a closed millinery. On a plank fence next to the elm-shrouded house, billposters had pasted a bright colorful notice for *Emmett J. Laswell's Traveling Circus Giganticus.* According to the advertisement, all the tent shows would open after the street parade on Friday. That meant this afternoon.

"I've never ridden a camel," remarked the dwarf, comparing the Arabian dromedary on the elaborately drawn poster to a notice in the morning paper he had purchased from a newsbutcher in the clubcar. "Have you?"

"Sure I did," Alvin lied. "It wasn't nothing special."

A black second-hand Chevrolet drove by in the rutted street. The farm boy put down his suitcase. He had slept better than he expected in the upper berth and woke just after dawn with the fever dissipated and his cough subdued. He was still tired, but not quite so enfeebled as he had been. The eggs he ate for breakfast in the buffet car had set him up just fine. Down behind the framehouse was a chilly creek hidden by dense cottonwoods and shagbark hickory trees where a pack of boys playing truant from school for the day rough-necked along the soggy embankment, voices chattering like nutty mockingbirds. Alvin expected to see hundreds of kids just like them at the circus by sundown.

Back near the depot, a steam whistle shrieked.

The dwarf asked, "Did Chester mention to you whether or not our flophouse puts up suppers? I'd rather save my card winnings for an emergency."

"I got pocket money enough for eats till the end of the week. If that don't do, he says we can wash dishes at a lunch counter."

Alvin picked up his tattered suitcase and started walking again. A cool breeze swept through the thick cottonwoods and brushed dust along the old board sidewalk.

"Actually, I'm quite good at dishwashing," said the dwarf, folding the newspaper under his arm. He rushed to keep up. "Auntie despised it, so she decided that doing them ought to be my after-supper chore. I also directed Bessie's weekly marketing and regulated many of the household duties when Auntie went on holiday. Why, in less than a month I learned how to prepare cowheel jelly and sausage pudding and rummeled eggs, while Pleasance taught me to improve boiled starch by the addition of some salt or a little gum arabic dissolved. Isn't that fascinating?"

"You said it." Alvin suddenly felt a strong piss coming on and didn't see an outhouse.

"Oh, I doubt we'll have any trouble at all earning our way if need be."

"Gee, that's swell," the farm boy remarked, hurrying his pace along the wooden sidewalk. "Maybe you can buy your own pie tonight."

The boardinghouse at Third Street and Borton was three floors high and dingy with flaking paint and missing roof shingles. Virginia creeper draped the clapboard siding, and thick patches of milkweed clustered to the foundation. Old sycamores shrouded the upper floors. A steep cement staircase led up from the sidewalk to a dusty veranda littered with apple crates and soiled cushions and potato sacks filled with discards. The screen door was ajar and a single electric light was lit in the entry. A stink of fresh turpentine issued from somewhere indoors and faint voices echoed throughout. Parked at the curb out front was a black truck with an advertisement on both door panels for ***Timothy Meyer & Co. Painting***. Scattered leaves blew about the dirt road. Alvin's stomach was going sour as he grew nervous again being in a strange town. What if he got sick here? Where would he go? The dwarf went indoors ahead of him, passing a small placard on the siding that read: **No Invalids!**

Upstairs, a radio set broadcast a jazzy dance program and the music echoed through the dark stairwell. The empty foyer for the big old house was gloomy and cool and smelled of linoleum and musty closets. Jade-green portières left of the entry hall across from the desk revealed a side parlor. A narrower hallway led to the dining room and kitchen at the back of the house. Overhead, the ceiling plaster showed cracks and water-blotches, and the brass light fixture had gone dark from years of tarnish. The front desk was unattended, so the dwarf set his suitcase next to a brass spittoon, then reached up from his tiptoes and rang the service bell. An office door behind the desk opened and a young blonde hardly older than Alvin came out. She was dressed plainly in a pale blue flower-print frock. Her hair was bobbed and curled and she had a darling face with brown calf-eyes. The farm boy's heart jumped when she smiled at him. "Good afternoon."

"Hello."

Her sweet face brightened further. "Why, you're with the circus, aren't you?"

Without hesitation, the dwarf nodded. "Dakota Bill, bareback riding and Indian knife tricks, at your service, ma'am." He bowed elegantly.

The girl smiled. "Pleased to meet you. My name is Clare." She looked across at Alvin. "You must be Melvin. Your telegraph arrived Wednesday evening."

"Yeah?"

"Of course, it's just lovely that you'll be staying here with us. Why, I adore the circus." Her brown eyes sparkled.

Alvin heard footsteps pounding down the stairwell from the second floor. A man's husky laughter echoed loudly out of the corner room above the parlor as a painter in lacquer-stained overalls came down the staircase into the foyer, look of distress on his face. He shouted to the blonde, "Honey, telephone Doc Evans, will you? I just swallowed some turpentine!"

"Oh, dear!"

"Tell him I'll be over his place in nothing flat!"

The painter hurried out of the boardinghouse and down to the sidewalk. The girl rushed back into the office and dialed for the operator. "Hello, Shirley? This is Clare." She nudged the door shut behind her.

Alvin walked to the front door and watched the painter running up the sidewalk. One block behind him, a postman strolled along with his mail sack while a delivery truck and a tan Hudson-Essex rattled past in the other direction. Tall shady elm trees blocked his sight farther on. A train whistle sounded in the distance.

The office door opened again and the blonde came out, shaking her head. "Would you believe that's the third call this week Doctor Evans has had for turpentine poisoning?"

Alvin walked back from the front door as a draft from the street swept up into the boardinghouse. A cough rattled out of his chest, making his eyes water.

"One cup of castor oil, two eggs, milk, flour, water and a little saccharate of lime," the dwarf announced, authoritatively.

"I beg your pardon?"

"It's a cure for turpentine poisoning, and quite effective, I should add." The dwarf beamed.

The blonde smiled. "Are you a doctor, too?"

Wiping his eyes, the farm boy spoke up ahead of the dwarf. "He ain't nothing but a mouth that walks. Don't trust him."

"My young companion is the skeptical sort," the dwarf explained, still smiling. "But, no, I am not a physician. Merely an interested by-stander in humanity's welfare." Rascal bowed once more. "At your service."

Clare laughed. "Oh, I'm sure we'll have a wonderful time while you're here. Did you speak with Mr. Farrell about your room? I'm afraid he's gone to Perryville for the day."

"No, but we'll pay cash-money," said the farm boy, pulling a wad of small bills from his pants pocket. He felt like Rockefeller himself as he counted out ten dollars.

"Well, he's given you a corner room on the third floor with a fine view. I think it's adorable. Why, it even has its own plumbing." She took the payment from Alvin and put it into a metal box beneath the counter, then brought out a pair of keys. "These are for you. Don't forget, supper's prompt at six."

"What's that cost?" Alvin asked, gruffly. "Spud ought to know we ain't kings."

"Why, it's included with the room."

"Oh, that's swell."

She offered Alvin a lovely smile. "I'll just bet your circus is a peach!"

The farm boy blushed. He knew he resembled a crummy hobo, but she was treating him like gravy. What gives? Did she like him?

Clare asked, "Will I see you there tonight? I'm through at eight."

Because she was so pretty, he chose to go along with the gag. "Sure, we'll be there. We ain't set up regular yet with a tent like them other acts, so just look around for us. It's a pip of a show."

She gushed, "Oh, I'm excited already!"

The room was at the end of the hall by a window that looked down onto a grassy backyard of goldenrod and sawtooth sunflowers and bleached white laundry suspended on a wire from the kitchen porch to the slatted fence at Weaver Street. Only a few tenants were in the half-dozen rooms hired for the month, and the house was quiet. Alvin put down his suitcase, then unlocked the door and went in. The dwarf trailed behind, his own suitcase in hand. Morning light glowed behind drawn roller shades at the back and side windows, brightening a bare room that had a wood floor, two small iron beds covered in ratty quilts, an oak dresser and mirror, and a pair of spindle chairs. The dwarf went to the closet while Alvin tossed his old suitcase onto the bed nearest the wall. He was tired of lugging it around. Another small door led to a toilet with an old tub and washbasin and a porcelain commode, which Alvin used immediately. In the room across the hall, he heard a fellow walking about reciting aloud from the Holy Bible.

"This sure ain't the Ritz," Alvin remarked, as he came out of the toilet, buttoning his pants. He raised the shade above the backyard to watch a coal truck rumble down a wheel-rutted lane toward the railyard crossing and saw a pair of carpenters laboring on a wooden scaffold next door and a woman in an old hoop skirt across the road scattering corncobs among muddy hogs in a small wire-fenced pen. Frenchy once had a painting job until he got drunk at noon behind a lunch wagon and fell off the scaffold and landed on a cow, breaking her back. It cost him three days pay. Aunt Hattie like to boxed his ears.

Fastening the linen shade, Alvin said, "I'll bet you that painter fellow ain't drank no turpentine, neither. It smelled like kitchen brew to me. I seen drunkards at home tackle a bottle of overnight that knocks 'em flat sudden. Some doctor's probably using the stomach pump on him right now. What do you bet that Spud fellow hired us a room in a booze flat?"

The dwarf closed his suitcase and shut the closet. "Oh, I suspect there aren't a dozen establishments in this town unfriendly to the contentious fluid. Although I'm quite immune myself, drinking's become quite the thing to do, you know. Why, this past year even dear old Auntie refused to go to bed without enjoying a good-night toddy. Shall we go visit the circus this morning?"

"Nope, Chester said not till after dark." The farm boy sat on the mattress, testing its firmness. He felt tired again; he'd have a nap if he weren't so hungry. He sniffed the quilt, wrinkling his nose at a damp musty odor. "Ain't this a swell dump? I bet you we got bedbugs."

The dwarf went over to his own bed and climbed onto the mattress and bounced up and down squeaking the springs. Then he rolled over onto his stomach and sniffed the blue quilt. He slid off the bed and peeked underneath. When he stood up again, he announced, "Blue ointment and kerosene, mixed in equal proportions, then applied to the bedstead."

"Huh?"

"A very fine bedbug remedy," said the dwarf.

Alvin got up and went to the door. "How's about we get us some eats and watch the street parade? I'm awful hungry."

Spud Farrell's boardinghouse was closer to the grimy neighborhood of stovepipe shanties and truck gardens than to downtown. Here the narrow streets were unpaved, and motorcars had cut a thousand tracks in the dirt, and occasionally horse-drawn wagons still lumbered along under honey locust and sugar maples where tired men wearing overalls and denim walked to work at the railyard and sawmill each morning, metal buckets in hand.

Smelling wood smoke from old cook stoves, the farm boy and the dwarf strolled Third Street toward downtown. Wooden fences on both sides of the dirt street advertised the circus, and tall ironweed grew in thick patches between fence posts and gates. Up on the corner, a woman in pink cotton and a white apron swept her porch with a flurry of tiny children at her feet. Just ahead on Elm, a postman walking his morning route shouted to a fellow in a flashy new Buick parked at the curb of a blue stick Eastlake framehouse where two elderly women shoveled manure from a wheelbarrow into a freshly dug spinach patch. Two blocks from the boardinghouse, Alvin smelled crap-foul backhouses and chicken coops and livery stables on the breeze. Farther on, he saw scrawny apple and peach trees in weedy backyards whose tin garages, cluttered with rusty junk, stood doorless to the brisk wind. Auto horns sounded through the sun-warmed elms and willows, and Alvin thought he caught scent of a fresh-baked cherry pie on a window ledge somewhere closeby. Whistling a Sousa march, the dwarf led Alvin down an alley shortcut where chirping catbirds nested in wild grape, and crabapple branches and dogwoods scratched at the plank fences. They paused briefly to listen to phonograph music droning from a third-story attic and morning voices exchanging airy greetings across kitchen porches. They stepped back against the fence as an empty milktruck rumbled by, and covered their mouths from the dust and exhaust that roiled up in its wake. Emerging from the alley, they discovered shrieking children running about at recess beneath a black oak in a dusty schoolyard on South Main near the creek. A slatted fence separated the square lot from a white high-steepled Lutheran church next door. On the stoop of the gray weatherboarded schoolhouse, a plump older woman was busy scolding a trio of boys in brown knickers. Behind her, a small girl in a soiled petticoat stood by the doorway sobbing. Waiting for a delivery truck to pass, the dwarf rushed across the dirt street into a prickly ash thicket that separated the schoolyard from the Ford garage on the other lot. There he spied on the children trading turns swinging from a rubber tire and skipping rope, playing jacks on a flat patch of dirt, throwing a scruffy baseball back and forth, wrestling and riding each other about pick-a-back. Alvin was content to observe from the sidewalk across the street. He hated school. Teachers were ugly and mean and assigned lessons not a fellow on earth could figure out by himself. He preferred shoveling horse manure to reading books. If a kid had a decent egg on his shoulders and wasn't afraid of work, he could find a job that paid enough to buy a new suit of clothes when he needed it and a movie every Saturday night and pocket money for emergencies without busting himself up over spelling words nobody knew how to use and stacks of numbers on a blackboard that usually added up to a horsewhipping on his bare bottom in the woodshed out back. What did the world care, anyhow, if he slopped hogs and went fishing instead of learning about Abe Lincoln?

After a few minutes, Alvin whistled to the dwarf and crossed the street to the Ford garage where he nearly choked from the odor of gasoline engines. Just ahead, a short bridge spanned the ravine. Tall sycamores rose beside thick cottonwoods from the creek bottom and Alvin bent over the iron railing halfway across and spat and watched his spittle disappear into the cold swirling water. Walking on alone up the slop-ing road to Main Street, he counted nineteen swallows perched on tele-graph wires between a Shell filling station and a Western Auto Supply store. He took a minute to study the ads for Goodyear tires and Mobil Oil on a barnsiding as three automobiles and a smelly fruit truck roared by. He watched a nurse in white guide an old woman up to a doctor's office in another clapboard framehouse where a hornet's nest was stuck under the corner eaves. Somebody yelled out his name and he looked behind him. Two blocks down the road, the dwarf was hurrying across the bridge. Alvin gave another whistle, and went on ahead downtown.

They sat at a small marble top table by the front window in Moore's Café next door to the Royale movie house on Main Street. Cigarette smoke and conversation filled the narrow dining room, dishes clanked, cooking grease hissed in the kitchen. Alvin sipped carefully at a cup of hot black coffee. It burned going down, but soothed his sore throat just the same. He was feeling better and better. The dwarf stirred ice about with a spoon in his glass of orangeade and watched the men and women passing by on the busy sidewalk outdoors. He remarked to the farm boy, "Those children are terribly excited over the circus. Why, it's all they could speak of."

"Nothing about arithmetic?"

"Oh, I'm sure most of them thoroughly enjoy schooldays. In-cidentally, did I tell you that my father's Uncle Edgar taught moral philosophy at Virginia with William McGuffey himself? Much of my inspiration for learning came from the collection of *Eclectic Readers* my mother left me. Why, those books were among my very best friends at that time of my life."

The dwarf put his spoon on the table and drank from the glass of orangeade.

Alvin noticed several customers were staring now. Whether it was at him or the dwarf, he didn't care; he thought it was rude, so he stared back until they were forced to look elsewhere. When he was in the sanitarium, visitors occasionally wandered into the sick wards and ev-ery so often Alvin would awaken from a nap to find himself the object of somebody's nosy attention. It made him feel worse than ever. He learned to despise people who couldn't keep their eyes to themselves.

The waiter came to their table, carrying a plate of lamb and sweet potatoes and another with pickled beets and chicken fricassee. As he set the plates down, lamb for Alvin, chicken for Rascal, he asked, "Are you two fellows with the circus?"

"Sure we are," Alvin replied, already set for a swell fib. "I'm a lion tamer and my friend here does some juggling in a clown suit. It don't pay much, but we get by all right, I guess."

The waiter looked skeptical. "Sort of late in the season for the circus, ain't it? We don't usually see you folks much after Labor Day."

Alvin nodded. " 'Course it is, but business was scarce this summer. Come wintertime, even circus people got to eat like everyone else, ain't that so?"

"I suppose it is."

Downtown was filling up. Looking out through the window, the waiter said, "Got a swell parade today, do you?"

"Sure." Alvin stuck his fork into the lamb like he was starving. "Sells a flock of tickets."

A group of homely women dressed in black stopped at the window to peer in. One of them tapped on the glass and held up a placard upon which was written in thick black ink: **BOOZE**. The stocky woman next to her showed another placard reading: **Prisons, Insane Asylums, Condemned Cells!** Two more hatchet-faced women stepped forward and pressed tall placards to the glass: **Good Riddance to Bad Rubbish** and **DRY or DIE.** Their grim focus was directed toward the farm boy and the dwarf. The waiter tried shooing them away, "Go on! Beat it!"

Not one of them budged.

The dwarf offered a salute and a pickled beet.

Flustered by the unwanted attention, Alvin blurted out, "How come them ladies are doing that? Who the hell are they?"

"Temperance Union," replied the waiter, waving at them again to go away. "They don't care much for your sort."

The waiter put the bill on the table and left. Most of the customers were watching now with considerable amusement. Several laughed out loud. Alvin had lost some of his appetite. The dwarf, however, ate his chicken fricassee as if he were alone in his own kitchen and hadn't a care in the world. Soon, after tapping sharply once more on the window glass and displaying their placards, the temperance women moved on. A hearty round of applause from the restaurant patrons cheered their departure. Once they were gone, the farm boy drank his cup of coffee and ate half the plate of lamb and sweet potatoes without any idea at all why he had been given the bad eye.

Main Street was paved with bricks and its buildings were tall and dignified. Telephone wires crossed above motor traffic along six blocks of prominent enterprise. A loaded trolley ran up the center of the street, bell clanging at each intersection. People shouted and waved and dodged automobiles to reach F.W. Woolworth's five-and-dime or Piggly Wiggly and the postal telegraph office at Fifth Street. Businessmen in wing collars came and went from the First National Bank as sewer diggers labored to repair a broken water main next to a Rexall drugstore. The farm boy and the dwarf strolled in and out of the late-morning crowd from block to block, admiring show window displays under striped awnings, buying pears from a vendor on Sixth Street and a hot pretzel at a stand on Seventh, stopping briefly in front of a German bakery to enjoy the aroma of hot cinnamon buns, then watching a pack of scrawny dogs struggle over spoiled pork chops in the narrow alley between Clarke & Son's hardware and the butcher shop. Halfway up Main, the dwarf ducked into Oglethorpe's Boots while Alvin stared at a group of pretty secretaries and lady typewriters on midday lark by the wide cement steps of Schaick, Pilsner & Allyson - Attorneys at Law. The farm boy walked up the block to the pool hall next door to McKinney's barbershop and found it jammed with young men in shirtsleeves and suspenders, the odor of cigarette smoke and hair tonic and liquor stiff as a saloon. Earlier, at the Ford garage, Alvin had seen two boys with flasks in their hip pockets, and noticed a box of quart bottles in the passenger seat of a Dodge coupé parked out front of Vickers Apothecary next to the Family Welfare Association at Fifth and Main. He presumed that Icaria was ankle-deep in liquor like any other town. Who had stopped chasing booze when the saloons closed? Most fellows his age thought it was sporting to drink and take joyrides around the county and get a girl going with a bottle of hootch in the dark. He knew a youth named Henry Sullivan from Arcola not sixteen years old who drove a liquor truck for George Remus until a gang of hijackers stiff-armed him one night behind a Diamond gas station in Indiana and broke his jaw. Alvin decided he was allergic to booze himself because of how sick he got after hardly a swallow, worse yet since the consumption; but his cousins of both sexes were drunk on canned heat more than once behind the dance hall in downtown Farrington and none of the adults seemed to care much at all, themselves occupied day and night hiding hootch in the rubber collars of wagon horses or filling empty milk bottles with raw corn whiskey. Not more than a dozen arrests for liquor traffic had been made in Farrington since Christmas, yet each Sunday morning Reverend Whitehead of the United Methodist church and Dr. E.G. Fortune of the Episcopalians reminded their flocks how proud the Lord was of them for staying dry.

At the corner of Main and Seventh, Rascal stopped in front of a shoeshine shop to admire a pair of Gold Bond oxfords on the work counter. A hand-painted lithograph advertising the circus extravaganza was posted in the window. The farm boy studied a jewelry store across the street and thought about investigating a wristwatch; he had seen a gold-filled Illinois watch back at Stantonsburg for forty dollars that he fancied quite a lot.

"Why, look," the dwarf remarked. "There's the Belvedere Hotel."

He directed Alvin's attention to an elegant four-story brick building across the street in the next block where men in business suits crowded atop the cement steps to the front door and a pack of shiny automobiles were clustered out front. Rascal stepped back off the sidewalk to let a woman pushing a baby stroller get by. "Let's go scout the rooms. Perhaps we can improve our situation."

Watching a flock of pigeons silhouetted on the cloudy sky across the hotel's rooftop, Alvin shook his head. "Chester ain't checked in yet. He won't get here till tomorrow and he didn't say nothing about us dropping up to see him, neither. He told me that Spud fellow'd let us know when he got into town."

A column of black Ford sedans and a loaded melon truck and a blue delivery van roared by, trailing a cloud of smelly black exhaust. People along the sidewalk were staring at the dwarf. So, too, was a crowd across the street under the awning of Brown's clothing store. Just behind him were a couple of osteopath patients waiting to see Dr. Kessler, their faces pressed to the plate-glass. When the farm boy gave them his own evil eye, they turned away.

"Well, I still want to go have a look."

Alvin shrugged, preferring to remain out of doors in the sunlight. He was sick of hiding in the shadows. "Suit yourself, but I'm staying right here. Parade's coming any minute now."

"We wouldn't miss a trick."

"I ain't a-going with you."

"Well, so long, then."

The dwarf gave a farewell salute, and shot off the curb behind a loaded autobus.

"Hey!"

Alvin watched him dodge through traffic and disappear into a sidewalk crowd in front of the Lotus Café. Uptown, the trolley bell clanged. A new yellow Oldsmobile rolled by with two men balanced on the running boards smoking cigars. One of them held up a Republican placard. The driver honked the horn as he passed the I.O.O.F. building.

Alvin walked up the block to the Orient Theater on the corner of Eighth and Main where a freckled young newspaper boy in a flat cap and brown trousers leaned against the lamppost, a scrawny beagle at his feet. People stepped around him as they hurried past. A stack of unsold copies of the *Icarian Mercury-Gazette* sat on the dirty cement beside the curb. The boy was counting pennies into his front trouser pocket. Feeling a chill, Alvin walked under the marquee to get out of the draft. Framed-in glass next to the polished double doors held the theater program. Tonight, the Orient featured a beauty contest, a minstrel show, two Vitaphone melodramas, and a Western thriller. Beside the program in the glass case, a posted handbill promised wholesome recreation under the new ownership of the refurbished theater. Next week a series of lectures on current events would be sponsored by the Family Relief Society — Admission 10¢.

"Are you in the circus, mister?"

Alvin turned around and saw the newspaper boy standing next to the empty ticket booth, his beagle behind him. The boy's brown trousers were dusty and his old roundtoed shoes covered with mud.

For the third time since breakfast, Alvin told his new lie, "Sure I am."

The boy's face brightened. "Gee, that must be swell. Is that one of your clowns?" He pointed across the street to Rascal walking just then under a giant pair of spectacles that advertised an oculist near the Belvedere Hotel.

" 'Course it is."

"Why, I bet he's awful funny, ain't he?"

"So long as he ain't mooning up that ol' beer jug of his."

"Huh?"

"You never mind him," Alvin instructed the boy. "He woke with a grouch on today and ain't talking sense to no one. Say, how come you ain't in school? Waiting on the parade?"

The newspaper boy shook his head. "Naw, I got fleas from ol' Spike here, so Miss Othmar sent me home. My pop says I got to sell all my papers or I can't go to the circus tonight. We're busted, I guess."

Alvin watched the dwarf enter the Belvedere Hotel. A cold gust riffled the stack of newspapers at the curb. The boy bent down to scratch his dog's nose.

"Can't you dig up some dough nowhere?" Alvin asked him. "Why, I met a swell girl this morning at a flophouse where we hired a room that might let you do a basket of laundry for her. That'd be worth something, I'd bet."

The boy screwed up his face like he'd just swallowed a bottle of castor oil, then spat on the sidewalk. "Nothing doing! I ain't washin' for no dame. Momma whipped me last week 'cause Spike got mud on her clean sheets and made me scrub 'em all white again. No thanks!"

"Well, how come your daddy won't kick in a nickel or two? Is he a skinflint?"

The boy gave a shrug. "Pop's a crapshootin' fool and he got the craze again. Momma's fed up, but she don't want to be a joykiller, neither, so she don't say much." His expression changed to an eager grin. "Jeepers, it must be swell to ride all over in a circus wagon. You ain't got a sideshow for a kid whose dog eats tacks and razor blades, do you?"

"Naw, we ain't got nothing like that."

The newspaper boy lowered his head and kicked at the dirty pavement. "Aw, gee whiz, me and Spike never get a break."

"Tacks and razor blades?"

The newspaper boy nodded. "Pins, too!"

"Kid, you're almost as big a fibber as someone else I know."

The boy's face reddened. "If you got any tacks or pins on you, we can prove it." He rubbed his dog's neck. "And how!"

Alvin laughed out loud, and then coughed till his throat hurt.

The newspaper boy scowled and knelt down beside the scrawny old beagle and hugged him tightly. Alvin noticed a commotion across the street. A tall clown in greasepaint and blue polka dots encircled by shouting children was distributing heralds along the sidewalk by the Belvedere. Straightaway, Alvin heard the faint song of a steam calliope in the distance.

He looked back at the scruffy newspaper boy. "I guess a fresh kid like you'll probably never amount to nothing, huh?"

"Aw, phooey on you, too."

The farm boy took a fistful of dimes from his trouser pocket. "Here, kid." He put them into the boy's hand. "Go to the circus tonight. Take your folks with you. Have a swell time."

The newspaper boy shot to his feet. "Gee, mister! No kidding?"

"You said it." Alvin swatted the boy's cap. "See you later, kid."

Then he rushed across the street to join the crowd at the Belvedere Hotel. People were standing three or four deep now at the sidewalk and Alvin had to shove his way up the cement steps to the entrance. Next door, men and women leaned out from the upper floor windows of a radio and appliance store, shouting and waving to people on the street.

The lobby of the Belvedere was carpeted in Oriental rugs and rich with palms, stuffed easy chairs, gilded pier mirrors, and china cuspidors. A group of businessmen in black waistline coats stood at the registration desk, chatting with the clerk. Cigar smoke and conversation bloomed from the adjacent dining saloon. A pianist played "Shaking the Blues Away."

Alvin crossed the narrow lobby in search of the dwarf. The elevator opened and a young bellboy wearing a crimson monkeyjacket came out with a pair of Louis Vuitton bags. Alvin removed his cap and sneaked around a potted palm into the noisy dining saloon where thirty or forty well-dressed men and women sat enjoying lunch. He looked carefully table by table and past the end of the mahogany bar to where the downstairs toilets were located, but didn't see the dwarf anywhere, so he went back across the lobby to the registration desk and waited to speak to the clerk. When the gentlemen in waistcoats walked off, the clerk nodded for Alvin to step up to the desk.

"May I help you, son?"

"I'm looking for a friend of mine that come in here a few minutes ago, and I was wondering if you seen him at all, a little fellow with suspenders and blue trousers?"

"Is he a guest here?"

"No, sir. He ain't. We already got us a room across town." Briefly, the farm boy considered lending Chester's name to the discussion, but thought better of it.

After the clerk scribbled a series of names and numbers into the ledger, he said, "Describe your friend for me again, please."

"Well, like I said, he's about this high, with sort of — "

The clerk interrupted. "Is your friend with the circus?"

Alvin nodded. "Yes, sir."

Frowning, the clerk shut the ledger. "In that case, I can assure you he's not here. Our policy no longer permits circus people of any sort at this hotel. I suggest you look elsewhere. Good day."

The clerk walked off with the ledger.

Humiliated once again, Alvin slunk out of the Belvedere. He knew he'd made a fool of himself, but didn't care this time. He was sweaty and felt his fever rising. He coughed hard and wiped his mouth with his shirtsleeve. Atop the busy steps, he jostled for a decent view of upper Main Street. More painted clowns mingled along the downtown sidewalks, passing out handbills and distributing free admission tickets to pretty girls and small children. Just across the street, Alvin saw a rangy emerald clown with hair like a cotton candy rainbow seated at the curb by the Orient Theater, his elastic arms wrapped tightly about the newspaper boy and the scraggy beagle. Music from the circus band echoed on the wind. Uptown, the grand parade had begun.

The farm boy climbed up onto the stone balustrade and balanced against the building façade high above the crowded sidewalk. He held his breath when he saw the great Indian elephants lumbering down the street under black walnut trees three blocks away at Potter and Main. Astride each was a royal Nubian princess in peacock-blue silk and glittering sapphires. Marching ahead of the majestic pachyderms, flutists in green tricorn hats and scarlet plumes led a team of sixteen brown ponies from Lilliput drawing a gilded carriage wild with lavender roses and firebreathing dwarves. The crowd on Main roared with delight as the circus band played *"Entry of the Gladiators."* Policemen cleared the street ahead. A big bass drum boomed a martial rhythm as imperial trumpets heralded the arrival of gold-turbanned equestrians performing tumbling tricks atop prancing white stallions, while a curious menagerie of strange caged beasts and terrible human phenomena in painted wagons were tugged along by plodding mule teams and silver-collared draft-horses. From his stone perch, the farm boy witnessed a euphonious parade of the fabulous and the bizarre, an alchemistic history of the known world. No mere child's torpid dream of Bengal tigers and gypsy sword swallowers: here, Caesar's grand war chariot salvaged from those dusty storehouses of Leptis Magna rolled again behind proud Arabian steeds under the hand of a dour Russian Cossack as crimson pantalooned dwarves from Cairo and Bombay flung knives and spun cartwheels between great dancing bears, and a Sultan's rosy harem escorted a camel caravan of Iberian jugglers and giraffe-necked giants and Chinese magicians and tattooed snake charmers. Next came Gloucester's sea serpent swimming in a glass turquoise tank wagon with three lovely mermaids rescued from a fisherman's net off Martinique, then Wellington's triumphant Waterloo marching band in red dresscoat and gold braid with a rousing chorus of "Rule Britannia," and thirteen antiquarian bandwagons carved and gilded by druidic gnomes recounting in painted mythological tableaux wondrous stories of golden geese and fairy kings, enchanted nightingales and ancient jinnis, sleeping princesses and shipwrecked sailors. Block after windy block, midget clowns and fat clowns and giant clowns juggled fiery torches and somersaulted off shoulder tops and strode upon stilts and dove through flaming hoops and tossed bags of warm peanuts and fresh Crackerjack to howling children until every zebra, ostrich, llama, buffalo and gazelle had passed in revue, and the Wild West bareback riders and rope dancers and spangled Prussian acrobats had exhibited feats of daring and wonder, and the great thundering steam calliope, *Seraphonium*, that deafening shriek of melodious pipe whistles, had summoned the brave and the curious to follow the wagon parade of Emmett J. Laswell's Traveling Circus Giganticus back to Icaria's showgrounds, and not one solitary child had been left behind on Main Street.

The dining room was lit with oil lamps for supper. Nine dishes were set at the table and the portières drawn to keep out the hall draft. By six o'clock, all the boarders were seated and grace was spoken by Virgil Platt, a gaunt narrow man with gray whiskers on a weary face whose Bible reading Alvin had heard through the wall that morning. A hint of tears welled in the fellow's eyes when he thanked the Lord for such daily blessings as the living and penitent require. Seated across from Alvin were the oddest pair of middle-aged twins in Lord Fauntleroy dress: Eugene and Samuel Szopinski. Both wore pince-nez over powdered cheeks and smelled of fresh lilac water and talcum. Next to them was matronly Eva Chase from Vicksburg, dressed in pine-green cashmere and tortoise-shell eyeglasses. Beside the dwarf were two older fellows with slicked-back hair, black dinner jackets and smart linen collars: Percy Webster and Russell James. To Alvin's left on the parlor end opposite from Virgil Platt was silverhaired Mrs. Celia Burritt, overly elegant in a grenadine dress and satin mantel. Ox-tail soup and haricot mutton and sweet rice croquettes were on the table with hot coffee and a kettle of peppermint tea when Alvin sat down. He bowed his head with everyone else during grace, then listened to introductions by Mrs. Burritt, helped pass the serving plates around the table, and attended to a conversation begun by Eva Chase and the dwarf while Alvin was still upstairs napping after the parade. It was the strangest story he had ever heard.

"Now, those days," said Eva Chase in a reedy drawl, "my dear Carl had a marvelous gift for limerick which kept all the troupe in stitches when it rained and there was no show. He was the handsomest man I ever knew, yet so devoted to theater that only the feebleminded thought him capable of performing his tragic soliloquies in a fusty Barnum exhibit. And, oh, those dreadful drafty halls Mr. Forepaugh thought to hire for Carl's famous Gilbert & Sullivan stunts, quite unimaginable! I remember once in Nanty-Glo, the entire troupe went out after midnight and left free tickets on stoops all over town for the coal miners. Carl had such a fervid audience the next evening, he sent a telegraph to Jimmy Armstrong and another to the Manhattan Opera House. I was so hopeful for him back then."

Still drowsy from his nap, Alvin watched Virgil Platt scoop a warm helping of mutton and croquettes onto his plate and pass the silver platter to the Szopinski twins. Percy Webster slurped the ox-tail soup. Russell James examined his water glass for spots.

Mrs. Burritt remarked, "Love is deception's most potent elixir, darling. You see, few men truly intend anything remarkable in life. Distinction is much more the result of circumstance and good fortune than we've all been led to believe. Why, if Adam hadn't forgotten his breakfast that day, I'm quite certain none of us would've drawn our first wicked breath in the world."

"That's silly," said Eugene Szopinski.

"Entirely absurd," his brother Samuel added, cutting into the mutton.

Careful not to burn his fingers, Alvin took the serving plate of sweet rice croquettes while the dwarf poured himself a steaming cup of peppermint tea. He was starving to eat again, which meant he was sicker than ever.

Unbowed by Mrs. Burritt's needling observations, Eva Chase continued, "When I was still a girl of sixteen, Carl traveled down from Baltimore to see my performance of 'Evangeline' in a nickel tent show and he brought purple lilacs and champagne and offered to marry me once the show left Pearl River. He paid two dollars for a photographer to record my image on glass, and purchased a lovely old brass frame and a scented teakwood box to store it in. Later we had our fortunes told by a blind swamp gypsy who took Carl's hand by candlelight and traced upon it with a yellow fingernail a path of starry dreams and love priceless and pure."

"No such thing," Percy Webster interrupted. He set down his soup-spoon. "Dreams, that is. Why, I've been in love so often, quite naturally I know it like sunshine. But dreams are mere rumors, untrustworthy ones at that, scandalous and wretched insinuations that serenade our bed chambers with such fevered promises as only children and canaries ever endure."

"Eternal love is a figure of speech," said Mrs. Burritt. "If I'd been born mute, perhaps my girlhood room on Summer Avenue would yet host private teas and slumber parties for the fragile of heart."

"Oh, I just adore slumber parties," the dwarf interjected, stirring sugar into his tea. Alvin smothered a rising cough with his cotton napkin, far too intimidated to utter a word. He had never been around folks like these before and didn't want them to think he was a dumbbell.

Russell James said, "Well, of course, Percy is far too reckless a fellow to admit a fault, but nobody who has actually dismembered on Phineas Barnum's own stage a creature as delightful as May Wallace ought to expect his sleep to be blissful and unadorned."

The farm boy quit chewing.

"Such a tragedy," lamented Eugene Szopinski, as he cut apart the sweet rice croquette with his fork.

"Utterly grievous," Samuel Szopinski agreed, raising a stained napkin to his lips.

Virgil Platt ate supper vigorously with eyes locked firmly on his dinner plate.

After enjoying a sip of hot coffee, Eva Chase began again. "Once long ago, I traveled around the world with Father's old steamer trunk and my mother's lavender parasol and felt happy as a lark. In a hundred foreign cities from Rangoon to Constantinople, my sweet Carl was hailed as the greatest performer on earth. He danced in silver shoes with shiny green buckles and plucked emeralds and rubies out of thin air and sang like a nightingale, and one impossibly marvelous evening at the Maryinski Theater, he received a white rose bouquet and a private note of admiration from Empress Alexandra herself. When we left Paris to sail again for America, my desperate heart became so haunted by joy and fear, I counted every star fleeing heaven for the nightblack sea and scribbled secret wishes onto tiny scraps of paper and scattered each upon the cold waves. No girl ever born loved as I did then. By August, we'd traveled up the Mississippi to Memphis where Carl performed sixty-two lantern shows aboard a grand old Dixie paddle steamer that floated like a fancy wedding cake on the summer twilight river. There I was struck down by fever, pitifully bedridden two floors above a garden café of sweet blossoming honeysuckle and Spanish guitars. For half a month, I suffered that awful delirium alone lying prostrate beneath a frayed scrapquilt of calico rose petals, nibbling on overripe tangerines until juice stained my gown. Each night, flamenco melodies and mad fluttering moths tortured my dreams, those few that I recall because so wicked a fever inebriates the brain with rustling murmurs of unspoken desire, and once engaged these cruel phantasms fly about like ghosts. I remember rising from bed to stare into a beveled mirror on the chamber suite where I saw my reflection dressed smartly in diamonds and lace for a honeymoon trip somewhere, a wayward angel in waiting. Desolate with need, I called out for my precious Carl, but by then, you see, a vagabond circus had come down from Cairo toting flying-act rigging and tightwire, and he'd gone whispering across the water by moonlight."

"He'd met the pretty aerial ballerina," observed Eugene Szopinski, stabbing at another forkful of mutton.

"Miss Alice Vandermeer," Samuel Szopinski added, smiling wanly as he sipped his tea.

Mrs. Burritt put her rice plate aside and poured herself a cup of coffee. Somewhat theatrically, she remarked, "Who among us is not born to tragedy and sorrow? Love withers and our hearts dry up. Milk-white skin shrivels and goes gray. Disappointment hounds our every step. Who wakes each morning unaware of this?"

Quietly, the dwarf reached for the serving bowl of ox-tail soup, while Alvin listened to Virgil Platt chew his food, a most unpleasant noise like boot heels in mud.

Russell James said, "My beautiful daughter Lulu quit Ringling Brothers to go traipsing about with a vacuum cleaner salesman after her marriage to Mr. Zû had rotted away. She became so disagreeable I was forced to throw her wormy old chifforobe into the street and nail the back door shut."

Percy Webster lowered his fork. "Well, honey, you wrote her such nasty letters, what on earth did you expect?"

"Aggravation," said Eugene Szopinski.

"Impertinence," his brother Samuel suggested.

Eva Chase tasted a rice croquette, then dabbed her rosy lips delicately with a cloth napkin. She spoke in a voice sweet as ether: "Once when I was a girl, I slept for a whole year believing I'd been locked away in Mother's musty old cedar wedding chest, blessedly hidden from a grown woman's delicate powders and rouge and a gentleman's ardent correspondence. Instead, I'd drowned in leagues of sorrow more common than autumn rain, that awful solitude, and true hope no more than pale dewdrops. Too often I'd dreamed of a lovely white dove in a spangled cape dancing on the aerial rigging high in the big tent above a thousand delirious upturned faces, my dear Carl's adoring eyes among them. Then, one day, Mother hired a detective to poke about muddy carnival lots, eavesdropping at tent flaps for clues. He relayed news a month later from Louisville of a terrible accident at the matinee tightwire performance, a perfect swan dive to the sawdust, a mangled beauty. I rode the train all night guided by vaporish tea leaves and prayer. Arriving by dawn at a wet tent-littered fairgrounds, I worried that my memory of our journey around the world together was only a pierglass hallucination, a rhymeless delusion, for which a renowned artist such as he had no natural use. Hugo the Strong-Man sent me to a painted wagon by the Big Top where a plum-colored pygmy named Missus Bluebell guarded the door. Hearing my story, she shed a tear for both of us, then showed me inside. My belovéd Carl lay shrunken in the smoky shadows beside a burning oil lamp on a cot of embroidered pillows, dressed for theater footlights in green silk sashes and Chinese slippers, a chewed sprig of deadly nightshade and an ivory fan from Singapore on his red satin chest. A note in India ink waited for me atop his costume portmanteau, scribbled perhaps when I was still aboard the train. He wrote that love was ruthless, discordant, unworthy of our defenseless hearts. Be quick now and flee it. Forget its deceitful embrace. I buried him on a grassy hilltop in Vicksburg facing the summer Ferris wheels and the happy crowds."

A parlor clock chimed the half-hour as Alvin poured himself a cup of hot coffee to soothe his throat. Finished with his croquettes, the dwarf gingerly sipped peppermint tea. The spicy aroma of warm raisin pie under a checkered cloth on the walnut sideboard filled the narrow dining room.

Eugene Szopinski said, "We fell from the highwire at Buffalo when we were thirteen years old."

"Too young to appreciate the distance to earth," his brother Samuel explained as he cut up his last bite of mutton. "Now we're both scarred for life."

"Indeed," Russell James said, "one evening in my own youth, a passing mesmerist persuaded me that my heart had become a cold desiccated husk decaying within my chest, utterly devoid of normal human inclinations. Thus entranced, I toured for years with Sells-Floto as the Fossilized Man until Lulu's mother purchased me from the sideshow and brought me home with her."

"You see, my dear, that far perch eludes us all now and then," said Percy Webster, folding a napkin beside his supper plate, "yet blindfolded we proceed across heaven's great expanse determined to prove ourselves worthy of this brief moment."

Mrs. Burritt added, "I've always been grateful for those blessings that seem to come to us from far away."

Carefully, Virgil Platt put down his cup of coffee onto a polished china saucer. He rose from his chair at the head of the supper table and turned to Eva Chase. He said: "Only the empty-hearted lament those days of carnival and renown once they're gone. A man's gift maketh room for him, and bringeth him before great men. This, I believe, is the elation for which he was born."

The farm boy and the dwarf stalked through the damp woods four blocks from the rotten stink of old stockyards west of town. Lights burned yellow in the upstairs of houses behind them. A cold wind rustled early autumn leaves and Alvin felt a rising chill in the dark. He heard the lilting gaiety of a carousel somewhere up ahead as he followed the scurrying dwarf along a rutted path, sidestepping ripe clumps of poison ivy and fending off errant branches as he went. Lights from the circus glowed like will o' the wisps across the hidden wood. Up a short hill they went crouching Indian-fashion through patches of elderberry and silky dogwood. Alvin stopped to catch his breath at the top as the carnival wind gusted. The dwarf's chirping voice was senseless and joyful as he trampled tall stalks of grass toward the distant circus tents. Crowds of people from town swarmed the bright showgrounds entrance. Alvin, too, ran as best he could toward the sparkling galleries of merriment.

A hundred yards away he smelled hot roasted peanuts and fried onions on the evening wind. The greeter's call drew him closer still. Colorful flags and banners rippled and flapped. Pipe music shrieked. Two pairs of painted clowns clasping colored balloons danced a silly jig beside the ticket taker whose booming voice carried across the dark.

"STEP RIGHT UP! STEP RIGHT UP! WONDER OF WONDERS! MIRACLES, MYSTERY AND MAGIC!"

Burning ash from the fellow's cigar scattered on the wind as Alvin purchased tickets for himself and the dwarf and joined a line of people from town at the entry gate. He watched one of the green balloons escape a clown's idiot grasp in a gust of wind and rise drunkenly into the cold black sky. A plaintive cry rang out from a pack of children by the steaming popcorn stand as another clown on stilts attempted to catch the fugitive balloon, but already it had wafted up too far and soon vanished beyond the fancy circus lights and the fluttering banners high away into gray evening clouds. Wherever Alvin looked, people jammed exhibits and canvas tents. Pinwheels and Roman candles fizzed and sparkled in the night sky. A troupe of clowns on unicycles wheeled toward the Big Top. Jugglers in jester hats and Nubian sword swallowers performed feats of grand dexterity near the chariot cages and gilded Museum wagons. Bombastic sideshow talkers shouted above the crowds. Alvin stopped briefly to buy a fluffy stick of pink cotton candy next to a dart-throwing booth, then followed the dwarf past the Topsy-Turvy House toward the carousel where giggling children mounted high on regal steeds went round and round to a Strauss waltz while smiling mothers and fathers stood by in the sawdust admiring the painted wooden horses and the gilded poles under the electric canopy.

Wiping his sticky mouth on a shirtsleeve, Alvin watched a top-hat-ted midget in a painted sandwich board advertising a dog and pony show march past the carousel, yelling: "COME ONE! COME ALL! COME ONE! COME ALL!"

More skyrockets exploded over the tent circus.

Alvin felt a tug on his shirt.

"Look," the dwarf said, directing the farm boy's attention between tent exhibits to a collection of circus midgets fixed out in medieval silks: seven noblemen and a charming lady-in-waiting. They appeared to be gathering for a performance of some sort. One of them carried a lute and another held juggling pins.

"What of it?" He'd witnessed plenty of freaks acting up already. They made him jittery.

"My goodness," Rascal sighed. He crossed his legs oddly and bit his lip.

"Let's go see something," Alvin said, feeling impatient. He didn't know how long he had until fever wore him out or another coughing fit struck and he wanted to have some fun for once.

"You go along, if you like," the dwarf said, his roaming eyes stilled by the tiny maiden. "I believe I'll stay here awhile."

"Maybe we ought to have a look in that funhouse back there," Alvin suggested, reluctant to go off alone. What if he had a coughing fit like he did at that carnival in Galesburg last summer?

"Isn't she a knockout?" the dwarf remarked, as the darling midget performed a short melody on the penny flute while executing a dainty pirouette for her audience.

"Yeah, sure," Alvin replied, beginning to feel febrile and wobbly again. He watched one of the midgets breathe fire through a golden ring and another strummed the lute. "But what do you say we go have ourselves a good time? Why, I'll bet there's something doing in one of them big tents. Let's go have a look-see."

"No, thank you," the dwarf demurred, sounding moony now. "It's plenty wonderful right here." He sucked in his breath and folded his fingers together in a squirmy knot.

"Well, I ain't coming back for you," Alvin groused. "I'll be too busy hunting up some real fun."

A dreamy smile on his lips, the dwarf replied, "I'll look you up later on."

Disgusted, Alvin went off on his own, hoping to find the girl from Spud Farrell's boardinghouse. Without the dwarf to keep him company, nobody paid him any notice at all as he walked alone under the gusting banners and electric lights. The farm boy jostled and shoved with circus-goers at tent openings and game booths, and grew dizzy admiring the mechanical Whirly-Gig and the bright electric Ferris Wheel. He ate a steaming hotdog and a bag of popcorn while watching Tessie the Tassel Twirler perform for a noisy crowd of men in a 10¢ tent behind the marionette show *("She wiggles to the east, she wiggles to the west, she wiggles in the middle where the wiggling is best!")*. In the Topsy-Turvy House, he chased a gang of kids tossing half-chewed Crackerjack at each other through the dizzying Rolling Barrel and the Mad Tea Party in candlelit Upside-Down Room and out the slippery Shoe-Chute where Alvin tripped on the Crazy Stairs and skinned his knee. Outdoors again, more children ran past, screeching like wild animals. Fireworks boomed overhead. A cold wind blew across the sky, chasing the farm boy deeper yet into a glimmering sawdust land.

The citizens of Icaria swarmed the high-grass circus, clustering at Laswell's mysterious tent shows and cage wagons, awed by his Chinese magicians and Egyptian mummies and ferocious Bengal tigers, his wild black cannibals nine feet tall. A thousand tales of wonder in a single evening of blue fire and rolla bolla. For a nickel a head, the curious pack Charon's Tent of Sorcery to see a pale spook in a silken cloak grace Cleopatra's throne whose fragrant apparition roils from clouds of purple smoke by the bleak light of the sideshow conjurer's font. No sad angelfaced harlequin in pearls, but a proud Ptolemy rid at last of Antony and the asp. Tent flaps rustle as she strums a golden lyre: white doves fly forth: flower petals fall. Women faint and a few men yell "Cheat!" and "Humbug!" and half a dozen red-hot cigar butts are hurled across the amber haze of burning candle wax. A trio of fresh towheads who'd wriggled under the tattered canvas walls for a peek, crawl back out of the dusty shadows and race down the windy night to the elevated platforms under the square tent of Laswell's torch-lit Hall of Freaks where the gathered crowd is restless but timid.

"That's right, folks! Come in a little closer! She won't hurt you!"

At a rap of the sideshow talker's cane upon the podium, Sally Victoria, the Two-Headed Girl, dressed in a lavender and silver lamé tea gown, steps out from behind a woven brown curtain and begins to sing in harmonious duet a waltz lullaby called "Dreamy Moon." Her darling faces are dolled up with show-lashes and ruby-red lipstick and a fancy French hairdo. Harvey Allison from the hardware store on North Main falls in love by the second stanza and immediately begins composing a love sonnet to sweet Sally Victoria. When the song ends, the rural crowd hurries off to the growling Dog-Woman from Burma who swallows full-grown rats with shotglasses of Kentucky bourbon ("In her own land she is considered a great beauty, but she's a long way from home!"), and on to the next row of platforms where a mated pair of steely-clawed Stymphalian birds from the marshes of Arcadia squawk and hiss at photographs of President Hoover, and the recently unearthed Peking Man demonstrates his astonishing knowledge of algebraic equations, and the Human Pin Cushion from Iranistan receives one hundred forty-two needle punctures from audience volunteers while reciting "Ode on a Grecian Urn."

Then the bronze torches dim and the anxious crowd is invited to the platform draped in Oriental carpets at the back of Laswell's Hall of Freaks where a silken gold shroud is withdrawn from a glass aquarium revealing the Turtle Boy paddling in foamy brine and pink coral with the strange man-sized Bishop Fish: a queer pair, indeed.

A dark-bearded lecturer in black top-hat and tails steps out from backstage to address his audience: "Ladies and Gentlemen, listen to a tale of woe from distant maritimes, a fable for the ages. Here in this crystal tank a remnant of moral tragedy resides, for in truth these two sad creatures were once as human as you or I. Many years ago by the shores of an ancient sea dwelt a humble tinker of little means. Such was his station in life that even beggars took pity on him and shared what meager portions of bread and fish they had, knowing without such mercy the poor tinker would surely starve. By that same barren shore was a small chapel whose devout cleric ministered to all who sought comfort and delivery from the harshness of the world. He knew the tinker well and regarded him plainly as another child of God who had lost his way. Each morning the cleric watched the lowly tinker pass along the shore with his sack and his old nets. Each evening he watched the tinker return, his scant accumulations in tow. Perhaps he envied the tinker's perseverance. Perhaps he despised the tinker's disregard for pious fellowship. Who can say? From a nearby village the cleric had taken in a wayward youth to look after the chapel grounds and garden. Now, this youth, too, watched the tinker come and go and had little patience for hardship, believing that life was a blind drawing of lots and fortune simply a matter of will. One evening after vespers, the youth approached the cleric with a remarkable story. The meandering tinker, he claimed, had cast his ragged net upon the waters that morning and retrieved a treasure of uncommon degree. He had hidden it somewhere under the floor of his straw hovel, intending to tell no one, nor share even an ounce of his newfound prosperity. The cleric agreed that it was indeed characteristic of the selfish tinker to obscure so great a discovery and reminded the youth that all men are born stewards of this earth and that what belonged to one, belonged to all equally and without distinction. Therefore, the cleric determined that the tinker's vanity was in fact a sin whose absolution required the forsaking of his prize. Furthermore, he and the youth would go to the tinker that very night and remind him of this obligation. Now the cold sea was fitful and blustery as the cleric and the youth went along that ancient shore with lanterns to light their way in the dark. Few thieves from iniquitous Calcutta ever conspired so unmercifully as this cleric and the callous youth to plunder such a guileless mark. In his drafty hovel the tinker slept before a dull kindling fire, while outside the cleric searched the sky for providential indications and saw instead a great black tempest rising off the sea. The youth stole into the straw hovel and shook the tinker awake and demanded he reveal the whereabouts of his treasure. The tinker replied that he no longer possessed it, that a dream he'd had persuaded him to cast it back into the sea, and he showed the youth an empty hole in the floor where the treasure had been hidden. Now the cleric, too, entered the bleak hovel and accused the tinker of deception and warned that blind avarice provoked a particularly harsh wrath from heaven. The poor tinker acknowledged that the greed of men was, indeed, insatiable, threatening of immorality and ruin. Better, he had decided, to be rid of wealth than remain its fearful servant. Furious, the youth stepped forward and bludgeoned the hapless tinker and dragged him from his sad hovel out into the storm and threw him to the raging sea. Then the youth returned to the straw hovel and began digging in the floor while the cleric sought guidance from heaven and the great dark tempest surged ashore with sea waves mighty and deep."

The top-hatted lecturer pauses to gaze briefly at the two curious creatures paddling lazily in the shallow coral water of the glass aquarium. A woman at the back of the tent who had fainted rises again to take her seat. The surrounding audience remains hushed by the lecturer's tale.

"At daybreak, a merchant passing along the barren shore caught sight of a fisherman's net half-buried in wet sand and straw. As he drew closer, the merchant spied a figure wriggling in the old net, a slimy fin, a long scaly cloak, a pair of drooping eyes shrouded in kelp: our pious Bishop Fish. Working to liberate this creature, the industrious merchant discovered another cowering beneath, this sad Turtle Boy, limpid and weak, limbless, wallowing in fear. Soon enough the merchant freed both from their entanglement in the old net, then seeing how curious was their appearance, how grotesque and godforsaken, he loaded both together atop his donkey cart and brought them along with him on his travels throughout the world. When he died, a good-hearted gypsy took possession of both creatures, and after many exhibitions in many carnivals in many lands, we present them here tonight. Legend has it that every creature on earth possesses its twin in the sea, a doppelgänger of the soul, a perfect likeness of its truest nature. Who knows? What is certain, however, is that the tinker and the cleric and the youth were never again seen on that distant shore, and if miracles are, indeed, indications of divine will, let no one leave this tent tonight unmoved."

The lecturer departs the stage as a pair of platform torches flare brightly, further illuminating the two strange creatures who paddle sluggishly about the aquarium, occasionally grazing each other, seemingly indifferent to the slackjawed audience. The pale Turtle Boy flops onto a flat stone perch and belches loudly enough to be heard at the back row. That trio of towheads who lie under the tent walls giggle while the plump Bishop Fish folds his fins together on a miry lap as if in prayer and

shuts his eyes. The surrounding coral glistens in the flickering orange light. Eventu-
ally the platform torches dim once more and this tent crowd is shown to the rear exit
in favor of another curious audience waiting out front. The show goes on.

Late in the evening, Alvin wandered through the Palace of Mirrors whose drafty corridors shimmered a pale winter blue and mocked his sorry reflection. The ceiling was hidden in black drapes that billowed like the wingéd shadows of great birds. Mechanical voices tittered laughter in the dark. Ticket stubs and dead cigarette butts littered the floor. A stink of bathtub gin and witch hazel and burning tobacco fouled the sparkling corridors. Alvin Pendergast strolled a crooked path and went nowhere while odd voices chattered here and there and the draft grew colder. In one mirror he resembled a pale blimp, in another a ridiculous string bean. He was elongated and squashed, his nose flattened, his smile wide as a pie, his eyes like saucers, his hands and feet swollen as if by a summer bee sting. His mouth looked sloppy and mean, his arms slithered like rubber snakes. Shadows of passersby darted from the corner of his eye. Soon he felt dizzy and stopped walking. Fever chilled his skin. He sat down and stared at a trio of reflections across the filthy corridor, each joyless and shriveled, sour with sweat. His head throbbed and his legs were numb and he felt faint. Alvin had expected to die in the sanitarium. He had seen blood in his sputum and imagined thousands of rancid tubercles growing like weeds beneath his ribs. For days on end he lay hushed in bed listening to the ashen wheezing of his own invalid lungs in hopeful anticipation of swan-winged angels descending to the gloom-gray ward. Doctors came and went, jotting notations on daily charts while muttering to themselves in Latin. Nurses spoke most cheerfully to the doomed. No more fishing under slants of drowsy sunlight. Alvin napped in septic clouds of waste and rude medications. Gurneys wheeled in and out. Homesickness for the farm persisted through numerous belladonna plasters and daily treatments of cod liver oil. A dozen series of X-ray photographs failed to reveal his despair. *These sanitarium corridors are dark and drafty, too, traveled by consumptive patients like himself whose bleak faces re-*
flect malignancy and hemorrhage. The floor is cold on his feet and his gown flutters

as he proceeds. No one speaks, but many faces seem familiar. Passing the children's ward he sees old schoolmates seated in a circle eating biscuits and custard pie, each exhibiting the scrofulous habit of watery eyes and translucent skin, glands swollen up like walnuts. Across the hallway, Mrs. Burritt and the Szopinski twins are taking the sun cure, bathing euphorically in a shower of bactericidal ultra-violet rays under bright tungsten lamps. They see his reflection in the mirror and wave as he passes. He pretends not to notice, so ashamed is he of being there. Why among all Pendergasts did he alone become infected? Aunt Hattie maintained his fate was sealed at birth. Uncle Henry argued in favor of invasive bacilli corrupting a glass of raw milk. What does it matter now? Down this dark angled corridor, the fortunate expectorate lung stones and weave baskets for exercise while the ill-fated lie in tub-baths with cloths of black silk shrouding their eyes or endure the gruesome treatments of the artificial pneumothorax apparatus. Looking into a mirror ahead, he sees Rascal administering an injection to Clare from a hypodermic needle flooded with a solution of gold and sodium. Both are dressed in white sanitarium gowns. Quivering with fear, Clare calls to him for help, "Melvin!" while the draft in the corridor rises like a wintry spook. He feels as if he is suspended upside-down.

"Melvin?"

Wilted flower petals blown on the cold wind from the nearby woods showered the carnival darkness as Alvin lay on his back staring up at a poster of Jupiter the Balloon Horse nailed onto a two-by-four in front of an exhibit called Cirque Olympic. Clare knelt above him in a plain yellow print frock and cloche hat. She held a small beaded handbag at her side. A sudden gust riffled her dress, forcing her to cover herself from the scurrying sawdust. Across the way, a quartet of polka dot clowns and trained poodles turned cartwheels for a cheery group of children. Swarms of townspeople hurried by. High-arching skyrockets burst upon the cloudy night sky.

"Oh, Melvin, are you all right?" Clare asked, concern in her eyes. "I've been so worried."

Alvin's head swam as he sat up. He felt confused and had no idea where he was. He mumbled, "I was just having a nap."

"In the mirror house?"

"Huh?" Alvin's eyes watered and his head hurt. He thought he might be sick to his stomach.

"You were lying on the floor in the mirror house when Mr. Hughes from the radio shop found you. Are you sure you're all right? Maybe I should fetch a doctor. You look awfully pale."

"I got lost."

Clare giggled. "Why, you silly! You were only a few steps from the exit!"

"Oh yeah?" Alvin replied, still feeling bewildered. He looked back over his shoulder and saw the rear exit to the Palace of Mirrors. He hardly remembered a thing. "I guess it was dark."

"When Mr. Hughes and that other fellow carried you out of the mirror house, they said you felt light as a bird." Wind blew in her hair. "Have you been eating well?"

Alvin rose slowly, keeping his eyes focused on the poster of Jupiter the Balloon Horse. He was sorely feverish. "I got fixed up with a bad radish last week and it gave me a whopping bellyache. I suppose I was pretty sick for a couple days there."

He stood still for a moment to take his bearings. The Big Top was just ahead along the midway. Clare held him gently by the arm, close enough for Alvin to smell the fragrant Orange Blossom perfume she wore.

"Be careful," she said, keeping him steady.

"I'm all right now," Alvin lied, his dizziness easing. "I ain't sick no more."

"I'm awfully worried. You look so pasty and thin."

"Well, I guess I been working too much inside them tents," he told her, as a pair of gypsy swordsmen led a baby elephant past. He tried changing the subject. "This circus is pretty swell, ain't it?"

Clare's expression brightened. "Oh, it's so marvelous I'm just lost for words! It's absolutely grand! Why, I'll bet you've seen a million shows, haven't you? It must be wonderful to be in the circus."

"It's a panic, all right," he replied, watching the noisy crowds. "But see, we've got to put it over big every night and that ain't so easy, let me tell you. Some nights, well, even for those of us that got sawdust in our blood, it just ain't in the cards and whatever you do ain't half enough." The farm boy kicked at the dirt, uneasy with fibbing her.

Clare tugged at his arm. "Oh Melvin, let's go see the lions, can't we? Please?"

"Why, sure we can," he replied as the wind gusted, fanning up dry leaves and paper scraps. "If that's what you want." He knew he could honey her up if she gave him half a chance.

"Oh, it is!"

Alvin looked through the noisy crowds to the ticket booth at the opening to the Big Top. "Say, wait here, will you? Let me talk to that tooter over there."

"All right." Clare smiled sweetly. "Hurry!"

Alvin went across to the derbyhatted ticket taker. Keeping his back to Clare, he said, "I need two tickets."

"It's ten cents." The fellow's eyes were bloodshot and his teeth to-bacco stained. He raised his eyes and nodded in Clare's direction. "Is she your sweetheart?"

Still feverish, the farm boy dug the change out of his pocket and handed it over on the sly. "Yeah, what of it?"

"She sure's a peach," said the ticket taker, his attention stuck on Clare. "I'll bet she's nice to smooch, too, ain't she?"

The farm boy scowled. "Say, maybe you ought to button up your face. I can scrap pretty good and I ain't afraid to, neither."

"Oh yeah?" The fellow snickered at Alvin.

"Yeah."

"Get on along, buster, I'm busy." Turning away from Alvin, he be-gan his spiel again to the passing crowds. "STEP RIGHT UP! STEP RIGHT UP! NOW UNDER THE BIG TOP! FEROCIOUS LIONS TAMED BY THE INCOMPARABLE BALDINADO THE GREAT! WITNESS THE BEAUTIFUL JENNY DODGE PERFORMING THE MOST ASTOUNDING MID-AIR SOMERSAULTING EX-PLOITS ON EARTH! WONDER OF WONDERS! STEP RIGHT UP! STEP RIGHT UP!"

The farm boy waved and Clare came over and he led her under the fluttering banners at the entrance to the Big Top, the ticket taker whistling rudely at Clare as she went by.

Once they were inside the tent, Alvin told her, "That fellow gives me the creeps."

She agreed, "He seems awfully fresh."

"That ain't the half of it."

By the crowded plankwood bleachers, Clare squealed, "Oh, Melvin, look at all the pretty ponies!"

The Wild West show had filled the big tent rings with Apache bareback riders and sturdy soldiers in blue cavalry outfits amid deafening gunfire. A frightful massacre! Siberian Cossacks and Arabian swordsmen emerged from the wings to join the fray. Wild horses stampeded over flaming hurdles. Guns boomed. Steel sabers flashed. The audience shrieked with delight at an Indian war cry and another round of booming cannon fire.

Alvin's ears were ringing when he felt Clare pinch his arm.

"Isn't it just wonderful?" she said.

"Sure," Alvin replied, "but I don't see nowhere to sit."

Since fainting in the mirror maze, he had become terrifically worried about getting stuck in a crowd. He guessed his fever hadn't reduced much at all and his stomach felt rotten. He watched a band of feathered Apaches riding bareback ponies away from the battle to a large cheer while a troupe of friendly clowns passed out sticks of cotton candy to eager children in the front row. More people shoved past. The ringmaster in red tails and black top-hat bounded into the center ring to a chorus of brass trumpets. High overhead a glittering troupe of blue-sequined aerialists crowded the lofty tightwire perches. Flaming torches flared. Smells of fresh popcorn and steaming horse manure and gun smoke filled the air. The ringmaster addressed his audience by megaphone: "LAD-IES AND GENTLEMEN! EMMETT J. LASWELL PRESENTS THE GRANDEST, MOST COLOSSAL, SPECTACULAR, SENSATIONAL SHOW OF THE AGE!"

"Didn't your little friend say he was with the Wild West show?" Clare asked, entwining her arm with Alvin's.

The farm boy shook his head as he coughed. "Naw, he laid an egg in Joplin with that fool knife trick of his and got canned. Now all they let him do is juggle apples on the midway for a kiddie show. I guess he'll be blowing the circus pretty soon now."

"Gee, that's too bad. But you'll still be performing tonight, won't you? I'm awfully anxious to watch. Remember, I'll be pulling for you."

Alvin cocked his head at her, feigning his best expression of puzzlement. "Ain't you seen my act? Why, I put it on an hour ago."

Clare's jaw dropped. "Oh dear!"

"It went over swell, too. First stunt of the night. Why, I never heard such a racket as when I gave them Bengal tigers the ol' whip. Laswell himself said it was just about the swellest performance he ever seen and he ain't usually that liberal with his compliments. Says he might even star me in the next show."

The farm boy looked off toward the prancing ringmaster. He scouted the bleachers again for somewhere they could have a better look at the string of gargantuan India elephants parading into the three-ring circus as the daring highwalkers balanced beneath silk parasols and formed pyramids across from the great trapeze. A huge cheer went up from the surrounding crowds. Tramp clowns danced and tumbled on the sawdust. A slim fellow in a silver suit was shot out of a giant black cannon and sailed across the tent into a rope net, saluting to the grandstand as he flew by. Zebras and camels and trained bears appeared in the wings with a family of Turkish acrobats. The ringmaster doffed his hat. When the farm boy turned back to Clare, she was gone. Alvin called her name and walked forward to the edge of the wooden bleachers and searched the audience there. When he didn't see her, he looked back toward the Big Top entrance and the flocks of people crowding around Zulu the Cannibal King who had come into the big canvas tent juggling six bleached human skulls.

"Melvin!"

Clare's voice, nearly drowned out by the commotion in the center ring, came from the musty darkness beneath the old bleachers. Crouching down under the fifth row planks, the farm boy saw Clare kneeling in the damp sawdust with a frilly bundle of white in her arms, a little girl dressed in Sunday lace wearing a cute baby bonnet on her head. When the child noticed Alvin staring at her, she cried out, "Mama! Mama! I want my mama!"

Clare smiled at the farm boy. "The poor dear's lost."

"How'd she get under there?" Alvin asked, crawling a few feet forward. A Phunny Phord clown car backfired over and over as a pile of midgets in police uniforms chased a pony-drawn firewagon around the outside of the rings and a trio of midget firemen parachuted down from the tent peak. The crowd roared with delight.

Alvin backed up as Clare guided the little girl out from under the bleachers. "She ain't hurt, is she?"

Clare shook her head. "No, but she's awfully frightened. And listen to her voice, it's so husky. I think she's caught a cold."

The child whimpered and buried her face in Clare's bosom.

"Well, where's her folks?" Alvin asked, searching the crowds nearby for a worried face. There were so many people jammed together under the tent, he wasn't surprised a little kid could get separated from her parents. Glancing up to the white canvas tent top, he watched a Chinese cyclist riding across the tightwire with a pair of squealing red-capped monkeys on his shoulders.

"Why, Melvin, I think she wants us to take her to her mother!"

The farm boy saw that Clare had let go of the child and was being tugged toward the tent exit. "What if her mama ain't left yet?" he asked. "What if she's still looking in the tent?"

The little girl pointed to the exit. "Mama! Mama!"

"You see?" Clare said. "I think she wants us to go with her, the poor dear. She seems to know where her mother went."

"Well, gee whiz, we ain't hardly seen nothing of the show yet," the farm boy complained, staring at the child who was about the homeliest kid he had ever laid eyes on. He wished she'd stop her sniveling. There were lots of worse places to get yourself lost than at a circus.

Instead, the little girl whimpered again, "I want my mama! I want my mama!"

Clare picked her up and gave her a hug. "Sweetheart, we'll find your mama, I promise." She looked up at Alvin. "Don't you see what I mean? Oh honey, I guess we'll just have to find her mother."

The crowd roared as the Great Baldinado strode into the lion cage and cracked his leather whip at the King of Beasts, inspiring the bandmaster to strike up a rousing chorus of "Cyrus the Great."

A troupe of Egyptian contortionists emerged from a sequence of tiny drums. Gold-spangled acrobats soared on swaypoles high above as Clare led the little girl out of the Big Top with Alvin trailing reluctantly behind.

Wind blew across the busy midway, scattering wastepaper and errant balloons. Music from the carousel rang like distant choral bells. Alvin felt a chill and buttoned his shirt up to the collar. What a switch! An hour ago he had been alone and now he had himself a family. The thought crossed his mind that perhaps he might marry this girl one day if consumption didn't kill him. She was pretty and smelled like spring flowers. He thought he would go with her as often as she'd stand for it. They passed the musical Whirly-Gig as it discharged another group of breathless passengers. A roustabout in a flat cap winked at Clare as he took tickets for the next ride. On a platform a few feet away sat pasty-faced Minnie the Fat Lady eating a ripe watermelon. The little girl whined again for her mother and pointed Clare to the showgrounds entrance, crowded with newly arrived circus-goers. Alvin smelled steamed hotdogs and mustard and watched an old Negro in suspenders and a tarnished derby lead a pair of spotted ponies toward the lot of painted bandwagons. More boys from town hurried by, stuffing popcorn and Crackerjack into their mouths as they ran.

"Why, I think she wants us to take her home," Clare said to Alvin, as crimson skyrockets lit the black sky. "She's awfully insistent."

Across the midway, a skinny concessionaire's tiny white poodle rolled over and jumped up and did a backflip off an apple crate next to the soda pop stand. An audience of children clapped loudly.

The farm boy frowned. "Well, that just don't seem at all fair. You hardly been here yet and there's still lots to see."

"Oh, but there'll be other shows, and you said yourself that you're finished. Isn't that right? Meanwhile, this poor little tot's frightened half to death and can scarcely wait to get back to her mother." Clare knelt down to give the little girl a kiss on the nose and received a kiss on the lips in exchange. She giggled and the little girl pinched her cheek. Clare picked her up and hugged the smiling child to her bosom. "You see what I mean? Isn't she the cutest thing you ever saw? Oh Melvin, you're looking all blue. I suppose you've got your heart set on seeing the rest of the show tonight, don't you? Well, why don't I take her home myself? It's silly for both of us to leave so early and I'm sort of played out, anyhow, so I'm sure I wouldn't be good company."

Her dainty yellow frock tousled in the wind. Somewhere across the dark showgrounds, a trumpet blew. A troupe of sequined acrobats marched out of the fluttering shadows beside the cage wagons.

His head hurting now, the farm boy shrugged. "If you say so."

Clare smiled. "Maybe we could go on an auto picnic tomorrow?"

The child grabbed at Clare's breast. "Mama!"

"I ain't got a motor," Alvin answered, gazing down the dark windy midway where a familiar figure emerged from the belly-dancing side-show, hat in hand. Chester Burke took a cigar from his breast pocket, lit it, then crushed the dead match in the dirty sawdust underfoot.

"Oh, we'll have a grand time," Clare promised, "but now I have to see this little dear home to her mother. You won't be sore at me, will you, Melvin?" She stared him in the eye, noticed his disappointment. "Oh, it's not as bad as all that, sweetie. I really do hope you'll look me up tomorrow, honest I do."

"Sure." The farm boy watched a pink-haired clown approach the gangster. They shook hands and the clown began speaking with Chester like they were pals.

Clare leaned forward and gave Alvin a soft peck on the cheek. "You're absolutely topping!" She hugged the little girl. "Say good night to Melvin, sweetheart. Bye-bye! Bye-bye!"

The child kicked and shrieked, "Mama! Mama!" and urged Clare toward the showgrounds gate. Clare waved back to Alvin as she passed under the rippling flags. A fresh gang of young people reeking of moonshine liquor bought tickets to the circus. The wind gusted hard as Clare vanished across the dark summer fields toward town. When the farm boy turned to look for Chester again, he found himself surrounded by half a dozen midget clowns dressed like Keystone Kops.

The circus wagons were parked trailer fashion in a large dirt lot behind the Big Top. Performers came and went, some dressed in costumes, others stripped down to workshirts, leotards and robes. A cookhouse next to one of the empty animal wagons drew plenty of attention with the circus so far from town, sideshow curiosities waiting in line with highwire artists and billposters and harness makers and sweaty roustabouts for a hot meal. Noise from clown alley echoed through the performers' painted wagons, lewd insults and elaborate gags traded back and forth for a laugh or a stiff jolt of booze. Inside the gilded wagon, *King of Lilliput*, a proud elderly midget dressed like Sir Lancelot and seated upon an overstuffed silk pillow under a shuttered window by a small cookstove offered his candid opinion of life with the circus to the farm boy and the dwarf.

"Now, if you were to have asked me thirty years ago how far I'd be willing to travel for riches and fame, why, I'd have said 'To the moon and back, my friend. To the moon and back!'"

He reached into a basket of fruit at his feet and drew out a ripe banana. Alvin sat on a narrow wood stool next to a cupboard full of old photographs and embroidered handkerchiefs and little knick-knacks. Still feeling feverish and wan, he ate from a bowl of Crackerjack in his lap and tried to pretend he was all right, though his breathing was disturbingly labored. Rascal, dressed up as Napoleon at Waterloo and grinning like a sloppy drunk, reclined on a lavender fainting couch beside tiny Josephine who wore a pretty taffeta ballgown of her own and a powder-white pompadour. She was perhaps half a foot shorter than the dwarf with a grown woman's face and lovely opaline eyes. She and Rascal held Japanese fans and shared sips from a cloudy bottle of schnapps.

"But men are not trained seals," said Sir Lancelot, slowly peeling his banana. "We require more than a steady diet of fish and exercise to show our best. Yet how many exhibitors have ever appreciated this simple truth? Dan Rice died a drunkard when Spalding turned him out. Tom Thumb passed away rich but childless." He sniffed the banana. "Oh, how wonderful it once was to be young and hopeful."

Another dozen or so midgets wearing a variety of absurd theatrical costumes had stuffed themselves about the flowery interior of the painted wagon — Betty Boop with the Keystone Kops shoulder to shoulder on a feather bed, Emperor Nero on a footstool with a cup of tea, Billy the Kid dressed in chaps, six-guns, and a ten-gallon hat on a padded bench-seat beneath two flickering kerosene lamps with Merlin and Kaiser Wilhelm and Chief Crazy Horse — a scene utterly bewildering to the sick farm boy.

The dwarf remarked, "My companion and I have traveled quite a lot recently. Constitutionally speaking, it's been perilous, of course, but my Uncle Augustus always held to the opinion that getting out of bed every morning is well worth the risk."

Betty Boop giggled.

Alvin saw Merlin produce a silver hipflask from thin air and have a drink. The wagon was humid and smelled of fried onions and stale cigars. A bouquet of marigolds in a crystal vase on a carved bookshelf was already wilting in the heat from the stove. Alvin felt dizzy.

Smoothing his toga, Emperor Nero said, "I have led parades through countless hamlets whose populace imagines we exist only for the amusement of children. This is the harlequin's secret. He pretends to believe the audience adores his featherbrained antics, then weeps false tears of unhappiness when sentiment turns against him. Frivolity is bittersweet. It buys our meals, yet leaves the audience believing us fools: a dubious bargain, indeed."

Alvin listened to the wind gust through clown alley. He heard an angry row developing near one of the lion cages. Rascal hiccuped and sweet Josephine patted his back.

Merlin snapped his fingers and a miniature deck of playing cards appeared in his tiny hands.

"Do a trick," Kaiser Wilhelm requested, his spiked helmet tipped askew.

"Yes," agreed Chief Crazy Horse, "let's have some stunts. I'm feeling awfully low this evening."

Merlin addressed the farm boy: "Young man, are you clever at riddles?"

A titter of laughter swept through the Keystone Kops. Betty Boop clapped a hand across her mouth as a black eyelash sagged.

Too ill to appreciate the joke, Alvin shrugged. "I ain't heard one yet."

"He's rather slow on the uptake," said the dwarf, stifling a giggle of his own. "Better make it easy."

Alvin snapped back, "No, I ain't." He coughed harshly, muffled by his sleeve. The wagon was stifling and he began to feel faint once more. He wondered if the midgets kept a doctor handy.

"Go ahead, tell him your riddle," ordered Sir Lancelot, busy uncorking a bottle of wine. "Let's try to be gracious to our guests."

Merlin nodded while shuffling rapidly through the playing cards. He thought for a few moments, then quoted: *"A mighty black horse with gallant white wings, within his grand paunch bears many strange things."*

"Oh, that's so simple," said Billy the Kid, drawing his toy six-guns. He cocked both silver triggers with his thumbs.

"Don't tell, don't tell!" cried one of the Keystone Kops. "Let him guess!"

"He won't get it," Emperor Nero advised. "Ask him an easier one."

"Oh, let him try," said Josephine. She took another nip of schnapps and passed the bottle to the dwarf whose gray eyes lolled oddly.

"I ain't got any idea," Alvin growled, embarrassed by all these circus midgets staring at him like he was slow. Worse, he knew most of them were tipsy. It seemed all they did was drink once their act was over. He hated drunks, no matter what size they were.

"Don't be sore, honeypie," cooed Betty Boop. "Merlin's got a million snooty riddles and even we ain't heard 'em all. But here's the gag: If you guess one, the poor dope's finished."

"You're darned right he is," one the Keystone Kops put in gleefully.

"Go ahead, kill me," said Merlin, flourishing the deck of cards. "You're all a bunch of shallow-waisters, anyhow."

"I think Merlin needs a diet for his head," said Betty Boop. She blew him a kiss.

"I ought to give you a shiner for yours," Merlin shot back, riffling his playing cards like a loud ugly fart.

"Go ahead, rave on, you big horse. You can dish it out all right, but you sure can't take it."

"Oh, quit quarreling with him," Sir Lancelot told Betty Boop. "Can't you see he's tight?"

"It's a ship," Rascal proposed after imbibing another sip of schnapps. Josephine kissed him on the cheek. The dwarf smiled. "If I may help my young companion."

All eyes switched back to Merlin whose flamboyant posture drooped dramatically. The deck of cards vanished in the wink of an eye, replaced by a scowl and a muttered obscenity.

"Well, I'll be!" Emperor Nero laughed. "He got it!"

A boisterous cheer went up from the Keystone Kops. "HURRAH! HURRAH!"

"The little fellow's a credit to his race," declared Betty Boop.

"You said a mouthful!" Billy the Kid cackled. He tipped his ten-gallon hat to the dwarf. "Attaboy!"

Sir Lancelot lit a Cuban cigar.

Alvin heard the steam calliope roar to life across the windy show-grounds. Near clown alley, someone began practicing scales on an old violin. The farm boy ate a fistful of Crackerjack and tried to forget how sick he felt. Why couldn't he go home? He was tired of all this nonsense.

Rascal burped, then remarked to no one in particular, "When my Uncle Augustus was just a boy before the Civil War, he was employed by a puppet show aboard the *Floating Palace* in the Gulf of Mexico, so I know all about boats. Once I determined the 'gallant white wings' were sails, it all made perfect sense. Also, Auntie and I played riddles quite often at supper, some of the cleverest you ever heard. Whoever guessed correctly won a glass of sherry, though I must tell you I preferred Coca-Cola, especially during the summer when the heat in our kitchen was simply dreadful. To be honest, I believe I won more often than not."

"Living straight keeps down the weight," Josephine remarked with a smile. She gave the dwarf another kiss on the cheek. "Aren't you precious?"

"Getting fresh, eh?" Billy the Kid snapped at her. He twirled a six-gun on one finger. "Maybe you better cut out wine tonics after the show, honey."

"She's after him, ain't she?" said Betty Boop. "Like mama and papa. I'll bet he's even got a decent stake somewhere."

Emboldened by nightfever, Alvin blurted, "Didn't he tell you he's a millionaire? Why sure, my little pal's got loads of dough. Just you ask him."

"Oh, I'll lay he doesn't," said Chief Crazy Horse. A yellow feather fell off his war bonnet. "Look at his patent leathers."

"What of it?" Josephine protested. "At least he ain't so nickel and dime! What's your aim in life besides getting a forkful of those dames you been chasing around with?"

Chief Crazy Horse laughed. "Josephine's motto is, 'Get 'em young, treat 'em rough, tell 'em nothing.'"

"Oh yeah? How about that skunk you dragged in here last week?" she snapped back. "All your taste is in your mouth!"

Sir Lancelot shushed her. "Aw, easy kid, easy."

Wind shook the circus wagon again. A pair of muleskinners walked past cursing Laswell. Alvin heard a flat ukulele join the practicing violinist across the dirt lot. Then he watched Merlin roll a silver dollar over his knuckles and remembered how Frenchy used to be able to do that before he got his hand caught in Uncle Henry's thresher.

"I guess you think the well-to-do got it all sewed up, don't you?" Kaiser Wilhelm cut in, finally. "Well, I was rich once, too. Like Midas, I tell you. Houses, boats, dames, swimming pools, you name it, and everything according to Hoyle. I played the market right out of school like a Morgan and nobody could say I wasn't liberal, neither. Why, they got plenty of orphanages and old folks homes these days in Philadelphia thanks to the charity bureaus I started up back then. Yessiree, it was all going so grand, and me the one that put it over. Well, when you pull down that kind of dough, you got to keep your eyes peeled for those that like to take it from you. In my case, I had my brother Frank who was always shooting off his head about how stingy I was towards my own flesh and blood once I'd made the grade. He earned a fair enough wage with United Cigar to keep his pretty wife Peggy in a new dress every month and those five kiddies of his rolling in toys, so I tell you he had nothing to kick about. Now, Peggy had a sister named Helen who wasn't hard to look at and seemed willing to give a short weight like me a tumble if I played my cards right. She smelled like lilies-of-the-valley, I tell you, and kissing her made me shiver, so I married her and built her a castle at Newport. That cost plenty all right, but I was sweet on Helen and we got on well together — or so I thought. Well, here's the pay-off: it was all a double-cross. Frank and Helen hired a detective to follow me around until he brought back pictures of me and some dame in a hotel room that proved I was a cheat. They got a judge to bust off the marriage and give everything I owned to Helen. Didn't matter that the dame from the hotel room worked in the steno pool at United Cigar and the judge played golf on Fridays with Helen's Uncle Bob. After that, everything went on the bum. I got so cockeyed sore, I started drinking. See, I had to take it out on someone, and there wasn't anybody left to put me wise to myself. Helen knew how to sell her stuff, all right, but she never did love me and I only got word the day her lawyer sent me the telegraph. Now, I don't hold with misery drinking anymore because I don't want to end up an old soak, and I don't take up any of the financial papers, either. I had a good enough nut on my shoulders when I was young to play the market for all it was worth. After Helen, though, I figured out that all a fellow really needs is some bread to dunk in his coffee and a sweetheart to tuck him in at night, and that's the straight of it."

Another cold gust of wind shook the wagon. Fiddling with her sagging eyelash, Betty Boop squeaked, "You're all set now, though, ain't you, honey?"

Kaiser Wilhelm smiled. "Sure I am."

"You bet he is," said Emperor Nero. "That's the Kaiser you're talking to."

Sir Lancelot puffed on his cigar as the Keystone Kops shared a bottle of wine and a plate of meat sandwiches brought over from the cookhouse. Billy the Kid played with his six-guns. Josephine stroked the dwarf's hand while the farm boy listened to the piping of the steam calliope near the Big Top and tried not to get sick all over himself.

The wagon door opened to the cold draft and Alvin saw a grimy fellow wearing a tattered brown derby stick his head inside. He growled at the Keystone Kops, "The boss wants to see y'all over to the office, and he don't mean maybe." He pointed a finger at Emperor Nero. "That means you, pipsqueak."

Then he slammed the door and left.

Nero wiped his mouth. "Ain't Johnny a scream?"

"Aw, raspberries," said Billy The Kid, getting to his feet. "Let's shove off."

Wind hissed through the upper branches of the old sycamore trees that flanked the boardinghouse where Alvin lay sweating under a ratty wool blanket in the dark. A side window was raised to the night air and a lilac scent of damp gardens carried past the storm screen. Ragged shadows from the streetlights below fluttered across the walls and ceiling. A hound dog tied to an iron stake in the lot next door barked off and on at ghostly intruders. The boardinghouse felt dead and empty.

Drumming his fingers on the iron bedpost, the dwarf rested under the sheets in his own bed, stripped to his union suit. It was hours past midnight. When the farm boy came back from the showgrounds, he had hoped to find Clare working at the front desk, but the light was out in the office and nobody answered when he called for her, and he went up to bed feeling feverish and lonesome. Meanwhile, the dwarf was full of stories from his night at the circus. He admitted running off to the showgrounds after the street parade. At North Street, he explained, a lion had escaped from its wagon cage and gone on a rampage through a widow's tomato patch until it was subdued by a pair of animal trainers in Pith helmets. One of Laswell's funnymen was horribly mauled trying to protect a crowd of children and had to be driven to a hospital in the next county. According to the dwarf, it was the most exciting thing he had ever seen — until he crossed paths with Josephine behind the Big Top.

"I introduced myself to her by the corner of the snake house where I was struck dumb by Cupid's arrow. I'd never been in love before. Isn't that remarkable? Auntie always cautioned me against passion, warning that my heart was born frail, susceptible to poisons of many sorts. Well, she needn't have worried. I feel lighter than air."

"I seen Chester at the circus tonight."

"Oh?"

Alvin rolled over in bed, shrugging off part of the blanket. The sheets beneath him were damp with sweat. "He was talking to one of them clowns. I don't know what for."

"They've traveled ten thousand miles this year," said the dwarf, shoving back his own covers. The bedsprings squeaked as he kicked at his blanket. "Josephine says she once performed with a royal Hungarian wire walker and rode in a gilded wagon that had its own sink and phonograph and marble tub from Savannah. That was years ago, of course, but did you know Mister Laswell still pays three hundred a week for many of the sideshow acts, more for the Big Top? It's fascinating, isn't it? Why, I believe a fellow could do a lot worse for himself than joining a circus."

Falling leaves blown free by the cold wind pattered the boardinghouse roof like autumn rain. Alvin stared at the dark ceiling. Whenever he worried, his fever worsened. He thought about how far ten thousand miles was from home. He listened to the draft at the storm screen and the dusty leaves falling and the barking dog next door. The dwarf ruffled his sheets and sneezed. Alvin coughed into his pillow. He told Rascal, "You shouldn'ta gone there till dark."

"I found help."

"Beg your pardon?"

"We needn't be afraid now. While you were napping, my dear Josephine introduced me to the King of Lilliput who was quite gracious in showing me about the circus. You have no idea how many friends we've made here. I told them everything."

"Chester'll shoot you in the head."

The dwarf sat up in bed, casting his own odd shadow on the pale wallpaper behind him. He leveled his voice. "We were not made that we might live as brutes."

"I ain't fooling," Alvin warned.

"He has no hope who never had a fear."

"You're crazy."

Down on the front sidewalk below, a man whistled tunelessly walking Third Street toward the railyard. The dwarf sipped from the water glass he kept beside his bed. Once finished, he told Alvin, "You see, I'm done with Hadleyville forever. Auntie can keep my inheritance if she wishes. It is immaterial with me now. When Josephine was a tiny girl, her mother knew a witch who lived in a peach orchard just outside of town. She dallied with divination and brewed magic potions in her root cellar that amended one's stars in the heavens. Although Josephine was still no bigger than a cabbage at her thirteenth birthday, she was invited by Alice Roosevelt to dance a minuet on a tea table at Sagamore Hill for the President himself. Do you believe in destiny?"

A cold gust shook the storm screens. His fevered skin chilled by the draft, Alvin replied, "I believe it's a long walk home even if you don't get shot."

"I have faith in society." The dwarf leaned over onto his pillow. "We've never been alone. We've just imagined we were. When my mother gave birth to me, she intended that I belong to the world, not squander half my life hidden away from it. Auntie was cruel to tell those lies. I trusted her to know what was best for me and I was deceived. Tonight at the circus, Josephine and the King of Lilliput helped me discover a solution to the riddle of freedom. Would you care to hear it?"

The farm boy listened to the wind and thought about the wild pinewoods on the farm in Illinois, a distant call, indeed.

"'Tis true that we are in great danger," said the dwarf. "The greater therefore should our courage be."

"Don't joke me. I ain't in the mood."

The storm-shutters on the veranda downstairs rattled harshly as the dwarf told the farm boy, "Listen here: trust me, and I promise you that after tomorrow night, we won't have a worry in the world."

Morning light filled the lobby when Alvin came downstairs for breakfast. The dwarf had risen early and gone out on his own. All the windows in the lower boardinghouse were flung open to the morning air to let out the stink of turpentine fumes from the painters working on the second floor. The farm boy rang at the desk for Clare and another girl came out of the office and told him Clare would not be in until noon, so Alvin reluctantly left the boardinghouse and went downtown to eat. Trucks and automobiles rumbled along Third Street. The clouds were patchy now and blue sky shown through, warmer than yesterday. Alvin found a half-empty lunchroom two blocks from Main and bought himself hotcakes and ham and scrambled eggs and two cups of fresh coffee. He hadn't eaten much more than popcorn at the circus and woke with his fever gone but his stomach growling. The fainting spell he had suffered at the circus frightened him greatly. He knew he was sicker than last month and worried that sooner or later a relapse of his consumption might send him to the grave if he didn't watch out. He imagined the dwarf was back at the circus, honeying up his little sweetheart. Maybe he was busy working up a show of his own. Alvin had never seen so many half-pints at one place before in his entire life. The idea of them traveling around together wisecracking and putting on circus shows everyday didn't seem all that peculiar to him now after sitting in their wagon for an hour. He supposed it wasn't all that bad a life. The fact that a fellow doesn't come up much past another fellow's belt buckle shouldn't mean he doesn't deserve the best of what there is to be had.

When he finished with breakfast, the farm boy strolled around downtown for an hour or so, looking in store windows. The sidewalks were less crowded than yesterday and the trolley wasn't operating. A fresh bounce in his step from a full stomach, Alvin crossed the street to the jewelers where he bought a new wristwatch and stuck it in his pocket. Then he walked back to the boardinghouse. The painters were sitting out on the veranda drinking coffee and talking. One of them had a morning edition of the *Icarian Mercury-Gazette* spread apart on his lap and was reading a story to the others. A prominent businessman named Theodore Bowen had been robbed and badly beaten last night in his house on Cobb Avenue. His son had reported the matter to the police. Nobody had been arrested and no further details concerning the man's condition had been offered to the newspaper. When the farm boy came up the steps, the painters stepped back to let him by. He nodded and passed into the cool lobby. Behind him, the painter with the newspaper on his lap muttered a crude obscenity regarding circus people. Alvin checked at the desk for news of Clare again and received the same answer: she would be in for work at noon. A cabinet clock in the office chimed once. He went upstairs to wash his face.

In the third floor hallway, the farm boy listened to Virgil Platt reciting more Bible verses. Through the floor vents he thought he heard a woman performing "Beautiful Dreamer" a capella in a room somewhere downstairs. Maybe it was only the radio. A noisy delivery truck roared past the boardinghouse in the direction of the railyard. Alvin unlocked his room and went inside and found Chester standing by the raised window overlooking Third Street.

"Hiya, kid."

He had on the same charcoal-gray waistline suit and fedora from last night at circus. His face was drawn and tired. He held a white handkerchief to his mouth, dabbing a sore on his upper lip. The odor of turpentine had wafted up into the room through the vents, spoiling the sweet garden scent from the morning yard. Alvin smelled a trace of liquor, too.

"Sorry about this dump," Chester said, taking off his hat. He set it on one of the spindle chairs. His voice was cold and hoarse. "Spud's not the square shooter he used to be. When I knew him on the North Side before Prohibition, he drove a taxicab and wouldn't make a play on your sister for anything in the world. No cards or booze or dirty work with those switchboard girls, either. He led a clean life back then."

"I ain't got a sister," Alvin lied, trying to be funny. He was sick of Chester treating him like a hick. Besides, talking back didn't seem so risky anymore. They were all going to jail soon enough.

Shouts from the painters on the veranda to someone across the street echoed in the boardinghouse. Alvin closed the door behind him and sat on the dwarf's bed.

"I hear you boys were really whooping it up at the circus last night," Chester said, as he took out a cigarette and lit it. "Shooting the works."

He walked over to the sink and ran water over the smoldering match, washing it down the drain.

The bedsprings squeaked as the farm boy leaned forward. "You didn't leave off a message for us to pull out of going, did you? Nobody told us nothing about it, if you did."

Chester had a look in the closet. He nudged the dwarf's suitcase with his foot. "Hallie downstairs says you had a date to go out with her friend Clare last night."

The farm boy studied his shoe leather.

"Well, what's it all about?" Chester tapped hot ash off into the sink. "Is she sweet on you?"

"She says it's nobody's business."

Chester smiled. "I suppose that's so."

Alvin got up off the bed for a look outdoors. He wondered if Chester had in mind to call on her, too. "I ain't stuck on her or nothing. We talked about having a picnic this afternoon."

Chester exhaled smoke from his cigarette. "Did you meet her crowd? That'll tell you more about a girl than the hat she wears."

The farm boy coughed, then shook his head. "I ain't seen nobody yet but her."

Chester walked back over to the raised window. "It's a swell circus, isn't it?"

"We hardly seen half of it. There was a baby under the bleachers that wanted to go home with her. We missed the lions."

Chester laughed. "How's that again?"

Alvin kicked at the baseboard, and coughed again. "It was all a lot of nonsense."

"What a mob, though, eh? Why, I'll bet you Laswell was raking in the dough last night."

His expression blank, Chester watched a loaded fruit truck rumble by. The painters had gone back inside to work. A faint breeze rippled through the tall leafy honey locust next door.

The farm boy spoke up. "I seen a fellow without no arms or legs light his own cigar."

"He stood out, did he?"

"There was others, too. A fat lady with a flock of tattoos on her bosom and a monkey that played 'John Brown's Body' on a xylophone. Then they had a fellow from Indiana with a extra leg that kicked a football and danced a funny jig for us."

"I'll be damned."

The farm boy went over to examine the dwarf's water glass. There was a little puddle on the nightstand. He asked, "Did you hear about that fellow that got hisself knocked around last night?"

Chester blew smoke through the storm screen. "Sure I did. It was in the morning paper. That's rotten luck."

The farm boy rolled the water glass over in his hands. He was scared, but too sick anymore to worry about it. "You didn't have nothing to do about that, did you?"

"Are you asking if it was me that cracked him on the head and broke open his safe?" He chuckled. "I heard the cops found a clown wig under his desk and one of those phony red rubber clown noses in the backyard."

"So they think somebody from the circus did it?"

Chester nodded. "Sure, unless it's a frame-up."

"That'd work."

"Not for us. Brings too many cops to the circus, poking around, keeping their eyes peeled for any sort of funny business."

"I seen you talking with one of them clowns at the circus."

Chester snuffed out the cigarette on the worn rim of the window frame. He looked weary to Alvin, impatient. "Him? Fellow's name is Lester. He used to work in the Union stockyards before the War. He knew my pop from Market Street."

"Oh."

"Says he's finished with Laswell. Hates his guts. Wants to help us stick him up for a cut of the profit. Claims Laswell hasn't been to a bank since the show in Kirksville and Lester knows where he keeps the strong-box. The box office closes at midnight, so that's when Laswell collects the kale and stashes it. Well, tonight we'll be doing the collecting for him. Easy as pie."

"I don't know I'd trust a fellow I just met like that."

Chester walked back over to the toilet and flicked the burnt cigarette butt into the porcelain bowl and flushed. Then he washed his hands under the sink faucet and dried them on a rosy hand towel. When he finished, he told the farm boy, "My pop had the right dope about that. He didn't trust anybody he didn't owe. Lester's no brick, but he won't have the guts to pull out and he knows if he squeals he'll get what's coming to him. The fact is, you don't have to trust 'em if you know how to sell your stuff."

Chester wandered across the room and looked out to the house next door whose small attic window was propped open with a stick. A white fabric of some sort flapped across the shadowed frame like a ghost in the morning draft. The farm boy heard the boardinghouse telephone ring downstairs. Heavy footsteps tromped on the woodplank veranda. Somebody shouted.

Chester came away from the window with a bright smile. He told the farm boy, "I got a date to go out myself tonight, some gypsy dame who was giving me the once-over by the monkey show. I'd had a fair uplift already, but what a doll! I told her I'd drop over about ten. What I'll do is dope out the whole plan this afternoon and meet you at the ticket gate by half past nine. Get me?"

The farm boy nodded.

Chester looked him straight in the eye. "We're all set now?"

"Sure."

He broke a faint smile. "It's a cinch we'll knock it over. Tell the midget to pack his bags after supper."

Alvin nodded again. "All right."

Chester took his hat off the spindle chair. He had one more peek out over Third Street. As he left the room, he told the farm boy, "Our breaks is coming, kid."

The farm boy waited at the raised window overlooking Third Street until Chester came out of the boardinghouse and walked off under the green canopy of drooping willows toward downtown. Alvin watched a squirrel leap into the walnut tree from the rooftop next door and scramble down the trunk. He listened to one of the painters laughing downstairs. A pair of motorcars rattled past, one in either direction. Although Alvin felt tired enough to lie back down on the bed, he went to wash his face instead and use the toilet. He took the Illinois wrist-watch out of his trouser pocket and saw that it was almost noon, so he decided to go back downstairs and wait for Clare on the shady veranda in the fresh air. He saw Percy Webster entering a bedroom at the front end of the upper hall as he locked his own door. Virgil Platt had quit his Bible recitations, but Alvin heard the floorboards creak as the old man continued to pace restlessly about his room. The farm boy took the rear staircase down to the lobby.

The door to the back porch was tied open to a draft against the painters' turpentine. Alvin glanced inside the kitchen and found it empty and looked into the dining room and saw Mrs. Burritt at the table with a cup of tea and a small book. Then he heard the painters carrying another ladder up the main staircase and Clare speaking to the postman. He had butterflies in his stomach when he walked into the lobby and saw her at the front desk. She was dressed in a pink apron frock with a cherry blossom print and dainty gold earrings. She looked swell. The postman left a brown package on the desk with Clare and went back outdoors. Upstairs, the painters struggled to maneuver the tall ladder across the second floor landing.

Alvin approached the desk. "Hello."

She raised her eyes, yet barely smiled. "Oh, hello there."

"I ain't seen you this morning."

"Mother kept me home to help with the wash," she said, hardly looking at him.

"Oh yeah?"

Clare took the package off the desk and put it into the office. When she came back out again, she told Alvin, "I'm afraid I also ate too much cotton candy last night. I had the awfulest indigestion before breakfast."

The office telephone rang and Clare went to answer it, closing the door behind her. Alvin heard Mrs. Burritt's voice in the parlor. Then the dog next door began barking as a pack of boys ran past on the sidewalk out front. When Clare hung up the telephone and came out, the farm boy asked, "Did you see that little girl home all right last night?"

Clare sat herself on a stool behind the desk. "Well, now that was the strangest thing. Do you know she never said a word to me about where she lived? Not one peep. Instead, she made me bring her to my house and fix her a cup of hot cocoa and a plate of sugar cookies."

"Is that so?"

"And the little dear insisted on sleeping in bed with me. I was so confused. She wouldn't tell me her name or where she lived or her mother's name or anything about herself at all. But when I woke up in the morning, she was gone."

"Just like that?"

Her face brightened somewhat. "Yes, isn't it peculiar?"

"You bet it is." Alvin hated youngsters, particularly ones who did nothing but moan and blubber for their mommas. Everyone in the family thought he'd have a big family one day, but Alvin didn't pay them any mind because he knew he would probably be dead before he ever got married.

"Well, that's not all. After breakfast, Mother came into the kitchen claiming that some of her silverware was missing and that she was sure the child was a thief. I said, 'Mother, you're absurd,' but she told Father and he's already informed the police. Then there was that beating with poor Mr. Bowen and the clown on Cobb Street last night, you know."

"Yeah, I heard about it."

"Well, it's all quite a mystery, don't you agree? First the child and where she came from, and then that circus clown attacking poor Mr. Bowen?"

"It sure is." He wondered if Spud told her about Chester. Wouldn't that be a surprise?

Clare lowered her eyes. "I can't go with you on a picnic today. I'm sorry."

"Huh?" The farm boy felt another swarm of butterflies fill up his gut. "How come?"

"Father says that since Mr. Bowen was attacked by circus people, he swears to tan me with a willow switch if I have anything more to do with their crowd so long as they're here in Icaria. So that's why I can't go to the circus tonight and I can't have a picnic with you."

"Well, I ain't in the circus."

"Pardon?" Clare's eyes narrowed.

What else could he do now but tell her the truth? "Fact is, I ain't never been in a circus, neither. That was just a made-up story."

"I don't understand."

Alvin shrugged. "It's how come you ain't seen my act last night, 'cause I ain't got one. I had to buy a ticket to get in just like everybody else."

Clare's expression darkened. "You mean, you lied to me?"

"No, I let my friend do the fibbing. I just didn't set him straight, is all."

"Is he in the circus?"

"Nope."

Her voice quivered, grew angry. "That's so deceitful."

"I know it," the farm boy admitted, suddenly realizing his confession might have been a mistake. Aunt Marie had always told him that honesty in love was the best tactic, but maybe she was wrong.

"I don't know what to say."

"Well, how about that picnic?"

Clare rushed into the office and slammed the door behind her.

Alvin gave her a minute or so, then rang the desk bell, hoping she would change her mind.

She yelled at him to go away.

Dejected and feverish, he went out onto the veranda. Avoiding the clutter of boxes and wicker and potted plants, he walked to the side porch and watched a woman in a calico skirt and cotton shawl carry a basketful of green apples up the street. Next door, a man in a white jacket and trousers lounged in a hammock chair smoking a pipe. One of the painters came out with a bucket of dirty gray water and poured it into the mulberry bushes beneath the veranda, then went back indoors again. Alvin heard the telephone ring. He considered trying to explain to Clare about the dwarf and Chester and how they had come to the circus. All he wanted to do was go on a picnic with her and tell her how pretty she was and let her know he'd write letters to her even if he got sent back to the sanitarium. He had worked it all out before breakfast. If she asked, he'd tell her everything. Of course, the trouble now was that she was too cross at him to listen.

Looking up, he saw Rascal scurry along the narrow alley beside the boardinghouse toward the rear garden. Alvin shouted after him, then hustled down the front steps and across the lawn and followed the dwarf's path through the scraggly ironweed and wilting sunflowers into the backyard where he found Rascal on his knees behind a damp patch of rhubarb by the rear garden fence.

"What're you doing there?" the farm boy asked, tiptoeing past a summer growth of sweetpea and moss roses. The tool shed in the back corner of the yard was open. The dwarf stirred cow dung into the soil with a trowel next to a squat terra-cotta pedestal. Bees swarmed in the gooseberry nearby.

Without interrupting his labor, Rascal replied, "I'm planting red tulips as a declaration of my love for sweet Josephine, and blue hyacinths as a foreswearing of constancy."

"Do you remember this ain't your yard?"

"I've already obtained permission from Mr. Farrell this morning. In fact, he was pleased to grant me the favor."

"You seen Spud?" Alvin liked that name. He thought maybe one day he'd go by Spud Pendergast.

"Of course."

"Well, what's the big idea? We ain't stayin' past tonight."

"Home is where we hang our hat, don't you agree?"

The farm boy walked over to the back fence. Across the road in a poultry yard, chickens squawked at a small brown terrier chasing about in the dirt. After studying the surroundings to be sure no one was listening, Alvin told the dwarf, "Chester's got a plan doped out for tonight. He was just upstairs."

Rascal planted his autumn flowers and took up a tin watering pot and sprinkled the black soil. After that, he washed off his hands with the garden hose and wiped them dry on his shirt and got up. "Isn't it pitiable?"

"How's that?"

"To be at once a tee-total failure and utterly malign."

The dwarf stared at his planting ground with undisguised satisfaction. He emptied the watering pot, then collected the trowel and a muddy tan-fork and dropped them both into it.

"You ought to watch out what you say."

"I'm not at all worried."

"What're you so high-hatted about?" asked Alvin, irritation rising with his fever. What made the dwarf think he was all that brave? He hadn't stood up since Hadleyville. He was nobody's hero.

"Consider whether thou art not, thyself, the cause of thy misfortunes; if so, be more prudent for the future."

Alvin smiled. "Yes, we have no bananas."

He chuckled at his own joke.

The dwarf glared back at him. "This is quite serious! I've had a reading this morning and discovered how close is the link between jeopardy and fortune. Indeed, our very fates are defined through the subtlest of actions by ourselves and those with whom we've chosen to associate."

"Aw, go on."

"Associate not thyself with wicked companions, and thy journey will be accomplished in safety."

Alvin raised an eyebrow. "You seen a fortune teller today?"

The dwarf nodded gravely. "The preternaturally gifted Madame Zelincka, as peculiarly constituted an individual as I've ever encountered. She's invited us to a sitting in her parlor this evening. I assured her we'd both attend."

"Well, I ain't a-going. That's nothing but a humbug."

Rascal smiled. "Despair not; thy love will meet its due return."

"Beg pardon?"

"You see, I took the liberty of inquiring on your behalf. Through Madame Zelincka's reading, those incorporeal intelligences on the other side of the veil communicated a message of joy and confidence to your sorrowing soul. She counsels patience."

"She knew about Clare?" the farm boy asked, somewhat incredulously. Aunt Hattie swore by palmistry and spiritistic divinations, while Uncle Henry always maintained it was bunk.

The dwarf nodded. "Madame Zelincka interprets emanations from all brains, near and far. In fact, she says I may be able to speak with my mother this evening if the atmospheric conditions in her spirit-room remain constant. I'm very excited. Madame Zelincka met my mother several years ago during a mesmeric trance and says she is more than willing to remove the veil between our world and the ethereal plane to reunite a loving son with his mother. She's obviously quite experienced with spirit-communions."

"You mean, conjuring ghosts?"

"Spiritual intercourse," the dwarf corrected. "My friend, such manifestations have not been banished by the electric light. There's an unseen world that surrounds us, awaiting a purifying flood of influence from the spirits, radiant fore-gleams of our future informed by our past. Even Buster Brown says ghosts can't do us any harm. Nobody can do you as much harm as yourself. All that glitters is not gold and all that's mysterious is not ghosts in this world of wonders. I've decided I'm going to be good and find out all about it on the other side of Jordan."

The farm boy watched a scrawny goat chewing on tufts of grass in a pen next to the poultry yard. He shook his head. "That's a lot of hooey. If you ask me, there ain't no such thing as ghosts."

"Oh? How would you know that?"

"Well, I ain't never seen one," Alvin replied, giving the garden fence a shake. He guessed if there were any real ghosts, he and the dwarf would've been paid a visit by at least one of those unfortunate souls Chester had murdered this summer. Down the road, the post-man emerged from an old framehouse. Alvin watched a woman in curlpapers wave to him from the second-story window.

"Have you ever seen the Queen of England?"

"No, but I seen pictures."

"Well, Madame Zelincka has a grand collection of spirit photographs atop the secretary in her office. I'm sure she'll be happy to show them to you this evening."

Fatigued enough for a nap, Alvin shrugged. "What's the use?"

Taking up the tin watering pot, the dwarf looked him straight in the eye. "Listen here: in Hadleyville last March I hired a tarot reading in my bedroom that predicted, *'If thou goest to a far country, thy lot will be to undergo many perils.'* Isn't that remarkable? Actually, I thought I'd never leave that house alive, yet look how distant I've traveled since then, how many miles from that grave Auntie named my home. Has this all been hallucination? Although there are mechanisms in place at the circus tonight that will free us from the quagmire we've blundered into, what about tomorrow? What then? I've never been more determined in my life to see beyond the horizon. This evening, Madame Zelincka has promised to offer those of us seated in her spirit circle a vision of Jordan and immortal truth. When I hear my dear mother's voice, I'll be assured that there are, indeed, other lives and other purposes than this."

The farm boy swatted at a passing bee. "Talking ghosts?"

Walking over to the tool shed, the dwarf replied: "There are more things in heaven and earth, Horatio, than are dreamt of in your philosophy."

At twilight on Beecher Street, dried summer leaves blew uphill along the old plank sidewalk. Lamps glowed behind curtained windows of the tall elegant homes obscured under magnolia and sugar maples and flowering oak. Cats hid in poison moonseed and peeked out through iron gates. Bluestreaking meteors raced across the cold black sky. Near the top of the street, the dwarf climbed the narrow stairs of a dark Victorian and rang the brass doorbell. Alvin waited by a garden urn on the brick walkway below. A shadow clouded the stained glass side panel as a young man in denim and suspenders came to answer the door. Summoned by the dwarf, the farm boy followed up the wooden steps and past the young man into the house.

Effluvium of incense and amber-lit gasoliers filled the entry hall. Turkish carpet runners of indigo and crimson ran the length of the house and up a dark-wood staircase to the second floor. All the walls were decorated in olivegreen anaglypta and Morris floral patterns, and the ceiling overhead was painted with golden sunbursts and wild roses. The scratchy phonograph recording of a nocturne by Chopin played in the front parlor to the left where the dwarf hurried straight off upon entering the house. Welcomed by the young man, Madame Zelincka's son Albert, the farm boy was shown through a knotted rope portière into a formal parlor illuminated by electric tulip sconces and oil table lamps. Seated next to the phonograph cabinet on a rosewood chesterfield in the bay window were an earnest little man and his wife, both in elegant evening dress as if out for a night at the opera. Across the room, the dwarf occupied a velvet easy-chair by the fireplace whose mantelpiece of carved marble resembled the entablature of a Greek temple. Behind him, the double doors leading to another room were closed. Mahogany bookshelves and potted palms flanked the arching doorframe.

"So, this is Alvin," said the woman, her blue silver-beaded gown sparkling in the reflected light. "What a fine-looking boy." She offered a warm smile. "Dear, my name is Edith, and this is my husband, Oscar Elliotsen."

Oscar rose from his seat to greet the farm boy. His oiled-hair and thin-waxed moustache glistened as he crossed the carpet to shake hands. "Good to know you, son."

"Yes, sir." Alvin felt himself blush. They were treating him like a king. How come?

"I heard quite a lot about you this morning," his wife added, leaning over to remove the needle from the phonograph as her husband returned to the chesterfield. "It's so extraordinary."

"Thanks."

Wondering what all Rascal had told them, Alvin took off his cap and sat down on a rose tufted sofa near the dwarf. It had been a long hike from Third Street and he was glad to be off his feet. Fresh gardenias in a crystal vase on the side table beside him gave off a delightful scent. He decided this was one of the swellest houses he had ever been in. But who were these people?

"Although my dear friend here is a confirmed materialist," the dwarf remarked, putting his feet upon a stitched hassock, "I'm convinced he is more than fit for our kindred purposes."

Edith smiled at Alvin. "Well, doesn't that sound familiar? Oscar was quite the skeptic himself, weren't you, dear?" She patted him on the knee. "Why, for years he was utterly persuaded that spiritism was jugglery of the commonest sort."

"Pure imposture," her husband confirmed, crossing his arms. "Pabulum for crack-brained lunatics."

Edith added, "He believed that claims of spiritualist miracles were less violations of the laws of God and nature than fraudulent trickery."

Oscar nodded, sternly. "Ingenious deception."

"Well, ain't it the truth?" the farm boy blurted, maybe not so face-tiously. He still considered this whole business of setting up a pow-wow with the spirit world a lot of hooey.

Edith gasped. "My heavens, no! Those of us still in the flesh may well be persuaded that our side of the veil is all there is, that our lasting purpose is merely seed for soil, yet how can that be when a living gate such as Madame Zelincka informs us how strong our ethereal link is to those who've already passed over?"

"Our departed loved ones grieve for us in the idyllic realm," the dwarf explained, "longing to demonstrate the divine knowledge that death is not the end — "

"That light of perfect understanding," Edith interjected.

"Whose message," the dwarf continued, "brings comfort to the liv-ing and joy to the disincarnate spirit, finally unburdened of all regret and sorrow."

"Mental telegraphy is no humbug," said Oscar, straightening up. He gave Alvin a fearsome look. "Why, Thomas Edison himself knew more about etheric forces than all the sensitives in America. In-deed, I've been told he performed experiments at Menlo Park which proved that electricity is itself simply the manifestation of disembod-ied spirits."

Edith remarked, "Just last spring, my husband witnessed the use of an Ediphone to record spirit voices."

"It is our own vital electricity," Oscar explained, "our electrical emanations, that initiates the spiritual telegraph through which these trance mediums perform. There's no longer any recondite mystery about it. The science behind celestial guidance has become clear as day. In fact, I'm inclined to believe that anyone with the proper mental physiology should be able to achieve spiritual rapport."

Edith agreed. "It's true, of course. I've communicated clairaudi-ently with my sister Sara for years. She passed over with typhus when she was just nine and I missed her terribly before I learned what a lovely purpose she has now among the spirit spheres and how beautiful everything is over there."

The double doors parted behind Alvin, and he heard a woman's lilting voice issue from the back parlor: "Flowers whose fragrance lingers, whose bloom fades not, a summer's day of joyous youth."

Oscar Elliotsen and the dwarf got up and Alvin looked over his shoulder to where Madame Zelincka stood under the mahogany archway dressed in a flowing lavender robe.

Edith grinned and clapped her hands. "Oh dear, I had a crystal vision of you just yesterday evening, materializing for me like this in gossamer silk, spirit-spun!"

Quickly, Alvin stood, too, having decided to keep any further opinions under his hat. He didn't want these folks to hate him. People were being friendly for once and he didn't want to foul it up. Besides which, he knew he had good reason to make friends with the dearly departed.

Madame Zelincka smiled as she strolled into the parlor. "Then it would have been infelicitous of the spirits not to have called us together this evening." She surveyed the room. Her face was pale and lovely, her eyes blue as the sky. She was sober and statuesque, taller than her guests, and her brown hair, a graceful chignon of dark curls, hung down her back. "I'm so pleased you're all here."

Alvin smelled a scent of sweet verbena as the medium drew near. She winked at him and he blushed. Why hadn't he worn a suit? He felt like a hick.

Oscar Elliotsen said, "I've been waiting all week to tell you that Mrs. Tingley's temple dome at Point Loma was even more beautiful than you promised."

Edith said, "My husband's favorite shade is amethyst."

Oscar added, "We joined a harmonial circle on our final evening with Dr. de Purucker that got over to Madame Blavatsky herself. As she spoke to us of her celestial life now, we were inundated by a wonderful sprinkling of fresh violets from the summerland."

The dwarf remarked, "Oh, I've read that the pure dry air of California inspires the most startling manifestations."

Madame Zelincka's eyes sparkled in the golden light from the shaded oil lamps. She nodded. "That's quite true. Contrary to our original theories of vibration and mental regions, spirit magnetism appears to be invigorated by atmospheric conditions that most closely resemble the radiant fountains of sunlight those exalted souls enjoy in the seventh sphere."

"Madame Zelincka?"

A dainty older woman dressed in a white lace gown with a garland of pearls and a crystal pendant appeared under the archway. Alvin saw she had been crying lately, her powdered face drawn with tears of sadness.

The medium greeted her with a warm smile. "Lillian, come meet our friends." To the others in the parlor, she explained, "The disembodied spirit of Lillian's late husband Joseph has survived in an etheric body for three years now without knowing he's passed to a life beyond our own. Because he's still able to see and hear his loved ones, he thinks he's dreaming, a not uncommon spiritual infirmity for those whose physical lives were crippled somehow by disease or discontent. Tonight, this mental agony of Joseph's, shared faithfully by his dear Lillian, will be addressed by our psychic circle and the purpose of his life in spheres above, revealed to him at last."

Lillian remained in the doorway, her fingers knotted tightly together. "Can't we begin now?"

Madame Zelincka polled her guests. When each nodded a willingness to proceed with the séance, she smiled. "Well then, perhaps we should retire to the spirit room."

Edith agreed, rising from the chesterfield. "Indeed! There is no artifice to the odic flame. Mysteries will be revealed, enlightenment gained only when we commence our sitting."

"That light of heaven beaming through to us," the dwarf said, starting for the back parlor.

"The great truth," Oscar Elliotsen added, crossing the carpet arm-in-arm with his wife.

"There is no death," Edith affirmed.

The farm boy waited briefly by a potted palm on the side of the doorway where several unshelved books were stacked casually atop the flanking bookcase: *Scientific Basis of Spiritualism*, *Thirty Years Among the Dead*, *Gleams of Light and Glimpses Thro' the Rift*, *Somnolism and Psycheism*, *Proofs of the Truths of Spiritualism*, and a thick blue volume with the odd title *OAHSPE*. He hadn't seen any ghost pictures yet.

As Madame Zelincka entered the back parlor, her son Albert increased the illumination in order for everybody to see where they needed to go. The spirit room was a perfect octagon draped in burgundy silk at each wall, divided by bracket gas lamps with tulip shades tinted pale heliotrope, yet barren of furniture except for the round spirit table and six mackintosh chairs. Persian rugs covered the floor while the entire ceiling above shimmered with golden stars on an indigo sky.

The sitters took their places at the table with the dwarf seated between Lillian and Madame Zelincka, the farm boy to Lillian's right, Edith next to Alvin, and Oscar Elliotsen between his wife and the medium: a proper balance of men and women around the spirit circle. Once everyone was comfortable, Madame Zelincka placed a fountain pen and a stack of blank message cards on the table, then motioned to Albert who departed through the front parlor, drawing the mahogany doors shut behind him. Tulip-shaded gaslights were reduced to a faint purple glow and the sitters became still. The darkened spirit room was cool and the air dry and clean. Alvin remembered how his sisters had played with a Ouija board planchette and automatic writing when they were younger. For half a year, Mary Ann claimed to be clairvoyant and told everyone in the family she had received personal messages on a slate hidden in her closet from a ghost named Agatha. Both Amy and Mary Ann learned how to crack their toes like the Fox sisters and imitate spirit rappings under the dining room table. Only Grandma Louise was fooled. No one in Alvin's family had ever mentioned attending a genuine séance.

He heard Madame Zelincka's melodic voice speak out of the gloom: "Please place your hands on the table, palms down."

She waited a few moments for the sitters to comply, then began, "By the constitution of our universe, each of us exists in the all-pervading ether as pure spirit until we are born into the material world, which is itself the beginning of our individuality that persists after physical death when the spirit quits the body once more to join celestial spheres. Those of us who remain earthbound give off thought-rays that attract beings of an ethereal order to the gates between life and death. Because even the long-departed remember earthly pleasures, many would gladly forsake the highest realms of eternal glory for the joy of seeing families gathered together again for Sunday dinner or watching a belovéd child at play once more. This insistence upon re-visiting the earth-plane is achieved by the attracting odylic energies of a sympathetic medium, which permit direct communication with spir-its across the veil much like electricity is filtered through a galvanic bat-tery. These spirits experience a séance like a blissful afternoon dream, a pleasant interlude. They yearn to be called."

Madame Zelincka became silent.

After a few minutes, the farm boy felt a strange chill in the air, not unlike the dark draft in the Palace of Mirrors. His fellow sitters were barely visible across the spirit table, but the ceiling sky of stars seemed luminescent, floating gently in the gloom high overhead. He heard a faint tinkling nearby like the ringing of a tiny bell. A brief vibration rattled the table. Lillian drew a sudden breath. Alvin felt a mild breeze pass through the darkness behind him while the jingling increased to a delicate melody from a music box some garden fairy might possess. The spirit table shuddered and tipped. He heard Edith whisper to her husband. The table shook hard and the farm boy's arms tingled as if stung by electricity and the spirit table trembled and began to rise ever so slightly from the floor. Lillian squealed and briefly pulled her hands away. Strange knocking sounds circled the room. Raising his eyes, the farm boy saw an apparition of fireflies mingling with the stars. It sent a cold shiver up his back.

"Spirit lights," Edith murmured.

The table rose to a foot above the floor and hovered silently. Higher in the dark, the spirit lights glowed blue and flew about the room like burning phosphorous on a spectral draft. Alvin heard the ticking of a metronome somewhere and the beat of a snare drum. He held his breath as the table tipped precipitously toward Oscar Elliotsen who grunted but stayed in his chair. Then the music faded away and the spirit table descended slowly to the floor.

A violet aura formed about Madame Zelincka.

She spoke aloud, "Ethan?"

The spirit lights suddenly fled and the farm boy felt his hair ruffled by another chilly breeze. A single bird feather wafted out of the darkness overhead, drifting and spinning slowly downward toward the sitters.

It alighted precisely in the center of the spirit table.

Madame Zelincka spoke again. "Ethan?"

A minute of silence.

Another feather.

Then, like a distant tinny voice over the radio, *"I want my milk and johnnycake."*

The medium asked, "Are you hungry, Ethan?"

"Yes, ma'am. I sit by the river everyday without catching so much as a tadpole. The fishing is very poor in the spirit land."

Changing slightly the timbre of her voice, Madame Zelincka told the sitters, "Poor Ethan is an orphan child who drowned in the Potomac the night our great President Lincoln was murdered, so his physical remains went unsought, his passing disregarded. As Ethan waits to be claimed, his tragic predicament summons other desperate souls to the gate."

Madame Zelincka reached under her own chair and brought up a small paraffin lamp that she lit with a lucifer match and placed on the spirit table. Then she passed one of the blank cards to the dwarf, one to Lillian, and one to Edith. By now, Alvin had forgotten he ever had a fever.

Her violet aura dimmed by the lamplight, Madame Zelincka said, "I must tell you now that there are tramp spirits who infiltrate many sittings hoping to impersonate a familiar loved one for the purpose of instituting mischief. The messages from such beings only confuse true spirit teachings, like a ray of light deflected at its source. They can be hurtful and dangerous. Therefore, determining proof of a spirit's identity is essential. What I would like each of you to do now is to compose a thought or a question on your card that might only be addressed through direct writing by one who knows you best. When you've done so, place the card beneath your chair and leave it there until I ask for it."

Madame Zelincka took the fountain pen and handed it to Edith. "Mrs. Elliotsen, would you please begin?"

"Surely."

The medium raised her voice. "Ethan?"

"Yes, ma'am."

"Are the others here?"

"Yes, ma'am. They each wish to speak. Shall I let them?"

"Soon, dear."

"I learned a song by the river this morning. Would you care to hear it?"

"Of course."

"Ta-ra-ra-boom-dee-ay. Ta-ra-ra-boom-dee-ay."

The farm boy heard a faint giggling echo race about the spirit room. He watched Edith pass the fountain pen to Lillian, who began scribbling onto her card. The flame within the paraffin lamp flickered. Alvin squinted nervously into the dark, but saw nothing. His legs felt numb.

Madame Zelincka said, "That's very nice, Ethan. Can you sing another?"

"No, ma'am. The water's very cold today. I watched three squirrels fight over a walnut. I think it may snow soon."

"Ethan, may I please speak with Joseph Cheney?"

"Yes, ma'am."

Lillian handed the pen to the dwarf, and hid her message card. Oscar stifled a cough. The dwarf rapidly scrawled something and gave the fountain pen back to Madame Zelincka.

The medium extinguished the flame in the paraffin lamp, darkening the spirit room once again. She spoke softly, "Joseph?"

The sitters were each silent.

Alvin felt the barest prickling over his skin, but held his attention on the medium. For perhaps half a minute, Madame Zelincka gazed dimly into the purple shadows beyond the table.

Then, slowly, a green luminous effluence emerged from her eyes and ears and mouth, like a radiant fluid passing into the atmosphere.

"Emanations of ectoplastic strings," the dwarf murmured in the gloom, his own eyes wide with wonder.

"Ghost serpents," said Oscar Elliotsen.

"Pure etherium from across the veil," Edith said, with a smile. "Essence of the divine."

Alvin watched in awe as the glowing ectoplasm curled and floated about the spirit table, briefly caressing the stack of message cards, then winding in and out of the sitters, trailing away from Madame Zelincka like plumes of faint green smoke.

The medium spoke up, "Joseph?"

A man's husky voice echoed out of the darkness across the room. *"Yes, ma'am."*

Alvin searched quickly about for the source while Madame Zelincka said, "Lillian, please ask your question."

Lillian brought her card out from under the table. She spoke sweetly: "My husband Joseph was always quite a deuce with the girls. We first met during college at the Junior Promenade when I was on Reception Committee. Norris Webster introduced us to each other next to the coat closet where Joseph told a particularly clever joke."

"Which three members of our esteemed faculty most resemble a camp breakfast? Bacon, Dunn, Browne!"

The dwarf laughed aloud.

Oscar Elliotsen stifled a cough.

Nodding, Lillian passed her card to Madame Zelincka who glanced at it briefly with a smile. Then the medium inquired, "Are you feeling well, Joseph?"

"I'm not sure. My wife believes I ought to take more exercise. When I was a student at the university, I threw the hammer on Field Day and never lost."

Madame Zelincka smiled. "Joseph, do you know where you are now?"

"I see a table with chairs and a circle of people I've never met. Are you having a party? Was I invited? I suppose I must've been because I'm here, aren't I? Really, I can't quite remember."

The medium asked, "Do you feel lost, Joseph?"

"I've had peculiar forebodings recently. I've been confused and I haven't slept well. There's a strange darkness all about. Is this the Mohonk Mountain House? Lillian and I were married in the Parlor Wing twenty-three years ago. It was my wife's idea to return for our anniversary."

"Joseph insisted we make the same walk up to Sky Top cliff as we had when we were young," Lillian told Madame Zelincka. "The trail was awfully cold in the evening, black as pitch, and quite treacherous coming down. I should have known there would be an accident. My husband suffered terrible ulcerations after his fall, yet refused a physical examination until he was unable to rise from bed at the end of the week."

"I had an accident?"

"Don't you recall?" Madame Zelincka asked.

The husky spirit voice crossed the room. *"I have no memory. I can't think."*

Lillian said, "I prayed by your bedside and mopped your brow for thirteen days, my darling. I held you to the very end."

Softening her voice, the medium told Lillian, "Your husband is gradually losing his earth memories. His mental life now occurs in spiritual darkness which he's experiencing as a form of wakeful delirium." She spoke up. "Joseph?"

"Yes, ma'am?"

"Do you know what year it is?"

"Of course I do. It's 1926."

"No, it isn't," the medium replied. "This is now 1929."

"That's impossible!"

"Yet it's true."

"Where have I been? Am I insane?"

The medium asked, "Do you believe you are?"

"As a man thinketh in his heart, so is he."

"This is no mental derangement or dementia. Three years ago, you passed over to the spirit side of life. You've lost your mortal body, Joseph. Your earthly life is finished."

"I don't believe you. Why, it's utter nonsense. Now I'm sure this is all a silly dream."

"You've been wandering in a twilight state for quite some time now, unconscious of the truth. Do you still need to eat? Do you feel the chill of autumn? We've gathered here in our circle tonight to wake you from this sleep of death that has blocked the spiritual progression which is your natural destiny."

Alvin watched the tulip lamps briefly flicker across the dark. A slight breeze passed by the spirit table bearing a musky odor of shaving soap and cologne, but he saw no one. Were the other sitters not so calm, he'd have been utterly petrified with fright.

"*Oh dear! Lillian, is this not some hideous nightmare? Am I really dead?*"

"Darling, I've missed you so!"

Madame Zelincka said, "Joseph, nobody ever really dies. We simply pass on to an invisible world of higher mental spheres. The grave is not our final goal."

Alvin heard the voice shift again to another corner of the spirit room. "*If I've died, why am I not in heaven?*"

"Heaven is within you, Joseph, as it is with all of us. You're drawn here to the magnetic aura of the living perhaps because of a conscience stricken with discomfort over mistakes you made during your life on earth, or bothersome worries that should no longer concern you."

"*Have you considered the wisdom of disturbing the dead? Perhaps I'm an evil spirit. When I was a boy, I always thought I'd like to be a pickpocket or a highwayman. Perhaps I'm unfit for heaven of any sort.*"

"Rubbish!" Lillian scolded. "Why, darling, you're the most decent, kindhearted man I've ever known."

Madame Zelincka said, "Don't be downhearted, Joseph. This outer darkness you're experiencing is only the tomorrow of death from which each of us rises, sphere to sphere, in our spiritual progression to immortal realms."

"*I seem to have forgotten everything I ever knew about life. I feel so blue. I just want to sleep. Perhaps I'm better off dead, after all.*"

"Joseph, a spirit never dies. These sorrows you've known on the earth plane will all pass away while the flowers you once discarded will bloom again in the summerland. The hour for sleep is done."

"*Will I go sit up in a tree somewhere with Jesus and eat figs?*"

Madame Zelincka answered simply, "Where your treasure is, Joseph, there will your heart be also."

"*I hope to be with my dear Lillian again one day.*"

"You will. Do you see the spirit guides waiting for you beyond the veil?"

"*Oh, yes! Now I do! Great Scott, I hadn't noticed before.*"

"You've awakened at last," Madame Zelincka said. "Joseph, it's time for you to go."

"Is there sympathy beyond the grave?"

"Yes, indeed."

"Thank you."

"Good-bye, darling," Lillian said, her soft eyes bright in the green ectoplasmic glow. "Good-bye."

"Good-bye."

The husky voice faded away.

A chilly gust of air raced through the darkened spirit room and was gone.

Alvin fixed his gaze on the medium who seemed to be drowsing in her chair, both eyes shut, her lovely aura shimmering beneath errant strands of luminous ectoplasm. Was she done now? He was already frazzled and worn out. How long was this sitting supposed to last?

The tulip lamps appeared dimmer still.

Madame Zelincka spoke again, "Ethan?"

"Yes, ma'am?"

"Is Dena Elliotsen willing to speak with us?"

"Yes, ma'am. She's right here."

"Please let her do so."

The sitters waited.

Soon the farm boy felt a peculiar disquiet in the violet darkness. He heard a rustling of petticoats somewhere close by, and thought he smelled a scent of rosewater wafting through the spirit circle. Again he searched the dark and saw no one. He almost coughed, but stifled it quickly.

"Mother?"

A girl's dulcet voice.

Edith Elliotsen straightened in her chair. "Sweetheart, is that you?"

"Mother?"

Madame Zelincka spoke to Edith, "Take the card, dear, from under your chair and read to us now the question you chose, then confirm the answer written beneath it."

"Mother?"

The phantom voice rose in pitch, a strange inflection of urgency. Under a pale glow of writing ectoplasm, Edith retrieved her message card and stared at it through her reading glasses, then gasped.

The girl's voice echoed across the spirit room. *"Mother, are you there?"*

Edith spoke aloud: "Is kitten in the closet, dear?"

"No, ma'am, she's in father's drawer."

"Oh, dear me!" Edith cried, "It's her! My little darling!"

Alvin watched Oscar Elliotsen take the card from his wife and read the ghost script beneath Edith's handwriting. When his chest heaved forth a sob, Edith gently placed a hand on her husband's coat sleeve.

Madame Zelincka spoke into the gloom: "Dena Elliotsen?"

"Yes, ma'am."

"Can you see your mother here across the gate?"

"No, ma'am, it's still so very dark."

Edith explained, "My daughter was blinded by typhoid fever the week of her fourteenth birthday. The poor little dear. It broke our hearts."

"Yet it was I, Mother, who bore the burden of sightlessness thereafter, confined to the downstairs of the house on Porter Street like a helpless infant when my soul so desperately sought the ardor other girls my age already knew."

"That deceiver of tender youth," Edith cautioned, "from which our only wish was to protect you."

"By hiding me away from that most beautiful sorrow? Oh, Mother dear, have you never learned? Desire is the blood of life! Alone at night with my knitting, I hungered for the glow of youthful love and plotted my flight to Boston with no fear that I recall. How often these long years I've wondered if the courage I found to board that train came unexpectedly from my blindness, apart from which I might not have dared enter that vile garment factory on Lincoln Street nor the cold flat I took alone. Yet now I see how the remnants I sorted morning till night all that winter long were woven scrap by scrap into a tawdry lace that came to be my own design."

"You're being cruel," Edith said, her voice quivering. Oscar Elliotsen took his wife's hand.

"No more so than the vain echo of dreams that murmur hope when life promises none. That light of day I felt from my window facing the eastern sky brought sanctuary from unanswered prayers and led me to Robert Watkins in whose arms my heart at last took flight."

"I've always refused to speak his name aloud," said Edith, dabbing one eye with a handkerchief. Alvin heard a faint breeze ripple the burgundy drapes about the room. He thought of those birds in the dark rafters of Uncle Henry's barn.

"A woman loves at her own peril. I hold no bitterness, no remorse. Denying myself that sweet flowering of love for which each of us is born would have been far more shameful. Suppose he had not been destitute of character, and marriage his aspiration, do you imagine me in a pleasant cottage somewhere, belovéd of my own children and content? But that was not my fate. Mother dear, I never shared your unwavering faith in the mercy of the world. When Robert withdrew his love, my sorrow was complete. Alone and bed-ridden with grief, I refused to treat a simple cold until the pneumonia that grew one night out of a sudden fever swept me away from that wretched circumstance."

"Darling, we prayed so hard that you'd come back to us," Edith said, weeping now. "When your father brought me the letter from St. Elizabeth's Hospital, I believe my heart stopped beating altogether."

Alvin noticed a dim gray light in the darkness above the spirit table behind Madame Zelincka. He held his breath as it became a gleam of white that drew nearer the circle.

"Mother, these quiet meadows sustain all my memories of life: the pretty orchard blossoms and sweet clover, that shady brook in the dell, the larks that sang for us each morning, and you and Father whispering beside my cradle and my casket by twilight. Awakening here, I found my blindness merely a fading dream. I walked all day without need of instinct and saw the wind pass through the catalpa trees by the river. I know now, Mother, the soul is like the perfume of the flower, its splendid bloom rising unseen, its essence lovingly savored, its worth beyond beauty."

Dumbfounded, Alvin watched the white luminance descend over the table by the Elliotsens like a cloud of light. Within the heart of that silver radiance, a hazy shadow emerged in the form of a graceful spirit hand that reached down to Edith and gave her a wild rose, still damp with dew.

"I'll always be with you, Mother."

Then the luminous cloud faded away to darkness while Edith and Oscar Elliotsen huddled together, weeping. Across the table, Alvin heard the dwarf whisper something to Lillian about teleplasmic arms and spectral phosphorescence after which the spirit room was quiet once more.

Another couple of minutes passed.

Alvin's heart quit drumming. He let out a breath, shifted his shoes on the carpet, hoping to leave. Then he heard Madame Zelincka speak firmly into the gloom, "Ophelia, are you here?"

Rascal sat up on the parlor cushion he had brought for his chair.

"Your son has come a long way to speak with you," said the medium. A light breeze passed across the room, fluttering through Madame Zelincka's robe. The spirit table trembled and thumped.

The dwarf spoke aloud, "Mother?"

A harmony of whispered voices, nearly inaudible, entered the dark and Alvin thought he heard the faint strains of a piano hymn like those Aunt Hattie played after Sunday dinner on the farm.

Madame Zelincka asked, "Ophelia? Are you here?"

The dim tulip lights flickered and a rhythmic knocking chased along the walls as the spirit table slid half a foot sideways while Edith's white rose and the stack of message cards briefly levitated.

The dwarf called into the dark, "Mother? Is that you?"

A warm draft fragrant with sweet honeysuckle swept into the spirit room and the knocking ceased and the table became still once again.

A pleasant female voice spoke from the shadows. *"Arthur?"*

Madame Zelincka indicated for the dwarf to remove his message card from beneath the chair. Doing so, he read aloud, "We seek at the end of life's rainbow, a treasure we hope to find there — "

"And wealth we do find, but not of the kind we expected, no, something more rare."

Across the room stood a woman dressed in white, her features indistinct as if bathed in morning mist.

"Ophelia Glynn Burtnett?" the medium inquired.

"My mother," confirmed the dwarf, handing his message card to Madame Zelincka.

"Your father wrote that poem in our wedding album a long while ago when we were very young. Do you know he was the handsomest man I ever saw? I felt so proud to sit in his carriage. When I was a girl, I dreamed of white peonies and bridesmaids all in a row and beautiful oaths of love and duty foresworn. To be blessed throughout my life with the endearment of those nearest my heart gave me such joy. Yet good fortune so often leads to forgetfulness. The road is always best on the other side. What I cherished most, your father held in disregard, and what he sought, I never wanted. Do you

believe we can know our destiny before the evidence of it becomes clear? You were my only child, Arthur, born on a summer evening beneath the nursery Grandfather Burtnett built. I needed three days and a wealth of prayer to bring you into this world, and I remember worrying that if I didn't hurry you along, your aunts and uncles would all give up and go home. I wasn't afraid for myself. Augustus said I had a true mother's fight in me and would surely prevail in that good struggle. Early in the season, a family of bluejays had nested in the walnut tree outside my bedroom window and I listened to their chattering all the while. I waited for you longer than anyone thought I could and only when you came forth and drew your first breath as my wonderful child, did I pass on to a life and a purpose that still seems mysterious to me."

"I grew up without you, Mother, all these years," the dwarf said in a trembling voice, "only a photograph of you and a poem on my bedstand."

"You've been very brave."

"I've tried to be a decent and faithful son, though I admit I've had my trials."

"Arthur, human nature hasn't changed a particle since I passed. All we know of morals, high and holy, we find in our own hearts. There is no aristocracy of merit on earth or in heaven absent of that goodness. You've walked in a state of grace all your life, and I've been proud to call you mine."

The farm boy held his gaze on the woman in white across the room whose shimmering spirit garments seemed translucent in the violet dark, her lovely face and slender hands paler than alabaster. Despite the clear white fire of her ghostly countenance, somehow she appeared to Alvin as substantial as anyone else in the spirit room.

The dwarf lowered his eyes. "I've always worried that you'd have been greatly disappointed at seeing me, how I was born to this stature — my deformity. It seems no one in the family had ever in memory … well, I'm told I was quite unexpected."

"Shame on you, Arthur. Your birth was my greatest joy, my love for you more perfect than heaven's gleam. If all your life were a breath of honey, and heartache left to others, would you have had the courage to come seek me here? One day years from now when your morning room is quiet and the blanket that warms your legs has become thread-worn and faded, you'll know that our truest blessings can never be soiled by vain utterances and that in the eyes of those who love us well, our spirit suffers no lasting stain."

The dwarf hesitated, his voice fractured by emotion. Then, like a child seeking favor, he asked, "Will I marry?"

Alvin saw the tulip lights flicker while the manifestation appeared to ripple like pond water under a passing breeze.

"That heart which is penetrated by love for thee will indeed prove true."

Madame Zelincka lightly squeezed the hand of the teary-eyed dwarf who hesitated over his next question, brow furrowed with consternation. What did a loving son require most of his mother's eternal spirit? The farm boy watched intently as the dwarf asked the apparition across the room, "Will my life prove worthy of your sacrifice?"

The woman in white raised her hands toward the spirit table and answered with a radiant smile, *"Arthur, my dear, your life's greatest glory is yet to be revealed."*

With those words, she began to recede into the dark, her lambent spirit form evaporating to a pale translucence like a bright light extinguishing from within.

The dwarf cried out and rose from his chair and stood with his knees at the table as the glowing apparition gradually faded back into the darkness and disappeared. A draft redolent of honeysuckle ruffled the silk curtains and the spirit room fell silent, each of the sitters mute in the wake of the strange spiritistic occurrences.

Alvin heard a creak overhead as somebody walked the floor upstairs.

The dwarf sat back down on his pillow.

After another minute or so, Madame Zelincka spoke up: "Ethan?"

"Yes, ma'am?"

Her lovely violet aura diminishing, Madame Zelincka collected her stack of message cards together and glanced at her guests around the spirit circle. Then she said, "Ethan, may we ask you one more question?"

"Yes, ma'am."

The farm boy stared at the medium.

Lillian Cheney shut her eyes.

"Is this world of strife to end in dust at last?"

Edith Elliotsen squeezed her husband's hand. The dwarf looked toward the curtained shadows where that perfect reflection of his mother had vanished. Alvin noticed a faint odor waft past his face like a child's breath of sour milk.

"Ethan?"

A songbird warbled from a distant tree.

"No, ma'am," a small boy's voice echoed in reply. *"Life is everlasting."*

Alvin Pendergast waited near the ticket booth at the showgrounds entrance in a dusty wind. By the hour on his new wristwatch, half past nine had come and gone and Chester hadn't yet appeared. Circusgoers passed through the gate flushed with glee as the ringing song of the carousel swept across the early autumn dark. A flurry of gold Roman candles boomed among the stars to the cheers of small children, but tonight the farm boy disregarded the hot popcorn and the bellowing barkers. He had seen the elephant and now he wanted to go back home to the Pendergast farm. In the sanitarium, Alvin had witnessed a slight woman named Anna Cates pass away so beset with chronic phthisis that gangrene had developed in one lung, which alternately hissed and gurgled when she spoke. The doctors pronounced her ghastly infections unmistakably hopeless and left her in the consumption ward to die. Rumor had it she owned a house in Ohio tended to by a trusted neighbor, and two calico cats who slept beside her pillow at night, but no surviving family in the world. Her discharge from the sanitarium back to Oberlin was implacably denied by the administrator, so she retired to bed that last week of her miserable life, refusing to rise day or night until she was called to heaven, *"half to forget the wandering and the pain, half to remember days that have gone by, and dream and dream that I am home again."*

Feeling light-headed, Alvin watched a stocky marshal ride past on horseback wearing a white ten-gallon hat and shiny six-guns on his belt. Deputies from Icaria wandered in and out of the showgrounds, trailed by painted clowns holding seltzer bottles and nickel balloons. He watched two schoolboys in blue denim overalls light a thick firecracker and toss it over the fence into the wagon circle. When it went off with a noisy bang, both ran away to hide in the grassy meadow. Another quarter of an hour went by without Chester showing up and the farm boy grew cold and anxious. He feared both the known and the unknown. His fever rose steadily with a hacking cough he fought to subdue. Windblown grit stung his eyes and drew tears. Buttoning up his jacket, Alvin turned away from the ticket booth and the flapping banners and stared out across the wooded meadow toward Icaria, lit yellow beneath the evening clouds.

Soon, Chester waltzed out of the dark, looking dapper in a striped gray suit with a white carnation on his lapel. He was whistling a smart "I'll Say She Does," with a hint of satisfaction on his lips. Circus-going kiddies from downtown dodged around him like he was a king. He lit a cigarette and tossed the match into the damp grass. Alvin gave him a short wave, then regretted it when Chester frowned. The gangster angled away from the main gate and Alvin followed him, trying to act more casual now.

Once they were in the grassy shadows away from the big crowds, Chester stopped and gave the farm boy a once-over. "Say, kid, you're looking a little giddy around the gills. You just get off the Whirly-Gig or something?"

"I ain't been nowhere at all," Alvin answered, wondering how pasty he really looked. Was it so clear? He tried to stiffen up, act ace high like he knew Chester expected.

"Well, don't worry. We won't be here much longer." Putting his back to the crowds at the showgrounds entrance, Chester told Alvin, "I got it all taken care of after supper. I doped out the plan with Lester over a couple of steaks, and paid a visit to Spud Farrell. He's got an office in the icehouse out by the trainyards. Not half bad for a dump like this. Back in Cicero, he was selling rock candy under a crumb box at the Starvation Army. Of course, now that he's a big wheel out here in hickville, well, some fellows seem to have it in mind these days to turn every square racket into a shakedown, I don't know why." He stared Alvin straight in the eye. "Do I look like sucker bait to you, kid?"

"No."

Chester smiled, then took a drag off the cigarette and exhaled into the cold breeze. "I guess good ol' Spud thought he could fry the fat out of us once we tipped over the joint, like he'd nabbed us jaywalking and was going to blow off to our mommies. I don't mind sharing the gravy train, but we haven't been dough-heavy all summer and everyone knows it. When I offered to kick in a third and he wouldn't give, I figured it was time to knock off the song and dance and tell him the bad news. He made a lousy choice. I'm letting you and Lester divvy up his cut."

The farm boy's limbs went numb. "You killed Spud?"

"He was a menace to my peace of mind. Now he's out of the game. Soon as we're through here tonight, I want you and the midget to get your bags and beat it out of that flea trap. I'll be waiting for you in a motor over on Ash Street. Just don't shout it to the world when you're leaving. Get me?"

Alvin felt petrified. "Sure."

Chester flashed a grin. "I tell you, kid, this circus is the softest touch I've ever seen. When the tents close at midnight, Lester'll kick in the box, and we'll take our split and do a Houdini. Laswell won't know up from down."

"Nope."

"All I need you to do is keep an eye on his trailer for me until I do the honors with my little hotsy. She's expecting me any minute now and a smart fellow doesn't keep a sexy dame waiting. Just keep track of the comings and goings at Laswell's trailer so nothing queers the deal before we pop him."

"Which one's his?" Alvin asked, utterly confused about his role in all this. Did Lester know about him and the dwarf?

"Did you see those old firewagons back of the Big Top?"

Alvin nodded. "Yeah, I guess so."

"Well, Laswell's trailer is right behind them. It's painted up orange and blue top to bottom like a French whore, with a crocodile eating a naked Chinaman on the side. You can't miss it."

"All right."

"Just keep your eyes peeled for anything fishy going on there. Think you can handle that?"

"Sure."

Chester took a drag off his cigarette. "Where's the midget?"

The farm boy shrugged. "Fooling around somewhere, I suppose."

"All right, well, just make sure you two are there when it's time to bug out. I'd hate to leave you behind. If the cops get hold of you, they'll break your guts before breakfast and pretty soon they'll turn on the heat for me, and that'd make us both a couple of very unhappy fellows."

"Don't worry," Alvin said, scared to death now. "We'll be there."

"I believe you. Just be on time."

Chester took another puff off his cigarette, then flicked it away and went into the circus. Alvin waited a couple of minutes, then followed through the main gate. Sawdust blew everywhere in the cold wind. Confetti spun up out of Clown Alley as a piping steam fiddle played a rambunctious melody. Alvin crossed the showgrounds toward the Big Top, oblivious to the costumed apes on camelback, golden-horned satyrs trailing black-eyed hermaphrodites, the glint of ancient wares in a makeshift Pantechnicon. All he could think about was whether or not his disease would kill him before Chester did. He guessed now that he ought to have gone back to the sanitarium, after all. Truth was, Doc Hartley had always been kind to him. It wasn't his fault Alvin had a relapse. Lots of folks did. Some got better and others died. That was just how life played out. It wasn't anybody's fault. Not like the deliberate killings of Rosa Jean and her daddy, that bank clerk at Stantonsburg, the preacher at Allenville, and that poor kid he and Rascal buried in the muddy stall last month. Now Spud, too. How many others as well? For shame, for shame! Frenchy would tell Alvin he was caught between a shit and a sweat, all for having crossed the river with Chester that night. Frenchy also used to say there's no use in sticking your neck out till you know what the score is, but Alvin hadn't paid any notice to that and now he was on the run with a cruel stonehearted killer who would likely shoot him over a hamburger roll.

A tiny hand tugged at the farm boy's right sleeve.

Turning about, Alvin found the diminutive Emperor Nero just behind him, white toga splotched with burgundy wine stains, laurel wreath tipped slightly askew.

Suppressing a burp, the clown midget told the farm boy, "Your presence is requested at the wagon of Mademoiselle Estralada."

"Pardon?"

"It's dreadfully important."

"I ain't supposed to go nowhere but here. I got an appointment I can't pull out of."

"It's been called off."

Alvin frowned. "Says who?"

"Says I, but it ain't just my opinion. Let's go."

Another harsh gust kicked up, further soiling Emperor Nero's white toga with grime. A pair of African elephants wailed under the Big Top. Circus cannons thundered.

Emperor Nero whistled to Alvin from beside the ticket booth. "What in thunder are you waiting for? You're not afraid, are you?"

The farm boy walked closer. In fact, he was quite a bit afraid. "Maybe. I ain't seen nobody put one over on him yet."

Emperor Nero sneered. "Aw, there's nothing to it! We'll fix that big stiff, all right. You just wait. If he starts any trouble, I tell you, I used to be pretty handy myself. What do you say?"

The farm boy shrugged. Why not? Any choice he made now was the same as another. Besides, he had already taken plenty of orders from Chester and what good had it done him?

Banners flapped loudly in the wind. A fresh crowd of towners lined up at the ticket booth. On the other side, Emperor Nero stepped back to let Alvin pass, and then kicked the bottom of the booth to draw the barker's attention. "Say, hatchet-face, what's the dope? I hear you got bitched by Little Flora last night. Ain't that a shame?"

The fellow handed out a pair of tickets, refusing to look at the circus midget. "You ought to scram before I push your face in."

Emperor Nero gave the ticket booth another hard kick. "She says getting familiar with you scared the life half out of her."

Someone in the crowd heard that and laughed aloud.

The fellow threw aside the ticket punch and slid off his stool. "Say, who do you think you are, shooting off your head? I'll poke you in the nose!"

Emperor Nero put up his fists. "Oh, you want to rough it up a bit, do you? Why, that'd be swell by me. I'll be laughing myself sick in nothing flat."

The barker started away from the ticket booth. "You'll start squealing when you get what's coming to you. Just stay right there. I'll fix you, you little pop."

"Aw, go sit on a tack, Nellie!" Emperor Nero kicked a cloud of dust up toward the barker, then ran past the farm boy, shouting, "Come on, kid, let's beat it!"

The midget rushed off through the scattered crowds, Alvin hurrying right behind him. People in line at the soda pop concession laughed as they went by. More rockets fizzed and boomed and schoolchildren ran toward the sparkling lights of the ringing carousel. Emperor Nero led Alvin between twin tents of the giraffe-necked Negresses, Zira and Lot, and a snaggle-toothed sorceress named Fatima who wore smoke-dark glasses and blew green fire off her fingertips at passersby. A stink of trained pigs and filthy pony punks overwhelmed the warm roasted peanuts and popcorn as the farm boy chased Emperor Nero behind the cage wagons where a lion tamer in safari suit and Pith helmet smoked a fat cigar and recited his spiel for a later performance while the jungle cats paced and growled amid swarms of black flies.

Crawling under a rope line behind the museum wagons and elephant tubs, Emperor Nero chortled, "Oh, that companion of yours is a very wicked fellow."

"Huh?"

"I tell you, he's got all the angles."

The farm boy banged his foot on a tent stake next to the Apple Family's dog and pony show. He heard drum taps inside the tent and a clash of cymbals. Emperor Nero crossed a narrow alley of manure and sawdust toward a painted gypsy wagon parked beneath a leafy cottonwood tree at the north boundary of the showgrounds. Lilac bushes curled under the rear iron wheels. Oil lamps glowed behind linen shades within. On the wagon steps, Josephine sat beside Chief Crazy Horse, and Alvin thought he saw a couple more circus midgets lurking in the shadows by the fenceline. The carved front door was shut.

"You're late," said Crazy Horse, getting up. His great feathered war bonnet drooped onto the wooden step above him.

"You're darned right I am!" Emperor Nero replied, fixing his laurel wreath. "That big horse Johnny Mills tried to kill me back there. Ain't it so, kid?"

The farm boy nodded. "Sure it is."

Tiny Josephine spoke up, "Mademoiselle Estralada invited the gangster to call on her at half past the hour. Merlin says they're still with Billy the Kid and a bottle of Scotch behind the Big Top. What if he figures out it's a stall to get him pickled? Just thinking about it gives me the cold shivers. I believe this is very dangerous."

"Aw, you're imagining things," said Chief Crazy Horse. "We're all set now, ain't we? What's the trouble?" He straightened his war bonnet. "We'll put it over, all right. Don't you worry."

"I ain't following any of this," Alvin remarked, more nervous by the minute now. Going back on Chester scared the hell out of him. He coughed as the wind gusted. "What's it all about?"

"Beg your pardon, dear?" said Josephine, smoothing her blue satin gown as she rose from the wagon step. Her tiny feet were pinched into gold satin mules with silver nightingales painted on the toes.

"Well, nobody's told me nothing yet," the farm boy growled. "Chester ain't no dumbbell. Try to cross him, he'll shoot the whole lot of us in the head."

"Maybe so," said Chief Crazy Horse, "but we can't poop out on a pal. Why, if you fellows don't do nothing, sooner or later you're both liable to get pinched, and Ol' Sparkie'll be the finish of that."

Josephine added, "I wouldn't see my little sweetheart hurt for anything in the world."

"Oh, he's got a marvelous plan," said Emperor Nero, knotting the wine-stained toga into his fist. "I just know we'll knock it over."

Chief Crazy Horse told Alvin, "Don't forget, kid, these thicknecks ain't so tough they can't get remunerated like the rest of us."

Alvin saw a pair of Keystone Kops crawl out from beneath the painted wagon. One of them with an oddly familiar babyface gave him a grand stage salute. When Alvin waved back, the midget blew lightly on his police whistle and chased after his partner through the thick sumac and prickly ash that cluttered the fenceline.

Kaiser Wilhelm hurried out from the alleyway behind the cage wagons, waving his tiny arms. "They're coming! They're coming!" The spiked helmet fell off the Kaiser's head into the dirt and he stooped to pick it up.

Josephine stole a quick look at her gold watch pendant. "Oh, dear! It's time!"

"I tell you, we'll panic 'em," Chief Crazy Horse told Alvin, jumping down off the wagon steps. "Just you wait and see."

Emperor Nero grabbed the farm boy by the sleeve. "Come on, kid. The show's starting."

"Where're we going?"

"The best damned seat in the house," he said, shoving Alvin underneath the painted wagon where the farm boy saw a trapdoor hanging open. "Go on, climb in."

"What?"

Emperor Nero gave Alvin a stiff kick in the pants. "Make it snappy!"

"Ain't you coming, too?"

"Nope, I got to shove off. The gypsy ain't so liberal with the rest of us."

The farm boy crawled next to the trap door and had a peek up into the shadowy interior of the gypsy wagon. "There ain't room enough!"

Alvin looked behind him and saw the circus midget had already gone. Scared of Chester finding him where he didn't belong, he reached through the opening, grabbed for a handhold, and pulled himself upward into the dark. As he rolled clear, someone jerked the trap door closed.

A match flared briefly, illuminating the dwarf who giggled and blew the match out again.

"What the hell is this?" the farm boy grunted, shifting his knees to get comfortable. It was so dark he couldn't tell up from down. He smelled a peppery odor of incense and burning kerosene, and when he leaned backward he felt the brush of clothes hanging on a rack behind him.

"Shhh! We're in a costume closet," Rascal murmured. "Will you please be quiet? They'll be here any minute."

"Well, I can't see nothing. It's dark as pitch."

"Shhh!" The dwarf crept forward and slid open a thin foot-wide rectangular slot in the closet wall that revealed the wagon's lamp-lit interior. "Here," he whispered, "have a look."

Peeking through the narrow slot, Alvin saw a cozy boudoir draped in paisley textiles and bamboo like a Turkish harem, a pillow-heaped divan, Chinese lilies in cut glass flower vases, hand mirrors and Japanese fans on a tea table, muslin curtained windows, and a beaded portière concealing the front of the wagon.

"It's lovely, isn't it?" the dwarf remarked. "Why, I could easily imagine myself — "

"Shhh!"

Alvin heard voices from the wagon steps, an iron key turning in the door lock. He shrank back from the slot as the floorboards trembled under the heavy footfall. The dwarf shoved by for a look.

Chester Burke spoke as the door swung shut. "Go ahead, sweetheart, argue me out of it."

The farm boy pushed the dwarf away from the slot as Mademoiselle Estralada slipped through the beaded portière, her blue glass-crystal earrings and silver bracelets jingling. She was dressed head to foot in shiny indigo and gold silk sashes, her skin coffee-brown, eyes brighter than wet pearls. She spoke to Chester while unlocking the bottom drawer of a teak cabinet. "I just knew you were thirsty."

"Maybe I should get a haircut instead." Chester lit a cigarette as he came into the boudoir. "I ought to cut out getting drunk, start leading a clean life, and all that."

"It's not healthy to deny oneself pleasure," the gypsy remarked, reaching down into the cabinet. Alvin watched her draw out a pale blue decanter of ice water and a pair of tall heavy fluted glasses. "I've always believed intoxications to be borrowed dreams."

Chester exhaled a plume of smoke. "Sweetheart, I can see you and me are going to get on swell together. What do you say we take a hootch bottle and go hire a car for a joyride, just the two of us?"

"Oh, there's no need to go anywhere," the gypsy said, sliding open a drawer in the upper cabinet for a china saucer and a pair of silver vented spoons. "I'm sure I have everything you could ever want right here in this wagon."

"Oh yeah?" Chester cracked a grin.

"Be contented with thy present fortune," said Mademoiselle Estralada as she opened a tiny porcelain bowl atop the cabinet. "Constancy on thy part will meet a due return."

She placed a handful of sugar lumps on the china saucer with the vented spoons. Alvin muffled a cough with his sleeve, and the dwarf dug an elbow angrily into his ribs. It was stifling in the closet and Alvin wasn't sure how long he could remain crowded into there without getting sick.

"Say, didn't I hop into my best suit to date you up tonight?" Chester asked, picking up a scratched glass daguerreotype in a faded green plush frame. He examined it intently for a few moments. "I tell you, I'm a dandy fine fellow, once you get to know me."

Mademoiselle Estralada smiled. "You're a very pretty man."

Chester replaced the daguerreotype, and tapped ash into a silver ashtray. "Well, it's not all that often I get taken in hand by a sweet peach like you, too. Maybe tomorrow night you'll let me blow you to dinner, what do you say?"

"Why, that would be wonderful." Among the stuffed satin pillows on the divan were beaded pincushions embroidered with fancy chenille and pearls. Mademoiselle Estralada made room among these for Chester. "I hope this is comfortable."

"Oh, sure it is." He brought the ashtray with him as he sat down, then eased back onto one of the stuffed pillows. "It's swell."

Wiping sweat from his forehead, Alvin watched the gypsy take a round wicker basket from behind the divan and draw out a cloudy green bottle which she placed on the teak cabinet with the water decanter and fluted glasses, the vented spoons and sugar lumps.

Chester had a drag off his cigarette. "What're we drinking, honey?"

Mademoiselle Estralada smiled. "La Fée Verte."

"Beg your pardon?"

She showed him the bottle whose label read *Pernod Fils - 60°*.

"I'll be damned, that's 120 proof."

"Too strong for you?"

"Hell no, I've been drinking alcorub all week. I'll be all right. I'm full of pep. You like this hightoned liquor, do you?"

The gypsy smiled again. *"Avec les Fleurs, avec les Femmes, avec L'Absinthe, avec le Feu, on peut se divertir un peu, jouer son rôle en quelque drame."*

Chester laughed. "Gee, I ain't parley-voo'd fran-say with a dame since the war." He tapped his cigarette over the ashtray.

"Oh, were you in France?" the gypsy asked, pulling the cork from the bottle of Swiss absinthe.

"Me and 'Black Jack' Pershing himself at Saint-Mihiel with the Austrian 88's." Chester sung, *"It's the wrong way to tickle Mary, it's the wrong place to go."*

He laughed.

Mademoiselle Estralada said, "That's very nice."

She poured the absinthe into the first glass, filling about a third of it with a lovely emerald liquid that glimmered in the lamplight.

Chester smiled. "Thanks a million. I tell you, that war was the graft of the century. All I got out of it was a drink habit and some cheap chromos for a souvenir." He winked. "Don't worry, honey. I came back clean."

"Did you kill anyone?" the gypsy asked, pouring an inch less absinthe into the other glass. A sweet scent of licorice filtered into the sweltering closet. Alvin had never seen such pretty liquor in his life. Just looking at the green drink made him thirsty.

"Naw, I'm a pacifist. I didn't hold much for shooting scrapes. I preferred bourbon and dice with my pals in the drinkeries. It was a hell of a lot safer."

"That's very sensible."

Mademoiselle Estralada put a lump of sugar in one of the vented spoons, then took the pale blue decanter, placed the spoon over the fluted glass, and dribbled ice water onto the sugar, gradually dissolving it through the spoon into the emerald absinthe below.

Chester took one last drag off the cigarette butt, and snuffed it out in the silver ashtray. "Say, that reminds me, this beauty pageant you were telling me about, that wouldn't have been at the Navy Pier, would it? See, I went out to a speakie on the South Side one evening to shake a hoof with a dame from Halstead Street. You know, the sort a fellow wants to slick up for even if he's just taking her downtown to a ping-pong parlor."

The gypsy lightly stirred the mixture, her spoon making a pleasant tinkling sound as the swirling green liquid became a cloudy opalescent. Then she gave the glass to Chester. "À votre santé."

"Thanks." He sniffed it, and took a sip. "Say, that's not half bad."

"It's sweet, no?"

He took a longer sip and licked his lips. "Yeah, sort of minty."

"I'm happy you like it."

"Sure I do." Chester took a long swig, draining half the glass. "Anyhow, trouble was, this dame's pop was one of those old-timers who thinks nobody younger than himself'll ever amount to anything. If a fellow dating his little girl wasn't rubbing elbows with the well-to-do, he thought she'd laid an egg for letting the fellow pay a call on her in the first place."

Chester took another drink of absinthe while the gypsy stirred her own glass. "Well, she wasn't exactly a society dame herself, but when I bought her a fox neckpiece, he acted like I hadn't done anything more than have her down to a sweetshop for a couple of chocolate drops. Told her I was a missing link! Well, that made me pretty sore, so I fibbed to the cops that his alleydog'd bitten me in the back of the leg and they came and took it to the pound. I tell you, that old goat cried like a dame when he found out."

Chester finished the glass of absinthe. He studied it briefly, and gave the glass back to Mademoiselle Estralada. "Gee, that was swell. How about another?"

"Certainly."

Alvin watched the gypsy set her own glass aside and fill Chester's half up with absinthe. She took another lump of sugar with the vented spoon and slowly dissolved more ice water into the gangster's glass.

"At any rate," Chester said, settling back on the divan, "I got nothing to kick about tonight."

"You seem very happy."

"Sure I am."

The dwarf scuttled away from Alvin into the wardrobe of dresses where he covered his face with one of the gypsy's gowns and sneezed. Then he crawled back to the slot just as Mademoiselle Estralada returned Chester's glass to him. "Here you are."

"Thanks." He drank half of it down in one long gulp and broke a grin afterward. "Gee, that's refreshing."

The gypsy sipped her own absinthe, then sat down next to Chester on the puffy divan. A wind gust outside shook the wagon windows. Lamps flickered. She remarked, "Lester says you're from the Big Town."

Chester took another drink. "Not lately. I had a run-in last spring with some mental defectives mucking around Lauterbach's saloon in Cicero. They were pretending to be snoopers in their Sunday blacks while hijacking two dozen barrels of rum a month out of the storehouses in Skaggs grocery trucks. Too bad none of 'em were any too good at it."

Alvin watched Chester finish off his second glass of absinthe, and wipe his lips with the back of one hand. Madamoiselle Estralada asked, "You were a watchman?"

He shook his head. "Naw, I worked for a messenger service Lauterbach hired to send these sports a notice about how unhappy he was with the job they were doing. After me and some of the boys delivered them a valentine to a garage at North Clark Street, I decided I ought to get away from the liquor traffic for a while, maybe buy a second-hand motor, go see some of the country."

The gypsy smiled. "What a marvelous idea. Would you care for another drink?"

Chester gave her the empty glass. His eyes had drooped a fair amount since entering the painted wagon, his speech deteriorated to a mild slur. "Don't mind if I do."

Mademoiselle Estralada filled his fluted glass more than half full with absinthe. Once again she performed her ritual with the sugar lumps and the vented spoon and the dribbling ice water. Alvin began to feel closed in and worried that Chester had a cast-iron stomach and could probably drink arsenate of lead without getting knocked flat.

Chester picked up one of her Japanese fans and waved it about. "Say, I thought you were gonna tell my fortune."

Mademoiselle Estralada stirred the drink. "Would you still like me to?"

She tapped the spoon clean on the rim of the absinthe glass and set it aside. Her painted eyelashes glittered in the kerosene shadows.

"Why sure, it'd be swell."

The pretty gypsy gave Chester his third glass of absinthe, then sat down again beside him on the divan and took his free hand in her own and gently traced the map of his palm with her fingertips while he drank two-thirds of the sweet liquor. "Let not distrust mar thy happiness."

Chester kept his eyes on her as he took another drink. He waited for her to speak again. When she didn't, he frowned. "Is that all? Nothing about me and Sunshine Charlie and a basement full of mazuma? I thought you were a fortune teller. You sure ain't no Evangeline Adams, honey. Go on, try again, but this time tell me how big my fortune's going to be."

He drank the rest of his absinthe and let the fluted glass roll off his fingers onto the divan. In the closet, the dwarf started to whisper something until Alvin hushed him.

Mademoiselle Estralada frowned. "Please don't scold me. When I was a child, I tamed lions for the circus in Budapest and charmed the king cobra."

"Sister, I don't know that I'd hire you to train a flock of seals if you weren't any better at it than you are at telling a fellow's fortune."

Narrowing her eyes, the gypsy took his other hand and rapidly retraced the lines across his palm. Then she advised, "If thou payest attention to all the departments of thy calling, a fortune awaits thee, greater than any treasure within the country in which thou residest."

Chester cracked a sloppy grin. "Gee, now that's more like it, sweetheart. Sounds like I ought to break into the foreign oil game, what do you think?"

The dark-skinned gypsy leaned over and retrieved Chester's empty glass from the divan, then stood up, her jewelry tinkling in the shadowy boudoir. She told him, "As the seasons vary, so will thy fortune."

Chester laughed. "Oh yeah? Well, here's one for you, sweetheart: As long as dandelions bloom, as long as fruit ripens, as long as grain grows, just so long will men drink! Now, go ahead and fill 'er up again. I'm getting thirsty."

"If you like," the gypsy replied, taking Chester's glass back to the bottle of Pernod Fils.

"I sure do."

Alvin watched Madamoiselle Estralada sip briefly from her own drink, then pour more absinthe from the green bottle into Chester's glass. Black wisps of burning kerosene diffused the lamplight throughout the boudoir.

Chester spoke up from the liquor trance he had been lapsing into for the past quarter hour. "What do you say you come over here and we tell each other some smutty stories?"

The gypsy stirred the absinthe into another milky green cloud. She arched an eyebrow. "You wish to be naughty?" The spoon clinked on the inside of Chester's glass.

"You bet I do."

Mademoiselle Estralada put down the vented spoon, brought him the glass of absinthe, and kissed him on the cheek. He grabbed her by the elbow and kissed her on the lips.

"Sweetheart," he murmured as he let go, "you just drain me up."

The gypsy smiled.

Chester drank half the glass, then burped. "Say, what do you got in this liquor of yours? Gasoline?"

"Elixir of wormwood," Mademoiselle Estralada replied, "grown in the Val-de-Travers."

"You don't say." Chester drank another gulp, his mouth smeared crimson with the gypsy's evening lipstick. "Well, it's got one hell of a wallop, whatever it is."

"I'm so glad you enjoy it."

"A good cocktail sure makes the evening go, don't it?" Chester poured more absinthe down his throat, then stared cockeyed at the gypsy. "How come you ain't sitting here beside me, honey? Got a tummy ache?"

He giggled like he was daffy.

Mademoiselle Estralada reached behind her to the tea table between the closet door and the divan and drew out a Chinese lily from the cut glass vase.

Chester said, "Make love to me, honey, and I promise I'll take you to Jelly Roll Morton's show at the Cotton Club next week. Cross my heart." He gulped more absinthe and started blinking strangely. "You see if I don't."

The gypsy sniffed the delicate lily as she swayed in front of Chester. "Darling, I'm afraid I'm awfully done in tonight."

Alvin watched Chester drink to the bottom of his fourth glass of absinthe. The gangster groused, "Aw, so that's how it is, sweetheart, you don't love me, do you?" His voice had degenerated now to a sad drunkard's slur.

"Of course, I do, you pretty man. You know I do."

Chester dropped his empty glass onto the Persian rug in front of the divan. "I'm not a bad sort," he mumbled. "I tell you, we'll have packs of fun, won't we?"

"Sure we will, darling," Mademoiselle Estralada murmured in a soothing tone as Chester passed out. "Beautiful fun."

The farm boy and dwarf waited silently behind the hidden closet slot, hardly breathing in the dark. Wind rattled the wagon as they watched Mademoiselle Estralada stroke Chester's forehead with her fingertips. After a few minutes she quit and whispered something into his ear. Then she turned toward the closet and nodded.

"Let's go," the dwarf said, nudging Alvin away from the trapdoor.

"Huh?"

The wagon's front door opened and Alvin heard a flurry of footsteps. One of the Keystone Kops poked his head through the beaded curtain. He held a cotton cloth and a red rubber clown nose, which he handed wordlessly to the gypsy. The farm boy watched bug-eyed as Mademoiselle Estralada went back to the divan and stuffed the fat clown nose into Chester's mouth and tied a fierce gag around the back of his head with the cotton cloth. Both Kaiser Wilhelm and another Keystone Kop slipped into the boudoir.

"Are they going to kill him?" Alvin whispered to the dwarf who had already dropped down through the trap door.

"Oh, heavens no! That would be murder. Hurry up!"

The farm boy heard the circus midgets dragging something into the gypsy's boudoir, then the dwarf tugged on his ankle and Alvin wriggled his way back down out of the closet and dropped onto his knees in the sawdust beneath the painted wagon. As he crawled out into the cold wind, the farm boy told the dwarf, "When he sees what we done to him, he'll shoot us all in the head."

"No, he won't."

Across the showgrounds, the shrill music of the grand calliope, *Seraphonium*, piped into the night air with the noise of the gleeful crowds. By the front stairs, Emperor Nero and Chief Crazy Horse and Merlin and Sir Lancelot and Billy the Kid had gathered with more Keystone Kops, all bearing grave expressions. A wild animal cage had been rolled up next to the gypsy's wagon, its iron door swung open.

The dwarf took Alvin by the arm. "Come on now, we have to leave."

A chill ran through the farm boy, fear needling his spine. He said, "I tell you, this is all a lot of nonsense. He'll kill us for sure."

"Let's go."

They left the painted wagon to head off in the direction of the noisy midway. Nearby, a great cheer went up as someone rang the big steel gong atop the Strongman Pole. After Alvin's confinement in the dark closet, the glittering lights of Laswell's Circus Giganticus seemed wildly incandescent, a dazzling barrage of electric merriment. The farm boy's head swam, his legs tingled, as he chased the dwarf past the Palace of Mirrors and Laswell's shivery Hall of Freaks toward the whirling Ferris Wheel where lovely little Josephine sat waiting for them atop an apple crate between the dart throw and the shooting gallery. The hot roseate lights dyed her powdered pompadour a glittery pink like cotton candy and she held a paper fan at her chin to protect her show makeup from the windblown grime of the evening midway. When she saw the dwarf emerging from the crowd by the penny pitch, she shot to her feet with a squeal. The dwarf rushed forward to receive an embrace.

Josephine kissed him on the cheek. "My darling, you were so brave!"

Catching his breath as he came up behind her, the farm boy remarked, "Aw, he ain't done nothin' but watch."

The pretty circus midget smiled. "You were both very brave."

"Well, I guess that's so."

With a solemn voice, the dwarf told Josephine, "This is the beginning of the end."

She nodded. "Then we ought to be very careful."

Behind them, the glittering Ferris Wheel stopped briefly to discharge a load of rowdy passengers, mostly young people anxious to rejoin the midway crowds. Perhaps a hundred yards away, just beyond the nickel games and the hootchy-kootchy tent, a big roar went up in the direction of the animal cages. Alvin heard a round of applause amid the buzzing "oohs" and "aahs" of delighted children. The fresh tide of strolling circus-goers along the midway shifted immediately toward the excitement. Even the sideshow talkers and pitchmen paused in mid-spiel, looking somewhat quizzical.

"Let's all wait here," Josephine advised, her hand on the dwarf.

He shook his head. "No, dear. My friend and I must see this through to its conclusion, but perhaps you should stay. It'll certainly be perilous."

"What're you cooking up now?" Alvin asked as he watched a pack of panting schoolboys rush up the circus midway toward the commotion. His own head was buzzing with fever and excitement.

"You and I have one last duty to perform," replied the dwarf. "I'm afraid it's unavoidable."

"If I stay here," Josephine asked, "will you promise to come back safely?"

"You have my word."

"Then I won't go. Please be careful, darling."

She leaned forward and kissed the dwarf and hugged him tightly. Once they broke apart, the dwarf turned to the farm boy. "We mustn't be cowards."

"I ain't saying nothing till you feed me the dope on where we're going."

"This way," the dwarf said, directing Alvin into the weltering crowds up the midway, which resembled a street parade of circus-goers and roughnecks and curious tent performers in silken capes and silver spangles. Half the distance to the furor, a bearded albino magician stood high on a gilded stool, casting white doves into the night sky. Here and there, somersaulting clowns zigzagged toward the hubbub. Farther ahead, the farm boy saw a mob of people jamming together near the Topsy-Turvy House. The dwarf cut a path closer yet until he and the farm boy drew at last within sight of the ballyhoo — a hulking caged gorilla hauled out from the menagerie onto the crowded midway for all to see. Atop the iron cage, a sign read:

CONGO THE GREAT!
FEROCIOUS MAN-EATING BEAST FROM DARKEST AFRICA!!!

A gang of boys had already encircled the exhibit, banging on the bars and taunting the creature with sticks. No trainer showed his face. The burly gorilla lolled in one squalid corner of the wild animal cage, heedless of the clamor. People shouted filthy curses and hurled garbage. Arriving from the Big Top, the Dixie Jubilee Minstrels played a stirring "Invictus" to exuberant cheers. Then Alvin saw a boy with a hefty firecracker light it with a safety match and toss the firecracker into the cage beside the gorilla. When it exploded with an ear-jarring bang, the monster awoke with a vicious roar, sweeping most of the crowd back from the iron cage. A tall boy carrying a long stout stick jabbed the gorilla from behind. Two deputies from Icaria emerged from the crowd to chase the boy away, but another youth tossed a second burning firecracker at the gorilla. It detonated an instant after hitting the beast, driving the creature into a frenzy. Howling with rage, the huge gorilla threw itself at the bars, side to side, then leaped for the front of the cage whose iron door, when struck by the angry beast, simply swung open to the riotous midway. A red-haired fellow in a plaid tam o'shanter standing next to Alvin and the dwarf fainted dead away as the gorilla climbed down from the iron cage and bellowed at its tormentors. Women screamed. Children ran. The gorilla moved toward those too frightened to escape as a strident voice from the gallery behind the Topsy-Turvy House shouted, "SHOOT HIM! SHOOT HIM!"

Which the deputies certainly did, emptying both their revolvers into the crazed beast from a dozen feet away, firing and firing and firing, until the gorilla toppled over backward.

When the echo of gunshots had fled across the dark, a strange hush permeated the midway.

Not a soul moved.

Only the colored flags and banners flapping in the cold wind over the Big Top disturbed the quiet.

Then one of the deputies approached the fallen gorilla and poked the carcass with the toe of his boot. He holstered his revolver and walked carefully around the perimeter of the beast whose blood soaked the dirt. He paused at the gorilla's head, then bent down for a closer look. He frowned. "Well, I'll be damned."

He leaned forward and undid two buttons poorly hidden in the fur at the neckline.

"Looky-here, Tom!" he called to his partner.

Then the deputy slipped off the head of the fallen beast, exposing the ashen lifeless face of Chester Burke. "Why, this ain't no gorilla. It's just some fellow in a monkey suit."

One morning in early October, Alvin Pendergast sat in a prairie grass meadow watching the old trucks and painted wagons of Emmett J. Laswell's Traveling Circus Giganticus load up along a narrow dirt road that led west beyond the woods to a farther country. He had packed his own suitcase in the upper dark of the boardinghouse and left by the back door without saying a word. He brought three apples and a handful of crackers in the pockets of his coat and ate one of the apples while he sat there. His brown Montgomery Ward suitcase lay beside him in the damp switchgrass. Except for the spare cash-money Chester had neglected to collect from the dwarf, the farm boy believed it contained all he owned in the world.

Half a year ago he had left home for fear of being put in the grave, woefully ignorant of life. He had thought to escape somehow the relapse of consumption that raced through his blood by going away where nobody he laid eyes upon would judge him according to the prognosis of his decay, where each day would be a clean slate upon which brave new adventures would be written. Instead, some secret corner of his heart longed for familiarities unaffected by disease: a bee-swarmed path behind Culbertson's lumber shanties, goodnight melodies from his daddy's radio set, that old signalman on the Burlington railway staggering along the tracks at six o'clock each evening with a load of hootch in him, the damp Illinois corn wind in autumn. Guarded mercies too numerous to evade. Six months of sneaking in and out of these strange towns had left him lonely and tired, reconciled to worsening nightsweats and a malignant guilt. On the wooded path back to the boardinghouse after Chester's death at the circus, Alvin had asked the dwarf about the disposition of the gangster's departed spirit, if he knew where such sinners reside in the afterlife. The dwarf explained that their late companion was a moral imbecile whose criminal passions had consigned him forever to a lightless Hades, incapable of inflicting further pain and misery on fellow souls yet held slave by his habitual desire to do so. He would thirst but never drink, complicit in his own agony. There is no peace for the wicked and the damned, the dwarf assured Alvin, and left it at that. They were free now, their torment resolved, and that would have to be enough. He refused to utter another word on the subject. What he had failed to clarify was what Chester's fate meant for Alvin, to where the farm boy's own spirit was tending, shamed as he was by unforgivable behavior all this past summer long. Contrition was meaningless; what's done was done. How was he supposed to live out what days remained him now, infected body and soul? That secret corner of his heart provided the answer: He would go back home to the farm where he belonged, after all. He would take up a tin pail and fling oats to Mama's chickens and sweep potato bugs off the porch after supper and help old Uncle Boyd dig that ditch along his driveway and repair Uncle Henry's barn floor and fill a bushel peach basket for Aunt Hattie and another for Auntie Emma and learn to whistle a dandy ragtime jig outside Granny Chamberlain's window where autumn's shadows are thatched with maple branches and moonlight, for it was she who told him once that the answers to all life's riddles are found within a box of tricks hidden up in this good earth, God alone knows where, and nothing of truth is revealed until all our days here have run their course. Some tomorrow he would put on his work-clothes at dawn and breathe the field smoke of burning corn stubble and share another dinner plate of fried catfish with Cousin Frenchy and tell his sisters a pretty swell bedtime story; and when his own time came, be it sooner or later, he would go to his rest, safe at last in the bosom of his family.

Alvin left the chewed-over apple core in the thick grass and wiped his hands on the back of his trousers. Most of the circus wagons were loaded. Rumbling truck engines spewed exhaust into the cold morning air. He saw the dwarf on the road by the great steam calliope, a black derby hat on his misshapen head. Rascal carried a flat wooden box under one arm as he left the circus caravan and crossed the road down into the grassy meadow toward the farm boy. A chilly breeze rippled through the autumn maples, scattering old dried leaves all about. The farm boy smelled burning ash on the morning air. He picked up the cheap matting suitcase and began walking toward the wagons. The first couple of trucks started rolling forward. Fifty yards from the road, he met the dwarf who told him, earnestly, "They were quite disappointed."

The farm boy set his old suitcase back down in the wet switchgrass. "You know I didn't promise nothing."

"Of course I do."

"I ain't got an act like you. I'd be shoveling manure like some hick."

The farm boy kicked at a muddy clump of grass. His fever was gone for now, but he still felt tired. Up on the road, another truck engine roared to life.

"Why should our endeavor be so loved, and the performance so loathed?"

"Beg your pardon?"

Rascal smiled. "My dear Josephine asked me to give you this."

He handed Alvin the wooden box.

"What is it?"

"See for yourself."

Alvin undid the brass latch that held it shut. Inside the box he found a polished steel throwing-knife with a leather handle.

The dwarf told him, "It's a souvenir from Buffalo Bill Cody's Wild West show where my very own Josephine performed the treacherous Wheel of Death on two continents. She risked her mortal life for six dollars a day and meals, and when the show closed, a Pawnee warrior by the name of Gideon White Cloud gave it to her in celebration of her extraordinary courage. Josephine wishes you to have it in appreciation of your own."

The farm boy took the knife out of the wooden box and rolled it over in his fingers. "Ain't you ascared no more?"

"Of course I am," replied the dwarf, "but when there's no peril in the fight, there's no glory in the triumph. Fear is bravery's stepchild. Hiding under the floorboards of my bedroom last spring, I'd resigned myself to the sorry prospect of scavenging and disrepute because I was ignorant of the steadfastness of hope. Auntie always imagined me incapable of sorting out my own affairs and too weak of heart to seek my way in the world without her constant guidance. She mistook my natural hesitancy for cowardice, and perhaps her stingy opinion informed my own ridiculous behavior these past few years. Well, no matter, because, you see, what I've learned since crawling out from under that tacky old house is that we needn't be children to fix our sights past tomorrow, or the day afterward, and be brave enough to call that our rightful place."

A dark flock of sparrows sailed over the meadow toward the morning woods as the farm boy thought about Hadleyville and how big the sky looked west of the Mississippi. "We seen a lot."

The dwarf grinned. "Oh, but there's so much more."

Up on the road, the pipes of the gilded calliope shrieked and steam rose into the hazy morning sky. Flanked by a few last scrambling roustabouts loading on, the painted circus caravan had begun moving.

"You won't change your mind?"

The farm boy shook his head. "There ain't much sense in it."

He squeezed the knife handle tightly, kicked harder at the clump of grass. What's done was done. Somebody rang an iron ship's bell mounted atop one of the circus wagons. The clanging echo shot out across the autumn meadow.

"My friend, you've been a wonderful traveling companion. Perhaps one day we'll find each other in another circumstance more fitting our best ambitions. You know, Uncle Augustus always told me the journey provides its own possibilities."

"I hope so."

The dwarf reached into his back pocket and took out a small shiny-black arrowhead. "This is a token of my own admiration. I dug it out of a beaver dam on the Belle Fourche River on my first excursion out West and have held it for luck ever since. I want you to have it." He handed the arrowhead to the farm boy. "Thou art now the favorite of fortune."

Alvin smiled, deeply touched by both gifts. "Thanks."

"Well, good-bye, my friend."

"Good-bye."

They shook hands, the farm boy and the dwarf, then parted as the autumn wind swept out of the east, chasing fallen leaves across the meadow.

Alvin Pendergast watched Rascal hurry away through the damp switchgrass, watched until the dwarf joined the long caravan of rolling circus wagons heading to another horizon.

Then he, too, started for home.

NEW JERUSALEM

I N THE SUMMER OF 1893, when Harry Hennesey was seven years old, he and his father traveled eighteen hours by train and steamship to the White City at Jackson Park, site of the greatest fair of the century: the World's Columbian Exposition.

"Sit up here and have a look." Jonas Hennesey propped his boy up onto the forward deck railing of the whaleback steamer Christopher Columbus *plying the blue waters of Lake Michigan toward the Casino Pier one brisk morning in mid-July. "Son, you'll never in your life see anything more beautiful in the world than this."*

On the shoreline ahead, a magnificent dream of gleaming white palaces and flag-topped towers appeared out of the morning mist. A roar went up from the passengers aboard the steamship. Harry gripped the deck railing as the White City grew larger and larger. Wind rippled across the lake. All month long he had been fearful of the train ride and getting aboard a lake steamer, but now he thought this was the most wonderful thing he had ever done. Who at school wouldn't envy him?

Once the steamer docked, Jonas led his wide-eyed son beneath the ivory pillars of the Columbian Arch into the Court of Honor where the gilded Statue of the Republic seemed to rise from the glittering waters of the Great Basin. Crowding the wide promenades were more people than Harry had ever seen in his life. Loaded motor launches passed in and out of the harbor beneath the arched white balustrade. Swan-beaked gondolas drifted here and there across the lagoon. On either side of the basin were the gigantic alabaster palaces of Manufactures and Liberal Arts, and Agriculture. Straight ahead in the distance rose the shining gilded dome of the great

Administration Building high in the morning sky on a scale young Harry hadn't dreamed possible. Like a gleaming city of heaven.

Jonas guided young Harry down the stairs into a flurry of ladies dressed all in lavender with fringed parasols and pretty sunbonnets, each carrying a map of the Fair as they strolled onto the grand promenade that led west along the Great Basin. High atop the Agriculture Building, Saint-Gaudens' statue of Diana the Huntress shifted about, restlessly tracking the direction of the morning wind. There was so much to see, Harry felt dizzy with excitement. Where should they go first? Jonas suggested they share a sack of candied popcorn, and Harry agreed with great enthusiasm. They crossed the bridge beside the Columbian Fountain at the North Canal, and down a wide elegant street between the Electricity Building and Mines and Mining, toward the densely foliated Wooded Island in the lagoon and the stupendous Transportation and Horticulture buildings beyond. In the plaza by the lagoon, Jonas sat his son on a park bench before he went off to buy them a snack.

"Don't leave here," he warned, "or you'll get lost and I won't be able to find you. Not in these crowds."

But no sooner than Jonas disappeared into a flock of fair-goers, emboldened by his own curiosity, Harry rushed to the lagoon to watch an ancient Norse sailing vessel manned by a crew of men in helmets and fur navigate the inland waters around Hunter's Island. Sheer excitement got the better of little Harry as he dashed along the railing of the lagoon, dodging in and out of the morning crowd, cheering and waving to the men on the boat until he reached the towering glass pavilions of the Electricity Building. He wandered inside to see the great dynamos from around the world. Sparks crackled and dashed above him, luminous balls of electric magic chased along cornices, leaping pillar to pillar as automatic wands drew words in thin air overhead. Awed to distraction, Harry failed to realize how far he had run from the park bench. He had no idea how long he had been gone, nor how to get back. So many people circled about that he lost his sense of direction and began to cry. What if he couldn't find his way back to the bench? What would he do all alone? His mother had warned that strangers might take hold of him and put him in a steamer trunk. He hurried back outside to the promenade. Which way had he come? He remembered the boats he had chased, and ran to the lagoon railing, then followed it back over the bridge, praying his father hadn't gone off and left him. The bench was empty. Frightened, Harry began weeping hysterically. How could he possibly survive on his own? Who would take him home? A firm hand caught his shoulder and spun him about.

His father shouted in his face, "Was it so difficult to mind yourself for two minutes? I ought to take you back to the hotel right now! Your mother was right! You're too young to be here!"

Harry had never seen his father so angry. What could he do but offer his abject apology, followed in tears so desperate he could scarcely breathe. Jonas dragged him back to the bench and exacted a promise that Harry be good for the rest of the day or get sent back to the hotel for the duration of the trip. Afterward, calming down, his father gave Harry a small sack of candied popcorn and peanuts and sat beside him for a few minutes, patiently describing how the fair had come to Jackson Park. He recited some of the names of the patrons and artists and architects whose genius was responsible for all Harry saw: Daniel H. Burnham, Bertha Palmer, Frederick Law Olmsted, Augustus Saint-Gaudens, Francis Millet, and Louis Sullivan. He told Harry that this Exposition was evidence of a New Jerusalem, which would one day rise on the American shore. That was why, his father explained, he had brought Harry to Jackson Park this summer, so that he might see with his own eyes the possibilities of an American future guided by men of art and wealth and vision.

From the lagoon, they passed by the high-arching Golden Doorway of Louis Sullivan's grand red Transportation Building, glittering in the morning sunlight. Along the western edge of the lagoon were gardens of palms and tree ferns, bamboo, flowerbeds, and a variety of small quaint statuary symbolic of the four seasons. Harry felt happy now that his father's anger had faded and they were walking together again in this wondrous place. Beyond a great dome flying Old Glory, Jonas took Harry to watch a parade of fair-goers from countless nations streaming in and out of the Midway Plaisance. Turks and Arabs in colorful Oriental dress passed by, a Singhalese tea merchant and his son, a family of Laplanders with a pair of dogs on leashes, Chinese from the Joss House, Boushareens from Cairo Street, Austrians in lederhosen, Negroes in long cotton robes from Dahomey Village, and a lovely dark woman from Nazareth. Jonas reminded Harry to smile rather than stare at strangers, then explained to him how the Exposition had invited peoples from all the Seven Seas to participate in this greatest of World's Fairs.

"Every nation was sent a notice to come to Chicago and take part in the Fair. Everybody on earth was welcome. It's what makes America so special, you see. Our good fortune is intended by God to be shared, and always will be. Don't you ever forget that."

After buying orange cider from a soda-fountain pavilion, his father asked Harry if he could keep a secret.

"What kind of secret?"

"Well, we're meeting a very dear friend of your mother's here today. Her name is Esther and she's a very nice lady. But you can't breathe a word about her once we're home."

"Why not?"

"Because Esther wants this to be a surprise, so we can't say anything unless your mother mentions it. All right?"

Harry nodded, too afraid to ask why. Besides, his father seemed happy now.

"Do you promise?"

"Yes."

"Cross your heart and hope to die?"

Harry crossed his heart.

"Because if you keep this secret, I won't see any reason at all to tell your mother how you ran away this morning. Do we have a deal?"

Glad that his mother wouldn't hear about the mistake he'd made, Harry agreed, and he and his father hurried off toward the State buildings, a dignified neighborhood resembling grand wealthy homes where Jonas told him Esther was waiting. They met her on the Texas verandah amidst a crowd of Quakers. She was dressed in a black silk cape over a green striped gown and wore a frilly hat with tiny feathers. When Jonas introduced them, Esther gave Harry a pinch on the cheek and commented on how nice his jacket and pants looked that morning.

"He's such a darling, Jonas."

"Yes, he is." Jonas put his hand on Harry's shoulder. "You're going to make me proud one day, aren't you, son?"

"Yes, sir."

Together, they wandered back down the walkway past the Louisiana State Building where a Creole symphony played music for the restaurant serving opossum stew and rice gumbo. It was near midday now so Jonas bought them each a bowl of gumbo and a lemonade, and they sat watching a steady crowd of fair-go'ers pass by while Esther and Jonas spoke of people whose names Harry didn't recognize. They laughed and laughed, and Harry was glad because his father seemed in great spirits again.

The three of them went on to the bohemian Midway where the noontime crowds were thick and noisy. Eskimos in Arctic dress mingled with fair-goers, half-naked

Dahomeyans posed for Kodak photographs in red-bricked Cairo Street, drums beat constantly, and rattling tambourines and melodic lutes heralded the passage of one exotic procession after another. Jonas guided Harry and Esther to George Ferris' great revolving wheel ride and paid their fee to board one of the thirty-six passenger cars, each the size of a Chicago trolley.

At first, Esther was afraid to ride the big wheel. "It's awfully high," she worried. "What if we should fall off?"

"Oh, we won't let that happen," Jonas told her, "but if it'll make you feel better, dear, we'll hold your hand, won't we, son?"

Harry nodded, glad to be helpful because he knew it pleased his father.

"Why, that's very sweet of you," Esther said, as they boarded the car, arm-in-arm. "I feel so much better now." She smiled at Harry, and gave Jonas a soft kiss on the cheek that made Harry blush. He had never seen anyone but Mother kiss his father before. When they reached the top of the great wheel, young Harry pressed his face to the window of the car and looked east over the Midway where the minarets of the Moorish Village and the Streets of Cairo grew smaller and smaller. Farther off, he could see the dome of the Illinois State Building and black smoke drifting slowly over Lake Michigan from a departing steamship at the Casino Pier. This grand panorama thrilled Harry. He was a cloud potentate, ruler of all he surveyed. But then Esther complained again about being up too high.

"It just makes me dizzy, Jonas. Why, I could faint any moment now."

"Here, darling, put your head on my shoulder." He winked at Harry who smiled back, but felt confused over Esther's behavior. She was acting like a little girl and his father didn't seem to notice. As Esther laid her head on Jonas's shoulder, the Ferris wheel began at last to rotate downward, and Harry decided this had been his best time yet at the fair.

Back on the ground again, they entered the Streets of Cairo amid dogs and donkeys and fortune-tellers and a troupe of Nubians and Soudanese in full costume. Jonas wanted to see the Mummy of Ramses II, "The Oppressor of Israelites," an exhibit next to a replica of an ancient tomb. Afraid of mummies, Harry chose to stay outside with Esther to watch a demonstration of martial expertise by a pair of Egyptian swordsmen in scarlet silk turbans, and saw a procession of boys pass in revue led by Solomon Joseph and his donkey Ta-ra-ra Boom-De-Aye. Once Jonas came out of the mummy show, they hurried over to the "Wild East Show" of blazing swords and daring riders atop bright steeds at mock war in the Arabian desert.

When the show ended, Jonas paid 50¢ for Harry to have a camel ride of his own. Afterward, weary of the crass bustling Midway, they all agreed that a ride across the Exposition lagoon by gondola would be the perfect way to relax until supper.

They walked down to the docks at the south entrance of the glimmering Art Palace. Jonas paid the fares to a red-jacketed Romanian whose fellow gondolier played a folk melody on the mandolin as the vessel shoved off from the boat landing. Jonas and Esther sat arm-in-arm beneath the shaded awning at mid-vessel, while Harry edged close to the bow to see any fish that swam by. Gliding beneath the bridge into the north lagoon, he watched crowds of people on the Wooded Island streaming about the lush thicket maze of paths lined with pretty trellises of climbing roses and honeysuckle, orchids and Parmee violets scented of heaven. The gondola drifted through a fleet of motor launches and past a pair of lovely Venetian sailboats whose passengers waved to Harry as they streamed by. The air now was warm and slightly breezy, the water cool in the silvery blue lagoon. Jonas identified for Esther those many countries whose colorful flags and banners and pennants fluttered in the breeze off the lake. Wearing a big smile, Esther told Harry that his father was the smartest man on earth. "Don't you agree?"

"Yes, ma'am."

Jonas laughed. "That's my boy!"

"It is wondrous, isn't it, Jonas?"

"Yes, it certainly is, dear."

"Don't you agree, Harry?" she asked. "Don't you think this is the most marvelous place in all the world?"

"Yes, ma'am," Harry enthused. "I wish we could stay here forever."

Esther smiled at Jonas. "So do I."

The Venetian gondola glided ahead of a South Sea islander's canoe into the quiet waters of the South Canal toward the great Obelisk, and the gondolier on the bow oars sang a ballad and his companion at the stern strummed the mandolin before steering the boat in a lazy arc to dock at the steps below the gleaming portico of Machinery Hall. There, Esther used her Kodak to take a snap of Harry and Jonas that she would later mail to them at Christmas within a gilded frame inscribed:

Sweet memories of the fair

Eventually, as sunset reddened the sky over the White City, Harry stood beside his father and Esther on the west end of the Convent de la Rabida, staring across the calm golden waters at the perfect reproductions of the three Caravels that had brought Columbus to America four hundred years earlier: the lovely "Niña," "Pinta," and the flagship "Santa Maria." Each had been built at the expense of the Spanish Government and brought to the White City for the Exposition in recognition of the honor shown the "Admiral of the Ocean Sea" by the fair organizers. That these small vessels had sailed so far into the unknown, Jonas told Harry, was testimony that Providence had guided the navigating hand of Columbus, that it was his destiny to discover the New World, that these Caravels were evidence of Progress and Civilization, and that here at the White City were expressed modern humanity's finest achievements, proof in America of the New Jerusalem.

— **2** —

"Hennesey!" A man's voice called from across the cold warehouse. "There's a fellow out here to see you!"

Harry put down the issue of *Collier's* he was reading and glanced at the clock on the wall. It was ten a.m. straight up. His only morning appointment was already an hour late. Since dawn it had been raining and was so chilly out, Harry had worn his winter overcoat on the trolley, half-expecting to see a flurry of snowflakes on the wet wind. Autumn was just around the corner, all right. Frustrated and uncomfortable, he got up from his desk and went to the office doorway and saw Joe Phelps next to a short dark Italian fellow in blue denim overalls, a brown derby hat, and leather work-shoes soaked from the morning rain. The Italian had a pair of big steamer trunks and an apple crate with him, just unloaded from an olive-green Whippet Six sedan. He lit a Camel cigarette when Harry came out to greet him, rubbing his hands from the cold. If this was another joke, Harry decided he'd punch Phelps in the nose.

"You're quite a bit late," Harry told the Italian, holding back his irritation. "I've been sitting in that freezing office over there since half past eight and all I had for breakfast was toast and coffee."

Phelps laughed. "Harry, your pal Salvatore here don't speak a word of English."

Joe Phelps, born Guiseppe Alfredino after his maternal grandfather, spoke briefly to the Italian in his native language. The fellow nodded as he puffed on the cigarette. Phelps told Harry, "Sal's cousin Francesco was in the papers last month for falling out of his stateroom window in the middle of the Atlantic Ocean. Had to be rescued by a launch from the *Conta Grande* and wound up in the hospital at Naples for a week. Sal said his aunt nearly had a stroke when she heard about it."

"Is that so? How awful." Harry wondered why they thought he'd appreciate that little story. He'd heard worse. What was life anyhow, but a series of episodic affairs?

Phelps spoke again to the fellow who shook his head vigorously and tapped ash off the cigarette onto the wet cement floor, then gestured toward the steamer trunks while nodding at Harry. The Italian gave the old apple crate a kick.

Phelps explained, "Sal's hoping to put over a big sale here, Harry. He just says to me before you come out, 'Wait'll Mr. Hennesey gets a load of what I got for him!'"

Taking his cue from Phelps, the Italian fetched a key out of his coat and unlocked one of the trunks. When he flipped open the lid, Harry saw immediately what Joe Phelps was referring to: four boxes of El Producto cigars, a dozen tubes of Iron Glue, Wanamaker's silk stockings, six cans of Berry Brothers Liquid Granite floor varnish, a dozen boxes of Venus pencils, two dozen boxes of Ace combs, an Ansco Royal camera, and nine Burgess Snap-Lite flashlights. It was quite a load, all right.

Phelps said, "When you make your pile, Harry, I hope you'll toss me a couple of peanuts."

"Do you suppose this is on the up-and-up?"

"Why, sure! I'd say it's in the bank."

Well, Harry doubted that, but only a fool walks off without taking a peek. At Phelps' nod, the Italian unlocked the second steamer trunk and flung it open. Inside were a pair of Temple Radios with the new electro-dynamic speakers, boxes of Duco polish, Beeman's Pepsin Gum, Pepsodent dentifrice, Palmolive shaving cream, seven bottles of Wildroot hair tonic, a tube of Pazo ointment, a box of 5¢ Rocky Ford cigars, and five B.V.D. union suits: another bonanza of merchandise. The Italian displayed his wares with a broad smile.

Joe Phelps scratched his head.

Harry was suitably unimpressed. If these goods are clean, he thought, I'm the American Beauty.

Just then, a large black delivery truck dripping rainwater off its bumper backed into the warehouse, spewing a cloud of exhaust. When it rolled to a stop, two boys in flat caps and denim overalls jumped out of the rear. They folded the wet canvas to one side as a blue uniformed driver got out holding a clipboard and a lit cigar. In the back of the truck were stacks of unmarked barrels.

"Bootleggers," Phelps remarked, watching one of them pry open a wooden barrel with a crowbar. "Probably Lou Faralla's boys. They're selling the barrels. Can you beat it for nerve? Right under Follette's nose. Unless, of course, Charley's working this racket himself." Phelps whistled softly. "What I wouldn't do to get a flash at Follette's old ledger."

Dubious of the whole proposition, Harry said, "All right, Joe, let's come down to cases here. How do I know if any of this merchandise is on the level?"

Phelps answered with a laugh. "Well, as a matter of fact, it ain't. Sal here and a couple of his cousins hijacked it out of the Pittsburgh train yards just last week. These aren't brainsharks, Harry. Sal hasn't peeked at a mirror since he got off the boat. Why, he thinks he's an up-and-coming fellow, a regular American like you or me. When a pal of his told him about your ad in the *Sentinel*, he figured it was a cinch you could help sell this stuff of his without anybody getting nicked for it. Trouble with you, Hennesey, is you think you're just too straight for that sort of thing. Well, I don't mean to be fresh, but you could do a corking big store down in the wholesale district with Sal if you weren't so damned yellow."

"Oh, is that a fact?" For an instant he considered giving Joe a swift kick in the shins. It was insulting of him to bring this Italian fellow here.

"Look, Harry, aren't you always poking me up to do more to get along? Let's get this clear, see, because ordinarily you couldn't hire me to join a crowd of sapheads like Sal here. Well, maybe it's not such a crank idea to think a fellow like him's worth his salt to you and me both."

"Who the hell do you think you're talking to? I'd have to be off my nut to do business with a pack of thieves, and I tell you, I'm not." It was the same old story since the day he stepped off the train. They offer you advice on how to get rich and every piece of that advice leads back to their own racket.

"Aw, you can't kid me, Harry. You've been putting on the dog for Follette all summer long, soaking clients with that same slick pitch of yours, and all he's given you is the same glad eye like any other mucker. Fact is, you and Sal and me got a swell deal here, so don't try to skin out of it."

"Go to hell, Joe, and take your goddamned pals with you!"

Infuriated, Harry rushed back to his office and slammed the door. He sat down at his desk, thoroughly disgusted. He had never been so mad in his life. That sonofabitch Italian had no business bringing a truckload of hot merchandise to him. Who the hell did he think he was? And Joe Phelps was a goddamned idiot. Harry leaned up to see out of the office window. Phelps was still there running through the Italian's inventory, listing it piece by piece in his own stupid little book. Well, Joe could rot in hell for all he cared.

The telephone rang.

Keeping an eye on Phelps, Harry picked up the receiver. "Hello?"

Silence.

"Hello? Who is it, please?"

He waited a few seconds more. Hearing nothing, he replaced the receiver and stood up. His knuckles were numb from the cold. He looked out his office window again. Astonishingly, Follette's nephew Benjamin was in the warehouse now, dressed in an olive-tan belted raincoat and hat, walking side-by-side with the uniformed driver of the bootlegger's delivery truck. Phelps walked over to greet him. Now what? They stopped beside the barrels at the back of the truck where Benjamin shook hands with the two youths and gave Joe a big smile. Were they pals?

The telephone rang again. He picked it up. A muffled voice inquired, *"Mister Harry Hennesey, please?"*

"Speaking! Who is this?"

"Will you hold the wire, please?"

"Of course!"

Harry continued to watch the gathering out in the warehouse. Benjamin looked every inch a Follette. His father, Major H.P. Follette, had been killed by an artillery shell at the Argonne and Charles Follette had taken the poor boy under his wing. Harry felt sure Benjamin was being groomed for the Follette fortune: educated at Princeton like his uncle, shown the inside ropes from the mailroom to the executive offices, assigned his own territory and clients, privileged to develop new accounts by himself, urged to assume responsibility. Yes, sir, Charles A. Follette was certainly proud of his nephew. How wonderful it must be, Harry thought, to know you'll be rich no matter which way fortune rolls.

The wire went dead.

"Hello? Operator? Hello? Anyone there? Hello?"

Nothing.

Bewildered, he jammed the receiver back down onto the hook. There was a knock at the door. "Come in!"

When the door opened, Benjamin Follette stood on the threshold, clipboard in hand, a friendly smile on his face. "Good morning, Mr. Hennesey."

"Hello, Benjamin." Harry tried to be pleasant. After all, it was not this boy's fault whom his uncle associated with these days. Besides, Benjamin had always been decent to him.

"Well, what do you know, sir?" Benjamin lowered his clipboard as they shook hands. He had a man's grip, firm but polite. You certainly couldn't argue with that.

"Care for a lemon drop?" Harry always kept a bowl of candy on his desk for clients. People seemed to like that. It gave off an air of generosity, never a bad tune to sing.

"Well, I don't mind if I do," Benjamin replied, then popped one into his mouth.

Harry rolled another chair over to the desk. He tried to look confident. This was likely to be something difficult. He just had that sense. "Have a seat."

"Thank you." Removing his hat, Follette's nephew sat down. "It's cold as the dickens out there, isn't it?"

"Yes, it is. But we're supposed to see some sunshine later on."

"I hope so. Uncle hates rainy days. Nobody wants to do any work."

"Well, how can I help you? You're not here for the rent, are you? Because I mailed that last Tuesday. I'm sure it's arrived, hasn't it?"

The boy chuckled, dismissing Harry's concern about the rent with a casual wave. "Of course it was on time. Uncle says you've never been late. He's always greatly impressed by that."

"Well, it's important to be reliable."

Benjamin noticed the book on the desk, a title Harry had purchased just last night: *Barron Ixell, Crime Breaker* by Oscar Schisgall. "Are you in the Book of the Month Club?"

"No," Harry replied, rather surprised Benjamin had heard of it. The Follettes didn't seem the reading sort. "Actually, I found this at Gutenberg's Book Shop on 31st Street. It and Ellery Queen's new novel, *The Roman Hat Mystery*, were reduced for Bargain Week, so I bought them both. They're pretty involving."

Benjamin smiled again. "I adore a good detective story. Mother only reads *Telling Tales* and *Woman's World*, but you can't persuade her to admit it in public." He picked up the clipboard, thumbing back several pages. "Well, Mr. Hennesey, Uncle has a proposition he'd like you to consider this morning."

"All right," Harry replied, sitting forward in his chair. Here it comes. "Shoot."

"You're on a nine month lease with us, is that correct?"

"Yes."

"That is to say, you're paid up for four months."

"Yes, that's true," he agreed, reaching for a lemon drop of his own, slightly confused by Benjamin's questions. "What are you driving at? I don't suppose your uncle's intending to raise my rent. I have a contract, you know."

Benjamin shook his head. "Nothing of the sort, Mr. Hennesey. Please let me continue."

"All right."

"Now, what would you estimate is the current market worth of the goods you're storing with us?"

"Well, as of today I suppose with a set of desks I just bought, I've got perhaps three thousand dollars in merchandise. That'll change later this week, however, as I've found a buyer interested in a collection of Harvard Classics and a Crosley walnut console. Thanks to Armstrong and Sarnoff, the best radio sets are quite popular these days, you know."

Benjamin scribbled a few notes onto his clipboard, worked out some figures, and looked up at Harry. "Mr. Hennesey, what would you say to an offer of five thousand dollars for your entire inventory and the rental space to the end of your contract?"

Not certain if he had heard correctly, Harry replied, "I don't follow you."

"Well, Uncle would like to offer more than a fair profit on all the merchandise you're storing with us, and full compensation for the seventeen weeks left on your contract here."

"You're joking."

Benjamin chuckled. "Of course not. Uncle's not the sort. Ask anyone who's know him more than a month. Have you ever heard him tell a joke?"

Harry felt confused, half-conscious of a manipulation occurring here. "What brought this on? Is your father selling the warehouse? He ought to know I put quite a few hours into collecting this inventory. I've got months and months of labor involved here. It hasn't been easy at all."

"Look here, sir. I don't want to bluff you out, but to be truthful, this has all been decided downtown. A week ago, in fact. Uncle's convinced he needs your space and that's all there is to it. I've come down here to settle up. We both believe the offer is more than fair. Indeed, with the rent factored in, your net yield will be somewhere near two hundred-fifteen percent. That's an A-1 good profit, by any measure.

My advice would be to sell the goods. Take a holiday. Go see your kiddies. Don't they miss you like the dickens? It must be tough having you
away like this. I know I wouldn't care for it."

Why is he talking to me like this, Harry wondered. I suppose he's
trying to throw me off balance, but I'm not that irrational.

"Son, I'm not quite clear about this business of giving up my lease.
Sure, the money's swell, but once it's spent, then what? Where do I
go? A biscuit factory? I'm no millionaire. One thing always leads to
another and bills need to be paid, not just tomorrow or next week,
but a month from now, and the one after that, and on it goes." Harry
rapped his knuckles on the desktop. "No, Benjamin, I don't mind selling you all the seltzer bottles you want, but I'd be a fool to give away
my table, too."

Benjamin looked out to the warehouse where Phelps and Sal
were helping those two young fellows unload the empty barrels.
Harry noticed, too. Christ, he thought, they've got the whole crowd
of numbskulls toadying up. This is what happens when you shift
your glance. Well, he'd be damned if they'd get him, too. He had a
contract, after all.

He noticed Benjamin's pleasant expression had changed. "Mr.
Hennesey, we're offering you almost twice cash-value for your merchandise, when, in fact, we don't have to pay a dime, and you'll still be
out on the street tomorrow. Don't you know that?"

Astonished at the impertinence, Harry straightened up. "Look
here, son, I've got a bona fide lease for this space, signed by your uncle,
which says I don't have to vacate until the first of March. Now, I don't
pretend to be able to match pennies with every hotdog stand you fellows are invested in, but I'm no bum on the bumpers, either, and I
know my rights and I'll protect them with the law, if I have to."

"Actually, we've already got a notice to terminate tenancy at will.
We'd rather not use it, but we're certainly prepared to if you force our
hand."

"On what grounds?"

"Negligence."

"That's absurd! What negligence?"

"A box of kerosene lamp oil you kept next to Phil Fermer's space leaked all over the floor, causing a terrible fire hazard. Ordinarily we might've called you down for it ourselves, but the fire inspector received notice this morning, so that's all she wrote."

Harry leaped out of his chair. "What on earth are you talking about? There's no leak! I was just over there not half an hour ago!"

"There will be."

At last he realized what sort of game this was. "Good grief, I ought to punch you in the nose right now, you sonofabitch! What kind of stunt are you pulling here? A dirty blackmail is all this is! You fellows want my space for bootleggers, don't you? That is, if you're not running the rum yourselves. God almighty, who would've thought the great Charles A. Follette was no better than a cheap racketeer?"

Benjamin stiffened. "Say that again, Mr. Hennesey, and that family circle of yours'll have a rough Christmas, if you get my meaning. Don't forget, Illinois is just a telegraph away these days."

"Get the hell out of here!"

Taking another lemon drop from the candy bowl, Benjamin told him flatly, "By four o'clock this afternoon, your job lot becomes our merchandise. We'll send a fellow down here to help clear out your inventory. After he telephones to us that you're packed up, there'll be a check waiting for you at Uncle's office no later than four o'clock on the 99th floor of the Empyrean Building." He stared Harry in the eye. "It's a swell chance to cash in, Mr. Hennesey. Just don't shoot your face off and everyone'll be happy."

Back when Harry worked at the Kansas City stockyards, a jobber named Rodale wormed his way into the office supply business by stealing boxes of catalogues and ledgers, then offering to replace them with his own inventory at half price. He had the game salted so expertly that when a colleague of Harry's, Bill Winslow, caught him at it, Rodale produced a book that somehow proved Winslow himself was the thief and if he made a kick about it, Rodale would take his case to the district attorney. Winslow was so terrified he wound up paying Rodale two hundred bucks a month to keep his mouth shut. What else could he do? If Rodale hadn't drank up his profits and driven his Dodge off a bluff into the Missouri River, Winslow might have lost his head and eventually tried to kill the sonofabitch. Nobody who worked in the office those days saw any other way out, but Harry thought Winslow ought to have simply quit the stockyards and started over somewhere else. Wasn't that another definition of moral eloquence in business? Have the courage to cut the most agreeable acquaintance you possess, when he convinces you he lacks principle. Rodale certainly wasn't agreeable, by any means, but earlier this summer Harry thought that Follette seemed to be everything he had ever aspired to. Now Follette was threatening harm to his wife and children. But if Harry cracked his idiot nephew on the head, which is what the sonofabitch deserved, then what? There'd be other days to even the score. After all, he had Olive Blanchard. That could pay off sooner than Follette thinks.

Getting hold of himself, Harry asked calmly, "You say the check's downtown? Is that on the level?"

Benjamin smiled. "Sure, it is. You can telephone, if you like. Meriwether-1389. Ask for Heddy."

"Maybe I'll do that."

"Just be there by four o'clock."

"I will."

Despite the rotten circumstances, Harry certainly needed the money for Marie and the kids, who would soon be back home again with the Pendergasts simply because he had attempted a leap from a dangerous height and fallen on his face. So in a few short minutes Harry put his reluctance aside and agreed to assign everything he had purchased over the past year to Follette's company, then use the part of the profit that did not go directly to Marie to secure another office space in which he could do business. Benjamin Follette produced the paperwork that nullified Harry's rental contract and showed a receipt for all his merchandise in storage.

Once Harry had put his signature on the agreement, Benjamin offered his hand to Harry, who accepted it gracefully. What good would it do to beg off now? "Well, Mr. Hennesey, I guess that winds it up. Oh, by the way — " He reached into his coat and took out a small envelope. "A delivery boy handed this to me on my way in here. It's for you."

"Thank you," Harry said, taking the envelope. It had his name scribbled on the outside, but there was no postage stamp. "I presume Kelsey and Fermer are each being offered a similar arrangement." He doubted that sonofabitch Phelps was getting the air. That louse-hound probably gave Follette the idea about leaking the kerosene. It just shows you, doesn't it?

"Sure they are. It's all in the selling game. Everyone seems to be quite satisfied. Well, good luck, sir."

After Benjamin had walked out of his office, Harry went to the door where he saw Follette's boy greeted by Joe Phelps and the Italian and the cigar-smoking truck driver in the blue uniform. The empty barrels had been unloaded for delivery to corrupt, arrogant bootleg-gers. All four were laughing loudly.

— 3 —

The whistle from the iron foundry at 113th Street shrieked, signaling the noon hour. Walking through a cold gray wind near the muddy train yard, a quarter mile from the river, Harry heard the clank of freight cars coupling, a donkey engine whining, furious steam drills digging into concrete. Across the rough waters, the white marble cenotaphs in the city cemetery, "Elysian Fields," gleamed in streaks of sunlight less than a mile upriver from the gray monolith of State prison whose barred windows glistened, too, like a gilded tomb. He saw streetcars on the hill above the river slums, tall apartment houses under construc-tion, an errand boy on a bicycle hurrying through icy gusts atop the sandy bluffs.

Once upon a time, Harry Hennesey had thought of himself as one of those opportunists who see life differently than others: intensely and with greater clarity and egotism of personal destiny, by no means a prima donna, but someone to be reckoned with. He had worked hard for many years to accumulate all those practical things that show a standard of living that is always rising. He did not want to beat the system. It was too cumbersome and contemptuous of the individual to be beaten. He believed that we are just too primitive to conquer that machine of our own creation, and our lifetimes are too brief. We simply do the best we can and, in the end, when everything is finished, we take our rest, confident that we have done our fair share, and perhaps a good deal more. Because nothing is really hidden. Memory is a great leveler of reputations. We become less impressed by personality than real achievements, and less and less often judge character by pretense. But it is our capacity for feeling which saves most of us before it's too late by gradually killing that conventional desire to succeed at any cost. It also saves us lying to ourselves unnecessarily.

This was in the air when Harry opened the envelope Benjamin had given him at the warehouse. It held a note inside which read:

> *I got the works from one of those dollies at winterhill so you and me got something to talk about at the show tonight and dont be late — TC Cobb*

Now, six weeks had gone by since that ugly night at the roadhouse without any sign at all of Cobb. Harry presumed the murder of Fred Markle had something to do with that, but he could not be certain. He had felt melancholy himself for days and had horrible dreams and woke one night with a terrible sweat. Of course, Harry had expected Cobb would come back, but there was still a feeling of unreality about it. Ill-fortune so often seems to arrive when we are hopeful of better days ahead. Maybe this is because the most remarkable things we do in our lives somehow persuade us there is a beautiful breeze at our backs whose inspiration offers a special advantage over everyone else. Languishing in the doldrums, we watch for umbrellas to billow and leaves to flutter far out of proportion to our need.

But September had been a wonderful month so far. Business was going smoothly with a number of sales to rental outfits, secondhand stores, and a tiny Dutch woman up in Franklin Heights who had apparently been aching for just the sort of painted peacock lamp stand

Harry happened to have scrounged up at a yard sale on Morris Avenue. Now that he had cash in his pockets, for his mental well-being he'd kept Pearl sleeping on his sofa the past couple of weeks, cooking breakfast at his kitchenette, talking his ear off. He had given her strict rules regarding domestic activities and the sanctity of his possessions, including his bed where she was not permitted under any circumstances. He ached enough for her without carrying this lovely affair across that final threshold. Also, there'd be no smoking or drinking in the room, and no nagging. He would not tolerate excuses. He was tough. But she had taken to these conditions with only a few complaints and was not difficult to live with.

About a week after their melancholy visit to Tarryton Crossing, he invented a story that the missing Olive had been found in the cellar of a small house on Long Island Sound. He told Pearl the stolen money had been recovered and the case closed. Last week, he had gotten Marie's telegraph announcing that she and the children were through with Texas and intended to go back home to Illinois where they belonged. She had been expecting a fight from him, but instead Harry agreed with her and admitted it by telephone the next morning. So that was settled, too. Cissie and Henry would be safe and happy again. Everything was sailing along wonderfully.

Except now he had this stupid note to worry over.

A mile and a half from the drafty warehouse, he folded his wet umbrella and sat on a sheltered bench at a damp trolley station off Quinan Road and re-read the note. Bloom's files had sprung a leak. That sounded very peculiar. A girl had confided something she did not quite understand and, thanks to her irresponsibility, Harry's beautiful breeze had receded to a puff. Damn the sanitarium, anyhow. There was nothing distinctly high-minded or sentimental about confidentiality. You were either careful, or you were not. He felt a sudden disgust over Bloom and his messianic obsession toward insanity and terminal illness. What right did he have to interfere with people's lives? Damn him, too. And which show was Cobb referring to? There must be a hundred theaters in the greater metropolis. In any case, Harry had no intention of striking some sordid agreement in a dark balcony. Cobb was crazy if that's what he expected.

Though the sky was still cold and misty, sunlight cracked through the gray clouds here and there, suggesting better weather, so Harry changed his mind about riding the streetcar back downtown. Convinced he needed a good long walk to refresh his perspective, he left the trolley stop and headed down a steep alley slope next to a vacant shoe factory with busted out doors; by a dilapidated tin shed where wet smokebushes bloomed beside a Waverley electric motorcar rusting in the dooryard of a gray framehouse whose windows were raised open to warm the cold rooms of an immigrant attic; past a pale spinster in a blue cotton dress wrapping cigars on the back stoop of a Methodist church and rain-soaked Negro yardmen toiling with rakes in the grassy lot; descending to a crumbling flight of cement steps behind a block of fish markets amid the pungent smell of hot-tar on patched rooftops, tunes from a hurdy-gurdy, the rumbling jingle of one last empty milk wagon rolling home.

Harry wandered through the tenement back alleys west of the marsh where the great river was visible from the slope of weedy sand-lots and irregular termite-ridden fences. There, laundry lines extended from parcel to parcel, and threadbare children ran about freely, barely conscious of the dreadful poverty upon which their frail lives teetered. Walking along, he saw itinerant ragpickers with makeshift fishing poles in hand trudging up wordless and empty-bucketed from the muddy waterfront below. He watched a well-dressed young man in a flashy new Stearns-Knight motorcar handing stacks of week-old magazines to a pack of kids, and a beefy patrolman beside a fire hydrant putting a stiff boot into an old brown dog that cowered at his feet. He saw a collection of derelict woodsheds and old corncribs on a slant in a carpenter's yard behind an old livery stable, each sagging downhill under the mean weight of its own roof beam and eaves. He saw the ancient shingles on a coalhouse roof rippling loose in a gust of wind off the cold river, black oil-smoke drifting out of smoldering brick incinerators by an old paint factory, manufactured goods of all shapes and purposes used up, broken, discarded, forgotten; and flies, everywhere flies, inheriting the foul occupancy of less fortunate creatures.

Strolling in a nasty mood along soggy Front Street, Harry counted ships behind the great wharf houses: masted schooners, windjammers, ferryboats, freighters, sandscows, tugs, brick barges, cattle boats. Yellow quarantine flags flew beside a string of pennants on a passenger steamer out on the cold river. A pair of lifeboats bobbed on the current of dirty water near the crusted pilings of the old wharf beaten on by the tides. A white sloop tacked toward the far shore. Gulls flocked the upper railings or wheeled on the stiff breeze above the current. All along these stark docks, the current lapped gently, glutted with dumpings of refuse. On a poster just past a narrow wet gangplank near the ferryhouse, where a blue one-night boat slid gently past the old piers toward deeper, cleaner waters, Harry read:

JOIN THE NAVY AND SEE THE WORLD

Between the busy docks from Lower York Street to 73rd, he watched jobbers and longshoremen, fishmongers, laborers, ironworkers, and sailors in pea-jackets visiting barbershops and hashjoints and saloons, seedy lodging houses, and brothels: those wooden whorehouses that looked like tourist cabins where grim prostitutes, seasoned and weary, miserable with fear and vice, bent over washtubs in the sunlight or hung laundry on wire lines only a short distance from outhouses whose loathsome odor of feces and stink of ammoniac urine infected the fresh air. Mulling over his own troublesome situation as he hurried through the gray wind along each block of this cold harbor of waterfront slums and ruin, Harry saw drunks asleep in narrow alleyways, and young thugs crowding lampposts, hands thrust in worn pockets, soot and insolence on wary faces. Police whistles blew up and down the long wharf. Alarm bells clanged. Coalwagons and delivery trucks and taxicabs rumbled by. A stench of ash and rot remained.

At 62nd Street and Landon Place, where the brick bulwark first rose beside the old granite drainpipe, Harry Hennesey leaned on the iron railing and raised his collar against an icy breeze and looked downriver past the distant spiderwork of cables on the suspension bridges and trestles as a large steamship and a Norwegian freighter charted the cold brown current south. Trailing both ships, a slow flatbarge chugged across the swirling eddies, smoke billowing high into the gray sky from its funnels. Thirteen miles down the shore, by the Burlington Lighthouse, each of these vessels would disappear to sea as more arrived bound for the crowded wharf by way of waters that had once witnessed God's bright morning, that first light, and a bird's song echoing above the river flood basin long ago. Now that prodigal harvest, that lilac night, is a memory forever gone on the cold current, as the river carries memories away with silt and leaves, memories of birch-bark canoes and wood smoke in autumn, memories of drums and voices in the ancient wilderness, memories of people drawn to the flood of the river. Once, these moraine ridges and drainage basins and forested plains, thick with porcupine grass and tall hickory trees, red oaks, and squirrel corn and prairie parsley, were noisy with wild fowl and bold summer winds. Then wooden sailing ships entered the muddy river navigated by clever Frenchmen, traders in pelts and maps and warfare. A crude fortress built of hewn logs and stone guarded the waterway from the bluffs above. Cannon fire echoed across the fog at dawn. A lonely village grew in the wilderness, a sparse settlement gradually edging down from the dense forest to the sandy riverbank below. Flatboats and paddlewheelers maneuvered upstream. Violet-filled swamps were dredged, the forest lightened, wilderness subdued by ax and plow. A brave American city of red brick and granite rose atop the bluffs. Horse drawn wagons and gilded carriages rolled along cobblestone streets. Steamboat whistles and brass bands greeted new arrivals. Gaslights lit the bluffs at dusk. Bridges spanned the river. Buildings grew taller. More people arrived. Machines of industry and commerce invested the city with wealth and fortune. Smokestacks were raised up along the soot-smudged skyline. Electricity lit the bluffs at dusk. More people arrived. Train whistles and opportunity welcomed each fresh face; so did factory whistles, motor horns, a million voices, day and night. More people arrived. Now the years pass away like wood smoke on an autumn wind. A new century dawns. The past is buried in concrete, the familiar brown earth, unfenced, raw, wild, hidden beneath the crowded avenues and boulevards, the harsh tenement buildings and cold steel mills. Gunshots echo across the fog at dawn, and nobody greets the dry half-starved faces of immigrant children lost in the filthy streets. *He is a fool who only sees the mischiefs that are past.* That voice of kindliness whose conciliatory purpose once gave rise to nations is choked by the rough and ugly. As the great city celebrates the glory of skyscrapers and airplanes, the iron-breast of this modern Babylon-by-the-Euphrates is slowly rusting, crumbling into a gray relic above the tides, the swift cold current. More people arrive. The river carries memories away with silt and leaves.

— 4 —

Once the morning rain had quit and the sun was out again, Harry arranged to meet Pearl beneath the Grand Arch of the Republic at two o'clock outside the east gate of Legion Park where pigeons swarmed the monument square. Heading there along Wellington Avenue from a busy lunch counter on Upson Street, he had purchased an early evening edition of the *City Sentinel* and scanned the Want Ads for office space and business opportunities. Most of the blackmail Follette intended to pay him for vacating Transfer & Storage had to be wired straight away to Illinois; the children needed new clothes and books for the fall term, and Marie would soon have fresh household expenses Harry did not want those damned Pendergasts to pay for. What was left he would invest in fresh inventory and a new location in which to store it. So far, this real estate listing seemed the most attractive:

LARGE GARAGE

Buchanan Street near 32nd. 35,000 sq. ft: modern fireproof bldg, lowest ins. rate; large elevators, excellent light; suitable for showroom, stock rooms or mfg; For particulars, apply Homer L. Spence, Inc., Central Station. Phone Lexington 1530

He had also circled several employment ads for females: telephone work, hostess services, those sorts of positions that might fit someone with little technical training or education. Naturally, jobs with stenographic, bookkeeping, or typing services were out of reach, but perhaps if —

He stopped himself. Who was he hoping to fool? Any job in this city was out of the question for that poor girl. She needed a margin of absolute safety and nothing would fit here anymore. Maybe he should go to the police, tell them the whole story, beginning with those fellows in Sylvester's office. If he couldn't quite recall their names, maybe he could still remember what was said, and if someone gave him a list of Follette's associates, he might still be able to figure out who was who. No doubt Follette's got top-drawer connections at City Hall, but they couldn't all be taking a fix, could they?

The shrill whistle of a peanut wagon shot through the sunlit square, echoing under the great Memorial Arch whose marble walls were carved with patriotic scenes of Americans in battle. Across the busy street, a spewing hydrant drew a flock of children to play. An immigrant fruit peddler stopped his cart to watch. Crowds of amused pedestrians skirted the cold flood. Farther up the block, a black patrol wagon swerved out of the long ranks of autos on Langston Avenue to park at the curb. In front of a Piggly Wiggly grocery store, a bearded man wearing a sandwich board that read END OF THE WORLD? stood on a soapbox, ranting, "PRAISE GOD!" and "GLORY TO THE LAMB!"

Within a few minutes, Harry watched Pearl emerge from a crowd of elderly women near the yellow rose bushes that encircled the marble Fountain of Armistice. She wore a breezy blue frock and a silk scarf and cloche hat. Those brown silky curls about her ears, soft rosebud mouth, that trembling little chin. *Love in her sunny eyes does basking play.* Good heavens, she was beautiful. Close enough to be heard now, she shouted, "Did you see him, honey? Did you?"

"See whom?" Harry called back above the children racketing about under the spray of water, shrieking with delight. He smiled affectionately and thought to himself: Don't tell her your troubles. Let her be gay and frivolous today. Tomorrow always comes too soon.

She darted forward to kiss him warmly on the lips. "Why, Shipwreck Kelly, you old goat, that's who! He's put on a sitting back at the Hudson Street flagpole and says he ain't coming down 'til Thanksgiving. Ain't it the cat's nightgown?"

"Thirteen days, thirteen hours, thirteen minutes."

"How's that again?" She took a breadstick out of her bag and bit off the end.

"It's precisely how long that fool said he'd be up there. It was in all the morning papers. Some bigger fool by the name of Kozlowski is paying him one hundred dollars a day to beat Hold 'Em Joe Powers' record of last summer."

"Well, ain't it a yell?" she laughed, stepping backward when a pair of giggling young girls on rollerskates swept past under the Arch. A brown terrier chased behind them, barking loudly, scaring the pigeons. The elevated trolley clanged on approach to the 34th Street crossing.

Smiling, Harry folded the newspaper under his arm. "So, I suppose one day soon that'll be you perched on top of some flagpole, won't it? Honestly, isn't that Avon Foreman boy just about your age? I think he was just given an award by the city of Baltimore for his ten days of foolishness aloft. Well, now he certainly made his mark, didn't he?"

"Aw, you needn't go to pieces, honey. I don't want to mash my head. Besides which, Shipwreck Kelly ain't the only show in town, see?" She gave Harry a theater handbill.

Looking it over, he read:

Shamrock Theater

THE COREY BROS PRESENT LILLIAN FAYE

IN

"LOVE'S LOST ILLUSIONS"

WITH

MISTER JULES WELCH

"THE TRAMP WHO STOLE VIRGINIA'S HEART"

PLUS

VENTRILOQUIST SOCRATES OGG

Moran AND Mack . Ignatius THE Great . Sweet Lorelei

AND

"THE Shamrock Girls"

TWO EVENING SHOWS

"What is this?"

She circled behind his back, brushing her fingers across his collar. "Honey, I got the most wonderful news in the world!"

"What's that, dear?"

"Oh, it's so marvelous I can hardly tell you. Mr. Corey gave me a dancing job! He picked another jane at the audition for the chorus last month, but had to give her the air on account of the trouble she was laying up for herself with some of the other girls. When I seen they were holding another audition, I went down there and told Mr. Corey if only he'd give me the chance, I'd smack it over for him every show." She chewed off another piece of breadstick. "So, how's about that, honey? Ain't it the swellest news you ever heard? Why, I'm a genuine hoofer now." She added, "There's a change of bill twice a month and Mr. Corey says a dame with real talent's as scarce as a Chinese policeman, so if I can put this act over, why, it's a cinch I'll be famous in nothing flat. You'll be there, won't you? Our first show's at eight."

"Tonight?"

She kissed his cheek. "Wait'll you get a load of my costume, honey. It's an eyeful!"

Harry would have been perfectly happy without this piece of news, because now he certainly knew what Cobb meant by talking at the show. If they were to meet at the Shamrock theater, Cobb might decide everything had been settled but the cost of the agreement, and only he knows what that would be. This is all a great advantage for him, Harry thought, and a trap for me. There'd be consequences for taking the wrong perspective.

Pearl tapped his shoulder. "Say, honey, I got an idea. There's a swell Jew by the name of Louie Nash, works for Rogers Peet at the corner of 52nd and DeKalb. He'll hire you some natty duds for the show to-night, see, and won't soak you, neither, 'cause he's a pal of mine. What do you say? Why, you'll be a regular Joe Brooks."

She rubbed the back of his hand.

Across the street, a couple of detectives in long coats and badges climbed out of the patrol wagon and walked down to Schaefer's drugstore on the corner. A uniformed patrolman followed them inside, and two others remained behind at the curb, nightsticks in hand. More children ran by headed for the gushing hydrant while mid-afternoon traffic roared in the street.

"Darling, I've already got a coat and trousers being pressed at the Chinese laundry on Gardner Street. Not to mention the fact that I have an appointment at the Empyrean Building within the hour. Honestly, dear, things have become very complicated today."

"Aw, honey," Pearl moaned, tugging lightly on his sleeve. She rubbed her bosom against his arm. "You got to promise to see me knock 'em dead this once. Please? What do you say? I'll even buy you a bowl of chop suey after the show, if you like. I got the dough now on account of finding myself a real job. Just like I said I would. Ain't you proud of me, honey? Even a little?"

Good grief, this was difficult. "Of course I am, darling, it's just that I've got so much to do. I know it doesn't seem fair."

"Hey, I know that kid! That's Herbie Shaw! "

"Who?"

Harry saw a youth in a flat cap and suspenders race out Schaefer's drugstore with a revolver in his hand. The patrolman waiting up the sidewalk barked an order for the youth to drop the gun. Another patrolman chasing out of the drugstore clubbed the youth in the back of the head with a riot stick, knocking him to the sidewalk. Next he kicked the boy hard in the ribs and snatched the revolver from his grasp. He pulled out a whistle and blew it. A detective rushed out of the drugstore carrying a shotgun. The injured boy lay face down and bleeding on the sidewalk, watched over by one of the patrolmen. The other detective led a white-coated druggist out of Schaefer's carrying a box of liquor bottles. He had a grin on his face and the druggist was weeping. The detective pushed him up the sidewalk to the patrol wagon. His partner went back into the drugstore. When the boy tried to get up, the patrolman stepped on his hand.

Pearl shot across the street like a bullet, dodging between two Fords and screaming like a banshee. Harry could hardly believe his eyes. She ran up onto the sidewalk and gave the patrolman a shove in the back, almost knocking him over. A passing grocery truck blocked Harry's sight, but he heard her yelling, "YOU DIRTY SONSABITCHES! GET OFF ME!" When the truck drove on, she was wrestling on the sidewalk with two patrolmen. One of them was trying to pin her arms. Then they both got hold of her. Seeing them drag Pearl into the drugstore, Harry lost his temper and rushed across to help her, nearly getting rundown by a lady in a Ford sedan before reaching the curb. "HEY THERE!" he shouted after those two cops. "WHAT DO YOU THINK YOU'RE DOING?"

Another patrolmen stepped forward and stuck his hand in Harry's chest. "Step back, mister."

"That's my meal ticket you fellows just dragged inside! If you know what's good for you, you'll get her out of there right now!"

"Says who?"

"Listen here, if one of you sticks his hand up her skirt, the whole damned lot of you'll be trading those nightsticks in for broom handles! She's the mayor's niece, for heaven sakes! Don't you know that?"

Did the mayor even have a niece? Good grief, where'd that come from?

"Are you on the level?" The cop looked down into the drugstore where Pearl was yelling her head off.

"You're damned right I am!" Harry insisted, half-convincing himself. "Now, bring her out of there before she takes it personally. No use sticking your neck out. She's trouble, I tell you. If I weren't running from the bill collectors, you wouldn't catch me down here playing nursemaid to that little hellcat."

As a large coal truck rumbled by, the cop gave Harry a good hard stare, then shrugged. "Aw, what do I care, anyhow?" He called down to the patrolmen inside the drugstore. "JOHNNY?"

Another voice came back. "YEAH?"

Pearl shouted a particularly vulgar obscenity Harry had never heard before.

"BRING HER OUT!"

"WHAT FOR?"

"JUST DO WHAT I SAY!"

A round of bickering began indoors, one cop begging the other to let him crack Pearl on the skull. *Don't let her talk you over! She's asking for it like nobody's business!"*

Harry told the patrolman beside him, "If one of them knocks a tooth out, you're all sunk. I'm not joking. You better drop it. She's his favorite niece."

"FOR GODSAKES, JOHNNY! BRING THAT DAME OUT, PRONTO! AND DON'T GET FRESH WITH HER, NEITHER!"

Back at the patrol wagon, the druggist called out, "Hey, I'm the mayor's brother-in-law! He'll cash you in if you turn me loose!" Then he laughed until the detective banged his head against the wagon.

How do these fellows tie their own shoes in the morning? Harry watched the patrolmen grab the injured boy and drag him up the sidewalk to the patrol wagon beside the druggist who had quit laughing. Motor traffic slowed when it passed the drugstore. The bearded Jeremiah with the sandwich board had abandoned his soapbox and gone elsewhere. Another lively flock of pigeons settled across the monument square.

"Here's your dame," the cop told Harry as the other detective brought Pearl out of the drugstore. Her hair was mussed, her paint smudged. She looked dazed and distressed. When the cop handed her over, he said to Pearl, "Sorry about this nonsense, honey."

She spat on his shoe. "Says you, buster! Why, I ought to crack your jaw!"

Harry grabbed her arm tightly.

She squirmed to free herself. "Hey, lemme go!"

"Oh, just stop that." Harry faked a pleasant smile and dug in harder, astonished that his bluff had held. Who would've taken that bet? "Let's go, darling. Your bib's waiting at home." He nodded to the patrolmen. "Thanks, fellows. You're awfully good sports."

Harry hurried her past the crowd that had gathered to see someone get shot. Once they were far enough from the drugstore, he let go of her.

She lurched away from him. "Jeez, what'd you do that for? You hurt my arm!"

A bus drove by. Traffic thickened at the neck of Langston Avenue and 34th Street. Two of the patrol cars roared off past the monument square, sirens wailing. Once they had gone beyond the elevated rail, Harry heard an airplane droning high overhead and blocked the sun with the back of his hand to get a better look. A long white banner with black lettering trailed off its tail, but was too high to read clearly.

Pearl growled, "I ain't afraid of those big shots, honey."

"Well, you ought to be. They could've thrown you in jail. Who was that boy, anyhow?"

"Some kid who used to be stuck on me," she smirked, "until I cut him out for wearing my clothes. Now he's a sneaker for Winking Willie who does him the big favor of letting Herbie share a pillow at the Fairchild when he's not bird-dogging jobbers down on the waterfront. Those cops didn't need to club him like that. I tell you, they're all ginks, every last one of 'em."

Harry checked his watch and saw it was nearly half past two. If he didn't hurry now, National City Bank would close before he could deposit Follette's check. He told Pearl, "Look, darling, I have to go."

"Where?"

"Downtown."

"Well, I ain't got nothing to do 'til rehearsal at six. I'll go with you."

Take her to Follette's office? Now, that'd pay, wouldn't it? "It's a business appointment, darling, nothing you'd be interested in. Believe me."

"Aw, honey, you can trust me. I'll be good. You won't even know I'm there."

A mail truck stopped at the curb just ahead of them and a postman got out to retrieve the mail. When he saw Pearl, he gave her a wink. She blew him a kiss and the fellow dropped his sack.

A raw gust of wind tumbled through her hair.

Harry watched a taxi chase a silver Packard through a red light up the street.

Arguing with Pearl was hopeless. Just exasperating. Then come the kisses and embraces when she knows you're beaten. She just seemed to get everything she needed. Well, he couldn't stand on the diving board all afternoon, so once again he relented. "If I let you tag along, you have to promise there'll be no funny business, and when I ask you to wait for me, you'll do so."

"Sure, darling." She kissed him on his lips. "I'll do anything you want."

— 5 —

Pantheon Avenue ran through the financial heart of the metropolis, the high-minded district of banks and stock exchanges and great corporate offices from whose boardrooms and dictographs and stock tickers and pneumatic tubes was distributed daily a fervent accounting of the modern American Dream. Only two miles from Baskin Street, fortune and prosperity were linked by confidence and optimism to the big Bull Market whose erratic momentum had mesmerized the nation for most of the decade culminating this summer in heights of illusionary wealth few Americans could distinguish from genuine earnings and profit. In this rapacious atmosphere of inflated portfolios and buying on margin, cab drivers and waiters and doormen and shoeshine boys, sign painters and barbers, traded stock tips and conversation on freight loadings, radio expansion, automobile output, mail order and crop yields even as guileless suckers and shrewd con-men willingly swapped hats hour-to-hour according to vacillating levels of faith in the daily financial news.

The Empyrean Building stood in the geographical center of the city, its radio antenna atop the majestic glass-crystal spire rising precisely 1,114 feet above the bright fountains of Elysium Plaza. From within this greatest of the city's shining skyscrapers, myriad corporations and brokerage firms and national syndicates brought the wealth and culture of the Republic to the millions. Avery P. Anthony, one-time protégé of Louis Sullivan, designed his modern version of the towering Ziggurat and introduced it to the aerial age in the steaming summer of 1927. Glittering audacity provoked a passion in the young architect for this jazzy, flamboyant blend of Beaux-Arts and Machinery and Bronze Age aesthetics in an American skyscraper whose one hundred floors of sunbursting, zigzagging Art Deco ornamentation electrified the era that provided its lofty air-minded inspiration. Huge crowds on Pantheon Avenue greeted the dedication of the glorious building on the Fourth of July. George Gershwin himself performed "Rhapsody in Blue" on piano with Paul Whiteman and his Concert Orchestra in the warm sunlight of Elysium Plaza. Airplanes crisscrossed the silver-blue skies above downtown. Vice-President Charles G. Dawes delivered a stirring speech. When the great twelve-foot lobby doors swung open to a polished green serpentine marble foyer, trumpets blared, flashbulbs popped, and one thousand helium balloons tinted gold to resemble champagne bubbles were released into the atmosphere from the windy observation deck. Afterward, giant white-hot beacons emblazoned the uppermost floors late into that exuberant summer evening while fireworks and jazz showered the metropolitan dark and extravagant parties took the celebration higher and higher into the building until paper festoons and silk scarves and top-hats were cast fluttering from windows into the rarefied air, and champagne glasses were hurled over the stainless-steel railing of the riotous Seventh Heaven Club on the 100th floor to watch their descent through the clouds.

At dawn, J.P. Morgan and Company moved in. By the end of the week, Radio Corporation of America, Allied Chemical, General Electric, U.S. Steel, Pennsylvania Railroad, Montgomery Ward, American Telephone & Telegraph, National City Bank, Galaxy Features Syndicate, United Press, and Charles A. Follette's American Prometheus Corporation occupied the greater part of the skyscraper. Soon, the frantic energy of Elysium Plaza summoned investors and speculators, business lawyers, diamond and insurance brokers, exporters and importers, editors and cartoonists, doctors and dentists, accountants, bookkeepers, typists, stenographers, filing clerks, secretaries, receptionists, messengers and window washers to 2771 Pantheon Avenue for the privilege of earning a dollar within the greatest building the city had ever seen. Every newspaper in the Republic that month led with a feature on the skyscraper, every magazine from *Life* to *American Legion* had an angle on some facet of its design or an interview with somebody's uncle who had wired the elevator call buttons on the 73rd floor while Garbo or Mencken or Babe Ruth looked on. All the newest automobiles by Packard and Chrysler and Studebaker and Buick were photographed in front of the Empyrean Building to prove how modern they were. Radio broadcasts from the Seventh Heaven Club invariably drew huge audiences to the nightly airwaves. Indeed, many felt that public affiliation of any sort stood one in with the era's most advanced thinkers.

Despite how dreadful his day had been so far, Harry himself felt the thrill of Elysium Plaza upon stepping off the trolley with his young sweetheart in the broad sunshadow of the towering skyscraper. Street traffic was dense and smelly and loud, individuals hurrying in and out of the skyscraper, flustered and breathless. Hardly a soul now paused to admire the wingéd aluminum finials on the four corners of each rising setback or the reflective silver terra cotta that shone high into the cloudy metropolitan sky. Who had the time? Instead, traffic roared and men snarled while checking their watches, quite aware that opportunity waited for no one.

Harry and Pearl dodged and shoved and angled leeward with the hustling crowds, eventually accompanying a group of Oregon timber brokers into the central lobby where a great bronze sphinx greeted visitors. People streamed by. Elevators hummed and rang. Doorways framed in polished aluminum and black carrera glass led off in several directions toward a newspaper and cigar stand, a barbershop, candy store, lunch counter, travel bureau, a haberdasher and Florsheim Shoes. Well aware of the precariousness of bringing Pearl here this afternoon, Harry hustled her past the sphinx pedestal into the middle of the marble foyer. Thirty feet overhead, a ceiling mural of airships and aviators from Montgolfier to Lindbergh, surrounded by paneled chevrons and sunrays and prisms rubbed aquamarine and gold with metallic paint, was lit by rows of lotus-inspired light sconces. Across the foyer a huge reproduction in bas-relief of Maxfield Parrish's oil painting *Air Castles* occupied the north wall, while high on the west wall a large clock with chrome lightning bolts for hands displayed the hour. Harry directed Pearl immediately to the elevators ahead of a group of businessmen where she pressed the call button, and stood close to him as several people gathered behind. The elegant doors were fit with inlaid wood veneer to resemble Nile papyrus in bloom and he assumed each was buffed and polished daily since the entire row gleamed like a new pair of shoes. A pyramid-shaped light above the express elevator shone a bright rose. After a few moments, a bell chimed softly and the doors parted. Harry entered after Pearl. The elevator-runner was a boy perhaps a little older than Pearl, his fresh face scrubbed and pink.

He was dressed in a royal-blue monkey jacket with gold braids and epaulets and a matching round stitched cap. Gripping the crank handle,
the boy asked Harry, "What's your floor?"

"Ninety-nine."

Just saying that number was a pleasure. Who's a big shot now? Maybe
he could turn this over somehow, make it all come out for the good. You
do have to be confident there is a shape to these enormous challenges,
because the steps up and the steps down are often so closely related you
won't recognize the difference unless you accept that there is one.

A small group of men in business suits crowded in, each giving the
floor number of his own destination. The boy swiveled the crank and
the elevator began to rise. One of the men rustled open a newspaper.
Others murmured conversation nearby. The mahogany walls were ornamented with radiating bronze sunbursts; obsidian speedlines framed
the ceiling; amber lotus sconces high in the corners provided a golden
luminance. The elevator-runner stared at Pearl who stood beside him
along the wall near Harry. The boy smelled of cheap shaving soap and
witch hazel and looked sleepy. As the elevator passed the tenth floor,
Pearl frowned at him. "Do you mind awfully?"

The boy smirked. "Say, what's a dollface like you doing downtown?
Selling hankies?"

She raised her chin, sliding a step closer to Harry. "We got us an
appointment upstairs, if it's any concern of yours."

The boy chuckled. "A big cheese, eh?" He worked the brass crank
as the elevator slowed.

"I should say so," Pearl replied, with a scowl. "You little peanut."
She took out her compact and checked her lipstick in the mirror. Harry considered putting his arm around her waist to let the boy know
Pearl was out of his reach, but decided against it. Who could say what
the other fellows in the elevator might think, a girl that young in his
company? He was no moral reprobate, but some people are entirely
unprepared for certain thoughts about love and romance. In any case,
whose fault was it if a fresh beauty adored him?

A bell chimed, the doors slid apart, and two of the businessmen
exited the elevator. When nobody else got on, the doors eased shut and

the elevator rose once more. Harry began to feel nervous. Why hadn't he just asked Benjamin to mail the check? He was facing a whole new world here without any introduction.

Behind him, the man with the newspaper said to someone nearby, "Did you read Lardner's column this morning?"

A voice replied, "No, I didn't."

"Well, I've got a sawbuck says the day after the Cubs cop the pennant, McGraw quits baseball."

"Phil heard from Selden Hughes that McGraw bought a pair of yearlings at auction last month from Middlebury Stables. Hopes to race them at Saratoga, eventually."

"Say, didn't Hughes have 'Clyde Van Dusen' at the Derby?"

"Just to show," replied the voice. "Somebody told him McAtee'd been seen with a bottle of gin the night before and swore he'd never be able to stay in the saddle long enough to win. That stupid fellow cost Selden a cool ten grand."

"Lousy bastard."

Both men laughed.

The elevator stopped at the 32nd floor and the man with the newspaper got off. Harry leaned out for a look down the hallway where a pudgy redheaded receptionist for the Galaxy Features Syndicate office sat at a single desk. Through the window behind her, Harry saw men in suspenders and loose neckties strolling about waving papers and gesticulating at each other. A gray haze of cigarette smoke hung beneath the ceiling. Then the office doors burst open and a trio of men rushed toward the elevator, shouting to the boy, "Hold the door! Hold the door!"

All three were carrying scratchpads scribbled on in black ink. They crowded the front of the elevator, nudging Pearl closer to the elevator boy.

"Sixty-three, kid! Step on it!"

Harry felt a slight spell of vertigo as the elevator lurched upward. The machinery hummed in the walls. Poor Marie hated elevators. A couple of years ago, he had taken her to Chicago on a short business trip and hired an eighth floor room at the Drake Hotel with a stirring view of Lake Michigan. But she was so scared to ride the elevator, they had to climb a hundred stairs twice a day, which put hell on his mood. He left her home after that.

Holding the crank, the elevator boy murmured something to Pearl.

"Let me alone," she growled, pressing her shoulder into the bronze sunburst on the elevator wall. Harry was amused by the boy's hopeful flirtations. She really was irresistible, wasn't she? Certainly every fellow in the elevator wanted to make love to her. Each sneaking glance betrayed that desire. If it were not for all this other nonsense, he thought, I'd be the luckiest fellow in the whole damned city.

"I tell you, it'd be slick," the boy persisted. "Why, I ain't such a bad scout."

Pearl laughed. "That's a hot one."

"Aw, come on, dollface. When are you through? I won't steer you wrong. Honest!"

One of the men facing the door said to the man beside him, "If Nelson telephones to Bessemer City before suppertime, you be sure he reminds those NTWU people that Gastonia won't tolerate a union meeting tonight. If Ella May wants to sing her songs, let her do it at home. It's not safe in Loray or Marion, either. They ought to know that by now."

"Beal sent a telegram to Harrelson's office yesterday claiming Gardner told the papers in Raleigh he was a communist and ought to fry."

"Oh, that's absurd. Why, I heard Gardner gave a speech in Charleston only last week arguing for reform over anarchy. Beal's just frightened by Aderholt's cronies. I'll see that someone talks to Hays and settles the poor fellow down."

Somebody coughed at the back of the elevator and the men in front stopped talking, except for a last remark concerning Lillian Gish touting Clicquot Club ginger ale aboard the White Star liner *Majestic* while playing Ping-Pong with Dr. Annie Besant. The elevator rushed to a stop at the fifty-ninth floor and a man from the rear of the car with a stack of catalogues under one arm hurried off to the Felton Insurance offices.

As the elevator ascended to the top third of the skyscraper, the boy said to Pearl, "You ain't engaged, are you?"

"Why, sure I am," she replied and held out her left hand, absent of any jewelry. "You ain't blind, are you?"

The elevator boy snorted, "Well, I been engaged once."

"She didn't answer to 'Dora,' did she?"

"Say, that's rich." He swiveled the crank and the elevator came to a stop again. "Sixty-three!"

When the doors slid open, the men with the scratchpads exited with two others from the back of the elevator. Harry recognized the office immediately as United Press. He considered getting out just to change their situation. Nobody would expect them to jump off on this floor, would they? The roar of typewriters and reporters on telephones and shouting editors cascaded through the windows into the elevator. He wondered what these fellows might think of Follette's little sex drama. A crowd of men in white shirts with rolled up sleeves gathered around the receptionist, yelling at each other. A lovely blonde secretary with an impressive bosom stood beside the door, weeping. Beside her waited a young messenger boy in knickers holding a large brown parcel. Two other men came around the corner from the switchboard operators and entered the elevator, one with a camera hanging around his neck, the other wearing a straw hat and carrying a thick stack of newspaper clippings.

"Eighty-five!" said the photographer.

"Seventy-nine!" said the one with the clippings.

Harry stayed put as the doors closed and the elevator rose. Well, what would have been the point of getting off there, anyhow? Who would've believed him? Instead, he tried to think of what he intended to say to Follette when they reached his office. Stay away from her, you sonofabitch, or I'll go to the papers? He certainly couldn't let those fellows think they could get away with anything. If he did, they'd never lay off.

The man with the clippings said to the photographer, "Anyhow, like I was saying, I hired a bird from Mary Duncan Stenographic last Tuesday. Nicest eyes you ever seen. Of course, she won't touch me for anything. Says she's in love and has to remain pure for some fellow she met typing form letters in a collection agency last summer. What a card! Normally I won't hire a girl just for her sex appeal, but this little sweetheart couldn't write her own name without a hint. If I can't make her soon, I'll have to let her out."

"Red roses and pink champagne," suggested the photographer.

"Not on a stringer's salary."

"Walt Wilwirding says the *Herald-Dispatch* pays by the inch," the photographer remarked. "If that's so, you ought to be able to rent a houseboat on Biscayne Bay for a week with what you've got there in your hand."

"Say, is that a joke? I tell you, for what I've been earning since McBride took over the city desk, I'd be better off writing copy for the Motor License Bureau."

A voice shouted from the back of the gold-lit elevator, "Hey, son! You just missed my stop!"

Harry almost laughed out loud. That's what you get, sonny, for flirting on the job! The boy promptly halted the elevator at the next floor. A bell chimed and the doors parted. Nobody moved. The elevator boy looked at a short dumpy man in a Weber & Heilbroner hat at the back of the car. "Ain't you getting off?"

"This isn't my floor."

Harry looked out and saw a sign indicating Rosenberg Brothers, a commodities investment firm. He knew a fellow named Steinmetz who used to work for that outfit. Took a transfer to Cleveland and bought a big house on the lake. He made a fortune in bond sales, but his daughter fell out of a boat and drowned. A stack of financial journals from Wall Street sat next to a Monroe adding calculator on a fine oak desk. A telephone was ringing loudly, although Harry didn't see anyone rushing to answer it.

"It ain't that long a walk down," said the elevator boy, trying to hide the embarrassment of his error while Pearl snickered at him. The boy's face was red as a tomato.

"Do you know which floor is mine?"

"I forgot."

"Then how would you know how far down I've got to walk?"

Another voice spoke from behind Harry, saying, "Look here, I have appointments at Lehman Brothers. If this fellow's not getting off, then please shut the bloody doors and take me up to eighty-one!"

Murmurs of agreement persuaded the elevator boy to start the lift up again, despite a flurry of obscenities from the man whose floor he had missed.

The photographer said to the man with the clippings, "I'm taking Jenkins' picture tonight."

"In the chair?"

"Naw, sitting in a holding cell next door. McMurtry's got fifty bucks for me if I can sneak a flash of Joey with the priest."

"I covered Charlie Becker at Sing Sing for *Harper's*. Damnedest thing I ever seen. The poor fellow smoked like a Franklin stove for five minutes before they switched off the juice. I haven't done one since."

When the lift stopped again, Harry heard Pearl snarl at the elevator boy, "Aw, you're all wet. Why, a girl'd have to be crazy not to fall for a sweetheart like him." She entwined her fingers into Harry's and gave them a warm squeeze. He gave serious thought to kissing her. Why not? Whose business was it, anyhow, if they wanted to make love? Were it not for that idiot elevator boy, he'd certainly give her a good hard kiss just to make these other fellows jealous.

"I tell you, he's a sissy," the boy replied, adjusting one of his gold epaulets as the doors slid open. "Seventy-nine!"

"Well, so long," the man with the clippings said to the photographer before he got off the elevator. A scrawny clerk wearing a green eyeshade passed by. Trailing just behind him, a towheaded office boy labored with a new Mimeograph machine and a stack of empty brown file pockets. Harry heard the clattering of stock tickers. The man with the clippings turned around. "Oh, incidentally, McMurtry wanted me to tell you that George Pipal spoke well of those pics you took of Sandburg at Elmhurst last year. 'Right out of the top drawer,' he said."

"Gee, thanks. That's swell."

The doors slid closed. Meanwhile, the dumpy man shoved past Pearl to the front of the elevator and stood next to Harry facing the polished doors as they rose again, nervously shuffling his feet. His suit was rumpled and he needed a bath with a fresh bar of soap. The elevator boy looked away. Disgusted with these delays, Harry checked his pocketwatch: ten minutes to three. If this stupid elevator didn't hurry up, he would be late to the bank. Pearl gave his arm a light tug. She had her lips pursed for a kiss. When he furtively shook his head, she pinched his wrist.

The ivory light sconce above Harry flickered briefly. Out of the blue, the dumpy man remarked loudly, "Why do we have to stop at every floor? Doesn't anybody understand the purpose of the express elevator?"

From behind him, a voice replied, "Look here, you're not the only one with appointments this afternoon."

Without looking back, the dumpy man scowled. "I'm telephoning long distance to Elias Cohen in five minutes with one million dollars at stake. I should say that's likely more important than whatever silly transactions with Remington Rand you've engaged."

"Well, I'll have you know I'm a lawyer retained by Clarke Brothers, and I'm expected at Central Station within the hour. I doubt very much the firm would consider the triflings of another real estate purchase as an excuse for my having missed this afternoon's train to Atlanta."

Sure, Harry thought, let's have a scrap over elevator stops.

The elevator slowed to a stop at the 81st floor where a man carrying an armful of stamped envelopes got off, glaring at the dumpy man as he left. When the doors slid open again, both the dumpy man and the photographer exited, the former to a loud raspberry from someone in the middle of the car. Now only three young patent lawyers remained, each carrying calf-bound law books and a leather briefcase, success evident in their dress and demeanor. As the doors slid shut and the elevator rose toward the top of the skyscraper, the elevator boy said to Pearl, "So, what do you say, dollface? Me and you and the Marx Brothers tonight at the Paramount. I'll pick you up at eight o'clock."

"Aw, go fly a kite, you little pipsqueak. You're lucky I ain't already socked you in the eye for that smart crack about Rudy Vallée."

"Try it and see what happens, sweetheart."

Now these two? Good grief! Harry grabbed Pearl's arm and drew her close to his side. Behind him, one of the lawyers said to the others, "Listen here, I finally bought Dorothy that new Marmon Roosevelt for her birthday. She'd begged me for a month and you know how weak my resolve is when it comes to my best girl. Well, imagine this: She cracked it up last night on a lamp pole driving to the City Symphony."

"No!"

"Cross my heart! She stopped at the Xanadu Club for a highball with Eva and was so corked when she left, she forgot her coat and hat. Well, she hit the pole trying a turnaround at thirty miles an hour in the middle of Sutton Street. I told her, 'Darling, next time it's a Ford!'"

Laughter filled the elevator. Then the first lawyer added, "I suppose you've heard about Felix, haven't you?"

"No."

"Not a word."

"It's cancer," said the lawyer. "They spotted it on the X-ray yesterday morning. Bessy's beside herself. She doesn't give a damn about honorary degrees or statues to Civic Virtue. She says if Felix goes, she'll swim out into the river and drown herself."

"How awful."

"Yes, what a shame."

The elevator came to a stop at the 99th floor; a soft bell chimed and the doors parted. Harry stood back to let the patent lawyers get off ahead of him. One of them stuffed a dollar bill into the elevator boy's pocket as he passed. Harry let Pearl by, too, then nodded a thank-you to the boy and got off. Behind them, the boy whistled to Pearl. When she looked back, he called out, "Say, dollface, wasn't that you I seen yesterday baring her fanny down at Fletcher's Beach?"

Then the doors slid shut.

Harry and Pearl arrived in a square elevator lobby facing a carved granite archway whose frieze of Machine Age inventions and Industrial achievement framed the words:

AMERICAN PROMETHEUS CORPORATION

An oriental rose carpet led beneath the granite arch to tall double doors of polished walnut, where a radial sunray transom reflected the illumination from a glass and silver chandelier fifteen feet above the floor. The lawyers had already rushed off to their appointments. The lobby was quiet. Two other elevators with identical Nile papyrus veneer flanked the dim lobby, east and west. Mayan-inspired motifs decorated the lobby walls, painted stars and clouds filled the sky-blue ceiling. Utterly frustrated by the duration of the elevator ride, Harry hurried under the arch to the double doors. Chasing him, Pearl groused, "Why ain't you felt like taking my part, honey?"

God, is she still on that? "You mean because some silly elevator boy passed a slighting remark? Don't be childish!"

"It ain't only that, darling. A girl needs to feel she's — "

Harry stopped at the door. He'd had just about enough of this. "Maybe I ought to go back there and knock him down! Would you like that? Would that make you happy?"

"That ain't what I meant."

"We're late," he said, losing patience. "If you can't behave, maybe you ought to go downstairs until I'm finished. I told you, there's no fooling around in here. This is an office with some very important clients of mine. I'm not joking. You either sit quietly or I'll have to show you out now."

Bringing her up here, he knew, could be a great mistake. The men on this floor of the building were enormously wealthy, and saw little consequence in those who were not. It was hard to realize the truth in that, but scarcely a week went by without some calculated business shift that put a small-timer out on the sidewalk. You could argue the insinuation is unfair, that each fellow is possessed by the same plan to get rich and live comfortably, and if that's so, then what could possibly be wrong with succeeding? Well, we want what we want, and if good fortune resolves it into view somehow, we make sure to get what we can for ourselves without concern for those who may have wanted it, too. If there is anything left over, the best of us may even share it.

"Look here, darling," he told her, "this fellow I'm seeing today hates doing business after lunch, but if I can't put myself over to him, I'll lose an opportunity that could mean the difference between eating at

Eckleburg's next month or kicking over trash cans on Parker Street. Do you follow me?"

"Sure, honey."

"Once I'm through, we can do whatever you like, but you've got to be careful to keep out of trouble for now. Do I have your word?"

"Will you buy me a flower?"

"Yes, dear, if you behave yourself."

Charles A. Follette's office was situated at the end of a rectangular Sienna marble foyer lit by clamshell sconces. A plum-colored oriental carpet covered the middle of the foyer woven with the defiant Titan as its center medallion. Fresh palms in brass pots beneath framed oil paintings of clouds and angels decorated the hall between the doors. A fancy varnished mahogany desk occupied the northeast corner of the hall next to Follette's door where an older woman in a beige dress and somewhat gaudy emerald lorgnette sat talking on the telephone. On the receptionist's desk was a fruit bowl of ripe summer apples and a fluted vase of pink magnolias.

Pearl wandered about the lobby while Harry waited for the receptionist to finish her telephone call. Terrified that he would be late to the bank with Follette's payoff, he checked the time on his pocketwatch once again, hoping the receptionist might notice his concern. When she continued to ignore him, he strolled over to one of the wall niches to examine a silver Roman wine pitcher. Harry had little doubt Charles Follette was as wealthy as anyone in the city. He'd read once in the *Star Herald* that a significant portion of the financing for Elysium Plaza had been paid directly out of Follette's personal fortune, that Avery P. Anthony spent part of a summer with Follette at Grossinger's in the Catskills revising the interior design to suit the industrialist's whims, and that only a guarantee to Follette by the city commissioners that he be granted the honor of occupying the 99th floor allowed the Empyrean Building to exist.

A door on the east wall opened and two of the lawyers he had just seen on the elevator came out carrying a thick blue sheaf of law papers and headed for the lobby.

"Would you please put that back?"

Harry turned toward the receptionist and smiled when he saw Pearl replacing a shiny green apple from the fruit bowl.

"Thank you very much."

The receptionist went back to the telephone while keeping an eye on Pearl who lingered nearby. Now Harry felt awful about snapping at her in the lobby. He should have stuck up for her when she needed it, put that stupid elevator boy in his place. He watched Pearl fiddling with the palm fronds, her delicate figure more gorgeous than any of those fanciful angels. She was the most beautiful thing in this entire building.

Follette's office door swung open and the industrialist himself marched out with a short fellow in a blue pinstripe suit. They strutted across the foyer side-by-side, chatting amiably about flying hydroplanes into the Alaskan wilderness. Once Follette had escorted the man through the tall doors to the elevator lobby, Pearl hurried over to Harry, wide-eyed with excitement. Trying to keep her voice down, she told him, "Honey, that was Roscoe Merriman!"

"Who?"

"The sheik of all bootleggers. Why, he owns the Pelican Club, Tony and Lou's, Sallie's Oasis, and the Alhambra. Old Roscoe's floatin' in gin-soaked dough."

"How do you know that?" For a minor, her knowledge of the nefarious comings and goings in this city really was astounding. She was practically a tabloid unto herself.

"Oh, I seen him a couple of times at that Italian spaghetti parlor on Becker Street with Frankie Gambino and Albert Hupp. Ain't nobody in town crookeder'n them two."

Follette came back into the lobby wearing a big smile. Wrapped tightly in his fist was a copy of the *Evening Dispatch*. Well, this is it, Harry thought. If I'm really no milquetoast, I'll go right over and give him a piece of my mind. He's no more royalty than I am. The worst that can happen is he'll throw me out of the building. But I won't bow down to him, and he better know it.

Taking a deep breath, Harry called out, "Sir?"

Follette turned about as Pearl strolled past toward the elevator lobby. He studied her intently for a moment, then shook his head and smiled at Harry.

"Why, Hennesey, old man!" Wearing his usual ingratiating smile, Follette walked over and they shook hands. "What brings you up here today?"

Holding his temper, Harry replied, "Benjamin told me there'd be a check waiting for my space at Transfer & Storage. Apparently that was all decided this morning."

Follette woke up. "Oh yes! You've decided to leave us. Sorry to hear that. I presume opportunity's knocking elsewhere. I certainly can't blame you for taking advantage. It's just unfortunate we couldn't have discussed this earlier, offered you another situation, perhaps. Well, I suppose it's somewhat my fault. I've been away at Grossinger's and Forest Hills where my lovely friend Miss Helen Wills just won another championship. Marvelous tournament! Splendid tennis! Of course, once it was all settled, I was forced to give her quite a spanking on my own court at Newport. It's been many years since my day at Princeton, but I showed her I can still whack a decent backhand!"

He's either joking, Harry thought, or a terrible liar. Or maybe nobody tells him what decisions are made in his name. We're just all commodities, aren't we?

Meanwhile, the industrialist reached into his coat pocket and drew out a fat cigar and bit the end off. After searching his breast pockets for a match without success, he called out, "Heddy!"

The receptionist stood up. "Yes, Mr. Follette."

"Could you help me, please?"

"Certainly, Mr. Follette."

She came around from the desk with a box of matches and hurried over to light his cigar.

"Thank you, dear," said Follette, puffing smoke into the air. He gave Harry a wink as though they shared a common bond.

"You're quite welcome."

"Heddy, do we have something on accounts payable for Mr. Hennesey?"

"Indeed, we do," she replied, heading back to the desk for a white envelope that was lying with a stack of other envelopes near the bowl of apples. She brought it to Follette who slit it open with his thumb and had a peek inside, then handed it over. Harry tucked the envelope into his coat pocket. He saw no sense in counting blood money in front of Follette, nor would he let Follette see him grovel like that.

"Will that be all, sir? I have Mr. Farnsworth waiting on the telephone."

Follette laughed. "Philo can wait all week if he likes, but he won't get another penny for that silly contraption of his. You can tell him I said so, too. The very idea of it scares me half to death."

Harry decided to lay out his cards. It was too late for cowardice. "Look here, sir, I hope you realize I'd rather have worked out an arrangement to stay with Transfer & Storage. There wasn't any great advantage in moving elsewhere, not when I have family responsibilities, you see, a wonderful wife and two lovely children who depend on me to keep them clothed and fed. It isn't fair to look down the road and not expect some bargain waiting for a good word or two after all the hustle and bustle I've been chasing this year. That lost niece of yours, for example, the one you put me after. Well, I've kept my ear out for your benefit as much as mine, and not that I've minded, either, because I believe in loyalty, as little as that's appreciated in this day and age. Now, I'm not saying Benjamin's offer wasn't generous, because it certainly was, so that's not — "

"Benjamin's quite a boy, isn't he?" Follette exhaled a ragged smoke ring.

"Yes, he is," Harry agreed. "But that's just what I'm driving at here. Don't you see? It's how he persuaded me to give up my space that's got me in a bind." Good grief, this was tough. Would he be ill-advised to mention Benjamin's threat? Whose game was this, anyhow? "You can't say I haven't done my best to help you out with this niece situation. Sure, I admit I haven't turned her up yet, but it's a big city and I've still got a few irons in the fire, you ought to know, and I doubt anyone is doing much better, so I just can't see why you fellows have decided to let me out like this."

Follette's expression changed, his round brow furrowed, eyes firm. "Hennesey, I've always thought of you as a terrier."

"Oh?"

"You're a businessman, aren't you?"

"Well, I certainly like to think so."

"Of course you are." Follette removed the newspaper from under his arm, and folded it open. "Listen here." He began reading from somewhere in the middle. "*My personal belief is that much of the crime we now have is hatched in speakeasies. I remember a speakeasy on Hicks Street that was raided recently, where we found not only liquor but narcotics. Incidentally, there were men of twenty-four different nationalities on the premises at the time. We have little trouble in getting convictions in narcotic cases. With a nod of the head the Federal attorney usually can influence the jury. We do have a great deal of trouble with juries in liquor trials.*"

Follette folded the paper closed once again. "How does that strike you, Hennesey?"

"Well, I'm not sure," he replied, confused with this turn in the conversation. "I'd need to have another look at it." What the devil did liquor have to do with any of this?

Follette shook his head. "Prohibition's finished, Hennesey, because it's no damn good for anybody but bootleggers and the Anti-Saloon League. Did you know that I just took a three-year lease on a grocery store at Lennox Avenue that's costing me $1350 a month?"

"No, I didn't."

"Well, Heddy's just received a notice from the city attorney's office reminding me that if the store is operated as a speakeasy, not only is my lease immediately terminated with no recourse to action, but that according to the Jones law I can be fined ten thousand dollars or do five years at Iron Hill. It's preposterous."

Trying desperately to be agreeable, Harry nodded. "I admit it certainly does sound unfair." My God, how on earth does Follette think he'll be elected governor, running rum out of his warehouses? You don't strike a bargain like that except out of desperation, or insanity.

"Well, it's more than that, Hennesey, it's damned nonsense! A fellow ought to be able to do business in America however he sees fit. Did you read last month that legal reserve life insurance in American companies passed one hundred billion dollars? Those fellows are rich as Croesus, which proves there's still a fortune to be made in this country. Now, I hold no brief for the Exchange, and certainly our stocks on the market are somewhat irregular these days — nobody knows how high 'up' will finally be — but I watch the broad tape all day long and still haven't the least idea how much this damned corporation'll be worth tomorrow. Benjamin believes we ought to increase our investments in tobacco stocks and urban properties. The board wants me to buy banks and Hollywood movie studios. My mother wants a bungalow in Connecticut. It's all a damned muddle. Oh, some people say it's the Jews who are trying to skin us alive, but that's a lot of baloney. I tell you, any Wobbly, Presbyterian or Shriner'll cheat you just as quick. That's the world these days. Why, a fellow who goes into business today to earn some money'll end up spending half his life trying to prevent the other fellow from taking it away!"

Harry was baffled as to what in the world any of this had to do with Benjamin and the warehouse? Why should he cry if Follette or any of his rich pals do a fold up over some slump in the market?

He glanced about nervously. Where had Pearl gone?

Follette puffed rapidly on his cigar and ranted on, "That Airvia mess with Gerald Tiffany finally scared Benjamin into disposing of our connection with Hadley & Company, and it cost me a small fortune. Now, this afternoon, my sister Margaret's telephoned to tell me her friend Edna is sitting in jail for bringing a hip flask of gin to Saint Peter's Cathedral last Sunday evening. Margaret claims the city attorney intends to prosecute this young lady to the fullest extent of the law on the same day our illustrious mayor is expecting the Prometheus Corporation to purchase eleven million dollars in bonds for his new subway system. I tell you, it's the limit."

"I should say so," Harry agreed, feigning commiseration. This was all becoming tiresome. Four short months ago he had hoped the great Charles A. Follette would find him industrious enough to want to strike a bargain to do business together one day. Now he decided that if being rich shortened one's nose so much as to pay little notice to his fellow man, how could wealth be something to strive for? Then again, why scrabble for the big bonanza at all when you can't take it with you?

Follette frowned as he blew another foul smoke ring. "Hennesey, do you belong to the Rotary Club?"

"No, sir, I don't," Harry admitted. "Frankly, I haven't had the time for social activities this summer. Business has kept me occupied day and night since I arrived in the city." Actually, he hated clubs of all sorts. Who needed a secret handshake when the fellow's other hand was stuck in your pocket? He didn't need stock tips and had no interest in golf.

"Well, it's a damned shame because an organization like that ought to engage a fellow like you to push them along, make a big noise. That's what I meant when I called you a terrier. I've watched you, Hennesey. Quite a lot, in fact. You're a regular fellow. You work hard, got a good egg for selling. An honest one, too. True as tomorrow, and that's damned remarkable for this day and age."

"Thank you."

"Trouble is, you're still a terrier among wolves."

"I beg your pardon?"

"Look here, Hennesey, a fellow like you'll never be rich." Follette took another puff on his cigar. "Now, don't get all out of sorts. I'm just stating a fact as I see it and most people in this city'll tell you Charley Follette sees it pretty damned straight! You're not a crook, Hennesey. You take the Eighteenth Amendment and the Sullivan Law to bed with you every night, and I admire that. Why, if this 'city of the good time' had a few more steady fellows like you, it'd be a hell of a lot smarter place to live. Instead, it's shysters like Piersall and Riesling and Hupp who muck around in the dark trying to pry a buck loose from their neighbors that are getting rich. They're the wolves, see, and they don't give a damn where that buck comes from, whether it's liquor, graft, rackets, you name it. And if it means dropping a few fellows into the river every so often to get it, well, that's fine, too. City Hall doesn't care much for the 'up-and-up,' either. All the hushdope in town says the mayor's got his own hand in the cookie jar. For Christsakes, half the barrels of Canadian whiskey Eddie Barker's agents took off those trucks on the Lewiston Bridge last week still wound up in somebody's cellar! Do you get me?"

Before Harry could answer, the door to Follette's office opened part way and a bespectacled young man with slicked-back hair leaned out. "Charley, they're at it again. Mitchell and Cutten. And Livermore claims he's leaving. You better get back in here."

Follette gave him a nod, and blew another smoke ring as the door closed. Dropping his voice, he told Harry, "Hennesey, old man, the plain truth is that it was me who told Benjamin to deal you out of the warehouse. Believe it or not, I did it for your own sake. A bum like Joe Phelps would eat you alive in no time at all, and he's not the only one, either. Like I said, you're a regular fellow, a good citizen, and a hell of a lot better than that mob up town. They don't know morals from marbles, and that's the plain truth. My advice is to take the five thousand and put it somewhere it'll help you earn an honest living. Leave all the rest of this nonsense to us wolves. All right? What do you say?"

At the last now, Harry tried his own bluff. "But what about your niece? Like I said, there's a trail to be followed here and I haven't lost the scent. As a matter of fact, I've got a fellow over in Kingston who seems to know a thing or two about this situation, and I was hoping to take the train out there tomorrow to see what he had to say."

Follette shook his head. "Don't bother about that, anymore. I'm afraid she's out of your league. We've hired half a dozen snoops from the Burns Agency who've promised results within thirty days or our money back, so you can put that girl away now and buckle down to business. It's over the dam. Believe me, you're better off putting her behind you."

"Are you absolutely certain?" No matter how rotten a bunch this was, Harry despised being cut out before he had the chance to quit.

Looking him straight in the eye, Follette cracked a millionaire's grin. "Hennesey, old man, glad you dropped up." Then the great industrialist gave Harry a friendly clap on the shoulder and walked back to his office without saying another word.

Harry felt like a damned fool. Now that he had been given his dismissal, that sinking he felt in his heart was humiliation, not disappointment. Where had he gotten the idea that Follette ever really admired him at all? What is more deplorable: being disillusioned by others or deceiving yourself? Follette was only a symptom of a peculiar disease that infected more men today than ever, so there really shouldn't have been anything to be ashamed of. Yet he remained where Follette had abandoned him on the woven medallion of the beautiful plum oriental carpet, until the receptionist spoke up, "Your little girl went to the ladies room."

He lifted his eyes. "Oh, thank you."

"Is there something else I can help you with?"

Utterly dispirited, he asked meekly, "Is it possible to tour the Seventh Heaven Club?"

The receptionist shook her head. "It's exclusive to members."

The telephone on the desk rang.

"What about the observation deck?" Maybe he could throw himself off.

"Go back out into the lobby and use the east elevator."

Then he asked the receptionist, "Will you tell the young lady where I went?"

"Of course."

The telephone rang again and Harry left.

A brisk wind rippled the flags on the aluminum finials a thousand feet above the great metropolis in a late afternoon sky streaked with white clouds and droning mail planes. Sunlight flashed off the glass-crystal spire whose ninety-foot radio antenna whistled high in the cold wind. Gray wisps of smoke from excursion steamers and coal barges drifted above the Broad Street trestle and the Washington Bridge. Harry stood at the northwest corner of the observation deck behind a stainless-steel safety railing watching a river of motors fill the great arteries of the city from the Avenue of the Republic to Empire Boulevard and the needle-thin sidestreets between Highland Park and Burlington Point. From this bright continent of the air, the old architecture below seemed to him clustered and sooty, the voices of the grounded millions rendered mute by distance, this Eden of clowns, as Mencken called it, no longer such a triumph of optimism.

Once on business trip to Knoxville, Harry paid a nickel to visit a camera obscura in an old frame building overlooking the Tennessee River. The consumptive brother of a gypsy fortuneteller whose carnival had left town led Harry into a small black room and in the darkness parted a curtain over a hole in one wall admitting a thin beam of light that projected a picture onto a flat plate of polished silver suspended from the ceiling. This reflection revealed a glittering metropolis of alabaster towers and golden minarets, the true nature of the city, claimed the rasping gypsy, denied fulfillment by God solely because of the foolishness of its inhabitants whose blasphemous infidelities and transgressions against His laws divided them from their own glorious inheritance. When the gypsy let the curtain fall closed once more, blocking off the beam of "divine light," he opened a small blacked-out window just to the left of the hole from where Harry was able to see the Knoxville he knew across the cold water, a city bleak and gray whose promised charms were that day fugitive at best. Why that image of two cities, one blessed and the other degenerate, so possessed the invalid gypsy Harry never knew, nor the secret of the camera obscura that revealed it, as both were gone a year later when Harry next stood on the sandy bluffs above the Tennessee River, staring at Knoxville across a hazy dusk.

"It's a miracle, ain't it, honey?" Pearl spoke from just behind him, a fresh green apple in her hand. She joined him at the railing and offered him a bite. When he declined, she polished the apple on her dress, and ate a big chunk out of the middle. Her silk scarf fluttered in the late wind as she admired the grand panorama of the broad blue summer sky from one hundred stories up. "He's a case, ain't he?"

"Who?"

"That old Charley Follette," Pearl replied, sliding over beside him until their arms were touching. She rubbed up against him. "Aw, I heard the line he was giving you, honey. I tell you, it's a load of bunk. Why, I had to take a sneak so's I wouldn't be tempted to give him a good sock in the eye."

Sincerely touched by Pearl's show of loyalty, Harry smiled. "You're very considerate."

Though, really, what did she know about Follette, except that perhaps men like him were likely responsible for too much of the sorrow girls like her endured in this city? Her courage shamed them all. If she went into the river some dark night, this whole crackerbox ought to throw in the towel and be done with it.

"Just don't let 'em high-hat you, honey," she counseled, brushing the scarf off her face as the brisk wind swirled up, a chill raising goose-flesh on her bare arms. "Darling, they ain't no better than you are. They just got lots of dough, that's all. You still got more smarts than the whole pack of 'em taken together."

Pearl ate another chunk out of the fresh apple.

Harry shrugged, unconvinced in his own heart that what she had said was the truth. Certainly he'd had sufficient faith in himself that night he crossed the dark plains of the Republic aboard the *Twentieth Century Limited*, writing up inventories of all he intended to buy and sell in the Big Town, the fair profits he intended to win. He had brought with him a large corded trunk packed solid with honest merchandise and the addresses of prospective clients. He traded stock quotations and business cards in the dining car with men in five-button vests and inquired about advertising boards on roadways leading in and out of town. Had his wallet allowed it, he would have hired skywriting pilot Jack Savage, or a series of witty notices in the *Society News*, maybe a smart word or two of self-promotion on a radio show. His enthusiasm for the marketplace had been boundless, reckless probity his desired reputation. While his competitors were out chasing skirts day after day, Harry had telephoned to the managers of stores and warehous-es, mailed hundreds of letters of introduction to potential customers, posted clever business advertisements in each of the city newspapers, walked miles in the industry district laboring for advantages that he had surely earned only to have Follette make him out to be another befuddled Roy Riegels at the Rose Bowl. Apparently four months in this city operating as a good straight fellow had garnered for him less profit than derision among his peers. So what was left for him to do? Speculation? Painting the tape? He had little faith in this new era of permanent prosperity. Buying on margin was nonsense, nor could ev-erybody in America be rich. Harry Hennesey had been taught by his father that the work was the thing. Blue skies now and then would be his reward.

A short while later when his darling Pearl offered him the last of the ripe summer apple by one of the nickel telescopes at the east end of the observation deck, Harry ate the few bites that remained and flung the core over the lofty railing.

— **6** —

Late in the summer night, Harry Hennesey's taxicab delivered him to the corner of Clancy and 89th street in front of the old Aeolian Hall where the names of Burns & Allen, Ed Wynn and George Jessel were highlighted on the bright electric marquee, and the enthusiastic crowd to the box office spilled out into the noisy street, reeking of gin and perfume.

The cabdriver hadn't been familiar with the Shamrock Theater so Harry was forced to walk south along stone-paved Clancy Street past raucous dance halls and nickelodeons, dodging knots of scabby-headed drunks and roving sailors until he discovered the Shamrock across from the old Olympia Theater where Eddie Cantor, Edgar Bergen, Jack Benny and Fred Allen were headlining that week. He bought a ticket from a sleepy boy in a black coat and went indoors. The theater lobby was grim and drafty. Gilt-framed placards beside the doors to the music hall commemorated some of the famous acts that had once appeared at the Shamrock: the mysterious Harry Houdini, Georgina Smith and Olga Petrova, Maurice Barrymore, John T. and Eva Fay, Vesta Victoria, Horace Goldin, Sober Sue, Ching Ling Foo, the Polka Dot Trio, Nat Goodwin, and the famous levitationist Harry Kellar. A tarnished brass ash receiver by the lavatory was overfilled with dead cigarette butts and burnt-out cigars. Two oily-haired young theater ushers in dress trousers and patent leather shoes stood shoulder-to-shoulder browsing a well-thumbed copy of *Zitt's Weekly*.

Harry went on into the music hall and chose a seat in the center rear against one of the cracked calcimined walls. The velvet curtain was closed and an ebony grand piano at stage right yet unattended.

Flanking the empty stage were pots of white begonias and a placard that read:

Jimmy & Ethan Corey

P · R · E · S · E · N · T

THE SHAMROCK VARIETY SHOW

A man in a brown serge suit and a tan felt hat sat alone ten rows back from the piano, chewing Chiclets. A handful of wiseacres in business suits who might have been salesmen from a Ford Agency took seats nearer the middle of the theater, cracking dirty jokes and laughing as if they'd drank their suppers earlier that evening. Another pair of fellows who looked to be dirt farmers in work-shoes and cloth jackets hurried in carrying sandwiches and bottles of cream soda and went immediately to the front row, a whiff of bay rum and liquor trailing behind them. An older man with mutton chop whiskers in a tuxedo and silk top-hat entered accompanied by a slightly younger woman in a rose organdy dress and big pink leghorn hat. They sat just down the opposite aisle from Harry. A pale young girl, barely older than Pearl, wearing a white dimity dress and a silver cloche hat joined them, chattering excitedly as if she hadn't been to a show before. It was almost eight o'clock now. A few more men and women straggled in, sitting here and there about the old music hall. Voices echoed faintly from backstage and Harry thought he heard a violin tuning. Dingy light bulbs atop a gaily-painted wood proscenium glowed dull amber. The high-beamed ceiling was dark wood and dusty, charcoal black at the roof pitch from half a century of gaslight fumes and steam heat and cigar smoke.

Now where was Cobb? Sitting this far back in the theater gave Harry the great advantage of spying into every row, and apparently his nemesis had not yet arrived. This seat seemed well concealed in the rear shadows and he doubted Cobb would notice him before he spotted that little rat, so long as he did not make himself too evident. He had felt a distinct fear, however, since climbing into the taxicab half an hour ago on Jackson Street, because he really had no idea what he expected to do once Cobb arrived. Given the kind of stakes he'd overheard in Sylvester's office that night, this could go very badly. He wondered what sort of fellow Cobb might really be. Was he a gangster or an errand boy? Was he dishonest, or could he be counted on to stick to a fair bargain? You could never tell with fellows like that. He's not really a businessman, so he couldn't be expected to behave like one. He was probably more underhand than smart. In any case, Harry realized that he simply needed to have a strategy. Once you're tangled up with a circumstance of someone else's making, you can't easily retreat to your previous life. What you do must be extraordinary. It must be something you would never conceive of otherwise.

Soon the ceiling lamps dimmed and two tall fellows in tuxedos crossed to the center of the stage from either wing. Those two dirt farmers and the man in the serge suit applauded. The hot-lights rose to a yellow cast and the two tall red-haired men's smiling faces became visible. When they spoke, their voices in perfect unison carried to all corners of the music hall.

"WELCOME, LADIES AND GENTLEMEN, TO THE SHAM-ROCK REVUE!"

They took a deep bow together and the pianist in a black bowler hat began to play a jaunty Irish melody and the plush velvet curtain rose on a chorus of eight girls dressed in emerald skirts and polished white shoes and frilly white blouses with ribbons and emerald bows. A pudgy violinist beside the piano player raised his bow and joined in as the twin masters of ceremonies sang an old Pat Rooney standard, "Biddy the Ballet Girl":

> *"On the stage she is Mamselle La Shorty*
> *Her right name is Bridget McCarthy.*
> *She comes at night and from matinees*
> *With baskets of flowers and little bouquets*
> *She's me only daughter*
> *And I am the man that taught her,*
> *To wear spangled clothes*
> *And flip 'round on her toes*
> *Oh, the pride of the ballet is Biddy!"*

Behind the Corey Brothers, the toe line of Shamrock girls danced a nifty waltz clog in ballet style, sixteen bars of clever footwork and choreography that Harry found impossible to believe Pearl (third from the left) had learned in less than a day and a half of rehearsals. He was frankly astonished. Her dancing was quick and sprightly, perfect in tempo and style, and she was every bit as pretty in lashes and mascara as the other girls. Had he known Pearl was so accomplished, he might have brought her to the Baghdad Gardens for a night of dinner and dancing. He loved a good Fox Trot. Once Marie did, too, but for so long now she seemed to prefer staying home to herself and the children. Why this was, he had no idea. As a girl, Marie had adored dancing. Then after the children were born, most of her youthful enthusiasms seemed coldly reconciled to the past. Lamentably, that was where he and Marie were different. He had never lost that desire to put his hat on. It's the rare fellow who would rather sit by a family hearth than venture out in the company of convivial spirits. Ham and eggs were swell to eat, but not for every meal. Watching his darling Pearl do her steps with such charm and expertise, Harry felt somehow justified in his blushing fondness for her. Although he knew she couldn't see him in the shadowy hall, he nodded to her proudly as if she were his own, an odd feeling indeed.

> *"Last Saturday night I got paid,*
> *I thought I'd go to the thee-ayter,*
> *And take the old woman along,*
> *In the parquette in front I sate her.*
> *When Biddy came out on the stage,*
> *My son Terrence was up in the tier.*
> *He cried — sister, Biddy, go in — but*
> *They waltzed Terry out on his ear."*

When the tune ended, the audience laughed, and the Corey Brothers took a bow while the piano player and violinist played on and the chorus of Shamrock girls did another four bars before dancing off the stage behind the Corey Brothers to a loud applause. Then the proscenium lamps dimmed and the musicians began a soft duet of parlor music, a soothing melody of desert romance in old Arabia. Lighted cigarettes burned crimson among muted voices here and there.

During supper at a small bistro on the corner of Lennox and Bond, Pearl had told him this engagement at the Shamrock Theater would earn her fifteen dollars a week. Of course, he assumed she was fibbing. Having now seen her dance in this shabby theater, he thought she was worth twice that. She had a genuine stage presence, a fresh and innocent quality that stood out from the other girls. He hadn't been able to take his eyes off her.

Just as Harry began another search for Cobb among the narrow rows, the theater hall went entirely dark and the two musicians stopped playing. He heard the curtains rustle apart and footsteps cross to the front of the wooden stage. Somebody in the audience burped. Then a single bright ceiling spotlight flashed down upon the stage revealing a man dressed in a black swallowtail suit seated upon a tall stool. His hair was slicked back and he wore nose-glasses and a Vandyck beard and supported on his right knee a ventriloquist dummy in plain red suspenders, brown work trousers, and button shoes, whose painted expression resembled that of the bearded man himself. Once the casual murmurs in the audience subdued, the ventriloquist spoke in a strangely tired and hollow voice that resonated throughout the steamy hall:

"I am Socrates Ogg, father of the new Adam. From the trunk of a mighty oak, I have carved a Modern Man. No past has he but the afterbirth of sawdust and glue collected through his creation, no soul but that which I have painted onto his wooden face with my own hand. The new Adam has neither conscience nor aspirations. He is an entirely Modern Man born to serve the Republic, accepting of his fate without complaint nor protest nor anger nor envy. He has no family but his employer and his Maker. He is tireless and loyal. He requires neither food nor drink nor spiritual sustenance. He suffers no vices and seeks no virtue greater than a desire to serve — "

"Freedom!"

A fluty tenor's voice echoed across the music hall as the ventriloquist's dummy rose up from the lap of Socrates Ogg and swept the hushed audience with a moon-eyed gaze. Swiveling his head slowly, the dummy searched out into the dark for the Chiclet-chewing man in the serge suit and the dirt farmers and the Ford Agency wiseacres and Harry himself hidden in the shadows of the back row where the ventriloquist's dummy met his gaze and Harry blinked nervously until the dummy's eyes continued on across the aisle. A wry smile crossed the dummy's wood face and one painted eyebrow raised and that lovely crystal voice spoke again: *"The first of earthly blessings, independence!"*

Socrates Ogg clutched the dummy tightly to his ribs. "Quiet!"

Ignoring the admonition, the dummy spoke more loudly. *"I suggest to you, the cause of freedom is the cause of God!"*

Somebody close to the stage laughed, and the ventriloquist addressed the audience with a light chuckle. "My dear Adam has never known true want nor deprivation. Does he now seek the independence of the destitute and the idle?"

The dummy slipped free of Ogg's tight grasp and cried out with a brave smile, *"Freedom has a thousand charms to show that slaves, howe'er contented, never know!"*

The ventriloquist studied the dummy's modest apparel up and down, and sadly shook his head. "Can a man take fire in his bosom and his clothes not be burned?"

With a wink to the audience, the dummy confessed, *"You should never have your best trousers on when you turn out to fight for freedom and truth!"*

Harry joined the rest of the crowd in a hearty round of laughter. This really was a good act, he thought. Maybe it was a little eccentric, but who needs another sawdust joke, anyhow?

Quick as lightning, Socrates Ogg thrust his left hand into the dummy's trouser waistline and drew out a silver hip flask. "Aha! So, freedom and whiskey do indeed hang together! Drunkenness, my little friend, is a careless disruption of gratitude and discipline that leads foolish men to anarchy!"

The painted dummy threw back his small wooden head in a loud guffaw. *"Freedom, and not servitude, is the cure of anarchy!"*

"Ladies and gentlemen," the ventriloquist enjoined, "does not common sense require the Modern Man to admit that selfish independence serves no greater good than his own vain desires? By whom will the needs of the many be served?"

The dummy thrust a defiant fist into the air. *"Slavery, they can have anywhere! It is a weed that grows in every soil! Thus freedom now so seldom wakes, the only throb she gives is when some heart indignant breaks to show that she still lives!"*

Socrates Ogg thundered a reply that echoed throughout the hall, "There is no honor in the abandonment of Society! Only the reckless independence of want and starvation and pitiless death!"

"That sweet bondage which is freedom's self!"

The ventriloquist leaped to his feet, hoisting the painted dummy up with him. "Then be free, my little fellow, to know the independence of solitude and isolation from the Republic of Man!"

The theater went black.

Murmurs rippled across the audience in the dark. Harry heard a brief shuffling from the stage, then a pair of white-hot ceiling spotlights shone down revealing Socrates Ogg alone on his stool and the painted dummy seated in a small chair on the far side of the stage. The illumined ventriloquist held an impassive gaze upon his face, hands folded resolutely in his lap. Harry felt a chill run up his spine.

His wooden eyes shut tight, the painted dummy's sweet voice issued plaintively from sealed lips: *"With a great sum obtained I this freedom!"*

Socrates Ogg calmly observed, "He did not think that it was necessary to make a hell of this world to enjoy Paradise in the next."

"What stands if freedom fall?"

A broad sneer crossed the ventriloquist's lip. "For he on honeydew hath fed, and drunk the milk of Paradise. Whither now the new Adam? No wiser than the old, I fear."

The wooden ventriloquist dummy's eyes popped open and he rose awkwardly in his chair, struggling upright to his tiny feet once and for all like a man of flesh and blood, and once risen proclaimed loudly to the startled audience: *"These things shall be! A loftier race than e'er the world hath known shall rise with flame of freedom in their souls and light of knowledge in their eyes!"*

The theater went black once more and a hush swept the crowd. Harry was stunned by the illusion. My God, how on earth did he do that?

When the stage-lights came up again, Socrates Ogg stood with "Adam" tucked into his arms beneath the proscenium. The bearded ventriloquist took a bow with his painted dummy to a scattered round of applause, then disappeared behind the velvet curtain.

The stage-lights dimmed to amber and the pudgy violinist took up his bow and began playing "My Blue Heaven" for the murmuring crowd. From the corner of his eye, Harry saw two older women stroll into the theater to his right. As they went by, he saw Cobb seated in the next aisle.

It was a stupendous shock.

Good grief, Harry hadn't even noticed him come in! Cobb tipped his derby hat with a wry smile on his face. This fellow's a mile ahead of me, Harry realized. There's nothing I could have done. It was all a set-up.

Cobb rose and started over. He looked pleased with himself.

"Psst!" One of the young ushers came down the opposite row of seats toward Harry.

"Huh?"

The usher asked, "Is your name Harry?"

His voice trembled. "Yes, it is."

"I'm supposed to show you backstage."

"Pardon?"

"Some dame's asking for you."

Harry noticed that Cobb had stopped at the aisle entrance. He appeared confused. Harry stood and nodded to the usher. Onstage, the velvet curtain parted for a dreadful comedy routine Harry had seen once at a vaudeville hall in Cincinnati. They were called "Moran & Mack" and did a silly blackface act with one portraying a dullard, the other a smart-aleck. The pianist bowed them on with a rousing ragtime melody as the usher led Harry across the aisle to a stage exit on the west wall. Already, the two comics had begun playing to a crowd of lively upturned faces.

At the upper rear of the theater, Cobb sat back down.

"Moran: I hear you folks are getting rid of all your horses.
Mack: Only the white ones, they eat too much.

Moran: You mean to say the white horses eat more than the others?
Mack: Yes, the white horses eat twice as much as the black horses.
Moran: How do you explain that?
Mack: There's twice as many of them. We have four white horses and two black horses. So we're getting rid of the white horses and are going to get black ones..."

Laughter rippled through the crowd as the stage door slammed shut behind Harry. He felt a tremendous relief, but no certainty at all that his lucky escape had changed a thing. He'd only been postponed. The Shamrock was connected to the Mercury Theater next door by an old alleyway between the thick brick walls covered by a simple plank-walk ceiling overhead. A string of electric bulbs provided only adequate lighting, and a cold draft from the grassy back lots behind Clancy Street rustled at a canvas curtain that blocked entry to the dressing rooms in the rear. In front of the curtain was a thick sweaty man in an old blue suit. He was sitting on a packing crate by the brickwork smoking a cigarette and reading the funny papers. When Harry approached to go backstage, the man shook his head, "No visitors."

"A boy just said I was invited by one of the dancers to come back here. I don't think he was joking me."

The man flicked ash off his cigarette and let the funny papers drop to his lap, a grimy hot-eyed scowl on his ruddy face. "Your name ain't Ethan Corey, is it?"

"No, it's Harry Hennesey."

"Then I can't let you in." He dropped the cigarette to the cement floor and squashed it cold under the heel of his shoe and rustled the funny papers straight to begin reading again.

There it was. Harry felt like part of a Punch and Judy show. To his discredit, he had no idea what to do next. Maybe if he'd had a cocktail earlier.

A woman's voice rang down the hall. "Gustav? If there's a swell-looking fellow with you, let him come on ahead. He belongs to Babyface."

Without looking up from the funny papers, the man shouted back, "I ain't heard nothing of the sort and he ain't getting in without me hearing it's jake, either from Wendell or the Coreys!"

Harry heard the clacking of high-heels on concrete as somebody hurried toward him down the drafty hall. The canvas curtain parted and a blonde with green eyelids and her hair in old-fashioned curlpapers peeked through. "Hello, darling. Are you Harry?"

"Yes, I am."

She smiled. "Well, it's about time you turned up. Babyface's getting sick in the latrine."

"This fellow ain't got permission," grumbled the man with the funny papers.

The blonde, wearing only a lavender wrapper, stepped through the canvas curtain and grabbed Harry by the hand. "Come along, honey. Don't pay Gustav any attention. He's just an old picklepuss."

The man dropped the funny papers onto his knees. "Gee, Fanny, have a heart, will you? Corey'll make some dust fly if I let this fellow go back there on account of you dames ain't couchayed with enough stagedoor johnnies already this month."

"Aw, stick it up the sewer, you old gasbag!" The blonde dragged Harry behind the canvas curtain. In the narrow light, a score of busy stagehands and wardrobe women were working amid freshly painted stage scenery and wooden props and tired costume racks.

"She's a hot little sketch, ain't she?" the blonde asked Harry, leading him down the hall beneath the leaky steam pipes and iron catwalks that connected the attics of the two theaters.

"Who?" His voice was still jittery from that near catastrophe back in the hall.

"Why, Babyface, of course," said the blonde, stepping over an empty brass birdcage. "You ought to know she's absolutely cuckoo about you."

They passed one of the back rooms in the Mercury Theater where a pianist and a trio of crooners rehearsed a fresh rendition of "Do, Do, Do." Just beyond, a man roughly Harry's age wearing a gray flannel suit and felt fedora stood attaching theatrical notices onto a section of cardboard next to a closed dressing-room door belonging to Ignatius the Great and Lillian Faye. Harry slowed briefly at the ventriloquist's dressing room. An oil lamp glowed dimly inside and a theater poster on the back wall advertised a long-ago engagement at the Paris Opera House. The peculiar voices of the ventriloquist and his painted dummy murmured in the dark. My God, how on earth had Ogg made that thing stand up?

The "Shamrock Girls" were in the second door from the back entrance near a zigzagging iron staircase where a telephone was ringing. The blonde went straight into the dressing room and left the door open for Harry. Across the threshold, a horse-toothed redhead was standing nose-to-nose with another curly blonde wearing a blue cotton bathrobe.

"Why, I wouldn't give that four-flusher a lay if he set me up to champagne and lobster at the Ritz! Once I seen him in his dinner clothes with that counter girl from the cafeteria, he couldn't have made me with a case of barbital and a sledgehammer."

The cramped dressing room resembled a Baskin Street gown shop, with the assortment of show hats and tea gowns, pink corsets, silk stockings, Japanese fans, feather boas, silver-fox fur capes, and quilted dressing gowns folded atop wardrobe trunks or hung sloppily on a single iron garment rack. Toilet water, brushes, combs, jars of beauty cream, vermillion powders, postcards and studio photographs were scattered in front of the long dressing mirror. The room reeked of curling irons and cocoa butter and greasepaint, cigarettes and liquor. Radio music played from a small Philco set perched on a trunk at the back of the room, the volume down low and tuned to the Wonder Bakers Orchestra.

The redhead tied the silk sash on her maroon silk kimono. A haze of cigarette smoke hung in the dressing room from a couple of girls in sapphire-blue kimonos who were sitting on a stuffed couch against the wall to Harry's right, puffing on Egyptian Deities and skimming over copies of *Billboard* and *Variety*.

Impressed by the sight of so many girls in skimpy dress, Harry felt his nervous dissatisfaction dispersing. A lovely young blonde holding a highball glass and a bottle of Canadian ale at the dressing table noticed him in the doorway. "Say, girls, ain't this one an eyeful?"

A champagne pail and a vase of pretty blue hyacinths sat by her elbow beside a pair of gold satin mules with silver nightingales on the toes. She'd just had a henna rinse and her hair was still damp. When she smiled, Harry saw a gold tooth in place of one of her upper incisors.

The short brunette seated on the far end of couch in a pink charmeuse winked at him with spidery black lashes. She was painting her fingernails with red liquid polish. "How's tricks, big boy?"

Lighting a cigarette from a package of Meccas, Fanny shook her head at the henna-blonde. "Forget it, Stella. This is Babyface's friend, Harry. Poor fellow just threw up his job today."

Stella asked, "So how come he ain't looking that down on his uppers?" She poured three fingers of Canadian ale into the highball glass. "Say, how's about a little bite to drink, honey? I bet you ain't had a lift all day."

Harry took off his hat to look more cheerful. He smiled. "No, thank you. I'm trying to stay dry tonight. Orders from my doctor."

Fanny told the other girls, "Babyface's been trading deep dope on Harry here all week. She says he's afraid of getting in wrong with the concerns, but won't take a job pearl diving in a lunchroom, neither. Isn't that true, honey?"

He frowned. Where did they pick that up? "Yes, it's been a rough month, but I guess I'll make out all right. There's always another connection, isn't there?"

On the couch beneath a poster of Sarah Bernhardt at the New York Palace, a raven-haired dancer with a rubber ice-pad on her head spoke up. "Well, any dame can see he's pretty steady. Why, I just bet him and Babyface have packs of fun."

"Oh, like hell they do," the henna-blonde cackled while studying her penciled eyebrows in the dressing mirror. "Why, Babyface still thinks it was the stork. Get a load of this: Yesterday, when I sent her to the drugstore for some safeties, Babyface came back with a box of pins."

All the girls laughed.

Harry blushed and loosened his tie, wishing he could get off a few funny ones himself. Ordinarily he'd be lively with this set, but seeing Cobb had probably put an end to that tonight.

Fanny told him, "Babyface'll be back any second, honey. You sure you won't have a drink?"

"No, thank you, dear. I'm really not thirsty."

Harry eased into the dressing room and away from the door, so he couldn't be seen from the hall in case Cobb poked his nose through the curtains back there. Opportunity seemed born with that stupid fellow.

Grabbing a scarlet lipstick, Stella remarked, "Well, Mickey didn't take precautions with Irene and now he's sore as a crab."

"He caught a dose?" Fanny asked, flicking ash off the cigarette onto the cement floor.

"Nope, Irene says he got her in trouble. Ain't he a numbskull?"

The horse-toothed redhead sat down in a straight-back chair across the room and smoothed out the wrinkles on her kimono. She reached into a paisley hand valise and took out a box of gingersnaps. "Why, Stella, only last month you called Mickey a humdinger."

"Oh, that's just 'cause he looked so down in the mouth after busting up housekeeping with Maggie. I swear he was ready to turn on the gas before I gave him the dope about that dumb cluck. Why, even when she was sleeping with him in that rattletrap hotel on Garber Street, I still seen Maggie making sheep eyes at those straphangers in the peanut row. How's I supposed to know he was ogling and flirting around with Irene all along?"

"Mickey's been chasing floosies ever since I known him at the Republican," said the redhead, jamming her hand back into the box of gingersnaps. "He'd come backstage fussing that Jacobs ain't hired any spring blood and what's the use of working a show if it ain't for getting a fellow all the nookie he wants."

Fanny laughed. "Well, this ought to put him wise about getting confidential with the wrong dame."

Calming down a little, Harry watched Stella drink another shot of ale from the highball glass. He wasn't surprised to see girls like these on the liquor-go-round. That night in Kansas City, he'd watched Gloria down one gin after another before she finally flopped him onto her bed. Maybe she imagined it helped her sex appeal, but after the fifth Collins, she hardly remembered what to do with her brassiere.

Stella said, "I guess Daisy here's been hoping Mickey'd comb 'em all out of his hair so's he'd date her up instead."

The homely redhead frowned. "Don't go smart-aleck on me, honey. That stupid Irene's just raking up the past, half of which ain't even true. Why, when Mickey offered her the name of a doctor in Morrisville who'd give her some pills, she threw a glass at him."

"She ought to try castor oil and quinine first. One of those doctors'd rook a nitwit like Irene."

Fanny said, "She's so jumpy from sin I bet she'd take a situation in some bum little tank town if Mickey gave her enough pocket money to hire a room for a year."

Closing the box of gingersnaps, Daisy shook her head. "I tell you, Irene's a nasty little bitch who's only trying to hold him up for blackmail. Mickey says her rattle-brained family's hired a lawyer. It's all hellishly sordid."

"Aw, you're wilting my collar!" A freckle-faced red-haired boy roughly Pearl's age with a cigarette stuck behind his ear leaned into the dressing room from the drafty hall. He had on a cheap ill-fitted brown suit and carried a notepad and pencil. "Why, I ain't met a dame yet who ain't lost the curl in her hair on account of our sex life, and I ain't been played false yet, neither."

"Zowie!" Fanny shrieked. "Why, if it ain't Rudy Valentino himself back from the boneyard! Say, sweetheart, Percival just filled us in about those fairies over at the Columbia putting the bitches' curse on you in old Poodledog's office Friday night. Gertie thinks you'll be worrying her now to fit you into a change of her spiffiest clothes."

"Oh, I bet he's crazy for my rabbit fur coat, too," said the raven-haired dancer with the rubber pad on her head. She giggled at the boy, and Harry got a strong whiff of beer wafting off him.

Daisy added, "Mary Borden says her cousin Ollie's hellishly attracted to you." She gave him a sly wink. "Ain't that hinky-dinky?"

Stella raised the bottle of Canadian ale. "Say, girls, let's take a drink to our own little king of the pink powder puffs!"

"Aw, you dames know what you can do about that," the boy groused. His voice was reedy and slightly immature." Why, it's a sure thing I'd fight any of those birds that says I got to take a leak with 'em. I ain't no Ethel."

He noticed Harry by the wall. "Say, you look familiar. You ain't one of 'em, are you?"

Harry smiled. "Not since breakfast." He could already see this kid was a nut. "Why do you ask?"

"None of your business, but I'm warning you, too. Keep your mitts to yourself."

Fanny giggled again. "Girls, we better get out the paraldehyde. Valentino's got an edge on tonight."

"Poor kid's sour as a pickle," Stella remarked, filling her highball glass. "I guess he's been on the shelf too long."

"I'd bet he's been drinking paregoric out back again," said Daisy, sticking the box of gingersnaps back into her hand valise. "He ought to at least get on the wine wagon with Gustav."

"Aw, I ain't been stiff since Tuesday," the boy grumbled, taking the pencil down from behind his ear. He nudged past Harry. "Now, any of you glamour girls want some eats from the hash joint, or can I go set them Woolworth dolls up to gin rickeys with Ignatius?"

"Get me a peach melba," said Stella, taking a scarlet silk kimono off the rack.

Daisy stood up to brush gingersnap crumbs off her lap. "I want cinnamon toast."

The boy scribbled down her order, too. "Check."

"A plate of noodle soup and schnitzels," said the raven-haired dancer, shifting the rubber pad on her head.

"Check."

The sandy brunette reading *Billboard* lowered the paper. She told the boy, "Gertie wants some buttered toast with a piece of cheese on top, and you can have me a cup of cocoa and some apple cake."

"Check."

Harry felt somebody pinch his hand.

"Hiya, honey!" Pearl giggled from the doorway, still wearing her frilly emerald costume. She gave him a kiss on the cheek. "Did you meet my new pals?"

Fanny answered on his behalf. "He's been hearing all the dirty talk, Babyface. That's twice as good as any howdy-do!"

Pearl slipped her arm affectionately around his waist. "My sweetie here don't drink much liquor and he won't cuddlecoody, neither, but I guess he's a pretty good egg!"

Daisy agreed, "Harry's got the stuff that gets 'em, sweetheart!"

"You having anything to eat, Babyface?" the boy asked Pearl, as he finished scribbling down the other girls' requests.

Pearl shook her head. "I got a jumpy tooth." She took Harry by the hand and parked him over on a stool near the end of the messy dressing table next to a pot of pale lemon narcissus wrapped in tissue paper. Then she sat on his lap. "I ate a flock of aspirin before we went on and it ain't done me any good yet. On second thought, how's about a couple ponies of gin? Make 'em longsleevers, sweetheart, and I'll cut you in."

She nudged Harry so he'd know she was kidding, but he really didn't care if she drank an ocean-full tonight so long as he could get her out of here safely. Cobb was no fool. He had to be somewhere close by. Harry just had that sense.

"Not on your tintype, sister! This ain't a lush lounge! I ought to tell Wendell to keep a bottle of smelling salts handy for you dames that can't keep it corked during the show."

"Don't be a rotten pear," said Fanny, lighting up another Mecca. She dropped the burnt match into a dirty tin ashtray on the dressing table. "We're hungry, and we ain't eating supper at a dog wagon for thirty a week. So, how's about beating it down to Maury's before Jimmy gives you the air?"

"Aw, keep yer pants on," the boy griped as he prepared to go. "I'll be back with the eats soon as I can."

Once he was gone, Daisy borrowed one of Fanny's cigarettes and lit it up. She walked over to the door and leaned out into the drafty hall. Shaking her head as she came back in, she told Fanny, "Gustav says that poor kid's been hitting the hop since he was in diapers. He's got nits in his hair from sleeping on that attic cot Wendell hired him in bedbug alley and he's always bothering someone for a dollar just so's he can have another rye whiskey for breakfast. The kid's no bum and a loafer, neither, yet I never seen him with enough kale in his pocket to set a girl up to a bottle of pop."

"Wendell's got a pretty good graft going with that kid," Fanny agreed, exhaling smoke. She tapped ash off the cigarette into an old Campbell's Soup can.

Daisy frowned. "Oh hell, Wendell's so crooked he has to go through a door edgeways, and he's a skinflint, too! If you ask me, Valentino oughta quit this scrimpy joint before he finds himself on the bum roasting murphies in a trashcan somewhere." Abruptly, Daisy switched her attention to Pearl. "Sweetheart, why ain't you freshened up your face like we told you to?"

"I went upstairs to look for Stella's katy," she explained, "and all of a sudden I wasn't feeling in the pink no more, so I went to the toilet and got sick." She shrugged. "I guess I forgot after that."

Fanny said to Harry, "Honey, you better set Babyface straight about her looks. This show's been hell on wheels all summer and the Coreys didn't hire Babyface for her dancing."

"Actually, I thought she was quite good."

Pearl giggled. "Gee, thanks, darling!" She kissed him on the cheek.

"That dopey routine ain't paying nobody's back bills, dearie." Daisy laughed. "Why, it's so pokey, the whole show'd go belly-up if your skirt weren't so short."

"We oughta be tossing cream pies at those dead cats in the orchestra seats," said Stella, fiddling with the tuning knob on the radio which wasn't broadcasting anything but static now.

"I'll tell the world," Fanny said, brushing past Harry to go out into the cold hall. Her stale gardenia perfume bloomed sickly sweet in his nostrils. "Why, sure as fate this act'd be hitting the headlines."

"Or the highyallers'd give us the horselaugh," said Daisy, "and Corey'd cut us all out of the show for good!"

"Gee, that'd be tough." Pearl smiled, checking her makeup in the dressing mirror. "Why, I ain't even a star, yet."

"You will be, darling," Harry assured her. "Just ask those fellows in the peanut row."

As the chorus girls laughed, he heard a loud commotion from down the hall, voices shouting back and forth. Then Fanny called out and someone answered and she rushed back into the dressing room, yelling

like a lunatic, "CHEESE IT, GIRLS! THERE'S A FIRE AT SHEP-
HERDS ISLAND!"

— 7 —

Across ten miles of marsh grass, a fierce glow like the ruddy haze of
sundown lit the dark horizon. Sitting hand-in-hand with Pearl, Harry
stared out an open window of a Pelican Coast Short Line interurban
crowded with city people anxious to watch the great amusement parks
burn to the ground if the hook-and-ladder companies were unable to
extinguish the flames. It was after nine o'clock now and the west motor
road was jammed with automobiles whose headlamps glimmered in
the night. To the east, steamboat whistles echoed over the cold water
as loaded passenger ferries glided upriver obscured by groves of black
willow and hackberry and seedling home orchards under the hazy yellow moon sky.

Crossing the last interurban trestle over Roanoke Creek half a mile
from Pelican Station, Harry smelled hot ash on the draft and saw the
shimmering Wonder Wheel in the distance revolving slowly on the
windy summer sky, backlit by a terrific fire. He felt unusually nervous.
Cobb had disappeared, but Harry had no confidence that they had
eluded him. He seemed ghost-like and eagle-eyed. Harry expected
him like the striking of a clock.

The noisy crowd in the interurban packed the windows as a flurry
of fire trucks from Oxon Hill and Bethany township maneuvered the
motor road with sirens wailing to join the Shepherds Island companies
already laboring with the conflagration. Pearl wrapped her scarf over
her nose and mouth and leaned on Harry's shoulder. The motorman
rang the bell again and again to warn vagrants off the rails who were
slogging up through damp hogweed from the Bethany railyard jetty.

At Pelican Station, the conductor announced that the fire marshal
was terminating all scheduled trains to Shepherds Island at half past
and that anyone who did not wish to walk back to the city was advised
to return now by the interurban. Less than half of the riders remained

on board. Pearl told Harry that a man named Billy Morgan who worked a shooting gallery at Starland had an automobile they'd be able to ride back to the city in when it was time to go. But she needed to let him know where to pick them up, so the plan was for her to tell Billy while Harry followed the fire engines. They didn't have a lot of time. The second show at the Shamrock Theater was scheduled for ten o'clock, but since Ethan Corey had elected to drive his old Stanley Steamer out to see the fire for himself, his brother Jimmy had posted a delay on the marquee announcing the late show to commence at eleven. Agreeing to rendezvous in half an hour under the garden pavilion on the Jordan Recreation Pier, Harry and Pearl emerged from the depot's electric arch into a gigantic crowd of people, more than fifty thousand strong, swarming the wide half mile of lighted boardwalk from Sand Avenue clear down to the old steamboat pier at Pelican Bay where the fabulous Egyptian Obelisk of Thebes was now fully engulfed in flames and a lovely summer sky of stars had disappeared behind dense clouds of black smoke and burning cinder. Starland's famous electric Funny Face had gone dark and a skinny clown on ten-foot stilts marched about with a megaphone, announcing to the noisy crowd that Wormwood's Monkey Theater and the Steeplechase circuit and the Grand Casino Hippodrome and Blowhole Theater were all closing.

"Somebody'll be in a pretty pickle if it all goes up," Pearl said, clutching Harry's arm. A troupe of costumed midgets in greasy black-face and painted sandwich boards scurried past toward the loud Bowery where a barker on a tall stool by Nathan's Red-Hots was offering the last one hundred hotdogs at a penny a customer. Harry drew her close beside him, worried she would be trampled. He'd grown deathly afraid for her now and panicked at his responsibility. *Giving ourselves over to self-indulgence is a terrible conceit when we choose to involve someone else in our own moral truancy.*

At the far end of Sand Avenue, the lights atop the Elephant Hotel went out. Wind scattered paper trash and rattled the tin sign above the Original Turkish Harem. Under the lamppost halos of pink light that lined the boardwalk, tabloid reporters scribbled notes in frantic interview with anyone willing to discuss the unfolding catastrophe. Small gasoline boats and green skiffs piloted by boys in blue workshirts and flat caps drifted on the cold currents off the Jordan Pier.

"Maybe I oughta skidoo," Pearl said, as a throng of raucous sailors and Oriental acrobats wandered out of the rowdy Bowery. "Billy ain't gonna stay open all night."

"All right," Harry nodded, though he worried about losing her if the fire spread. What if she couldn't reach the Jordan Pier? Where would she go? He doubted she appreciated this situation like he did.

A thin Arabian boy wearing a blue silk turban led a short caravan of camels out of Starland with several pretty girls in harem costumes trailing behind. Harry noticed their bosoms were half-exposed and he watched a gaggle of cute little bottoms wiggle as they went by.

Rubbing Harry's hands, Pearl worried, "You won't get burned up in the fire, will you?"

He smiled and kissed her forehead. "Of course I won't, dear. I'm not that adventurous. Besides, why get myself killed when I have you waiting for me?"

"I love you, too, Harry," she told him, leaning so close he could smell the flowery perfume on her neck. "Don't monkey with a buzzsaw."

He took her into his arms, gave her a terrific hug and a reverent kiss. "You be careful, young lady. A fire's nothing to fool with."

Her lovely eyes glistened. "I promise, darling."

Then she quickly disappeared into a long line of women by the Guess-Your-Weight machines. Moving off, too, Harry heard pilothouse whistles from the water and saw a passenger ferry arriving out of the dark from downriver, its twin-decked railings jammed with spectators. By now, the raging inferno at Thebes had illuminated the sky over the amusement parks, and smoking ash wafted down like winter snowfall. Motorcycle policemen drove back and forth, urging people to depart. Sirens wailed in the distance. Harry crossed the boardwalk to the iron railing above the sandy beach where young men in bathing-suit uppers and khaki pants huddled on blankets with girls in summer dresses and street-makeup, faces lit orange by the flaring light. Overhead, the rose arc lights hissed and flickered. A stray dog chased and worried his ankles, then scampered off. People shouted and laughed nervously while rushing about in a hundred directions. Harry passed the frenzied Bowery where acrid smoke had killed the carnival smells of saltwater taffy and caramel popcorn and mustard-drenched red-hots. He almost expected to see Fat Ollie and Lucifer and that stubby guardian angel, Billie Fry, wandering about, choosing marks for another con-game. He looked for Cobb, too, in every face. Running off from the Shamrock had been a crazy thing to do. If they had really angered Cobb, who could predict what he might do? Harry was more afraid of that little fellow than being burned alive in the fire.

A roar went up from the stupendous crowd as the colored lights atop Edmund Tingley's Wonder Wheel and the dizzying Loop-the-Loop roller coaster at Starland winked out. The crowd roared in protest. Then Hell Gate went dark. So did the Oriental Scenic Railway and the Venetian Lagoons and the Old Mill House and the Japanese Garden. Up and down the Bowery, pavilions, arcades, burlesque theaters, shooting galleries, and circus animal exhibits closed. At a quarter past nine, a collective gasp surged through the crowd when Nightingale Park's Elevated Promenade and the fifty thousand bulbs of the Kaleidoscope Tower dimmed, then went black, leaving mile-long Sand Avenue lit only by the roaring flames devouring Karnak's Temple. The great fiery holocaust had begun. Thousands began to panic and head for Pelican Station.

Harry felt the searing heat on his skin as he stood in a flood of water with an anxious crowd beside the Jordan Pier, watching frantic companies of firemen in rubber coats labor with long hoses and ladders beneath the gargantuan pillar of fire that only a few hours ago had been W.A. Harrington's magnificent Theban Obelisk. Wooden barricades separated the spectators from the city hook-and-ladder companies, and policemen with nightsticks patrolled the lines to keep out the foolhardy. Harry was jostled and shoved by people hoping to get as close as possible. Falling ash stung his eyes as he stared high up at the towering flames. Somewhere above him, he heard a pack of young boys scrambling along the roof of the garden pavilion. Thebes was a smoldering blaze of cinder and sparks, only the three-story black metal skeleton of the Osiris rollercoaster still recognizable. The awful heat was suffocating. Removing his jacket barely helped. A mean gust of hot wind knocked his hat off. Behind him, hundreds had already retreated to the sandy beach to watch fountains of water from the hose-wagons drench the flames that crackled loudly across sixty acres of phony Egyptian temples and tombs and grand palm-lined colonnades of Cleopatra's Garden. Rather than escaping, Harry crept closer to the barricades, avoiding the hoses and frantic firemen. Clouds of warm soot dampened his face.

"BEAT IT, MAC!" one of the firemen yelled at him, then shoved past into the Garden. Cops ran up and down Sand Avenue with bullhorns and clubs, trying to clear the boardwalk. Some spectators scattered, others dodged closer to the fires. Harry joined half a dozen fellows scampering down to the entrance of the pier where a fire hose split open spraying water like a geyser. A teenage boy ran under the water soaking himself head to foot and giggling like a fool until a fireman came out of the smoke and slugged him in the jaw.

The fire raged through the painted lathe and plaster gardens. Carved parapets and terraces ignited, curled and collapsed. A searing heat shoved the crowd nearer to the river. Harry repeatedly checked his clothes for sparks. Wherever he looked, Shepherds Island burned with a terrible ferocity, yet Harry stayed put, anxious to see what came next. He just hoped to God that Pearl had sense enough not to come here looking for him.

At half past nine, while he was watching a dozen young firemen struggle with a broken hose, a thunderous boom shook the boardwalk under his feet. Rocked off balance, he stumbled to his knees, and an instant later the night sky brightened as a great plume of fire surged upward through the burning Obelisk, and Harrington's four-hundred-foot electric tower of light exploded like a colossal skyrocket. From far below, Harry thought the night heavens themselves had combusted into a fiery holocaust. He scarcely drew a breath before the flaming Obelisk blew outwards across the sky, flinging hot meteors of iron fragments and raging timber over Sand Avenue. Screams filled the night air. A giant blast of heat roiled out, igniting splinters on the wooden barricades and raining hot sparks and ash down on the boardwalk, incinerating half the fire company laboring below. Thousands bolted over the railing toward the water. His own face singed by the fire wind, Harry dropped off the pier onto the sand at the waterfront. Half a dozen boys leaped from the pavilion roof, clothes and hair smoking, and ran howling for the cold river. Harry smelled burning wood above him and ducked under the pier, frightened nearly out of his wits. Another explosion rumbled across the boardwalk and the hot wind blew millions of sparks into the darkness. From beneath the pier Harry watched the boardwalk ignite plank to plank toward him. Covering his head, he crawled through the sand between the pylons toward the wide water where dozens of men and women blackened by smoke cowered in the flickering shadows.

Harry sloshed away from the pier, putting his back to the intense heat. People were splashing into the current by the hundreds now, faces soiled with ash. Harry watched a pair of firemen drag a filthy man to the waterline, wrap him in wet blankets, and lay him flat on his back in the sand. A plump woman in a lavender dress hurried out of the dark to join them, firelight reflecting on her pale skin as she arrived at the river's edge. One of the fireman spoke to her and his partner drew a sooty blanket over the man's face. Hysterical, she plunged into the water only to be hauled out again by a fellow in a black derby. A flake of burning ash fell on Harry's arm and he brushed it off. Another fell on his shoulder and he brushed that off, too, and waded farther out into the cold water.

Black incandescent smoke clouded the night sky. The wounded fire companies on the boardwalk retreated a hundred yards back from the nightmarish inferno to a skirmish line at the Nightingale Park hydrants, and showered the old wooden boardwalk behind them with a thousand gallons of water. The upper beams on the pier sparked and flared as a fireboat steamed close and let loose a cannon of water. Soaking his handkerchief in the chilly current and pressing it to his face, Harry Hennesey sloshed downriver.

The night sky was pitch-black with smoke, and emergency sirens wailed across the summer dark. Harry waded ashore in the swampy reeds a hundred yards or so south of Pelican Station. Utter confusion swept Shepherds Island. With the electric trolleys no longer running, the mile-wide sandspit of land swarmed with thousands fleeing the hot cinder and ash. He huddled in a dense grove with a strange troupe of performers expelled from Starland when the lights went out. From the shadows in the damp thicket, a tiny female voice sang one of Harry's favorite tunes.

"Meet me tonight in Dreamland
Under the silvery moon
Meet me tonight in Dreamland
Where love's sweet roses bloom.
Come with the love-light gleaming
In your dear eyes of blue
Meet me in Dreamland,
Sweet dreamy Dreamland
There let my dreams come true."

Princess Wee Wee strolled to the water rehearsing her whimsical number accompanied by the Mexican Siamese Twins and another female dwarf in a lacy old wedding dress. Behind them on the sandy beach, Thebes' famous "Congress of the World's Greatest Living Curiosities" idled in the dark brush. Creeping back of a rotten log, Harry watched 689 lb. Jolly Trixie delicately pluck a ragged bouquet of birdfoot violet and butterfly weed which she sniffed once and presented as a gift to mule-faced Myrtle Breckinridge, "The Ugliest Woman in the World." Emmanuel Gunther, exhibitor of the carnival sideshow, paced about the beach in strident debate with the Blue Man and the Prussian Skeleton Boy, while a group of tattooed ladies and strong men shared a pack of cigarettes and the feral Monkey Girl built a storybook castle in the wet sand aided by chirpy pinheads in polka dot clown suits and a circle of giggling child midgets. Isit, a retarded Negro boy still dressed in his hairy Wild Man of Borneo costume, stood high on the dark grassy dune watching another fireboat steam toward the Jordan Pier.

"You needn't hide, dear."

In the sandy brush a few yards away, the bearded Lady Olga wore an evening gown of black valenciennes camouflaged by shadow. Her murmured voice startled Harry. He rose slightly from back of the fallen log to see her more clearly. Her ghastly appearance startled him. A mean trick of nature, a fluke of biology, a singularly unkind fate.

Lady Olga said, "I've grown this beard since I was two years old. It's paid my livelihood for half a century. Today I earn eighty dollars a week exhibiting myself on a platform. Should I be ashamed?"

Not once in Harry's life had he been the least infatuated with those horrid tent shows, nor had he ever blamed the unfortunates who inhabit them. Isn't our natural superiority of fortune sufficient, however unremarkable? Why belabor those sad souls?

"Did you know I've married twice and given birth to children of my own?"

He shook his head.

"I tell you, not one survived."

"I'm sorry." The awful crush of losing his dear little boy unbalanced him for years, irredeemably souring every advantage he had gained in life since that sad gray afternoon.

A bell began clanging far away at Pelican Station, its pealing echo rising and falling as the wind shifted. Listening momentarily, Harry thought he heard his name called somewhere across the smoky distance. Was he hallucinating all this?

Speaking firmly above the frolicking midgets and a rustling wind, Lady Olga told Harry, "Since the day my mother sold me to the Mohammedans of the Great Orient Family Circus when I was only four, my life has been occupied in dime museums and carnival sideshows. Audiences have always adored me. Every so often I feel miserable, yet I've never envied those who come to stare. Do you know why?"

A gleeful quartet of pinheads enjoyed a game of Ring-Around-the-Rosy, splashing wildly in the black oily tide. High atop the dunes, Isit clapped and danced.

"No, I don't." Disoriented in the night wind, Harry felt oddly confused, lost for words.

Lady Olga approached the thicket where Harry stood silently in the dark. There, as a girl's urgent voice called again across the windy beach, the bearded woman confessed, "It's because I believe that here in the land of Nod, if the truth was known, we're all freaks together."

— **8** —

His trousers still damp and soiled, Harry Hennesey sat close beside Pearl in the backseat of a green Ford sedan as it raced down a narrow road past worn-out farms and weathered mill wheels, back to the city. The automobile smelled of liquor and cigarettes, and a draft from a broken window whistled near his ear. The Negro behind the wheel was Pearl's friend Billy Morgan; another in the passenger seat had introduced himself as Reuben Felloneau. Both had been drinking since supper.

Six miles down the road in a quiet neighborhood of gimcrack houses and truck gardens, Billy Morgan stopped the car at a closed Standard Oil filling station and got out with Reuben Felloneau. Across the road, a signboard next to a street lamp advertised **RIVER DAY LINE — BOSCAWEN RD. PIER —** *Start That Vacation By Boat!*

Mumbling about a need to fill up with gas and oil, Billy Morgan lit a cigarette, and followed Reuben Felloneau past a rickety wooden gate around to the rear of the station. Harry remained in the Ford with Pearl as dust swirled about the empty motor road. Fatigue muted his exhilaration over having survived the great conflagration. He had the feeling of being ridden about with no direction of his own. If I'm not soaking in a bathtub soon, he thought, I'll keel over.

"That sure was a narrow squeak, honey," Pearl remarked, brushing flakes of ash off his damp coat. She kissed his ear. "You could've been fried like toast."

Harry forced a smile. "You just said that five minutes ago." She'd thought his story of the destruction of the Theban obelisk and his adventure downriver to the narrow sandbar was the most remarkable thing she had ever heard.

"That's 'cause I never felt so bum in my life like when I thought you'd got yourself burned up." She took his hand, pressed it adoringly to her cheek. "Don't you know I worry about you, honey?"

A light came on inside a back room of the filling station. Harry took out his pocketwatch. It was just past ten o'clock. He felt sober and cold. Before the fire happened, he had intended to go back to his room after supper and listen to the Sylvania Foresters musical variety show on the NBC radio network, perhaps tune in *Amos 'n' Andy* and *Slumber Music* while he did his toilet before bedtime. Also, a dozen tardy correspondences awaited his attention, dunning notices and letters he needed to answer. He watched Pearl fidget with her compact as a noisy Mack truck rumbled by. Dry grass under the signboard swayed in the draft.

"I guess we ought to've hired a hack downtown," she remarked, rolling open the window to a smell of dust and oil. Her own scent of perfume had mostly evaporated, yet she smelled fresh as a daisy. How did she manage that?

He told her, "I'd have preferred the Pelican Bay passenger ferry myself."

Pearl laughed. "That old teakettle?"

"Sure, why not? At any rate, it'd be quicker than this." All evening long, he'd imagined sitting beside her on the ferry ride downriver. Tonight when she came back to his apartment, he thought he could very well put her between his sheets and make love to her. He had never felt so certain about anything in his life, not since asking Marie to marry him. But why tonight? Why not tomorrow, or the day after? He had no cancer eating him up that he knew of. Was he afraid that if he didn't take her tonight, a devouring guilt over all his sordid indiscretions would prevent this from ever becoming more than a final whisper at bedtime?

A crash like glass breaking echoed into the night from back of the filling station. Somebody hollered out. Dogs began barking down the road. Harry heard a heavy thud and another splintering crash and a husky voice speaking rapidly in the dark. In a grove of trees back behind the building, a porch light switched on. More dogs started barking. Billy Morgan hurried around from the rear of the filling station, carrying a paper bag filled with clanking bottles. He climbed into the front seat and cranked the engine to life. Reuben Felloneau strolled casually out the wooden gate, then closed it and fastened the latch. He lit a cigarette as if he had the whole night to kill and nowhere else to be. Then he got into the Ford and Billy Morgan swung the automobile back out into the road and headed south past tall ranks of poplars and shuttered framehouses.

"Did you forget the gas and oil?" Harry asked, leaning forward. He had a sudden fear of becoming stuck on the roadside in the middle of the night. Who could tell what these fellows were up to? They acted a little shady. Pearl said she trusted them, but they were Negroes, weren't they?

Eyes fixed hard on the dark highway ahead, Billy Morgan replied, "Ain't got the need no more."

They sped past coalfields and slag heaps and cement factories that indicated those grimy industrial towns surrounding the metropolis. Reuben Felloneau hung his right arm out in the draft, letting hot ash from his cigarette blow by Harry's window while Pearl prattled on about how "ripping" the show was at the Shamrock Theater and didn't Harry think she'd be a star one day. They passed a trash dump and more painted signboards and parked grain trucks in a fenced-in lot near an old train shed where Billy Morgan veered off the main highway and drove through a leafy neighborhood of streetlights and simple dwelling houses. Reuben Felloneau flicked the spent cigarette away and rolled up his window and brought out a gold hip flask and Harry smelled gin in the car. Crossing a series of intersections into the business district, they drove past a beauty shop and a laundry and a bowling alley and a movie house and a Studebaker agency, then onto a lighted avenue past a long row of stores and settlement houses and narrow sidestreets that led back down into the great city. Each block smelled of garbage and wooden backhouses and old brewery wagons and chimney smoke from factory blast furnaces near the river. Automobile traffic grew and Harry saw people on the streets, too, collected in small packs on the sidewalks in front of poolrooms and alleyways, mostly Negro faces now as Billy Morgan drove into the century-old Ashford Street precinct, miles closer to the sooty coal wharves and rusty freighters than the quiet streets of Empire Boulevard and Edison Heights.

Harry heard the music from blocks away, syncopated jazz and booming bass drums and raggy piano melodies in crowded jazz clubs, young people dancing and carousing on the sweltering rooftops of Ashford Street late into the night. For years he had watched Pathé Newsreels that described the Negro's city, his flophouses and rusty tenement buildings, one-room flats with no carpets on the floors, faulty plumbing, busted radiators, brown rats in the boiler rooms, leaky attics. In the metropolitan newspapers, Harry had read about the junk heaps and dope parlors and streetwalkers and vicious gunmen wearing fancy coats and suede shoes. He had seen tabloid pictures of dead bodies washed ashore below the Concord Bridge, faces blasted by sawed-off shotguns, throats slashed with automatic knives. After eight o'clock on any evening, trolley conductors for the Green Line saw few white customers north of the old Haarlem Wharf and the traction companies repeatedly petitioned City Hall for permission to discontinue service at ten o'clock sharp, despite the knowledge that every other streetcar line offered transportation until midnight. Since the trolleys were owned by the interests, there were no picketers on display for news photographers and passersby, no printed handbills or wooden barricades or soaring oratory to swelling crowds. Instead, Negro congregations appealed weekly for a higher arbitration on all issues of fairness and race, while several thoughtful editors at *The New Republic* and *World* and *American Mercury* trumpeted a striking renaissance in Negro art and society, offering the persuasive observation that tolerance and curiosity invariably dignify the public good. In fact, not all whites avoided Ashford Street after dark.

The glittering Jamaica Club reminded Harry of New Year's Eve in Kansas City, men and women of both races in ritzy evening dress, polished cream-colored limousines bumper to bumper at the curb, Fats Waller and Mamie Smith headlining theater cards on both sides of the lobby. If it was true the Negro could not yet sing and dance himself off Ashford Street, Harry saw that had certainly not stopped others from coming here to celebrate his unusual talents. Billy Morgan drove past the exuberant congestion to the next block where he parked the Ford under a fire escape in a grimy alleyway between a movie house and a pawnshop. All four got out into the noisy dark. Reuben Felloneau grabbed the paper bag of bottles and Billy Morgan lit a cigarette and walked out to the sidewalk. Somewhat nervously, Harry and Pearl kept close together holding hands. Most of those fellows he had gone to school with in East Texas would have been rubbing their eyes in disbelief. A stream of headlights glowed in the street. Horns honked. Negro drivers shouted at both Negroes and whites on the curbside. When Harry was young, he used to cross the river every so often to Shantytown where he fished with a smart colored boy named Asa who could bait a hook with a bandanna tied across his eyes. Then an ugly rumor regarding Asa's older brother Sewell led to that family rushing out of Shantytown late one night by Locomobile. A month afterward, Harry's father Jonas lost a fine colored clerk to a ferocious beating by two drunken oil workers behind a saloon on Talbot Road, which caused his father to suggest at church the next Sunday morning that man's opinions of faith and race divide the soul from God's best intention; better that kindness and mercy guide our imperfect hearts. But Harry seemed to recall that few minds were changed.

Walking to the front of the alley, Pearl told him, "Billy's going to drive me back to the Shamrock, but he ain't got time to take you home, so he says you got to go with Reuben."

"What do you mean by that? Where's his motor?"

"He ain't got one," Pearl confessed, "'cause he can't drive."

"Who says?" Harry had no desire to be trapped here, and he began fishing in his trousers for pocket money. He came out with nine cents, not half enough.

"Billy told me," Pearl replied, rubbing the back of Harry's hand, reassuringly. "He said Reuben never learned how."

They watched a convertible Chrysler full of white collegiate-looking boys and girls roll past followed by a new Willys-Knight and a Cadillac limousine transporting a swank dinner crowd uptown. The kids in the convertible were yelling loudly and singing as if returning from a football game. Somebody up the sidewalk flicked a lit cigarette at the car as it passed, but no one in the Chrysler seemed to notice. Meanwhile, Harry wondered how he was expected to get back to his apartment six miles away in the middle of the night with no automobile and insufficient pocket money for a taxi. This was absurd. How did he let himself get talked into these things?

As if interpreting the frown on his face, Pearl told Harry, "Billy says Reuben'll walk you down to the cross-town trolley at Powell and 40th."

He frowned. "Are you joking, dear? That's nineteen blocks!"

"Aw, don't be a sis, Harry. It ain't that far and nobody'll bother you none with Reuben along. I tell you, it's plenty safe." She smiled. "Just remember to be cool and look hot."

As Harry worried himself silly over this new round of nonsense, Billy Morgan stood just up the block telling dialect stories with a crowd of black men in blue silk suits and derby hats beneath the marquee of the Lyric movie house. His pal Reuben Felloneau was still in the alleyway fiddling with the bottles in the paper bag. Harry heard a bluesy saxophone playing in a cabaret across the street where theater placards advertised Eubie Blake and Noble Sissle. More automobiles rolled past, including a patrol car driven by the first Negro policeman Harry had ever seen in the metropolis.

He decided to beg. "Darling?"

"Yes?"

"Honestly, I'd rather stay with you," he pleaded, hopefully. "You see, I'm feeling sort of abandoned right now, and I wonder why we couldn't just go up to the Jamaica Club for a little while? What do you say, dear? Wouldn't that be wonderful?"

Harry was more scared now than ever to be left alone on Ashford Street. What did he know about Felloneau? Nothing, that's what. Who was to say this fellow wouldn't drop him off on a street corner ten blocks from here where he'd get his skull cracked open for no good reason except that he wasn't a Negro?

He felt a sudden pressure rising in his chest. Good heavens, maybe he was having a heart attack! Did they have any doctors up here?

Pearl kissed him gently on the lips. "Aw, don't pull a long face, honey. I guess maybe Reuben's got you all wrought up, but I tell you he's a swell fellow, honest he is. He just got a summer layoff from the Butterfly Club and he's feeling every which way 'cause most stores won't let a colored fellow kid 'em along like the rest of us."

Feeling his head floating away, Harry tried another tact. "I love you, darling. Do you know that? It's true. If you go off without me, I don't know what'll I do, but I won't be as happy as I am right now with you standing here in front of me."

She kissed him again, and gave him a tight hug. "Gee, honey, sometimes you just panic me." Pearl smiled at Billy. "Ain't my honey bunch marvelous?" She kissed Harry like she wanted to be taken. "How's about we have a big time after I get off? What do you say, honey? Just me and you?"

"Sure, darling," he said, feeling utterly flat now. "If you say so." Why on earth couldn't she forget about the late performance and stay with him? Why couldn't they go off somewhere together tonight? Maybe take a train down to Miami Beach. Marie didn't have to know. He could tell her there were fresh clients from Cuba he needed to see. He wondered if Pearl had ever seen the ocean from a sunny strand. They could make love under a palm tree by moonlight.

She pursed her rosy lips, feigning a pout. "Honey, let's not be cross at each other. Do you promise?"

"Yes, darling." Resigned to his fate, he kissed her sweetly.

Pearl smiled. "You're awfully swell, honey."

Reluctantly, he stepped away, nodding bravely. "Show 'em how, dear."

She giggled.

Another row of motorcars roared by and Reuben Felloneau strolled out of the alley with the paper bag. Pearl called to Billy Morgan and he came down the sidewalk, smoking a fat Cuban cigar a man at the Lyric had given him. Feeling both scared and melancholy, Harry watched them climb into the car.

As Billy Morgan backed the Ford out into the street, Pearl rolled down her window. "I'll give you the lowdown on the show, honey, when I get back."

Then he waved good-bye and she blew him a kiss and Billy Morgan swung the green sedan into traffic and drove off up the street, honking the motor horn as he went.

Reuben Felloneau handed the paper bag to Harry, lit a cigarette, and looked over the street in both directions. Then he gave a nod to Harry and they started off down the sidewalk away from the gala crowds surrounding the Jamaica Club, where Fats Waller's jazzy floor-show in the Kingston Ballroom was already in full swing. Harry heard the bottles clanking in the bag as he walked and felt like a drugstore delivery boy. He considered asking Reuben Felloneau what they contained, but resisted the urge. What business was it of his, anyhow? He decided to just keep his mouth shut and do whatever Felloneau said.

People were out all over, enjoying the summer night, and Harry felt a thousand curious eyes on him as he and Reuben Felloneau hurried past the noisy Merlin Club and the Congo and the Regency Palace. He realized this was not the dreary tabloid Ashford Street of sallow-faced dope peddlers and cripples with pushcarts and Negro gangsters he had been reading about all summer. Although the industrial city encircled Ashford Street — its tall gray factories looming over the neighbor-hoods as freight whistles drowned out children's laughter and the odor of coal gas blended with liver and onions cooking in hot kitchens — the intrusion was certainly far less evident after nightfall. In fact, other than the color of people's skins, he decided that it was hardly different from York or Baskin or any other precinct in the white immigrant city.

Reuben Felloneau finally spoke as they crossed a quiet 52nd Street, twelve blocks south of the Jamaica Club. Harry hadn't heard him utter a syllable since Shepherds Island. Reuben Felloneau said, "I got a bird to see up here. Won't take more'n a minute or two."

On the other side of the street a billboard read, *Watch the clouds — Julian is arriving from the sky!* A Negro newsvendor for black magazines and newspapers like *Crusader* and *The Crisis* and *The Messenger* and *Negro World* was closing up for the night. In the middle of the next block was a book distributing company between a cigar store and a machine shop. A lamp glowed in a third-story window behind a linen shade. The ground floor of the building was leased to a certified accountant named Dubé and an employment agency whose jobs were chalked onto a blackboard out front. Next to it were advertisements for night school and Bible classes. Another offered expert instruction in paper-hanging.

"Don't go nowhere," Reuben Felloneau told Harry near the door-way of the building. "Some folks up here'll treat you mean if they catch you alone, beat you with a razor-strop, maybe cut your throat, send you off to stony lonesome."

In the yellow glow of the corner streetlight, Reuben Felloneau looked as if he were suffering an advanced case of tuberculosis and knew it. His brown face was gaunt, his eyes cold. Harry nodded and shifted his grip on the paper bag and felt a terrific case of the jitters. Nobody had told him about a stop. Good grief, this was ridiculous. He should've borrowed some money for a taxi. Reuben Felloneau rang the doorbell and stepped back for a look up and down the street. A blue La Salle drove by with a Negro youth at the wheel. A green Haynes sedan passed in the opposite direction. Harry heard the thump-thump-thump of heavy footsteps descending a staircase just inside the building. Pointing to a stack of garbage cans, Reuben Felloneau told Harry, "Stand over there so's he can't see you. I like to surprise him."

Harry did as he was told.

Reuben Felloneau waited with his back to the brick wall, one hand inside his coat. The sidewalk was empty. Another pair of automobiles drove by.

When the door opened, a fat black man in gray suspenders and baggy trousers and a pair of stub-toed iron-plated shoes came out to see who had rung the doorbell. Reuben Felloneau stepped forward and shoved a hand into his gut and the door shut behind them, not a word spoken by either man.

Alone on the sidewalk, Harry waited impatiently as more mo-torcars passed, stirring dust up in the street. Behind the book dis-tributors' building, a man's drunken voice shouted curses out a high window. A woman called back. To confirm a suspicion he'd had back at the Standard Oil station, Harry unfolded the paper bag and dis-covered that he had indeed become a bootlegger. He sniffed at the bottles and detected a peculiar odor, more gasoline than gin or whis-key, probably due to the paper bag having come from inside the filling station. At Transfer & Storage one afternoon, George Lancaster had brought in a moonshiner's recipe for corn liquor that included granulated sugar, corn meal, tomatoes, raisins, malt hops in syrup, and yeast. Others dumped refuse like banana peels and eggshells into the mash, ignorant of the hazardous chemistry involved with the careless distilling of drink paraphernalia. Just last week, Harry had read a magazine article regaling the dangers of home alcohol distilled in garbage cans and barrels and copper pots that left a poisonous residue of metals in the liquor. The same article described an immigrant Irish family of eight on Baskin Street discovered to have been bathing regularly in a tub used for making gin that was being sold by bellhops at all the grand hotels along Roosevelt Boulevard. Joe Phelps always got a kick out of telling the joke about two former college roommates meeting at a lunchwagon:

"Hello, Sam. What are you drinking these days?"

"I often wonder!"

Harry closed the paper bag and went back to the machine shop and put the bag on top of the garbage cans. Perhaps gasoline was used now like ether to needle beer or soak into handkerchiefs at the smelling parties Pearl had been telling him about. Did anyone in the city pay even the slightest heed to temperance or Prohibition?

Farther up Ashford Street, three or four blocks away, he saw a crowd of nattily dressed Negro youths come up onto the sidewalk from a cellar staircase and head off uptown. A taxicab turned off at 53rd, a block up from where Harry stood. He gave brief consideration to chasing it. Where was Reuben Felloneau? This was idiotic. He strode out to the front of the book distributing building and looked up. A lamp was lit behind a linen shade and Harry saw someone outlined near the window frame. Was that where Felloneau went? Another drinking party? He shook his head, and took out his pocketwatch to check the hour. Almost ten o'clock. If I'm not in bed soon, he thought, I'll fizzle out after breakfast.

A truck rumbled down the street, making the bottles clank in that paper bag. Afraid of them breaking, Harry went over to pick them up. As he took the sack in his arms, someone called out from behind him, "Well, well, well, look what we have here: Charley's delivery boy, bringing home the groceries."

Harry turned and saw Cobb standing in front of the cigar store. He was wearing a long coat, that derby hat, and a cold smirk.

Cobb said, "So, what do you know, Romeo?"

Harry thought his heart had stopped.

Strolling closer up the sidewalk, hands in his pockets, Cobb said, "That was pretty savvy of you back at the vaude hall, how you skipped out on me with that kid and I couldn't do nothing about it. I tell you, I'm not used to getting the walk-around. I have to give it to you, pal, you got your nerve, all right."

Harry felt panicked. How on earth had Cobb found him? Had he been following them all night? Harry shifted the sack of bottles to toss them and run if he had to.

Cobb stopped next to the employment agency blackboard. "You're giving me the dog-eye, Hennesey. How come?"

For God's sake, what does he want? Harry asked, "How do you know who I am?"

A pair of black Ford sedans gunned by in opposite directions, gassing a cloud of dust and exhaust fumes. He heard more angry shouts echo from a couple blocks away. Some dogs began barking.

Cobb said, "I guess you think you're a pretty slick article, don't you? Why, sure you do. I seen you up at Sylvester's party on the Heights, acting palsy-walsy with that ritzy crowd like you was one of the big cheeses. Well, you didn't fool nobody, I tell you, 'cause even a cheek like me can get in aces with the first-raters and see what spills out. So, yeah, I know plenty about you, hot shot. And I ain't the only one, neither."

Harry felt his muscles tense. If he ran now, could he get away before Cobb shot him? "Look, this must be some awful mistake. I don't even know who you are. What's this all about?"

"Your little dame ain't nothing but baggage, pal, just like that sack you're carrying, that's what. She ain't worth taking a wallop for. Throw in with me and we can pull a split that'll make a big noise for both of us, and I tell you, it's a lot more than five G's. The way I see it, you got the goods and I got the plan. We ought to be a team, me and you. What do you say?" Cobb took a few steps closer, his face shadowed in the lee of the old brick building. "Look, I know what you're thinking. Why should I trust you? We don't know each other from Adam, so how can we be partners? Well, when you think about it, why not? For starters, you wouldn't pull a double-cross like maybe some other fellows, because you know that birds like me and you ain't going to outlive our times unless we get in the game, and that little dame's our ticket."

"And what kind of game do you think we're playing here?" He stared at Cobb. "Money isn't everything, you know. Sometimes we ought to just let it go."

"You got something against getting rich, is that it? What are you, a communist?"

Harry bristled. "Are you a Swede?"

"You got a smart mouth, pal, and I don't think I like it."

"Well, I don't care what you like." Those words came out of his mouth as if someone else were speaking. Obviously, he'd just gone insane. "And that girl's none of your business, either, so keep away from her. I won't warn you again."

Good grief, what sort of threat was that?

Cobb grinned like he was at a birthday party. "I didn't get that last part. If you got something to say to me, pal, go ahead, spill it."

"I don't like you, is that clear enough? So why don't you just leave me alone?"

For God's sake, where was Reuben Felloneau?

"It's clear as a bell, big mouth," Cobb told him, "and I got your answer right here." He produced a small Iver Johnson revolver from his coat. "Fact is, tailing you all summer's put a crimp in my style, Hennesey, and I'm fed up with it. So I think we're going to take a little stroll, just me and you, and settle our score. Don't worry, I'll make it quick. POP-POP. Any complaints, you can take up with St. Peter."

"Go to hell, you sonofabitch."

Cobb lifted his revolver. "You first."

Harry's throat constricted. "Look, I have a family." He suddenly felt cold and pathetic. He barely murmured, "They need me."

"Well, I got kiddies, too, pal," Cobb growled, "but I ain't left mine home to chase skirts. Maybe they won't miss you as much as you think.

Now, get moving or I'll plug you right here."

Terrified, Harry took one step backward. Good God, he's really going to kill me!

Then:

A loud BANG from high inside the building drew his eyes upward in time to see a brilliant flash behind the linen shade as the third-story window exploded outward, raining glass down onto the sidewalk, and a stuttering Tommy gun thundered within the room and a revolver fired four times and a shotgun boomed and Reuben Felloneau's name linked with vile obscenities echoed into the street.

Cobb lay flat on his back, sprinkled with broken glass.

Another pair of shots were fired.

Somebody indoors yelled, "I SEEN A WHITE FELLOW OUT HERE WITH HIM TOTIN' THE BOMBS WHEN HE COME UP THE BLOCK!"

A Negro with a .38 in his hand leaned out the shattered window.

Cobb sat up, dazed, then looked around.

Harry threw the sack of gasoline bottles at him.

And ran.

A wild shot clipped the brick building just off his right shoulder. Another banged the garbage cans behind him. Harry heard Cobb shout, and the shotgun boomed by the door stoop, and half a dozen more guns roared as Harry ducked around the corner at 51st Street. Scared half out of his wits, Harry hid for a moment. When he snuck a peek back up the sidewalk, he saw Cobb lying on his side in front of the machine shop, a Negro dressed in a smart gray suit with a felt hat standing over him. The Negro shot Cobb twice in the head.

Harry ran again.

— **9** —

The lobby of the Warsaw Hotel was empty when Harry staggered up to the desk and rang for the night clerk, Mortimer Watt. He was shut in his office practicing polka tunes on a piano accordion he had bought for three dollars from a former tenant who had given up a fifth-floor apartment to move back to Toledo. Harry rang the bell again and Watt came out, flushed and wheezing. "Hennesey, you look as if you been put through the washing machine."

Watt's breath reeked of sauerkraut juices, a homemade remedy he had been drinking all week for pleurisy. He went back to the postal slots and took out Harry's mail, a handful of business correspondences and a pair of dunning letters. "Say, you been listening to the airwaves tonight?"

Harry shook his head. "No, I've been out all evening." Sitting by himself at the radio? Was that a joke? Any version of the evening's facts would've knocked Watt over backwards.

"Well, Winchell's still raising Hail Columbia about Runyon chasing the old phedinkus in the Babe's Pullman car."

His legs worn out and aching from running on cement sidewalks, Harry grimaced. "Thanks for the mail, Mort."

"You ought to watch out for yourself, Hennesey," Watt wheezed, as Harry crossed the lobby to the elevator. "You're looking pretty rocky."

Upstairs on the sixth floor, Harry stopped outside Arnie Silberberg's room and removed a business card from his wallet that read:

Harry L. Hennesey
Artist's Agent

Silberberg was a seldom-employed cartoonist seeking representation in the metropolitan marketplace. Deciding to try and help the poor fellow along, Harry had ordered four dozen cards printed up. He slipped this one under the door, then urged himself down the hall to his own room and found a telegram from Western Union lying on the floor. He tore it open. The telegram was from Farrington.

TRIED TO TELEPHONE YOU AT OFFICE HEARD YOU BUT YOU
DID NOT HEAR ME FOUND LOVELY HOUSE ON PARKER STREET
NEED CONFIRMATION PLEASE DONT MISS HENRYS BIRTHDAY
THE CHILDREN SEND THEIR LOVE WE MISS YOU
    YOUR LOVING WIFE MARIE

Harry laid the telegram on his desk next to the typewriter, draped his coat over the chair, and went to the toilet. His bladder had been aching since Ashford Street. When he came out again, he sat down at the desk and re-read the telegram, then carelessly studied the dunning letters and the other business correspondences and scribbled brief notes on each for later. Two blocks away, the Ibbetson Street elevated trolley clanged and rolled off into the night. In ten minutes, the last city owl cars would close down and the metropolis would rest. Still horribly shaken from his encounter with Cobb, he got up and ran a bath for himself, then went to the window and raised it open a foot to admit some fresh air. What would his family have done if he had gotten himself killed? Good grief, their lives might have been ruined. A salesman he knew from Peoria by the name of Henrici drank a couple highballs too many one afternoon and ran his motor into a tree at fifty miles an hour. His family was forced to sell their home and live at a tourist camp where one of his kids got run over by a truck. He could never tell Marie what happened tonight. First of all, she wouldn't believe him. Secondly, she'd know somehow a woman was involved. What else could he have been doing there? She would be right, of course. His behavior had become absurd. He had fallen in love with a girl half his age and left his brain at the curb. What had gotten into him? God almighty, if he had any hope left at all of getting back home to Marie and the children, his stupidity had to stop tonight.

Looking out above Jackson Street, Harry watched a man in a long coat hurry up the sidewalk as a coal truck rumbled by. Twelve blocks east of the hotel, the crystalline string of lights atop the Washington Bridge glimmered above the wide river. A rising wind scattered trash about the empty streets. Shocked by his own erratic behavior all evening long, how close he had come to being murdered, Harry stood at the window for a while listening to motor horns in the distance, voices echoing across rooftops, freight whistles by the waterfront, howling alley cats in a bitter dispute on the next block. Upstairs in the apartment overhead, a tenant named Fink rose from his bed to pace the floor. Downstairs, Isabel and Minette Dantino's thirteen Swiss clocks began chiming midnight. Steampipes rattled and hissed in the old hotel walls. Across the hall, Ernest Owen's radio set broadcast the "Silver Slipper Orchestra." Harry left the window to shut off the bathtub water.

Long ago when he was young, Jonas Hennesey traveled three days and nights by train and carriage to Syracuse, New York, for the privilege of paying fifty cents to see the Cardiff Giant. Newspapers across the Republic had touted the petrified discovery as the "8th Wonder of the World." The morning Jonas arrived in Syracuse, a paleontologist from Yale proclaimed it a hoax, which lured an even larger crowd than the day before. Fraud or relic, Jonas Hennesey spent his fifty cents and stood in line to see the ten-foot antediluvian stone giant and afterward went home, satisfied that he had been witness to something miraculous. Maude told Harry this story about his father as an object lesson in gullibility. In her opinion, all of Creation was revealed in a glance, and a bird was a bird whether its beak was long or short, and there is no new thing under the sun. Regardless, Harry knew he would have paid a dollar himself to see the Cardiff Giant because the miraculous in this life seldom disappoints. He considered his father to have been a decent, hardworking individual who had sacrificed his portion of life's adventure for those he loved. Jonas Hennesey operated a mercantile in downtown Bellemont for the better part of four decades to keep a roof over his family's heads and food on the supper table while taking precious little for himself. Other than his trips to Syracuse and Jackson Park, and a pilgrimage to see the Atlantic Ocean from the rainy shores of Cape Hatteras, Jonas Hennesey stayed in Texas his entire life. Every Saturday when the bluebonnets were in bloom, he fished on the river with his old friend Homer. Once a year, he spent a week with his sister Frances and her husband Rollo at Matagorda on the Gulf of Mexico. He read books and Wide World Magazine *and* The Century *and* Scientific American *and* The Literary Digest, *and wrote poetry and debated Socialism with the Wobblies at union hall meetings. He taught a Baptist Sunday School class attended by Harry and Rachel, and occasionally sat in for a hand or two at the organized poker games held during lunchtime at the feed merchant. Jonas Hennesey voted Social-Democrat and served a term as Notary Public and another as Postmaster and twice ran for mayor. When oil was struck in Texas cow pastures, he rode a train to Amarillo to join the petroleum game by purchasing leases in a couple of respectably profitable wells. The money he earned in four years allowed him to buy the mercantile building he had worked in half his life to facilitate income for his family's future.*

Harry adored his father. When he was still a boy in knickers, they flew kites together among the wheat and alfalfa plots out on the windy prairie and went to the dog races in Longview and shared a basket of Maude's popovers next to the chinaberry tree after summer evenings downtown. Jonas bought his young son a cowboy suit and read detective stories to him at bedtime and taught him code pleading and how to make change from a dollar. When Harry used cusswords, his father punished him with a hickory switch behind the barn. When he brought home good marks from school, his father took him fishing on the river or bought him a cherry phosphate at Hooker's drugstore and a lemon candy. On Harry's tenth birthday, Jonas gave him a Kodak "Brownie" camera. On his fifteenth, Jonas secured Harry a position at R. W. Raymond's department store in the mercantile building where he began to learn the selling game from men in the wholesale dry goods business. Jonas Hennesey bought his first motorcar the day after Harry's twenty-sixth birthday, a 1912 Elmore Torpedo, in which he drove about the county debating advocates of scientific management and the Income Tax Amendment and the use of common drinking cups on trains. At Maude's urging, Jonas lent his convincing oratory to the cause of women's suffrage, and against eugenic marriage, bloomers, and the Lincoln penny. Somewhere up in the Pendergast barn in Farrington was an old Mason jar containing one hundred fifty-three Indian head copper coins, the final present Harry ever received from his father. That week of Harry's twenty-seventh birthday, Rachel came down with diphtheria and was bedridden for three days after receiving the antitoxin and Harry put off his return to St. Paul when Jonas told him he had business in Port Arthur and needed Harry to stay at the house with Maude to watch over his young sister. Thirteen hours later in the middle of the night near the Gulf Coast, with a woman from Corpus Christi named Zelma beside him in the passenger seat of his Torpedo Roadster, Jonas Hennesey drove into a ditch, killing them both.

After climbing out of the tub and toweling off the residue of bath salts, Harry put on a blue cotton robe over his union suit, brushed his teeth and straightened up the toilet articles in the cabinet above the sink, then filled a hot water bottle and switched off the bathroom light. Pearl's ratty pigskin suitcase lay next to the easychair, latches left unfastened from early morning. In another couple of hours or so, she would be back from the late show at the Shamrock Theater. For almost three weeks now, Pearl had been sleeping over nights on the couch in his apartment, a situation Harry knew to be entirely inappropriate, however much he adored having her there. He had only intended it as a temporary arrangement until Pearl found herself a safe bed at a rooming-house or the Y.W.C.A. on South Jefferson Street. All summer she had hinted about the perils of vagrancy while refusing to reveal where she slept at night. One afternoon up on McKinley Avenue within the shady concrete edifice of the Tomb of the Republic, Pearl let slip an oblique reference to bedding down on wooden pallets away from gandy-walkers and men in black frock coats, while recounting a horrible dream she had of being chased across the dark city by an invisible man. That afternoon at the memorial monument, Harry deduced a grave fear in sweet Pearl's offhanded remarks that persuaded him she held no true fidelity to a life of scarcity and discomfort. Indeed, her professed dread of that nameless invisible man pursuing her through the shadowy nocturnal streets confirmed this. A week later, at Harry's request, she carried her suitcase into his apartment with a promise to respect both his privacy and the sanctity of her own virtue. Yet he had spooned with her on the couch in his union suit more than a dozen times already. What had gone wrong?

Maude's family refused to travel from Waxahachie to attend the funeral. Her mother insisted that the circumstances surrounding the fatal automobile accident were so utterly disgraceful that Jonas Hennesey ought to be dropped into an unmarked hole somewhere and buried like a dog. The Baptist minister from Tyler who performed the ceremony offered no mention of the wreck in his words of condolence, asking instead of the mourners to remember the goodness present in every man's heart, then appealing for forgiveness from a higher authority: "O God, whose mercies cannot be numbered; accept our prayers on behalf of the soul of thy servant departed, and grant him an entrance into the land of light and joy, in the fellowship of thy saints, through Jesus Christ our Lord. Amen." Harry placed a twig from the chinaberry tree on his father's casket as it was lowered into the earth. Rachel added a bouquet of lavender lilacs, and cried incessantly for the rest of the day. Maude stayed in her room until twilight when she came out and began cleaning the house like a penitent shamed. Harry spent all night sorting through several trunks of his father's books and magazines and knick-knacks, packing into a small box all he felt he ought to keep, and left at dawn by train for St. Paul. Not until his own son David was born two years later did he return to Texas.

Disconsolate and fearful over everything that had happened today since Benjamin Follette's visit to the warehouse, Harry fixed himself a lukewarm cup of cocoa and condensed milk, switched off all the lights in his apartment and slumped into the easychair with the hot water bottle across one sore leg and listened to the distant whistles of the great ships moving downriver. He sipped his cup of cocoa as a chorus of voices murmured in the conjoined walls of the old brick hotel. On the first floor, a woman named Nellie French counted her savings aloud to $7.53 from a week of mending rents in longshoremen's trousers. Across the hall from Nellie lived a family of Germans who worked together in the cannery on Killion Street and sold safety razorblades and watch chains out of the apartment at night. Thirty-two year old Pat Plepler on the fourth floor gave parlor music lessons at a dollar and a half an hour and baked angel cakes for McDonald in exchange for rent credit. A shingle maker named Tutt from Cleveland sang arias in a second-floor shower every morning at four-thirty and came back to the hotel each evening by a quarter past nine blind drunk and rowdy, moaning into the walls how the filthy Hun had gassed him at Belleau Wood. This Warsaw Hotel stood among a thousand crossroads within the city for the nomadic and weary seeking purpose somewhere in the great Republic, their comings and goings noted by furniture trucks at a sidewalk curb, scribbled nameplates on postal boxes, suitcases in a narrow lobby.

Nor had young Pearl's appearance on the sixth floor elicited any unusual questions or attention from the other tenants, after all; hers was just another curious face in a dingy hallway, another murmuring voice in the old brick walls. Harry was no invisible man, yet he had few illusions regarding her presence in this room. How could he? Was not hypocrisy the homage vice pays to virtue? Guilt had long ago wormed into his heart a persistent reminder of past infidelities. Perhaps he had orchestrated this liaison, seeking by carnal abstention to rid himself of older sins. Another abject failure. Day after day this lovely wayward girl floated in his thoughts, weakening his concentration and resolve. The marriage vows he had spoken fourteen years before offered less obstruction than a shameless fear of ridicule, or disease. Yet now a young girl inhabited his apartment at night like a dear forsaken spirit, whispering honeysweet affections across the shadows, professing promises of fidelity he pretended each sunny morning not to have heard. Who appreciated her sadness and daring more than he? Who saw more clearly the pathetic course her young life revealed, the ripe possibilities his own love offered? *I hear a voice you cannot hear, which says, I must not stay.* Each day at dawn, Harry listened to her bathing in the tub, rehearsing show melodies in a reedy bird's voice, talking to herself, tittering at some silly joke. One morning after her bath, with the curtain to his bedroom parted slightly by a draft, he watched her lean nude and pale beside the raised window frame for a quarter of an hour, gazing silently out across the sooty rooftops toward the cold river, radiant sunlight in her eyes. For months she was his patient guide through the narrow alleyways and crowded boulevards of the great city, his urchin Beatrice. Now this darling girl slept in his care. Had it been her imagination, or his, that suggested they required each other equally?

Worn to the bone, Harry stared out the window toward the Washington Bridge as he sipped his cocoa. He thought about that telegram. Henry's birthday. A little boy dreaming of shiny new toys in a dark, distant room. *Upon my soul forever their peace and gladness lie like tears and laughter.* Not three hours ago, Harry had been desperate to make love to Pearl. Those sweet lips, that glorious young bosom, beckoned him mercilessly. Her honey-scent filled his nostrils, electrified his senses. He had felt feverish with desire for her, reckless and tumescent. Nothing would do but that he have that girl to his bed, caress her youthful skin, part those supple thighs at last, and make unpardonably exquisite love to her until dawn. Only three hours ago, he gladly intended to break that bloodless oath of sexual abstinence he had sworn to himself upon arriving in the metropolis. God, did he feel sick now, panicked with guilt. He dreaded his own incautious thoughts. What on earth had brought him to this? Last year on dear little Henry's birthday, he had been in downtown Chicago entertaining a woman named Greta Corbin he had met outside the Trianon the night before. He bought her a steak dinner, then kissed her up in his hotel room. She had three kiddies at home with her sister on the West Side and a husband dead in his grave from a railroad accident. When Harry confessed he was married with children of his own, she slapped him. Then she took him to bed and made love to him for half the night. When Harry arrived home two days later, Marie told him Henry had cried himself to sleep when Daddy hadn't come to his birthday party. Thoroughly ashamed, Harry walked himself to exhaustion that night, crisscrossing town from one end to the other. *All men that are ruined, are ruined on the side of their natural propensities.* He had always told himself that we are responsible in equal parts to ourselves, our families, and the society to which we belong. True pride arises from the knowledge that we are admired by loved ones and fellow citizens alike for both our behavior and deliberate contributions to the common good. *Let thy deeds deserve praise, and posterity will applaud them.* Since boyhood, he had tried to lead an exemplary life. Once when he was young, he kept a ledger of sins and virtues and graded his performance as mediocre. He had lied too often at home and peeked over Tommy Maxwell's shoulder during arithmetic tests for which he had failed to study. He atoned as best he knew how by refusing to pinch candy from Hooker's drugstore, never cheating a schoolmate at marbles, or sassing his parents. Perfection eluded him, but he charged toward adulthood with the noble conviction that how one lived was more important than how one earned a living. *Let us be moral.* He had always made a dollar, fair and square. He treated his fellow man with courtesy and respect, and hadn't once ignored the Sunday collection plate. Only love had led him astray, tipped the ledger against him. *Let us contemplate existence.* This is what he considered as he sat in his easychair in the dark: If vain sexual transgressions had stained that Ideal he held up as the best way to conduct a life, then all he had gained in a quarter century of labor and devotion had fallen away, and little Henry's birthday would soon become a bitter reminder that no man can truly make a change in his nature.

Shortly after one o'clock, Harry finished his cocoa and retired to bed.

A week after his father's funeral, Harry received a telegram at St. Paul from his roommate Victor Ferguson who had been traveling in Europe on business. It read simply: "Now is the virtue of manhood passed without dispute from father to son."

That humid summer on Summit Avenue, Harry accepted invitations to every festive lawn party and elegant soirée he was able to attend. Under the striped canvas tents of the wealthy and consequential, Harry Hennesey strolled about listening to the concert musicians entertain men with firm handshakes and their lovely wives in fine dresses and sparkling jewelry. He ate their catered food, drank their expensive wines, and waltzed in the freshly mown grass with their pretty daughters. When Ferguson returned in late June from France, he and Harry hired carriages together in which to steal kisses from Lutheran co-eds along the banks of Lake Harriet when the stars were bright and the clear waters lit silver by summer moonlight. One night at Loring Park in a secluded arbor near the cycle path, Harry made love twice to Eustace Griffith whose father had just that afternoon offered him a sales position with Pillsbury-Washburn Flour Mill Company. The same week, Ferguson persuaded Harry and two buxom secretaries from North Star Shoe to wade nude with him at sundown in the reedy shallows surrounding Christmas Lake. Later in August, a sweet debutante by the name of Pauline Constance Bennett from Portland Avenue gave herself to Harry after dusk on the old dam at Minnehaha, while farther along the creek a quite inebriated Ferguson attempted unsuccessfully to spawn under the laughing waters of the cold Falls themselves with young Gladys Cook of Lake Minnetonka. Each night that summer, before going to sleep in the corner room upstairs of the Ferguson brownstone, Harry wrote a tender love letter to Marie Alice Pendergast expressing his imperishable affections for her. If he had indeed arrived on the homestretch, if his halcyon youth had truly flown, then he also believed the responsibility of marriage and family provided the surest foundation for manhood. By September, firmly convinced that all those orgiastic pursuits of the summer past were reckless exceptions to his heart's truest desire, Harry began to woo Marie in earnest with flowers and unexpected telegrams, secret gifts and ardent notes delivered to the Pendergast farm outside of Farrington, Illinois. And when at last she accepted his proposal in a rented canoe on that windless April evening eight months later, much of the grief he suffered at his father's death evaporated in her lovely smile. His wedding present to Marie was the house at 119 Cedar Street.

Now and again, sadness abides like a lingering season. Until Harry came back to Bellemont with Marie and David after Armistice, Maude had chosen not to disturb the locked contents of Jonas Hennesey's rosewood writing desk. She had hidden the key to the main drawer in a sewing basket and pretended it was lost and forgotten. One year later, Harry retrieved the tiny iron key from Maude's bedroom closet after supper and unlocked the drawer. Jonas Hennesey's private papers and business correspondences had been long since reconciled, his personal effects distributed among family and old friends — except for the contents of the drawer. A familiar sentimentality whose motive not even Maude fully appreciated had kept the rosewood writing desk shut and locked since the accident. That evening, Harry carefully unfastened the brittle clasp on a small leather case he had located at the back of the drawer and drew out his father's "Isabella" quarter: a rare commemorative coin from the World's Columbian Exposition. Jonas Hennesey had purchased it as a souvenir on the last day of their stay at the Fair and had willed the silver coin to Harry as a memento of their grand trip to Jackson Park that summer long ago. Rachel took away an old photograph of her father on the plank sidewalk out front of the mercantile building on the day he assumed ownership. Maude kept for herself a pair of gold cuff links Jonas had worn to the Maypole cotillion at Waxahachie in 1884 when by lamplight he had first asked her to dance. Harry brought the "Isabella" quarter back to Cedar Street where it remained locked in his own writing desk through the long season of Cissie's difficult birth and the terrible drowning that so cruelly stole young David's life on Lake Calhoun, a cold gray windy afternoon when Harry preferred a flat business appointment at St. Paul over a day at the park with his wife and little boy. Alone and distracted by a gust of wind, Marie failed to see David sneak into a fisherman's flatbottom boat. A tether slipped its knot, floating her child out onto the lake. Panicked, she shouted for him to come back. Overbold and terrified, young David dove into the water and drowned. Marie's cousin Emeline reached Harry by telephone an hour later. He collapsed where he stood. For over a year, Marie wept for her first born in private, inviting nobody to the house, cooking and cleaning in mournful silence, retreating each evening to the front porch after Cissie was in bed to rock alone in the wicker swing with a cup of hot tea in one hand, a slender volume of Longfellow's poetry in the other. Her profound sorrow haunted them both until little Henry was born and Harry accepted a low-paying bookkeeping job with Consolidated Milling of Farrington in order to be home by suppertime as his own father had done. Harry dearly loved Marie and the children. Unfailingly after David's death, he took his family to church with him on Sundays, played the piano for them after dinner, read funny stories and shared gentle affections with each at bedtime. By then, however, Harry had also broken his marriage vows with a woman from Davenport, Iowa, who assured him that virtue has forever inspired more loneliness in this life than comfort.

But infidelity can be a heartless sin. Shamed by Jonas Hennesey's betrayal, Maude refused even to acknowledge its painful occurrence. Nor had Harry any clear idea whether or not Marie suspected his own pathetic indiscretions. After each incident, he wired a telegraph expressing his love for her and the children. Often he had flowers delivered to her as well, or a pretty gift. Did that signify love to her, or guilt? He never asked because Marie always acted grateful, as if domestic harmony were a sign of forgiveness. Even after he quit his menial bookkeeping job with Consolidated Milling and went back to selling on the road again, she continued to fix his meals and wash his clothing, offer sweet smiles across the porch shadows at twilight, a warm gentle touch in the dark of the bedroom when the children were fast asleep down the hall. Yet fear worried his thoughts when he lay awake before dawn. If he passed away quietly one night between heartbeats, or bled to death in a weedy ditch on a rural motor road, who would care that once he, too, had been young enough to harbor grand hopes and expectations for a life of goodness and consequence? Patience is a cultivated virtue gratified only by accomplishment. The experience of failure in business and marriage reminded him of Elijah's cry, "I am not better than my fathers." Fourteen years after purchasing the house on Cedar Street as a present to the woman he would love his entire life, Harry sold it to rid himself of the responsibility of regret, to try somehow beyond these constant trials and discouragements to resurrect some measure of faith in the certainty of his own rise one day to a state of grace and prominence in the great Republic. Belief in that resurrection had brought him to the city this summer.

He woke as the apartment door clicked shut. A draft from the hallway rippled the curtain near the foot of the bed. It was late, just past three o'clock. Pearl was in the bathroom, running water from the sink. She had the door closed so as not to disturb him, but a light was visible under the threshold. He heard her humming a popular radio tune as she washed off her show paint and prepared for bed. What could he say to her tonight after everything he had seen and done? None of this was her fault. *What can innocence hope for, when such as sit her judges are corrupted?* Love should beget love. It should be a harbor of refuge from a miserable world. How tragic life would be without it. Listening to her in the dark, he felt so blue. What did it mean to love another human being? Was it not the rarest of all gifts, perhaps the very reason for life itself? Once long ago, he had given his heart to Marie Alice Pendergast, and offered his love to her forever. Years passed as she bloomed with children while Harry strayed here and there to other arms. His affection for her wilted, his heart soured to that old promise. He would always love his dear Marie as a woman full of grace and goodness whose presence in his life seemed irreplaceable. In bed, though, in the dark, her loving touch no longer shook the ground beneath him. Smiles faded, joy dispersed. He began believing sex had so little to do with love that he could bed down with any number of women and risk nothing of his heart which he had convinced himself must belong forever to Marie. Into this delusion, Pearl had wandered that rainy night at the Orpheum Theater. Harry fell in love with her without even knowing it. They kissed under the emerald glass dome and his resolve vanished without a trace. If he made love to her now, what sort of fellow would he be? Somehow Harry imagined he had fooled that sweet young girl into believing he might give his heart away for just the right kiss. But was she really that naive? My goodness, who'd been deceiving whom?

After the bathroom light went out, Harry heard Pearl close the window to the street where whistles from the river were still audible across the summer night. Downstairs, a toilet flushed. The ancient plumbing rattled up the walls as Pearl undressed in the dark. When Harry heard her flip open the suitcase latches, he shut his eyes and fell asleep again. *Maybe tomorrow I'll ride the trolley down to Buchanan Street and hire that loft to store the inventory I can buy with Follette's check. Why get run out of the fair selling game? If Joe Phelps chooses to hock his reputation for a brass check and winds up one day borrowing from Morris Plan, so be it. Harry Hennesey won't be satisfied peddling vacuum cleaners door to door.*

Pearl sat down at the foot of his bed as a chilly draft redolent of soap and stale perfume swept through the parted curtain. She squeezed his foot to wake him. Gripping the blanket to his chest, Harry lifted his head.

Pearl drew closer. "Honey?"

When his eyes met the pale moonlit darkness, Harry found a most delightful young girl seated nearly beside him on the bed, dressed in a wornout raccoon coat with nothing but her pale nude skin underneath. One rosy breast was exposed, a shadow of pubic hair. So this is how it was to be seduced? He forced a joke. "Why are you wearing that coat?"

But that wasn't what he meant.

Pearl answered brightly, "Fanny gave it to me after the show 'cause she said I got across so swell tonight." She smiled. "Ain't that slick?" She wiggled her hips, squeaking the bedsprings.

Trying hopelessly not to stare, Harry nodded. "Yes, it's wonderful."

In the apartment upstairs, Fink was awake and pacing the floor again. Harry had left a dozen notes at his door since June, apparently none read at all.

"Stella says we laid an egg, but she got so pickled during the fire," Pearl giggled, "she fell off the stage and landed on a fellow in the orchestra seats and broke his arm."

"Oh, that's awful." His eyes pried between the folds of her raccoon coat, that gorgeous young body beneath. Was he supposed to pretend to resist? *Ask not of me, love, what is love?* You can't pretend to be human. You either are, or you aren't. It's one of those facts of life to be marveled at.

"Weren't you proud of me, Harry? I socked it good tonight, didn't I? Fanny says I got real talent, too."

"Of course you do," Harry agreed, as Fink's pacing upstairs slowed to a stroll. "But don't forget, darling: talent without hard work won't grow a potato in Ireland. It's important that you knuckle down and keep at it. That's the surest formula for success." Good grief, now he was sounding like his father. He should never have bought a ticket that night to the Orpheum Theater.

"*If you want the rainbow,*" Pearl sang slightly off-key, "*you must have the rain.*"

"Hmm?"

She sighed. "It's just swell of you to watch out so's I ain't taking any sort of misstep with my life." She leaned forward and gently rested a hand on the bedcovers atop his knee. Within the folds of her raccoon coat, both pale breasts hung freely now, taunting him. "Billy told me about Reuben. Ain't that a shame? Nobody said nothing to me about him trying to spot them other fellows tonight, or I wouldn'ta let you go. Just thinking about it gives me the horrors. I'm awful sorry you got mixed up with ginks like them, honey. Honest I am."

Her rueful voice trailed away as the curtain fluttered slightly in the draft. Harry gazed at her in the dim light from the street. Her tender young skin still looked much too white. He had grave doubts about her health. She had scarcely eaten a bite of stew and dumplings at supper.

Down the hall somebody operated the elevator, descending slowly to the lobby. The iron bed creaked as Pearl shifted her weight. Softly, she sang, *"Blue skies smiling at me, nothing but blue skies, do I see."*

Her grip on the musty raccoon coat loosened, exposing a slender portion of her nude belly while she sang, *"I never saw the sun shining so bright, I never saw things going so right."* Between truant officers and casting offices, who could have blamed her if she'd been ready to turn on the gas? Instead, she greeted each new morning like Valentine's Day, as if her young life were, in fact, perfect as heaven. *"Noticing the days hurrying by, when you're in love, my how they fly."*

Outdoors, a man's hoarse voice shouted at the barking dogs as Pearl finished singing, *"Blue days, all of them gone, nothing but blue skies from now on."*

Fluttering her eyelids, she remarked, "I just can't make you out, honey. Why, I thought you'd be sore as a pup that I ain't a check girl or knitting scarves and mittens like most other dames. Fanny says that if she had a red cent for every fellow who told her to quit dancing, she'd be living at the Ritz. She says a bachelor girl ought to shoot the moon if she can."

"Just the same, darling, you ought to know a steady and reliable income is equally important. Starvation isn't all it's cracked up to be. You ought to know that as well as anyone."

"Aw, I ain't got the stuff to be a telephone girl, honey. Honest I don't. Sure, I know you're only trying to help me, but gosh, when I'm not dancing, I miss it like the mischief, and I ain't smoked a cigarette since Corey gave me the job, and Fanny won't let me use cusswords no more, neither, 'cause one day I'm gonna be a star."

The barking of the dogs near Franklin Street persisted as a series of automobiles motored by toward the river. Harry averted his eyes from the soft nude curve of Pearl's lovely thighs. He felt guilty and mean and wished he were somewhere else. Why are we so cruel to those we love? Most of our lives are driven by that inexpressible curiosity. Maybe there is no answer except in the asking. He wondered how had it all come to this. Why couldn't he have simply left her in the swan-boat at Shepherds Island that night in May? Any fellow with character wouldn't have blundered into this pathetic situation. He wondered how Marie had tolerated him all these years. He was such a louse, after all.

"Oh, honey, I promise if you let me keep this job, you won't have any call to bawl me out, not ever again."

"Look, darling, I've only offered my opinion. You really ought to make your own decisions. I'm certainly willing to give you my best advice, but that's all it really is. You see, as you go along in your life, you're going to meet lots of people who will try to tell you what to do, but just remember that most of what they'll say is really only gossip. They believe themselves because they've never had anything better to go on."

A police siren shrieked in the direction of the river. A motor horn honked down the street and another dog began barking. Pearl slid off the bed and darted back through the curtain. Harry heard the suitcase latches snap open and Pearl rummaging among her possessions.

She came back into his bedroom with a fresh red rose in her hand. "I had an awful head after the show tonight and almost forgot to bring this home with me. A fellow threw it on stage when we took our final bow and I picked it up 'cause nobody ever threw me a rose before. I felt like a queen." She held the rose up to his nose. "Ain't it beautiful?"

"It certainly is," he agreed, shifting uncomfortably under the blanket. As aroused as he had been just five minutes ago, now he felt flat and cold. "I just don't follow what this has got to do with — "

Pearl gently placed a hand on his stomach and the raccoon coat fell open to her nudity, daring him to refuse her. "We gotta stick together, see? You know how fond I am of you, honey. Please don't be conventional. Why, if it wasn't for us falling in love, maybe I'd just be some silly bird checking hats at the Blue Onion. Now I got a swell future, honey, a real job so's I can make good on all you been doing for me since we met, and I won't let you down, neither. Honest I won't. Why, it'll be me and you, darling, forever and ever."

Her bright hopeful smile showed Harry what a fool and a hypocrite he truly was.

Upstairs, Fink had quit pacing and gone back to bed.

A pout crossed Pearl's cherubic face in the night blue shadows, her bosom swelling scant inches from his chest, parted thighs exposing her womanhood, a honeyscent of perfume everywhere. She murmured, "Don't you want me, darling? Ain't I pretty enough?"

Harry sighed. This was the stupidest thing he had done in his entire idiotic life. When she awakened him, and he saw beneath the folds of her raccoon coat, he desired her more than any girl he had ever known, but there's nothing more indiscreet than lying. "Darling, I rather doubt Marie would appreciate my helping you further your aspirations by allowing you to sleep here in the apartment with me, night after night. She's no fool, after all."

"Nobody's getting wise to us, honey," she argued, "and it ain't like I been advertising downtown. Why, none of the girls even asked if I let you love me up, and they know I ain't a faker." She threw her arms around his neck, burying her face in his nightshirt. "Now you're just trying to cut me out, honey, and it ain't fair. Oh, darling, I can't stand this anymore. Please don't stall. I know you got a crush on me."

She kissed him frantically, pressing her nude body against his, offering herself flagrantly. Frustrated by his own stupidity, Harry tried to lift her off his chest. "Please, darling — "

"Why, sure you do, honey!" she cried, clutching him even more fiercely. "And I got one on you, too, bigger'n the Ritz! Oh, darling, don't throw me over just when my luck's changing. Ain't you got any sense? Maybe I ain't part of the best bunch yet, but I tell you it's a cinch I'll learn all the steps, why sure I will. And when I do, I bet you I'll smell more roses than anyone ever dreamed — " Pearl's voice choked up, her violet eyes soaked with tears. She sagged. "Oh, what's the use? It's all gone to smash, ain't it?"

She began sobbing.

Any other night, Harry might have hugged her tightly to his chest, kissed her like mad, taken her under the blanket. But it just was impossible now. She had to hear the truth, that terrible story.

"Darling, did you hear me when I said I almost got killed tonight?"

"Yes!" she sobbed, rubbing her eyes. "And I told you that was a mistake! Those pluggers were laying for Reuben, not you. Billy said so. He was awful sorry, but you're safe now, honey." She hugged him tightly.

"But, you see, I'm not talking about those colored gangsters. There was someone else on that sidewalk tonight, a fellow named Cobb, who was laying for me. In fact, he'd been on my trail all evening. Except that it wasn't just me he was after. It was you, too. He wanted to put a bullet in my head because of something both of us have gotten ourselves involved in without even knowing it." Harry looked her straight in the eye. "Do you hear me? That Cobb fellow was working for Charles Follette who's had a big search put on for you all this summer long. He's sent up a reward worth five thousand dollars for the fellow who turns you over first, and that would've been Cobb if he'd gotten rid of me tonight, and he nearly did. I was damned lucky to escape."

Pearl stopped crying. Her look of incredulity told Harry she'd had no inkling of what he was telling her. "Five G's? Is that right?"

"I'm sorry, dear. It's my fault for not telling you sooner. The truth is, Follette offered me the reward way back at the beginning of the summer and I didn't see anything wrong with it because he said he was looking for his long lost niece. That's why I'd asked you to help me. I thought it was a swell deal until I found out what his pals intended to do with the poor girl once she turned up. I'm no killer, darling, I hope you believe that, and when I saw your name on the patient ledger at Winterhill, I realized you were the one they were looking for, and then I knew I had to protect you, but now I don't think I can. If Cobb could figure out who you are, so can somebody else. It's not safe for you here in the city, anymore, and that's all there is to it."

She seemed puzzled by everything he had just told her, baffled by her role in a sensational scandal. He tried to read something of that in her eyes.

But then she spoke, "Honey, I tell you, that's more dough than I ever seen in my life, and I got a crazy idea. We ought to go back to-morrow morning, soon as we get up. I'll tell him who I am, see, and I'll prove it, too, so he won't think I'm a gold digger. He'll be nuts not to believe me, and then we'll be rich, honey, both of us. What do you say? Ain't that a swell idea?"

My God, was she deaf?

"Look here, darling, you're still not listening! This isn't some reward to be collected. It's a bounty, and you're the prize. Somehow Charles Follette's become convinced that he's your father by a long-ago liaison he skipped out on before you were born. He got a helpless young wom-an into trouble, your poor mother, and now he plans to run for governor, and because of that he's terribly frightened of how your existence will appear to the blue noses in this state who treat any hint of scandal with the worst consequences. If your face shows up on the front page of the city news dailies, that's it; he's finished. In short, you're a threat to his political future, and a fellow like him simply won't have it."

Harry felt awful having to tell her all that, but she had to know the truth if she had any hope of surviving this mess.

"But, honey, don't he miss me?" Pearl asked so childishly that Har-ry almost wept. *What is life, when wanting love?*

As gently as possible, he told her, "Charles Follette doesn't know anything about you, darling. You're just another worry on his agenda that needs resolving. It's nothing personal. He simply doesn't care the least about you or anything regarding your life."

"But he's really my pop, ain't he?"

"Maybe he is, dear, but I doubt that means anything to him one way or the other. It's just not on his horizon. Fellows like him hardly know more than a few of us by name because we're not on the tip sheet."

This all felt so foolish now, Harry was tempted to switch off the light and give her a hug, listen to the ships passing the river, let her sleep on his pillow beside him. But that would be even more ridiculous, wouldn't it? She wasn't listening, anyhow. Her obsession with being loved had completely taken over.

Pearl draped her arms around his neck. "Honey, maybe if I was to go there and he got a really good look at me, it'd be different, don't you think? Why, I know I'm pretty and I can be awful sweet when I want to. Don't you think him seeing me in the flesh'd change his mind?"

"No, darling. I don't."

"Why not?"

Exasperated with her naïveté, Harry told her flatly, "Because he doesn't want a bastard daughter, that's why. Good grief, dear, if for one second I thought he did, I'd ride you up to his office myself! But he doesn't, and there's no use pretending otherwise. Look here, darling, I made a terrific mistake not telling you any of this when I realized you were the girl his men have been scouting around for. I hadn't thought it all out until this evening, and maybe I imagined somehow I'd be able turn this situation into something favorable for both of us. Well, I was wrong. Honestly, darling, you're in a very precarious position, much worse than I could've guessed. That fellow Cobb knew all about us. Maybe he told someone else. Maybe he kept it to himself. I can't be sure either way. At any rate, if they're not onto you yet, they will be, which means you'll either have to go into hiding or get out of the city altogether, the sooner the better. I've thought about this all evening, and I want to put you on a train, maybe out to Larksburg. We could hire you a room in a hotel there, keep you out of sight until we decide where it's safest for you to go. I'd come and get you when that happens, see you off to a new life, a better one. We've just got to be sensible about this because — "

She snapped back at him. "Look here, honey, I ain't going nowhere, and that's the straight of it! I ain't scared of nobody. They can come looking for me all they like. Boop-boop-a-doop."

"Darling, they'll tie a weight around your neck and drop you into the river."

"Oh, I'd like to see 'em!"

Harry began to realize that this poor young girl wouldn't concede her defect of caution because this was how she had been surviving since her mother had taken ill. What right did anyone have to tell her how to live now? He heard the elevator rasping up from the lobby. The gate clanged open, and footsteps padded to the end of the hall. The back door creaked and slammed shut. A wolf whistle called in the alley behind the old brick hotel. Somebody laughed across the street.

"Do you love me, honey?" Pearl cupped her hand softly over his. "I'm awfully afraid you don't, and that's how come you're throwing me over. I couldn't stand it if you didn't love me, darling. Do you?"

Now he had proof of how big a fool he had been for allowing her suitcase into his apartment. But that wasn't the whole story, was it? Not for himself. Yes, he loved her. She was the most adorable girl he had ever kissed, but that tenderness and affection he felt for her had blown far out of proportion to something he'd always known was desperately inevitable. Quite plainly, as much as Harry loved this preposterous, stubborn, intriguing young girl, he simply loved his own dear children that much more. Those beautiful little faces. He was their dear old dad. His love for them was joyous, purer, unencumbered by guilt or threat. Because a child's love holds no conditions, wants only reciprocity: a new toy now and then, healing comfort during illness, hugs and kisses at each homecoming, a little story at bedtime with a happy ending. Far away at night, he could not hope to provide all that, yet he had to try, or risk forfeiting a love that should have no natural bounds. If need be, would he break someone's heart to save the lives of his children? Would he do it without hesitation or second thoughts? Without regard for his own happiness?

"Of course I love you, darling," he told her tenderly, "and I'm not throwing you over at all, but you're not safe here in my apartment, anymore, and that's saying it plain as day."

Pearl sat up straight on the bed. "I tell you, honey, I won't go. I'm not leaving you, and that's all there is to it. You need me to look out for you, see, and I won't let you down. Maybe you think I don't stand a chance with brass nuts like them, but it just ain't so. I tell you, they don't scare me one bit."

"Darling, that's foolish. Follette's crowd owns most of this city. They can go wherever they choose, and do whatever suits them. You're only here right now because they don't know your mother's wedded name. You were born before she and your father married. As awful as this sounds, being illegitimate has kept you alive."

"Don't talk about her like that, honey. It ain't nice."

"It's the truth, dear."

"Well, it ain't nice."

Harry threw up his hands. "Good grief, I'm just trying to help you, darling, but honest to goodness, there's only so much I can do if you won't take my advice. Are you listening? It's just not smart for you to be here any longer. Let's admit it, you need to go away soon, maybe even tomorrow. Let me buy you a train ticket. It doesn't have to be to Larksburg or St. James. Tell me, dear, where have you always wanted to go? How about Philadelphia? Have you ever been there? It's a wonderful city."

As she blinked, a tear dribbled down her cheek. "Make love to me, darling, toot sweet." She flopped over on top of him, nuzzling his ear. "I tell you, I can't wait another instant." She sloughed off her raccoon coat and jammed a hand inside his union suit.

That was the limit.

"Stop it, darling." He grabbed her wrist. "It's too late for that now. I'm all run down, and it's no good like this, anyhow."

"Says you." Panting suddenly, she tugged at his buttons with her other hand and kissed him hard on the mouth. Her breath was gin-sour and hot. She forced her hand deep into his drawers. "I know you love me, honey, I just know you do!"

He thought she'd gone insane. She fought like a cat to undress him, scratching his stomach and thighs as they grappled furiously. Finally, he forced his hands and knees underneath her and shoved upward, hurling her off the bed. She landed sideways on the floor, banging her head on the nightstand. He threw off his blanket. "Goddamn it, I said, STOP! Have you lost your mind? Good grief!"

She whimpered.

"Why did you do that?" Harry sat up and put a foot on the floor. What a mess. He stared at her. His heart sank. "Gosh, dear, are you all right? I didn't mean to be rough. I'm so sorry."

Naked and barefoot, Pearl collected her raccoon coat and got up, her pretty face stained with tears.

Embarrassed by every last bit of this, he told her, "Look, darling, you're just worn out. Everything'll be better tomorrow. You'll see. We'll figure it out together. I promise." He offered a sunny smile.

Retreating to the curtain, and dabbing her eyes with one sleeve of the musty raccoon coat, Pearl told him quietly, "I love you, Harry, and we ain't done nothing wrong."

Then she eased the curtain apart and slipped through.

"Do you know, darling, the tears stand in my eyes now as I feel my heart warm to yours. If only you knew how light my heart was when I thought of your love and devotion as we sat so near together. Do you wonder that I wanted to kiss you over and over again?...

"You are so good to me, sweetheart. Where in all the world could I find such another dearie? I couldn't have any good in life if it were not for you. What lots of things have happened since we began to love each other, and what lots of things are yet to recur. But through it all we won't lose faith in each other. I want my darling to be the darling of all these years, the beautiful simple pure girl and the noble virtuous woman...

"Your love is great, but your pride is greater. I believe in you, and trust you without a shadow of questioning, but it came to me all of a sudden: You are everything to me now, suppose if you should cease to love and think no more of me? But I know that time will never come. You will always love me, and I, you, and we will live many happy useful years together...

"My heart warms toward you this morning and I would just like to put my arm around you and give you an old-fashioned hug. I don't believe that all love each other as we do. You will probably say that I am conceited, but I think that we are a pair of model lovers, two love sick youths as some people would say...

"How I do wish that I was fixed so that we could get married. Every time I come near a jewelry store, I stop and look in at the window if they have any ladies' rings in sight and it makes my heart ache when I see so many nice costly ones that I would like to present you with one of them. You are mine and I am yours and we belong to one another. I am about as poor as any young man and yet, I think that I am the richest. I look at those better-situated than I am and wonder if they have a treasure similar to the one that I have, and if they haven't, then who is the richest? I am, of course, and always will be as long as I have you...

"We are the wise ones, dear. That is, you are wise and I reflect your wisdom as the moon reflects the light of the sun. I am no longer drifting aimlessly through

the world. I am working for you. Work is going to take on a new look; labor will
be sweet; all, and everything that I do, will be for you. Some day in the great future
when you and I are enjoying prosperity and I am bending over and kissing you, I
will say these words, my darling: I am kissing you now because you kissed me when
things looked dismal and I had nothing but hope. Come what will, my sweetheart,
we will love each other until the end of our earthly pilgrimage. Marie, you are the
best girl in the city."

— **10** —

Harry woke at sunup to a cold draft in the apartment. Rising to use
the toilet, he found the front window open to a gray-violet dawn,
the smoke-mist of breakfast fires hovering over city rooftops. He
also discovered that Pearl had gone during the night and taken all
her possessions. He supposed she was angry and hurt, and why not?
Bumping her off the bed like that was inexcusable. Why he had re-
acted so violently to her mashing, he didn't know. He'd been awfully
tired and horribly shaken up by that business with Cobb. Good grief,
those Negro gangsters had shot the fellow dead on the sidewalk in
plain sight of the street, and gone back indoors as if they hadn't
done more than pay a newsboy. Pearl refused to grasp the seriousness of all this, and he had failed to get it across to her. Permitting
him to buy her a train ticket to Philadelphia or New York or Boston
could've been the greatest thing she had ever done. Instead, she preferred to let him rut on her with no thought of tomorrow. Finally,
he'd showed some better sense. Last night had been a point of no
return. Escaping disaster on Ashford Street had certainly changed
his outlook, offered him a fresh start; he'd be damned if he wouldn't
take it. Once Pearl had left his bedroom, all he could think of was
telephoning Marie to see that she still loved him and wanted him
home with the children where he belonged. Gosh, he prayed that
was so. He'd bought a new Oz book for Cissie, and had something
even more special for little Henry's birthday. As for Pearl, he hoped
she wouldn't hold a grudge. What he'd done was necessary for both

of them. She ought to be able to see that. Certainly he loved her. Of course he did. But he was a married man, after all, who had made a dreadful mistake and admitted it. Nobody was perfect. Anyhow, being young, she would likely get over this disappointment and realize he was right about how dangerous it was for her to remain in the city. If a cheap hoodlum like Cobb could manage to figure out she was Follette's bastard daughter, someone else could, too. Likely sooner than later. The trouble had been persuading her to listen. Why did she have to be so damned stubborn?

Shading his eyes to the morning light off the river, Harry leaned out the window and saw Jackson Street busy with milk trucks and loaded pushcarts and noisy automobiles, people on cement stoops trading lively conversation in the chilly air. He closed the window and went to the toilet. After a hot bath and a shave, he heated up a cup of coffee on the stove while he dressed and considered the telegram to Marie he wanted to compose at the Western Union office later that morning. She had been awfully patient with him. Whenever he felt a little tough or indisposed, she would lay her head on his shoulder and offer that comfort so true to her good nature. Even when he acted rather cold and indifferent, and couldn't even bring himself to say he loved her, her quiet kindness left no doubt that she always loved him. What on earth had he ever done to earn that dear heart?

After Harry finished his coffee, he went to the elevator. Down in the hotel lobby, a pair of men in gray waistline suits stood by the desk browsing a pink extra edition of the *Metropolitan Herald* whose headline in bold print announced the terrible fire on Shepherds Island. Harry located a shivering newsboy at the corner of Lafayette and 16th Street and bought a morning *Sentinel* and walked four blocks to a lunchroom where he ate wheat cakes and Virginia ham, and read the paper. Afterward, he returned to the Warsaw Hotel to review the stack of business correspondences in order to determine how best to reorganize his strategy. Only when he decided to go make up his bed did Harry notice the folded paper note fallen on the floor beside his nightstand. Scribbled in pencil on light blue stationery, yet quite legible, it read:

Dear Harry,

I bet you didn't think I could write my own name, did you? I told you I'm no dumb Dora. I hoped someday I'd be rich as mud and you'd come to tea and give me a diamond and say I'm pretty. Isn't that a laugh? Now my heart's broke so I guess I'll jump. I love you.

So long,
Pearl

The four blocks to the river were jammed sidewalk to sidewalk with automobiles, green busses, red motorcycles, coal trucks, and hundreds of hurried men and women. Dodging in and out of the crowds, Harry ran most of the way to the Washington Bridge, arriving just as a loaded ferryboat and a raffish steam yacht decorated with a rainbow of tiny flags passed by underneath. He stopped momentarily to catch his breath in the broad shadow of the Herald Street masonry tower, a soggy odor of river tide and wood smoke and stale beer rising from the filthy vagrant camps near the gray breakwater below. Across Herald Street, grimy-faced truants played follow-my-leader atop a lumber pile at the back of a sandlot where an Italian and his son on makeshift wood scaffolding repaired the roof of a tarpaper cook shack. High overhead, heavy steel suspension cables sung in the morning gusts.

Terrified that Pearl had already jumped off into the swirling wake of a large freighter, Harry hurried up the walkway along the iron railing toward the center of the great bridge, looking over the edge every few yards, praying silently not to catch sight of the gasoline boats that routinely dragged bloated corpses from the muddy waters. What had he done to her? If she'd jumped, it was his fault for letting her out like that. *I must be a monster.*

Directly beneath the gothic arch of the nearest suspension tower, a stocky policeman stood in a crowd of bridge workmen smoking a fat cigar and laughing loudly enough to be heard above the steam whistles. Harry quickly waded in among them, providing a brief description of Pearl and asking whether or not anyone had seen her on the bridge this morning. The policeman answered Harry by inquiring if he had knocked her up.

"Are you joking?" Harry replied, insulted by the innuendo. "I'm a married man!" These fellows didn't need know his relationship to her. It was beside the issue now.

"My friend, some husbands kiss all day — they start with the kiddies and end up with the maid. Is that why she jumped? Somebody gave her the dope on your little lady at home?"

The circle of bridge workmen laughed.

Furious now, Harry shot back, "I'm simply asking if any of you've seen her on the bridge this morning."

"What's she look like again?" asked one of the workmen in patched denim overalls. His thin face was gray with soot, eyes bloodshot from fatigue. A smell of turpentine rose on the wind. Impatience rife in his voice, Harry described Pearl once more, though he knew they didn't care.

Scratching his chin, the workman frowned. "Naw, I ain't seen no dames like her jumping today. Maybe you oughta come back tomorrow."

The steam whistle from a sandscow plying the cold river upstream drowned out more raucous laughter. Harry stepped forward and kicked over one of the garbage pails, dumping a pile of scrub brushes onto the bridge walkway. The nearest workman lunged forward, grabbed Harry by the lapels, and gave him a shove. Frustrated, Harry shoved back. Straight away, the crowd of workmen moved toward him. Retreating along the high iron railing, he shouted, "For heaven sakes, isn't anyone here capable of answering a simple question? There's a girl's life at risk!"

The policeman interceded as dust kicked up from a passing coal truck clouded the roadway. "Look here, Mac, if some poor jane's taken a dive on account of you treating her bad, well, that's tough all right, but nobody up here likes a smart-aleck, either, and you don't seem to know when to pull the chain. Now, none of these fellows've seen any dames jumping off this bridge today, so why don't you make yourself agreeable and go home?"

Disgusted, Harry left the Washington Bridge, terrified with guilt. Last night, Pearl had come to him so filled with glee from her show performance, so full of love and true affection for him, and what had he done? He had shown her out with little regard for the damage he had inflicted on her young heart. What would Marie think if she knew he'd caused a girl to leap to her death? How would his children fare in their lives forced to grow up with the knowledge of their dear old dad's unforgivable behavior? *My God, I ought to be locked up.*

Catching the yellow bus line at Columbia Avenue, Harry rode to Clancy Street, disembarking on the corner of 36th in front of the Victoria Saloon. The morning street was mostly empty. He hurried down the sloping sidewalk that led to Gable Lane. Behind the oldest theaters were grassy lots divided by fences. Laundry fluttered on lines in the midmorning wind. Following a narrow path pockmarked by the summer hooves of truck horses and old flour wagons, Harry jogged along until he recognized the connected Shamrock and Mercury Theaters and climbed over the plank fence and headed up the grassy slope to a back porch. The door was open so he went inside and knocked at the dressing room door where he had met Pearl's fellow chorus girls. When nobody answered, he tried the knob and found it locked. He heard someone playing the piano out front. Large props from the late show were still behind the curtain where they provided a South Seas backdrop of palm trees and sunshine and blue waves. Entering silently from backstage, Harry recognized the pianist as the same one in the black bowler hat who'd played last night. Seated beside him on the piano bench was a sweetheart brunette wearing a blue dress and a cloche hat and a fox neckpiece, singing an Eva Tanguay standard.

> *"When I was but a baby,*
> *Long before I learned to walk,*

While lying in my cradle,
I would try my best to talk,
It wasn't long before I spoke,
And all the neighbors heard,
My folks were very proud of me,
for 'Mother' was the word."

Her voice was accomplished, her smile engaging, and she had quite a nice bosom, too. She sung with her eyes on the pianist who seemed equally enraptured with her. Finishing the song, the pianist leaned over and kissed the girl on the cheek and told her she was marvelous. Standing at stage left, Harry clapped for them both, hoping to ingratiate himself.

The pianist turned on the seat. "May I help you?"

"I'm looking for Babyface. Have you seen her recently? It's quite important."

"I'm sure it is," replied the pianist, sounding testy, "but we're rehearsing here. Do you mind awfully?"

Holding his temper, Harry hesitated, and asked again, "Have you seen her this morning?"

"No, I have not." The pianist stood abruptly. "Did you notice the sign out front?"

"No, but if you'd just tell me where I might get hold of Babyface, I'd — "

"Are you able to read?"

"Yes, of course, but I came in through the back door. You see, I've been looking for Babyface all morning. I need to speak with her. It's urgent."

The pianist stared toward the front of the theater, then called out, "GUSTAV!"

"Listen here, it's very important that I see Babyface as soon as possible. It's life and death!"

"The next show's at eight o'clock this evening. If you buy a ticket, you can see her then." While the pretty brunette played her fingers lightly over the keyboard, the pianist walked to the curtain and shouted backstage, "GUSTAV!"

Then he disappeared behind the curtain for a few moments. When he came back out, he shouted again, "GUSTAV!"

Noticing that Harry hadn't yet gone, the pianist frowned. "Haven't I already told you she's not here? Do you prefer to be arrested for trespassing? I'll call the police this very instant, if you like."

"No," Harry told him, so angry now he could hardly stand it, "but why won't you answer my question?" *I'll bet if I cracked his nose he'd give me a minute.*

"Good! That shows you're not a complete fool. Now, please leave."

The pianist switched his attention immediately toward stage right. "GUSTAV!"

Realizing that stopping here had been a colossal waste of time, Harry rushed out the back of the theater.

It was six blocks to the cross-town trolley station at Parkhurst Memorial Church. He paid his fare and rode four miles along Roosevelt Boulevard past the Union Theater and the great City Museum of Art and the Carnegie Library and Roman Club, the Imperial, Morgan, St. Petersburg and Olympus Hotels, and the Fabrini Castle where carriages still parked under shady elm trees and the broad sidewalks were swept daily and doormen in elegant suits greeted passersby with a smile and a kind word. Halfway up the block between the Public Library and the Audubon Fine Arts Society, Harry left the trolley and entered the western gate of Washington Park through a pleasant grove of rain trees from Waycross, Indiana, that flanked the mausoleum of Charles Whitaker Hastings and attracted flocks of birds and squirrels and morning park-goers. If Pearl hadn't jumped, after all, and simply wished to hide away from him, Harry had few illusions about locating her. The vast geography of the city was daunting and she knew its dark corners far better than he. However, if she had simply chosen to go somewhere merely to sulk, well, maybe the odds were somewhat better — provided she still loved him. In fact, he bet she'd be back tonight. He knew her that well. She was probably out of her head right now, but by supper time, she'd miss him like the dickens and he'd have a second crack at persuading her to take that train ticket and get out of here for good.

Resting for a few minutes under the portico at Athena's Dome where that small glass window in back had been replaced, Harry mulled over Pearl's note once again. Why on earth would she write something like that? It was so confusing. For starters, why would she choose to commit suicide by jumping off a bridge into the river? The poor dear was afraid of the water. Once when they toured the old public bathhouses on the Villard Flats Recreation pier, Pearl refused to let go of his arm, fearing if she slipped, she'd be "swamped in the seapussies and drown like a rat." He'd laughed for an hour over that. Why subject herself to needless terror in the final act of her life? In any case, the simple truth was that if Pearl had taken her own young life because he'd thrown her over, he could never forgive himself. Perhaps old Collingsworth was correct, after all, when insisting that the instruction of guilt is what divides virtue from desire.

Harry left Washington Park through the Gate of Nations and boarded the trolley at the corner of Stokes Street and Thumann Avenue, next to the Academy of Music. Utterly miserable, he rode the twelve blocks to Knapp Avenue where he bought a cup of coffee at a busy lunchwagon across from the Metropolitan Institute of Arts & Sciences, then climbed the hill to Drinkwater Street. His intent was to leave one of his business cards in Margaret Stelinger's chart-book so that when Pearl next visited her mother at Winterhill, she would be given it. While riding the trolley, Harry had scribbled a short note on the back of the card:

all my fault. Please forgive me. Come back?

How that silly girl with a drink habit had so managed to disrupt his summer he had no idea, but perhaps what he botched so badly last night could still be repaired, or so Harry prayed as he strode past the twin griffins, up the granite staircase into the sanitarium.

The reception foyer was just as cheerless as Harry remembered it from August, still smelling of wood varnish and disinfectant, its sea-blue linoleum floor scrubbed spotless. The elderly nurse who had greeted them on Harry's first visit to the sanitarium was there now at the front desk, sorting through a tall stack of papers. He went straight over to her, asking to speak with Dr. Bloom.

"I'm sorry, dear," the nurse shook her head, "but he's with patients for the rest of the morning. Is there someone else who might be able to help you?"

Harry wracked his brain for the name of the woman who escorted him to Margaret Stelinger that afternoon. "Well, there was a nurse whose name I don't recall, but she was very pleasant. I met her here last month. She works with the Parkinson patients."

"Miriam Kaye?"

"Why, yes, I believe that's her. Is she here today?"

"Let me ring her office." The nurse went to use the telephone behind her. Still familiar in his memory were those resounding voices of the pained and desperate echoing through the bleached sanitarium walls. Was Christopher the hummingbird wrapped happily this morning onto a table in the dank basement? Did poor Gilda still triumph over her checkerboard upstairs?

"Sir?" The nurse had come back to the desk. "Miss Kaye wishes to know with which patient you're concerned."

"Margaret Stelinger."

Returning to the telephone, the elderly nurse repeated the name into the mouthpiece. A few seconds later, she blanched. "Oh my." Her eyes raised to meet Harry's at the desk. "Yes, of course... Pardon? Oh yes, I believe it's here... Yes, yes, of course. I'll let him know... Thank you, dear." She hung up the phone and searched briefly in a file cabinet and withdrew a sheet of paper. Before Harry could speak, the nurse asked, "Are you a member of the family?"

"No, but I'm a close friend of Mrs. Stelinger's daughter, Olive. Is there something wrong?" He felt strange saying her real name. Maybe if he had used it sooner, none of this would have happened.

"Dear, I'm awfully sorry." The elderly nurse softened her eyes with compassion. "Margaret Stelinger suffered a stroke during her evening meal last Monday. She passed away in the infirmary at midnight."

Harry stood in cold silence at the desk.

"It appears her daughter was informed Tuesday morning when she arrived for her weekly visit." The nurse placed the sheet of paper on the desk in front of Harry. "She claimed the body for burial at Elysian Fields."

Tuesday morning? Good grief, she had known of her mother's death for almost a week. Why hadn't she told him? His thoughts raced back furiously over the past several days, attempting in hindsight to detect her grief. *I see a hand you cannot see, which beckons me away.* Of course, she had hidden it cleverly beneath that fresh and eager veneer of youthful optimism. Why do we try with such great desperation to keep from confusing what is and is not real in this life, while persisting to believe so many things we just know are not true? She must have been utterly terrified of being truly orphaned now. Certainly that was why she had begged him to hurry back with her to the Empyrean Building, so she could throw herself onto Follette's lap. Instead of encouraging her to believe she wouldn't be alone, he'd tried to send her away on a train by herself somewhere. The very thought must have horrified her. But, honestly, how could he have known? Each of us has a terror of something so intricately disguised that we normally refer to more conventional phobias when describing what scares us most. Her mother's death must have tremendously distorted Pearl's dream of dancing through the jeweled city to the rising applause of thousands whose affection for her would be breathtaking and unconditional. When we lose that wonderful sustaining innocence of hope that somewhere, someone loves us with all his heart, we stop believing in the extraordinary, and after that we simply disappear.

A cold ache in his chest, Harry took the sheet of paper and read over it quickly: a death certificate stamped at Winterhill six days ago. It was signed at the bottom by Dr. Cornelius H. Bloom. On the line beneath the doctor's signature was another name in a familiar scribble alongside the word "daughter:" *Olive May Stelinger*

Five hours later, Harry stepped off the drafty interurban at Pelican Station next to the water tanks that had been tapped almost dry during the terrible conflagration the night before. Twenty-two fire companies had fought unsuccessfully to save Thebes. Now a fine layer of ash half an inch thick soiled most of Sand Avenue, and the two great surviving amusement parks looked desolate in the late afternoon mist. Photographers wandered about completing a record of the disaster. Reporters collected in small groups sharing anecdotes or badgering county marshals for more grisly details of the deaths of the sixteen firemen incinerated beneath the collapsed Obelisk. Asking fruitlessly here and there for a while regarding the whereabouts of Billie Fry or a fellow named Rocky who wore the Lucifer outfit at Hell Gate, Harry strolled the littered boardwalk past the silent Wonder Wheel and the soot-shrouded Funny Face at Starland and the Bowery where dozens of performers and barkers and shills worked hard at cleaning up. The wind had changed to save Nightingale Park. Though many of the frightened animals liberated from the Persian Circus were still free in the swamps near Roanoke Creek, architectural damage had been confined largely to the gilded domes and minarets of Sultan's Palace blistered by the fantastic heat from ruined Thebes. Sadly, most of William Astor Harrington's grand panorama of ancient Egypt was reduced to acres of gray smoldering rubble. Harry stopped in front of the charred Karnak Gate where a notice posted by the wealthy entrepreneur himself read:

> I had troubles yesterday that I have not today.
> I have troubles today that I had not yesterday.
> On this site site will be erected a bigger, better Thebes
> Admission to the Burning Ruins -- 25 cents.

A large canvas tent was raised near the partially burned Jordan Pier surrounded by clown-faced midgets on stilts and Indian elephants and bald strongmen raising pyramids of female trapeze artists upon indefatigable shoulders. Draped like a sash across the entrance to the big tent was a wide linen sheet announcing to all:

THE CONGRESS OF THE WORLD'S GREATEST LIVING CURIOSITIES FROM THE WRECK OF THEBES A LITTLE DISFIGURED BUT STILL IN THE RING!!

After discovering the sad fate of Margaret Stelinger at the sanitarium on Winterhill, Harry had taken a streetcar to the Orpheum

Theater where he and Pearl first met, calling her name upstairs and down in the musty flickering darkness while the owl-eyed organist played with enthusiasm and the audience roared at a straw-hatted fellow on a sagging flagpole. Later, he searched for her in the old carbarns at Doyle Road and on the lower bulwark at Columbia Avenue among the foul morass of lean-to's and tattered old A.E.F. tents along the windy breakwater. He hired a taxi to drive him slowly past the terraced gardens of the Sylvester mansion on Mulberry Avenue, and ridden the Tarryton County interurban out to Pearl's old hometown to see if perhaps she had returned again to Stuyvesant Street. By the fence there in front of her childhood home, he spoke to a middle-aged woman in a peach pink dress and flounced apron who assured him she had never seen anyone at all resembling Pearl in that neighborhood. Behind her, the shady yard had been neatly raked and all the house windows thrown open to the fresh morning air. As Harry walked off, a little boy wandered out from the garage with a wooden aeroplane and began calling for his mother.

When Harry Hennesey was a boy, his father had a motto framed on the wall above his oak desk at the downtown mercantile building that read: *"It's easy enough to be pleasant/ When life goes by like a song/ But the man worth while/ Is the man with a smile/ When everything goes dead wrong."* During those years at the stockyards and along the selling road, through high times and low, Harry asked himself: Have I ever been pleasant enough to those I loved? What capacity of feeling sets any of us apart from another? I love my wife and my children and my sister and my mother. Their love is the foundation of my life. I owe them more than I can hope to repay. Can fidelity to a needful heart ever be constant? *To be trusted is a greater compliment than to be loved.* All summer long, he held a vivid memory of Marie sitting on the wisteria-draped porch at Cedar Street in the lavender evening and his children's sleepy faces pressed to the glass of a second story window, waiting for him to arrive from the train depot at the end of a long business trip. One night aboard the Soo Line, he overheard a fellow from General Motors remark that our moral compass points to the penthouse or the notchhouse, but not both. It's a test of our character to detect the difference. To do something worthwhile during our brief time in the world means detecting the difference. He wondered: Why do we so often fail ourselves? Is it so terrible to wake up each morning believing there is nothing more important that day than to let those we love know how much they mean to us? Love is our last best hope of enduring the tragedies of this existence. Without love, everything becomes uncertain, and the end of each day seems to stretch away out of reach.

Exhausted now and heartbroken over a beautiful orphan child whose best desire was simply companionship in this modern age of selfishness and disregard, Harry Hennesey walked out onto the ash-sodden pier past groups of beaten-down vagrants huddled together on the damp benches, their downcast faces laden with despair. Most of the heavy planks beneath his feet were blackened from smoke, and those familiar obscenities scratched with penknives into the wood railing were obscured by soot. Under the pier, cold river currents lapped calmly at the old pilings. Yawl boats and wooden canoes drifted on the water. Gulls wheeled across the gray afternoon sky. He strolled alone to the end of the Jordan Pier where he stared away downriver toward the great metropolis on the distant shoreline.

In the five months since Harry had stepped eagerly from that morning train at Central Station, he had heard voices in alleyways throughout the city, lewd and sullen voices, whispering to passersby with all the conviction of experience that to read widely, to pray, to cultivate the companionship of good people, to be kind and thoughtful, may be the sum of virtues, but the business of the Republic is business, and all the law courts that ever were, all the ledgers of profit and fortune, confirm the privilege of greed to determine the worth of any man's life. That first day in the city, he had met a sad lunchroom counter man from Waukegan by the name of Buster Harlow who had lost his insurance job after attempting to raise profits by shady means. Now he was dead broke and his wife had left with his little girls. He told Harry that once he had sought the great honor of setting up a home with a wife and children who found in him qualities that make a good and true husband and father, one who could be loved, and who would be loved. With a bitter voice, he confessed: *This is life's greatest disappointment; not my failure to achieve financial success or a position of power, which I admit I wanted, but to have married with the ideals I had, with the overwhelming desire to be loved — and now to be deprived, cheated, of that realization. To be married to a woman who never really loved me, to live a lonely life, that is tragedy, for the years cannot be rolled backward. I cannot try again.*

A man's hopeful gaze is forever cast upon a life of joy and inspiration. He labors tirelessly in field and factory, stokes the hot furnaces of giant industries, hauls cotton and wheat on the wet docks of a hundred ports of call, walks another man's product down ten thousand rainy streets to knock on doors hour after hour, town after town, for the most meager of rewards, bravely confident that tomorrow holds more promise than yesterday. Not so long ago, he spent hard-earned savings to book passage aboard a fast express whose thundering locomotive carried him from the worn-out fields of the old Republic to the bright modern metropolis where the redemption of opportunity and success awaited. He dwells there alone, occupying a small apartment in the artless squalor of a drafty old hotel with a bed and a radiator, a closet and a sink, and a cloudy window facing a noisy street, nearly invisible from the heights of the great skyscrapers in whose long shadows he follows to work each day. At night, he wanders among his fellow men downtown. On a lighted street corner during an early autumn rain, he watches a tired young newsboy quote stock profits from the Exchange off a soggy newspaper he's waving to traffic. Long sleek automobiles splash and motor onward into the dark. Packs of wisecracking men wearing pearl-gray fedoras and expensive waistline suits crowd together under the neon marquee of the Rivoli movie house, smoking cigarettes and eyeing pretty girls in street makeup and silk dresses at the box office. These are sluggers and gunmen, cheap racketeers, purveyors of bootleg liquor and relentless violence; he's seen them in every block of the city. He walks on alone. Ahead, klieg lights crisscross on the rainy sky. Fire companies raise ladders to the smoke-filled fourth floor of a glittering ballroom whose patrons shriek from the upper windows to be rescued. Several lose hope and jump. Some are captured in flight by roving photographers. Hands in pockets, he huddles under the canvas awning of an all-night cafeteria next to a rain-soaked boulevard busy with taxicabs and dashing jaywalkers until a ruddy-faced policeman whose blue uniform is soaked nearly black from the evening rainshowers comes down the sidewalk and orders him to move along. Vagrants and small animals rummage through barrels of garbage blocking a dank alleyway as the elevated trolley arrives with a violet flash above the wet street. He produces a brass token from his pocket and climbs on board. The lights of downtown whiz by as the streetcar transports him across the city. Billboards flicker atop apartment buildings and darkened factories. Radio towers wink beneath the clouds. He rides the streetcar to the end of the line: a contemptible district of gurgling gutters and storm-drains clotted with filth where he watches for strangers in old coats and drooping hats who murmur obscenities to him from sheltered doorways and old brick stoops. He navigates these flooded streets in the dark, crossing from sidewalk to sidewalk, block after block, of industrial ruin and decay, until he reaches a familiar clapboard framehouse a quarter mile from the freight yards. A kerosene lamp glows in a second-story window. He knocks at the front door. After a few minutes, a woman in a lavender tea gown invites him inside. Downstairs is heated only by a gas burner on the kitchen stove and the hardwood floor is bare and cold, so she leads him upstairs where a table phonograph scratches out a fox-trot melody in the burgundy gloom of a chintzy parlor. She offers him a glass of Canadian Club whiskey and a seat on a threadbare sofa. He tells her a new Ford joke and she laughs and takes his hand when he finishes the whiskey and brings him into her bedroom. He's still nervous as he removes his blue serge suit and thinks about a girl he knows back home who once loved to play the "Melody in F" and go canoeing on summer lakes and read over and over the touching parts in novels. She was kind of shy, but he felt true inward love for her and knew it right along and married her as soon as she would have him. They went auto-riding in Michigan for a honeymoon and bought a house afterward and had a family. Then his business failed and the money ran out and he left home to find more profitable work, and after a long while humiliation brought him to this old house by the freight yard when he couldn't get affectionate to anyone else. He stands still as she bathes him quickly from a hot-water pitcher and a tin basin on the nightstand beside the bed. Then he slides between the sheets under the cracked plaster ceiling and watches her remove the lavender tea gown and her silk stockings and her hairpins, then closes his eyes as she extinguishes the red kerosene lamp. He's been in the city long enough now to know that a couple hours of rutting in the dark with a perfumed woman will not erase all the savage chaos of the crowded streets, the blind unthinking brutality, the drunkenness, poverty, envy and sorrow he sees every day. Yet he firmly believes that somewhere in this great Republic wild roses still bloom freely on the banks of a quiet river, and when the true story of the metropolis is written, those vivid dreams of wealth and prosperity that now power the great dynamos will fade away in sober remembrance of all the violence and bitterness and injury, grief beyond pity or forgiveness, that built this New Jerusalem, and grew a huge debt of the human heart, yet to be repaid.

— CODA —

HARRY SEARCHED FOR PEARL nearly a month, took ads out in the newspapers, left urgent notices about, inquired daily of the police. It was in vain.

At the end of September, he sent four thousand dollars of the check he accepted from Charles A. Follette in an express money order to Marie in Illinois. With what remained, he paid McDonald all he owed, then gave two weeks notice of his intent to vacate the apartment at the Warsaw Hotel. To celebrate little Henry's birthday, Harry mailed his son the "Isabella" quarter.

He did not rent the garage on Buchanan Street.

Instead, he purchased a ticket for a Pullman berth aboard the *Twentieth Century Limited*. On Columbus Day, 1929, Harry Hennesey left the Big Town and never returned.

A REPUBLIC OF DREAMS

CHARLIE PENDERGAST

IN THE LONG, LONG AGO, Mother and Father took me to the fun-fair for my tenth birthday. This was autumn, so we bundled up with blankets and rode out in the Ford with the chilly November wind blowing through our hair. Mother brought a jug of hot cider and a small picnic basket packed with apples and fresh cinnamon cookies. We made silly rhymes and jokes and sang the whole way there, but when we arrived the fun-fair was already over. The exhibition and game booths were dismantled, all the great tents drawn back to earth and folded up. We spread one of Mother's wool blankets out on a grassy hillock and opened the picnic basket and watched the trucks come to load up the flags and the booths, the tents and show horses, and take them all away. At dusk, Father lit a cigar and Mother wrapped her arms around me and we sat on the harvester blanket in the dark, this little family of ours, content simply to be together that autumn evening under a sky of stars that belonged just to us.

These precious incidences cross our lives like an errant draft before retreating, never to occur again. Each of us has a private history filled with high moments of unbridled gladness and equally bitter sorrows that pierce the heart and make of fleeting memory a salve for many wounds. When we are little, so much is hidden from us. Who are these people who come to supper and pinch my cheeks? Mother says they are her relatives from Wisconsin which makes them mine. Also, I am to remember Uncle Wesley in my prayers, though strictly speaking he is not my uncle. Old shoeboxes atop Father's closet shelves contain letters and collected paraphernalia so mundane I am unable to fathom the reason for their preservation. What is this moldy feather? This collar? This eyeglass? This marble? Father says he was once a boy, but how can that be? Where was Mother? I am not to touch anything in her medicine cabinet. When I do, my hands smell of powders and perfume. After the fun-fair, Mother bakes lemon pie with meringue for Sunday dinner. Later, she and Father share a secret I am not supposed to hear. Mother has cancer. She is not expected to live. On Saturday night, we pack up our things with a friend we call Desterhoff and drive to a lake in the northern woods where we spend the night in his cabin. Mother and Father love to go fishing. They rise at dawn and I see them wading arm-in-arm by the lakeshore. I think my mother is the most beautiful woman in the world. She cleans the walleye pike father catches and fries them in a pan for breakfast while I throw the baseball with Desterhoff who smokes a pipe and tells me I have a strong arm. On the drive home that evening, I ride in back with Mother. She lets me sleep with my head in her lap. The next morning, a doctor comes to our house and I am sent to the park to play. When I return, Father has moved a folding cot into my bedroom so that Mother can have her peace and quiet. He brings her medicine from the druggist twice a day and in the dark sometimes I hear her crying. One night, Father takes me to her room before I go to bed. Mother asks me to sit beside her. She holds my hand and says she's proud of me. Then she tells me that we should say good-bye to each other. And so we do. When Father wakes me for school in the morning, he says Mother has gone to heaven.

Childhood is a wonderful mystery. It is perhaps akin to a long ride home at night in the back seat of an automobile with Mother and Father up front to keep us safe so that we can sleep with no worries because they are always up front to do the worrying for us. And, of course, it doesn't last. Nothing of true innocence lasts. Too soon we're grown, and Mother and Father are gone, and we can never sleep in the back seat again. But we are born to this, and lose our youth willingly. We discard our kiddie clothes and silly talk and point our sights upward. Everything else falls away. During the Great Depression, I threw the javelin in high school and joined a club of young men. Father cut hair at the barbershop on Second Street from eight in the morning till eight at night, six days a week, and still fell five months behind in the rent. Uncle Cy was killed when he drove his car off a cliff in California. I gave my pin to Mary Armstrong at the senior ball and worked for a time as an usher at the Regent theater downtown. Auntie Emma died of a stroke in her backyard. Frenchy ran out on his family. Money became scarce. Father rented the spare room to a nice fellow named Selby who was a Jew. Uncle Monroe went out for a loaf of bread one afternoon and was run over by a truck as he walked along the roadside. Another war came. The army shipped me to Camp Campbell for basic training the week Aunt Hattie died of appendicitis. Roy Gallup went bankrupt. Cousins Rubin and Russell quit the farm and I was sent to Europe with the Seventh Army. Father wrote me a letter every day I was gone. He described the weather at home and who came into the barbershop, and ended each letter by saying it was time to take the dog out for a walk. I saw more of the world than I cared to, although the German forests were pretty and I made a lifelong friend of a policeman from St. Louis named Elmer Hagemeyer. On V-E Day, I drank my first and only beer, and wondered what all the fuss had been about. After the war, I came home and took a sales position with a furniture store. Cousin Bebbins moved to Florida where he died of liver disease. Father was elected head of the barbers union. One summer evening at a country club in northern Illinois, I met a girl, Lois Chase Freeman, who granted me the favor of marriage in 1951 and eventually bore me three lovely children. Father sold the house on Maple Avenue and moved to a downtown apartment near the barbershop. Uncle Henry gave his farm to a niece from Ohio who was a member of the Church of God. Aunt Clara passed away at one hundred and one years old. I was promoted to vice-president at Hudson Furniture. Our oldest, Janey, started kindergarten. Each Sunday evening, Father came to dinner and watched television with us and did card tricks for the kids. He gave my two boys their first haircuts. Lois joined a bridge club and began talking about Arizona as some place we might like to live one day. Uncle Boyd died of lung cancer in 1959. Auntie Eff died of pneumonia in 1960. Uncle Harris died of stomach cancer in 1962. The following spring, Lois and I found a beautiful home in a piñon grove just outside Flagstaff with a riding ring and a swimming pool. We bought a new Ford station wagon, loaded up the kids, and met Father for supper after work. That night, he told me the future is a constant blessing, but I knew he was hurt to see his grandchildren leave Illinois. In the fall, Lois re-designed our new home to suit her eye, and I was hired by an insurance office at Sedona. The kids rode horseback after school and I built a backyard barbecue and on the weekends we went camping. The next summer, I invited Father to come see us and have a look at the Grand Canyon. He drove down that August in his old Studebaker. We sat outdoors by the pool his first night on the desert while Lois washed the supper dishes and the children got themselves ready for bed. They had a hike planned for us in the morning. As he smoked his cigar, Father told me the barbershop was finished and that he was retiring. He'd had enough. It was time to go fishing. Before Lois and I went to bed that night, I looked in on Father to see if there was anything he needed, and found that he had died.

One day we wake up and we are old. That call to glory quiets and all our tomorrows are spoken for. We find so many loved ones visit us now in our dreams, we are glad to remember even those wounds that refused to heal. Looking backward only to make sense of our cruelties and chastisements seems irreverent. No man can be perfect in this world, nor do we expect it. There is some good in each of us, though, and we see it from time to time in the great and the obscure. A life reveals more than the glands of our bodies and the constitution of our brains. We are bound firmly and completely, perhaps even our ends shaped, by the eloquent traits of those stubborn and ageless strangers, our ancestors, who tilled the ground of their birthright, so their children might inherit fitter soil. Time was, a garden bloomed in Paradise. Far wanderers are we, and hope our faithful companion, ever longing to find a contented heart at rest in the fullness of days.